ROSEWOOD HIGH

#1-4

TRACY LORRAINE

THORN

A NOTE

Amalie is British so therefore her points of view in this book are written in British English. This may appear incorrect to some readers when compared to US English books.

1

AMALIE

"I think you'll really enjoy your time here," Principal Hartmann says. He tries to sound cheerful about it, but he's got sympathy oozing from his wrinkled, tired eyes.

This shouldn't have been part of my life. I should be in London starting university, yet here I am at the beginning of what is apparently my junior year at an American high school I have no idea about aside from its name and the fact my mum attended many years ago. A lump climbs up my throat as thoughts of my parents hit me without warning.

"I know things are going to be different and you might feel that you're going backward, but I can assure you it's the right thing to do. It will give you the time you need to... adjust and to put some serious thought into what you want to do once you graduate."

Time to adjust. I'm not sure any amount of time will be enough to learn to live without my parents and being shipped across the Pacific to start a new life in America.

"I'm sure it'll be great." Plastering a fake smile on my face, I take the timetable from the principal's hand and stare down at it. The butterflies that were already fluttering around in my stomach erupt to the point I might just throw up over his chipped Formica desk.

Math, English lit, biology, gym, my hands tremble until I see something that instantly relaxes me, *art and film studies.* At least I got my own way with something.

"I've arranged for someone to show you around. Chelsea is the captain of the cheer squad, what she doesn't know about the school isn't worth knowing. If you need anything, Amalie, my door is always open."

Nodding at him, I rise from my chair just as a soft knock sounds out and a cheery brunette bounces into the room. My knowledge of American high schools comes courtesy of the hours of films I used to spend my evenings watching, and she fits the stereotype of captain to a tee.

"You wanted something, Mr. Hartmann?" she sings so sweetly it makes even my teeth shiver.

"Chelsea, this is Amalie. It's her first day starting junior year. I trust you'll be able to show her around. Here's a copy of her schedule."

"Consider it done, sir."

"I assured Amalie that she's in safe hands."

I want to say it's my imagination but when she turns her big chocolate eyes on me, the light in them diminishes a little.

"Lead the way." My voice is lacking any kind of enthusiasm and from the narrowing of her eyes, I don't think she misses it.

I follow her out of the room with a little less bounce in my step. Once we're in the hallway, she turns her eyes on me. She's really quite pretty with thick brown hair, large eyes, and full lips. She's shorter than me, but then at five foot eight, you'll be hard pushed to find many other teenage girls who can look me in the eye.

Tilting her head so she can look at me, I fight my smile. "Let's make this quick. It's my first day of senior year and I've got shit to be doing."

Spinning on her heels, she takes off and I rush to catch up with her. "Cafeteria, library." She points then looks down at her copy of my timetable. "Looks like your locker is down there." She waves her hand down a hallway full of students who are all staring our way, before gesturing in the general direction of my different subjects.

"Okay, that should do it. Have a great day." Her smile is faker than mine's been all morning, which really is saying something. She goes to walk away, but at the last minute turns back to me. "Oh, I forgot. That over there." I follow her finger as she points to a large group of people outside the open double doors sitting around a bunch of tables. "That's *my* group. I should probably warn you now that you won't fit in there."

I hear her warning loud and clear, but it didn't really need saying. I've no intention of befriending the cheerleaders, that kind of thing's not really my scene. I'm much happier hiding behind my camera and slinking into the background.

Chelsea flounces off and I can't help my eyes from following her out toward *her* group. I can see from here that it consists of her squad and the football team. I can also see the longing in other student's eyes as they walk past them. They either want to be them or want to be part of their stupid little gang.

Jesus, this place is even more stereotypical than I was expecting.

Unfortunately, my first class of the day is in the direction Chelsea just went. I pull my bag up higher on my shoulder and hold the couple of books I have tighter to my chest as I walk out of the doors.

I've not taken two steps out of the building when my skin tingles with awareness. I tell myself to keep my head down. I've no interest in being their entertainment but my eyes defy me, and I find myself looking up as Chelsea points at me and laughs. I knew my sudden arrival in the town wasn't a secret. My mum's legacy is still strong, so when they heard the news, I'm sure it was hot gossip.

Heat spreads from my cheeks and down my neck. I go to look away when a pair of blue eyes catch my attention. While everyone else's look intrigued, like they've got a new pet to play with, his are haunted and angry. Our stare holds, his eyes narrow as if he's trying to warn me of something before he menacingly shakes his head.

Confused by his actions, I manage to rip my eyes from his and turn toward where I think I should be going.

I only manage three steps at the most before I crash into something—or somebody.

"Shit, I'm sorry. Are you okay?" a deep voice asks. When I look into the kind green eyes of the guy in front of me, I almost sigh with relief. I was starting to wonder if I'd find anyone who wasn't just going to glare at me. I know I'm the new girl but shit. They must experience new kids on a weekly basis, I can't be that unusual.

"I'm fine, thank you."

"You're the new British girl. Emily, right?"

"It's Amalie, and yeah... that's me."

"I'm so sorry about your parents. Mom said she was friends with yours." Tears burn my eyes. Today is hard enough without the constant reminder of everything I've lost. "Shit, I'm sorry. I shouldn't have—"

"It's fine," I lie.

"What's your first class?"

Handing over my timetable, he quickly runs his eyes over it. "English lit, I'm heading that way. Can I walk you?"

"Yes." His smile grows at my eagerness and for the first time today my returning one is almost sincere.

"I'm Shane, by the way." I look over and smile at him, thankfully the hallway is too noisy for us to continue any kind of conversation.

He seems like a sweet guy but my head's spinning and just the thought of trying to hold a serious conversation right now is exhausting.

Student's stares follow my every move. My skin prickles as more and more notice me as I walk beside Shane. Some give me smiles but most just nod in my direction, pointing me out to their friends. Some are just downright rude and physically point at me like I'm some fucking zoo animal awoken from its slumber.

In reality, I'm just an eighteen-year-old girl who's starting somewhere new, and desperate to blend into the crowd. I know that with who I am—or more who my parents were—that it's not going to be all that easy, but I'd at least like a chance to try to be normal. Although I fear I might have lost that the day I lost my parents.

"This is you." Shane's voice breaks through my thoughts and when I drag my head up from avoiding everyone else around me, I see he's holding the door open.

Thankfully the classroom's only half full, but still, every single set of eyes turn to me.

Ignoring their attention, I keep my head down and find an empty desk toward the back of the room.

Once I'm settled, I risk looking up. My breath catches when I find Shane still standing in the doorway, forcing the students entering to squeeze past him. He nods his head. I know it's his way of asking if I'm okay. Forcing a smile onto my lips, I nod in return and after a few seconds, he turns to leave.

2

JAKE

"I don't see what the big deal is," Chelsea whines to her friends. "She's not even really that pretty. Look." I can't help but follow her finger as she points across the quad. My eyes find the tall blonde girl immediately. My lips press into a thin line and my blood boils. Feelings that I've fought for years to keep locked down threaten to bubble up.

Ripping my eyes away, I stare down at the bench below me. My heart races and my vision blurs. Suddenly, I'm a six-year-old boy again watching my world fall apart.

The girls continue bitching but I zone them out, too lost in my own turmoil to care about their pathetic opinions on the looks of the new girl. She won't fit in here. I'm going to make damn sure of it.

"I have no idea what they're chatting about. She is fine with a capital F," Mason, my best friend says, his stare still focused on the blonde everyone seems so fascinated with.

"She ain't all that."

"What the fuck is wrong with you? It's the first day of senior year, it doesn't get any better than this."

"If you say so. I'm outta here."

"Jake, hold up."

I ignore him and jump from the bench. I must only make it two steps when a gasp makes me look up. When I do, I watch as New Girl collides with Shane, one of our players. His hands grip onto her upper arms to steady her. The sight of him touching her, protecting her has fire erupting inside of me. Just looking at her makes me feel vulnerable, and that's not something I ever want to experience again.

"What's going on?" Mason and Ethan flank my sides and stare at the same car crash that I am.

"You calling her?" Ethan asks, following my stare.

Not having a fucking care in the world has resulted in one thing at least. My reputation. I do what the fuck I like, when I like and everyone around here knows it's best to just let me do my thing. That means not turning up to class, getting off my ass drunk, and most importantly, I get first pick of the girls. The others can have her once I'm done if they like, I don't care about passing them down once I'm done. But I never get sloppy seconds. Ever.

"She's off limits."

"I fucking knew you wanted her," Ethan mocks before I turn and fist his shirt. The blood drains from his face as he prepares for the hit he's expecting.

"I don't fucking want her. I'm saying she's off fucking limits. You got that?"

"Yeah-yeah. Off limits, got it."

"And make sure everyone fucking knows it. That bitch don't belong here and we're about to show her."

"Are we done here?" Mason asks. He's always been the slightly cooler headed one out of the three of us. He pulls my arm away from Ethan and steps between us, but not before a confused look passes between the two of them.

Staking claim on a girl isn't unusual, but what I just did. That shit isn't normal and without intending to, I just showed both of them a side of me that I don't want anyone to ever witness. Weakness.

"Are you sure everything's all right?" Mason asks once again when we fall into step in the direction of our first class.

"Yeah. Just feeling the pressure, I guess."

"This year's gonna be great."

Raising an eyebrow at him, I wait for him to explain how that's going to happen. Rosewood High's football team has never been all that. We have all the passion and dedication we need, but historically, it doesn't help all that much. Every year Coach gives the speech that this year is going to be the year but as of yet, we've never progressed more than a few games into the state playoffs. I can admit that our team is performing better than ever, but I don't want to set my hopes on anything epic.

For me, football's a release. A way to work out the tension and to forget about my bullshit life. I might give it my all, but I'm under no illusion that it's my life. Some of the guys have high hopes of getting scouted for college and I'm sure for a few of them it'll happen but I doubt we'll ever see their names on the NFL team sheets.

"Don't give me that look, Thorn. You know as well as I do that this is our year. With you in charge, there's no way we won't make it to the end."

I can't criticize his enthusiasm, that's for sure. It's just a shame I don't feel it. And *her* arrival sure isn't going to help matters.

3

AMALIE

Aside from the constant stares from the other students and crashing into Shane, my morning is pretty uneventful. Classes are... fine, and much to my relief, I get set homework in every single one. That should help keep my mind active once I get home. The last thing I want to do is dwell on what my life has become so the more I have to do the better.

I was desperate to start here as a senior and do just one year, but Principal Hartmann point blank refused and explained to my gran that I would have missed too much and it would make getting into college harder than it should be, so in the end I didn't have much choice. I'm stuck here for two years.

Other than graduating, my main goal is just to put my head down, get good grades and focus on the future. A future in which I get to call the shots, not social services, investigating police officers or financial advisors.

I follow the main flow of students as I step out into the hallway before lunch in the hope it'll lead me toward the cafeteria. It pays off and in only a few moments I'm standing in line waiting to see what delights I might get.

When it's my turn, the lady serving looks at me with raised eyebrows.

Glancing down at the food, nothing looks appealing. Nothing has since the moment I found the police standing at the other side of our front door, but I promised my gran I'd eat, so here I am.

"Whatever's meant to be the best," I mutter, my voice is hollow in a way I'm becoming all too used to.

"Sure thing, sweetheart. My burger and fries will turn your day right around." Her smile lights up her face and I do my best to reciprocate but it falls flat. I get the impression she wants to say more, but when she looks up to hand my food over and notices the waiting students behind me, she just smiles and calls, "Next."

Grabbing my tray, I turn and a shiver runs through me. Lifting my eyes, I find that I'm once again under the watchful eye of the group of guys from earlier, who I'm assuming are the football team and front and center is the guy with the piercing, blue, angry eyes.

My stomach knots as he once again narrows his eyes at me.

"Will you get out of the way," someone snaps behind me before my shoulder is shoved and a group of girls storm past me. I barely catch my tray before it slips from my hands and stand to the side.

When I look back toward the entrance where they were stood, I find it empty. But the tingling of my skin tells me that I'm still very much the focus of his hate-filled stare.

Looking around the cafeteria, I find all the groups of students I expect to find. The artistic ones still wearing shirts covered in paint, the nerdy ones, the shy girls sitting quietly in the corner, and then the group I think I need to be as far away from as possible. The 'it' crowd. The football players and the cheer squad who are crowded around a couple of benches like they own the place. Well, let's be honest, they pretty much do. I might not be able to see the crowns sitting atop their heads, but they are very much Rosewood royalty.

Spotting an empty table between the nerds and the shy girls, I head over, drop my tray down and fall onto the bench.

I'm not really sure what I expected to happen today. But this isn't really it. I've barely spoken to anyone aside from Shane all day and I already have a bunch of haters, one in particular, it seems.

I understand that they probably don't want a new girl coming in. Hell, I don't really want to be here as much as they don't want me to be, but I've got little choice. My life was ripped from under me and this is where I ended up.

"There you are. I'm soooo sorry about not finding you this morning, my car wouldn't start and my parents had already left. Nightmare. Anyway... how's it been?" Camila says, dropping down beside me and pulling a sandwich from her bag. Camila is the one and only person aside from Shane who's really given me the time of day since I arrived. She's one of Gran's friend's granddaughters that I was introduced to. She's great, a real sweetheart and I feel awful that I've been kind of forced on her. She must have friends that she'd rather be spending time with right now.

"It's been... fine." I poke a chip into some sauce on my plate, but I make no effort to eat any of it. I already feel a little sick, I'm not sure adding food will really help.

"Wow. That good."

"Cam. What are you... oh hey, *Amalie*," Shane says, coming to a stop at the edge of our table.

"You two have already met?" Camila asks, looking between the two of us.

"Yeah, we crashed into each other earlier."

"I'm really sorry about that." Embarrassment colours my cheeks.

"No need. I could think of worse people to crash into. It was my pleasure." The way his eyes assess me as he says this makes my heart drop. I really didn't think I gave him any kind of idea that I might have been interested, but I can see hope and excitement in his eyes. I know we only spoke briefly earlier, but I kinda thought we could be friends. I'm not interested in anything else.

"Are you coming to join the others?" he asks after I look back down at my plate.

"Maybe in a bit. I think today's already been a little overwhelming, right?"

"Something like that," I mutter. "You can go. I don't want to keep you from your friends."

"It's fine. I promised you I'd show you the ropes and I've already failed. Although, it sounds like you were in capable hands."

"Damn right," Shane says, falling down onto the seat opposite me. His stare burns into me but I keep my eyes down, not wanting to lead him on.

"So, what classes do you have this afternoon?"

4

JAKE

All morning the only thing I've been able to see is *her*. It doesn't matter how many times I tell myself that she's someone else entirely, it doesn't matter. The devastation and betrayal I remember all too well burns within me. I'm powerless to do anything but let it rage. By the time lunch rolls around, I'm just about ready to smash someone's face in.

"What the fuck's eating you?" Ethan asks the moment he falls into step beside me.

"Fuck you."

"I'd rather not."

My fists clench as I try to talk myself down from shoving him up against the wall and letting out some of my frustration.

I knew going to the cafeteria was a bad idea. I should have walked out of school and fucked off. But I didn't. Instead, I continue walking beside Ethan, the majority of the rest of the team joining us at some point until the scent of the crappy food filters down and the vast room opens before us.

My steps falter the moment I see her just about to turn away from the counter. I may only be able to see her back, but I know from the thick blonde hair hanging down her back that it's her. It's like a fucking red flashing beacon to me.

"Shit, sorry," someone mutters behind me, they're not looking where they're going and crash into my back.

My feet refuse to move. It's torture just looking at her but it's like my body is quite happy to send me to Hell and back and insists I wait for her to turn around so I can get another good look at her face. It's not like I need to, they look so similar and I'm never likely to forget the face of the woman who abandoned me without so much as a backward glance.

"Thorn?" someone asks behind me, clearly wondering why I've stopped dead in my tracks.

The second she looks up, her eyes find mine. She looks like a deer caught in headlights, the thought has the smallest of smiles twitching my lips. She should be scared. I have every intention of running her out of this place before she gets too settled.

This is my school. My life. I'll be damned if I'm going to spend what should be the best year of my time here being tormented by her.

It's not until someone bumps into her that she's forced to drag her scared eyes away from mine and I'm able to move. Taking a step, I walk toward our usual area as if nothing happened. When I sit and wait for the others to join, I notice that the majority don't realize anything just went down, but Mason and Ethan's stares both burn into me. They both know me better than anyone, better than my pathetic excuse for a family, so they know something's seriously adrift. I don't expect them to understand. Fuck, I don't really understand it but they're not keeping a huge part of themselves hidden away in their bottom drawer like she never existed. They have no real reason to appreciate how much New Girl looks like that ghost I try to hide.

————

Practice is exactly the kind of distraction I need, aside from my desire to plant my fist into Shane's smug fucking little face. I resist the urge, for now. As our team's quarterback and captain, they all look to me for my ability to make quick decisions and lead them to what might hopefully be a successful year. Of course I want that too. I want more than anything to have some kind of reason to celebrate, hell knows I haven't had many reasons to do so throughout my life. But one thing I have learned is that life is generally better if you're realistic, and I'm realistic enough to know that we probably won't be winning the state championships this year either. That doesn't mean I'm not going to fight like hell to try to make it happen.

Standing beside Coach, I feel like I belong, like I'm making a difference and I can't help my chest swelling with pride. This is what I need right now.

Coach has already warned us that he's hitting us hard this year and this practice session is no exception. Our first game might not be until Friday night, but he's going to make damn sure we're ready for it.

Standing under the spray of the shower once we've left the field, I allow the water to pound against my shoulders in the hope it might relieve some of the tension.

"What the hell is up with you and that new girl, Thorn?"

Panicking at the mention of her, I look up, but the showers are empty apart from Mason, whose eyes are drilling into mine as if he's going to read the answer within them.

"I just don't like her." I shrug, turning off the water and reaching for a towel.

"That's bullshit and you know it."

The sounds of his light footsteps right behind me tells me that this isn't over. I know that if anyone were to understand, it would be Mason, but that doesn't mean I'm willing to talk about it.

"Whatever. I don't have to explain myself to you."

"No, you don't. But as your best friend, I kinda hoped you would."

Guilt twists my stomach. He's had enough of his own shit going on recently and I've made him talk when he least wanted to, I should have seen this coming.

"I just... I don't like the look of her. She doesn't fit here."

"Beautiful and sexy doesn't fit here? Oh knock it off. You'd normally be all over that. You're going to have to try harder if you want to pull the wool over my eyes."

Ignoring him, I turn and start pulling my clothes on. I don't have time for this. I'd just about managed to forget about her blue eyes and blonde hair while we were out running plays but now they're right fucking there again.

"Come on, I'll buy you a burger. It might soften you up a little."

Flipping him off, I follow him out toward his car so we can head to our usual hangout, a diner on the shorefront.

5

AMALIE

"I was intending on going home and getting a head start on my homework," I say to Camila when she tries convincing me to go with her, Shane, and a couple of their other friends to a diner.

"I'm sorry, but that's not happening. I promised my gran that I'd help you settle in."

"Really, it's okay. I'll make sure she knows that you did as she asked. I don't want you to feel like you need to babysit me."

"Enough," she snaps but her eyes shine with amusement. Threading her arm through mine, she pulls me forward toward the car park. "I'm not taking no for an answer. Plus, one of Bill's milkshakes will make all your worries disappear."

I don't think that could possibly be true, but I'm up for testing it out. I really don't want to spend the next two years being the social outcast I've felt today. But I'm equally as unsure if I'm really up for socialising and pretending that everything is good with my life.

"Wow, this is like a home from home," I say, my voice tinged with sadness as I climb into Camila's Mini.

"She's awesome, right? Well, when she starts. Keep your fingers crossed." She winks before making a show of pushing the key into the ignition and turning the engine over. Breathing a sigh of relief when it rumbles to life, she looks over at me and laughs.

"Aces on the first day of senior year is tradition. Anyone who is anyone will be there."

I groan, not only am I a junior but there's a whole group of kids who really won't want me there.

"I'm really not sure about this."

"Did something happen today? Did anyone say anything about your parents or..." Quickly glancing over at me, her eyes narrow as she tries to figure me out.

"No, no one said anything. I barely spoke to anyone aside from you and Shane." I keep the hateful stares I received that I think might have been worse than someone saying something hurtful to myself. At least if he'd said something it might give me a clue what his problem is.

The car park is packed when we pull off the main road. There are kids loitering all along the seafront and spilling down onto the beach. Camila really wasn't kidding when she said everyone will be here.

"The guys already have a table for us. Noah skipped out on his last class to get it."

"Seriously?"

"Yeah. Being here this afternoon is a big deal. Ready?" She gives me a smile I attempt to match after she's reapplied her lip gloss in the visor mirror and fluffed up her hair a little. She jumps from the car and I rush to follow suit.

Some of the other kids who are loitering around turn toward us, but thanks to Camila's obscenely short skirt, I'm thankfully not the focus of their attention. I do cause a few whispers once the onlookers have had their fill of her legs.

"Oh, there they are."

I follow behind as she heads toward a table full of students I don't recognise. It's immediately obvious why this place is called Aces. It's all black, white, and red with playing card memorabilia everywhere. Shane spots us walking their way and smiles at me like we're long-lost friends.

"Amalie, good to see you." The enthusiasm in his voice is a little too much as he slides from the booth he's sitting in to allow me to join their group of friends. Camila takes the seat opposite me and cuddles up into Noah's side. I can't take my eyes off him as he gazes down at her and drops his lips to her temple. She looks up at him with such adoration and love that it makes my heart ache and a lump to form in my throat.

I'm soon distracted when a boisterous crowd comes stumbling through the entrance. My stomach drops when my eyes find *him*. His obvious hatred of my mere existence radiates from his every pore.

Once again, his steps slow as he stares at me. His lips set in a thin line, his eyes dark and haunted. As he continues staring, I can't help but feel like he's not really staring at me but through me, as if I'm a ghost he can't believe he's seeing. I don't know about him but I sure as shit haven't seen him before. I'm pretty sure I'd have remembered if I had because although his presence sends a tremor of fear through me, I can't deny that he's hot.

His dark hair is short at the sides then longer on the top, his haunting eyes that have studied me from afar today I can now see are royal blue, and his body. Well... let's just say that it's obvious he's part of the football team because he is cut. His white t-shirt is pulled tightly across his wide shoulders showing off his sculpted chest and flat abs. I'd put money on there being one seriously impressive six-pack under there.

Thoughts of a man's body has thoughts popping into my head that I'd rather not think about right now. I already feel vulnerable around all these strangers who already know too much about my life and how I ended up here, I don't need the past and the emotions it comes with making me even weaker. Especially while my skin's still prickling from his stare.

"What the hell?" Shane asks, looking between me and the guy. "Do you know him?"

"Nope. Never seen him before until this morning. He seems to have some kind of issue with me though."

Dragging my attention back to the people surrounding me, I see that everyone is looking between the two of us expectantly.

"You sure you don't know him?" Camila asks. "He seems pretty interested in you."

"I'm very sure. Who is he?"

"Who is he?" Alyssa, another of Camila's friends, repeats much like I would imagine she would if I'd just asked who Donald Trump was. "That is Jacob Thorn. Captain of the football team. King of Rosewood High and every girl's wet dream."

"Not *every* girl," Camila quickly adds, looking up at Noah like he just hung the moon.

Eventually his friends must get fed up with the hold up and they drag him off and over to the empty table at the other side of the diner. That doesn't mean I lose his attention. I might refuse to look over, but I feel his eyes on me. My skin heats and butterflies flutter in my belly at knowing he'd rather stare at me than have fun with his friends. I know it's because he clearly hates me but my traitorous body doesn't care right now.

"If I can teach you anything about Rosewood High, Amalie, it's to stay as far away as you can from *that* lot. They're nothing but trouble."

"You sound like your gran."

She shrugs, not in the least bit offended. "I'm serious. I have no idea what's going on with you two, but you'd be best to shake him off as soon as you can and forget him and any of the other football players exist."

"Hey," Shane complains. "We're not all bad guys." He nudges my shoulder to make sure I hear his words.

"Good to know." Although, I must admit that I'm more shocked than relieved. I guess he has the body to fit the image, but that doesn't explain why he's sitting here with the 'nobodies' when he could be over there with his team, living the high life.

"I don't know how you can put up with playing for those assholes."

"I don't play for them."

"Whatever," Camila says, waving him off like she's heard the same argument a million times.

Their conversation soon turns to the year ahead, what parties are meant to be happening and the pep rally on Friday before the first game of the season. They all look at me like I've got three heads when I ask them to explain what exactly a pep rally is. They seem to forget that I come from a completely different world.

Camila bounces in her seat as she runs through what I can expect followed by demanding that I'll be there because not attending is a sure-fire way to get myself on the 'bullied list.'

I refrain from explaining how I couldn't really give a crap about all that, but I figure that if I've got to spend two years here, then I might as well not paint a target on my back.

"Anyway, you've got to be there so you can attend what happens after."

"What happens after?" I ask with trepidation. The excitement dancing in her eyes makes me nervous.

"You'll have to wait to find out, but it's epic. The party of all parties. Plus, you'll get to do it twice. Not many people get that chance."

6

JAKE

Mason's words don't leave me the entire ride to Aces. He's right of course. She is beautiful and sexy, no one with a pair of fucking eyes could deny that. She's too beautiful. That's the fucking problem. Anyone with looks like that can only have evil on the inside. I've experienced it and it's not something I have any desire to repeat, which is why she needs to go. We don't need that kind of poison around here. We've already got enough assholes roaming the halls at Rosewood High.

The place is packed but I'm not concerned we won't find seats. The booths at the back are practically reserved for us. We own this place and Bill knows it. If it weren't for us and our reputation, then his place wouldn't be filled with kids day in and day out.

Holding my head high, I walk through the diner entrance with Mason and Ethan close behind. The entire fucking diner turns to look as we enter and for a fleeting moment, the buzz I usually get knowing that I own this fucking place starts to race through my veins. Then my gaze lands on a wide pair of blue eyes, the exact ones that have been haunting me all day, and that previous elation sinks. That bitch sucks every last bit out of me.

"Keep moving," Mason instructs, but I'm powerless. As I stare at her, one event from my past, that changed everything about my future, plays out in my mind like a fucking movie. My chest constricts and my lungs burn as I try to drag in the air I need. No matter how hard I will it to go, the image of her face as she walked away from me is right at the forefront of my mind. My bullshit excuse of a life is her fault, but sadly she's not here to experience the consequences of her actions. But *she* is.

As my vision starts to clear and New Girl comes back into focus, I notice a few subtle differences from the woman who ruined my life. But I can ignore them. What's more important is that I get to rid myself of the anger and desperation I've carried with me since that day.

I'm so lost that my entire body startles when a hand lands on my shoulder. "You're starting to make a scene."

"Let 'em fucking look." I don't give a fuck what everyone thinks right now. All I know is what I need, and I need to see her broken.

By the time I get to our booths, I've managed to pull on the mask I walk around wearing on a daily basis and it ensures that no one will question me. There are only a couple of people on this planet who've ever seen the real me, the pain and ugliness that festers inside me and I'll happily keep it that way.

Mason gives me a concerned smile before turning to the waitress and giving her our usual order. I can only hope he's right and that one of Bill's burgers will sort me out.

She's only been here for one day and already I'm a fucking mess. This situation needs resolving and fast.

The guys around me talk excitedly about our first game while the girls discuss their cheer routines for the pep rally. I couldn't really give a shit about either, I've got more important things to deal with.

"What's wrong, Jake? The stress of being a senior at last getting to you?" Chelsea purrs, her fake tan encrusted hand landing lightly between my pecs and descending over my abs.

Why I ever allowed myself to go there is beyond me. But it seems Chelsea thinks that just because I've fucked her that she has some kind of claim on me.

"I'm good, thanks," I state, gripping her wrist a little too tightly and removing her from my body.

"Ow," she complains, turning her giant eyes on me like seeing the tears in them will suddenly make me give a shit.

"Don't fucking touch me."

"Aw, come on. You weren't saying that—"

"Enough," I bark. Getting up from the booth, all eyes follow my movement. "I'm done here."

Sliding out, everyone's eyes follow me, but I pay them little attention. They might think I'm leaving to get away from Chelsea or what-the-fuck-ever, but in reality, I'm leaving because of a certain blonde. She was escorted out by Camila, but she's just shot back in for something, so now's my chance to introduce myself.

Shoving open the side door with more force than necessary, it slams back against the wall. The bang reverberates through me and pushes me forward. My skin's still prickling from Chelsea's touch and my muscles are still pulled tight from the memories *she* dragged up earlier.

I spot her instantly leaning up against the diner wall with her foot propped up against the brick.

Excitement and anticipation bubble up in my stomach as I watch her for a moment. It's clear she's got a lot on her mind as she stares off into the distance, but I couldn't give two fucks about her worries right now. Mine are the only thing I care about.

My fists clench and a deep line forms between my brows as I take a step toward her. She might not be the woman who ruined my life, but right now, she's the closest thing I've got.

7

AMALIE

The milkshake is almost as good as Camila promised, although I don't forget about my worries for even a second, not that I really expected to. My life is a clusterfuck right now and no amount of strawberry milk, ice cream or sprinkles is going to rectify that.

"Good, right?" Camila asks when she sees my eyes roll back the moment the sweetness hits my tongue.

"So good."

"I got you the extra special one seeing as today's kinda important."

My stomach drops and my eyes fly to hers thinking that she's going to spill the secret I've been holding in all day. It's not like it's been hard work or anything and it's also not like I have any inclination to celebrate.

She winks before turning back to her friends. They're trying to include me the best they can, but our worlds are so far apart that I think it's going to take more than a trip to a diner for me to start fitting in.

Pulling my phone from my pocket when it starts vibrating, I find my gran's name staring back at me. "Shit."

I thought you'd be home by now. Is everything okay? Do you need me to come and collect you?

She may have insisted she drive me to school this morning, but I was even more insistent that I take the bus home. I'm very aware of how much I've already changed her life in a matter of a few weeks, and something as simple as getting the school bus is an easy way for me to allow her to continue living her life.

I'm good. Home soon x

Thinking it's the perfect excuse to get away from this place and the pair of eyes that are still taunting me from across the diner.

"I'm sorry, but I need to make a move. Gran's waiting for me. Is there a bus I can get from here or should I just ring for a taxi?"

"Don't be silly. I'll take you."

"No, you said it yourself how important it is you're here. I'll be fine."

"I can come back. Just let me take you, it'll make me feel better." She stares at me, her kind eyes telling me that I've not got a choice until I cave, stand and slide from the booth.

I hear her tell the others where we're going before she starts following me out of the diner. I keep my eyes focused on the door, fighting the need to turn around and confirm that the tingles coursing through my body are courtesy of being under his intense stare once again.

"Shit, I'll be right back. Noah's got my damn cell. Wait there."

She rushes back inside leaving me a few minutes alone to try to make sense of everything buzzing around my head.

The sensation that I'm being watched settles over me, and my heart starts to race. Looking around, everyone seems to be busy doing their own thing. I'm just about to blow out the breath I was holding, feeling ridiculous for feeling vulnerable, when a shadow falls over me. I go to squeal, but hot fingers grasp my chin and I'm forced to meet the dark stare of the eyes that have been haunting me all day.

My body temperature picks up and my hands start to tremble. Fear licks at my insides as he stares at me with dark impenetrable eyes, the blue almost black.

I expect him to say something, but the silence seems to drag out for the longest time. Instead, his gaze flits over every inch of my face, almost as if he's committing me to memory.

When his eyes meet mine, once again my breath catches. I tell myself that nothing's about to happen. We're in a busy public place and Camila is coming back any second.

My chest heaves as his body heat prickles my skin. Lowering his head, his breath tickles across my ear and down my neck. My traitorous body reacts and covers my skin in goosebumps. Something I don't think he misses if his deep, unamused chuckle is anything to go by.

"You don't belong here, New Girl. I'd take this warning very seriously if I were you because I can make your life very, very hard."

I try to swallow but my throat is too dry. Just when I think he's going to add more or do something else, his grip on me releases and he steps back. My body sways in relief but it's only a second later I realise what happened.

"Amalie, are you okay?" Camila asks, walking around the corner with her phone in hand.

"Uh..." I hesitate, my breathing still erratic and my head spinning.

"I was just welcoming her to Rosewood."

She looks between the two of us briefly before pinning her stare on Jacob. I follow her eyes and take him in. His body's mostly relaxed but the hardness of his face tells me that the threat he just made was no joke.

"Whatever you say, Jake."

"Keep your nose out. I know Mason won't take too kindly to you sticking your nose in our business."

Shaking her head, she reaches for me and I allow her to wrap her warm hand around my forearm and pull me away from him.

His stare burns into my back as we walk away. I tell myself not to look back, but my head moves without instruction from my brain and I find myself locked in his stare once again. His lip curls up in an evil smirk and my stomach drops.

I knew starting over here wasn't going to be easy, but I never expected this... *him.*

"Are you sure everything's okay?" Camila asks once we're in the safety of her car. My breathing has almost returned to normal, but his angry eyes are still the only thing I can see and the skin on my chin is still burning where he held me in his tight grip.

"Y-yeah. Everything's fine." Glancing over at me, I can tell she doesn't believe a word of it, but she doesn't push me for more and I'm grateful. "Just promise me you'll stay away from Jake. He's not a good person."

I desperately want to ask more but I fear coming across a little too interested, so I mumble my agreement and keep my lips shut.

The drive is short and we're soon pulling up outside my gran's bungalow in a quiet part of town. I first thought I might be lonely surrounded by Gran and all her neighbour friends but the longer I've been here the more I like being able to hide. I think I'm only going to appreciate it more now that school's started.

"Thank you."

"Anytime. If you need anything, please call, yeah? I know how hard it is starting your life over, if you need an ear or a shoulder, I'm here. Okay?"

"Yeah, thank you, Camila. I really do appreciate it."

"You're welcome. Have a good night. Oh and... I know you don't want to celebrate but happy birthday."

A lump forms in my throat. I'd mostly been able to put what today represents to the back of my mind. I have no intention of celebrating without my parents, so I made Gran promise not to tell anyone and not to make a fuss. It seems she may have broken that if Camila knows.

I nod at her, unable to respond for fear of bursting into tears.

Standing on the driveway, I watch as she backs out and waves just before she leaves my sight. I think the two of us could be good friends. We seem to have plenty in common, we have similar kinds of personalities, I'm just not sure I have the energy to let anyone in. Especially as I don't really know what my future holds after two years here. At the moment, my heart is still set on returning to London, but I must admit that after being here a few weeks, I do quite like the sun and the sea. It makes everything feel a little more possible without the dirt and grime of the city I'm used to.

Sucking in a deep breath, I turn and take a step toward Gran's front door. I soon realise that my warning to forget about what today is has been totally ignored because the kitchen is full of balloons and banners.

"I know, I know, you don't want a fuss. But it's your eighteenth birthday, sweetheart. You'll regret allowing it to pass you by." Her eyes are full of love and hope, I don't have it in me to argue, so I allow my eyes to take in the sight before me and the giant number eighteen cake in the centre of the table and force my lips to smile. I walk over and wrap my arms around her thin shoulders. She might be getting older now, but she's no less beautiful. It's obvious where both Mum and I got our height and looks from.

"Thank you, Gran." I really hope it sounds sincere because I don't want her thinking that I don't appreciate all the effort she's put in since the day I moved in. I'm not sure being guardian to her teenage granddaughter was what she had planned for her retirement, but here I am.

"I made your favourite. Fish and chips. Go and freshen up and I'll finish it off. I even did the mushy peas like you talk about."

Thoughts of home have tears burning my throat. I swallow them down, give her another smile and turn toward my room.

I hate being upset in front of her. I know it's meant to be her job to look after me now, but I hate the shadows that fill her eyes and the slight tremble of her lips when she thinks about her daughter. The last words they said to each other weren't ideal, but it's now something Gran is going to have to live with.

Dropping my bag and books on the little desk Gran set up in my room, I fall down onto the bed and squeeze my eyes shut as I try to block everything out. It might work with some of the crap in my head but unfortunately it doesn't work for *him*, Jake Thorn. What the hell is his problem? I'm new, I get that. But his reaction today, his warning was a little over the top. The skin covering my jaw burns as I remember his harsh grip and the anger oozing from his eyes as they bore into mine. Pure unadulterated hatred poured from them.

8

JAKE

Slamming the door on Mason's truck, I storm toward the house, although there's no fucking way I'm actually going in there. I live around the back. Hidden in the shadows so that my aunt and uncle can pretend that I don't exist. That's fine by me. I'd rather be out here knowing they don't care than be inside their house seeing them treat their own kids like royalty. Why the fuck *she* thought this would be the best place for me when she fucked off, God only knows.

Sliding the key into the lock of my trailer, I slip inside and lock the door. I don't really need to worry about anyone coming to bother me. Every single person in that house ignores my existence. Well, everyone aside from Poppy, my eldest cousin. She's tried to make an effort time and time again, but I shoot down every attempt she makes. My aunt and uncle don't want me to have anything to do with their kids, it's in their eyes every time they see me so much as look at one of them. I've got nothing against Poppy, she's a junior at Rosewood and is a great kid, but for her own sake, I stay out of her way. I don't want to cause her trouble with her parents and as they've told me plenty of times, that's all I am, trouble.

Pulling my cigarettes and a lighter from my top drawer, I fall down onto my built-in couch and light one. Taking a drag, I allow it to burn my lungs as I watch the smoke fill the space around me.

I try to clear my mind, to focus on my movements and breaths but it's no fucking good. All I see is her, all I smell is her sweet scent. The moment I was nose to nose with her, her stark differences to the woman she reminds me of were obvious. Her hair was totally natural, not the peroxide I remember, her eyes are a slightly darker blue, and close up have flecks of green in them that only became brighter with her fear. She's got a smattering of freckles covering her round little nose and high cheekbones, and she had this cute little mole just above and to the left of her top lip. The hate that had been festering within me since my eyes landed on her first thing this morning suddenly morphed into something else, something I refuse to acknowledge because I need the anger. I've waited years to expel it and her similarities are enough for me. They're enough to allow me to believe I'm hurting the woman who hurt me more than should be possible.

Dropping the cigarette butt into an empty beer bottle, I immediately light another but I already know it's not going to be enough to clear my head, to make me forget.

When Mason found me fighting to catch my breath and leaning back against Aces back wall after she left, it only confirmed to him that something was seriously up with me. He'd been digging all day, but he should know me better than to expect me to spill all my problems. We've been friends for almost as long as I can remember, and I've never once told him all my secrets. I have every intention of taking those motherfuckers to the grave. No one needs to know the truth about how impossible I am to love and who my mother really is. A shudder runs through me at just the thought of my friends finding out. That would be the only thing that could possibly make my life worse right now. New Girl's arrival is one thing but the truth coming out.... No, that can't happen, and I'll do anything in my power to stop it.

Stuffing my second cigarette butt into the bottle, I fall back into the couch wishing I had something stronger here.

My cell buzzes in my pocket and when I pull it out, I wonder if Ethan can read my mind.

Parents gone out of town. Get your ass over here.

Dropping my cell to the cushion, I stand and start stripping out of my clothes as I make my way to the bathroom. I turn the shower on as hot as I can and step under the stream of water. Closing my eyes, I let it rain over me, hoping it'll wash everything away but the moment I close my eyes all I see are hers. The fear in them has my heart rate increasing and my cock swelling.

Wrapping my fist around my length, I fall back against the cold tiles and release some of the pressure built up inside of me. It barely takes the edge off of my restlessness, but until I can get my hands on what I'm hoping Ethan will have at his house, it's the best I can do.

As I walk past the main house, I take in the family sitting around the table together laughing and smiling as they eat their evening meal. The sight used to hurt, it used to be like a baseball bat to the chest, but as time went on and I learned to lock everything down, all I feel is pity. Pity that they can so easily cast me aside like I don't exist. They're just as bad as *her*. Just as selfish as *her*.

Just as I'm about to look away, Poppy glances over her shoulder. Her eyes lock on mine and a small, sad smile twitches at her lips.

Ripping my eyes away, I continue to the sidewalk and make my way toward Ethan's.

———

"How many of them do we need to give you before you start talking?" Mason asks, handing me another bottle.

Releasing the hit I was holding, I look over at him. The buzz from the joint Ethan handed me is mixing with the alcohol and giving me the release I was craving.

"When has that ever happened before?" They know me better than that. No amount of weed or alcohol will get me to unleash the ugliness I hold inside.

"It's gotta happen one day, Thorn." He sits back and tips his bottle to his lips, swallowing down the last of his beer.

A knock sounds out around the house and Ethan jumps up excitedly. He's by far the wealthiest of the three of us. Not that it's all that difficult to have more than me, the guy who lives in the hidden trailer and mostly lives on handouts from my friends or ramen noodles. It's not something I'm proud of, but it's my life nonetheless.

He runs from his den, leaving Mason and I slumped on his giant couches. The sound of excited girly chatter filters down from the front door and my stomach drops.

"He didn't say he'd invited them." Mason looks at me like I've just sprouted another head. "What?"

"Nothin'. It's just not like you to turn down any offer of pussy."

"Yeah, well. Maybe today's different."

"Fuck me, man. That girl's got you all tied up, hasn't she?"

"Girl?" I ask, trying to play it cool but when his response is just to roll his eyes, I know I haven't succeeded.

"Maybe Chelsea can distract you, help you chill the fuck out."

Just as he says that, she slides herself onto my lap and helps herself to my beer. "Who needs distracting?" Her voice is high and squeaky, and it makes my skin crawl.

None too gently, I push her from my lap and she lands on the polished tiled floor with a thud and a squeal. Slamming *my* beer bottle down on the coffee table, she turns to me, pushes her chest out and rests her hands on her hips.

"What the fuck, Jake?"

"You okay, Chelsea? It looks like you've had a little accident," Mason asks, nodding down to the wet patch on her micro skirt.

Her cheeks flame red and her eyes darken before she huffs out a breath and storms away.

"I'm gonna need more of these if she's planning on sticking around."

Mason fixes his stare on me but one look at my narrowed eyes and tense shoulders and he seals his mouth closed.

Looking out over Ethan's garden, I watch as some of the other girls strip down to their bikinis and jump into the pool. Ethan soon follows their lead and in minutes has two backed up into the corner. I shamelessly watch as he thrusts his tongue into one of their mouths quickly followed by the other. Normally I'd be doing the same, or better, dragging one off to one of the guest rooms. But I'm not interested. Tonight I want to sit in a dark corner surrounded by bottles of beer and a handful of joints.

9

AMALIE

By some miracle, I make it to the end of my first week at Rosewood High without too much drama. Jake has kept his distance. I've caught his piercing eyes across the hallway more than once, but he's never come any closer. I'm not sure how I feel about that. A huge part of me wants to think that his warning on Monday was just a joke, his sick way of welcoming the new girl. I was there though, it was my chin prickling under his hard grip, there wasn't anything jokey or light-hearted about the move. He meant every word he said to me outside the diner and although I try to push the concern down, I know he's waiting in the wings, planning his move. If only I could figure out what his issue is, then I might stand half a chance of seeing it coming.

"For this assignment, you're going to pair up. I want detailed research and then some kind of presentation, I don't mind what form that takes, use your creativity. We'll start them next Friday." There's chatter amongst my classmates as they start planning their new history assignment. "I'll be choosing the pairings," the teacher barks causing everyone around me to groan.

He starts rattling off names, I've no idea who they belong too but I sit back and watch either the happy or pissed off expressions appear on their faces as they accept who their partner is.

"Amalie," he says, meeting my eyes. "You're with Poppy."

A girl with dark hair and even darker eyes turns and offers me a soft smile. I relax slightly when at first sight she doesn't appear to be a wannabe cheerleader or football player groupie.

The teacher reels off the rest of the names on his list before instructing us to sit in our pairs and start planning.

"Hey, I'm Poppy," she says, dropping her bag to the floor and falling down into the now vacant seat beside me. "You're in my film studies class, right?"

"Maybe. Sorry, this week's been a little overwhelming."

"S'all good. Lucky for you, you just acquired an excellent partner for this project."

"Is that right?" I say with a laugh, realising that I like her already.

We make a start, but the bell goes before we make much progress.

"So I'll meet you after school Monday and you can come back to mine?"

"Sounds good to me."

"You at the pep rally tonight?"

"Apparently so."

"You sound really excited about it." She laughs and pulls her bag up over her shoulder before we start making our way toward the door.

"It's not really my kind of thing."

"Na, mine either but my cousin's on the team so I go to support him." I smile but the mention of family has my heart sinking into the pit of my stomach. "So I'll see you Monday?"

"Sure thing." I give her a wave as she heads off toward her next class and I turn to do the same.

———

"Today is draaaaging," Camila complains when she finds me hiding in the back corner of the library at lunch. "You know," she says, looking around at the dusty shelves, "I always thought unquestionable stuff happened at the back of libraries. You're kind of ruining that for me."

"Sorry to disappoint. I'm definitely not up to anything *unquestionable*." In reality, I'm surrounded by art books trying to come up with an idea for our history project.

"That's a shame. You could use some excitement. I bet Shane would be up for it."

"You've noticed that too, huh?" I drag my eyes from the book I was flicking through and look into Camila's knowing eyes.

"It's hard not to. He's practically followed you around like a lost puppy since you arrived. It's kind of cute."

"It might be if I were interested."

"He's hot, what's the issue?"

"I'm just not interested in a relationship. My life's a mess right now, I don't need a guy making it worse."

"I'm sure the right guy could make it better. Relieve some of that tension you're carrying around." I scoff at her, close the book and add it to the pile next to me. "Wait... you are single, right? Or have you got the whole long-distance phone sex thing going on with some British hottie?"

"No, no hot phone sex."

She picks up on the sadness in my tone that I was trying to hide. "But there was a guy, right?"

"Yes, no... I don't really know. We were just messing about, I guess. It wasn't anything serious."

"But it could have been?"

"Who knows," I say with a shrug. "Guess I'll never find out now."

"I'm sorry," Camila says, her eyes darkening as my sadness seeps into her. "Any news from the detectives?"

"Not that I know of. They promised to call if they found anything."

I've been trying to put the idea out of my mind that my parents' deaths might not have been an accident, it makes the whole thing worse to think someone on this planet wanted them gone. I blow out a breath, fighting the tears stinging my throat from filling my eyes.

"Fuck, I'm so sorry. Come on, let me buy you a piece of cake to make up for it."

"I'm okay here."

"Amalie, you need to stop hiding. Or if you refuse to stop then you at least need to tell me what's bothering you."

The image of his harsh eyes as he dished out his threat that's been haunting me all week pop into my head again, but I refuse to admit that he's sent me into hiding. I've endured the worst life can throw at me over the last couple of months, I refuse to admit that I'm scared, and the school's bad boy has me cowering like a wimp in the library.

"Nothing's bothering me. This week's just been a bit much is all."

"I can't even imagine how you're feeling and I'm not going to pretend I do. If I push you too hard, you need to tell me, but you only live once, Amalie. I might never have known your parents but I'm pretty sure they wouldn't want you hiding in here when you could be out there living."

My stomach twists and I fight to drag air into my lungs. The sudden wave of grief that hits me threatens to break me. But I'm stronger than that. I spent the first month of my time here locked in my room at Gran's, hiding from the world and drowning in grief. My life was good, it was settled and then what was meant to be just another trip to Milan for my parents ended in tragedy when their helicopter got into trouble and unexpectedly came down over some French countryside.

Squeezing my eyes shut, I focus on my breathing and will the panic attack I'm on the verge of away. No one needs to see that side of me.

"You're right," I announce once I'm feeling strong enough and jump to my feet. "Let's go and find that cake."

"I should warn you that the cafeteria cake will probably be dry and as hard as a rock."

"How bad can it really be? Cake is cake, right?"

"I'll let you be the judge of that." Camila threads her arm through mine and I somehow manage to walk out of the library with my head held high, with someone who's quickly turning into a very good friend beside me.

As we stand in line, she catches me up on her week so far and the dumb shit Noah's been up to.

With our cake in hand, I'm starting to feel like everything's going to be okay and that it might actually be possible to enjoy my time here, that is until I look up and lock eyes with him. My steps falter and Camila all but crashes into my back.

"Amalie, what's—oh!" I feel her stare flit between the two of us and when I manage to pull away from his tormented eyes and look back to her, her brows are drawn and her lips are pursed in anger. "What the fuck's his problem? Hold this." She shoves her plate at me and storms off in Jake's direction. Every single one of his friends turns to watch her journey, some are amused by the angry brunette marching his way, other's lust-filled eyes trail over her body, but it's one set of eyes in particular that catches my attention. Mason, the guy who seems to be Jake's right-hand man is staring daggers at her.

I'm busy wondering what the hell the story is there when she comes to a stop, places her hands on her hips and rants at Jake. Fair play to her because I can't imagine many students in this school would willingly go up against him.

Eventually, his lips curl up in an unamused smirk and he waves her off. She takes two steps back, her eyes not leaving his before she quickly glances at Mason, turns and storms back to me.

"That cake had better be bloody good."

"What did he say?" I ask, racing after her when she takes off for an empty table at the other end of the canteen.

"Just a load of bullshit. Didn't believe a word of it."

"Bullshit like what?"

She stares at me and chews on her bottom lip. "He really doesn't like you. But seriously, don't sweat it, he'll get over it."

I'm not sure whether her words are meant to be comforting or not, but they don't make me feel better in the slightest.

"Yeah, we'll see. So what about you?"

"What about me?" She keeps her expression blank, but the darkening of her eyes tells me she knows exactly what I'm talking about.

"Oh come off it. Mason looked at you like he wouldn't piss on you if you were on fire. I might not have known you all that long, but it's enough to know you wouldn't hurt a fly. What's his deal?"

"Our moms are best friends. We used to be, we're not now. That's about it?"

Lifting an eyebrow, I wait for her to elaborate but she just fixes me with a stare before totally changing the subject. "Are you looking forward to your first game?"

"Um..."

"It'll be awesome, you'll see." She gives me her megawatt smile, but it does little to kickstart any excitement.

10

AMALIE

Turns out that Camila's car is already packed with everything she's going to need tonight so when we pull up outside Gran's house after school, she climbs out and pulls her giant-ass bag from the back.

"Coming in, huh?"

"I'm not letting you out of my sight. You know as well as I do that given the chance you'll bail on tonight and I won't allow that to happen."

"Maybe." Her brow lifts. "Okay fine, probably."

"You need to let your hair down and that's what tonight is about. Just for a few hours you can let go and just be you, the eighteen-year-old high school student. Get drunk, have fun, maybe have a kiss...or two," she says with a cheeky wink.

I can't deny that just the thought of what she's proposing doesn't make it sound a little appealing. The fun and drinking part anyway, I have no intention of kissing anyone. That kind of thing will only lead to making my already messed up life more complicated.

"Come on then. I've no idea what I should be wearing to this thing."

"Sexy, Amalie. Always sexy."

Gran's on the phone as we walk through to the kitchen to grab something to drink. She smiles at me and it's so genuine that it makes tears burn the back of my throat. She's been desperate for me to integrate myself with life here and finally accept that this is my home now. She never said it out loud, but I think she was worried that I was going to jump straight on a plane the second I turned eighteen and could legally look after myself. Of course, I thought about it time and time again. It would be so easy to go back to London, crash at a friend's house. I might even be able to get myself into university, I've got enough money sitting in my account to make it possible. But do I want to go back and be alone? I might have only been here a few weeks really, but even that is enough to know that I need to be here. I tell myself it's for Gran, my presence lifts the dark shadows her daughter's death has clouded her eyes with, but I also know that being away from London and all the places that will remind me of them is helping me too. I've no idea how I'd be able to go back to my old life when they're not there. In reality, they weren't around all that much, the business took up the majority of their time, but they were only ever a phone call away, even if they were off in a different country.

"There are freshly baked cookies in the tin," Gran says, having hung up the phone.

Camila immediately turns toward the tin Gran nodded at, pulls the lid off and stuffs one in her mouth. "You're a legend, Peg."

Gran and I both laugh as she stuffs her face. "So, game night?"

"Apparently so."

"You'll love it. I used to live for game nights as a kid. The excitement, the thrill of the win, the hope of catching one of the player's eyes." She gets this faraway look and I can't help wondering what she was like as a young woman. She's always been in my life, and we visited quite a few times, but it's only now that I'm living under her roof that I'm really getting to know her.

"I do not want to get anywhere near a football player."

"Oh yeah?" Gran's eyebrows rise in interest and sadly Camila can't help herself.

"She's already got two under her spell, Peg." I groan, grab a couple of cookies and leave the room.

"Of course she has, she's her mother's daughter. She'll have them all tripping over themselves."

My stomach muscles clench at the thought of my mum and I race faster toward my room, afraid to hear any more. I know that Camila's only winding me up, but I don't need reminding of everything I'm trying to ignore at school. Shane's interest and more importantly, Jake's anger. I don't need either of them in my life right now and I'd rather Gran didn't get involved, because if I've learned anything about her it's that she's a hopeless romantic who will jump at the chance of helping to set me up.

"I'm sorry, I didn't mean to—" Camila says a few minutes later having followed me down to my room.

"It's fine. You don't need to apologise."

"Your gran made us hot chocolate. It's not quite the start to the evening I had in mind, but I'm not one to refuse chocolate." We're both silent as we sip from our steaming mugs. "I think he really likes you, you know."

Catching me off guard, I turn to her, my brows pinched together. "Who?"

"Shane," she says with a roll of her eyes, like she could be talking about anyone else.

"Oh, right. He's not really getting the idea that I'm not interested."

"Why not? He's hot. And I have it on good authority that he's pretty talented...if you know what I mean." She wiggles her fingers in the air and I groan.

"Magic fingers or not, I'm not interested."

She gives me a disappointed look. "That better not be because another member of the team—*the captain*—has captured your interest."

Fighting to swallow the chocolate in my mouth, my eyes widen to the point I think they might pop out. "Please tell me you're joking. He hates me, and I must say, the feeling's kinda mutual."

"So something *has* happened?"

Shit. Every time I've seen her after the incident at Aces she's questioned me. It was obvious that something happened in the few minutes she was gone but I still refuse to relay the events of those couple of horrible moments.

"No. Can we please not talk about him? He doesn't deserve our time or attention."

"I couldn't agree more." She puts her mug down and jumps from the bed. "Let's find you something to wear. I've been dying to get in your wardrobe." I watch as she pulls the doors open, and a smile splits her face. "OMG it's even more than I imagined."

"You can borrow anything. If it fits," I add because our body shapes are very different. While I've got my mother's supermodel body, Camila is a super sexy hourglass and a whole head shorter than me.

"You serious?" She turns to me, a smile almost splitting her face in two.

"Sure." I'm not stupid, I know the cost of what she's looking at is beyond most people's imagination but to me, they're just clothes. I was never that fascinated by the designer labels who used to give my mum free clothes just so she could be photographed in them. I always knew we had money, more than most, but it wasn't until I moved here that the differences became more noticeable.

There's plenty of money in this town, mostly on the east side but it's nothing compared to the people Mum and Dad used to spend time with. Money means nothing to me, I'd much rather have my family than anything in the bank, but that decision was taken from me. It's one of the reasons why anger fills my veins every time I see someone look at what I'm wearing with jealousy oozing from their eyes. Clothes and designer labels aren't anything to be jealous of, they come and go and mean nothing, family though, parents...you only get one lot of those and I'd give anything to have mine back.

Movement at the other side of my room drags me from my morose thoughts and I sit back and watch as Camila pulls out item after item from my collection while making all kinds of ohhs and ahhs. That is until she stops, pulls something out and then turns to me.

"You have to wear this tonight."

"We're going to a football game, Cam, not a club."

Her shoulders shrug. "So? You want to look hot, don't you?"

Not really. "I just want to blend into the crowd. Jeans and a t-shirt will be just fine."

She rolls her eyes but instead of arguing like I was expecting, her shoulders drop in disappointment. "I guess it doesn't really matter what you wear, you'll still look stunning." She drops the silver sequined dress she was holding up. It's the one my mum bought me to celebrate finishing sixth form, but I never got to wear it. I probably never will either now, but there's no way I could ever get rid of it. It was the last thing she chose for me on the last day out I ever spent with her.

"What are you talking about? You're stunning, I'd love to have your curves." I push down the emotions that dress dregs up and walk over to my wardrobe. "What about something like this?" I ask, pulling out a playsuit that would really show off her full cleavage and shapely legs. "I guarantee it'll make Noah's eyes pop out of his head."

"You think?"

"I do. Try it on."

"Okay. And you can totally wear whatever you want *but*—" I groan. "I'm doing your makeup."

"Deal."

An hour later and Camila is standing in my playsuit looking like a knockout while I've got on a black pair of jeans, trainers, and my favorite t-shirt. It's white with 'with pleasure' in a bubble font across the front. Camila has done an excellent job of my simple makeup and adding some loose curls into my blonde hair.

"Shane's gonna blow his load when he looks at you."

"Cam, please don't."

"What? I'm just saying that you're rocking that look. You're gonna turn heads tonight."

"I don't want to turn heads. I just want to blend."

"I know you do, but trust me when I say that you'll never blend into a crowd." A sigh passes my lips but I don't say anymore. "Are you packed for tonight?"

"Packed?"

"Yeah, for the midnight dash party."

"If it's just a party, why do I need to pack?"

"Oh, Amalie." She pulls out a Louis Vuitton bag from the top of my wardrobe. "It's not just a party. The Midnight Dash is a long-held tradition, a rite of passage, type thing. It's an all-night party at the end of the beach. It's a night where you can let go, blow off steam and act crazy before the seriousness of senior year really begins. Plus, what happens at the Midnight Dash stays at the Midnight Dash." Her eyebrows wiggle in excitement and my stomach drops.

"I'm not a senior."

"Maybe not, but you're coming as my special guest. We're gonna get drunk, dance and enjoy ourselves. Now hurry because the pep rally is gonna start soon and we don't want to be late."

She stands with her hands on her hips and an impatient look on her face as I stand from the bed.

"What do I need to pack?" I ask on a sigh.

"Normal camping shit."

"What does that entail?"

"You've never been camping?" She looks at me but doesn't give me time to answer. "I don't know why I'm even asking that, of course you haven't been camping!"

"What? I'm not some stuck up rich kid. I can camp."

"We'll find out tonight. Change of clothes, bikini, and a pillow should do it." Turning from her amused face, I start shoving stuff in my bag, "Oh don't forget wet wipes, they are essential. And condoms if you have any."

"What? I do not need—"

"Oh shhh... it's Midnight Dash, anything could happen...and it probably will."

Dread twists my stomach at the excitement in her eyes. "If tonight's going to basically be one big orgy, please tell me now so I can stay home."

"Now you're just being silly. Come on." She zips up my bag for me, threads her fingers through mine and pulls me from the room.

"You two look beautiful. All ready for your big night?"

"I am," Camila answers proudly before turning toward me. "This one's a little more skeptical."

"You'll be fine once you're there. Here, I got you this," Gran says pulling open a cupboard and revealing a bottle of vodka. "Now, I trust you both to be sensible with it, I do not want a phone call from anyone to come and rescue your drunk butts from the beach. But I want you both to have fun, *you*," her eyes find mine. "Deserve it."

I thank her, give her a kiss on the cheek and the two of us make our way to the car. Camila bounces with excitement while I desperately try to drum up some enthusiasm for anything but making a start on the bottle of vodka in my hand.

11

JAKE

The roar of the crowd as they celebrate our win with us vibrates through me. This is it. This moment is what I live for. Being part of something so huge that my bullshit life no longer matters. No one cares where I came from, how I live or about the anger that resonates inside. All anyone cares about in this moment is that I'm their king. I'm the reason they have something to celebrate. Every single football fan wants to be me right now and every single female set of eyes on me wants a piece. I fucking love it.

"You were on fucking fire tonight," Mason says slapping his hand down on my shoulder. He's not wrong. Everything about tonight just fell into place. All our well practiced plays were executed with the exact precision Coach expects and we ran rings around our opponents. For the first time ever, the guy's words about this year being our year start to sound a little more possible. This might only be the first game of the season, but it's a fucking good start.

"I need a motherfucking drink and a nice piece of ass. Who's with me?" Ethan shouts into the locker room and there are calls of agreement and hollers of excitement. We've all been looking forward to tonight since we were old enough to understand what a party was. The senior year dash pretty much sums up how your final year of high school's going to go. Don't attend, or even worse, not allowed to attend and you're basically an outcast. Turn up and kinda participate and you're accepted but turn up and do exactly what's expected of you and you're set for the year. Tonight's about proving yourself, proving you have what it takes to be a senior at Rosewood high. It's tradition and at fucking last, it's our turn.

"Get that junk good and clean, boys. The girls are gonna be fucking lining up for us when we arrive. But choose wisely my friends, choose very wisely." Laughing at Ethan's antics, I head for the shower and do exactly as he just suggested because I don't intend on spending tonight without getting my cock sucked at least once.

As planned, we're the last ones to the beach. The smoke from the bonfire bellows up, pointing us in the right direction, not that we didn't know where we were going. The second I push Mason's passenger door open the music from below fills my ears and my heart picks up pace. I'm so fucking ready for this. My first week of senior year has been... fucked up to say the least. The new girl's arrival stirred an anger within me that I thought I'd managed to rid myself of but it's back with a vengeance, taunting me, pushing me forward. I've stayed out of her way the past few days, but that doesn't mean I'm not watching her. I see her getting closer to Shane and the way he looks at her like she's something fucking special. I see her walking around like she's got all the world's fucking problems on her shoulders. Well guess what, princess? The rest of us have our own shit to deal with and in order to release some of what I'm carrying I'm about to make your life even worse.

"Let's do this shit." Pulling coolers from the trunk, I follow both Mason and Ethan down to the beach.

A cheer starts up the second we appear, and my chest swells with fucking pride. Most of the cheer squad immediately jump up and our teammates who got here first come running at us. Chelsea makes a beeline for me but unlike I have the rest of the week, I welcome her excitement.

Her hand goes straight for my cock, rubbing it through the fabric of my jeans like the desperate slut that she is. "You're getting lucky tonight." Her high-pitched breathy moan does little for me, but I can't deny that her stroking isn't feeling good right now.

Running her other hand up my chest, she sneaks it around the back of my neck and reaches up on her toes, it's like she thinks I'm going to kiss her. She should know better than that by now. I don't kiss. Ever.

Just as her lips move toward mine and I'm about to shove her away, a flash of blonde catches my eyes. She fucking wouldn't. Would she?

At the sight of her, my body freezes, fury erupts in my stomach as my veins fill with fire. Clenching my fists at my side, ready to march over there and demand she leaves. I don't see her movement until it's too late and Chelsea's full lips press against mine.

She must feel my stare because her eyes lift and immediately lock onto mine. They widen in surprise before darkening when they take in the hussy who's pressed up against my body. Chelsea moans as my cock gets harder under her touch, only it's not for her. I'm hard because of the excitement racing through my body, the excitement for the revenge and pain I'm going to cause.

Ethan, the fucker, hollers at me for getting lucky and unfortunately causes a scene that has every set of eyes turning our way. Ripping my eyes from *her,* I grasp Chelsea's upper arms and force her away from me. She pouts, sticking her bottom lip out like I should be sucking it back into my mouth. She looks up at me and her face pales. I know why, the tension that she's seeing has my entire body pulled tight. My need to storm over there and drag New Girl's sorry ass from the beach is all-consuming.

Mason must sense where my head's at because his hand lands on my shoulder, turning me away from the eyes of every other senior on the beach.

"Why the fuck is she here? She's not even a senior," I spit when what I really want to do is punch something or someone.

"No idea. I guess she was invited."

"Fucking Camila. You need to sort that bitch out." His eyes narrow at me, but he wisely keeps his fucking mouth shut. He might be my best friend, but I have no issues turning him into my punching bag right now.

"Let's go set up camp and get a beer... or five."

Handing me the tent and a few bags that he and Ethan must have grabbed from the car while I was lip-locked with Chelsea, I haul them up on my shoulder and march off toward our spot. The best spot on the fucking beach.

Chelsea skips off as if I didn't just kick her to the curb. Her perky ass and overly big tits bounce in her almost pointless bikini as she moves, almost every male set of eyes follow her movements. Breaking my eyes from her, I take in the rest of the girls. Most are showing off as much skin as possible in the hope of bagging their guy of choice tonight. Dash night is a free for all. All bets are off as you go after the one you want. Not only are a lot of relationships made on this night, but a lot are broken too. The guys are mostly sitting back right now, watching their prey, waiting for the right moment to pounce. Excitement begins to erupt in my stomach as I consider my options for tonight. The thing is, the guys down there might think they have the pick of the bunch, but the truth is, the only people to get that privilege are the team, everyone else gets our sloppy seconds. As my gaze falls over the girls and they start to notice, tits are pushed up, asses get stuck out a little more, none of which do it for me. They all know they're hot and they use it to get exactly what they want. No different to Chelsea.

"Fuck me. Them lot are well up for it," Ethan rumbles behind me. "How are we meant to choose?"

As he and Mason start debating their options, my eyes once again fall on one person. Unlike every other girl here, she's dressed in jeans and a fucking t-shirt. As if she's not already enough of an outcast, it seems that whoever invited her also didn't give her the memo about the dress code. A smile twitches at my lips. She may not be the one I'm going to spend the night with, but she's got a target on her head all right. She isn't going to make it until midnight. I'll make fucking sure of that.

It takes us no time to get the tents up and the beers flowing. "Who are you all tagging?" Mason asks. It's a tradition at any party that we announce our targets for the night. There's no reason other than for bragging rights the next day when we tapped our target.

"I propose different rules tonight, seeing as it's Dash and all."

"Go on," I say, tipping my bottle to my lips and downing the contents, waiting for Ethan to explain his plan.

"I propose we name a tag for each other. Then you've got until dawn to do the deed."

The guys' eyes light up at the dare-like suggestion. "Fuck yeah," someone slurs having had one too many beers already.

"Sure. Name 'em."

Ethan lays back on his elbows and gazes at the party going on slightly farther down the beach. The giant bonfire roars, bathing everyone in an orange hue and the music booms from the speakers someone's set up.

He starts rattling off names, the guys either beam in delight or groan at the epic challenge they have ahead of them. Me? I don't have any worries. Most of the girls down there would do just about anything to be able to say they spent the night with me.

"Mason, you can have Chelsea." A laugh erupts when I noticed the disgusted look on his face.

"Fuck off. I don't want his used cast-offs," Mason snaps, flicking his eyes to me.

"You won't be complaining when she's got her lips around your cock later." Chelsea may be many things, but I can't deny that she sucks good cock, and if she thinks I keep her around for any other reason, then she's got another thing coming.

"You're fucking serious, aren't you?"

"Okay I'll give you a choice." The others groan because they weren't given that option. Mason lifts his brow, waiting to hear what Ethan's got to say but by the look of the wicked smile on Ethan's lips, I don't think he's going to like what he's got to say. "Chelsea or..." I swear everyone holds their breath, no more so than Mason as we all wait. "Camila."

"Fuck you, asshole," Mason seethes. "I'll stick with Chelsea."

"Thought you might." Ethan laughs while Mason sulks and slugs him in the shoulder.

"S'all in good fun, bro."

"Don't fucking bro me." Mason drags himself up and storms toward the cooler for another beer.

"He grown a fucking pussy or what?" A few people laugh, but mostly Ethan's comment is ignored. "So that leaves you, cap." I keep my eyes on the crowd below, watching them laughing and dancing, that is until my eyes zero in on one couple dancing and my anger starts to boil over. Right in the damn middle is

Shane and he's dancing with *her*. It was obvious he was interested when he first saw her, but the way his hands are currently resting on her hips and the look in his eyes pisses me off. It should be common knowledge by now that she's off fucking limits. If anyone's going to put their hands on her, it's going to be me.

My growl of frustration comes out louder than I was anticipating, and Ethan turns to me before looking back out at the crowd.

"Thorn," he practically sings he's so fucking excited and if I weren't so distracted by the sight in front of me then I might see his next words coming. "Because you're an overachiever, you get two. Shelly," he says, nodding toward where she's downing shots with Chelsea. I turn to him, his eyes dark and mischievous. "Amalie."

I'm just about to ask who the fuck that is when it dawns. My eyes find her in the crowd but this time she's not just dancing with Shane because as her hips move against his, she's staring right at me.

"Game on, asshole. Game. On."

12

AMALIE

As the alcohol starts to take effect, I realise that this probably isn't the worst idea I've ever had. It's been forever since I've had a night where I've been able to truly forget everything and just be me. Camila was right to drag me here.

I smile up at Shane as we dance together, still not all that happy about the lust I find in his green depths. I've no intention of leading him to think anything will happen between us, but my body can't help but roll with his in time with the music.

The panic that consumed me the moment I first locked eyes on Jake when he arrived has almost been replaced with enjoyment, which is a strange feeling after all this time.

The song changes and Shane spins me around so my back is to his front. The moment I look up I find him once again. His group has set up camp slightly up the beach so they can look down on us peasants like they own the place.

His eyes narrow and drop to where Shane's holding my hips and pulling my body so it's flush against him. Fire burns in their depths and my heart starts to pound. I'm not welcome at this party, that much was obvious when he first arrived. I'm surprised I've lasted this long, but looking at the disdain on his face right now, I fear my time might be up.

"I need to get a drink," I say, resting my head back against Shane's shoulder. Disappointment is written all over his face, which just proves that I need to put some space between us. Letting loose and having fun is one thing, but he's a sweet guy and I don't want to make him think this is more than it's ever going to be.

"I need to pee."

"Do you need me to hold your hand or something?" Camila asks with a laugh where she's dry humping Noah, her eyes bright with the alcohol she's consumed.

"No, but where are the toilets?"

"This is the beach. There aren't any."

"So where do we..."

"Just go into the trees and do your thing."

"The trees?" I glance up at where the beach ends and the greenery starts.

"This really is a different world for you, isn't it?"

I don't get a chance to say anything because Noah pulls her attention back to him and shoves his tongue in her mouth.

Shaking my head, I walk past the other kids who are too busy enjoying themselves to look up at me.

The second I step into the trees, darkness surrounds me. Pulling my phone from my back pocket, I put the torch on and use it to guide my way deeper into the undergrowth. It might be a little extreme but the last thing I need is someone stumbling across me mid-pee.

Once I'm confident I've left all the partygoers behind, I find a spot behind a tree and do my thing.

It's not until I'm fighting my way back toward the beach that a noise, or more a moan, stops me in my tracks.

Knowing that I need to get away from here before I look like a right creep, I continue forward but before I find the beach, I stumble across the owner of the moan.

A loud snap sounds out as I stand on a stick and his eyes snap to me. The anger I'm used to seeing is there, but it's been overtaken by desire. His full lips are slightly parted and his bare chest is heaving. When I lower my eyes more, I find a blonde on her knees with her head bobbing back and forth while his phone is in his hand like he's filming the event.

My stomach twists in panic. I really don't need to be standing here right now. "I'm so sorry," I whisper going to step away but he's clearly not thinking the same thing because as I move, he barks, "Stop."

Without instruction from my brain, my legs freeze but I keep my eyes downcast, not wanting to intrude on what should be a private moment.

The movement I can see out of the corner of my eyes tells me that the girl hasn't stopped. *She must be enjoying herself more than him right now,* I think and I have an internal battle about what to do. I should run, that would be the easiest thing to do but there's something about his commanding voice that forces me to stay stock still and wait to find out what he wants.

"Look at me."

Hesitantly, my eyes lift until I find his tormented stare. He pins me to the spot with his hate-filled eyes, and while my brain screams at me to move, to run, to do something. My body stays exactly where it is, fascinated, as pleasure washes over his face. His eyes narrow and darken further, if that's possible, his chin drops and the most erotic sound I've ever heard falls from his lips.

My teeth sink into my bottom lip as I watch the show. I'm more interested in watching than I should be. The heat coursing through my veins angers me because the guy I'm currently watching like he's the most fascinating thing on the planet hates my guts. But I can't not watch now I've got this far.

With his hand in the girl's hair, he pulls her back until she hits the floor. I wince but she doesn't seem too bothered. By the time he turns to me, he's tucked himself back into his pants and any pleasure that was on his face is long gone. It's hard once again with the muscle in his jaw twitching in anger.

"Enjoy that, did you? Watching me get my cock sucked. Hopefully it gave you some pointers because you're next. Although, I doubt you need any lessons, girls as beautiful as you are always at home being on your knees."

"Fuck you," I spit, taking a step back as he gets in my personal space.

"You'd be so fucking lucky. I don't fuck whores."

My breath catches at the same time my back bumps up against a tree. "Don't talk to me like you know anything about me. You don't."

"I know all too well how women like you operate, what you do to get what you want. It disgusts me and I intend on proving it." His body moves closer still and I press back into the tree. My heart thunders in my chest, fear making my hands tremble but I refuse to back down to this arsehole. He's no idea what the fuck he's talking about. "I intend to show the entire fucking school what an untrustworthy whore you really are."

"What the fuck is your problem? I haven't done anything."

"Not yet, you haven't. But you will. Girls like you always show their true selves eventually."

"I don't—"

Leaning forward, his chest brushes my breasts and my breath catches at the sensation. "See, you're doing it right now." He moves his chest again and my nipples pucker with the friction. "You'd do anything right now to get your way. Your body is craving it."

"Fuck you." My hand comes out to slap him, but he catches it, his hot fingers circling my wrist so tightly I swear it'll leave a mark.

His fingers grip my chin, making my lips pout. His hate-filled eyes bore into mine before they drop to my lips. His tongue sneaks across his bottom one like he's considering his next move. My heart continues to thunder so hard in my chest that my head starts to feel a little fuzzy.

Moving to the side he leans in, his hot breath tickles around my ear. "No, but I am going to break you. Show you exactly what you are."

The second the final word is out of his mouth, he releases me and steps back into the shadows. I don't waste any time and run in the direction of the beach.

My lungs are burning for air and my legs are shaking by the time I step foot onto the sand, but instead of the escape I was hoping for, I run straight into a solid wall.

A large pair of hands land on my waist to steady me but I fight to get away thinking he beat me out of the trees.

"Amalie, it's okay." The voice is unfamiliar yet kind, it has the desired effect because I stop fighting. That is until I look up and find Jake's right-hand man, Mason. Then I pull myself from his hands and take a giant step back. "Are you okay?" It looks like genuine concern on his face but seeing as he's friends with the arsehole I just left behind I highly doubt he actually cares.

"I'm good. Thanks." My voice is hard and cold and his eyes narrow.

"Did something happen in there?"

"No, nothing. I just went to pee."

A smile twitches at his lips. "Why didn't you just use the toilets?"

"The toilets?" I whisper. "But Camila said..." I trail off when his entire face twists as if he's in pain.

"It was a joke," her slightly slurred voice comes from behind him.

"Oh."

"Amalie, please tell me you didn't actually—" Her words falter when she spots Mason standing next to me. "What have you said to her?" she barks.

"Me? I haven't done anything. I wasn't the one who sent her into the trees to use the bathroom."

"I thought she knew I was joking. We parked next to the restrooms."

"Well, she didn't." Mason steps toward Camila, I could cut the tension between them with a knife as they stare at each other, both refusing to back down.

That is until someone else appears from the trees. We all look over as Jake walks out from the darkness with his usual swagger and general aura of hate surrounding him. Both Camila and Mason look between him and me. I can practically hear their thoughts running at a mile a minute in their heads.

Jake ignores both of them and walks over to me. His eyes run the length of my body before his hand slides into my hair and his rough cheek rubs against mine. "Watch your back, Brit." To our spectators, it might look an intimate move, but the reality of the situation is so very different.

He pulls back almost immediately, winks at me and starts walking backward, not taking his eyes off my body until he's forced to look where he's going. I know the moment his eyes are off me because the tingles that were following his gaze instantly vanish. I tell myself that it's the burning hate coming from him that causes it, but after having his hot and hard body pressed up against mine, I know it might not be the case. Jake Thorn might be a bastard, but he's a bloody beautiful one at that, and all my body sees is his hot one.

"What the hell was that?" Camila asks, Mason is too busy studying my reaction to say anything.

"It was... nothing."

"Nothing? What the hell happened in there?"

"Nothing happened in there. I just went for a pee, that's all. If you'd told me where the toilets were in the first place, then I wouldn't have been in there."

"I'm sorry. I thought you knew I was joking." Camila looks horrified that I actually listened to her and went in there, but really, why wouldn't I believe her? She'd not given me any reason to think it would be a joke.

"I need a drink." Storming through both of them, I march back toward the party and grab two bottles of beer from a cool box.

I've almost downed the first one when I feel her presence behind me. "Amalie, I'm so sorry. I didn't really think you'd... I thought you'd seen the restrooms."

"It's fine, honestly. None of that was your fault."

"What happened?"

"Five minutes!" someone calls from the other side of the group and cheers erupt from the crowd but at no point does Camila take her eyes from mine.

"Are you two ready?" Noah asks. When I look up, I find Shane at his side, his eyes alight with excitement and probably a little too much alcohol.

"Ready for what?"

"You're gonna love it." Camila practically bounces on the balls of her feet. I truly hope it's more enjoyable than her last 'surprise'.

13

JAKE

The second I saw the fear in her eyes when she found us, I almost came down Shelly's throat. Her appearance at that moment couldn't have been more perfect if I'd planned it myself.

My cock twitches in my jeans as I think about the way her eyes dropped down to my chest and ran over my abs. She might hate me after what I've done to her, but fuck if she didn't wish she was Shelly in that moment. And fuck if I didn't want that too. The thought of it being her throat I was punishing makes my cock weep with excitement. I may want to end her, but shit if I don't want to enjoy the ride, and the ride will certainly lead to her being on her knees, I can guaran-fucking-tee that.

The sweet scent of her perfume mixed with the fear in her eyes was exactly what I needed to feed the fury that fills my veins every time I look at her and remember what she represents. Weak, beautiful women who'll use what God gave them to get whatever they want no matter who they trample or abandon in the process.

My fists clench with my need to have her sinful, slender body pressed up against mine again so I can show her that her allure won't get her anywhere around here. *You're falling into her trap,* a little voice inside me shouts but I drown it with another swig of beer. I'm not falling into anything, I'm teaching the bitch a lesson. I'm getting vengeance for what another version of her did to me years ago.

"What the hell?" Mason asks, dropping down beside me.

"What?"

"Don't play fucking dumb with me. What the hell happened with Amalie in the trees?"

"What do you think happened? And for the record, she sucks like a fucking vacuum cleaner."

His eyes narrow and his teeth grind. "You're talking shit, she's not one of them." He waves his hands toward most of the cheer team who drop their panties for a look alone. "There's no way she did that willingly."

"Who said she was willing?"

"What the fuck is wrong with you right now? This isn't you, bro."

"This is me doing what needs to be done."

"We've been friends since we were in diapers, Jake. If you think for one minute that I can't see what's going on here, that I can't see exactly what you see when you look at her, then you're a fucking idiot. Your issues have nothing to do with her, she's not the one you need to punish for how your life turned out. She's going through enough shit of her own right now, the last thing she needs is you on her case. Now back the fuck off."

Standing, needing to do something to shake the tension taking over my body, I stare down at him.

"The fuck, Mase?" My muscles lock up as I fight the need to wipe the warning he's giving me right off his fucking face. Best friend or not, he's no right saying that kind of shit to me. Climbing from the sand, he stares me right in the eyes, taunting me.

"Go on, hit me. Take your anger out on me, better that than her."

"Why the fuck are you standing up for her?"

"Because she's done nothing other than have her own life ripped out from under her. Don't pretend like you don't know exactly what happened to her parents. You really think she needs you on her case just because she unfortunately looks a little like—"

"Don't say it. Don't fucking say it." I'm right in his face, our noses only a breath apart. One punch from me and the pussy would be down like a stone and he knows it, but yet he still stands toe to toe with me defending her.

My chest heaves, my hands clench but somehow I manage to keep them at my sides. "How was Camila?" I ask through gritted teeth remembering them stood together.

"Fuck you."

"Na, you're all right. I might go and find her though, I bet she needs a good pounding because that fucker she's with clearly isn't capable."

I don't see his fist coming but I sure as shit feel it as it slams into my jaw. I knew mentioning Camila would get him just as riled up as me.

"Don't you dare go anywhere fucking near her."

"Or what?"

His fist hits me again, but at no point do I retaliate. I need this. I need the pain.

"What the fuck?" Ethan shouts, pulling Mason off me.

"It's nothin'," I mutter, spitting out the blood that's filling my mouth from the split that's stinging my lip.

"Don't look like fucking nothin'." His stare flits between the two of us, making sure we're not going to get straight back to it the second he steps away.

Mason shrugs before inspecting his knuckles and walking off in favor of finding more beer. I knew mentioning Camila was an asshole move. But what can I say? I'm an asshole.

"How's it going with your girls?" Ethan asks after we both watch Mason walk away.

"Done."

"Both of them?"

"Both of them," I confirm.

"Wow, I thought Amalie was going to be a challenge too big, even for you, hotshot."

"What can I say? The girls just can't resist."

"You're fucking deluded."

"Don't give a fuck. I got some. Did you?"

"I'm still working on it." After he dished out all the names for us, Rich, another guy on the team gave Ethan an almost impossible challenge with his girl. There's no way he's getting any from her tonight.

"You ready? It's nearly time."

"Always ready."

Ethan chuckles and we both stick our beers in the sand, getting ready to move.

Someone shouts the signal and every single body on the beach starts moving. Clothes are thrown in all directions, some more than others depending on how brave they are and they start moving for the sea.

Dropping my jeans, I keep one hand over my junk as I continue watching the students lower down the beach. My eyes find her almost instantly, not that it's hard with her platinum blonde hair. I can't tear my gaze away as she watches what everyone's doing around her before gripping the bottom of her t-shirt and peeling it up her slim body. Even from here I can tell that her pale skin is as flawless as I expected it to be. Her small, pert breasts are covered in two small black triangles of fabric that tie behind her neck and back. My fingers twitch with how easy it would be to remove it from her body. Flicking the button on her jeans, she pushes them down her legs, bending over slightly to free her feet, the sight of her barely covered ass has my cock threatening to go full mast. Needing a distraction before my need is obvious to those around me, I follow their lead and take off running.

Midnight Dash is a test of bravery and courage. Those who want to prove themselves strip down to nothing and run full pelt into the sea. As expected, most of the guys drop everything whereas it's mostly just Chelsea and her slutty friends who bare all and flaunt everything they've got like shameless hussies.

Sadly, the water's not cold enough to cool off the image of her ass that's still burned into my head.

"Holy fucking shit," someone squeals behind me as water gets splashed and people laugh and mess about.

I stand waist high in water and watch their antics suddenly feeling totally deflated about tonight and the year ahead.

"This is fucking stupid," I mutter to Mason when he comes near.

"Right? Wanna go grab a beer?"

"I've got a better idea."

He eyes me nervously but being the loyal best friend that he is, he nods and follows me from the water, leaving the rest of our class behind to enjoy themselves.

14

AMALIE

"Where the hell's our tent?" Camila complains once we've made our way back to dry off.

The space next to the boy's tent where we pitched ours is completely empty. "He wouldn't, would he?" I don't mean for the words to be said aloud but I realise they are when Camila, Noah, and Shane all turn to me.

"Who?" Camila asks but by the narrowing of her eyes toward the football team I know she doesn't really need me to answer the question. "I'm gonna fucking kill them." She strides off toward where they're all sitting around drinking, mostly with the cheer team on their laps.

"Babe, wait," Noah says in a rush, grabbing her arm and pulling her back. "You going over there and making a scene is exactly what they want. Don't feed the animals."

"But they have all our stuff, our clothes, our underwear."

Noah's teeth grind but he doesn't release his hold on his girlfriend. Leaning into her, he whispers in her ear quiet enough that I can't make out the words. When he pulls back, she stares at him for a few seconds, a silent argument passing between the two of them but eventually, her shoulders sag and she says, "Fine. But I will make them pay for this."

"Here," Shane says, handing me his towel so I can dry off. I hesitate to take it, aware that I don't want him to think there's more to this but in reality, I've not got many options right now. "You guys can crash in with us. It's a four-berth, they'll be plenty of space." The excitement that shines in Shane's eyes makes my stomach twist with dread. I really don't want to hurt him, he seems like one of the good guys, despite his involvement with the football team.

"I think maybe I should just go home."

"What? No. Noah's right, that would mean they win and I'm not losing to those assholes."

"I get it, Camila, I do. But you don't need to fight this battle with me. I can just go, and you can continue like I was never here bringing this kinda drama into your lives."

"You about finished?" She stands toe to toe with me, her hands on her hips, her head tipped back so she can look into my eyes. "You're not going anywhere. I invited you because I wanted you here, *we* want you here. Fuck them and their childish games. Let's show them you're made of stronger stuff than that. I know you've got it in you because you wouldn't be here right now if you weren't."

She's right, I know she is, but that doesn't stop me wanting to run home and hide under my duvet from the arsehole that's trying to ruin my life more than it already is.

"Come on, have a drink and let's try to enjoy the rest of the night," Noah encourages, handing Camila one of his t-shirts.

When I turn to look at Shane, he's also holding out a shirt for me to wear. I take it from him, grateful I don't have to spend the night in only my bikini, but I question my decision to put it on when I realise it's his football jersey with his number on the back. I may not know all that much about American high schools yet but one thing I do know is that giving a girl your number is a big thing.

"Don't you have anything else?"

"That's my only clean one."

After a few seconds of staring at him and a little encouragement from Camila, I slip it over my head, feeling better about myself almost immediately having some skin covered. My string bikini might be massive in comparison to what some of the other girls are or aren't wearing, but it doesn't mean I'm comfortable having that much of my skin on show. I might have grown up in the fashion industry and around models who are more than happy to pose in next to nothing, but that's not me. I'd much rather be hiding behind the camera with my dad, than front and center of the attention with my mum.

With Shane's giant number ninety-nine on my back, I settle myself on the sand with the others and accept a bottle of beer when it's handed to me.

I didn't have any expectations for what tonight was going to be like. Hell, I had no idea what was going to happen seeing as Camila kept the details a secret from me in her attempt to build my excitement, but I can honestly say I didn't expect any of it.

As I look around at the students still splashing about in the sea, the ones who have coupled up and are rolling around in the sand, and then the separate party that the football team seems to be having higher up the beach, I wonder how this became my life.

Even though it happened to me, it's still hard to believe that your life can change in the blink of an eye. The friends I thought I had in London that would be my friends for life are mostly now gone. Even Laurence, the guy I thought I might have had a future with hasn't been in touch for weeks. While I'm here starting a new life, they're all embarking on theirs at their chosen universities and moving on...without me. It stings that we've already lost touch but really, I didn't expect it any other way. I can only hope that the guys I'm surrounded by now might be a little more loyal, or at least stick around long enough to help me through the next few months as I settle in and hopefully find my place. If they don't and whatever this thing is with Jake gets too much, then I'm not sure what my future might look like.

I've always been the kind of person to look forward and see the positive in things, but as I sit here wondering, I can't help thinking for the first time in my life that going backward is a serious possibility.

"Hey," Camila says, lightly elbowing me in the arm to drag me from my thoughts. "Everything okay?"

"Sure."

"I really am sorry about earlier. The joke kinda backfired on me."

"It's fine." It already feels like it happened a lifetime ago.

"Here, have a drink and come dance with me, this is meant to be a party."

Taking the plastic cup from her hand, I swallow it down in one and allow her to pull me from the sand. We make our way to the makeshift dancefloor, Noah and Shane hot on our tails.

A shiver runs through me as I turn to start dancing and when I flick a look over my shoulder, I find exactly what I'm expecting. His eyes on me.

Ignoring him, I turn back toward my new friends, plaster a smile on my face and attempt to do exactly what I should be doing, enjoying myself.

15

JAKE

It seemed like a good idea in my head but now that I'm sitting here watching her wearing his fucking number, I realize that I've screwed up.

Something possessive that I don't want to identify sits uncomfortably in my stomach and causes my muscles to bunch. The need to go and rip that fucking bit of fabric from her slender body is all-consuming. My fingers wrap around the bottle in my hands with an almost painful force.

"What the hell is wro—" Mason follows my line of sight. "Oh."

"Yes, fucking oh."

"I told you it was a bad idea."

"I expected them to lose their shit not just continue like they don't care."

"You can never predict girls, bro. You should have learned that by now." My teeth grind, I can usually predict girls like Chelsea and Shelly perfectly, they almost always do what I expect. But the new girl, she's different. Yes, there's fear in her eyes every time I get too close, but she doesn't back down. She's not afraid to go toe to toe with me and fight for what she believes is right.

Maybe she is right, a little voice in my head says. So what she looks just like the bitch who abandoned me, that doesn't mean she's anything like her.

Downing the beer in my hands, I reach for another, needing to drown out stupid ass thoughts like that. The hatred and anger has been festering inside me for years, now isn't the time to start questioning my intentions. The frustration I'm feeling needs to drive me forward, not turn me into a fucking pussy.

"You were right about Chelsea," he says, dropping beside me.

"Oh yeah?"

"Like a fucking vacuum cleaner."

Throwing my head back, I laugh at the shocked look on his face. "I told you it was good."

"I think she might have ruined blow jobs for me. No one else is ever going to compare to that."

"So what you saying? You gonna tie the bitch down?"

"What after she's had half the school's cocks in her mouth? Na, I'm good thanks. I need to figure out a way to find a good girl who can suck like that."

Shaking my head at his noble intentions to find himself a nice little girlfriend, I refrain from pointing out that he'll probably need to stop acting like such a dog before that happens. All the good girls are going to turn their noses up just like he is at Chelsea.

"You didn't really get her on her knees in the trees earlier, did you?" He nods toward where she's still dancing with Shane and my heart squeezes painfully in my chest.

"I'm not one to kiss and tell, Mase."

"Only because you don't kiss 'em but you always get sucked and tell."

Shrugging, I cast my eyes over the others, looking for some girls to watch who don't make me want to murder anyone. "Nothing to tell. She sucked, I came. Dare done."

"Bullshit. She wouldn't touch you with a ten-foot barge pole after the way you've treated her. And to be honest, I don't blame her."

"I don't need your opinion about this. Surely you've got enough of your own issues to be worrying about what I'm doing. After all, your girl's sucking *his* cock tonight instead of yours."

"She's not my fucking girl."

"Exactly, and that's the whole problem, isn't it?" He blows out a calming breath. It should be enough to stop me baiting him, but I'm in full-on asshole mode tonight. "I don't even know what you see in her. She's nothing special."

He turns his murderous eyes to me, they're almost black with his anger. For a second I think he's going to come at me again. But at the last minute, he throws his beer bottle down the beach and climbs to his feet.

"Fuck you, Jake. Fuck. You. When this all blows up in your face don't come crawling to me."

He storms off, going to join some of the other guys in the team. My eyes narrow on the Rosewood Bears jersey below me, and fury fills my veins. All of this is her fault. My life was...fine before she showed her face. Now I can't escape the anger of my past like I was once able to and my best friend since childhood just turned his back on me.

All. Her. Fault.

And I'm going to make sure she fucking well knows it.

16

AMALIE

The bright dawn sunlight filters through the thin fabric of the tent and when I come to, I realise that I'm hot and seriously uncomfortable. Trying to move, I soon figure out why that is. Shane is wrapped around me like a freaking snake, his arm hanging over my ribs, the weight causing an ache through my chest. The ground we're on, after giving up the air mattress to Camila and Noah is solid and I've got a lump of sand pressing into my hip.

Trying my best to slide from his hold, my arse rubs against his crotch. A low moan rumbles up his throat, his length grows against me and his arm tightens. I panic. There's no way I want him waking up and discovering we're in this position. Every time I look at him, his eyes darken with desire that has my stomach knotting for all the wrong reasons. The last thing I need is for him to think I wanted this.

Once I think he's fallen back asleep, I try moving again. He had much more to drink than me last night, almost everyone did. I was more concerned with keeping alert in case Jake decided to give me another visit and to really finish off trying to ruin my night. Thankfully, his burning stare from the other side of the beach was all I was subjected to. He needs to be careful, if I were any other girl, I might start to think his constant attention meant something other than hate. I mean, who in their right mind spends all night staring at a girl they supposedly hate so much when they could be having fun with their friends? Jake Thorn, that's who.

A shiver runs down my spine at the thought alone.

Feeling confident, I go to lift Shane's arms off me but I still the moment I hear his hushed voice.

"What are you doing? Go back to sleep." Dropping his arm once again, he pulls me back tighter against him. Every muscle in my body tenses as his morning wood presses harder against my arse then before.

Nothing about this is right, and it only goes to prove that nothing is ever going to happen between us, no matter how much he might seem to want it. Shane and I are only ever destined to be friends.

"I'm sorry, I really need to pee."

"Really? Now?"

"Really." He allows me to lift his arm again and I quickly jump away from his body.

"Be quick."

I don't respond because anything I might say to ensure he stays where he is would be a lie.

I wasn't lying when I said I needed the toilet, but I have no intention of getting back inside that tent.

Pulling the zip shut, I cast my eyes around the beach and my breath catches. The bonfire's still glowing, and it's surrounded with passed-out bodies of varying array of dress and empty beer bottles.

There are going to be some serious hangovers when they all start waking up.

Tugging down the bottom of Shane's shirt, I make my way across the sand and sadly, in the direction of the football team so I can make use of the actual facilities. There's no way in hell I'm going back in those trees, especially when the sun is only just starting to rise.

My steps slow when I approach a familiar sleeping body. I almost laugh to myself when I realise he's still facing toward where I was. Creepy fucker.

Taking a risk, I stand there for a few seconds taking him in. He looks much less vicious in his sleep. The almost constant scowl has gone and his forehead isn't creased in anger. He just looks normal, no... beautiful.

Shaking the crazy thought from my head, I lower my gaze, taking in his sculpted chest and abs before his V lines disappear into his jeans.

His tattooed arm moves and I almost jump a mile. My heart pounds and I immediately back up. The last thing I need while my head's lightly pounding from last night's beer and still a little sleep-fogged is to deal with a hungover Jake.

My legs move of their own accord and I find myself practically running toward the toilets and away from any danger.

As I expected, the toilets are deserted although the evidence that there's been a party is everywhere. Bottles and shot glasses are all over the countertops as well as discarded makeup and dirty wipes while a perfectly good bin sits beneath it all. There's nothing suggesting it was them, but my mind immediately holds Chelsea and her posse of cheerleaders responsible.

Lowering myself to the toilet, I drop my head into my hands. I have no intention of going back down the beach. I need to find a way to get home and away from the disaster this place is going to be when everyone starts coming back to life. The majority of people here I doubt will even notice I've left.

I wash my hands without looking up, I'm afraid of what I'll see when I do. Over the past couple of months, I've had to stare at my broken reflection and I've just about had enough of the sad, pathetic look in my eyes that I know has returned. *Returned?* I'm not sure it ever actually left. More like morphed into a different kind of misery. One where I've mostly accepted, although not dealt with, the loss of my parents but hate the life I've now been thrown into. I prayed that I could start at Rosewood high, blend into the background, graduate and move on. But it seems that was a little too much to ask. While I might have found myself a couple of friends, I've made one much worse enemy and I can't see him letting up anytime soon. He's intent on ruining my life here and something tells me that he's not going to stop until he gets what he wants. The only thing I can try to do now is to not show that his actions and vile words affect me.

I am better than the bitter person he could turn me into. My gran deserves for me to be strong and not to bring more drama down on her shoulders. My parents would expect no less than for me to laugh in the arsehole's face. I deserve so much more than this.

With my shoulders a little wider, I walk out of the public toilets with a new lease of life. The sun makes me wince and I allow myself a couple of seconds to enjoy the warmth of it on my face. I'm not used to this kind of weather and I hope it's not something I'll take for granted too soon.

Looking down at my bare feet, I suck in a deep breath and prepare for the painful walk home. I know that I should go and wake the others in the hope of a ride, but the thought of having Shane pull me back down to our little bed and wrap his arm around me is enough to keep me moving. I really don't want to lead him on, but it seems that he's intent on seeing something that isn't there.

I'm not one-hundred percent sure on the way home, but I figure as I get farther inland that I'll start recognising stuff and eventually figure it out. If it weren't so early, or if some arseholes hadn't stolen all our stuff, I could have rung Gran for help but that option is out too.

Thankfully, it's early enough that hardly any cars pass me, and only one has beeped at me so far. I understand why, I'm clearly doing some kind of walk of shame wearing only a Rosewood Bear's jersey that exposes almost all of my legs.

An unsettling shiver runs down my spine knowing what a stupid decision this was. This town is pretty quiet, but that doesn't mean there isn't some nutcase out prowling the streets waiting for their next prey to almost fall into their lap. I'm the perfect target right now.

The rumble of an engine slowing behind me vibrates through my body and my heart starts to pound a little faster.

It could be anyone, a rapist, murderer. Images of what could be about to happen to me play out in my mind like all the films I've seen over the years. My palms sweat and my muscles prepare to run as the car gets ever slower behind me.

Eventually, my fear gets too much and I have to look over my shoulder. The moment the passenger of the car becomes clear, a laugh falls from my lips.

"Are you shitting me?" I ask as I continue walking.

"Get in, Brit," Jake barks through the open window.

"Fuck you."

"Get. In. The. Fucking. Car. Now."

"Fuck. You."

His nostrils flare at my defiance and his lips press into a thin line. He's jolted forward as the car accelerates and I breathe a sigh of relief. That is until the car abruptly stops slightly in front of me and the passenger door is thrown open.

Turning on my tender feet, I go to take off running but strong, tattooed arms wrap around my waist. I still on contact and gasp in surprise when the entire length of his body presses against my back.

"I said, get in the fucking car," he growls, his voice is terrifying. My body trembles, there's no way he misses it and I curse myself for allowing him to feel my fear right now.

Before I get to argue, my feet leave the floor and I'm carried toward the car where Ethan holds the back door open to allow Jake to throw me in.

I squeal as I fly toward the leather seat, quickly scrambling so I can make my escape before the car moves, but when I sit up, I find Jake staring down at me. His eyes are dark and angry but there's a smug smirk playing on his lips.

"Let me the fuck out."

"Feisty this morning, aren't you?" His head tips to the side like he's trying to figure me out and fuck if it doesn't make him look even better. Heat unfurls in my belly as I go to force him out of the way. He sees what I'm planning and before I get a chance to do anything, he's leaning into the car, hands on the seat behind me, caging me in.

He doesn't say anything for the longest time. Instead, his eyes bounce between mine before dropping down to my lips. I bite down on my bottom one, my nails digging into the leather beneath me.

"What the fuck is your problem?" I seethe, hoping to get him out of my face and looking at me like he is right now.

An unamused chuckle falls from him. "My problem? I've got a fucking million, *sweetheart*. But right now it's that you're walking along the side of the road looking like a whore who's been kicked out after a good night."

"Sorry, am I bringing the tone of the area down a few notches?" I ask, and by the darkening of his eyes and the grinding of his teeth, I'd say it only fuels his anger. He wants me to argue, he doesn't know how to respond to me basically agreeing with him.

"Your night with Dunn and his small cock so disappointing that you had to run?" All the air leaves my lungs as he leans closer, his lips only millimeters from mine. His scent fills my nose and I can't help wondering how he smells so damn good after a night on the beach. My eyes focus on the darkening bruise on his cheek and the cut on his lip. I wonder who was on the other end of that fist? They should have done a better job. "Did you spend the whole time thinking of me? Thinking about how I'd fill your pussy to the max and bring you more pleasure than you've ever known."

My stomach knots and I try convincing myself it's with disgust but I'm not stupid and I hate myself for my reaction to him.

"Leave me alone." I try to keep my voice strong but neither of us miss the crack toward the end.

"You don't mean that. I see the way your eyes dilated when I got close to you. You want this. You might hate me like I do you, but you can't deny that you want me to fuck you."

"Get the fuck away from me." I try again but I know it's pointless. My words mean nothing to him.

"Me fucking you wouldn't achieve what you want. You want pleasure, but all I've got for you is pain, baby."

"Enough, Thorn," Ethan barks from the front seat and Jake pulls back a little, allowing me to suck in a few much needed breaths.

"Pain, Brit," he whispers menacingly. "Pain is all I've got for you."

I reach for the handle the second he slams the door shut, but it's useless, they've locked me in.

"Where are you taking me?"

"Home," Jake barks.

I want to ask why. If he hates me so damn much like he keeps expressing, then why not just leave me to cut my feet to shreds on the pavement? But I keep my lips sealed shut and with my arms folded over my chest. I sit back and watch the scenery pass as we head toward home.

"How'd you know where I live?" I didn't think to tell him the address when Ethan pulled the car away from the curb, but not long later he's bringing it to a stop outside my gran's house.

"We know everything that happens around here."

"Riiight. Well, thanks for the lift, I guess. I'd like to say it was a pleasure but...it wasn't."

"Should have left you to be fucking abducted," comes from the passenger seat.

"Ignore him," Ethan says. "He's PMSing or some shit."

A smile almost makes it to my lips as I push the door open. I bite back the urge to thank them properly because they really did rescue me when they could have left me to find my own way, but instead I slam the door and storm toward Gran's bungalow.

I really don't want to ring the bell and wake her up, but I don't know any other way to get inside without my keys. I could really do without all the questions that are going to come with me standing at her front door looking like I am.

With a wince, I press my finger down on the button and the ring sounds out through the house. I'm just starting to think it hasn't woken her when movement by the window to my left catches my eye seconds before the door's pulled open.

"Amalie, what on earth..." Her words are cut off by the loud rumble of an engine behind us. Her eyes lift from mine and she smiles as the car pulls away and disappears down the street.

"I'm so sorry to wake you. You can go back to bed."

"I was awake anyway. What's happened? Where's Camila? Why are you wearing a Bear's shirt?"

"I need coffee first," I say, shutting the door behind me and heading toward the kitchen.

17

JAKE

My body knew the moment her eyes were on me. Fire burned in my belly and my blood turned to lava under her intense scrutiny. As much as I wanted to open my eyes and scare the shit out of her, my need to know what the hell she was about to do was bigger. I expected her to hurt me after everything yesterday. I've got no doubt that she knows it was us who stole their tent and all their stuff.

To my surprise, she just stood there staring.

Coldness engulfed me when she eventually walked away and I knew I couldn't fight it any longer, I had to see her.

I regretted it immediately when my eyes ran up her long legs until they found the bottom of his fucking jersey she was still wearing. The fire raged within me knowing that he's spent the night with her. That motherfucker should have been warned she was off limits, yet he still does whatever the fuck he wants. Same as how he spends his time with his dumb ass friends instead of with his team like the rest of us. We all know where our loyalties lie, but Shane Dunn? He needs to be taught a fucking lesson and I've got the perfect ammunition. He's got a weakness for the new girl and I'm about to use it against him.

"Where to now?" Ethan asks after we've watched her walk into her Gran's house. Waking him up and demanding we follow her was probably a dumbass move, but I couldn't ignore the fact I'd seen her leave the bathrooms and head off toward home wearing only that fucking jersey and no damn shoes. I might want to hurt her, but I'll be fucked if I'm letting anything else happen to her.

"Aces."

"You wanna swing back by the beach for Mason?" I think back to our argument last night and I know he wouldn't come. He made his feelings very clear and as much as it might hurt, I'm not fucking bowing down to him right now. He might think he knows what my life's like, what goes on in my head but he doesn't know the half of it. So what, he knows what my issue with her is? That means nothing.

"Na, he's got plans."

"Wanna talk about it?"

Glancing over at him, I lift a brow.

"Fine. Fine. I was just offering."

"Just buy me coffee and we're good."

Dropping into our usual booth, silence descends as we wait for the waitress to come over.

"That game last night was epic."

Jesus, was that only yesterday? Being on the field feels like a million years ago already.

"It was a great start to the season."

"The fuck, Thorn? You're our captain. Our quarterback. You're meant to be even more excited about our first win than any of us."

"I am excited. I just don't want to get ahead of myself. This isn't the first time the Bear's have won the first game and crashed out soon after. I'm just gonna take each one as it comes."

"I get that, but shit, a little celebration wouldn't go amiss."

"Don't sulk, Ethan. It doesn't suit you." He flips me off as the waitress comes back with coffee. "How'd you get on with your girl last night? She cave in the end?"

"No." His point stays firmly in place. "You?" He was either too drunks to remember he asked me this last night or quite rightly didn't believe me.

"Yeah, man. You know I always get the girl."

"You got the new girl on her knees?" The shock in his voice should be enough to make him question me, but he never does.

"Something like that," I mutter, not wanting to outright lie to him.

"Daaaamn. That definitely deserves breakfast." Two plates full of sweet pancakes and salty bacon are dropped in front of us right on cue and my mouth waters.

———

"You didn't come home last night," my aunt hollers across the yard as I head toward my front door.

"And?" I bark back, it's not usually like her to give a shit about what I'm doing, hence the reason I've been banished to a trailer in the backyard.

"Just worried is all." *Yeah, fucking right she is.* She's probably more concerned that the money she gets for putting up with me will stop if I fuck off. As much as I'd love to do just that, I've not got enough money and she damn well knows it.

"I'm in one piece, as you can see." Fury at her pathetic attempt to look like she cares starts to bubble within me. "Did you need anything else?" I ask through clenched teeth.

Some movement behind her catches my eye and Poppy comes to stand in the doorway and looks between the two of us, her brows pinched together.

"Okay, well..." My aunt trails off before disappearing inside, shaking her head.

Giving Poppy a weak smile at best, I turn away and let myself into my trailer. None of this is her fault, it's not like she asked for me to be shoved into the middle of her happy family all those years ago.

Throwing the small bag I dragged from Ethan's truck a few minutes ago on my bed, I pull my shirt over my head, drop my shorts and march toward the bathroom. I need rid of the sand that's coating my body and reminding me of everything that happened over the past few hours.

The dribble of water from the showerhead does little to release the tension locking my shoulders tight.

Standing with my hands on the wall in front of me, I allow the water I do have to run down my back. I squeeze my eyes shut and regret it instantly. The image of her terrified eyes as I leaned over her in the car are right there, taunting me. Since the day she fucking turned up all she's done is fucking taunt me. Everywhere I look, every time I close my eyes, there she is bringing back everything I try to forget, teasing me with her body and reminding me that she's the reason Mason told me to fuck off last night. We've never fallen out. Yeah, we've thrown plenty of punches over the years but never has it ever come to what it did last night.

Her face fills my mind, the darkening of her eyes as I leaned in closer, the way they dropped to my lips like there was even the slightest fucking chance I was going to kiss her. Her floral scent, even after a dip in the sea and a night on the beach filled my nose and fuck if it didn't make my mouth water, making me wonder how bad that kiss might be.

My cock swells and twitches, catching my eye. Dropping one arm, I fist the length with an almost painful grip. Holding my weight against the wall with one arm I pump my cock, reveling in the escape as my mind empties and my body chases mind-numbing pleasure.

My balls draw up and as I come into the shower tray only one face fills my mind. It immediately ruins any high I might have just found.

Punching the wall in front of me so it leaves a decent dent, I growl out my frustration. How is that bitch managing to bury herself so damn deep under my skin when all I want is to get rid of her.

"What the hell are you doing?" I bark the second I find Poppy sitting on my couch. I'm not surprised, I pretty much expected it after she heard the exchange between her mom and me earlier.

"Just checking in and I brought you some supplies." She nods over to the two bags full of stuff on the counter. I don't need her bringing me stuff from the house, I'd actually rather buy my own food, but she insists that it's what her parents should be doing for me, so she makes it happen.

The corner of my lips twitch when I find a bottle of vodka at the bottom of the bag. "How'd you sneak this out?"

She shrugs, her face dropping. "Just took it after they went shopping last. They're so busy arguing that they probably even forgot they bought it."

My heart aches for her and her situation. I might fucking hate living here but I think I've actually got the better end of the deal being out here away from it all.

"You could keep it. Go out and have some fun."

Screwing up her face in disgust, she says, "No, it's okay. You can keep it. I'll stick to beer thanks."

I can't help laughing at her as I twist the top and take a swig, it makes her face twist even more.

"You should probably water it down with something."

"Yeah, I probably should."

I unpack everything else she brought me before falling down beside her. I used to sneak whatever she gave me back into the house but ever since I got caught and they thought I was actually stealing the shit I decided to stop. I don't want Poppy in trouble for doing something nice for me.

"So, how was Dash?" She tucks her legs beneath her and looks at me excitedly.

"It was..." I trail off as I try to decide what last night was. *Frustrating, painful, a total let down...* "It was fun, you'll love it when it's your turn."

"I can't wait. Another step closer to getting out of this shithole."

"You and me both, kid." She frowns and her lips part ready to rip me a new one for using the nickname she hates, but she obviously decides against it.

"You got homework to do?"

"Probably," I admit.

"I'll go get mine, we'll do it together. We need the grades if we're ever going to get out of here."

I want to say no. To send her back up to her house to leave me to wallow in self-pity alone but the sparkle in her eye at the idea of spending the afternoon here with me is too much to refuse and I find myself going in search of some actual fucking homework as she runs to the house. *Well, this will be a fucking novelty.*

18

AMALIE

"Amalie, you've got a visitor," Gran calls.

Closing the lid of my laptop, I place it on the bed beside me and climb off in search of who the hell's come knocking. I assume it's Camila since I ran away from them all this morning, although why Gran wouldn't just send her down to my room is a little weird.

I understand why when I round the corner and my visitor comes into view.

"Mason?" I ask, thinking that I must be seeing things. Why the hell is he at our front door? Then a thought hits and fire rages through me. "If you're here to do his dirty work, then you can think again. Just because you follow him around like he's God it doesn't mean I'll bend at his commands."

Gran blanches beside me but slowly starts to back away and I'm grateful she's going to allow me to fight my own battles.

"What? No, no. He has no idea I'm here."

"Okay. So why are you here?"

"I've got all your stuff in my car. Thought you might need it."

"Why?" I narrow my eyes at him, not trusting one bit that he's just being nice. Jake and his crew don't do nice.

Putting his hands up in defeat, he holds my eye contact. "Just being nice, I swear. Jake's acting like a jumped up asshole. You don't deserve that, so I thought it was time to do the right thing."

"Okay," I say, still not wanting to trust him as far as I could throw him.

"Come give me a hand?"

"Sure." Slipping on a pair of flip-flops I'd left by the front door, I follow him out to his car.

"I've got Camila's stuff too, would you mind taking that?"

"Why don't you take it to her. You know where she lives, right?" I've no clue if this is the case or not, but I'm desperate to know what the story is between the two of them.

"I don't think she'll take too kindly to me turning up unannounced. It'll be better if you take it." His shoulder slumps a little as he says this, only serving to make me even more suspicious of what their deal is with each other.

We both grab armfuls of bags and head back toward Gran's.

"Would you both like a drink? I've made cookies."

"I should really get go—"

"You can stay for a few minutes, can't you?" The words are out of my mouth before I have time to decide if I mean them or not, but having him here and seemingly willing to help me, I want to make the most of it. Who knows what information I could glean from my enemy's best friend.

"I'll leave you to it," Gran says, grabbing one of her cookies and disappearing into the living room.

The tension's heavy between us as I make two coffees and lead Mason out onto the patio.

"Why are you doing this?"

"Because you don't deserve any of that shit?"

"Yet up until now, you've been a part of it. So what gives?"

"For the record, I never agreed with anything he did."

"So why follow? Just because he's your captain doesn't mean you need to follow him around like a sheep."

"Trust me, I know. He's just been my best friend forever, and it's always been the two of us. Sometimes it's easy to forget maybe those closest to you don't have other's best intentions at heart."

Sipping on my coffee, I allow the words he just said to register.

"So what's this then? Peace offering?"

"I guess."

Silence descends once again as we both look out over Gran's garden.

"What's the deal with you and Camila?"

His body visibly tenses beside me as he blows out a shaky breath. That alone tells me that I'm right and that there's a definite story there. "There is no deal. We were friends, now we're not."

"Hmm..."

I keep my eyes on the flowers ahead of me but that doesn't mean I don't know the second his stare turns on me. "What does that mean?"

"Nothing. She just said the exact same thing."

"That's because it's true."

"Why aren't you friends any longer?"

"I didn't come here to talk about my life." His voice is suddenly colder, telling

me that he really doesn't want to talk about this.

"Okay, so tell me why your best friend hates me so much then."

"Not my story to tell. If he wants you to know then he'll have to tell you himself."

"Well... that's helpful."

"Sorry. I might not agree with him, but that doesn't mean I'll be going behind his back."

"Like being here right now? I'm assuming he has no idea you're here or returning our stuff."

"Uh... not exactly."

"So seeing as you know him so well, what's your advice? How do I get him off my case so I can just get on with my life?"

His hand comes up to rub his jaw as he thinks. "You're under his skin more than he'll ever admit and I don't think he realises that it's not for the reason he thinks."

"Wow, that helps," I say with a laugh.

"Just don't let him walk over you. Stand up for yourself. He'll respect that."

"I don't need his respect," I snap.

"No, but he needs to know you're strong. That you can look after yourself and handle things when needs be."

Narrowing my eyes at him, I try to read between the lines but really, I've got no idea what he's trying to tell me. "That cryptic message is all you're giving me, isn't it?"

"Like I said—"

"It's his story to tell. Got it."

His phone starts ringing in his pocket and he uses it as the excuse he needs to escape my questions.

"Something I should know about?" Gran asks, wiggling her eyebrows suggestively once I've seen Mason out.

"No, really not."

"Aw that's a shame. He's a good-looking boy. If I were forty years younger." I shudder on the inside, but I clearly don't manage to keep my disgust from my face because she starts laughing at me. "I'm kidding, I'm kidding. I think," she shouts as I turn my back on her and start back toward my bedroom with all mine and Camila's stuff. "You're totally allowed to date, by the way," I hear seconds before shutting my door.

Groaning, I drop everything into the corner and fall down onto my bed.

Grabbing my phone, I make the call I've been dreading. She's going to want answers and I'm not sure I'm ready to explain.

"I've got your stuff," I say, interrupting Camila when she starts demanding to know where I went this morning the second she answers her home phone. I feel bad about making her worry but even after my encounter with Jake, I know I made the right decision in leaving. Last night might have been bearable when there was alcohol coursing through my system, but waking up pretty much sober with Shane wrapped around me was a big enough sign that I didn't belong there.

"What? How?"

"Mason just dropped it all off. So I guess our suspicions were right about it being them who took it all."

"Why did he bring it back? That was *nice* of him." She says the words as if he's not capable of doing something like that and it only makes my curiosity grow more.

"I just need to shower then I'll come around to pick it all up. Fancy a milkshake?"

"I can't, I've got an English lit paper to write."

"Oh come on, you've already bailed on me once today."

The sadness in her voice forces me to agree. "Okay fine but only for an hour because I've got to get this done."

"Fine. See you in a bit."

Camila pulls up outside Gran's house a little over thirty minutes later. After filling her boot with her stuff, we head toward Aces. I try convincing her to go somewhere else, thinking about how half the school seems to hang out there but she won't have any of it.

Thankfully, he's not there. There are a few faces I recognise from the school halls and Camila says hello to a couple but we're able to find a booth in peace.

"Shane thinks you left because of him. Did you?" Camila blurts out after sucking down half of her milkshake.

"Yes and no."

"Why? You two seemed to be getting along really well last night."

"Yeah, we were... as friends. Then I woke this morning with him wrapped around me and his..."

"Cock?" Camila supplies helpfully.

"Yeah, that, pressing into my arse."

"I love the way you say *arse*," she says, mimicking my accent. "Sorry, sorry. Not important right now. So he was hard? What do you expect from a teenage boy when a girl's in touching distance?"

"It's not that. I'm just not interested and I don't want him to start thinking there could be more. There won't be."

"You sound so sure."

"That's because I am."

"You barely know him."

"I know enough to know that he doesn't do it for me."

"Shame. I was totally hoping we could double date. So who does do it for you? Don't tell me you need someone a little more... asshole-y."

My eyes almost pop out of my head at what she's suggesting.

19

AMALIE

"Hey," Poppy calls as she heads toward the bench I'm sitting on waiting for her. "You had a good day?"

I think back over the last few hours. It started off pretty well when Camila turned up with fresh donuts, she said they were a peace offering after the 'joke' she played Friday night. It wasn't necessary, but I wasn't going to refuse a sugary treat first thing on a Monday morning. My day soon started to go downhill the second I spotted Jake across the car park the moment she pulled into a space. One look into his eyes and I may as well have been back in Ethan's car on Saturday morning. My stomach knotted, my fists clenched and my temperature soared. Camila noticed where my attention was and immediately dragged me off in the other direction as she instructed me to ignore him. If only it was that easy.

"Yeah, it was fine." Pushing images of him aside. "Yours?"

"I had a surprise pop quiz in Math. I thought surprises were meant to be good things," she says with a roll of her eyes. "Plus a massive lab report to write up for biology. Nothing like easing into the new year gently. Come on, my car's this way."

I follow behind while Poppy continues chatting away about her day and before long we're pulling out of school and heading toward wherever she lives.

Her house sits on the boundary between the east and west parts of town. The building itself looks like it should belong on the wealthier east side with its colossal size, but the area most definitely looks like the west side.

"Wow, your house is stunning."

"We're pretty lucky to have this much space. I'm sure it's nothing compared to what you had in England." The reminder of home is like a punch to the chest. She's right, my parent's house in Chelsea was opulent and massive but it was just a house.

"I guess," I mutter sadly. "It's different here though. We could never make use of the outdoor space like you can."

The second she pushes the front door open we're met by a loud shout and the vibrations from a slamming door somewhere upstairs.

"Shit."

Footsteps pound down the stairs before a very pregnant and very stressed woman reveals herself.

"Mom, is everything okay?"

"Of course, sweetheart. Hi, I'm Tammi, Poppy's mom," she says turning to me with a wide, fake smile on her face.

"Hi, nice to meet you."

"Amalie's just come over to work on a project with me."

"That's fantastic. Why don't you both go and work outside. I'll bring you out some snacks in a few minutes."

"Thanks, Mom." Poppy turns to me. "Do you want to go and find a seat. I just need to run up to my room quick and grab my stuff."

"Sure."

"It's just this way, sweetie," her mum calls as she walks off, so I follow. Making my way through the house it's obvious that although it's huge, they don't really have the money to keep up with maintaining it. "Soda okay?"

"Perfect, thank you."

"Just grab a seat anywhere, I'm sure Poppy won't be long."

As I step out into their back garden, the late summer sun makes me squint and I pull my sunglasses down from the top of my head. Glancing around, I take in the few flowers that are dotted around but the most eye-catching thing is the pool. The blue water glitters in the sun and my body practically begs me to strip down and dive in.

Not being able to resist the temptation, I slip off my shoes and go to sit on the edge. The water is so warm after the summer of sun and I sigh in delight as it laps at my calves.

Resting on my palms, I tip my head back and close my eyes. The sound of birds and the rustling of the trees in the distance is so relaxing, it makes me wish Gran had this. I could lose a lot of time doing just this.

Just when I think I'm as relaxed as I possibly could be without lying on a float in the middle of the pool, a voice sounds out around me.

"What the fuck?"

My spine goes ramrod straight. I don't need to turn to know exactly who it is but what the hell is he doing here? Has his obsession with ruining my life now extended to stalking me?

I don't do anything, just pray that he'll leave as quickly as he arrived, but I'm not so lucky because in seconds his woodsy scent fills my nose and his body burns my hyperaware skin.

His eyes run down the side of my body and down my legs to where they're dangling in the water.

"Why?"

His vague question is enough to have me turning to look at him. I take in his creased forehead as he frowns at me like I can't possibly be here, his pursed lips and tired eyes.

When I don't respond, he continues. "Why? Why are you always fucking here?" He taps at the side of his head making me think that it's not my actual presence that's irritating him so much. "Everywhere I fucking turn, there you are, reminding me of everything, fucking me up like no years have passed."

My eyes narrow as I try to piece together what he's saying, but he might as well be talking gibberish.

His chest heaves as he stares at me, his eyes flitting around my face almost like he's committing my features to memory, but that really can't be the case as he's so fed up of me.

He reaches out and I gasp in shock as his hand lands on my lower back and pushes just enough to have my butt sliding across the tile beneath me and toward the water's edge.

"Jake," I squeal, my fingernails digging into the edge in an attempt to keep me out of the pool.

"Give me one good reason why I shouldn't."

"Because," I squeak, scrambling to come up with a reason. "Your cousin's about to come back." My brain suddenly puts two and two together after what Poppy said about supporting her cousin at the football game Friday night.

The pressure at my back reduces and the long breath he blows out tickles down my neck, making my nipples pebble beneath my vest.

"You need to stay out of my fucking way."

"Trust me, I'm not trying to get in your way."

His fingers grasp my chin and I'm forced to turn to look at him once again. He leans in so our noses are almost touching. "Then why are you always fucking here?"

I open my mouth to respond but another voice fills my ears.

"Jake, what the hell?"

At the sound of Poppy's voice, he gives my chin one final squeeze and stands, leaving me to drag some much-needed air into my lungs.

"Just saying hello to your new *friend*. You want to watch who you spend time with, Pop. People aren't always what they seem."

"What the hell is that meant to mean?"

"Just watch your back, yeah?"

No more words are said and after a second he turns on his heels and storms down the garden.

The air's heavy until he's vanished from sight and a bang sounds out.

"Are you okay?" Poppy asks, placing her books down on the table and walking over.

"Yeah, I'm fine."

"Is there something I should know about?"

I glance over at her kind face and I wonder how much I should tell her. Jake's a part of her family, I've no clue how close they are other than the fact she supports him on game nights.

"I don't think he likes me very much."

"Yeah, I got that vibe. Why?"

"I was hoping you could tell me that."

20

JAKE

Slamming the trailer door, I roar out my frustration into the empty space. I've managed to avoid her all fucking day. Every time I saw the flash of her platinum hair across the hallway, my fists clenched with my need to go over to her. I'm not sure exactly what I would have done if I did, I had no intention of finding out. But fuck if she doesn't call to me in a way no one else has before.

Then here she is, in my fucking garden.

My heart thunders in my chest with my need to go back out there and finish what I started. The image of her with her clothes soaking wet, her white vest see-through enough to give me a clue as to what she's hiding beneath makes my temperature soar.

"Fuck," I shout, the word echoing around me.

I make quick work of changing and grabbing my headphones before heading back out and to my make-shift gym. The trailer is right at the bottom of the garden and tucked into the mass of trees that separates this property from the bungalows behind. That's where my homemade gym lives. It's also my quiet place when I need to escape when things just get too much.

Climbing through the undergrowth, I stomp down some brambles that have grown since I was last in here until the small clearing opens up.

This place might not be anything like the gym we've got at school and it's a mile away from the one I sometimes go to with Ethan, but it does the same job. I've even now got an exercise bike that I took from someone's skip down the street over the summer.

Jumping, my hands wrap around the rough branch and I fight to pull my chin up. My muscles burn, reminding me that I haven't warmed up at all, but I don't give a fuck right now. I need to feel the burn, the pain that only I can cause. No one can tell me what to do here. I make the rules and push my own boundaries and limits.

I continue until my arms are trembling and begging for reprieve. Releasing my grip, I allow my feet to hit the floor once again, the ground crunching as I land on old sticks and fallen leaves.

Throwing my leg over the old bike, I turn up the tension.

Sweat pours from my skin as I push harder and harder. My head's filled with images of my past. I push my legs as fast as I can go as I try to escape. I picture her face the day she said goodbye and walked away from me. The way her lips were in an almost permanent smile because of the filler she'd had shoved in them, the ridiculous lashes that were stuck to her eyelids and her damn near yellow peroxide blonde hair. She was about as fake as she could probably get and I'm sure it's only got worse as the years have gone on.

I've done my best to steer clear of ever seeing her face again, but with the job she does, sometimes that isn't possible. I've always steered clear of opening any kind of magazines and walking away when any of the girls at school pull one out. If I have to ever see her face again, then it needs to not be when I have company. Thankfully the day I discovered her most recent career of choice I was alone in the safety of my trailer. No one was around to witness the fallout of that clusterfuck.

The music booms in my ears but I don't hear a word of it. I'm too focused on escaping the memories, the pain, the desperation I still remember all too well.

Almost every single one of my muscles tremble with exhaustion by the time I've finished. Pulling my sweat-soaked t-shirt from my body, I wipe my face and throw it over my shoulder as I head off in search of water.

Soft female voices drift down to me as I step toward my trailer and at the last minute, I change my mind and head toward the main house. I don't really have any desire to go inside but the temptation to torment her is too much.

When they come into view, they've both got their heads down, a pile of books, pens and notepads in front of them as they do their homework like good little girls. A little nagging voice in the back of my head shouts that it's probably something I should also be doing instead of filling my need for vengeance using the innocent new girl but that's all I seem to be able to think about these days.

"I hope you realize that nerds have no fun," I comment once I'm close enough for them to hear me clearly.

"And those who skip class end up flipping burgers. Problem?" Poppy says, her eyes coming up to meet mine, full of amusement. It might not be the first time she's mentioned my destiny being in a fast food joint.

A quiet whimper beside her drags my attention away, and I'm so fucking glad I do because New Girl is playing right into my hands. Her chin's dropped as her eyes roam over my naked skin. If it's possible, my body heats even more under her stare but I don't allow her to see any reaction from me.

"You about finished?" I bark, making Poppy blanch at my outburst.

Her cheeks flame red and I don't miss that it creeps down onto her chest and even as low as the swell of her breasts and she sheepishly looks back down at the book in front of her like nothing ever happened.

Falling down in the seat in front of her, I keep my attention on Poppy. "Any chance you could get me a bottle of water, Pops."

"I...uh..." she stutters, looking between the two of us. I understand her hesitation, I probably wouldn't leave her with me either.

"Please." I smile sweetly and lean forward, placing my elbows on my knees.

Moving my eyes away from Poppy as she hesitantly gets up and leaves us alone, I stare at the bowed head in front of me.

"What? You shy all of a sudden? I didn't think whores got embarrassed."

"Fuck you," she spits, standing up so fast that the plastic chair she was sitting on goes crashing backward.

I stand, her breasts brushing against my chest where we're so close. Her breath catches at the same time some weird spark shoots through my veins.

"We've been through this. I don't fuck whores."

"Yeah, so you keep saying, but here you are. Again."

Fury bubbles within me at her referring to herself that way. It's irrational because I started it but still, I fucking hate it.

Standing only a few inches shorter than me, she stays stock still, her blue eyes boring into mine. The hate I've been putting on to her suddenly feels insignificant as other urges start to take over. It's easy to imagine that she's someone else at a distance. It's easy to picture another face and fake blonde hair, but up close she's just a girl who's just about as lost as I am.

My eyes drop from hers in favor of her lips and I start to imagine how sweet she actually might taste, how soft her lips might feel pressed against mine.

"Back off, Jake." The harsh sound of Poppy's voice is enough for me to break my stare.

Looking up, I find her in the doorway with the bottle I requested poised like she's about to throw it at me.

The mortified look on her face is enough to distract me, so much so that I miss the movement of arms in front of me and by the time her palms slam down on my chest it's too late.

I take a step back to try to steady myself but there's nothing there. My stomach jumps into my throat as I start falling. I just hear the sound of her evil chuckle before I hit the water and go under.

Fucking bitch.

By the time I resurface, she's kneeling down at the edge waiting for me with a shit-eating grin on her face. Pride swells in my chest. I think I may have underestimated this one. She's not as weak as I first thought her to be and it's only going to make this thing between us more fun.

"Oh, Brit. You just seriously fucked up."

"Is that right? Because as far as I see it, you're the one losing right no-ah!"

The sound of her scream before the splash might be the most satisfying thing I've ever heard.

She fumbles around, arms and legs flailing in her panic. I eventually take pity on her and reach out.

Her waist is so damn small that my fingers almost meet at her spine. I pull her up and she sucks in a lungful of air while simultaneously fighting to get away. That is until I pull her flush against me. The temptation of feeling her curves against my hard planes is too much.

Her hands come up to brush away the wet hair that's sticking to her face and the second our eyes connect she stops fighting.

My fingers tighten around her in my need to show her just how much she's fucked up my life. Close up like this, she's nothing like the woman who caused me the real pain, so I focus on the present. This girl's the reason my life's gone to shit this past week. She's the reason why Mason is still avoiding me and why my nights are filled with dreams of times in my childhood that I'd rather forget.

Leaning in, my rough cheek brushes against hers and her entire body shudders against me. "You want to fight dirty, Brit? I can guarantee that you're going to lose. You have too many weaknesses that I can exploit whereas nothing can touch me." My tongue runs around the shell of her ear and she gasps in shock, every muscle in her body locking up tight.

To outsiders, like my cousin who's stare I can feel burning into my skin, it might look intimate, like I'm whispering sweet nothings into her ear. Well... I guess I am whispering promises as such.

Her chest swells as she sucks in some strength to respond. "I'm not the weak, pathetic girl you think I am. I'm not going to bend over and take it."

"Maybe you should, it'll all be over quicker."

"I didn't think you fucked whores."

Her words make my breathing falter.

Wrapping the length of her sodden hair around my fist, I pull her head back so I can ensure her eyes stay on mine and I lift and press her into the pool wall. I'm confident that she has no idea her legs automatically come up to wrap around my waist, but the moment her heat lines up with my semi-hard cock I'm not going to point it out.

I press harder into her, ignoring the fact that she'll know she's making me hard right now. I allow myself a few seconds to take her in. The darkness of her blue eyes giving away her anger and desire, the droplets of water that are littering her face and blending in with her freckles, her wet hair, pushed back from her flawless face. She's soaked yet there's no makeup running down her face, it only proves that she really is naturally this flawlessly beautiful.

"Don't," I warn, my voice deep and haunting, my mouth running away with me. "Don't ever call yourself that."

"But it's okay for you to?" Her voice is no more than a breathy whisper. My heart thunders and my cock threatens to go full mast knowing I'm affecting her as she is me.

"I do what I want, Brit. I thought you'd realized that by now."

My eyes drop to her lips because if that statement were actually true, they'd be pressed up against mine right now.

That realization is enough to make me let go and step back. I don't kiss girls. I use them for what I want and cast them aside. This right now, it confuses the fuck out of me and that only leads to more frustration.

"Amalie, are you okay?" Poppy calls. I spot her running toward the corner of the pool where I just was as sounds of water splashing fills my ears.

Jumping from the pool, I keep my back to both of them and begin to walk away to the sounds of their panicked voices.

"Hey, Brit," I shout over my shoulder just before I know I'm out of sight. I don't wait for a response, the silence is enough to tell me that they're listening. "Remember, I never lose." And with those final words, I get the hell out of there and away from the girl messing with my head.

21

AMALIE

"L et's go and find you some dry clothes and then I think it's probably best we get out of here."

I couldn't agree more as I follow Poppy into the house and up to her bedroom.

My head spins with everything that happened in the last few minutes. I thought I was being smart pushing him when he was distracted but I should have known it would come and bite me in the arse, and if his warning as he walked away was serious then I think I may have just upped the ante where he's concerned.

A long sigh falls from my lips as we walk into Poppy's bedroom. "Bathroom's there if you want to go and dry off. I'll just find you something to change into."

"Thank you," I mumble, heading in the direction she pointed. She's not asked me any questions yet but one glance in her eyes and I know they're on the tip of her tongue.

I make quick work of stripping out of my sodden clothes and drop them into the basin to wring out. Goosebumps cover my chilled skin but it does little to reduce the heat within my body. I should have hated the feeling of his palms burning into my skin, the pressure of his body being pressed tightly against mine. My head was screaming at me but my body had other ideas. There's something about that arsehole that calls to my body while in my head, I'm imagining a million ways to end him. It was confusing before he pressed the length of his body against mine and manipulated me into wrapping myself around him.

"Wanker," I mutter to myself, resting my palms on the basin and looking up into my darker than usual eyes. I hate him. I fucking hate him. Yet why do I have this constant need to try to dig just a little beneath the surface and find out what's really going on inside his head, what it was that really got his back up about me on my first day that he can't let go of.

"Here you go." Poppy's hand pushes inside the door and I take the clothes she offers. "I hope they fit."

"They're perfect, thank you."

Thankfully, Poppy and I aren't all that different body-wise although she is a few inches shorter than me. If this happened while I was with Camila, then I might have had issues.

I unfold a loose-fitting vest and a denim skirt before quickly sliding them on and wringing out my own clothes. Finding a hairbrush on the shelf above the basin, I make quick work of brushing through my wet, matted hair before piling it all on top of my head out of the way.

With my damp clothes in hand, I pull the door open, expecting to find Poppy waiting for me, only the room is empty.

Not really wanting to snoop around her house, I hesitate at the door but hearing sounds from downstairs, I make my way down.

I find Poppy gathering up our books from the table.

"I'm so sorry for ruining everything."

Turning to me, her eyes narrow in confusion. "You didn't ruin anything. He's the one with the issues. He's always been a little screwed, but that was... shit, I don't even know. You wanna get out of here?"

"Yes." The relief in my voice makes her laugh and once we both have our bags in hand, we head toward her car.

"Do you want to go home or..." She trails off.

"We've still got loads of work to do and I'm not sure I'm ready for all the questions yet," I say, knowing Gran will take one look at me in someone else's clothes and not let up until I give her answers.

"And you don't think I have any?" She chuckles making me groan. "Where do you want to go?"

"Anywhere but Aces."

"You got it."

I stare out the window as the car travels toward the seafront but luckily Poppy parks at the opposite end to Aces and once we've collected our stuff, she directs me to a small cafe that sits a little back from the sea.

"This place is cute." My eyes flit around the place thinking that I could easily step out of here and be back in London.

A long sigh leaves my lips. Poppy turns to me, her face full of sympathy like she knows exactly what I'm thinking.

"I thought you might like it."

We find ourselves a table and grab the menus, my stomach rumbling right on cue.

Once we've ordered, Poppy almost immediately pulls all the books out that she shoved into her bag before we left her house so we can continue where we left off. Or at least that's what I expect her to do so my stomach knots when she places her elbows on the top of everything and her eyes find mine.

"Go on then?" she prompts.

"What?"

"Don't give me what," she laughs. "You're sitting there in my clothes because my idiot of a cousin dragged you into our pool after you pushed him in. You can't tell me nothing's going on there. It was like the ultimate school ground flirting I've ever seen."

I scoff. "I can assure you that that was not flirting." My mind flicks back to the moment he stared down at my lips like he was going to kiss me, my temperature spikes at the memory but I push it down. I read that all wrong, surely.

"I'm pretty sure the tension between you was definitely sexual."

Someone at the next table glances over, my cheeks heat with embarrassment. "Shush. That was not what it was. He hates me. I've no idea why. Can we just forget all about it and get on with this?" I ask hopefully.

She's silent for a moment as I start to think that maybe she'll allow the subject to drop. Sadly, I'm not that lucky.

"My cousin's a little..."

"Fucked up," I offer when she pauses.

"I was going to say cut off or distant, but that works. He hasn't had the best childhood. I know that's not an excuse," she adds quickly when I open my mouth to argue. "I think his perception of how to act normal at times is a little skewed. He acts out so he doesn't have to deal with his emotions or feelings, well I think that's what he does. I've never managed to make him talk about it."

"What happened to him?" The words fall from my lips before I have a chance to stop them.

"His mother's a total fuck up. I don't really know the whole story, I was too young to understand, and no one talks about her ever. Enough about him, we've still got a ton of work to do."

Relieved that she steers the conversation away from him, I grab one of the books she's been leaning on and we get to work.

Thankfully by the time Poppy drops me home, Gran's already gone out. Monday night is bingo night with her friends and I couldn't be more grateful that I get to have a few hours to myself as I attempt to dissect every moment of my afternoon. My head's a mess after those short few minutes with Jake in Poppy's pool. He was his usual arsehole self but there was something else. The seriousness behind his warning about me calling myself a whore, the way he stared down at my lips like he wanted to suck them into his mouth.

Stripping out of Poppy's clothes, I step under the shower and allow the warm water to wash away the scent of chlorine that still covers my skin from my unexpected dip and pray that it's enough to wash him out of my mind too, although I think that could be wishful thinking.

His final words as he walked away repeat in my head over and over as I lie in bed attempting to get some sleep. *"Remember, I never lose."* I don't doubt for a second that those words were true. He wouldn't hold the position he does at school if he dishes out empty threats. Every other student seems to have him on some kind of untouchable pedestal. The girls quite clearly want to shag him and the guys want to be him. Fuck knows why, he's a wanker. A shiver runs up my spine reminding me that although that might be true, he's a beautiful one. The image of him hot, sweaty and dripping in water is etched on the inside of my eyelids and when sleep eventually claims me, it's still right there, inspiring my dreams.

———

When I wake the next morning, it's with dread sitting heavy in my stomach. I've no idea why, it's like a premonition or something. But something about his final words still haunt me and I just know he's going to keep that promise.

Camila pulls up right on cue and once again there are fresh doughnuts sitting on the passenger seat.

"I accepted your apology, you know that, right?"

"Yeah, but they were so good yesterday that I couldn't help myself. Plus, Noah complained I didn't get one for him so..."

Picking up the box, I climb into the seat and rest them on my lap. "I'm not complaining," I say, grabbing one up and biting into it. The sugar immediately makes my mouth water, it's exactly what I need.

"How'd you get along with Poppy last night?"

"Fine."

"That good?" she says with a laugh.

Blowing out a sigh, I remember last night's events once more. "Did you know Jake's her cousin?"

"Yeah."

"And you didn't think to warn me?"

"I didn't think I'd need to. Why, what happened?"

Much to Camila's amusement, I recall the events of the previous night.

"You ended up in the pool?" she laughs.

"Yeah, I should have seen it coming, really. Pushing him was a stupid thing to do."

"So how'd it end?"

"With him warning me that he never loses. I think I've managed to up the stakes. Fuck knows what I've got heading my way."

"I'm sure it'll be fine. What exactly can he do?" By the slight wobble of her voice, it's obvious that even she doesn't believe the words that just fell from her mouth. She slows at a set of traffic lights and turns to look at me. "Don't be so worried. It's not like he's got any dirt on you. It'll just be pathetic schoolyard gossip whatever it is."

I mumble my agreement, but her words do little to ease the dread twisting my stomach the closer we get to school.

Everything's fine until about ten minutes before lunch. I'm in English lit, hiding at the back and getting on with the assignment we've been set when someone's phone goes off. The teacher barks at whoever it was but I ignore them and go back to what I was doing. That is until I feel eyes burning into me.

Looking up, I find three sets of eyes staring right at me, amused smirks playing on all their lips. Narrowing my eyes, I try to figure out what the hell's going on but before I get a chance to do anything, more eyes turn my way. My cheeks burn with everyone's attention on me.

"Class," the teacher snaps. "Pay attention. I'll be taking these in and grading them once the bell rings."

The majority of students turn back around and continue writing but a couple of the guys apparently find me much more interesting and their eyes stay on me. My skin prickles uncomfortably as their eyes run over me, checking me out.

The second the bell goes, I grab my paper, slam it down on the teacher's desk and attempt to get the hell out of there. Sadly, someone calls my name right before I make my escape. Turning to look over my shoulder, I find the amused eyes of one of the guys who was just staring at me. "You free this lunchtime? I could really do with a little release."

Students surrounding him splutter with laughter and a couple of his mates slap him on the shoulder, jostling him forward.

My brows draw together but the moment his eyes drop to take in my body once again, I run from the room. This is the exact kind of attention I was hoping to avoid.

Seeing as I'd promised Camila last week that I wouldn't spend my spare time hiding in the library, I head toward the cafeteria to meet her.

The second I step foot inside, silence descends as almost every head in the room turns to look at me.

What the fuck is going on?

"There she is," I hear a familiar voice say from behind me and when I turn, I find Camila running toward me. "Are you okay?" Her eyes are wide and she looks manic.

"Yeah... why? What's going on?"

"Have you checked your phone in the last ten minutes?"

"No, why?"

"Hey, Brit. How much do you charge for thirty minutes?" a male voice calls.

"Fuck. We need to get out of here."

"What the hell is going on?" I ask again. Camila looks up at me, her face tight with anger.

"Not here. Come on."

Her fingers thread through mine and she pulls until I fall into step behind her. Stares follow our every move and catcalls and random questions about my prices fill the hallway.

When she tugs me through the entrance to the library, I know things must be bad. She refused to allow me to hide in here anymore, yet here she is dragging me toward the back of the room to do exactly that.

"You need to start talking."

"Okay, so..." she hesitates, bouncing from foot to foot and worrying her hands in front of her.

"Camila, just spit it out." I want to say that I've probably already lived through worse this year, but I push any thoughts of my parents from my head.

"There's this photo that's basically been sent to every student in the school."

"Right?" Wishing she'd just get to the fucking point, I gesture for her to continue.

"It looks like it's you." She pulls her phone from her pocket and holds it up for me to see.

"What the..." My words trail off as I snatch it from her hand and stare down at the girl's head in the photo.

I know exactly when it was taken, I guess I could say I was there at the time but the top of the head I can see is most definitely not me.

"It's from Dash," I whisper.

"You're telling me that is you?" Camila's eyes widen to the point they might pop out of her head.

"No, that is not me with Jake's cock in my mouth."

"I didn't think so. Hang on, how do you know that's Jake in the photo?"

Letting my back hit the wall, I lower myself down until my arse touches the floor. Camila follows my move and is soon staring at me waiting for answers.

"I went into the trees for a pee."

She winces, realising that this is all a result of her 'joke.'

"I did my thing and on the way back I stumbled across Jake and some cheer hussy on her knees. That's her in the picture."

"Her hair's darker."

"It's not hard to edit that on Photoshop, Cam."

"Shit."

"Show it to me again." Reluctantly, she hands her phone over and I stare down at it. "You remember what I was wearing that night?"

"Of course, jeans and a t-shirt."

"You can see the skin of her shoulder under her hair. I was wearing a white t-shirt."

"Doesn't mean you couldn't have taken it off in a moment of passion."

"Wait, you're accusing me now?"

"What? No. I was just pointing out what everyone else will say. I knew this wasn't you the moment I saw it. I didn't know it was Jake, but even still, I didn't think you'd got that close to anyone since you arrived."

"Damn right I haven't and I intend on it staying that way, and I'm certainly not selling it like this suggests." I read the text again. *Brit sucks your crown jewels for a bargain price,* and then my fucking phone number.

I daren't pull it out of my bag and find out just how many horny guys think they're going to get lucky.

"This is a fucking nightmare. Why would he do this?" Camila asks, taking her phone back so I don't have to keep looking at it.

"Because he never loses."

Dropping my head into my hands, I focus on my breathing. How the hell am I meant to go out there and hold my head up high. Every student in the building thinks I'm a slut who drops to her knees for money and no amount of denying it is going to work. It's my word against his, their king. I stand no fucking chance.

"What classes do you have this afternoon?"

My head spins just thinking about what's going to happen when I step foot out of the safety of the library. "I've no idea but I'm pretty sure that whatever they are, that I'm not going to be in them."

"You're gonna skip?"

"What do you suggest I do?"

She shrugs. "You'll look guilty if you run from this."

"Let's be honest here, they'll all think I'm guilty no matter what. I could climb up on the school roof and plead my innocence and no one would hear a word. Jake Thorn rules this school and if he says I'm a whore, then that's what I'm going to be."

"You're going to let him win, just like that?"

"For now, yeah. Not sure what else I can do."

"This is bullshit."

"You're telling me." A laugh falls from my lips but there's no amusement in it.

22

JAKE

My need for revenge as I walked away from the pool dripping fucking wet was all-consuming. I managed to ignore the fact my cock was rock fucking hard after being pressed against her soft but toned body under the water and focused on my need to ruin her. She doesn't get to call the shots around here, that's my job and if she thinks she can humiliate me, even if it's only in front of Poppy, then she's got another thing coming.

Swinging the door open on my trailer, I stormed inside, my muscles still screaming after my workout and I head straight for the shower, my mind running a mile a minute trying to come up with how I'm going to end her.

In the end, I gave up brainstorming and pulled out what was left in the bottle of vodka Poppy gave me the other day and a fresh joint I stole from Ethan and lit it up.

The alcohol and weed running through my system helped to relax me, but the images of her wet body were still front and center of my mind.

Needing someone else to be the reason for my constant hard-on, I pulled out my phone and flicked through some of the photos I'd taken over the previous months. Some totally innocent, others not so much and it was those I needed. Faceless girls, soft curves and hot little mouths. That's what I need right now.

If I hit call on the right number, I've no doubt I could meet one in only minutes and get exactly what she's left my body craving.

I'm scrolling through the photos when one catches my eyes. It takes me a moment to remember when it's from. The head full of blonde hair as she quite obviously sucks on me is all I can see of her. My breath catches as the wrong blonde girl pops into my mind. My veins fill with lava just thinking about her and the effect she has on me.

Opening up my messages, I forward it to someone I know can help.

Can you Photoshop this chick's hair so it's a much lighter blonde.

The three little dots appear immediately.

Give me five.

Taking another swig straight from the bottle, I place my phone on my thigh and wait. It lights up in half the time he said and the result staring back at me is perfect. My cock weeps at the thought of it being the Brit on her knees choking on my cock.

I save the image and wait until the perfect time. I want to be around to witness the fallout and that won't be possible while I'm hiding out in this shithole that I call home.

Knowing the image is sitting on my cell is fucking torture. I almost hit send a million times before school the next morning, but I know it'll be pointless. I want to see her face when everyone thinks it's her. The thought of seeing her pain and embarrassment has my mouth watering and my muscles twitching. It's exactly what I need to settle the angry beast that's festering inside me.

———

"Mr. Thorn, where do you think you're going?"

"I've got shit to do," I shout over my shoulder as I head for the classroom door, leaving the rest of my classmates completing their task like good little children.

"You can't just walk off —"

The door slams behind me, cutting off whatever it was that she was going to say.

Walking into the deserted lunchroom, a couple of the ladies laying out lunch look up at me, but no one questions me. Sitting on top of our usual table, I pull my phone from my pocket along with the new SIM I picked up on the way here this morning. I spent most of first period loading it with all the numbers I'd need, thanks to Ethan handing over his own phone at my demand. He has the number of everyone worth knowing so I know this will hit as I intend. Plus, gossip goes around this place like wildfire on the best of days so I've no doubt that those whose numbers we don't have will have it forwarded to them. No one likes missing out on the latest Rosewood drama.

I quickly slip my usual one out and replace it with the new one. I'm fairly certain that everyone is going to know this has come from me, but I thought it probably best not to be totally blatant about it.

Opening up my messages, I find the image and select send to all. My thumb hovers over the send button. A moment of doubt hitting me, making me reconsider what I'm about to do to her but I picture the reason for all this. The woman who ruined me, Brit might not be her, not by a million years, but she stands for the same thing. She's from the same world and that's enough for me.

With anger beginning to fill my veins once again as I think about the poor little boy she abandoned, I tap the button. A shiver runs down my spine as realization of what I've just done hits me. If she didn't hate me already, then she will after this. Hopefully then she'll stay as far away from me as fucking possible and I can attempt to continue with my bullshit life.

Even though everyone's still in class, I start getting replies almost immediately and it's when I get my first inkling that this might have been a massive mistake.

She can suck on me anytime she likes.

Shit, I'm hard just looking, man.

Come to daddy.

My stomach knots at the thought of her touching someone else. Of someone else's fingers gripping her hair tightly as they fuck her mouth. I know the photo isn't actually of her, she'll know the truth too, but my guy did such a good job that everyone else will believe it's her. I know for a fact that the guys won't be looking that closely at the photo to spot any obvious issues.

Jesus. I'm so fucked.

My hands tremble slightly as I pull the new SIM from the back of my phone and shove it deep in my pocket, hoping that I'll be able to shove the memories of those replies down with it. It's only a few minutes later that the ruckus of students leaving classrooms and heading this way filters through the mostly silent cafeteria.

No one pays me any attention as they come piling in, they're too busy chatting with their friends or more importantly, staring at their phones and showing it to the people they're with.

My fists clench and my muscles burn knowing exactly what they're looking at and exactly what the guys are feeling as they do. They're picturing her with her full red lips wrapped around their cocks.

My heart pounds in my chest and my teeth grind with my need to walk over to every guy who thinks they're staring at my Brit.

My Brit.

"Fuck this shit." Jumping from the table I'm sitting on, I storm toward the exit before the rest of the team or cheerleaders appear. The last thing I need is them trying to dig into what's wrong with me. As if I have a fucking clue. I'd like to know why I'm so screwed up just as much as they do.

23

AMALIE

I just about manage to keep the mask on my face until I step through the front door. Thankfully, Gran's out so she's not there to witness my meltdown the second I slam the door behind me.

"Motherfucker," I scream, my voice shaky with emotion that's bubbling up from the stress of the past hour.

How can he manipulate that photo to make everything think that's me? He's the fucking whore out of the two of us, not that anyone would ever look at him badly for his escapades.

My chest heaves as I suck in deep breaths and I desperately try to calm down. He doesn't deserve my tears.

I get myself a glass of water before heading toward my room. One look at the photo of my parents on my nightstand and the tears I'd banished instantly fill my eyes once again.

Perching my arse on the edge of the bed, I reach for the frame and run my finger over my mum's flawless face.

"Oh Mum," I sob. I'm fairly sure that no matter how much time passes, there are always going to be moments like these that all I need is a hug from her. I need the reassuring words that only a mother can give to tell me that everything's going to be okay. That I'm not about to become even more of a social outcast than I was already by being publicly humiliated by the school's bad boy.

What would she tell me to do? I wonder as I continue staring at the photograph. My dad would probably be threatening to go to his house and knock him into next week for treating his baby so badly, while my mum simultaneously calmed him down and supported me. Her reaction would be much less dramatic, telling me not to allow one boy to make me think less of myself when he's the one who should be embarrassed by his actions. She'd tell me that I'm better, stronger than this and to go out there with my head held high and allow people to think what they like because I know the truth.

It all sounds so good in my head but in reality, I want to hide and never show my face in that school again. I know that photo that's currently doing the rounds isn't of me, but everyone thinks it is.

Trying to shake the image of what I've left behind in the canteen from my head, I pull out a bikini top and a pair of shorts and head into the bathroom. If I'm going to spend the rest of the day hiding, then I might as well get a bit of a tan at the same time.

Grabbing my book and water, I leave my phone deep inside my bag, not wanting to even look at the kinds of messages I've probably received.

The only bit of the garden that's still in the sun is right at the bottom, so after dragging one of Gran's comfortable loungers down, I settle myself in the warm rays and try to block out the world.

I'm lost in my book and just as things are about to get interesting, the strangest noise hits my ears. It's almost as if someone's acting out the goings-on in my book with the heavy breathing and grunting that seems to be coming from the trees behind me.

Trying to ignore it, I go back to my book, but I can't block it out and end up re-reading the same sentence three times.

I sit there for a few more minutes but when the sounds continue, my curiosity gets the better of me. Putting my book down, I head toward the trees. This place is a kid's heaven, I can imagine all the dens that have been built down here over the years, it's almost a shame that most of the houses that run along the thick undergrowth are old people's homes.

My heart races as I descend farther into the shadows and I start thinking that this is probably the stupidest thing I've done in a while. I'm either about to stumble across a couple going at it or some ax murderer is going to finish me off. That would sure be a dramatic end to Jake and his stupid photo.

The panting continues and just when I'm convinced that I'm going to find a couple of teenagers stealing a moment of passion, I stumble across the real reason for the noise.

My eyes widen and my body stiffens as I watch a half naked, sweaty Jake pull his chin up to a tree branch above his head.

"Ugh," he grunts as he manages it, before lowering back down and repeating.

It might be dark in here with only a little sunlight filtering through the leaves above but the sweat running down his back glistens before soaking into his waistband that's sitting low on his hips.

My stomach twists and tingles fill my entire body. I want to say it's anger, this boy's got his heart set on ruining my life but I fear what I'm feeling right now is more than that.

I should turn to leave, he'd be none the wiser that I was even here but my body refuses to move.

My eyes stay locked on him as he pulls himself up so his chin hits the branch a few more times before he lets go with a growl and drops to the ground. Sticks snap and leaves rustle where his feet land.

I hold my breath, afraid of what's going to happen when he turns and finds me because it's inevitable.

He places his hands on his knees and sucks in a few breaths but even still, my legs stay put refusing to listen to my head and get the hell out of there.

It's not until he stands and turns that his eyes find me standing beside a tree like a stalker.

"What the fuck?" he barks, his eyes widening in fright and his hand coming up to cover his heart.

It's only now that my feet agree to move and I take a step back just as his eyes narrow in anger.

"What the fuck are you doing here? Shouldn't you be at school?"

My eyebrow quirks up. "Shouldn't *you* be at school drinking in all the praise from your posse after showing me for what I really am?"

"And what's that exactly?"

"A whore who sucks off anyone for the right price."

His chest swells as he sucks in a deep breath before releasing it on a growl. Then he's stepping forward toward me. I should probably be scared but for some reason I know that he's not going to hurt me. Not physically anyway.

"What did I tell you about calling yourself that?"

"It's a little late to be concerned about what people think of me, don't you think? The whole school is probably back there talking about what a slut I am while wanting to congratulate you on being able to get me on my knees mere seconds after meeting you. I hope you achieved whatever it was you were aiming for with that little stunt."

"Nowhere fucking near." His voice is so quiet that I'm not sure I actually hear right.

"What exactly is your problem with me, Jake? I've done nothing to you. All I did was turn up after having my life turned upside down. I don't deserve any of this bullshit from you and you know it."

"My problem. Oh, Brit, I have so many that I don't know where one ends and another begins."

Placing my hand on my hip, I jut it out, waiting because what he just said is nowhere near enough for me to back down.

"You didn't do anything, okay? It's what you stand for, where you've come from that I've got an issue with."

"London?" I ask, lines forming on my forehead in confusion.

"No, not London," he says, mimicking my accent. "Your world full of fake, plastic, privileged assholes who think the world owes them something just because they're beautiful."

"How's that my fault? I was born into that."

"It just is." His voice is so low and menacing that it makes my mouth go dry.

He takes one more step toward me and I've no choice but to step back if I don't want us to collide, only when I do, I crash into a tree.

His eyes drop from mine and take in my barely covered chest. My breasts swell under his intense scrutiny and my nipples pucker against the thin fabric, much to his delight.

"So what are you going to do about it, Brit?" He closes the space between us, and I fight to drag some air into my lungs.

"I have a name, you know." My voice is a breathy whisper and I chastise myself for falling under his spell. He knows he's hot and damn him for using it to his advantage.

"I know. You have a lot of other things too."

"Wha—" My words are cut off as his nose runs along the line of my jaw. I drag in a shaky breath and he chuckles.

"You love how much you hate me." It's not a question, so I don't bother responding, not that I think I'm capable right now.

He continues toward my ear and when his warm breath breezes past the sensitive skin, my entire body shudders.

"I bet you're so fucking wet for me right now. Just like you were in the pool. Shall I find out if I'm right?"

His words are enough for the fog to clear for a few seconds. He must sense the change in me because he pulls back and his dark, dangerous eyes find mine. "You don't touch whores, rem—"

I don't get to finish the sentence before his lips slam down on mine and they get lost. His tongue sweeps into my shocked, open mouth and finds mine. My head screams to pull away from him, to slap him for being so presumptuous but my body, that sags back against the tree, my knees damn near giving way. Thankfully, he pushes his knee between my legs and presses his body tight against mine, keeping me in place.

His hands skim up my sides. The gentleness of his touch causing goosebumps to erupt across my entire body.

A low moan vibrates up his throat and I swear I feel it down to my toes. Lifting my arms I place them over his shoulders, my fingers twisting in the short hair at the nape of his neck and I fall further and further under his spell.

My lungs are burning for air when he eventually pulls away from my lips but he by no means stops. Kissing down my neck, his fingers run down the edge of my bikini top, slipping inside to pinch my pebbled nipple.

A loud gasp fills the air around us, but I don't realise it falls from my lips. "Oh fuck," I moan when his fingers are replaced by his hot mouth and my sensitive peak is sucked deep, his tongue circling and sending a strong bolt of electricity down between my legs.

Knowing exactly what I need, his fingers brush the skin of my stomach and slip inside my shorts when they find the waistband. There's no hesitation in his actions, he knows exactly what he wants and exactly what he's doing.

"Oh fuck, oh fuck," I chant, focusing on what's about to come and forgetting every ounce of reality that I should be focusing on right now.

We're just two young adults, hidden under the darkness of the trees in a moment of unadulterated passion. Just two bodies taking exactly what they need and forgetting the consequences of real life and what could happen when this is all over. Regrets mean nothing as my body races toward finding the release I didn't realise I was desperate for until his hands landed on me.

His fingers push inside my knickers and almost immediately find my clit.

"Jesus, Brit," he moans, finding me totally ready for him. He kisses across my chest, pulling the other side of my bikini away and giving that breast the same treatment as his finger delves deeper to find my entrance.

Dropping my hands, I run them down over the muscles of his stomach reveling in the fact they dance under my fingertips. When I meet the top of his shorts, I slip them inside but slide my hand around to his arse, squeezing tightly and pressing his erection harder into my hip. He moans, his hips thrusting against me to find some friction.

"Fuck, you're tight," he moans, slipping another digit inside me and bringing my release almost within touching distance. "Fuck, yes, Come on my fingers, Brit."

His lips find mine once again, his tongue slipping past my lips to explore everything he can, his thumb presses down on my clit and my muscles tighten down on him. He groans. The sound along with the vibrations is enough to push me over. He swallows down my cries as pleasure races through my body. His hand grips my waist and his body presses me harder into the tree to keep me upright, the pleasure threatening to floor me.

I've just barely come down from my high when he pulls back slightly. His usually dark blue eyes are black with his desire, his face pulled tight, and it's enough to have little aftershocks shooting around my body.

Jake looks down at his hand where he's just pulled it from my shorts, I'm not sure if he's considering cutting it off after touching me or what, but what I'm not expecting is for him to lift it to his lips and suck them deep into his mouth.

I can't help myself. I reach for him, not ready for this truce between us to be over. I run my hands up his chest and wrap one around the back of his neck. Lowering his hand, he stares down at me. His eyes run over every inch of my face, it's almost like he's seeing me for the first time which is crazy.

"Jake, I need—"

My words are cut off by a loud shout from the other side of the trees. "Thorn, you in there, man?"

"Fuck." Releasing his hold on me, he backs away. I hate the disappointment that races through me, but losing his touch causes a coldness to hit me that I wasn't expecting.

"Jake?" His name is merely a plea on my lips, and I hate how desperate I sound for a boy I hate.

"Don't," he snaps, looking toward where the shout came from.

"Thorn?"

"Yeah, I'm coming. Wait in the trailer, yeah?"

"Sure thing, man."

Trailer? What?

Turning his hard eyes on me, I swallow as a little fear creeps up my throat. "This never happened."

"What?"

"Just forget it," he barks, leaving no argument. "Take it as an apology for that fucking picture." Reaching out, he takes my chin in his hand, his grip stings but I'm powerless to pull away. His lips crash against mine for one more knee-weakening kiss before he pushes away with such force that I stumble on something and tumble to the ground.

His eyes flash with concern as I moan in pain, but he does nothing. Without another word, he picks up his shirt that's been discarded on the dirt and disappears from my sight.

"Fuck," I grunt, falling back to the ground. *What the fuck did I just do?*

24

JAKE

My chest heaves and my head spins as I make my way out of the trees and away from her. Confusion runs through my veins. I shouldn't have touched her, I should have just left the moment I found her watching me, but I couldn't fucking resist. The tempting swell of her small but perfect breasts hiding behind those tiny scraps of fabric, the smooth, toned skin of her stomach that had my mouth watering and the pathetic excuse for a pair of shorts. I didn't get a chance to check from behind but I'm pretty sure they did a shit job of covering her ass.

As I emerge into the afternoon sun, I can tell myself as much as I like that I shouldn't have done it, but the reality is that my body is demanding that I turn around and finish the job I started. No, if I'm really honest then I want to go back and make sure she's okay after I pushed her away. The little squeal of pain she let out when she hit the ground rings in my ears. I know she hurt herself and I'm a total asshole for leaving her. *But isn't that what you want her to think?*

Shaking the thought from my head, I focus on what I'm about to walk into. Holding my t-shirt in front of the raging hard-on she caused that's still tenting my sweatpants.

Ethan and Mason's voices rumble through the thin walls of my trailer. I've not spoken to Mason since Dash so I can only assume that he's here to give me another asswhipping for my recent actions.

Pulling the door open, I make sure I'm covering my lingering excitement, although I'm fairly sure it'll vanish the second my eyes land on those two.

Their conversation stops the moment I step inside the trailer and two narrowed pairs of eyes turn to me.

"What the fuck happened to you?"

"Just working out."

"Really? Wanna try telling us that when you haven't got girl all over your face." Panicking, I lift my shirt to rub at my lips. "Fucking hell, Thorn, really?"

"What the fuck ever. I'm going to shower."

"I don't want to hear you sorting that little situation out, man."

Flipping them both off, I head toward the bathroom, turn the shower on and drop my sweats. My cock bobs between my legs, taunting me with memories of how I ended up in this state in the first place. I can still taste her sweetness on my tongue, the softness of her skin, the soft moans and mewls that fell from her lips as I brought her to orgasm.

My cock's hard as fucking steel again but nothing short of her touch will relieve it and that pisses me off more than anything. Not only can I not get her out of my head but now I need her, and I never want to need anyone in my life, ever. Needing someone means handing a part of you over, a part that can be smashed to pieces without a second thought. I will not allow anyone to have any part of me, no matter how small.

Turning the water to cold, I stand there thinking about anything but her body that might allow my cock to return to normal so I can go out and face whatever those two have come to talk about.

"Who was she?" Mason snaps the second I reappear.

"Oh... uh... Chelsea?" I don't mean for it to come out like a question, but it's the only name I can think of without revealing the truth.

"Fuck off, do you really think we'll believe that?"

Shrugging, I grab a couple of beers and toss them over to my pissed off friends.

"One..." Mason starts. "Chelsea was in my class last period, so I know she wasn't here. And two, you don't kiss, and you certainly don't kiss sluts like Chelsea. So come on, out with it before we start jumping to conclusions."

"It was no one."

"It was her, wasn't it?" Ethan asks.

"Enough," I bark. "Did you two just come here to give me a hard time about who I kiss or was there a point to your visit?"

"We came to knock some sense into you."

Placing my bottle down on the counter, I look between my two best friends. I take a step forward, hands by my side. "Go on then."

"We didn't mean literally, Jake."

"No? I probably deserve it."

"Fucking right you do. That stunt you pulled today was unforgivable."

She didn't seem to have a problem with it a few moments ago. The words are right on the tip of my tongue, but I somehow manage to keep them in. No one aside from the two of us needs to know what happened in the trees this afternoon.

Shrugging once again, I grab my beer and fall down onto the couch now that I know they're not going to take a swing at me.

"This is fucking ridiculous, Thorn. You're ruining her fucking life. How can you not care? I know you're an asshole, but this is insane."

"I care. I care about her dragging up stuff that I'd rather was left in the past."

Ethan's face twists in confusion, but Mason knows more than most.

"None of that is her fault," he fumes. "Just leave her to get on with her life."

"You want her?" My voice comes out calmer than I'm feeling as the realization hits me as to why he's always trying to defend her.

"What? No, I don't fucking want her."

"You sure? You seem to be on her side a lot of the time."

"Yeah, because you're acting like a prick and I'm ashamed to be your friend right now."

"No one's forcing you." Taking a swig of my beer, I look away from him so he can't see how I really feel about that suggestion.

"Fuck you, Jake. You won't listen to my advice, then carry the fuck on. Ruin that girl's life just to spite yourself. All you're doing is trying to cover up how much you want her, we can all see it. I've no problem allowing you to fuck all this up so badly that she'll never look at you again, let alone touch you."

"I don't fucking want her," I seethe, standing like Mason so I can stare right into his eyes.

The fucker has the audacity to laugh. He full-on chuckles in my face. It makes my blood boil.

"So that wasn't her lipstick smeared all over your face when you walked in then? Don't forget, we also know where she lives."

My hands clench with my need to wipe the smug look off his fucking face as he prepares to continue.

"What if I were to tell you that I did want her? What if I were to tell you that I'd already invited her to Shane's party Saturday night and she'd said yes? What if I told you that I intended to fuck her into next—"

"Argh," I roar, flying at him and slamming my fist into his cheek.

"Enough," Ethan demands from behind me, his hands wrapping around my upper arms to pull me from my best friend.

Turning me, his hands slam down on my chest, forcing me to back up and away from Mason.

"You need to pull your head out of your ass, Jake. You want her, so stop fucking around before you screw things up so badly that you regret it."

I push forward against Ethan, but his hold is too strong.

"I might not want her, but there are enough guys at school who do. You put her front and center of their thoughts today and all of them want a piece of her, none more so than Shane. You need to make her yours before someone else does."

"I don't fucking want her," I lie, the words falling seamlessly from my lips.

"I give up," Mason says, his hands up in defeat before disappearing from sight, the door slamming and the trailer shaking with his departure.

Ethan lets up his hold, walks back over to the couch and pulls a pre-rolled joint from his pocket. Flicking his lighter, he takes a drag before offering it to me.

I take it from him and take a long hit, my muscles immediately start to relax. "So what have you got to say about all this?" I ask, realizing for the first time that he mostly sat there silently while Mason went off on me.

"I feel like I'm missing a huge part of this picture, but I also agree with Mase. You just need to fuck her and get it out of your system."

"Is she really going to Shane's party Friday night?"

"Fuck knows, man. But if he has anything to say about it, then she'll be there, he's been following her around like a lost fucking puppy since she arrived. And if you ask me—"

"I didn't."

"If you ask me, at the rate you're going, she'd be better off with him."

"You're probably right."

"Really?" he asks, his eyebrows practically hitting his hairline.

"Yeah, I won't allow it though."

A small smile twitches at the corner of his mouth and my stomach drops. I may as well just have admitted how badly I want her.

25

AMALIE

"**S**hit, what happened?" Camila asks the second I drop down into her car the next morning. I'm not surprised, the huge bandage on my arm is kind of impossible to miss.

When Gran got home and found me trying to patch it up with gauze, she was insistent that she took me to the ER and get it looked at properly. I tried arguing but stood little chance against her, especially when she started going on about how it would be what my parents wanted.

Turns out she was right though because I ended up with a few stitches on the deeper part of the cut. I've no idea how falling on a few fallen branches made such a mess. I guess it was karma for kissing the Devil or something, all I do know is that it hurts like a bitch and kept me awake most of the night. I guess I should just be grateful that I didn't break it.

"I fell."

"You fell?" she asks incredulously. "Where?"

"I went for a wander through the trees at the end of the garden and tripped over branches. It was stupid." My face burns red and I'm grateful that Camila is too focused on where she's going so she misses it.

"You don't say." Thankfully, she accepts my lie and moves on, although it's to another topic that I'm trying my best to avoid. "You sure you're ready for this? Things didn't die down at all after you left yesterday."

Groaning, I slump down in the passenger seat of her Mini hoping that it might swallow me up.

"Can't wait."

At some ungodly hour last night when my arm was throbbing, I made the mistake of dragging my phone from the bottom of my bag. Aside from concerned messages from Camila and Shane, all the rest were guys asking when I was available and to my utter shock there were a few very unimpressive dick pics waiting for me as well. None of that pointed to the fact things had already blown over. I know from living a life surrounded by celebrities that gossip is only gossip until something else happens, I was just hoping something crazy would have happened after I left yesterday and that I'd be old news already. I guess that was wishful thinking. Until something else happens, I'll be seen exactly as Jake intended, a whore. Although, after what happened yesterday in the trees, I can't help feeling like there might be a little truth in it.

I'm ashamed that he affected me so much that I allowed him to put his hands on me. I'm also confused as fuck because what he did to me, how he made me feel in those few moments went against everything he's been trying to make me out to be. He told me he'd never touch a whore yet he didn't bat an eyelid about getting me off at the first opportunity.

I think back to the previous evening in Poppy's pool and I can't help thinking that he'd have done the exact same thing if given half a chance.

My body heats as I replay yesterday's events in my head. I can still feel the rough skin of his hands scratch across my stomach as his fingers dived into my shorts. I can still taste him on my tongue and remember his rough voice as he whispered in my ear.

Fuck.

"Are you okay? You're muttering to yourself."

"Yeah, I'm good. Just remembered that I forgot some homework."

"I'm sure the teacher will let you off. No doubt they know all about what happened yesterday as well."

"Fantastic."

"Shit, I didn't mean it like that."

I feel their eyes burn into my skin the second I step from Camila's car, but I keep my head high and focus on where I'm going.

"Amalie." My name being called by a familiar voice drags my attention from the building in front of me and when I look up, I'm relieved to see it's just Shane and not a guy wanting to book a 'date'. "Hey, how are you doing?" His eyes drop to the bandage on my arm, but he doesn't ask about it when I shake my head and roll my eyes like it's nothing to worry about.

"Great, I love being the school bike."

"Don't," he growls, stepping a little closer to protect me from prying eyes.

"You sure you want to be seen with me? You know everyone will think you're paying for my time." I don't mean for it to come out sounding quite so bitter but catching a glance of Jake's group laughing and joking over Shane's shoulder pisses me off.

"I don't give a fuck what they think. We know the truth, that's all that matters."

"You know that it wasn't me?"

"Of course."

"How?" I ask, my eyes narrowing suspiciously.

"It's not the kind of thing you'd do."

"But you barely know me." His confidence in my morals does make me feel a bit better, making me wish everyone could see the same thing.

"I know enough. Can I walk you to class?"

"Your funeral," I whisper, but it's not quietly enough.

"Amalie," he warns once again. "I can feed you to the wolves if you like but I'm thinking you'd rather stay in the shadows."

Just the mention of shadows is enough to bring Jake back to the forefront of my mind. Why don't I feel like I did with him last night when I'm with Shane. He's a good guy, he treats me right. He'd show me exactly how he felt and never do the kinds of things Jake does.

There's something seriously wrong with me that I can feel nothing but the support of a friend as I walk beside Shane.

The catcalls of Jake's group of friends filter down to us. Glancing over, I spot Chelsea and a few of her followers but he's nowhere to be seen.

"Just ignore them," Shane says, encouraging me to keep moving with a gentle hand on my back. "Come on."

Plastering on a smile for my friend, I chance a look over at him. He's smiling down at me with a sparkle in his eye that has me swallowing in concern. No matter how platonic I try to keep things between us, seems his imagination keeps getting the better of him. His fingers twitch on the small of my back and I step away slightly. His lips curve into a frown but he doesn't say anything.

"If you're going out of your way, I can walk myself."

"Kinda, but I need to know you get there without being harassed by any of these idiots."

"I really appreciate the support."

"And I really fucking hate the way all these horny fucking guys are looking at you right now. It's like they think you're a piece of meat for them to play with. Jake's gonna fucking pay for what he did yesterday."

"Please, don't do anything stupid," I say with a wince knowing that going up against his captain will never end well.

"I can't promise anything."

"Hey, happy birthday, man," a guy I don't know says, walking up to Shane and slugging him playfully on the shoulder.

"Thanks, man."

"Can't wait for your party Friday night, it's gonna be epic."

"Yeah, it should be a good night." Shane's reply is really lacking any excitement.

"Well," he says awkwardly looking between the two of us, probably wondering what his friend is doing with the school bike. "Hopefully we'll be celebrating a win too."

"We can only hope. I'll see you later, yeah?"

"Sure thing." Nodding his head at both of us, he walks away and disappears into the crowd.

"It's your birthday?" I ask, my steps faltering a little with the realisation.

"Yep, I'm all legal and shit now." I look over just in time to see his eyebrows wiggle and a cheeky smile twitch his lips.

"Well, happy birthday. I had no idea so I... uh... haven't—"

My awkward excuse as to why I haven't bought him a gift is cut off when he grabs my forearm and turns me to face him.

"Have dinner with me."

"Oh... uh..." My heart starts to race with the thought that even though I've been trying really hard not to give him any ideas that he might have just got them anyway. Biting down on my bottom lip, I stare up into his hopeful eyes and my stomach drops. I really don't want to hurt him.

"Not like a date or anything." Although by the way his face drops when he says this, it's obvious that it's exactly the opposite of what he wants. "Just friends. You can pay as my birthday present."

"Just as friends?" I ask, feeling like the shittiest person on the planet for turning down such a sweet guy. He's going to be an incredible boyfriend for someone one day, just not mine. As much as I might wish that he was the one to set my blood on fire and cause an eruption of butterflies in my belly, he doesn't. I also doubt he ever will. Shane and I are destined to be friends and the sooner he comes to terms with that, the better.

Awareness heats my left side, glancing over I find the students who were in front of us have parted and at the end of the hallway, seething in anger, is Jake. His eyes are dark and murderous as he stares between Shane and me. Trying to swallow down my apprehension, I turn back to Shane as he talks.

"Yeah, just friends. No pressure, Am—"

Pain sears through my shoulder as my back and head slams back against the wall.

"What the fuck is your problem, man?" Shane barks as he stumbles back a few steps.

"How much does she charge for dinner? I doubt she's worth it."

When my eyes focus, I find the two of them nose to nose. Jake is an inch or two taller, usually it would be unnoticeable but right now he looks like a giant compared to Shane. His chest is puffed out in anger, his shoulders wide as he tries to intimidate him but fair play to Shane because he holds his head high and gives back as good as he gets.

"You'd have to care about getting to know a girl to understand."

"I care," Jake growls so quietly I almost miss it.

"Yeah about getting between their legs and leaving as fast as possible."

"Watch it." Jake's hands slam down on Shane's chest and he steps back once again. "You need to remember where your loyalties lie." With one final hard stare and a flick of his eyes over to me, Jake storms off down the hallway. It takes a couple of seconds but the bystanders who watched the whole thing soon continue with their earlier conversations and turn their attention away from us.

"Fuck, are you okay?" Shane asks, rushing over to where I'm still standing, back up against the wall. I blink for what feels like the first time since I saw him standing feet away and it's enough to force a couple of tears out of my eyes. "Fuck, did he hurt you?"

It's only as his words register that I remember my head bouncing off the wall behind me as Jake slammed into me. But it's not the pain from that which is causing the tears, it's the memory of how gentle with me he was last night. Yes, his touches were demanding and confident but at no point was he rough or careless.

Blinking a little faster to force the tears away, I push myself from the wall. "I'm fine. Honestly," I add when he looks at me with a raised brow.

"That guy's an asshole. If I never had to see him again, it would be too soon."

I mumble my agreement, although even as I say it something inside me twists painfully. I should be fully on board after everything he's done to me, but there's a part of me even after what just happened that wants to follow him. To try to find out what his problem is and... *help maybe?* Chastising myself for the thought alone, it's clear that Jake Thorn is long past being rescued and that if anyone were capable, then it wouldn't be me doing it.

"Yeah, same." My agreement is weak at best and it causes Shane's eyes to narrow at me with suspicion. "So when are we having this dinner?" I ask, trying to get the heat off me.

"Thursday night? We can't do Friday because of the game and party."

"Party?"

"Yeah, my house after the game. It's kinda tradition, didn't anyone tell you about it?"

I shrug, there's a good chance someone might have but football parties aren't exactly high on my priority list right now.

"You'll be there though, right? At the game and party?" The hope that shines in his eyes is enough to tell me that the right answer would be no. I should say no right now, but when his face drops and a sad puppy dog look appears, I have a really hard time refusing.

"Come on, let's get you to class." The rest of the walk is in silence and I'm afraid I might have hurt him when the only thing I want to do is the opposite.

26

AMALIE

The rest of the day, and the next, is exactly as I expected. Full of stares, pointing, hushed whispers and propositions. By the time I meet Camila at her car Thursday afternoon, I've just about had my fill of bullshit.

"How you holding up?" she asks, glancing over at me as I climb into her car.

Letting out a giant sigh of frustration, a quiet chuckle falls from her lips. "That good?"

"Worse."

"It'll blow over soon. With the game and Shane's party this weekend, someone is bound to do something stupid and take the limelight off you."

"I can only hope," I mutter as she pulls away from school.

"Ready for your big date tonight?"

"It's not a date."

"Riiight."

"I'm serious, Camila. Stop getting any ideas about doubling with you and Noah out of your head. I'm not interested in Shane like that."

"So you keep saying, but he really likes you. Just give it a chance."

"That's not a good enough reason to lead him on. We're going out tonight as friends and that's all we're ever going to be." Even the thought of tonight has my stomach knotting in uncertainty. As much as I might plead that it's not a date, it's going to look like that to everyone else. As much as I don't want them to get the wrong idea, I also don't want Shane's reputation tarnished by spending time with me, the girl they all think charges by the hour.

"Do you know what you're wearing?" Camila asks, dragging me from my thoughts.

"Uh... jeans and t-shirt."

"Jesus, Amalie. I know it's not a date, but you could put a little effort in at least."

"Fine," I huff. "Want to come in and help?"

"I thought you'd never ask."

"How was school?" Gran asks as we walk into the kitchen to grab a drink.

"Yeah, it was good," I lie, feeling Camila's stare burning into the back of my head as I do. "What?" I mouth, turning to look at her, it's not like I came straight home and spilled every detail of the picture that's circulating that makes it look like me giving head. There are some things a gran and granddaughter never need to discuss, and this is one of them.

"You hear about Amalie's date?"

"It's not a date," I seethe, much to Camila's amusement.

"Aw, it's so exciting. I remember my first date. He was such a sweetheart. He bought me flowers, took me for a meal and we had the most romantic walk on the beach." Gran's eyes glaze over as she walks down memory lane. "And when he kissed me at the end of the night, I thought my life was never going to be the same again."

"There will be zero kissing going on tonight. We're just going out as friends."

"Yeah, yeah. Now let's go and find you something to wear that your *friend* will really enjoy."

"Make sure she wears a dress," Gran calls as we disappear down the hall.

"I am not wearing a bloody dress," I grumble, pushing my door open.

Camila goes straight for my wardrobe and begins pulling out suggestions, every single one I refuse. I'm not dressing up, I refuse to allow Shane to think that I made an effort to impress him. We. Are. Friends.

In the end, I relent on a smart casual summer dress with spaghetti straps and flowers all over. I rationalise that if it's casual enough to wear to school, then it's casual enough to wear out on my non-date.

Camila once again insists on doing my hair and makeup and when I eventually step foot out of my bedroom, I've got light but smokey eyes and loose curls hanging around my shoulders. The bandage that's wrapped around my arm does nothing for the look, but there's not a lot I can do about that, nor the constant reminder of the person who put it there.

"Whoa, you look beautiful. He's not going to know what hit him."

Groaning at Gran's words, I immediately turn around to change but unfortunately for me, Camila stands in my way.

"Uh uh... no way." Just as I go to step toward her, the doorbell rings. "It's too late anyway, he's here." The delight that lights up her face makes me want to stomp on her toe with my wedges.

"You're going to pay for this," I warn on a whisper but all I get in return is a joyful laugh.

"Just try to enjoy yourself, yeah?"

"Gran, no," I call when I spot her heading toward the front door. The last thing I need is her joining in on the 'wouldn't Shane make a great boyfriend' party. "Both of you just... disappear."

"He knows I'm here, he'll have parked by my car."

"Uh, fine. Gran, go hide." She pouts but does as she's told and slips into the living room.

Blowing out a long breath, I prepare to open the door. I'm not quick enough though because the bell rings through the house once again.

"Hey, sorry," I say, pulling the door open and plastering a smile on my face.

"No worries. I was beginning to think you'd stood me up on your own doorstep." His laugh that follows is a nervous one, and it doesn't make me feel any better.

"Whoa, you scrub up well." Instead of the standard jeans and t-shirt he always seems to wear at school, Shane's dressed in a pair of chinos and a smart-ish button-down. It's clear he's spent a little more time than usual on his unruly hair and he smells pretty damn good. His scent has my mouth watering, but it's still not enough to make me want him.

"You too, you look stunning." My cheeks heat at his compliment and I feel awkward for the first time in his presence since the day I crashed into him.

"Right then, have a good time, kids. Make sure you're back before curfew," Camila sings with delight, pushing past both of us and heading toward her car. With a little wave, she pulls away leaving the two of us alone for the first time.

"Ready?" He holds his arm out for me and I feel like a twat when I refuse but I already feel like this night is getting out of control.

"Where are we going?" I ask as his car speeds toward the seafront.

"For the best burger in town, of course."

"Aces?" I ask hesitantly.

"Of course. Where else? You said you wanted casual, and it doesn't get any better than Aces."

Shit.

I don't need to say anything, he must be able to sense my tension.

"It'll be okay. Plus, I refuse to hide you. I couldn't give a fuck what everyone thinks. I know that wasn't you in that photo and so do you. We also know that I'm not paying you to be with me, so fuck the rest of them and their small minds."

My fingers twist together in my lap as I try to believe what Shane's saying, but I can't help feeling like this night is only going to get worse.

Thankfully, Aces looks pretty quiet as we walk up to the entrance.

"Over here." Shane reaches out and takes my hand, pulling me over to an empty booth. I keep my head down but I don't miss the silence that descends around the diner. Quiet whispers soon start up but the buzzing in my ears means

I don't hear any of it. I do however feel Shane's hand squeeze mine tighter so I can only imagine what gossip is going around right now.

He leads me over to the booth and almost immediately a waitress comes over to take our drink order. I'm relieved that it gives me something to focus on other than the multiple stares I can feel tingling my skin. I've never felt more unwelcome in my life.

"I'm sorry, maybe you were right to be concerned."

"It's fine. They'll get bored eventually." Thankfully my voice sounds much stronger than how I feel about the situation.

Risking a glance up, I find Chelsea and her little gang of bitches at the table they were at the first time I came here. Most of them are staring at me but Chelsea has her head in her phone. I manage to contain my groan, knowing that she's probably summoning the rest of her troops including one I really have no intention of seeing tonight.

Things quieten down for a bit and we manage to eat our burgers without being interrupted, although at no point do I lose the interest of the rest of the customers. Even the ones I'm pretty sure don't attend Rosewood seem interested in me. I guess that photo didn't stay within the school population.

I'm just ordering a sundae for dessert when a shiver runs down my spine. I don't need to see the look on Shane's face as he glances at the door behind me to know who's about to walk in.

I tell myself to keep my eyes down on the menu, giving him any attention will only spur him on but my traitorous body has other ideas because only seconds later I find myself looking over my shoulder.

His piercing stare is directed right at me. The moment he realises that I'm staring right back at him, his eyes widen in surprise before they drop down my body. He can't see much seeing as I'm sitting in a booth but that doesn't stop them darkening.

"Well, well, well, isn't this *cute*."

"Leave us alone, Thorn."

"Or what?" he taunts, causing Shane to slide over to the edge of the booth toward him. "You gonna make me?"

"Shane, just ignore him," I plead, but it's too late. He's already standing toe to toe with Jake. Standing alongside them, I place my hand on Shane's forearm much to Jake's horror if the widening of his eyes and gritting of his teeth are anything to go by. "Sit back down, please. He's not worth it." I'm not above begging right now so that we don't cause more of a scene than we already are.

Taking a step back, Jake turns his eyes on me. They drop down my now exposed body and slowly take in every inch of my bare legs. Without looking over, I sense Shane's muscles tense as he prepares to physically remove Jake's eyes from my body, but he doesn't get the chance.

"Wasted on him, Brit. Wasted." He slowly steps back, taking his time to run his eyes over me once again before turning and going to join his gang of douchebags, which as usual these days seems to be minus Mason.

27

JAKE

hy the hell am I even here? I was asking that question before I even walked through the door but the second I got Chelsea's message telling me that she was here with *him* I didn't have a choice but to see it with my own eyes.

I thought it would be fun to come and taunt her but one look at her sitting there, dressed up all pretty for him and I knew I'd made a huge fucking mistake. A sharp pain pierced my chest as the image of pressing her up against that tree fills my head. My mouth waters as the memory of how sweet she tasted hits me. My muscles tighten with the need to feel her body against me and her tongue dueling with mine once again. The little summer dress she's wearing is just begging to be ripped away from her lean, sexy body and that's not being done by anyone's hands but my own. Teammate or not, Shane needs to understand who she belongs to.

My eyes widen as she reaches her hand out to stop him squaring up to me, the sight of a fresh bandage wrapping around her upper arm makes my stomach twist. Please tell me I didn't cause that?

I desperately want to ask her, the words are right on the tip of my tongue but thankfully her words about me not being worth it are the dose of cold water I need to remember what the fuck I'm doing, and admitting that anything happened between us can't happen again. It was a mistake, a mistake I might have been dreaming about repeating since, but a mistake nonetheless.

Sitting down with my friends, I fight to keep my eyes on the table in front of me and not the couple on a date just a few feet away. Why the fuck is he dating her anyway, I thought I made it pretty clear she was off limits.

"Who the fuck does she think she is? Does she think she's something special because she's got a fancy accent and famous, rich parents," Chelsea fumes.

"Dead parents," Victoria chips in.

"That don't give her the right to come storming in here and taking the guys right out from under our feet."

"Why, did you want Shane for yourself?"

"Fuck no. He's too much of a goodie-two-shoes. I bet he's a fucking virgin too."

"So what's the problem?"

"Who she's going to go after next is my issue. She'll soon realize he's a square and move on."

My skin prickles as Chelsea turns her gaze on me. "What?"

"You got plans tonight?" Her eyes flit between my eyes and lips.

"Yeah, and they don't involve you." I push her from my lap.

"Ouch."

"Fuck off."

Chelsea seethes, turns her back on me to give another of my teammates some attention.

The movement of Shane getting up and heading to the restrooms catches my eye. As tempted as I am to follow him and ensure he's unable to return to his table, I ignore him and zero my eyes in on Brit, who's stirring the remnants of her ice cream around the dish like it's the most fascinating thing in the world.

Unable to help myself, I push off the chair I'm sitting in and drop down on the bench opposite her.

"I think we should get—what the fuck are you doing?" she asks in a panic when she lifts her head and finds me staring back at her. "Shane's only gone to the toilet."

"Shame. What did you do?" I nod toward the bandage on her arms and she tries twisting away so I can't see it. "No point hiding." I drop my eyes down to where the juncture of her thighs are beneath the table and delight in seeing the color of her cheeks redden.

"It's nothing. You need to leave."

"Did I do it?"

"Why do you care? You want to hurt me, remember?"

"Not physically. Fuck." Rubbing my hand over my face and rough jaw, I stare into her soft blue eyes. Eyes that not so long ago I never wanted to see again but I'm starting to realize that they're nothing like the ones in my memory and everything like ones I want to look into over and over again. "I'm sorry."

I'm taken aback when her only response is to laugh at my apology.

"What's funny?"

"You apologising. That's a joke, right?"

My mouth opens to respond, although I have no fucking clue what to say when a shadow falls over us.

"Do you mind? You're sitting in my seat."

"I'm pretty sure you're actually taking my place right now."

"How's that exactly? Correct me if I'm wrong, but weren't you the one who just sent a very questionable photo around the entire school just to shame her? So why exactly would you want to be sitting here if you hate her so much?"

Isn't that the fucking million dollar question?

"You're right. She's all yours." Bile burns my throat just saying the words, but like fuck am I letting anyone know how I'm really feeling about this little date I'm witnessing.

"Wanna get out of here?" Shane asks Brit, totally ignoring that I'm still sitting here.

"Yeah. The unwanted company is kinda ruining the mood."

I have no idea if she says it for my benefit or because something really is developing between the two of them. Either way, I'm not fucking happy about it.

Reaching his hand out, I almost lean over and slap it away but to my horror, Brit reaches out and allows him to pull her from the booth and hand in hand they walk out of the diner. My stomach turns over like I could puke right on Bill's checkered floor, that is until she turns back and looks over her shoulder at me at the very last minute. That one look tells me everything I need to know. She's not with him, not in the slightest because just like me, her head's still in those trees and the body she wants next to her is mine.

"You want to get out of here and get drunk?" Ethan's voice filters through the haze that had descended and when I glance up, I find him staring at me with concern written all over his face.

"Yes."

Jumping into his car, we take off and I feel like I can breathe once again now I'm nowhere near her. But at the same time images float around my head about what she could be doing right now... with him. Is she allowing him to touch her, is she going to let him kiss her?

My teeth grind as the images keep coming. I should be the one fucking kissing her. *She's mine.* The sudden realization of how much truth is behind those two words hit me like a truck. Lifting my hand to try to soothe the pain radiating from my chest, I suck in a deep breath.

"You okay?" Ethan asks, glancing over at where I'm fighting to breathe.

"Yeah, just keep driving. You'd better have some fucking good weed."

"What the fuck's that girl doing to you, man?"

"Fuck if I know."

"You want me to try to track them down so you can claim what's yours?"

"She's not fucking mine," I grunt.

"Riiight, Thorn. Whatever you say." He grins, making me want to wipe it off his face. "I'm starting to understand what Mason's problem is, you really are fucking blind, dude."

"Are you just about finished?"

"Not getting involved, man. Whatever you need, I've got your back."

I appreciate that more than I want to admit seeing as Mason's fucked off. He's been my best friend for as long as I can remember, the calming influence to my hot head. He's followed me around like a fucking dog forever, I didn't think I'd ever piss him off. Seems I got that wrong. I miss him, but not enough to go fucking groveling. I'll have to come up with something else to get him on my side.

"Not going to yours?" I'm disappointed when Ethan takes a turn toward my place instead of his.

"Na, my parents are back for a few days. It's gotta be yours if you wanna light up."

"Great."

I tell myself that being so close to Brit won't be an issue. That at no point tonight am I going to want to go through the trees to find out if he brought her home safe.

Fuck, I need a drink.

———

Relaxing back, I allow the weed to flow through me, chilling me the fuck out while the beer warms my belly.

"You think they're back yet?"

"Who?" Ethan asks sleepily from his side of the couch.

"Shane and Brit." I roll my eyes like it should be fucking obvious.

"How should I know? If things went well, then he probably took her up to Head Point to get busy in the back seat of his car."

My entire body locks up tight at the suggestion. "He wouldn't... would he?"

"If he doesn't, then he must have a pussy because she's—"

"Do not finish that sentence."

"Fucking hell, Thorn, you've really got it bad, don't you?"

"I haven't got anything, I'd just rather not think about what they might or might not be up to." It's a barefaced lie and we both know it. Thankfully, Ethan drops it, he shrugs and goes back to his joint and whoever it is he's messaging.

I'm so lost inside my own head that I don't realize how much time's gone by or that Ethan's passed out next to me, snoring like a motherfucker.

Glancing over, I take in his peaceful sleeping face as he drools on my couch. My mind once again wanders to Brit and I find myself jumping up without putting much thought into my actions. I look back at my sleeping friend when I get to the door to make sure he's still out cold, then I push it open and step out into the night.

The weed and beer means my legs are a little unstable as I head toward the trees, but now I've started, I won't turn back until I find what I need to shut my imagination off.

I maneuver my way to my homemade gym without much consideration, I've made the trip a million times. But I find myself having to pull my cell from my pocket to make use of the flash when I trip over a stick as I try to make my way out the other side.

My cell illuminates the space just enough that I don't end up on my ass and before long I'm walking up an unfamiliar back yard toward a tired looking bungalow.

Walking up to the closest window, I find exactly what I was hoping for, Brit fast asleep in her bed. Glancing to my left, I spot a door that I assume leads directly into her bedroom.

Wrapping my fingers around the handle, I gently push down, my heart pounds as I wait to find out if it'll open. A soft click fills the air around me and my stomach twists in anticipation.

Slipping inside the dark room, I'm as silent as possible as I make my way over to her bed, the room only illuminated by the moonlight streaming in through her open curtains.

Crouching down beside her, I take in her beautiful, sleeping face, her long, light eyelashes rest down onto her cheekbones, her cheeks are a rosy pink, almost as if she knows I'm here, and her full lips are parted just slightly as her soft breaths slip past.

My eyes run over every feature, my cock hardening more with each second that passes. Unable to stop myself, I reach my hand out and tuck a lock of hair that had fallen onto her cheek behind her ear.

The moan she emits when our skin connects makes my balls ache and my veins fill with fire. It would be so easy to take what I need with her like this. I might be an asshole but that really isn't my style, even as much as I want to feel her body pressed up against mine right now.

Brushing my knuckle down her cheek and across her lips, she shifts and moans, and I panic, that is until I hear something that has my body frozen to the spot.

"Jake." Her voice is a breathy whisper, just like it was when I had my fingers inside her, and I almost come on the spot. Is she fucking dreaming about me?

But why? I've been nothing but an asshole to her since the day I first laid eyes on her. It's bad enough that I take up any thoughts in her head during daylight hours, but at night as well? That's fucked up. Just like how she never should have allowed me to get a taste of her the other night. Just that one taste has turned my slight obsession with her into something I'm now struggling to control, hence the reason I'm standing inside her bedroom like a creep while she sleeps.

She stirs again and reaches out. Her light fingertips trail down my t-shirt covered chest and my entire body shudders at the contact. I stay stock still, waiting for her to wake up and freak out at any moment but that doesn't happen. Instead, she drops her arm and drifts back off into a deep sleep.

Knowing I need to get out before I'm caught, I stand and make my way toward the door. Spotting a pad of paper and pen on her desk, I stop at the last minute and leave her a note.

28

AMALIE

Waking the next morning, my entire body is burning and covered in a light sheen of sweat. My nipples brush against the fabric of my tank and my core aches. The lingering images of my dream come back to me and my face heats with embarrassment as the picture of Jake sneaking into my room and taking exactly what he needed slams into me. It was so vivid, so much so that if I didn't know I'd just woken up, I'd be questioning if it really did happen.

I need to do something to get him out of my head. I had a great night with Shane last night, why isn't it him who can be starring in my naughty dreams? Why's it got to be the school's arsehole who's set on ruining my life?

After we thankfully left the diner and Jake's angry eyes behind, Shane took us for a drive around the town before we ended up back at Gran's. Knowing she was out, I invited him in and we sat out in the garden with some of her homemade lemonade and chatted away about school, our friends and other nonsense topics. At no point did he try to bring up my past life or my parents, or even Jake, and I was more than grateful to not have to think about such heartbreaking and painful subjects for an hour or two.

If he thought that me inviting him in was code for something more happening between us, then he didn't give them away and he also didn't look disappointed when the night ended with only a friendly hug between us. Even still, I went to bed with a heavy heart knowing he was feeling more for me than I was for him, but I can't help it, I can't force myself to fall for him.

I fell asleep like I have done every night this week with memories of my time in the trees with Jake playing on my mind. Those memories are to blame for the vivid actions of my dirty mind during my sleep and just another reason why I need to block the whole thing from my memory. Nothing good can come from obsessing over it. It's not like I'm going to allow it to happen again even if the opportunity presented itself.

Swinging my legs from the bed, I stand and walk over to the door that leads to the garden so I can swing it open and allow the cool morning air to fill the room. I love the scent of the end of summer mixing with the faint sea air.

A rush of air surrounds me, causing goosebumps to prick my skin as something fluttering to the floor behind me catches my eyes.

Bending down, I reach out to pick up the paper that floated to the floor but the second I lay my eyes on it my entire body freezes.

Lock your fucking door.

Looking around, I search for clues that anyone was here, but nothing seems out of place. Then I'm reminded once again of my dream. Of his gentle touch, the warmth of his skin.

"Fuck." Placing my palm on my cheek where I remember his trailing fingertips, I stumble back until I fall down on my bed. *Was it all a dream?*

Camila questions me on my 'date' the whole way to school, thankfully distracting me from my potential late night visitor but the second we arrive and I step out of her car, he's all I can think about. I look around and for the first time since I started here, I actively look for him, hoping to find any kind of evidence for the truth about last night. But sadly, aside from his bunch of idiot friends, I don't see any sign of him.

Pushing thoughts of him avoiding me to the back of my head, I head for my first class. He's Jacob Thorn, king of Rosewood High, why would he feel the need to avoid me? For all I know, he did come into my room last night and he's got more damning evidence of me on camera that he's in the process of shaming me with.

My heart races at the thought. If that's the case, he could have done anything. My stomach twists and my breakfast threatens to make a reappearance.

I'm the first into my art class, I stumble toward my desk and fumble to pull the chair out as I try to convince myself that I'm allowing my imagination to get the better of me. I know he's a dick, but he wouldn't take things that far, would he? I try not to focus on what the answer to that question could be.

"Hey, how are you holding up?"

"What? Why? What's happened?" I practically bark at Poppy when she falls down beside me.

"Uh..." Her hesitation has my heart racing and my head spinning. Her eyes narrow and her head tilts to the side in confusion. "Nothing, I don't think. I just meant after the beginning of the week, plus I heard a rumor you had a date last night."

Blowing out a huge sigh of relief that nothing else has happened, *yet,* I drop my head to my hands. "It wasn't a date. Just two friends getting some dinner."

"Does he know that? Even I've seen the way he looks at you."

"Yes, he was fully aware and nothing untoward happened. Not that your bloody cousin would have allowed it."

"Jake was there?"

"Yeah, always everywhere I turn driving me freaking crazy." My cheeks heat as memories from last night hit me once again but thankfully Poppy either doesn't notice or just ignores it.

"He needs to get a grip. He's acting like a crazy man."

"You're telling me. Did you get your bit of our presentation finished?" I ask, changing the subject.

"Yep, all done. We still meeting at lunch to go through it?"

"Yes. Library?"

"If you want."

By some miracle, I manage to keep my head down and avoid almost everyone all day. I spend my free period in the library along with the entire lunch break with Poppy running through our presentation for later that afternoon.

I hear no gossip that anything else has happened and there's no evidence of any new footage of me, so by the time I walk out of school after my last class to meet Camila, I'm starting to relax a little.

"Ah she lives," she chuckles. "I thought I was going to have to come and drag you out from that damn library."

"I had loads of work to do."

"So you weren't avoiding Shane after last night?"

"No. Why would I?"

She shrugs, but it's not enough to make me forget her comment. "What's happened, Cam?"

"Nothing, nothing. He just seemed even more interested this morning. Couldn't stop talking about you."

"He has no reason to, we had a nice night, like I told you this morning. Nothing happened, and I gave him no idea that it would."

"Well, from what I could tell, he's certainly got that idea."

"Fucking hell. Maybe I shouldn't go tonight."

"No chance. It's his birthday, you have to go."

"No, I really don't. I really don't want to spend a night with the football team and the cheerleaders, and I especially don't need to spend the night watching everything I say or do in case I lead him on."

"It'll be fine. Apparently Jake's not going, so that's one less thing you need to worry about."

Fuck. My. Life. How did things get so damn complicated?

"Come on, let's get out of here. We've got a game and a party to prepare for."

———

"So you're telling me that we have to wear school colours tonight?" I ask Camila when she pulls out multiple items of clothes that are all red and white.

"Yep, tradition."

"Fantastic," I mutter, pulling my wardrobe open and looking at my options.

I'm shoved aside as Camila takes over my wardrobe choices. "Hmmm... what about... this," she says, pulling a short white skirt from a hanger. "And... uh... this." A barely-there red handkerchief top swings from her finger. Both items are things I wouldn't have thought twice about sliding into when I was back in London, but here things are different. I know I'm going to be under the watchful eyes of most of the Rosewood High students tonight and it's something I'd rather avoid as much as possible.

"Or this?" I drag out a pair of white skinny jeans and a red t-shirt.

"Nope, too boring. I allowed you to wear what you wanted to the Dash, and you stood out like a sore thumb. Trust me, you'll look hot."

I refrain from explaining that I want to look the opposite of hot so I don't attract attention, but I know it's pointless, Camila doesn't understand.

Taking the clothes she's still holding out toward me, I turn on my heel and head into the bathroom to change.

My legs look a mile long in this skirt even to my own eyes, it most definitely isn't going to help me blend in and the top, although sexy, is even smaller than I remember.

With a huff, I throw the bathroom door open and storm toward Camila. "Can we compromise? The skirt and a t-shirt or the top and jeans?" I ask, exasperated.

"Whoa, you're not serious?" Her eyes almost pop out of her head when she turns and runs them over me. "I'm not into chicks, but I'd totally do you."

"That's the problem, Cam. I don't want anyone to look at me and want to 'do me.' I just want to hide." My frustration about this is beginning to get the better of me.

"Even Jake?" Her serious eyes hold mine and my stomach twists. *Can she read my mind?*

"No, especially not him."

"Really? Don't think I haven't clocked the change in the two of you. The air between you crackles even from across the school."

"I don't know what you're talking about. Anyway, you said he wasn't going tonight."

"That's what I've heard."

Narrowing my eyes at her, I suddenly get the feeling that she might be stretching the truth slightly.

"It's what I've heard," she repeats, her hands up in defeat. "Don't shoot the messenger."

———

When we walk into the stadium ready for the game a few hours later, it's with red and white face paint across our cheeks and Rosewood flags in our hands. I felt ridiculous in Camila's car but as we join the rest of the school and I realise it's not just the two of us looking like this, I feel a little better.

She eventually relented and I manage to get away with wearing the white skirt with a simple red t-shirt. I feel a little more comfortable, but I also didn't miss some of the stares in my direction as we walked from the car.

The game is much like last week's. The excitement is through the roof, the chants are so loud that it makes the stands beneath my feet vibrate and the elation when we score first is beyond belief.

I've still no clue about the game so while everyone oohs and ahhs around me, I try my best to join in and learn what it is they're so excited or disappointed about.

As we're beginning to get toward the end of the sixty minutes we're winning, but only just. That's when everything starts to unravel. The crowd goes quiet as the ball flies up in the air toward the other team's end of the field. The sound of Shane's name being screamed fills my ears as he takes off toward it to defend their current winning position, but just as he should grab it, he fumbles. The ball hits the ground right before one of the other team's players picks it up and scores.

Shane's shoulders drop in defeat as a couple of his teammates slap him on the back in support while the other team celebrates. Everything seems fine until Rosewood's quarterback comes storming across the field in Shane's direction. The stadium falls silent, Jake's intentions obvious from his body language. The second he steps in front of Shane his hands come out and he forcefully pushes against his chest. The rest of the Rosewood team turn to find their captain taking out all his frustrations on Shane. It takes a couple of seconds for them to react and when they do, it takes two of our guys to pull Jake away.

It all happens so fast, but one moment he's wrestling with Shane and the next he's been sent off and is disappearing from sight, I presume toward the locker rooms.

"Well that was dramatic," Camila comments beside me as the teams get ready to continue for the final few minutes. Rosewood is now behind and tensions are running very high for them to pull off this win. "Don't look so worried, they'll do it," she says when she glances over at me.

"Oh, I'm not worried."

"You might want to tell yourself that. You look as tense as a virgin at an orgy."

"What!?" I balk, dragging my eyes from where Jake disappeared to look at her.

"Ohhh," she sings like she's just figured something out. "You totally want to go after him, don't you?"

"Huh?" I try to come across confused, but I know exactly what she means and I'm having a hard time not doing exactly what she just suggested. It's crazy, I know, but something is calling for me to follow him. To find out what his problem is and if he's okay.

"Don't play all innocent. You know as well as I do that his issue with Shane is you. You said yourself that he was a pain in the ass at Aces last night during your date—"

"It wasn't a date."

"Ugh, whatever. He wants you, and Shane's standing in his way."

"There's nothing going on with Shane." My voice is exasperated. How many times do I need to repeat this?

"I know this. You know this. But does Jake?"

"Why would he care? He hates me."

"Does he?"

Suddenly a roar erupts around us, Camila's head whips toward the field and I follow to find the team celebrating a very last-minute touchdown which gives Rosewood the win seconds before the end-of-game whistle.

My chest swells with pride as I watch the guys on the field celebrate, but something tugs at my chest when I see Mason pull off his helmet and look around for his absent best friend. He's soon distracted when Ethan pulls him in for a celebratory hug. I've no idea if Camila's right and all of that was basically my fault, but I feel awful nonetheless. I don't want to get between anyone, especially if it's going to affect so many others like a loss here tonight would have.

"Let's get out of here. It's time to party!" Camila sings, grabs my hand and pulls me from the stands along with everyone else who's rushing to get out of here and start celebrating properly.

As we exit the stadium, I can't help looking back toward where I know the locker rooms are. I wonder if he's still in there?

29

JAKE

My entire body is locked tight with frustration. I've spent most of the day with that fucker in all my classes and then out on the field tonight. Every time I look at him, all I can see in his eyes is *I have something you want*. The image of him laughing with Brit last night in Aces is burned into the back of my mind. At least I know she didn't spend the night with him.

My cock twitches once again despite the tension taking over my body as the image of her peacefully sleeping comes into mind. I've regretted walking away since the second I silently closed her door behind me. If I'd have woken her, what would she have done? Would she have made me leave or would I have got another taste of her? The way she moaned my name certainly hinted toward the fact she might have allowed me to take what I needed.

As I storm away from the school with the sound of the entire student body shouting and screaming with what I hope was our win, my muscles ache. I'm screwing everything up, and as much as I want to blame her for everything, I know it's all my own doing.

If I'd ignored my burning need for revenge on another woman the first time I laid eyes on her, then none of this would have happened. If I wasn't so screwed up because of that previously mentioned woman, then I might have been able to deal with all the bullshit in my life. But no, one look at a girl who represents the same thing *she* did, and I lose all fucking sense of what I'm doing. One thing's for fucking sure, I wasn't supposed to want her. I wanted to hurt her, not want to make her fucking mine.

"Argh," I scream out my frustration into the night.

I should have stuck around for the team to come back into the locker room and for my ear bashing from Coach for losing my temper against one of our own, but I couldn't stick looking into his eyes once again. That fucker's got something that belongs to me and I'm not going to roll over and watch it happen.

When the lights of a store come into view in the distance, I decide to try my luck.

I nod at the cashier as I enter and breathe a sigh of relief that it's a young guy who looks like he might just understand my need for an escape tonight.

I grab a bottle of vodka, a couple of bags of chips and a few pre-made pasta dishes to shove in my fridge once I make it home tonight and carry the lot to the register praying that he'll just ring it up and let me be on my way.

The guy scans the food, obviously leaving the bottle until the end and my stomach knots. Now I've got it in touching distance, I need it more than ever. The relief from my fucked up reality is right there, but he holds all the cards. If he IDs me then I'm fucked. I've got a fake at home for these exact situations, but I didn't think I'd need it tonight.

"Bad night?" the guy asks, his fingers wrapping around the neck of the bottle.

"Like you wouldn't believe."

"I've got girl issues myself, I know how that can be, man." His assumption that my issue must be because of a girl pisses me off but sadly, he's spot on.

"Sucks, huh?"

My mood brightens just a little as the little beep from the register rings through my ears and I watch as the guy drops the bottle into the bag with the rest of my purchases.

"Good luck with your girl," he calls once I've paid and started heading toward the door.

"You too, man."

Things look up a little as I head toward the beach with my new purchases under my arm. I'm about to forget everything and it couldn't be more welcome.

I make sure I'm hidden from any passersby and drop down between a couple of dunes. I pull the bottle from the bag and twist the top.

I wince as the first mouthful burns down my throat, but aside from someone punching me in the face for being a total waste of fucking space it's the exact pain I need.

I swallow another and another until the events of tonight start to get a little hazy. I'm ashamed of my actions. I'm supposed to be the team captain for fuck's sake. I should have all our guy's backs and be fully focused on the game, but I let that slip and all because my head's too full of her. I thought hurting her would get her out of my head, block the memories she dragged back to the surface, but I was so fucking wrong. She might have dampened down the memories, but she's most definitely still in my fucking head.

I have no idea how long I sit in the dunes taking shot after shot of the vodka while munching my way through the first bag of chips I picked up, but eventually the ringing of my cell gets impossible to ignore.

Pulling it from my pocket, I look up for the first time and see that the sun has long set and the moon is reflecting in the inky black sea beyond.

I've got a stream of missed calls and texts from a range of people, I'm not surprised after my disappearing act but it's Ethan's name that once again lights up my screen.

"What?" I bark, the fact I've even bothered answering pisses me off.

"You coming to celebrate our win?"

"No. No one will want me there, I almost fucked it up."

"Enough with the self-pity, Thorn, no one gives a shit. We won in the end, that's all that matters."

"I'm good thanks," I say, looking down at my party for one surrounding me.

"Oh come on, there's booze and pussy for miles. You know that Shane's parties are the best bit about having him around. Plus, Amalie's here and she looks fucking smoking."

That final statement has me a little more interested and fire beginning to burn in my belly. "Should I care?" I hope the words come out as uninterested, but I have no idea if I succeed. The vodka's starting to make my head spin to the point I'm losing focus.

"Fuck yeah you should, she's dancing with Shane, and the way he's looking at her, man. It's like he wants to—"

"Enough. That's enough." I hang up to the sound of him laughing down the line. The fucker knew how to get me there. If I were sober, I might care about being played but right now all I care about is making sure her body isn't rubbing up against Shane's.

Dragging myself from the ground, I collect up my shit and start making my way along the beach.

Shane's house parties are pretty legendary, although not by his own doing. He's got older twin brothers who went off to college two years ago who are the ultimate party animals and two parents who always seem to be in another state. Oh and wealthier than I can only dream of. Their house is huge and sits right on the beach. His dad was one of the biggest NFL stars this country has seen, and the oldest Dunn boys lived for the celebrity status they were gifted with. They've both gone off to an Ivy League university with full sports scholarships, not that they needed it. Rumor had it that all the top college teams were begging for them, they wanted a slice of the fame too, understandably. It pissed me off more than I'd ever admit that they get a free ride just because of their dad while I'm here with nothing and with no chance at a college education. Yeah, so everyone knows my mother's name, but her reputation isn't going to get me fucking anywhere in this world.

Walking up the street full of massive, pretentious houses, my stomach knots with how my life could have been. Another shot from the bottle I'm carrying soon helps to drown the thoughts. Cars fill the street outside the Dunn house and the closer I get, the louder the music is. The neighbors must fucking hate these parties.

As I round the house there are kids everywhere, many I recognize from school, some that must be college kids, that's only confirmed when I spot the Dunn twins playing beer pong at the other side of the garden with girls hanging off them. Luca nods at me when he spots me but soon gets distracted by the girl who places her hand on his cheek and turns him to kiss her.

Rolling my eyes at them, I head inside to try to find Ethan. When I do, he's got some brunette I've never seen before pressed up against the kitchen counter with his tongue down her throat.

"Hey," I call out but he's clearly way too distracted by the girl. Lifting my hand, I slap him across the back of the head. "Oi, Savage."

Pulling away from the chick, he turns to look at me at the same time he rubs the spot on his head I just hit. "Hey, asshole. Good to see you."

"Fuck off. It's not like you gave me much choice. Where is she?"

"No idea. I hope you're not too late, she was getting pretty wasted."

Fire burns through my veins. If Shane or any other motherfucker have put their hands on her while she's drunk, I'll fucking kill them.

I go to say something back, but when I turn to Ethan, I see that he's distracted again. "Get a fucking room."

He flips me off over his shoulder before pressing even harder into the girl.

Swiping a beer from the side, I set about trying to find my Brit.

My Brit.

Fucking hell, that vodka's affecting me more than I thought. Why do I keep claiming her as mine?

A few of the guys clap me on the back in greeting as I pass, others try to drag me into conversation about tonight's game, but I'm not interested, not until I find her.

I spot Camila with her pussy of a boyfriend first. Wrapping my hand around her forearm, I pull her off his lips, much to her displeasure. "Where is she?"

"What the fuck?" She looks between me and where I'm still touching her with disgust filling her eyes. There's no love lost between the two of us since all the shit went down with her and Mason a few years ago. I know where my loyalties lie and so does she, it seems.

"Where. Is. She?"

"Fuck you, Jake. You must be fucking crazy if you think I'll feed her to you. You've already done enough damage." Noah, her fucking puppy dog boyfriend, wraps his arm around her waist, pulling her back against him, clearly not man enough to step out in front of her to deal with me himself.

"Just tell me so I don't have to waste time searching this place," I ask, already fed up with this conversation.

"Not a fucking chance." Luckily for me as she says this, her eyes flick over my shoulder. Following her stare, I find exactly what I wanted, or didn't, seeing as Shane's hands are currently on her body. "Shit."

Turning back to Camila, she swallows nervously.

"You fucking hurt her and—"

"And what? What the fuck are you going to do?"

She visibly pales, yet her boyfriend still does fuck all. "I haven't got time for this shit."

By the time I turn around, Brit and Shane have gone. "Fuck."

Glancing around, I find a door to the kitchen but there are so many bodies in the way that I doubt they made it through that quickly or ahead of me is a set of stairs. My heart pounds as images I don't need fill my head.

30

JAKE

Wasting no time, I run up, my slightly wobbly legs take the stairs two at a time with ease until my feet hit the first-floor landing. Working my way down the long hallway, I throw open door after door revealing a mixture of empty and occupied rooms with couples in varying states of dress. I don't bother saying anything until I get to the last room on this floor and swing the door open.

"Get your fucking hands off her."

Shane stills, his hands holding Brit around the waist as if he's about to run them up her stomach toward her... *Shit.*

My fists clench at my sides as I wait for her to say something about my interruption, but at no point does she lift her head from Shane's shoulder.

Narrowing my eyes at his panicked expression, I take a step forward, trying to figure out what's going on.

"What the fuck are you doing?"

"N-nothing. She's wasted, I was just going to lie her down to sleep it off."

"For your sake, I really fucking hope that's true." My voice is low and menacing. The muscles in his neck ripple as he swallows down his nervousness.

It's not until a soft groan comes from the limp body in his arms that I remember what the fuck I'm doing right now.

Slipping my arm between the two of them, I make quick work of pulling her from him.

"What the hell. Just put her on my bed. She needs to sleep."

"I'm not letting her stay within a mile of you."

Shane's face burns red with anger, a vein pulsing in his forehead. "That's not your decision to make. She fucking hates you."

"She's gonna fucking hate you if I leave her here for you to do whatever it was you were just about to do."

"I wasn't..." His hands fly up in exasperation. "I was just getting her away from the party. I wouldn't hurt her."

"Don't believe you," I bark, swinging her body up into my arms. She immediately wraps hers tightly around my shoulders and snuggles her face into my neck. My chest swells but I know it's not the time to focus on that. I need to get her out of here.

"You can't just walk out with her. How do I know you're not going to hurt her?"

"Because I wouldn't hurt a fucking hair on her head."

"Says the guy who sent a photo around the school making her out to be a whore."

"Have you just about finished sticking your nose into my business?"

"Nowhere fucking near, especially when you've got the girl I want in your arms."

"She's not yours, Dunn. Never was and never will be."

"And you really think she's yours?" he calls, but he's too late, I'm already walking away with my girl in my arms.

"Yeah, yeah I do," I whisper to no one.

Heads turn the second my feet hit the ground, a few chins drop and eyes widen as they take in the two of us.

"He's got to be fucking kidding me," I hear Camila fume, but I don't hang around long enough to hear what else she's got to say.

The sea of people part as I head toward the kitchen and thankfully at the end of it I find Mason nursing a glass of water.

"I need a lift."

"What the fuck are you doing, Thorn?"

"Getting her away from his wandering hands." His brows pinch but he doesn't argue. Instead, he places his glass down and leads the way out of Shane's house.

"Wait, wait," Camila calls after fighting her way through the crowds who obviously didn't move for her. "What the hell's going on? What's wrong with her?"

"Drunk? Drugged? Fuck knows. All I do know is that I found her in his bedroom with his hands on her. Not. Fucking. Happening."

Camila blanches, I assume at my overprotectiveness, but really I don't give a fuck.

"Shit, is she okay?"

"She will be."

Camila looks between the three of us, confusion written all over her face. I can see that she wants to take care of her friend, but she also understands that she's not got a chance in hell right now.

"Can I trust you with her?" I understand her concern, hell if the roles were reversed, I'd do anything I could to stop this from happening right now but Camila's not me, and I'm not one to back down.

"You can. I won't hurt her."

"I'm not sure that's true," she whispers.

"I won't touch her, you have my word."

"It wasn't her body I was worried about."

My mouth opens to respond but no words pass my lips.

"Are we fucking going or not. I didn't intend on spending my night out here with her." Mason's eyes flit to Camila and as always, I can see his conflicted feelings for her. He wants to hate her, I understand that more than most, but he can't really make himself do it.

"Yeah, open the back door."

It takes a bit of maneuvering but eventually I manage to get myself and Brit into the back seat of Mason's car. I lay her across with her head in my lap.

Staring down at her sleeping face, I run my fingers through her soft hair, taking in the array of shades of blonde beneath my fingers.

"I hope you know what you're doing," Mason says from the front seat.

"Not a fucking clue, bro. The only thing I know for certain is that I couldn't leave her there. The way he was touching her." My muscles lock up as I remember it.

"Are you sure you weren't just seeing what you wanted to see? Shane's not like that. He wouldn't touch a fly."

"Even if I was, I'm still not happy about her being in his room."

"Fuck me, Jake. You've really got it bad, huh?"

"What?"

All he does is laugh, telling me he knows just as much as I do how I feel for this girl. He knew before I did, hence why he was calling me out on my bullshit.

"You know she has every right to never forgive you for what you've done, right?"

"Yep, I'm aware."

———

Silence fills the car, the only sounds that can be heard is that of our breathing as Mason navigates away from the coast and into the town.

"Where the hell are you going?" I bark when he takes a wrong turn.

"Taking her home."

"No fucking way. We're going to my place."

"You expect me to leave her with you after everything?"

"Uh, yeah. You've just pointed out how I feel about her. I'm not going to touch her." His eyes hold mine in the mirror but after a few seconds, he's forced to look back to the road. "We can't take her home, her gran will be asleep, and she'll want to know what's wrong with her."

Blowing out a long breath, Mason white knuckles the steering wheel. "I'm not fucking happy about this."

"I don't need you to be. I just need you to take us to my place, and to trust me."

"Fine. But if you fuck this up, I'll knock your fucking teeth out."

"I'd like to see you try."

Mason laughs but the tension in his shoulders remains as he turns the car around and heads toward my trailer. In reality, it's the last place I want to take Brit, she's better than my damp fucking trailer but I don't have much else to offer her.

He brings the car to a stop in front of my aunt and uncle's house but doesn't kill the engine as he gets out and helps me pull a passed out Brit from the backseat.

"You okay from here?" Hesitation about allowing this to happen fills his voice. Part of me hates that he's questioning my motives but a bigger part of me is happy that he cares about her and feels the need to be concerned.

"Yeah, we're good."

"Don't make me regret this."

"Thanks for the lift, man. I really appreciate it after everything."

With a quick nod of his head, he gets back in the car and speeds off. I'm under no illusion that things between us are not going to go back to how they were before the girl in my arms appeared and threw my life into turmoil, but at least we've made progress.

I take each step toward my trailer carefully, although most of the effects of the vodka vanished the moment I saw her in his arms, I know I'm not sober by any means.

By the time I've dug my key out of my pocket and got her inside, my chest heaves with exertion. Maybe I should have asked Mason for help, I wonder as my breath rushes past my lips.

Walking straight through to my bedroom, I gently lower her down. My breath catches at the sight of her blonde hair fanning my dark pillow and her long, slender body lying across my bed. No girl's been in my bed before, fuck, other than Poppy, no girl's been inside my trailer. I wouldn't want any of the girls at school seeing this shithole. Somehow I already know that Brit's not going to judge. Hell, she's probably going to be too hungover, or angry, to even notice.

Dropping to my knees, I carefully slip her sneakers from her feet and place them on the floor. My eyes run up the smooth, muscular lines of her legs and my balls ache to feel how soft her skin is. But I won't. I won't touch without her permission.

Grabbing a clean pair of boxers, I go to leave the room for a shower. I didn't hang around long enough to have one after I got kicked out of the game and I stink. I'm actually surprised the stench didn't wake her from her drunken slumber.

I have the quickest shower possible, totally ignoring my cock that's happily bobbing between my legs hoping that she'll wake up and pay it some attention, I'm too impatient to be with her. Knowing just how much I need to be laying beside her in my bed freaks me the hell out, but I try not to dwell on it. I tell myself that I'm just concerned she'll wake up and not know where she is or that she'll be sick and choke on her own puke. The thought of that happening in my bed makes me shudder, but I'd deal with it for her if I had to.

31

AMALIE

My head's spinning before I even open my eyes. It takes me a few seconds to realise that the last thing I remember from the party was dancing with Shane and feeling my eyes starting to get heavy.

Bolting upright, I drag my eyes open and look at my unfamiliar surroundings.

Where the fuck am I?

It's certainly not Shane's mammoth house. I didn't have him down for a rich kid, or a kid who had a famous football-playing father, just goes to prove that you can't judge a book by its cover.

I'm still trying to piece together what's happened when some movement in the bed beside me startles me.

"How are you feeling?" The rough, sleepy yet familiar voice breaks through my panic. Looking down, my eyes almost pop out of my head.

Why the utter fuck am I in his bed?

"No, no, no, no," I chant as I shove the covers off me and scramble from the bed. "This can't be happening."

In my haste to get away, my foot gets tangled in his sheets and I fly headfirst toward the floor. Clearly, he's got a much clearer head, because just before my nose makes contact with his dingy carpet, two large hands grab on to my waist and I'm pulled back up.

"Get the hell off me," I snap, starting to fight to get away once again. When I'm released, he's not only saved me but deposited me into his lap.

When I glance to my left, inches upon inches of his tanned skin greets me and I feel a little flutter of something between my legs.

No, no, this is not happening.

"Why the hell am I in your bed?"

"You know," he says, placing his fingers against my cheek and forcing me to look up into his sparkling blue eyes. "You should probably be thanking me, not shouting at me?"

His fingers slip around the back of my neck, allowing his thumb to caress the edge of my jaw.

"O-oh yeah?" I hate that his touch makes my ability to think and speak falter. "And why's that?"

"I was your knight in shining armor, baby." Butterflies erupt in my stomach, but they almost make the sick feeling I've been trying to ignore more apparent. It must be written on my face because his eyes soften a little before he begs, "Please don't puke on me."

"It would be no more than you deserve." When I go to get off him, he allows me. I'm not sure if it's because he didn't really want me there in the first place or if he's afraid I am about to cover him in last night's dinner. I stumble back to the wall and allow it to help hold me up as my head spins and my stomach rolls.

"Fair enough," he mutters, his calm demeanor making my brows draw together in confusion.

"I'm sorry, but am I dreaming or am I really in your trailer with you being nice to me?"

"Don't worry, I'm about as shocked as you are."

"You say that, but you're not the one who woke up here with no memory of the journey."

"That's probably for the best."

"Really? Why? What did you do?"

"Me?" he asks, sitting up against the headboard and allowing the covers to pool low across his waist.

Eyes up, Amalie. Eyes up.

"Yeah, you. Did you manage to get me into some compromising positions so you've got some new images to spread around? I might be clothed right now, but I wouldn't put it past you to—"

"I didn't fucking strip you, Brit. I didn't fucking do anything other than bring you here to make sure you were safe." His voice deepens and I know I've touched a nerve.

"Well that was big of you but what exactly were you rescuing me from?"

"Shane."

"What? That's insane. Why the hell would you need to rescue me from him?"

"How much did you drink last night?"

His sudden topic change gives me whiplash. "Uh... a couple of beers and two or three shots."

"So not enough to be totally out of it?"

"I wouldn't say so, no. Why?"

"Because when I found you, you couldn't even open your eyes and Shane was just about to—" He stops himself saying anymore but I don't miss the clenching of his fists at his sides or the pulsing muscle in his neck.

"He was what?"

"Touching you."

"Shane? Really?"

"I can only tell you what I walked in on."

"You're fucking delusional, do you know that?"

"Maybe, but I couldn't risk it."

I really need to get the hell out of here and away from him, but I can't help myself. "Risk what?"

"Knowing someone else has their hands on what's mine."

"Yours?" An unamused laugh falls from my lips.

There isn't a hint of amusement on Jake's face as he swings his legs from the bed, stands and moves toward me. The way his stare stays locked on me reminds me of how a lion might stalk their prey.

He doesn't stop until he's nose to nose with me. I fight to keep my lips closed as my breathing increases knowing that if my breath smells as bad as it tastes then I'll probably turn him off in an instant, not that that would necessarily be a bad thing.

His hands land on either side of my head and his own, much fresher breath, brushes over my face as he continues to stare.

When he speaks, it's so quiet and low that I start to think I imagined it. "Yeah. Mine."

His head lowers, his lips closing in on mine and I panic.

"You're fucking delusional, you know that?" I ask once I've slipped under his arms and made it to the door.

His shoulders drop when he realises that our time is over. That is until he pulls on the mask that I'm used to. His features harden and I suck in a breath to prepare for what's going to come next. "You're right. I have no fucking idea what I was thinking. I should have left you there. Let them pass you around like the little fucking whore you are."

Tears immediately burn at the back of my throat and climb up toward my eyes. "I hate you," I scream, my voice cracking with emotion before I run through his trailer to find the door.

The sound of his angry roar and a loud crash behind me makes my steps slow a little, but it's not enough to make me turn around. Nor is the fact I realise the second I hit the grass beneath his trailer that I don't have any fucking shoes on.

I run until I get to the trees, then I have to start taking it a little more carefully as I navigate the twigs and stones underfoot.

I just get to the clearing when a snapping twig behind me catches my attention. I prepare to run despite how much it's going to fucking hurt but I don't get a chance. A strong arm wraps around my waist and I'm pulled back into a hard body.

His increased breaths tickle my ears and send a shiver down my spine. "I'm sorry, okay?"

Sucking in a large breath, I prepare to turn around and face him. "No. No, it's not fuck—"

My words are cut off as his lips slam down on mine. I forget all about the state of my mouth as his tongue teases at the seam of my lips and I allow him entry, too keen to experience all he has to give.

Just like before, he's pent up and angry. One arm stays wrapped around my waist while the other threads into my hair, tilting my head so I'm in the perfect position for him. The length of his body presses against mine, his length pressing into my stomach.

It takes at least a minute or two before reality seeps back in. Lifting my hands, I push against his chest.

"Jake, stop," I mumble against his lips. He steps back putting his hands up in surrender.

My eyes drop from his and I realise he came chasing after me in just his tight pair of boxer briefs, which quite clearly show exactly what he's got beneath, and a pair of trainers. As I stare down at the tented fabric, my tongue darts out to wet my bottom lip, my core flooding with heat.

I look back up just in time for his mouth to open. I expect some smug comment about being impressed by his size to fall from his lips so I'm shocked by what I do hear. "Have breakfast with me?"

"What?" His total three-sixty from his attitude as I ran from his trailer totally throws me for a loop.

"Have breakfast with me. It's still early, your gran won't be up yet, will she?"

"No, but... I need to shower and..."

"I have a shower. Plus I know the best place to get rid of your hangover."

I stare into his eyes, waiting for him to tell me that this is a joke, but he doesn't. He just patiently waits for my answer.

I want to say no. I know it would be the sensible thing to do, but the temptation of food eventually gets the better of me.

"Okay, fine. But the second you turn back into the arsehole you usually are, I'm leaving."

His lips curl up into a smile that hits me right in the chest. Why do I get the feeling this breakfast is more for him than it is for me? But that's crazy, after everything, why would he want to spend time with me in public?

Reaching out, he takes my hand in his. The small amount of contact warms me all the way to my toes.

"We're not going to Aces," I warn as we emerge from the trees.

"I wasn't even going to suggest it."

Everything is wrong about this, yet as I step up into his old trailer hidden at the bottom of the garden, everything feels so right.

"Make yourself comfortable. It's not much and I'm sure nothing like what you're used to but it's all I've got." For the first time since I saw him across the school that very first day, I see a little of his insecurity slip in. By some miracle, I've managed to peel away just a corner of the impenetrable mask he always wears. I'm not sure why, or what I did to deserve it but right this moment, the guy I'm seeing in front of me isn't Thorn, king of Rosewood High, but Jacob, an eighteen-year-old guy who's just as unsure about life as I am. Maybe we're not as different as he thinks.

"It's perfect, thank you."

"I'll go and find you a clean towel so you can shower, I'll be back in a bit." He goes to leave but stops before he's out of the kitchen area. "Here. I suspect you need these." I couldn't be more grateful for the little packet of painkillers that falls into my lap.

I wait for him to disappear and listen to his crashing around for a few minutes before I get up, pull the fridge open and grab a lukewarm bottle of water. Downing half of it, I throw a couple of pills into my mouth and hope they get to work fast on the pounding at my temples.

Falling back onto the inbuilt sofa, I prop one of the cushions under my head and close my eyes, trying like hell to drag up any memories from last night.

I must doze off because the next thing I know, a droplet of water hits my cheek and runs off into my hairline.

"What the—oh." I open my eyes to one fine sight. Jake's standing over me, his hair dripping wet from his shower and only a towel hanging low on his waist.

Biting down on my bottom lip, I try to fight the temptation to reach out and tug it from his body to properly discover what's hiding beneath.

"Go on, do it," he taunts.

"Do what?" I ask innocently, looking up at him through my lashes.

Dropping down to his haunches so his head is almost level with mine. "If you think I can't read your thoughts then you need to think again. How are you feeling?"

I take a second to focus on the throbbing in my head and realise that it is actually starting to subside.

"Better, thank you."

He stares at me for a few more seconds. I start to think he's going to kiss me again, but right before I'm about to move my head toward him, he stands and walks to the kitchen. "The bathroom's all yours. I should warn you that the showers not much more than a dribble and it never really gets that hot, but it kinda does the job. I left a new toothbrush on the side for you."

I cringe knowing that he has firsthand experience of just how disgusting my mouth is right now.

"I won't be long."

"Take your time. I'll make coffee... you like coffee, right?"

"I do."

"Maybe you're not so weird after all," he says as I make my way down to his bedroom.

I didn't pay much attention to the room before I stormed out earlier, but I saw enough to know that he's since tidied up and made his bed.

Looking back over my shoulder, I find his naked back as he reaches up into a cupboard and I can't help trying to figure him out. He clearly makes every effort to hide this part of his life, but why? Why does he live down here alone? Where are his parents?

The million and one questions I have about him swirl around my head as I chase the pathetic spray of water around the cubicle in an attempt to wash the remnants of last night off me.

32

JAKE

My body's practically vibrating with nervous energy as the water running in the bathroom sounds out around the trailer.

I have no idea what the fuck I'm doing. All I do know is that she's currently naked with water running down over her slender curves mere feet away, and I can't forget the pain that twisted my stomach almost in half when I watched her run away from me earlier. I wasn't ready for our time together to be over, even if she had no idea it was happening or why she was here. I try to ignore the fact that I'd basically kidnapped her, she had every right to want to run as far away as possible.

I'm sitting on my couch with my elbows resting on my knees and my head hanging between my shoulders when she steps into the kitchen. Glancing up, I find her hair piled on top of her head, one of my t-shirts covering her tiny frame and tied at her waist. Her long ass legs are still on full display in her short white skirt. My eyes damn near pop out of my head.

"I hope you don't mind, my top smelled of last night."

"N-no of course not. It... uh... looks better on you than it does on me."

She smiles shyly before glancing down at the counter. "This mine?"

"Yeah. Is it okay?"

"Do you have any milk?" I think she realizes her mistake the moment the words fall from her lips. "Actually, it's perfect."

Lifting the mug, I'm fascinated as she delicately blows across the top and then places her lips to the edge. She sips at the black coffee and does her best to look like she enjoys it but she falls a little far from the mark.

"You don't have to pretend to make me feel better," I say, pushing myself from the couch. "Come on, I'll buy you one you actually want to drink."

"Thank you."

It's still early and the only sounds that can be heard as we both step down from my trailer is the birds up in the trees.

Thankfully, there's no movement inside the house as we slip past and head out to the main road. I can sense Brit's stare as we make our way down to the bus stop at the end of the road. If I've got my timing right, then it should be here to take us away from this place any minute.

"Wow, Jake Thorn rides the bus." Her voice is light, she's clearly only joking but still, my stomach twists and my muscles lock up at her mocking.

"Things aren't always as they seem, Brit."

She opens her mouth but soon decides better of it. When she does eventually speak, she changes the subject, but I can see her desperation to figure me out deep in her blue depths. "I've got a name, you know."

"I'm aware."

I don't give a reason and thankfully she doesn't press me for one because the bus comes around the corner.

Tapping my phone to the pad by the driver, I pay the return fare for both of us and we head toward the back of the bus.

"I can't remember the last time I was on a bus," she muses, watching the houses pass us by out the window.

"Don't tell me, you had a Range Rover or two and couldn't possibly use public transport."

Her eyes are wide and her chin drops at the bitterness in my tone.

"Actually, I didn't have a Range Rover—or two. I had a Mini, but I used to get the tube to college every day. Driving in London was... actually, I'm not defending myself to you. You seem to have me all figured out, so I'll just leave you to it."

Jesus, even when I'm trying to be nice, I end up putting my fucking foot in it. "I'm sorry, I didn't mean it like that."

She shrugs and turns back to look out the window. I feel like a douchebag for snapping at her, but it's not an unusual feeling these days.

The rest of the journey is silent. Tension comes from her in waves and I can only imagine that she's already regretting agreeing to this. She could be at home, sleeping off her hangover instead of sitting here beside me. She only moves when she hears me press the bell, indicating that we're about to get off.

"I'm only following you because I'm hungry. This place better be good," she sulks as she follows along beside me until I come to a stop outside a little backstreet diner I found a few years ago.

"It is good. Best pancakes in the state."

She mumbles something under her breath but I don't say anything. She's got every right to be pissed off with me.

I find us a seat in the back and a waitress with about twenty cans of hairspray coating her dreadful hair do and a little red apron comes running over.

"Good mornin'," she sings way too happily. "What can I get for you both?"

"Two coffees, one black, one with cream, and two chef's special breakfasts."

Brit's eyes drill into me, I ignore them and continue looking up at the waitress who finishes writing our order before looking between the two of us. I'd love to know what's she's thinking right now.

"Okay, coming up."

She turns on her heels and races toward the kitchen.

"I can order my own fucking food, Jake," Brit fumes, her shoulders tense and her lips twitching in anger.

"I know, but trust me. It's the best."

She slumps back against the chair and drops her attention to her nails.

I'm not entirely sure how we went from kissing in the trees to her ignoring my existence, but I do know that it's all my fault.

33

AMALIE

I try to ignore it but his stare burns into the top of my head as I look down at my hands.

Why the hell am I here?

I can only put my stupidity down to whatever it is that still running through my system after last night. I know I didn't have enough to drink to be so out of it that Jake was able to get me back to his place without me even being aware of it. I think it's pretty obvious that someone must have spiked my drink.

But who?

The most obvious suspect would be the guy sitting opposite me, but something tells me that this wasn't his doing. Something deep inside me really wants to believe that he was doing exactly what he said he was, looking after me, protecting me. But again, why? He's made it clear time and time again that he hates me. So why do it, and why chase me this morning and bring me here?

The waitress returns with our coffees and as much as I want to be frustrated with him ordering for me, I can't be because I'm just grateful to have something drinkable. What he tried giving me back at his trailer was like treacle. I love my coffee, but it has to have milk.

Lifting the mug to my lips, my eyes meet his dark stare and a shudder runs through me. Any signs of the sweet and caring guy who looked after me both last night and this morning have gone. The Jake Thorn I know and... hate, is staring right back at me.

Taking a sip of coffee for courage, I ask the question I've been drying to know the answer to since the first time he looked at me.

"What exactly is your issue with me?"

He's silent for a few seconds and I start to think he's going to ignore that I've even asked a question when his elbows rest on the table and his eyes scan my face.

"It's not you exactly. You just remind me of someone I wouldn't piss on if they were on fire."

Whoa, okay.

Pure hatred fills his eyes and I realise that in reality, he might have let me off easily with the bullshit he's caused. There's something dark living inside him and it's just waiting to explode.

"Who?"

He shakes his head, clearly unwilling to divulge any more details. That's not going to stop me asking though.

"Okay, so how do I remind you of them?"

"At first, from a distance, I thought you looked like her. But... but now, it's just what you represent."

"And what is that exactly?"

"A rich, pretentious, privileged life that's full of fake, plastic, self-absorbed assholes who think anything important is only skin deep." It's not the first time he's said it, but it's the first time I really think about it.

"Wow. And that's the kind of person you think I am?"

"It's the world you came from."

"Maybe so, but I was born into that world. I didn't have a choice about it. But I've always had my own opinions of the industry my parents were a part of."

"Don't try to tell me that you didn't love it. All the attention, free designer clothes, being in front of the camera."

Part of me doesn't want to defend myself when he seems to have decided that he's already figured me out. But at the same time, I hate the judgmental look he's giving me like he knows me, when in reality he doesn't have a fucking clue. "I couldn't give a shit about the designer clothes. They're just clothes. They do the same job whether they cost twenty quid or two-thousand. And not that it's any of your business, but I've never been in front of the camera."

He snorts and I rear back.

"What's that supposed to mean?"

"Come off it, Brit. You've got supermodel written all over you, just like your mother. You're worth too much money not to force you into that world."

Pushing the chair out behind me with a loud screech, I stand and place my palms on the table. My breath races past my lips as I fight to keep control of my anger.

"For your information, my parents were good people. Yes, the industry they were in can be questioned a million ways and trust me when I say that I've done so, many many times. And yes, I might have the right look, but my parents would never, ever push me to do something I didn't want. I have always refused to be a part of that world. No amount of money could get me on that side of a camera doing some of the things those models do."

Jake visibly pales, but I don't want to hang around to find out why. Instead, I dart from the table and toward the exit, only he's quicker. His warm fingers wrap around my wrist and I'm forced to stop.

His body heat burns my back as he steps up to me and his breath tickles my ear. I shudder when his fingers tickle across the sliver of skin his tied up shirt reveals at my waist.

"I'm sorry. I was being an asshole."

"I'm getting used to it," I snap.

"Please come and sit back down. Just to eat and then you can go and never look back."

Something aches inside my chest at the idea of walking away from him for good. It's what I should be doing because he's right, he's an asshole. But for some reason, I'm a little bit addicted to him. A glutton for punishment or some shit because despite knowing better, I just keep coming back for more.

"Fine, but only because I'm hungry."

He releases me. I hate myself for it, but I immediately miss his contact.

When I turn back toward our table, the waitress is just placing two giant plates down. The sight of the food has my stomach rumbling. The scent of the bacon, eggs, and pancakes hits my nose as I retake my seat and my mouth waters. He might be right about something, this looks amazing.

We eat in silence, but that doesn't mean I don't feel his stare every time he looks up at me. I refuse to meet his eyes in fear he somehow managed to stop being pissed off and looks at me with his vulnerable eyes instead. I knew he was jumping to some kinds of conclusions about me. If I'm honest, I thought it was to do with money. It's no secret that my parents were very successful and wealthy, whereas it's becoming more and more obvious that he doesn't have all that much.

"Why do you live at the bottom of your aunt and uncle's garden?" The words are out before I have a chance to stop them.

"It's where I belong," he says sadly.

"Jake, that's not—"

"It's exactly what it is. You're not the only one who thinks I'm a waste of good oxygen." The honesty in his words is enough to kill any response that was on my tongue. "I'm not what everyone at school thinks I am. But pretending is better than reality. I just need to graduate and then I'm out of here."

"To where?"

"Anywhere. I don't care, I just need a fresh start somewhere no one knows me."

"What about college?"

My brows draw together when he laughs. "You really think I can afford to go to college? You've seen where I live."

"I know but—"

"No buts. It is what it is. The second I'm done with high school, I'm starting again. I don't give a shit where or what job I work to pay for it."

"Surely you could get a scholarship or something," I muse, not really understanding how it all works yet.

He shrugs. "Doubt it."

"Have you even looked into it?"

"Can you drop it, please?"

The desperation in his eyes means I do as he asks, for now. I don't know him all that well, but I do know he's better than to throw away the idea of college quite so easily.

The rest of our time in the diner is in silence. But it's not uncomfortable like it could be. Jake has slipped back into his softer side, the one I know he doesn't show a lot of people. It makes me wonder why he's dropping his guard with me.

"I should get you home before your gran worries."

"It's okay, she knows I went to a party last night. I can't imagine she was expecting me."

Jake swallows nervously. "About last night."

"What about it?"

"Someone spiked your drink."

"Seems that way. I'm pretty sure it wasn't Shane though. Please don't do anything stupid." I feel like the stupid one the second the words fall from my lips. Why would he do something stupid to protect someone he hates?

"I will find out who it was and they'll fucking pay."

Reaching over the table, I place my hand down on his, the warmth spreading all the way up my arm. "No, Jake. Just leave it, please. I don't need you fighting my battles."

"What if I want to?"

The waitress returns with the bill and Jake pulls out his wallet.

"Fuck," he mutters, obviously finding it emptier than he was expecting.

"It's okay, I've got it."

Handing over some cash, he stiffens at the other side of the table. His lips pressing into a thin line and the muscle in his neck pulsing.

I want to ask about his last comment but I don't get the chance because a shadow falls over us.

"Well, well, well, isn't this cozy."

I know the voice, I don't need to look up to confirm who it is. Instead, I keep my eyes on Jake's. They harden instantly, his shutters coming down putting an end to whatever kind of moment we were just having.

"Brit's just leaving."

My chin drops in shock.

"What are you even doing? Having breakfast together?" Chelsea asks. Total disbelief for what she's seeing clear in her voice. "Your looks might get you whatever you want in London, but they won't work here."

Chelsea juts her hip out, impatiently waiting for me to move but I ignore her and focus on Jake.

"What the hell are you doing?" I whisper but it's not quiet enough.

"Jesus, you really are a whore, begging for him to want you."

Jake's eyes stay locked on mine but I can't read anything in them. The boy who was here expressing his need to protect me has long gone. Taking three calming breaths, I push myself from the seat, preparing to go nose to nose with the school bitch.

"You're in my seat."

I stand and just like the first time we met in the principal's office, she has to look up at me and I can't help the smirk that twitches at my lips. She must fucking hate it.

"I thought you'd be too good to be spending time in this part of town."

She visibly pales. I might not really have a clue where we are right now, but it was obvious on the journey here that it's not the nicest area. I didn't think too much of it after Jake said he wanted to get away but as I stare into Chelsea's emerald eyes it suddenly dawns on me. He's ashamed. He came here with me so we could hide.

"I'm done with this bullshit. You're more than welcome to him."

"Like he'd ever go anywhere near someone like you. He's always been mine."

My body stills, my need to argue with her threatening to get the better of me. My shoulders tighten and my emotions burning the back of my throat creeps its way up to my eyes. When a guy starts heading my way, I'm forced to move and thankfully it's toward the door. I don't need the kind of drama Chelsea can bring in my life.

I briefly glance back over my shoulder, I find the guy who walked in with his arm around Chelsea. He's vaguely familiar, I wonder briefly who it is seeing as he's obviously older than her but the stare I feel from the booth I just vacated is too strong to ignore.

Our eyes lock, something flickers through his but it's gone too quickly to be able to read.

The tears that were burning my eyes threaten to drop and I run. Racing down the street, I find an alley and slip down it to allow me a little privacy to fall apart.

My back hits the wall and I slide down until my arse hits the dirty ground. A sob erupts from my throat and I drop my head into my hands. How could I have been so stupid to believe he actually wanted to spend time with me. He just wanted to use me as a dirty little secret.

I think back to how sweet he's been, and it only makes me cry harder. I shouldn't like him. I shouldn't care. But there's so much more to Jake Thorn than he allows the world to see. For some reason he's given me a glimpse of the broken boy hiding beneath the surface and I can't help but want more.

Stupid, stupid girl.

Once my tears subside, realisation hits me. I've no idea where I am and no clue how to get home.

Pulling my bag onto my lap, I dig around until I find my phone at the bottom amongst a load of receipts and coins. Thankfully, the battery's not dead, although it is at fifteen percent thanks to the stream of messages, missed calls and voicemails that I've totally missed from Camila and Shane.

Guilt sits heavy in my stomach that they've no idea where I am or if I'm okay or not. Do they even know I left with Jake last night?

Hitting call on Camila's number, I put my phone to my ear and listen to it ring.

When she eventually picks up, it's clear I've woken her. Her voice is deep and rough with sleep but she soon sobers when memories of last night must hit her.

"Amalie? Where the hell are you? Are you okay?"

"Yeah, I'm good. Is there any chance you could do me a favour?"

"Of course."

I explain briefly where I am, listing of a few places I can see from my hiding place. Thankfully, Camila knows and promises to be there in no more than thirty minutes. I can already tell by the tone of her voice that I've got a million questions coming my way.

I want to go and get more coffee but the thought of running into Jake again is enough to make me stay put. Seeing him in school is going to be bad enough after everything that happened between us.

34

AMALIE

It's only twenty minutes later when I spot Camila's car pull up to the curb. Dragging my exhausted body from the ground, I brush the dirt from my butt and head her way. As instructed, she stays in the car and in seconds, I'm pulling the passenger door open and climbing in.

"What the fuck is going on, Amalie? You get carried out of a party off your fucking face by your worst enemy and now I'm here picking you up. You've got some serious explaining to do."

"Take me somewhere quiet for coffee and I'll explain. Not Aces," I quickly add before she even suggests it.

So for the second time this morning I find myself in another backstreet diner with another waitress pouring me coffee.

"So he marched in all alpha-like and demanded to know where I was?" I ask, my brows drawn together in confusion. "Why?"

"Who the hell knows? But according to Shane he lost his shit with him, dragged you away from him and out of the house."

"He thinks Shane spiked my drink and was going to..." I trail off not needing to say the words out loud.

"Shane? Shane Dunn?"

"I know. I told him that he was crazy and that Shane would never do anything like that. But he found me in his room with his hands on me."

"Shane was just going to put you to bed to sleep it off."

"That's what I said, but Jake's having none of it."

"Okay, so what happened with Jake?"

I'm silent for a few moments as I try to figure out how to answer that question.

"Oh my god, something happened with him, didn't it? OMG did you fuck him?"

"What? No, I didn't fuck him." My cheeks heat knowing that although that's true, I'm not totally innocent. I did kiss him this morning and unbeknown to Camila, it's not our first either.

"But..." she encourages, scooting forward on her seat waiting to get the juicy gossip.

"We kissed."

"Oh my god," she squeals, clapping her hands together in delight. "It's like in the movies. He hates you to cover up the fact he really likes you."

Rolling my eyes at her romantic heart, I sigh. "No, I'm pretty sure he just hates me. I was probably just some stupid bet to him or something to see if I'm pathetic enough to fall for it. Well, ding a ling, I clearly am because look what happened. Ugh... I fucking hate him."

"Really?"

"Yes. No. I don't fucking know. There's just something inside him that calls to me. I wish I couldn't see it and just focus on him being an arsehole, but I can't help feeling like he needs help. He wants me to see it even though he's scared."

"So going back to my earlier comment..."

"You're a nightmare. How's Noah?"

"He's good. I told him when I was a little drunk that his birthday night is the night," she says with a wink.

"Wait. You guys haven't..."

"Nope. I told him I wanted to wait, and he respected that. But I'm bored now. Everyone else is at it so..."

"You can't do it just because everyone else is."

"I know and that's not the reason. We've been together for ages and I feel it's right. It's time to take it to the next level before we start stressing about college and all that."

I'm still not totally buying it. "You love him, right?"

"Of course." Narrowing my eyes, I try to figure out what she's hiding, but it's pointless especially because I'm not sure she knows it herself. I've seen them together plenty of times now. On the outside, they appear to be the perfect couple, but I can't help feeling like something's just not quite right.

"So what's next with Thorn?" she asks, dragging the conversation back to me.

"What's next is that we stop talking about him. I'm done with him."

"Liar. I can't believe he kissed you. Rumor has it that he doesn't kiss anyone. Ever."

Hearing that changes my mind about talking more about him. "Oh come off it. He's the ultimate school player, he must have kissed loads of girls."

"Nope never, apparently."

I think back to Dash night, which feels like a million years ago now, and his reaction to Chelsea putting her lips on him. Maybe what Camila's saying is true. But if it is, why did he kiss me?

———

I'm no less confused about the whole Jake situation when Camila drops me back at Gran's later that morning. She takes one look at me in a boy's t-shirt and raises her eyebrows.

"So not what you're thinking," I mutter, walking past her and heading straight for my room.

"When you're ready to talk, you know where I am."

My stomach twists as I fall back against my bedroom door. I don't want to shut Gran out after everything she's done for me but how am I meant to explain all of this to her. Even running the events of the past few weeks over in my head makes me feel like a crazy person. How the hell will it sound to her?

I take my time showering and washing his smell from me. It seems that no length of attempting to do that will be effective, his unique scent still lingers in my nose.

After pulling on a pair of pajamas and throwing an oversized jumper over the top, I pile my hair on top of my head and head out, expecting a million and one questions from Gran.

"You hungry?"

"I can make myself something. You stay there." She's sitting on her sofa reading one of the trashy magazines that she loves. I've no idea how she can keep reading them after some of the lies they've published about my parents and their colleagues over the years.

"Don't be silly. Take a seat and I'll make you a grilled cheese. Sound good?"

"Sounds amazing, thank you."

Silence falls around us as she works, and I sip the glass of water she passed over for me.

"Amalie, I know I'm old and you probably think that I couldn't possibly understand but please, I'm begging you. Talk to me. I'm worried about you."

The lies are right on the tip of my tongue, but when I do speak, the exact opposite fall out. "It's a boy."

"I assumed as much. Anyone I might know?"

I ignore that question, nowhere near ready to admit who it is in case she doesn't approve. If she knows who he is and where he lives, which I'm confident she does because nothing gets past my gran, then I've no doubt she wouldn't approve. Why would she? Jake's the school's notorious bad boy who's mostly treated me like shit since the first day I started at Rosewood.

"I shouldn't like him. He hasn't been exactly pleasant since I started." I skirt around the reality of the situation. "But there's more to the guy than he allows the outside world to see. He's hiding but I can see his vulnerability and I wonder if that's why he doesn't like me all that much."

She smiles at me, and a mysterious twinkle in her eye before turning to plate up my sandwich.

"What's the look for?"

"He's scared, Amalie. He knows you can see deeper than anyone else and he's scared of it being used against him."

I consider her theory for a few minutes and although I can't argue because I think she might have nailed it. I'm not sure that's all of the problem.

"There's more than that. He said something cryptic about Mum and Dad's lifestyle and it being the reason he doesn't like me."

"What's his name?" she asks again.

Laughing at her second attempt, I just shake my head at her. "Nice try."

"What?" The innocent look on her face might work on others, but it's not fooling me one bit.

"I'm not telling you because you probably know every single detail about his life and I don't want secondhand gossip."

Gran gasps, placing her hand over her heart like I've wounded her. "I'll have you know, young lady, that my knowledge of our town and its occupants is factual. No gossip passes these lips."

Laughing at her, I pull the plate she passed over toward me. The smell of the melted cheese making my mouth water. "Riiight," I say, humouring her before groaning in delight when I get my first bite.

"You want my advice?"

"Sure."

"If you think there's more to this boy, then you're probably right. If you think it's worth discovering, then keep digging but just be aware that what you could find might be ugly. If he's not worth the pain, then walk away... if you can."

Gran walks from the room, leaving me with that little nugget of advice. That question rolls around my head for the rest of the day. Can I just walk away? It's one hundred percent what I should do after the way he's treated me. But what we should do and what we want to do are often at either end of the spectrum.

Standing in front of my full-length mirror, I brush my hair out before retrying it up and out of my way so I can sleep. The light breeze from my open window causes goosebumps to cover my exposed skin and I quickly dive into bed.

Gran's got air conditioning throughout the entire house, but I can't get used to sleeping in it. The Brit in me much prefers the warm breeze coming from the window at night. I know I should shut it, especially after my late night visitor the other night but I can't bring myself to do it.

Anticipation mixes with Gran's words from earlier and I'm left tossing and turning for hours, hoping that sleep will claim me. But eventually a noise that I was expecting—hoping—for sounds out around the room.

The crunch of feet against the ground outside has my heart jumping into my throat.

He came.

I lie as still as I can, hoping I look like I'm fast asleep. I missed his visit last time and I'm desperate to know what he's going to do.

The click of the door opening makes me jump even though I'm expecting it. I fight to keep my breathing steady as he slips inside the room.

"Motherfucker," he whispers, sounding frustrated. I can only imagine it's because I didn't lock my door like I was requested to do.

His footsteps slowly get closer, before he kneels down beside me. His scent surrounds me once again. My heart threatens to thunder out of my chest as I wait for what he's going to do next.

"I'm so fucking sorry, Brit. You should wake up and send me away for being such a fucking screw up. I wasn't ashamed to be with you earlier, I just... I fucked up."

His voice cracks with desperation and I can't help my eyes flickering open.

He's left the door curtain open enough that the moon lights him up like he's under a spotlight. His head's hanging between his shoulders, he looks as broken as he sounds. And instead of anger filling my veins like it should, I find my fingers twitching at my sides to reach out to touch him.

"I shouldn't fucking be here. I just needed to know you were safe."

His head lifts and my breath catches as I wait for his eyes to find mine.

His lips part when he realises that I'm not asleep like he was expecting.

"Fuck, I—shit." He stands, his hands going to his hair and pulling to the point I think it's going to come out. "Fuck, I'm..."

He steps toward the door and I panic.

"Jake, wait." My voice is barely a whisper, but it's enough to stop him.

He stills but doesn't lift his gaze from the floor.

"I shouldn't be here," he admits, sadly.

"But you're here anyway."

Flipping my covers back, I push up onto my elbows and look at him. His shoulders are slumped in defeat, his hands hanging loosely around his hips.

"Jake," I breathe.

Something in my voice makes him turn, his eyes find mine before they drop down over my scantily clad body.

"Fuck."

His feet eat up the space between us and in mere seconds his hand is sliding into the back of my hair and his lips find mine.

I sense the change in him as we connect. Gone is the broken boy who just stood before me instead the man kissing me is lost to his need.

His tongue plunges into my mouth and I hungrily suck it deeper. I shouldn't allow this after what he did today but the second he puts his hands on me, it's like everything aside from the two of us in this moment exists.

Jake climbs onto my bed, his knees pinning my thighs in place as he continues to kiss me like it's our first and he can't get enough.

When we're both desperate for breath, he pulls back. His eyes are dark and hooded as he stares down at me. My core throbs for more as his fingers tickle over my chest and run along the hem of my tank causing my nipples to pucker behind the fabric.

"Tell me to leave. Tell me that you hate me and that I need to leave."

His fingers ghost lower and brush over my nipples, making me shudder.

"You're right, I hate you but—"

I don't get to tell him that I don't want him to leave right now because he lowers my vest and pulls my nipple into his hot mouth.

"Oh, fuck." My hips buck involuntarily but it doesn't achieve anything as Jake's still pinning me to the bed. His lips twitch in delight at my reaction.

He moves to the other side, exposing that breast as well so he can do as he likes. He licks, nips, and sucks while I moan and writhe beneath him.

I want to scream at him when he moves up my neck and runs his tongue around the shell of my ear.

"I'm going to make you feel so good, Brit."

My response is a moan as he starts crawling down my body. He licks at my breasts once again before lifting my tank and kissing down my stomach.

By the time he curls his fingers around the edge of my sleep shorts, they're soaking, my need for what he's got to give too much to bear.

"Jake, please."

"Fuck. Say that again."

"Jake," I breathe, his lips landing on my hipbone and trailing toward my center. "Please, I need... ohhh..."

Before I know what's happening, my shorts are gone and his breath tickles against my most sensitive part.

"So fucking sweet," he mutters, pushing my thighs wider and licking up the length of me.

"Oh, shit, shit, shit, Jake," I squeal, forgetting where I am and that we could be heard.

His tongue presses down against my clit before he starts circling, building me higher and higher. My hands alternate between fisting the sheet beneath me and sliding into his hair to keep him in place.

I shamelessly buck against his face, needing everything he has to give to wash away the anger and rejection he caused within me earlier. I've no idea if this is an apology of sorts, but right now I really don't care as pleasure like I've never experienced tingles at every single one of my nerve endings.

Lifting his fingers, he circles my entrance while continuing the blissful torture of my clit with his tongue.

"Jake, Jake," I chant as his fingers plunge deeper. My muscles pull tight as the beginnings of an earth shattering release begin to consume my body. "Yes, yes."

He continues for a few more seconds before something inside me snaps and I fall into an all-consuming bliss as he continues to lick at me, dragging out every last drop of pleasure.

My chest heaves, my breaths rushing out past my lips as I try to get my heart under control.

Jake sits up, wipes his mouth with the back of his hand, a shit-eating grin on his face at what he just achieved.

"Do you need to look so smug?"

"Brit, I—"

"Amalie, are you okay?"

"Fuck." Jake moves faster than I thought possible and flies into position hiding behind the door. His ability to know exactly what to do makes me wonder how many times he's got caught sneaking into a girl's bedroom.

A sick feeling bubbles up in my stomach at the idea of him doing what he just did to me to others but I don't get a chance to linger on it before a light knock sounds out and my bedroom door is pushed open.

I just manage to grab the sheets to cover up before Gran's head pokes around the door.

I'm lying with one eye cracked open just enough to see what she does. She briefly looks around the room but when she thankfully finds nothing suspicious, she silently closes the door once again and her footsteps head back down the hallway.

Breathing a huge sigh of relief, I watch as Jake appears from the shadows and kneels at my side.

He reaches up and cups my cheek in his warm hand. "I should go."

As much as I want to say no, I know it's not the right thing to do. This has already gone too far and we've come too close to getting caught.

I nod and his face drops, his mask has gone and I'm once again allowed to see the real boy hiding beneath.

When he stands, my mouth opens to argue but I can't. He needs to get out of here before Gran comes back or I do something I'm going to really regret. He's already under my skin, us spending anymore time together right now will only cause me more pain in the long run because it's not like he's going to take my hand at school tomorrow and walk around proudly that I'm his.

The thought alone frustrates me. I don't want to be his, do I?

Silently he backs toward the door. My muscles twitch to reach out for him but I manage to keep them at my sides and allow him to disappear into the darkness, leaving just the taste of his kiss and the fast beating of my heart as evidence he was ever here.

35

AMALIE

"Did you sleep well? You look better," Camila says the second I drop down into her car for our daily drive to school.

"Uh...yeah," I lie. In reality, it took hours for me to fall asleep after my nocturnal guest left and when the alarm went off this morning, I was far from ready for it. "You think anyone's forgotten about what happened at the party yet?"

"What, that someone drugged you and you were rescued by none other than Jake Thorn?"

I wince, I really don't need the reminder of how I ended up on Friday night. "Yeah, that's it."

"Shane feels awful, he's been texting me all weekend seeing as you're ignoring him. He really didn't do it."

I shrug, because although I was adamant that it wasn't him at the beginning, I don't really know him. Just look at Jake, I thought he was an arsehole through and through but he keeps proving to me that there is a little nice in there somewhere. Maybe Shane is the opposite.

"I just want to forget it now and not go to another party again for a long time."

"That might be a problem because Homecoming and Noah's birthday is this weekend."

"No one will miss me at homecoming and just tell Noah I'm busy or something."

"Nope. Not happening. Whether you like it or not you're a part of this school now, so Homecoming is non negotiable. You can wear that sexy little silver dress, and as for Noah's party, I'm sure I can convince you."

I mumble my frustration because sadly, she's probably right.

As we both walk toward the school, I feel eyes on me. Only they're not just on me because they flick back and forth between me and Jake where he's sitting in his usual spot surrounded by his posse.

His gaze follows me and burns a trail across my entire body.

"That's weird," Camila comments.

"What is?"

"Jake's not looking at you like he wants to kill you, he's looking at you like he wants to—"

"Enough."

Turning her curious stare on me, her hand lands on my forearm and comes to stand in front of me.

"Did something else happen that you're not telling me about?"

My cheeks heat and I know I've got no chance of hiding the truth.

"Maybe, but it's not a big deal."

"Anything that turns your face that color is most definitely a big deal."

"I'm going to be late for class."

Glancing at the time on her phone, she groans. "I'm only letting this go because you're right."

"Great, see you later," I call, sidestepping her and marching toward the building for my first lesson of the day.

The morning passes without any drama, it's almost how school should be, so naturally I'm on high alert waiting for something to happen.

I'm heading toward my locker before my meeting with the guidance counselor when I feel him. Jake's standing at the other end of the hallway with Chelsea practically hanging off him and Mason and Ethan flanking his sides.

Something crackles between us when our eyes meet, but I refuse to allow anyone else to see it. Dragging my eyes away, I open my locker. A small square of white paper catches my eye. Glancing around me to make sure I'm not being watched, I unfold it.

Same time tonight? J

My breath catches and anger ignites in my belly. Have I just turned into his dirty little secret?

Taking a step back, I go to turn toward where they were just standing but I don't need to look far to find him because the four of them are right behind me.

"How are you feeling, lightweight?" Chelsea snarls, her fake smile firmly in place.

"I was better before having to look at your face."

Mason snorts in amusement while Jake stands there with tense shoulders and his face set in his usual mask. Only when I look into his eyes, I see more. My broken boy is still in there.

"Give it a rest, Chelsea," Jake demands. My eyes almost pop out of my sockets at him defending me in public.

"Don't tell me you actually like the skank."

"No." That one word kills every little bit of hope that was bubbling up that things might be changing. "I just think it's time we lay off."

Flinging her hair over her shoulder she mutters a, "whatever," before waltzing off.

Jake goes to take a step forward but I refuse to allow him time to try to apologise for that. Slamming my locker, I storm past him, shoulder barging Ethan in the process.

"Brit?" Jake calls. I hate that the sound of his voice has butterflies erupting in my belly, but I refuse to turn around and acknowledge him. I've got a meeting to get to.

I head toward the library but stop a little short at Miss French's office. I've been putting this meeting off since I started because I knew she'd want to discuss my future, but it's become obvious all these weeks on that I'm no further forward with what I might do when high school comes to an end.

I knock lightly, hopeful she won't hear and I can pretend she wasn't here but I know that's just wishful thinking when she calls out for me to enter.

"Amalie, it's so good to meet you at last. You've been a little elusive to pin down."

"Sorry about that."

"No need to apologize. I understand that thinking about your future after everything you've been through is difficult. I just want to help focus your mind and answer any questions you might have. I know the education system here is different from what you're used to."

"Yeah, I should be at university right now," I say with a sigh, dropping down into the chair in front of her desk.

"I know and I really do understand your frustration at seemingly going backward, but I can assure you that this is the right thing to do."

"I get it, I do. It's just... frustrating."

Miss French flips open my file and quickly scans the information she's got in front of her. "Your grades are looking really good. It seems your teachers are really impressed with your progress."

"I've been working hard, the last thing I need is to be behind before I've really started."

"If only all our transfer students thought that way," she muses. "Anyway. It says in your transfer document that you were going to study photography in college. Is that still your plan?"

I'm silent for a few moments as I consider the answer to the question I knew was coming. "I don't know."

"And why's that?" I'm pretty sure she must know the answer. It seems that she has all my details in that folder so she must know why I'm here.

"I was always inspired by my dad. He was a genius behind the camera and he always said I had it too. I was taking photographs before I could talk apparently, like it was in my blood."

"And now?"

"I haven't picked up my camera since they died," I admit quietly, fighting the lump that's threatening to block my throat.

"Do you think that's what he would want? You to give up something you loved."

"No. never. It's just... hard."

"Amalie, I lost my parents at a young age too, so trust me when I say that I know how you feel. It's the hardest thing you'll ever have to go through, but you can't lose sight of what makes you happy, no matter how much the memories might hurt. Although painful, memories are good. They take you back to happier times and ensure that you'll never forget them. Your dad was a very talented man, I won't lie and say that I didn't look both your parents up. They were both very inspirational people, they achieved so much. I know they'd hate for you to give up because of them."

I wipe at my eyes, trying to clear away the tears that have dropped at her talking about them. One of the things I've mostly managed to avoid since moving here is having people talking about them. Other than the few days with the rumours about why I was here, it's only Gran who brings them up really. It just shows that although I've been feeling like I'm coping better, I fear I might just be hiding it instead of properly dealing with it. We're still waiting for news on the accident and whether it was actually an accident and I think I might be burying how I feel about it all until we get that verdict.

Miss French continues talking, dragging me from my dark thoughts. "If you decide to continue down the photography route then there are so many colleges with great photography programs both in and out of state. Have you thought about if you'd like to move away from here?"

Part of me wants to say yes, to start over somewhere I've chosen to be but another more nagging part knows that my only family is here, so why would I leave to be alone?

"I don't know," I answer honestly. "I can see pros and cons to both."

"I hope you don't mind, but I took the liberty of printing out some of the best programs just to give you something to think about. These ones are spread across the country, and here's a couple in state. Just give them all a read, check out the college websites. See if any of them speak to you. I know it's still early and you've got plenty of time to make a decision but there's no harm in starting to get ideas and having something to work toward."

"Thank you," I say, gathering up all the paperwork she's just spread across the table. Seeing some of the college names at the top of the printouts makes my heart race a little. I'm not totally naïve on this subject, in fact, studying for my degree in America was something I'd discussed with my parents more than once. They thought it would be good for me, and some of these institutions have incredible courses that could really help kick-start my career, along with my name, of course. But in the end, I decided that I didn't want to go that far away. I looked up some of Dad's suggestions though and I couldn't deny that what some of them could offer was incredible, plus the opportunity to live in stunning cities like New York was very tempting.

I'm walking out into the corridor when raised voices coming from the entrance to this part of the school make their way down to me.

"I'm sorry, but I can't just allow you to march into the building."

"But he's my son. I have every right to see him."

"Yes. Once classes are over, you may do as you wish but I won't have you disrupting my school or my student's education."

"This is infuriating. Do you know who I am?"

I round the corner right as she says those words and my chin drops.

Kate Thorn. Supermodel. Porn star. Drug addict. *Jake's mum.*

Fuck.

How did I not see this coming?

My movement catches her eye, and she drags her stare from the principal to me. Her eyes narrow as she looks me up and down.

"I know you."

"I'm Amalie Win—"

"Windsor-Marsh. I know who you are." Her lips curl in disgust as if I'm nothing more than a bit of dog shit on her shoe.

Turning away from me, she continues where she left off. "I don't know how long I'm in town for. I need to see my son."

As they stand and continue arguing, it gives me a chance to take her in. She looks completely different from the last time I saw her in person and everything like the images that have been plastered all over the gossip magazines for the past year or so. She used to be one of the industry's most sought after models. She was gorgeous, had the flawless face and the slim figure every designer wanted. Dad had photographed her more than any other model in his career, he was her favourite to work with and she often demanded it was him shooting or it wouldn't happen. But as with so many young success stories, the fame and money got to be a little too much. She was burning the candle at both ends and something had to give. She started drinking, snorting too much cocaine and lost job after job. According to the gossip, she'd snorted and pissed away every penny she earned and after a sex tape leak, she obviously realised there was money to make in sex and turned to that. I've not seen anything, but the screenshots and comments that have graced social media haven't been pleasant.

Her once porcelain skin is now almost grey, her cheeks sunken and her eyes tired and bloodshot. Although she was always very slim, her skin is now hanging from her bones. But it's her blue eyes and blonde hair that stand out to me. Although that blonde is anything from natural. It's peroxide yellow and even from this distance, it looks as brittle as straw.

Everything Jake's ever said to me suddenly makes so much sense. His hatred of where I came from, my parents' industry, even my looks to a point.

His mother is Kate fucking Thorn. I feel like an idiot for not putting two and two together. But why would I? I'm sure there are a million eighteen-year-old kids with Thorn as a surname who could have been the son she abandoned as a young child. The little boy she left behind was regularly mentioned when they were slating her in the press.

It should have been obvious, the voice in my head screams. But as I stand and berate myself, still eavesdropping on their increasingly heated argument, I spot movement over by the benches.

Jake rounds the corner, the shouting in the distance catching his attention and he looks up. Everything happens in slow motion. It takes a second or two for reality to hit him, but when it does, I've never seen a look on his face like it. I thought he'd looked at me with pure hatred but I'm realising that I was let off lightly because as he stares at his mother, he looks murderous. His entire body tenses, his fists clench at his sides like he might just walk up to her and punch her in the face. I step forward, needing to go to him but Kate sees where my focus is and her eyes land on Jake.

"Jake, my boy. Come here."

I drop my bag and books and race toward Jake as his chest swells and his entire body vibrates with fury.

"Come on, baby."

"Don't baby me, you fucking whore." With that, he spins on his heels and runs. I attempt to chase him but he easily outruns me and I'm left panting, bent over with my hands on my knees trying to catch my breath.

"Fuck," I mutter between heaving breaths. Looking back, Kate and the principal are gone.

I should leave him to his own personal hell but now I've got an understanding of why he is the way he is, I know that I won't be able to.

Walking back toward the school, I pick up everything I dropped and try to figure out where he might go.

I don't give school a second thought as I walk off-campus. I catch a bus toward the seafront. My first thought being Aces, although I'm pretty sure he won't want to be around people right now, but it's close to my second guess, the beach. If I'd just had my world turned upside down, I think I'd head straight for the ocean. There's something so relaxing listening to the waves crashing.

I come up short in both places, so with nowhere else to turn, I head toward his trailer. Even if he's not there right now, hopefully he'll reappear at some point.

I get the bus to his house, not wanting to be caught by Gran. I sneak through the driveway and down to the bottom of the garden. I forego the trailer, thinking that he might be in his make-shift gym, but it's empty with no signs he's been here.

Thankfully, his trailer door is unlocked, so I pull it open and step inside.

It looks exactly as it did the other day. It's much tidier than I would have expected knowing an eighteen-year-old lad lives here. I'd expect to find beer cans, clothes, and all sorts lying around but in reality, the only thing out is an ashtray.

Not wanting to pry into his life too much, I take a seat on his sofa and wait.

I must fall asleep because when my eyes flicker open, the sun is beginning to set and I have a very angry pair of eyes staring down at me.

36

JAKE

Dismissing Brit like I did in front of Chelsea was physically painful. Why couldn't I just grow a pair and admit that things had changed? The girl I'd quite happily have never seen again when she first arrived has somehow managed to bury her way under my skin and no matter how hard I try, I can't get her the fuck out.

I'm so used to playing the part of the carefree asshole at school that the act just comes naturally. No one questions the mask I wear, no one, aside from Mason, even knows it exists. They think this douchebag is actually me. They have no idea I use the persona to cover up what's really festering inside me. The anger, the hurt, the betrayal. It's been years, but it doesn't seem to make any difference, that little abandoned boy still lives inside me.

I should be in class but I managed to find out that Brit has a meeting with Miss French and with everyone else busy learning, I decided I'd surprise her and make up for being an asshole. The taste of her coming against my lips last night is the only thing I can taste and, fuck, if I don't need more of that. She has every right to tell me to go fuck myself, which I did multiple times with my hand once I got back to my trailer last night, but my need for her means I make a pathetic excuse to my teacher and march out of her room. I didn't even hang around to find out if she'd given me permission or not. Who gives a fuck. It's not like anyone in their right mind would question me.

When I spot the principal at the end of the hallway, I go to duck into the shadows so I can get to Miss French's office another way. But the figure standing in front of him has me stepping out in the open.

My heart races and an uncomfortable knot forms in my stomach.

It can't be.

Thinking that I must be imagining things, I take a few steps closer, my eyes locked on the woman who I now realize is going batshit at Principal Hartmann.

Fuck.

I've imagined a million times how I would react if I were ever to see her again. A million and one ways I could hurt her after what she did to me. But in that moment, before she sees me, everything inside me freezes.

She looks nothing like I remember, or like the one and only photo I have of the two of us together. She's no longer the stunning supermodel that I picture every time I think of her but some haggard old woman. The fact that life clearly hasn't been easy on her makes me feel a tiny bit better about everything, but it goes nowhere near making any of the anger or hurt go away. She left me without a backward glance for a life of glitz and fame. I will never forgive her for the selfish decision she made when I was a child. Maybe I could possibly consider going easy on her if she had made the decision with my best interests in mind, but it soon became clear that my happiness was not a factor in her decision. She left me with two people who quite obviously didn't want me and who had no time for the disaster child she'd turned me into.

As was inevitable, she turns to look at me. Red hot anger pours through my veins and my fists clench to make her feel just an ounce of the pain she caused me over the years. But as much as I might want to acknowledge her, I won't give her the pleasure.

When she opens her mouth and calls to me, my stomach turns over, threatening to empty itself on the concrete at my feet.

How fucking dare she call me *her boy* after everything? So what, her fancy life didn't go as planned and she's now a coked up, washed-up, old porn star? I'm not here to fall back on when everything's gone to shit and there's nowhere else to go.

My body trembles with the adrenaline racing through it. Fight or flight kicks in and after replying with words I don't even register, I run.

I run as fast and as far as I can. Just like she did to me all those years ago. Sadly, I don't have the kind of money I'd need to skip the country to get away from her. Instead, I find myself at the end of the beach between the dunes just like I did a few nights ago after getting thrown out of the game.

I rest my elbows on my knees as I drag in much needed deep breaths. I clench and unclench my fists, trying to release the urge I have to punch something—or someone—until that bitch can no longer affect me. I should be over this. It's been years, but still she's up in my fucking head, screwing me the fuck up.

Hitting my fist against my temple, I try to force her out. I haven't even laid eyes on her in over ten years, yet she has this power over me. Exactly why I've always refused to date. I don't want another woman to have this power.

Only you have, dipshit. Brit weaseled her way in despite what a douche you've been. Seeing the woman who gave birth to me once again only pointed out the alarming differences between her and Brit that I really should have acknowledged that very first day I saw her, but I was too blinded by her past and the life she came from. In reality, I should have seen her for who she is, not who I made her out to be in my head. She's proven time and time again that she's nothing like the woman I just left behind. No matter how many times I've hurt her, she's come right back like she knew there was something inside me she needed to drag out. With every insult I threw at her, she came right back. It's why I can't stay away. She challenges me like no one I've ever met before and she makes attempting to look indifferent to my advances a full-time job when all it really does is make me push harder to break her.

The thought of Brit has the anger and tension starting to drain from my body. It's enough to tell me that she's what I need right now.

Jumping up, I set about going to get her. She's probably still at school, and like fuck am I going back there right now, or ever again if she's going to keep turning up. Instead, I head home for a shower to waste some time before she comes home and I can get to her.

I focus on her as I make my way to my trailer. I don't bother catching the bus, the long walk is exactly what I need to attempt to clear her from my head. It's not lost on me that not so long ago I'd have been walking to get Brit out of my head and now I'm restless because I need her.

Fuck. I need her so fucking bad and I'm just about fed up trying to hide it.

My legs burn and sweat runs down my back by the time I walk down the garden toward my trailer.

Reaching behind me, I drag my shirt over my head, ready to go straight to the shower as I pull the door open and climb in.

I step toward the bedroom but something to my left catches my eye.

Fuck. She's here.

How did she know I needed her?

Dropping my shirt to the counter as I pass, I drop down to my haunches as I take in every inch of her beautiful face. How could I ever compare her to that old hag? There's nothing even remotely similar between the two of them. *Her* looks are mostly fake, Brit is a pure, natural beauty.

As if she can sense me, her eyes flutter open. She sees me immediately and her breath catches in fright.

"Jake, shit. I—"

I don't allow her to say anymore. My fingers thread in her hair and my tongue delves into her mouth. All I need right now is her. Her kiss to remind me that not everything in my world is totally fucked up.

She sags in my hold and allows me to take what I need. Little does she know though, it's never going to be enough.

"I need you," I say between heaving breaths when I pull back and rest my forehead against hers. I stare down into her blue eyes and it's the first time I admit to myself that I never want to look into any others again.

"Anything," she breathes. The honesty in her voice throws me for a moment. My fingers twist harder in her hair as I try to accept what she just said.

"Why? After everything, why are you still here and willing to give me anything?"

"I've no idea, I just know it's where I need to be."

"Fuck," I bark, releasing her and taking a huge step back.

"Jake, what—"

"Let's go somewhere."

"Okay, sure. Where do you want to go?"

"I don't mean for dinner or for the evening, I mean let's get out of here. Just me and you. What do you say?"

"I say... are you crazy?"

"Probably. I just... I can't be here right now." It's the truth. If she came to find me at school, I'm sure here will be the next place she visits. Fuck, she might even be up in that fucking house right now. "I need to go. Now."

"Uh... yeah. Okay. Can I go and get some stuff first?"

"You've got ten minutes to get back here or I'm going without you." I have no idea if that's true or not, the way I'm feeling right now, I'd wait forever for her to come back to me.

"Okay." Jumping from the sofa, she slips her feet back into her Chucks and takes a step toward the door. At the last minute, she turns back to me, wraps her fingers around the back of my neck and presses her nose gently against mine.

"I'm nothing like her, I promise," she whispers before placing a sweet kiss to my lips and running from the trailer.

My hands tremble as realization dawns.

She knows.

37

AMALIE

I run through the undergrowth, the thistles scratching my bare arms but I don't care. I need stuff and I need to get back to him before he leaves. He wasn't expecting me to be waiting at his trailer but one look into those tormented eyes and I knew it was exactly what he needed, just like this trip. I know he wants to get away before she finds him which is why I sigh with relief when I find Gran's bungalow empty, allowing me to shove a few things in a bag before running back toward Jake.

When I break through the trees, he just opens his door.

"Ready?"

"Yes."

I loiter for a few seconds while he locks up, then he takes my hand and leads me toward the house's driveway.

"What are you doing?" I whisper-shout in shock when he goes straight for his uncle's old car.

"We're getting the hell out of this place as fast as we can."

I watch in horror as he pulls the driver's door open, throws his bag in the back and jumps in.

"You coming or what?"

"Shit. Yeah. I'm coming."

I follow his lead by throwing my case with his and falling down onto the seat right as he leans forward to jump start the car.

"What is this? Grand Theft Auto?"

"Something like that. You ready for a wild ride?" He glances over at me and winks, making me think that he's not talking about the drive.

"Can't wait. Show me what you've got."

Jake groans as if he's in pain before doing whatever you do to hotwire a car. The engine rumbles to life, and he backs out of the driveway at record speed.

"I'm assuming that wasn't your first time."

"You'd assume right. Anywhere you want to go?"

"Nope. Just drive."

"Done."

I lower the window and sit back, allowing the warm breeze to flow past my face. I might be in a stolen car with Jake Thorn, a guy I would have quite happily thrown under one when I first encountered him, but as we drive along the coastal road with the radio blaring and the windows down, I feel freer than I have in a very long time.

"How did you know?"

"About your mum?"

"Yeah, but please don't call her that."

"I saw her arguing with Hartmann when I came out of my guidance counsellor meeting. I had no idea until then though. I feel a little stupid for not figuring it out."

"How would you have figured it out?"

"Just from some stuff you've said. Seeing her, it all made so much sense."

"I'm sorry."

"Sorry, what was that? You're going to need to repeat that, I didn't quite hear properly."

"I'm sorry, for everything. I was projecting all my hate for her onto you because of your parents and where you came from. It wasn't fair."

"I understand."

"You shouldn't. I was an asshole."

"I can't deny that, Jake, but you had your reasons. I'm glad I know the truth now. You should have told me."

"I don't talk about her, Brit. Ever."

"Will you?"

"Will I what?"

"Talk... about her. About what happened?"

His fingers tighten on the wheel with a white-knuckled grip.

"Everything I know about her is from magazine gossip or snippets I overheard when she was talking to my parents."

"From the bits I've seen, the press didn't get it too far wrong." He falls silent, the muscle in his neck pulsing steadily. I allow him the time he needs to gather his thoughts. "I don't have many good memories of her, she was always pawning me off anywhere she could so she could go out. But I guess, looking back, at least she was there. The day she turned her back, I'll never forget. She dropped me at my aunt's, kissed my forehead and turned away without even a glance back at me.

"I was young, I assumed my aunt was just looking after me, but she never came back. To this day, I have no idea if my aunt knew she was stuck with me from then on or what. She put me in the guest room and her and my uncle mostly just carried on with their lives like I wasn't there. The only difference for them was a little extra washing and another plate to put food on. If *she* was hoping that by leaving me there I'd have a better life, then she was mistaken. She might have been neglectful, but at least she was my mother.

"I used to overhear my aunt and uncle talking about things they'd seen she'd been up to and I used to sneak down to their office and use their old shitty computer to Google her. Even at that age, I was embarrassed. Some of the shit I used to find. I stopped looking the day the sex tape was leaked." A shudder runs through him at the thought.

"She's a fucking waste of space. All she cares about is herself. She never sent me a penny of her hard-earned money or ever came to visit when she was in the country. She just left me with them, not giving a fuck if I was dead or alive. I fucking hate her." The strength of his feelings for his mother comes off him in waves. His arms shake as he tries to control himself.

Needing to do something to help, I reach over and place my hand on his thigh. His muscles bunch before he relaxes slightly.

He glances over at me, the slightest hint of a smile on his lips. "What the fuck did I do to deserve this? You?"

I shrug because I really don't have the answer. "I saw something in you, I guess."

"Oh yeah?" he asks, his usual jack the lad persona slipping back into place.

"Something in your eyes."

"Oh? I thought you were going to say that it was my abs."

"Shut up, you idiot."

He laughs and after the tense conversation we just had, it sounds incredible.

The sun's setting and casting an orange glow over the sea.

"It's beautiful here," I say, totally lost in the view, my hand still firmly in place on Jake's thigh.

"There's a motel up ahead, you want to stop here?"

"Sure. Won't your uncle be mad you stole his car?"

"Probably. I don't really care. They all think I'm a total fuck up. I may as well act the part."

"Wouldn't you rather prove them wrong?"

"Why? They had me nailed as the bad kid they got stuck with from that very first day. Nothing I've ever done has changed their minds."

"That's really sad."

"Maybe, but it's my reality. It's why I'm leaving the second I finish school."

He kills the engine and jumps from the car. I stay seated and watch as he stretches his stiff muscles. It's not until I look at my phone that I realise how long we had been driving for.

Grabbing my handbag from the back seat, I join him at the front of the car.

"Let's go and see if they've got a room," I suggest. I take a step but don't make it any farther. Jake's hand slips into mine and I'm pulled back until I'm flush against his chest.

He stares down at me causing butterflies to start up in my belly. His hand cups my cheek, his thumb brushing gently over my skin.

"Thank you," he whispers. It's by far the most sincere thing he's ever said to me and it immediately brings tears to my eyes. His eyes bounce between mine. "Shit. That wasn't supposed to make you cry."

"It'll take more than that to make me cry, Thorn." His eyes narrow at my use of his nickname. "Come on, let's get that room."

A smile twitches at his lips, his eyes darkening. I can only imagine what he's thinking, and I can only hope it's somewhat in line with what I am.

———

Ten minutes later, Jake is pushing the key into our room for the night. He shoves it open, then steps aside allowing me to enter first.

"That's very gentlemanly of you," I say, looking over my shoulder at him.

"I'm not always an asshole."

"Really? I'll look forward to that. Ahhh," I squeal as his hands land on my waist and I'm thrown onto the double bed in the middle of the room.

I land with a bounce before I flip over to find him looming over me. He crawls onto the bed and pushes my legs apart so he can settle between them. His hands land on either side of my head and he drops down slightly, closing the space between us.

"I meant what I said outside."

"I know." His eyes roam over every inch of my face, the intensity in his eyes making me want to clench my thighs.

"Am I in the way?" he asks, his eyes sparkling with delight.

"That all depends."

"On..."

"What you're intending on doing."

"Oh, I've got plans. There are so many things I want to do."

Heat floods my core as memories of how good his mouth felt on me last night.

"The first thing I want to do." He lowers even more so our lips are brushing. "Is get some food. I'm fucking starving." He jumps from the bed, chuckling with amusement as I groan in frustration. He holds his hand out for me and I pull myself up so I'm sitting. "I saw a pizza place just down the street. Up for it?"

"Oh, don't worry. I'm up for it."

"I change my mind. I'm not hungry now."

"That's a real shame because now you've mentioned it, I'm ravenous. Come on."

I turn back when I get to the door, just in time to see him rearrange himself in his jeans. Fuck, maybe we should just stay in here.

38

JAKE

All I wanted to do was get back between her legs, but I knew she deserved better than that. She didn't have to agree to this little impromptu trip, but she did so without any second thought. Fuck knows what I did to deserve her support right now because I know damn fucking well I don't deserve it.

As much as I want to spend the night doing all the filthy things that are filling my head, I'm more than willing to allow her to take the lead. I don't want to push her into more than she's ready for.

We both sit back in our chairs after polishing off a pizza each. "That's better," I say, grabbing my soda and draining the glass. I almost spit it all over her when she lets out the most unladylike burp.

"Oops," she says, covering her mouth with her hand, her cheeks turning a light shade of red.

"You're ruining all my first impressions of you, you know that, right?"

"Well, seeing as you hated me on sight, I don't think that's a bad thing."

"I... I just saw her. I know it's crazy because really, you're nothing alike but... fuck. I was a dick." Pulling my eyes from hers, I stare across the small diner, regret consumes me.

Brit reaches across the table and laces her fingers with mine. Dragging my gaze back to her, my breath catches in my throat at the hungry look in her eyes.

"Let's go back to our room."

I'm powerless to refuse her suggestion. After throwing a few bills down on the table that definitely covers the check, we stand and hand in hand we walk from the diner.

There's something so freeing about being somewhere where no one knows either of us. While we're in Rosewood, we'll always find someone who'll recognize us. And it's not that I'm ashamed to be seen with her like she thought at the diner. I'm more concerned about her and what people will think when they see her with me. I've got a reputation and I know they'll judge her, make her out to be as bad as one of the cheer sluts. I can already predict what the gossip mongers will spread around.

We're both silent on the short walk back to our room but the tension crackles between us. I know she can feel it too because every minute or two she'll look over at me. Concern creases her brow and I know she wants to help but I'm not sure what she can do right now but be here. I know that I'm going to have to go back and deal with my mother. If she's made it this far to see me, then I can't imagine she's going to get back on a plane and disappear all that willingly. She's done the hard part, she's made her presence known after years of avoiding the place, avoiding me.

Pulling the key from my pocket, I unlock our door and allow Brit to enter before closing and locking the door behind me.

Turning, I take a step forward but stop just short of crashing into her.

She stares at me, her eyes assessing as she chews on her bottom lip. "What are you doing?"

"Trying to figure out the best way to make you get out of your own head. You wanted to escape but you've spent the whole time with your head back in Rosewood worrying about what you left behind."

"I know, I'm sorry but—"

Stepping closer, her body heat burns into my chest. "I wasn't looking for an apology, Jake. I understand. Family shit can be... hard."

"Shit, Brit. I'm so s—"

"No. We're done talking." Her voice comes out harder and I start to panic that I've pissed her off again and that she's about to run. Thankfully when she moves, it's the very opposite.

Her hands rise and link behind my neck, our mouths just a breath apart.

"You think I can take your mind off it?"

Our noses press together, her lips just tickling lightly against mine. My cock stirs in my pants at just the thought of tasting her again.

"I don't know. Do you need me to leave and then sneak back in when you're not expecting it?"

"I'm not really a fan of time-wasting."

"Maybe not, but you can't deny that having someone sneak into your room at night and get you off isn't hot as fuck. You know you owe me, right?"

"No, you most definitely owed me those."

I nod, there's no way I can disagree with that after everything I've put her through.

Our breaths mingle as our chests heave and we continue staring at each other. Her blue eyes darken the longer we stand here. It's almost as if we're daring the other to make the first move. It's hot as fuck but my need for her is at a breaking point. Every muscle in my body is locked up tight and my fingers twitch at her waist itching to explore every inch of her perfect fucking body.

It's almost like someone counts us down because the second I break, so does she. Our lips collide, our teeth clash as we fight to get closer. My hands slip inside her t-shirt, my need to feel her skin against mine too much to deny.

Finding the clasp of her bra, I flick it open and run my hands around the front to get what I really need. Her breasts might be small, but they fill my hands perfectly.

She moans and I swallow it down as I pinch both her nipples between my fingers.

Her hands find their way under my shirt and she lifts until I'm forced to break our kiss so we can pull it over my head. I immediately drop it to the floor, pulling her body back to me, wasting no time.

With one hand under her t-shirt, I wrap the other around her waist and walk her backward until her legs hit the bed.

"Amalie, fuck. I need you."

She stills in my arms and pulls her head back so she can look at me.

My stomach drops. She's just changed her mind. *Fuck.*

"W-what's wrong?" My cock throbs against her, willing her not to put an end to this right now.

"You said my name," she says softly, her cheeks heating when she realizes what she said. "It's just, you've never used it before."

"Using it meant accepting what I really wanted."

She wants to ask, it's right on the tip of her tongue but I'm not ready to express everything I've been keeping buried since she first walked into my life. I've bared enough of myself to her today. So instead of allowing her to say anything, I grip the bottom of her shirt and pull it off her quickly followed by her bra.

"Fuck," I grunt as I'm greeted by her rosy pink stiff nipples. They're as perfect as I remember.

Dropping my head, I suck one and then the other into my mouth ensuring I run my tongue around each one. Her hips thrust toward me as she moans my name and fuck, if it doesn't make my cock leak for her.

"Need more," I demand, dropping to my knees, I kiss down her flat stomach before flicking open the fly of her jeans.

Feeling her stare burning into the top of my head, I look up as I begin to pull the fabric of her jeans and panties down her legs.

She looks so innocent as she bites down on her bottom lip, my balls ache for her as she waits to see what I'm going to do.

With our eyes still connected, I lean forward and place a kiss to her hipbone. Her eyelids flutter but they don't close fully.

I can't fight it any longer and I have to pull my eyes from hers. Sitting back on my haunches, I stare at her body.

She might have the body of a supermodel, but that doesn't mean she doesn't have curves. And fuck me if those curves don't bring me to my knees.

"Sit on the bed."

She follows my order but instead of staying upright, she falls back onto her elbows, giving me an incredible fucking view.

Reaching forward, I wrap my hands around her thighs and pull her so her ass is hanging over the edge, then I lower myself toward her core. Her scent makes my mouth water before I suck her swollen clit into my mouth.

"Jake," she cries, and I feel like a goddamn king.

Fuck ruling the school, the only person I want to be a king for is her.

39

AMALIE

J ake doesn't pull back until he's allowed me to ride out every second of the orgasm he gave me.

He stands from his position on the floor and goes for his waistband. Not wanting to miss anything, I sit myself up on my palms and watch intently as he pushes the fabric of both his jeans and boxers down his thighs.

His cock springs free and my eyes widen. I'm not a virgin, but shit, that's bigger than I've experienced before.

Before he drops the fabric to the floor, he digs into his pocket and pulls out a strip of condoms.

"Wow, someone was optimistic."

"Better that than being caught shor—" His words falter when he looks up and finds me staring at him.

"Jesus, Amalie. Could you be any more beautiful?"

The sound of his deep voice saying my name causes even more butterflies to erupt in my belly. I never knew hearing my own name could affect me so much.

He takes a step toward me and my heart pounds inside my chest.

"I need you... so fucking badly, but if you don't then—"

"Stop." I place my finger against his lips as he begins to climb over me. If I wasn't sure about this, then I wouldn't have put myself in this position. I'm laying here naked willingly. It might be the stupidest thing I've done to date because all the sweet stuff he's saying to me could be one big fat lie, but after seeing his mum earlier and the effect it had on him, I'm pretty convinced that he's telling the truth. He was too vulnerable to bullshit me when he first found me earlier.

Placing my hands against his rock hard abs, I skirt them up and over his chest and then up into his hair. My nails scratching his head slightly, making him moan.

"Fuck. I don't deserve for this to happen. You should kick my naked ass to the curb and make me walk back to Rosewood."

"You're right. That's exactly what I should do. But I'm not."

"Fuck." Settling between my legs, he drops his lips to mine and kisses me like he'll die without it. His tongue plunges into my mouth and tangles with mine as his hips thrust in an attempt to find the friction he needs.

Scratching my nails down his back, I grab on to his arse and pull him closer to where he needs to be.

"Condom," he mutters against my lips.

"I'm covered, it's okay."

"No," he says harshly, sitting up straight. "I'm not taking any chances on my life being turned upside down again, not yet anyway."

I can't argue, he's just being sensible.

Ripping one of the squares from the long length he pulled from his pocket, he opens it with his teeth and quickly rolls it down his cock. I watch his every movement, my pussy clenching to feel what it'll be like pressing inside and filling me to the hilt.

Lining himself up with my entrance, I fall back onto the bed and wait.

"How slow do I need to take this?"

I know it's his way of asking if I'm a virgin and I can't help smiling to myself. "However you need. It's not my first rodeo."

"Fuck," he barks, a conflicted expression crossing his face.

"Hey," I say, reaching up and cupping his cheek. His eyes find mine and he seems to come back to himself.

He pushes forward and I wince a little. I might not be a virgin, but it's been a while.

"Holy fuck, you're tight," he groans as he slowly continues to push inside until he's as deep as he'll go.

I expect him to fuck me. To take all his frustrations over everything that's happened today out on me, but that's the exact opposite of what he does. In reality, he drops his face into my neck as he slowly grinds into me.

It's not long before his well-considered movements begin to awaken another release within me.

"Jake, Jake," I chant, my nails scratching down his back as my muscles lock up ready to fall over the edge.

Pulling his head up, he finds my lips as he holds himself up with one elbow while the other caresses my face. It's softer and more emotional than I ever could have imagined with him.

My muscles clamp down on him as my release crashes into me. He sits up and stares down at me. My eyelids are heavy as wave after wave of pleasure races through me, but I can't break my contact with him. Something is happening between us and I don't want to miss a second of it.

"Fuck, Amalie."

Before my orgasm fades, he slides his hands under my arse and lifts me. Then, much like I was expecting, he thrusts hard and fast into me. His head falls back as his muscles pull and ripple before my eyes.

The sight of him taking what he needs is enough to bring on the tingles of another release. One he ensures he drags out of me by pressing his thumb down on my clit.

"Fuck," he roars before I feel his cock twitch. "Amalie," he cries as he empties himself inside me.

Pulling out, he drops the used condom over the side of the bed and then rolls over and pulls me tightly into his body.

Our chests heave with our exertion and my muscles continue to twitch with pleasure. I know I'm not alone in wanting more because I can feel his still semi-hard cock against my arse.

We lie there in silence for the longest time, neither of us ready to give in to sleep quite yet.

"You still awake?" he whispers eventually.

"Yeah. You?"

"Yeah," he chuckles. "Amalie?"

"Yeah?"

"I never said it before because I was an asshole but, I'm really sorry about your parents. That must have been really hard."

The mention of my parents immediately has tears burning my eyes and only reminds me of the conversation I had with Miss French earlier today.

"Thank you. It's—" My voice cracks and he clearly notices.

"Shit."

Turning me so I've no choice but to face him. He kisses the two tears that fall and pulls me tighter to his chest.

"I'm so fucking sorry."

I've no idea if he's apologising for the loss of my parents, which he clearly had nothing to do with, or for the shit he pulled over the past few weeks. It doesn't really matter what it's for specifically because I accept it, nonetheless.

"Do they know how it happened?" he asks after a few more minutes of silence between us.

"They're still looking into whether or not their helicopter had been tampered with. I'd hoped they'd have the answers they need by now. It's taking forever. I just need it to be done so I can attempt to move on."

"If it helps at all. I think you're doing a pretty incredible job already. What you've been through would have broken most people."

"You did a pretty good fucking job."

"Which I'll probably regret for the rest of my life. I was so stuck in my own problems that I didn't even give what you've been through a second thought. I was so fucking pig-headed."

Rolling him onto his back, I throw my leg over his waist and lie on top of him with my chin resting on his chest.

"It's in the past. No point in beating yourself up over something you can't change."

"I need to let go of the past. Seeing her today showed me that. I need to look ahead, figure out what the fuck I want to do with it."

"Have you had a meeting with Miss French?"

"Plenty." I hate to bring up the idea of college again because he shot me down pretty quickly last time but there must be something he can do to get there.

"And what does she say about college and stuff?"

"That I should look into it and stop ruling it out. Don't give me that look," he says when I raise my eyebrow at him in an 'I told you so' way.

"How about we look into things together?"

"Go to college together?"

"Whoa, hold your horses there, Thorn. We just had sex, not got married." His face drops and it makes me wonder if he's more serious about this thing between us than he's letting on. "I meant just do some research, try to figure out the future together."

"I guess we could do that."

"Do you have any idea what you'd like to study?"

"Hmmm... how about your body?" he asks, flipping us both over and sucking one of my nipples into his mouth.

"I'm not sure that's an option." I laugh as he tickles my sides before settling between my legs once again like it's his new home.

"I want to do photography so I could most definitely make use of your body."

"Is that right?" he asks with a wink.

"I learnt a few tricks from my dad, I'd be able to take a few inches off you."

He gasps in mock horror. "See I was right, I knew you were a bitch."

"That might be a little more convincing if you were to say it when your hard cock isn't poking me between the legs."

"You can take photographs of me any day. I'm not shy."

"So I see." My gaze drops to where his fist is stroking his cock slowly.

———

It's safe to say that we leave our stamp on that motel room, and the bathroom, when we decide it's probably time for a shower.

By the time I swing my legs from the bed some time long after sunrise the next morning, I swear every muscle in my body pulls.

"You okay?" Jake asks, looking over at me with the covers pooling across his waist. It sure is a sight to wake up to. His hair is sticking up in all directions and his lips are still swollen from our hours of kissing. Something inside my chest swells at the sight of him, but I put the feeling to the back of my mind, afraid that if I focus on it too much, it'll only result in heartache.

I smile at him but it's anything but convincing.

I've no idea what's going to happen once we walk out of this motel room, but I know things between us are never going to be like there are in here.

There are too many obstacles that will get between us once again when we get back to Rosewood. Jake's mum is the most obvious issue but I can't forget all the kids at school who are going to be less than impressed if something were to happen between us.

"Why do you look so worried?"

"Because we've got to go back to reality soon."

"So? I should be the one stressing about that. It's my whore of a mother that's waiting for me." I rear back for a number of reasons and I think he realises his mistake because he rushes to apologise. "I'm sorry. I wish I could trade mine for yours."

"It's okay," I say, reaching my hand out and squeezing his. "But..."

"But what?"

"What happens between us when we walk out of here. Last night was—"

"Incredible. Mind-blowing. Earth shattering," he says, pulling me back down to the bed with him and kissing me on the tip of my nose.

"Yeah but—"

"But nothing, Amalie." Goosebumps prick my skin at the sound of my name, and it makes him smile. "We can walk out of here hand in hand and it can continue for as long as you want it to, if that's what you want."

"It's not that easy though."

"Why isn't it? In case I didn't make it obvious enough last night, I want you, Brit. I'm done with the bullshit and the pretending. I'm yours, if you'll have me."

"But what about everyone else?"

"No one else matters."

"I'm not sure everyone will see it that way."

"Like who?"

"Chelsea for one."

"Fuck Chelsea. She has nothing to do with what's between us."

"No, but she'll have an opinion and she'll make sure others do too."

"Fuck 'em. All of them. If I need to stand on the fucking school roof and announce to the world that you're mine, then I fucking will."

"I'm not sure that's necessary," I mutter, getting embarrassed just thinking about him doing something so ridiculous.

"How about we just take it as it comes. I need to deal with Kate when I get back, no doubt she's waiting for me and we'll just go from there. Maybe you'll let me take you out."

"On a date?"

"Yeah, if you like."

A smile twitches my lips at the thought. "Have you ever been on a date before?"

"No, never. Never dated and never kissed anyone."

"That rumour was true?"

"Until you, baby." My eyes widen in surprise. "I meant it. I'm serious about this, about us."

"Me too," I admit, putting my heart on the line.

"Okay then. Shall we get this show on the road? We've probably got people looking for us at home, well you will have at least." He's right, it's a school day and neither of us are there. I left a very brief note for Gran yesterday saying I was sleeping elsewhere but I'm sure she was still expecting me to turn up to school today, Camila too.

"Fancy a shower first?" I ask, quirking my eyebrow at him.

"Fucking right I do." He's up from the bed faster than I can blink and then I'm in his arms and we're making our way toward the bathroom.

"Argh, that's fucking freezing," I squeal when he turns it on and we're both blasted with ice cold water.

"I'll warm you up, baby."

He's not wrong. Those few words are enough to do just that, but he ensures he finishes the job by backing me up against the wall and surrounding me, inside and out, with his heat.

40

AMALIE

Pulling my phone from my bag, dread sits heavy in my stomach when I find a load of missed calls and texts from both Gran and Camila.

"Fuck," I mutter, putting my phone to my ear as it starts ringing.

"Amalia? Where the hell are you? I've had the school on the phone telling me that you haven't turned up."

"I'm so sorry. I'm just with a friend who needed me." Jake's elbow jabs me in the arm and his eyebrows rise as he mouths 'friend?' to me.

"I trust you, Amalie, which is why I told them that you're ill, but I'd appreciate the head's up in the future."

"I'm really sorry. We just got carried away. We're on our way back. We'll be there in a couple of hours."

"Okay. I'll see you soon. You might want to speak to Camila before she finds you first."

"Will do. See you soon."

"Friend?" Jake asks, looking pissed off with my description of him.

"It just wasn't a conversation to have over the phone. I'll introduce you properly in person when we get back if you like." He swallows nervously at the thought. "What?"

"I've just never done the whole meet the family thing before, plus she'll know who my mother is and—"

"And nothing. Gran's pretty open-minded. She'll be fine."

"If you say so."

Looking at the clock, I know Camila will be in class but not wanting to freak her out more than she probably already is, I ring anyway.

It goes to voicemail but not five minutes later she's returning my call.

"Where the utter fuck are you? And don't tell me, you're with Jake?"

"Um... not sure where we are exactly, but yeah, he's here."

"Jesus fucking Christ, Am. I've been going crazy."

"We're both fine. We got a motel room for the night."

"Okay, so... I expect to hear every detail from that later, but for now, I'm just glad he hasn't killed you and sent your body out to sea."

"I heard that," Jake calls with a laugh.

"Good, I hoped you would. You fucking hurt her, Thorn, and I'm coming after you."

"I'd like to see you try."

"Don't tempt me. She's already too good for you."

"I couldn't agree more."

"Okay as fun as this has been, I am here and listening to this conversation. Come by Gran's after school, yeah?"

"Uh of course. We're going dress shopping remember?"

"Um...no."

"Shit, I might have forgotten to tell you, but I need your help getting something sexy for both homecoming and Noah's birthday because, well... you know."

"Yeah, I know. That's fine. I'll see you later. You can buy me dinner."

"After the stress you've caused me today? I don't think so."

"Whatever. Bye."

"What the hell was that about?"

"Camila's been saving herself."

"Her and Noah haven't..." He trails off. "Wow. I bet Mason doesn't know that."

"What's it got to do with him?"

Jake rolls his eyes like it's so obvious that I shouldn't even need to ask the question. "He's been in love with her forever. He just won't admit it."

"I knew there was something between those two. They both refused to talk about it when I asked."

"They're both as dumb as each other. Pretend they can't stand each other, but in reality, they're exactly what the other needs."

"That's rich," I say with a laugh.

"Hey, at least I got my shit together."

"Yeah, just make sure you keep it that way."

Reaching over, I place my hand on his thigh, but he grabs it and brings it to his lips. "Always." His promise makes my heart flutter, but I fight to keep my head in charge of what's growing between us. He's got the power to break me and we've only been officially whatever we are for a few minutes.

We chat about random shit all the way home but it's nice. I know hardly anything about him, so I soak up mundane things like his favourite food and colour.

It's not until he pulls up to his aunt and uncle's that the reality of the situation makes itself known. There's a twitch at the living room curtains before his uncle comes flying from the house, closely followed by his aunt who waddles with her giant pregnant belly.

"What the fuck were you thinking, boy?"

"I just borrowed it for a few hours. No harm done."

"You didn't borrow it. You stole it. You should be fucking lucky we don't have the cops on your ass right now."

"Like they'd give a fuck. Have you seen the state of that thing?"

"That thing is my '91 Pontiac Sunfire. I'm gonna do her up and she'll be a classic."

Jake scoffs. "A classic piece of shit."

"Just because we allow you to stay on our land doesn't mean you have the right to take our shit whenever you feel the need. What if your aunt went into labour?"

Jake glances at his aunt and then to the other car in the driveway. "She looks pretty pregnant to me. Come on," he says to me, grabbing my hand and leading me away.

"Fine, walk away, but you haven't heard the end of this, boy."

Jake flips his uncle off over his shoulder.

"Shouldn't you at least apologise? He does kinda have a point about you stealing it. You hotwired it."

"I would if I cared. They're no better than the bitch I ran away from. They've done fuck all to help me. Why should I help them?"

I refrain from pointing out that it works both ways and that if he was a little nicer, then maybe they would be. I have a feeling that too much time has passed for Jake to attempt to fix any relationship he once might have had with his family. It's sad, especially seeing as I'd do anything to have mine back, but it is what it is. I can't hold his irresponsible family against him just because my loving ones died.

"Are you ready to meet my gran?" I ask as we emerge into her garden from the undergrowth. When he doesn't respond, I glance up at him. "Jacob Thorn, are you nervous?"

"What? No. I don't get nervous. Life's too short for that shit."

"Whatever you say."

"Hello," I call when we step in through the open back door.

"Why are you coming in from-ooooh," Gran says, her eyes dropping to our joined hands. "So this is the friend you skipped out on school for?"

"Gran, this is Jake. Jake, this is my gran, Peggy."

"It's nice to meet you."

"You too," Gran manages to get out once she's wiped the shocked look from her face.

"I'm so sorry if we caused you any concern with Amalie's disappearance. It was totally my fault, I needed to clear my head, and she agreed to go with me."

Gran's eyes assess Jake the whole time he's talking, and I can't help wondering what she's thinking.

"Would you both like something to drink? You can tell me about your little trip."

Thankfully Gran turns away to pour us both a lemonade, so she misses the colour that hits my cheeks as I think about what our trip mostly entailed.

Jake stays for almost an hour before he excuses himself. "Walk me out?" he asks, reaching out for my hand. I slide mine into it and he pulls me from my seat and out to the garden.

He comes to a stop just before the trees that hide his trailer from Gran's bungalow. He pulls me to him and rests his arms around my waist.

"I don't think she likes me."

"She hasn't had a chance yet. Give her time we kind of ambushed her."

"She's only seeing my reputation and my surname."

My gossiping Gran is probably well aware of who his mother is and what his life is like.

"Just let her see the real you. The person you show me, not the arsehole the rest of the town see."

"You really think I'm an asshole?"

"Jake," I say with a sigh, lifting my arms over his shoulders and linking my fingers behind his neck. "That is you surviving. I get it. I understand why you wear the mask you do but I think maybe that it's time to start shedding it." I make a rash decision and one I hope doesn't come back to bite me on the arse. "It's Homecoming on Friday. Will you be my date?"

Terror flashes over his face and I immediately regret the question. I'm forcing too much on him too fast.

"It's okay. Forget I said anything. It was stupid."

"No, no. It wasn't stupid. I just didn't see it coming. If you want me to be your date, then that's what I'll be." He lowers his head and brushes his nose against mine. Butterflies flutter in my belly at the thought of him announcing what's between us to the world.

"Are you sure? Everyone will be there."

"More people to be jealous that you're mine then."

My heart tumbles in my chest before he presses his lips to mine in a soft, simple kiss.

"I'll see you later. *Don't* lock the door."

Heat pools between my legs at the prospect of a late night visitor.

"Okay. See you soon."

He drops another kiss to the tip of my nose and disappears into the trees.

———

"You know who his mother is, right?" Gran says the moment I walk back into the house. The second I turn from the direction Jake went, I saw her looking through the window.

"I do now. She turned up at school demanding to see him yesterday."

"She came back?"

"Yep. It knocked him for six."

"Amalie, come and sit down a minute."

I follow her order, although it's with a ball of dread in my stomach.

"I'm not going to tell you what you can and can't do, or who you can and can't see. But that boy, from what I've heard, is bad news."

"Trust me, Gran. I know exactly what Jake is capable of. I know about his reputation and how he's forced to live his life. Our relationship wasn't all flowers and hearts when we first met but for some reason, we keep finding ourselves drawn to each other."

"And that kind of connection shouldn't be fought," Gran says, the old romantic within her bubbling up once again. "I just need you to be aware of who he is. His mother is—"

"A disaster?"

"Yeah, something like that," she chuckles. "I trust you, Amalie. You've got a smart head on your shoulders and if you say he's worth it, then I'll welcome him into this house with open arms."

"Thank you, I really appreciate that."

"So, Homecoming dress shopping with Camila later then, huh?"

"How do you know about that?"

"She wanted to know if you'd be back for it when she came to pick you up for school this morning. She looked pretty excited about it."

"She is."

"Are you going?"

"It looks that way."

"You should probably be a little more excited about it."

"I know. It's just that parties and I don't seem to mix all that well so I've no reason to think this one will be any different."

"I'm sure it'll be fine. You'll have a strapping young man on your arm this time."

My lips curl up into a smile at the thought. "Yeah, I just hope that won't bring me any more trouble."

I fill Gran in on some of the high school drama that is now my everyday life before going to get ready for Camila to pick me up for dress shopping.

She ends up dragging me into every single clothes shop at the mall. And in true female style, the dress she buys was the very first one she sees.

As promised, she makes me buy her a burger and chips for dinner and nags me for every minute detail of my time with Jake.

"You know all the girls at school are going to want to kill you, right? Not only has Jake Thorn kissed you, but he spent the entire night with you."

"Yeah, I'm aware."

"It'll be fine. If he's as into you as he says, then he'll kick them all into shape. No one will say anything to you if they've got half a brain."

"I bloody hope so."

———

As I lie in bed later that night waiting for my late night visitor to appear, I run through the events that led up to us skipping town yesterday. I still feel stupid for not putting two and two together, especially after he explained that it was where I came from and my parents' industry that he really hated.

I'm just starting to drift off to sleep when the phone ringing fills the bungalow. I listen as Gran walks down the hallway to get it before her voice filters down to me.

"Amalie, are you awake?"

"Coming."

Pulling a hoodie over my shoulders, I make my way down the dark hallway to where she's standing by the phone with just a lamp on lighting the room.

"It's the detective from London. I thought you'd want to hear first." My stomach drops into my feet.

"Shit." Blowing out a slow breath, I try to prepare for whatever he might have to say to me. I take the phone from her and lift it to my ear. "Hello?"

"Miss Windsor-Marsh, Detective Griffin. I have some news regarding your parents' crash."

"Okay," I say, my voice shaky as my hand trembles at my ear.

"The crash has been deemed as a horrific accident. Our investigators can't find any evidence of anything on the helicopter being tampered with."

"Oh my god," I breathe.

"It's over, Amalie. I know it won't be easy, but I hope that now you have the answer you've been waiting for that you'll be able to move on with your life. You'll need to speak to your solicitor but your parents' possessions and accounts etcetera will now be released. I'd advise setting up a meeting as soon as you can."

"Thank you."

"I know it's late there, but I wanted you to know as soon as I got word to tell you."

"I really appreciate that. Thank you so much."

He says his goodbye, I place the phone back on the unit and fall back against the wall. My knees give out and I crash to the floor.

Tears stream down my cheeks, but I don't sob like I'd expect.

"What did he say?" Gran asks impatiently.

"That it... that it was an accident. No evidence of anything untoward. It's over, Gran. It's done and they're gone." It's those words that make my dam break. Gran drops down beside me and holds me to her as we both cry for everything we've lost.

I've no idea how long we sit there crying on each other's shoulders, but all of a sudden, a thought hits me and no matter what, I can't make it go.

"I need to go back."

"What?"

"I need to go back to London." The thought of being able to pick up some of the things I was forced to leave behind has me on my feet in seconds.

"Let's try to get some sleep and then we'll look for flights in the morning."

"No. I need to go now."

"Don't be crazy, Amalie," she says, but I'm not listening, I'm already halfway to my room to grab my laptop. In minutes I have the website open and searching for flights.

"There's one for tomorrow." Grabbing my card from my purse, I book it and slam my laptop closed.

"You can't just run to London. What about school?"

"I'll just be a couple of days," I say as I fill a holdall with clothes. "I just need to be there. I need to... I need to say a final goodbye now that we know."

"Hold your horses and I'll come with you."

"I'm sorry, I don't mean to sound harsh, but I need to do this alone. I need to figure out a way to put my old life behind me."

"Okay," Gran says with a nod and a sad smile. "I understand. I'll drive you to the airport. Just promise me something."

"Anything."

"Promise me you're coming back."

41

JAKE

I should have been expecting it, but when the knock comes on my trailer door, I call out for whoever it was to enter, stupidly assuming it's Ethan or Mason. But when I look up, my blood runs cold as I watch my so-called mother step up into my home.

"Jake," she whispers as if I'm a wild fucking animal that's going to bolt at any second. If she wasn't blocking the door waiting for me to run, then I might consider it, but I've spent the last decade planning what I might say to her should she ever reappear and now it's my chance. "I can't believe how big you are, and so handsome."

"Because that's all that matters to you, isn't it? Looks. You couldn't give a fuck about what's in the inside because your heart is black."

"Jacob Thorn," she scolds and it just fires me up more.

"No. You don't get to come storming in all these years later and attempt to parent me. You gave up that responsibility the day you walked out of my life, leaving me with those two cunts."

"How can you say that about them? They took you in when I couldn't do the job properly. I was ill, Jake."

"Bullshit, *Mother*. You weren't ill, you were just fucking greedy. Someone told you that you had a pretty face, offered you a decent paycheck and off you went like you had no one depending on you. And as for those two." I point up toward the main house. "They were so good at looking after me, they shoved me down here on my own when I was barely old enough to look after myself."

"I'm sure there was more to it than that. From what I heard, you were a bit of a terror."

"So they removed me from their house and left me down here to do as I wished. Are you fucking surprised?"

"I've made mistakes, Jake. I'm only human."

My muscles tense and my chest heaves that she can stand there and make such claims after everything. My fists clench with my need to hurt something, mainly her but I won't give her the privilege of calling the cops on me, because I've no doubt she would, followed by selling the story of her abusive, uncontrollable son to the press.

"No. You've not just made mistakes. You've ruined my fucking life. You had one job the day you gave birth to me. To put me first. To make me your priority. But you failed. You failed every step of the fucking way. So I'm sorry if you expected to walk back into my life and I'd welcome you with open arms but that is never going to happen. If you came back a few weeks, even a month later, I might have considered forgiving you. But now, no fucking chance. Too much time and too much pain has passed." Taking a step toward her, she visibly cowers like I'm about to hit her.

I swing my fist, but it ends up nowhere near her face. Instead, it smashes through the kitchen wall and into the spare bedroom.

"Please, Jake," she cries.

"Your pathetic tears won't work on me."

"Please, I want to make up for everything. I'm not going anywhere this time."

"Well, I am. I've got nothing more to say to you."

Pushing past her, I jump down from the trailer and run.

She has no right getting up in my space and trying to make up for mistakes. No fucking right.

I run until my legs burn with pain and my lungs aren't capable of sucking in air fast enough. What I need is Amalie, but I'm no good to her showing up like this.

Instead, I come to a slow jog as I head up Mason's drive. Other than Amalie now, he and Coach are the only ones who know about my mom. I do my best to keep her a secret for fear of the guys Googling her and watching her fucking porn videos. I'm not stupid enough to think they're all oblivious. When she was riding high, this town loved to ride her fame coat tails. Weird how it all came to a grinding halt when she was caught snorting cocaine off dirty old toilet seats in some backstreet bar.

I bang on the door as I try to get control of my breathing. Thankfully, it's Mason who comes to the door, I'm not sure what anyone else would make of the state of me.

"Glad you're still alive," he says, opening the door wider for me to enter. "Where the fuck you been?"

"Uh..." I follow him down to his kitchen, the sound of kid's TV blasts from the playroom as we pass. "Your mom here?"

"Na, she's... out."

Mason likes talking about his home life and family situation just as much as I do. So I just nod in understanding and continue following him.

He pulls two beers from the fridge and passes one over.

"Kate's back."

The bottle stops halfway to his mouth and his chin drops.

"Please tell me you're joking."

"Be a fucking hilarious joke, right?"

His lips twitch up but seeing as he lived through the whole thing with me, he finds it about as funny as I do.

"She turned up at school yesterday afternoon demanding to see me."

"Shit, man. What did you do?"

"I ran. Seems Brit saw the whole thing and when I got back home, she was waiting for me. We stole my uncle's car and fucked off for the night."

His eyes widen in surprise, but I swear I see a little bit of pride in them too.

"And how was that?"

"Fucking mind-blowing, bro. But I don't kiss and tell."

"Fucking knew you were in love with her."

"In lov—" My words falter as I consider his statement. Am I in love with the girl who I thought I hated? "Fuck."

"Took you long enough to figure out, bro."

"Jesus." I scrub my hand over my chin as a child screams bloody murder.

"Mason, Charlie keeps hitting me with his truck."

"Fucking hell. Let me go deal with them."

Mason walks back down to the playroom and has a stern word with his two younger brothers before coming back looking exasperated.

"Is your mom ever planning on investing in a real sitter so you can get out and live your life?"

"She keeps promising things will change, but I gave up hope of that ever happening a while ago. Just gotta keep going. One day we might win the lottery or some shit. Anyway, my issues aren't the most pressing right now. What the fuck are you gonna do about your mom?"

"Other than hope she fucks off as quick as she did last time? Stay out of her fucking way. I can't be dealing with her bullshit."

"Na, not now that you've got a girlfriend to worry about."

"Fuck. I've got a fucking girlfriend."

"Bro, the chicks at school are gonna lose their shit. They've all been vying for your attention for years and then Amalie walks in and sweeps you right off your feet."

"She didn't sweep—"

His eyebrows almost hit his hairline.

"Fine. Okay, maybe that happened a little bit."

I drain my beer as Mason chuckles.

"Another?"

"Gimme all you got. Gotta drink that bitch out of my system."

I hate that I miss sneaking into Amalie's bedroom when I told her specifically to keep her door unlocked. But getting fucked up with my best friend is exactly what I needed. Even if he did spend the night playing daddy to his kid brothers.

———

When I wake the next morning, it's with a banging head but Mason ensures I'm up by ripping the sheets off and threatening me with a bucket of cold water.

"If you don't get your ass off my floor, get dressed, and show up for practice, Coach will have your balls."

"I know, I know," I mutter, trying to get my arms and legs to work enough to get me off his rock hard floor. I already know I'm going to be in his bad books for missing the previous two days of practice.

Coach isn't the reason why I drag my ass off the floor though. It's Amalie that has me stumbling toward Mason's bathroom so I can shower off the scent of last night's alcohol consumption. Day two into our relationship and I'm already going to be groveling after not showing my face last night.

The thought of her waiting in bed for me wearing a tiny pair of panties and a shirt thin enough to see her nipples though makes me wonder what the fuck I was thinking staying here last night.

I avoid our usual spot when I get to school. The last thing I need right now is fucking Chelsea pretending to care where I was yesterday. Instead, I head straight toward Amalie's locker. Only, she's not there.

I have no idea what her schedule looks like, I've spent the past few weeks trying to pretend that I don't care, something which I'm now regretting more than ever because it would help me find her faster.

Knowing who I need to ask, I walk toward Camila and her small group of friends. Sadly, that also involves Shane, someone who never needs to cross me ever again. Everything inside me begs for me to hit him for what he did to my girl at that party, but something tells me she wouldn't be happy if I did. She seems to be under the illusion that he's a good guy and couldn't possibly be the one who drugged her.

Ignoring his death stare, I place my hand on Camila's shoulder and turn her my way.

"Where is she?"

"Wha..." It takes her a few seconds to register it's me. "Amalie?"

"Yeah, Amalie. Who the fuck else would I be asking you about?"

She just shrugs and it pisses me off.

"Where is she?" I spit.

"Don't you know?" She's baiting me, I know she is, but I can't help but let it get to me. I fucking need her.

"Does it look like I fucking know?"

My raised voice is starting to cause a scene, but I don't give a shit.

"She's gone to London."

My head spins as I try to accept what she's just said to me. I spent practically all of the past two days with her and she never once told me she was leaving. My heart starts to race as panic begins to take over. Why wouldn't she tell me she was leaving?

"When's she get back?" My voice is rough as I fight like hell to keep myself in check.

"I don't know. Her gran said she booked a one-way flight."

My chin drops in shock. "One-way?"

"Yeah, probably trying to get the hell away from you," Shane bravely pipes up, giving me the perfect excuse to do exactly what I was craving the second I laid eyes on him.

"Motherfucker."

My fist flies and I hit him square on the jaw. He stumbles where he wasn't expecting the hit but manages to catch himself before he tumbles to the floor.

The next thing I know, a pair of large hands wrap around my upper arms and I'm being pulled back while Shane groans in pain.

The taste of copper fills my mouth telling me that he must have got a few of his own hits in but my body is too pumped up with adrenaline to feel anything right now.

I'm forcefully shoved forward as people start to surround Shane.

Fuck him. I hope it hurts like hell.

"You don't deserve her," he calls out above the commotion.

A smirk curls at my lips. *Ain't that the fucking truth.*

By the time I'm pushed through the door to Coach's office and shoved onto the seat in front of his desk, I'm starting to come down from my high and my face is starting to ache.

"You need to start talking, boy. First fighting during a game, then missing practice two days on the trot and now this. I'm this close to benching your ass, Thorn. This fucking close." When I glance up, he's holding his thumb and forefinger about a centimeter apart. "What's going on? Please don't tell me all of this is over some skirt."

"She's not just some skirt," I seethe.

"So it is a girl. Who is it that's got you all strung up?"

Dropping my eyes to my lap, I keep my mouth shut.

"I can't help you if you don't talk."

"It doesn't fucking matter who she is, okay? She's gone. Fucked off and left me behind like the trash I am."

"Well, this one really has got herself under your skin."

"It's not just her, Coach."

He leans back and crosses his arms over his chest, waiting for me to spill. I'm surprised he doesn't know. Gossip spreads through the teachers here just as fast as it does around the kids. "Go on."

"Kate showed her face."

He nods, waiting for me to spill, which I do. Coach is the one and only parent figure I've had for most of my life so unlike most of the world around me, he knows all my dark and dirty secrets. He's also bailed me out of the shit more times than I can count.

"You need to get her out of your head or you're going to be useless Friday night. It's our big game against Eastwood, in case you've forgotten. We win this one and we're well on our way to state. But I need you, Thorn. I need you and I need you fully focused. No screwy mother, no girl issues. Get them out of here and focus," he says, tapping my head. "Now get the fuck out of here and go sort out your face. I'll see you on the field after class."

"You're not benching me?"

"Not yet. I need you Friday, you're just going to have to keep your nose clean until then or my hand might be forced. Now fuck off before you get blood on my office floor."

No sooner am I released from Coach's office and I'm hauled into the principal's office and given an ass-kicking for my actions. Much like Coach though, he also knows he's relying on me for Friday night's game, so in the end, he goes easy on me.

——

By Friday night, my bruising is starting to reduce and my cuts on my knuckles healing, shame the ache in my chest is yet to abate. I tried phoning her when I first discovered she'd left, but it didn't even connect. So after fucking up my trailer a little more than it already was after my mother's visit, I sent her a text that I regretted the second I hit send. In reality, I didn't mean any of the harsh words. Her sudden disappearance just hurts so fucking much, her actions are exactly what I accused her of when she first arrived. She's no better than my mother who ran at the first hint of a better life. Was her few hours with me so fucking bad that she had to leave the country?

The last thing I want to do is go to school and get cheered on as we hopefully thrash Eastwood's ass. They're our closest rival and almost every year they fucking beat us, leaving with smug as fuck smiles on their faces.

The entire school body fills the stadium for tonight's game. Homecoming is a big deal, hopes are high after our last couple of wins and all eyes are anxiously on us as we hit the field. The roar of excitement from our fans makes me wince, but it helps to push aside everything I'm feeling and allow me to focus on what I should be doing right now.

Fuck her, if she doesn't think this place is good enough for her then good riddance. This place is mine and right now my people need me.

The game's fucking hard and not helped by the fact that Shane taunts me with overly amused eyes or a shove in the shoulder if he thinks he can get away with it. He's pissed that I had her, even for a short amount of time but he's equally fucked off that I made her leave. I might gloat that I had Amalie to myself, but at least I didn't have to drug her to get her into bed.

Coach notices the tension between us and mouths over to me to calm my shit down. We both know that I shouldn't be on this field right now after I jumped Shane the other day. I'm determined to finish this game and not have him ruining it, like he's attempting to do.

We win, but only just, and the excitement is off the charts as we make our way back into the locker room.

"Fuckin' yes, boys," Ethan hollers. "Now let's shower this shit off and go find the pussy."

Everyone else cheers but I just start stripping my uniform off and it doesn't go unnoticed.

Mason and Ethan appear at my sides.

"You're coming, right?"

"Do I look like I want to go to a fucking dance?"

"Aw, come on, you'll get the crown and then you'll have even more girls hanging off you than usual."

Neither of them so much as flinch when I raise my arm and slam my fist into the locker in front of me.

Pain radiates up my arm, but I welcome the distraction from my heart.

"I don't want other fucking girls," I whisper, not wanting the rest of the team to overhear that I've grown a fucking pussy.

"Fine, well how about you come to celebrate with the team. You don't have to stay all night. We can leave early and get fucked up."

Now that sounds more like an offer I can't refuse.

"Fine, but only because you're offering something to kill the memories of it after."

"That's my man." Ethan slaps my shoulder before heading off to the showers.

"You still haven't heard from her?" Mason asks, sounding more concerned about me than just missing out on tonight.

"She's gone. I hope she's laughing her fucking tits off. She played me at my own game, made me want her and fucked off."

"Na, man. That's not her style. Have you even gone to speak to her gran, find out what's going on?"

My silence clues him in to the fact I've done no such thing. I ain't chasing her and allowing the whole fucking town to see that she's got me on my knees.

I shower and then pull on a white button-down with some black pants and shoes. Dressing up is the last thing I want to do, but I don't want to let my team down more than I already have.

I can plaster on a fake smile for an hour before someone hopefully hands me a bottle of something strong.

42

AMALIE

Walking back into my parents' house is the weirdest feeling. It's exactly the same as when I left. The housekeeper that's still employed has kept it sparkling clean.

My heart ached more than I thought possible as I look at all their belongings, their lives.

I shouldn't have run like I did, but the need to be surrounded by them was too much. I miss them more than words could ever express and hearing the news that no one wanted them dead made me need this final closure.

This place might feel familiar in so many ways, but it's obvious the minute I step inside that it's no longer my home. The two people who made this place feel like a loving family home are gone, leaving it as no more than a house.

I spend my first day wallowing in the loss of my parents and going through all their stuff. As much as I hate to remove pieces of them, I know it needs to happen to help me move on. I select a couple of my favourite items from my mum's wardrobe and jewellery collection and I let go of the rest. It's time to move on.

Once the house is mostly cleared, I feel a little better and like this trip was actually worthwhile and not just a crazy spur of the moment decision that I'm going to regret.

It wasn't until I turned my phone off ready for the flight, I realised that in my haste to pack I didn't pick up the charger.

I told myself that there was a reason I forgot it and when I walked past the shops at arrivals in Heathrow Airport, I didn't stop to get a new one.

Miss French kick-started thoughts about my future, I need this time to figure out what I want to do. It might be selfish to shut myself off from the world, I know Jake won't be happy about it, but I'd hope he'd understand my need for a little time. My life's been crazy, and I just need a minute to take a breath. I need everything to slow down, all the changes to stop just so I can be me.

I organise a meeting with my parents' solicitor to discuss what happens next along with another at the bank as I try to figure out what the hell to do with the money they've left behind. I knew they were well off, but having the reality of the situation on the screen in front of me was a little overwhelming. As their only child, everything, including their business has been left to me. Thankfully they've got very capable people running it which means I don't need to do anything. They were sensible enough to have things set up just in case the worst were to happen. So apparently, I just get to sit back and reap the rewards my parents would have got. If I'm honest, I'd rather just have my parents, but it's a bit late for that now.

The second I step from the bank I know what I need to do. Since the moment I landed, I think I knew that this place wasn't my home and more time here has only proved one thing. I left my heart behind in America. It's firmly in the hands of a hard-headed, sexy and broken guy who I think feels the same way, despite every way he tried to prove otherwise.

Allowing thoughts of Jake in, my heart aches to see him again. To feel the security of his arms around me.

Flagging down a taxi, I rattle off my old address and tell him to hurry the hell up. I've got a flight to book and hopefully catch.

———

The flight back is excruciating. Once I'd made the decision, I wanted to be back there that instant. So sitting for almost an hour even waiting to take off took its toll.

I called Gran the moment I booked my last minute flight, and she agreed to pick me up at the other end.

I purchased a phone charger at the airport and made use of the onboard power supply to charge it.

When I turn it on at the other end, it goes crazy with messages and voicemails. Almost all of them from Jake and Camila.

I ignore every single one. My focus is on one thing, and one thing only.

Gran greets me at arrivals like she hasn't seen me in years, not just a couple of days.

"I missed you too," I say into her hair as she holds me tight.

"I was so scared you wouldn't come back," she admits, making my heart ache.

"I think I needed to go back to realise where I really wanted to be. I love

London but this place has become home to me now. There was never a chance I wasn't coming back."

"Thank God for that." When she pulls back, her eyes are swimming with tears. "I love having you here, Amalie. I didn't realise how lonely I was before you came."

Emotion clogs my throat and only confirms something I'd pretty much decided on in London. I'm not leaving her to go to college. Once I've got tonight out of the way, I'm going to get out the paperwork that Miss French gave me for the local colleges and check out their courses. This is where my heart and my family are, so this is where I need to be.

"I really like it here too. I didn't realise quite how much until I left."

"That's so good to hear. Now, let's get out of here, I understand there's a dance tonight and I'm pretty sure there'll be a boy waiting for you."

"I'm not so sure," I mutter, walking out of the terminal beside Gran.

"No?"

"I haven't spoken to him since I left," I admit with a wince. I know it probably wasn't the most sensible thing to do where Jake is concerned but I needed the time.

"Well, even more reason to get dolled up to the nines and sweep him off his feet."

The second I'm through the front door of Gran's house, I run toward my bedroom.

I have the quickest shower of my life before blow drying my hair and throwing a little bit of makeup on. I might be in a rush, but I still need to look like I've made an effort.

Pulling open my wardrobe, my eyes land on one dress. The little silver one that my mum bought me for my end of sixth form night out.

Pulling it out, I allow myself a few seconds to admire it. I've no clue if it's the kind of thing girls wear to Homecoming but right now, I don't really care, it's exactly what I need to give me the confidence to walk into that gym and claim my place in this school.

I forgo the fancy arrival seeing as the dance has already started and allow Gran to drop me in the car park.

After waving her off, I walk up the short path toward the gym. My hands tremble and butterflies flutter so hard in my belly that I think I might take off.

I'm terrified that he's going to turn me away after I left him. It's exactly the kind of behaviour he roasted me for when I first arrived, but I'm determined to make him see that it was a one-off, that I'm back and one of the biggest reasons is him.

Blowing out a long breath, I shake out my arms and lift one to pull the door open.

The sound of the chatter and excitement inside filters down to me, but to my surprise, there's no music.

My curiosity along with my need for Jake has my feet moving. I walk down the short corridor and the reason behind the lack of music soon becomes clear.

"And your Homecoming queen is..." There's a brief silence before whoever is in charge of the microphone announces Chelsea's name. *Of course she fucking is.*

I roll my eyes and inwardly groan before continuing.

The gym is filled with balloons and streamers to make it look less like a sports hall and more like a room to celebrate in, but my eyes don't focus on any of that or the hundreds of kids staring at the stage because it's just one man on the stage who captures my attention.

He's dressed in a white shirt with the collar undone at the neck, sans tie. His black trousers are skinny enough to hug his thighs and make my mouth water, but it's his eyes that I get lost in as he stares into space. They look haunted in a way I remember all too well. They're just like the first day he saw me, and then again when he looked at his mother only a few days ago.

Chelsea flounces up on stage making a right song and dance about receiving her crown and being objectified by everyone.

Jake doesn't so much as glance her way as he stands there like he wants the ground to swallow him up. I'm not surprised he's been crowned king because that's exactly what he is. He rules this place. He knows how much they need him for any potential football success, and he uses it to his advantage.

I'm frozen to the spot watching this little ceremony playing out in front of me when every muscle in my body tenses as Chelsea slides up next to Jake. She has a twinkle in her eye that I don't like as the photographer gets a couple of shots of them. Just as he takes a step to leave, she blocks his path and crashes her lips to his. His body stills, his eyes widen, but it's that moment he finds me standing in the doorway.

It takes about a second too long for him to react. I'm just about on the verge of walking up there myself and pulling the hussy from him when his arms rise, and he forcefully pushes. The entire student body gasps in horror as she loses her footing and falls from the stage.

I've no clue what happens to her because my focus is solely on Jake's angry eyes. As the commotion continues in front of the stage, Jake effortlessly jumps down and sidesteps the crowd that's formed.

My heart pounds with every footstep he takes toward me. I've no idea what he's going to do, but the look in his eyes and the hard lines of his face terrify me.

At no point does he break our contact and I think that's even more unnerving. He wants me nervous.

My entire body is trembling by the time he steps up to me and I prepare for what abuse about my leaving is going to fall from his lips, but nothing happens.

He's inches from me, his eyes locked on mine, his chest heaving almost as mine is. His arm lifts and I flinch, not that I really think he's going to hit me, more that the movement surprises me.

Then he does something I really wasn't expecting. His hand cups my cheek before his fingers slide into my hair.

"Thank fuck," he mutters, his voice is broken and defeated before his lips land on mine.

I've no clue if it's because I shut off the world around me to focus on his kiss or if the gym really does turn silent as he kisses me in front of the entire school.

His hand tilts my head to the side so he can plunge his tongue into my mouth and totally consume me.

The arms he has around my waist tightens, pressing our bodies together and the unmistakable feeling of his length pressing into my stomach ignites something inside me that I'm not going to be able to ignore.

Pulling back, he rests his forehead against mine, our increased breaths mingling, his eyes softer than they were previously but still full of hunger, just this time he's not hungry for pain or revenge he's just hungry for me, that knowledge only makes my need for him even stronger.

"We need to get out of here."

43

JAKE

I thought I was imagining things when I looked up and saw her standing like a fucking angel in the doorway.

I blinked, expecting for her to be gone when I opened my eyes, but she was still there. Unfortunately, Chelsea took advantage of my moment and not only was Amalie still there, but fucking Chelsea was attached to my lips.

The force I used to get her away with was stronger than necessary, but she's pushed her luck with me one too many times. The only girl I want touching me is currently chewing on her lip, looking unsure of herself in the sexiest dress I think I've ever seen.

I thought I'd be angry seeing her again but all I feel is relief. She's back, and she's here for me. That's all I need to know, that she's mine.

Marching over, the only thing I can think about is having her lips on mine. And the second I get my wish, everything that has been wrong with me this week suddenly rights itself.

"We need to get out of here." With her hand in mine, we walk out of the gym and away from everyone but not before I spot a delighted Poppy smiling at us. I wink and she laughs lightly before giving me a little wave.

It's already dark out, but the sky is full of twinkling stars. I've never paid much attention before, but I swear they're brighter tonight.

"Can you walk in those shoes?" I come to a stop and look down at her feet. I don't want to have to walk home. I want to be the kind of guy who can help her into my car to get her back to my bedroom as fast as possible, but unfortunately, that guy isn't me. The best I've got to offer is a moonlight walk along the beach on our way back to my shitty trailer.

"I'll walk as far as you need me to." My heart races hearing the words I had no idea I was longing for.

Giving her arm a tug, she falls back into step beside me as I head toward the beach. We walk for quite a while in silence, just soaking up each other's presence.

"I'm so sorry for leaving like I did."

"I'm sorry for the message I sent. I didn't mean any of it."

She's silent for a few seconds and I panic. I regretted that message the second I sent it, but it was too late. The vile words were already out in the wild.

"I haven't read any of them. My phone died and when I got back my first priority was getting to you. I realised something while I was away."

"What was that?"

She stops as she slips off her shoes and we step down onto the sand.

"The detective rang to explain that there was nothing suspicious about my parents' crash and my first instinct was that I needed to go home. Only, the moment I stepped foot on English soil, I realised that it was no longer home to me. The place I'd left behind was home now. The people I'd left behind were my home."

I bring her to a stop in my hidden spot between the sand dunes and take her cheeks in my hands.

"Me?" I ask, hating the hesitation in my voice. But seeing her again tonight only solidified the strength of my feelings for her. I'd barely survived a couple of days without her, it's pretty clear that I can't live the rest of my life without her by my side.

"You, Jake. I just need you."

"Fuck." A ball of emotion I'm not all that used to clogs my throat and the backs of my eyes burn as I stare down at her beauty. "I love you, Amalie. I love you so fucking much." I don't give her time to respond, instead I slam my lips down on hers, intent on showing her just how much I mean those words.

When I eventually let up her for air, tears are streaming down her cheeks, but she has the widest smile on her face.

"What?"

She chuckles and I can't help but join her. "I'm pretty sure you're the biggest arsehole I've ever met, Jacob Thorn. But do you know what?"

I shake my head, hoping to fuck she's going to say exactly what I said to her. My heart feels like it's bleeding out not hearing the words.

"I love you, too."

EPILOGUE

Amalie

Telling Jake how I really felt was like a huge weight lifted off my shoulders. The look in his eyes as I said those three little words to him is something I'll never regret. I wanted to sob like a baby when it hit me that there's a very good chance he's never been told them before. Thankfully, he saw the onslaught of fresh tears coming and quickly distracted me.

With his lips on mine, he lowered us both to the sand and right there, under the stars and in the privacy of the dunes, he set about proving just how he felt by making love to me until neither of us could stay awake any longer.

I've no idea what time we eventually stumbled off the beach, both grinning like loons and laughing like we had no cares in the world. It was the most incredible feeling and one I have no doubt Jake will continue to make me feel for a long time to come.

When we got back to his trailer, we both showered the sand off together in his tiny cubicle, it was cozy but neither of us had any intention of separating anytime soon, so it was kind of perfect, before we both fell into his bed.

———

"Are you ready for this?" I ask, standing outside Noah's house where his party is spilling out into the backyard and the music's blaring so loud there is no doubt as to what's going on inside.

"I'm so ready. It's time to show everyone exactly who you belong to."

With his hand firmly holding mine, we walk into Noah's house.

The eyes of our intrigued classmates follow our every move. The girls lock their gaze on our hands before their death stares find me. They all gossip amongst themselves, but I refuse to cower down to their petty jealousy.

I don't react other than my smile growing wider with every step I take. That is until we come across a group of girls sitting around the sofa. When a couple of them part, it becomes obvious why they're all sitting there because in the centre with her newly cast ankle propped up on the coffee table is Chelsea.

"You broke her ankle," I whisper to Jake, trying my best to keep any amusement out of my voice.

"I wouldn't have pushed her if she didn't take advantage of me. My lips are for you and you only. It's time all these assholes know it."

He wraps his arm around my waist and pulls me up against him. He doesn't need to say anything to get the attention of everyone in the room. He's Jake Thorn, he commands everyone's attention just by breathing.

Once he's confident everyone is staring our way, he slams his lips down on mine. He kisses me like it's our first time before bending me backward and really giving our audience a show.

"I love you, Brit," he whispers when he pulls me back upright.

"And I think everyone in the room other than you hates me," I say as a joke, but his eyes harden in anger.

"If any fucker gives you a hard time, you've only got to say the word."

"I'm a big girl, Jake. I can look after myself."

"Don't I know it," he mutters with a laugh.

I open my mouth to respond but a commotion in another room drags everyone's attention from us.

"Mason, no," someone screams, and Jake takes off running. I'm forced to follow seeing as his hand is still holding mine.

The crowd parts for him and it's then we get our first look at Mason throwing punch after punch into Noah's face.

"What the fuck just happened?"

Jake races forward to pull his friend away, when I look up, I find the horrified eyes of two girls. One belongs to my best friend and the other a girl I barely recognise as another senior and one of Chelsea's crew. Whatever's happening right now, I sense is going to change Camila's life in a way she wasn't expecting.

Keep reading to discover Camila and Mason's story!

PAINE

1

CAMILA

"What the hell are you doing?" I scream, running toward where Mason has Noah pinned to the floor. There's blood streaming from his nose and a split in his lip, but the most striking thing is that he's not trying to fight back. He's just taking it.

"Motherfucker," Mason growls, his voice is so low and menacing that a shiver races down my spine.

What the hell has gotten into him?

Reaching out, I place my hand on his forearm right before he's about to throw another punch into Noah's broken face.

"Stop," I shout. "Mason. Stop, please," I beg, my voice cracking.

My contact is obviously what Mason needs to bring him out of his trance. He lifts his eyes to find me. The darkness in them makes my breath catch. If I didn't know better, I'd think he wanted Noah dead. But that's not the Mason I know. Well... the Mason I knew. But it seems the boy from the end of the street is long gone these days.

"What the hell are you doing?"

He stares down at Noah a few seconds longer before allowing Jake to pull him up and away.

"I—" He looks up at me and I swear I see pain pouring from his eyes. "He was kissing that skank." His voice is low, so only I can hear as he tips his chin in the direction of Tasha, a member of the cheer squad. Her eyes are wide and she's as white as a sheet, but then so is everyone else as they stare at the scene unfolding in front of them.

"What the fuck is your problem? Not satisfied making me an outcast, now you've got to get involved and ruin my relationship too?"

"No. He was... they were in the bathroom together."

My heart pounds in my chest. He wouldn't, would he? Noah loves me, that I'm sure of. This is a joke. Mason's had too much to drink and has decided to throw his weight around, show me who's boss.

A low moan comes from Noah, and it drags me from my fog. Why am I focusing on Mason right now when my boyfriend is groaning in pain from being on the wrong end of his fists?

"Get him out of here," I bark at Jake, who immediately jumps into action. Amalie looks between the two of us, not knowing which way to go. "It's fine. Go with him. I'm just going to get Noah cleaned up and put him to bed. Everyone out," I shout, knowing that our entire class is currently watching this play out in front of their eyes.

Dropping to my knees, I place my hand on Noah's warm chest. His eyes flicker open and a small smile twitches at his lips.

Some movement to my left catches my eye, and, when I look up, I find everyone still standing there.

"Get the hell out," I scream. That, along with Alyssa and a couple of other friends starting to usher people from the room, seems to get them moving at last.

My hands tremble as I stare down at my broken and bloodied boyfriend.

"Are you okay?" I whisper.

"Yeah, never been better," he grunts.

"Can you get up? We'll go and get you cleaned up."

"Yeah, I'm good. He didn't hit that hard."

I don't point out that the state of his face right now doesn't confirm his story.

With his arm around my waist, I lead his limp body toward the stairs as the movement of people leaving sound out around us.

No one comes to help, which kind of pisses me off, but I understand that they probably don't want to get in the middle.

"Sit," I instruct when we make it to Noah's bed. "I'll be back in a few minutes. Don't go anywhere."

I walk past his adjoining bathroom, knowing I won't find anything I need, and instead go to the main bathroom.

With a first aid box in hand, I head back toward Noah.

I come to a stop in his doorway and take him in. He's pulled his shirt off and is laid back on his bed. Blood and darkening bruises color his cheeks.

Noah's been my rock. We'd never really had much to do with each other despite being in the same classes for years, but we found each other when I was at my lowest, thanks to my inability to use a computer competently.

We were supposed to be making spreadsheets, but me and numbers aren't a match made in heaven and I was on the verge of throwing the mouse across the room when he offered his help. Grateful didn't even come close to expressing how I felt as he explained how the formulas worked in such a simple way that I couldn't not understand while our teacher focused on Mason and his gang of jocks, ignoring the rest of us.

Anger burned in my belly and I glanced over my shoulder at the special attention they got just because of their position in the school. It was just another reminder of why things turned out the way they were meant to be. Girls like me were never destined to be friends with guys like him. I guess it's just a good thing I discovered that before my heart got in even deeper. We may have been young, but I'm not naïve enough to ignore that fact that I gave part of my heart to Mason Paine long before I even knew it was a thing.

Noah's eyes flutter open like he can feel me standing there. Even with all of the swelling, I can see love in them.

Mason's lying. Noah would never do that to me. Especially not tonight.

"Babe?"

"Sorry," I say, forcing myself from my musings and walking toward him. Perching myself on the edge of his bed, I dip a washcloth into the bowl of warm water and start to clean up his face.

He winces in pain as I gently dab at the corner of his lips.

"I didn't—"

"I know."

I trust Noah with my life. He's been nothing but the perfect boyfriend since he asked me to homecoming a few weeks after that class. Another boy had consumed all my time and thoughts up until that point, and I had no idea that anyone else existed or might have been interested. He totally swept me off my feet, and I haven't had a moment of regret since.

At the beginning, I missed Mason. I was desperate to know what he thought about Noah. I was just so used to talking to him about everything, but Noah soon showed me that I didn't need Mason the way I always thought it did. I had the sweetest new boyfriend and my best friend in Alyssa. I didn't need the boy who turned his back on me when things didn't go his way.

I work in silence, cleaning up Noah's poor face.

"Where do your parents keep the painkillers?"

He tells me where to go, and, after disposing of the bloodied washcloth, I go in search of something that might help him sleep.

When I get downstairs, Alyssa, Lisa, Wyatt, and Shane are all busy tidying up the mess the rest of our class abandoned on their way out.

"Thank you so much," I say, walking into the kitchen.

"You're welcome. Is he okay?" Alyssa asks, concern shining from her eyes.

"Yeah, he'll be fine."

"What did he do to deserve that? Mason totally flew off the handle. I've never seen him like that, even on the field," Shane says. He knows Mason the best out of any of us these days, seeing as he's on the football team with the douchebags. Fuck knows why, he's nothing like any of them and actually a good guy. Things have been weird for him at school since he was accused of drugging Amalie and having the shit kicked out of him by Jake for it. He's kept his head down and avoided everyone—aside from this party, seeing as Noah's his best friend. I can still see the dark shadows that night left behind in his eyes, but he made the effort tonight. I know he's innocent, Noah too, but that doesn't mean anyone else at school agrees. Jake Thorn pinned him as guilty, so that's what he'll be unless someone's able to prove otherwise.

"Fuck knows. Mason is probably just trying to make my life harder than necessary; it seems to be his thing these days," I mutter.

"What actually happened between you two?"

"Nothing. It's nothing." It's the same excuse I've given ever since shit went down between our families. I have no desire to live through it again, and I can't see things ever going back to how they once were between us.

"You guys can get out of here if you want. I'll finish up."

"Really?" Alyssa asks, looking concerned.

"Yeah. I don't want to give him the satisfaction of ruining everyone's night. Go to Aces or something."

"As long as you're sure."

The three of them finish off what they're doing before saying goodbye and heading out.

Noah's parents wisely booked themselves into a hotel for the night, so I've got plenty of time to get the place back to normal before they get home—not that it's too bad. The party hadn't really had a chance to get going before Mason ruined it. So much for Noah's eighteenth birthday being his best ever.

I throw a few more cups into the trash before grabbing a box of Advil and going back up to Noah.

He's out cold when I walk into his bedroom. Even with just the moonlight illuminating his face, I can see that the swelling has only gotten worse and the bruising darker. He's even got a purple patch emerging on his ribs.

Mason really did a fucking number on him. My fists curl at my sides in anger. How dare he put his hands on Noah? It's like he's intent on ruining everything about my life. I'm surprised he wasn't more onboard with pushing Amalie out of town before Jake realized he was in love with her. Getting rid of someone who's fast become my best friend is just something I can imagine he'd do to piss me off.

Placing the glass of water and painkillers on the dresser, I walk over to pull the curtain.

"Come here," Noah says, barely managing to hold his hand out for me.

"I don't want to hurt you."

"You won't."

After slipping my shoes off, I climb into his bed beside him, fully dressed. This wasn't exactly how I planned on spending his birthday night.

His arm wraps around my waist and he pulls me back against his chest. I don't miss his sharp intake of breath as he does.

"I'm so sorry, Noah."

"Hey, none of this was your fault."

His soft lips press against my shoulder before he drops his head to the pillow and falls back to sleep.

2

MASON

My entire body vibrates with anger as Jake leads me away from that motherfucker's house.

I didn't particularly want to be there in the first place, but Amalie had convinced me seeing as it was her and Jake's first appearance as an official couple. I knew I should have worked the fucking shift I was offered instead of showing my face in there.

Almost our entire class was in his house and almost every set of eyes watched as I pulled his sorry, cheating ass from the bathroom and slammed my fist into his face.

I only went for a piss. The last thing I was expecting was to find him with his tongue down Tasha's fucking throat. I expected it of her, she's one of Chelsea's little crew. But Noah? He might be a total computer nerd I'd happily never look at again, but I thought he was faithful.

If I thought I disliked him before, then I fucking hate him now.

In hindsight, I probably shouldn't have defended her. It was what she fucking deserved after everything, but still, my need to end him for betraying her got the better of me.

I flex my fingers as Ethan drives away from the scene of the crime.

"Where to, ladies?"

"Just take me fucking home. I'm done with tonight."

"But I've got the goods at my place."

"He said home," Jake barks from the backseat, managing to come up for air from devouring Amalie.

"I know you two are in love and shit, but is that necessary?"

"Wow, she really does turn you into a crazy man, huh?" Ethan muses.

"I've got plenty of fight left in me if you want a pop, Savage."

"Nah, man. I was just saying."

"Well, fucking don't."

"You'll understand when you meet her," Jake pipes up.

"Her? Who's her? Camila?"

"No, not Camila, dickwad. I mean *her*. The one."

"Fuck off. You have full permission to shoot my ass if it ever looks like I'm gonna hand my balls over to a chick. They're mine, thank you very much."

"Aw, it's not that bad. Amalie takes very good care of my— ow," he complains after the sound of a slap rings through the car. "Once you find her, my friend, everything changes. Right, Mase?"

"No fucking clue what you're talking about," I grunt, already over this fucking conversation.

"Riiight. Of course not. I forgot. You hate her."

My teeth grind. He's baiting me to admit that I've got feelings for Camila, but he's going to have to try harder than that because anything I felt for her died the moment my life fell apart.

Turning to stare at the sea as Ethan heads back to my side of town, I ignore whatever else is said. The only thing I can see and hear is that motherfucker as I pulled him away from the trailer trash and he started trying to defend himself.

I'm not sure I've ever been so fucking angry. And for what? Her?

The tension in the car is heavy. They all pretend they know how I'm feeling, but none of them have a fucking clue. Even Jake doesn't know the whole story.

I grunt some kind of a thank you before slamming the car door. My eyes catch Amalie's in the backseat now that Jake's released her, and I see a million questions in her eyes. She's desperate to fix this thing between me and Camila, but she has no idea what she's dealing with.

I once thought I'd spend my life with Camila, just like our mothers plotted from the day we were born, but the reality of the situation is very much different.

The car idles behind me. If they think I'm going to change my mind, then they've got another thing coming.

The house is silent as I walk down the hallway aside from the quiet sound coming from the TV in the living room.

"Hey, Diane. You can head off if you'd like," I say when I round the corner and find my brothers' babysitter curled into the corner of the couch.

"You're back early. Everything okay?"

I keep my aching fists behind my back. I don't need our next door neighbor prying. It's bad enough I have to rely on her to look after Charlie and Ollie so that I can attempt to have something of a normal life. "Yeah, I just wasn't really feeling it tonight."

"That's a shame. You deserve to let your hair down every now and then."

Don't I fucking know it. "There will be plenty more parties," I mutter.

"Ah, I remember it well. Senior year was the best year of my life. No commitments, no worries. Shit, sorry." She winces as she realizes her mistake.

"It is what it is. Thank you so much." I pull some money from my wallet and hand it over.

"Mason, how many times do I have to tell you. You don't need to pay me. I'm happy just to help out."

"I take up too much of your time as it is. You should be at home with your own family, not babysitting mine. Use it to take your kids out or to buy them something nice."

I could take her up on her offer of free childcare but then that would make me just as bad as my mother, and I refuse to be that person who takes everything and everyone for granted.

"Did the boys both go to bed okay?"

"Yeah. Charlie was complaining of a tummy ache, but he was acting fine."

I thank her again and see her out.

Spinning back into the home I've lived in since birth, I hate it just that little bit more.

My bloody fists catch my eye, and I head to the kitchen to clean them up and inspect the damage. Coach is going to have my balls at practice on Monday when he sees I've been fighting. Football is my only escape, and I hope it's my way into college, but I'm also very aware that it's the first thing that might have to give if things get tougher. If Mom can't find a better job, or at least more hours, then it means that I'm going to have to start picking up more of the slack, and finding a job that's flexible around school and games isn't easy to come by.

I just want to be a fucking kid and enjoy senior year while I still have a chance. Is that too much to ask?

I wince as the warm water runs over my knuckles, sending the blood spiraling down the drain. It pretty much sums up my life.

I shouldn't have hit him, I tell myself again. I should have left him there and allowed Camila to find him. She deserves a little bit of the pain I go through every day because of her fucking family.

She walks around like she doesn't have a care in the world, not giving two shits about the mess they left behind just down the street. We might still be living in this house, just, but the people who are left inside are far from the people she knew.

Turning off the water, I rest my palms down on the counter and stare out at the garden. The garden my dad used to spend his evenings and weekends maintaining when he wasn't out helping me train for my next game.

Now, it's overgrown, uncared for and totally unruly. He'd hate it—if he ever bothered to come back and see his kids, that is.

Burning anger fills my veins and I push it away, not wanting or needing the reminder of him.

Taking the stairs two at a time, I quickly check that my brothers are both sleeping soundly in their rooms before ripping off my shirt over my head and dropping it to the floor. I find a bottle of Jack I'd hidden at the back of my closet and twist the top off before falling down onto my bed. Lifting it to my lips, I shudder as it burns down my throat. I hardly ever drink, so it hits me pretty quickly. I'm usually stronger than this and focus on my responsibility, but tonight I need it gone. I need the memories and what could have been out of my head.

My room is bathed in darkness. Not even the light from the moon shines in with the curtains that are permanently closed. If I open them, all I can see is her house, into her room. It used to be great. Everything used to be great.

Darkness consumes me and images of her standing in her bedroom window fade away.

The next thing I know, my eyes flutter open and a blinding light sends a piercing pain through my head.

Motherfucker.

"Mason." A little voice filters through the alcohol haze surrounding me. "Charlie's been sick. He's really upset."

"Fuck." Sitting bolt upright in bed, my head spins and my own stomach turns over. Lifting my arm, I find my fingers still wrapped around the now empty bottle.

"Isn't Mom home?" My voice is slurred even to my own ears.

"I don't think so. Can you help me clean him up?"

"Of course, dude. Lead the way."

Case in point as to why I don't drink.

The desire to drop to my knees and crawl into Charlie's room is high, but somehow I manage to keep upright with a lot of help from the wall.

Charlie's sobbing hits my ears long before we enter his room. That along with the stench is enough to sober me up a little.

He needs me, and I need to not be a total fuck-up right now.

I dry heave as I step into the room and get a sight of the mess he's made.

"It's okay, buddy. We'll get this cleaned up and you'll be as good as new."

"I'm so sorry," he wails.

"It's not your fault. You don't need to be upset."

"You can come sleep in my bed, Charlie."

My head spins and I fight to keep the contents of my own stomach down as I begin stripping his bed, but my heart swells in my chest for these two boys. Neither of them asked for their life to be like this, to have to spend so much time looking after themselves and each other, but there's only so much I can do without totally ruining my own life and future in the process.

After throwing all of Charlie's dirty sheets into the washer, I head back up to make sure they're okay. I find them both curled up in Oliver's bed, fast asleep.

A smile twitches at my lips as I stare down at them. They might cause me more stress than most seniors are forced to endure, but I couldn't imagine my life without them. I'm pretty sure I owe them both everything, because without them, I know I could have lost myself pretty easily over the past few years.

3

CAMILA

"He said Noah was kissing Tasha?"

"Yep, apparently so," I say to Amalie over a milkshake the next morning after leaving Noah to deal with his parents.

"And you don't believe him?"

"No, not one word of it. This is Noah we're talking about. He's never been anything but totally loyal, faithful, and honest."

"I know but—"

"There are no buts, Ami. Mason hates me. It's not the first time he's done something just to hurt me for breathing the same air as him."

"Mason? Mason Paine?"

"Yes." I sigh, getting pissed off with her opinions on this situation.

"But he's always been so sweet to me."

"Yeah, well, you didn't 'ruin his life' or whatever shit he spouts at me for the reason behind his douchebag-ness."

"That's not a word."

I quirk an eyebrow. "Do I look like I care? I just want to forget all about this and move on. He totally fucked with my plan for last night. I need a new one."

"So, you and Noah didn't get it on after he was accused of cheating and beaten within an inch of his life?"

"Do you have to find this all so amusing?"

She does have the decency to look slightly regretful. "I'm sorry, it's just that I'm glad this kind of drama isn't directed at me. It's nice to see someone else with boy issues."

"I don't have boy issues. Noah is my boyfriend and Mason is…"

"Mason is..."

"No one. He's no one and needs to back the fuck off."

"You ever going to tell me what happened?"

"He just blames me for how his life turned out."

"That's all you're giving me?"

"Sure is. You want more, ask him."

She wraps her lips around the straw sticking up from her milkshake as she thinks. I know she's desperate to learn more about what happened, but I really just want to forget about the whole thing and that Mason Paine even exists. It's bad enough I've got to walk past his house every day and stare at his bedroom window every time I open my damn curtains. I don't need him to be the focus of my every conversation today.

"Have you even asked Noah about it?"

"Of course."

"And?"

"And he said he loves me and that I'm the only girl for him."

"Convenient."

"What do you have against Noah all of a sudden? You seem to be suggesting that he's guilty here."

"I have nothing against him, Cami. I'm just intrigued. Mason doesn't strike me as the kind of guy who starts fights for no reason."

"No offense, Amalie, but you don't really know him. You've only met the Mason who'll do anything for his best friend. To be honest, they're about as fucked up as each other." Her mouth opens in an attempt to fight for her boyfriend, but I cut her off. "Don't you even think about trying to defend him. Some of the shit he did to you should have been unforgivable."

"Can't help who you fall in love with, Camila."

"Christ, you sound like your gran," I mutter, reaching for my own milkshake.

"I know that, and I'm not criticizing you for it. It's just... Mason is part of my past. Do I miss the sweet boy from down the street? Some days. But life has turned him into an asshole, and my life is better off without that kind of drama in it."

"Okay. I'll drop it." I don't believe a word of it. Her eyes are still assessing me like she can see something I'm not aware of.

"Good, because Noah's been so good to me. The perfect boyfriend. He's the one for me."

Her eyes hold so much, but thankfully she keeps her mouth shut. I don't need to spend the rest of the morning rehashing this.

"What's going on with Jake's mom? She still around?" I ask, desperately needing to change the subject.

"Sadly. Jake's refusing point-blank to talk to her, hoping that she'll up and leave again, but it doesn't seem to be working."

"You think she's serious about fixing everything she fucked up?"

"I have no idea, honestly. I think too much damage has been done. Jake's never going to give her the time of day."

"Understandable." Silence descends around us as we slurp our milkshakes. "So... how's the college search coming?"

"I'm still trying to convince Jake to come and have a look around Florida U and Maddison with me but—"

"Whoa, hold the phone. You're going to college together?"

"No decisions have been made. He just promised me he'd look into it. I found his grades stuffed at the back of one of his drawers in his bedroom. Any college would be stupid not to let him in. Plus, he's got the obvious bonus of being a fucking awesome quarterback."

"Aw, look at you getting all involved in the game. I'm so proud of you," I say with a laugh. It took enough convincing when she first got here to even see a game, let alone understand it enough to know just how talented Jake is.

"Shut up. Anyway, Maddison has potential courses for both of us, so if we did decide to go together then we could. That's still a long way off though, and I don't want to freak him out too much. He still doesn't think he has a shot at a scholarship or being accepted."

"That's crazy."

"That's what I keep saying. Plus, he could defer a year if he wants, get a job, save some money, and we could start together."

She might think the idea of going together hasn't been made yet, but the way she's talking, I think it's kinda set in stone. I'm happy for her. She had her life turned upside down but somehow, she's managed to create something pretty fantastic here, not to mention snagging Rosewood's most eligible bachelor. I never thought I'd see the day that Jake Thorn handed his balls over to a woman, but Hell must have frozen over because he is seriously whipped by my new best friend.

"What about you? Noah still want to go to Virginia?"

"Yep," I say sadly. "I still have no idea, really. I've applied for a bunch of places, but the idea of moving across the country scares the crap out of me."

"You'll figure it out."

"I guess." I shrug, feeling the pressure landing on my shoulders. Everything at the moment seems to be about college. It's all everyone is talking about, no one more so than my parents, and I don't know what to tell them. I want to go to college, of course I do, but I have no idea what I want to do with my future. English is my thing. I love reading, writing reports, that kind of stuff, but do I want to do it for a job for the rest of my life? I have no idea. The decision seems so huge and I don't feel at all prepared to make one yet.

I drop Amalie back home after our little morning rehash of the night before and our possible futures.

"Morning, sweetheart. Good night?" Mom asks as I head for the kitchen for a glass of water.

"Uh... yeah," I lie. It was entirely *not* what I was expecting, not to mention that I'd planned last night to be *the* night with Noah, and here I am, still a virgin.

"That's good. I'm glad you had fun." She gives me a kiss on the cheek as she passes and heads for her home office. Mom's job is being a social butterfly. If there's an event running in Rosewood, you can bet she's had a hand in it. Dad had a promotion a few years ago that allowed her to give up her job and focus on what she loves: party planning. It's great knowing she's enjoying herself, even if it does mean they're almost always out of the house, attending events.

"I'll be up in my room if you need me."

Pulling a packet of chips from the cupboard, I take them and my water up to my room. I turn my speakers on and stop in front of the window.

As always, his curtains are shut. It makes me sad to think that his room must always be as dark as his heart's turning out to be. He was so much fun as a kid. I have so many memories of bouncing out of bed and running down the street to find out what trouble we were going to get into that day.

But that's all it is now: memories. That Mason is long gone. In his place is someone I'd rather forget.

He's angry.

Cold.

Cruel.

4

MASON

"You've got to be fucking shitting me." Walking into school Monday morning, the first thing I see is them. Together. Like nothing fucking happened.

Noah's got her pressed up against the lockers and is staring down at her like she's the most precious thing in the world.

She looks up at him in a way I remember all too well, and it makes my blood boil.

He was kissing someone else while she was mere feet away. What the fuck is wrong with her?

"Just leave it," Jake says, noticing the tension that must be radiating off me.

"But he—"

"I thought you hated her. Why do you care if she's not dumped his cheating ass?"

"I do hate her. I'm just shocked, is all."

"Really?" he asks, a knowing twinkle in his eye.

"Yes. Now stop looking at me like that."

"Fine. Fine." He wants to say more, I can sense it, but thankfully Amalie appears out of nowhere and cuddles into his side.

His hands immediately wrap around her waist and his lips go to hers. I'm happy for them, even happier that he's stopped being such an asshole.

I let out a sigh as I watch them. Something twists my stomach, watching how close and easy they are with each other. I haven't made a secret of the fact that I want that. The guys all think I'm crazy, although Jake should have a better understanding now he's been whipped by Amalie.

"You okay?" she mouths, placing her hand on my forearm and dragging my eyes away from the car crash happening in front of me.

"Never better," I mutter, grabbing a couple of books from my own locker and slamming the door as I head out toward our benches.

Chelsea and a few of her girls are already there. She immediately gets up when she sees me walking her way, but it's not her I'm interested in.

"Tasha," I greet, a wide fake-ass smile on my face. "Enjoy the party on Saturday night?" All the blood drains from her face.

She knows what she was doing in that bathroom. So do I, and so does Noah.

Wrapping my hand around the back of her neck, I pull until she has no choice but to stand. She shudders against me as I drop my mouth to her ear. To anyone else, it might look intimate as I dig my fingers into her waist.

"Didn't have you down as a geek lover. I thought you all only went for jocks."

"I, uh..." Her voice quivers, and I can't help the smile that tugs at my lips. "I was drunk."

"Sure you were."

When I pull back, I find exactly what I was expecting: Noah looking this way from his spot by the lockers. He's far enough away that no one around him would think anything of it. But I know.

The second our eyes meet, he looks away.

You're going down, motherfucker.

"Mason, please don't—"

"Tell anyone? Oh, Tash, you're going to regret that."

She's a good head shorter than me, and as she stares up at me with panic in her eyes, they fill with tears.

"Play with fire and you will get burned."

My hand lifts to her chin and I crash my lips to hers. I know he's watching, and I need to make this as painful for him as possible. I hold still for a second before I drop her as I step away. She stumbles backward and lands awkwardly on the bench. Her friends are too distracted by the rest of the team who've descended to notice her.

Running my eyes over each of them, I shake my head. Ethan's got Shelly on his lap, his hands tucked up the back of her tank. The other guys either have one or multiple girls' attention, and I wonder what it must be like for your only concern to be about which cheerleader you want to bang. It's no secret that I've spent private time with more than one of them in the past, but it was only to blow off steam when things got a little too much.

Backing away from the group, I look to where Noah was only a few seconds ago, but their group has dispersed, leaving only one behind.

I move toward her without really thinking about it.

"What the—" she squeaks, trying to free her wrist from my grip, but I'm stronger. Much stronger.

I drag her along with me until we reach the girls' bathroom.

"Mason, what the hell are you doing?"

"Out," I bark at a handful of students. Some I recognize and some I don't, but all scramble for the door. One benefit of being on the team and Jake Thorn's best friend is that if I say jump around here, students immediately ask how high.

Pulling Camila in front of me, I run my eyes down her body. She's hot. There's no denying that. Her curves were designed for a man, not that fucking pussy.

My fists clench as I think about him having his hands on her body. A body that should have been mine to take, if her family didn't fuck everything up.

Her chest heaves, keeping my attention on her larger than average tits. My mouth waters and I take a step toward her. She has no choice but to take a step back, making her hit the tiled wall with a thud.

Resting my forearms on either side of her head, I stare down at her, taking in her gold flecked brown eyes that plead with me to let her go.

"Mason, please," she begs.

It never used to be like this. I'd have given my life for this girl in a heartbeat. But then she had a hand in ruining my life and everything changed.

"You think Tasha begged on Saturday night?" Her eyes flash with disbelief. "How much effort do you think she had to put in to get Noah to put his lips on her?"

"Stop," she demands, her tiny hands coming up to push on my chest. Nice try. I might be one of the slimmer guys on the team, but I still have at least fifty pounds on her tiny body and a fuck load more muscle. She's got no chance in making me go anywhere.

"Do you think he used the same moves he uses on you?" She swallows as I reach out and take a lock of her dark hair between my fingers. "I've watched the two of you. This is his move, right? He grabs a piece of your hair and you melt into him. Do you think it worked on her?"

She wants to fight. Her body is practically trembling with the need to scream at me right now, but for some reason, while she's locked in my stare and surrounded by me, she's frozen.

Dropping my head slightly, I hover only a centimeter or two from her. Her increased breaths race past her parted lips.

"Looks like he's not the only one who'd willingly stray. Get your head on straight, Lopez. Do you even love him?"

Taking a step back, I put some space between us.

"Fuck you," she spits, able to speak now that she's not cornered. "You have no right to drag me in here and ask me that. You made your choice years ago and walked out of my life. You don't get to keep dropping back in when it suits you."

Her words are rushed, her eyes flitting around the room trying to figure out what to do and how to get away from me. Her uncertainty only fires me up more. That is until the door opens, and someone joins us.

"What the hell is going on?" Amalie asks, looking between the two of us.

"We were just having a little heart to heart. Nothing to worry about." With one final look at Camila, I walk out of the girls' bathroom. Principal Hartmann is right outside, but if he's at all bothered about watching me leave, he doesn't show it.

I'm late to class, but after an apology and what I've discovered is a panty melting smile, even to fully grown women, the teacher waves it off and I take my seat between Jake and Ethan at the back of the room.

"Where the hell did you go?" Ethan whisper-shouts, but I don't get a chance to reply because Camila comes rushing into class.

"A problem getting out of bed this morning, Miss Lopez?" Mrs. Peterson asks, her brows drawn together in frustration.

A smirk curls my lips. She didn't even bat an eyelid at my tardiness.

"I'm so sorry, I had to use the bathroom." Camila's cheeks flush and I sit back to enjoy the show. Her eyes briefly flick to me before she focuses back on Mrs. Peterson once again.

"What the fuck did you do?" Jake asks.

"Me?" I lift my hand to my heart as if just the suggestion that I had something to do with this wounds me.

"You might act all sweet, but I know you, Mase. I know the deal between the two of you. Back off her."

"Oh, that's rich." I laugh.

"Listen to some of your own advice. You remember telling me to leave Brit alone?"

"Different situation."

"Is it?"

"Yeah. Amalie was innocent. Camila ruined my life."

He lets out a frustrated breath but doesn't say any more. He should know it would be pointless.

5

CAMILA

His eyes burn into me as I try to defend the fact that I was late to class. I didn't really think Mrs. Peterson would be too bothered; it's not like I show up late often. I'm a good student. I do my work, keep my grades up and contribute to school life however I can. Just because I'm not part of a sports team shouldn't mean I get treated differently. If I were Chelsea, or Tasha, right now I'd already be sitting down and getting on with my work.

Eventually, Mrs. Peterson puts an end to me being the sole focus of her class and allows me to find my seat. Unfortunately, said seat is right in front of Mason. I'm always aware that he's there. His hate filled stares aren't new to me. But something's different today. There's more to his attention, and it has something tingling right under my skin.

I chalk it up to the way he made me feel as he pinned me to the wall in the bathroom. He was angry. He always is these days, so that's not exactly a surprise, but there was a heat in his eyes that I haven't witnessed before.

He was enjoying himself as he threw Tasha in my face. He can do that as much as he likes; my loyalties lie with my boyfriend, who thankfully isn't in this class. The last thing I need is a pissing contest between the two of them. I think we all know who'd win that anyway. The football god everyone loves verses the IT geek. Yeah, there's only ever one winner in that situation.

I try to focus on what we should be doing, but my mind keeps taking me back to the bathroom. The heat in his eyes keeps my temperature higher than it should be, and the memory of how close his body and lips were has butterflies fluttering in my belly.

It's so wrong.

He's gone out of his way over the past four years to prove how much he hates me. He totally ignored me to start with, and although it was excruciating at the time to go from having my best friend by my side to nothing, it was easier than what was to follow. He's put me down and belittled me at any opportunity. Yet as he lowered his head, I swear he was just a second away from kissing me.

Did I want him to?

There's the million-dollar question.

In that moment, closing my eyes and letting him sweep me away would have been so easy. My body was begging for it, my fingers pressed up against his chest and begging to grip on to the fabric of his jersey and pull him in the last little bit.

Lifting my fingers to my lips, I allow my mind to wander back to a time in my life I've tried to forget.

My first kiss.

I was fourteen. I'd missed curfew and was getting a roasting from my parents for disregarding their rules. I'd been with Mason, just hanging out in his garden, and we'd totally lost track of time before he walked me home.

He must have heard them shouting at me for being irresponsible and making them worry, because when I made it up to my room with tears streaming down my face, there he was.

I had no idea how he got in, but when he opened his arms for me all I could do was to run at him.

He was my safe place. My sanctuary when things weren't going right.

I had a good life. My parents loved me and gave me everything I needed, but as their only child, they could be a little overprotective.

Mason was my release from the pressure they put on me.

My tears soaked into the fabric of his jersey. He was tall, even then, so my head rested against his chest. I felt so safe in his arms, like nothing or nobody could touch me. Our friendship had been solid for as long as I could remember. We'd never argued or fallen out. I always thought I was so lucky when I used to see others at school falling out with their best friends. I truly believed that would never be us. When I was brave enough and lifted my head from his chest, he stared down at me with such love and adoration it made my breath catch.

"Mason," I whispered.

"Shhh." He lifted his hand and stroked the backs of his knuckles down my cheek. Right there and then was the moment I fell head over heels for my best friend.

He lowered his head and his lips pressed against mine. It was the single most perfect moment of my life.

We stayed still for a few seconds before his tongue snuck out and teased the seam of my lips. My heart was thundering in my chest. I'd talked about kissing a boy with my girlfriends time and time again. I'd imagined what it might be like, how nervous I'd be when it happened, but standing there wrapped in his arms, reaching up on my tiptoes, there were no nerves. It was just so... right.

I opened my lips and his tongue hesitantly slipped past them until he found mine. I knew this was his first time as well. We'd talked about it before, but I never expected to experience our firsts together. It was everything and more that I'd ever hoped it would be. Until it was over.

"Dinner," Mom called from the bottom of the stairs, and we jumped apart as if we'd been caught.

His chest was heaving, his eyes dark and hooded. I knew he was turned on. I knew about sex, but I was still naive enough to be shocked by it.

It was the perfect time and one I've wished to go back to many, many times over the past four years so I could ensure what happened next turned out differently.

I was still feeling out of sorts when I got down to the dinner table. My parents looked stressed, more so than they should be for me missing curfew. I would soon discover why, but I never could have imagined how it was going to change my life.

The next time I saw Mason, everything had changed. Gone was the sweet, caring boy I'd fallen so hard for, and in his place was a cold and callous teenager who hated the world and everyone around him.

———

"Earth calling Camila." When I look up, I find the concerned stares of Noah, Alyssa, and Shane all staring back at me.

"I'm sorry," I whisper.

"Where'd you go? Anywhere good?" Alyssa asks, elbowing me in the ribs.

"Nah, just planning an assignment I was given this morning." The lie rolls off my tongue a little too easily, and I hate myself for it.

In truth, I can't get that memory of Mason and me in my bedroom four years ago out of my head. I have no idea if that's what he was trying to achieve this morning, to get under my skin, but shit if he hasn't succeeded.

"You sure you're okay?" Noah asks, as perceptive as ever. His hand squeezes mine under the table.

"Yeah, promise." Lifting my free hand, I gently run my thumb over the cut on his lip. "Does it still hurt?"

"Not enough to stop me from doing this." His lips brush over mine and I lose myself in his kiss, only in my head it's not him I'm kissing.

Damn him and his games.

6

MASON

Fuck this shit.

Getting up from my seat, I swipe my tray from the table and deposit what's left into the trash on the way out.

Fire burns through me as I think about finding him on Friday night with Tasha pushed up against the bathroom wall. I fucking hate cheaters, even if the person they're cheating on is someone I don't care about.

That's not true, a little voice says in my head, but I push it down.

"Mason, where you going, man?" Ethan shouts as he passes me on his way into the cafeteria.

I ignore him. I'm not in the mood to have a heart to heart right now. Instead, I head to the gym. I need a distraction, and short of spending next period inside a cheerleader, this is my only option.

There are a few freshmen working out when I walk in, but they mostly keep their heads down and ignore me. I can only imagine it's the murderous look on my face that ensures that happens.

Heading over to the bench, I load up some weights and lie down. My whole football career I've had grief about my size. I've spent the past few years working tirelessly on building myself up so I don't look like the weed of the team. It's worked to a point—I'm bigger than I've ever been, but I've also managed to find something to keep me focused along with football. When I have the time.

I push my arms until my muscles burn. I love the pain. It makes me feel alive and like one day I might be able to leave this bullshit life I'm forced to live.

If he was still here, everything would have been different, only *they* sent him away. Thoughts of the hand that the Lopezes had in my dad's absence from my life spurs me on.

By the time I drop the weight back onto the stand, I'm alone in the gym. I find my phone from the bottom of my bag, shove in some earbuds and turn it up as loud as I can stand.

Memories that I managed to shut down years ago have started to threaten to bubble back up to the surface. I might have wished that karma would come and bite her in the ass, but witnessing it with my own eyes has stirred something within me. My need to protect her is slipping back in. It's a feeling I remember all too well, seeing as when we were kids it was my one and only focus. She was the most precious thing in my life, and I'd have done anything to keep her safe. I'd have happily taken her pain as my own in the hope to save her from it.

Then everything changed and my need to protect her soon turned into a need for revenge. But even that started to wane as time went on and I realized that I didn't really have it in me to hurt her. I wanted her to suffer, sure. She needed to know what they'd done to me, to my life. Will exposing her scumbag boyfriend settle that little need for revenge that still lingers inside me or, like earlier, will it get me too close to her once again?

I turn the speed up on the treadmill as the image of her large, dark eyes as she stared up at me earlier fill my mind. I haven't looked at her like that for years, or more so, she hasn't looked at me like that for years. The want, need, adoration that I remember all too well was right there in her eyes, or maybe I was imagining it because after the way I've treated her over the past four years, she'd be right to hate me.

When I first discovered the truth about what happened, I ignored her. I was too angry to even be able to mutter a word to her. I could see how much it hurt her, I could see her devastation as she looked at me from across the classroom or cafeteria, her need for me to wrap my arms around her and tell her everything was okay. But it wasn't okay, because my world was on a downward spiral that would only get worse. It hurt when she stopped searching me out in the crowd, supporting me at games and finding any excuse she could to try to talk to me. That's when things changed. She started to look happy; all the while I was continuing to fall apart.

I never wanted to humiliate her, not in the public way that Jake did to Amalie, but my need to make her suffer just a little bit of the pain I'd experienced was too much to ignore. I'd do pathetic stuff, stuff I'm even embarrassed to admit, but mostly belittling comments that I knew would eat at her. Having my best friend turn into my enemy meant I knew exactly what to say to get a rise out of her. I knew that calling her out in class, in front of a crowd, would piss her off, so I did it. I knew how much she hated being the center of attention, so I forced her into it any chance I got. The redness of her face and the hardness of her eyes as everyone looked at her made it so worth it. It helped to squash down my memories of just how important she once was to me.

"You been in here all afternoon?" Jake asks when he sticks his head into the room. I wasn't supposed to be in his last class, but there's no doubt Amalie's already filled him in on what happened with Camila earlier, so he was probably worried I'd gone to do something stupid, like shove Noah's smarmy face down one of the toilets for disrespecting her.

"Yeah, I needed to escape."

He narrows his eyes at me but doesn't say anything. "You'd better not be too exhausted for practice or Coach will be pissed."

"I'm good," I say, although in reality, my muscles feel like jelly as I follow him out to the locker room. He's yet to see my fucked up knuckles, so that should distract him if I'm a little sluggish.

Our practice session is grueling. Coach doesn't let up for even a second, but knowing our away game against Penshore is approaching, I can't blame him. The Chargers are the ones who ended our season before it even really began last year and ruined any chance of us getting to the playoffs. Thankfully he takes one look at my scabbed up hands, tuts and shakes his head.

I can barely put one leg in front of the other by the time he lets us leave the field. In hindsight, my hours in the gym might not have been my best move.

"Fuck, man. If he keeps that shit up we'll all be dead by Friday night."

"He knows what he's doing," Jake grunts, slapping Ethan on the shoulder.

"I know, but fuck, it hurts."

"Growing a pussy or something, Ethan?"

"Nah, just worried about my stamina for the girls tonight."

"You're so full of shit," I mutter, following both into the locker room and then into the showers.

"Aces?" Jake asks. "I told Brit I'd meet her there."

The thought of sitting and watching the two paw all over each other doesn't sound like my idea of fun, even if I could. "Nah, got plans tonight."

"Okay, well... I'll see you tomorrow then."

Jake knows exactly what I mean by 'plans,' and being the loyal friend that he is, he never outs me.

Slinging my bag over my shoulder, I head out to the parking lot on shaky legs. I desperately want to just go home and fall into my bed, but that won't be happening for a few hours yet.

"Evenin', Mason," Heather sings when I walk through the entrance to the store I work in, now fully dressed in my yellow and green Price Chop uniform.

"Sorry, I'm a few minutes late. Practice ran over."

"No problem, sweetie."

I dump my bag in back before heading toward the checkout to find out my list of jobs for the night.

I should be at home starting the homework assignments I was given today, but instead I'm here making sure we've got enough money to feed the boys. It shouldn't be my concern, but sadly this is my reality.

Thankfully it's fairly busy for a Monday night and time passes quickly. That is, until my entire world grinds to a halt and three girls enter.

I look around for Heather but she's out back on break, leaving me to keep an eye on the small store alone. Normally that wouldn't be an issue, but then on any other day no one I know walks through the front door. There's a very good reason why I found a job as far out of Rosewood as possible.

Turning my back, I make it look like I'm busy stacking stuff behind the checkout as they pass, praying they don't find what they came looking for and leave just as fast as they entered.

7

CAMILA

"Aces?" Amalie asks when she finds me after school.

"And here I was thinking you hated the place?"

"I did, when I hated Jake. Things change." She shrugs. Yep, they sure do. And in the blink of an eye if you're really unlucky. "I told him I'd meet him there after practice. Where's Noah?" She looks around as if she's expecting him to be following me.

"He's got his computer club thing this afternoon."

"Just the girls it is, then," she says when Alyssa joins us.

"You still okay coming to that art shop with me later?" Alyssa asks me.

"Yeah, of course." I plaster a smile on my face. In reality, I'd totally forgotten.

"Oh, art place?" Amalie asks, and the two of them start chatting away. Leaving them to it, I head toward my car and wait for them to join me.

"As long as Jake doesn't have plans for me, I'll come too."

"Of course Jake will have plans for you," I say with a wink in my rearview mirror as she settles in the back of my car after Alyssa calls shotgun. "When the trailer's a rockin'." Her cheeks flame red but her eyes widen in horror and my stomach drops.

"Trailer?" Alyssa asks, and I immediately feel awful. Amalie trusted me with that bit of information about Jake's life that he keeps close to his chest.

"Yeah, it's their little love shack. All sorts of unmentionable things go on in there."

"Every Rosewood girl's dream, time in a trailer alone with our star quarterback," Alyssa swoons.

"I thought you were more of a basketball fan?"

"I am. Those guys are banging, but you can't say you'd turn down one of the football team if you had half a chance."

My mind wanders back to the bathroom earlier. Did I have half a chance? What would have happened if I closed that tiny amount of space between us?

"Hey, you okay?" Amalie asks, poking her head between the front seats. "You've turned as white as a sheet."

"Yeah, I'm good." She eyes me curiously. "You both know I've got more of a thing for the geeky guys. At least they've got a better reputation."

"Do they?" Amalie whispers, sitting back and thankfully shutting the hell up. I don't need everyone else judging Noah after Mason's false accusations.

"You find out what the hell went down between Noah and Mason Saturday night?" Alyssa asks as if she can read my mind.

"It was just Mason being a dick," I mutter, hoping she'll change the subject and soon.

"Really? It didn't look like he was playing around."

"Who the hell knows with Mason these days. His mood changes with the wind."

Alyssa accepts my comment and starts talking about some gossip she heard earlier. Thankful that the heat is off me, I focus on where I'm going and try to banish thoughts of Mason from my mind.

Alyssa and Amalie chat away, but I hear none of it. My mind is still in the girls' bathroom with Mason's dark eyes staring down at me. Taunting me.

Our usual table is free, and the second we're seated the waitress comes over to take our order.

"These are on me," Amalie announces. "I never really thanked you both for taking me in on my first day and not allowing me to be an outcast."

"It was nothing," I say, waving her off. "We should be thanking you. Our lives were pretty boring until you turned up."

"I'm sure there are people who say otherwise." Amalie turns toward the entrance where Chelsea and Tasha are walking through the doors, Tasha holding it open for her hobbling captain.

"Shouldn't they be out on the field trying not to fall from the top of their pyramid?" Alyssa mutters, taking in their scantily clad bodies.

"Ignore her," Amalie mutters when she notices me follow Tasha across the diner. "If you're so adamant that Mason's lying, there's no need to drag her into the drama."

Just before they get to their usual table, Tasha looks up and directly at me. If she's surprised by my attention then she doesn't show it. She gives me a wicked, fake smile and continues to their booth.

"What the hell's her problem?" Alyssa spits.

"No idea," Amalie responds, but she doesn't take her eyes off me. The fact she doesn't share the confidence I have in my boyfriend pisses me off. I'm just going to have to prove somehow that he's only got eyes for me.

Three strawberry milkshakes are placed on our table and all conversation halts while we enjoy the creamy treat. I don't care how old I get, I'm pretty sure I'll always feel like a little girl while drinking one.

I relax with a full belly and enjoy some girl time. We chat about school, homework, last week's Homecoming and upcoming parties.

"You're coming to the game Friday night, right?" Amalie asks.

"Um..."

"Oh come on, Cami. You can't let him stop you from enjoying yourself. You love football games."

It's not the game I enjoy so much as it is the atmosphere and knowing that I'm part of something. I've never really been one for group activities or sports, so I've never really got involved in any other way than supporting those who do.

"I'll think about it," I mutter, much to Amalie's disappointment.

Of course I want to go. I love the buzz of game nights and I love supporting our team. Minus a certain number eleven, of course.

"Oh, here they come."

Silence descends on Aces as most of the team comes barreling through the front doors. The Rosewood Bears are like royalty in this place. They all head in the direction Chelsea and Tasha went earlier and fill the diner with loud chatter and banter. It's weird, but the place doesn't feel right unless they're here.

My eyes scan each of them as they walk past our table, giving us little to no attention until Jake and Ethan follow behind the rest of the team. But it's just the two of them. Mason's nowhere to be seen.

Unlike the others, they stop at our table. Jake drags Amalie from the booth and pulls her into his arms, his lips immediately seeking hers out. Ethan rolls his eyes at the pair of them before glancing at me and then turning his sights on Alyssa.

"Whatcha say, sweetcheeks." He wiggles his eyebrows, much to Alyssa's horror.

"I say no thanks, hotshot."

"Aw come on, you know you want a piece of this." He lifts his shirt, showing off his chiseled six pack, a smug grin on his face.

"Please tell me that move doesn't work on the likes of them?" She flicks her eyes toward the huddle of cheerleaders, a disgusted scowl on her face.

"Them? Nah. One look in their direction and they're begging for a ride."

"Jesus," Alyssa mutters, clearly unimpressed by both Ethan and the cheerleading team's slutty ways. "And this is just one reason why I prefer basketball."

Ethan's hand comes up to cover his heart. "Ouch, you wound me. Actually wound me."

"Oh, get over yourself. You ready to go?" she asks, turning to me.

"Sure. Can't wait." Alyssa rolls her eyes at me but doesn't let me off the little trip I agreed to.

"You coming, or are you too busy sucking Jake's face off?" she says with a laugh as she squeezes past the loved up couple.

"I'm coming. Just give me two minutes."

"We'll be in the car," I call over my shoulder.

It takes almost ten minutes for Amalie to remove herself from Jake's hold. We've just about given up on her when she appears through the doors.

"You're just as bad as her with Noah, you know that right?" Alyssa says to Amalie when she gets into the car.

"You're just jealous," I call back.

"Yeah, and...?"

"Maybe you should have taken Ethan up on his offer. Bet he'd show you a good time."

"After he's already showed most of the female population at school one too? No thanks. Where was Shane? I expected him to show his face."

He always used to. It was fairly standard that he wouldn't arrive with the rest of the team, seeing as he makes no secret of the fact they're not his friends, just teammates. But ever since Jake accused him of spiking Amalie's drink, he's kept his distance. Although, I'm with Amalie on this one; I've known Shane since we were little kids, and spiking someone's drink isn't really his style although I must admit that not showing his face does make him appear a little guilty.

I back out of the space as Alyssa puts the address into the GPS.

"You didn't say we were going west."

"I didn't think it would matter. It's not like we're staying."

"True," I mutter. I just hate going to the west side of town. I know it's probably stereotypical of me, but I feel like I'm going to be offered drugs or get mugged every time I go there.

Before I know it, I'm pulling my car to a stop in a dark and dingy looking parking lot behind a row of shops. I might offer to stay with it to ensure I keep all my wheels, but that would mean I'd have to stay here alone and there's no way in hell that's happening.

I rush to get out when the others do and double check I've locked it before walking away.

"You think you're being a little paranoid?" Amalie asks.

"Have you heard any of the local news recently? This place is a ghetto."

"Really?" she asks, one eyebrow raised in question. "It wasn't that bad when Jake brought me here for breakfast."

"I'm sure everything is a little less scary with Jake Thorn on your arm." Alyssa laughs.

"Yeah... that could be it." Amalie gets this far off, wistful look on her face which makes me want to puke. I'm starting to understand why she always used to complain about mine and Noah's PDAs.

"This is it. You're going to love it, it's like Aladdin's cave," Alyssa says to Amalie as I follow behind, clutching my purse tighter to my body than necessary.

An hour. I'm dragged around a damn art shop for a whole hour while Alyssa and Amalie fill their baskets. The only good thing about the experience is that they had quite an extensive notebook section and I was able to feed my addiction.

"Can we run into the store? I promised Mom that I'd pick up a few things for her."

We follow Alyssa across the road and around the discount food store while she selects what she needs. I don't pay all that much attention to my surroundings until we head toward the checkout and Amalie elbows me in the ribs.

"What?" I snap, rubbing the sore spot.

She nods her head toward the register. I'm about to ask what the issue is when my legs stop working.

Standing behind the register dressed in a hideous yellow and green polo shirt is Mason.

"What the fuck is he doing here?" I whisper.

"Working, by the look of it," Amalie adds helpfully, as if his uniform wasn't a dead giveaway.

"Fuck, Alyssa's..." I don't finish my sentence. I don't need to as both Amalie and I watch her walk up to him, much to his horror, and place her basket on the counter.

He's frozen as he stares down at the items in front of him, but eventually, he must realize that no one else is going to ring it all up.

Blowing out a long breath, he reaches out and scans each item before dropping them into a bag. At no point does he look up and register that Amalie and I are standing here, but I have no doubt that he's aware that Alyssa's not alone.

Mason takes the cash for her purchases and all but shoves the change back at her before turning around and attempting to look busy. Unfortunately for him, it's obvious to all of us that he's not actually doing anything.

Alyssa looks over her shoulder at us, her brows drawn together in confusion, and together we follow her from the store.

No one says anything until we're safely back inside my car, and even then it takes a few seconds for Amalie to break the silence.

"Well... that was weird."

"Right?"

"Did you know he had a job over here?" Amalie asks, once again poking her head between the seats and looking at me.

"Me? Why the fuck would I know. He hasn't spoken to me like a human being in four years." I slam my lips shut, aware that I've said too much.

"Four years?"

"It's nothing," I say, trying not to make a big deal out of it.

"It's really not, Cami. You were best friends. How do you go from that to nothing for four years?"

"Shit happens. You of all people should understand that. Things happen for a reason. I'm sure it's better this way."

"You really believe that?" Amalie's voice is full of disbelief, and I can't say I blame her.

I shrug. "What else is there to think?"

"He really didn't want us to see him tonight, did he?" Alyssa chips in. "He looked seriously pissed to have been spotted."

"Yeah. Probably best we keep this to ourselves."

"And now you're protecting him?" I should have known that Amalie would call me out on my bullshit.

"I don't want any more drama than necessary. He's clearly got a job on this side of town for a reason, so let's just let it be."

"Okay, whatever you want." She sits back and thankfully ends the conversation.

It's not until we're approaching a burger place that Alyssa breaks the silence, suggesting we go and get something to eat. I can't really say I'm feeling all that hungry after seeing Mason, but when Amalie agrees, I don't have a lot of choice.

It's later than I was expecting to be home when I let myself in through the front door. Kicking off my shoes, I walk through to the kitchen to grab a drink before heading up to do some homework. My parents are sitting at the dining table in silence, both looking stressed as they turn to me.

"Sorry I'm late. I went to an art shop with Alyssa and Amalie and then for food. Are you both okay?" I ask hesitantly, taking in their deep frown lines.

"Uh... yeah. We were just hoping you'd have been home before now. We need to discuss something with you."

"Is it urgent? Because I really need to complete my English assignment for tomorrow."

They both glance at each other before Dad nods and turns to me. "Not at all, sweetheart. You do what you need to do and we'll all have dinner together tomorrow night. How does that sound?"

"Sounds great." I grab a bottle of water from the refrigerator and head for the stairs.

"Why did you put it off?" I hear Mom snap.

"School's more important."

Mom scoffs. Now I'm desperate to know what's going on but equally afraid to find out. It didn't look like they had happy news.

8

MASON

Angry doesn't even begin to describe how I feel as I watch the three of them walk out of the store. I got a job in this part of town for a very good reason, so the fact they've just found me pisses me off more than I'm willing to admit. My life is one big series of fuck ups and the fact I even need to be working this shitty job is just another one, but it's the only place I could find that would be flexible enough for me to work around school and football games.

It's almost midnight when I eventually pull up at home. The lights are all out aside from the living room, where I'm assuming tonight's babysitter is currently hanging out, waiting for either Mom or I to appear. But to my surprise when I get there to let them off for the night, the person I find laid out on the sofa with a bottle of vodka in their hand is none other than my mother. She shouldn't be here yet. Her shift at the bar doesn't finish until two AM.

"Mom," I shout, louder than necessary seeing as she's asleep. I have no qualms about waking her. She sleeps most of the day and does whatever the fuck she likes whenever she feels like it.

"Shit, fuck. Yeah, what is it?" she asks in a panic, sitting up and pulling the bottle to her chest protectively.

"It's all right, I'm not going to fucking steal it. Shouldn't you be at work?"

"I... uh... got laid off."

"I'm sorry, you fucking what?" Red hot fury explodes through my body. She only works a handful of shifts each week as it is. She needs to be picking up more hours to support her kids, not losing her fucking job.

"It's a total misunderstanding. I didn't steal anything."

Rolling my eyes, I take a step from the room. "You're a fucking joke," I spit over my shoulder. "How about you lay off that bottle so you're sober enough to find a new job in the morning, eh?"

I take the stairs two at a time as I head for the safety of my room. Of course, I stop to make sure my brothers are sleeping soundly before I shut myself away. I'd put money on the fact *she* didn't do the same when she got home. The only thing she wants to ensure is okay is her fucking vodka.

I crack my knuckles as I walk through my bedroom door in an attempt to release some of the frustration that's pulling at my muscles. It does fuck all to help, but the sound is somewhat soothing. I could really do with hurting someone right about now. I picture the terror on Noah's face as I drove my fist into it on Saturday night and something inside me settles just a little bit. That is until the image of who I was misguidedly doing it for pops into my mind.

"Fuck." Rubbing my hand down my face, I scratch at my rough jaw as I think back to her finding me in Price Chop earlier. I've gone out of my way to hide my reality since the day my dad walked out and I was forced to step up to the plate.

Without thinking, I rip my curtains open and stare down the street. Her curtains might be closed, but there's an obvious light shining behind them. She's awake. That's all the invitation I need.

Turning on my heels, I race from the house and down the street. I don't bother knocking on her front door, it'll only alert her parents. They know full well that things went south between us, so there's no way they'd allow me inside at this time of night, even if they are up.

Instead, I walk around the side of the house and across the grass. I'd always wanted to try climbing up here, but there was only one time I actually attempted it. I'm fairly sure after the kiss it led to that if things didn't play out the way they did, I'd have done it time and again if it meant I got another taste of her.

Memories of that night threaten to bubble up, but I do my best to swallow them down. I don't need to remember the sad look in her eyes as she stared up at me that evening. I felt terrible. It was totally my fault that she was late home and ended up in trouble. I was being selfish and didn't want to let her go. It broke my heart to hear her getting laid into by her parents for breaking curfew. When her first sob sounded out through the barrier of the front door, I knew I couldn't leave her. I made my way around to this trellis, I gave it a tug, much like I do right now to ensure it's secure, and I pulled myself all the way to the top so I was able to climb into her open window. A window that was always damn open. I'd warned her about it before, knowing how badly I wanted to climb up meant others would too, but she never shut the fucking thing. It was almost as if she was inviting me to join her. That's what my fourteen-year-old hormone filled body imagined, anyway.

Opening her window wider, I throw my leg over like I've done this a million times and silently slip into her room.

The only sound I can hear is that of my heavy breathing, and it's not until I poke my head out from behind the curtain what I realize why. She's scared of sleeping alone in the dark. My heart threatens to pound out of my chest as I run my eyes up the bump in her sheets until I find her dark hair that's fanned out on her pillow.

Walking over, I allow myself a second or two to look at her peaceful, sleeping face and imagine things weren't so fucked up. That the last time I was in this room was the beginning of something incredible, when in reality it was the end of everything I'd known. The events of the weeks following that night will forever be burned into my mind as the worst weeks of my life, and although Camila didn't personally have a hand in it, it was the actions of her dad that threw both mine and my little brothers' lives into meltdown. Charlie was only a baby, Oliver not much more; neither of them deserved to lose not only their father but practically their mother as well.

Thoughts of that time ignites a fire in my belly and reminds me why I'm here.

Finding a glass of water sitting beside her bed, I pick it up and raise it above her head.

My hand trembles slightly as I tip it, but the sight of the small stream of water pouring over the edge mesmerizes me enough to continue.

"Argh, what the fu—Mason?" Her eyes are wide as she sits up and pushes my arm away with so much force that the glass and the remainder of the contents crash to the floor. "What the fuck is your fucking problem?" She scrambles from the bed, wiping at her wet face, and stands tall in front of me. I want to laugh at her attempt to square up to me—like she'd be able to win anything with her tiny size. My eyes drop from the fire lighting her usually dark ones in favor of her body, and the moment I do, any amusement falls from my lips.

Fuck. She's standing before me in a ruby red satin cami and tiny short set. The top is twisted around her body, her left breast all but falling from behind the fabric.

My eyes lock on to that smooth, porcelain bit of skin. How easy would it be to reach out and expose the rest, to be able to get just one look at the body that's featured in so many of my dirty teenage dreams? My temperature soars and my cock begins to swell inside my pants at the thought of how perfect her pink nipple is bound to be. I wonder if it tastes as sweet as I always hoped, or sour like I'd be tasting a rotten piece of fruit?

"Why the fuck are you here?" She tries again, her hands going to her hips, sadly dislodging the fabric and allowing it to fall back into place.

"I'm..." Standing in front of her dressed as she is seems to have zapped my brain. I fight to remember why the hell I'm here, but I come up short. My only thoughts are of her and how quickly I could get that satin on her bedroom floor.

No. You can't have her.

My sudden realization drags tonight's events to the forefront of my mind and reminds me why the hell I am here.

I take a step forward. "You look like you were expecting company, dressed in this sexy little outfit." Lifting my hand, I run my fingers along the soft scrap of fabric resting on her shoulder. Her shoulders tense at my contact, but I don't miss how her nipples pebble behind the satin. "Did he stand you up? He's probably got better company. I hear Tasha is a stellar lay."

Her arm flies out, but before her palm connects with my cheek, I wrap my fingers around her wrist. I trained my entire life to catch that vital ball, I'm not going to miss her arm.

Her eyes harden and her teeth grind.

"Get out of my fucking bedroom."

"Why? Don't you want to give him a taste of his own medicine? He seems to be more than happy playing away. Maybe you should see what the fuss is all about." I tug her arm. She tries to fight, but she's no match for me and I get my way. Her soft breasts press against my chest and I all but moan out loud at the sensation it causes within my body.

Dropping my head, I brush my lips against her ear. "We could even send him some evidence if you like. Really hit him where it hurts."

"Fuck you." Her knee lifts, but I'm expecting it and jump back before she makes any contact.

"You're going to regret that."

"Am I?" She rolls her eyes before reaching for the hoodie that's hanging over the back of her chair and wrapping it around herself. I'm not ashamed to admit that it's a damn shame to hide that banging little body away.

"Are you always this clueless? Your boyfriend's banging a cheerslut and here you are, letting him get away with it."

"He's not. Fuck." She shoves her hands into her hair, pulling it away from her face and allowing the hoodie to fall open. My eyes have a mind of their own and once again drop in favor of her curves. "I'm not talking about this with you. It's none of your fucking business. You gave up any right to have an opinion on my life years ago. Now do me a fucking favor and get the hell out." She gestures toward the window with her outstretched arm and widens her eyes in impatience.

"Don't I fucking know it."

"What's that supposed to mean?"

"Nothing. Listen, what you saw tonight. I need you to keep it locked."

She laughs, actually laughs in my face. "Hang on, let me get this right. You've broken into my bedroom, thrown water over me, harassed me, told me I'm an idiot, and all because you need a favor. Fuck you, Mason. Fuck. You."

"First, it's not breaking in if the window is open." Her eyebrow quirks, but I

don't give her a chance to argue. "Second, I'm only telling the truth. Not my fault if you choose not to believe me."

"And third?"

"Third. I just... I just... I need it kept quiet. No one else needs to know about my life."

"You've got a job, so what? You're not the only one out earning a bit of their own cash."

"It's..." Her eyes bore into mine as if she's trying to read my mind, and for a second I'm worried she might just be able to. We were always on the same wavelength. We'd finish each other's sentences, blurt out the same ridiculous idea simultaneously. It only makes sense that she can see right through my bullshit. "You're right. No biggie. I just wanted to sneak in to try my luck. I mean, if your boyfriend's out getting his dick wet then there's no harm in me doing the same."

Her face damn near turns purple with anger. "Get the hell out of my room, Mason, before I scream for my parents."

It's an empty threat. I'm pretty sure she wouldn't bring that kind of drama down on either of us, but just in case I'm wrong, I take a step toward the window.

"I'll see you soon, Cami-bear. And if you're still dressed like that, then even better." I wink, allow myself one last trip around her body despite the fact she's now pulled the hoodie around herself as tight as it'll go, and climb from the window.

I let go when I'm halfway down the trellis and jump to the grass. Her burning stare tingles down my spine as I make the short walk back to my house, but I refuse to turn around. That is, until I know I'm about to disappear from her sight. Then I turn and face her window. Just as I suspected, her face is tucked between the curtains, watching me. Once she realizes I've caught her and the fabric falls in front of her face, ending our connection. I can't help laughing as I let myself back inside.

I might not have got what I went over there for, but I left with much more. If this morning in the girls' bathroom wasn't evidence enough, then tonight was: if I were to so much as drop my lips while I was touching her then she'd cave to me.

9

CAMILA

After securing the window and changing my pillow for a dry one, I have the worst night's sleep I've had in a long time. I know that shutting the window doesn't change the size of my room, but the second I pull it closed, I can't help feeling claustrophobic and like the walls are closing in on me. It's crazy, I know, but I guess it's true what they say: fears are irrational. I feel like I can't breathe without that small amount of fresh air flowing in, and I hate him for it.

When I do manage to fall asleep, it's only two hours before I need to be up for school, and when my alarm goes off, I'm in a bitch of a mood.

The second I push through the doors into school, I see him. He's standing at his locker, which is unfortunately directly opposite mine, as Chelsea and a couple of her sluts surround him. One of them runs their fingers down his arm while Chelsea presses her palm against his chest, laughing at whatever he just said. I throw up a little in my mouth at the sight.

I don't take two steps when my skin starts tingling with awareness. I don't want to look up at him. I want to ignore him and show him that I'm indifferent to his attention. Sadly for me, but although my brain might want this, it seems my body has other ideas because as I come to a stop in front of my own locker, my head twists and I find myself locked in his dark stare. His blonde hair is falling over his face where he's bent down attempting to look interested in what the girls are saying, but they don't have his eyes. They're firmly burning into me.

Even with the distance between us I can see how incredibly dark they are. A shudder runs down my spine as I'm transported back to last night when he

stared down at me with such intensity. I couldn't help but think he was about to devour me, and in that moment, just for a second, part of me wished he would.

"Good morning, beautiful," Noah sings, coming to a stop beside me and wrapping his arm around my waist. I freeze and he notices. "You okay?"

My eyes betray me and flick over to Mason, who I find staring daggers at the back of Noah's head. His words from last night slam into me.

"Are you always this clueless? Your boyfriend's banging a cheerslut and here you are letting him get away with it."

Looking back into Noah's kind eyes, he smiles at me, clearly concerned with where my head's at this morning. Reaching out, his fingers twist around a lock of my loose hair and he leans in toward me.

"Missed you last night," he murmurs against my lips before pressing them against mine.

I don't kiss him back immediately like I usually would, and he soon notices. He pulls away, and I panic. Lifting my hand, I wrap it around the back of his neck and pull him down to me. The last thing I need is him questioning my resistance. It's not his fault that Mason's lies are on repeat in my head. Because that's what they are... lies, right?

Fuck, I hate this. I trust Noah one hundred percent, and that asshole is making me question everything. If he'd told me these things about a boyfriend four years ago, I'd have dropped them like a stone, but Mason's been nothing but a pain in my ass all this time, trying to ruin my life for something I had zero control over. So why I'm giving his accusations head space I have no idea.

When Noah's tongue slips between my lips, I move mine to join it. His kiss is the same as always, but I can't help but feel something's changed.

When he eventually lets me up for air, his eyes are heated, his eyelids slightly lowered, and an excited smile plays on his lips.

My stomach drops. I never told him about my plans to lose my virginity on his birthday night, but I had told him that it would happen soon. He's been the perfect gentleman waiting for me. I know many teenage boys who wouldn't have been so patient, but I also feel like it's starting to wear thin. We've done... stuff. Or more so, I've done stuff. He hasn't got past the odd hand roam with me. I knew that once things started getting too serious, it was likely to go from zero to one hundred in the blink of an eye. I don't know why I've been holding off, it's not like everyone around us isn't doing it. But, I don't know. Something just hasn't felt quite right.

I stare off over his shoulder as my mind races with all these crazy thoughts, but I'm soon pulled from my misery when I lock with that pair of brown eyes. Only it's different this time. The girls have gone, leaving Mason standing alone, and the way he's staring at me, he looks kind of vulnerable. It's unnerving and not a look I've seen on him for a very, very long time.

"You coming to my house after school?" Noah asks, pulling my attention back to him.

"I'm sorry, I can't tonight. I promised my parents that I'd be home. They've got some drama they need to talk to me about."

"Is everything okay?" he asks, genuinely concerned.

"I have no idea. They looked a little stressed last night, but I didn't have time to chat. I still hadn't finished that English assignment."

"Still? I thought you were planning on finishing it over the weekend?"

Yeah, I was, but then Mason beat the shit out of you and I was left with my head spinning out of control. I don't want to admit that though. Instead I go with, "I ran out of time."

"That sucks. Maybe tomorrow then?"

"Yeah maybe." Turning away from him, I open my locker and switch out some books from my bag, ready for the day.

Noah seems to get the idea that we're done, and after a quick kiss on the cheek and an 'I'll see you later,' he turns and heads off in the direction of his own locker.

I let out a breath I didn't know I was holding and stare at the picture that's pinned to the back of my locker. It's of Noah, Shane, Amalie and me at Dash earlier in the year. Noah's standing behind me with his arms around my waist, a huge smile on his face as he stares down at me and not at the camera like everyone else. A smile twitches at my lips, but it's not enough to put to rest the confusion swirling around my head.

I give myself a talking to and swing the door shut. What I'm not expecting when I turn and take a step in the direction of my first class is to find Mason still watching me from his side of the hallway.

Anger surges through me and I turn toward him.

"What? What is your fucking problem? Breaking and entering and scaring the shit out of me not enough? You've got to be a creepy stalker too?"

His lips thin and his jaw ticks with frustration. "Just watching you fuck your life up."

"Don't you have your own life to lead? Why are you so interested in mine all of a sudden?"

I didn't think it was possible, but his features harden even more at my words.

"Don't worry, I've got enough of my own bullshit without adding yours to it."

I'm silent for a few seconds, trying to figure out if there's some secret message I'm supposed to pick up in those few words, before I decide to be the adult in the situation and walk away.

"That's it, run away from what's right in front of you."

My spine stiffens as his parting words settle into my body, and I fight myself not to react further. He doesn't need to know his words affect me.

I only get a few minutes of relief because it feels like only moments after having sat in my seat and pulled my books out that he joins me in our chemistry class. I keep my eyes down, but that doesn't mean I don't feel his stare burning into the top of my head as he passes to take his seat at the back of the room.

By the time it gets to my AP English class before lunch, I'm starving and can barely keep my eyes open. I hand my assignment in that I finished sometime before midnight last night, only to be handed another.

"The title of the piece is to be *Against All Odds*." Miss Phillips points to where she's written it on the board before fully explaining that she wants a piece of creative writing in any form we wish to convey that title.

I'm so tired that my mind fails to come up with a single idea and I panic that he's going to have ruined my creativity as well as my night's sleep.

Writing the task in my diary, I pray the clock will tick around so that I can eat.

If I had the energy, I might cheer with delight when the lunchtime bell rings out through the school. I rush to pack up my stuff and leave the room as fast as my legs will carry me, hoping to get a spot at the front of the line.

I practically inhale my burger and fries once I've placed them on our usual table. I'm over half done before I sense someone coming to join me. Glancing over my shoulder, I find Shane making his way over.

"Hey stranger. How's it going?" I mumble around a mouthful of fries.

"It's... going." He lowers his tray and himself to the bench opposite me, blowing out a huge breath.

"You still moping about what happened at your party? We all know it wasn't you, you don't need to sweat it."

"You might, but does everyone else?" he asks sadly, glancing around at the students now filling the cafeteria. "I keep getting these accusatory, disappointed looks from everyone. That's not me, Cam. I wouldn't ever do that, especially to someone I—" He cuts himself off, pain and regret filling his eyes. We all know he liked Amalie, he made no secret of that fact. I think he was hopeful that she'd warm to him, but unfortunately for Shane she fell head over heels for the captain of his football team instead. I'm pretty sure that outcome didn't feature in his plans whatsoever.

"Those who matter know it wasn't you."

"I feel like an outcast. No one wants me around anymore in case I'm a threat."

My heart bleeds for him. Although he has a spot on the football team, Shane is one of us. He's fought for years to be accepted by both parts of his world, but whoever it was that spiked Amalie's drink and framed Shane has managed to shatter both in one fell swoop. I feel for the guy, I really do, but I'm not sure what to say other than to wait for someone else to do something that'll take the heat off him, because this is high school: gossip only lasts for so long before someone trumps you and steals the limelight.

"They think I drugged her. That's not going to go away easily. I'll never be invited to a party again."

"It'll pass. Just focus on showing everyone how kind and caring you are and everyone will soon realize that you're not capable."

"Shane, my man. How's it hanging?" Noah says, dropping down beside me. He doesn't bother waiting for Shane's response. Instead he pulls me into his side and slides his fingers into my hair so he can drag my lips to his. His kiss is over the top and excitable, and it puts me off even more than I was this morning when he kissed me.

"What's up with you today? PMSing or something?"

"Yeah, something," I mutter, turning back to my fries.

He nudges me in the arm. "Hey, I was only messing. Are you okay?" he whispers a little more softly, his hand sneaking around my back to wrap around my waist.

"I'm—" I don't get to make my excuses because Shane cuts me off.

"I should go." His voice is broken and defeated at best.

When I look up, I find him staring over my shoulder with sad eyes. Following his gaze, I find Amalie and Jake walking in, hand in hand. The entire room seems to fall silent for a second or two as their king and his queen arrives.

Jake Thorn was always Rosewood's bad boy, but as I watch him pick up two trays, one for himself and another for Amalie, I wonder if we all hadn't gotten him very wrong. He's so sweet with her, like a totally different person to the Jake we've all seen over the past few years. They stand in line, their trays resting on the rail, and he wraps his arm around her waist, pulls her to him and kisses the top of her head. He lingers for a beat too long and I swear my heart nearly explodes on the spot. He's fallen so hard for her, it really is a sight to behold. I also know from how she talks about him that he's it for her. There's absolutely no doubt in her mind.

Everyone's chatter seems to start again, and I turn back to Shane who's just about to push up from the bench he's sitting on.

"Please stay."

"No one wants me here, Camila. *They* don't want me here." He flicks his eyes to where the couple are waiting for their food.

"She knows it wasn't you."

"Doesn't stop him wanting to take my teeth out... again," he mutters.

"He had his pop at you. He's moved on to other, more satisfying, things," Noah helpfully adds while Shane visibly pales at the thought of what the girl he wanted is now up to.

"I'll see you guys later." Before we can argue, he's gone, lost in the crowd.

I turn my eyes back to Amalie, who gives me a smile before returning to concentrate on whatever her boyfriend is saying.

Something twists uncomfortably inside me. Is that... jealousy? Why would I be jealous of Amalie and Jake? I'm sitting here with my boyfriend. I've got what they have, I've had it for quite a while now. *Have you?* a little voice in my head asks, but I push her away and turn to Noah. I smile at him, but it doesn't reach my eyes. I fear Mason's words might be making more of an impact than I want them to, and every time I look into Noah's eyes, I wonder more and more if he is indeed hiding something.

———

The last thing I want to do when I get home is to have a heart to heart with my parents, but it seems I don't get any reprieve because when I walk into the kitchen, they're already sitting at the table waiting for me. The fact that my dad should be at work doesn't even really register as I drop my bag and get myself a drink.

The atmosphere in the room is heavy as I make my way over to join them. The morose looks on their faces don't help the ball of dread that's sitting heavy in my stomach. Are they about to tell me they're splitting up? No, surely not. They're happy, right?

My mind runs a mile a minute as I wait for one of them to put me out of my misery.

"Darling, we need to discuss something with you," Mom starts.

My heart pounds as I wait for her to ask me who I want to live with, as if I'd have that answer easily to hand, but when my dad takes over, it's very different words that fall from his lips.

"Our office is closing."

"Oh my god," I gasp. I'm equally shocked and happy that they're not separating. "I'm so sorry. You can get another job though, right?"

"That's what we need to discuss."

"Okaaaay."

"The company is relocating everything to their main office in New York. So I've still got a job if I want it, it's just—"

"In New York," I say, guessing where this is going.

"Yeah."

Anger burns within me that they've already made this decision. "So this isn't a discussion, this is you telling me that we're moving?" I snap, pushing the chair out behind me in frustration.

I'm in my senior year, they can't just tell me they're going to drag me halfway across the country and think I'll be okay with it. And it's not only school. What about my friends? What about Noah? *What about Mason?* a little voice adds, but I ignore her because I don't give a fuck about him.

"Sit down please, Camila. That's not what this is." I look between the two of them. Both have encouraging expressions on their faces and I slowly lower myself back down, hoping they really have thought this through.

"We're not expecting you to up and move to New York, sweetheart. Unless of course, that's what you want. Your dad has been given a very generous offer for him to work four days a week and to commute, but before any decisions are made, we wanted to discuss it with you. We know this won't affect your life like moving would, but we're both very aware that it will disrupt your senior year and our priority, as ever, is your happiness and success."

"Right, okay." I sit back and let that sink in for a few seconds. "So, what happens if you turn down this offer?"

"Honestly," Dad says with a sigh, "I have no idea. There's nowhere close that does what I do. So right now I'm faced with the decision of travelling or changing my career."

"Neither is an issue. We've got investments that we're in the process of liquidating so that we have money should be need it. Money isn't really the issue here, it's more our happiness and our quality of life as a family."

I nod, understanding where they're coming from before I turn to look at my dad. "What do you want? Like, really want?" I know how much he loves his job. He's a total IT geek and lives for everything computers.

"If I'm being really honest, and probably selfish then... I'd love to take their offer. Working in New York has always been a dream of mine and it will give me a lot more opportunities to climb the ladder. But the most important thing here is my girls. I need both of you to be happy no matter what."

I hate to say it, but I refuse to be the one to hold either of my parents back, especially because in less than a year I'll be off at college somewhere. The thought has a ball of dread forming in my stomach because I'm still none the wiser as to what I want to study or where, but time is closing in on my decision. "Then you should do it."

"But that would mean Dad wouldn't be here most of the time, and if I'm also being honest, I don't want to always be left behind. I'd really like to experience city life too."

"I'm nearly eighteen. I'll be at college soon without you both. I'm sure I can cope."

Mom and Dad look between each other, a silent conversation happening in front of my eyes, but I have no idea what they're saying.

Eventually Dad nods and they both turn to me. "We trust you, Camila, and we know that you're more than capable of being alone sometimes. I won't go all of the time, but I wanted you to be aware from the outset that I might not always be here like I have been."

I bite down on the inside of my cheek to stop from saying that she's not here all that often as it is. All the social events that she organizes have her out more than she's in. I can't remember the last Saturday night we all spent as a family.

"It'll be fine. I want you guys to be happy. I'll be too focused on school to notice."

"Nice," Dad says with a laugh. "Seriously though, I'm so proud of you, Camila."

"Thanks. Are we done? It's just, I've got homework to do."

"We are. I need to pop out for a bit but then I'll sort dinner when I get home, okay?" Mom says.

"Sure thing."

After grabbing a fresh drink, I make my way up to my room and pull my books from my bag.

I stare down at the assignment I got from Miss Phillips and think about what I'd like to do.

10

MASON

All day I waited for someone to walk up to me and mention my job, but by the time the bell rang signaling the end of the day, no one had. After everything that I've done to Camila, I really thought she'd tell the entire school my little secret the first chance she got. I'm amazed that she hasn't spilled.

She was angry with me this morning after what I did last night. Her dark eyes had a fire burning in them that I've never seen before as she stood in front of me with her hands on her hips. I can't deny that her temper didn't fire me up a little too. I remember all too well from when we were kids that she could have a temper if she wanted to. It wasn't directed at me all that often, but when it was, I knew about it.

"What are you smiling about?" Jake asks when I join him in the locker room ready for practice.

"Oh, nothing."

"You get a hand job during history or something?" Ethan adds. He really does have a one-track fucking mind.

"No, sadly not." His words make me realize how long it's been since I did receive that kind of attention. "Chance would be a fine thing."

"You're shitting me. You've seen the girls who drool after every step we take, right? Just look at one of them the right way and they'll drop to their knees."

"I'm well aware. But it's not one of them I really want."

"Oooh, does Mason have a little crush?" Ethan's eyebrows wiggle in delight that he might be about to discover a secret.

"No. I just don't want a cheerslut who's already sucked on yours."

"Why not? I'm clean."

Rolling my eyes at him, I pull my locker open and start getting ready for practice. Truth is that just a few months ago I wasn't really all that bothered about who was on the other end of my cock as long as they made me come at the end of it. They were the perfect distraction from my bullshit life. But as time goes on, I've realized that those experiences were pretty meaningless. It might make me sound like a pussy, at least it does in Ethan's eyes, but I want more than a quick, dirty fuck with a girl who's already done at least one lap of the team. I want... I want what Jake's found with Amalie. I want someone who's going to stand by my side despite what my life is, despite what my family situation is. I want someone I can rely on when times get hard, not just someone who turns up when they want something.

Practice is fucking killer. I swear we'll all be broken by the time Friday night's game comes around if Coach keeps up with this level of craziness.

I probably should have seen if I could snag an extra shift tonight, but knowing that I need to speak to Mom meant I didn't pick up the phone and beg for extra hours. It's coming though. I just know that Mom's not going to be proactive as she should be about finding another job.

I'm proved correct when I pull up outside our house not long later to find her car parked in the driveway and then her sitting in front of the TV with a tub of ice cream in her lap. At least it's an improvement on the vodka from last night.

"I see you're busy looking for a way to pay the bills," I mutter as I pass her heading to the kitchen. "We need to talk."

A few months ago, when Mom's hours were cut, I forced her to sit down with me so we could write down a list of all our expenses and the day each bill needed to be paid. It's now pinned to the front of the refrigerator in the hope that seeing it might spur her into action. Clearly that was wishful thinking, seeing as she has no job whatsoever now.

I pull it from its clip and sit down at the breakfast bar with that and a can of soda praying I can figure out a way around all of this. I have a little bit of money in savings ready for college, but it's nowhere near enough to keep us afloat until Mom gets off her ass and brings in some money.

"What are you doing now?" she mutters, eventually joining me in the kitchen.

"Trying to figure out a way to ensure we're not evicted and forced to live on the streets."

She lets out an amused sigh which only adds to my irritation levels. "That's not going to happen."

"Why not? We've got no way of paying all of this." I wave the piece of paper in her face. "So why wouldn't we be kicked out?"

"Just trust me, okay?"

"You're fucking joking, right?"

She narrows her eyes at me before pulling the refrigerator open and reaching for a bottle of wine.

"So I'm assuming you haven't got another job yet?"

"It's only been a day, Mase. Calm down."

"Calm down? Calm down? Am I the only one who cares about those two boys playing upstairs? Have you even fed them since they got home from school?" Guilt twists her face and I get my answer. "You're meant to be our fucking mother. You should be the one worrying about paying the bills, about whether we all eat correctly or not. It is not my job to be their father," I call when she decides she'd rather spend her evening alone with her bottle of wine. "Fucking waste of space," I mutter, staring back down at the list of numbers.

Pinning it back up where I found it, I set about making dinner for myself and my brothers. If she doesn't care enough to do it, then she can fend for herself. I'm not making her life even easier for her.

After making sure Charlie and Ollie have a bath, I leave them in their rooms with the understanding that they can play for another thirty minutes before they must be in bed. Thankfully, Ollie is a pretty responsible kid and I'm confident that when the time comes, he'll ensure Charlie does as I said and climbs into bed. My blood boils that my seven-year-old little brother has to take on that kind of responsibility. But I can't do everything myself. I need to keep my grades up if I have any hope of graduating and going to college. I also need to be out on that football field, but I fear that might have to go by the wayside if I need to pick up more hours to keep this roof over our heads.

Thankfully, it seems to have gone quiet down the hall. I get up to go and check on them but at the same time, there's a knock at the front door. I turn to go and answer it but soon realize that I don't need to, seeing as Mom's footsteps sound out before female voices fill the air. The other woman's is one I recognize well. I've almost heard it as much as my own mother's.

I should head back to my room and leave them to it, but my need for another drink gets the better of me and thank fuck it does because if I don't overhear what I do, then fuck knows when Mom would ever have told me the truth.

"I'm really sorry to have to do this, Nicky, but we're selling the house," Mrs. Lopez says.

My spine immediately stiffens, but I stay out of sight. *Sell the house? Why does she need to apologize for selling their house?*

"What does that mean for us?"

"I don't know, Nic. Do you have enough to rent somewhere else? I'm sure you could get something a little smaller that you could afford on your salary."

Wait... what?

As I storm around the corner, both of them look up at me. Shock covers both of their faces that they've been caught.

"Oh, hello Mason. I didn't realize you were home."

Bullshit, seeing as my car's parked in the drive.

"Cut the crap. What were you both just talking about?"

"It's nothing, baby. Just go back to your homework."

I'm already fighting the fury that's filling my veins. The last thing I need is her patronizing tone, talking to me like a goddamn child.

"No, I think I need to hear this, seeing as I'm the only one bringing money into this house right now."

Mrs. Lopez's mouth drops open as she looks between the two of us.

"What happened to your job, Nic?"

"They let me go."

Mrs. Lopez lets out an exasperated sigh. I've always wondered why these two are still friends. They're polar opposites in every way, but even after everything that happened that ripped our family in two, they're still as close as ever.

"Why didn't you tell me that just then when we were discussing..." She trails off.

"Yeah, about that. Who owns this house, Mom?" She visibly pales before looking down at her feet. "Mom. Who owns this fucking house?"

"They do." It's so quiet that I almost miss it, but I already knew the answer. Her opening her lips was only to confirm it.

"Motherfucker."

"Language, Mason."

When her eyes find mine, they're hard and disappointed. She's disappointed in me? That's fucking rich.

"So the mortgage I've been busting my ass to help pay isn't our mortgage. It's just rent, and rent to *them*." I don't even try to cover the disdain in my voice. Everyone in this room knows exactly how I feel about the Lopez family and how they ruined my life, I'm not going to start sugar coating that shit now.

"You don't pay any rent," Mrs. Lopez admits before my mom fires a few daggers at her and she promptly slams her lips shut.

"Fucking hell." Lifting my hands, I run them through my hair and tug. This is not fucking happening. So not only did the Lopezes ruin my life by running my dad out of town, but they basically own my life.

"We'd like to do some renovation before we put it on the market. So I'm sorry to ask, but we really need you to move out as soon as possible."

I stand stock still and watch the panic start to cover Mom's face. So it appears being on the verge of homelessness is what it takes to make her realize what a dire situation this is.

"But... but we have no money," she whispers.

"What happened to all the money I thought you were paying the mortgage with?" I ask and watch her pale even more.

"It's gone."

"Gone? That would have been thousands of dollars. How can it just be gone?"

"I spent it."

"On what?"

"Stuff. Nights out."

My fingers tug at my hair impossibly hard until I think I'm going to start pulling it from my scalp.

"So what you're saying is that unless by some miracle you find a seriously well-paying job in the next few days, we're homeless. Well, isn't that just fucking great." A cold laugh falls from my lips because, really, why didn't I see something like this coming?

"Nic?" Mrs. Lopez questions. When I look back at Mom, at least she has the decency to look upset by this. Tears fill her eyes, and fair play to her because her bottom lip actually trembles a little.

"So come on. You must have a plan. When you decided to spend every penny we had, you must have had a backup plan. You're our mother, after all. You're supposed to have our best interests at heart. You can't possibly be standing here and telling me that you're about to make us all homeless because of your stupidity." My words might be cruel, and just a tiny bit of regret hits me when she starts to sob, but fuck it, she deserves everything I can throw at her right now.

She shakes her head as she cries. Mrs. Lopez is clearly softer than I am, because as I stand there with my arms crossed across my chest waiting for her to fill me in on her big plan, she pulls Mom into her arms and rubs her back.

"I know it's been hard since he left," she soothes in her ear.

"Fuck that. It's been four years. She's an adult. She's supposed to be a mother," I seethe.

"She's ill, Mason. Give her a break."

"Ill?" I ask, an unamused laugh falling from my lips. "Don't make excuses for her."

She opens her mouth to respond but clearly thinks better of it, not wanting to get into an argument with the person who somehow manages to keep this family barely above water.

"Come and move in with us—"

"No, Gabriella, we can't—" Mom tries to weakly argue, lifting her head from Mrs. Lopez's shoulder.

"You can and you will. Just until you get yourselves sorted. Clint and I won't be there all that much while we get him settled in New York."

"No, no, we—"

"No," I state, my heart slamming against my chest. I can't live in their fucking house. I can't live with Camila. Fuck. If it weren't for the Lopezes then my dad would still be here, and we wouldn't be in this fucking mess.

"Mason. We have no other option." There's hope shining in Mom's eyes, but

I'm not stupid. I know it's because she just got offered an easy way out. Having a roof over our heads means she can fuck about for a while longer. She doesn't care that that roof might be the last place in the world I want to be. I think I'd actually rather be homeless. The image of me living in a cardboard box pops in my mind and I realize I'm being a little dramatic, but I really don't want to have to move into that fucking house.

"I'll stay with Ethan or something," I mutter, turning to leave them to it, unable to listen to any more of this bullshit. I have no idea if the Savages will put me up, but seeing as he lives in a huge house and his parents are almost never there, I doubt anyone will even notice.

"Think about your brothers, Mase. They'll need you."

Spinning, I pin my mother with a searing look.

"Think about my brothers. Are you fucking joking? All I do is think about them. I'm risking my future, my career, my everything for them right now, not that you have any fucking clue what I do *for them.*"

She balks, but not as much as Mrs. Lopez who looks like she wants to take a swing at me. I guess that's the benefit of me avoiding her and her only spending time with my manipulative mother: she doesn't really know the whole truth about what plays out inside this house.

Storming away from both of them, I poke my head into the boys' room to make sure they're sleeping peacefully before silently making them both a promise. *I won't allow her bad choices to ruin your lives. I swear it.*

The second I close my bedroom door behind me, I pull my phone out and call work. If we're going to get through this and get out of the Lopezes' before I do something stupid then I'm going to need money, and to get that money I need more hours.

Heather's hesitant to agree to my plans, but I know she's struggling for other options seeing as two members of staff have quit recently. That seems to be the only thing about my life that's falling into place right now.

Tomorrow I'm going to have to make some concessions for my new work schedule. My stomach is already in knots knowing what I'm going to have to give up, but I'll do anything for those two little boys, to ensure they grow up with at least one person looking out for them.

Picking my phone back up, I message both Jake and Ethan.

I need a drink. You free?

Almost immediately three little bouncing dots appear and replies start filling my screen.

Ethan: Fuck yes. Get your asses over here. Free house.

Jake: Sure thing. Mase, pick me up?

I reply telling Jake that I'll be twenty minutes before jumping into the shower and trying to ignore everything that happened downstairs.

Tomorrow everything's going to change, but tonight I can enjoy spending time with my friends. I have no idea when I'll get the chance again, so I need to make the most of it.

11

CAMILA

I stayed up too late working, and when my alarm first goes off the next morning, I turn it off and roll over. Bad idea.

When reality comes crashing down, I sit bolt upright in bed and realize that I've only got thirty minutes to get to class.

"Fuck." I jump from bed, drag some clothes on and pull my hair up into a messy bun. I'm still brushing my teeth as I run for my car and throw it into reverse.

The hallways are empty as I run toward my physics class.

Everyone turns to look at me as I crash through the door, and I want the ground to swallow me up. I look terrible, I'm well aware of that. That last thing I want is everyone judging me for it.

"Good morning, Camila. How nice of you to join us."

"I'm so sorry, sir. Problem with my alarm."

"You haven't missed much, go and take your seat."

I breathe a sigh of relief that he's not going to roast me for it and do as I'm told. All sets of eyes in the room follow my journey. Well, all but one. The set of eyes I expected to torment me, or to be filled with joy that I'm once again in trouble, stay locked down on the desk in front of him.

Don't get me wrong, it's not that I wanted to look into Mason's dark, hate filled eyes after the morning I've had, I just find it bizarre after the interactions I've had with him the last few days.

Ignoring whatever it is that twists at my insides, I drop down into my seat at the desk next to his and pull my books out.

I'm just reading through the information on the board, hoping I can catch up, when I feel his stare.

Glancing at him out of the corner of my eye, my breath catches at the look on his face. He looks exhausted. His eyes are dark, the shadows around them even darker, and his mouth is turned down at the edges. It's so weird seeing that look on his usual cheerful, if not tormenting, face.

The sudden urge to ask if he's okay is all-consuming, but I force my lips to stay firmly shut for two reasons. One, I don't want to be caught talking after already being late, and two, I shouldn't care.

His eyes bore into mine as our connection holds, and I can't help but wonder what he sees staring back at him. I fear it's just the girl he hates who he thinks ruined his life. He's not stupid, he must know I had nothing to do with that. I guess it's just my connection to the man who had a hand in everything.

I let out a sigh and turn back toward the board. I don't want to fall even more behind than I already am.

I don't see Mason for the rest of the day, but when I catch up with Amalie outside her locker at the end of school, I learn the reason for the look on Mason's face. It seems that he, Ethan, and Jake had one too many last night.

"They're all hanging out of their arses," she says in her British accent that always makes me smile.

"On a school night? I thought they were more sensible than that. Did something happen?"

"Not that I'm aware of. Coach has been pushing them hard for Friday's game. I think they just needed to blow off some steam. They're all regretting it today though."

If I had any sympathy for how Mason looked this morning, then it's gone the second Amalie told me it was a hangover. Fucking idiots.

"Have you decided if you're coming Friday night?"

"No, I—"

"Come on, Cami. Don't miss something you love because Mason's being a dick."

"It's not him, it's…" I wrack my brain for a reason before the conversation with my parents last night comes back to me. "My dad's kinda lost his job."

"Oh shit, I'm so sorry," she says genuinely as we make her way to my car.

"It's not quite that dramatic, I don't think."

"Oh?"

I wait until we're in my car until I explain about New York.

"Woohoo, house party at Camila's," she says with a laugh. "You must be buzzing about getting some time to yourself."

Truth is, I am. My parents can be a little overbearing, but as it is, they're hardly home when I am. I doubt I'm going to see much of a difference aside from them not stumbling their way into the house in the early hours of Sunday morning after whatever event they've attended has come to an end.

"It'll be good. I'll be able to focus on homework and graduating."

"Plus, you can have me there whenever the hell you like."

"As if you have time, you're always with Jake."

She's silent for a few moments, forcing me to look over to make sure she's okay.

"What is it?"

"I've been thinking about something recently, but I can't help thinking it's crazy."

"Go on, I like a bit of crazy."

"I've had all my parents' inheritance come through, and I want to invest some of it."

"Invest it how?" If she's about to ask me for stocks and shares advice, then she's going to be bitterly disappointed.

"In property."

"You want to buy a house?"

"Yeah. I figure that I'm eighteen and don't have to live with Gran, and Jake, well, he doesn't exactly have the world's greatest home, so I thought—"

"Hold the fucking phone. You're not talking about investing in a rental here, are you? You're suggesting buying a house for you and Jake to... live in?" The idea sounds so absurd coming from my mouth, but I realize that as I say the words, it's also actually kind of perfect.

"You think I'm insane, don't you?"

"If I didn't know you both then I'd say hands down yes. But actually, for the two of you, it could be incredible. So long as you don't fall out."

"We won't," she says with every confidence in her boyfriend. My stomach drops a little because it's the kind of confidence that I used to have in Noah, but seeing as he blew me off for his friends this afternoon after we agreed to spend time together, I'm starting to get more and more suspicious after everything that's happened.

"Does Jake know about this?"

"No, I haven't said anything yet."

"What about college?"

"That's what we need to figure out, but I'm pretty set on staying close so I can be here for Gran. There's a lot to consider."

"It all sounds very grown up."

"If I was still in London, I'd be living on my own right now at university. I don't really see it as any different, and Jake's basically been living on his own for years, so not much will change for him." Every time she mentions Jake's hidden life, my heart aches for him a little. Much like everyone else at school, I just thought he was a cold asshole. I had no idea what had been happening to him behind the scenes. Almost everyone still thinks that about him, there's only a select few of us that now know the truth about his life, and I can't help thinking that a stable life in his own home with Amalie will be incredible for him. Being abandoned in your uncle and aunt's damp trailer at the bottom of their garden is no way to live.

"You meeting Noah tonight?"

"Apparently not. He's busy."

"Oh right. Have you spoken to him properly about what happened at the party?"

I'm not sure what she means by properly, but no, I haven't brought it up again, or my growing suspicions that something isn't right with him.

"Nothing to talk about."

"If you say so. Fancy a milkshake before we're forced to do more schoolwork?"

"I don't think I can say no to that."

I chuckle as I make the next right and head toward Aces. The boys are at practice, so I know I've got my best friend to myself for the next couple of hours and I intend on making the most of it.

We end up going back to her possible house purchase and find ourselves searching for houses on the outskirts of town so that it would be a reasonable distance to both Rosewood High and Maddison if they do end up going there. It's crazy that I'm not even eighteen yet and I'm sitting looking at houses. I thought this kind of thing was meant to happen way in the future. I guess it is for 'normal' kids, but with everything Amalie has been through and the amount of money sitting in her bank account, I guess she's anything but 'normal.'

By the time I get home, I know that I need to start on my homework if I've got any chance of getting a full night's sleep tonight.

I don't bother going to the kitchen and risk being distracted by whoever is crashing around in there and instead head straight for my room.

I'm not a nerd. Well, I don't think I am, but I'm also not one of those students who leaves everything to the last minute and hope that it's going to be okay. I pride myself on being organized, on doing my homework the night it's assigned then sitting back knowing that I'm sorted and can enjoy my weekends. Alyssa is the former, which is one of the reasons we started to grow apart even before Amalie arrived in town. She wanted to hang out every night of the week and then would spend all weekend trying to catch up. I hated it. So when Amalie appeared and turned out to be on my wavelength, I couldn't be happier. It's just a shame she was forced to start at Rosewood as a junior. If she were a senior, I think we'd have been great study partners.

My mind wanders back to when Mason and I first started at Rosewood. We'd hop off the bus and head for one of our houses so that we could do our homework together. My strength has always been English whereas his leaned toward math. We were a match made in heaven as we helped each other out and studied for tests together.

I let out a sad sigh. I miss those times. When I allow myself to think about it, I miss a lot of things that used to involve Mason.

Pushing my thoughts aside, I look down at my calendar to see what I'm going to do first when a knock sounds out from my bedroom door.

"Yeah," I call seconds before Mom pokes her head inside.

"Hey, sweetie. Good day at school?"

"Yeah, not bad. You had a good day?"

She lets out a sigh that tells me all I need to know and falls down onto my bed. "Sorting out your dad's stuff. It kind of feels like he's moving out. I hate it."

I walk over to the bed and wrap my arm around her shoulders. "I thought you were okay with this?" She seemed so set on the idea when we all spoke yesterday.

"I am. I think it's a fantastic opportunity for your dad. I'm so proud of him. I just want to be a part of all his new experiences."

"He'll make sure you are. Plus, you can go with him and experience it firsthand as often as you like."

"I don't want to abandon you."

"Mom," I start but pause to consider my words. I don't want to hurt her; it appears she's already having a hard enough day. "Please don't take this the wrong way, but you're not here all that much now. You spend evenings and weekends either planning or attending events, and Dad's been working more late nights than ever."

"You're right," she breathes, regret filling her voice. "We haven't been here enough for you."

"No, that's not what I'm saying." And exactly why I wanted to choose my words carefully. "You're both incredible parents. I'm lucky to have you." That's been proven so much more obvious as I've learned of Amalie and Jake's reality. I really am lucky to have two supportive parents who just want the best for me.

"Aw, Cami-bear." My heart twists at the nickname Mason made up for me back in the day that my mom picked up somewhere along the way. "Anyway, you're not going to be totally alone while we're gone." She glances at me nervously and I lift a brow at her, waiting for her to spill the beans, although from the glint in her eye, I don't think I'm going to like it. "It's just temporary, but the Paines are moving in. Just until they get themselves sorted," she rushes to add.

"No, no, no," I say, getting up from the bed and pacing in front of her. "I can't live with them... with *him*."

"Camila, I know it's not ideal but we're having to sell their house and I kind of sprung it on them, so it's only fair we help out where we can."

"Wait, *you're* selling *their* house?" Confusion mixes with my anger and I come to a stop in front of her.

"We bought it as an investment property when things got tough for Nicky when David left."

"Wow," I breathe. I really didn't see this coming. "So why can't they just go and rent somewhere else?" I spit, not wanting to have to deal with Mason on a daily basis.

Mom's face drops and I fear there's a lot more to this than she's letting on, or that she even knows. The image of Mason in his Price Chop uniform floats back into my mind. He was mortified at being discovered. I guess their issues run deeper than being abandoned by David after he lost his job. Suddenly his school night drinking session last night makes a little more sense. Is that how he decided to deal with this?

I shouldn't feel any sympathy for him. I don't want him here... I think. But knowing that his family is falling apart does tug at my heartstrings a little.

"They don't have anything, sweetheart. I'm pretty sure I speak for Nicky when I say that they'd rather not move into our house. But sometimes life just gets too tough and we all need to do things that we'd rather not."

"I get that, Mom. I do. And I'm all for helping out in their time of need but—"

"Mason," she finishes for me. "I can assure you that he wasn't all that thrilled by the idea either. That boy is so different to the sweet one we used to know. I don't expect him to cause you any issues, he wants to be here even less than you want him here."

"Not sure that's possible," I mumble. Falling down on the edge of my bed, my head falls back as I try to process all of this.

"Who knows," she says, staring off into space. "You might even find a way to rekindle your friendship."

"Yeah, maybe." Really un-fucking-likely, but I refrain from telling her that when she's got that twinkle of hope in her eye.

"You two were so sweet as kids. I really thought he'd end up being my son-in-law one day."

Me and you both.

"When are they moving in?"

"They're going to move stuff over the next few days with the intention of being in completely over the weekend. We've got builders starting renovations next week."

"Does it need a lot of work?" I ask. My memories of the place are that it wasn't all that different from this house. Warm, cozy, welcoming. But I guess that was a while ago.

"It just needs a little TLC. We'll have it on the market in no time and the money should help if your dad's job doesn't go as he's hoping."

I nod, because what else can I do? This decision has already been made, and me kicking up a fuss right now isn't going to change anything. They're probably all over there now packing up all their stuff ready for the big move.

A large ball of dread sits in the pit of my stomach. It's hard enough seeing Mason at school every day and wondering what the hell's going to come out of his mouth every time I pass him in the hall. What's it going to be like with him down the hall in my home?

Disaster.

It's the only thing it can be.

"I'm sorry to spring this on you. I know it's less than ideal, but everything will work out." She taps my thigh and stands. "Dinner will be about thirty minutes, sweetie. Do you need help with anything?" She glances at my books spread out across my desk.

"No, I'm good. I've got a report to start."

"Okay." She gets up and walks to the door, leaving me standing like a lost sheep in the middle of my room. "Everything will work out for the best, Cami. Everything happens for a reason, right?"

That's her little motto. And I must say that I'm usually happy to go along with it. But right now, I can see absolutely no good reason for Mason and me living under the same roof. It's got disaster and pain written all over it.

She closes the door behind her, and after blowing out a very long, frustrated breath I fall down onto my chair. I stare at my diary but no thoughts of what I might write fill my mind. I'm too lost to my memories.

We were nine, maybe ten. My parents had gone away for the weekend to celebrate their wedding anniversary. The Paines had agreed that they'd look after me so they could have an adults only weekend. I was buzzing as I packed my small bag and tucked my pillow and teddy bear under my arm, ready to walk down to their house. It wasn't the first time Mason and I had had a sleepover, but it was the first time we were allowed to be left alone for a few hours and to order in our dinner. It felt so grown up and my innocent mind wanted to pretend we were practicing for the future when we might have a house of our own and order takeout every night of the week.

His mom and dad were just going out for dinner. I think they were testing us to see if we could actually be left behind, but neither of us cared. We had the whole house to ourselves, free rein on the takeout menus and a stack of DVDs to get through.

There had been a storm warning all week, but we have yet to see any of it, and it was looking like it was starting to veer away from us, so no one thought any of it. We'd eaten our body weight in Chinese takeout and downed enough soda to rot every single one of our teeth, but we were on top of the freaking world as we ran around the house, dancing to music louder than we were usually allowed and just generally being crazy kids. It was incredible.

Until that storm hit.

Mason's parents were still out as the wind started roaring through the trees outside, some of the branches hitting the windows, making harrowing noises. The rain lashed down and from our seats on his couch we watched as it bounced off the ground outside. It was fine. We were in the house. We were safe and we were together. Then the lights went out.

I hate the dark. I always have. But being in the dark during a storm is so much worse. My heart was racing, my palms were sweating as I sat trembling beside Mason, who was vaguely aware of my fear seeing as he knew that I slept with a night light, but he had no idea the severity of it. The wind blew stronger, and noises that I was unable to identify sounded around us. We had no idea if the house was about to collapse on us or if some madman was about to crash through the front door and tear us limb from limb. I knew the thoughts were irrational, but the second darkness falls around me, even now, I'm frozen with fear as all these crazy images about what could happen to me fill my mind.

"I can't find the flashlight," Mason admitted after a quick search of the usual places.

"Candles?" I whimpered. I needed anything to cast a little light in the house, anything that could stop me falling headfirst into a debilitating panic attack.

"I don't know where the matches are."

"I'm scared," I admitted in a soft voice.

The next second, there he was, his body pressed up against mine, his arm around my shoulder.

"It'll be okay, Cami-bear. I'll keep you safe. I'll always keep you safe."

He held me until the lights eventually flickered back on. I have no idea how long we were in darkness for but thankfully the storm passed and his parents were able to make it home. The house didn't crumble around us and no one tried to kill us, but even to this day, being in the dark terrifies me. Those exact thoughts still haunt me. But that night, he made it all better. He distracted me with his warmth, kind words, and endless support.

I wonder what happened to that boy? I think as I stare out the window at his— my parents'—house. Is he still in there or has he been banished for good? His curtains are shut like always. It'll be weird to see them open again when someone else moves in.

"Dinner," Mom calls and I'm forced to abandon my pathetic attempt at starting my homework in favor of her tacos. It's no secret that they're my favorite and I wonder if she's done them tonight to soften the blow of the news about our new lodgers.

12

MASON

Mom's weirdly organized for this move. I wish she was as proactive about getting a fucking job, but as I arrive home from work late that night there seem to be boxes everywhere. This is the only house I've ever known. It's going to be weird walking away. I've got so many memories here, although not all of them good. Maybe a fresh start wouldn't be a bad thing. There's still evidence of my dad in the fabric of this building; maybe being away from that will have a positive influence on Mom. It's a long shot, but I can only hope. I worry that the reason she's so excited to move down the street is that she's expecting to have a few more babysitters for the kids she should be looking after. She's going to be seriously pissed off because it sounds like Gabriella and Clint are going to be spending most of their time in New York. I hope that doesn't mean she's going to expect Camila to pick up the slack in her childcare. I don't really want my brothers getting too attached to her.

"Can you make a start on your bedroom please, Mase?" Mom says when she sees me standing in the kitchen doorway watching her box up plates.

"Sure. What are you doing with all that?"

"Clint said we could store this kind of stuff and any furniture we want to keep in their garage."

"That was nice of him," I mutter, but she still hears it.

"Can you promise me something?"

"That all depends on what it is." Pulling the refrigerator open, I find a bottle of water and twist the top.

"Can you please be nice to them? They're doing us a huge favor... they've done us a huge favor. If they didn't buy this place after your dad walked out, then I have no idea what we'd have done."

"They only did it out of guilt."

"No, they didn't. They did it because they are nice, honest people. Mason," she says on a sigh, placing a bowl down and turning toward me. My breath catches because she looks more like the mom I remember than I've seen in years. "You need to stop blaming them for what happened. It was your dad who fucked up. He deserved to be caught and to be laid off."

"I don't disagree, Mom. It was just the way it was done. They went behind his back. That didn't need to happen. If they were more considerate about it all then he might still be here. This might not be happening right now." I wave my arm around at all the boxes.

"We're better off without him. He'd have ruined us no matter what."

"You really believe that?" She makes it out like it was all his fault. She seems to forget that the final nail in the coffin for Dad firmly rests on her shoulders.

"I do. Your childhood memories of him aren't the man he was."

I don't believe a word she says. My dad was a good man until everything went to shit. Okay, so he didn't have to leave, but Mom didn't give him much choice in the end.

When I allow myself to think of him, I see afternoons on a football field as he supported me either from the sidelines, out in the garden as he helped me practice plays, or on the computer as he taught me how to play games and baffled me with his tech knowledge that I didn't have a chance in hell of understanding, but it was what made him tick.

Leaving Mom behind with a couple of flat boxes in my hand, I head to my room. My entire childhood—my life—is in this one room. The thought of packing it all into the boxes propped up against the wall fills me with dread, although not as much dread as the prospect of where we're going to be moving to.

Falling down on my bed, I make the mistake of closing my eyes.

The next thing I know, the sun's pouring in around the edges of my curtains and my alarm is blaring loudly next to me.

Sitting up, I realize that I'm still in my Price Chop uniform and the boxes I left by the door are still there waiting to be filled.

"Fuck," I shout, dropping my head into my hands and scrubbing them down my face.

I'm fucking exhausted, but I can't see it getting better anytime soon. Heather was reluctant, but she agreed to let me pick up shifts at the store every day after school until closing. I promised her it was going to be a short term thing until I could get enough cash together to at least give us a deposit on a place. I refuse to allow my brothers to live in someone else's house because their parents are fuck-ups for too long.

Coach was less than pleased when I went to his office yesterday morning to explain that I was having to step down from the team. He was rightly concerned. He knows as well as I do that my only shot at college next year is a football scholarship, but what choice do I have? My family has to come first. I can always go to college in the future, but my brothers will never get a second chance at their childhood.

Ignoring the boxes, I drag my weary body toward the shower and start getting ready for another long ass day where I've not done the homework that's going to be expected of me and I work in a shitty discount store until I can't put one foot in front of the other.

Mom's nowhere to be seen when I eventually get downstairs with both Charlie and Ollie in tow. Thankfully, Ollie has a friend in the next street whose Mom picks them both up to take them to school. I have no idea how I'd cope if I had to do more than get them up and dressed.

"Good morning, my gorgeous boys."

"Mom? What are you doing up?"

"Don't looked so shocked, Mase. I am capable of getting up and making my boys breakfast."

"Really?"

Her eyebrows almost hit her hairline, although I have no idea why she's surprised. I can't remember the last time I saw her this side of midday. I know she worked late, but I'm sure there are other parents out there who do nights and still manage to be a parent.

"I thought I'd take my little men to school today."

A look passes between Ollie and Charlie. They look anything but pleased. What I wouldn't give to know what they're thinking right now.

"It's okay, Mrs. Richmond can take us."

Mom pales. "Oh, okay. Well, I'd like to pick you up."

Ollie blows out a frustrated breath, but he doesn't refuse.

I have no idea what she's up to, but quite frankly I don't have the time to sit around to find out. "Well, if you're making these guys breakfast, I'm going to head out."

Playing happy families was not on my to do list today. If I can get into school early, maybe I can hit the library and attempt to do some of the homework most other kids will manage while I'm working my ass off.

———

"What the fuck's going on?" Jake demands when he falls down into his seat in History later that morning. Our teacher is standing at the front of the class ready to start, but in true Jake Thorn style, he doesn't give a shit and stares me down until he gets the answers he wants.

"Not now," I mutter, knowing we're going to have people listening around us.

"Yes. Right fucking now. Let's go."

He's up and out of his chair with his bag over his shoulder waiting for me while Miss White's face turns beet red in frustration.

"Mason and I have another engagement," he barks as he all but pushes me through the doorway and away from our bewildered teacher.

"We can't just walk out."

"Why the fuck not? You can't tell me you actually wanted to be sitting in there." I open my mouth to respond, but I don't really have an argument. Where I really want to be is in bed sleeping, but knowing my luck, it's probably already been moved into the Lopezes' garage.

Silence hangs heavy between us as we walk out toward the field. The stadium's deserted and I realize that was Jake's plan. To get me alone and get the truth out of me.

"Coach said you'd bailed on the team. What the fuck don't I know, Mase? I know I've been spending more time with Brit but fuck, man. If you need me, you know where I am."

I blow out a long breath, turning away from his assessing blue eyes and stare across the field.

"Everything's fucked up. Mom's lost her job. The Lopezes own our house and are selling it, and with no other fucking option we're all moving in with them."

Jake doesn't respond immediately, and when I turn to him, he's sitting with his mouth agape as if he can't find the right words.

"I've had to increase my hours at the store in an attempt to do something. I can't fucking stay under the same roof as them."

"You mean as her?"

"Yes. No. I don't fucking know." I stand and shove my hands into my hair. "I don't know anything right now other than I've had to give up the one thing that keeps me going in order to bail my fucking mother out again. This is my senior year. It shouldn't be like this."

"I know, man. Trust me, I know."

I turn to look at my best friend with frown lines marring his forehead. I know that out of everyone, he understands, but his sympathy isn't going to help me right now.

"How much do you need? Maybe you could ask Bri—"

"No. No fucking way am I asking your girlfriend for a handout. I'm not a fucking charity case."

"I know that, and it would only be a loan until you get yourself sorted."

"And how exactly would I pay it back? We need every penny I can earn for rent, bills and food."

He blows out a breath. "I just need you on the field."

"I know. I need to be there too, but something's got to give."

"This is bullshit."

I fall back down beside him as the silence stretches out as we contemplate the lives we've been dealt, even though Jake's is very much looking up these days.

"How long do you think it'll be before you fuck her?"

"What?" I blanch. "I'm not going to fuck her. Kill her maybe," I muse.

"Whatever. Getting a bit of action might help chill you out a little though." I give him a side eye and he just shrugs. "You coming to Ethan's party Friday night? Maybe you could pull and blow off some steam."

"I'll be working."

"Come after. You know it'll be an all nighter if Ethan has anything to do with it."

The thought of going and having fun with our class and watching them all down drink after drink and act like they've got no cares in the world doesn't thrill me with joy, but what's my alternative? A night in the Lopezes' guest room?

———

The next thing I know, it's Friday night, my stuff is all packed into boxes in my room ready to be moved up the street, and I'm standing behind the checkout in Price Chop when I should be on the field with my team trying to kick Penshore's asses.

Amalie keeps messaging me and I keep checking my cell to see the score even though it kills me to know what they're achieving without me. Seeing that they're winning is bittersweet. Of course I want them to win. I want them to walk all over the Chargers after they knocked us out last year, but I hate that they don't need me. Being a Rosewood Bear gave me something to belong to when my life has felt like it's spiraling out of control, and I don't want to be disposable to them much like I am to some of the people in my life.

Yes, my mother relies on me, but it's not me she needs, she just needs someone. Camila doesn't need me. She moved on with her life pretty fast after I gave her the cold shoulder. My brothers need me, but that's only because our parents are fuck-ups. What they really need is a decent Mom and Dad.

A couple of customers walk up to me and I'm forced out of my depressing thoughts so I can scan their items.

My cell vibrates in my pocket again with another update, and my fingers twitch to pull it out midway through checking, but the last thing I need is to be caught and fired.

I end up with a line, and by the time I get to pull my cell out again, it's vibrated at least six times and the game's long over. Shame my shift isn't.

A smile curls at the corners of my lips when I look down at Amalie's penultimate message telling me that we smashed it. My chest swells with pride for the team, who for all intents and purposes are my family, but sadness that I'm not a part of their elation right now sits heavy in my stomach.

Amalie: We'll see you at Ethan's, yeah?

I stare down at her message. I'm tempted, but I'm pretty sure it's the prospect of drinking my body weight in alcohol that makes Ethan's party seem appealing more than spending time with my classmates who'll probably spend the night asking where I was tonight.

The rest of my shift drags on until eventually the clock hits midnight and at least I'm able to help Heather close up for the night and head home.

My eyes are heavy as I drive from the west side of town toward our street. The only house I've ever called home looks different as I pull up in the drive. We haven't even moved out and yet it feels like it should belong to someone else already. The connection I've always felt to the place, to my dad, has already been broken. That feeling is only strengthened when I step into my sparse bedroom. The only thing that remains is my bed; everything else is gone. Mom told me that Clint and a few friends were coming today to clear the place, but I didn't want to believe it. I wanted to believe that this was all one big joke and I'd come home to Mom laughing about it while telling me about her new job. Sadly, that's not the case. After poking my head into my brothers' room, I find that totally empty along with Mom's, and I know they've already moved out.

I stand surrounded by nothing but old memories and realize I have two options: I stay here alone and miserable, or I find alcohol and a distraction or two. The second option wins out.

13

CAMILA

It takes all of about five seconds after the Bears hit the field to notice something—or someone—is missing.

"Where's Mason?" I ask, turning toward Amalie who's shouting and screaming along with the crowd. It a far cry from the girl I dragged along to the first few games of the series.

"He uh..." A conflicted look crosses her face. "He wasn't able to play tonight." I narrow my eyes at her but don't press the issue. It's obvious she knows more than she's letting on but has promised Jake she'll keep Mason's secrets. I should respect that she's being loyal, but mostly it just pisses me off.

Mason's not one to miss a game. It took everything we all had to stop him playing with a broken collarbone back when we were friends. Nothing short of a disaster would keep him from the field.

I briefly wonder if his reaction to having to move in with us is enough to do it, but I can't imagine he's anything but thrilled that he gets to torment me under my own roof for the foreseeable future.

The game is incredible. Our Bears are all over their Chargers, and Jake is on fire as he leads our team to an outstanding win. Amalie screams beside me for her man until her throat must be hoarse. He's in for a good night once she gets her hands on him, that's for sure. Jealousy stirs within me knowing that neither of them are going to be able to keep their hands off each other whereas my boyfriend didn't bother traveling for this away game. I know it's out of town, but I was driving no matter what, he could have at least showed his face. He's been irritating me more and more this week, and I hate that it's Mason's words that ring out in my head every time I even think about him.

We usually hang out quite often, but I feel like I've hardly seen Noah this week. I know I've had stuff going on and some of that's on me, but still, I haven't seen him long enough to even begin to explain about Mason moving in, and I need to because he needs to hear from me that his presence in my house isn't going to affect us. Noah's never been the kind of guy to get jealous. Our relationship's been so steady and easy that neither of us has needed to. But equally, neither of us has had to live with our ex-best friends who could quite easily have been more, either. If he finds out from someone else and assumes that I've been lying to him then it's really not going to look good.

When I asked him if he was going to Ethan's after we all get back later, he just mumbled a maybe. Not exactly the kind of response I was looking for.

"Come on, we need to meet the guys."

"You mean you need to shove your tongue down Jake's throat the second he appears."

"Yeah, that." She doesn't even attempt to apologize, instead just grabs my hand and drags me from the stands. Penshore clearly has more money than Rosewood does. Its football stadium is seriously impressive and huge in comparison to ours, and while it would take us barely five minutes to find where the guys will exit at home, here it's almost fifteen.

Much to Amalie's delight, we're just in time and the guys come barreling out all fresh from their showers with wide smiles on their faces as they laugh and joke with each other, celebrating their win.

Jake takes one look at his girl heading his way and takes off running until he scoops her up in his arms and spins her around while she squeals.

I smile as I watch them, but it doesn't get rid of the heavy feeling in my stomach.

Because Jake is a law unto himself, he manages to get both himself and Ethan excused from traveling home in the school bus with the rest of the team. I soon discover why, because I haven't pulled out of Penshore's parking lot before he's got Amalie pinned to the backseat.

"Really?" I bark.

"What? I'm celebrating our win. You watched, it was fucking epic. I deserve this."

"I'm not denying that, but maybe you do deserve it in private later."

Jake flips me off over his shoulder and I blow out a long, frustrated breath.

"You jealous? I'm sure we could solve that, baby." Ethan's hand stretches between the console between us as if he's going for my thigh. I slap it away like it's a wild animal.

"Ow," he complains, rubbing the back of his hand. "You only had to say no." He sulks while the lip smacking behind continues.

"No," I state. "Not in a million years." I glance over at him, ensuring disgust fills my eyes.

"So where's your *lovely* boyfriend tonight? Too busy to escort you to the game?"

"Busy with friends."

"Well at least we know he wasn't with a certain cheerleader, seeing as she was shaking her pom poms for a crowd with us."

A loud slap rings out around the car before Ethan complains once again.

"Shut the fuck up, man," Jake says between his heavy breathing.

"What? I was just saying what we were all thinking."

My stomach turns over to the point I think I might puke in my lap. Is that what everyone thinks of me? Am I that girl who just turns a blind eye to my boyfriend's actions because I'm stupid and trust him?

"He's just being a dick, Cam. Ignore him." Amalie's hand lands on my shoulder in support. Although from the things she's said about the situation, I suspect she's on Ethan's side.

"You all think I'm stupid, don't you?"

"Only you know the real situation and the real Noah," Amalie soothes. "If you say he's trustworthy, then we support you, one-hundred percent. Right, guys?"

"Right," Jake agrees. Not that he has much choice. He's more clever than to go against Amalie and end up with blue balls until the end of time.

"Sure. But if it all goes south, hit me up. I can make you feel so good about it all, baby."

My lips curl in disgust. "You're a dog."

Conversation turns to tonight's game and I mostly zone everyone out as I stew on my current situation. That on top of not knowing where Mason was tonight is enough to have the beginnings of a headache throbbing at my temples. I want to ask about him, I'm desperate to, but I know how it'll look to the guys, so as much as it pains me, I keep my lips sealed.

"Pizza. I need pizza," Ethan suddenly chirps when we head toward a restaurant.

"Don't you need to be back to let people into your house?"

"Nah, they all know what they're doing. Come on, you guys must be hungry."

Sounds of agreement ring out around the car, and I find myself pulling into the parking lot so we can feed the beast.

I try to allow their excitement over their win to filter into me, but the truth is that Ethan's words about Noah are on repeat in my head. We know he wasn't with her, but where was he tonight? Where's he been all week?

I fucking hate questioning him. He told me he was meeting friends to do some homework. Never before would I have questioned him. He's got a plan for next year and he needs the grades, I've always appreciated that, but now, after what Mason did and accused him of, I just don't know anymore. Everything's festering inside me and it's making what I feel for my boyfriend turn sour, which is ridiculous because he's not done anything wrong. Or has he?

"Mason would have fucking loved tonight. I hate that he's not here." Those few words from Ethan are enough to drag me back to the present.

"I know, but he's got to do his thing. Hopefully he'll be back," Jake says sadly, but from the tightness of his features I'm not sure I believe him.

"What the fuck's he got going on? Banging some hot chick we don't know about who's more important than us?"

My spine stiffens and Amalie doesn't miss it. I shouldn't give a shit. Just like Ethan, it's no secret that Mason's made his way around the cheer squad and half the female population at Rosewood. Hearing this isn't unusual, but why do I suddenly care so much?

"Ha, nothing like that, man. Just family shit, you know how it is."

If I wasn't watching Ethan quite so closely for his response then I might miss the brief darkening of his eyes and the way his muscles tense for the slightest moment. He shakes himself out of whatever it is quickly before saying, "Yeah. I get that. Sucks though."

"What family shit have you got to worry about? Your dad's filled your bank account and leaves you a mansion of a house to party in most weekends?" Jake says it lightheartedly but Ethan pales nonetheless.

"It's not all about money."

"Don't I know it."

The atmosphere around our table suddenly takes a depressing turn. I glance at Amalie, who shrugs a shoulder at me.

"So... one step closer to the playoffs then. You think you guys can hit top spot in the division this year?"

It takes a few minutes, but eventually, with the subject back on football, the air lightens and their previous excitement wins out.

With my belly bloated with pizza and soda, we head back to the car, ready to hit Ethan's house to party.

I'll admit that I've never really thought about him and his home situation that much. He's always living it up with his lavish parties and throwing money around, but hearing him talk about his parents' absence, it suddenly makes me realize how lonely his life must be aside from the wild parties. It makes me wonder how much of the real Ethan we all actually see. He's the joker, the one who gives zero fucks about everything; is he hiding his reality just as much as Jake was?

His mammoth house appears before us as the gravel of his driveway crunches under my tires. There are already people everywhere, and all the lights in the house are glowing from the windows. It looks like they've started without us.

I park my car, blocking in about five others when Ethan tells me just to stop in favor of jumping out.

"I can't just leave—"

"It's fine. None of these people will be leaving until morning," Jake says, also getting out and dragging Amalie with him.

This might be my first time attending one of Ethan's parties, but I'm not naive as to what they're like. Stories fly around for days after one of his blow outs. I can't say that I haven't been curious about experiencing one for myself, but being in the wrong friendship group as well as staying as far away from Mason as possible meant that I've never stepped foot inside Ethan's house before.

"You coming?" Amalie shouts back, making Jake pause halfway to the house.

Dragging my eyes away from the building that must be at least four times the size of my parents' house, I pull the keys from the ignition and step out.

Kids loiter around the outside of the house, some just chatting to friends, others clearly already so drunk they can hardly stand up straight. *How long has this party been going on for exactly?* I wonder as we walk past everyone and follow behind Ethan, who throws the door open and holds his arms out in a 'the king is home' stance.

People look our way immediately, as if they can feel both his and Jake's presence, and cheers erupt.

Even from behind, I watch as Ethan's chest puffs out in pride while Jake pulls Amalie into his side and they duck off to the right. Not wanting to be part of the 'Ethan show,' I trail behind them until they come to a stop by a keg and Jake gets us all a drink.

"So this is an Ethan Savage party then?" I look around the room as the pounding music rattles my bones.

Scantily clad women fill the vast space, some hanging off guys, others dancing and drinking together. When I find Ethan again, he's in the middle of a group of girls wearing only bikinis. They all rub themselves up against him and he eagerly kisses one. My eyes widen. I know he's got a reputation, everyone at Rosewood knows that, but to see it with my own eyes is a bit of a shock. It seems I may have lived a somewhat sheltered life with my group of friends.

A red Solo cup is thrust in my hand, and in only a few minutes, I find it's empty. Turning back to Jake and Amalie, I find them tongue tied again, so after getting myself two more cups of beer, I head off on my own to explore the place in the hope I find some other friends who aren't going to spend the night sucking each other's faces off.

As I make my way through the house, I find I recognize about fifty percent of the people here. Fuck knows where the others have come from. I can only assume they're from the west side and living it up east style.

I don't find any of my friends, and even after the rest of the team appears, it soon becomes clear that Shane's also swerved this party.

The beer goes down a little too well, and by the time I find Amalie again in the kitchen she's watching Jake and a couple of other members of the team lining up shots of tequila.

"Hey, beautiful. How's it going?" Zayn, our wide receiver, slurs, wrapping his arm around my waist.

"Fine," I reply, my spine stiffening as I try to remove his hands from my body.

His hold tightens and I find myself pressed up against his body. "I haven't seen you here before."

"No, but you're in my math class and I've got a boyfriend."

"That won't stop him," someone calls from behind me.

"Well, it matters to me." I finally manage to escape his hold and move to the other side of Amalie.

Reaching out, I grab one of the shots in front of her before downing it and going for another. I hope like hell that the alcohol helps me find the fun in this party, because right now I can't think of anything that could make this evening worse.

I just knock back the second shot when silence falls over the room.

"Mason, my man! We missed you tonight."

Every muscle in my body locks up tight just hearing his name. I haven't been this close to him since the morning after the night he found his way into my bedroom. Yeah, I've seen him around school and in classes, but he's mostly kept his head down. I can only assume that's got something to do with his new living accommodation. I can't forget about the fact that in only hours, he's going to be moving into my house.

His eyes find mine and a shudder runs down my spine. How the hell are we going to survive each other living under the same roof?

"Yeah well, I couldn't let you fuckers party without me as well. Who's got the good stuff?" Prying his eyes away from mine, he glances around the room.

I spin on the spot, reaching for another shot and downing it instantly. I don't even feel the burn like I did with the previous two.

My head spins but I welcome the distraction. The sensible thing to do right now would be to call an Uber and leave, but something tells me to stay. Some fucked up part of me wants to experience this party and all it has to offer. I tell myself that's got nothing to do with the guy who's just entered, but I'm not so sure that's true. I'm desperate to know why he bailed on tonight's game but is seemingly okay to turn up here ready to drink.

A shiver runs down my spine seconds before his scent fills my nose. I suck in a deep breath and hold it, not knowing what's about to happen.

"Why the fuck are you wasting this stuff on the likes of her?" Disdain drips from his words, making Amalie's mouth drop open and the muscle in Jake's neck pulsate.

"Play nice," Jake barks. "Hopefully this will chill you the fuck out." He hands Mason a shot.

He lifts it in the air as if he's going to make some big speech, but when he doesn't say anything, I stupidly look over my shoulder. His eyes find mine and they hold for a second too long, his dark ones becoming almost black as something unpleasant crackles between us.

Every dread I had about what we've got to come once he moves in quadruples in those few seconds before he drags his eyes away and downs his shot. The muscles in his neck ripple as he swallows, and I hate myself for not being able to look away.

"I need more than that."

Jake sets about fulfilling Mason's request to get steaming drunk as the song booming from the speakers in the other room changes.

"Come on, let's dance." Amalie grabs my hand and drags me away to where we can see a makeshift dance floor.

"Did someone say dance?" Zayn calls. I look back to see him bouncing toward us like an overexcited puppy, but the heated stare coming from behind him that burns into me soon catches my attention.

I knew coming here was a bad idea. It's a real shame that I'm already too drunk to really care or do anything about it.

Amalie drags me in front of her, and, with our hands locked together, we start moving to the music. Zayn comes up behind me, places his hands on my hips and joins in. I should push him away. I should be thinking about Noah, but in that moment, all I think about and feel is the beat of the music pounding through me and the way my body moves.

One song blurs into another. Zayn continues to grind behind me, and eventually I feel Amalie move away from me. When I drag my eyes open I understand why when Jake pulls her back into him and they move smoothly together.

My heart aches as I stare at them so in sync, so connected, so in love. Whereas I'm here dancing with a guy I barely like and no idea where my actual boyfriend is.

The thought is sobering at best, and after detaching myself from Zayn, I head back to where the alcohol was. The tequila bottle is laying empty on the counter, so I'm forced to take a beer when someone offers it to me.

"Careful who you take drinks from. You don't know who's been here before." I look up to find a junior with a smirk on his face. "Oh, that's right. Shane's not here."

"Shane didn't do that," I seethe. "He's not like that."

"Facts speak for themselves though, don't you think."

"Fuck you."

The guy's eyes widen slightly but he doesn't respond, instead grabbing two cups of his own and stalking from the kitchen.

With two cups in hand, I lean against the wall and watch the bodies dancing and gyrating against each other. Some of the scantily clad girls from outside seem to have appeared and are hanging off most of the football team, hoping to get lucky. Seeing all the bare skin makes me realize that the cheer team are nowhere to be seen. I can't believe they'd miss one of Ethan's parties.

Someone walking through one of the many doors that leads to the garden catches my eyes.

"Noah?" I ask, even though he's too far away and the music's too loud for him to hear me. My brows draw together as he sways his way toward me, looking three sheets to the wind already. So much for him not coming, it seems he's been partying for quite some time.

He doesn't say anything as he steps up to me. Instead he wraps his hand around the back of my neck and pulls my lips to his. He's forceful in a way I've never experienced before, but I put it down to the alcohol and allow myself to melt into him.

His other hand grips my hip as his tongue delves into my mouth. The taste of strong alcohol explodes on my taste buds, and that's saying something because I've had enough now to make the world spin around me.

I must have somehow managed to get the cups I was holding onto the table beside me, because the next thing I know, I'm back on the dance floor moving against Noah. My body follows orders but for some reason my brain screams that I shouldn't be doing this.

Why isn't it as fun as when I was dancing with Zayn?

I look up to find Noah's kind eyes in the hope it'll settle whatever is going on in my head, but I don't make it that far. Instead my gaze falls on Chelsea and her team's grand entrance. I stifle a giggle because she can only be so grand while hobbling along on two crutches. The image of Jake pushing her from the stage at Homecoming fills my mind, and my previous laugh falls from my lips. It really was a fall from grace for our queen bitch.

Flanking her sides is Tasha and Shelly followed by the rest of the team. Everyone but Chelsea is only dressed in their bikinis, and water droplets from the pool glisten under the spotlights.

There's a lull in the noise level as they enter, exactly as Chelsea would want it, and almost every set of eyes turn their way. Breasts get pushed out and hair is flipped over shoulders. It's really quite a sight to behold, and it only makes me glad I never pursued wanting to be a member of the team. When I was seven or eight, I thought it would be a great idea, especially because it would keep me close to Mason, but it wasn't long before I discovered that I wasn't the kind of girl that belonged on the squad. I don't care all that much about my appearance and I certainly have no intention of sleeping my way around the entire class, evidenced by my intact virginity. I wonder briefly if that's what Noah's intensity tonight is about. Is he hoping that I'll get drunk tonight and give it up? Well, if that's the case, he can think again. I've got too many questions running around my head about him to do that. Until I can get Mason's warning from repeating in my mind that most definitely isn't happening. I don't care how blue his balls are.

I follow the squad's progress as they make their way through the room. A couple drop off to find their boyfriends or the guys they're dating, but Chelsea seems to have a destination in mind because she doesn't stop hopping until she reaches it.

Oh fuck.

Mason.

He's standing at the edge of the room watching everyone, much like I was a few moments ago, but the crowd hid him from me.

Chelsea somehow manages to maneuver herself so she's pressed right up against him while Shelly takes his other side. It leaves Tasha standing somewhat awkwardly in front of the trio. She hovers for a few seconds in her skimpy red bikini before looking over her shoulder and directly behind me. Noah noticeably tenses as their eyes meet. Mine narrow at her but at no point does she look at me before she flicks her hair over her shoulder and saunters off.

I should say something. I should accuse him after letting him off so easily at his birthday, and with the alcohol fueling my thoughts I'm just about to—that is until Chelsea frees one of her hands and threads it into Mason's hair. His body stills for a beat like he's not really all that happy about her attention. He glances up and our eyes collide. I shouldn't be watching this car crash, and that one look he gives me really shouldn't hit like a baseball bat to the chest, but I'm powerless to pull my eyes away as an evil smirk appears on his lips before he lowers his head and gives Chelsea exactly what she wants.

My stomach turns over, threatening to expel the alcohol sloshing around in it as even from here I watch his tongue slide in her mouth.

Suddenly I'm fourteen again and I'm watching my best friend, the boy who gave me my first kiss, flaunting how much he hates me in public. Anger bubbles within me, my veins turning red as lava fills them, and I spin in Noah's arms.

Concern twists his features. He watched every moment of what happened just like I did, but also unlike me, he's not questioning any of it. *It's because he's covering something up*, a voice screams in my head, but at this moment, I ignore her.

Reaching up on my tiptoes, I find his lips and kiss him as eagerly as I was just subjected to watch Chelsea kiss Mason.

My heart pounds, my temperature increases, but it's got nothing to do with Noah and everything to do with *him* and what he may or not be doing behind me.

I'm still kissing Noah when I drag my eyes open, and to my shock I find his wide and staring over my shoulder.

Is he watching us?

Breaking away, I drag some much needed air into my lungs. I wait what I think is a suitable amount of time, but in reality, I'm drunk as fuck and it could be immediately that I look over my shoulder to find what, or who, has his interest.

There's no one there.

I scan the room, but I can't see Mason, Chelsea, Shelly or Tasha anywhere.

Noah's phone vibrates in his pocket between us. I look back to him as he pulls it out. His eyes are swimming with desire, but there's also something else in their depths that I'm too far gone to decipher.

"It's one of the guys wanting to know where I am. I'll be back. Get us a drink, yeah?"

Then as quick as he appeared, he's gone, disappeared into the crowd, leaving me standing alone with my chest heaving and my head spinning with confusion and anger.

What the hell just happened?

Not wanting to stand like a loner, I walk toward the drinks and grab myself another beer—not that I need it. My previous drinks are swirling around my stomach and making my head spin pretty bad. I've been drunk before, but I don't remember my surroundings moving quite this much.

I drink the beer faster than I intended as I try to find someone I actually like, but I come up short. The only person I spot that I know and would possibly talk to is Ethan, but he's otherwise engaged with the three—yes three—girls he's dancing with and molesting. They're lapping up his attention as they practically strip him naked on the couch.

He must realize he's got another's attention because he looks up and finds me staring.

"Always room for another, Cam-Cam." He opens his arms wide as if trying to prove his point, but all it achieves is making my feet move faster.

With my need for the toilet starting to get the better of me, I go in search of a bathroom. I find a huge line for the one in this floor, but knowing just how big this house is I know there's more.

I just about manage to put one foot in front of the other to climb the stairs, and with the help of the gold handrail I eventually stumble into the second floor hallway.

"Jesus," I mutter as I stare down the long hall that's lined with doors.

There are a few people up here, most kissing and stumbling toward what they're hoping are empty bedrooms.

Ignoring them, I set out on my quest. Avoiding any doors that are shut, fearing what I might find behind them, I go for the open ones. I get an eyeful when I poke my head into a couple that I was not expecting, and even the ginormous family bathroom has a couple going at it on the tiled floor, but eventually, right at the end I find an empty bedroom with what looks like an en suite.

Breathing a sigh of relief, I stumble into the room, managing to catch my toe on the corner of the bed and face planting the floor.

"Ow," I complain, trying to grab my toe to inspect the damage but not managing to find it.

Giving up, I crawl to the door at the other end of the room.

My fingers don't want to follow instruction and it takes me about a year to pop the button on my jeans and shimmy them down my legs. But eventually I manage to do my business. I have no idea how long I sit there for, but when a noise sounds in the bedroom I just came through, I can't be sure I didn't fall asleep a little bit.

I manage to get my jeans up without making friends with the floor and step from the room when the two people that crashed inside become clear.

"Mason?"

14

MASON

I know the second I walk into Ethan's back garden that this is a bad idea. The cheer team are slutting it up in the pool—well, all but Chelsea, who's sulking with a drink on a lounger seeing as she can't get her cast wet.

They all shout for me to join them as well as questions about where I was tonight. Ignoring them in favor of drinking everything about my life away, I go in search of the alcohol. I know Ethan's house well, and if something doesn't get placed in my hand the second I walk into the kitchen then I'll go and find my own. His dad might think his office is secure, but the three of us know differently.

She's the only person I see when I walk into that kitchen, and damn her because the second I look into her eyes and see just how drunk she is, my need to get obliterated is overtaken by my stupid need to protect her. It's been four years. At what point can I actually stop caring?

I take the shot that Jake hands me, but after we watch both Amalie and Camila leave the room, I refuse any more. Jake doesn't question it. He knows I like to stay sober in case my brothers need me.

The whole night is a waste of fucking time, but it only gets worse when I stumble across Camila with her fucking boyfriend. Their hips grind together in time with the music like I'm sure they've done a million times before. My fingers twitch to rip her away from him for ever getting to touch her like that. They've been together for years now, I'm sure he's well acquainted with her body. My lips curl in disgust that someone else has been able to explore what should have been mine.

Because my life isn't already bad enough, I stay exactly where I am, leaning against the wall watching them. It's fucking torture but no less than I deserve.

The second the noise level dips and the sea of people in front of me part, I know I'm in trouble. Chelsea's eyes lock onto mine, and like a lion stalking her prey, she hops over to me.

Something burns down my spine as she gets closer, and a glance over her shoulder confirms that I've managed to get Camila's attention.

Happy to flaunt your cheating boyfriend in my face? I can do better.

Chelsea's a slut, almost all the cheer squad are, but she's one I've only had a few 'moments' with seeing as prior to Amalie's appearance, she only had eyes for Jake. Since he's now quite obviously taken, she seems to have set her sights on me. I, however, have no intention of receiving anything from her aside from the odd blow job if she really insists because damn, she's fucking good at them. Must be all the practice she's had.

I'm not proud of my actions, but with Camila's stare burning into me, I slam my lips down on Chelsea's. I regret it the second her sickly sweet perfume fills my nose and her fake ass nails dig into my skin.

It's worth it for all of a second when I see the mortified look on Camila's face. But that second is soon over because she firmly plants her lips on that motherfucker's, and I'm forced to watch him kiss her while he stares longingly across the room at Tasha.

Anger has my body trembling. My need to go and rip him from her and rearrange his face again is strong. But she chose not to believe me the last time, so why should I waste the energy in trying to show her what he really is?

Instead, I rip myself away from both Chelsea and Shelly, who's now joining in and rubbing my cock through my jeans, and storm from the room. I leave Chelsea sulking behind me but Shelly must decide it's her turn for a bit of one on one time because she follows me.

I need a drink, but the last thing I want is to not be aware of what I'm doing right now. I've made plenty of bad decisions in my life, but I don't want tonight to be one of them.

I walk around the house hoping to find Jake and Amalie while Shelly follows me like a lost fucking puppy. It's sad, really fucking sad, but I allow her to trail me thinking that I might be able to make use of her.

The moment I see Camila attempting to climb the stairs, I realize that she could be about to come in very handy.

"You wanna head upstairs?" Shelly's eyes light up like I've just offered her my lottery win, but I don't feel bad about using her weakness. I'm probably saving her from one of the assholes down here who'll really use her if she gives them half the chance.

Taking her hand, I pull her up the stairs, making sure I stop to find an empty room, but I know the one I want. Ethan's is right at the end of the hall and everyone knows it's off limits. Everyone aside from the person I've just seen disappear inside.

"Mase, we can't, that's Eth—" Case in point about his room being off limits.

"I'm his best friend. The rules don't apply, baby." My stomach turns with saying those words to her, and to make my point, I tilt her head up and kiss her as I back her into the room. She soon sags against me, willing to give me everything I want.

I worry about Chelsea and her squad of hussies. They're going to get themselves into some serious trouble one day if they continue being so free and easy.

I slam her back against the door to make our appearance known, and it works like a fucking charm because only a few seconds later, Camila appears in the doorway.

"Mason?"

I glance at her, my lips still attached to Shelly's, and I don't miss how her face pales at finding us together.

"Perfect," I drawl when I pull away from a panting Shelly. "You fancy adding another to our party, Shell?"

"The more the merrier."

With my arm around her waist, I pull her over to where Camila's frozen on the spot. I reach for her but stop the second she looks like she's about to throw up, and thank fuck I didn't grab her because she bolts to the bathroom and heaves into the toilet.

"Ew," Shelly complains, backing up toward the door. Clearly I wasn't all that important if she's going to run before she's even got any action.

I let her go—I didn't even want her here, really—before stepping inside the bathroom to check on Camila.

She's slumped next to the toilet, her eyes are closed and her head lolled to the side. She's out of it.

"Camila?" I flush the toilet before bending down in front of her. "Cami-bear?"

She moans as if she can hear me but doesn't respond.

"Where's your useless cunt of a boyfriend? He should be looking after you right now."

"I dunno," she slurs. "Gone."

"Motherfucker." I slam my palm down on the tiles behind her and she doesn't even flinch. "When are you going to realize what a waste of fucking space he is, huh?"

She doesn't respond other than to snore lightly.

I should leave her here. After everything, it's what I should do, but that's not who I am. I can act like I hate her, like she single-handedly ruined my life, but even I know that it's a lie. And telling myself that I stopped caring about her after her family ran my dad out of town and sent my life into a spirally mess is an even bigger lie I tell myself most days. Underneath all my hate and frustration at the world is still the little boy who would do anything for his girl.

Forgetting about my need for revenge and my mission to hurt her, I scoop her up in my arms and walk from the room.

"Where we going? Noah, need Noah."

Just hearing his name falling from her lips when the fuck-up is probably balls deep in Tasha as we speak pisses me off beyond belief and almost has me dumping her on Ethan's bed for him to deal with later. But when I glance down at her conflicted sleeping face, something bigger tugs at my heart and I find myself walking from his house and laying her across the seats in the back of my car to get her home.

Thankfully, knowing Ethan's house as I do, I take her out the back and only a handful of people spot us.

It's long past midnight when I pull up outside her house. Seeing my mother's car parked in her driveway brings reality crashing back down on me. This isn't just her home now, it's mine too for the foreseeable future.

How am I supposed to look at her every day? How am I supposed to deal with her fucking boyfriend coming around and playing nice with her parents, which I'm sure he does? He's just that kind of smarmy fucker.

Knowing everyone will be fast asleep by now, I pull the key out that my mom gave me and let us in. The house is in darkness as I carry her up the stairs. She stirs, telling me that she's not completely comatose, but she's still had way too fucking much to drink. Where the fuck was *he*? It's his job to ensure she's safe. He must have known how much she'd had to drink when he was dancing with her. This right now, it's not my fucking job.

I kick her bedroom door open and step inside, managing to flick the light on without dropping her. I'm immediately hit with memories I'd rather disintegrated with our friendship. The walls are the same shade of soft pink they always were, and everything's in exactly the same place.

I remember sitting at her desk, working on homework. Lying on the floor, playing with our toys. Snuggling under her duvet watching films that were too old for us. My heart aches for what we once had and what we could have been if it weren't for me and my need for revenge.

This girl was my everything and I ruined that. The realization is startling. That first kiss we shared in this room, it could have led to something incredible. Or did everything work out as it should? Would we have always ended up hating each other in the end?

She stirs in my arms and I'm reminded of why I'm standing here right now, wondering what if.

"Mason," she moans. I have no idea if she's realized it's me holding her or if she's dreaming, but the sound of my name falling from her lips does something to me. My veins fill with fire and my cock swells. "Mase, please." There's heat in her words, a heat I don't need to hear, ever.

"Fuck," I grunt, placing her on the bed and backing up to the door.

I have one more night where I'm able to put space between us, so instead of heading to my new room, I leave the house and go home for my last and lonely night in the only home I've ever known.

15

CAMILA

When I come to, I soon realize that I'm lying in a puddle of my own drool and that my head is fucking pounding.

What the— "Oh fuck," I whisper into the silence of my room as hazy images from last night start to hit me.

Shots of tequila.

Noah.

Mason.

Bathroom.

Mason and Shelly.

Fuck. My stomach churns and I prepare to puke over the side of whoever's bed I'm currently sleeping in.

I remember being carried and being laid out on a comfortable bed, but I don't have the fucking slightest of clues as to who did that. Noah, maybe? Jake? Did Amalie find me and look after me?

My head spins as I try to make sense of anything other than the fact that I drank way too much. I went to that party wanting to forget, but before I've even opened my eyes, I'm regretting the stupid decision.

I suck in a few deep breaths through my nose, and once the swirling of my stomach has subsided, I crack my eyes open.

What the—

I'm in my bedroom. I blink a few times, thinking I must be still asleep, or my alcohol fuzzed brain is making me see things. But I really am in my bedroom. Looking down, I find that I'm still in my Rosewood Bears t-shirt and my jeans that I pulled on before last night's game, although they now have puke on them. Gross.

Whoever it was who got me back here last night certainly did not see me at my best.

I prop my pillows up against my headboard and lie back. My usual glass of water is sitting on my nightstand, but unusually there's a packet of Advil sitting next to it. The sight makes me smile, but it doesn't help me figure out how I got here.

A thought hits me and my head snaps to the side, expecting to find I have a bed partner, but that part of the bed definitely hasn't been slept in.

Reaching for the tablets, I pop two out while thanking whoever was thoughtful enough to leave them and wash them down with the water.

Slinking back down under the covers, I will them to kick in soon so I can get up without worrying that I might puke on my feet.

I lie there wondering how much of a fool I made of myself last night as the sounds of people moving around and chatter downstairs filters up to me.

Fuck. Today's the Paines' official moving in day. Groaning, I roll over and somehow the pounding in my head subsides enough for me to fall back to sleep.

Eventually banging from the other side of the wall wakes me back up. Thankfully, the pounding inside my head has lessened and I don't want to puke the moment I sit up, so I take that as a positive. Looking at my alarm, I blanch when I see it's almost lunchtime. I love sleeping, but I'm not one to sleep in this late.

Swinging my legs from the bed, I grab a change of clothes and head for the bathroom.

I feel like a new woman once I've brushed my teeth. It's almost like the simple task washes away my hangover. I turn the shower on nice and hot, strip out of yesterday's clothes, and step under the spray, hoping it'll wash away the memories as well as the stench of alcohol that seems to be clinging to me.

With my dark hair freshly blow dried and straightened, and a fresh white tank with a simple pair of sweats where my dirty old clothes once were, I pull the door open and step into the hallway.

The banging I could hear had totally passed me by in my need to get clean, but the second I round the corner I almost crash into reality.

There in front of me, topless and showing off what seems like miles of rippling muscles, is Mason attempting to single-handedly maneuver a double bed into the bedroom next to mine.

I'm powerless but to stand and watch as he tries to twist it this way and that to successfully get it into the room that used to be my dad's home office. It had been emptied a few days ago for our new tenants. I'd hoped that maybe his mom or brothers would be allocated that room, but apparently the universe wants to torture me some more by making him my neighbor.

His muscles ripple and stretch as he continues to fight with the huge wooden base.

What I should do is sneak back into the bathroom before he sees me, seeing as I need to pass him in order to get to my bedroom. But obviously that isn't what happens. I move, but it's not to hide. Instead I lean against the doorframe and watch, too fascinated to drag my eyes away from his body.

A guy's body isn't an alien thing to me, but seeing as Noah's more of a computer geek than a jock, it's safe to say that I'm not used to the kind of definition my eyes are feasting on right now.

I have no idea if I make a noise, there's a very good chance as he bends to try to lift the bed over the doorjamb that I moan or something else equally embarrassing, because he does have one fine ass. Even if the guy attached to it isn't all that pleasant. There's got to be something good that comes out of this arrangement, and if it's that I get a bit of regular eye candy then I guess I can live with that.

His head pops up and he immediately finds me watching him. Even with the distance between us, I see his eyes darken and drop as they take in my scantily clad body. I immediately regret not putting a bra on under my tank when I feel my nipples beginning to pebble under his intense stare.

"You just gonna stand there staring or are you going to fucking help?"

"Oh... uh... yeah, sure." I drop the dirty clothes I'm holding on a pile on the floor and race over.

"Can you squeeze through that gap and pull from inside?" He nods toward the tiny space between the bed frame and the door, but he must realize it's probably impossible when his eyes drop to my breasts once again. They definitely aren't getting through that gap.

"How about you squeeze through. That way if it falls, it'll only fall on you." His eyes widen in shock, although I swear I see a little pride in there too.

Over the past four years I haven't made all that effort to stand my ground with him. I figured there wasn't much of a point. He was going to hate me whether I bit back or not. I just preferred it to be over quicker so I could attempt to move on with my life. Things have changed over the past couple of weeks though, especially with him now moving in here. I'm not going to sit back and accept whatever shit he wants to throw at me. This is my house, and if he thinks he can walk all over me, then he's got another think coming.

"Sounds good. I always prefer the girl on top anyway."

The image of him with his hands and lips all over Shelly last night hits me out of nowhere, and I sway slightly with the sheer force of it.

"What?" he asks when he notices a change in me.

"Bet Shelly fucking loved that last night. She's probably spent all morning bragging to her pathetic friends about riding number eleven." I don't realize my mistake until I say his number. He didn't play.

He blanches but covers it quickly. "She fucking better be. I rocked her fucking world."

"'Course you did, hotshot."

His eyes narrow. "You're just jealous because you'll never get to find out."

"Ha, yeah. Jealous. How'd you figure me out?" I roll my eyes so hard they actually hurt, but the way my blood heats beneath my skin makes me wonder how true his words might actually be. Seeing him with both Chelsea and Shelly last night did something to me. Shaking my thoughts from my mind, I find that Mason's slipped through the gap. "We doing this or just stroking your already fucking massive ego?"

"It's not my massive ego you should be thinking about, Cami-bear."

"Fuck you, Mase. Do you want my help or not?"

"Fine, but only so I can have a bed tonight."

"For sleeping," I add. "I refuse to listen to you banging your conquests on the other side of the wall from where I sleep."

He tugs the frame and the whole thing moves forward. I hold it but barely, allowing him to do all the work and get it into place. He gently lowers it to the carpet, and I stand back to watch, still too fascinated by his body than I should be. Nothing's said between us. My last statement hangs heavy in the air. Until he turns and pins me with his dark stare.

He takes a step toward me and I take a huge one back. He looks like he's a lion stalking his prey, and I get the feeling he's about to have me for lunch.

"You'll fucking love it, lying there listening to the moans I drag out of them. Imagining it's you beneath me. Imagining it's my hands bringing you more pleasure than you've ever experienced before."

My back hits the wall, but he keeps coming. I glance over his shoulder but I have no hope of ducking him and getting to the door.

"We both know that I'd be more capable than that waste of fucking space boyfriend of yours. I would say I bet he hardly knows where to put it, but we both know that's not true because he's sticking it to Tasha pretty well, so I hear."

"Fuck you." My arm flies out to slap him, but just like the last time I tried this move he catches it before it makes contact and pins it to the wall above my head.

The move makes my back arch, my breasts thrusting forward. He closes the space between us, his heat burning through my thin clothing.

"If only you stopped resisting." My head spins for a few seconds, trying to figure out what the fuck I said, but the moment I realize, my cheeks heat and I fight to get away.

"Yeah, because you're an asshole," I spit. "Now get your fucking hands off me." I push from the wall, but all it achieves is for us to press closer together. My skin tingles and something explodes low down in my stomach.

His manly scent fills my nose, and I'm powerless to stop the hitch in my breathing as he stares down at me.

"You fucking love me being an asshole. That's why your heart's racing, why your nipples are fucking begging me to suck on them, and I bet you're wet as fuck for me right now." His free hand lifts and he trails one fingertip along the edge of my tank.

Sure as shit, my nipples tighten almost painfully as goosebumps skate across my skin. He hooks his finger in the fabric at my cleavage and pulls. My breath catches that he's about to expose me, but his eyes don't leave mine. He releases the fabric in favor of running the same finger around the waistband of my sweats.

"Shall we find out if I'm right? I bet you're wetter for me than you ever are for him. What do you think?"

"Mason." I wanted his name to be a warning, but fuck if it doesn't just sound needy.

My pussy throbs for attention and I'm almost at the point of demanding he does something about it when he removes all contact from me and stands back.

An evil smirk tugs at his lips. "Wow, Cami-bear. I thought you'd at least put up a bit of a fight. Seems you and your boyfriend deserve each other if you'd give yourself over to me that easily. Now get the fuck out of my bedroom."

I push from the wall and all but run to the door.

"And Cami-bear?" I shouldn't turn around but fuck if it's not what my head does the second I hear him say my name. "I don't want to hear you strumming one out next door now that you're all hot and bothered."

"Fuck. You." I don't hang around long enough to hear his response. Instead I run to my room and slam the door.

Why doesn't this door have a fucking lock on it?

16

MASON

I'm equally amused as I am fucking horny after watching Camila run from my new bedroom. It was true what I said, I was shocked she allowed that to go as far as it did and fuck if I wasn't about two seconds from sliding my hand into her fucking hideous sweatpants to find out what she really thinks of me. She was begging for it, that much was obvious. It makes me hate her fucking boyfriend that much more for not taking care of her as he should be and putting all his efforts into his cheerslut.

I think back to last night and the state she was in. Where the hell was he? He was at the party, I'd already seen Camila sucking his fucking face off. What guy in their right mind disappears on a girl who's all over them like she was him?

"Fucking idiot," I mutter as I throw my mattress on top of my bedframe and fall down onto it. My chest heaves from the exertion it took to get the fucking thing over here. Mom had help from Clint and his friends to move all her shit. It seems no one cares how I move in. In fact, they've already settled in so well that they've all gone for a fun family day out. I wasn't even invited.

Dragging my cell from my pocket, I pull up my recent messages and find our group chat.

Me: Workout?

It's probably the last thing the guys want to do after the game last night, but I'm agitated and storming into Camila's room and finishing what we started up against my bedroom wall isn't really an option, so I go for the next best thing.

Ethan: Fuck that, man. Still got two chicks in bed.

I shake my head at my best friend. I want to be disgusted with his ways, but right now even I can admit that I'm jealous as fuck. I didn't want to fuck Shelly last night, but damn, that doesn't mean I don't need to. My balls are so fucking blue right now they're almost fucking ice.

Jake: I'm in. If Ethan's busy you'll have to put up with my gym though.

By his gym, he means his little set up behind his trailer. We both kinda rely on Ethan to get us into his decent gym, seeing as neither of us has the money for the membership that he does.

Me: Perfect. Give me twenty.

I'm not fussy. I don't need a fancy weight bench or an all singing, all dancing crosstrainer. A tree branch and the rusty bike Jake pulled from a skip a few months ago is all I need to burn off a little steam and try to get the idea of how fucking up for it Camila was just a few moments ago from my head.

Despite the fact that I'm going to work out, I head for the shower first before pulling on my own pair of sweatpants and a fresh t-shirt. My hair's still wet as I walk into the Lopezes' kitchen to fill up my water bottle.

I'm expecting it to be empty, so I startle a little when I turn the corner and find Camila bent over the oven, her ass on full display.

"Now you're just starting to look as bad as *them*, trying to flaunt it and rub it in my face."

She jumps up and backs away from me.

"How long is it you're staying exactly, because it's been a few hours at the most and I'm already sick of the sight of you." The way the gold flecks in her eyes sparkle, I know this isn't entirely true.

"Fuck knows. You'd be better off asking my mother how long before she pulls her head out of her ass and does her fucking job." I don't mean for so much to pour from my lips. It seems that even being around Camila this long is dragging the old Mason out who used to tell her everything once again.

She opens her mouth to respond. I shouldn't really need to worry about spilling too much, because with us all living in one happy house, everything I've been trying to cover up is going to be out in the open in mere days.

"Just forget I said anything. We'll be gone as soon as I can do something about it."

"It's not your job to do anything about it." Her voice is softer than it was a moment ago. "That's why you didn't play last night, wasn't it? You were working."

"It doesn't fucking matter why I didn't play. And you need to keep your nose out. You've already done enough damage to my life."

"Fucking hell, Mase. How long is it going to take you to realize that none of that is on me? I had nothing to do with what happened with your dad. Why are you still punishing me for that?"

My chest heaves as she takes me back to the day my dad walked out. My mom was sobbing behind me where I stood in the doorway, watching him head to his car with just one suitcase of belongings to his name.

"Blame your dad, blame my dad, blame your mom. Who the fuck ever but me. I was as innocent in all of that as you were. They might have been the ones to push your dad to leave and for your mom to fall apart, but *you* are the only one to blame for ruining this." She gestures between us. "*You* single-handedly ruined the friendship we'd built for years. *You*, Mason."

Her index finger jabs me hard in the chest, and when she looks up and meets my eyes, hers are full of tears. "You weren't the only one who lost something, Mason. Okay, so it might have been worse for you, but you weren't the only one to have your life turned upside down, and that's something I don't think I'll ever be able to forgive you for. Now get out of my fucking way."

I can't move. I'm frozen to the spot as the words she just said to me filter into my brain.

"Move," she demands, her voice cracking on that one word alone. Keeping my eyes on the tiled floor, too afraid to see the emotion on her face, I stand aside and allow her to pass with her lunch.

"Fuck." My hands lift to my hair. I should follow her. I should attempt to fix something, but as I look around her perfect family home, I'm reminded of everything she still has. She lost me, so what? I lost everything.

I get to Jake's trailer in record time in my need to get the fuck away from that house and everything it represents.

I know he's here waiting for me, so I pull the door open and step inside. If I wasn't so lost in my own head, I'd probably be able to predict the scene I walk in on. At least they're fully fucking clothed, I guess.

"Ever heard of knocking, asshole?" Jake mutters, pushing himself up from Amalie and none too discreetly rearranging himself in his pants.

Jealousy burns through me faster than I'm able to control. I fall down on the opposite couch, rest my head back against the wall and wait for them to sort themselves out.

"What the fuck's eating you?" Apparently my torment is obvious to my best friend.

"I moved in this morning."

"Moved in where?" Amalie asks. Her soft, innocent voice makes me look up at her.

"You don't know?"

She glances over at Jake with narrowed eyes, but I know she's not pissed he kept my secret.

"Into the Lopezs' house."

Her brows are drawn together in confusion when she looks back at me.

"The Lopezes' house? As in, Camila's house?"

"The one and only."

"Why?"

With a sigh, I give her the basics so she understands just a bit of the disaster that is my life.

"That might explain why she's been ignoring my calls all morning. She just disappeared on us last night. I assume Noah got her home safe."

"Not exactly," I admit but regret it instantly when their intrigued eyes turn on me. With a sigh, I resign myself to explaining. "He disappeared too. I found her drunk off her ass in Ethan's bathroom."

"Where the hell did Noah go?"

"You took her home, didn't you?"

Jake and Amalie ask at the same time.

"I have no idea," I say to Amalie to address the issue of Noah. "Balls deep in Tasha, probably. And yes, I took her home. She doesn't know it was me, though, and I'd appreciate if you didn't tell her." I turn my stare back on Amalie.

"Why? She might go a little easier on you if she knows you looked after her."

"She just doesn't need to know," I snap, not really wanting to dissect the issues between Camila and me. It's bad enough that I can't get her and her practically see-through tank out of my head.

"Right, well. If you two are heading to work out, I'm going to go and see Camila and make sure she's okay. Maybe see if I can convince her to dump Noah's arse."

"She won't listen," I mutter.

"She'll figure it out eventually."

"Come on then, let's attempt to get her out of your system," Jake says after giving Amalie a kiss goodbye with a smug as fuck smile, as if he knows exactly what he's talking about.

17

CAMILA

"How's the hangover?" Amalie asks when she strolls into my bedroom later that afternoon.

"Fine," I mutter. "Don't ever let me drink tequila again."

"Yeah, because you'd have listened to me last night if I'd told you to stop."

I shrug at her because we both know she's right.

"So..." she starts, falling down onto my bed behind where I'm sitting at my desk, attempting to make a start on my 'Against All Odds' paper. "Were you planning on telling me about your new housemate?"

"I was hoping that if I didn't acknowledge it, then it wouldn't happen."

"How'd that work out?"

"Fantastic. He moved his stuff in the room on the other side of that wall this morning." A smile that she tries to fight tugs at her lips, her eyes shining with delight. "Do you need to enjoy this quite so much?"

"I'm sorry, but it is quite entertaining. He was wound as tight as a spring when he turned up at Jake's earlier."

"You've seen him?"

"How did you think I found out he'd moved in, seeing as you didn't want to tell me?"

"Jake. What did he say?"

"Not a lot. Why? Has something happened in the short few hours he's been here?"

"No." She raises an eyebrow. "I just helped him move his bed in and he was an ass. He keeps going on about Noah, accusing me of being dumb."

"Can you blame him?"

"Noah's not cheating." Even I can admit that the argument is weak at best.

"Right, so what happened to him last night then?"

"He brought me home when I was too drunk to keep my eyes open."

"Did he?"

I open my mouth to tell her that it was him, but her cell ringing cuts me off.

"Shit, sorry, it's Gran. I promised her I'd be home to help with something this afternoon. We will be continuing this conversation though."

"Fantastic. Can't wait." She gets up and heads for the door. "Wait. If it wasn't Noah then... was it you and Jake?"

She laughs, and it makes my blood boil. "What do you think, Cami?" Her head tilts to the side like she's talking to a cute little kid and then she's gone, leaving me even more confused about what's going on than I was before she arrived.

Pushing thoughts of last night's party and my new neighbor aside, I focus on the task at hand.

Against All Odds. The only person who I can think right now who's done anything even close to the title is Jake. The hard to crack, ultimate player, bad boy, finally reformed, against all odds, by my new best friend.

Tapping my pen against my chin, I consider how I might play this.

In the end, I turn what is a very real story into a somewhat fictional newspaper article set in the future about an NFL player overcoming his adversities and making it despite his early years.

By the time I hit print and shut the document down, I'm proud of what I've achieved. My back's stiff from sitting in the same position for so long, and my shoulders ache.

The sun's long set, and as I sit back and stretch, I realize that I'm starving.

The house is still quiet. My parents told me yesterday that they intended on taking Mason's mom and brothers out for the day in the hope that the boys will be distracted from having to move from their family home. I like their positive thinking, but I'm not sure how much it's going to help in the long run. I might not know them all that well—they were only babies when I used to spend most of my time around them, but just from hearing Mom talk about them over the years, I know they're perceptive kids. There's no doubt, even at their age, that they don't know what's going on with their lives right now.

I find myself some dinner before settling on my bed for an evening of binge watching some trashy TV. Mason has not reappeared since our interaction in the kitchen earlier today, and I couldn't be happier. The last thing I need is for him to turn back up, demanding we continue where we left off. Whether that's from his bedroom or the kitchen, neither fills me with joy. Okay, that might be a bit of a lie. Something is still tingling just beneath my skin after he backed me up against the wall earlier, even though I know I should have forgotten all about it already.

I'm just losing myself in the latest episode of *The Bachelor* when my phone buzzes on the side. I assume it'll be Noah, seeing as I haven't seen nor heard from him since last night despite sending a couple of messages to him this afternoon to try to dig into what actually happened. I snatch it from the side and look down at the screen. But instead of my boyfriend's name staring back at me, it's an unknown number.

555-617-9764: Are you ready to learn the truth?

My finger hovers over the reply button, but in the end I think better of it. Whoever this is is just using me for some cheap entertainment.

I'm just putting it back on the nightstand when it vibrates in my hand once again.

555-617-9764: Shane's house. First bedroom on the right. Now!

My hand trembles that this might be something serious, or at least the answer to the question that's been spinning around in my mind since I watched Mason slam his fists into Noah's face about this time last week.

My hands tremble as I get off the bed. I still. This could be one big joke and I could find Mason at the other end, laughing his ass off. But why would he be at Shane's? They've never got along, even less so after the whole spiked drink situation at Shane's last party.

I decide that I need to find out for myself, knowing that if I sit here thinking 'what if' then it's going to eat me until I do shift my ass, and by then it could be too late.

Pulling a zip up hoodie on over the top of my tank top, I slip my feet into the first pair of shoes I find and go to leave the house.

Just as my foot hits the bottom step, the front door opens and Mason walks through. As if he knows I'm there, he looks up and finds my eyes immediately. Amusement fills them, especially after he's taken in my outfit.

"If that's what Noah asks you to dress in for a booty call, then he's even weirder than I thought."

"I don't have time for this bullshit," I mutter, storming past him and snatching my keys from the sideboard as I pass.

"Have a good night. Don't do anything I wouldn't do."

Flipping him off over my shoulder, I slam the door behind me and head for my car.

Thankfully it starts the first time, and in seconds I'm on the road heading for Shane's house to find out what awaits me.

By the time I pull up on his street, my hands are shaking uncontrollably and my stomach is knotted so tight I fear I might not be able to stand straight. It's clear there's a party going on inside, but I don't register the fact that my friends are partying without me. I just need to know what I'm going to find in that bedroom. Mason's at home, or at least I assume that's where he stayed, so I'm pretty confident this isn't a prank he's organized.

Turning off the engine, I suck in a deep breath and step from the car.

The walk to his house feels like the slowest of my life, but all too soon, I'm pushing down the door handle and stepping inside.

There's no music like I was expecting, and the house isn't full to the brim like the cars lining the street led me to believe.

Laughter filters down from where I know Shane's den to be, and I can only assume it's a boy's night and they're all down there watching whatever sport's on the TV.

Ignoring them, I take a step for the stairs.

With each step I take, I tell myself that this is just a joke. Noah is probably waiting for me, expecting me to hand myself over to him. Why is it that the thought of that being about to happen makes me more anxious than any other alternative?

The dread that's sitting heavy in my stomach tells me that whatever I'm about to find behind that door is going to turn my world upside down, but I'm powerless not to keep moving toward it.

I lift my hand to the doorknob, my heart racing, my head spinning as I consider that Mason is about to be proved right.

I twist it as slowly and as quietly as I can. I have no idea what I might find, and I haven't decided if I want my presence to be known.

I push the door open just a crack and squeeze my eyes closed tightly as I pray that I'm not about to witness what I think I am.

A loud moan has my eyes flying open, and when I look up, I find exactly what I feared. My boyfriend thrusting as hard as he can into a cheerleader.

I gasp but quickly cover my mouth with my hand, not wanting to be caught standing here staring.

Noah's head is tipped back in pleasure as his fingers grip onto Tasha's hips, who's on all fours in front of him.

"Fuck, fuck," he grunts, and I start to back away from the car crash in front of me. Tears burn my eyes, but initially it's not for what he's doing or even what I've lost, it's for the fact that I didn't trust the one person who I'd have given my life for not all that long ago.

Mason told me what is happening almost right in front of my eyes, and I chose to ignore him. To call him a liar, time and time again.

A sob rips from my lips as I fly back down the stairs, my stomach clenching and my mouth watering like I'm about to lose the contents of it any moment.

I can't get to the front door quick enough, but a throat clearing as me halting my retreat and turning around.

Standing in the far corner of the room is Shane. His eyes are soft and full of sympathy. My fists clench with my need to run over and slam them into him. If he knew about this and didn't tell me, I'll never forgive him.

He opens his mouth, but knowing I'm not going to be able to deal with whatever he's about to say, I turn back and race from the house. The front door slams behind me. I'd like to think it might alert the couple upstairs that something might not be right, but I doubt it.

I don't remember the drive home. I have no idea if I run any lights or cut off any other drivers. With my tears threatening to spill over, my only focus is locking myself inside my bedroom so I can fall apart in the safety of my own space.

I race through the house and up the stairs, praying that I don't run into my parents on the way, wanting to know what's wrong. The last thing I want to do is explain what I just witnessed.

18

MASON

It seems that the Lopezes could be a good influence on Mom, because I was expecting her to bail the second they all got back this evening, but to my total shock she bathed them both and put them to bed. The relief I felt knowing that I didn't need to worry was huge and just showed how much pressure I'd been under over the past few years, not only looking after myself and trying to keep the house running, but playing dad to my brothers. It was exhausting. I didn't pick up any shifts this weekend seeing as we were moving, and I had no idea how that was going to go. If it went as badly as I was anticipating, then I fully expected to need to escape to Ethan's to get drunk and high instead of running to work. As it is, it hasn't been too bad. I mean, I can hardly say that my encounter with Camila this morning was a bad one. Much the opposite with the way she longingly stared at me, practically begging me to put my hands on her. The way her breasts swelled in her tank. Fuck, I'm getting hard just thinking about it.

Sitting up on my bed, I look around the room. It's nowhere near the space I left behind up the street. Gone are my navy blue walls and the wonky shelves my dad had put up badly when I was a kid that held my football trophies from over the years. Instead, they're in boxes, stacked with a load of other stuff in the corner. I've only unpacked the necessary stuff in the hope that if I don't move in completely, it means we're not staying all that long. It might be wishful thinking.

This room's been Clint's office for as long as I can remember. It was always off bounds to us as kids. We made it our top priority to break in and find out why on many occasions. We assumed, the naive kids that we were, that there was something worth finding. We were disappointed every time we snuck in here to only find a bookcase of boring IT books, a huge computer with more monitors that I'm sure any one person actually needs, and old coffee cups that had been there so long they were growing things.

The last time was the only time we found something to make the risk of sneaking in worthwhile. There was a bottle of half empty whiskey sitting on the desk next to Clint's keyboard.

"You ever wondered what that stuff tastes like?" Camila asked.

We were probably twelve or thirteen at the time, both of us had had the odd sip of wine that our parents had allowed with our dinner and both of us at that point had turned our noses up, not understanding why our parents were so fascinated with it.

Hard liquor though, the amber liquid that our dads drank when they got together for an evening. Not a drop of that stuff had passed my lips and I'd be lying to say I wasn't curious.

Giggling like the naughty kid she was, Camila wrapped her slim fingers around the neck of the bottle and twisted the top.

Both of us kept an eye on the door the entire time. We were alone in the house, but we had no idea how long it would stay that way.

I watched as she lifted the bottle to her lips and poured a generous amount into her mouth. The second she swallowed, she started sputtering, her eyes going wide as it burned down her throat.

"Oh my god. That's..." She coughed, her eyes watering. "Awful. Here."

I laughed at the fact I had to join in even though she so obviously regretted drinking it. I was a little more hesitant when I lifted the bottle and only took a small sip. Honestly, I didn't think it was so bad, but when I looked up to find Camila staring at the bottle in my hands like it actually offended her, I followed her lead. "Yuck."

I lowered the bottle as something flashed in Camila's eyes.

"It couldn't have been that bad, maybe I had too much." She waved her hand out for the bottle and took another sip.

Thirty minutes later and we were both drunk, although we had no idea at the time. Life was great as we laughed and messed about in Clint's office before we were caught.

To this day, I remember the look on Camila's face as Clint and Gabriella took me by the arms and marched me back down the street for my own parents to reprimand me, not only for breaking and entering but stealing and getting drunk. She looked at me like her parents were taking her right arm from her. Her eyes dropped and her bottom lip trembled. She didn't care we'd been caught, she just wanted us to serve our punishment out together, but our parents all knew that the best way to punish us was to keep us apart.

Pushing my memories back down, I swing my legs from the bed to take a shower and head to Ethan's. He might have only had a party last night, but seeing the messages that have come through in the past hour, it seems he's at it again. Twice in a weekend is unusual for him, but I may as well go and see what the hell's going on.

I pull the door open and step into the quiet hallway, ready to head for the bathroom when something, or someone, slams into me.

"Fuck," I grunt, the force of the collision making my breath catch.

Her sob hits my ears before I get a chance to look down, my arms instinctively wrapping around her, and I hold her against me for a beat. The feeling is too fucking good but when she starts fighting I don't resist. It shouldn't feel that good.

"Get the fuck off me," she wails, loud enough to wake my brothers. I want to tell her to be quiet, but the look on her face as she takes a step back steals my words.

"What's wrong? What's happened?" She has tears streaming down her face and her eyes are red. This hasn't just started.

She sucks in a few shaky breaths as she stares down at the carpet beneath our feet.

"Don't make me say it," she whispers so quietly that I have to lean in toward her to hear. Her strawberry scent fills my nose, and that mixed with her state tugs at my chest in a way I'm not all that happy about.

"Say what?" My brows draw together as I stare at her, trying to figure out how I should know what's going on right now.

"Oh don't look at me like that." She lifts her hands and wipes her cheeks with the back of each. "Like you're concerned. You've been waiting for this to happen."

"Waiting for what?" I ask hesitantly, slowly putting two and two together in my head.

She huffs out a frustrated breath. "You were right, okay? Does that make you feel better? Make you feel like the winner? You were right, I was an idiot and look where it got me. You happy seeing my world fall apart?"

"What happened?" I seethe, ignoring all her other comments and needing to know exactly what I'm dealing with.

"Noah," she sobs, her bottom lip starting to tremble again as her memories of whatever's happened hit her. "He's fucking her."

"Motherfucker," rumbles up my throat. My fists clench with my need to lay into him again for ever hurting her.

"Why are you so fucking angry? You wanted this."

My mouth drops as a humorless laugh falls from my lips. "I didn't fucking want this." I wave my hand around in front of her but keeping it far enough away from her that I won't be tempted to pull her into my arms once again. "I warned you. I told you what he was up to but you chose not to believe me."

She stares at me, her eyes turning hard, argument forming, but it never leaves her mouth.

"I'm so fucking stupid."

She drops her head into her hands and cries. "Excuse me," she mumbles into her palms and goes to move past me. But she doesn't get to take a step before my arms shoot out to stop her.

I push her back against the wall when she tries to run from me. "Mason, don't. I don't need—"

My hand cups her cheek and forces her to look up at me. The sadness swimming in her eyes guts me. No one else should have the power to hurt her like this. Noah's a worthless motherfucker, and I'm so fucking glad she's learned the truth.

"Mason?" My name is almost a plea on her lips as she stares up at me. There're only inches between us, our increased breaths mingling as the silence stretches out around us.

"You need to forget him. He doesn't deserve your tears."

"I—"

The sound of footsteps on the stairs beneath us filters up and I panic. Gripping Camila's arms, I pull her into my room and shut the door behind us.

I push her back against the wall and step into her. My foot lands between hers and my arm rests on the wall beside her head. Her eyes, although still sad, hold a fire that wasn't there before.

"He shouldn't be the only one enjoying himself, Cami-bear."

My fingers lift and find the zipper that runs the length of her hoodie. I pinch it between my thumb and forefinger and pull. The sound of the metal separating is the only sound filling the room besides her increased breathing.

"How did you find out?"

She tenses as I get to the bottom of her hoodie and it falls open, exposing her tank covered breasts. Pushing my hand inside, I wrap it around her hip.

"I... I saw them."

My jaw pops at her admission. *Motherfucker.*

19

CAMILA

Mason stares down at me, his dark eyes wild as he tried to control his anger. If the situation were different, I might be scared. He's directed almost all his anger at me for four years over how his life turned out, but right now I'm not even on his radar, not for his anger at least.

His fingers tighten on my hip to the point that he'll probably leave bruises, but the way he's looking at me right now, I really don't care.

There's a promise in his eyes. A promise that he can make me forget even if just for a few moments.

The image of Noah's bare ass as he plowed into Tasha is burned into my eyes. I'll do just about anything now to remove it. So when his hand releases me to run his fingertips along the bare sliver of skin between my sweats and tank, I don't stop him. Instead, I stupidly allow my head to fall back against the wall as tingles erupt throughout my body. My thighs clench and my core throbs as anticipation races through me.

Surely, he's not going to...

I shouldn't even let him.

I should run. Run and lock my door—if it had one—but that image that's on repeat in my head and the prospect of it happening is too much.

His eyes stay locked on mine as his fingers slip just slightly under the waistband of my sweats. The skin around them crinkles slightly as he narrows them, giving me an out, but it's only for the briefest of seconds because no sooner have I registered the warning than his hand is sliding lower and into my panties.

I gasp when his fingers part me and press against my most sensitive place.

"Oh...oh..." I moan when he puts more pressure on my clit and starts to circle. "Oh..." Heat floods my entire body as a knot tightens in my lower stomach.

His breath hits the skin of my neck, and goosebumps break out across my body. His eyes stray from mine to my lips when my tongue sneaks out to lick across the bottom one, but at no point does he make a move to kiss me.

The realization of what this is hits me harder than the sight of them on that bed tonight. Mason doesn't want me. He's merely taking something from Noah in his need to punish him for what he did to me. I'm under no illusion that Mason's about to step in and take his place.

My fingers wrap around his wrist, ready to push him away. I don't want this because of some fucked up male rivalry that he can use against Noah. I should only want this with someone who wants it with me, someone who's going to treat me with the respect and love I deserve, but just as I go to push him away, he reaches lower, a finger circling my entrance and slipping inside.

My grip loosens at the sensation and my hand falls away in favor of what he's doing to me. It feels so fucking good. My head goes fuzzy, all the thoughts, the devastation of tonight melting away as my chest burns for more air and my body gets ready to tip over the edge of the pleasure he's holding me on the cusp of.

His head leans in closer to my ear and I shudder. I can't see his mouth but I know he's smiling at the reaction I'm having to him.

"Come for *me*, Camila." His fingers thrust deeper and my body snaps. My hips jolt forward, allowing him to get even deeper which only strengthens the explosion racing through my veins.

My nails scratch against the wall at my back, my knees threatening to buckle beneath me.

The high fades almost as fast as it hits, and I'm left with my chest heaving as Mason slips his hand free of my clothing. He pulls back and stares at me once again. Only this time, instead of the concern for me that was there before, his eyes are full of achievement.

Heat stirs in my belly, but it's not lust this time. It's anger.

"Fuck you, Mason." I slam my hands down on his chest and force him to back up. Surprisingly, he does allow me to push from the wall to make my escape. I'm mortified that I just allowed him to put his hands on me like that but fucking furious for his reasons for doing it.

Reaching out, my fingers wrap around the handle ready to drag it open and leave him behind. But the sound of my name falling from his lips behind me has me stalling. My brain screams at me to run, but my body betrays it. It seems to naturally respond to the deep timbre of his demand, and I fucking hate it.

Unable to stop myself, I look back over my shoulder.

"I bet he never made you come that hard."

My eyes narrow. I'm desperate for a quick comeback, but the second he lifts the fingers that were just inside me and sucks them into his mouth, his eyes fluttering closed, all words vanish. My chin drops, my cheeks heat and all thoughts leave my head. My breathing catches once again, but it's not until he pulls his eyes open that I find it in me to run. And I run as fast as my shaky legs will allow.

———

I barely leave my room, only sneaking out for the necessities like the bathroom and stealing chips and ice cream from the kitchen when I'm confident I won't be caught. I know he's in the room next door—the beat of his music has been quietly filtering through the wall all morning—but I've yet to see anyone. I know I'm on borrowed time though.

It can't be thirty minutes after that thought when a soft knock sounds from my bedroom door. I look down at the pajamas that I'm still wearing despite the fact it's long after lunch. I don't bother getting out of bed or trying to make myself look anything but the mess that I currently am when I call out for them to enter.

As expected, Mom slips inside my still darkened room. She takes one look at me and the closed curtains and a deep frown mars her usually smooth face.

"Camila? What's wrong?"

All morning I've fought my tears, but one look at my mom's concerned face and they spill over. Whether they're for Noah or just my stupidity for what happened with Mason last night, I have no idea. At this point, my turmoil has just mixed into one. She rushes to me and pulls me into her arms.

"It's okay, baby." I cry like I should have when I got home last night, only I was distracted.

When I eventually pull back, Mom's shoulder is soaked with my tears.

Her face is still full of concern when she takes my cheeks in her hands and wipes away the tears with her thumbs.

"N-Noah…" My words get stuck in my throat. "He…He…" I shake my head, not able to vocalize the words, especially to Mom. "It's over."

"Oh, baby." She pulls me back into her arms but it seems that I've run out of tears—for now, at least. "I remember it well," she says on a sigh. "I know it feels like the end of the world right now, but I promise you, it'll get better." She rubs my back as she tries to console me, but it only makes me realize something. Although I'd been adamantly defending him for the past week since his birthday party, I think on some level I knew because as much as last night was a shock, it's not hurting as much as I think it probably should right now. What's hurting more is knowing I allowed Mason to take advantage of my emotional state. I should have been stronger. I should have pushed him away. Told him no. But I did none of those things. I actually fear that I may have even encouraged him.

Now he's got ammunition, something he can use against me, and I have no doubt he will.

"Don't move," Mom instructs before rushing from the room, leaving the door ajar.

I have no idea where she disappears to but I don't put much thought into it, especially when the music next door stops and the sound of his door opening has me on full alert.

When he starts walking and his footsteps only get louder, my breath catches. It's ridiculous because the bathroom's right there and he's probably just going to use that, but my fucked up brain's convinced he's coming here.

The footsteps slow and my heart threatens to beat out of my chest as I wait for him to appear in the gap.

I blink and he's there. I may only be able to see a couple of inches, but every muscle in my body clenches at the sight of him in his black shirt and light ripped jeans. His hair's flopping down in front of his face so I only get to look into one eye as he finds me sitting cross-legged on my bed. His eye drops as he leisurely takes in what I'm wearing—or not, as the case may be. My body heats under his scrutiny, my nipples pebbling and my core clenching as memories of how easily he played me last night slam into me.

His attention eventually comes back up to my face and his mouth opens like he's about to say something, but lighter footsteps sound before my mom's voice has Mason turning away, allowing me to suck in a much needed breath.

"You heading out, sweetie?"

"Yeah, party at Ethan's." Mason's deep voice rumbles through me, reminding me of when he whispered in my ear last night.

Another party, and on a Sunday night? I know Ethan likes to enjoy his freedom, but shit.

"Well, I won't get in your way. You deserve to go out and enjoy yourself."

"T-thank you." With the briefest of glances back at me, he's gone. His footsteps thunder down the stairs.

"Here we go," Mom announces, pushing the door open wider and revealing her carrying a tray loaded with freshly made nachos, a bottle of what looks like mojito, and a couple of glasses.

Now this is something I can get on board with. My resolution to never drink again after Friday night's disaster goes flying out the window. I'm with my mom, she won't allow me to get trashed.

"Oh my god, I need this," I say, my stomach grumbling as the aroma of melted cheese fills the room.

I scoot over in bed to allow her space, and, once she's comfortable, I pull up *Mean Girls* on the TV and we sit back and enjoy a little girl time.

Mom suggests calling Amalie and Alyssa to join in, but as much as I love spending time with them, this right now is perfect. She's going to be off next week to help Dad set up his apartment in New York, so this might be the last time we get to spend some quality time together in a while. Anyway, I have no idea about Alyssa, but I could pretty much put money on Amalie being otherwise engaged right now with a certain star quarterback.

"What's that look for?" I didn't realize thinking about how happy Amalie is caused my face to change, but apparently it did.

"Nothing. Just thinking that Amalie will be with Jake. You haven't seem them together yet, but..." I sigh, trying to find the right words. "You know when you just look at two people and know it's it. That's them. They're just so... connected. It's weird."

"I know exactly what you mean, baby. I was one of the last of my friends to meet the man who was to become your dad. I know how it feels to think you're being left behind."

"No, that's not it. I know I've got plenty of time. I'm not even eighteen yet. I don't know, it's hard to explain." Or hard to admit just how jealous I am of them when I once thought I had exactly the same with the boy next door.

"Speaking of your eighteenth, young lady. The table is all booked for Friday night. Are you sure you just want it to be just the three of us? You're more than welcome to invite some friends or—"

I cut her off before she suggests the Paines. It's bad enough living under the same roof, I'm not dealing with anything else. "No, just us. I'll be seeing the girls all day Saturday, so it's fine."

She eyes me curiously. When she first brought up my birthday a few weeks ago, I think she was expecting me to want a big party like Noah and invite my entire class, but honestly, I couldn't think of anything worse than spending the night worrying about someone damaging the house or throwing up god knows where. A nice quiet weekend with my favorite people is all I need.

One chick flick soon leads onto another, and before we know it, Dad has to come to find where his wife's disappeared to. He makes a joke about her sneaking out of the living room to cheat on him. My stomach clenches, and although I never said the words to her, Mom reaches over and squeezes my hand in support.

Once she's disappeared off with Dad, I make the most of knowing Mason is out and head for the bathroom for a shower before bed. All my homework's done, so I can hopefully get an early night so I'm ready for whatever drama is sure to come my way this week.

The thought of having to see Noah and Tasha has my stomach turning, but not as much as having to be in the same room as Mason. My need to hurt him might just get the better of me.

I end up tossing and turning for what feels like forever before I give up and turn my TV back on. I never had issues sleeping until all of this kicked off last weekend; now every time I close my eyes, all I can see is Mason staring at me as he told me how stupid I was, Noah as he nailed Tasha, and imagining everyone's looks of sympathy when the truth comes out. I put my cell on silent before I made the journey home from Shane's yesterday and I've stopped myself looking at it ever since. I'm pretty sure he'll have texted, but I have no idea if he's aware he's been caught or if he still believes he's getting away with it. Either way, he's not concerned enough by my radio silence to turn up here looking for me. I take that as a sign that this is probably for the best.

It's sometime after midnight when my world falls into darkness. I was watching some late night chat show with some reality star I'd never heard of when there's a click and everything goes out—the TV, the ceiling light, my night light, and the hall light. Everything.

My chest immediately constricts as I stare into nothingness. There's not even any moonlight filtering through the curtains.

My hands tremble and my heart races as I sit in the middle of my bed, wrapped in my sheets, and rock, praying that everything will come back on any second.

The seconds stretch into minutes and my panic begins to get the better of me. Realizing that sitting here in the dark is more terrifying than seeing what Noah has to say for himself, I find myself leaning over the side of my bed to find my purse. Digging around blindly inside, I wrap my fingers around my cell and pull it out, only when I go to wake it up, nothing happens. I press the power button and the only thing I get out of it is the little red flashing battery telling me that it's dead and absolutely no help whatsoever. I did have a flashlight in my top drawer, but I took it to Dash and I can't remember what happened to it.

My fear increases, my breaths coming out scarily fast, but I don't seem to drag any air back inside. Everyone else must be sleeping, and even in my panicked state, I feel ridiculous for even considering waking them. I'm almost eighteen for fuck's sake. It's just a little power outage, nothing's going to ha—

The front door slams shut and my heart jumps into my throat. I sit perfectly still, trying to hear what's happening. I feel my pulse in every inch of my body as I wait.

There are a few bangs before feet hit the stairs. With each step, my body flinches. I grip the sheets tightly to my chest, my nails digging into my palms despite the fabric between them.

My door's shut, but I still see the flash of light that appears underneath. I'm torn between running out there and confronting whatever it is that's making light or hiding under my bed in case it's a man who's come to murder me under the cover of darkness.

I'm still trying to convince myself to stay on the rational side of my imagination when it's gone. The light goes out but there's no noise. That is, until the click of my door has me scooting up the bed in an attempt to get away.

The sheets raise to my mouth. Only my eyes would be showing if anyone could actually see me as I sit trembling in fear.

The sound of another person's breathing fills the room and I bite down on the inside of my cheeks to stop me from screaming.

If he's here to kill me, I hope he makes it quick, I think as footsteps get closer.

"M-Mason, is that you?" I whisper so quietly that even if it is him, the chance of him hearing me is slim.

Whoever it is doesn't respond as they make their way around the bed. It's not lost on me that they must know my room, seeing as it's pitch black and they haven't bumped into anything.

"Mason?" I snap a little louder, my fear getting the better of me.

Oh my god, oh my god, I chant to myself when the bed dips.

His familiar scent fills my nose as he gets closer, but I don't release the breath I'm holding. Nor do I relax. I'm still frozen in fear and waiting to see what he's going to do.

His hot breath sweeps over my face. The faint scent of whiskey fills my nose, but it's not enough for him to be drunk, I don't think. A shiver runs down my spine when his lips brush against my ear. Then softly he whispers words that take me back to another night when we were cloaked in darkness.

"I'll keep you safe. I'll always keep you safe."

A whimper falls from my lips. I hate to admit it, but having him here with me allows me to breathe since the lights went out.

He sits up and I hear rustling before the sheets are tugged from around me.

"M-Mason, w-what are you doing?"

"Shhhh."

My heart races, but suddenly it's for an entirely different reason as I'm pulled down the bed so I'm lying on my back in only my silk cami and short set. Mason pushes my thighs apart with his hand, and the second they part, he settles himself between. The roughness of his jeans brushes the sensitive skin inside my thighs and my core tightens at the sensation.

What the hell is he doing?

The mattress dips again as he falls on top of me, his hands resting on either side of my shoulders. My breathing is incredibly loud in the silence of my bedroom, and it gives away everything that I'm feeling right now.

Everything about this moment is so wrong, but being here in the dark with him hovering above me, I can't help but want everything from him. Everything that was ripped away from us all those years ago.

I. Want. It. All.

He dips down, his lips brushing against the soft skin of my neck. My back arches at the contact, and my thighs pin him in place.

This is wrong, a little voice screams in my head, but I push her aside and focus on the electricity racing around my body. I flex my fingers, feeling it all the way to the tips as he continues to kiss me.

"Mason," I moan when the heat of his tongue runs across my collarbone.

Lifting my hands to find him, they connect with the hot skin of his back. I guess that explains the rustling of fabric before he climbed between my legs.

I run my palms up his bare skin and don't miss his entire body freeze and his breath catch at my contact. It's nice to know he's as affected by this as I am.

He comes back to himself barely a second later, his lips descending toward the lace that lines my cami. My nipples pebble at the thought of him revealing them, and my cheeks heat. It doesn't matter that it's totally dark and he can probably only just make out the outlines of my body like I can him. The thought of being exposed to him still has butterflies erupting in my belly.

"Mason... w-what—" His finger slips one strap from my shoulder and he pulls it low enough that the soft fabric skims over my nipple. I can't help but arch a little at the sensation, my body begging for more.

"Stop overthinking. Just feel. Just forget."

"Oh god," I whimper, powerless to do anything but what he just instructed as the scorching heat of his tongue licks around my breast before zeroing in on my sensitive peak and sucking it deep into his mouth. A bolt of lust shoots straight down between my legs, and I fight to squeeze them together to get some friction.

"All in good time."

My other strap follows the same path as the first, and he's soon giving my other breast the same treatment. I writhe beneath him, desperate for more, for everything.

Crazy thoughts start filling my head, despite my attempt to do as he said and forget.

Am I willing to give myself over to the boy who's hated me for the past four years?

Is this the reason I held off with Noah?

Was it always meant to be Mason despite what's happened between us?

By the time he starts kissing down my belly, I only just about hold myself back from pushing him lower. I may not have done this before, but I know damn well what I need, and if last night against his bedroom wall taught me anything, it's that I need him between my legs right fucking now.

Not even a second later, his fingers wrap around the waistband of my shorts and he tugs them and my wet panties down my thighs.

Instead of telling him no, like I probably should, I lift my hips to assist him with his mission.

My cheeks burn so much that I feel it on my neck as he crawls down the bed, lying on his front so he's in line with my core.

Holy shit, this is happening.

He blows a stream of air across me and I damn near fall apart from that alone. I moan, rolling my hips, needing some kind of friction to put an end to this delicious torture. Of all the horrible things he's done to me over the past few years, holding out on me right now might be the worst. If he were to stop and walk out right now, I'm not sure I could be held accountable for my actions.

Just as I start to believe that's actually going to happen, his fingertips dig into my thighs as he reaches forward and runs his tongue up the length of me. He moans like I'm the most delicious thing he's ever tasted before moving closer and flattening his tongue against my clit.

I cry out, totally forgetting where we are and who I could wake up. Grabbing the pillow beside me, I cover my mouth as he starts to increase the tempo. He licks, sucks, bites, and teases my entrance with both his tongue and fingers. He builds me up until the tension in my body is at breaking point before slowing his movements down and allowing it to subside.

"Mason, please, please." My cries for more are muffled by the pillow still covering my mouth, so I have no idea if he can hear me or not. If he can, he sure doesn't listen. Why am I not surprised?

His fingers thrust deep and he curls them inside me as he goes to town on my clit. I scream and allow myself to fall at his skilled touch.

My back arches, my hips grind against him and my nails dig into my pillow as I ride out wave after wave of pleasure. My fear about the dark forgotten, my anxiety about what tomorrow brings long gone, the only thing I feel right now is what he's done to me. It's an incredible feeling until I start to come down from my high and realization sets in.

What the fuck did I just do?

20

MASON

The second my tongue connects with her clit, I realize something. I'm addicted.

If I thought tasting her off my fingers last night was mind blowing, then I don't even know what this is.

It wasn't my intention to come in here, drag her down the bed and have her basically ride my face as I licked at her, but the second I stepped into the room with the noble intention of making sure she was sleeping soundly in the darkness I came home to and the sounds of her labored breathing hit my ears, I knew there wasn't any chance that she was asleep.

I remember all too well how scared of the dark she is, and I might be an asshole but there was no way I could be on the other side of the wall and try to ignore the fact that she'd be here terrified.

I thought I probably owed it to her to make her feel safe. I stupidly thought that if she was awake maybe she'd just let me sit with her to keep her calm like when we were kids, but it was all shot to shit when I discovered how worked up she was.

Her cry of pleasure is unintelligible, but I like to think it's my name she's screaming into the pillow. Her legs try to close around me, but I press my palms down against them and continue licking at her gently until she's come down from her high.

I think it's safe to say that this is one blackout I'm not going to forget for a very long time.

My cock strains against the fabric of my pants, desperate to find the same relief she has from the fucked up foreplay we've had going on recently.

I know I don't deserve to be here right now, but my need to try to make her feel safe was too much to bear, especially after discovering what Noah's really been up to only last night. She needs this escape more than ever, and if I'm being totally honest, last night wasn't enough for me. I needed this, and fuck if I don't need more.

She slowly stops twitching against me, the pillow falls from the face, and her fingers thread into my hair to drag me up. My heart pounds and my cock aches to find out if she's going to continue this, if she's going to give me everything I've wanted since I was a horny fourteen-year-old boy.

I pull back, a smug smile on my face at what I just got to experience. Lifting my hand, I wipe the back of it across my mouth but it doesn't reach the other side because a click sounds and then we're both blinded as the bright lights of her room come back to life.

Neither of us says anything, but our eyes immediately lock. Embarrassment, and, I hate to say it, regret fill her. Her hands fly up to cover her breasts, and I almost groan in frustration.

"Cami." I fight like hell to keep my eyes on hers and not allowing them to drop to her exposed body like I'm desperate to do. I've had my hands on almost every part of her body, I know exactly how she feels; now all I need is to see her incredibly sexy curves without the cover of clothing.

"Get out," she whispers, her eyes widening even further. She fights to get away, but my hands land on her hip, pinning her in place. Her chest heaves and her breaths race past her lips as her eyes search mine, trying to read me.

"Cami, don't—"

"I said get out." Her voice is stronger this time, and I start to believe that she really means it. My stomach drops with disappointment. "That was probably the biggest mistake I've ever made. Now get the hell out of my bedroom. You're not welcome in here."

"But I—" She pins me with a vicious look and my words falter. Nothing I can say right now is going to change her mind. Camila might be a lot of things, and stubborn is most definitely one of them.

The second I begin crawling from the bed, she reaches out for the sheets and wraps them around her. Only her head pokes out the top.

My cock tents the front of my pants, and when I look over, her eyes are zeroed in on the bulge. *Well, what did she expect after allowing me to taste her?*

I'm pulling the door open when her soft voice fills the room. I don't look back, I don't dare to, because I know all I'll want to do is climb back under those sheets with her and continue.

"Don't get the wrong idea about this. *This* is nothing, and it will not be happening again."

I hear her warning loud and clear, and I can't help that it fires me up to prove her wrong.

Camila Lopez was mine from the first moment I laid eyes on her. It was always inevitable, and it's about time I started proving that she feels the same.

With the weight of the world on my shoulders, and a raging hard-on, I head straight for the bathroom in the hope that jacking off in the shower might at least take the edge off.

It's wishful thinking, because as I stand under the cold stream of water with my length in my hand, the only thing I can think of is how tight she'd be as I slide into her. How she'd feel as she came around me.

Tingles run down my spine and my balls draw up and I spill my seed into the shallow water at my feet. But her taste is still on my tongue, so the second I come, I'm fucking hard again.

I had girls hanging off me at Ethan's the past two nights. I could have easily taken one of them up to a bedroom to help clear my mind, but something stopped me. I hate to admit it, but that someone was *her*. Especially tonight, knowing that she was probably sitting at home still thinking about Noah and how he could betray her like that. I shouldn't have even gone to Ethan's. My heart ached to stay home and make sure she was okay, even if it was from the safety of my bedroom while she was next door.

"Fuck," I roar when I get into my bedroom with only a towel wrapped around my waist. I slam my fist into the solid wood and revel in the mind numbing pain that shoots up my arm.

I don't give a shit if it wakes anyone up. I don't give a shit about anything but trying to get these fucked up thoughts from my head. I've spent the past four years trying to push her away. My life exploded the day her dad exposed the fraud my dad was committing at work. It was wrong, Dad was in the wrong, I'd never dispute that, but he and Clint had been friends for years and he just went behind Dad's back with all the evidence he'd compiled and watched as his best friend was marched from the office, changing his, and all our lives, forever. The only saving grace, I guess, was that it was never reported to the police. I don't know the reason for that. I can only assume that he was understanding and didn't want to ruin our lives any more than necessary. I do know that the money Dad had stolen was paid back, forcing us into even more debt.

Dad lived for his job, and for his family. We were the reason he was doing what he did. Mom was falling apart. She wasn't earning an income, and because of her, we were drowning in debt. He was just trying to support us, and if Clint had bothered to ask his friend what was going on instead of marching straight to the boss with his little secret mission, then things could have turned out very differently.

I was young. I didn't understand, still don't, the finer details of what happened. All I saw was my parents and my family falling apart, and it was all their fault. The family up the road who were meant to be part of our support network. How could they betray us like that?

They watched as Mom began drowning herself in vodka, staying out all hours and leaving Dad to dive headfirst into his own depression while I was forced to bring up my brothers single handedly. I was a child, yet everything fell on my shoulders.

I so desperately needed the support of my best friend, but every time I looked at her, this uncontrollable hate bubbled up within me. She had a hand in this. Not physically, but she stood beside her parents and watched us fall.

Dad couldn't find a job—he now had a record—Mom was drunk all the time, and I was ripping apart at the seams. If it weren't for Jake, Ethan, and football, I'm not sure I'd have gotten through it all.

As if all that wasn't bad enough, Mom had to bring home one of her drinking buddies. Dad had taken us out to get some food and when we came home, there they were, going at it in the middle of the living room.

They were so drunk, fumbling around each other that they had no idea they'd been caught.

I remember vividly the coldness in my dad's eyes as he turned to me and told me to take my brothers upstairs. I rushed to do as he asked, terrified by the vacant look in his eyes.

I have no idea what was said, but shouting and screaming from below bellowed up as I put some cartoons on the TV in an attempt to cover the noise. Once I knew they were okay, I snuck to the top of the stairs and listened to everything unfold from then on out.

Dad was wild, Mom was manic. There were thuds, grunts, screams, pleading. I could go on. It was exactly what no fourteen-year-old should ever have to endure after everything that had already happened.

Dad left that night. He packed a bag, told me that he'd see me soon, kissed my brothers on their head and he was gone. To this day I've not seen or heard from him.

I had no choice but to try to stay as normal as possible for my brothers while Mom fractured. She was a shell of the woman she used to be, and I was terrified someone would find out and we'd all be split up and shipped off to foster homes around the country. With that thought constantly in the back of my mind, I just kept going.

Even after everything, Gabriella still came around. It seemed that no matter what, she and Mom were still as close as ever. I was grateful for the support; she helped Mom somewhat get herself back together, but I'm pretty sure that to this day, Mom never told her the whole truth. I think that Gabriella still thinks she just fell apart when Dad left, not that she was the catalyst that made it happen.

I hated seeing Gabriella at the house. She and her family represented everything I used to have and everything I craved to have back. A stable home with loving parents, but I feared even back then that neither were something I'd ever have again.

Seeing Camila happy after I turned my back on her hurt. It hurt almost as much as watching my dad leave that day, but what could I do? Her face was a reminder of where it all started. I knew that if I gave her the chance she'd wiggle her way back in and see the ugliness that I was forced to endure on a daily basis, and I couldn't do that to her. One of us deserved to live a good life and to be happy. So I let the hate that had taken up permanent residence under my skin fester and I turned it on her.

I laid awake most of the night, my cock throbbing for some action and my head spinning as thoughts of my fucked up past mix with my equally screwed up present.

Everything I tried to keep hidden was crushed the second I had no choice but to move in here, under their roof. I tried to keep her out of it, to allow her the freedom from getting involved, because I have no doubt it's what she'd have done if she'd have been given the chance. She'd have helped me babysit. She'd have used her own money to buy us food when we had none, and she'd have ensured I focused on the positives. But fuck the positives. Everything, including myself, was poison, and I wasn't allowing her to be touched by it too.

The last thing I need is a sleepless night, seeing as I've got school and work every day and night this week, but when my alarm goes off and my eyes are still wide open, it seems that I don't have much choice.

Knowing that she's not going to take too kindly to seeing me, I do us both a favor and get the fuck out of the house before I even hear movement from her room. I take my gym bag and hit the machines before anyone one else.

By the time I'm joined by a few other members of the team who all look at me with curiosity, I'm covered in sweat and still trying to outrun my memories of last night. Not sure any amount of fucking miles will help with that one somehow.

I ignore each and every one of their stares as I make my way to the showers to get ready for class.

The moment I step out of the locker rooms, Noah is the first fucker I see. He's walking along with a couple of his computer geek buddies, laughing like he's got no cares in the world. My fingers twitch to feel his neck compressing beneath them as I force him to accept what's coming to him for hurting her. I refuse to do it with a fucking audience though. It's definitely a conversation we need to have with a little privacy.

Your time's coming, you fucking waste of space, I promise as I silently trail behind them.

21

CAMILA

om was super sweet to me this morning and made me pancakes for breakfast before school. I know she feels bad about my breakup, but she's equally feeling guilty about leaving me on my birthday weekend for New York. I don't know how many times I've told her that it's fine, but I've given up now because I'm sick of repeating myself. She keeps offering for me to go with them and I've been adamant about staying, but after last night, I can't help being tempted by the offer. Being in a different state might be the only thing that will keep my mind off Mason at this point.

Did I do the right thing by sending him away last night? Yes, I can say with complete certainty that I did. Do I regret it, however? Yes, yes, I fucking do.

The reality check that hit me upside the head when the lights came on and I saw him for the first time between my legs was nothing short of painful. My chest constricted so hard I was worried I might have broken a rib or two. How could I have allowed him in to do that to me? I know it was Mason, but I barely batted an eyelid before I allowed him to strip me half naked and have his way with me.

I pull my cell from the charger I plugged it into sometime after Mason left my room last night and power it up.

One single message comes through.

555-617-9764: Girls like you never win. Enjoy the fall.

What the actual fuck? I throw my cell into my purse, angry at whomever is at the other end of those messages and equally confused and hurt by the fact that

Noah seems to be ignoring me. I assume that means he knows he was caught and is hiding. A fucking apology at least would be nice.

The drive to school is silent, and it makes me yearn for the mornings not so long ago when I'd pick up Amalie and we'd shoot the shit together about whatever drama was going on. Now she's spending so much time with Jake, she doesn't need me to pick her up, seeing as she's hardly ever home. That'll be even more true if she goes through with her plans of buying them both a place to live.

Suddenly, a feeling of loneliness washes through me. My parents are about to head off to New York to embark on the next part of their lives, my best friend is busy planning hers, my boyfriend is... well, we all know what he's doing. Where does that leave me? Alone in a house with a guy who appears to be torturing me on an hourly basis. Just hearing the water running in the bathroom last night after he left me was fucking hard work. My imagination was running on overdrive, imagining what his body might look like as the water ran down over his muscles. He was obviously hard as he left my room. Was he in there fixing his situation? Fuck if the thought of that didn't have me on the verge of breaking the door down so I could find out.

I'm later to school than usual. Students are already making their way to their first class of the day, and the hallways are starting to clear out.

I go directly to my locker, keeping my eyes locked on the floor. I have no idea if anything's got out yet, although if the silence of my cell is anything to go by then it's still very much a secret.

I'm just swapping some books when I sense someone behind me. Glancing over my shoulder, I don't find who I was expecting.

Shane looks seriously sheepish as he stands with his hands shoved deep in his pockets while he chews on his bottom lip.

For the first time since Saturday night, I wonder if those messages came from him. He clearly knew what was happening under his roof. He was there waiting for me.

Shaking my head, I push the thought aside. That's crazy. He'd never do something like that.

"How are you doing?"

"I've been better, but glad I'm not walking around with my head in the clouds anymore."

"I'm sorry you had to find out like that."

"How long have you known?"

"Not long. I've suspected something for a while but never had any evidence. Then after Mason kicked his ass, I started to look a little deeper. We were supposed to just be having a guy's night, watch the game, have a few beers, but the second the girls showed up, I knew he had other ideas. Sadly, it didn't take long to watch him lead her upstairs when he thought we were all distracted."

"So you called me there?"

He casts his eyes away. "No. I was just going to talk to you about it. I didn't want you to find out like that. But it was taken out of my hands."

"By whom?"

He shakes his head. "Doesn't matter. What matters is that you know the truth and you can do what needs to be done."

"Does he know I know?"

"Not that I'm aware of. I thought I'd leave that to you."

I'm not sure if I'm grateful or not. The thought of standing in front of Noah after all the time we've spent together and telling him it's over when he has no idea it's coming, even after what he's done, fills me with dread.

As it turns out though, I don't get the chance.

I was so focused on what Shane had to say that I didn't realize that the hallway around us was not completely empty. Well, that is until an almighty crash sounds from just around the corner. A deep grunt follows before a very familiar voice sounds out.

"This isn't even half of what you deserve, you motherfucker."

Shane and I run around the corner, and what we find is exactly what I feared.

Mason has Noah pinned up against the lockers by the throat as he growls like a wild fucking animal in his face.

"This is going to hurt," Shane mutters, sounding way too amused about this situation.

Mason's fist connects with Noah's cheek, and his head snaps to the side. Both of them seem oblivious that they've got company. I can only hope that the words that fall from Mason's mouth wouldn't if he knew others were listening.

"You know, I probably should be thanking you. If it weren't for you fucking up, then I wouldn't have spent most of last night between her legs." Noah visibly pales, while my lips purse in frustration. This is just one big pissing competition to him. Noah screwed up, so he made it his first priority to take something from me that Noah never managed to.

I feel Shane turn to look at me, but I can't take my eyes off the car crash happening in front of me.

"What I can't figure out is why you'd play away with a slut like Tasha when you had her with her sweet, tight little pus—"

"You're lying. I know you're lying, because that frigid bitch won't let anyone touch her. I've been dating her for years, I should fucking know."

Mason turns a strange shade of purple, and I know I need to put an end to this before he kills Noah.

"Enough," I bark, having had enough of listening to this mortifying conversation.

"No. You're a fucking liar." Noah struggles to get out of his hold as I reach them. Neither of them turns to me. They're both locked in their stare off.

"Put him down, Mason. This isn't your issue, or your fight to have. Now back the fuck off."

"Like fuck it isn't. You know—"

"Just shut up. I think you've already said enough, don't you?"

Reluctantly, Mason releases Noah's neck and he falls down with his hands on his knees as he catches his breath.

"You're going to fucking regret ever touching that whore," Mason warns. I sense he's got more to say, but he soon shuts his mouth when I turn my stare on him.

"He's lying. Tell me he's lying, Cam," Noah begs, clearly not able to handle that while he was off getting his rocks off, I was able to give someone else what I never gave him.

I look back to my pathetic excuse for a boyfriend. Does he actually think he has any kind of right asking that question?

"It doesn't matter."

"You're lying," he snaps, looking up to Mason. "You never would have let him touch you. You hate him."

The sound of Mason's quick intake of breath at this statement is hard to miss, but how he can be surprised after the way he's treated me over the past four years I have no idea. Noah's been by my side through all of it and knows as well as I do how Mason's treated me.

"Yeah well, I never thought you'd cheat, but I guess we can all be wrong at times."

He blanches, but he must had been given a clue that his indiscretions were out in the open when Mason flew at him not so long ago.

"Just in case you need it spelled out for you, we're over. The cheerslut can have you. I hope she chews you up and spits you out like they all do."

"Camila, wait."

Ignoring Noah's pleas for me to hear him out, I turn my back on him and start off down the hallway toward my first class. That is, until Mason reaches out. I tug my arm away before he makes contact. I can't deal with him being this close having done what he just did, let alone touching me.

"Don't," I snap.

"What he just said... does that mean—"

"It doesn't mean anything, Mason. Just leave me the fuck alone. You've already done enough damage."

His face drops, and I almost take every word back, but when I recall what he just did and said to Noah, my back straightens and I leave the three of them behind me.

I intend on going straight to class, but instead of turning left toward history, I find myself heading straight for the exit. After a short drive, I order myself a takeout milkshake from Aces and take it down onto the beach.

I find myself a spot on the last bit of dry sand and sit and watch the waves crashing in.

My fingers grip the cup a little too tightly as I replay those horrendous few minutes in the hallway. Mason had no right doing or saying what he did. Noah was my mess to fix, yet he stormed in like a bull in a fucking china shop. What exactly was he trying to achieve? Does he want to be seen as the big man who always gets what he wants so badly that he had to go after Noah to tell him what he spent his night doing before I even got the chance to look at him?

Digging a little hole for my cup, I drop my head into my hands, trying to figure out where I go from here.

Two things are for sure. One, things are over with Noah, and two, I need to stay the hell away from Mason.

I hang around town for the rest of the day, not feeling prepared at all to face the music, but I know that the gossip will have spread around Rosewood like an out of control wildfire by now. My cell's been vibrating almost constantly in my purse, but I've ignored it, preferring the distraction of shopping for a new outfit for my birthday meal on Friday night.

I don't venture home until I know school's out, knowing that the chances of both my parents being home is high seeing as they're busy packing for Dad's move. But when I pull into our driveway, I find that it's not only their car waiting for me but there's also a red little sporty thing parked there. Knowing it can only belong to one person I know, I suck in a deep breath and prepare for the questions that are about to come my way.

"Hey, sweetie. Did you have a good day?" Mom asks the second I walk into the kitchen. She pulls the refrigerator open and hands me two cans of soda.

"Yeah, it was..." I don't get to finish because Mom's sympathetic eyes find mine.

"It'll get easier, I promise." They're the same words she said to me last night. Just like then, they don't fill me with any kind of confidence for what the next few days and weeks might be like. "Amalie's up in your room starting on her homework. Here, I bought you doughnuts to cheer you up." She passes me a box and my mouth waters.

"Thank you."

"You're welcome, baby. If I can do anything, just let me know."

"Will do." I'm not sure that extends to kicking the Paines out, so I take everything she offers and head up to my room.

I pass Mason's brothers' room and poke my head in to find them playing with their cars, so I leave them to it in favor of the one-on-one session that's about to commence.

"Hey," I say, dropping onto my bed when I find Amalie sitting in my desk chair working.

"Ah... here's the little skiver."

"Skiver?"

"Yeah, you skived class." When I raise an eyebrow, she translates it for me. "Ugh, you skipped class. That better?"

"Much. And yeah, well... you would have too in my position."

"Hey, no judgment here. I've done it a time or two if you remember. That was because of a guy as well."

I groan, choosing to focus on the doughnuts as I ask my next question. "Does everyone know?"

"That Noah's been shagging Tasha? Sadly, yeah. I'm so sorry, Cami."

"Yeah, well, it's not like I wasn't warned it was happening."

The bed dips as she joins me. "Don't beat yourself up for wanting to trust him. It fucking stinks what he was getting up to, but at least you know the truth now, I guess. Is it true that you walked in on them?"

"Sadly."

"How'd you know where to find him?"

"I got a message telling me to go to Shane's house."

"Who from?"

I shrug. "I don't know for sure, but it was one of them."

"One of them?" Amalie asks, but I'm fairly sure she knows the answer. She's had enough run-ins with certain members of the squad.

"The cheerleaders. I had a message saying something like 'girls like you never win' or some crap. They're just jealous. You've got Jake, my boyfriend screwed me over with one of theirs. They're probably seeing it all as one big game."

"I bet it'll go down like a lead balloon then that Mason's been on your side of this whole thing."

"That's not the half of it," I mutter, not really expecting it to come out loud.

"Oh? Is there something I should know about?"

"They might have other reasons to be pissed at me."

"Oh my god, oh my god," she squeals, clapping her hands and bouncing on the bed. "Have you and Mason—"

"Not gone all the way." I wince, dropping my head into my hands.

"But you've done... stuff?"

"There might have been stuff, but I really regret it and would rather not talk about it," I say into my hands in a rush, hoping we can drop the subject.

Amalie's fingers wrap around my wrist and she pulls my hands from my face.

"Firstly, stop hiding. Secondly... how was it?" Her eyebrows wiggle in delight and I want to die a thousand deaths as my mortification from last night when the lights came on consumes me once again.

"It was... a mammoth mistake. We had a power outage, I'm terrified of the dark, he claimed he only came in to make sure I was okay but one thing led to another and..."

"And…" Amalie's eyes are wide as she waits to hear more.

"And I let him… do stuff. But it was a mistake," I add in a rush, just in case she missed it the first twenty times I said it.

"Say that it was a mistake one more time and I'll start to think you're only trying to convince yourself. So he let himself in during a blackout and went to town on your body, just like that?"

"Kind of," I admit with a wince.

"So this wasn't the first time something happened?"

I shake my head. "There was a… moment, Saturday night when I came home after finding… *them*."

"Mason seems like a really good guy to have around in times of trouble, I'll give him that." Her lips curl in an amused smirk and I swat her shoulder for turning this into a joke, but I can't help but allow myself to laugh along with her.

"Well, distraction or not, it shouldn't have happened, and his behavior this morning only served to prove that."

"I heard he confronted Noah."

"It was worse than that. He basically bragged about what happened, rubbed it right in his face."

"And? The guy was shagging Tasha behind your back, why does it matter if Mason shares what you've been up to?"

She's probably right. Why should I care after what he's done to me? But I do. I also care because I don't want to be branded with the same label of 'slag' as the rest of the girls that offer themselves up to the football team without second thought.

"I don't need everyone thinking I bounced straight from one to the other. It really isn't like that, even if it kinda looks that way." I blow out a long breath, wondering how I ended up in this situation.

"I get, Cami. I do. But this is Mason we're talking about. The guys who's been in l—"

"Don't. Don't say it, don't even think it." I narrow my eyes at her but I know it's too late. She's had crazy ideas in her head about the two of us since the day she first met us. "It's not happening. It doesn't matter how good last night felt." Amalie's eyebrow rises in an 'I fucking knew it was good' gesture, but I press on. "He's been nothing but an asshole to me for four years. I doubt that just because he's gone down on me that's going to change. He's set on making my life hell. He'll just use this against me too."

Her eyebrow lifts, and it makes my stomach twist in frustration. Why does she always have to stand up for him? "Do you really believe that?"

I've got to, because I can't allow myself to think about the alternative.

22

MASON

"Motherfucker," I growl, planting my fist firmly in the mirror hanging in the boy's bathroom. Glass shatters, ripping my knuckles to shreds, but I don't give a fuck. I don't feel it. All I can feel is the clenching of my heart and my burning lungs as I fight to drag in the air I need.

"That frigid bitch won't let anyone touch her. I've been dating her for years, I should fucking know."

His words from only a few minutes ago repeat in my head. What he's implying would mean... No. No, she can't be. She wouldn't have allowed me into her room last night to do what I did. She wouldn't have allowed me to slide my hand beneath her panties the night before if she's a virgin. Would she?

"You never would have let him touch you. You hate him."

My chest constricts as I hear those words over and over. They're not news to me. In fact, I've heard them before, directly from her own lips, but having someone else tell me how she feels about me... fuck. I rub at my chest, hoping to ease the ache, but it does little for the organ that's fighting to keep going beneath my ribs.

She should hate me. It's what I was trying to do when I set out on my 'ruin Camila's life' mission. I wanted her to suffer like me. But hearing it, and from him...

I crash back against the wall and slide down to my ass. My head bangs back against the grimy wall behind me, but I don't even feel it.

I'm too lost. Lost to her.

First period is almost over when I eventually emerge from the bathroom with my knuckles cleaned up as best as I can.

"Mase, what the fuck, man?" Jake calls down the hallway. Fuck only knows why he's not in class where he should be.

"I'm good. I'm just...uh..."

His eyes scan my face. Fuck knows what he sees staring back at him, but the second they drop they find my busted up hand. "Who was on the other end of this?"

"No one. Well, not the time that caused this."

His eyes narrow. "So who was it before that?"

"Noah." I admit quietly.

"Again?"

"Can you just leave it?"

"Not likely. Especially when you're bleeding out on the floor. Wanna get a burger?"

"It's barely ten."

"And? You know Bill will cook us what the fuck ever we want the second we stroll in."

I can't really argue with that, so with a small nod in his direction we head out.

"Pull over here."

"What are you—" I stop asking when the pharmacy comes into view.

"Just shut the fuck up, yeah?" Jake says with a laugh, jumping from my car and running toward the entrance.

In only a few minutes he reappears. "Hand," he demands.

"This is very domesticated."

"Yeah well, maybe Amalie's rubbing off on me." I raise an eyebrow. "Oh yeah, she's definitely rubbing me that way." I want to punch the smug motherfucker in the face with the hand he's nursing. He must sense it because he holds tighter, making it sting. "Oh stop being a pussy. You punched a fucking mirror, I'm just making sure there's no glass in it."

"What happened to Jake Thorn, the guy who didn't give a shit about anything or anyone?"

"He fell in love, man, and she cracked his heart wide open."

"I think I like this new version of you better."

"Yeah?"

"Yeah. Just... keep the touchy feely shit to this though. I don't want you turning into a hugger."

"Fuck off am I hugging you. You need a shoulder to cry on, you call my girl. She's good at that shit. Actually, on second thoughts, call your own."

"I don't—"

"Oh that's right. You don't need to call her, you live with her. Just smash her door in and take what you need."

Staring out the windshield, I swallow as the memories from last night hit me.

The feeling of her thighs pinning my head in place, the sound of her cries, her taste.

"Mason?" Jake asks, reading me correctly. I don't need to turn to look at him to know he's got a smile on his face right now.

He's probably the only person who knows how I felt about her all those years ago. We were young, I didn't really understand my feelings for her, but he did. He always has, and I hate how fucking perceptive he is. He's given me so much shit for what I've done to her, but I know it's only been his way to attempt to make me admit that I still have feelings for her.

I've shot him down every single time, but I'm not so sure if that's because I was trying to convince him that he was wrong or myself. It's becoming more and more obvious that I've never forgotten how I felt at only fourteen every time I so much as glanced Camila's way, and I fear it's only been getting worse, not better.

"What did you do?" He finishes whatever the fuck he's doing with my hand and allows me to pull it back to the wheel. I slam my foot down on the accelerator and speed down the street in the direction of Aces.

He allows me the silence, but I know he's only going to let me get away with it for so long.

Seeing as we should be at school, our booth at the back is empty and Bill's eyes widen in shock when we walk in.

"Your Monday going that well?" he asks with a laugh, coming over to serve us himself.

"Something like that," I mutter, then groan at Jake's response.

"Mase has girl problems."

"Ah, I see. Well, if you need any advice, I've had plenty of experience."

We both smile at him before ordering. He turns to leave and I fall back against the bench with a sigh. My hand is fucking throbbing, I flex my fingers, wincing when it only gets worse.

I picture Noah's panic as I pinned him up against the lockers this morning and I know without a doubt that I'd do it again. Even now knowing what I learned soon after.

"So..." Jake encourages once our sodas have been delivered and we're left alone once again.

"I took something that didn't belong to me."

His brows pull together as he studies me.

"You're gonna need to give me more than that."

"Camila caught Noah fucking Tash at a party."

"Shit." Jake winces. "She okay?"

"What do you think?"

"So what's this got to do with you punching a mirror?"

"I might have... distracted her. Twice." A smug smile twitches at his lips and I look away, not wanting to witness him being so happy about the situation. "But it seems that the reason that Noah was banging someone else was because he wasn't her..." I trail off, hoping he'll put two and two together. The last thing I need to do right now is spill any more of her secrets.

He's silent for a few seconds and I look back up at him. I see the second the penny drops. "No fucking way. They've been together for like..."

"Two years," I helpfully add. "That doesn't excuse his cheating though."

"I'm not saying it does, I'm just shocked is all. They've always seemed so... close."

"I know. I didn't even think. I just barged in and..."

"And..." He wiggles his eyebrows, wanting to drag the dirty details from me.

"Distracted her."

"So what? You took her V card. It was always meant to be yours anyway, even you can't deny that."

"It didn't get that far. She kicked me out."

"So what's the fucking issue then?"

I'm silent as I consider his question. I pushed her further than she's comfortable with without a second thought. I might have been horrible to her, but that shit's not me. I don't take without knowing my partner is with me one hundred percent.

"Ohhh... you're pissed you didn't get all the way."

"What? No. I'm pissed because she didn't want it and I did it anyway. What the fuck, man? I thought you were here to help." I push from the bench and go to leave.

"Sit your ass back down, dickhead."

Without instruction, my legs bend and I hit the seat.

"I know Camila, and I can assure you that if she wasn't into it, she'd have kicked you out long before you touched her."

We're both silent as Bill approaches with our food and places two huge plates of burgers and fries in front of us. We thank him and he leaves us to it. All the while, Jake's words spin around in my head. He's right, I know he is. Camila is headstrong. She hasn't backed down to any of the shit I've given her, and she's not likely to just roll over now. But it doesn't change the fact that she's clearly been denying Noah any action but quite happily allowed me what I thought she needed.

I poke my pile of fries as my head races.

"This is so fucked up," I mutter. I don't even really mean for Jake to hear it, but he does.

"Is it? As far as I can tell, you're on the cusp of getting everything you've ever wanted. It just depends on what you do next and if you fuck it up."

I look up at my best friend, my jaw dropped in surprise. When the fuck did he become so wise?

―――――

We don't return to school. Instead we head to his trailer and hide out in his little makeshift gym. My muscles scream at me to stop after my workout this morning, but I welcome the pain. Anything in an attempt to keep my mind from Camila and what's going through her head after what happened this morning.

Once we've both run out of energy, we collapse on Jake's sofa. He lights up while I make do with a bottle of water from his lukewarm fridge.

"Amalie's talking about buying a house for us to live in," he blurts.

I splutter with the water I was attempting to swallow. "Shit, man. That's like... serious."

"You're telling me." He pulls himself so he's sitting up straight.

"What's the problem? You love her, right? Want to be with her always?"

"Yeah, I don't even need to think about that. It's just..."

"Just?"

"She's got all this money just burning a hole in her bank account, and what do I have to offer?"

"Besides your outstanding personality and sharp wit?"

"I'm serious. She's, well... everything, and this is all I have." He gestures to his old trailer.

"She doesn't care, Jake. She wants you, not what or what doesn't come with you. She loves you, what's in there." I nod down to his chest and he blows out a long breath.

"I know. It's just so huge."

"Agreed. But there are no rules. Trust her to know what's right for her and trust yourself to make the right decision. If moving in together feels right, then do it. You've both experienced enough shit over the years to be able to make a serious decision about this. Just do what feels right."

"You know, I could say the same thing to you."

"We're not talking about me."

He shakes his head but thankfully keeps his mouth shut. We hang out at his place for the rest of the afternoon before Jake has to head back to school for practice.

"When are you coming back?"

I shrug, bending down to pull on my shoes. "Whenever Mom pulls her finger out of her ass and gets a real job."

"Never, then?" he says sadly. "We need you if we stand any chance in our next few games."

"I'm doing my best, man."

"I know. It just fucking sucks."

I drop Jake back at school before heading to work. I change in my car before pulling my cell out of my pocket. I've got a few messages, most from Ethan asking where the fuck I am, and a few are from the other guys on the team, but there's nothing from Camila. Not that I really expected there to be.

Should I have left her to deal with the fallout of what I did this morning? No, probably not. But I couldn't hang around and be forced to look at Noah after what he admitted. I equally couldn't look at Camila, knowing the truth. Seeing the regret in her eyes would kill me. It's most definitely something I can live without.

With a sigh, I climb from the car. This is my life now. I'd better man up and deal with it.

———

Every day that follows is just a repeat of the one before. I somehow drag my body from bed just in time to get to school before the final bell. I spend all day with my head down, ignoring Camila in the few classes we share. I've already done enough damage. If she wants to bring up what happened then she's going to have to come to me, not the other way around. I'm still undecided if I actually regret going to her that night or not. On one hand, I still remember how she reacted to my touch, but on the other, I remember Noah's face as I filled him in on what we'd been up to, and guilt consumes me that she might not have been as into it as I remember.

The second I walk out of the school building after class, I head straight for work. Each night is the same, even down to some of the same customers buying the same items every day. It's monotonous, but it it's exactly what I need.

By the time Friday rolls around, I want to give up. When I head downstairs before leaving for school, there are birthday balloons and banners everywhere and a pile of gifts the size of a small mountain on the dining table.

Rolling my eyes at the sight. I grab a cereal bar from the cupboard and leave before any of the celebrations start. They're definitely something I don't want to be a part of. As if living here as it is isn't a constant reminder of the stable family life I don't have, I don't need to see them spoil Camila on her special day.

23

CAMILA

"Happy birthday, baby!" Mom calls the second my foot hits the bottom step. She comes rushing over and wraps me in a hug. A ball of emotion clogs my throat as I embrace her back. It's exactly what I need.

This week's been... weird. She and Dad have either been out or packing getting ready to head to New York tomorrow, and I've either been in the house with Mason's brothers or at school being ignored by the guy himself. I was expecting him to corner me after he tried to talk to me in the hallway but nothing. I lie awake every night after he gets home from work, expecting him to let himself in so he can ask me about what Noah said, but again, nothing. Whenever I see him at school, he just looks down as if I don't exist. I don't fucking get it and it's frustrating the hell out of me.

I thought it would be worse with him moving in, but this week I've seen him less than ever. I should be relieved after everything, but I'm far from it.

"I can't believe my baby is eighteen." Mom pulls back, her eyes swimming with tears. "Come on, I made you waffles."

I take her hand and allow her to lead me toward the kitchen where Dad, Nic, Ollie, and Charlie are waiting.

"Happy birthday," they all sing in unison. I thank them, looking around, wondering if I'm the only one who notices the person who's markedly absent.

Shouldn't he be here for this too?

I don't want to ask. I want to ignore him as much as he has been me, but I find the words tumbling out nonetheless.

"Where's Mason?"

"He'd already left when I knocked. Probably got practice or something."

My chin drops at his mom's excuse. "He's not on the team anymore, so why would he be at practice?"

"He's... what?" She's totally taken aback, and it ignites a fire in my belly. Does she really have no fucking clue what he's doing for her? For his family?

"He quit," I spit, taking a step toward her, my fingers curling into a fist. "He quit to pick up more hours so he could look after his family."

She swallows and breaks our eye contact. At least she has the decency to look guilty about it.

"But—"

"But what? Are you going to find a job so he doesn't have to work so hard, or are you going to continue fucking around?"

"Camila," Dad snaps, but I ignore him.

"Bringing money into the house shouldn't be his responsibility. It should be yours," I seethe. "He's risking everything for you. College. His future. All because you can't be bothered to do your job and support your kids." I'm only assuming the bit about college is true. The guy I used to know used to spend all his time talking about playing college football, so I can only assume that hasn't changed, and him not being on the team at the most vital time of the year is not going to help. They've got three games left before the playoffs. Three games he should be playing in.

"I'll fix it, I promise," she whispers.

"Really. When is that going to happen? His team needs him on the field tonight. The season is almost over already. I'm afraid it's going to be too little too late."

"He'll play the last two games. I'll make sure of it." She puts more conviction into those words than I've heard from her in years, so I can only hope they're true. "Tell him to sort his hours so he can play."

"Do your own dirty work," I snap, finding my chair and ignoring the atmosphere I've created around the breakfast table.

The second I've forced down my waffles, I run for my car, desperate to not have to look at Nicky any longer. I'm starting to understand why Mason suddenly changed. His mom was never like that when we were kids. Maybe things were worse than he allowed any of us to see.

I'm met at school by Amalie and Alyssa, who are holding out a tray full of doughnuts with candles poked into them.

"Happy birthday to you, happy birthday to you," they sing, but the fact that now both Shane and Noah are missing doesn't pass me by. First I lost Mason, then Shane, and now Noah. I know the reasons for each absence, but it doesn't mean it hurts any less. Okay, so after everything, maybe I'm not all that bothered about Noah.

"Thank you." I plaster on a smile that I don't feel. So much is already changing, and we're not even that close to the end of the year and the end of our school careers. As always, that thought makes me think of what I'm going to do next. Everyone tells me that I'll figure it out and not to worry, but how can I when everyone seems to know exactly what they want to do and I'm like a lost little sheep running around the field, trying to figure out which way is up.

I take a pink-striped doughnut from the box and cram it into my mouth in the hope it covers how I'm really feeling. I'm eighteen today. An adult at last. I should be celebrating, but my uncertain future along with everything has me feeling nothing like doing so. It makes me glad I decided on a quiet evening with my parents tonight and a day with my girls tomorrow. I don't have it in me to party.

I'm gutted to miss tonight's away game, but it's a little too far to travel and I knew my parents wouldn't have any of it if I tried demanding to go. It's the first and hopefully the last game of the season I'll miss. I know that I'll go to college next year and have a new team to support, but the Bears have been my team for as long as I can remember, and to be able to see them succeed this year under Jake's leadership would be everything.

"I'm so excited for tomorrow," Alyssa says, bouncing toward our lockers. "A day to chill, no boys."

"Something you need to tell us, Alyssa?" Amalie asks before I get the chance. As far as I'm aware, she's still free and single—but things can change fast, as I'm beginning to learn.

"Nah, I'm still working on the basketball team. Any day now, one of them will figure out that their life is not complete without me."

Amalie and I laugh at her serious expression.

I pull my locker open the second I get there to pull some books out, but when the door opens, a squeal rips from my lips as something flies out at me.

"Fucking hell," I say, my heart racing as an 'Eighteen Today' balloon rises into the hallway. "Was this really necessary?" I ask, turning to look at the girls.

They glance at each other, questions filling their eyes.

"I wish it was us, but we just brought the doughnuts," Amalie admits.

"So who?" I mutter, pulling out the weight, hoping there might be a note, but there's nothing. "Weird."

"I bet it was him," Amalie whispers in my ear.

Tingles run down my spine at her suggestion, and I know he's looking at me. I close my eyes for a moment, not wanting anyone to see the water that fills them. His absence has hurt this week. I know I was the one who sent him away, but is it wrong to have expected him to fight? He's never been one to go down easily; that's what makes all this worse. He's not himself, and I fear all this might have hurt him more than he'd ever let on.

When I turn and look over my shoulder, Jake and the team are at their usual benches, but Mason's not with them. I quickly glance around, but I see no sign of him. I do, however, spot Shane, who's hovering a little down the corridor, looking like he wants to come over but is unsure because of Amalie's presence. My heart aches for him once again that he feels he needs to keep his distance for something he didn't do.

I wave him over. He hesitates, but when Amalie notices who's holding my attention she smiles at him.

"Happy birthday," he says, giving me a hug.

"Thank you."

"Hey," he says to both Amalie and Alyssa. I hate the uncertainty in his eyes, and as he looks up to where Jake is, I realize that he's more scared of him than anything else.

Following his line of sight, Amalie turns back to Shane. "Just ignore him." She reaches out and places her hand on his forearm encouragingly. Jake immediately jumps from the bench and starts making his way over.

"Watch out, caveman incoming."

Amalie rolls her eyes but doesn't make any effort to put space between her and Shane, and why should she? They're not doing anything wrong.

"Let me walk you to class," Shane says, turning my way.

"You don't need to be afraid of him."

"I'm not, I'd just rather not be in his way."

I grab what I need and step into Shane's side, saying a quick goodbye to both Amalie and Alyssa. "Everyone knows it wasn't you," I say, looking up to Shane. It's not the first time I've said the words, and I'm sure it won't be the last.

"People will believe what they like." He shrugs.

"But you're giving them the power to make you hide, make you run away."

"I'm not doing anything I don't want to do, Cam. I never have wanted to spend time with Jake, and I still don't. Nothing's changed."

"But the parties."

"Meh... my brothers have held parties most weekends since I was a kid. They're nothing new."

I look up to him, trying to read if he's telling the truth or not.

As we close in on the math department, almost all the cheer squad seems to emerge from the girls' bathroom.

"You should have seen her face," one of their high-pitched voices screeches over the rest.

"She so had it coming to her," someone else adds.

Shaking my head, I go to side step them, but sadly I'm noticed before I get to escape.

"And people call us the sluts," Chelsea says, rolling her eyes at me. "I know it's only Shane, but seriously, how many guys do you intend on getting your claws into this week? Noah was doing the right thing, if you ask me. Do you know how long it was going on for?"

The blood drains from my face. It's a question I've tried not to think about, knowing the answer could only make the whole situation a hell of a lot worse.

Shane's stance changes beside me before he steps up to Chelsea. "That's enough," he barks. I can't deny my opinion on Shane changes in that one instant.

He's always been the quiet one who does anything he can to stay out of trouble. Unfortunately, who he is and the life he's been born into means he's often dragged right into the middle of it all.

Chelsea's eyes widen in shock, her chin dropping. Is she... is she lost for words?

"Camila's not in the wrong here. *They* are." He flicks his eyes to Tasha, who's cowering behind her leader. "I don't care if she's a cheerleader or the fucking President, she shouldn't have gone after someone else's boyfriend. End of."

Shane holds Chelsea's eyes captive as he stares down at her. It's as if he's willing her to bite back. His chest heaves, his fists clenching at his sides as his frustration gets the better of him.

I wait, hardly breathing to see what's going to happen next, but after a silent, and tense, few seconds, Shane releases her and turns to me.

"Shall we continue?" It's almost painful to drag my eyes away from a shell-shocked Chelsea and over to him, but when I do, it's worth it because his eyes are glittering with accomplishment, and so they should. He just silenced the queen bitch, and in front of her team.

"That was fucking awesome." I practically bounce all the way to my math class. "Did you see her face? She was so fucking shocked. Man, if people stood up to her more it would knock her down a peg or two." Shane remains silent beside me. Noticing the tense set of his shoulders, I slow our pace and come to a stop in a quiet part of the hallway. "Are you okay?"

"Yeah, I'm good." He doesn't look down at me, just stares off over my shoulder. When I turn to see what has his attention, I find an empty hallway.

"I know things are weird now Noah and I aren't..." I trail off, not wanting to think about all that. "But I'm here, if you need to chat or anything, you know that right?"

His eyes finally find mine and I breathe a sigh of relief when I find his usual green happy-go-lucky ones looking back at me.

"Come on, we're going to be late."

Both Noah and Mason are in my second class of the day, so just as things start to settle down in math, I know I've got a potential storm brewing. We should have all had a class together on Monday, but I skipped and since found out that I wasn't the only one.

I slip down in my chair, hoping it makes me invisible as Noah walks in. My stomach twists and my heart aches. There's so much familiarity there. I could so easily get up and go and sit on his lap. It would be second nature. I've spent so much time with him by my side, in my corner, or so I thought. But then his betrayal hits me like a bat, and I have to fight to keep my waffles down.

It's weird. Not even a week's passed since I found them, but already, I don't think I hate him. I'll never forgive him, I know that much, but I just can't find it in me to give him the time or energy it takes to hate him.

With a sigh, I pick up my pen and start doodling in my book in an attempt to look busy. I don't think he'll try to talk to me—he hasn't all week, so I can't imagine he will today even if it is my birthday.

To my utter shock, as he passes my desk, he drops a white envelope down, but he doesn't stop.

I should stuff it in my bag, or the trash, and forget it exists, but only after a few seconds my curiosity gets the better of me.

Pulling the lip open, I slide out the birthday card. On the front is a vintage typewriter with happy birthday typed on the paper sitting in it. It's pretty but nothing special. It's not until I open it that my breath catches.

I'm so sorry.

A silent sob rumbles up my throat. The fuck load of emotions I'd been managing to keep shoved down threaten to bubble up and spill over.

Sucking in a long, slow breath, I attempt to calm myself down. I'm in the middle of class, and I'm not the kind of girl who just cries during a school day, I'm stronger than that.

I close my eyes and will myself to pull it together when the atmosphere in the room presses down on my shoulders. I don't need to look to know why, but I do, nonetheless.

Mason's hard and cold eyes are locked on Noah, who squirms in his seat. He's not a fighter, so I'd imagine being pinned against the lockers and punched in the face the other day terrified him.

As Mason steps farther into the room, he seems to suck all the air out. I fight to drag in the breaths I need, but as he passes my desk all I get is a lungful of his scent. My body betrays me and sends me back to being laid out on my bed with him between my thighs. I squirm in my seat but it's for a very different reason than with Noah, although both involve Mason's hands.

When I was with Noah, the idea of going further was always on my mind, but that was mainly because I knew he wanted it, although I was a little curious. But now, after experiencing just a taste with Mason, it's all I can think about. And I'm pretty sure it's not just the act or the pleasure, but the person who delivered it.

I'm fucked.

He doesn't stop. His steps don't even falter as he passes me. I turn my head away from him to ensure he can't see the emotion swimming in my eyes.

He doesn't walk much farther, seeing as he sits directly behind me. The scratch of his chair against the floor makes my teeth grind.

It's another five seconds before I hear anything else from him. The rest of the class have gone back to their previous conversations, so they're probably totally unaware he even says anything to me.

"Please don't tell me one pathetic I'm sorry card will send you running back."

My spine stiffens. I didn't even realize I'd dropped the card on the desk in front of me. Quickly reaching out, I close it and shove it into my notebook.

"I thought now that you'd been shown what it could really be like, you'd realize that you can do better than that—"

"Enough," I snap, turning to face him. A satisfied smirk plays on his lips as my eyes narrow at him. The rest of the room silences and turns toward us to watch the show. They're all well aware that there's no love lost between the two of us. This isn't the first time we've had a standoff in school in the past four years, so they're probably waiting for their next installment of the Camila and Mason show.

"What time shall I stop by later for your special birthday surprise?" His words drip with sex, and I wouldn't be surprised if all the girls within a ten-foot radius aren't wet right now from the deep rumbling of his voice and the promise in his tone.

"Fuck you." My voice is low and angry, but he doesn't miss it. His smile curls up wider.

"What's that? You want to go all night this time?"

I swear steam nearly blows from my ears. My teeth grind as my fingers twitch to lash out at him. If it weren't for the fact that the rest of our class are all staring at us, waiting for something to kick off, then I might just do it.

Something crackles between us as our stare holds. I want to say it's hate, but even I'm not blind enough to recognize that it's laced with desire, a need that I'm not sure either of us is going to be able to deny forever.

I open my mouth to say something, fuck knows what, when our teacher slams the classroom door. Rustling fills my ears as everyone turns to look to the front of the room.

"Miss Lopez, Mr. Paine, do we have a problem here? I'm sure it could all be sorted out in detention."

I blow out a frustrated breath and turn toward Mr. Lawrence, who's standing with his hands on his hips waiting none too patiently to begin his lesson.

"N-No, sir. We're good."

I take my seat, but Mason's stare burns into the back of my head, and the second Mr. Lawrence turns to write on the board, I look over my shoulder to find that he is indeed staring daggers into me. His eyes might be narrowed and hard, but I see more within them. I see the twinkle of delight, the promise, the lust that sends tingles headed straight between my thighs.

The second the bell goes, I scoop up everything from my desk and run. I don't know if I'm running more from Noah or Mason—not that it really matters. I don't want to talk to either of them.

Thankfully, the rest of the day is uneventful. Well, unless you count the huge chocolate cake that Amalie appears with in the cafeteria at lunchtime with eighteen candles lit and ready to be blown out by the birthday girl.

With the majority of the school making the trip to Eden Falls for the game tonight, it means that Aces is pretty dead after school when I walk in with Amalie and Alyssa flanking my sides.

"You know you could have gone tonight, right?" I say to Amalie, who's missing the game to have a milkshake with me.

"We can be apart sometimes, you know."

"Really?" I ask, my eyebrows almost hitting my hairline.

"Anyway, I'm having dinner with Gran tonight. Going to broach the subject of me moving out."

"That sounds like fun."

"I'm pretty sure she knows it's coming. I'm hardly ever there and living in Jake's trailer. She knows how much money I inherited, so I'd be crazy not to use it."

"You found a place yet?" Her face transforms at my question. "You have?"

She pulls her cell from her pocket, swipes the screen and then turns it to me. I look down at the small but perfectly formed newly-built duplex on the outskirts of town, and my heart drops. I feel selfish that it's my first reaction. It's not all that far away, but it will put the final nail in the coffin for any more morning trips to school together. Not that they'd been happening recently. It's just another thing that's changing, and I don't like it.

"It's cute."

"You could sound a little more enthusiastic."

"I'm sorry. It really is nice. I can totally see you living there." That perks her up a little.

"Really?"

"Yeah. Have you viewed it?"

"We're going Sunday. I'm so excited. A place of our own, no worrying about damp or my gran walking in on us."

"As if everyone at school didn't envy you enough already," Alyssa helpfully adds.

"Yeah, the girl with dead parents who had to move halfway around the world. All they see is the good stuff, they ignore the pain it took to get there."

"I-I know that. I was just saying."

An awkward silence settles over us.

"So you think they're going to do it tonight?"

"Of course they are. Jake was confident they were ready. Still pissed Mas— sorry," she cuts herself off when she sees the grimace on my face.

"What's up with that anyway? He suddenly gives up the team and starts fighting your battles for you. Has he had another personality transplant?" Alyssa asks, and I feel guilty that we're not as close as we were when Mason changed the first time. She experienced it all with me back then, knew every little thing he did to me, but now she's barely on the sidelines of what's going on.

"He's got some family stuff going on. He's had to stop playing, but it's only temporary. He'll be back before the end of the season." I want to believe what Nicky said to me this morning but honestly, I'm having a hard time doing so.

Our conversation turns to another of my favorite topics right now: college applications. I just about manage to hold in my groan as Amalie explains that she's managed to get Jake to a meeting with Miss French and he's finally beginning to accept that college could be an option. It makes me realize that I'm not the only one dealing with everything changing in my life and that I should suck it up and get on with it like everyone else around me seems to be doing.

Once our milkshakes are empty and we've exhausted our college chat, they both agree to meet at mine tomorrow morning before our date at the spa. I just hope that our conversations tomorrow while being pampered can stay on the lighter end of the scale. We're supposed to be relaxing, not stressing about our futures.

My parents are both in their bedroom getting ready for our meal when I get in, but I find Nicky, Ollie, and Charlie playing in the living room. The second I see she's alone I turn to escape, not wanting a rerun of this morning at breakfast.

"Camila, please wait."

I pause halfway to the stairs, but I don't turn around.

"I wanted to apologize. I was out of order this morning. You were right, everything you said about me as a mom. You're right. I've failed. I've failed Mason, and if I'm not careful, I'm going to ruin those two in there too. I'm going to fix it though."

"How?" I ask, spinning on the balls of my feet and pinning her with a look I hope comes across as threatening.

"I-I... uh... I've got a job."

"Just like that? How convenient."

"I had been looking, just not putting as much effort in as possible." I raise an eyebrow, not believing a word of it. "It's a bar over in East. I start after the boys' bedtime and will be home to make them breakfast and take them to school. The wages are so much more than my last job, so hopefully we'll be able to get back on our feet sometime soon and out of your hair. I know life's not been easy for you with us all—Mason—living so close."

"It's—"

"Don't try to pretend that it's anything other than it is, Camila. I've leaned on your mom too much, relied on her to help me, but she's my best friend, not my keeper. I start tomorrow night and I've arranged for the boys to have a sleepover, so the house is yours if you wanted to celebrate your birthday without any adults around." The reminder that my parents leave in the morning doesn't fill me with joy. I'm also not sure how I feel about the prospect of Mason and me having the house to ourselves. Anything could happen. I fight to keep the wicked smile from my lips that threatens to break free at the prospect. "I won't take up any more of your time. Go and get ready, I just needed to tell you that you're right and I'm sorry."

With a nod, I turn back to the stairs, but before I lift a foot, I say over my shoulder, "I'm not the only one you need to be telling this to."

"I know. I'll speak to him, I promise."

The only thing I can do is take her word for it, so I continue up to my room. Before pulling out the dress I bought for tonight, I grab my cell and send both Amalie and Alyssa a text.

Me: Got the house to myself tomorrow night. Want a girls' night in?

I avoid adding *to keep me away from Mason if he's here,* but I'm pretty sure Amalie will be able to read between the lines. And I'm proved right ten minutes later when I get a reply.

Amalie: Sounds like fun but if you want him, go get him!

Groaning, I throw my cell on my bed and take my outfit with me to the bathroom.

24

MASON

"Get your ass over here now. I had this party for you," Ethan complains when I answer his sixth call after finishing work and replying to his message that I'm not coming to his house to get wasted.

"Fuck off. That's bullshit and you know it."

"But we won," he whines like a little bitch. "You know how horny I get when we win."

"Fucking hell, if I agree, will you stop talking?"

"Yes! I've got a row of shots waiting for me and a gaggle of girls all wanting a piece. You might not even find me when you arrive."

"A gaggle?" I ask, although really, I don't need any more detail than that.

Ethan seems to be diving headfirst into whatever bottle and willing girl he can find recently. He claims to be having fun, but there are shadows in his eyes that tell a different story. He's friends with the wrong two guys if he thinks that Jake and I can't see that it's all a cover for something. For what though? We have no idea.

"Yes, now get your ass here. There's plenty to go around."

The idea of touching another girl besides the one I can't get out of my head is anything but appealing, but knowing Ethan needs me has me putting my car in drive and heading to his place. I know Camila was going out with her parents tonight, so I can only hope she won't be there so we won't have a repeat of last week.

The music's pounding when I step through Ethan's front door, and, as usual, there are people everywhere, quite a few of whom I don't even recognize. Making my way to the kitchen, I try to find Jake. I'm sure he wants to celebrate as much as Ethan does after another win. I try to push aside that it's another win that they managed without me.

"Mase, my man. Get over here," Ethan calls the second he spots me. "Here." He hands me two shots of something dark. I hesitate in knocking them back, unlike him. "Live a little," he says, having another before leaning in and whispering, "She's not here. No rescue mission needed tonight. Kick back."

Without a second thought, I tip the small glass to my lips and allow the liquid to burn down my throat before warming my belly. It feels good. But not as good as the haze that begins after the third... or fourth one. Damn, it's been too long since I felt this free.

I hang around with Ethan for a bit before a couple of girls come over and drag us to the living room to dance. I have no clue who they are, but as I watch Ethan shove his tongue down one of their throats, I guess he does, or he just really doesn't care.

I drink, I dance, I fight off multiple advances from different girls. I must admit that by the end of the night when people are either starting to leave or pass out, the temptation of those who are still interested is high. I haven't had sex for-fucking-ever, and the thought of sliding balls deep into a willing girl has my cock thickening in my pants. But then the image of Camila with her fingers gripping onto my hair so tightly I thought she was going to pull it out hits me, and the temptation to drag one of them upstairs wanes a bit.

I'd gotten a text from Mom when I'd left work to tell me that she'd organized for the boys to have a sleepover tomorrow night and that she'd be out, so I know I don't need to worry about my responsibilities tonight. Knowing that is such a weight lifted from my shoulders, but my desire to go home to her only gets stronger the more alcohol I have.

"I need to go home," I slur to whomever's listening.

"Nah, man. You've had too much." I squint my eyes at the face which has just said that. I vaguely recognize him. A member of the team? Who the hell knows.

"I need... I need her."

"I'm sure I can find you someone suitable." As he says that, someone I do recognize comes hopping around the corner. "Hey, Chels. Mason needs a girl."

She licks her lips and eyes the length of me. Any desire that was coursing through my veins instantly vanishes. She hobbles over and attempts to look sexy as she falls onto the sofa.

"What can I do for you?" She winks, and it makes me want to bring up the drink I've consumed.

"I think I'm good."

"Here, have a drink with me."

I oblige because there's nothing else I want to do with her, even if she does suck good cock.

———

A sharp pain to my shin wakes me up. My eyes fly open in shock as it radiates up my thigh.

What the fuck?

Rubbing at my leg, I look around a room I recognize as being one of Ethan's guestrooms before dropping my eyes to the bed beside me.

Oh no, no, no.

My heart starts to pound and blood rushes past my ears in panic as I stare down at a sleeping Chelsea.

No, no, no, no.

I slide from my bed on still drunk, wobbly legs and back away. Did I drink that much? Looking down at myself, I'm relieved to find that I'm still wearing my jeans and boxers, although my fly is undone.

I look around the room, hoping to find my shirt, but I come up empty. *Fuck.*

Chelsea stirs and I panic. Rushing from the room, I don't look where I'm going and stub my toe on the corner of the dresser.

"Motherfucker," I cry, grabbing my toe in agony as my eyes water.

"What's wrong, baby?" Her sweet, sickly voice has bile racing up my throat.

Please tell me I didn't. Please, dear fucking god, tell me I didn't.

"Come back to bed. I'll make it all better."

Glancing over my shoulder, I find her sitting up in bed with the covers pooled at her waist.

"Put them away, Chelsea. I'm not interested."

"Not what you said last night."

"You're lying," I state, reaching for the door handle to get the fuck away from her. There might be a pair of tits ready for the taking, but knowing who they're attached to doesn't make the risk worth it by a long shot.

"Am I?"

Not being able to stand her voice any longer, I close the door behind me and go in search of my shirt and some painkillers.

"Yo, sick night, man," Ethan says, stumbling into the kitchen while I'm rummaging through his cupboards with a bottle of whiskey in his hand.

"Please tell me you're not having that for breakfast."

"What?" he asks, lifting it to his lips and downing a generous shot. "Hair of the dog."

"What the fuck's going on with you?"

"Enjoying life, just like you should be."

"Who says I'm not?"

"Your face." He looks up over my shoulder, his eyes lighting up. "Wait a minute, is there something you want to share?"

Before I get a chance to ask or even look around, arms slip around my waist and Chelsea appears at my side wearing... my fucking shirt.

"Give it back," I demand, removing her from my body.

"Aw, I thought you left it for me, baby."

"Un-fucking-likely. Give it back."

"Okay," she says with a shrug and a salacious smile. She props her crutch against the counter and curls her fingers around the bottom of the fabric. "If you insist."

As she peels it up her body, Ethan's eyes go wide as saucers.

"Damn, girl. What were you wasting your time on him for?"

"Fucking have her," I spit, pulling the fabric of my shirt over my head and cringing when I realize it smells like her pretentious perfume.

"Come here, baby. Let me show you how a real man does it."

Chelsea takes Ethan's outstretched hand, not giving two shits about the fact that she's standing there stark naked. Girl's got no shame or morals, and the further away I am from her, the better.

Reaching into my pocket for my car keys, I find something else first. I pull the foil free from the fabric to find an empty condom wrapper.

Anger bubbles up inside me. Storming back over, I wrap my fingers around Chelsea's arm and pull her from Ethan's grasp.

"I don't know what game you're playing, but it needs to stop." I flick the wrapper in her face. "You might be a bitch, Chelsea, but this isn't you. I know I didn't fuck you last night. I wasn't even capable of getting up the stairs, so cut the shit and stop pretending. You're only trying to convince yourself."

She opens her mouth, but I've had enough of her bullshit and storm from the house.

Why the fuck did I come here last night? I should have just gone home to bed, or even better, the bed next door.

The house is in silence when I arrive home. Camila's parents have left for New York, she's at her birthday spa trip with Amalie and Alyssa, and Mom's pawned the boys off on a friend, presumably so she can have a night out. I roll my eyes. Taking myself straight to the bathroom, I strip out of my Chelsea scented shirt and throw it at the wall like this whole mess is its fault. Turning the water up as hot as it goes, I step underneath. I'm fairly certain nothing happened between us last night and she's just playing her usual game, probably trying to make some poor guy jealous by making it look like everyone else wants her. I'd like to have hoped she'd grown up enough to realize that that shit don't work, but apparently not. The water burns but I ignore it, wanting to wash away every second of last night. The less I remember the better.

Once I get back to my room, I fall onto my bed with the intention of getting some more sleep but I end up just lying there staring at the ceiling, wondering what time Camila's coming back.

I eventually get fed up of just wasting time and pull some homework from my bag and attempt to catch up a little after another week of working late. The sooner Mom sorts her shit out and I can cut down, the better.

I get lost in what I'm doing, and whoever it is at the front door ends up ringing incessantly before I give up and climb from the bed to find out who it is.

"Wassup, man!" Ethan booms, stepping into the house with a crate, followed by Jake and the rest of the team.

"What the hell are you doing?"

"Bringing the party to you, what's it look like?"

"I said no to this," I call over my shoulder, but he ignores me. Racing after him, I stop him in the kitchen just before he starts raiding the cupboards. "This isn't my house. You can't party here."

"Camila won't care. I have it on good authority that you two have it to yourselves for the weekend so... here we are. Got things to celebrate, man."

I blow out a breath. "I don't want all the guys knowing I had to move in here," I admit quietly.

"Don't sweat it. We told them it's Camila's thing. Wanting a blow out after Noah and all that shit. We got your back, man."

Music comes on as the sound of the guys' banter from the living room filters down to us.

"Okay fine. We'll order pizza," I say, slapping his thieving hands away from the cupboards. "But just the guys, okay?"

"Yeah, whatever you want." He winks at me and my stomach twists. He's so not telling the truth, but I roll with it—for now, at least.

Beers and pizza with the guys soon turns into shots and beer pong, and beer pong soon turns into body shots with the cheer squad and a few other girls Ethan managed to drag here from fuck knows where. I can't help but notice Chelsea's absence though. I'd have thought she'd have been first here after last night.

"Hey, handsome. Ethan said I should come over here and show you a good time," a soft voice whispers in my ear. I turn to look over my shoulder and the room spins at my movement.

She's pretty and her voice isn't like nails down a chalkboard like Chelsea's. She walks around me and makes herself at home on my lap.

"Nice house you've got here."

"Thanks. Can't say I pay much attention."

Her hands run up my chest and over my shoulders. Leaning in, her nose brushes against my neck. "Hmmm... you smell so good. I bet you taste even better." Her lips hit my skin and the world vanishes around me as I focus on her attention. Fuck if it doesn't feel good.

25

CAMILA

Seeing as both Alyssa and Amalie are coming back to my house for the night, we make the most of the spa's restaurant before heading home. We've had an incredible day. We've been scrubbed, buffed and tanned, and I haven't felt this relaxed in ages. A day with my girls to talk about mindless crap and gossip (that didn't involve me) from school was exactly what I needed today. It also helped take my mind off the fact that we're going home to a house without my parents. They're probably living it up in New York without me. My happiness wanes a little, but I try to cover it. I'm so proud of my dad. He deserves this after all his hard work, but it's going to be weird with them being in a different state most weeks. At least when they've been absent in the past I know they've only been a phone call away.

"That was incredible," Alyssa says, pushing her dessert plate away from her and rubbing her belly. "I don't think we did enough exercise today."

The two of us laugh with her. I can't help but agree. The food here has been almost non-stop all day; my belly feels a little bloated and my eyes are getting heavy with my need to curl up and sleep it all off.

"Ready to head back?" I ask them both.

"I'm not sure I ever want to leave here," Amalie complains. "It's pretty incredible."

"Aren't you used to this kind of thing from before?" Alyssa asks. Amalie's still quite tight-lipped about her past life, and I must say that I assumed this would have been a weekly event in her glamorous life.

"Mom and I used to go to a spa maybe once a month. It was our thing."

I immediately feel awful when her eyes water a little. "Shit, you should have said. We could have done something else."

"No, don't be silly. I'm not going to stop doing something I enjoy just because it's something I used to do with them." I frown at her when a tear escapes.

"Really?"

"Really. This is good. I don't want to spend my life hiding from my past. I need to push myself. This is now, that was then. I'm good."

I'm still skeptical as we emerge from the hotel entrance to find Amalie's little red car. She insisted on driving, seeing as I've been her taxi almost since she arrived. I wasn't going to argue about sitting back and enjoying the ride.

I don't think I even make it five minutes into the journey before my eyes fall closed and I drift off into my food coma.

"Camila. Cami." A hand shaking my shoulder is what eventually drags me from my slumber.

"Yeah, I'm awake."

"Cami, I think you might have an issue."

"What's that?" I ask, opening my eyes and seeing we're parked out front of my house but we're surrounded by other cars and... "Motherfucker." Movement from inside proves that my assumption is correct. That fuck wit is having a party. In my house. Without my permission. "I'm going to fucking kill him."

"Camila, wait, don't you think that—"

I don't hang around long enough to hear the end of her sentence. I push the front door open with such force it slams back against the wall and knocks a vase full of flowers in the hallway over, but I don't so much as flinch as the anger that's descended over me forces me forward.

I storm past a couple of guys from school until I spot Ethan fondling a girl in my kitchen.

"Where is he?" I seethe, my lips pursed, my hands on my hips.

"Calm down, baby girl. He's allowed to celebrate too, you know." At no point does he remove his hand from the girl's top. I want to scream at her to get some morals, but she looks too drunk to care right now.

"Where the fuck is he?" I spit out. He casually looks around, feigning making an effort to find him and pushing me right to my limit. "Ethan?"

Slowly his eyes come back to me. Amusement plays on his lips, making me want to punch him in the face.

"Ah... now I remember. I last saw him dragging a girl upstairs." My stomach turns over at the suggestion, my fancy dinner threatening to make a reappearance at the thought of him being with someone else. Although, that's not enough to stop me from turning on my heels and running for the stairs.

"Camila, what's—" I don't stop to allow Amalie to finish her question. Instead I storm up the stairs, ensuring my angry footsteps can be heard. I might not bat an eyelid about going after him, but I will give him some warning that a storm's brewing.

Wrapping my fingers around the cool metal of his door handle, I don't even wait long enough to think.

"Mason, what the fuck do you—" My words falter when I find him sitting on the edge of his bed with his bare back to me. At the intrusion, a female head pokes around him. She's sitting on the floor. I can only imagine what I'm interrupting right now, but I don't give a fuck. I'm too angry that he thinks this is okay.

"Get out," he growls, but he doesn't turn to me. Not giving in to his demands that easily, I take a step further into his room. "I said get out." His voice is low and rough as he repeats his demand, but I hold my ground. I'm not going to be bossed around in my own home by this asshole.

I soon realize that I wasn't the one being demanded to leave when the girl makes a show of getting to her feet and storming from the room. At least she was fully clothed.

Mason stands and I swallow, a ball of dread forming in my stomach.

"What do I think I'm doing?" he asks, turning his dark, angry stare on me.

"Yeah. This is my house, you can't just—"

"You think I don't know that?" His voice echoes off the walls of his small bedroom. "I'm reminded every single fucking day that I'm not in my own house. That I don't have a fucking home." He steps right in front of me. His scent fills my nose and the heat coming from his bare chest seeps into me. "Trust me, I don't need you of all people pointing this shit out to me."

"You have no right to have a party here."

"So everyone has to do what you want because it's your fucking birthday? What the fuck about mine? Don't I get to fucking celebrate too?"

My body sags. Of course I knew today was his birthday. For years we had joint birthday parties, every single year until, he abandoned me.

He shrugs when I don't come back with an answer, and it really fires me up. "Don't fucking shrug at me."

"Why, what would you rather I did?" He steps closer. "You want me to touch you again? Do things to you that no other has? Make you scream my motherfucking name?" My back hits the wall in my attempt to keep distance between us.

"Fuck you."

"Didn't get the chance, Cami-bear."

Before I know what's going on, Mason's fingers tangle in my hair and his lips descend on mine. He's still for a second, I guess waiting to see what I'm going to do. I intend to fight, on pushing him away and causing him some physical harm for touching me, but then his tongue runs along my bottom lip and mine part to allow him entry without instruction from my brain.

His tongue sweeps into my mouth, teasing mine until it begins dancing with his. The taste of alcohol mixes with him and makes my muscles relax. He steps into me, one of his thighs coming between mine and pressing against my core. My need to grind down on his is all-consuming, especially when the solid length of his cock pushes against my hip.

My shirt is lifted and the rough skin of his hands lightly scratches as he explores. He moans and grinds his hips into me, but the noise has reality hitting me full force.

"No," I shout, slamming my hands down on his chest until he backs up and away from me.

We stare at each other for a few seconds, our chests heaving, his cock straining against his pants.

Words elude me, so instead of coming at him with some smart remark, I just push from the wall and walk away.

"That's it. Run. Run away like there's nothing going on here. Clearly he was right—you are a frigid bitch."

I gasp in shock, turn and run toward him. He doesn't see it coming this time, and my palm connects with his cheek. The sound of skin hitting skin echoes around us. His eyes darken and my stomach clenches in fear. The muscles in his neck pull as he holds himself back. From what, I have no idea, and I don't intend on hanging around long enough to find out, because I run.

I practically fly down the stairs before pulling the plug on the sound system and sending the house into almost silence. The few people I can see turn and stare, looking slightly shocked before I make an even bigger spectacle of myself.

"Get the fuck out of my house," I scream as loud as my lungs will allow.

People start moving, but not as quickly as I expect.

"Get out. Get out. Get out," I shout, racing through the house, repeating myself until everyone gets the hint that I'm not fucking joking.

It feels like forever before Ethan eventually gets his ass dragged out by an apologetic Jake. I give him a thankful smile just before he kisses Amalie and closes the front door behind him.

With a large sigh, I fall down on the sofa. Amalie and Alyssa drop down beside me and each take one of my hands.

"Are you okay?"

I'm silent for a few moments as I consider what just happened. "I'm sorry. I think I kinda freaked out a little bit."

"What happened upstairs?"

"I... uh..." I'm not sure how much I want to share, but when I turn and find Amalie's kind eyes, I find it all spilling from my lips. "I walked in on Mason with a girl. Shouted at him. Kissed him and then slapped him."

"Whoa. Rewind," Alyssa demands. "You kissed him."

I shrug. "He was obviously horny, I was mad, it just kinda happened."

"You said he was with a girl."

"Well, I assumed he was. She was on the floor by his feet and he was sitting on the edge and she was—"

"Not giving me a blow job," a deep voice finished for me. "If you're going to give them the gossip they might as well get the whole truth."

I refuse to turn around. I refuse to even acknowledge him with an answer. Both Amalie and Alyssa turn around but the silence is deafening.

"Cami." Amalie elbows me in the ribs, but I ignore her. I'm not dealing with him, not when I'm still so angry. "Fine. I'll be back in a minute."

We listen to her soft footsteps before hearing the low mumbling of their voices from the kitchen.

"You know, I didn't believe the gossip at school that started going around about you two. After everything that he's done to you, I really didn't think you'd ever go there. But I see I was wrong."

"It's nothing, Alyssa."

"You just kicked everyone out of your house because you found him with a girl."

I fume, turning to look at her. "No," I snap. "I kicked everyone out because he had no right inviting them all here without so much as asking."

"I know that he takes the piss, a lot actually. But shit, Cam. It's his birthday weekend too. Doesn't he deserve to have a little fun too after everything?" Alyssa doesn't know the whole story when it comes to Mason's life. Hell, even I don't know the whole story, but I can't deny she doesn't have a point, much like he did upstairs.

I blow out a long breath as the sound of Mason's feet thundering up the stairs fills the space around us before Amalie returns with drinks.

"Mojito? They're strong."

"Yes," I say, jumping up so fast I almost knock the tray from her hands. I pour myself a glassful before downing the glass in one swallow.

"Whoa, slow down, I don't need to get Mason to carry you to bed again."

I pause for a second, then swallow what's in my mouth and look up at her.

"What?"

"That night you passed out at Ethan's. You do know it was Mason who got you home, right? Not Noah."

I mumble some kind of agreement. My memories from that night are still hazy at best, but I never believed he would have looked after me like that.

"You've really got under his skin. That's if you ever really left. I think you should go and apologize for tonight."

"I will," I agree, pouring myself another drink. "Later."

The first jug soon turns into the third as the three of us trawl through Netflix, watching all the chick-flicks that have been released recently. No one says a word about the guy hiding upstairs, but every time I hear a creak from his movement, my stomach knots knowing that I really should do as Amalie suggested and apologize for ruining his night.

The problem is, I'm scared. Not of him. I could never be scared of him. I'm scared of being alone in a room with him. He's going to be as angry, if not more so, than he was earlier, and look how that ended.

What comes next?

26

CAMILA

We head up to bed before we're drunk enough not to be able to set about getting beds made up. I let Amalie and Alyssa use the bathroom while I find something to watch on the TV and grab a clean pair of pajamas.

I take a very quick shower to freshen up, seeing as I can still smell a whiff of chlorine from the jacuzzi earlier, then I let my hair down and brush it and my teeth before pulling the door open.

I expect the hallway to be empty, but when I lift my eyes I find that it's very much not.

"Shit," I mutter under my breath as he just stands there, taking up all the space with his wide frame and sucking all the air out. "Excuse me."

"Why?" he taunts. "Want to finish what we started?" His scent hits my nose and my mind takes me back to earlier. I remember how it felt when he put his hands, his lips, on me. My knees weaken, and I fight the urge to lean toward him to do as he just suggested.

"Get out of my way. I've got friends waiting." I duck under his arm, and surprisingly he allows me to escape. That is, until he opens his mouth.

"Ah, that's right. Birthday girl Camila is celebrating the big one eight. What fun that must be to be able to have a good time."

My muscles lock as guilt overwhelms me. I shouldn't have flown off the handle earlier. He's right, it's not fair that I get to do whatever I want for my birthday and ruin the only thing he had. I haven't even seen any presents around the house pointing to the fact that his mom remembered.

I reach out and grab the doorframe, suddenly feeling very sick at the realization that no one's done a thing for him.

"I hope you all have fun," he spits before disappearing into the bathroom where I just was.

I blow out a long, slow breath. I feel awful. It doesn't matter how horrible he's been to me or what he's done, the truth of the matter is that the boy I knew and loved is still buried in there somewhere, and he's crying out for something special today. My eyes burn with emotion as I rack my brain for something I can do to make his day not a complete waste, but it's so late. I guess I could get in touch with Ethan and restart the party, but something tells me he wouldn't want that now anyway.

With a huge sigh, I push my door open and crawl onto my bed.

"Hey, you okay?" Amalie asks, dragging her eyes away from what's on the TV.

"Yeah, I'm good. Just tired."

"You want us to turn this off?"

"No, no, it's okay."

I cuddle down under my sheets with the lights from the flashing around me and the noise barely registering. The sound I do hear loud and clear though is that of Mason leaving the bathroom and shutting himself back in his room.

I have no idea how long I lie there, tossing and turning with the weight of what I did today pressing down on me, but eventually the TV gets turned off and the sound of the girls sleeping around me fills the room.

There's still a low beat coming from Mason's music next door. It's not loud enough to keep me awake, but as I lie here, it's all I can focus on.

He's in there. Alone on his birthday. It's wrong. So wrong.

Making a snap decision, I throw the sheets back and let my feet drop to the carpet. I'm silent as I make my way to the door and ever so slowly crack it open. The glow from the light out here fills the room, but no one stirs and I slip out into the hallway.

My heart's hammering to get out of my chest before I get anywhere near his door. My temperature rises as I consider what I'm about to do, but I don't let it stop me.

My hand shakes as I wrap my fingers around his door handle. The click of the lock seems like the loudest thing I've ever heard and I still, thinking it might have woken the girls. When I hear nothing, I push on. I twist more. The door moves, and my time for backing out vanishes as the soft light from the room beyond appears.

One inch. Two. Three. My eyes drift across the carpet until they hit the base of his bed. Then, sucking in a huge breath of confidence, I look up.

I find him immediately, sitting in the middle of his bed with school books around him. My heart physically aches to see him doing his homework on a night he should be celebrating.

His hair's falling over his face and he looks up at me through it, waiting for me to announce what the hell I'm doing if the hard set of his muscles are anything to go by.

"Y-You were right. I'm sorry."

His head tilts to the side to show he's listening and I take a step forward, pushing the door closed behind me, halting a quick escape.

"Go on," he encourages.

"I-I...I was wrong. Today is your day and I freaked out and ruined it. If you wanted a party, then you had every right to one."

He's silent for a beat. His intense eyes bore into mine as he digests what I've just said.

"I didn't want a party."

"Then why—"

"Ethan." He rolls his eyes at his friend's antics.

"Oh. Okay, well still. I ruined your night. I stormed in and sent the girl—"

"There was nothing going on with the girl."

"But she was—" His eyes narrow. "Doesn't matter. Not my business," I say, feeling ridiculous for thinking this could even be a good idea.

"Why are you here, Camila?"

"Because... Because it's your birthday, and you're in here alone when you should be celebrating."

"And what exactly are you going to do about it?" he taunts, his eyebrow lifting as he waits for my next move.

I take another step toward the bed, and then another until I'm over halfway across the room.

Mason drops his pen to the bed, and, pushing the books away, he rests back on his hands as if he's about to enjoy a show.

For the first time since I entered, his eyes drop from mine. A trail burns down my body as they run over my breasts, my nipples pebbling as if he's touching them. My stomach clenches with lust as he drops lower down my satin covered body until he finds my bare legs.

He makes his way back up, an amused smirk playing on his lips, but the heat in his eyes is unmistakable.

"You just come here to tease me? To remind me of what's usually right on the other side of the wall that I can't have." He nods his head toward the wall that separates us from each other every night.

I shake my head, my nerves getting the better of me.

"So what then, Cami-bear?" He sits forward and scoots to the edge of the bed. He could touch me if he reached out, but he doesn't. "You must have come in here with a plan. I know you remember. I know how you think."

Isn't that the fucking truth. Four years of not being friends, but he can still read me as well as he did back then. It's how he's managed to hurt me. He knows my weaknesses, my fears like the back of my hand, and he's used them against me so many times. Yet, despite all that, here I am basically offering myself to him. No... to the boy I know that's hiding inside. The little boy who's scared he's lost his family and has no one to turn to. The little boy who thought the best way to deal with everything was alone. Well, I want to prove tonight that that isn't the case. I once loved that little boy with all my heart. I'd have done anything for him, but I'm realizing that when times got hard and he backed away from me, I allowed it. I didn't fight for him like I should have done. I didn't drag him kicking and screaming out of the pit he'd fallen into so that we could fight it together. Well... now's the time to make all that right.

With a new sense of determination, I lift my hands and curl my fingers around the lace trim on my cami, and, with a deep breath of air, I lift it up. As it leaves my body, cool air replaces it. My hair falls down onto my back and I drop the fabric to the floor.

His eyes hold mine, pride swelling in them as he waits me out.

With my heart trying to beat out of my chest, I take a hesitant step forward. His knees part so I can stand between them. His chest heaves beneath his shirt, and the muscles in his neck ripple when he swallows.

"Fuck."

He stands, his chest crashing into mine as his hand grips the back of my neck and his lips find mine. His part almost instantly, and I find myself following his movements. Our tongues duel and tease as we devour each other. It's a kiss that's been a long time coming, eighteen years to be exact, and right now, standing crushed up against his body, I don't ever want it to end.

His fingers grip my hip. It's bordering on painful, but I don't care. I need more. I need everything.

My hands find their way up and under his shirt, and his muscles bunch as I make contact and I smile into his kiss, knowing that he's as affected by this as I am.

His hand drops lower and slips inside my shorts and panties so he can grip onto my ass. The move pulls our bodies closer together, and the feeling of his cock pressing into my stomach has a wave of heat racing through me.

Ripping his lips from mine, he trails kisses along my jaw before descending my neck. He sucks on the sensitive skin beneath my ear that makes my entire body shudder with pleasure before he stills.

He breathes me in with his lips still pressed to my skin, but he doesn't do anything and I start to panic. Doesn't he want this? Me?

His fingers tighten against the back of my neck before he blows out a breath and whispers in my ear.

"If this continues, I won't be able to stop. I need you to tell me now if you don't want this."

The only sounds that can be heard are our heaving breaths as I fight to find the right words to answer him with.

"Mason." He groans as I say his name, his grip on me tightening once again. "I want you."

"Fuck."

He stays where he is with his face tucked into my neck for a beat before he pulls back and looks deep into my eyes. All I see is him. The boy I remember with his silly jokes, supportive, kind nature, and insecurities. He really is still in here.

His large hands wrap around my waist and he moves up until it's my legs against the edge of his bed. With one hand on my back, he slowly lowers me down, never once taking his eyes from mine. It's like he's trying to tell me something that he's too afraid to admit with words.

With his knee on the mattress next to my hip, he reaches behind his head and pulls off his shirt. My eyes drop in favor of enjoying the inches of toned skin he's just revealed. Apparently, I don't have the restraint that he does.

Once he's dropped the fabric, his palm connects with my stomach before brushing upward until he finds my breast. He squeezes gently, and it's like a direct line to my clit. It throbs as a wave of heat hits me, practically melting my panties right off me.

His lips find mine again as his fingers continue to drive me crazy, moving from one side to the other, pinching and palming my breasts until my hips start lifting from the bed in search of more.

"Mason," I moan when he pulls his lips from mine in favor of my neck.

"Never thought I'd hear you moan my name," he admits quietly as he descends over my collarbone. "Never thought... fuck." His eyes fly up to mine. The heat in their depths has me squirming, but I can still see his hesitation. He's still not convinced I'm in this fully with him. It's like he's thinking it's a joke or something, and I'm going to run at any moment. Little does he know that I'm deadly serious about this.

Taking his moment of hesitation. I place my hands on his shoulders and flip us over so I'm straddling his waist. I sit up straight and throw my hair back over my shoulders, giving him a full view of everything. On the inside I want to curl up and die with embarrassment, but Mason's always had this way of making me feel brave.

"Happy birthday, Mase."

I trail my fingertips down his chest and over the deep ridges of his abdomen until they hit his waistband. His muscles twitch with my contact and I can't help but smile. If possible, his cock grows even harder beneath me. I lick my lips and glance up at him. He doesn't miss the move, his own lips parting in anticipation

My fingers make quick work of undoing the tie around his waist, and in seconds he's lifting his hips from the bed to help me pull them and his boxers down his thighs.

His cock springs back and rests up onto his stomach. My eyes widen slightly before the corner of my mouth curls up. Maybe he does have a reason to be such a cocky asshole if he's rocking junk like this.

Dropping to my knees, I pull the fabric free of his feet until he's bare before me. It's not the first time over the years I've seen him naked but fuck, he was a boy then. Now, he's most definitely all man.

Excitement bubbles up in my stomach as I settle myself between his thighs and he props himself up on his elbows to watch the show.

"Ready for your present?" I ask in what I really fucking hope is a seductive voice.

His chest heaves and he bites down on his bottom lip, but at no point do any words leave his mouth. He never was a chatterbox like me, and I guess that extends to situations like this.

Knowing that his lack of response doesn't match his interest level, I reach forward and take his steel length in my hand. My fingers wrap tightly around, causing him to suck in a breath through his teeth.

His eyes are locked on where we're connected as I start to move. His teeth grind and his jaw pops, and I feel more powerful than I ever have in my life.

His eyes start to shut as the feelings take over. Leaning forward, I lick the tip of him. His eyes fly open as he stares at me with disbelief. With my confidence growing, I wrap my lips around his head and suck him into my mouth.

He groans and sits up. His hand finds my head and his fingers dig into my hair to hold me in place. He guides me slowly until his cock's swelling even more.

"Cami," he warns, wrapping his other hand around my forearm. I look up at him. His pupils are blown, his cheeks flushed and his lips parted. It's the most erotic sight I've ever seen, and it pushes me forward.

I suck him deeper, almost gagging when he hits the back of my throat.

"Cam, I'm... I'm gonna—" I lick around the head and suck him deeper. His words falter as his cock twitches. His roar that follows makes my chest swell with pride and my panties even wetter.

"Fuck, Cami-bear," he says between his heavy breaths.

Helping me up from the floor, he immediately seeks out my lips and captures them in another earth-shattering kiss.

I'm not aware I'm moving until my back hits the bed and my shorts and panties are pulled down my thighs. My muscles clench as I remember how incredible he made me feel last time he touched me. I'm not waiting long for a reminder because his hands land on my inner thighs and they're spread wide, exposing every inch of me to him.

"You're so fucking beautiful. So much more than I ever imagined."

"You've thought about this?" I ask, my voice coming out stronger than I was expecting.

"Only every fucking night before I fall asleep." I'm not expecting that, and words fail me to respond. Although it soon becomes apparent that he wasn't expecting one, because he dips his head and rubs his tongue up my seam.

"Oh shit."

"You can't tell me you've not thought about getting a repeat."

"Every second since you walked out." He stops and looks up at me, and I immediately regret my words.

He opens his mouth but no words form. Instead he goes back to the job at hand. He parts me, finds my clit and licks and sucks until I'm chanting his name.

"Come on, Cami-bear. Let me feel you coming." His words rumble through me, setting off the first sparks of my release. His fingers push higher into me and touch a part of me that has stars flashing behind my eyes. "That's it. Let go. Show me how good it feels." He licks faster, circling around my most sensitive spot as he thrusts deeper, and it's only seconds later when my body quakes and I come with his face between my legs.

"Holy fucking shit," I pant, one arm thrown over my face as I try to catch my breath.

"Good?" I don't need to look at him to know he's got a shit-eating grin on his face.

27

MASON

S tanding up, I wipe my mouth with the back of my hand and stare down at her laid out naked on my bed.

Fuck knows what made her decide to walk in here tonight, but fuck if I'm going to put too much thought into it.

It was obvious she turned up with a mission in mind. Her eyes we set and her body ready, despite the obvious nerves that were racing through her. She might think she can hide it from me, but I can read her like a book. I always could.

My eyes run up from her feet, which are placed on the end of my bed, over her bent legs to her swollen pussy. My cock weeps for more despite being inside her hot little mouth only moments ago. I skim up over the curve of her waist, pause at her breasts for a few seconds taking in her tight, rosebud nipples which taste like fucking candy, until I find her face. As if she knows where my attention is, she lifts her arm.

Her breath catches when she finds me staring down at her.

"Hey," she squeaks, suddenly looking unsure of herself.

"Hey."

She lifts herself up on her elbows and I panic that she's about to run. I warned her what would happen if she allowed this to continue. We're not done. Not by a long shot.

I kneel on the bed, caging her legs in, and land with my hands beside hers, bringing our lips almost within touching distance. My eyes flit down to them. I desperately want to take them again, but I need to know she wants this.

"You sure?" I don't want to ask, I just want to do it, but I know this is a big deal and I need to know she's serious and not going to regret it once it's over. She only gets one shot at her first time, and whenever she thinks of it, she'll be forced to think of me. My chest swells at the thought.

Her hand wraps around the back of my neck and she pulls me down. She lies back and I follow, my weight pressing her into the mattress.

I kiss her like I should have years ago. I pour everything I've ever felt for her into it and pray that she can feel my desperation, my regret, my love.

"It's okay, Mase." She pulls back and looks into my eyes. "It's okay." She thinks I'm doing this to ensure she's ready, but she has no idea that all I'm doing is making up for lost time, replacing all the kisses she gave that motherfucker with my own because we both know that her lips should have only ever touched mine.

"Aren't I allowed to take my time with you?"

Biting down on her bottom lip, she shakes her head. "I need to feel you. *All* of you."

"Fuck." There's no fucking way I can deny her that.

Reaching over, I pull open my top drawer and feel around for a condom. I pull out a box and tip the contents on the bed beside her.

Her eyes widen in horror. "I didn't agree to needing that many."

"We'll just stick with the one for now. These can be for tomorrow," I add with a laugh.

Just like when we were kids, when I'm with her, everything seems that little bit easier, that little bit more possible. My reality washes away. The fact that I was sitting in my bedroom alone doing my homework on the night of my eighteenth birthday has vanished, because all that matters right now is her.

She watches intently as I roll the condom down my length.

"Lift up and lie back against the pillows," I instruct, pulling the sheets from beneath her when she follows orders. I flip them back with a little too much enthusiasm and they fall to the floor, my school books disappearing inside. I ignore them, it's not like I have any intention of needing them anytime soon. I've got a naked Camila in my bed, the one good thing I've allowed myself to fantasize about over the years. It's actually happening, right now, and I intend on making the most of it.

Her dark hair fans out on my pillow and as she gets comfortable, I find myself exactly where I've always wanted to be. Between her legs. I push them wider to allow me the space I'm going to need before taking myself in my hand and rubbing the head of my cock through her wetness. She's soaked from her previous orgasm, so I have no question as to whether she's ready for this or not.

Her body trembles beneath me with a mix of lust and fear, and her eyes never leave mine, as if she's finding the strength she needs within them.

"I'll take it slow, I promise."

I've never taken anyone's virginity before—well, not that anyone admitted to —and I'm just as terrified as she is of hurting her.

Dropping lower, I push inside her. Her eyes widen, but she doesn't do anything to stop me.

Leaning over her, I grip onto the back of her neck and crash my lips to hers. Pushing into her a little more, I kiss her harder, hoping that I'll be able to mask any pain. I know it's wishful thinking, but I do it nonetheless.

"Just do it," she mumbles against my mouth, and I do exactly as I'm told.

I thrust forward and all the way inside her. My muscles lock tight as her walls ripple around me, trying to accommodate my sudden invasion. I'm fucking desperate to move, to feel more, but her little whimper beneath me puts an end to my selfishness.

When I pull my eyes open that I didn't realize had slammed shut, I find hers staring at me with tears pooling at the edges.

There are so many things I want to say to her, to reassure her that it'll get better, but I push all of those aside in favor of showing her. My tongue delves back into her mouth as my fingers go in search of her clit. The pain's going to fade, or so I've heard, and hopefully it'll soon turn into pleasure. I fucking hope so, because if I don't get to move soon, I might fucking explode.

I play her body the only way I know how, and soon she starts to relax under me. I test the waters by flexing my hips slightly, and she gasps.

"Sorry, I'm so sorry," I whisper into her neck.

"No. It was... it was good, I think."

"You think?" I ask with a smile.

"Do it again and we'll find out."

So I do, and she makes this incredible little noise that I want to hear for the rest of my fucking life.

Sitting up so I can see her, see where we're connected, I stare down at the vision below me. She reaches for my hands and our fingers intertwine as I start to rock into her faster.

"Mason," she moans, her eyes getting heavy with pleasure.

Letting go of one of her hands, I go back to her clit. Pressing down with the pad of my thumb, I gently start to circle. Her hips lift, her back arching as she cries out. Her muscles clamp around me and tingles shoot up my spine.

I continue what I'm doing, increasing the pace with each thrust, and before long, she's chanting my name.

Just before she falls, I take her lips once again to muffle her cries. Her fingers grip onto my sides, and, as she finds her release, her nails dig in. That little shock of pain along with the tightening of her pussy pushes me over the edge with her, and I roar my release.

I fall down beside her, our chests heaving with exertion. I remove the condom, dropping it over the side, and I pull her into my body and hold her tight.

"That was some fucking birthday present." She laughs, her body jolting in my arms with her amusement. "Are you okay?" I drop a kiss to her shoulder as she thinks.

"I don't know," she admits quietly. Rolling her over, I give her no choice but to have to look at me.

She reaches out and tries to tuck a bit of my hair behind my ear, but like always, it just falls forward once again.

"Was I totally crazy coming in here tonight? Have I just made the biggest mistake of my life?"

"Why would you say that?" My thumb gently caresses her cheek as I try to hide the fact that her questioning what just happened between us cuts.

"Things haven't exactly been easy sailing between us, have they?"

"Nope. But no one said love was easy."

Her lips part to respond, but she must decide better of it. "I should probably go."

"Go, like run back to your room?"

"I was thinking more the bathroom, but yeah, I should probably do that too."

Dropping my head, I whisper in her ear, "Don't make me your dirty little secret, Cami."

I know it's probably what I deserve, but I'm not ready to give her up and I'm certainly not ready for other guys to now think she's single. Our history is common knowledge around Rosewood, and I have no doubt I've pissed off enough guys who would willingly go after her if they got the chance just to piss me off.

She doesn't respond, just drops a quick kiss to my lips before climbing from my bed. She looks around at the floor before quickly finding her discarded pajamas and pulling them on. Every inch of me wants to demand that she gets back into bed, but I need to allow her some space if that's what she needs. She'll come to me when she's ready. At least I hope she will.

The second she closes the door behind her, I roll onto my back and throw my arm over my eyes.

I just fucked Camila. I just took her fucking virginity.

A smile twitches at my lips. I always thought it would be the two of us. We kind of went a long way around to get here, but it happened. I now just have to hope she doesn't regret every second of it and hate me more than she should.

The silent seconds stretch out into long minutes, and I start to think that she's snuck back into her room and I'm going to have to spend the night in my bed alone. The thought doesn't thrill me.

I've given up hope and I'm just drifting off when the sound of a door opening brings me back around. I've turned the light off so I can only see her shadow with the sliver of moonlight shining through the curtains.

The sheets lift and she climbs in next to me, immediately tucking herself into my body.

"Do you need me to turn the light on?" I whisper, knowing how much she hates the dark.

"I'm good as long as I'm with you."

My heart damn near explodes in my chest. I remember her saying the same words when we were kids, but I didn't expect her to still feel the same all these years later.

I kiss the top of her head and hold her a little bit tighter, because in the cold light of day, this could all just be a memory.

28

CAMILA

I wake up hot with my legs stuck to something.

What the—

And then it hits me. I'm not stuck to a thing, I'm stuck to a person, and that person just so happens to be Mason.

Memories play out in my mind like a fucking movie. Me walking in here bold as brass and telling him in not so many words that I was his birthday present and whipping my top off. My cheeks flame and my temperature increases as embarrassment at my forwardness hits me full force.

My personal movie continues, me with his cock as deep in my mouth as I could get it, the taste of him on my tongue. Me writhing in his bed as he pushed me toward my release with his tongue and fingers. The biting pain as he pushed all the way inside me. My muscles clench at that memory. I knew it was going to hurt, but I wasn't disappointed with what came next. Fuck, that was mind blowing. The way he felt moving inside me, stretching me.

Jesus. I need to get out of here.

With him snoring lightly beside me, I somehow manage to unattach myself from him and slide from the bed. He doesn't so much as stir, just proving that the hours he's been putting in to support his family really are taking their toll.

After using the bathroom, I sneak back into my room and slide between my cold sheets. It's only then that I wonder if I just made a very bad decision. He's going to wake and find I've left. Is he going to hate me?

I don't get to dwell on my decision, because fabric rustling fills my ears before my mattress dips and someone climbs in beside me.

"If you even think about lying to me, then I'm going to drag you next door and demand answers from the man himself," Amalie whispers, her eyes twinkling in the morning sun.

"I wasn't going to lie," I whisper back.

"So you didn't just do a very short walk of shame in the hope I didn't know you slipped out last night and rocked Mason's world?"

"Shush, Alyssa might hear you!"

"Are you kidding me? She snores louder than a fucking rhino. If she can sleep through that and you screaming last night, then she certainly can through our whispering."

"You heard me screaming?" I cover my face with my hands, mortified that my best friend heard everything. "Oh my god. Oh my god."

"No, I didn't actually. The bed banged against the wall a bit, but that was it. You shouldn't need to worry about your parents knowing what's going on under their roof when they return."

I peek through my fingers at her.

"So how was it? I'm assuming you gave him a fine birthday treat."

"It was..." I trail off, trying to find the words to describe what my time with Mason last night was. "What I'd always hoped it would be."

A wide smile breaks across Amalie's face. "I always knew you two were meant to be together."

"Whoa, hold your horses. Just because we..."

"Fucked," Amalie helpfully adds.

"Yeah, that. It doesn't mean we're together."

"Really? You're going to lie there and try telling me that you've not been secretly yearning for him for the past four years."

"I was mostly hating him."

"Yeah, trust me when I tell you that I understand how quickly that can change."

I open my mouth to tell her that she's not all that far from the mark, although I'm only just starting to understand how I've been feeling myself when another voice pops up.

"What are you two whispering about? It sounds juicy." Alyssa's head pops up over the mattress.

Amalie looks to me. I widen my eyes and shake my head slightly. I'm not ready for the world to know about this yet.

"Just talking about Jake."

"Ugh, of course you are. You know those guys don't need their egos boosting any more, right?"

Amalie laughs. "I'm aware."

"Come on, I want pancakes," I announce, sitting up and putting an end to any more of Alyssa's questions.

I throw a hoodie over my pajamas and leave them both to get washed and dressed.

Pausing at Mason's door, I press my ear to the wood and listen, but only silence greets me, so I assume he's still sleeping.

I make my way to the kitchen, opening the curtains we'd shut on our way up last night and turning the radio on as I pass.

With all the ingredients I need out on the counter, I get started making my batter just like my granny taught me. She made the best pancakes. I smile as I think of the lady who taught me to bake as a kid and fire up the stove.

By the time the girls join me I'm dancing around the kitchen and have a stack of pancakes that almost hits the counter above.

Amalie immediately reaches for the jug of orange I'd pulled from the refrigerator and downs half a glass.

"If I didn't know any better, I'd think you got some last night," Alyssa says, watching my hips wiggle in time to the music.

Amalie snorts mid swallow and sprays the kitchen in juice as she starts coughing and spluttering.

"Oh my god. I'm so sorry. It... uh... went down the wrong pipe?" Thankfully Alyssa buys the lie. I, on the other hand, can't help laughing as she begins cleaning up.

Once the counter is clear of juice, Alyssa and Amalie grab the items I've got lined up and take them to the table. I'm just about to join them with the pancakes when the atmosphere in the air changes. It's suddenly hard to breathe, and I don't need to turn around to know the reason why.

"I must have missed my invite for pancakes." His voice rumbles through me and hits me right between the legs. I can't deny that I'm not feeling a little sore down there this morning, but I like the reminder of what happened last night. Looking over my shoulder, I watch him stalk toward me and I stiffen. "I didn't like waking up alone."

His hand slips around my waist and I jump away, grabbing the plate of pancakes and holding them in front of me like a shield. His entire face drops at my reaction to him, and it breaks my heart. I didn't mean to hurt him.

"Oh, I see." Without saying another word or picking up anything from the kitchen, he disappears and storms back up the stairs.

A lump forms in my throat and my eyes burn with unshed tears. That wasn't how I intended our first meeting the morning after to go.

"Cami, come on, we're starving to death in here," Alyssa shouts, and I shake my head to get it together. I'll give them breakfast, point them in the direction of the front door and then go and sort Mason out.

Amalie gives me a sympathetic look when I appear, probably looking a little worse for wear. She'd have seen Mason storm past this room on his way back to the stairs. She knows that something is off between us.

"Thank god. I'm dying for one of your pancakes—or five."

They both eat more than their body weight in syrup and fruit covered pancakes while I push one around my plate, my mind repeating that short interaction with Mason in the kitchen. The second I jumped away from him, I regretted it, but I didn't want Alyssa walking in. It's stupid, I know. If I told her not to say anything, she wouldn't. I trust her, but this is all so new, so scary and potentially serious that I don't know which way is up.

Alyssa sits back, downing the last of her juice, and lets out the most unladylike burp before announcing that she needs to get home because she's got a family meal this afternoon for her grandparents' wedding anniversary.

The three of us take all the plates to the kitchen and they help me fill the dishwasher and clean up before we head upstairs to get the girls packed.

Alyssa shoves all her stuff in her bag, says her goodbyes and is gone before I even blink. Amalie hangs around a little longer. Once she's sorted, she sits on the edge of my bed with me and takes one of my hands in hers.

"Just go and talk to him. Explain how you're feeling. He'll understand. Chances are, he's feeling the same."

I nod. "I will, if he'll listen."

"Of course he will. That boy's been in love with you forever. It was in his eyes the first time I saw him look at you."

I give her a smile but I don't share her enthusiasm. Things between Mason and me are more complicated than anyone else understands. "I'll do my best."

"I'm at the other end of the phone if you need me. And he might be his best friend, but if I promise sexual favors, I'm sure Jake would knock him out for you, should you need that option."

"Thank you," I say with a laugh, smiling for what feels like the first time all morning.

Amalie gives me a hug and assures me that she can see herself out. I stand at my window after she walks out and watch as she climbs into her car and drives off.

The house is still empty besides the two of us. I have no idea what time Nicky and the boys are due back, but I know that we need to make the most of the peace. With the number of people living under this roof right now, times without threat of interruption are going to be hard to come by.

Thinking against knocking and walking into his room, much like I did last night, I decide on trying a different tact.

Grabbing a fresh set of clothes, I carry them down to the bathroom. I turn the shower on and strip down before dropping a bottle into the shower tray, ensuring it's loud enough that he'd have heard before I grab my phone and send him a message.

Me: Any chance you could help me please?

29

MASON

Waking up alone kinda hurt, but in the end I tell myself that she just woke up earlier than me and got bored. Why she wouldn't wake me to keep her entertained plays on my mind, but I rationalize that she's got friends sleeping over in her bedroom so I guess she needs to be social. It still pisses me off though.

But that was nothing compared to the way she jumped away from me when I touched her in the kitchen. It was like my touch physically burned her and she couldn't get away fast enough. I thought last night was the beginning of something, something that should have happened a long time ago, but it seems that I might be the only one who feels that way.

Pushing aside the books I'm trying to focus on, I throw myself back on the bed. The need to work out my frustration pulls at my muscles, and I tug my cell from my pocket to see if either Ethan or Jake, or both, are free to work out. I'm missing out on my daily practice with the guys and I'm desperate not to ruin the hours of work I've put in. I might not be on the team right now, but that doesn't mean my dream of college football has died.

I let out a sigh. I sent my applications in as early as possible. I know it's still way too early to hear anything back, but the radio silence makes me feel a little sick nonetheless. My stomach twists that college might not even be an option at all if I don't get a scholarship. Getting a roof over my brothers' heads is more important right now. This place isn't exactly a long-term home for them.

The sound of Amalie's car backing out of the drive sounds out over my music before Camila's small feet move down the hallway. I hold my breath, thinking she might come storming in, but she walks straight past my door. My heart drops but I refuse to go chasing after her. If what happened between us last night meant nothing to her, then so be it. I'm not being one of those pathetic guys who goes begging to the girl. No fucking way.

The bathroom door bangs shut before the shower turns on. *Fucking tease.* My imagination gets the better of me as I picture what her sinful curves might look like covered in white fluffy bubbles. My cock swells and I fight to stop my need for her getting the better of me. It's something I've become a fucking master at, so it shouldn't be all that hard.

But you've made her yours now, a little voice says in my head, but it's forgotten when a loud crash comes from the bathroom. I sit bolt upright, trying to hear if she's okay.

Chastising myself for caring so much when she clearly doesn't, I open my messages but before I find the chat, a new message pops up.

Cami bear: Any chance you could help me please?

I stare down at my cell, blinking a couple of times just to make sure I'm not hallucinating. A wicked smile turns up the corner of my lip. This is karma kicking her ass for this morning.

Running my hand through my hair, I climb from my bed and head toward the bathroom, hoping like hell I'm about to walk into something that can go straight into my wank bank.

My smirk still firmly in place as I walk into the bathroom, half expecting her to be curled up in a ball on the floor having tripped over the toilet or something stupid, but what I actually find makes my eyes widen and my jaw drop.

Camila's standing under the torrent of water, her hair soaked and sticking to her shoulders and down onto her chest. Rivers run over her breasts, down her stomach and over her hips. I'm instantly hard, my cock tenting my sweats.

"What are you waiting for?" Her voice is like pure sex, and I don't waste a second. Pulling my shirt over my head, I drop my pants and step into the shower. But I don't touch her. I keep an inch between us and just stare into her eyes, my need to know what the hell she's playing at only marginally more important than her body right now.

"I'm so sorry," she whispers over the sound of the running water. "I just... I didn't want Alyssa finding out something before we even know what's happening here. She was in the other room and—"

"What about Amalie?"

"She... uh... she knows everything. I can't hide anything from her, she's too damn percept—ah." Her back hits the cold tiles behind her and I sweep the hair away that's sticking to her cheek. My lips slam down on hers and she instantly opens for me.

All my panic and frustration from this morning instantly settles. I skim my hand up from her hip, over her waist until the weight of her breast sits in my palm. I pinch her nipple between my fingers and she gasps, pulling my body closer so I'm pressing her against the wall.

I kiss along her jaw and nip at her earlobe as she shudders beneath me.

"Show me how sorry you are," I growl in her ear.

Her head pulls back in shock and hits the wall, but she doesn't do anything about it. She stares into my eyes, hers narrowing as she tries to figure out if I'm serious or not. I don't respond to her silent question. I don't need to, because a sly smile turns the corners of her lips up before she leans forward and presses them to my chest. She kisses a line down the center of my torso before dropping to her knees. The sight is exactly as I pictured it in my head.

Her delicate fingers wrap around my solid length and my skin erupts in goosebumps as she slowly starts pumping. My knees threaten to buckle. Resting one hand against the tiles and threading the other into her hair, I stare down as she wraps her lips around my cock. Best fucking sight in the fucking world.

It's all too soon when my balls start to draw up, but it's not ending this way. Slipping from her mouth, I lift her to her feet and push her back against the wall. The cold makes her breath catch again, and I make the most of her shock by plunging my tongue into her mouth.

Lifting her leg up around my waist, I tease her with my fingers.

"So fucking wet," I murmur against the sensitive skin of her neck, making her shiver.

She moans, flexing her hips forward, seeking more.

"Tell me you're on birth control."

"I... I am."

"I've never gone bare before, I fucking swear to you."

"O-Okay."

I pull back and look at her, unable to keep the wide smile off my face.

"Yeah?"

"Mason, please." Her lids are heavy with desire, her usual rich chocolate eyes almost black with need.

"I could never say no to you."

Hiking her leg higher, I pull her hips from the wall and find her entrance. I slide in slowly, assuming that she's probably still sore from yesterday—not that she's said anything if she is. I push in an inch at a time, studying her face for any kind of discomfort, but there's none. Instead her head drops back and her eyelids flicker shut as she absorbs the sensation.

I drop my head into the crook of her neck once I'm fully seated. The feeling of her, skin against skin, is fucking mind-blowing, making me so fucking glad I've never been stupid enough to go bareback with anyone else. There was never supposed to be anything between us, but I allowed life to break us apart. Well no more. Camila is mine, and there won't be a fucking thing separating us ever again.

I roll my hips and she starts to moan, her nails digging into the skin over my shoulders, but I don't let up. I increase my tempo, gripping her tighter as she begins to clamp around me.

"Fuck, Cami. Fuck. You feel so fucking good."

Her cheeks flush at my compliment, and it makes me smile that she can be embarrassed by my words while she's full of my cock.

Her body starts to tremble in my hands, and I drop one of mine to find her clit. I barely touch her and she cries out my name, her pussy clenching me so fucking tight that it sends me over the edge with her. My orgasm slams into me and I empty myself inside her, making her mine from this day forward.

"Well, that was unexpected," I say into her sopping wet hair after I've lowered her leg and pulled her into my embrace.

"I really am sorry," she mumbles into my chest.

"I know. I wouldn't be here otherwise." My fingers thread into her hair and I gently tug until I can take her lips.

By the time we step from the shower, I'm hard again and ready to be inside her. I pass her a towel and then wrap another around my waist.

"Already?" she asks, staring down at the tented fabric.

Taking her hand in mine, I pull her up against my chest. If this is happening, then I intend on going all in with the honesty. "The second I learned what sex was, there was only one person I wanted to be doing it with. I've had to wait a fucking long time for that to happen, and I intend on making up for it now."

She looks up at me, and the emotion in her eyes hits me right in the chest. It's exactly how I've wanted her to look at me for the past four years while I was on self-destruct mode.

Slipping one arm around her back and the other under her knees, I sweep her up into my arms and carry her toward her bedroom.

I lay her down on her bed before pulling the towel from around her body and setting about making her chant my name once again. I always feared this girl would be the death of me, and I'm finally discovering why.

I have no idea how much time passes, and while I've got my lips and hands on Camila's body, I really don't give a fuck. But eventually the sound of the front door closing filters up to us along with the excited chatter of my brothers.

"Looks like our peace is over," I say, pulling back from her lips and propping myself up on my elbow so I can stare down at her beautiful face.

Her wide, awe-filled eyes stare up at me. She studies me like she hasn't looked at me a million times before with a soft, satisfied smile on her lips.

Lifting her hand, she cups my cheeks. "What happens next, Mase?"

"Well, I'm kinda hungry, seeing as I didn't get any pancakes this morning."

"That's not what I mean. I meant with us. What happens from here?"

"Anything you want," I say.

"Anything?"

I nod, wondering what she could possibly be thinking. "What do you want?"

"Me? I want more of you, any chance I can get," she says.

"So this is just a sex thing for you?" I ask.

"What? No, not at all. Why, are you just using me for my body?"

"I might just be." I wink and move over her.

"Hmmm... I think I can handle that. Should I warn the others?" Her eyebrows nearly hit her hairline. "I'm joking, baby. There's only you. There's only ever been you."

"You're serious, aren't you?"

"Deadly."

"But what about the last four years, the—"

"The way I've treated you? I was a dick, Cam. My life went to shit, and I saw you in this house playing the perfect family. You had everything I wanted, you were everything I wanted, but I couldn't handle it. So I made myself hate you. It was easier to hate than it was to allow you to see what was festering inside me. I mean, it's still not pretty, but I think I'm finally understanding that I can't continue like this, hiding from who I am and what I really want."

"And what do you really want?" she asks, and I realize that she really needs me to spell it out for her.

"I want you, Cami-bear. I've only ever wanted you." I lift her hand and rest it over my heart. "You were in here long before I even realized what it meant." She gasps, her eyes filling with tears. "I'm sorry for all the bullshit. I'm sorry for all the pain I caused you. I was lashing out at my bullshit life, and I targeted it at the person I loved the most."

"You... you love me?"

"I've loved you since the first moment I saw you, Cami. It was always meant to be us."

A sob rumbles up her throat, but her hand drops from me.

"If this is a game... If you're playing me right now, I swear to fucking god that I'll hurt you."

I can't help but laugh at her. She looks too cute, trying to threaten me.

"The only thing you can do to hurt me is to walk away. I need you, Cami-bear, and I'm fed up with trying to convince myself of anything else."

Her eyes bounce between mine as she tries to decide if she can trust me. I hate that she has to hesitate, but I can hardly blame her. I see the moment she decides. I feel the change in her even before the words leave her lips. "I love you too, Mason. Always have, always will."

"Fuck." Her words make my chest constrict to the point of pain. Dropping my weight on top of her, I kiss her like I should have been doing for the past four years instead of trying to send her life into the pits of hell like mine was.

I have every intention of taking her again, but that's all shot to shit when Mom calls my name up the stairs.

"Fuck." Dropping my head to Camila's shoulder, I drag in a few deep breaths.

Mom calls again, and this time I shout back that I'm coming, much to Camila's amusement. "Are you?" she asks with a raised brow.

"Don't tempt me."

"Up you get. You need to hear what she's got to say, and I've got homework to do."

"I can think of better things to do than homework."

She climbs from the bed and walks over to her drawers to find some clothes. "I'd like to still be able to walk tomorrow if possible."

"Walking's overrated."

"Go and get dressed, your mom wants you." She throws a pair of panties at me and I catch them and bring them to my nose.

"I know they're clean, but really?"

"Yep. In fact, I think I'll keep these."

"Weirdo."

"I'll be whatever you want me to be."

"Right now that would be dressed so you can hear your mom out."

"Do you know something I don't?"

"I might, but if you want to know for sure then you need to get some clothes on and find out."

Reluctantly, I leave her in her room getting dressed to find some clothes of my own. I don't waste any time, and the second she steps out into the hallway, I join her.

"Ready?" I ask, holding my hand out for her.

"Have you even washed them?" She nods at my hands, that have spent a significant amount of time inside her in the last hour or so, with her nose screwed up.

I wink at her and she flushes bright red. "Ah, Cami-bear, we're going to have so much fun." Despite my potentially dirty hands, she threads her fingers through mine and together we descend the stairs.

"Do you have to call me that?"

"Sure do, sweet cheeks."

"Ugh, that's worse. Maybe Cami-bear isn't so bad after all."

We're both laughing as we walk into the kitchen. There are a couple of presents sitting on the counter beside a football cake. My brothers are sitting at the breakfast bar while Mom leans against the worktop with a coffee in her hands.

Her eyes lift from our joined hands and a wide smile spreads across her face. "Have you two... are you two...?"

"We are," Camila announces happily as a shit-eating grin spreads across my face. This incredible girl by my side is fucking mine. How did my life go from one big disaster to, well... this?

"Oh my god, I'm so excited. You might get to be my daughter-in-law after all." I swear Mom's eyes get a little wet at the prospect.

"One thing at a time, yeah? She's only just started talking to me again."

Mom laughs, pushing one of the presents toward me. "Happy birthday, baby. I'm sorry I wasn't here to celebrate yesterday, but I thought you'd want to spend it with friends over me. Plus, I worked an extra long shift."

"It's fine, I—wait, you worked?"

"Yep, I've got a job. A well paying job that means you don't need one. I was looking, I swear, but it wasn't until your girl here had a few choice words for me that I really started taking it seriously."

I squeeze her hand in mine for fighting for me.

"It's still nights, so I'll need a little help with the boys but I'll be back for the school run and I start after their bedtime. Hopefully in a couple of months, I'll have saved enough to get us our own place again and we can restart our lives.

"I can't possibly thank you enough for everything you'd done for me, for us. I'll never be able to repay you for everything you've done to keep our family going, but I need you to call your boss and tell them that you need your life back. Friday night, I expect you to be out on the football field where you belong."

Emotion clogs my throat. "You serious?"

"Yep. Being here, it's been a bit of an eye opener. I haven't had a drink in... well I can't remember, and Gabbi convinced me to start taking the pills the doctor gave me months ago. I should have done it years ago. I finally feel like I can be the mom the three of you deserve."

"That's awesome, Mom. I'm proud of you."

"New starts from here on out for all of us." She lifts her coffee in the air in a toast we all agree to.

I open the gifts—a new bottle of my favorite cologne, some boxers, and some chocolates. To most people it wouldn't be anything, but to me, it's everything. Mom's been so lost over the past few years that she's barely realized my birthday had happened, so these few gifts are just proof that the speech she just made could be true. I really fucking hope it is.

30

CAMILA

The next morning, hand in hand, Mason and I walk into school. The second we approach, everyone turns our way. Most people are shocked to see us walking side by side, but when their eyes drop to find our fingers connected, their eyes almost bug out of their heads. Our four-year feud hadn't been private after Mason made every attempt to humiliate me as possible in front of the people we'd grown up with. They knew us as the untouchable two-some, but suddenly, almost in the blink of an eye, he turned on me and everyone was witness to my misery.

The few people who know us better look much less surprised and way happier for us. Amalie and Jake are the first to greet us as we head for the main doors.

"About time, man," Jake says, slapping Mason on the back while Amalie smiles and winks at me.

"Well, fuck me if Mason Paine hasn't handed his balls to Camila at last," Ethan announces as we descend on Mason's locker. His voice booms down the hallway, but there's an unmistakable slur to it which has all our brows drawing together. "I guess there's only me now to serve all these wonderful ladies of Rosewood High."

"Ethan, are you drunk?" Mason asks, bringing us to a stop in front of him. The answer is obvious the second we're close. He stinks of alcohol.

"Just enjoying my senior year."

"It's Monday morning."

"And who are you? My mom?" A bitter laugh falls from his lips.

"What the hell?" Jake asks, releasing Amalie and getting in Ethan's face. "Do not tell me you fucking drove here in that state."

Ethan shrugs, and every muscle in Jake's body tenses while Mason's grip on my hand becomes painful.

"Come with me," Jake demands, wrapping his hand around Ethan's forearm and pulling him away from the lockers.

"Or fucking what, asshole?"

"Don't you fucking question me right now." Jake's jaw tics as he goes nose to nose with Ethan. "You wanna stand here and get caught, get suspended and miss the rest of the season?"

Ethan pales slightly but doesn't back down. "So what if I do? Not like you two would care. Too fucking busy getting your dicks wet to notice what the hell I'm doing."

"Yeah, and that's why we're standing here now trying to make you see fucking sense, because we don't fucking care. Now. Let's. Fucking. Go."

Ethan allows Jake to move him this time.

"I'll be back," Mason says, dropping a kiss to my temple.

"It's fine. Stay with your girl. I'm just gonna get him sobered up," Jake says, already making his way down the hallway.

"You sure?"

"Yeah, man. I got this."

"What the fuck's going on?" Amalie asks like she's been left out of the secret.

"Fuck knows. Something's been going on a while though. He's been partying more than usual, getting drunker..." Mason trails off as he watches his two best friends make their way down the hall. "He's not said fuck all, though."

"Jake will get it out of him. Plus, he's drunk, so I'm sure his tongue will be a little loose."

Mason turns his attention back to me, pushing me up against his locker. "I know he said not to, but I'm going to go and find them. But first, they need showing exactly who you belong to."

"Mase, I think—" My words are cut off as his lips find mine.

There are a few hollers of excitement behind us, but I block them out. How could I focus on anything else other than his lips when they're consuming in a way only he can?

"About fucking time," a familiar voice says when Mason pulls back.

"I'll see you later." He kisses my knuckles and I practically melt into a puddle on the floor. I watch as he walks away, my eyes fixated on his body and the rippling muscles of his back.

It's not until he's out of view that I turn to Alyssa, a wide smile on my face.

"Ugh, do you have to look so fucking happy?"

"Sorry, can't help it. I had one hell of a wake up this morning." I wiggle my eyebrows and she rolls her eyes.

Movement behind her catches my eyes, and when I look up, I find Chelsea standing in the entrance, staring daggers at me.

Making a snap decision, I push away from the lockers and stalk toward her. She doesn't move as I approach, not that it would really matter if she did. She might have lost one crutch, but she's still got a boot thing on her foot.

"Looks like you were wrong," I say once I'm confident she can hear me. I don't stop moving until I'm right in her personal space. Leaning into her ear, I whisper my final words. "Girls like me do win, after all."

She gasps as if it's a shock that I knew it was her who sent me after Noah. Who else did she really think I'd think it was?

"Only Ethan left now, but even he has standards." I stand back and run my eyes down the length of her. "Have a great day." My smile is wide and fake, but fucking hell, I've never felt better.

Flicking my hair over my shoulder, I turn and walk away from her with my head held high. That won't be the last we hear from her, of that I'm sure, but right now, I feel on top of the world.

Amalie and Alyssa smile at me as I stalk past them and toward my English class to get the day started.

Miss Phillips sets us up with a task before sitting behind her desk and calling us all up one by one to give feedback on our "Against All Odds" paper.

"Camila," she calls halfway through the class.

Pushing my chair out behind me, I make my way to the front of the class. A few sets of eyes burn into me. Apparently, I'm much more interesting since Mason's public claiming of me this morning, but I ignore them and take a seat.

"I really enjoyed this, Camila. Your writing was engaging, creative, descriptive. I was really impressed."

My smile grows as pride swells in my chest. "Can I ask what you're thinking about majoring in at college?"

"Honestly, I have no idea. English has always been my strength, but I don't really know what I want to do, or if I have a career in it."

"Have you considered journalism? After reading this, I think it could really suit you."

I pause for a few minutes, letting her suggestion roll around in my mind.

"Obviously, this paper was based on football, but I'm confident you could turn your hand to a different subject quite easily—unless, of course, sports is your thing." I'm not sure if she takes my silence as me ignoring her. Possibly, but that's far from the truth. In reality I've got tingles of excitement that have so far eluded me whenever I've thought about college.

"Okay, well... I've made a few suggestions but really nothing much. I was really impressed, Camila. Think about what I said, okay?"

"I will. Thank you so much." I walk back to my desk with a wide smile on my face and hope bubbling up inside me. Things are starting to turn around. Hopefully, I can stop focusing on everything that's changing but embrace all the new things. Mason, college, our future.

By the time lunch rolls around, I'm desperate to see Mason and tell him about what Miss Phillips said. The more I've thought about it, the more excited I've gotten at the prospect of a journalism major. I spend most of my last class looking up colleges—well, that was until I realized that I have no clue what Mason's plans are and that I don't want to set my heart on anything until we've at least had a conversation about it. For all I know, he wants to move halfway across the country, although if I know Mason at all, then I'm pretty sure he'll want to stay fairly close for his brothers.

His usual table is still empty when I get into the cafeteria, so I grab some food and take a seat at our spot. It's only a few minutes before Shane joins me, shortly followed by Alyssa. As expected, they both grill me about Mason. They look at me skeptically when I don't have all that much to tell, but it's only been a few days and I'm still trying to get my head around it all, if I'm being honest. I went from slapping him when I was so angry on Saturday night to walking into school as his girlfriend this morning. It sounds crazy even thinking it, but it's my reality.

I know the moment he and the rest of the team walk in because a brief silence falls over the students and they all turn their way. It's easy to see Jake, Mason, and Ethan as normal guys when you hang out with them outside of school, but to everyone else, they own this school. Realizing that I'm now a part of that is a sobering thought.

Looking over my shoulder, I find him immediately. His dark eyes lock on mine and he moves away from his crowd and directly over to me.

"Come sit with me?" I look over to Shane, seeing as Alyssa already excused herself to hit on the basketball team when they arrived. Mason watches my movement before coming a little closer. "It's okay, we can stay here. How's it going?" he asks Shane, dropping to the seat beside me and wrapping his arm around my shoulders. His lips land on my temple and a wave of heat washes through me.

"I'm good. Congrats, man."

Mason nods at Shane.

"I called my boss earlier," Mason says so only I can hear. "She's allowing me to start later so I can do practice, but until she gets a replacement, she still needs me Monday and Tuesday night."

My heart drops. "That sucks."

"It's okay. I didn't want to just quit. Who knows how long Mom's new job could last. We need a fall back. Plus, I like earning my own money."

"So I won't see you after school?"

"No, but I was hoping for a sleepover maybe."

A smile twitches my tips. "I would say that's a sure thing."

"On that note," Shane says, grabbing his tray and standing from our table, "see you later, Cam. Mason." He nods at Mason before disappearing.

"He's all right, you know."

"I know."

"And he didn't drug Amalie, that's not his style."

"Never said it was. I didn't think he had it in him either, to be honest, but with no other suspects what's everyone supposed to think?"

"I know, it just sucks. He's basically gone into hiding." A silence descends around us but I soon remember what I was so excited to tell him about. "So, Miss Phillips thinks I should consider journalism."

"That's awesome. Where have you applied?"

"UFC, Maddison, a couple out of state, but I'm not sure I really want to move away. You?"

"I want Maddison. Their team's awesome, plus they have a fantastic teaching department."

A soft smile finds its way to my lips. "You want to teach?"

"I think so. My brothers have shown me how awesome kids are and how rewarding it is watching them learn. Why are you looking at me like that?"

"Because I equally hate that I didn't know this but at the same time love that I get to know you all over again."

"I feel the same, Cami-bear. But deep down, you were the only one who ever really knew me, and I haven't changed, not really. I might be a little tougher skinned now, some might say an asshole, but I'm still the boy you used to play hide and seek with in the woods."

I swoon at his words and tuck myself into his side.

"I still see him," I admit quietly.

A couple of seconds pass as I enjoy being in the warmth of his arms before he speaks. "I'm taking you out Wednesday night after practice."

"Out. Like a date?"

"Exactly like a date. Be ready at six."

Excitement blooms on my belly before the sight of Chelsea and her gang of bitches catch my eyes as they arrive in the cafeteria.

"Ugh," I complain when she locks eyes with me.

"What's wrong?"

"Chelsea's not thrilled about us."

"Chelsea can fuck off. She acts like she and the rest of the squad own us. She needs to realize that the guys only keep them around because they're so easy."

"Nice. So tell me, boyfriend. How many of the squad have you been easy with?"

"Can I have a pass on that question?" I lift a brow at him. "I can say that I've never fucked Chelsea though. I always drew the line there."

"Good to know you had some standards." I laugh, because it's easier than being pissed off that he didn't answer my question. Not that I'm really sure I wanted the answer. There's a lot to be said about ignorant bliss at times.

31

CAMILA

I don't see Mason for the rest of the day as we're in different classes, and then he heads straight to the locker room after school so he can talk to Coach and hopefully grovel for his place back on the team. I get a brief message saying everything's fine and that he'll see me later, but that's it, and I hate it. I know it's greedy and selfish, but now I've got him back I want him all to myself. I want to continue learning all the new things about him, the things I've missed out on in the last four years.

"You're thinking about him, aren't you?" Amalie asks, dropping in the booth in front of me and pulling what's left of her milkshake back in front of her.

"N-No, I was thinking about the homework," I argue.

"Fuck off, were you. You've got this soppy, heated look on your face. You're so imagining what you'll do to him when he gets home from work tonight."

My cheeks burn. "I'm so not," I try to argue but Amalie has none of it.

"So, Wednesday night date? Did he say what you were doing?"

"Nope, just that I had to be ready at six."

"Mysterious. I like it."

I laugh at her and finish my milkshake.

I spend the rest of the evening doing homework and then keeping an eye on Mason's brothers once Nicky heads to work. I can't wait for him to get his hours sorted, not just so he has to work less but so he can lose some of the worry in his eyes. He hates not being here for his brothers when his mom can't be. It's not his job, but he feels that it is. I just hope Nicky manages to stick with her new attitude and she finds a way to work and support her kids that allows Mason to live the life he deserves.

Thankfully, both boys stay in bed and asleep, so I'm not really needed. They know me well enough now, but I'm not sure I'm who they'd want if they woke up with an issue.

I climb into bed ten minutes before Mason is due home, wearing my sexiest nightwear. It's a black lace slip that's almost see-through. I bought it a few months ago when I thought I was going to go all the way with Noah. I shudder at the thought now, but I'm so glad I stuck to my guns and held back. I know that I'd have always regretted doing it with him, especially knowing that it could have been Mason.

My heart pounds in my toes and fingertips as I wait. He never said he'd come to me, but I can't imagine he wants to get into his own bed alone. I'm just wondering if I should have waited in his bed instead when his car pulls up outside. By the time his feet thunder up the stairs, I'm trembling with anticipation.

His footsteps pause at his room, and my heart drops. But then the floorboard creaks and my door is slowly pushed open.

I've got my nightlight on so I can clearly see him slip into the room. He glances over but must assume I'm asleep. Turning away from me, he toes his shoes off before pulling his work uniform from his body. His back muscles ripple and pull as he undresses, and heat floods me knowing that body is going to be pressed up against mine at any moment.

He's still got his back to me when I sit up, allowing the sheets to pool at my waist. And I wait.

He turns, takes a step forward and then looks up. "Oh shit." A wicked smile curls up his lips as his eyes drop from my face in favor of my barely covered breasts. The slip is cut down low, revealing almost everything—not that the sheer lace hides much.

He stalks toward me, my panties getting wetter with each step he takes.

"Maybe working late and missing you was worth it." He steps up to the bed then drops his last item of clothing, revealing his hard length to me. If I wasn't sure enough already then it most definitely confirms that he likes what he sees.

He crawls up my body, taking one of my breasts in his hand before finding my lips.

"Missed you tonight, Cami-bear," he mumbles when he kisses down my neck. "My night was long as fuck. If I knew this was waiting for me then it would have dragged even more."

His lips trail over my chest and down the valley of my breasts before slipping the fabric aside and sucking my nipples into his mouth, alternating between the two.

"Oh god," I whimper, my hips grinding, desperately trying to find some friction.

He pulls the covers from the bottom half of my body and throws them off the bed in his desperation. Before I know what's happened, he's the one lying on his back and I'm sitting across his thighs.

"Now that's what I'm fucking talking about." He links our hands and tugs me so I fall forward against his chest. My nipples brush against his skin and sparks of lust shoot straight for my core. My hips flex without any instruction from my brain, and Mason groans when the heat of my pussy rubs his length.

"Need you, Cami-bear. Ride me."

My eyes fly open at the demand and nerves hit me out of nowhere. I've not had a moment's hesitation with him so far, but that's because he's been in charge, he's been the one calling the shots. But he's just given me the power, and the realization that he's been with others who are more experienced than me hits me full force.

I look away from him and close my eyes.

"Hey, what's wrong?" His hot palm rests on my cheek and I'm forced to look at him. "Get out of your head, Cami. The only place in the world I want to be right now is here, inside you. Forget about the past and just go with it." His fingers slip inside my panties and he moans when he finds me ready for him.

"How long have you been lying here, waiting for me?"

"Long enough," I whisper, enjoying the feeling of his fingers teasing my entrance too much to hold a conversation about this.

"Lift up."

I do as I'm told, and in only seconds, Mason has the lace of my panties pushed aside and he's impaling me on his cock.

My muscles clench as I slowly lower myself down on him.

He hisses as I get lower, his teeth grinding and his jaw popping as he tries to restrain himself.

"Don't hold back. I want everything you've got." His eyes flash with heat.

With his fingers gripping onto my hips, he thrusts himself up until I'm so full of him, I swear I'm going to split in two.

"Oh, fuck."

"You okay?"

"Yeah, yessss," I squeal when he thrusts again.

I move with him and begin to meet his movements like for like until the sound of our skin connecting and our heavy breathing is the only thing that can be heard as we both chase our releases.

"Cam, I'm gonna—"

"Let go."

His hips get even faster, his face tensing and the muscles in his neck straining. It's fucking fascinating to watch. I'm totally lost to him, but the second I feel the first twitch of his release, my own hits me. My upper body sags as I'm consumed by my orgasm and the incredible guy who delivered it.

At some point, I end up on top of his chest with his arms wrapped tightly around me. His cock still twitches inside me, reigniting my own pleasure each time.

"Did you have a good night at work?"

Mason smiles and tucks a lock of my hair behind my ear. "Not really, but coming home to you certainly makes up for it."

We lie locked in each other's embrace, a comfortable silence falling around us. The events of the day run around my head when a thought strikes me. "Is Ethan okay?"

Mason lets out a long, pained breath. "I have no idea. Coach ended up taking him home after ripping him a new one for showing up to school in that state, but we never got to the bottom of why."

"He'll talk when he's ready." It's the only thing I can think to say. I don't know Ethan well enough to know how he deals with stuff, aside from getting drunk it seems.

"I've never seen him like that this morning. Yeah, he likes to party, he likes to drink, none of that is news to anyone, but he's been going to the extremes recently. I'm worried about him."

"Do you want me to try talking to him?" I offer.

"Yes. No. I don't know. I think you're right. We'll only get to the bottom of it when he's ready to talk."

Eventually we drift off to sleep in each other's arms, and we're exactly the same when we wake to the sun streaming in the next morning.

As promised, Nicky is there to get Charlie and Ollie up. She actually makes us all breakfast. I'm surprised, but Mason is astounded if the look on his face is anything to go by.

"I like this look on her," he says to me while she goes to refill the coffee pot. "I hope it continues."

"It will," I say, hoping to keep up the positivity. Things are turning a corner for all of us. We need to start embracing it, not fearing things changing.

Ethan doesn't show his face, and I can see the concern on Mason's and Jake's when they try calling him and get no answer. Something serious is going on and it's bothering them so much, two guys who like the world to think they care about nothing, that it's really starting to worry me. But short of showing up at his house, I have no idea what I can do to help.

———

I'm desperate for our date to start by the time Wednesday evening rolls around. I'd fallen asleep when Mason go home from work last night after our eventful night previously, and we haven't had any classes together today.

I stand in the hallway waiting for his car to pull up to find out what he's planned. I had no idea what to wear, and after standing in front of my closet for the longest time I went with a black denim skirt, a plain white shirt and a pair of boots. I didn't want to dress up and look like an idiot. Equally, I didn't want him to think I hadn't made an effort.

I pull my blazer on, hoping it's enough to dress up my outfit should I need it. My stomach clenches when I look out the window and still find it missing Mason's car. I blow out a slow breath. He'll be here.

When a car does pull onto the driveway, it's not the one I was expecting. Pulling the front door open, I walk toward the little red car and lean down to talk to the driver.

"Get in."

"I can't, I'm waiting for Mason."

"I know. I'm your taxi. Get in."

"Ooookay." I do as I'm told and drop down into Amalie's passenger seat. "Where are we going?"

"My lips are sealed."

Sticking my tongue out at her, I sit back and wait to see where she takes us. "So, I'm assuming you helped plan this, whatever this is?"

"Nope. It was totally him. I just agreed to pick you up."

I start to tick things off as we drive through town as I attempt to guess what he's been up to. We pass the cinema and bowling alley, so they're out. We continue past Aces and a couple of other restaurants I thought could have been possibilities. When Amalie pulls into a deserted beach parking lot, I start to wonder if she's made a wrong turn.

"Okay, out you get," she says, dismissing me with a flick of her hand like she's bored of me.

"Here?"

"Yep."

"But there's nothing he—" Just as I say that, a figure appears over the dune. "Mason," I breathe. The sun's just set and the horizon is still a dark orange hue that makes him appear larger than he really is.

"So are you going to get out now?"

Without taking my eyes from him, I unbuckle myself, thank Amalie and climb from the car. My feet eat up the space between us in only seconds, but still it feels too long. Amalie's tires crunch against the gravel as she leaves us.

"Surprised?" Mason asks, grabbing my hand and leading me toward the beach.

We're right at the end, the same place Dash was all those weeks ago. I think back to that night briefly as we walk. I was flying on the excitement of starting senior year with my boyfriend by my side and making sure Amalie took hold of her new life with both hands. I really had no idea that the next time I'd be here

Noah and I would no longer be together, and that I'd be holding on to Mason's hand like I need it to survive. I truly believed our relationship was dead. He sure made it seem that way. How things seem is a funny thing. Jake seemed like he was an asshole who had the world at his feet. Wrong. Mason seemed like he was going to forever hate me. Wrong. Ethan? Well, we all know he's a party boy, but what's he hiding right now while everyone's assumed he's just enjoying himself? I guess only time will tell.

"Oh my god," I gasp when we hit the top of the dune and I get a look at the beach beyond. A bonfire sits in the middle of the sand. Tiki torches mark a path toward it and a blanket and picnic basket that sit in the warmth of the fire.

"You like it?" The hesitation in his voice has me turning toward him.

"It's incredible. Thank you."

"Anything," he says, reaching for my cheek and resting his forehead against mine. "Anything to make you smile."

My heart damn near shatters in my chest. I'm just about to tell him that the feeling is mutual when he takes my hand and leads me toward his bonfire, telling me that he's starving.

I take a seat on the blanket while Mason unpacks the basket, showing me everything he's brought for us to eat.

"Wow, were you planning for others to join us?" I ask with a laugh but soon realize that I'll be gutted if he says yes.

"No, I just wasn't sure what you'd want."

I look down at all the food before glancing back up at him from under my lashes. "How about you?"

He reaches forward and runs his knuckles down my cheek. "All in good time, Cami-bear."

Desire that was already sitting heavy in my belly races through my veins. "Here?" I ask skeptically, looking around at all the open space.

"Anywhere you want."

I sit up straight and glance over my shoulder. The excitement of getting dirty down here where anyone could find us has me more excited than I'm willing to admit.

"Food first. We'll see what happens later."

With all the food laid out between us, Mason passes me a plastic cup before popping the top of a bottle of pink champagne and filling mine up. "This is fancy."

"It didn't cost much more than juice. It probably tastes like crap."

"It's only the company I care about." He smiles at me before chucking a chunk of cheese into his mouth. I focus on his lips as he chews and realize that I'm really not interested in food at all right now.

"Eat," he demands, and I'm powerless but to reach out and take something.

"How was your day?" he asks, distracting me from my need for him as I run through my classes and the gossip I'd heard.

"Any more issues with Chelsea?" he asks begrudgingly.

"Nah, she's steered clear since I ambushed her."

"Good. If she knows what's good for her, it'll stay that way."

32

MASON

My beach date was everything I hoped it would be. When I told Camila that I wanted to take her out, I didn't have a fucking clue where we were going to go. As I ran through the normal options, I soon realized that none of them were good enough for her. The little effort that goes into arranging dinner and a movie just wouldn't cut it. I can tell by the way she looks at me that she's still a little dubious about my intentions with her, and it guts me every single time. I deserve it. No, I deserve worse than that. She should still hate me, not be agreeing to dates with me, let alone allowing me to spend every night in her bed, but that's just who Camila is. It's why I fell for her all those years ago and why I was never truly able to rid myself of her.

I breathe a sigh of relief when I walk out of the locker room on Thursday afternoon. My work hours might not be quite back to normal, but I'm already feeling the benefit of cutting back. I told Camila to be at home waiting for me when I finished; I have no idea what she's expecting when I show up, but I plan on spending the evening with my girl in my arms, pretending to watch shit movies on TV while we make out. Knowing that Mom will sort out dinner for my brothers is a huge relief, although if I'm honest, it has left me feeling a little lost. I used to operate on a such a strict regime in order to function and not crack that I don't know what to do with my sudden free time.

As I drive past my old house, movement around the back catches my eye. Pulling up in the driveway like I've done a million times before, I get out and walk around to make sure everything's okay.

What I'm not expecting when I get to the back of the house is to find a woman, probably Mom's age, staring in through the window with her hands blocking out the light in the hope of actually seeing something.

"Can I help you?" I ask, my voice booming across the space between us.

"Oh shit. Fuck." She jumps back like I've just shot her, her eyes wide, her hand covering what's probably her racing heart. "I'm-I'm so sorry. I'm not going to break in or anything. I just... I came looking for you."

"For me?"

"Yeah. You're Mason," she states, her eyes softening. "You look exactly as I was expecting."

My eyes narrow in curiosity and suspicion. "Who are you?"

"I think we should probably sit down." She nods toward our old swing bench and I reluctantly follow her lead.

I sit but she hesitates despite this being her idea. Eventually, she blows out a shaky breath and lowers beside me. She stares ahead at our old overgrown garden that my dad would hate if he ever saw it.

"I'm... um... I guess I'm your stepmom."

My jaw drops as I turn to stare at her.

Her blonde hair is in tight curls and hangs just above her shoulders. She's got light makeup on, but to be fair, she doesn't really need it. She's pretty. If what she's saying is true, then I could understand why my dad would be interested. I notice that her looks aren't all that different from Mom's. It's a slightly unsettling thought.

"How's that?" Dumb question, and I almost regret asking it, but I'm going to need more information than her 'guessing she's my stepmom.'

"I first met your dad about three and a half years ago at a rehab group. We chatted a bit, but due to both our reasons for being there, it was never more than that. Then two years ago we quite literally bumped into each other in the store. We started meeting up regularly—dating, I guess."

I'm silent as I listen to her tale, trying my best to read her expression to figure out if she's telling the truth or not, but I can't help but believe her.

"Six months later I discovered I was pregnant. Your dad asked me to marry him and we had a city hall wedding a few weeks later."

I've got another brother or sister? "Boy or girl?" The question is out before I realize. I need to know, but equally I don't want to fall into her trap by being distracted. This could all be bullshit. "This little trip down memory lane is nice and all, but why are you here telling me about it? If you're married to my dad then you'll know that he's had no contact with me or my brothers since he walked away."

"Sister," she says, her eyes softening as she thinks of her. "I promise you that is something he battled with every single day."

"Because that fixes everything. Why are you here?"

"He..." She pauses, her chin trembling, her eyes filling with tears. Dread twists my stomach. "He died."

Those two words are like a baseball bat to the chest. "No. No, you're lying. How do I even know you know him? You could be making all this up."

"W-Why?" She sniffles. "Why would I do that?"

"I don't fucking know. People do all sorts of crazy shit."

"I-It's true. Look." She rummages in her purse and pulls her wallet out. She opens it and turns it toward me. My world crumbles in on itself as I stare at the man I used to idolize standing with a new family.

"Fuck." I stand, looking out at the jungle of a garden, unable to stare at that picture any longer, although when I close my eyes, it's right there, burned into my memory.

"I'm so sorry to spring this on you like this."

"Really? If you were that sorry then you wouldn't have bothered," I snap.

"He wanted to come and see you himself. He'd been putting it off for years. But then he got ill and—"

"This is bullshit. It's so easy to try to convince me of all this crap now he's gone."

"It's true, Mason. Not a day passed when he wouldn't talk about you or your brothers. I've never met you before but I feel as though I know you, know this place," she says, waving back toward the house. "Things weren't supposed to end as they did, but your mom broke him. He loved her so much, Mason. When he discovered..." She trails off, not that I need her to fill in the gaps. "It broke his heart. When we first met, we were in a group session trying to find our self-worth once again after being in a relationship that almost ended us. I may not know everything that happened between your parents, Mason, but trust me when I tell you that I know how he felt about leaving you, how much it gutted him."

"Then he should have come back."

"I know, and I can't argue. I tried to get him to do it, but he was scared. Scared you'd hate him."

"Well, he should have been. Are we done here? I've got shit to be doing."

Her mouth opens but she doesn't say anything. I take two steps before her words make my legs stop working. "He's left you and your brothers everything." I turn and pin her to the spot with my stare. "H-his parents died last year. He got all of their estate. Now it's yours." Anger swells within me. He never spoke to his parents. I've never even met them. Why would I want their money?

"I don't want anything from him. He left us. He found a new family. He. Chose. You."

"He didn't. He found himself with us. His heart never left this place. He yearned to be back here, and I prayed every day that he'd love me like he did her. He loved me, in his own way, but it wasn't like it was with your mom. He loved

Megan, but she could never make him forget you. If anything, it made him worse."
She digs into her purse and pulls out an envelope. "Here. It's from him. Please, take
it. He was planning on seeing you, he got tickets to your final game. He wanted to
watch you play, tell you how proud he was of you but... he didn't make it."

My heart pounds in my chest so hard that I start to feel a little lightheaded. Is
she telling the truth? Was he really going to come?

"What killed him?"

"Brain tumor. He'd been complaining of headaches for weeks, months even,
but refused to go and see a doctor. By the time I convinced him to go, it was too
late. They gave him six months at best. That was only six weeks ago." She sobs,
her hand coming up to cover her mouth. "I'm sorry, I just had to see you. To
explain to you that he never forgot you, or your brothers. Take it, please."

My hand trembles as I raise it to take the envelope. I stare down at it the
second she releases it.

Mason.

Seeing his handwriting makes my knees buckle, but I force them to hold my
weight, taking a step back instead. She doesn't say anything as I walk away
from her.

Yanking my car door open so hard I'm surprised it doesn't come off its hinges,
I rev the engine and gun it onto the street. I have no idea where the fuck I'm
going, but I need to get the hell away from here—from her.

I have no idea how long I drive around town for, trying to make sense of all
the bullshit that's running around my head, but at some point, my need to drown
it all out has me pulling up to Ethan's house.

I don't bother knocking, we never have in the past, and it's only his car sitting
in the driveway. I make my way past all the empty yet perfectly presented rooms
before climbing the stairs and walking toward the end of the hallway.

I knock on his door but only in the hope it'll alert him to a visitor and stop
me from walking in on something I'd rather not see if he's got a girl in here.

To my shock, when I open the door I find Ethan alone, sitting on his bed and
resting back against his headboard. He's got a cigarette in one hand and a bottle
of whiskey in the other. The room is in darkness aside from the glow from the
light in the en suite at the other side of the room. There's no music, no TV, just
Ethan.

"What the fuck do you want?" he barks without even looking at me.

"I get it, you don't want to talk, nor the fuck do I." Walking into the room, I
fall down onto his sofa and rest my head back. It still spins with everything she
told me, and the photo she showed me is still front and center. "What are you
waiting for? Chuck me the bottle, asshole."

He doesn't move, and when I eventually pull my head up to find out what the fuck his problem is, he's staring right at me, deep frown lines between his brows.

"You fuck things up with Camila already?"

"I said I don't want to fucking talk. Drink. Now."

He complies with my demand this time and I reach out to grab it as he throws it at me. Twisting the top, I lift the glass to my lips and swallow, one, two, three shots. By the fourth I don't feel the burn and my head slowly starts to swim. Exactly what I need.

33

CAMILA

All fucking night I sat there waiting for him, but he never showed. He never answered his phone, and when I spoke to anyone else who I thought might know where he was, they hadn't seen him either.

By the time he doesn't show up to school Friday morning, I'm starting to go out of my mind.

"Where the fuck is he?" I ask Jake, coming to stand toe to toe with him. It wasn't so long ago that I was terrified of being anywhere near him, but now I don't bat an eyelid at confronting him.

He swallows, and it tells me everything I need to know.

"What do I need to make Amalie withhold from you to get the answer?"

"Hey, don't drag me into this," she complains.

Ignoring her, I continue to stare into his mesmerizing blue eyes. "Tell me."

"Ugh, fine. He's with the other idiot who's skipped all week. Happy?"

"Not at all." I storm off down the corridor.

"Camila, please don't do something stupid," Amalie calls, but I know for a fact that if it were Jake hiding that, she'd be there demanding he speak to her.

I'm at Ethan's in no time, feeling stupid for not thinking he'd be here before. I pull up next to his car and jump out of mine, leaving the door wide open in my haste to find him.

I slam my fists on the door but I know it's pointless. The music inside is so loud that there's no chance either of them will hear me.

With my frustration growing, I march around the back of the house, but finding those doors also locked, I growl in frustration.

What the fuck happened for him to go from messaging me about waiting at home for him to locking himself in Ethan's house?

Some movement catches my eyes and my heart jumps into my throat that he's about to walk into the kitchen, but when someone appears, it makes my stomach falls to my feet.

A girl, dressed in only a guy's white shirt, pulls the fridge open and grabs a six-pack before disappearing the way she came.

"You're a fucking asshole, Mason Paine," I scream, tears streaming down my face as I try to tell myself that everything between us this week wasn't one big joke to him. I told him I loved him, for fuck's sake.

I don't remember the drive home, but when I get there to find my parents' car parked outside, I almost reverse back out. The last thing I need is them digging into what's wrong with me and why I'm not at school where I should be.

Wiping at my face, I pull my visor down and attempt to clean my face up, but my red-rimmed eyes practically shine like a fucking homing beacon.

Blowing out a long breath, I wrap my fingers around the door handle and prepare for what's to come.

The house is silent when I step inside. I go to the kitchen but find no one. It's not until I walk toward the stairs that I spot my parents' heads out on the love seat in the garden. They're laughing together and the sight makes my heart ache. Is that kind of happiness so hard to find? I've been screwed over by two guys in less than two weeks. Can things get any worse?

Shutting myself in my room, I crawl under my sheets fully dressed and hating that I can smell his presence. With the sheets over my head, I allow myself to cry for everything I've lost in the past two weeks.

Mason was right: I am a fucking idiot. I didn't see what Noah was doing right under my nose, and now I've opened myself up to him, the guy who's spent the last four years making my life misery. So. Fucking. Stupid.

At some point I must cry myself to sleep, because the next thing I know I'm being gently shaken awake by a hand on my shoulder.

"Camila, Cami. Come on, I'm worried about you," a familiar British accent says from the other side of the sheets.

"Go away," I mutter. I'm not ready to deal with the situation. I'm happier just hiding under here and locking it all out.

"Not a chance." Slowly, the sheet is peeled away from me. The light makes me wince. I scoot up so I'm sitting with my arms wrapped around my knees. "What happened?"

"He's having lock-in with Ethan and a barely dressed girl." My voice shakes with every word. "I thought he was telling the truth about how he felt about me. How could he do that to me?" I sob.

"You don't know he's done anything, Cami. That girl could have been there for Ethan."

"Why else would he be there?"

She shrugs, and I hate that she doesn't have an argument. She's usually so quick to defend Mason, and right now I need her to make me think I'm wrong. I need to be wrong. I need to know the boy I fell in love with really is the man I see now. I can't cope thinking it was all an act to play me.

"It might not be how it looks. I know it's hard, but you need to reserve judgment until you've spoken to him." I look to her and narrow my eyes in frustration. She reaches out and smooths my hair down. "Are you going to get changed?"

"For what?"

"Uh... the game, silly."

"I'm not going." I reach for the covers, but Amalie's quicker.

"There are two games left. I'm not allowing you to miss one of them."

"I don't care. I don't want to see—"

"Him?"

"Anyone. I'm fed up with everyone judging me. I'm the poor girl Noah cheated on, then I was the girl everyone hated because I turned straight to Mason, and now I'm the idiot again."

"No one's judging, Cami. Hold your head high and show the world you're stronger than that."

Amalie gets up from the bed and I start to think I've won and that she's going to leave. Unfortunately, she just goes to my wardrobe and pulls my Bears shirt from inside.

"Now go to the bathroom, freshen up, put some makeup on and let's go. I refuse for you to make me late so I miss seeing Jake in action."

Rolling my eyes at my best friend, I let out a sigh and climb off the bed. After everything she's done for me, attending this game is the least I can do for her. Then the second it's over, I'm coming right back here and not leaving.

The atmosphere at school is electric. We've never had such a successful season, and if it were any other night I'd be shouting and screaming with the best of them. Unfortunately, my heart's just not in it.

"They've so got this in the bag tonight," Amalie says beside me, bouncing up onto her toes.

"Even if Ethan and Mason turn up drunk?"

"They wouldn't do that to Jake, or Coach, for that matter. They also know it would get them benched for the final game and none of them want that, Mason especially after missing the last couple." I try to share her enthusiasm, I really do, but her words fall flat.

It's only a few minutes later when the roar of the crowd makes me wince and everyone is suddenly on their feet as the Bears run onto the field. My eyes zero in on our players, trying to find number eleven. I shouldn't be surprised when he's

last out along with number eighty-nine, Ethan, after what I saw earlier but I am, and I'm even more surprised they both turned up.

"See, I told you it would all be fine. Maybe Ethan was just having a meltdown or something."

"You say that like you don't know already." Jake knew exactly where Mason was earlier, so am I really supposed to believe that Amalie is clueless in all of this?

"I don't know anything. Jake doesn't tell me all his friends' secrets, just like I don't tell him all yours." I want to argue with her, but I know she's right. "Now, try to relax and enjoy the game."

It's a good game. We dominate for most of it and manage an easy win, thanks to our opponents losing their quarterback to injury only a few minutes in. But there's something different about our team, and it's all because of two players. Mason and Ethan. It's obvious to everyone, especially Coach and Jake who are constantly shouting at them to focus, that there's something wrong with them. Mason especially as he slams into the opponent's players with as much strength as he has. He's not usually rough player, but tonight he's on the verge of being sent off more than once.

"See, I told you something's wrong," I say to Amalie when Coach gives Mason another ear bashing. "That's not how he usually plays."

"I know. You need to find him after and talk to him. You're coming to Ethan's, right?"

"No, I'm really, really not."

"Camila," she sighs. "Rip the plaster off. Talk to him and get it over and done with. Find out the truth before you drive yourself crazy."

"Fine. I'll talk to him and then I'm leaving."

"Fine," she says, mimicking me.

———

"Come on, I told Jake we'd meet them at Ethan's," Amalie says, walking past the entrance to the locker room and toward her car. I kind of hoped I'd be able to see Mason before getting to party central to save me from having to step foot inside.

We're one of the first ones there, so the house is still quiet when we walk through the front door.

"Something's different here," I say as we make our way to the kitchen for a drink.

"In what way?"

"All the family photos are gone." I look around the room, making sure I'm not going crazy and they've just moved. Previously there were pictures of Ethan and his mom and dad everywhere over the years, but now, every single one is gone.

"Weird. Although family issues would explain how he's been acting recently."

We find bottles laid out in the kitchen and Amalie helps herself to one before the sound of everyone else arriving fills the house. Dread sits heavy in my stomach. I shouldn't have come here. I should have gone home and hidden.

I've barely lifted the drink Amalie made me to my lips when Jake sweeps across the room and pulls Amalie into his body for a celebration kiss. She eagerly returns it and I turn away, not wanting to intrude on their moment. Most of the rest of the team head our way to find drinks while others put the music on and start chatting and dancing around us.

With the intention of slipping out the back, finding my car and disappearing, I head down the hallway. I've got the exit in my sights when a hand reaches out from one of the rooms and grabs my forearm. My heart slams against my ribs as I prepare to look into Mason's eyes, only when I look up, I don't find his dark ones boring down on me. Instead, I look into Noah's.

"What do you want?" I spit. "I was leaving."

"Trouble in paradise already?"

"Fuck you, Noah. You don't get to judge or have any opinion on what I'm doing anymore."

"You're right, I'm sorry."

"So what did you actually want? I'm assuming you dragged me in here for a reason."

He takes a step forward and I take one back. Unfortunately I bump into the wall, stopping me putting any more space between us.

He reaches out and takes a lock of my hair between his fingers. The move is so familiar, but unlike every other time he's done it, I want to slap his hand away from me. He has no right touching me after everything he's done.

"I just wanted to apologize properly. I never got the chance to tell you that I never meant to hurt you."

"Really? So you fucking a cheerleader behind my back wasn't meant to hurt?"

"No, that's not what I meant." He leans a little closer. The smell of alcohol on his breath is obvious.

I glance to the side, thinking that I could side-step him and still get out of here when movement by the door catches my eye. There's a flash of blonde hair, but it's all I need to know that it was Mason.

Fuck.

As I turn back to Noah, it registers to me how this must look to an outsider. Pushing my palms against Noah's chest, I force him to back up.

"I don't want to hear it. Go and find your cheerslut if you want to talk to someone."

I'm walking away when my cell pings in my purse. Pausing for a moment, I pull it out hoping that it's Mason, but when I find *that* number staring back at me, my heart picks up pace. Nothing good ever comes out of that number.

My hands shake as I swipe to unlock it. I could be about to read anything, but what I find shocks me even more than I was expecting.

Photo after photo flashes up on my screen of Mason and... Chelsea. My stomach turns over, my hand automatically lifting to my mouth.

His promises that he'd never slept with her ring through my mind and fire me up, and when my feet move, it's not in the direction of the exit. I storm through the house looking for him. Or her. I don't really care if I should happen to find her first and show her what I really think of this little stunt.

It seems I'm in luck because when I do find them, they're together. Red hot anger fills my veins as I watch from the doorway as Chelsea walks over to Mason with two drinks. He already looks pretty out of it, but he accepts the cup and tips it straight to his mouth. He watches her as she steps into his side. I see red when she places her hand against his stomach and runs it up to his neck.

Marching over, my hand lands on her shoulder and I pull her away from his body.

"What the—oh, Camila's joined the party."

Mason looks between the two of us, his eyes wide, and he places his cup on the table next to him.

"You're a filthy fucking slut, you know that?" My hand goes flying out, and I'm so ready for the satisfying sound of my palm connecting with her cheek, but just as I'm about to swing, fingers wrap around my wrist.

"Whoa, she's not worth it." Jake's deep voice fills my ears and I spin on him.

"You." I narrow my eyes and poke him in the chest. "You need to get out of my way. That bitch needs a fucking lesson. She thinks it's okay to interfere in our lives just because we have what she wants, what she seems to think she deserves."

"Trust me, I know and I agree, but you don't want to do this with an audience."

"Why? Give me one good reason why I shouldn't."

A loud crash from behind us has us all turning around, and when we do, we find Mason in a heap on the floor.

"What the hell?" Jake's on his knees by his side, instantly turning him into the recovery position. I've only been here a few seconds but one image stands out in my mind. Reaching over, I grab Mason's drink and thrust it under Chelsea's nose.

"Drink. It," I demand.

She stares down at the cup before looking up at me. Guilt flashes in her eyes and everything falls into place.

"I said drink it."

"Camila, what are you doing?"

"Finding out the truth."

I can feel everyone's eyes burning into my back, but I don't look away from Chelsea.

"It was you, wasn't it, at Shane's party?" Amalie comes to stand beside me, waiting for an answer. But we don't get one, not yet anyway. "Those photos you just sent me. They're staged, aren't they?"

Chelsea has the gall to actually roll her eyes at me like what I'm suggesting is actually ridiculous.

"Fine," she mutters. "Yes, it was me, and yes they're fake." The attitude on her face doesn't falter, and this time when I move, there's no one behind to stop me.

My palm stings like a bitch as it collides with her face.

"What did you give him?" She continues staring down at the floor, my handprint glowing on her face. I close the space between us. "Tell me what you gave him and we might make it a little easier on you. Not that anyone's going to want anything to do with you after this."

"Ugh, it's nothing much. It'll just knock him out for a bit. No harm done."

"No harm? No fucking harm?" This time Amalie comes to stand between the two of us.

"Get the fuck out of here, and if you're lucky, we won't call the police." Without batting an eyelid, Chelsea turns and runs—well, hobbles.

"She's so fucking done here." My chest heaves and my fingers continue to curl into fists as I stand and watch her.

"We should probably try to get him to bed," Jake says from behind me, reminding me of what's actually going on here.

Running over, I fall to my knees and place my hand on Mason's cheek. "He's going to be okay, right?"

"I'm sure he'll be fine. It shouldn't hit him as hard as it did Amalie."

Ethan walks past at that moment, his arms around some girl I've never seen.

"Savage, a little help here?" Jake barks, catching his attention. He does a double take of us crowded around a passed out Mason before walking over.

"Jesus, how much has he had?"

"Not enough to do this," Jake seethes. He's barely holding himself together, and when I look up to his eyes, I see that they're wild with fury. He's wanted someone's blood for what they did to Amalie that night. He was so convinced he'd got it when he plowed his fists into Shane's face, but Amalie and I told him that he was wrong. Shane wouldn't do that. As nice as it is to be proved right about my friend, I'm not about to point it out anytime soon. "Help me get him up."

With Jake and Ethan at his sides, we manage to get Mason up to one of the guest rooms.

"Do you want me to stay?" Amalie asks once he's laid out.

"No, it's okay. I'll call you if I need you."

She's hesitant to leave, but after a few seconds she turns and closes the door behind her. I make quick work of pulling Mason's shoes from his feet and then crawl onto the bed beside him.

"What the hell is going on, Mase? Why did you disappear?" I'm staring at the ceiling, not expecting a response, so I almost jump out of my skin when he speaks.

"Cami?" His voice is rough and slurred. It hits me right in the chest despite wanting to hurt him for abandoning me for no reason.

"I'm here. It's okay."

"I'm so—"

"Just sleep, Mase. We'll talk tomorrow when you're more with it." It seems that's all the encouragement he needs because he's out like a light again.

I don't leave his side, and I toss and turn all night. Despite the light being on, I can't settle, too many thoughts racing around my mind trying to come up with why he could have hidden from me.

I eventually drift off when the sun starts to rise, and I'm only woken by footsteps a while later.

When I open my eyes, I find Mason sneaking toward the door.

"You're leaving?" I ask, my voice rough with sleep.

"I've got something I need to do."

"I'll come, just wa—"

"No. I need to do this alone."

"What the hell's going on, Mason?" I demand, swinging my legs over the edge of the bed and standing in front of him.

"It's... it's..."

"Is there someone else?"

"No. Although I could ask the same thing. I seem to remember you getting up close and personal with your ex last night."

"Oh yeah, I'm cheating on you with him. Don't be so ridiculous." I can't help rolling my eyes. "A little trust would be great."

"Yeah, same here. I'll see you later."

"You said that before," I call out as he makes his way down the hallway.

He looks back at me, his eyes haunted and sad. Unease fills me, and it's probably the wrong thing to do seeing as we just talked about trust, but I rush to pull my boots on and follow him out of Ethan's house. There are passed out bodies everywhere downstairs. I quickly step over them and get to my car without being spotted by Mason.

I sit tight while he backs out of the driveway and then I follow. I hate that I'm doing this, but that look in his eyes haunts me.

I follow him to the east side and then out to the next town. When he eventually indicates to turn off the main road, my brows draw together.

It's a cemetery.

I hang back, allowing him to turn around if necessary, but he doesn't come back. Instead, when I drive into the parking lot, I find his car with the engine off and him walking down the path toward the graves.

I fight with myself for long minutes as to what to do. I should just drive home and wait, I do know that, but my need to know he's okay is bigger than my need to do what's right.

I push my door open and follow the path he disappeared down. There are rows and rows of gravestones and a few people are scattered about, placing down flowers or just having a morning chat with a lost loved one.

I keep walking, looking left and right, trying to spot him. Just when I think he's vanished I find a figure sitting on the ground in the distance, facing a gravestone.

I gasp when I see his shoulders shaking and his head lowered in pain. My heart breaks for him and I have no fucking clue what's going on or who's died.

My legs carry me to him without instruction from my brain. My need to comfort him is too strong to deny.

I have no idea if he hears me coming, but when I sit down on the damp ground beside him, he doesn't so much as flinch.

He blows out a long breath, and I wrap my arm around his shoulders in comfort. It's then that I look at the stone in front of him.

David Michael Paine.

Beloved husband and father.

Oh fuck.

"Mason, I'm so sorry."

It's then he lifts his head from his knees and looks at me over his arm. His dark eyes are almost black with grief and full of tears. That sight has my own burning the back of my throat.

A sob rumbles up from his chest and I crawl closer. He uncurls himself and pulls me onto his lap. I wrap my arms around him and hold him as tight as I can as he cries on my shoulder. I rub his back and whisper that I love him in his ear, hoping that it does something to help.

I feel utterly useless, but as he clings to me, I know without a doubt that I did the right thing following him here.

"How did you know?" he eventually whispers in my ear.

"I followed you," I admit. "When you turned and looked at me, I knew something was seriously wrong. I couldn't leave you."

"I'm so sorry. I-I didn't mean to... get lost but fuck—" Some more tears fall and I catch them with my thumbs as I rest my forehead against his.

"It's okay. I wish you'd told me. I could have helped, supported you. I thought... I thought..." I trail off. It doesn't matter what I thought right now. What matters is Mason and how he's feeling. "How did you find out?"

"I had a visit from my stepmom."

"You've got a stepmom?"

"Apparently so. He was going to come and see me, but he didn't make it. He wrote me a letter. She wanted me to have it so..."

"She brought it to you," I finish for him. "Have you opened it?"

He nods. "But I haven't read it. Inside was the address for this place, her address, and his folded letter. I didn't have it in me to read his words, not yet."

"That's understandable."

"But I woke up this morning and I knew I needed to see him. I needed to put everything behind me. I've held onto the past for long enough. It kept me from you for too long. It's time to face up to it and move on."

I nod, allowing him time for his thoughts.

"She said he's left everything to me and Charlie and Ollie."

"Wow," I breathe.

"I mean, *everything* could mean a beat-up old car and a twenty-dollar bill..."

"Or it could be enough to secure your future."

34

MASON

"He could give you everything you need to start your life properly. It might be a little late, but in the end, you'd know he had your best interests at heart."

I didn't know that the only thing I needed after running from my old house the other day was to feel Camila's arms wrapped around me, but the second she appeared at my side my muscles relaxed and everything that woman's appearance disturbed inside me settled instantly.

I woke up this morning with a raging headache and a need so strong to get out of that house that I can't even describe it. I thought I needed to get lost, to drown myself alongside my best friend and forget everything I'd discovered. Turned out I was wrong, because Ethan is hell bent on ruining his life right now whereas I just needed a distraction. What I'd discovered wasn't going to disappear anytime soon. I knew that I'd need to poke my head back into the real world and deal with it all.

The moment I saw Noah leaning into Camila, I knew I needed to pull my head out of my ass and talk to her, but then Chelsea happened and the next thing I knew I was in bed with Camila at my side.

I could have told her everything this morning, but my head was so fucking fuzzy and the last thing I needed was for everyone in his house to start waking up and questioning me on everything.

"So, what now?"

"I think I need to go and see her. I wasn't exactly polite the other day."

"She turned up and told you your dad had died. I'm sure she understands."

"They've got a daughter, Cami. I've got a sister."

"Oh."

"Do you want to come with me?"

"If you want me to."

"Always." I can see the skepticism in her eyes, thinking about the fact I decided that I didn't need her when I first found out all this. But after a second, she takes my hand and together we leave my dad behind and head toward our cars.

Pushing her up against her car, I press my body into hers and stare down into her eyes. Lifting my hand, I tuck a lock of her hair behind her ear, brushing my knuckles down her cheek and onto her neck. I wrap my fingers around the back of her neck and hold her to me, our foreheads together, our breaths mingling.

"I'm so fucking sorry."

She looks away and I hate that she feels the need to. "Mase." She pauses and it makes my heart thunder in my chest. "Do you remember what happened last night?"

"I had a few too many and you guys put me to bed?" It's the only explanation I have for how I went from Jake ripping me a new one for my behavior on the field to being in bed fully dressed with Camila beside me.

Slipping her hand behind her, she pulls her cell from her back pocket and opens it up.

"Do you recognize these at all?" She turns the screen to me and my eyes almost pop out of my head. Taking it from her hand, I swipe to see more of the same. Chelsea with her hands all over me, her lips pressed against mine and her hand... "What the fuck? This never happened. Cami, I haven't... I didn't..."

She lets me stew for a few seconds before she opens her mouth. "I know. She staged them. She's been going after me since she called me to Shane's the night I discovered Noah. That girl's got some issues."

"You don't fucking say." I scroll up through the other messages she's received. "Why didn't you tell me about these?"

"Because they're nothing. Just a pathetic girl trying to play games to get her own way."

"True, but you shouldn't have to deal with this." I look back at the photos and my stomach turns over. I know exactly which night these are from. I was so fucking drunk that I passed out. I never thought she'd pull something like this.

She shrugs. "It could be worse. Those could actually be real."

"I don't even remember getting up to the bedroom that night. There's no way I was capable of this."

"I know. She drugged you."

"She fucking what?" I ask, thinking I must have misheard her.

"That night, last night, did you accept a drink from her?"

I think back. "Yeah, but—"

"It was her. She was the one who drugged Amalie at Shane's party."

"Fucking hell." My hands lift to my hair and tug. "What the fuck was she playing at?"

"I don't know, but I'm pretty sure she needs some help. The shit she does isn't normal."

"You're fucking telling me."

Camila's hands run up my chest and I'm dragged from thoughts of Chelsea as I look into her dark eyes. "Her issues aren't our responsibility. Everyone is going to know what she's done after last night. Hopefully it'll be the reality check she needs."

"We'll see." I can't help feeling like she's always going to be the way she is. She's so desperate for attention that it seems she stops at nothing.

"Shall we go then?" Camila asks, reminding me where we were heading.

"Yeah. I'll put her address in my GPS if you want to follow me."

"I'm right behind you."

"Thank you, Cami-bear." I don't know if I mean for chasing me, for believing in me or for giving me a pass after my behavior the past two days, maybe a little of all of it. I drop my lips to hers for a quick kiss. I'm afraid if I allow it to go on for too long that I'll use it as an excuse to get out of here and not do what needs doing.

It's only a short drive to the address I found inside the envelope. It's a cute little duplex home with flower boxes under the windows. I stop the car out front and Camila pulls up behind me. I don't move as I stare at the house my dad had called home for the last years of his life. Regret fills me that I never made the effort to find him. I told myself it wasn't my job, seeing as I was a kid, but if I'd made that effort then maybe I'd have seen him again, maybe we'd have had the chance to rebuild our relationship. All the possibilities of what could have happened swim around in my head until Camila appears at the window beside me.

I open the door and look up at her. Sympathy fills her eyes. "I can't even try to imagine how you're feeling right now, but whatever you need, I'm here. You need to leave, just give me a sign and we're out of there."

After releasing a slow and steadying breath, I climb from the car.

Maybe they're not in, I tell myself as we make our way up the small front garden.

Camila raises her hand to the door and knocks three times. It becomes immediately obvious that someone is inside, because the sound of a young child crying filters through the door.

I suck in a breath when I hear footsteps heading our way. Camila must hear it or sense the tension within me because she reaches for my hand just before the door's pulled open.

"Mason." She's shocked to see me, that much is obvious. "It's so good to see you. Hi," she says, turning to Camila. "I'm Julie, and this munchkin is Megan."

"Hi, I'm Camila. I'm Mason's girlfriend."

"Camila, it's so good to meet you. I've heard so much about you."

"Really?" Camila asks, sounding shocked.

"Of course. David used to tell me what you two used to get up to, how you were both attached at the hip. He always hoped you'd end up being his daughter-in-law." Camila's chin drops but no words pass her lips.

"We've just been to see him," I blurt like an idiot.

"Would you like to come in? I was just making us some lunch."

"Oh... um..."

"That would be lovely," Camila answers for us, and when Julie moves aside, Camila all but drags me inside. This is why I needed her here, because I'd have bolted by now otherwise.

My hand slips from hers as we make our way through the explosion of toys in the living room in favor of looking at a photograph that's hanging from the wall.

"That's from our wedding day," Julie says from behind me, not that it really needed explaining with her in a white dress and Dad in a suit. "It was just a small thing. He'd have loved to have had you there."

I nod. Hearing things like that doesn't really make any of this better, because at the end of the day, no matter how much he'd have liked me there, he never invited me.

Dragging my eyes away, I look at the other photographs scattered around her house. Most of them include my dad, whether it's the two of them together or him with Megan. My heart aches more with each one I look at. I was desperate to see him, to ask him why he never came home, to tell him that I understood why he left, but here he was only one town over, living a new life with a new wife and daughter. Why weren't we good enough?

"It's only cheese sandwiches, I hope that's okay."

"It's perfect, thank you so much," Camila answers as I trail behind her, trying not to let it show just how much I'm struggling with all of this. "Just say the word, Mase, and we can leave," Camila whispers in my ear after Julie's placed Megan in her highchair and turned to the kitchen

"I'm okay." In reality, I'm anything but, but now I'm here I want to find out more.

"Megan's almost nine months old. I never thought I'd have kids, but she was the best thing that ever happened to me. I'm not sure how I'd have got through all this without her."

Julie gives me some more detail about how she met my dad and what their lives were like together. I'm torn as I listen to her happy stories. Of course, I wanted him to be happy and to restart his life after everything that happened, but at the same time while I was drowning at home, trying to keep his family above water, a part of me hoped he was struggling just as much. I guess the fact that they met at rehab means his life wasn't always like this.

I let out a sigh and both Camila and Julie turn to look at me.

"I know this is a lot to take in, Mason. I just... I had to come and find you. That letter and everything he left you deserved to be in the right hands."

"I don't need his money," I say sadly.

"I never said you did. Nor did he. When his parents died, they left quite a big estate behind, and him being an only child meant it all went to him. He never spent a penny of it. He wanted you to have it all. He'd already written it into his will before meeting me. Everything's all ready for you, our lawyer just needs somewhere to send the money. Your brothers' shares have been put into trust ready for when they're eighteen."

I nod, still unsure about how I feel about all of this.

We stay just over an hour before Camila makes our excuses. She can see I'm struggling and thankfully makes the call for me.

I follow her out to our cars after saying goodbye to Julie and agreeing that I'll consider coming back one day to get to know both her and my sister better. I haven't decided if that will happen or not. My head's spinning too much right now to make any kind of serious decisions. I left my bank details with her so she can forward them to Dad's lawyer, so all I need to do now is wait to see what he wanted me to have.

I hate that Camila and I are about to get into different cars right now to head home. I desperately want her beside me as I try to process everything.

"We'll be back in no time," Camila says, reading my thoughts. "We could order pizza and watch a movie, maybe."

"Sounds perfect. Thank you for this."

"You're more than welcome."

I pull her into my arms and hold her like it might be the last chance I get. "I love you, Cami-bear," I whisper into her hair. I'm really not sure how I'd have handled this today if it wasn't for her.

"I love you too. Come on, let's get back." I nod, dropping my lips to hers for a chaste kiss before allowing her to climb into her car. Once she's strapped in, I close her door and make my way to my own car.

I set the GPS to home. I should be able to navigate my way back, but with the way my head's spinning the last thing I need to do is think about anything else.

In forty-five minutes, we'll be back and I can pull Camila into my arms and never let go. The last few days have been stressful at best, and I need to lose myself in her more than I need my next breath right now.

My head's still back in Julie's house as I stared at the photos of my dad living a life I didn't know existed as I make my way out of town. I'm so focused on getting back that I'm not paying enough attention. I look up and see the red light I should have stopped at and slam my foot down on the brake, but it's too late.

35

CAMILA

Mason's a mess. Every time I looked at him in Julie's house I could see his internal conflict about even being there. He was trying, but it was taking its toll on him. Unable to see him suffer any longer, I make our excuses and get him away.

The drive home should be easy. It's one straight road back to Rosewood. I trail behind Mason, wishing that I was sitting in his passenger seat and holding his hand in support instead of being all the way back here.

The lights change up ahead, but Mason makes no attempt to slow down. He flies toward them and my heart jumps into my throat as his car speeds toward the intersection.

"Brake, Mason. Brake," I shout, but obviously he can't hear me.

My heart thunders in my chest as he continues forward as a car comes into view from the left. It's not slowing down either, but why would it? It's got a green light.

Fuck, fuck, fuck.

I can't drag my eyes away from the inevitable. Mason's brake lights finally shine bright but it's too late. Both cars are going too fast, and I have no choice but to watch as the two collide. The sound of crushing metal echoes around me as I sit frozen, my hands gripping onto the wheel, my foot pressing so hard down on the brake it's hitting the floor, but I stopped long ago.

Get out of the car. Get out of the fucking car, I repeat over and over as I stare at the wreckage, but I know it's wishful thinking. There's no way either driver is walking away from this one.

A few other witnesses go running toward the cars, but I can't make my body move. I can't do anything. My fear for what this means locks my muscles tight. The only thing that seems to still be working is my heart as it pounds against my ribs.

Mason please, come on. Just get out of the car. GET OUT OF THE CAR.

I have no idea how much time passes. All I know is that I'm still in the exact same position in my car and Mason hasn't emerged when the flashing lights of an ambulance race toward the scene.

Knowing that help has come gets me moving. I'm like a robot as I climb from the car and slowly make my way over. I'm not aware of my body moving, but I'm not aware of the distance I've traveled until I'm standing just in front of Mason's car.

I'm not able to see him, but the soft tone of the paramedic fills my ears.

"My name's Devon, I'm a paramedic. Can you hear me? You've been in a accident. We need to get you assessed and get you out of this car." I start to assume he's awake and listening. I begin to relax a little until he speaks again. "If you can hear me, squeeze my finger."

I don't feel anything as my knees hit the concrete, or the stones digging into them.

The sound of a scream hits my ears, but it's not until a policewoman bends down in front of me that I realize it came from me.

This can't be happening. I just got him back. He's got his whole future ahead of him. This cannot be happening.

"Shhh... calm down, sweetheart." The policewoman joins me on the ground and rubs my back, encouraging me to suck in a deep breath and release it through my nose.

"M-My-My boyfriend. He-He's—" I can't get the words out past the giant lump in my throat and the panic crushing my chest.

"He's being looked after by the best. You just need to stay back and give them space to do their job."

"Is he...is he alive?"

"I don't know anything right now, darling. I know it's hard, but you just need to be patient. Those guys are the best, they'll do everything they can for him, I can promise you that. Would you like me to call anyone for you?"

I think for a moment. The only person I need is in that car. A sob erupts from my throat at the thought of losing him like this.

I shake my head. "Okay. It would be really helpful if you could give me his details to pass on."

I nod, because moving my head seems to be the only thing I'm capable of right now. "M-Mason Paine. He's eighteen." I rattle off my address, phone number and his mom's name before she runs over to one of the paramedics.

Two other ambulances arrive along with a fire engine, and I sit frozen on the ground as I watch them begin to cut people from cars. It's the most surreal experience of my life, sitting there waiting to find out if the person I love more than anything in the world is dead or alive.

"Camila, fucking hell," Amalie's scream fills the air but I don't move, I can't rip my eyes away from what's happening in front of me. Her body falls down beside me and her arms wrap around my shoulders, but I still don't move. I vaguely remember texting her with my location, but I did it on autopilot. I have no idea if I even gave her a reason for it. "It's going to be okay. *He'll* be okay."

"You don't know that. He could... he could be—"

"No, you need to think positive. He's going to be fine."

"But what if he's not," I wail, not able to process that thought. "What am I supposed to do then?" She pulls me tighter to her and I soak her shoulder with my tears.

When I eventually pull back, I find Jake looking between the two of us and the wreckage beyond with concern written all over his face. When his eyes don't come back to us, I can't help but see what's caught his attention.

I'm horrified as we watch the firefighters cut the top of Mason's car away before the paramedics rush in to tend to him.

"Oh my god," I whimper, my hand covering my mouth as even more tears pour from my eyes.

What will I do without him?

"Where are you going?" Amalie shouts and I manage to drag my eyes away from where Mason is to see Jake talking to the police.

"They'll be taking him to Rosehill Hospital. Let's go there so we're ready for him when he wakes up." Jake talks to both of us but I refuse to look at him.

"No. No, he needs us here. I need to be here."

"You can't do anything right now, Cam. You need to allow them to do their jobs and be ready for what Mason's going to need from you when he wakes up." She must see the fear on my face. "He'll wake up, Cami. He'll be fine."

"She's right. He's stronger than this."

I want to scream at them to look at the wreckage in front of us, but I know they're just trying to keep me calm. They see the devastation, they know how bad this is, they just don't want to voice it.

"Look." Jake points over my shoulder. "They've got him on a gurney. They'll be heading to the hospital any minute and they'll be faster than us. We need to get there now."

"What about my car?" I look over to where I abandoned it in the middle of the road.

"I'll go and pull it into the shoulder. You two go and get in the car. Take my cell, call his mom." He hands it to Amalie and runs toward my car.

Amalie does as she's told and pulls me along with her. I'm still trying to process his first statement to know what I should be doing right now.

The blue flashing lights illuminate the interior of Amalie's car. I climb into the back, my nose pressed up against the window as I fight to see him, to see if he's okay, but they all move too quick. One second they're running toward the ambulance and the next they're slamming the door and one of them is jumping in the driver's seat.

"He's leaving, we need to go now."

"Jake's coming. Try to stay calm, we'll be there as soon as possible."

———

The second Amalie brings the car to a stop, the three of us take off running. There are two ambulances already out front of the building, one of which had Mason inside it.

"We're here for Mason Paine, he was just brought in my ambula—"

"Camila," Nicky cries, and I turn just in time for her to collide with me and wrap her arms around my shoulders.

We hold each other for the longest time. When she eventually releases me, I find myself swept up into my parents' arms, who are also here waiting.

"Any news?" Amalie asks.

"Nothing. Did they say anything at the scene?" I shake my head, although I have no clue if anyone's actually addressing me.

Eventually all of us find seats and we begin the long wait to find out if he's going to survive or if we somehow have to find a way to continue on without him.

When someone eventually walks through the double doors and heads our way, a collective gasp sounds out.

"Family of Mason Paine?" We all stand, and the doctor looks along the line of us. "Immediate family."

Nicky and I stand forward. I don't give a fuck what they consider immediate family. I'll lie through my fucking back teeth if it gets me past those doors and to his side quicker.

Nicky looks to me and takes my hand. "We are."

"Okay, follow me."

Just before we disappear through the doors, I look back. Everyone is still on their feet, desperation on their faces. I feel for them but not enough to stop me walking through and hearing firsthand what's happening.

"Please take a seat." The doctor gestures into the room and we both shuffle inside and drop on to the edge of the chairs. "Mason has been very lucky—"

I don't hear any more. Those five words repeat through my mind long after the doctor has finished explaining whatever might be wrong with him, because right now I don't care about any of that. He's alive and that's all that matters. We can work through anything else as long as he's still here.

I drop my head into my hands and sob tears of relief.

"When can we see him?" I eventually ask when the doctor finishes.

"Not yet, but it won't be long. Someone will come and get you when he's ready."

I nod, although I'm far from happy with the answer. I need to see with my own two eyes that he's going to be okay.

Silence descends around us after the doctor closes the door to give us some privacy.

"What did he actually say?" I ask Nicky after long minutes when I realize I heard nothing.

"Um... broken ribs, collapsed lung, concussion, b-broken something else... I think." She breaks down, unable to say any more as her emotions get the better of her. Wrapping my arms around her, I hold her while she shatters. If she thought she had a wakeup call when I gave her a few home truths not so long ago, then this should really open her eyes to what's happening around her.

"I should go and let the others know he's going to be okay."

She nods at me and releases my hands that she was holding for support.

The second I push the doors open, everyone runs at me. At some point they were joined by Ethan, who looks equally as distressed.

"He's going to be okay." I go on to explain what I can remember Nicky told me about his injuries.

Amalie and my parents hug me and I fight to keep my tears in. I need to start getting myself together and so I can be strong for him when we're allowed to see him.

It's another two hours before Nicky and I are allowed into his room. We follow a nurse down toward him, but my feet stop moving when I get to the door. We've already been warned that he's under sedation because of his head injury and that his face has been cut up from the glass that shattered around him. I can't cope with the images that have been filling my mind, let alone see the real evidence of what this has done to him.

"Camila, are you okay?" Nicky asks, turning to see where I've gone.

"I-I don't know if I can do this," I admit quietly. Watching the crash and him getting pulled from the car from a distance was one thing. But having to sit next to him while he's unable to do anything, seeing him so vulnerable... I'm not sure I can hack it.

"Of course you can. Mason needs you right now. He needs you to be strong, he needs you to hold his hand and help him get through this."

My chin trembles as I picture sitting vigil at his bedside for however long it is until he wakes up. The doctor said they'll reduce his sedation tomorrow if things are moving in the right direction, but there's no guarantee he'll wake up that quickly.

Nicky looks between me and the door behind which her son lies, and I feel like the worst person in the world for keeping her from him.

"It's okay, you go. I just need to catch my breath."

"I'm not going in there without you."

I blow out a breath. I can't keep her from him.

Sucking in a deep breath, I take a step forward. Her arms wrap around my shoulders and she pushes the door open. She releases me the second we're in the room and races over to Mason's side, a sob ripping from her throat.

I'm frozen in the doorway, watching as if this is just one big nightmare and that my boyfriend, the boy I've loved since I was old enough to know he made my heart race, isn't lying in a hospital bed with wires and tubes coming out of him and attached to some really scary machines.

"I know it looks scary, sweetheart, but it's all okay. It's just helping him. Mason is still Mason," a nurse says softly, her eyes full of compassion. "He might be able to hear you if you talk to him. He'd love to know you're here."

I nod slowly and take a step toward him. My eyes stare at his sheet covered feet and slowly I make my way up his body. The sheet stops mid chest and then his body is hidden by his hospital gown. His body just looks like he's sleeping, but then I get to his face. A small cry passes my lips as I take in the cuts, the dried blood, the stitches.

"Oh my god." Racing toward him, I find his hand and lift it to my lips. I manage to push aside the hospital smell, and when I breathe in, it's all Mason. He's here. He's going to be okay.

Dropping down to the chair behind me that the nurse pushes forward, I keep his hand clutched in mine as I drop my lips to the back, staring at his battered face.

When the doctor came back after his initial visit, the panic of not knowing if he was dead or alive had alleviated and I was able to focus when he repeated Mason's injuries. He's broken two ribs which had caused a punctured lung. He has a concussion from his head injury. But other than that, it was just cuts and bruises. He was very, very lucky because with the speed both of the cars were going, it could have been much worse. Hopefully if all is well, he'll wake up once they reduce his sedation and he could be home in a week. God, I really fucking hope so. We've only been here a few hours and I'm already ready to get him out of here.

36

CAMILA

It's been two days. Two days since I watched that car plow into the side of Mason's. Two days since I watched him get cut from the wreckage. Two whole fucking days since I looked into his eyes, since I heard his voice, and I feel like I'm fucking dying. Every breath is a fight to drag in. Every movement is heavy, not that I've moved far from his side. People keep bringing me food and trying to force me to eat, but I can't stomach it.

The doctors said he should wake up once they reduced the meds, but other than a few movements, he's yet to do so and it's scaring the shit out of me.

Crazy thoughts keep running through my head like, what if they got it wrong and he's not okay? What if his concussion is worse than they think and he's not going to remember anything, not going to remember me? The thoughts have my heart racing and the room around me starting to blur.

Everyone keeps telling me to stay positive. To trust the doctors. But as each hour passes, I find it harder and harder to do so.

"Camila, you really need to come home, baby," Mom says softly from her spot by the window.

"I've already told you that I'm not leaving him."

"Please, just let us look after you. You need a shower, you need sleep and you need a decent meal inside you."

"I'm not leaving." This isn't the first conversation like this I have had with my parents, and I'm sure it won't be the last.

"Nicky is here. If anything happens, she'll call right away, won't you, Nic?"

"Of course. But your mom's right, Cam. Mason needs a better version of you than you are right now."

Something unpleasant stirs in my stomach that I'm not what Mason needs right now. I always want to be what he needs.

With a sigh, I allow my mom to pull me from the chair I've turned into my home. I don't take my eyes from Mason as she gently pulls me toward the door. I don't want to leave him. If he wakes and I'm not here, I'll never forgive myself.

The car ride home is in silence. I just stare out of the window, regretting that I allowed them to take me away from him. He needs me there. He needs me by his side.

"How about I run you a bath and then I'll make your favorite dinner, sound good?"

I don't respond, because how could anything sound good right now? Selfishly, I don't even want to hear the words 'he's awake,' because it would mean I'm not there by his side.

I robotically follow her up the stairs and sit on the edge of my bed while I listen to her run the bath. The last thing I want to do is sit in there alone with only the images of the crash and Mason's broken body filling my mind, but I also don't have it in me to argue right now either.

She comes back in to tell me it's ready before pulling some clean clothes out of my closet and some underwear from my drawer. I'm grateful she's not expecting me to think for myself and thankful to get some fresh clothes. I might not be totally with it right now, but I know I'm still in the same clothes I was wearing Friday night, and they most definitely do not smell good.

She leaves the folded-up clothes on the counter, kisses my forehead and then leaves me to it.

With a sigh, I strip down and climb into the tub. The hot water surrounds me, and where I'd usually enjoy the feeling of the soothing water relaxing me, I feel nothing. I'm numb. It's like I left a part of myself on that road where I abandoned my car. I fear that without him waking up, I'm never going to find it again.

The silence around me is deafening, and it only makes the questions in my head louder. I'd put music on but have no idea where my phone is—not that I really want to listen to anything.

I allow myself to slide down until I'm fully submerged. I don't resurface until my lungs burn for air, and when I do, I make quick work of washing my hair and body. When he does wake up, he deserves for me to at least look like I've tried.

"Camila," my mom's panicked shout fills the room, and I jump from the bath. Something about her tone has me moving and flicking a towel around me as fast as I can. "We need to go, Nicky just called. He's waking up."

Fuck, fuck, fuck. I'm not there. I told them not to make me leave. I knew it was wrong.

My legs tremble as I try to pull on a pair of leggings. My skin's still damp and I end up crashing to the ground in a heap in my haste to get back to the hospital.

"Are you okay?"

"Yeah, I'm coming. Get the car started."

Thankfully I manage to pull the rest of my clothes on slightly more efficiently, and, with sopping wet hair that's dripping down my back and soaking my hoodie, I run to the car.

My heart threatens to pound out of my chest and my nails dig into the leather beneath me. My legs bounce with my need to make my dad go faster, but there's no point in me demanding him to do so. He's the world's most cautious driver, even in these kinds of situations. According to my mom, he even drove like Miss Daisy when she was in labor with me, a story that I've always found amusing until this very moment.

I'm out of the car before he's even brought it to a stop. I hear them shouting behind me, but I don't stop. My only focus is getting up to his room as fast as I can.

I stumble up the stairs, my legs moving faster than my body can cope with, and by the time I crash through into the ward, my muscles are burning with exertion. There's a reason I don't make an effort to do sports, and this is why.

The nurses look up from their station as the door crashes back against the wall, but they all stay put when they see it's me. I've become part of the furniture the past two days, so they all know who I am at this point.

I race down the corridor, almost overshooting the door when I get to it. Swinging around the door frame, I come to an abrupt stop at the end of Mason's bed.

But he's not looking at me. His eyes are still shut.

"What happened? Mom said he woke up." I can barely get the words out between my heaving breaths.

"He was. He moved, he squeezed my hand, he moaned. I thought it was it, it was more than we've got from him so far, but then he just fell back to sleep."

"Fuck," I bark, the realization that our wait is going to continue for longer slamming into me. I fall down into the chair at the opposite side of Mason's bed to Nicky and take his hand in mine. "Come on, baby. Wake up for me, please," I beg, more tears slipping down onto my cheeks. I'd have thought I'd have run out by now, but it doesn't seem to be the case.

"I'm just going to grab a coffee," Nicky says, dropping a kiss to Mason's head and leaving me alone with him.

"It's time to wake up, Mase." I rub my thumb over his rough jaw, being careful of his cuts and bruises.

The machines have been taken away now. There's no beeping, nothing apart from the sound of his shallow breathing as he heals.

I stare at him, praying that he'll do something to show me he's coming back to me. I'm so focused on the stillness of his face that when his eyelids flicker, it actually scares me.

"Oh my god, Mason. Can you hear me? I'm here, baby. I'm right here. Everything's going to be okay."

There's nothing for long seconds and I start to wonder if I imagined it. But then, right as I'm starting to believe I hallucinated, he does it again, only this time they open. Not a lot, but they open nonetheless.

I move closer, taking both his hands in mine. "Can you hear me? Squeeze my hand if you can."

Then the most incredible thing happens. His fingers tighten in mine. "Oh my god, Mase." A sob rips from my throat and I carefully prop myself on the edge of his bed, being careful of the tubes he still has coming from his chest.

"They made me go home. Can you believe that? I've been here since the moment you arrived, and when they make me go, it's when you start waking up. Are you trying to tell me something with that?" I ask with a laugh, because I'm fully aware that he has no control over what his body does right now.

"Everyone's been here. Jake and Amalie, Ethan and his whiskey bottle, your mom, my parents. We're all here for you, Mase." I sigh when there are no other signs of him waking up.

"What the hell were you playing at?" I ask. "Do you have any idea how fucking scary it was to watch you run that light and a car impale itself in the side of yours? I thought you'd fucking died, Mase. I thought that was it. I already lost you for four years. I only just got you back and I thought you'd fucking died on me." My tears make my vision blurry, but when I look up from our joined hands, it's not enough to hide the pair of eyes that are staring back at me.

"Mason, fuck. Oh my god." I wipe my eyes with the backs of my hands and wait to see if he's going to do anything. The second I connect our hands once again, he squeezes them tightly.

His lips part, his tongue sneaking out to wet his dry lips.

"Wait, hang on." I reach over for the cup and straw that's been sitting unused for the past two days and fill it with some water. Lifting it to his mouth, he sips a little before I pull it away again and place it down.

I look into his dark eyes, my heart thundering in my chest as I read everything he wants to say to me. I see his fear, his confusion but also relief, and I hope that's there because I'm here with him right now.

When his lips part again, one single word manages to break free.

"Sorry."

The small amount of control I had on my emotions snaps and I cry. I'm desperate to crawl in beside him and feel his arms around me, proof that he's here and that he's awake, but I know I can't and it kills me.

"It's okay, baby. You're here and you're going to be fine. I love you. I love you so much."

His own eyes fill with tears, and when one trickles from the corner, I reach out and catch it with my thumb, cradling his cheek in my hand.

"Everything's going to be okay," I repeat, sensing that he needs to hear it again.

We're still staring at each other when Nicky comes back in, cradling her coffee in her hands.

"Mason? You're awake."

A small smile twitches at the corner of his lips when he sees her, but his eyes are starting to get heavy, and after another few seconds he's drifted back off to sleep.

37

MASON

I was aware that everyone had been here. I'd heard their voices, I'd felt their touch, I just wasn't able to open my eyes. It freaked me the fuck out the first time it happened, but hearing everyone around me talk and a few hazy memories, I quickly figured out what had happened and where I was.

No sooner had I got frustrated with the situation than I'd fall back to sleep and forget all about it, until the next time I woke again.

I knew Camila was here. I'd heard her voice many times and I could feel her tiny hand in mine. She was all I needed, and every time I heard her say that everything was going to be okay, I believed her. But it was one thing she said that gave me the strength to finally open my eyes and see her.

"I already lost you for four years. I only just got you back and I thought you'd fucking died on me."

The guilt that hit me hearing that statement had my eyes flying open. How could I be so fucking selfish? I should have been paying attention to where I was going, not busy thinking about the past, my dad, but instead, I once again caused Camila pain. Pain that I'm not going to be able to do anything about, other than to apologize, and that is nowhere near what she deserves after witnessing what she did and sitting beside me all this time.

Over the next few days, I manage to stay awake longer and longer. Every single time I open my eyes, she's there, sitting in the same chair, wearing the same clothes, looking equally as beautiful as she does exhausted, and I wish she'd take some time to look after herself.

"Hey, you're awake," she says, pulling her chair closer before standing and dropping a kiss to my lips.

"Hey," I say, my voice rough and croaky after being asleep for fuck knows how long.

"How are you feeling?"

"Better actually. I feel like I can breathe again. My head kills though."

"I'll call the nurse. Get you some more painkillers."

I want to say no, to keep it just the two of us, but I know she's doing the right thing. If I want to get out of this place anytime soon, then for once I need to learn to listen to those around me and do as I'm told.

I have no idea how many days might have passed. Sometimes I wake up and it's dark out, other times it's light. I have no sense of anything, and it's seriously disorientating.

"What day is it?" I ask Camila when I wake up once again to find her sitting in the chair beside me on her tablet.

"Friday."

I think for a few minutes.

"The game." Tonight's the final game of the season and the one to seal our fate. We've already secured our place in the state playoffs, but if we win tonight, then we finish as district champions, something none of us thought was even a possibility when Coach started getting us excited for it all those months ago.

Jake's aim was the playoffs. He said he didn't care if that meant we came first or fourth, as long as we placed, but we all knew that he was desperate for that top spot. And he deserves it after the work he's put in. He deserves to be able to celebrate something.

"What do you think I'm doing? Amalie is sending me updates. It's a tight game by the sounds of it."

She turns the screen to me and hits play on a video that she's sent through. Every muscle in my body aches to be out on that field with them. After missing those games because I had to work, I'd hoped that we'd be able to finish the season as a team, but it seems fate had other ideas for me.

"You've still got the playoffs. There's still a chance you'll be okay to play."

"I know. It just sucks that I can't even be there."

"You've got loads of games ahead of you yet, Mase. Just think of all the college games to come."

"If I get in."

"You'll get in. Stop worrying. Your grades are good, and you're shit hot on the field. Maddison would be crazy not to accept you."

I let out a sigh, hoping that she's right. From as early as I can remember, Dad and I talked about me playing for the Panthers and that dream is now in touching distance and the risk of fucking it all up is getting higher and higher.

"I need that fucking scholarship." I've got no hope without it.

"You'll get it, but you might not need it after all. We still have no idea what your dad's left you."

The memory of sitting in Julia's house slams into me, I gave her my bank details. I wonder if she's already passed them on?

A more pressing thought takes over. "Have you told my mom?"

She nods. "I have. I hope that's okay. They wanted to know why we were where we were and in separate cars. I didn't have it in me to make something up."

"No, it's fine. How'd she take it?"

"She was upset. Shocked. She hasn't said so, but I'm pretty sure she's been out to his grave."

I nod, wondering how she's really taking it. She's been managing to get her life back on track since moving in with the Lopezes. I fear hearing about Dad might send her spiraling back down again.

"She's doing okay though. Work gave her this week off to be with you and the boys, but she hasn't touched a drop of alcohol. She's good, Mase. Just worry about yourself, yeah?"

I can't help it. After spending the past four years basically doing her job for her when she was unable to look after herself, let alone her kids, I'm scared of going backward. We might be living under someone else's roof right now, but my life is better than it's been in a really, really long time, and I don't want that to change.

Sucking in a deep breath, I prepare to ask a question I'm not sure I want an answer to. "Cami?" She turns her eyes on me and my chest aches that I've put her through this after everything else. "W-what happened to the other car— the people in the other car?"

She reaches for my hand, and I panic. "She's fine, Mason." Relief bubbles up to the point I think I might actually burst into tears. "Your mom has seen her and spoken to her. Everything's going to be okay."

I nod, images of how different things could have been playing out in my mind.

My thoughts are put on hold as Camila suddenly jumps up from the chair. "They did it. They fucking did it."

A smile breaks across my face.

"They won?"

"They did. *You* did. You're a champ."

"I didn't—"

"Don't you fucking dare. You've given your all to that team, don't you dare downplay this right now."

———

Two hours later, we hear them before we see them. But seconds after there's a commotion out in the corridor, Jake, Ethan, and the rest of the team come crashing into my hospital room. Their excitement is infectious, and for the first time since Camila told me, a sense of pride and achievement races through me.

"We fucking did it," Jake cheers, coming over to my side and pulling me to him, albeit carefully. "We're fucking champions, bro. We did it."

I might hate that they were forced to do it without me, but Camila was right, I am a part of this, and as the excitement reaches a whole new level inside my tiny hospital room, I can't help but get carried away with it. Even Ethan seems to have left his issues at the door as he laughs and jokes with the rest of the team.

"Not that I don't want you guys here, but aren't you supposed to be celebrating your win right now?"

Everyone but Jake, Ethan, Amalie and Camila have left, and I've been waiting for them to make their excuses to leave as well.

"We are," Jake says, pulling Amalie down onto his lap.

"No, you're hanging out in a shitty hospital room when you should be fucking shit up."

"It can wait," Ethan says, shocking the hell out of me.

"You're telling me your place isn't party central right now?"

"Nope, not without you, man."

"Don't stop enjoying yourself because I'm stuck in here. You guys deserve it."

"Yeah, well, we'll still deserve it when you're out of here and can celebrate with us." I smile at my two best friends. They might be their own brand of fucked up in certain ways, but fuck, I couldn't ask for two better boys to have my back.

"I appreciate that, but I really don't want to stop you."

"It's all good. Plus, I think we can probably all agree that I need to slow down at bit."

"Yeah, about that."

All eyes turn on Ethan as he lets out a huge breath. "I'm sorry I've been a bit of a fuck-up recently." Jake goes to say something, but Ethan doesn't give him the chance. "My dad's been cheating on my mom. She left a few weeks ago."

"Oh fuck. I'm so sorry."

Amalie reaches over and places her hand on his shoulder in support when he drops his head into his hands, and I don't miss the look that passes between her and my girl. It makes me wonder if they'd already figured this out.

"Where's she gone?"

"To my grandparents in Connecticut. She wanted me to go but..." He blows out a breath. "My home's here. I couldn't leave but—fuck."

Silence falls around us.

"I just needed to get it off my chest. I know I've been acting like a dick and I'm sorry, I just—"

"It's okay, Ethan. We get it. Families are hard fucking work. Parents are hard fucking work. All of us in this room know that. Whatever you need. We're here."

"I appreciate that. Anyone want a drink? I just need to get some air." The girls ask for a coffee, but Jake and I go without.

"Fuck."

"Well I guess that explains the missing photographs." My brows draw together at Camila's words. "You locked yourself in his house for two days. Don't tell me you didn't notice all their family photos had gone." When my face stays blank, she rolls her eyes at me.

"What? My dad had died, I needed a release."

Seeing as no one looks shocked, I assume that Camila has filled everyone in on what's happened in my life and excuses my lack of attention. Not that I ever really gave Ethan's family photos a second glance. I do feel for him though, a family breakup can be seriously fucking tough.

"I wish he'd have said something sooner," Amalie muses.

"Explains a lot though. He idolizes his dad for the success he's had, so knowing he's betrayed his mom must be a serious kick in the teeth."

"I wonder who the woman is," Camila adds.

"I'm sure he'll tell us when he's ready," I say, knowing exactly how he's feeling right now.

"Well, that seriously soured the mood, huh?" Jake says with a laugh, seeing as we're supposed to be celebrating.

"We're in a hospital, it's not exactly the best place for a party."

"We'll make up for it once you're back on your feet."

Ethan reappears about twenty minutes later. His shoulders seem wider than when he walked out, and I can't help but wonder if having the weight of his secret lifted was exactly what he needed.

They stay for another hour, the guys filling me in on every play in tonight's game and how they managed to turn things around at the last minute to take the lead and the title.

"Playoffs, here we fucking come!" Jake announces, slamming his closed fist to his heart.

"We've got this. Well, you guys have. Only time will tell for me."

"You'll be there. I won't have it any other way."

When they see me starting to fade, they make their excuses and leave us to it. I feel bad that they're only heading to Aces for a burger and not to a party, but I can't exactly make them.

"Can I?" Camila asks, nodding to the space on the bed next to me.

I shift over the best I can, the pain from my ribs taking my breath for a few seconds, but we just manage to squeeze on. Having her in my arms feels so damn good, and I never want to let her go.

EPILOGUE

CAMILA

M ason ended up staying in the hospital for eight days in all. After the fourth day, my parents demanded that I leave each night so I could get some sleep. I argued, of course, but in the end, they won and I can't deny that I felt a hell of a lot better after a full night's sleep in a bed and not just a series of catnaps in a hard hospital chair.

I did put my foot down, however, when my parents and Nicky started talking about getting Mason's room ready for him. The three of them looked horrified when I announced that he would be moving in with me, but to be fair to them, they didn't argue. They must have known it wasn't one they were ever going to win.

They told me that they'd allow it for now, while he recovers, but that it would need to be readdressed in the near future. I fought hard to hide my eye roll. I have no clue what's going to happen when Nicky decides to move out, but until then, I have no intention of allowing Mason to sleep anywhere but my bed.

My dad had to go back to New York. Mom was planning on going with him again, but with everything that happened, she insisted on staying home and helping Nicky out with Mason and the boys. We both told her it wasn't necessary, but she wouldn't have it.

So the following Monday morning, the three of us escorted Mason home and up to my bedroom. I hadn't told him about his sudden bedroom move, but the smile that curled at his lips as we moved slowly to my room told me that he was happy about it.

I refused to go back to school, much to my mom's horror, but I'd already missed one week. What was another really going to do? I emailed our teachers and got schoolwork so neither of us fell behind, and we spent the afternoons working.

Spending time together was incredible. We were able to make up for our lost time and talk about everything that happened during our years apart, and Mason totally opened up about what happened after his dad left.

My heart bled for him, and I so wished he could have just talked to me at the time instead of building his walls up so high that I had no choice but to be pushed out. I might understand why he did it, but that doesn't mean I'll ever be happy about the years we lost.

True to his word, Ethan held off the celebration party until Mason was able to attend, and that's where we're headed tonight. Mason's still in pain, mostly with his ribs, but he's insistent that he's well enough to go. As much as I want to demand he stays in bed until he's fully recovered, I also know that being stuck inside the house is driving him crazy. I can't really argue with him that sitting on Ethan's sofa won't really be that much different from sitting at home.

He's not able to drink due to the pain meds that he's still on, but he's not all that bothered about drinking anyway. Something tells me that's a side effect of Chelsea taking advantage of him the last two times.

Without being at school, we've missed the gossip firsthand, but Amalie was very quick to tell me that Chelsea never reappeared the Monday after Ethan's party. No one knows where she's gone—not that anyone really cares. I can't help but feel sad for her. Yes, she's a bitch, but there's a reason she does what she does, and I get the feeling that her life could be very different to what we all assume it is. She's all designer labels and caring what everyone thinks, but underneath that, I think there's a girl who's just desperate to be liked and fit in. One day we might get the chance to know the real Chelsea. I guess that all depends if she decides to show her face again.

Stepping out of the shower, I dry myself off, slather my body in my favorite moisturizer and slide my new dress up my body. Mom and I went shopping the other afternoon to give Mason and Nicky a little time together. The moment I saw it, I knew I needed it. It's nothing special, just a short little black dress with a lace overlay. It's simple, fits me perfectly and makes me feel like a million dollars. I also have a sneaking suspicion that Mason will like it too.

After blow drying my hair and applying my makeup, I make my way back to my bedroom to see what he thinks.

Pushing the door open, I find him sitting on the edge of the bed dressed in real clothes for the first time since his accident. After ditching the hospital gown, he's lived in joggers, not that you'll hear me complaining because they certainly look good on him when they're riding low and giving me a hint of what he's got hiding beneath.

His eyes lift as I step inside the room and they widen as they take me in.

"Fucking hell, Cami-bear. Are you trying to kill me?"

"You like?"

"I more than fucking like. Come here." He stands from the bed. It's awkward and I can tell by the frown that mars his forehead that it hurts, but he doesn't complain. Instead, he holds his hand out for me and I slide mine into it. I take a step toward him before he lifts his arm, encouraging me to spin for him. I do it because I'll do pretty much anything he asks of me.

"Do you have any idea how badly I want to bend you over and fuck you in this dress?" I bite down on my bottom lip and look up at him through my lashes. "Don't fucking do that," he growls, reaching down to rearrange himself in his pants. "How long did the doctors say until these ribs will be healed?"

"A while yet," I say with a laugh. "We'll just have to be creative."

"Hmmm..." He drops his head into the crook of my neck, breathing me in. "I like the sound of that." His hand slips around my waist and down to my ass. He pulls me up against him until he hisses with pain, but the unmistakable length of his cock presses into my stomach.

"We do not have time for that. Amalie will be here any minute to pick us up."

"I'm sure it would be quick. It's been over two weeks since you touched me."

"Even more reason to make it even more memorable by waiting a little longer."

He groans as I step away from him and slide my feet into my shoes. "I'll make it worth your while," I say with a wink.

"How's that?"

I move to leave the room, but I stop to whisper in his ear on the way out. "I may not be wearing any underwear." I am, but he doesn't need to know that right now.

"Fucking hell." He bites down on his knuckle, a pained look in his eyes. "Come on. I think I just heard her car."

He mutters something behind me, but I don't make the words out as I start to descend the stairs.

"Whoa, Ethan really pulled out all the stops for this one," I say as we attempt to get near his house. There are cars lining the road leading toward it, and when we walk up the driveway, we find it full. The music booms from inside and there are people everywhere who've come to celebrate the team's win, or to just make the most of the free alcohol courtesy of Ethan's dad who's been even more free with his credit card since the truth about what he's been up to has come out.

Turns out he's been seeing a woman from Michigan for months. His mom had known for a while before she handed him divorce papers and announced she was leaving. Ethan was totally blindsided by it all. According to Ethan, his dad's still seeing the woman. He's tried to convince Ethan to meet her, but he's point-blank refused, although Ethan's worried he's not going to have much choice in the matter soon because his dad has been talking about moving her in. He's angry, understandably so, and he has no idea how to release it other than to get fucked up and fuck anything that moves. He's trying to rein it in, but he's struggling and none of us really know how to help him other than to listen when he is willing to talk.

We make our way through the house and we head out to the kitchen. "I see what you mean about the photographs. I have no idea how I didn't notice before."

"You had other things on your mind."

A few days after Mason got home, he logged onto his internet banking to find out if Julie had organized for whatever his dad had left him to be transferred. His eyes nearly popped out of his head when he saw the figure staring back at him. He got on the phone immediately to her to find out if there had been some kind of mistake, but Julie assured him it was correct. I literally watched the weight of worrying about paying for college and having to support his family leave him. It was incredible. Since then, he's been smiling just like I remember from before his dad left and his life spiraled out of control. He's truly been the Mason I remembered and always hoped was still in there somewhere, even if he is a little battered and bruised right now.

"Are you okay? Do you need to sit down?"

"I'm fine. Stop worrying. Let's get you a drink, you need to relax."

"I'm just—"

"Trust me, if I need to sit down then I will, but right now, I just want to try to be normal."

I nod, continuing beside him and following Jake and Amalie to the kitchen where we find Ethan.

"The party's really starting now, ladies and gentlemen. The captain is in da house!" He lifts his drink in salute to Jake before downing it. The rest of the team who are all huddled in the kitchen cheer while Jake laughs at Ethan's antics. It's nice to see him being his usual crazy self.

I have a drink with Amalie while Mason catches up with the guys before he turns to me. "Dance with me."

"Are you sure—"

"Stop it." His fingers press against my lips. "I just want a normal night with my incredible girlfriend to thank her for being by my side through all of this."

My heart swells at his words. "I'd love to dance with you."

He slips his hand into mine and he pulls me toward the living room turned dance floor. He twists me into his body and wraps his arms around my waist. We don't really dance. I can tell by the slight narrowing of his eyes that he's in too much pain, but he refuses to let it stop him. I'll humor him for a song or two, and then I'm going to make him sit his ass down to rest.

Goosebumps prick my skin as he runs his hands up my waist until he threads his fingers into my hair and tilts my head so he can capture my lips. We stand in the middle of the dance floor and kiss like we're the only ones in the room. I pour everything I've always felt for him into it. It was always meant to be Mason and me. We may have had a few bumps in the road, but we finally found where we're meant to be.

Pulling away from my lips, he tucks his face into my neck. His breath races over my sensitive skin, and I shiver in his arms.

"Cami-bear?" he whispers into my ear.

"Yeah?"

"You're going to be my wife one day. I hope you know that." A wide smile curls my lips and my heart sings. I thought I'd lost my best friend, the one who made my heart beat a little faster and every second of my days better, but it seems our time apart might just have been to prove one thing. We were always meant to be together.

———

I eventually manage to get Mason to sit on one of Ethan's giant sofas. The others join us along with some girl that's attached herself to Ethan like a fucking rash. She's not Chelsea, so I guess we can't really complain.

I'm busy watching everyone around us when a girl catches my eye. She doesn't look like a typical Rosewood student, and she's definitely not someone I've seen here before. She's dressed head to toe in black with leather cuffs around her wrists and fishnet tights with giant holes on her legs, finished off with a pair of biker boots.

Her eyes run over our group before she stalks over. I knock my knee against Mason's to get his attention, and he soon spots who I'm pointing out and watches her approach.

"So, these must be your dumb jock friends. Jesus, you're so cliché it actually hurts to fucking look at you," she says, glaring at Ethan.

Whoa, who the fuck is this chick?

Ethan's eyes turn hard, the muscle ticking in his neck as he stares up at her. Jake tenses beside Amalie, who looks as shocked as I feel.

"And you are?" Jake asks, his chest swelling as he stands and stares her down. She's short, probably shorter than me, and she has to tip her head back to look him in the eyes, but she doesn't cower one bit.

She laughs in his face, proving that she has no idea who he is. Well, that or she really doesn't give a shit.

Ethan shifts the girl on his lap to the other side. "This..." He points up to the biker chick with a snarl on his face. "This is Raelynn, my darling never-to-be fucking stepsister."

"Your what?" Mason asks, his mouth gaping open.

"Don't get too used to her being around. She's not staying. Not if I have anything to do with it."

They stare at each other and something crackles between them. Ethan was already struggling enough; she's surely the last thing he needs. Only time will tell.

Things are about to get SAVAGE!
Keep reading for Ethan's story...

SAVAGE

1

ETHAN

The sound of his car pulling up in the driveway fills me with dread. I've avoided spending any time with my father since his secrets were exposed a few weeks ago, and, being the spineless prick that he is, he's allowed me the space. Any decent dad would force me to sit down to hear him out, but no... he ran. Ran back to *her,* no doubt.

My parents have been even more absent than usual recently—not that I'm complaining. It meant I had the place to myself and was able to do what the fuck I wanted whenever I wanted, just the way I liked it. But I had no idea that they weren't just on another one of Dad's work trips. The reality of it was that Mom had moved back in with her parents in Connecticut, and my dad was banging his assistant in Washington.

I shake my head, still refusing to fully accept what he's done. I'm not ashamed to admit that he is my idol, and the fact that he's just screwed my mom over in the worst possible way shakes me to my core. The man I've always looked up to, who I thought was a god, just pissed all over everything I ever believed. I thought he was honest, trustworthy, honorable. But it seems that all of that was an act, a lie. All it took was a woman in a short skirt with an easy smile, and he ruined everything we had.

My fists curl as the sound of the front door slamming shut echoes through the empty house.

"Ethan?" My name booms up to me. I want to pretend I'm out, but he's just parked next to my car. There's no chance I'm going to get away with this. "Ethan?" he shouts again, his feet pounding on the stairs as he makes his way to my room.

His knock on the door is strong and assertive, and it makes me want to slam my fist into his ribs just to show him how fucking strong he really is.

When he still doesn't get a response from me, he pushes the door open anyway and walks inside.

"There you are, son. Didn't you hear me calling?"

Keeping my head down for a beat, I then turn toward him. He's wearing his standard suit and tie duo, the one I thought always made him look so powerful and successful, but now, I just roll my eyes. He's a joke.

I don't respond. He knows full well I heard but that I have no intention of talking to him. He didn't just betray my mom when he stuck his dick in that whore, he betrayed our whole family. Our name. Everything we stand for.

Ignoring the fact that I clearly have no interest in what he's got to say to me, he continues nonetheless. "I've got tickets to today's game. Thought it would be good for us to spend some time together."

Although the thought of the game is appealing, especially knowing that he'll have fucking epic seats, if it means sitting next to him and pretending everything is perfectly fine, then no thank you very much. "I'm good, thanks. I'm busy." I turn back to stare out the window. In reality, I'm doing fuck all, and the fact that I'm sitting on my bed with nothing turned on or even my cell in my hand should clue him in on that.

"Really?" he asks, the amusement in his tone pissing me the fuck off.

"Really."

"Ethan, come on. Don't be like that. I know you're pissed at me, but not everything is as it seems."

"Oh, really so you weren't dipping your pen in the office ink while being married to Mom, then?" He pales. "If I've got it so wrong, please, enlighten me, Father." I stand, stepping right in front of him. I'm taller and wider than him now, and I know how much he hates it. His neck ripples as he swallows. It's not with fear. This motherfucker's not scared of anything, especially not me.

"You wouldn't understand."

My teeth grind, and my chest swells with anger. "I'm not a fucking child," I seethe. Relationships are complicated, I get that. Things happen, I get that. But what I don't get is why he couldn't be a fucking adult about it and talk about it instead of fucking the first woman who crossed his path.

He stares me down, daring me to say exactly what's on my mind, but I refuse to acknowledge his behavior with that kind of attention.

"I had to pull some serious strings to get these. Are you coming, or what? It's supposed to be an outstanding game." He waves the tickets in front of my face.

I haven't been to an NFL game in forever with him out of town, and the temptation of the roar of the crowd, the shared excitement, the knowledge that I can forget about my own bullshit life for sixty minutes is enough to have me agreeing, although I'm not happy about it.

A smile of achievement curls at Dad's lip, and I regret it instantly.

"I'll meet you downstairs in twenty. We'll go for steak after, too." Damn him, he knows I can't refuse the offer of steak.

With a nod of his head, he ducks out of my room, leaving me to stew in my anger some more.

Pulling my shirt over my head, I drop my joggers and step into my en suite. It might have been different if I'd have seen it coming, but my parents have always seemed so happy, so solid. While I watched my friends at school fall apart over the years when their families were ripped in two, I always felt grateful knowing that that would never happen to me. I was that confident in the love my parents had. So the day I got a tearful phone call from my mom, it wrecked me in a way I could never imagine.

"I'm so sorry, baby, b-but I'm not coming home. T-Things are over between your father and me."

I've watched people break when their girlfriends have split up with them, when their teams have lost, when they've failed the test they spent weeks studying for, but I never thought it would feel quite like it did in that moment.

She begged me to leave and move to Connecticut with her, pleaded with me that she couldn't lose me as well, but my life is here. Everything I have—besides her—is here. I can't just up and leave everything I've worked so hard for, or my friends who I know have my back no matter what.

As much as it gutted me to do it, I had to tell her that I was staying put. I had plans for my future, none of which included moving in with my grandparents. Although, now thinking about it, following my dad's footsteps to study business at UFC isn't all that appealing. I always wanted to be just like him, but now, I'm thinking being the opposite might not be so bad.

The drive to the stadium is in silence. Only the sound of Dad's V8 engine could be heard as I kept my eyes on the world passing by outside the window. I might have agreed to this, but I don't want him under any illusion that there's been any kind of truce between us. There's a very good chance I might never forgive him for this.

The game is exactly as I hoped. The excitement and roar of the crowd seeped into me the second we stepped foot inside the colossal stadium. My buzz as the cheerleaders shook their pom poms filled my stomach with the kind of tingles I only get when a football is involved. I live for this. Shutting the world out and focusing on one goal. I love the cheer of the crowd, knowing, whether playing or spectating, that I'm part of something bigger than just my little life.

I'm sure everyone around me thinks it's the attention of being a Bears player that I love, and yes that's part of it, but it's not all of it. Being beside my brothers, taking on the world together, means everything to me.

My focus is solely on the game and putting myself in the players' shoes.

Playing in front of the Rosewood High crowd is a serious buzz; I can only imagine how those guys feel when they run out to this exuberant crowd.

It's a tight game, and it keeps us all on our toes throughout. My heart's racing when the whistle blows for the final play, not knowing which way it's going to go.

I fall down onto my seat, the high from the game making me want to celebrate. It might not be my win, but fuck if I don't have the same response. There's nothing like a good party and a fuck after a successful game.

I glance around to see if there are any options for the latter, but when I look to my left, I find my dad looking back at me with a smile on his face and my excitement immediately vanishes. My mom has told me stories from what he was like in high school. They didn't get together until years after, partly due to his reputation. Am I just as bad as him? Am I destined to make the same mistakes when it comes to women?

"Ready to eat?" he asks as everyone starts to leave.

I'm not. The last thing I want is food right now, but I doubt I've got a chance of getting out of it. "Let's go." There's no enthusiasm in my voice, and the way my dad's eyes narrow, I know he doesn't miss it. It doesn't stop him from taking me to the most expensive steak house in the district though.

The atmosphere is heavy, the tension between us becoming seriously uncomfortable as he orders us both a fillet steak and sits back with his beer, practically waving it in my face after refusing to order one for me, claiming that I'm underage—which of course is true, but it doesn't stop him filling the house every weekend for me, or leaving his credit card for me to stock up with more should we run out.

"I know you're angry, Ethan. I understand that this was a shock, but things haven't been right between your mother and me for a very long time. We—"

"I don't care, Dad. You didn't need to cheat. There are a million ways to deal with a failing relationship, and fucking your assistant isn't one of them."

He rears back slightly at my blunt tone.

"It's not like that with Ash." I raise a brow, not missing the fact he's talking about her in the present tense, like she's still very much a part of his life. "She was there for me as a friend long before anything happened."

"Spare me the details of your sordid little affair."

"Keep your voice down, Ethan. The whole town doesn't need to know our business."

A spiteful laugh falls from my lips. "And you don't think the gossip is going to be rife when they realize Mom's not coming back?"

He opens his mouth to respond but nothing comes out. "Listen, son," he says eventually, and my stomach drops. I should have known he had a hidden agenda with this spur of the moment daddy/son bonding day. "I know you're not going to be happy about this but—"

I blow out a slow breath as I prepare for the next bit of information that's going to rock my world.

"Ash is going to be moving in with us."

"She's fucking what?"

"Look, I know this isn't ideal. I hadn't planned on asking her yet, but things are tough for her in Washington right now. She's lost her apartment and—"

"I don't give a fuck, Dad. We're not a fucking homeless shelter for women you randomly pick up."

His face turns beet red with anger. His eyes narrow and his lips twitch. I recognize it as the look he gets when he's trying to keep his shit together. "It's my house, Ethan. If I want her there, then she'll be there."

Well, isn't that just fucking great.

"It might be your house, but you're never there. Are you expecting me to play house with this woman, or is she going to disappear with you for weeks at a time?"

"She'll be with me, but—"

Fuck my life, there's another but. I stare at him, my expression blank as I wait for the next blow.

"Her daughter will be coming with her and enrolling at Rosewood. I'm going to need you to take care of her while she settles in." I wait for him to tell me that he's joking, but at no point do his lips twitch into a smile. "She's a lovely girl. I think you'll like her."

2

RAELYNN

"Hey, honey," Mom says, letting herself into our depressing apartment after working her second job of the day. "I hope you haven't eaten, I brought your favorite." The second she says the words, dread sits, heaving in my stomach. Mom only splurges on Chinese when she's got bad news to break. And more times than not, that news is that we're moving. Washington has been home now for almost eight months. It's the longest we've stayed anywhere that I can remember; I should have seen it coming.

Mom's been unusually settled, and I had hoped that I might get to complete school here, but as I round the corner into our living area to find her unpacking the takeout boxes, I know the reason we're about to up and move again. It's always for the same reason. A man.

Every time she promises that it'll be different. That this time, he's the one and we're going to lay down some roots and make ourselves a real home. But every time *the one* turns out to be a total douche and we end up leaving—or running, more like.

She's a serial fiancée. Almost every time things get serious enough that he buys a ring, and then he shows his true colors and it's all over. The one before last one was the worst. A shudder runs down my spine as I think of him.

Eric, though, seems like a good guy. He's the wealthiest of the men she's gone for in the past, and she does have a good nose for the ones with money. It's how she thinks she's going to make herself happy after years without anything to her name. I truly hope that one day she finds what she's looking for, but I fear it's all just one big fantasy.

"Smells good, Mom," I say, dropping onto our worn couch, breathing in the scent of real food. It's been a while since I ate something quite so substantial. "What's the occasion?" I ask, the words almost getting stuck in my throat.

She blows out a breath, stalling for time, and I realize that at no point does she attempt to look up at me.

"We're moving again, aren't we?"

"I'm so sorry, honey. But I think it's for the best."

I nod at her sadly, knowing the real reason she wants to move again right now but also knowing that she's not going to voice it. We never talk about that—about *him*. She just keeps trying to outrun the memories instead.

"Eric's got this amazing house by the sea. The local high school is incredible. You'll have so many more opportunities than you do here."

That is very true. The high school I'm currently at is the worst of all the ones I've experienced in the past five years. I certainly won't miss the place when she drags me across the country once again.

"When are we leaving?"

She swallows and pokes her chopsticks into her noodles. "He's coming to get us on Wednesday."

"Wednesday?" I almost snort rice out through my nose. "Wednesday? As in the day after tomorrow?"

At least she has the decency to look guilty.

"He's not sure when he'll be back at the office again, and he doesn't want to leave us here longer than necessary."

Jesus, the way she says that makes me think we're kids' toys sitting on a shelf, waiting for a new owner.

"We're more than capable of moving on our own. It wouldn't be the first time," I mutter.

Guilt fills her features. I know this isn't how she wants us to live, but unfortunately, it's our life. Maybe one day she will get the stability she craves. I hope she does, I really do. Is Eric Savage it? Of the possible stepdads I've had over the years, he's got to be up there in the top three of real possibilities. But who knows what the future could bring. It's not ceased to amaze me this far.

"It's important to him to help."

"I'm assuming his wife's moved out?"

"Raelynn," she snaps, her eyes finding mine for the first time.

"What?" It's no secret that Mom and Eric's relationship started while he was still married. The whole thing just sounds a little too cliché for my liking. He was unhappy in his marriage, got friendly with his assistant, and the next thing we all know, he's taking her out to dinners to thank her for her dedication to the firm and I come home from school early to find them on the bed I'm forced to share with Mom in our tiny one-bed apartment. But it's all okay, because said wife found out and left, and now we get to move into his castle that overlooks the sea. I just about manage to stop my eyes rolling thinking about it.

"This is the last time, I promise."

"Sounds great, Mom." They're not the words I want to say. I want to demand to know how she can sit there and say that after all her past ruined promises that we'd settle down. I want to scream about how I'm once again uprooted from a school I've barely had time to get used to.

Silence descends around us. We don't even have a TV to break the tension.

After finishing my sesame chicken, which I struggled to force down after having my assumptions confirmed, I place the box back on the coffee table. "I have a test in the morning I need to study for. Not that it'll make any difference if I pass or not."

I'm almost in the bedroom when she calls for me.

"Rae?"

I pause, but I don't turn around or even speak.

"This is going to be the last one, I really feel it this time."

"I hope so, Mom. I really do."

I ignore the textbook sitting on the dresser as I walk into the room. I couldn't give a fuck about the test; I just needed a little space, not that I get much of that in this barely five-hundred square foot apartment. I might not be all that excited about packing up the few possessions we have once again, but the idea of living somewhere a little bigger is definitely appealing.

Exactly as promised, when I get home from school on Wednesday afternoon, our apartment is missing its possessions—not that there's a lot of them—and Mom and Eric are waiting for me with a couple of suitcases next to the couch.

"Did you have a good day?"

"Fine," I mumble. I spent all day wondering where the hell she was dragging me to this time. Eric does appear to be truthful, but really, until I see the evidence of this house overlooking the sea, I'm going to be skeptical. Mom's fallen for some very convincing liars in the past, so just because he wears a fancy suit and flashes his black Amex about whenever he buys anything, it doesn't really mean all that much to me.

"Did you say goodbye to your friends?"

My mom's not stupid—she's actually a very intelligent lady, despite her obvious flaws—so how has she not realized that we move so often that not only is it impossible for me to make any friends but I'm at the point where I've actually given up trying? What's the point when in two, five, eight months I'm going to be dragged somewhere else in the country?

"Yeah," I lie. "They promised to stay in touch." I somehow manage to keep the bitter tone out of my voice. Getting into a fight with her now is only going to result in a tense journey to wherever it is we're going.

"Fantastic. Well, our flight leaves in two hours. Shall we go and get some food first? I'll have a driver waiting outside."

"Sounds perfect," Mom practically squeals in excitement.

"Do you want to change first?" Eric asks, running his eyes over my outfit.

"No, I'm good." I glance down at my ripped, paint-covered jeans and my slashed-across-the-midriff tee. I don't really give a shit if I don't fit into his fancy world. Mom's the one he wants, not me. He's only got to put up with me for a few months before I finally decide where I want to go to college and actually spend three whole years in the same place. I'm not one hundred percent on where I want to go, although I have a few definite no's after the places Mom's dragged me to.

"Okay then." He doesn't look happy about it ,but as I stand with my arms folded over my chest and my chin jutted out, he wisely shuts his mouth, clearly agreeing with me that an argument before boarding a plane is a bad idea.

With our suitcases and belongings in the back of his driver's car, we head toward the airport, stopping at a diner on the way. It's not the kind of place I expect Eric to choose, but he can hardly take us to a fancy restaurant with me dressed as I am. The thought fills me with joy. I might not get a say in where we live, but I do have control over some things.

"What did Ethan say about our arrival?" Mom asks, reminding me that it's not only Eric we're about to move in with.

"He can't wait to meet you."

The thing about having a million—or so it seems—men come in and out of your life is that you get really good at reading them. Mom's addiction to assholes has really helped me identify the bad ones way before she does, and right now, Eric is lying through his teeth.

"Really?"

"Of course. I've told him all about both of you."

I can't help rolling my eyes. He might know plenty about my mom—they've been seeing each other long enough to know the basics—but I would put money on him not having a fucking clue about the darker parts of our past that make us the way we are. Mom might be quick to fall in love and trust, despite having her heart shattered more times than I care to count. I, on the other hand, do not trust anyone, even my own mother to a point, with her terrible judgment. I will ensure no one knows enough about me to use it against me. I learned the hard way years ago that allowing someone in and trusting them only leads to pain, and it's not a lesson I'd like to repeat.

"I've enrolled you at Rosewood High. Ethan can show you around on Monday and help get you settled."

"Brilliant." I smile at him and he returns it, assuming mine's genuine. It's not. I've started over at schools so many times now that finding my feet is almost part of the fun. Plus, getting lost is always a good excuse for being late.

The rest of the journey is just about tolerable. We fly first class, obviously, and while Mom and Eric are otherwise engaged, I manage to snag myself a bottle of champagne. It's fancy as fuck—Christ knows how much it must cost him—but I don't care. I tip it back like it's sparkling water in the hope it helps me forget what's happening right now.

———

The second we're out of the airport, I know that Eric's words about where he lives and the money he has are true. There's a fucking limo waiting for us.

Mom squeals in excitement as he pulls her into his arms and kisses her sweetly. The champagne filling my belly threatens to make a reappearance at the sight.

It's so over the top and pretentious.

"I wanted you to arrive in style, sweetheart."

Jesus, I'm really going to hate this place.

Some poor member of the airport staff wheels out our cases on a trolley and proceeds to place them in the trunk. I follow his lead and grab the handle of the passenger door of the ridiculous car, much to the driver's horror. He's waiting patiently to greet his guests.

"What?" I bark. "Do *you* want to sit in the back with those two pawing each other?"

"Point taken, Miss. You are very welcome to join me."

"Thank you." I grace him with the first genuine smile I've given out all day and climb in.

I make quick work of changing his radio station to something a little more current and sit back and wait.

We've made it this far. All that's left is to see this house he's promised us.

The drive is longer than I was hoping for, and I find myself dropping off to the sound of the driver singing along with my music. If I cared, I'd ask how he knows the words when most of his passengers probably request classical or some other shit, but I don't.

I don't open my eyes until the ground under the tires starts to crunch. My chin drops as I stare at the house we're driving toward. It's fucking massive.

"Impressive, right?" the driver says, and I realize that I've moved forward in my seat to get a better look. The place is bigger than some of the apartment buildings we've lived in.

"It sure is something."

"I hope you're happy here, Miss. Rosewood is a great place to live."

Only time will tell. I don't respond with my reservations, instead I just smile and climb out of the car when he pulls it to a stop.

"It doesn't look like Ethan's here. I told him what time we were arriving," Eric grumbles. "Come on, I can't wait to show you around."

"Just point me in the direction of my room." I have no interest in a guided tour of his fucking mansion. If I have to live here, then I'm sure I'll figure out which room is which soon enough. Not that anyone could possibly need all these fucking rooms.

He pushes the doors open and a huge staircase is revealed. It's like those you see on wedding photos where the brides gracefully glide down toward her prince. The thought has the champagne sloshing around once again.

"Take the stairs, turn left. Your room is the last one on the right. It's got an incredible view and a balcony. You'll love it. I had Rachel make it all up for you, but if you need anything, please just ask."

I want to ask who the hell Rachel is, but assuming she's the maid or some shit, I just nod and follow his directions up the insane staircase.

3
———

ETHAN

"You know I love you, man, but are you planning on going home sometime tonight?" Mason says with a laugh. I turned up here under the guise of catching him up on the school gossip, seeing as he's been off since his accident last weekend.

"Dad's back," I say, hoping it'll be enough to stop him giving me grief for not wanting to go home. In truth, it barely scratches the surface of my reasons for not wanting to be there. No sooner had we got home after our father/son bonding day of horrors, he packed a bag and took off for Washington, promising to be back with my new ready-made family tonight. I'm even less willing to meet them right now than I was when he told me they were coming.

Anger burns within me that Mom's perfume has barely faded from the house yet he's totally fine with moving in his mistress and her daughter. Asshole.

"Trust me when I tell you that letting all this fester inside isn't the best course of action. I know you're angry. I'm angry for you. But you need to talk to him. Get everything out in the open."

I mutter some kind of response before standing from the chair I'd taken over in Camila's room a few hours ago when I made myself at home here.

"We're here if you need anything," she says softly from her spot tucked into Mason's side. It's a harsh reminder that I'm now the gooseberry in our group. I used to live for times partying with my boys, but they spend almost all their time with their girls now. And where does that leave me? Apparently at home with a replacement mother and a child to babysit.

I leave them to it, sadness and anxiety only growing stronger the farther I get away from them. My fingers curl around the steering wheel of my car with an unforgiving grip as I head toward home. Dad told me what time their flight got in—it was almost like he was expecting me to host a fucking welcome party. I shake my head. He's fucking delusional.

The lights are on when I pull up in the driveway and my stomach drops. This is really happening.

I sit out in my car with the engine off for longer than I'd planned. Dad and his new woman are in the kitchen, sitting at the table and enjoying a late dinner together. I watch as he reaches out and touches her arm, laughs at her jokes and smiles at her in a way I remember all too well.

Hatred that I've never experienced before begins to swell inside me until it's like an ugly monster wanting to escape. My hands tremble, my heart pounds, and my stomach turns over at the thought of having to go in there and accept them. It's not going to happen. It's never going to happen.

She and her daughter have ruined my family and my life, and I have every intention of ensuring they're aware that their presence isn't welcome.

After sucking in a few more ragged breaths, I push the car door open and make my way toward the house. The anger that's burning inside me fuels my movements until I'm opening the front door and marching inside the only home I've ever known that now feels like a stranger's.

Dad and his woman's laughter sound out from the kitchen. He'll expect me to come and introduce myself, so that's exactly what I do.

"Ethan, where have you been? I thought I told you what time we were arriving so you could be here."

I stare at him. The happiness on his face does nothing for my fury.

"I had better things to do," I spit, moving toward the cabinet that holds his precious scotch. The room is in silence as I pull the door open and grab a bottle from the back. One of his favorites.

Twisting the top, the sound of the thin metal breaking is almost deafening before I tip the neck to my lips and swallow down a generous mouthful.

Glancing at him over the end of the bottle, his eyes narrow in anger. I shake my head. What was he expecting? For me to welcome this woman into my life with open arms. She's the reason my mother has run back to her childhood home without so much as a glance backward in my direction. There's no way in hell he can really expect me to be okay with this.

His jaw twitches as he grinds his teeth before finally opening his mouth again. "Ethan, I'd like you to meet Ashlynn. Ash, this is my son, Ethan."

Her eyes sparkle with delight, and I about manage to keep the scotch I'd just swallowed in my stomach.

"It's so nice to meet you at last. I've heard so much about you."

I wince. She could have the softest voice in the world and it would still be like nails on a chalkboard for me.

"I can't say the same." With the bottle in my hands, I storm from the kitchen with Dad's frustrated words sounding out behind me. I don't register any of them as my feet pound up the stairs.

I bolt straight to my bedroom. My fingers just grip my doorknob when a noise from behind me makes me still.

I think it's time to introduce myself to my new 'sister.' I roll my eyes at myself. I intend on getting rid of these two before anything crazy like that happens.

Turning on my heels, I push open her bedroom door instead of my own. I don't bother knocking. I have no intention of being polite or considerate.

My brows pull together when I realize the room is empty, but that's only for a moment because the second water stops running I understand where she's hiding.

Dad told me that she was enrolling at Rosewood, but also that she's a lovely girl, so I'm expecting her to be a freshman, maybe a sophomore, if I'm lucky. Stalking farther into the room, I find a small suitcase sitting on the end of the bed.

Placing the bottle of scotch on the nightstand, I walk over, glancing at the contents. Some black lace catches my eye, and I hook my finger under it and pull. I reveal a tiny black thong and hold it up in front of me. Okay, so maybe not a freshman then. Not content on just invading her privacy a little, I dive back into the case and discover a matching bra. While the thong had hardly any fabric to it, the bra is the opposite, making me really hope she's not a freshman. Finding the label, I flip it over. 32D. Now that's something I can definitely get on board with.

"What the hell do you think you're doing?" The atmosphere in the room becomes heavy as I'm caught red-handed with her lingerie hanging from my fingers.

A smirk curls at the corner of my lips, knowing that when I turn around, I'm going to discover who exactly is occupying this room and just how much fun I can really have with her.

With her underwear still laced through my fingers, I spin on the balls of my feet.

My smile widens at what I find.

She's covered only in a white towel that's wrapped around her body, and her dark hair is hanging in rat tails around her shoulders and sticking to her face. Her skin is still covered in water, but what really captures my attention is her eyes. They're dark, almost black, and they're staring pure hate into me.

The feeling is very much mutual, sweet cheeks.

There's no way this girl's an innocent freshman, and I don't just mean that because of what I know she's rocking under the towel she pulls tighter around her. There's a depth to her that only comes with age and experience.

Her eyes narrow as our contact holds, something crackling between us.

"Have you about finished snooping through my stuff?"

"I just wanted to know more about my new neighbor."

"Nothing to know. Now get the hell out."

"This is my house." I take a step toward her, but she doesn't move. Brave girl.

"Actually, I'm pretty sure it's your father's house."

"That's where you're mistaken. I'm very much in charge of what happens under this roof." I close some more of the distance between us, and I don't miss the hitch in her breathing.

She rolls her eyes and something explodes within me at her defiance. I step closer and right into her personal space. My blood races through my ears, the anger and hate mixing with her freshly showered scent and heading straight for my dick.

Dropping my eyes from hers, I take in her full lips, her slender neck, and her heaving chest. Her minty breath hits my nose and I bite down on the inside of my cheeks in an attempt to restrain the devil inside.

Unable to keep my hands away, I run one fingertip along the edge of the towel.

"Do I need to show you just how true those words are? Do I need to prove that I am the one in charge here?" It would only take one small movement from me to make the towel drop to the ground, she knows it as well as I do, yet she still doesn't cower down.

Her dark eyes flash with contempt, and it makes it really fucking tempting to expose her.

Dropping my face so our cheeks brush, I whisper in her ear.

"You're not welcome here."

She shudders as my breath hits her ear, and the wicked smile it causes is still on my face when I pull back and look at her.

"You know," I say, taking a step back and allowing my eyes to roam over her. "I think that getting rid of you is going to be so much fun." I wink as I back up to her door, grabbing my bottle as I go. "I think I'll keep these." I bring her tiny panties up to my nose and sniff. They're clean and mostly smell like laundry detergent, but there's still a hint of her. It makes my mouth water and excitement fill my veins.

We're going to have so much fun.

4

RAELYNN

I breathe a sigh of relief when he walks out of my room and slams his bedroom door closed. Racing over to my own, I gently push it to and fall back against it. I have no idea what I was expecting from him. Everything that Eric had told me about Ethan was all positive. But what I just got... that was anything but.

I understand this is a big change. I totally get that his mom only left recently, and his life has been thrown upside down. He's underestimating one thing, though. My life is in a constant state of upside down, and him threatening me does not scare me.

I've experienced, and handled, worse than jumped-up little rich boys who think they can throw their weight around just because they live in some fancy house and get to do whatever the fuck they like with Daddy's money.

Oh Ethan, you might think you're in charge here, but you're about to be bitterly disappointed when I don't bow down to your greatness.

I push away from the door and turn to look at it, hoping I might find a lock, but sadly it doesn't exist.

The sudden boom of loud music from across the hall makes me jump. My fists ball and my lips purse that he's got the power to make me flinch like that. I tell myself there and then that I'll never allow him to see my fear. I've locked it down before; I can do it again just to prove to him that I won't be beaten.

I dig into my suitcase for some underwear. Thankfully I wasn't intending to put on the pair he just walked out with. *Fucking idiot.* I find a large t-shirt to pull over my head to sleep in. I brush out my hair and crawl into bed with it still wet. I'm not one of those girls who gives a shit how it ends up looking if by some small miracle I do actually manage to get to sleep tonight. I've been battling insomnia for a few years now, and if that wasn't bad enough, add the new bed, the different surroundings, and the asshole across the hall with his banging bass and I'm pretty confident that sleep is going to elude me. The one thing that I refuse to allow to mess with my sleep, though, is his threats. He can suck on those. He doesn't scare me.

I sit against the massive pillows with my back pressed against the ornate headboard of my bed and look around. The room itself is pink. *Do I look like a girl who likes fucking pink?* The fact that I can smell the slight hint of paint means this was done recently. Eric's known me for months, did he really think I'd want a pink fucking room? I thought he was supposed to be intelligent with this fancy-pants business empire.

Shaking my head, I look at all the furniture. There's more in this one room than Mom and I have had in any of our apartments put together. There's a hairdryer, straighteners, and products already lining the dressing table along with a fully stocked bathroom. Not a single thing has been overlooked. Probably modeled on the kind of hotel room he frequents, not that I'd have any clue what they would be like since the best I've experienced is flea-ridden motels when we've run away from another of my mother's terrible life choices.

———

The pounding music from his room must have eventually lulled me to sleep, because when I wake the next morning, it's with the sun streaming in through the curtains that I apparently didn't shut last night.

The house is in blissful silence as I walk to my en suite to start the day, although I can't say that I do it with much enthusiasm. The ball of dread that formed while his haunted blue eyes stared into mine that I didn't want to acknowledge is still there, only I think it's bigger.

Still dressed in my oversized t-shirt, I open the doors leading out to the balcony and find a small outdoor loveseat tucked into the corner, and a coffee table. As I look out over the beach and the blue sparkling sea, a smile finds its way to my lips for the first time since I learned of this move. I think I've found my favorite place here. It's still early, but the nighttime chill in the air covers my skin in goosebumps and I welcome them.

I stand, leaning against the railing for the longest time, or at least it feels that way seeing as I've yet to have my morning coffee. With the hope of caffeine giving me a little extra bounce in my step, I pull on a pair of jeans and a black shirt and go in search. With the amount of money Eric seems to have, I have every confidence that I'm not about to find a shitty discount store jar of coffee hiding in a cupboard but something that actually will hit the spot.

I'm proved right when I eventually find the kitchen and spot a scary looking machine built into one of the cupboards. I walk up to it, my head tilting to the side slightly as I try to figure out how the fucking thing works.

"It's not as complicated as it looks, dear," a soft voice says from behind me, and I practically hit the ceiling. I turn, my eyes as wide as saucers, my heart jackhammering in my chest. "Oh, I'm so sorry. I thought you saw me sitting here." She lowers her own coffee and pushes the chair out behind her.

"I'm Rachel, the housekeeper. You must be Raelynn." She's probably early forties with light brown hair with flecks of gray. She's short, although not as short as me, and a little plump around the middle. But she has the softest eyes and the gentlest face I think I've ever seen. "The mugs are kept up here." She reaches up and pulls one down. I look at the size of it, and I don't realize my thoughts are written all over my face until she speaks again. "Bigger?"

"Much, much bigger."

"How big things are is certainly not something you need to worry about in this house." His voice makes my spine go ramrod straight.

Rachel shakes her head and sighs, clearly used to Ethan's brand of inappropriateness. "Good morning, Ethan."

"It sure is."

I don't turn to look at him, instead standing frozen to the spot in the hope that I might suddenly have the power to turn invisible.

When the heat of his chest seeps into my back, I start to wonder if I actually am and he's about to walk right through me. But sadly, it's not the case. He presses his front against me as he stretches up to the cupboard and pulls down a mug. It's red with a huge B on it, I assume for his dumb football team, but it's not what really catches my attention because it's his hands that my eyes focus on. They're rough. His knuckles look like he punched something in the recent past, but there's something about them that just captivates me.

"I hope you had a good night," he breathes into my ear, causing my entire body to shudder against his. "If I were you, I'd start sleeping with one eye open. You might be forced to leave at any moment."

My breath catches as his huge hand lands on my hip and squeezes until it starts to sting.

"Ethan, I hope you're playing nice."

He takes a huge step back, and it's almost as if I imagined the whole thing as he comes to stand in front of me and begins making his own coffee, totally ignoring the fact that I was quite obviously about to get a lesson on how to use it.

His wide shoulders and muscular back block my view, and I chastise myself for thinking about how damn sculpted his back is beneath his skin-tight shirt.

It's not until the machine stops that he turns. He takes a sip, not even flinching when the boiling liquid hits his lips.

"Oh, I'm sorry. Were you waiting?"

I roll my eyes at him, but I don't miss Rachel leaving the room as I do so. Sadly, Ethan glances up and catches it as well.

"You don't scare me, you know."

"Is that so? I'd rethink that if I were you, because I'm about to become your worst nightmare, sweet cheeks. Whatever it is that keeps you up at night, that's exactly what I'm going to be." I swallow nervously as one face pops into my mind. One that is most definitely not welcome.

He steps forward and I have no choice but to take one back to stop us colliding. My back hits the wall and I flinch.

His huge frame towers over me, a low chuckle falling from his lips. His eyes bounce between mine as I fight to keep my fear from them. His, however, are cold, and the sight has a tremble threatening to race through me, but I fight it. I will not show this, this... *bully* that he affects me in any way. I have a right to be here. I understand the circumstances of mine and my mother's arrival aren't all that desirable, but we're here nonetheless.

Leaning forward on his forearms, he continues to stare down at me while his freshly showered manly scent fills my nose and kickstarts a bunch of traitorous butterflies in my belly.

He opens his mouth and my eyes drop to his lips. He leans forward and my heart skips a beat that he's going to kiss me. But at the last second, his face turns.

"Watch your back."

And then he's gone. He quickly pushes from the wall and disappears from the room and quickly out of the house.

I sag back, my breathing erratic and my hands trembling as I try to get my head in the game. He's trying his best to scare me, and although the emptiness in his eyes when he looks at me does instill a little of it in me, it's nothing compared to what I've experienced in the past. Nothing that Ethan can do will hurt me. He's all talk. He won't touch me.

"Good morning, honey," Mom says when she and Eric join me in the kitchen a while later. "Would you like a coffee?"

"Y-Yes." I've managed to move myself from the wall in favor of the chair that Rachel was occupying when I first walked in.

I watch as Mom practically bounces her way toward me. She's so fucking happy right now, it's sickening. I wonder what she'd think about the situation if I admitted to Ethan's less than welcoming treatment of me?

"We heard you chatting with Ethan. Did he already leave for school?"

"I-I guess so." All I know is that he's no longer in the house, and right now that's all I care about.

"That's a shame. Rachel's set us up a family breakfast. Sadly, they don't get to happen all that much with the traveling I do," Eric says, pressing the button that brings the coffee machine back to life. "What's your preference, Rae?"

It's only when he asks that I remember the reason I came down here in the first place was to get my morning caffeine fix.

"Black, please. No sugar."

"Sweet enough, huh?"

"Something like that," I mutter.

I follow both of them through to a different room, and my chin drops when I take in the fancy looking dining room, but what really blows my mind is the amount of food covering the fourteen-seat table. He's never here, Eric just admitted that, so why the hell they need a table for fourteen God only knows.

I hesitate in the doorway, feeling totally uncomfortable in this situation. I was much more at home in the tiny apartments that Mom and I have shared with half a loaf of moldy bread to eat between us.

"Come on, honey. Come and eat," Mom encourages, looking more at home than I think I've ever seen her. I'm glad this kind of wealth looks good on one of us.

I pick at a croissant while Mom and Eric chat away, but I have no clue as to what they're actually talking about. My brain is still trying to process how this is now my life.

"Rae, Rae, Raelynn..." Eric repeating my name eventually drags me from my inner turmoil, and I look up at him.

"Huh?"

"I was just explaining that Principal Hartmann is expecting you to start at Rosewood High on Monday, so you've got a few days to get a feel for the place before the hard work starts. Do you have any idea what you would like to do after graduating?"

"Um... no, not yet." That's not entirely true. I know I want to go to college, if I can afford it, and I know that I want to get out on my own. I'm aware that might mean me getting a job here and saving some money before I'm able to do so, but my dream is freedom, to find a home and to stay there.

"Well, that's fine. There's still time. Miss French, the guidance counselor at Rosewood, is fantastic. She's really helped Ethan try to figure out what he wants; I'm sure you'll find her just as helpful. Set up a meeting as soon as you can, yeah?"

"Sure thing. Are we done? Do you mind if I..." I trail off, hoping that my longing look toward the exit is clear enough.

"You've hardly eaten anything, honey. Are you okay?"

"I'm fine. I actually had something before you came down." It's a lie and one that I'm not proud of. The one solid thing that Mom and I have had over the years is our honesty. It's not always been pretty, but we've always told each other the truth, and I feel like I've just betrayed her. I walk out of that room with a heavy heart as well as a messed-up head.

I make myself another coffee before disappearing up to my room to try to figure out what the fuck I'm supposed to do with myself before I start school on Monday. I get what Eric was trying to do, but quite frankly, I think I'd rather be dropped in at the deep end and forced into my new life this morning. It's not like it would be the first time it's happened.

My coffee has long been drunk, and the sound of Eric's car has long since faded as it pulled out of the driveway. He'd promised to show Mom around town properly. I was invited, but aside from being forced to spend time with Ethan, quite honestly, I couldn't think of anything worse.

With the house all but empty, I eventually decide to go exploring. I poke my head into every single room I find. I swear they get bigger and grander with every door I open. I find countless bedrooms. A living room, a snug thing, a games room, even a fully kitted out home gym with indoor pool, along with all the other rooms I'd expect. After shrugging a jacket on and slipping my feet into my boots, I discover what outside has to offer. The infinity pool takes my breath away, but I can't deny that the glistening blue water doesn't beg for me to jump in. I don't even own a swimsuit. I guess that's something that's going to need resolving, seeing as this place has not one but two pools... and a jacuzzi, I find when I turn the corner. There's even a full-on pool house out here. If anyone had told me that this was going to be where I found myself at the end of this year, I would have laughed in their face.

Although it's obviously nice, I feel totally out of place and uncomfortable being here. I'm so far out of my comfort zone I can't even see it in the distance. I belong in a damp old apartment with barely-working appliances and constantly lukewarm water. Not here in what I can only describe as a mansion. Mom, on the other hand, doesn't seem to have had an issue settling into our new home if her smile as she bid me farewell earlier was anything to go by.

I leave one room to last. Do I feel like a creep as I twist his doorknob and push it open? I sure do. But do I care? Not one little bit.

In my head, I had images of a dark, musty smelling, messy room, but what I walk into is very much not that. The walls are painted light grey, the bedding and the furniture are black, but the curtains are all open, allowing the sun to stream in. There aren't clothes all over the floor and the surfaces aren't covered in dirty dishes and moldy food. It's just... clean. My brows draw together as I look around. This perfectly organized room doesn't go with my image of Ethan at all.

Pulling the door shut once I start to feel awkward for intruding on his space, I get myself ready, grab my purse, and head out. I've explored the house; now it's time to find out what this little town is really like.

5

ETHAN

I don't bother to see if anyone else is here yet. Instead I head straight for the gym before practice starts.

Every single muscle in my body is locked up tight after my interaction with *her* this morning.

I was expecting some young little kid to turn up, but it seems that what I've got instead is a defiant bitch who's brave enough to stand up to me. Stupid, stupid girl.

She might think that she's dealing with someone who's pissed off at the world, but she has no idea how deep the wound is that my dad's left me with.

I change into my sweats and a t-shirt and hit the weights. The pull of my muscles helps ease the ache in my chest that seems ever-present these days. The easiest way to get rid of it is to drink, but I promised both Jake and Mason that would ease up after turning up to school still drunk the week before last. I can't help it. It's the only thing that makes it all go away. To forget that Mom's left and Dad's moved his fancy woman, and her daughter, into our house. It's our house. My family's. Neither of them belong there.

My anger fuels me and keeps me pushing forward until a familiar face appears at my side.

"Well, I must admit that it's better finding you in this sweaty state rather than in any other you've been in recently."

Jake takes the weight from me and props it back up onto the bench. Sitting, I suck in a few deep breaths as the pain in my arms subsides.

"Come on, Coach is waiting."

I follow him out to the field where Coach embarks on another inspirational speech after our division win. We're on a bye-week this week so plenty of time to listen to him try to fire us up and to prepare for our first playoff game against Manor Crossing Bobcats next week.

We only get a few drills in before Coach calls time, telling us that he's going to grind our asses after class.

"If he talked less, we'd have time to do more," I mutter to Jake as we walk off the field.

"I heard that, Savage. Get your head in the game."

I glance over my shoulder at him, expecting to find his hard stare boring into me, but surprisingly I find a sympathetic look on his face. He dragged me into his office after he found Jake and Mason trying to sober me up the day I turned up drunk and demanded to know the truth about what was going on. I understood his, and the guys', concern. I've always been the pretty level-headed one. My life's always been stable, aside from my parents mostly being in another state to me. While the others on the team have dealt with deaths and separations, I've just continued never expecting my life to explode before my eyes.

"You done that paper for English Lit?" Jake asks as we're getting dressed.

"No. What paper?"

"Mrs. Bailey is gonna have your balls if you don't hand something in."

"What was I supposed to do?" I complain, ready to pull something out of the bag at the last minute. English Lit isn't until this afternoon, I'm sure I've got time.

The two of us head of the locker room once Jake's given me a rundown on what's apparently been a two-week project that's completely passed me by. I haven't even read the book we're supposed to be writing about.

"Just tell her the truth and get an extension. It won't be a problem."

Thankfully, he shuts up the second we come to a stop by our tables. The rest of the team has already congregated seeing as we were the last two out, and the cheer squad are already hanging off their every word. Don't get me wrong, I like the cheer squad, *a lot*, but Christ, they can be a bit much at times. I like a willing girl as much as the rest of them but sometimes, it's just too easy. Sometimes the challenge, the chase, is what it's all about, and all this group does is open their legs as soon as it's been suggested and do whatever we demand. I can understand why Jake and Mason haven't ended up with one of them.

"Hey, baby," Shelly sings, coming to sit on my lap the second my ass hits the wood of the bench.

"Not today." I push her off and she looks at me with her brows pulled together and a pout on her filled lips. She soon gets over it though because she turns her attention on Zayn.

With everyone chatting away, it's easy to see the two giant holes in our group. Obviously, Mason's out of action after his car crash. This place and the team aren't the same without him, but according to him, he'll be back next week. But the other missing person isn't someone that a lot of people are acknowledging right now after her true colors were exposed. Chelsea. We all know that Chelsea's got a terrible reputation. She's a slut, she's easy, she's a bitch of epic proportions, but the thing with Chelsea is that she's the master at wearing a mask. Everyone thought Jake was bad for hiding who he really is... well, they haven't met the real Chelsea. How do I know this? Because I have.

Chelsea isn't the mean bitch everyone knows her to be. I know she's done a load of bad stuff, and I won't forgive her easily for hurting some of the people I love, but I know that's not who she really is.

Dragging my cell from my pocket, I find our chat and send her a quick message. Everyone else might have happily forgotten she ever existed, but she needs to know she's got some friends, now more than ever.

Ethan: Missing you here. I hope everything's going well x

I close it down before anyone else notices. They all think I use Chelsea for one thing, just like every other guy she probably comes into contact with, but it's not the case. The times we've disappeared off together, we haven't had sex. In fact, I've actually never slept with her, never done anything with her. She always had eyes for Jake, and I made the sensible decision to stay out of the middle of that situation just in case anything were to happen, although Jake made it very clear it never would. I'm all up for having fun, but not if there's even a chance the girl could end up with one of my guys.

As the bell rings and everyone makes a move for class, I head in the opposite direction to the library. No time like the present to get that paper written—after I've read the damn book, of course. It's probably going to leave me either further behind with the classes I'm missing, but fuck it. It needs to get done, and I really don't want to be on the wrong end of Mrs. Bailey. She's one scary woman.

I find myself a quiet corner to sit in and pull out the book that I find hiding at the bottom of my bag. It seems that I was in class for the day it was all set. No excuses there. Fantastic.

I read the first two chapters. It goes in, but by the time I get to the third, I lose all concentration and the only thing I can think about is *her*. The more I try to forget her dark eyes as she stared up at me earlier, the more insistent the image becomes. My grip on the book in my hands gets tighter and tighter until my need to rip it in two starts to get the better of me.

Shoving the book back where I found it, I throw my bag over my shoulder and march from the library and quickly out of the school.

I put my car in drive and crank up the volume on the music in an attempt to get out of my own head. It works for all of two seconds before the guy singing starts going on about a temptress with dark eyes that won't let anyone in. It touches too close to home. Turning it off, I continue the rest of the journey to the seafront in silence with only my irritating thoughts for company.

I park in the almost deserted parking lot next to Aces and head inside.

I was in such a rush to get away from *her* this morning that I didn't grab anything to eat. I'm now starving after my stint in the gym and our, albeit short, training session.

There are a couple of people here having breakfast but, as expected, no one I recognize. I fall down into our usual booth and wait for Bill to notice me.

"It's not even ten am," he says, sliding into the other side of the booth less than two minutes later. "You having that good a day?"

"You have no idea," I mutter.

He's silent for a beat before he leans on his elbows, closing the space between us, and lowers his voice. "Have they moved in?"

I rear back in surprise. I wasn't sure anyone was aware of our new house guests. I want to say they're temporary, but just seeing Dad and his new toy so happy last night, it makes me wonder if he really is serious about this.

"How'd you—"

"Not much that goes on in this town that I don't know about, son."

"Great." I slump back in my seat, staring out the glass at the front of the diner to the beach beyond.

"Just give it time. I know it doesn't seem like it now, but things will feel normal again. How's your mom doing?"

"Honestly, I have no idea. She makes out that she's fine, but I can hear the sadness in her voice. I haven't spoken to her since I found out about them moving in. I have no idea if she's aware or not, and I don't want to be the one to tell her that Dad's moved in her replacement."

"You need one of my burgers. It'll sort you out right now," he says, clearly out of helpful advice for me.

"Give me the works, Bill."

"Coming right up, kid." He walks off but stops halfway to the counter. "Don't let this affect your schoolwork. We need you out on that field, you hear me?"

I nod because it's the only thing I can do, but trying to focus on bullshit assignments right now is the last thing I want to do. My need to cause some pain is burning hotter than my need to graduate right now.

I pull the book back out and attempt another two chapters while Bill cooks my food, but although I read the words, I couldn't tell anyone what they were about. Feeling hopeless, I push the book across the table as if its mere presence offends me.

I've never been the best student, or the most gifted in the classroom. I much prefer doing things with my hands than sitting with a book. I'm a practical person, logical and methodical, but only on my terms, and most definitely not with a shitty English book I'm forced to read. Dad's paid for tutors for me in the past, but honestly, they've made fuck all difference. They just wound me up, having to spend more time on stuff that frustrated the hell out of me.

I'll achieve enough to get into college, especially with my football skills, but I'll never set the world on fire like Dad hoped I would. I don't know what his issue is, he was a terrible student in high school. He's even admitted on occasion that he almost never finished college, but look at him now. He's got a business empire most people in this town are jealous of and earns more than he could ever spend in a lifetime. Why can't I do that?

I finish my burger, and when the diner starts filling up and getting louder, I grab my stuff and head out, hoping to find some peace to attempt this fucking assignment somewhere else.

6

RAELYNN

I walk down the street for a few minutes before I come across a bus stop. After discovering that one is due any minute, I hang around with my hip against the pole and wait it out.

The street that the Savage house sits on is a stunning tree-lined road. The houses get bigger the higher up the small hill you get, and, surprise, surprise, Eric purchased the house right at the top. The ones around me now are quite obviously smaller, but they're still stunning and way more than I've ever had the privilege of living in before.

I'm just starting to think the bus isn't coming when it appears out of nowhere and comes to a stop beside me.

Digging in my purse, I manage to scrape together the fare and walk to the very back of the bus, past all the elderly passengers who look at me with shock on their faces. I guess I don't fit the ideal of the uber-wealthy around here. Oh well, sucks for them, because it seems I'm going to be here for a while.

I keep my eyes on the passing scenery, attempting to remember the trip back. I have no clue where this bus is headed, but when it turns onto a street that runs along the beachfront and then slows to a stop where there's a whole crowd ready to get on, I decide it's my time to get off.

I thank the driver and step out into the morning sun. It's warmed up significantly since I walked on to my balcony. *My* balcony. What the hell has my life become?

The blue sea glistens in the clear sky above, and I'm powerless but to walk toward it. It's been a lot of years since I've been to the coast. Too many to actually count. I don't even remember what the place was called that Mom moved us to when I was probably seven, maybe eight, and we ended up in a trailer not far from the sea. We didn't stay there long. The boyfriend she found was a druggie and thankfully she found out sooner rather than later and off we went once again.

I shake my head at the memories. The best part about that place had been being able to sneak out when she was preoccupied and walking along the wet sand with the waves splashing at my feet. Everything seemed that little bit easier when the beach was involved. I wonder if it will feel that way here once I'm a little more settled.

I move along a little before finding steps down onto the beach. Dropping down, I place my boot covered foot on the soft sand. I make quick work of pulling them and my socks off until I feel the grains seep between my toes. I sigh with contentment and allow myself to drift back to the peaceful times I had on that beach as a kid. I was naïve back then, I had no clue what my life was going to be or how I was going to be dragged around the country like a kid carrying their favorite rag doll as my mom attempted to find what it was she wanted out of life.

I begin walking. I pass young families making sandcastles and wonder what it must be like to grow up with two parents whose main focus is their child. Don't get me wrong, my mom cares, it's just a little misguided. She's done her utmost to ensure I have everything I could possibly need over the years. I think her wanting to give me the best is one of the main reasons she goes after these supposedly rich guys who promise her the world. She wants me to have the best opportunities in life, the kind she never had. But without her realizing, I think she's turned into her own parents, the ones she swore she'd never be like, always chasing the possibility of an incredible life but never quite getting hold of it.

When I get to some sand dunes, I slip between them and make myself a little seat in the sand. I fall down and drop my boots beside me as I stare out at the crashing waves.

The sun heats my face, and after a few minutes, I pull my jacket off and lie back. I wouldn't be able to do this in the height of summer. My porcelain skin wouldn't allow me. It burns at even the mention of summer sun, but this November sun is perfect for me.

With the sound of kids playing in the distance and the water crashing on the sand mere feet away, I find myself drifting off in a way I never do when I lie down in an actual bed.

I relax for the first time since I found out about this move and drift off.

———

When I start to come around again, my skin prickles. I have no idea how long I've fallen asleep for, but my thoughts about the sun being safe might have been wishful thinking as I feel it burning.

Lifting my arm, I use my hand to shield my eyes from the sun before attempting to drag them open.

I startle when I do and find a shadow before me, but that shock is nothing compared to what hits me when I realize who that shadow actually belongs to.

He takes a step forward, his body protecting my face from the sun, although I'm sure he's not doing that out of the kindness of his heart. His face is blank, there's literally no expression. The only thing that gives away how he's feeling is the haunting look in his eyes as he stares down at me.

My heart begins to race as he comes even closer. I'm used to being at a disadvantage height-wise seeing as I'm a total short-ass, but being looked down upon while he looms over me is slightly terrifying, not that I'll allow him to know that.

"So turning up unwanted in my house wasn't enough. You need to ruin my peace and quiet out here too?" he fumes, his fists curling at his sides.

Pushing myself up so I'm sitting, I drag my eyes away from him. With the sun behind him, it makes him glow like he's some kind of fucking angel. What a joke. The guy standing before me is all devil. I think anyone would be hard pushed to find anything angelic.

I stand and close the space between us. I don't for a second think it's threatening at all, but I feel better for standing up to him and not cowering down like I think he's expecting me to.

"Shouldn't you be at school, little boy?" I tilt my head to the side in the hope that I look and sound patronizing as fuck.

His eyes run over every inch of my face, taking note of everything that's changed since he cornered me this morning.

"What's with the war paint? Don't want anyone to see your real face?"

As usual, my makeup is dark. My eyeshadow and liner are heavy and my lips a dark matte purple. My hair's the same though, pulled back from my face and out of the way. It might be long, but that's only because it's easier to tie up and forget about.

We stare at each other, neither of us saying anything as the air between us crackles with hate.

"You don't belong here. You need to go back to the trailer park you fell from."

A bitter laugh falls from my lips, an unamused smile curling at one side of my lips.

"Wow, that the best you can come up with, posh boy? If you want to get rid of me, you're going to need to try harder than that."

Out of the corner of my eye, I spot his arm come out moments before the warmth of his fingers wraps around my wrist. I gasp in surprise when his touch burns.

He tugs and I have no choice but to step forward. My breasts press against his chest, my temperature increasing as his warmth surrounds me.

I have to tip my head back in order to keep eye contact, but as uncomfortable as it is, I refuse to break it.

"You want me to try harder. Are you sure about that, trailer trash?" I swallow and try to keep any fear or trepidation from my face.

I lift a brow at him, and his fingers tighten on my wrist. "And what exactly are you going to do?"

His eyes narrow, pure hatred pouring from their dark blue depths as his chest heaves and his increased breaths fan across my face.

He releases my wrist, but he only loses contact for a second because that same hand is suddenly wrapped around my throat.

"What am I going to do?" He laughs, and it's the sound of pure evil. His fingers squeeze but only lightly. He's not cutting off my air supply—not yet, anyway. "I'm going to make sure you leave this place with your tail between your legs and tears streaming down your cheeks."

"And where exactly am I going?" I quip.

"Anywhere. I'm sure your whore of a mother will open her legs for some other poor mug and you can move in with him."

My teeth grind. "She's not a whore." His grip tightens, and for the first time, my eyes water and I start to panic a little. There are people not so far away, but I have no idea if they'd hear me scream. If I even got the chance to.

"Oh no. So she didn't seduce my dad while he was a married man?"

"Whatever has happened between our parents, it's got nothing to do with me. I'm unfortunately along for the ride."

"I. Need. You. Gone."

"And I need you to let me go."

His eyes hold mine. His jaw pops and the muscle in his neck pulsates with anger.

"I'm going to fucking ruin you."

"Do your worst, posh boy. I've handled worse than you before, I'm sure it'll be a walk in the park."

"Fuck you," he spits, releasing me with a shove that's just about hard enough to force me to the ground. "Now get the fuck out of here."

A huge part of me wants to fight him. I was here first and this is a public beach, but as he stands with his arms crossed over his chest, the fabric straining against his muscular forearms and shoulders, I decide the best thing to do is what he says—for now, at least.

Grabbing my purse and boots, I start backing away from him. I can still feel the pressure of his hand around my neck as if it's still there, and it irritates the hell out of me seeing as there are now feet between us.

"Just because I'm walking away, that doesn't mean this is over."

"Not by a long shot, sweet cheeks. Already looking forward to the next time." He winks at me and I turn on my heel, not able to look at his pained face any longer.

I get that he's unhappy with how his life is right now, but seriously, I didn't ask for this either. Okay, so I may have got the better end of this deal with the fact that I now live in a mansion overlooking the sea, but I didn't want to be here anymore than he wants me to be. I had no intention of starting my life over once again.

I walk past all the families playing and adults who've come to enjoy the warm sun, but unlike when I walked in the opposite direction I don't really take any notice of them. My head's spinning thanks to Ethan's warning, and I quite honestly can't get away from him fast enough. A little trepidation fills my veins, but I'm not scared of him—at least I don't think I am. He's a posh boy who's always got everything he ever wanted, I'd imagine. What's he really going to do to *ruin* me, as he keeps threatening?

After climbing the steps back up onto the sidewalk, I find a row of shops. I come to a stop outside a diner called Aces when the smells from its kitchen hits me. I pull my boots back on and push the door open. After not really eating anything at breakfast, I'm suddenly starving.

Trying to put my interaction with Ethan behind me, I walk inside, appreciating the decoration of the place.

Looking around, I find the sign for the bathrooms and head that way. Before I do anything else I need a second to sort myself out.

Locking myself inside one of the stalls, I lower the lid, place my ass down and drop my head into my hands. My breaths are unsteady as I replay what just happened with Ethan down on the beach. He's angry, I get it. But I'm not the one he should be taking this out on. I'm as innocent as him.

My stomach feels as if there's a ball of lead sitting in it. How am I supposed to live with him if our encounters are going to continue like that—or worse. I'm supposed to be starting at his school on Monday. I can only imagine how that's going to go. He'll have had a two-day head start to ensure everyone hates me from the get-go. I shudder as I imagine everyone's eyes turning to me. Being the subject of everyone's attention as the new girl is easy, but being the new girl who ruined Ethan's life, their beloved football player... yeah, that could be interesting.

Once I feel able to face the world once again, I wash my hands before risking looking into the mirror. My face is even paler than usual and the black makeup around my eyes is all smeared from the tears that pooled in them. Quickly tidying myself up, I hold my head high and walk back out into the diner.

No one even looks up at me as I pass. It's a welcome relief.

I ignore the table and booths and head straight toward the bar stools at the counter.

"Good morning," a slightly graying man says with a warm and friendly smile.

"Morning. What's good here?"

"What isn't?" he says with a laugh that is infectious enough to have the beginnings of a smile pulling at my lips.

Reaching into my purse, I pull out my wallet. "What have you got for... five dollars?" I ask sadly, the reality of my situation hitting me full force. I'm in yet another place I never asked to be, I'm being forced to live with a guy who hates me, and I'm broke.

"I'll see what I can do for you, sweetheart. I'm Bill, by the way." The friendly smile he gives me as he walks away doesn't make me feel all that much better.

I spin on my stool and take in my surroundings, from the black and white checkerboard floor to the red walls and chrome fittings. This place screams 1960s diner, and I kind of love it.

I sit, staring out the windows at the sea beyond, lost in my own world when a voice behind me startles me.

"Here you go."

Spinning back around, the last thing I expect to find is a huge plate with a giant burger and a massive stack of fries beside it and the biggest chocolate milkshake I think I've ever seen.

"Uh... I can't afford all this," I argue, knowing that it must cost way more than I have.

"It's on the house, Raelynn."

My eyes narrow. "How do you know my name?"

"I know everything in this town. And I know that things can't be all that easy for you right now. Just wanted to put a smile on that sad face of yours."

"I... uh..." I stutter, not knowing what to say. No one's ever this nice. "What do you want?" I snap, thinking that there must be a hidden agenda here.

Bill raises his hands in surrender. "Absolutely nothing. Just being welcoming."

"Are... are you sure?" I'm still skeptical, but now that it's in front of me, my mouth is watering for a bite.

"Of course."

I pick up a fry and throw it into my mouth, still waiting for him to tell me what the catch is, but he never does. Instead, he disappears to grab some plates when the chef calls.

That first fry turned into the whole pile, and before I know it, the plate in front of me is empty and I feel full and satisfied, and a little bit fat.

"That was so good," I all but groan when he comes back over to clear my plate. I still have the milkshake to start on, but I figure waiting a few minutes wouldn't hurt.

"So how have your first few hours in Rosewood been then?"

I consider my answer for a few moments. "Interesting."

"That good?"? He laughs.

"This is my tenth school in as many years. Moving and starting over is pretty much my life. I'm used to all this shit. Although..." I pause as I think about the guy in question. "With all the guys my mom's picked out over the years, this is the first time I've had to worry about their child. Nothing like throwing me in at the deep end."

"Ethan giving you grief?"

"You could say that."

"Give him some time. He was kinda blindsided by all this."

"How do you know so much?"

"I'm the eyes and ears of this town. Nothing gets by me."

"Thanks for the heads up. Seeing as you know everything, do you know anywhere that's hiring? I need a job, and I need one soon."

"Sure do, kid. How about you start on Monday?"

"Huh?" I ask, crease lines forming in my brow as I stare at his amused face.

"You want a job? I need a waitress. My last one quit only yesterday. It's yours if you want it."

"You have no idea if I can bus tables or not."

"You seem like a pretty switched on kid. I'll take my chances. What do you say?"

"I say that would be amazing, but I insist you take this out of my first pay check." I push the plate toward him and pull the milkshake closer.

"I'll see what I can do. Head over after school Monday and I'll get you up to speed in no time."

"Okay, sounds good." A little bit of happiness manages to poke its way into my otherwise miserable existence right now. At least if I have a job, I'll be able to afford to get away from Ethan when he runs me out of town. I shake my head at my thoughts. That asshole isn't going to see the back of me that easily. After the life I've lived, he's barely even a pussycat compared to the lions I've dealt with in the past.

He wants to fight? Bring it on, baby. Bring. It. On.

7

RAELYNN

After securing myself a job and walking along the rest of the promenade, I make my way home. *Home.* I'm not sure this place will ever truly feel like that to me. I know I've only been here a matter of hours, but I feel more like an outsider here than I have in any other place we've lived. I know that's Ethan's fault, and I hate that he has the power to make me feel that way.

Vowing to stand up to him and not allow him to ruin this new start, I begin making my way back to the mansion.

It takes longer than I expect to navigate my way back, but eventually I turn up the street I vaguely recognize as the one I left this morning.

When I get to the top of the hill, the Savage house comes into view and I breathe a sigh of relief. Although it's probably not hot to the locals, I'm melting in this late autumn heat.

The driveway is empty, hinting to the fact I have the house to myself. It's not until I have it confirmed that Ethan's not here that I truly relax. The last thing I need right now is to go up against him again so soon.

I briefly wonder what happened to him but soon chastise myself for even thinking about him. He could have been washed out to sea by the rising tide for all I care.

The house is blissfully silent. Even Rachel seems to have vanished. I have no idea if she lives here or just turns up from time to time or what. After pressing what feels like every single button on the coffee machine, I eventually manage to make myself a huge cup and take it up to my room.

The sun is still on my balcony, so I curl my feet up beneath me on the love seat and stare out into the distance.

My coffee's long gone when I glance down at the glistening pool water beneath me. The temptation to dip my body in that sun-warmed water eventually gets too much as I find myself depositing my dirty mug in the kitchen and heading out.

I don't have a suit, but seeing as I've got the house to myself, I pull my shirt over my head and drop my pants. I glance around, ensuring that I don't have an audience while I'm standing here in my underwear before diving in.

I sigh the second the water hits my skin. It's warm and relaxing, everything I hoped it would be.

I can't remember the last time I went swimming, but I soon find my rhythm as I paddle back and forth, my muscles starting to pull and ache and reminding me that I'm stronger than I think and that I can go up against Ethan asshole Savage.

I have no idea how many lengths I do or how long I'm in the water. All I do know is that my body aches to the point I'm unsure if I'll be able to walk back up to my room and my skin is all wrinkled.

With the sun starting to descend in the sky, I decide it's time to get out before anyone stumbles across me swimming in my underwear, and I slowly climb from the water. The sun kisses my wet skin as I emerge, and it feels incredible. Scooping up my dry clothes and boots, I hold them in front of me, trying not to get them wet, and I run back into the house. I'm just about to step through the door when some movement to my right catches my eye. I stop and stare, expecting someone to be standing there, but there's only a small tree blowing in the light wind. Assuming it must have been that, I head up to my room to shower.

Thankfully, the house is still as silent as it was when I first arrived back, and not wanting to have to deal with anyone, mostly Ethan, I spend the rest of the night locked in my room once I've grabbed a couple of bottles of water from the refrigerator.

Like I do most nights, I toss and turn listening to the sounds of the house around me. What I don't hear at any point is Ethan coming home. My mom and Eric do. She pokes her head in my room to make sure I'm okay but soon disappears to spend time with him after announcing that they're going out of town tomorrow.

That means I'm going to be alone in this house with *him*. Fan-fucking-tastic. I can't wait. That's probably the reason sleep eludes me most of the night.

I must drift off at some point because I wake with the sun streaming in and the curtains blowing in the light wind.

After visiting my en suite, I grab a bottle of water I didn't drink last night and take it out onto the balcony with me. It's not the coffee I crave, but I need to wake up a little before potentially having to deal with Ethan.

I look out at the view I'm already becoming used to and sit on the edge of the love seat. A splash below catches my attention and I lean over so I can see the pool beneath.

The second I see his muscular body cutting through the water, I freeze. He's got a huge tattoo covering almost his entire back. I squint as he moves, trying to make out the details, but he's going too fast so instead I focus on how his muscles ripple as he does length after length like a fucking pro. I'm fascinated watching him. I forget all about the person inside the body and lose myself in his repetitive movement as he continues.

I don't realize I've moved and am standing at the railing to get a better look until he comes to a stop at the edge. He must sense my attention because no sooner has he found his feet is he looking up at me. His hand lifts to push his hair back from his face and I freeze, my breath getting stuck in my throat as our eyes connect. I want to back away, pretend this never happened but I'm fucking frozen under his stare.

Still holding me captive, he puts his hands on the edge and pulls himself from the pool, revealing his toned and muscular body.

A bolt of lust hits my lower stomach. I can't help it. He's fucking gorgeous. His thick chestnut hair is soaked, and water droplets cover his tanned skin and run down to soak into the waistband of his navy swim shorts, which I now see are clinging to his body and showing me everything he has to offer beneath. Maybe his arrogance is warranted if he's packing in the downstairs department like he appears to be.

When I raise my eyes to his again, he's got a shit-eating grin on his smug as fuck face.

Okay, he's got me. He's hot. But the arrogance is such a huge fucking turn off.

He winks before blowing me a kiss. I just about come to my senses in time to flip him off before he disappears from my view.

I fall down onto the seat, my heart pounding and my panties damper than I'd ever want to admit from his little show. I need to remember that he's a massive asshole and not to get blindsided by his body.

I'm still trying to rid the images of him from my mind when my cell pings somewhere in my bedroom. Knowing it can only be Mom, seeing as no one else has my number, I go in search of it.

When I find it at the bottom of my purse surrounded by a few stray coins, hair ties, and a tissue, I pull it out and look at the screen.

Unknown number. I almost throw it back where I found it, thinking it'll be some kind of sales thing, but curiosity gets the better of me and I open it.

You can come and watch me in the shower if that's your thing.

My fingers tighten around my cell to the point of pain. How the fuck did he get my number? And why the fuck does he think I want to watch him shower?

My mind runs away with me and I picture his ripped body with water and bubbles making their way south, only this time, there are no shorts.

Damn him.

Fuck. You.

The little blue dots start bouncing immediately.

Not a chance, sweet cheeks. Not. A. Chance.

I growl, throwing my cell onto my bed. I shouldn't have responded, but it's too late now and he's found another way to torture me from afar.

He leaves his bedroom not long later, then the house. Eventually, my need for caffeine eventually gets the better of me and I'm forced out of hiding.

I find suitcases lining the hallway when I get down the stairs and I'm reminded that I'm being left here for Christ knows how long.

"Morning, honey," Mom sings when she sees me. "Coffee? Rachel's making pancakes. They are to die for."

"Sounds good." I look toward the stove when I enter the room and smile at Rachel who's standing there with an apron around her waist and spatula in hand. I'm not sure how I feel about being served food in my own home, or Eric's home at least, but Mom sure doesn't seem to have an issue with it as she sits there and stuffs a chunk of maple syrup-covered pancake in her mouth.

"When are you leaving?" I ask, dropping down at the table opposite her.

"In about an hour. Eric's just popped to his office to take a call."

"And how long are you going for?"

"I'm not sure. Eric's got business in a couple of different states, so we thought we'd make a bit of a vacation out of it seeing as I've got no work ties now."

"That's nice," I lie. Unfortunately, she sees straight through it.

"You'll be okay here, won't you? Eric's already spoken to Ethan about taking you to school on Monday and getting you settled. I'm sure he'll be around should you have any issues."

"Everything will be fine, Mom."

"I hear he's planning a party for tomorrow night. It'll give you a chance to meet some of his friends. That should make Monday easier, seeing some familiar faces."

"It'll be fine, really." I refrain from pointing out that starting a new school is almost as regular an occurrence as my morning coffee. Although, I must admit that the prospect of a house party fills me with dread. I can't imagine he'll want me attending.

"I've got something for you," she says, reaching for her purse that's sitting on the chair next to her. She rummages around before pulling something out for me and passing it over.

"What's this?"

"A bank card, silly." She shakes her head like I'm an idiot.

"I know what it is, I'm asking why you're giving it to me. I've already got a bank account."

"I know, but Eric wanted you to have this. It's to look after yourself while we're away."

"Mom, I don't want his money." I hold the card out for her to take back, but she just wraps her hand around mine and refuses.

"It's yours. The money in it is yours. Enjoy it, honey. Go and blow some of it on something you've always wanted."

I nod, but I already know that won't be happening.

Mom chats away while we both eat one too many of Rachel's pancakes, but before too long, Eric pokes his head into the room to say that they need to leave.

Mom's practically bouncing on the balls of her feet with the excitement of being able to go traveling with him. A small part of me is happy for her that she's no longer having to work a minimum of two jobs at a time to keep a roof over our heads. I can't help wondering what the cost of it all is though. While she thinks she's got everything she ever wanted, I'm already drowning in her decision and it's only been two days.

I spend the day lounging around the pool with my notebook and journal at my side. I found from a young age that if I write down my thoughts I'm able to work through them better. I'm pretty sure learning that is one of the reasons that my past hasn't screwed me up more than I am. It was only a year or so ago that I got into lyric writing, but I'm becoming more and more obsessed with getting my thoughts down in song form, not just the jumble of words that spew out into my journal.

I get everything down about my move here and try to make sense of Ethan's behavior, but even writing it all down doesn't help me try to figure him out.

I tap my pen against my notebook as I attempt to put the words I just poured into my journal to lyrics.

I don't get a chance to come up with anything because the sound of a car pulling up in the driveway and then a door slamming has me sitting up straight in the lounger.

"Shit," I mutter. I had every intention of being locked in my room when he got home from school, but looking at my cell, it seems I lost track of time.

I quickly gather everything up and run toward the door, hoping that he might stop off at the kitchen on his way to his room. Sadly, I'm not so lucky. As I race down the hallway toward the stairs, he steps out of the home gym, staring at his cell, and I collide right into him. Both of the books in my hand go skidding across the tiled floor along with my cell and two empty bottles with a half-full glass of water. It shatters at his feet after colliding with his chest, soaking his shirt.

"For fuck's sake," he barks. My eyes fly to his, and I retreat a little at the anger within them. He runs his palms over his stomach, trying to dry it off. Realizing it's a little too late for that, he reaches behind his head and pulls his shirt up and off in one swift move.

My eyes take on a mind of their own and drop from his to take in his sculpted body up close. If anything, it's even more defined than I thought it to be from a distance this morning.

He takes a step forward, and I don't have a choice but to take one back if I don't want him crashing into me. Sadly, instead of connecting with him, I do with the wall instead.

My eyes meet his as he continues to close the space between us.

His are full of hunger, but not the kind that excites me. The kind that terrifies me.

"You seem to like looking at my naked skin."

"I... I..." *Fuck.* I hate that he's turned me into a stuttering mess with his closeness.

"You want me?" He holds his arms out to the sides like he's offering himself up to me. But I already know him better than that.

"N- no."

"Really? Because that's not what your eyes are telling me. Or your nipples."

I look down despite the fact that I know that I put a padded bra on this morning and there's no way he'll be able to tell what kind of state my nipples are in right now.

His amused laugh has me looking back up at him. My lips are pressed into a thin line and my pulse thunders in frustration in my neck so hard I've no doubt that he can see it.

"Fuck you, Ethan. I wouldn't want you if you were the last man on Earth."

"Is that right?" He tilts his head to the side and lets his eyes drop from mine in favor of my body. Thank fuck for that padded bra, because the second his gaze lands on my breasts, they pebble beneath the fabric. Traitorous fucking body. "Because I wouldn't touch you with someone else's, sweet cheeks. Now." He leans forward once again, his scent filling my nose, and my mouth waters. He smells like weed, beach, and man. It's a heady mixture. "Pick up your shit and get out of my fucking way." His hand slams down in the wall next to my head and I gasp in surprise.

An evil smile curls at his lips. "You're too fucking easy, you know that? We're going to have so much fun, you and me."

"Is that another threat? Because I won't bow down to you."

"No, it's a promise, trailer trash. And don't worry about bowing, because you'll already be on your fucking knees with my cock in your mouth."

He steps back, accomplishment written all over his annoyingly handsome face while I stand with my mouth open in shock. Did he really just say that to me? I mean, I've heard plenty worse but still, does he really think this is how it's going to go between us?

I'm too stunned by his words to notice him reach down and pick up my journal until he speaks.

"Aw how cute. The trailer trash writes a diary about how pathetic her life is." He flips through it, and I panic. There are things written on those pages that I wouldn't even want my best friend reading, let alone my worst enemy.

I launch myself at him, trying to snatch it out of his hands, but being the asshole he is, he holds it high above his head and well out of my reach.

I'm pretty sure there's nothing more irritating to deal with being short than someone forcing you to jump like an idiot to get something that belongs to you.

"You're a fucking asshole," I bark, jumping again and hoping like hell I make some kind of contact. When I'm still miles away, I decide on another tactic. One that will be much more fulfilling for me.

I stop jumping around and stand in front of him, holding his eye contact.

"You think you're so fucking clever, don't you?"

He shrugs. "I have my moments, sure."

"You're not going to beat me, Ethan. You picked the wrong girl to go to war with."

"Is that right?"

I spot the moment he forgets about what he was doing and focuses too much on what I'm going to say next. I use his distraction to my advantage and swiftly lift my knee until it connects with his cock.

He grunts, bending forward and dropping my journal to the floor. "Fucking bitch," he whines as all his breath leaves him and he bends over in pain, dropping to his knees.

"Now who's on their knees, *bitch*."

He growls, but he's unable to do anything other than breathe through the pain as I collect up my stuff, leaving the glass in shards on the floor for him to deal with.

"Clean up the mess you made, won't you?"

8

ETHAN

Tears burn my eyes as pain radiates from my groin.

Fucking bitch.

I should have seen it coming really, and I feel like an idiot for leaving myself open to her abuse. She might show signs of fear every now and then, but she could well be right when she says that I've chosen the wrong girl to mess with, because there's something dark in her eyes. Something haunts her, stops her being afraid when she really should be. I intend on finding out exactly what it is. If I find her vice then I can use it against her to get what I want: my family back, not that bullshit one my dad is trying to palm me off with.

When I eventually get back to my feet, I stumble my way up the stairs and to my room. I hesitate at her door, but, still feeling the effects of our last encounter, I decide against now being the time to get my revenge.

Instead, I head for the shower and to change, ready to head to Zayn's to hang out with the guys.

It's been a long fucking week and I'm ready to chill the fuck out with some, booze, weed, and pussy. My body relaxes at the thought alone.

With my hair still wet from my shower. I slide my feet into my sneakers and pull my door open. I'm expecting to find the hallway empty and her hiding in her room, but the sight of her leaning against her door jamb startles me a little.

Her eyes stare at mine and then drop down my body once again. She can try and act the innocent with me all she likes, but her body screams that she wants me. A smirk curls at my lips.

"I'm fine, thanks for asking."

"I wasn't."

"Right, well. I'm out, you're not invited."

"Did I ask to be?"

"No, but even if you did, the answer would be no."

"Awesome."

I take two steps past her when she says my name.

"What?" I bark, already over this little... whatever the fuck it is.

"You got any weed?"

"Yeah, plenty. The fucking good stuff too. Thanks for asking."

I look over my shoulder. Her next question is right on the tip of her tongue. I can practically see it, but the second she realizes I'm looking at her, she locks it down.

"Have a good night," she says instead, turning back into her room and slamming the door on me. My fists clench at how easily she thinks she can hide from me.

With a shake of my head, I leave both her and thoughts of her behind.

The guys are already at Zayn's, seeing as they all went straight from practice. I, on the other hand, thought it would be a good idea to go home first. What a fucking stupid idea that was. My balls are still aching now. Readjusting myself as I walk up toward his front door, my mouth waters in preparation for what I'm hoping to find inside.

Zayn's house is smaller than mine, but then that's not hard seeing as my dad owns one of the largest in the town, but it's still a decent size. Ignoring most of the rooms, I head toward the back of the house where Zayn's den is. It consists of a giant flat screen, surround sound, and enough couches and beanbags for the entire team and a few chicks. Just perfect for tonight.

The guys are already lounging around with bottles of beer in their hands when I walk in. Someone almost immediately throws one to me that I just about don't catch at the last minute.

"Where the fuck's the pussy. We're division champs—I thought they'd already be sucking you all off," I say, falling down onto an empty couch.

"Probably gone home to shave, with a bit of luck," someone says from behind me.

I look around at the guys I consider my family, and it's immediately obvious that two people are missing. I never thought the presence of two people could make that much difference, but without Jake and Mason here, it's like two of our puzzle pieces are missing. We're no longer a whole unit, and I hate it more than I care to admit. It almost feels like being at home. There's a massive piece missing there too, although the two in its place most definitely don't fit the gaps.

I drain the first bottle of beer and have made a good start on the second when the sound of the door shutting and the clicking of heels filters down to us.

Thank fuck for that. I love the guys, but sadly they're unable to scratch the itch I've currently got.

Being the vice-captain of the squad, Shelly leads her girls in. I don't get a chance to see who follows her, because the second our eyes connect, she makes a beeline for me. Shelly's been my go-to girl for a while now. She's a nice girl, unlike some of the others. Although she'll still open her legs at the drop of a hat, she is a little more selective of who she gets with. As far as I know, since she started hooking up with me, she's not been with any of the other guys. At least not that anyone's admitted to, anyway.

"Hey, gorgeous," she purrs, shedding her cropped leather jacket and leaving it on a pile on the floor as she hikes her dress up and climbs onto my lap with her knees on either side of my hips.

"It's nice to see you too."

She's wearing a black halter neck dress that's cut low on her chest, giving me one hell of a view. Her tits aren't all that big. Ideally, I'd probably like a little more to play with, but I'm not one to complain when they're thrust right in my face like they are now. Unfortunately, I can't help comparing them to another slightly larger pair I've seen recently, although covered in clothing. The thought pisses me off to the point I consider removing Shelly from my lap. But knowing I need this distraction if I'm ever going to get her out of my head, I leave her be, grinding down on my semi.

Her lips go to my neck as she grinds down on me. Everyone chats around us and like always, ignoring what we're up to. This kind of activity is the norm around this group. None of us could be accused of being a prude, that's for sure.

It's not until someone clears their throat that I pay all that much attention to what's going on around me. When I look up to the entrance to the room, I find someone who is very much not used to our little get-togethers.

Noah.

He's got his arm wrapped around Tasha's shoulders as he looks around at all of us, the muscles in his shoulders pulled tight as he tries to figure out if coming here was the right thing to do, no doubt. Shane is standing behind him, looking a little more comfortable, but this isn't really his scene either. He's never come to hang with us before. Although he's part of the team, he's made it his mission to stay as far away as possible.

"You guys don't mind, right?" Tasha asks, walking into the room like she belongs. She does, I guess. She's one of us. Well, she was until she decided to steal Noah right from beneath Camila's feet.

"The more the merrier," Zayn says, slapping Justin on the shoulder to shift up a bit to allow Shane to sit.

The atmosphere in the room changes instantly. It goes from being easygoing and relaxed to everyone sitting a little straighter and watching what they say.

"You got any weed, baby?" Shelly whispers in my ear, dragging my eyes away from Noah who looks a bit like he's about to shit his pants, being surrounded by us. I guess he should have thought about that before sticking his cock in a cheerleader instead of his girlfriend at the time. I guess I can't be all that mad at the guy—it meant that Mason got what he's wanted since he knew what a vagina was in the form of Camila.

"Does a bear shit in the woods?"

Shelly's eyebrows pull together. "Uh…"

"Yes, I've got some," I say, putting her out of her misery when her confusion at my question only gets worse.

Lifting her up a little, I slip my hand in my pocket and pull out everything I'm going to need to roll us a joint.

"Take that shit outside, Savage," Zayn barks, noticing what I'm up to. Rolling my eyes at him, I place Shelly down on her feet and we head for the door. That's the one issue with this house: the hard no smoking inside rule.

I pull out two of Zayn's garden chairs and fall down into one, watching Shelly do the same. Flicking my lighter, I light the joint and put it to my lips. The first hit is like fucking heaven as I feel some of the tension locking up my muscles drift away. I forget about Dad and his new hussy, I forget about school and the upcoming playoff game. I just focus on the here and now. Almost.

I pass it over to her and watch as she takes a long pull.

"It's nice out here, eh?" She makes a show of glancing around at the pool area that's covered in twinkling lights.

"I guess." To be honest, I don't really give a shit where I am right now. My only focus is to forget.

I rest my head back and look up at the clear sky. The stars twinkle above me and everything washes from my mind.

Needing another hit, I drag my head forward and look to the girl in front of me. I find Shelly has propped her foot up on my chair, her legs spread wide open, showing me exactly what she's not wearing beneath.

My eyes focus on her pussy, and I bite down on my bottom lip as I wait to see what she's going to do. Her chest heaves as she tries to read me. Her eyes bounce between mine, but she's going to be disappointed if she thinks simply opening her legs is going to get me moving tonight.

She must eventually realize that I'm not all that impressed, because she lifts the fingers of her free hand to her mouth, sucks on them for a second and drops them down between her legs.

I can't lie. The sight of her playing with herself before me does stir a little excitement within me, and my cock begins to swell. The more I stare at her, the more I start to imagine her pussy and her fingers belonging to someone else. Someone much more closed off, someone much less willing to put this kind of show on for me.

"Fuck," I bark, startling Shelly, her fingers pausing as her eyes narrow on mine, probably wondering what the fuck's wrong with me. On a usual night, I'd be all over what she's offering, but I just can't find it in me right now to want to.

"What's up, baby? Was practice that tiring?"

"No, I..." I have no idea what my excuse is. I should be on my knees with my head between her thighs, but right now, it just feels wrong.

When I make no move to touch her, she pulls her hand away and stands. She unties the knot behind her neck and allows the fabric covering her tits to fall to her waist.

"I know you're more of a boob man." She cups herself, standing only inches from me, and her head falls back as she pinches her nipples. "You know, Ethan, you've never fucked me outside before. I think maybe tonight is the night under the twinkling stars. It's so romantic."

"I don't do romance," I bark, keeping my eyes on what she's doing to herself because she's not wrong. I'd do pretty much anything for a good pair of tits. *These aren't the ones you want,* a little voice says in my head. I shake it out, trying to focus on the here and now, because although my head's not in the game, I really could do with the release she's offering me.

She leans forward, her hands pushing my hair from my face and angling my head so she can kiss me. When her lips drop to mine, I don't push her away. I want to want this. I want her to distract me from my crazy thoughts and make me want to fuck her into next week. It's what I need. What my body craves. But still, I don't react the way I want.

She pulls away, kissing across my neck, her hand dropping down over my abs until she rubs at my cock over the fabric of my pants.

"Come on, Ethan. Where's my big boy, huh?" she purrs in my ear, and it's the final straw. I stand with such force that she stumbles back, landing on her ass with a thud.

"Shit, I'm sorry." When I glance up, I notice that we've got an audience. Or more, Shelly's tits do as half the team are staring at her as she sits there, exposing herself. I hold my hand out for her and pull her from the ground. "Cover up, you look like a dirty slut." With that said, I storm around the side of Zayn's house and down his driveway.

9

RAELYNN

Assuming I'm going to have the house to myself seeing as Ethan went off to his little party, I run myself a bath in the hope that it'll do something about my tense muscles and spend the evening watching shit on TV.

It's heading toward midnight when I switch it off and attempt to get some sleep. I'm lying in the dark with only the silent house for company when there's a crash outside.

I sit up, straining to hear if there's someone out there. It goes silent again before the unmistakable sound of the front door slamming rings out.

Fuck.

As I sit with my heart trying to beat out of my chest, I debate whether a burglar or Ethan returning would be more preferable. It comes to something when you'd rather face a criminal than your possible future stepbrother.

There's a crash, and then another.

I swing my legs from my bed and search for a weapon in case I need it. My eyes land on the bunch of flowers in a vase that I assume Rachel thought I might like, and I walk over. I pull the flowers out and throw the water over the balcony before heading over to my door. As silently as I can, I slip out and make my way toward the noise.

I creep down the stairs, noting that none of the lights are on.

If this is a guy robbing the place, then I probably shouldn't be heading his way with only a vase as a weapon.

Shaking the voice from my head, I continue down until I get to a doorway where I think the noise is coming from. There's another almighty crash followed by an angry growl.

Pushing the door wider, I tiptoe inside, raising the vase above my head. The guy's dressed all in black with a hood up over his head.

I'm just about to launch it at him when he turns. A familiar pair of blue eyes find mine a milli-second before my arms follow through with their intent.

Thankfully, Ethan is quicker and manages to stop the vase from connecting with his face, sending it crashing to the floor.

"What the fuck do you think you're doing?" he roars, his voice slightly slurred, possibly explaining why he was down here fucking this room up in the dark.

His hands slam down on my shoulder and I stumble back, tripping over something in the process and finally colliding with the wall. My head slams back against it, making the room go a little hazy and my eyes pool with water.

When I eventually pull them open, he's right in front of me, breathing down on me with his teeth bared.

"This is all your fault," he seethes. His voice is so menacingly quiet it sends a shiver of terror through me. We're alone in this huge house, he's drunk, and I stupidly left my phone upstairs.

"Me?"

"Yes, you." We're toe to toe. Our faces only inches apart. I can smell the alcohol and weed on him. It makes my mouth water for a taste and a hit of my own instead of the water I've been drinking all night. "You are ruining everything. Everywhere I go, there you are. Everywhere I turn. There you fucking are. Even tonight. There you fucking were."

"I-I haven't been anywhere tonight," I say, confused by his comment.

"You're in fucking here," he spits, poking his finger into his temple. "Fucking tormenting me. Driving me fucking crazy."

I open my mouth to respond, but when I realize I've got no words I quickly close it again.

"You're going to fuck everything up for me. I. Need. You. Gone."

His hand lifts, his fingers taking my chin with a painful grip and forcing me to look up at him.

"You hear me, trash?" I swallow, not able to speak when he's holding me so tight. "But you're not going to fucking leave, are you?" His eyes are wild as he stares into mine. It's a look I've experienced before, and I know nothing good can come of it. "So what am I going to do about it?"

I don't know if he realizes he's having a conversation with himself, but I don't point it out. Instead I just hope that the little voice in his head will have some reason in a minute and let me go.

Thankfully, after a few seconds, he does. But not so I can run. Instead, his hands find the top of my tank and in one swift move the worn, thin fabric practically melts under his touch.

My hands fly up to cover my breasts, but I don't get anywhere near before his fingers are around both of my wrists and they're lifted above my head. My back arches and the fabric that was still half covering my tits falls to the side.

His eyes hold mine for a beat before they drop. A smile pulls at the corner of his lips.

"At least there is something worthwhile about you, I guess."

"Ethan please, don't," I whimper, chastising myself for sounding weak and vulnerable when all I want to be is strong and in control of the situation. So what, he's looking at my rack. I'm sure he's seen plenty before.

My chest heaves as I try to get control of my racing heart and he eats it up. I'm playing right into the palm of his hands and giving him exactly what he wants. My fear.

"I wonder how you taste." He lowers down and looks from one nipple to the other, then up at me through his lashes.

Fuck, I hate to admit it, but with desire swimming in his eyes, I can't help but want him to lean forward and find out. My nipples harden as my core floods. I hate myself even more for the reaction, but I can't help it.

Here, in the dark with him almost hidden in the shadows and looking sexy and as dangerous as hell, I can't help my imagination running away with me, even though at the same time, I'm desperate for him to release me so I can go running back to my room.

He closes the space between us. His tongue sneaks out and flicks my tight bud. My entire body flinches with the contact and sparks shoot toward my clit, making it ache.

"Ethan." I intend for it to be a warning, but even I can admit that it comes out sounding needy as fuck.

I barely have time to blink and he's leaning forward once more, only this time he sucks me into his hot mouth, his tongue circling around me, making me crave more. My hands pull against my restraint, but he doesn't let up. He switches to the other side and I cry out despite fighting like hell to keep it in.

What the fuck is he playing at? Is this how he intends to ruin me? With pleasure?

His hands shift but only so he can free one of his own. He continues pinning both of mine above my head, ensuring he has full access to my breasts which he continues torturing.

My panties are soaked with my need for more, and the more he sucks, nips and licks, the worse the situation gets.

"Fuck. Ethan. Fuck, please?" I'm not aware of the words as they fall from my mouth, but the second I realize I'm begging for more, color stains my cheeks.

I shouldn't want anything from this asshole, yet here I am after one touch from him, sounding like a desperate whore.

"You want more, sweet cheeks?"

"Ethan," I cry when he bites down on my nipple.

"How close do you think I can get you to the edge? I'm going to watch you climb, make you think your release is in touching distance, and then I'm going to ruin it all just like you have my fucking life. Is that what you want?" His words blur, the blood rushing past my ears and the desire coursing through me meaning I make no sense of them.

"Yes," I pant. "Yes."

His free hand brushes the sensitive skin of my stomach before it disappears inside my sleep shorts, his fingers parting me and finding my clit almost instantly.

"Fucking hell, I knew you wanted me," he groans as if he's in pain when he discovers just how wet I am.

"Oh god," I moan as he pinches my clit between his fingers before diving deeper and finding my entrance.

"Oh no, baby. I'm not God, I'm the motherfucking Devil."

Ain't that the truth. A bitter laugh falls from my lips as he pushes two fingers inside me.

"Jesus," he grunts, and I can only assume that's a good thing.

With his thumb pushed against my clit and his fingers bent inside me, I'm racing toward a mind-blowing release in seconds.

He pulls back from my breast and watches me. I want to tell him to look away, but I don't have it in me as I fall headfirst into—nothing. Wait, what?

I drag my eyelids open, not knowing when they even shut to find Ethan backing away from me. My arms drop to my sides, my muscles aching where they'd been pinned in position for so long.

Ethan's amused yet hungry eyes hold mine as he lifts his hand and sucks his fingers into his mouth. My imminent release makes itself known once again, my muscles pulling tight as I watch his eyes roll back in pleasure.

"I've tasted sweeter." His eyes drop from mine to take me in, only this time I'm able to cover myself.

"I fucking hate you," I spit, but his only response is a wicked smile that plays on his lips.

I watch as he steps over the mess of the shattered vase along with whatever it was that he sent crashing to the ground before I walked in on him.

"Clean up the mess you made, won't you?" he says, repeating our words from earlier before he disappears from my sight.

The sound of his footsteps pounding up the stairs fills my ears as I slide down the wall until my ass hits the floor.

My body shudders with the coldness he left behind now that all the adrenaline has left my body. My core throbs with my need for a release, and my body trembles with the knowledge of what I just let him do to me.

I shouldn't have allowed it to get that far. I shouldn't have allowed him to take that much from me.

I'm unable to keep the tears that burn my eyes in and I sob on the floor of his den until my eyes sting and my ass goes beyond numb.

10

ETHAN

I slam my bedroom door with such force that I'm surprised it isn't falling from its hinges when I look back over my shoulder.

I pull my hoodie and t-shirt over my head in one fell swoop and quickly add my pants and boxers to the pile as I storm toward my shower. My rock-hard cock bobs in front of me, taunting me, reminding me what I just left behind downstairs. It's the exact reaction I should have had to Shelly, but the one that didn't appear until I turned around and found *her* wielding a fucking glass vase and about to smash it over my head. I guess I can't really blame her, I was walking around in the dark smashing shit up.

After marching from Zayn's, I stopped in a store who believe my fake ID and always serve me whatever the fuck I want, and got myself a bottle of whiskey. I spent the whole walk home drinking the fucking thing. By the time I got back here, my head was spinning and I was angry beyond belief with both myself and the way my life is right now. The last thing I needed was her, but there she was, and before I knew what the fuck I was doing, I had her backed up against the wall with her perfect fucking tits in my face.

I shouldn't have touched her, I know that. I *knew* that. Even with the whiskey racing through my system. But I couldn't help myself. The fear in her eyes called to me. Her rosebud fucking nipples called out to me. I should have walked away like I did from Shelly. But unlike with Shelly, my cock was fucking rock-hard and the only thing I could think about was how fucking sweet she'd taste. And fuck if she wasn't even sweeter than I could have possibly imagined.

My mouth waters, the taste of her still on my tongue. I picture what it might be like to have my head between her thighs and get the sweetness straight from the source. My cock aches with the thought, but as I step under the shower, I refuse to do anything about it. I tell myself it's punishment for being so weak tonight. My only saving grace is that she's just about as blue balled as me right now, seeing as I left her right on the brink of orgasm like the total fucking asshole I am.

I stand with my face tipped up toward the showerhead and allow it to rain down over me. It does little to cool the fire raging in my body even when I turn it to ice cold.

My cock's still rock hard when I step out and wrap a towel around my waist. As I walk through my bedroom, I kick my pants out of the way. The top of my foot connects with the corner of my cell, and I curse in pain. But it gives me an idea.

Pulling it from my pocket, I find our conversation.

Don't even think about finishing yourself off. You're mine now.

I expect her to reply, telling me where to go almost instantly, but the message doesn't even show as read. In the end, I get fed up waiting, and, with the amount of whiskey I'd consumed, I pass out naked on my bed.

———

When I wake the next morning, it's with a pounding head, my body soaked in sweat, and my heart racing from the dream I was in the middle of. A dream I need to forget about as soon as humanly possible. I don't need any more crazy ideas in my head about what could have happened last night had I not walked away when I did. I shouldn't have touched her. I knew before I even laid a finger on her that she was out of bounds, but I couldn't help myself.

"Motherfucker," I curse into my pillow, replaying the events of the previous night in my head. What was wrong with Shelly? She'd have scratched my itch perfectly fine. Why couldn't I have just used her like I usually do and stayed the night at Zayn's passed out on his couch?

The doorbell ringing through the house eventually drags my ass out of bed. I wait long enough in case she decides to go and answer it, but when I hear no movement, I'm forced to go myself.

I stare at her door as I pass, wishing I could see inside to know if she's in there and hiding from me or if she's run. The sensible thing to do would most definitely be the latter.

Pulling the front door open, I find a guy standing there with my alcohol delivery for tonight's celebratory party. We won the fucking division. I should be pumped right now. Our first playoff game is next Friday night. That trophy we've all coveted for so long is almost in touching distance, yet I can't seem to rid myself of the anger, the hate that seems to have taken over every inch of my body.

I point the delivery guy in the direction of the kitchen and walk down the hallway to the doors that lead to the garden while he does his thing.

At first glance, it's empty, but after a few seconds, I realize that the ripples in the water aren't that of an empty pool. Standing back behind the curtains so I'm out of sight. I watch as she makes her way across from one side to the other. It's not the first time I've watched her. I couldn't help myself when I got back on Thursday afternoon. Wanting to see what she was hiding under her clothes had me loitering in the bush like a fucking creep. It was fucking worth it, mind you.

With the guy unloading bottles behind me, I continue to stare, willing her to climb out so I can get another look at her banging little body. Not five minutes later do I get my wish, only it's better than I could have imagined. My lingering hangover immediately vanishes as other aches and desires erupt in my body. This time, she's not wearing her underwear, but a white tank that's gone totally see-through and a tiny pair of panties. My cock's instantly hard for her once again. The sight before me mixes with my memories from last night of her pleading with me to let her go.

Rubbing myself through the soft fabric of my sweatpants, an idea forms.

"See yourself out when you're done, man," I call to the guy in the kitchen before running up the stairs and pushing her bedroom door open.

I still the second I'm inside, because unlike last time, this room now smells of her. I jump onto her bed and look at the stack of books sitting on her nightstand. Each spine has a different year written on it. I go for one in the middle and pull it out. Resting back against her pillows, I flip it open to a random page and stare down at her writing. It's more feminine that I'd have imagined, and I can't help but smile when I turn the page again and find it written in pink. She really is a mysterious one, my new housemate.

Dear Diary,
Today's been great. Kurt took me out to buy some new clothes. I got the jeans I've wanted forever and the sneakers Mom said we couldn't afford.

I don't get a chance to read any more, because the sound of her footsteps out in the hall has me looking toward the door.

Seconds later, she's pushing it open. She doesn't spot me right away as she throws the towel in her hand into the corner of the room and peels her soaking wet tank up her body. She reveals her smooth skin and tiny waist. Her hair, as always, is tied up. She reaches up and pulls the band that's holding it hostage. It falls down her back like a wet curtain.

Unable to take the ache in my solid length as it presses against the fabric, I reach down in the hope of relieving it, but as I do, I must make more noise than I was expecting because she turns.

Our eyes lock and she screams in fright before bringing her hands up to cover her chest.

"Get the fuck out of my room, Ethan." She glances down at what's in my hands, and more fear than I've witnessed from her before creeps into her eyes.

"That's not a very nice way to welcome a guest."

"You're not a fucking guest. You're not welcome in here."

"My house. I do what I like."

"Get. Out."

"Not until I get what I came in here for."

"And what's that exactly?"

I pause, because other than to torment her a little more, I didn't really come in here for anything specific. I run my eyes down her body that's now starting to shiver from the morning breeze coming from the window.

"Strip," I order.

"W- what?" An unamused laugh falls from her lips as her eyes widen in shock.

"What? It's not like you're really wearing much anyway. It won't make all that much difference."

Her teeth grind, her face going beet red with her anger as she tries to decide what to do. I can see that she wants to fight, but surely she must know it's only going to get worse for her if she does. The best thing she can do right now is exactly as I say.

"Come on, sweet cheeks. I already know what it tastes like. Might as well give me the whole experience."

Still, she stands there like a fucking deer in headlights. Dropping my gaze, I go back to her diary.

"I only thought silly little girls wrote diaries. I'm starting to wonder if I got you all wrong, trailer trash."

"Ethan, please."

"Please what? Please touch you again? Please finish you off from last night? I hope you took my warning seriously and didn't immediately finish yourself off after I left," I say, having a flashback to the text I sent her. The blush that's already staining her cheeks travels down to her chest. "Maybe I should get you to do it now. Give me a nice little show to start my day off with."

"Please, just leave." Her voice cracks, and it makes me realize just how hard she's going to be to break.

"Where was I? *Dear Diary,*" I mock. *"He took me for ice cream, not the cheap kind Mom insists on, but the kind that comes in every flavor imaginable. I had toffee, he had chocolate. I regretted my decision when I saw the chocolate chips in his, but he let me try some.* I bet you had a good old lick, didn't you, you dirty bitch."

All the color's drained from her face when I glance up from her stupid diary.

"If it'll make you leave, fine." She shoves her thumbs into the sides of her panties and shimmies out of them until they're around her ankles. She holds her hands out to the sides, trying like hell to appear confident while completely bared to me.

I take her in, every single curve, hair, and dimple. I can't deny that, although short as fuck, she's got all the right things in all the right places.

Placing her diary back on the stack beside me, I push myself to the end of her bed. My eyes stay locked on her body. On her full tits and rosebud nipples that are just begging for attention. I run my eyes down her smooth stomach as I focus on the small strip of hair that leads to what I know is a hot and tight little pussy.

Her body trembles before me, but I'm not sure if it's with the chill or terror.

I stand, dropping my head so I can stare down at her. A smirk pulls at one side of my lips. "Until next time, sweet cheeks."

I leave her standing stock still, but I don't close her door behind me. The thing irritates me. Not knowing what she's doing behind it drives me insane.

The second I'm in my room, I pull on a clean shirt and hoodie, and drop my phone and wallet into my pocket before turning on my heels and marching straight out of the house. There's no way I can stay here knowing exactly what's right across the hall.

I could call an Uber, but I decide to walk the distance back to Zayn's to pick up my car. The time alone with only my thoughts might help clear my head. Now I'm away from her, my temples continue to pound with last night's alcohol, but still, I can't get her out of my head. The darkness of her eyes as she stared into mine, silently begging me not to hurt her. I must be doing a better job of scaring her than I thought if she's worried about me physically hurting her. I'd never hit a woman, and even she falls under that bracket. I may want to hurt her in other ways, but I'll never raise a hand to her.

I don't feel that much better by the time I walk up Zayn's drive. The only difference is that my cock's no longer trying to punch its way through my sweats. I don't bother going inside, knowing that it'll only invite questions about where I fucked off to last night when I had Shelly offering herself to me, quite literally. I have no intention of talking to any of those motherfuckers about what my issue is right now.

Jake, Mason, and their girls know the truth. Even telling them was hard enough. I'm happy to let everyone else think whatever the fuck they want as to my current state of mind and almost permanent pissed-off attitude.

Sliding into my car, I rest my head back and shut my eyes. My life is spinning out of control right now and I have no idea how I'm supposed to rein it back in. I need to stay away from her, that much is obvious, but I'm not sure I can. She's like that one thing in your house as a kid that you're warned never to touch, but no matter how wrong you know it is, you just can't resist.

Pulling my cell from my pocket, I find Jake and shoot him a message.

Ethan: Gym?

The little dots start bouncing, and in about thirty seconds I stare down at the response I was expecting.

Thorn: Can't. Doing house shit with Brit.

"Fuck," I bark, my hands slamming down on my steering wheel. It's always been the three of us. Jake, Mason, and me. But since things got serious with Amalie and Camila, it seems our party of three has almost immediately reduced to a lonely party of one. And exactly when I need them most.

Some movement from inside Zayn's catches my eye. I could go in there and invite one of whoever's left to join me, but it's not the same. Yes, they're my family, but they're not my brothers, not like Jake and Mason. I open up another conversation that I've been waiting for a reply on. When I look down at my last message I sent her, it shows as read. I blow out a breath, wondering if she's okay and getting the time out that she needs.

Deciding to send her another message, seeing as I could do with someone to talk to as much as I'm sure she could, I start typing.

Ethan: I'm here if you need to talk x

I stare at it, but it doesn't even show as delivered.

"Fuck it." I pocket my cell, put my car in reverse, and drive toward the gym I try to hit up a couple of times a week. I've got a pretty kitted out gym at home, but the wider range of equipment, along with the steam room and sauna drag me here. It's exactly what I need as I try to work through my issues. It also means I'm away from her, away from the temptation of doing something stupid again.

I work myself in the gym until I can't feel my limbs, then I drag my aching body to the sauna to sweat out the alcohol that's probably still in my system from the previous weeks' blow outs. Tonight should be fucking epic, and I need to be ready for it. I also need to figure out a way to keep her away. The last thing I need is her attempting to befriend mine, not that I think for a minute she'd fit in with them. I'm sure the cheer squad will take one look at her and turn the other cheek. She doesn't exactly scream joy and happiness, more dark, edgy, and will likely shank you in your sleep if you so much as look at her the wrong way.

I grab some food on my way home and then, despite the fact I only just showered at the gym, I have another and get ready for tonight.

Her door is shut, as usual, and the house is in silence. I have no idea if she's here or not, but I decide against finding out. I need to focus on tonight, on celebrating our epic win, getting drunk and having fun. The last thing I need is thoughts of her ruining it for me. We worked our asses off for that win and we deserve to let our hair down before the craziness of the playoffs start next week.

I spray myself with my favorite cologne, run some gel through my hair and pull on my lucky shirt. I tell myself that last night's disaster with Shelly was a one-off and that I'll be fully on board with any female who so much as looks my way tonight.

I've just done a lap of the house to make sure everything is as it should be before the crunch of car tires on the driveway sounds out.

Pulling the door open, I find cars everywhere and kids from school heading toward the house.

Almost all of them stop and greet me with a slap on the back or a slug to the shoulder. Some bring their own supplies, just to be polite, but everyone knows I'll have more than enough alcohol inside for everyone who arrives. They all walk in, assuming everything is the same. Little do they know that everything under this roof is very different from the last time they were here. Fuck, I'm different, thanks to our two new lodgers. The anger that's constantly burning away inside of me turns me into a person I don't like, but there doesn't seem to be much I can do about it, especially as *she* seems to be there no matter which direction I turn.

The house fills up, someone turns the music on, and everyone gets to it. I want to say their merriment is infectious, but it's not. I force a smile on my face and head to the kitchen for a drink.

Alcohol of every variety fills the counters. One good thing in all this bullshit is that Dad upped the spend on my credit card. I don't really want his guilt money, but I'd rather have my friends piss it down the toilet to fuck him off than not use it, I guess.

Most of the team are huddled together, some with girls clinging to their sides. The cheer team hasn't arrived yet, so it gives the others who are brave enough a chance.

"Hey, gorgeous," a girl purrs, coming up to me and running her hands up my chest until they lock around the back of my neck.

"Hey, I don't think I've had the pleasure of meeting you before." She's got bright red hair and wide hazel eyes.

"You're Ethan Savage, right?"

"The one and only, sweetheart."

A salacious smile curls up at her lips. "I've heard all about you and your... talents." She runs her tongue over her bottom lip, and I eagerly watch its movements before dropping down her body. She's wearing a small top that shows off both the swell of her tits and her stomach before a scrap of fabric wraps around her hips, barely covering her modesty. Something I can most definitely work with.

"Oh yeah?" I ask, stepping a little closer and wrapping my arm around her waist. Her sweet scent fills my nose. It's not unpleasant, but it's not exactly enticing either. She smiles at me, pushing her tits into my chest. "Play your cards right and you might get to find out tonight."

She leans in, her lips brushing the shell of my ear. "I'll let you do whatever you like," she all but moans.

My cock stirs at the thought, but only a little, and I'm pretty sure only because it's still after what was in touching distance last night.

I used to live for these shameless hussies who do anything on demand just because we're the kings of Rosewood High, but suddenly, I'm not finding the same appeal as I once did. A little voice in my head tells me I didn't have a problem until *she* turned up.

Anger races through me. She's ruining my fucking life, and she's not even here right now.

"How about we get a drink and talk more about that? I'd love to know what you can do for me."

11

RAELYNN

The second he walks through my bedroom door, I slam it shut behind him and pull the dresser in front of it to stop him from coming back.

My body is trembling from the memories he dragged up from just reading that small snippet of my diary. Why I thought leaving them on my nightstand was a good idea God only knows.

Racing over, I lift all but the one I'm currently writing in and spin. I don't exactly have anywhere I can hide them, but at least they'll be out of immediate sight if—when—he returns. I shove the whole stack into the ottoman at the end of my bed and close the lid, hoping it'll help to lock down the nightmares that are contained within those pages.

A cold shiver runs through me as a few flash backs hit me. Ethan will never find out about the horrors that are written in there. If he were to find out—no, I'm not even going there.

Picking up my wet, discarded clothes, I throw them into the laundry and head for the shower to wash away not only the chlorine but also the shame of what Ethan just made me do. I try not to dwell on it, but it's there, tingling at my spine.

I turn the shower up as hot as I can bear and stand under, hoping to wash away everything from both last night and this morning. It doesn't matter that this is my second shower, plus a dip in the pool since he touched me last night, I can still smell him as if he's standing right next to me.

All I want to do is keep my head down and do what I need to do here before I can graduate and move on. I've got no intention of making his life harder than I'm sure it's already been, seeing as his dad just left his mom for mine. Both of us have been caught up in the crossfire of their drama, and as far as I'm concerned, neither of us deserves it, but it's exactly where we've found ourselves. Unfortunately for me, I'm the one Ethan seems to be firing all his arrows at.

The sight of all the bottles covering every surface in the kitchen when I eventually emerge from my bedroom has my stomach in knots. The last thing I want is an enforced house party. Seeing as it's already late afternoon, I decide to go out and stay out as late as possible in the hope of missing most of it. I might be happy with only myself for company, but that doesn't mean I want to lock myself in the fancy bedroom for the foreseeable future.

I make the same journey I did the other day, only I don't bother with the bus, thinking that I need to waste as much time as possible if I'm going to avoid the party. I walk along the beach before heading for the promenade and pushing through the door into Aces. If I'm going to be working here then I may as well start getting a feel for the place.

It's much busier than it was the other day, but I manage to get a seat in the corner at a tiny table for two. I don't see Bill, but the waitress who comes over to take my order is really sweet, and thinking that she could be my colleague come Monday makes me feel better than I have since stepping foot on that damn airplane. Jesus, was that only days ago?

I eat but seeing as the place is so busy, I feel bad about hanging around when they could be serving a new customer at my table, so I pay and head out. The sun's starting to set over the ocean when I step out, so I head back down the beach once more.

I find myself a seat on the dry sand, staying away from the dunes I hid between yesterday, and pull my diary from my purse. I tap my pen against the page as I try to gather my thoughts about what's happened between Ethan and me in the past twenty-four hours. I recall last night, being totally honest with myself about how he made me feel. If someone would have told me that he'd have pinned me like that, and to a point pushed himself on me, I'd have thought I'd have freaked out, managed to somehow squirm out of his hold and hurt him as he deserved. But the reality of the situation was that I was powerless to resist. The fear I felt fused with a heady mix of desire and instead of fighting, I allowed it. My core throbs as I vividly remember how his fingers felt against my sensitive skin, the delicious stretch when he slid them inside me.

Fucking hell, Rae. Get your head out of the gutter.

None of that matters. What matters is that he's a fucking asshole who doesn't deserve my thoughts, let alone space in my diary.

Motherfucker.

I turn my thoughts to my new school and my new job. Aces is the one place that I've felt at home since being here, and it has a little excitement starting to tingle in my belly that at some point I might even fit in here.

———

That thought is soon wiped away when I get back to the house. Feeling like I'd exhausted my time aimlessly wandering around the seafront, I regretfully head back. There are cars littering the driveway, I discover kids everywhere, and music booming so loud that I'm sure the neighbors must be on the verge of calling the cops to shut it down.

I walk past two girls, one holding the other's hair back as she pukes into the flower bed. I turn my nose up at them as I pass, but they don't notice my attention. I have to shoulder barge a couple who insist on standing in the doorway, sucking each other's faces off as I attempt to get into my own fucking house.

Who am I kidding, this place is never going to me mine, or feel like home in any way.

The inside is packed with kids drinking, dancing, and getting high. My mouth waters for some alcohol and a joint between my lips. I look around, wondering how to go about getting both of those. Remembering the insane number of bottles littering the kitchen earlier today, I head that way. Ignoring the beer, I head straight for the spirits and pour myself one very generous shot of vodka and swallow the lot in one.

"Whoa, someone's ready to party," someone calls over to me. He takes a step in my direction, but one hard stare from me and he soon changes his mind. There's something to be said for the permanent scowl that seems to be on my face these days. It takes my usual resting bitch face to a whole new level.

A couple of the girls who are barely dressed on the other side of the kitchen run their eyes over my outfit of choice. I knew before walking in here that I wouldn't fit in in this world of rich kids. I have no idea if this whole town is full of "Ethans," but it's safe to assume it is instead of hoping for the best and being disappointed.

Dragging my eyes from their judgmental ones, I pour myself another giant drink and knock it back. It burns all the way down my throat, although not as bad as the first one did.

Heat from the vodka burns my belly and spurs me on. I think maybe it's time I introduce myself to Ethan's nearest and dearest.

I almost do an entire lap of the house before I eventually find him sitting on the couches in the vast family room with his friends and some slut wiggling around on his lap. My fingers twitch at my sides as I watch her run her hands through his thick hair and whisper something in his ear that encourages his hands to run up her thighs until he's gripping onto her ass that's pretty much on display for everyone, seeing the fucking ridiculous skirt she's wearing.

My teeth grind as I watch them, and eventually I manage to drag my eyes to the others around him. I've seen enough photographs around this house to know that Ethan's on the football team, so it's a pretty easy assumption that the guys he's spending time with are also on the team.

Bored of watching from the sidelines, I take a step forward in the hope that I piss Ethan off by my mere presence.

As I get closer, one by one their attention lands on me. The dark-haired girl is the first to look my way before she nudges the guy she's sitting beside, and he brushes his long blond hair from his face to find me. The stunning blonde is next to look up. She's curled into the side of the guy talking to Ethan despite the whore on his lap.

Coming to a stop in front of the group of them, I turn to Ethan. "So, these must be your dumb jock friends. Jesus, you're so cliché it actually hurts to fucking look at you."

His eyes are murderous when they turn on me, the blue darkening before me as I stand with my hand on my jutted out hip. His lips press into a thin line as a vein in his neck starts pulsing.

Did he really think I was going to cower away from him after last night and this morning? Just proves how little he knows me.

"And you are?" the dark-haired guy asks, looking from Ethan to me with an almost equally furious expression on his face as he stands.

I laugh at his attempt to intimidate me by standing tall. Does he not think I'm used to that kind of shit by now? Why do I get the impression that he's probably the captain and leader of their little group?

Ethan shifts his chosen one to the side before bringing his hate-filled stare back to me. "This..." He points at me like I'm a fucking zoo animal. "This is Raelynn, my darling never-to-be fucking stepsister."

"Your what?" the blond guy gawks.

"Don't get too used to her being around. She's not staying. Not if I have anything to do with it," Ethan spits, his eyes holding mine to make sure I hear the warning.

"Do your worst, hot shot. I'm not as fragile as you'd like to believe."

"Oh, I don't know," he muses. "You crumbled beneath my hands pretty quickly last night."

I fume, fighting the heat that threatens to bloom on my cheeks.

"What?" I question, trying to sound as innocent as possible. "When you forced yourself on me?" There's a collective gasp from his friends, and the girl, now at his side, tenses.

"Oh fuck off. You were begging for a piece of this." He lifts his shirt, exposing his abs, and I scoff.

"Oh please, your dad's are better."

I'm not sure I've ever seen anyone go a brighter shade of purple before. It's almost amusing if it weren't for the murderous look in his eyes.

He stands, pushing the girl away. Thankfully, or maybe not, thinking about it, the guy on the other side of her manages to break her fall as she heads for the floor.

"You fucking what?" He takes a step toward me. Every single muscle in his body tenses as he stares me down, hoping to get a reaction out of me. Sadly for him, I've had enough liquid courage now not to be affected by him in any way.

"Once a cheat, always a cheat," I taunt. "How many others do you think there have been?" Eric has never so much as looked at me the wrong way, unlike some of Mom's more questionable boyfriends, but Ethan doesn't need to know this. Nor that I'm pretty confident that my mom's been his only indiscretion.

"Shut. Up," he spits, getting right in my face, but I refuse to back down.

"He's probably been getting his dick wet on the side for years."

A menacing growl rumbles up his throat. He bares his teeth, closing the last bit of space between us, his nose almost brushing against mine.

"Your mom was probably—"

"Shut. The. Fuck. Up." He steps forward again, bumping into me and grabbing my arm to keep me pressed tightly against him.

"Ethan," someone calls from behind him, but his towering frame and wide shoulders are too big for me to see around. "Leave it, yeah?"

But he doesn't take the hint.

"Bro, she's not worth it." The guy I'm assuming to be their captain appears at his side, his hand landing on Ethan's shoulder.

"You've got that fucking right. You're not worth shit, trailer trash."

"Enough, Savage," he barks, successfully managing to pull him back from me, albeit slightly.

A smile curls at my lips. "That's it, Savage. Be a good little boy and do as you're told. Fucking pussy."

He lunges for me, but his friend is quicker and manages to hold him back. But when his eyes turn on me, they're almost as angry as Ethan's.

"Take a hint. Fuck off." He tips his chin to the door, as if he's got the fucking power to dismiss me.

"Who the fuck are you?" At no point am I going to cower down to these assholes like they want me to. Instead, I take a step closer, alternating my stare between the two of them.

"Me?" the guy asks incredulously.

"Yeah you, dickhead. Who. Are. You?" I ask slowly, as if he's an idiot who can't understand the English fucking language.

"I'm Jake. Jake Thorn."

"Well, Jake. Jake Thorn," I mimic, ensuring amusement dances in my eyes. "Keep your man here on a fucking leash. And maybe teach him a lesson in respecting women." I glance around him to his girlfriend, who's standing watching our interaction like she might need to jump in at any minute. "You seem to have a loyal girl over there. You could probably teach this asshole a thing or two."

Ethan spits out a laugh, but I don't hang around long enough to find out why. I do however hear Jake's voice as I head for the doorway.

"Oh man, you've got your fucking work cut out for you with that one." He chuckles, and when I glance back, I see him slap Ethan on the back and head over to his girl, who walks straight into his arms like she belongs there.

After pushing through groups of kids loitering in the hallway, I manage to get to the kitchen to find more to drink. The second I come to a stop by the bottles, silence settles around me. An unsettled feeling fills my stomach, knowing that when I turn around all eyes are going to be on me.

I pour myself another vodka, stares burning into my back as I do. Sucking it down, I try to drag up the energy to deal with more assholes, and I turn around.

As I expected, every set of eyes in the room are trained on me. But it's the group right in front of me who seem most fascinated.

"I think you might have stumbled into the wrong party, princess," a deep, rumbling voice says.

I smile, because he couldn't be more correct. "Yeah, I can see why you might think that. Sadly, this is where I'm apparently supposed to be."

"I'm sorry," a sweet voice sings, "but Ethan never would have invited you here."

I shrug, not wanting to tell my life story to these judgmental assholes. "Anyone got any weed?"

The girl snorts as if it's the craziest question she's ever been asked.

They all stand there, no one offering anything, before I decide better of it and turn to leave.

I'm almost out of their sight when someone calls out to wait.

"Zayn, what the fuck are you doing?" the sweet voice snaps, but he doesn't reply. Instead he steps up beside me.

"I think I've got exactly what you need." I breathe a sigh of relief and follow him outside.

The second he walks toward the sun loungers that sit around the pool, two other kids immediately jump to their feet and run off.

"Whoa, I need to learn that trick," I say with a laugh.

He doesn't comment, just falls back, pulls a joint from his pocket and lights it up. He takes a long drag. I focus on his pursed lips as he does so before running them over the rest of him. He's smaller than Ethan, although not by much, his hair is cut close to his head, and his skin is almost olive from the amount of sun he's clearly had this summer.

There's no denying that he's hot. The problem is that, just like Ethan, he damn well knows it and probably uses it to his advantage.

He holds it out for me before allowing the smoke to plume from his lips. I think it's meant to be seductive, but he's going to need to work harder to get me interested.

"Thanks," I mutter, making quick work of lifting it to my lips.

I sigh in relief when I inhale and my muscles immediately start melting into the lounger cushion beneath me.

This is what I fucking needed.

I rest my head back and allow my eyes to close as I absorb the feeling, wishing it was enough to make me forget where I am right now.

"So," a deep voice says beside me. "Who are you? I don't recognize you from Rosewood."

"That would be because I don't start there until Monday," I say, keeping my eyes closed despite the fact that I can feel his burning into the side of my face.

"Oh, so we'll be seeing more of each other then?" His voice sounds a little too enthusiastic for my liking.

"Have you moved far?"

"Washington."

"Where are you living?"

I open my mouth to respond, but I don't get a chance to say anything, which is good because I've no idea if I'm willing to admit the truth.

"What the fuck are you doing?" The joint that was happily pinched between my finger and thumb is ripped from me. My eyes fly open in time to watch it bounce along the tiles beside the pool before a large shoe lands on it and twists. My teeth grind. Such a fucking waste, I still had plenty left in that. *Asshole.*

Ethan grabs my wrist and pulls me from the lounger.

"Savage, what the fuck, man?" Zayn barks from behind me, his own lounger squeaks as he gets up covering Ethan's harsh breathing.

"Mind your own fucking business," Ethan barks, but at no point does he look up at the guy behind me.

"I would, but not while you're manhandling the girl I was getting to know."

"*She,*" he barks, his lip curling in disgust, "is no girl. And you won't be getting to know her because she's not staying. She's not welcome at this party. Trailer trash wasn't invited."

My entire body vibrates with anger as I attempt to put everything I hate about him into my hard stare. I have no interest in making a scene for the entire senior year of my new school to watch before I've even started.

"Ethan, seri—"

"Enough," he shouts. "*She's* leaving. Aren't you, trash?" Something crackles between us as both of us refuse to back down.

The longer we stand there, the more my temperature increases and the more my heart begins to race. I want to tell him to go fuck himself and spend the rest of the night at his pathetic party, but really, I want to be here about as much as he wants me here.

"I hope that skank gives you crabs." I step toward him, my shoulder slamming into his arm as he refuses to move out of my way. Pain warms the joint, but I refuse to show that he's had any effect on me.

I don't look back as I swing by the kitchen for a bottle of something to keep me company and then I head up to my room. As I pass each door, I find some of them being utilized, so I don't know why I'm surprised when I get to mine and find a couple writhing about on my bed. At least they're clothed.

"Get the fuck out," I scream like a banshee. Both of them turn, wide-eyed, to me before scrambling off and disappearing out of sight.

"Fucking hell," I mutter, closing the door behind them and looking around the room, wondering what I can utilize to keep my door securely shut for the rest of the night. The last thing I need are more horny couples turning up for a quick fuck.

Not seeing anything other than furniture, I put the bottle in my hand on the nightstand and start the arduous task of pulling the dresser so it's in front of the door once again.

My arms burn as I attempt to move the solid wooden piece, but eventually I get it over enough to stop anyone trying to join me.

Happy that I'm safe, I undress, pull on a tank and sleep shorts and get into bed with my bottle and the sound of the party downstairs for company.

Over the years, I've been alone, a lot. But right now, with people enjoying themselves like they've got no care in the world right beneath my feet, I think it's the loneliest I've ever felt. Mom's always been by my side, but now she's got Eric, even she's fucked off for better things.

I hate that a lump crawls up my throat, but eventually with the alcohol only heightening my emotions, I allow myself to succumb to the emptiness inside me. *Maybe things will get better come Monday*, I try telling myself, but I know it's unlikely. I don't need to be told that I don't fit in here. I already feel it. Worse than anywhere I've been before.

12

ETHAN

"**W**hat the hell was that?" Zayn asks, rightfully intrigued by what he just witnessed.

"Nothing," I bark, hoping he'll drop it, which of course he doesn't.

"Oh yeah, that totally looked like nothing. I wasn't sure if you wanted to kill her or fuck her right there before my eyes."

"Kill. Definitely kill. I wouldn't fucking touch her with yours." I look over his shoulder as I say this, not wanting him to see the lie I've just told. Even as the words fall from my lips I can see her up against the wall last night with her tits on full display and my hand disappearing into her shorts.

"Whatever," he mutters, clearly not believing me.

"You're kidding, right? You just saw her. She's not exactly my type."

"She's got a pussy. I thought that was your type."

"Fuck off," I bark, walking away from him in search of more alcohol, not wanting to accept that what he's just said is totally true. I have not been all that selective about who I spend time with. It just so happens that I've not come across anyone quite like her before. I think that's most definitely a good thing because despite the fact that she just did as she was told and fucked off out of my sight, she still won't leave my head.

Images of our short time together fill my mind along with her banging little body she exposed to me this morning as she stood there trying to look confident.

Finding a bottle of whiskey the second I walk into the kitchen, I tip the neck to my lips and swallow as much as I can until it burns too much.

The redhead who's been following me around all night appears in the doorway and saunters over. I let my eyes run over her curves, and although I appreciate her body, my cock doesn't stir like it usually would with a body like that stalking toward me with intent written all over it. Her hips swing, her tits bounce, and her eyes are begging me to fuck her.

"Hey, baby. Where'd you disappear off to? I missed you." Her voice is sweet and soft, and she gazes up at me like I've just hung the fucking moon but still, nothing happens. The only thing I desire for some fucked-up moment is for dark, angry eyes to be staring into mine, not these willing ones. It would be so easy to get this girl up to my room right now and take what I need. But that's just the problem. It would be too easy. Suddenly, the challenge that *she's* set is the only thing I can think about. The only thing that's getting my cock hard and my temperature increasing is the thought of breaking her down and proving to her that I can take whatever it is that I want.

Red's hand slips under my shirt, her long nails lightly scratching down my abs as her eyes alight with desire.

"Hmm..." she moans. "I can't wait to see these with my own eyes."

She turns her body into me, acting as a shield so her hand can drop to my crotch. She rubs my cock through the fabric of my jeans, and much to her delight, it reacts. Although it's partly due to the images in my mind about a girl who keeps defying me at every turn.

"Let's go upstairs," she practically growls in my ear. "I want to taste you, make you groan my name as you come in my mouth."

Fuck. Me. This one's not beating around the bush.

Part of me wants to deny her, to send her on her way with a big fat rejection. But in the end, my need for release wins out, and when she slips her small hand into mine, all it takes is a light tug from her and I follow her toward the stairs. I point her in the direction of my room and she eagerly makes her way down the hallway.

My footsteps falter when we pass *her* room. Part of me wants to burst in and insist she watches just so I can see her eyes darken with desire like they did last night, but something stops me. I have every intention of her being the one on the end of my cock when she's in the room while I've got it out, not some slut who's willing to give me what I need.

I push my door open and slam it shut behind us, just to be a dick. The second it's shut, I make quick work of undoing my waistband and pushing the fabric to my hips.

"What are you waiting for?" I don't mean to be such an asshole, but it seems I can't help it these days. He keeps appearing more and more.

Red looks from my eyes and down at my semi, which if I'm honest, is waning fast. If she doesn't hurry the fuck up and wrap her lips around it, then she's going to find herself on the other side of the door on her ass.

"But I—"

"But what? You said—"

"I know what I said," she barks, spinning away from me and taking a few steps. "I just thought—"

"Thought what? That I'd light a few candles and make love to you?" She stills at my words and I know I hit the nail on the head. "Un-fucking-likely, sweetheart. You offered to suck me dry. I only followed for that. I've no interest in anything else from you. So either kindly get on your knees or fuck off."

After tucking myself away, I move away from the door to allow her an escape. It only takes her twenty seconds to take it.

She leaves much quieter than we entered, and I can't help but smile thinking that *she'll* assume I've got some hussy in here doing fuck knows what.

Falling back on my bed, I twist the cap off the whiskey that's still in my hand and take another huge mouthful as my thoughts run away from me.

I have no idea how long I lie there drinking by myself as the party rages beneath me. I know we're supposed to be celebrating, but suddenly, being surrounded by people and pretending that everything is okay is the last thing I want to be doing.

I do have an idea for what might make this night worthwhile though.

Pushing myself from the bed, I pull my door open and take the few steps so I'm standing in front of hers. I remember the words she said to me in front of Jake and Mason earlier, and my need to teach her a lesson for trying to embarrass me starts to burn through my veins.

I do her the courtesy of knocking this time, wondering if she'll willingly come to the door. Nothing happens beyond. There's not even any movement.

"Trash? You in there?"

Silence.

"Sweet cheeks," I sing, attempting to sound less threatening, but still it doesn't work. That or she's not there. Something stirs in my stomach that she might have gone somewhere.

Wrapping my fingers around the handle, I push down. A rush of air passes my lips as I prepare to reveal the room beyond, but the second I push, nothing happens.

"What the fuck?"

The door barely moves enough for a slither of light to shine through the gap.

"What the fuck do you think you're doing? Do you really think this will keep me from getting to you?"

Silence.

"And to think, I brought you a new joint. I can hardly give it to you like this."

She's either playing a very good game, or she's fucked off over the balcony. Either way, it pisses me off that she's not at my beck and call. I'm also more pissed off than I want to admit that she's managed to put a barrier between us. Her door's pissed me off one too many times now. It's time to show her that I really mean fucking business about making her life her hell until she ups and leaves.

———

By the time I wake the next morning, the house is in silence, but the banging of my head more than makes up for it.

"Fuck," I grunt, rolling over and thinking on the reason for my current state. An empty whiskey bottle.

I lie on my side ,facing away from the light that's creeping in through the curtains and curl myself into a ball, hoping it'll be enough to keep my stomach from turning over. I didn't eat anywhere near enough yesterday for the amount of alcohol I drank.

As I lie there wishing I could fall back into a blissful sleep, memories from the previous night start hitting me.

Finding *her* getting comfortable with Zayn in the garden. Just a hint of the anger I felt at seeing them together licks at my stomach. She shouldn't be here, let alone trying to befriend members of the team.

The redhead flicks through my mind and how she ran at the first sight of my cock despite trying to climb my body like a tree most of the night. Fucking pussy. If she couldn't handle me then I guess she did us both a favor in the end, even if I'm still craving a release I'm afraid only one girl will be able to provide.

I think about her door being locked, or what the fuck ever that was about last night, and my fingers fist the sheet as I consider what I might have done if that thing had flown right open and given me the access to her I craved.

My cock weeps, desperate for the kind of attention it usually receives on mostly a daily basis, or it had until *she* turned up.

She's fucking ruining my life in every sense of the word.

I spend what's left of the daylight curled up in my bed, hoping that at some point the hangover will vanish. I know that Rachel is downstairs putting the house back together. Before I turned into the asshole I am now, I used to go down and help, feeling guilty even for the mess I'd made. But right now, I really don't give a fuck.

It's not until the sun's set that I emerge from my room. I make myself a protein shake in the kitchen before jumping in my car and heading for the gym. It's not unusual for me to do two good workout sessions two days running, but I don't usually head here for them when I've got a perfectly good gym at home. The need to get away is just too much though. I had no idea if she was in her room, or even in the house, but I wasn't prepared to hang around and find out.

She'll be immersing herself in every part of my life come tomorrow when she turns up at Rosewood High for her first day. I need just a few hours of peace before every secret I've been trying to keep is exposed by her appearance. I might have kept her and her mother's arrival under the rug, but I have no doubt she'll sing just who she is from the rooftops if it'll piss me off.

I head home, still feeling the effects of last night's drinking and desperate to fall into my bed. The sight of the familiar little red sports car makes me groan. I should have known they'd turn up at some point to drag information out of me after my confession last night.

Needing to get this over with, I slam my car door and head inside. I stop by the kitchen to grab three bottles of beer before making my way down to my den, where I know they'll be waiting.

I find them, exactly as expected, laid out on my two couches staring at the sports channel that's illuminating the huge flat screen on the wall.

"Ah, nice of you to join us," Mason says, slowly pulling himself to a sitting position when I walk through the door.

"To what do I owe this pleasure?" They both look at me with arched brows. "Ugh, fine. Hit me with it."

I fall down onto the couch on the other side of Mason and lift a bottle to my lips.

They're silent for a few seconds, the three of us just looking at each other.

"Just spit it the fuck out."

"Stepsister?" Mason asks. "Were you ever planning on telling us?"

"I told you he was moving the whore in."

"No you didn't. You said you were expecting to have to meet her. You never said anything about them living here or that there was a stepsister situation."

"It's not a situation," I mutter into my bottle.

"Oh, so that electric hate that was zapping between the two of you last night as you stared each other down was... nothing?" Jake asks, amusement filling his voice.

I blow out a breath through pursed lips. "I fucking hate her, okay? She needs to fuck off and leave me to get on with my life."

"And what's she done exactly?"

"Except turn up and not cower down to your bullshit."

"And look hot," Jake adds. "Don't forget that."

Mason nods, knowing smiles forming on both of their faces.

"She's not fucking hot. She dresses like a fucking hobo."

"Really?" Jake asks, his eyebrows almost hitting his hairline. "Because from what I could see she was a feisty little—"

"Unless there's an insult coming then I suggest you shut the fuck up."

"You really hate this girl?" Mason asks as if this needs clarifying.

"She's ruining my fucking life. She needs to fuck off."

"Just as we thought," Jake says, looking at Mason with a smile playing on his lips.

"Did you two come for any reason other than to piss me off with this bullshit?"

"Just thought we could hang out." Jake lifts his beer to his lips, but amusement still fills his eyes.

"So where is she now?"

"How should I fucking know? Back in the trailer park she crawled from hopefully."

I can tell by the way they're both looking at me that they don't believe a word that's coming from my lips, but I don't give a fuck. I intend on proving *her* just how much I hate her, then I can prove it to these motherfuckers at the same time.

Thankfully, they drop the subject in favor of the game highlights that start on the TV. All talk turns to football and our upcoming playoff match. Mason sulks the whole time that he's unable to play, but he gets little sympathy from me seeing as the fucking idiot ran a red light and almost killed himself. He came out of it pretty lightly if you ask me.

It's long past a sensible time to call it a night when they head off, seeing as it's a school night, and they've both got girls waiting for them when they get home.

As I head upstairs to finally hit my bed, I glance at her door, the girl who seems to always be in my head now. What I wouldn't give for it to be anyone else and to have them naked and waiting for me in bed right now like I'm sure Jake and Mason are about to find. As I push my door open, the image of her dark hair and curvy little body laid out in my bed fills my mind and all my blood rushes south.

I look back over my shoulder at her door but decide to hold off for now. She's probably inside holding her breath, waiting for what I'm going to do. I want to build her anticipation, that way she'll be even more ready for me when I make my move.

———

Dad told me before he left that I was to ensure she got to school this morning and to help her out getting her schedule and finding where she needed to be. He clearly couldn't see the darkness festering inside me as he delivered these orders because he left believing that it might actually happen.

I sent her a message before I crashed sometime after midnight last night telling her to be ready by eight am. She read it immediately, but she never replied. I've no idea if she'd even willingly get into a car with me, but I thought I'd at least try.

At two minutes to eight, I'm sitting behind my wheel with the engine ticking over.

Thirty seconds before I told her to be here, the front door opens and she emerges from behind. As usual, she's dressed in all black. Her skirt shows off her shapely albeit short legs and her oversized shirt has been ripped almost in half, revealing her slim waist. Her hair is piled on top of her head, and as she emerges into the morning sun, she lowers a pair of sunglasses over her eyes, cutting me off from seeing how she's feeling about today, not that I really give a shit. I just hoped to see a little fear or at least some nerves in them for what today might hold.

She blows out a long breath before taking a step and heading toward me. I watch her every movement as she gets closer, and fuck if it's now that my cock decides it wants some action because it starts to swell beneath my pants. Why's it her swaying hips that wakes it up? What was wrong with Shelly's the other day or Red's last night?

She reaches out and pulls the handle, and just as I'm expecting, she finds it locked.

Leaning down, she looks through the passenger window at me, her lips pursed in anger that I'd lock her out. When I don't do anything, she lets her arm fall back to her side as she waits for me to get my shit together. You're going to be waiting a lot fucking longer than you think, sweet cheeks.

A smile curls at my lips as pushed her sunglasses to the top of her head and stares at me. Something passes between us. A warning. A promise. Fuck knows, but it's there before I slam my foot down on the accelerator and speed from the driveway, leaving her behind in my dust. An evil laugh rumbles up my throat as I look back at her standing totally helpless in the center of the large space.

Fucking idiot. Did she really think I was going to make it that easy?

13

RAELYNN

Fucking asshole.

I don't know what I was expecting, and I feel stupid for ever thinking he might have taken me to school this morning like a normal fucking human being.

I was shocked when I saw the message, but I stupidly took it for what it was and made sure I was ready. I didn't have any other way of getting to school, so I took his olive branch. Only it wasn't one. I should have known better.

Dragging my cell from my purse, I pull up Uber and set about ordering a car, hoping I can still get there in time.

With the car only minutes away, I perch my ass on one of the steps leading to the house and wait.

Nerves rattle around in my stomach, but I swallow them down. This is just another Monday. Just another school.

Only this place isn't just another school, it's a school where I'm not wanted before I've even started.

I blow out a frustrated breath as a car pulls up into the drive.

The journey is in silence. I've no intention of making small talk with the driver.

At the first sign of the school, dread starts to weigh heavy in my stomach. The temptation to go running back to hide in my bedroom is high, but without graduating I've little chance in creating the life I crave. One where I'm in charge of my own destiny and where I live.

Sucking in a huge breath, I thank the driver and push the door open when he pulls to a stop at the edge of the parking lot. There are kids everywhere. It looks like just another high school. The buildings I can see look similar to all the others, and the kids loitering around fit the stereotypes I've found in every other school. Only this one includes Ethan.

Throwing my bag over my shoulder, I take off toward where the sign is pointing to the entrance to discover what this day is going to hold.

The second I start moving, heads turn my way. I'm sure after Friday night people are wondering who I am. I don't pay them any mind as I hold my head high and focus on the building I'm heading toward. That is until I feel *his* stare burning into me. My skin prickles, and a hint of fear runs down my spine, but like fuck am I allowing any of these motherfuckers to see it. I don't care if I come across like a bitch, none of these kids will get to see the real me. The only thing they're going to experience is the hard outer shell I've learned to shield myself with.

I refuse to look his way, or for my steps to falter. I don't want him to think he has any power over me.

Relief floods me when I pull the door open to the entrance, and I shut off all the curious eyes.

I stand at a little glass window and wait for someone to help me. The women beyond all tap away on their keyboards, none of them bothering to look up even after I ring the bell.

Eventually someone comes over. "Can I help you, love?"

"Yeah. It's my first day, I—"

"Ah... Raelynn, is it?" she asks after looking down at a piece of paper. "Principal Hartmann is waiting to meet you."

"Fantastic." The sarcasm in my voice is impossible to miss, but somehow it seems to go over her head as she directs me to his office before shutting the little window, halting anything else I might have had to say.

I'm standing at his door in seconds. I don't bother knocking—after all, he's expecting me.

He glances up from his desk at my intrusion, his brows creasing as he takes me in. I already know I stand out from his usual student like a sore thumb. I just saw most of them on my walk here and none of them quite have the style or aura about them that I do.

He clears his throat, I guess hoping to cover the fact that he was gaping at my outfit of choice. "I guess you must be Raelynn."

I fall down into the chair in front of his desk.

"Correct. Do you have my schedule?" I've been in enough of these 'welcome to the school' meetings that I don't need to hear the bullshit he's about to spew at me.

"Is Ethan not with you?" he asks, looking back to the door.

"No."

"His father assured me that he'd escort you here and show you around today."

"That was nice of him. But there's no need. I'm capable of fending for myself. Just give me my schedule and a map and I'll get out of your hair." I barely contain a snort when I look to the top of his head to find he has none.

"Oh... um... if it's all the same to you, I'd be much happier if one of our students welcomed you properly."

"Oh don't worry, Principal..." I look down at his name badge, pretending that I've already forgotten what his name is. "Hardmann, I—"

"It's Hartmann, actually."

"Right. Well, I can assure you that I've had quite the welcome already. None of that will be necessary."

He waves me off, turning to press the button on his intercom. "Sandra, get a cheerleader here. I've got a job," he barks before releasing it and turning back to me.

"I'll hear nothing of it. No student of mine starts at Rosewood High without a proper welcome."

"Fantastic," I mutter under my breath.

Thankfully, he passes over my schedule and releases me without much further bullshit and allows me to start my first day.

"Jesus fucking Christ," I say, looking at the chirpy blonde waiting for me in her red and white cheer uniform outside the principal's office. "This day's just getting better and better."

"Hi, I'm Shelly. I'm going to show you around, welcome you to Rosewood." She's so fucking happy it makes me want to puke on her pristine fucking uniform.

I snort at her, pull my bag higher up my shoulder and take a step past her. "You're dismissed. I can figure this shit out myself."

"Um... but Principal Hartmann said—"

Looking over my shoulder at her, I laugh. "And of course, you always do what *Principal Hartmann says*," I say, mimicking her chirpy tone. "I bet he's got you sucking him off on a weekly basis."

She splutters in disbelief, her cheeks brightening in anger or embarrassment, I'm not sure. "I... um... fine. Do your own thing. See if I care."

I arch a brow at her minor tantrum for being dismissed and take off. I look down at my schedule to see I've got English Lit first. I come to a crossroads in the hallway and glance down each corridor. *I've totally got this.*

It must be at least thirty minutes later when I find a door that has the right number on it. I suck in a breath and knock before pushing it open. As expected all eyes turn on me, but there's only one set I see. Ethan's.

Fuck my life. Of course, he's in my first class of the day.

His eyes hold mine and stop me from entering the room.

"Can I help you?" the teacher asks, turning from where she's writing something on the board.

It takes another full two seconds for me to rip my eyes from Ethan's.

"Sorry, I'm... uh... new here."

"You must be Raelynn. If you—"

"It's Rae," I interrupt.

"Okay, Rae. If you'd like to take a seat." She points into the room and I take a step in that direction. Karma once again bites me in the ass when I realize the only spare seat in the room is right in front of Ethan. Of fucking course it is.

Rolling my eyes, I make my way over as an evil smirk spreads across his face as I get closer.

"Nice of you to join us," he jokes, sitting back in his chair and crossing his arms over his chest. The guys around him join in with his amusement.

Huffing out a frustrated breath, I drop my bag to the floor with a bang and fall into the seat.

"You haven't missed too much, we've only just started this task so I'm sure you'll catch up." I nod at the teacher as she drops a textbook and exercise book in front of me. "Page ninety-two."

I flip it open and try to listen to what she's saying, but most of it goes in one ear and straight out the other.

Being able to hear the low rumble of his voice as he says fuck knows what to his friend about me doesn't exactly help with my concentration, and when something hits the back of my head, I give up completely.

Clearly not happy with the fact that I let his ball of paper fall to the floor, he tries again. This time it ricochets off my shoulder and drops down onto my desk.

I stare at it. He obviously wants me to open it. But as much as I might want to find out what vile message he's written inside it, I keep my hands in my lap and stare at it.

After a few minutes, my curiosity gets too much and I reach for it. I'm just about to reveal what's inside when the teacher stops beside me.

"That's not exactly the best way to introduce yourself, is it, Miss Pritchard." She snatches the note from my hand and pulls it open. She pales slightly at what's written before demanding to know who wrote it.

As expected, the entire class falls silent. I'm sure every single person behind me knows it came from Ethan, but equally no one is brave enough to go up against a member of the football team. It's the same in every school I've spent time in. It might not always be the football team that rules the school, sometimes it's the soccer or the basketball team, but ultimately it's a bunch of jacked up, arrogant assholes who think they're fucking gods.

I roll my eyes and slump down in my seat.

"I think maybe you and I need a chat after class, Miss Pritchard."

"Great," I mutter. First class of my first day and he's already getting me in trouble.

————

After getting a ten-minute dressing down from my English Lit teacher about how passing notes isn't what is expected of Rosewood High students, I'm late for my biology class. She doesn't seem to care that I clearly wasn't the one to write it. I mean, I'm hardly going to warn myself of what's coming to me. But then again, I guess no one ever pulls up the legends that are the football team for their appalling behavior. At least I can blame the fact that I'm new and lost for my tardiness. Could this day get any fucking worse?

Finding the cafeteria at lunch is much easier than any of my morning classes, seeing as almost every student in the school moves in that direction.

With a tray full of questionable looking food, I glance around for a table. Every one is taken, so I head to a half full one with two people sitting at it, purposefully ignoring the one full of football players and cheerleaders. Thankfully Ethan's attention is on the same girl who was forced on me earlier so he doesn't notice my arrival.

"I'm sorry, do you mind?" I point to the empty seats.

The guy nods. "Sure, go for it."

Dropping my tray to the table, I feel their attention on me, but I don't look up. I'm really not in the mood for people after my shitty morning.

"Hey, you're Raelynn, right? Ethan's..." The female voice trails off.

"I'm not Ethan's anything," I snap.

Glancing over out of the corner of my eye, I vaguely recognize the girl from Saturday night, but I've no clue who she is. The guy isn't familiar at all.

"Oh sorry. Yeah. So how are you finding your first day?" When I just stare at her without offering an answer, she opens her mouth once again. "I'm Camila, by the way. This is Shane."

"Great." I give her a very quick and equally fake smile before looking down to my plate.

An awkward silence settles around us before we're joined by another guy.

"Hey, baby. Having a good day?" I glance up to see the blonde guy from the couch on Saturday night very slowly and carefully lower himself down beside Camila.

"Are you sure you should be here? The doctor said—"

"Screw the doctor. I'm not sitting at home anymore."

"Fine. But if you do more damage, you know Coach won't let you play in the final."

"We've gotta make it there first. Don't you think you're being a little presumptuous, Cam?" the other guy says.

"Glad to know you're feeling positive about it."

"We're not the same team without you, man."

I roll my eyes, realizing that the other guy is also on the team. I look over to where the rest of the team and cheer squad are huddled around a few joined up tables, and I wonder why these two aren't over with them.

I know the second their eyes turn to me. "Mase, you remember Raelynn from Saturday night?" Camila asks, clearly pointing me out.

"Hmmm, yeah. That was quite an introduction."

"Thanks," I mutter, still refusing to look their way.

"I need to go and see the guys. You going to be okay?"

"Of course. I'll see you last period. Take it easy."

The sound of them kissing makes me cringe before he gets up as gently as he sat down and walks toward the team, closely followed by Shane, although he looks reluctant to join them all.

"So what's his story? Bad tackle?" I ask Camila when she turns back from watching her boyfriend's ass walk away.

"Car accident."

I feel a little bad for jumping to conclusions, but I don't show it because I don't give a shit what she thinks of me.

"Listen—" she starts, turning her dark, assessing eyes on me.

"No, I'm not sitting here listening to a lecture from Miss Goody Two Shoes. You don't know me, nor will you get the chance to. You're Ethan's friend. I get it. You don't want me making his life hard so he's distracted from the game. Whatever. I don't give a shit. You do you, and I'll do me, and if we're lucky, our paths won't cross all that often."

Her chin drops at my words. I take her moment of silence to grab my tray and walk away with a smirk on my face.

I'm not here to make any friends, and it's about time that nosey bitches like Camila realized that.

14

ETHAN

I'd have put money on her selling me out to Mrs. Harris so I'm pleasantly surprised when I get through the day without being called in to explain myself for the note I wrote. It wasn't pretty but I couldn't refrain from playing with her.

I'm just finishing a lap on the track when the girls come out onto the field for their gym class. I search through them. They're all wearing skin-tight gym uniforms in the hope of attracting one of us. All apart from one. *Her.*

A smirk pulls at my lips as I take in her oversized dirty shirt and the shorts that hang to her knees that have clearly been pulled from the spares cupboard. The ones we all dread wearing because they've been in there as long as the school's been here and smell as such. I couldn't have planned it better if I'd organized it myself.

"Savage, pull your head from your pants and focus," Coach calls.

"Sorry," I mutter, dragging my eyes away from the girls as they start warming up, most of them flaunting everything they have, trying to get us to look their way.

Coach sets us off again, and after a while the girls head off on their cross-country route. I watch as they run, staring at their asses sway and their tits bounce, but no one really catches my attention until she runs past. She's totally uncoordinated compared to the members of the cheer team who've sprinted off trying to show up the rest of the class. She's right at the back and plodding along like it's the worst day of her life.

I chuckle as I turn the corner and up my speed, pushing myself to my limits as I try to outrun *her.*

"Good, Savage. Use that aggression and push harder."

I put everything I have into my next lap, but the second the final lot of the girls come into view, I find I can't help but look up. They all run past me but one, the one I want to see. When I look to where they all appeared from, I find her bent over with her hands on her knees and panting like she's run a fucking marathon, not just the school's cross-country track.

"What's wrong, trash? Weaker than you think?"

Her eyes lift to find mine. They're narrowed, her hate for me shining bright.

"Maybe it won't take as much for me to break you as I was expecting. At least put in a bit of a fight." Fury fills her eyes as she sucks in deep lungsful of air.

"I'll outrun you if it kills me. You won't break me." She sounds so sure in herself but I don't share her confidence. She might act like nothing can touch her, but I've seen the hint of fear that fills her eyes. I fucking crave it more than my next tackle. I will see it again, and I will see her break before me. I'll put everything I have on it.

With one final hard stare, she finds some energy from somewhere and heads back toward the rest of her class.

I watch her progress as she makes her way across the field. Heat fills my veins that despite having a shit first day, largely thanks to me, she's still going.

Coach runs us ragged before dismissing the rest of our class but keeping the members of the team out on the field ready for practice to start.

Mason comes out, albeit slowly, after class and eagerly listens to Coach's pep talk before slinking back to the bleachers looking seriously pissed off at watching us all sweat out the weekend's alcohol consumption to ensure we're focused and ready for Friday night's game. The first one of the playoffs. I should be fucking stoked, I guess I am to a point, but it's not my main focus, thanks to my dad and his wayward fucking dick.

Zayn slams into me when I'm not paying attention.

"What the fuck, man?" he barks when I push back, slamming my hands down on his chest hard enough that he stumbles back. He's still on my shit list for giving her weed on Saturday night.

"Get out of my fucking face," I spit.

"That's enough, Savage. Leave the bitch fights to the cheer squad, eh?"

His warning is enough to stop me, but it doesn't put a halt to the death stare I have trained on Zayn. "Stay the fuck away from her, you hear me?"

"Loud and fucking clear. She's really not your type though, dude."

"Did I fucking say she was?" I step toward him again, but this time it's Jake that gets between us.

"Fuck off, Zayn." Jake stands in front of me, his hands on my shoulders. "I get it. I fucking get it." An understanding passes between us. "But don't let her fuck it up for you, for us. Keep her off the fucking field, yeah?"

I want to kick back. I want to ask him if that's what he did when Amalie was messing up his head, but I bite back the spiteful words because this thing with *her* is very different. Amalie was messing up Jake's head because he wanted her. That is not the fucking issue I have right now. The only thing I want from the trash that's moved into my house is her fucking gone. *After you've got your hands on her*, a little voice says in my head, but I push it down. I only want to get my hands on her to break her. To show her that she doesn't belong here. My home is not where pieces of shit like her belong.

By the time Coach lets us head for the locker room, my legs are like jelly. I've no doubt we're going to kick ass on Friday night—he's working us harder than ever knowing that it's now or never.

"We've fucking got this, boys. That fucking trophy is ours for the taking," Jake shouts excitedly into the showers where we're all washing off layers of sweat and mud.

A chorus of agreement sounds out around the team, and when I look over, I find even Shane getting caught up in the excitement.

"Who's up for Aces? I need a fucking burger the size of my head," Zayn calls.

I'm not sure why he asks, it's pretty much tradition at this point. Some of the guys make their excuses and fuck off once they're dressed, but the normal crowd, plus Shane, all head toward the parking lot together to get in their cars.

Mason is still with us, having watched the entire practice, although he's starting to look a little worse for wear. It's like he's forgotten he was almost fucking killed a little over two weeks ago. I know he's desperate to be part of our playoff games, but I'm worried he's pushing himself too much too fast.

"Um..." Shane starts looking totally uncomfortable. "My car's in the garage, any chance of a lift?" He looks between the three of us, I think half expecting us to tell him where to go.

I glance at Jake, his lips pressed into a thin line as he stares at Shane. We might now all know the truth about who drugged Amalie at his party, but he still doesn't trust the guy. I get it, he was after Jake's girl long before Jake pulled his head out of his ass and realized he wanted her.

"Yeah, man. Ethan's driving," Mason says, gesturing to the back door.

Shane nods but still looks hesitant, and the three of us pull open doors and jump inside.

"Not like you to join us, Dunn," Jake states, clearly not happy about it.

"Thought maybe it was time I joined in," Shane mumbles as he stares at the passing scenery.

"Don't you think it might be a little too late?" Jake barks.

"Leave it, Thorn. Shane's part of the team. He's welcome wherever we are."

"Would never guess you're banging his friend."

"Just the fuck up, Jake," I add, helping both Mason and Shane out.

He rolls his eyes but shuts his mouth.

The rest of the journey is tense at best. I'm not sure what game Shane is playing, but Jake's right with what he's saying, this is weird as fuck.

We pull up to Aces as the other guys do and pile out of the car. Shane immediately walks ahead, making me wonder who he's really meeting here.

The three of us hang back and allow the others to go ahead of us.

"Well, that was fucking weird," Mason says, echoing my previous thoughts.

"Oh, I thought you were on Team Dunn all of a sudden."

"I just don't think you need to be such a dick to him, he's not actually a bad guy. Just odd that he's suddenly latched on to us."

"He just wanted a free fucking lift."

"Whatever. Come on, I'm starving."

I march toward the entrance, Jake and Mason flanking my sides. I know they're just as eager to get inside because their girls are there. I roll my eyes to myself that I'm going to have to spend the next however long watching them suck each other's faces off and whisper sweet fucking nothings into their ears. Fucking pussies. I expected it from Mason. The way he and Camila fought like cat and fucking dog for years, I'm surprised it took so long. But Jake... I never thought he'd get pussy whipped, but he's like a soppy fucking puppy where Amalie's concerned.

My steps falter the second I step foot inside the diner, causing Mason to crash into me.

"Ow, fuck. Ouch," he complains as a flash of dark hair runs past me to his side.

I feel bad for causing him pain, but most of my mind is consumed with the fact that *she's* standing over our usual table setting plates down.

What the utter fuck is she doing here?

15

RAELYNN

By the time I finish that damn gym class, I'm a sweaty, hot, aching mess. The last thing I want to do is go and start my first shift at Aces. But knowing I can't use Eric's credit card for an Uber every morning to get myself to school, I force myself into the showers, ignoring the stares from the other girls around me wanting to know who I am and probably why I have 'bitch' written all over my face. Obviously, not literally, but I don't need to be told I've got a fantastic resting bitch face. I see it in the mirror most days. Never more so than since moving here. I'm not here to make friends, and I need everyone to know it before they start trying.

It works, because no one so much as asks my name. Fucking fine by me.

I call another Uber and jump in out front of the school when it pulls up. Looking at how short the journey is, I could probably walk it, but my first day isn't the time to show up late because I got lost. I already look a hot mess after doing a rush job of my makeup in the dirty, cracked school mirror I was left with after the cheer team monopolized the decent ones the second they pushed through the door into the locker room.

I'm still wearing the same outfit I was earlier. The only change I've made is to pull on a shirt that covers my belly; I'm not sure anyone wants their burger delivered by a girl who can't cover herself up appropriately.

A wave of trepidation flows through me as I step into the diner and find almost the entire senior Rosewood class inside. If I knew this was the school hang out, I might have chosen another place to work. Acknowledging that it's too late to worry about it now, especially as Bill's just glanced up at me and smiled, I walk toward the register.

"Good afternoon, Rae," Bill sings. "You're looking like a little ray of sunshine. Good first day?"

I bark out a laugh at his description of me. We both know that I'm about as far away from sunshine as physically possible.

"As far as first days go... I've had better."

He winces but thankfully says no more about it as he waves someone over. "Rae, this is Cody. Cody will be mostly working the same shifts as you, so he's pulled the short straw to show you the ropes."

"Hey Rae, nice to meet you," Cody says politely. I give him a quick once over from his sun-kissed shaggy surfer hair and down his slim, tall body. He's hot.

"You too." He smiles at me and only gets better looking. If I had to guess, I'd say he was a little older, maybe at college.

"Right, I'll leave you both to it." Bill wanders off, leaving me to follow Cody around as he points things out and tells me about protocols. This isn't my first waitressing gig, so most of it sounds simple enough.

"Here's your apron," Cody says, holding it out for me. "Notepads for taking orders are here, if you need them. I'll just show you how to put them through to the kitchen and then you should be good to go."

I nod and follow him over to the register. The system is exactly the same as one I've used before, so I instantly know what he's going to show me, not that I tell him that. He seems to be enjoying himself playing boss so I let him get his fill.

"This place usually gets a little crazy when the Rosewood kids finish for the day, so you'll need to get out of school pretty quick to beat them all."

"I'm sure I can cope." I glance around to make sure no one needs anything before asking the question that's been on the tip of my tongue since meeting Cody. "So are you from around here?"

"Nah, I'm a student at Maddison U," he says, confirming my suspicions that he's in college. "What about you? Rosewood born and bred?"

"Nope. Moved here last week. Mom shacked up with some guy who lives here and dragged me halfway across the country."

"Rough."

"Meh, it's pretty standard for me."

"How are you finding it?"

I look around the diner once again right as a group of cheerleaders arrive, the one who was supposed to be my chaperone earlier front and center. Her eyes find mine and they narrow in disdain before she elbows a couple of the others.

"Oh great. I've fitted right in." A bitter laugh falls from my lips.

"Oh yeah, so I see. I wouldn't worry about that lot. You're not missing out on much by not being part of their group."

"I'm sorry, you think I want to be a part of that?" I snap.

Regret covers his face almost instantly. "No, no. That's not what I—forget I said anything. Looks like they want to order."

I groan, following his gaze and finding the entire squad with their eyes on me.

"Feed me to the wolves, why don't you. I'm sure they'd much prefer you."

"Are you kidding? All they want is their football jocks."

"I think you and I might just get along fine after all."

Pulling the little notepad I shoved into my skirt back pocket earlier, I twist the pencil in my fingers and make my way over, much to their delight.

"Well, well, well... new girl seems to have got herself a little job," the ringleader sneers.

"What can I get for you?" I ask, ignoring her barb and plastering a smile on my face.

"Oh look, she does smile," another comments.

Everything in me wants to tell them where to go and refuse to serve them, but seeing as they're my first customers of the first day of my job, I can hardly do that, so instead, I force myself to keep my cool as they each rattle off their orders, looking pleased as fuck that I'm quite clearly beneath them being their waitress.

"Coming right up," I sing, walking away and ignoring their petty comments about what I'm wearing and the state of my hair.

"You okay?" Cody asks when I join him back at the register.

"Of course. I've handled much worse than those spoiled brats."

"I had a feeling you'd say as much. Things can only get better from here on out, right?"

I'd like to say I agree with him, but not twenty minutes later when I'm putting the cheer squad's plates down in front of them does it get a whole lot worse.

I'm expecting it, because where the cheer squad goes, the football team generally follows, so when the door bursts open and excited male chatter fills the relatively small diner, I know exactly who's arrived.

I don't want to look, but it's like my eyes have a mind of their own. Turning away from the table slightly, I watch as they all come barreling through the door —well, except for the one I'm dreading.

Breathing a sigh of relief that he's not shown his face, I spin back to drop the last plate down. That's the exact moment when my blood runs cold. The atmosphere in the entire diner changes and my spine stiffens.

Standing straight, I look around the table and plaster a smile on my face. "If you need anything else, please let me know." Glancing at one of the guys, I say, "I'll be back in a few moments to take your orders." Then I spin on my heels and get the hell out of there.

I race past Cody and out to the kitchen. Once I know I'm out of sight, I fall back against the wall and suck in a few deep breaths.

"Is everything okay?"

"Yeah, perfect."

"Ooookay." His eyes study me for a few seconds before I swallow down my apprehension and push from the wall.

"Right. I've got a job to do." I refuse to allow myself to shy away from that asshole. He has no right to have any power over me or to make me regret taking a job that I so desperately need.

"If you need anything, you know where I am." I nod at him and walk back to the table.

All eyes turn on me as I approach, the girls judging, the guys trying to place me and work me out. Good fucking luck with that. I imagine only the best shrink in the country would be able to sort my head out right now. The only person's attention I don't hold is *his*. I'm shocked. I thought this would be the perfect opportunity for him to humiliate me.

"What can I get for you all?"

I start with the guys I don't recognize before my eyes land on Zayn's, followed by the two guys who were sitting with Ethan on Saturday night. None of them acknowledge me, they just place their orders like they would with any other waitress.

Knowing that I can't ignore him and walk off without taking his order like I'm desperate to do, I wait for a beat, but the asshole still keeps his eyes focused on the menu in front of him.

"Ethan?" I prompt, pissed off that he's wasting my time.

There are a couple of gasps from the girls, as they look between the two of us. The ringleader stares at me.

"You know this girl, Ethan?" Her voice is the one that drags his eyes from the table. He looks to her before glancing over at me. The way he looks at me has my nails digging into the notepad. It's like the simple act of even looking at me is more than I deserve.

"*Her?*" he spits. His eyes run the length of my body, his lip curling in disgust. "Please, I don't spend time with skanks."

My brow arches as I glance at the kind of girls he does spend time with.

"Good to know. Now, can I get you any food?" I try to take the high road, but I don't think anyone around the table misses my voice crack.

He sits back, placing his arm over the back of the bench he's sitting on like he owns the fucking place, a smug smile firmly on his lips as he assesses me.

"Burger, fries, soda. You to leave us alone."

"Jesus, Ethan," his blonde friend mutters.

Rolling my eyes, I note it down, not that I'll forget, and turn my back on them.

"Was that really necessary?" a guy's voice says before one of the girls pipes up. "You sure you don't know her?"

Shaking my head, I walk to the register and put the order through to the kitchen.

"Friends of yours?" Cody asks with a laugh.

"Oh yeah. Can't you just feel the love?"

He laughs. "How have you done one day at school yet managed to piss off both the cheer squad and the football team already?"

"I have very special skills."

His eyes glance over my shoulder and his face drops a little. "Do you need me to take over that table? I don't mind."

"No chance. I'm not allowing them to think they've won."

He nods before leaving me to greet a few more familiar faces who sit in his booths. It's the two girls from Saturday night. There's some shuffling from behind me before the two guys walk over and sweep their girls into their arms.

I watch them for a few minutes before the bell from the kitchen rings out to tell me there's food ready.

Sadly, Ethan's is the first prepared, but that doesn't mean it's the first I deliver. I push it to the back of the counter and pick up every other one.

With it still getting cold in the kitchen, I head toward where the two of his friends are now sitting at the other side of the diner with their girls.

"You guys want this over here?" I ask, able to breathe a little easier being away from the main group.

"That's great, thanks. Listen—" the blonde guy starts.

"You don't need—"

He interrupts. "I do. Ethan's being an ass. This whole thing with his parents has rocked him more than he'll admit."

"I don't give a shit. You think all of this is what I wanted?"

"No, no, of course not but—"

"Do not ask me to go easy on him or give him the benefit of the doubt or some bullshit. Not happening."

He holds his hands up in defense. "Was going to do no such thing. You seem like you can handle yourself around him."

"So, as stimulating as it is, is there actually a point to this whole conversation?"

The other three around the table stifle a laugh.

"You know," the dark-haired guy pipes up, "I think the two of you might actually get along just fine. I'm Jake, in case you forgot. This is Mason. My girl's Amalie and this is Camila."

If he expects me to remember that, then he's got to be even more delusional than I think he is.

"You need anything, give these two a shout," Blonde says, nodding to the girls.

"Thanks." It's totally insincere, but I'm not really the kind of girl that other girls make friends with.

I leave them to it and head back to the kitchen. Ethan's food should be suitably cold by now.

I fight the smile that wants to spread across my face the entire journey toward him with his plate.

He looks up as I approach while everyone around him eats.

I drop it down in front of him a little harder than necessary, a few fries bouncing off the plate and onto the table.

His eyes narrow at me, his lips press into a thin line. He's desperate to give me a dressing down, but something's holding him back. I'm assuming it's his audience.

I smile at him. "Enjoy."

More and more students pour in through the front doors as they make their way from the beach once the sun starts to set, and I'm so busy that I hardly have a chance to acknowledge the hate stare coming from *his* table every time I so much as walk past, but he never tries to say anything and I avoid taking any more orders from them as they sit chatting.

It must be half an hour later that the noise of them all leaving fills the diner. I look back over my shoulder as I head toward the kitchen to see I'm right. Most of the girls have already walked out, leaving a few of the guys hanging back, sorting out the check

Breathing a sigh of relief, I continue forward. That is until warm fingers wrap around my wrist and I'm pulled none too gently into the dark bathroom beside me.

"What the—" My words are cut off as his hand comes down on my mouth. My eyes widen in shock.

He stands close, his nose only an inch from mine, his increased breath covering my face. I can only just make out his features with the emergency light illuminating the space around us. The rest of my senses are on full alert—it's how I know he smells fucking mouthwatering right now. Asshole. Why can't he smell as rotten as his personality?

"You have no fucking right being here. You're quitting. Tonight."

My eyes narrow. Who the fuck does he think he is, trying to dictate my life?

My chest heaves and my hands tremble slightly with his closeness and the evil hint in his blue eyes as he stares down at me.

16

ETHAN

T his is my fucking place. My fucking escape. Why the fuck does she have to have found a job here of all places?

I was desperate to say something, to do something as she stood at the end of our booth with her little pad of paper in hand, but I didn't want everyone around knowing there was anything between us. As far as I'm concerned, Dad will get bored and the two of them will fuck off out of our lives as fast as they entered and no one will need to be any the wiser.

Anger swirls within me as I watch her deliver everyone else's food bar mine. She thinks she's fucking clever. Well, she needs to think again because she won't win these games she's trying to play. I'm the fucking master here and she's merely the puppet.

I see my opportunity the second everyone starts to leave. I excuse myself to the bathroom and double back on myself, following her down the hall that leads to the kitchen.

I watch her ass sway in her short as fuck skirt. What was Bill thinking when he offered her a job? Like fuck does she fit in here.

Her little gasp of shock when I pull her into the dark bathroom makes my lips twitch in achievement. The dim light above reflects in her dark eyes. I swear I see a little fear in them. It makes my cock hard.

She flinches when I demand she quits, but I'm not stupid. She's not going to listen to anything I say. She's already proved that my words don't affect her like they should. This girl's all about actions, and I have plenty of things up my sleeve to prove to her that she doesn't belong here, that she doesn't belong in my life.

I take a step closer, my hand dropping from her mouth but only enough so I can take her chin in my fingers and pinch hard enough to make her fight to get away.

"I took it fucking easy on you tonight. But bringing me cold food... you're not going to get away with that, trash. I left my check on the side, I'm sure your wages tonight will easily cover it.

Her defiant eyes hold mine, but the small amount of water that's beginning to pool in them gives her away.

"You scared of me?"

"Never."

I close the space between us, my nose brushing hers. I don't miss her sharp intake of breath at our contact.

"You should be," I whisper. "And it's not just me you've got to worry about. All those guys out there, they do what I say, and they'll make your life a living hell if I so much as whisper the words."

She swallows, her slender neck rippling against my palm. "Bring it on," she taunts, her lips curling up into a smile. "I've dealt with worse than a rich prick like you. You can't fucking touch me."

"Oh, sweet cheeks. We both know that's not true. We both know I've already touched you, and we both know just how much you were enjoying it."

Reaching forward, I slip my hand under the tiny scrap of fabric that's wrapped around her hips. She's wearing fishnets beneath, and the second I push my fingers inside two of the holes they practically disintegrate. The rip sounds out and it's like music to my ears.

"Ethan, you can't—"

"When are you going to fucking learn? I can. I will. And I'll do it whenever the fuck I like."

I trail one finger over her center that's covered in soft cotton.

"What's this? Granny pants? I thought you were a lace kind of girl."

"What do you care?"

"You're right. None would be so much better."

"Ah, fuck," she cries when I tuck my finger beneath the fabric and immediately find her swollen clit.

"You've been waiting for this since I pulled back the other night, haven't you? And if how wet you are tells me anything, it's that you followed my orders. You didn't get yourself off, did you?"

"Y-you're not getting any of my pleasure."

Her eyes shine bright and her chest heaves as I continue teasing her nub.

"Is that right? Because right now you're dripping down my fucking fingers like you can't get enough of me."

If it were lighter, I'd love to see the color I know is staining her cheeks at my comment.

Slipping my fingers lower, I find her entrance and push two fingers inside her tight pussy. A groan climbs up my throat, but I catch it before it passes my lips. She doesn't need to know that I'm imagining just how tight she'd squeeze my cock.

I lean in, my rough cheek scratching her soft face until my lips brush her ear. She shudders, and I smile.

"Next time, I'll be the one taking all the pleasure."

I pull my fingers from her and step back. My cock's tenting my pants, but with the darkness in here, I doubt she can see the effect she's having on me.

Learning from my mistake when I lift my hand, I don't suck my own fingers like I'm desperate to do. Instead I lift them to her lips.

"Open," I demand. And in true trailer trash style, she keeps them firmly shut.

"I don't take kindly to you defying me. Open your fucking lips, or I won't wait until next time to push my cock between then."

I don't think she means to open her mouth, because she looks as shocked as I feel when her lips part and I'm able to push my fingers inside.

I realize my mistake instantly, and it makes me regret this even more than tasting her the first time.

Her lips seal around my fingers before her tongue licks around each one as she sucks.

My breath catches and my cock weeps. That is until just before she releases me and her teeth sink down into my skin.

"Argh, you fucking bitch." I pull my hand back, wiping her saliva off my fingers and pulling them up to see if she broke the skin.

"Put any part of your body in my mouth and that's what's going to happen, posh boy. Just because you've got money and a highly inflated ego, it doesn't mean I'm going to drop to my knees at the click of your fingers. Now, get out of my fucking way, I've got a job to do." She steps around me and pushes the door open. The move floods the room with light and she stops and looks back at me over her shoulder.

Her eyes run down the length of my body before lingering on my obvious hard-on. "Hmmm... looks like someone didn't get the message. Might want to tell your cock that I bite before you end up in the ER."

Her laugh fills the room as she steps out and allows the door to slam closed behind her.

"Fuck," I bark, lifting my hands to my hair and pulling to the point I think it might start coming out.

What the fuck is wrong with me? Why can't I just stay away from her? Leave her to do her own thing while I do mine? Why can't I just leave her the fuck alone?

Rearranging myself in my pants, I quickly wash my hands, not being able to cope with the scent of her lingering on my fingers. The memory of her hot mouth sucking on them is torture enough.

"Where the fuck did you go?" Mason asks the second I join him, Jake, and the girls outside the diner.

"Just went to the bathroom."

All four of them eye me suspiciously but wisely none of them say anything.

"Back to mine? There's still some booze left from Saturday night."

"It's a Monday night," Camila points out, looking a little shocked by the suggestion.

"Right, which means we've got the whole week still to get through before the game Friday."

"Even more reason why you shouldn't be drinking. We need you all sharp and focused if we're going to make it past the first game."

Rolling my eyes at her, I catch Jake's. His hold the same seriousness that Camila's do, but I already know he's reading more into this than I want him to.

The truth is that I just don't want to go home to an empty house right now. I can't handle the fact that they'll all head off home together to enjoy their evenings while I'm going to end up getting off- my-ass drunk just to escape reality.

"Yeah, let's head to yours. Cam's right, though. No alcohol and definitely no weed."

"Spoil sport."

17

RAELYNN

"**J**esus, Rae. You look like you've just seen a ghost," Bill helpfully points out when I stumble into the kitchen a few minutes later.

What I really needed to do was lock myself in the ladies' bathroom and take a breather, but I'd lost track of how long Ethan had me pinned in that dark room and I didn't want anyone to think I was taking the piss on my first night.

"I'm good. I'm good."

"Okay," he says, but he doesn't look convinced as he keeps his eyes on me for a few more moments.

"It's starting to quiet down out there at least," Cody says, joining us in the kitchen. Thankfully, he's too busy dropping off plates to notice my appearance.

My heart is still trying to pound out of my chest, and my veins feel like they're filled with lava from the way he was touching me. I'm not even going to start on the state of my panties, because he was right. I didn't get myself off after he had me on the edge the other night and now, after he's had another go, I'm fucking desperate for a release.

Thankfully, the rest of the night is much less eventful. We've had a steady stream of customers—some I'm sure are Rosewood students, but they're all polite and most tip me really well, which helps toward Ethan's unpaid check.

"Honestly, it's fine," Bill argues when I'm forced to explain why the register doesn't add up at the end of the night.

"No, I always pay my way."

"It's not your *way* to pay though, is it? I'll get it out of Ethan one way or another, don't you worry about that."

"But—"

"No buts. You've been great tonight, Rae. I think it's the beginning of a beautiful thing. Now get the hell out of here and go and do some homework or something that'll ensure you don't spend the rest of your life waiting on others."

"It's done okay for you," I say, now having experienced just how much he loves his place and his job.

"Maybe so, but I've seen the fire in you tonight. You're destined for greatness, kid. Not a diner. Now scoot. Both of you." Bill flicks a cloth in both mine and Cody's direction and together we head to get our stuff and leave for the night.

"See, I told you things would get better," he says as we walk toward the parking lot.

"I guess."

"Are you going to have an even bigger fan club by tomorrow evening?" he asks lightly.

"Probably. No one here really likes or wants me here."

"Hey, that's not true. I'm starting to think you might be pretty awesome."

"Oh yeah?"

He shrugs, a little color hitting his cheeks at his admission. "You need a ride home?"

"Uh... it's okay. I was going to walk, clear my head."

"It's dark."

"And?"

"Come on, I'll give you a ride." I go to argue, but he soon cuts me off. "It's just a ride, Rae. I'm not offering up marriage."

"I know, I'm just not used to anyone offering me anything."

His mouth opens to respond, but he soon changes his mind and closes it again. Awkwardness crackles between us until he comes to a stop behind a red Ford and points toward the passenger side.

The journey home is nice enough. Cody chats about college and his life here while I try to avoid any conversation about how I came to find myself in Rosewood aside from what he already knows.

"It's just up here," I say, wanting the seat to swallow me up when the houses that line this street start to turn into mansions.

"Up here?" he asks, skeptically.

"Sadly. This one." I point to the driveway, expecting him to pull up at the curb so he can make a quick escape, but instead he pulls right up in front of the house. The gravel beneath the tires crunches as we make our way up the ridiculously long track and come to a stop behind the cars here. My heart drops, that he's home, but knowing he's got company makes it that little bit better.

Risking a glance at Cody, I see his eyes widen as the house appears before him. "And you need a job at Aces why?"

"Don't be fooled. None of this has anything to do with me. I'm just an unwanted guest right now."

The car slows to a stop and the intensity of his stare hits the left side of my face as he turns to me.

"So how have you ended up here exactly?"

"My mom." I let out a huge sigh. "She's been seeing the man who owns this place. She moved us here out of the blue."

Peering at Cody out of the corner of my eye, I'm pleased when I find no evidence that he already knows the story of what's happening under this roof. After the way Bill seemed to know everything, I was worried the whole town was aware of Eric's affair which saw his wife run out of town and for us to be shipped in.

"That's tough. Nice digs though. Could have been a hell of a lot worse."

"Oh don't worry. She's dragged me to hell and back before." The words are out of my mouth before I have a chance to stop them.

I stare out the window at the giant brick build mansion and sigh. Movement in one of the downstairs windows catches my eye and my blood runs cold. Oh goodie, Ethan's waiting for me.

I have no idea how long we sit there in silence, but eventually Cody breaks it. "If you need to sit out here all night then that's fine. It would have been good if you'd have warned me though, could have got some food." His voice is full of humor, but it doesn't really hit his target.

"I'm so sorry," I say sadly. "You must have better things to do tonight than sit here."

I release the seatbelt and reach for the handle, but his soft voice stops any further movement. "If you need a friend, Rae. I'm here."

"You don't even know me." I don't mean to sound defensive, but no one's ever offered to be my friend before. They usually run as fast as they can in the opposite direction.

"I get good vibes. And forgive me for saying it, but I get the impression that you're kind of lonely."

A lump of emotion crawls up my throat at his words. "I'm used to it."

He stares at me for a beat, his mouth opening to say something but obviously deciding better of it. "Can I give you my number? Just in case you ever need a friendly voice."

"Sure." I pull my shitty cell from my pocket, open my contacts and hand it over. Cody does a double take on it before tapping in his details and then ringing himself. "Thanks," I mutter, taking it back. "I should probably go."

I push the door open and stand before leaning back in. "Thank you. I... uh... really appreciate it."

"Anytime. I'll see you tomorrow night, yeah?"

"Can't wait." An almost genuine smile twitches at my lips before I shut his door and wave him off.

I stand at the front door for a long few minutes, still putting off going inside, but I know I can't stay out here forever.

Eventually, I turn and push the heavy front door open. The sound of the TV and people chatting and laughing filters down to me as I make my way to the kitchen for a drink.

I'm standing behind the refrigerator door, about to pull out a bottle of water when a shadow falls over the floor beside me. My stomach twists, but fuck, if it's not fear laced with a hefty amount of desire after our encounter earlier.

Blowing out a slow breath, I pull a bottle out and prepare to face him. Shutting the door, I keep my eyes on the floor, hoping he'll allow me to escape unscathed. I know it's wishful thinking.

I take a step toward the door, but he's right there, blocking my exit. My skin prickles with his undivided attention on my body, but still I refuse to give him the satisfaction of looking at him. I've had my fill of him today. I just want to lock myself in a room and try to block out any memory of ever meeting him.

"Who is he?" His words shock me so much that my eyes fly up to his. I find his stare hard and piercing as he waits for his answer.

"Why the fuck do you care?"

He takes a step forward and I suck in a breath before he steals all the air from around me. It's a huge mistake because his manly scent invades my senses as he gets in my personal space.

"Ethan, let the girl get a drink, will you? She's been working all night," a soft English voice says from behind him, but with his wide shoulders blocking my view, I don't see her as she joins us.

Ethan's teeth grind as he continues to stare down at me.

"Ethan, for fuck's sake." A delicate hand curls around his upper arm before she forces herself between us.

"Would you like to join us?" she asks me, looking back over her shoulder.

"No," rumbles up Ethan's throat at her offer.

"We're just in Ethan's den. You're more than welcome."

"No. No, she's fucking not."

"Down, boy." She laughs at Ethan, but it does nothing for the raging inferno that's blazing in his eyes.

"Whatever," I mutter, taking a step back and finally able to breathe. "I've got better things to be doing than hanging out discussing high school gossip."

I leave the room, but it's not until I turn the corner to head up the stairs that I lose his attention.

"What the fuck is your problem?" she barks at him, and I can't help but smile at her attempt. My steps falter so I can hear his response.

"I fucking hate her. She needs to get out of my fucking house and my fucking life."

"Riiight. Ethan, I'm neither blind nor stupid, and you may recall that I've been in a very similar situation. I know exactly where your head is at right now, and I get it, I do. But—"

"But?" he barks. Most people would probably cower at his booming voice, but I get the feeling she doesn't even flinch.

"But stop being such a fucking wanker. She's new. It's hard. And it certainly wasn't her choice to be here, so give her a fucking break."

"Whatever." His footsteps get louder, and I run up the remaining stairs as fast as my legs will carry me. I don't need him knowing that I was listening.

Closing my door behind me, I hope that he's too busy with his friends for me to have to bother with dragging the dresser across, for now at least. I throw my purse down on the bed and start stripping out of my clothes for a shower. Ethan and his little pathetic posse aside, I enjoyed my shift tonight. It was awesome to be able to forget about the bullshit and chat to Cody and the other members of staff like I'm just a normal person. It was a bit of a novelty after the past few days of being treated like the scum of the earth.

I hang my head and allow the jets of water to thunder against my shoulders in the hope it'll release some of the tension pulling them tight, but I get little relief.

I run a brush through my hair, remove my makeup, pull on a tank and shorts, and climb into bed surrounded by the homework I was given today, ready to make a start.

My future is the one thing I have control of right now, and I intend to do everything I can to ensure I can get the hell away from here at the first possible opportunity. If Mom wants to continue living this life, then she's welcome to it. Ethan's right about one thing: I don't belong here. I knew that from the moment I stepped foot inside this house.

I'm just reading through one of the chapters I've been given when a knock on my door halts my movements.

I glance over, wishing I'd pulled the bloody dresser over before I crawled in here. My heart starts to race as I wait for what he's going to do. The second he realizes he can walk straight in here, he's going to, and Christ only knows what might happen once we're alone again.

Memories of his fingers moving against me earlier slam into me and my core clenches. Fuck him for making it feel so good.

Another knock sounds out before a voice I wasn't expecting calls my name.

"Rae, are you in there? It's just us."

"Fuck," I mutter under my breath, wondering how I'm going to get rid of them as fast as they appeared.

Climbing out of bed, I walk over to the door.

"Well if it isn't Barbie and Sindy. What a nice surprise."

The brunette bristles slightly, but the blonde doesn't seem affected in the least.

"Hey. We wanted to come and make sure you were okay. Introduce ourselves properly."

"No need." I push the door to close it on them, but the Brit shoves her foot in the way. I arch a brow at her, hating that she's so damn tall I almost have to break my neck to look at her.

"I know how hard it is starting over here. I was you only a few months ago. I know how it feels."

"Trust me when I say, you have no idea what it's like to be me."

"I'm not talking about you, I'm talking about your current situation."

"Ha, yeah, the Barbie doll who hangs off the football captain's arm knows anything about what I'm dealing with right now."

Something I must say ticks her off, because she steps toward me. Quickly followed by her friend. "By all means, judge away. Most people do. But I can assure you that what you're thinking is wrong, and you and I have more in common than you'd like to admit." She glances over my shoulder and her demeanor totally changes. It's so fast that I almost get whiplash. "So, what are you working on?" She sidesteps me and marches straight into the room, followed by her friend.

"Uh..." I stare at them both as they walk over to my bed and sit down.

"I've been assigned this too. Boring as hell, right?" I stare at her in disbelief. "I'm Camila, in case you forgot. I'm sure you've had so many names thrown at you today that your head's spinning."

"Um..." My eyes flick between the two of them as I try to figure out what the fuck is going on.

"And she's Amalie."

"Right. I don't know what it is you're trying to achieve here, but I don't do friends."

"That's good, because we've already got enough. Just thought you might want some company while the guys watch football replays downstairs. Come on, we can do this together, make it quicker."

And that's how I find myself sitting on my bed, surrounded by books and two girls that I'm fairly sure I'll never connect with on any level aside from being stuck in this house with someone they're friends with.

I can't deny that doing homework alongside someone else makes it a hell of a lot easier, and I hate to admit it, but slightly more enjoyable.

Both of them chat away while we work and give me some of the high school gossip that I really don't give a shit about but listen to anyway.

They tell me about Ethan and their guys, and the sappy looks that cover both of their faces when they do makes me want to puke on the carpet. They both see it but also refrain from stopping.

By the time they leave, my homework is done and I fear I've had my first ever girls' night in. It's a weird as fuck feeling, especially as I curl down into my bed with my diary and relive the entire experience.

I have no idea if they go back downstairs to hang out with the guys, I don't even hear Ethan come up, because by some fucking miracle I actually fall asleep before two AM and end up being woken by my alarm clock the next morning.

18

ETHAN

Getting a lecture from Amalie was the last thing I needed after the day I'd had. The only thing I needed was to relieve some of the tension that was pulling at my body, and there was only one way I wanted to do that. I wanted *her*. I wanted her so fucking bad I could hardly think straight. The image of thrusting balls fucking deep inside that tight little pussy I've had the pleasure of dipping my fingers into was so fucking tempting. Hearing the little noises she makes when she's getting close, hearing her demand that I stop, that I release her. Fuck. My balls were so fucking blue I was expecting them to shrivel up and fall off any moment.

I've no idea what the time is when the others leave. I'd lost focus a long time ago, even Jake's chat about strategies for Friday night didn't drag me back to the here and now. The only thing filling my mind was her. It fucking infuriated me.

Listening to Camila's advice from earlier, I forgo grabbing the bottle of whiskey that taunts me from the side in the kitchen when I take the dirty glasses through and settle for a bottle of water instead. She's right. I need a clear head for the game, even if it means my reality is clear as fucking day.

I hover outside her bedroom door when I get there. It's so tempting to see if she's locked me out again, but the aching of my muscles from our grueling practice session earlier and the stinging of my tired eyes after nights of lack of sleep get the better of me. I don't even bother stripping down, I just fall on to my bed and almost immediately pass out.

When I wake the next morning, the sun has long risen, and school has long started.

"Fuck," I groan, dragging my sore body from the bed and toward the shower.

I'm as quick as I can, but I feel like I'm moving in slow motion as I try to wake my ass up enough to function.

As I pull open my bedroom door, I find hers ajar. I want to go inside and dig around, but I've already missed morning practice. If Coach finds out I've also missed class because I was incapable of getting my ass out of bed, then there's a solid chance he could bench me Friday night, despite the fact we all know he needs me.

I force my feet to keep moving, I grab a black coffee as I pass the kitchen and make it out to my car to head to school.

She consumed my mind the entire day as memories from the fucking bathroom play out on repeat in my head.

Practice is a fucking killer, so much so no one suggests even going to Aces in favor of quietly dying at home before it all starts again in the morning. The way Coach eyed me as I walked into the locker room after school, I had a feeling it was my fault for bailing on this morning that he put the team thoroughly through their paces.

When I get home, I find dinner on the counter that Rachel has left for me and warm it up. I barely taste the chicken and veggies as I pack it away, desperate for the energy it will hopefully give me.

I dump the plate in the dishwasher and drag my pissed off, exhausted, and horny ass up to my bedroom.

Her door is ajar just like it was this morning, and I can no longer resist. She's been messing with my head all day, so it's about time I ensure the feeling is mutual seeing as we've had no classes together today and I've only seen a glimpse of her in the hallway.

Pushing the door open, I glance around the tidy space. I'm shocked she's not had the place redecorated black yet. The pink that adorns the walls sure doesn't suit her.

I pull open a couple of drawers and peer inside, finding nothing more exciting than a couple of her tiny skirts. It's when I open the first one on the opposite dresser that a smile curls up the corners of my mouth.

Her underwear.

I pick up the pair of panties on the top. They're exactly as I imagined what she was wearing last night at the diner. White, cotton and boring as fuck. A million miles from the sexy black ones I stole on her first night here that still sit on my shelf like a trophy in my room.

Moving them aside, I find the much more appealing lace that's hiding beneath. I pull a few out, imagining just how they'll look on her small yet curvy body. My mouth waters and my cock swells as I think of the body I've both seen and felt under my palms.

In a spur of the moment decision, I scoop the whole pile up, along with her bras that are in the next drawer. I kick the door open that's swung back almost shut when another idea hits me. That thing's been pissing me off since the moment she moved into this bedroom.

With a newfound energy, I dump her underwear on my bed and go in search of my dad's tools.

By the time I hear a car pull up in the driveway hours later than I was expecting, I'm lying on my bed watching TV after showering the remaining sweat from my body from my evening exertions.

I tell myself not to, but I'm powerless to resist going to the window to see if that motherfucker from Aces has dropped her off again. I can't see her, so I can only assume that she's standing at the doorway and waving because he lifts his hand and nods at her.

The cheer squad are all about us and getting their teeth into any member of the team possible, but I've heard them fawning over surfer boy waiter before now. Any of them are welcome to him as long as he keeps his paws off *her*.

The front door slams shut and after a few minutes, the sound of her footsteps on the stairs fills my room.

"What the fuck?" she barks when she finds her empty doorway. I picture her standing with her hands on her hips, her lips pursed in anger and her eyes darkening with her need to hurt me.

I smile as I wait for what's to come next.

Her footsteps storm my way before my door flies open and her small, angry body appears.

"Evening, sweet cheeks," I drawl, running my eyes from the top of her head all the way down to her toes and back again.

She's wearing a white shirt that's tied around her waist, exposing her stomach and a ripped denim skirt with her standard fishnets. The whole look is finished off with a pair of heavy biker boots. I shouldn't like the look, let alone find it anywhere near sexy.

"What the fuck have you done?" she seethes, her hands on her hips as her chest heaves in anger.

I shrug and rest back against my headboard. My indifference fires her up. Her eyes alight with fury and her teeth grind.

"Where is my fucking door?"

"Gone. Easier access."

I rest my hands behind my head and watch as she tries to stop herself looking down at my bare torso. Credit where credit's due, she lasts longer than I was expecting her to before her eyes drop.

"G-give it back," she stutters, finding my eyes once again.

"So you can hide from me? I don't think so."

I glance around her and find exactly what I was hoping. Her bed. She follows my stare, her body practically swelling with anger. She storms my way, but not before I swing my legs from the bed and stand. Her arms lift, her fists clenched ready to fight as I stare down at her. The scent of alcohol surrounds her and now she's close enough, I see the glassiness in her eyes.

"You've been drinking," I state.

"And?"

She shrugs.

"Have you been with *him*?"

"Why the fuck do you care who I've been with? I haven't been here, that's all you should be concerned with."

"Where. Have. You. Been?" I demand.

The tension between us crackles, but she still doesn't drop her fists. I take a step toward her until her hands brush my chest. I fight to keep the growl in that wants to rumble up my chest from the contact.

"What do I need to do to get the answer out of you?"

She quirks her head to the side. My fingers grasp her chin and hold her in place. Her breath catches and a little of the fear I crave mixes with the defiance in her eyes.

"I went to the beach," she admits eventually with a roll of her eyes.

"With who?"

"With *him,* and a few of his friends," she taunts. "We had a great time. A little booze, a little sand, a little—"

"Don't," I warn, my fingers tightening to the point her lips open. It would be so easy to slam mine down on them right now, to plunge my tongue between them and take what I need.

"Why? You don't own me. I can do what I please—*who* I please."

In one swift move, I have her backed up against the wall beside the door.

"What are you going to do? *Touch me?* Bring me to the edge and leave me hanging once again? Does that make you feel like a man? Does it give you the sense of power you crave?" My jaw pops and the muscles in my neck twitches in frustration. "Does it make you feel special?"

Wrapping my hands around her wrists, I pin them to the wall at her sides as I close the space between us. Her face only comes to my mid chest, so she has to tilt it back in order to look at me. Her soft curves press into my hard places.

"Seeing as your mom walked away from you without so much as a second glance, I'm sure you enjoy feeling special."

"Shut up," I bark, having had enough of her spiteful words.

"Or what? What are you actually going to do? Finger fuck me into oblivion?" Her brows rise in challenge. "Maybe you'll just go the whole hog and bend me over your bed and fuck me until I'm raw. Would that make all of this better, eh?"

"Shut. Your. Fucking. Mouth."

"And what if I don't. Are you going to shut it for m—"

My restraint snaps and I slam my lips down on hers just to make her stop talking. A growl breaks free from my lips and I hate that I'm showing any sign of enjoying this. But fuck, if she doesn't feel fucking incredible.

My tongue delves past her lips, finding hers. She resists for about ten seconds, but when I press my body against hers and squash her against the wall, she soon caves. There's no denying my enjoyment then, because my length's pressed against her stomach.

I release her wrists, my need to feel her body beneath my hands too much to bear as her taste and scent render me useless for anything other than finding pleasure.

I find her bare waist and slip my hands inside until I find her bra-covered tits. She moans, her head hitting the wall, but her kiss doesn't falter.

She sucks on my tongue and my cock jumps at the possibility it could be next. It's about time I got something out of this war we have going on.

Her nipples pebble beneath my touch, and I desperately pull at the fabric containing them, needing to feel her skin against mine.

Pulling back from her lips to drag in a few deep breaths, I trail my lips to her ear.

"Did he make you feel like this?" I whisper.

"Ethan." I'm not sure if it's a warning or a demand for more. I take it as the latter.

Dropping to my knees, I push her skirt up around her waist, exposing the tiny pair of panties she's wearing.

"Did you wear these for him? Hoping he'd notice when you bent over in the kitchen and take you from behind?"

"No," she whispers so quietly that I almost miss it.

"Or did you save showing it off until you had an audience on the beach? Give him and his friends a little show."

"No," she says louder.

"The things they could have done to you on an empty beach after you'd had a few drinks." I shudder at the thought. No one touches her besides me. My words might be affecting her right now, but fuck if they're not driving me crazy too.

Reaching up, I thread my fingers into her fishnets and pull until they practically disintegrate in my hands, leaving her just in her tiny red panties. They're almost too pretty to ruin. Almost.

"Ethan," she gasps as the sound of the lace ripping fills the silent space around us.

Pulling them from her body, I abandon them on the floor before dipping my finger into her heat.

"Oh god," she whimpers above me.

"You get so wet for me, sweet cheeks."

"How do you know it wasn't for him? For him and his friends," she grates out between heaving breaths.

I don't give her an answer. Instead I lift her leg over my shoulder, part her, and press my tongue to her clit.

"Fuck, fuck, fuck," she chants, her fingers threading into my hair and pulling so tight it starts to sting.

Her addictive taste fills my mouth and I breathe a sigh of relief like a junkie getting his next hit. I lick at her feverishly as she chants incoherent things above me. Needing more from her, I lift my other hand and find her tight entrance. I circle around it, making her cry out my name. Every muscle in my body locks up as I fight my need to throw her down on my bed and fuck her into next week.

This woman drives me to insanity. I shouldn't want to touch her, let alone crave her this fucking badly.

Pushing up inside of her, I bite down on my cheeks as her walls ripple around my finger and I imagine just how that might feel on my cock.

"Come, sweet cheeks," I growl, her hands gripping impossibly tight as I find the spot inside her which makes her tremble with her impending pleasure.

I want to punish her, make her pay for turning up here like she did, but as she climbs to the point of no return, I'm powerless but to allow her to fall this time. My name is barely a plea on her lips, and fuck if it doesn't make me want to know how it'll sound as she reaches climax.

My teeth graze her clit and she stills, her pussy flooding my fingers before she cries my name, her head slamming back against the wall as she rides out her orgasm.

Unable to fight my need to look at her, I pull back so I can take in the look on her face as she loses control. It's fucking breathtaking.

I continue fucking her with my fingers until she stops pulsating around me. I pull them out, suck them into my mouth and stand.

Her eyes are glassy with lust, her lips parted as she tries to catch her breath.

Allowing her eyes to drop from mine, she takes her time running them over the ridges of my abs and following my v lines down into my very tented shorts.

"Off," she demands, nodding toward my only bit of clothing.

I'm solely thinking with my cock, and I foolishly do as she asks, dropping the fabric to my ankles and letting my hard length spring free.

19

RAELYNN

I try not to focus on just how mind-blowing that release was as I struggle to get my brain to fire. That motherfucker has taken my bedroom door off— T=the only thing I've got that allows me to hide in this goddamn house.

He's going to fucking pay for this. And if he thinks the orgasm he just delivered goes anywhere toward making it better, then he needs to think again.

He has no idea, but he's just upped the stakes on this little game of hate we're playing.

I stare down at his cock as I try to get my breathing under control. I must admit that it was easier than I thought it would be to get him to expose himself. But then, guys do think with their cocks, so I'm not sure why I'm surprised.

It twitches under my stare as he waits for me to do something.

Tilting my head to the side, I make a show of biting down on my fingernail. "You know, I thought for all your arrogance that you'd be rocking something much more impressive." He snorts a laugh, assuming that I'm joking. Looking up to his eyes, I see a little vulnerability sneak into them. No better way to offend a hot-blooded male than to insult his manhood. "I've got dildos bigger than that. Come back when you've hit puberty and I'll consider it."

Spinning on my heels, I race back to my room, leaving my ruined panties on his floor as a reminder of my visit.

His growl sounds out behind me, quickly followed by his footsteps. I stop in my doorway and turn to him.

"Stop," I demand, putting both my palms up to him.

He's still gloriously naked, having shaken off the fabric around his ankles, but I'm unable to appreciate it due to the fact that I just lied and told him he wasn't all that. Our eyes hold, something sparking between us. My core aches for more of what he just gave me, but I'm not giving him any more than I already have. Even that was more than he deserves, but the second he put his hands on me, I was powerless to resist.

"You might have removed the door, but this is my space. If you know what's good for you, you'll allow me it. Fuck the privacy, you've already seen everything anyway. But you do not take a step past this door frame. Understood?"

His eyes narrow. He wants to defy me, as I was expecting. Really, I don't have a leg to stand on. If he insists on invading my room then he will, he's already proved that, but I want to see if there's anything redeemable about my asshole housemate.

I take a step back to see what he'll do, mostly expecting him to follow me, but he doesn't. He and his still hard cock stay on his side of the threshold. He lifts his arms and his fingers grip the frame above his head. The move makes his muscles ripple deliciously. It's almost painful to keep my eyes on his face.

"I suggest you go to bed, Ethan. It's late, and it's a school night."

"Didn't stop you drinking, did it?" he sneers, watching as my hand lifts to the bottom of my shirt.

"I'm a big girl, Ethan. I can do what the fuck I like."

His eyes widen in delight when I pull the fabric up over my head before undoing my bra and allowing it to drop to the floor at his feet.

A low groan rumbles up his throat and I just about manage to contain the smile that wants to make its way to my lips, knowing this is affecting him.

"Regretting it yet?"

"What?" he barks, his eyes locked on my bare tits. If the situation were anything else, I'd be cowering away, but something about Ethan makes me so brazen. It's probably my need to prove to him that all these little tricks he's playing, making me vulnerable by stripping me bare, aren't going to intimidate me.

"I could be hiding behind a door right now. You'd have no idea I was standing here almost naked."

His eyes darken. "I've got a fucking imagination, sweet cheeks."

"Good thing, really," I mutter, pulling open a drawer and dragging out an over-sized shirt.

"And why's that?"

"You're going to need it. You're getting no more from me."

"Is that right?" He lifts his foot to take a step forward, and my brow arches in warning. "Fine. But this isn't over."

"You're damn fucking right it's not."

His teeth grind and his jaw tics. After sweeping up my discarded bra, muttering something about having the set, he turns on his heels and storms to his room. My eyes feast on his muscular back covered in that stunning tattoo until he slams his door behind him so hard that the house rocks.

A bitter laugh falls from my lips. There's nothing amusing in the slightest about tonight, but I think the lingering alcohol from the beach along with the dying aftershocks from my orgasm make me slightly crazy.

I had no intention of going out drinking after work. I had homework to do, so as far as I was concerned, I was going to come straight back here and hope that I'd be allowed to get on with it. A small part of me even hoped Ethan's friends might be here. It was a weird feeling because I've never done homework with anyone in my life, but even I can't deny how good last night was as we worked together.

Cody had invited me to join him down to the beach earlier in the evening, but I'd declined. I thought he'd accepted it, but as our shift came to a close, he started rattling off reasons why I needed to kick back and enjoy myself. I couldn't really argue with any of his points, but after a day at school, I'd had my fill of judgmental assholes.

He assured me that his friends were nothing like that, and after promising me a lift home, I relented, his promise of beer and a joint if I was really lucky getting the better of me.

It was a good night. At no point did the team or the cheer squad appear like I expected them to. There were other kids I vaguely recognized from school, but without their leaders here to influence them, they were shockingly polite as I took their orders and delivered their food. I know they recognized me, it was right there in their eyes, but no one said a word.

Cody promised that his friends were different, and seeing as he'd only been kind to me during our very short friendship, I had no reason not to believe him.

The second we stepped down onto the beach, I realized he was right. His friends all glanced up at me, smiled, and said hello before continuing as if I weren't some crazy person with three heads, which pretty much sums up the looks I get within the walls of Rosewood High.

Someone passed me a beer, and just like that I was accepted into their group. They didn't care that I didn't belong here, they didn't care I was a high school student, they just accepted me for who I was and it felt so fucking wonderful.

While Cody sat there with a bottle of water, I accepted bottle after bottle until the world around me started to spin a little. It was only a few moments after I realized that, that Cody suggested getting me home. I told him that I was capable of looking after myself if he wanted to drink with his friends, but he was adamant he make sure I was home safe. I refrained from pointing out that I felt safer down on the beach with him than I did being in that house. And I was only proved right when I walked down the hallway to find my fucking door missing.

Despite having zero privacy, I fall asleep miraculously early for the second night in a row. When I wake the next morning, the sun is streaming in through my open curtains and the door opposite mine is open, but the room is seemingly vacant.

Rolling over, I stretch out my limbs and glance over at the clock.

"Fuck." I sit upright, my heart pounding. I'm late. Really fucking late. Why didn't my alarm... "Motherfucker."

Jumping from the bed, I pull some clothes from the closet before turning to my underwear drawers.

My heart drops and my breath catches when I find them both empty. The only thing inside the drawer where my panties were is a folded piece of paper. Unfolding it, I stare down at his rough handwriting.

For easier access.

They're the same words he used to explain my missing door. Anger burns in my belly before it explodes to a raging inferno through my veins and pushes me forward.

I storm into his room and start pulling drawers open. If I don't have any, then I'll have to make do with his. I find a brand new pack of boxer briefs at the back of one of the drawers, and finding something else I can make use of on the top of the dresser, I swipe it off and take it all back to my room.

They're going to be huge on me, I already know that, so I throw my shorts back into my closet and pull out a baggy pair of jeans and a sports bra that I had in a different drawer, thank fuck.

I totally miss the first two classes of the day, so when I eventually walk down the hallway toward my locker, there are students in all directions, switching up books and having a quick chat with friends before the bell rings once again.

I make quick work of shoving the books I need in my bag before slamming the door closed and taking a step toward my next class.

The second I look up, I spot a familiar set of eyes staring at me, accomplishment filling his light blues and a smirk playing on his lips. Anger from finding my empty drawers explodes within me, and I storm over.

"What the fuck is your problem? Not content on driving me fucking crazy, now you've got to start stealing as well."

"Like I said, sweet cheeks. Easy access."

"Like I'm letting you anywhere near me again."

He smiles, reaching out for my wrist and pulling me up against him before I get a chance to jump away. His head lowers so he can whisper in my ear.

"The sound of you moaning my name last night is still loud and clear."

My core clenches as I remember his fingers stretching me open.

"And now you're remembering it. Your breaths are increasing..." He reaches out and pushes the hoodie I'm wearing open to reveal my sports bra covered tits. "And I know your nipples are hard for me."

Desperate to wrap the fabric tighter around my body, I lift my one free arm to do just so, but before I get a chance, we're moving.

"Ethan, what are you doing?" His grip on my wrist is painfully tight as he pulls me down the hallway toward a door I have no intention of going in.

"Ethan, no." I try fighting, but he well overpowers me. Slamming my free fist into his arm that's dragging me along does little to stop his progress.

"Fucking pain in my ass," he mutters before turning and lifting me. I'm none too gently thrown over his shoulder. I just about manage to keep hold of my bag as his arm wraps tightly around the back of my thighs. I kick my feet in protest but I'm no match for him.

"Put me the fuck down," I bark as he pushes the door open and the smell of sweaty boy hits me. Amazingly, when I lift my head from being forced to look at his ass, the room is empty.

"You might as well stop fighting. No one will come and rescue you, trailer trash."

"I don't need rescuing, asshole. I can look after myself."

"Is that right?" His voice is almost amused as he lowers me to my feet and pins both of my hands behind my back in one move. My bag drops to the floor with a crash, a few books sliding from it.

My chest heaves with the effort I put in trying to kick him when I was in the air.

"When are you going to learn, trash? I get what I want when I want."

"Oh yeah? Because from what I saw last night, you wanted something." I glance down at his crotch before crawling back up his jersey to his darkened eyes. "But you walked away when I told you to."

A laugh falls from his lips. If I were a weaker girl it might have me quivering, but all I do is angle my chin to him in defiance. "Don't mistake my actions last night for me walking away, sweet cheeks. I was merely..." He waves his free hand around as if he needs time to come up with the word, but I know it's all an act. He is totally in control right now, and he knows exactly what he's saying. "Building the anticipation," he drawls eventually.

"There's nothing to anticipate. Nothing will happen."

He smiles, his eyes dropping to my own lips before he sucks his bottom one into his mouth briefly. I know he's thinking about kissing me last night, and I'm about to taunt him with it when there's a noise behind us.

I'm moving before I have a chance to blink. Ethan drags me around a corner to the farthest part of the locker room, the showers. He backs me up against the tiled wall, pressing his hips into mine.

Footsteps get louder before someone shouts out, asking if there's anyone here. My lips part a second before Ethan's large palm presses down on my face to stop any words that might be about to crawl up my throat.

"Don't. Even. Think. About. It."

His eyes drill into mine as I fight to drag as much air as I need into my lungs.

My breaths were already coming out in fast pants before he half cut off my airways.

"Where's the little skirt today, huh? I was looking forward to watching you bend over in class."

"Fuck. You," I spit the second he releases me.

An evil smirk curls at his lips. Standing back, he pops the button of my jeans open. The fabric falls away enough to reveal what's beneath.

"Fucking bitch," he whispers, his hand coming up so his fingers thread into his hair and pull.

"What?" I ask innocently. "Mine seemed to have vanished, so I had to improvise. They're a little big, I must admit, but they're pretty comfortable."

His eyes are full of pent up anger when he lifts them from the floor to find mine. I swallow nervously and wait for what's about to hit me.

"First you steal my mother, then my home, my peace, my motherfucking sanity, and now this? My fucking underwear."

"You know full well that I didn't—argh," I squeal when his hand slams down beside me and the shower above sprays me with ice cold water.

He watches in delight as the water soaks me through. The loose strands of hair that were flying around my face immediately stick, and I don't need to look in the mirror to know my makeup is already starting to run down my cheeks.

"And you're the one who's worried about the fact his life's been ruined." I laugh, but any trace of amusement is long gone. "You're a fucking joke, you know that?" I take a step toward him, but not away from the water. "A fucking waste of—"

My words are cut off as he takes a huge step forward. His chest crashes into my sopping wet body until I hit the tiles behind me. His fingers grasp my chin and my head's tilted so I'm at the right angle for him to slam his lips down on mine. He immediately pushes his tongue into my mouth despite me refusing him entry. He strokes my tongue but still I refuse. My tightly balled fists lift and rain down fury on his chest, but he doesn't so much as flinch. In fact, he's so unaffected by the attempts to fight him off that his hand skims the wet skin of my stomach and is inside his boxers while I'm still hitting him.

"Give in, sweet cheeks. You know as well as I do that you're desperate for this."

I gasp when he finds my clit, giving him the access he needs to my mouth to really take what he wants.

"Fuck," he groans into our kiss when he finds what he was expecting. Me wet and ready for him. "You really love hating me, huh?" he whispers in my ear before sucking on the sensitive skin beneath.

Still the shower rains down on us, although at least the water is a little warmer now.

He circles my clit for a few more seconds, driving me higher and higher before dropping lower to find my entrance.

"Fuck. One day soon it's not going to be my fingers stretching you open."

"No, no," I chant but my argument is weak at best. We both know full well that no matter how much I might deny it, the thought alone has more moisture heading south.

"I'm going to fuck you like you've never been fucked before. I'm going to make you fucking raw. You'll regret the day you ever fucking walked into my life. I'm going to fuck you so fucking hard that you'll never forget exactly how I felt inside you. No one will ever compare. Ever."

"Oh god." His words are like fuel to the inferno ready to detonate inside me.

"You'll remember my cock for the rest of your days. Always wishing you had another chance." He changes the angle of his fingers as he says this, and I break. My muscles tense before the first wave of pleasure hits me. Ethan slams his lips back down on mine to swallow my loud cries, but, not wanting to appear like I've just allowed him to take exactly what he wants, I suck his bottom lip into my mouth and sink my teeth into the soft flesh.

"Fucking bitch." He releases me, his fingers coming up to his lips to check for blood while I rest back against the tiles, dripping wet and fighting to catch my breath.

His eyes hold mine, the promise he just made me adding an extra spark, and fuck if it doesn't make my core clench for what he was describing.

Thankfully the water's stopped, but every inch of me is soaking wet. There's no way I can go to class right now.

"Get out."

"Or what?" I sass. "You going to follow through on your promise? Right here, right now?"

"Don't fucking tempt me, trash."

Holding the sides of my wet hoodie out, I show him the skin I've got on display. "But I'm already wet."

"Shut up," he barks.

"What? You going weak on me now? You ain't all that, you know. You're all talk. I doubt you could fuck me into the next hour, let alone next week."

"I said, shut the fuck up." His hand wraps around my neck, and I'm forced back against the tiles with a loud bang.

When he speaks, his voice is menacingly quiet. "You will get what I promised you. But on my terms. When I want it. Not when you're offering it up right in front of me like a whore."

He pushes away from me, reaches behind his head and pulls his wet jersey from his body. His back ripples as he moves, and I find myself motionless as I watch the ink covering his shoulder blades twist and flex.

"Why are you still here?" He doesn't look back at me. Instead, he continues the job he started. His hands lift to undo the waist of the jeans, and when he comes to a stop beside a certain locker, he pushes them and his boxers down, exposing his peachy ass.

He bends slightly to attempt to get the wet fabric from his ankles, and it's then that I see the black ink on the underside of his butt cheek.

"What the fuck is that?" I don't mean for the words to come out loud, but before either of us register, I'm close enough behind him to see it in all its glory.

A laugh bubbles up from somewhere within me. I feel fucking schizophrenic with the way my moods swing around this asshole, but seeing the tattoo on his butt, there's nothing I can do but laugh.

"Is that a fucking teddy bear?"

He spins, his angry eyes finding mine, but unlike last night I'm unable to resist the ripped body before me. He looks powerful when he's dressed, but like this, he's a fucking god. Not that those words will ever pass my lips, of course.

"And fucking what?"

"N-nothing," I stutter, staring down at his solid length. The head is purple and angry, proving just how badly he needs to do those things he whispered in my ear not so long ago.

"Either put it in your fucking mouth or get the fuck out."

I bite down on my bottom lips as if I'm even considering it and I take a hesitant step toward him.

"As tempting as that is, *Teddy*, I'm afraid it's a hard pass for me."

"Then why. Are. You. Still. Fucking. Here?" He's right on the edge of his control. I can see it in his eyes, and I've no doubt that if I hang around for even a minute longer, then I'm going to find myself in a position I've no intention of being in.

"I'm sure there's a cheer slut hanging around somewhere just desperate to gag themselves silly on that."

"GET OUT." His shout echoes off the walls around us, and it successfully gets me moving. I run over to where my bag and books are on the floor, gather them up, and head for the door. All the while, his eyes burn into my back.

Pushing the door open, I look back at him. He doesn't so much as flinch, knowing anyone could walk down the hallway and see him stark naked, but then I guess when you're as big a whore as Ethan Savage, most of the school's already seen your junk, so it really doesn't matter.

I nod once before disappearing from his sight and dragging in the first real breath of air I have since I locked eyes on him not so long ago.

"**F**uck," I bellow as the door bounces shut. Turning, I bury my fist into the locker beside mine.

What the fuck was I thinking, dragging her ass in here. *You knew she wasn't wearing any panties,* a little voice says, breaking through the haze of anger and desire that's clouding my head.

"Fuck. Fuck. Fuck." The skin covering my knuckles splits, but I welcome the pain. It's a needed relief from the lead weight that seems to fill my entire body these days.

My banging must disturb Coach, because seconds later I sense him appear behind me.

"Get dressed, son. I think we need to have a chat, don't you?"

My head hangs between my shoulders. Disappointment comes off him in waves that I'm in here fucking up his lockers instead of being in class.

"Just give me a minute, yeah?" My voice is rough and barely sounds like my own, even to my own ears.

"Two. You can have two."

Yanking my locker open, I drag out a dry set of clothes and tug them on. I run my fingers through my wet hair, pushing it back from my face, and with one loud slam of my locker door, I head toward Coach's office.

He's staring down at a clipboard with some plays drawn out on them, but despite my arrival, he doesn't look up. He just continues tapping his pencil against the plastic, seemingly deep in thought.

Coach is scary. He's intimidating, larger than life, and now, the only man I look up to. He's terrifying when he rips you a new one, but his silence is a million times worse than that. My stomach twists as I wait for him to acknowledge me.

"I'm ready when you are, son." Still, he doesn't look up.

I blow out a long breath, trying to figure out where to even start. Coach already knows the basics of what's happened, he knows I'm struggling, but fuck, putting this into words is harder than I thought it would be.

"I'm sorry, Coach. *He's* just fucked with my head. I'm so fucking angry all the fucking time."

"I get that, Ethan. I really do. But there's more to this than just your father. Tell me what's really going on." He sits back in his chair and finally looks up at me.

"He's moved her in. Her daughter too."

Coach lets out a breath. "Raelynn?"

My eyes narrow. "You knew?"

"Of course. Not much happens under this roof that involves my boys that I don't know."

I nod. It's all I can do. It's not the first time something like this has happened.

"She giving you grief?"

"No," I answer honestly. "The issue is all mine."

"As I assumed, seeing as she's started here and kept her head down. All the while you are spiraling out of control. Where is your father?"

I shrug. I thought they were supposed to be back by now, but as usual, he just does what he likes. It was always Mom who'd call or text to let me know what they were doing and when they'd likely be home, but now, I guess it'll all just be a guessing game.

"Okay, so let me tell you what needs to happen." He leans forward and places his elbows on his desk as he stares daggers into me. "You need to focus, get your head in the game. Forget her, forget him. This is about you and your future. We win these playoffs and any college who knows their shit will want you. Three games, Ethan. You've got to keep your head for three more games. Hell knows I already lost Thorn to a skirt, Paine too if he manages to get back on the field. I need my best safety fully on board. You got that?"

"Yes, Coach."

"I'm sorry. I didn't catch that."

I lift my chin. "Yes, Coach," I shout, my deep voice echoing off his walls.

"Good, now get your ass to class. And if I so much as find you in here when you should be elsewhere, alone or not," his eyes narrow, telling me that he knows more than he's letting on right now, "then so help me God."

Rising from the chair, I walk toward his door.

"Ethan."

"Yeah, Coach?"

"Make your mamma proud, son."

Emotion clogs my throat. Unable to swallow it down so that I can respond, I nod my head and leave his office.

The temptation to march right out of school and attempt to forget this day ever happened is high, but I've already fucked up twice now this week. I don't need any more reasons for Coach to ride my ass before our first game on Friday night. So instead of walking out, I stop at my locker, grab my shit, and head to class.

The second I step into the room, all eyes turn on me. I ignore the teacher, who barks something at me about my timekeeping before walking toward the back and my seat that's waiting for me beside Jake. I pass another empty desk, but it doesn't register. I'm too distracted by the look on Jake's face.

"Where the fuck have you been, and why is your fucking hair wet?"

"Don't ask," I mutter, pulling my books out and none too quietly dropping them to the desk.

"Don't tell me, it has something to do with that other empty desk."

I shrug. "How should I know?"

"Don't bullshit me, Savage. I can see exactly what is going on. You hate her. I get that, more than most. But don't pull the same shit I did to try to deal with it."

"This isn't the same." His comparison of this situation with his and Amalie's pisses me off.

"Fine, okay. But let me just say this one thing..." He stares daggers into me until I've no choice but to turn to look at him. "Amalie is the best fucking thing that ever happened to me, and I could have very easily ruined it before it even started because of my stupidity and misplaced anger. She's innocent in all this, just like you are. Maybe you're not destined for anything together, maybe you're right. But she could be a friend, your sister. Don't fuck it up, whatever your relationship could turn out to be."

My breath catches as his words hit a little too close to home. "You know. I think I liked you better when you were an asshole."

His laughter floats around me before the teacher stops whatever it is she's talking about to ask if we're listening. I just about refrain from replying with 'does it fucking look like it?'

The rest of the day fucking drags. The only good thing about it is that I don't see her again. It almost means I can lock down the memory of her in the locker room as if it didn't exist.

I'm getting changed for practice when my cell rings. Dragging it from my pocket, I find my dad's name illuminating the screen.

My thumb hovers over the answer button.

"Just do it," Jake mutters over my shoulder.

Blowing out a breath, my lips press into a thin line and I swipe and put it to my ear.

"Yeah," I bark.

"I just received a call from the bank questioning a transaction made this afternoon in the mall. Victoria's Secret was one of the shops mentioned. They flagged it as unusual and wanted to know if something untoward was going on." The fact that he doesn't even say hello or ask how I am isn't lost on me.

"I'm in school. I haven't been shopping in—" My words falter. Trailer trash hasn't been seen since leaving the room I'm standing in right now. I rummage through my bag, find my wallet and flip it open. No credit card.

Bitch.

"Actually, no. It's fine. It was... Rae." Her name sounds weird falling from my lips. It's not lost on me that I've not yet used it, but there was something about her having an actual name that meant she was real and not just some part of my fucked-up imagination.

"Rae went shopping in the mall with your credit card when she should be in school? What the hell is going on, Ethan? And why wasn't she using her own card?"

"Nothing. It's fine. She just had a wardrobe issue, and I don't know. Maybe she thought mine was hers, I don't know," I ramble, just wishing he'd get off the phone. This is the reason she used mine, so I would get this phone call and have to explain myself.

"Did it burn down or something? She's spent a hell of a lot this afternoon."

"Yeah, something like that. It's fine, don't worry."

"Okay well... make sure she's back in school tomorrow," he demands like it's my fucking job to parent the girl who's the same age as me.

"Whatever." Pulling the phone from my ear, I end the call and throw it into my bag.

"Everything okay?" Jake asks, but I barely register his question. My imagination is too busy running away with itself. *She spent all afternoon in Victoria's Secret.* My mouth waters and my cock begins to stir to life. I wonder what I'm going to find when she gets home from work tonight?

Easy access is one thing, but her curvy little body wrapped in lace... *Fuck.* My temperature soars at the thought alone. The image of her bent over with his ass on display, lingerie still in place as I slam into her fills my head and won't abate.

"Ethan?" It sounds like it's being shouted down a tunnel, but a quick slap to my head brings me back to reality.

"Get your fucking head together. Two days until this game, man. I need to be able to rely on you."

"We've got this, cap. Come on."

I make quick work of changing and head out onto the field for Coach to put us through our drills. He nods at me as I jog toward him, but I don't respond. I just get to work. I need the burn that only he can deliver if I'm ever going to successfully get that image out of my head.

———

My evening drags. I refuse the offer of heading to Aces, knowing that she'd be there working with fuck only knows what under her clothes. Instead, I head home, eat the food that Rachel's prepped for me and hang out in my den watching TV and attempting to do some homework. I'm not very successful at either and keep finding myself staring into space with only one thing on my mind. I know it's been a while since I got laid, but fuck. The permanent hard-on I seem to be walking around with isn't fucking necessary. I consider calling up Shelly or one of the other girls to come and relieve my situation, but the thought really doesn't appeal. The idea of someone else's mouth, on the other hand, I'm very interested in.

Pushing up from the couch ten minutes before I'm expecting his car to pull up on the drive to deliver her home—that's assuming she doesn't go out drinking with him again—I make my way up the stairs and into her room. I feel much less like I'm breaking and entering without there being an actual door to open.

The second I step inside, her scent assaults me and my mouth waters as I remember just how she tasted on my tongue last night.

Looking around, I find her diaries have vanished from the nightstand. Assuming they haven't gone far, I start opening the few pieces of furniture in here until I find them stacked neatly in the ottoman.

I pull out the same one I had the other day. I just lie back on her bed and flip it open when the front door slams.

Excitement fills my stomach as I wait for her to find me. She'll be pissed that I'm here again. Good. I want her fired up. She's more fun when she is.

21

RAELYNN

"Fucking hell, Ethan," I shriek, turning the corner to my room and finding him getting comfortable on my bed. "Get out," I mutter, my long-ass day getting the better of me. I've no idea why I'm so tired seeing as I've slept well the past two nights, which is something that hasn't happened in... forever.

"No fucking chance. I was just getting to a good part." Glancing up, I see what's in his hands that I missed when I first walked in and panic.

"How'd you find that?"

"You didn't exactly hide it, did you?"

"Where was I? Oh here... *Mom's sick, so Kurt took me out for the day so she could rest. He promised me a fun day, but I didn't think in a million years that it would have been as fun as it was. He took me ice skating. Mom's always refused, telling me she's scared, but I've wanted to go forever and now I have. It was awesome. Then we went for pizza and ice cream. It was the best day. Kurt is by far the best boyfriend Mom has had. I hope things work out for them. I can imagine him being my stepdad one day. Aww, how cute.*"

I have to fight like hell to keep my body from visibly shaking as he takes me back to that time.

Mustering up the courage to speak in the hope that it'll stop him from reading further, I storm over, dumping my bags on the bed as I do. "Enough," I bark, leaning forward to snatch the diary from his hands. But he sees it coming and moves it away before I get a chance to get my fingers on it.

"Ohhh... someone's got their panties in a twist. You'd better be careful with them, seeing as you maxed out my credit card buying them."

My mouth drops open. I knew he'd find out. Hoped he would, actually. But I wasn't expecting it to happen quite that quickly.

"Wondering how I know?"

"Don't care," I mutter, turning my back on him and kicking my shoes off.

"My dad called," he starts, disregarding my comment. "The bank called him about unusual activity on my card. Wanted to know why I was buying women's underwear instead of being in school."

I'm glad I've got my back to him, because I know guilt is written all over my face. I didn't want to spend Eric's money, but the second I saw his card sitting on his dresser this morning after discovering my missing underwear, I couldn't resist. At the end of the day, it might be Eric's money, but it was Ethan's allowance I was splashing on the most insanely expensive underwear I've ever seen, let alone purchased.

After walking out of school I continued with no destination in mind. When I came across a bus stop, I got on and just let it take me wherever while I stared at the passing scenery.

Everything was like a blur as I sat there, and that was fine by me. I needed to forget everything about this day that was entirely fucked-up from the moment I woke up late and discovered my missing underwear. But the second I saw that we'd pulled up to a mall, the stolen card started burning in my pocket and I was powerless but to walk toward the shops. I didn't intend to spend much, just buy some cheap underwear to tide me over until the asshole gave mine back, or I found it. But when the first shop I came across was Victoria's Secret, a wicked smile spread across my lips and I couldn't help myself.

"Yeah, well. If his asshole son hadn't stolen everything I own, then it wouldn't have needed replacing, would it?"

Thankfully, when I turn around, he's closed and lowered my diary to the bed, his focus solely on me.

"So..." he says, flicking his eyes to the bags.

"So what?" My eyes roll in frustration. All I want to do is have a shower and get started on my homework, not have to deal with his bullshit.

"I want to see what *I* bought."

"You want to see my new underwear." *Of course he fucking does. Creep.* "Why? So you know what you're stealing next time?"

"No because it's from Victoria's Secret and it's probably hot. I might even make you do a little fashion show for me."

"Make me?" I ask, my voice raising an octave in shock. "I hate to burst your little bubble there, hotshot. But you can't make me do anything."

"Now, that's where you're wrong, sweet cheeks." His voice drops as he says my one of many nicknames, and fuck if it doesn't make things flutter down south. "I can make you do a lot of things." He scoots to the end of the bed, his eyes roaming over my body. "One." He lifts his fingers to start counting, making me want to snap each one off. "I can make you want me. Two. I can make you scream my name when you come." My cheeks heat and I pray that he's too consumed with my curves to notice. "And three. I can make you beg for more."

"No fucking chance."

"You want to bet?"

I laugh. "No. I really don't want to make a fucking bet with you."

"Why? Are you afraid you'll lose?"

"No chance. I never lose."

"Well then it looks like we might have an issue." He stands from the bed and stalks over. "Because I also never lose."

My heart picks up speed at his closeness, the heat from his chest seeping into mine and making my nipples pucker. His hand lifts to the zipper on my hoodie, and he slowly pulls it down.

"F-fine. W-what is it?" I stutter as he parts the fabric to reveal my sports bra clad torso beneath. Although the way he's looking at my chest, you'd think I was naked. I regret the question the second it falls from my lips, but the moment his dark, hungry and angry eyes meet mine, I know I've made a huge mistake.

"I make you beg for more, and you get on your knees and give *me* more."

"There's something fucking wrong with you." Somehow, I manage to sidestep him and escape to the other side of the room until I'm in front of the doors.

"Many, many things, sweet cheeks. But right now, my problem is simple." I keep my back to him, looking out over the view across the beach and to the ocean that's the other side of the balcony.

His heat presses to my back, the hard ridge of his erection pressing into my ass and making me bite down on my bottom lip as a wave of desire so strong washes through me. I hate him, he's an asshole. His closeness shouldn't affect me like this.

He pushes us both forward until we're on the balcony and looking out over the view.

"You think anyone down there can see us?"

I look to the people he's talking about on the beach who are only illuminated by the bright moonlight and gasp as his calloused fingers trail down the soft skin of my stomach.

"We can see them, can't we? So there's no reason why they can't see us." I would imagine the fact that we're backlit from the light in my bedroom only makes us more visible to them. A shudder runs through me at being watched, but I'm afraid to accept that it's excitement, not the fear I should feel.

"Hmm..." The vibrations from his low moan seeps into my back. "That's what I was thinking. I was also wondering if they'd like a little show."

"Ethan." His name is meant to be a warning, but it sounds anything but.

"I can already taste this win. You're already moaning my name." His fingers tease across the waistband of my jeans before he pops the button and tucks them inside. "What happened to my boxers?" he asks when he finds the soft lace of my new panties.

"Burned them," I say between heaving breaths.

"Fuck," he groans before pushing deeper inside my panties until his fingers part me and find my sensitive nub.

I need to tell him to stop, to push his hand away. Anyone could look up here and find us in this position.

"Ethan, no." My argument is weak at best as he begins to circle my clit. My fingers wrap around his muscular forearm with the intention of pulling it from my body, but he presses a little harder, my body sagging against him as the pleasure races through me.

"You need to get out of my room." My voice is barely above a whisper and a far cry from the demand I was hoping.

"Is that right? So what I'm doing right now, with those people down there potentially watching, isn't turning you the fuck on?"

I shake my head against his chest, the only argument I have.

"That's weird, because what I'm feeling is very different. You're wet as fuck right now, sweet cheeks. And those down there," he threads his fingers into the back of my hair with his free hand and forces me to look down at the beach, "they're fucking loving it. Actually, I bet they're down there begging for more. You want to give it to them?"

"Ethan."

"Oh, baby. You've no idea what your begging voice does to me. You feel that?" he asks, thrusting his hips to ensure his solid cock presses into me. "It makes me hard as fuck just thinking about how hot that little mouth of yours is."

Oh fuck. My core clenches to feel something inside, his punishment on my clit not enough. But the second I start to think he's going to give me more, he removes his hand from me. My muscles go lax, and if it weren't for him at my back, I might fall to the floor.

"Nooo," I cry, immediately missing his attention.

His fingers grasp the shoulders of my hoodie, and in a blink, it's thrown back into the room somewhere.

"You think they want to see your tits?" he groans in my ear.

I shake my head, my panties impossibly damp at the thought, but it doesn't stop him. His fingers pinch the zip at the front of my top and slowly, so fucking slowly, he pulls it down until it releases my breasts. They were already swollen and desperate for his touch, but the second the cool breeze brushes over them, my nipples pebble and my back arches in the hope of more.

"You fucking love this, don't you, sweet cheeks? You like being put on display, being pushed to do something so sordid." His words dig up a memory that I spend months—no, years—trying to bury. The grip of the vivid flashback to someone else's words almost engulfs me, but as if he knows what I need, his warm palms cup my breasts and squeezes, bringing me back to the here and now.

I lean back harder into him and he palms them and pinches my nipples so tightly that a bolt of lust shoots straight to my core.

"You think all the guys down there are hard, watching me play with your tits?"

A low groan rumbles up my throat, my only answer to his question as my head rolls back on his shoulder, my eyes falling closed with the pleasure.

"Eyes open. I want you to watch them watch you."

In reality, everyone seems to be going about whatever it is they're doing down there, and although they can probably see our figures, I doubt they can see what we're doing or the fact that I'm topless.

"You want more, sweet cheeks?"

A "yes" falls from my lips before I even realize I've said it, my body so desperate for the release he can give me now he's started.

His hands leave my breasts in favor of my jeans. They're pushed from my hips, and in seconds they're pooled at my ankles. Ethan demands I step out of them before kicking them back into the room.

"Nice choice," he says, running his finger over the delicate lace of the G-string I'm wearing. "Did you know that red's my favorite color?"

I shake my head, although seeing as the school and his team play in red, it was a good guess that he'd like it. Not that that was why I bought it of course. *Bullshit,* a little voice screams in my head.

His hands stop on my hips, and I'm spun and pushed up against the railing. The cold bites into my bare ass, but I don't have time to think about it because the darkness in Ethan's eyes captures my attention. He looks wild. I've no idea if he's been drinking tonight. I can't smell it on him, that's for sure, but he looks like a man possessed. I wonder if it's desire or just pure hate that's running through him.

For the first time tonight, a slither of fear creeps in. Is he going to take this too far? Force me to do something that I'm not ready for? This game we've been playing, this push and pull is fun and all, but I'm very aware that it could turn into something very ugly very quickly, and if that happens then I'm afraid to consider the fact that he really could shatter me. He could drag me back to my past, and I'm not sure how I'd manage to get myself out of that dark hole I was once in. Especially while under the same roof as him.

His eyes bounce between mine, and for the briefest moment, I see something else in them. Something more than just the desire and anger. Something deeper. Something painful, and it's that I latch onto. He's acting out, trying to prove he has power over this house and the things that happen inside it, but deep down, his actions are coming from his pain over what's been forced on him. I get that. I understand that burning anger for something you have no control over. It's probably the reason I've allowed things to go as far as they have between us. The reason why I'm once again standing basically naked in front of him, giving him everything—or almost everything—he wants because I see more. I see deeper, and he fucking hates it.

No sooner has it appeared does it disappear, and his eyes harden once again before dropping to my heaving chest.

"Well, sweet cheeks. That's one sweet show you're giving those people down there."

I swallow my nerves as he takes a step toward me.

"You want to give them the finale?"

I swallow loudly and his eyes flick up to mine. They hold for a beat, and I swear he can see my fear for what comes next.

I'm out here, naked for all intents and purposes, and totally at his mercy. I could scream, but really, no one would hear it. He can do—take—whatever he wants right now, and as much as my body might be desperate for what he can give, I'm not sure it's worth it.

"Jump up," he demands. His eyes flick to where my palms are resting on the wide stone barrier that's stopping me from falling to the pool area below.

"Uh..."

"Do. It." He steps closer, looks at me from under his lashes, and helps me out by lifting my small frame from the floor.

I'm perched on the balcony. One wrong move and I'll end up a broken, probably dead, mess on the tiles below. My eyes hold his, too afraid to look around. Certainly too afraid to look down.

"I read something somewhere that fear only makes the pleasure better, more intense." A wicked smile curls at his lips and he leans around me to look at the ground below. "That's a long way down. Are you scared, sweet cheeks?"

I shake my head. In reality, I'm pretty terrified right now but have no idea if it's from possibly falling to my death or of him.

"Do you trust me?"

Again, the only thing I do is shake my head.

He laughs. It's deep and evil, and has a ripple of panic running through me.

"Wise. Very wise."

He pushes my thighs apart and stands between them. His own chest is heaving much like mine although covered in fabric.

"So what happens next then, eh?" Our eyes hold but no words form. "Are you going to give me what I want and beg? Or are you going to defy me, again?"

I tilt my head to the side slightly as if to say, try me. But I don't think he reads the move in the way I intend it, because he uses my angle to slam his lips to mine and force his tongue into my mouth. His hands slide down my bare back, goosebumps erupting in their wake as he drags my ass to the edge so he can press my core to his hard cock.

"Oh fuck," I moan, my head falling back. Pleasure takes over my fear as he rubs himself against me. His hardness and the roughness of the lace against my soft skin are too much to bear.

"Don't forget to hold on. I'd hate to have to clean up the mess when you hit the ground."

"Fuck you," I spit, suddenly finding my fire.

"Ah, so you're still in there then. I thought you were being too compliant." My teeth grind at his statement. Doesn't he realize how hard it is to keep my head on straight when his hands are on me? *Of course he does, it's why you keep ending up in this situation.*

I open my mouth to spit back some cutting remark about him being power mad, but he lowers his head and his lips wrap around my nipple. All thoughts leave my head in favor of feeling.

When he has his hands—or mouth—on me, all the voices in my head vanish. It's fucking addictive, which is why I'm here right now riding the very possibility of imminent death while desperately craving the lightness only Ethan can provide me with. My past vanishes, my present disappears, and I'm just a body craving release. We're just two people giving each other what we need to escape our reality. It's in that moment that I wonder if I should stop denying him more and allow him the same emptiness he must crave as much as me. If I can give him the same thing, would it make him easier to live with? Would he let up a little?

I don't get to dwell on those questions for too long, because he starts descending down my stomach. His fingers grip onto the lace of my panties and tug. I'm so lost to what he's about to do that I don't even chastise him for ruining them.

"I suggest you hold the fuck on if you want to see tomorrow," is his only warning before his fingers part me and he licks at my clit.

With the angle I'm at, I get to see everything. Every leisurely lick of his tongue against me, every time he grazes his teeth against my clit before he sucks it deep into his mouth and makes me cry out his name. I get to watch as he pushes one, and then two, fingers inside me. And I get a first look at my wetness covering his face when he pulls back to drag in some much-needed air.

When our eyes lock, I forget everything. Who we are, where we are, why I hate him so fucking much. The only thing I can think about is how much I need him to continue, how I need this and so much more from him. It's fucking dizzying how badly I need him right now and although I hate to admit it, let alone accept it, words start tumbling from my lips.

"Ethan, please." I'm desperate to reach out, thread my fingers in his hair and drag him back to me, but I daren't move my hand from holding me up. "Ethan," I moan, flexing my hips a little in the hope that it'll entice him back.

"What is it you want, sweet cheeks?" He's sitting back on his haunches, his eyes following his fingers, teasing a trail over my heated skin.

"You," I moan.

"Me what?"

"Y-your tongue. Your fingers. Please, Ethan. Please."

"Is that you begging for me, baby?" The achievement on his face doesn't even register as he keeps me on the edge of earth-shattering pleasure with his slow movements and deep plunges of his fingers.

"It's whatever it is to get your face back between my legs. Argh, shit, Fuck," I bark when he dives in.

I chant, scream, cry his name and many more things I'm sure as he pushes me toward the edge. I'm just about to crash when he stands, pulls me into his arms, wraps my legs around his waist and carries me into my bedroom.

I'm dropped to the bed only a second before my legs are parted once again and he's continuing his previous actions. Only this time he doesn't let up until I crash. And do I fucking crash. My entire body locks up as my release slams into me. I twitch and convulse on the bed, but Ethan doesn't stop. He doesn't pull back until I've ridden out every last second of pleasure.

He sits back, his finger still teasing me, sending aftershocks shooting around my body, his eyes locked on my pussy.

Once I regain the control of my limbs, I prop myself up on my elbows.

I expect him to immediately claim his prize for winning our stupid little bet. But instead, he's sitting there staring at me like he's lost in a daze.

"E-Ethan? A-are you—?"

Abruptly he stands, his hands lifting to his hair before he starts backing away from me.

My body fills with ice the second he moves away. Did I do something wrong? He seemed to be totally enjoying himself down there. Why's he freaking out?

He lifts his eyes. Our connection holds, desire crackling between us as I wait for him to come back and take what I now owe him. But he ever does.

He opens his mouth and closes it so many times to say something that eventually I lose count. The silence drags out between us, the only thing that can be heard our increased breathing, before he eventually pulls his thoughts together and speaks.

"You're ruining my fucking life." And then he's gone. He leaves my room and, soon after, the house.

22

ETHAN

Unable to stay in the same house, I head straight for the stairs and climb into my car. I've got the engine on and I'm backing out of the driveway before my brain's caught up with my body.

It's late, I've got nowhere to go, but fuck, anywhere is better than being in that house with her.

My hands tremble as I drive. I squeeze the wheel in the hope it'll make it abate, but nothing helps. The image of her laid out before me totally naked and at my mercy is burned onto the back of my eyes, and no matter how fast I drive, no matter how recklessly I take the turns, it won't fucking leave.

Eventually I pull up in the deserted parking lot beside Aces. I park so I can stare out over the beach and the calm sea beyond, hoping that the solitude will help clear my head, but it does fuck all.

I've no idea how long I sit there for. All I know is that it's too late to turn up on anyone's doorstep when I do leave. It doesn't stop me though.

I forgo going to Mason. He's still living with the Lopezes, and I doubt they'd be too pleased with a midnight visitor, so I go to the only other place I possibly can. Jake's.

As expected, the house where he lives is in darkness. I pull up on the street as I usually would and make my way around the house to his trailer at the bottom of the garden. I might think he's crazy to even consider moving in with Amalie, but one look at his dingy trailer and I realize why he's agreed. No one deserves to live in this shithole. We should all be grateful for Amalie for giving him a lifeline and being willing to help make his existence that much better. He's been screwed over from every angle all his life, it's about time he experienced some happiness.

His trailer is also in silence. I'm grateful it's not rocking, not that that would have stopped me letting myself in.

I flip the light on and I'm rummaging around his mostly empty fridge in the hope of finding a beer when footsteps make their way down to me.

"What do you—" Jake barks, probably assuming it's a burglar. Not that any burglar in their right mind would rob this place. "Ethan? What the fuck?"

I look over my shoulder to find him standing in only his boxers, his hair messed from sleep, although if Amalie's shoes by the door are anything to go by, I wonder if she had something to do with the state of him. I'm suddenly assaulted with the image I left behind. I could look like Jake right now, thoroughly fucked and sated, yet here I am, frustrated as fuck with the bluest balls known to man.

"Sorry, I needed somewhere to crash. You got any beer?" I ask, giving up on my hunt, shutting the fridge and turning to him.

"Your house not adequate enough? And no, it's game week. No beer. No weed. No—"

"Sex not on the banned list, I assume," I interrupt. The fucker doesn't even bother to hide his smugness.

"If you had a hot girl beside you every night, would you give it up?" His brow arches as if he really needs an answer.

"Fuck no. But you're our captain. We need you fully focused," I tease.

"I am. I'm fully focused on the game and fucking my girl into next week. Now, as nice as this little visit is, why the fuck are you here?"

"I needed to get out."

"Why? Your pare—dad back?" He catches himself at the last minute. The reminder of how much my life has changed in what feels like only a matter of days slams into me.

I stumble back with only a fucking bottle of water in my hand and fall down onto his sofa.

"No."

"So... oh," he sings as realization hits him. "What's happened?"

"Nothing."

"Okay," he drawls. "So really I should be asking what you've done." He sits on the other side of the couch, rests his elbows on his knees and looks at me, and I mean really looks at me.

"I..." I fall back and scrub my hands down my face. "Nothing. I've done nothing."

"Well that's bullshit, and you know it." The fucker has the audacity to actually fucking laugh. "You fucked her?"

"What? No. Of course I haven't fucked her." It's the truth, but fuck if it doesn't feel like I'm lying to one of my best friends.

"But you want to."

"No," I bark way too quickly and defensively. "I fucking hate her. Okay. That's it. She's in my house, in my life, in my face, and she needs to fuck off."

"Riiiightt."

"She doesn't belong there. They both need to fuck off, and my mom needs to come back."

"It sucks, man. I get it. Family shit is, ugh... a fucking nightmare. Relationships are complicated, and although I'm in no way condoning what your dad did, clearly there had been issues with him and your mom for him to do that. You know better than I do that he's always been loyal, always respectful. It's out of character for him, so there's clearly shit you don't know about. But ultimately what happened between them is exactly that: between them. What you need to focus on is them both finding happiness again, and if that needs to be apart and with other people, then so be it."

"Fucking hell, bro. When did you get so fucking deep with advice?"

"Having a family like mine puts things into perspective," he mutters. "You need to stop worrying about your parents. You'll be off at college soon, not giving two shits what they're up to or who they're fucking." I wince and he laughs. "Focus on you, not them. Focus on our final games, on your grades, on college. What the fuck ever. Just leave her the fuck alone. She's not worth fucking up your senior year over."

"Isn't she?" I mutter, and a shit-eating grin spreads across his face. Motherfucker.

"I don't know, Savage. I don't know her. But you do, and better than you're willing to admit, I'm thinking, if you're being here in the middle of the night is anything to go by."

"Fuck you."

"Nah, save it for your girl."

"My wha—no. Fucking no. I hate her."

"I know. I get it, I really do. I hated Amalie, remember." He looks to where I assume she is sleeping in his bed, and his eyes go all soft and glassy.

"You're so fucking whipped, man."

He shrugs. "Trust me, there are worse issues to have."

Silence falls around us. He continues staring at me as if I'm about to have some big epiphany while his words roll around in my head. I can't deny that some of his advice makes a lot of sense, not that I'm going to tell him that.

"So are you going to sleep here and let it spin around your head all night, or are you going home... *to her*?"

The image of her laid out before me hits me once again, along with the feeling that filled me in that moment. Since the day I learned of her existence and arrival in my life, I've needed to hurt her. Needed to prove to her just how badly she's fucking my life up. But in that moment, after she'd been begging for me to make her come, just like I told her she would, all I could think was that I needed her. I didn't need to hurt her, or teach her a lesson. I just needed her, and that was scary as fuck. She might have owed me a blowjob but like fuck was I taking it from her when I needed her. I'm taking when I need to hurt her, prove to her who's in control of this thing between us. I can't let the lines blur. She's my plaything. My ragdoll to tempt and tease when I so desire. She has no control in this situation. None. Zero. *So why do you want to go and crawl into her bed to feel her against you again?*

"Motherfucker," I shout.

"Keep your fucking voice down. You think I'm good with advice? You wake Brit and she'll give it to you all fucking night."

"Oh yeah?" I ask, my eyebrows wiggling suggestively.

"You want me to fucking hit you?"

"I'd like to see you try."

It's in that moment when we're staring each other down that a figure appears in the doorway, clad in only one of Jake's jerseys and looking as happy as Jake was when I first arrived.

"You two need sleep. Your game is only hours away."

"Two days," I argue, and she narrows her eyes at me.

"Jake?" She holds her hand out, and the pussy-whipped motherfucker immediately gets up and walks over.

I'm still shaking my head at him when he looks back over his shoulder. "Listen to the master, Savage. There's no hotter sex than with someone you think you hate. Maybe you should give it a try."

My teeth grind, but any argument I might have dies on my tongue because I already know from the tastes I've had that it will be fucking mind-blowing. She's feisty, brave, unbreakable when she's clothed. But strip her bare and there's an innocence about her that I'm not sure she realizes comes off her in waves, and it's so fucking sexy.

Fuck.

———

I end up crashing on Jake's couch. Thank fuck they both go back to bed and seemingly go back to sleep, the last thing I needed was to lie there listening to them have a fuck fest and reminding me what I potentially walked away from.

Jake has me awake at the crack of dawn so he can get a quick workout in before our morning practice, crazy motherfucker.

Reluctantly, I head home to change and grab my stuff. My heart's in my fucking throat as I climb the stairs and prepare to look into her wide, dark eyes once again, but to my utter shock, when I get to her room, her bed is made and she's nowhere to be seen.

A mixture of relief and disappointment hits me, and I fight to keep the latter at bay. There's no way I should be disappointed about not seeing her. I should be glad.

I have a quick shower, drag on some clean clothes and head for school, ready for Coach to put us through our drills for the first time today.

Her bedroom taunts me as I make my way back downstairs, and I start to wonder if taking the fucking door off was the stupidest thing I've ever done. For easy access, I said. But fuck, easy access to her has only led to my head being even more fucked-up.

Trying to push her to the back of my mind, I make my way to school via a protein shake from the kitchen and focus on the task in hand. Friday night's game. Coach deserves for me to be on the ball—hell, Jake and the rest of the team deserve it. We've worked fucking hard for his opportunity, I'm not going to let 'a bit of skirt,' as Coach would put it, distract me from my main goal: seeing Jake lift that motherfucking trophy.

I don't see her all day. By some miracle, she's not in any of my classes, and she must avoid the cafeteria at lunch because every time I casually look around I don't spot her. It's a relief, don't get me wrong, but there's this little nagging part of me that wants to know she's okay. That she's not as fucked-up as me after last night.

It was fucking hot though... my mind starts drifting over the events on her balcony the night before while I sit in last period. Watching her come undone and knowing we could have had an audience was a huge fucking turn on.

I shift in my seat, rearranging myself.

"Get her out of your head, bro," Jake warns, leaning over and winking at me. Motherfucker.

"She doesn't exist."

"Right," he says with a laugh. "That's why you're squirming around like a bitch in heat."

"Shut the fuck up."

"Focus, remember. F-O-C-U-S," he says slowly, enunciating each letter.

I flip him off, but right at the same second our teacher turns around and stops what he's explaining to rip me a new one. Fucking great.

Practice is fucking painful but no less than I expected, and before I know it, I'm dragging my ass back up the stairs toward my bedroom. One look at her still empty and open bedroom and I know what I need to do.

After dumping my stuff, I eat the fish that Rachel left and then I go and find her door that I dumped in the garage. I make quick work of putting it back on. Fuck easy access, what I need is to stay away from temptation. Nothing good can come of things going any further between us, so I need to put a barrier up.

I'm aching like a motherfucker by the time I take the tool bag back to the garage. The sight of the water glistening in the garden catches my eye, and the relief of the jacuzzi becomes too much to resist.

I strip down to nothing, not having the energy or the care to head back upstairs for some swim shorts, and I lower myself into the soothing water. This is my fucking house and no one is home, so I tell myself that I can do as I fucking please.

I twist the top off the bottle of water I brought out with me and drink down half before resting my head back and allowing the bubbles to take away the ache in my muscles.

It's not until I hear a bang that I realize I must have fallen asleep. I sit up with a start, my heart racing as I try to figure out if I'd managed to drown myself or not, but thankfully my head's still above water and aside from the moon and stars twinkling brightly above me, everything else is the same.

I rest my head back once again and stare at the stars.

Focus, Ethan. Focus on the game. Block everything else out.

Movement above me catches my eyes before she rests her arms on the railing of her balcony and looks out over the beach beyond. My cock immediately hardens as I think about what the view from down here might have been like this time last night.

Reaching down, I take my length in my hand. I've resisted this long, but my need for release is becoming too much and I've told myself time and time again today that she won't be the one relieving it.

I keep my eyes on her, wondering if she's reliving last night once more as well. What I wouldn't give to know her thoughts right about now. *I wonder if she'll write them in her diary.*

My hips thrust up as I remember just how she tasted last night, just how tightly she squeezed my fingers when she came. My grip tightens as I near the end, a low moan ripping from my throat. She turns as the noise hits her, and she finds me immediately. Her mouth parts as her eyes drop to the water. The bubbles finished long ago, and I have no clue if she can see exactly what I'm doing or not, but I'm so close to the end that I really don't give a fuck. With her eyes back on mine, my balls drag up and I groan out as my release hits me. My eyes are desperate to shut, but I fight it and keep them on her instead.

"Fuck," I pant, my heart racing as I come down from my high.

She doesn't say anything. She doesn't move. We're locked in our stare.

Something's different. I've no idea what it is. The tension that's always between us crackles like normal, but there's been a shift and I worry it's me after my realization last night.

I desperately want to look away, to break whatever connection there is between us, but I'm powerless to do so. So instead, I push myself from the water and sit on the edge. I forget all about the fact I'm stark naked—not that I really care, she's already seen everything. Her eyes drop and release me from the daze I was in as she takes in my body. My temperature spikes and my cock twitches once again, knowing it's receiving attention from her.

Pushing myself to my feet, I turn my back on her. I know that if I continue looking at her dark come-fuck-me eyes as she stares at my body with desire oozing from them that I'll march straight up to her room and do just that. But I can't.

Instead, I scoop up my clothes, go straight to my own bedroom and lock myself in my en suite as I shower. The whole time thoughts of her rattle around my head, but at no point do I leave my room or see her, and that's the way it should be.

———

Between classes and practice, Friday seems to pass by in an exhausted blur. The excitement for our first playoff game has exploded to the point it's all any of us can think about. It's welcome relief from having her front and center of my mind, that's for fucking sure.

She hasn't paid me any attention since I was in the jacuzzi last night. Any crazy thoughts that she was going to appear in my room and do good on our bet were soon smashed when she didn't so much as knock on my door, let alone step inside. She just seems to be getting really good at avoiding me. It's something I'm allowing for my own sanity but equally something I'm intending on putting an end to very soon. She might think she's lost my attention but it's very much the opposite. After lying in bed for hours after my late night nap, I managed to convince myself that I didn't really feel how I did when I had my head between her legs. My need is still there, still as strong.

I watch her in the couple of classes we share together, trying to figure her out, trying to figure out my game plan when it comes to getting her out of my life.

I know that Amalie and Camila tried reaching out to her the other night, despite the fact I told them not to, but other than the odd smile in their direction, it doesn't seem like she's making any effort to make any friends. It makes me wonder if she really has as much intention of hanging around in Rosewood as she claims.

I shake my head, focusing on what tonight is going to bring. The whole day has been a buzz of excitement. All anyone can talk about, including the teachers, is how we are going to smash the Beavers' asses tonight and move on to the next round.

I stand in the locker room, surrounded by the team with Jake beside me. He's fucking pumped, there's no other way to describe him. His eyes are firmly set on the end goal, and he's not letting anything slip until he has that trophy in his hands.

"This is it, boys," he says, taking over from Coach's pep talk. "This is what we've worked our whole lives for. We are so fucking close I can almost feel that cool metal in my hands as we take victory. This fucking season is ours, *motherfuckers*. Who's with me?"

A loud roar of agreement echoes around the locker room. We bump fists and slap each other's shoulders in excitement before Jake leads us out on the field.

The roar from the crowd is deafening as we run out to the cheer squad shaking their pom poms in delight.

This is the biggest crowd we've ever played for, I swear. The stadium is filled to the rafters. I can only imagine how epic it's going to sound in here when we pull off our win.

I glance over at the bench to find Mason watching from the sidelines, and my heart sinks a little. He keeps telling us that he'll be back for the final. I know that six weeks' rest should be okay after broken ribs, but shit, he almost died. The last thing I want is for him to push himself and do more damage than necessary after everything he's been through.

I nod at him and he gives me a weak smile in return. I'm pretty sure he'd give anything to be standing with us right now.

I quickly glance around at the rest of the crowd. I spot some of the guys' parents cheering them on, but as expected, I don't find my own. Even *she's* not bothered to turn up, instead preferring to work instead of support her new school team.

I blow out a breath before Coach pulls us in for our final pep talk.

23

RAELYNN

"Shouldn't you be at school right now, getting into the spirit of things?" Cody asks as I lean my hip against the counter. Aces is dead tonight. We've had no more than three customers all night. Bill may as well have shut the place instead of paying both Cody and me to be here.

"Do I look like the kind of girl who'll wiggle her pom poms for the football team?"

Cody snorts with a mouthful of soda. "I wasn't suggesting you join the squad. Just thought you might want to—"

"Want to what?"

"Try to fit in."

"Meh, fitting in is overrated. I much prefer to be a social outcast. Makes things more interesting."

"I'll have to take your word on that."

"Oh god, you've always been the popular one, haven't you? Should we end our friendship now so I don't ruin your rep?"

"I wouldn't say I was in the popular crowd. That was reserved for the football and basketball players at my school, but I was never as disliked as..." He trails off. We both know what the end of that sentence is but still, because I'm a bitch, I gesture for him to continue.

"As who?"

"Err... you."

"It's really quite a skill, but by the time you've done ten schools in almost as many years, these things get easier." Cody pales slightly at my admission.

"Ten schools in ten years?"

"Not quite. More like eight, I think."

"You think?"

"Lost count after six." I shrug like it's no big deal, but really it is. A lot of my issues stem from my lack of a stable home. If I stayed anywhere for any decent time, maybe I'd have actually made some friends, have someone other than myself that I could rely on. But that's not how my life is, so I don't dwell on these kinds of thoughts. Well, I don't anymore.

Cody and I keep ourselves busy filling up the condiments and rearranging the cutlery tray, anything really to make the time pass. He offers time and time again for me to go and enjoy my evening but each time I refuse. I'm more than happy there with him, and I feel much more at home than I'm sure I would at school with the others right now. I even feel more comfortable here than I do at home. Ever since Ethan walked out the other night, I can't settle. I've no idea where he went. All I do know is that he didn't come home. I can only imagine that he went to find a cheer slut after deciding I wasn't worth it. I still have no idea what went wrong, but I'm trying not to think about it. I shouldn't care. I should be glad that he seems to have given up on me, left me be to get on with things.

I blow out a long breath. Cody looks up, and I'm expecting him to tell me to leave once again, but as he opens his mouth, his eyes flick over my shoulder. "Looks like the game must be finished."

My stomach drops. The last thing I was expecting was for them to all turn up here. I thought they'd go straight back to the house to start on the insane amount of alcohol that's been delivered. I've no idea how Eric allows Ethan to just do whatever he pleases with an open credit card.

Unable to resist looking, I glance over my shoulder. Only, I'm not met with either the exuberant or disappointed members of the football team like I was expecting, there's just one girl who pulls the door open and steps inside. She glances around, noting that it's basically empty before walking right up to me.

"Hey, Rae. Do you have five minutes?" I want to hate her, but her soft accent tugs at something deep within me.

"Um..." I hesitate, looking back at Cody for support, but the fucker doesn't help one bit.

"I think I can cope," he says, nodding toward one of the empty booths. "I'll bring you both a milkshake to give me something to do."

"Thank you." Barbie flashes him her megawatt smile and glides over to the seat. I'm not nearly so elegant as I follow behind.

"So to what do I owe the pleasure? Shouldn't you be sitting on the sidelines screaming as we take the win?"

I stare at her. Her lips twitch as if she's trying to keep her excitement locked inside, but it doesn't seem to be a fight she's winning. "They've already done it. They fucking smashed them. It was incredible." Her excitement is palpable, and her eyes go all soft as she most probably thinks about the captain.

"Okay, so you should be celebrating then, right? I assume that's what the brewery's worth of beer is for at the house."

"Yeah, I'm heading there in a minute. I just thought that maybe we could have a chat first."

"Why?" I ask, surprised that she's taken time out of such a big night to talk to me.

"Ethan's..." She pauses as she tries to find the right words.

I have a few choice ones that I could fill in for her, but I keep my lips sealed, preferring to wait and see what she's got to say.

Cody appears at my side before she gets a chance and delivers two strawberry milkshakes that Barbie instantly reaches out for. I watch as she purses her pink lips around the straw and sit back to wait for her.

"You were saying?" I ask, ensuring it sounds as bored as I'm beginning to get.

"Ethan's a mess."

I snort. "You're telling me."

"No, I don't think we mean in the same way. Look, I've not been here all that much longer than you have, but those guys are already like my family. Yeah, they have their quirks, like everyone, but deep down, they're really good guys." I open my mouth to argue, but she cuts me off. "Ethan too. Ethan's this larger-than-life character who just wants everyone to be happy. He thought he had everything and then suddenly, his dad pulled the rug from under him and he's not stopped falling since."

"We all have shit in our lives. Why should he be given a pass because he can't handle it?"

"I'm not saying he should. I'm just saying that..."

I cross my arms over my chest and wait.

"Okay, look. When I first turned up here, Jake hated me. And I mean *hated* me."

"Please, that boy looks at you like you've just hung the moon."

A smug smile curls at her lips.

"Now, maybe. Then? He wanted me gone. He was hurting, badly, and he projected that onto the wrong person. Luckily—or maybe unluckily, I guess it depends on how you look at it—I gave him shit right back. I pushed harder when he tried to hurt me. I could see more. I could see the broken boy beneath who was desperate for love. Shit," she says, glancing away. "I probably shouldn't be telling you all of this."

"No, it's okay. Go on," I encourage.

"All I'm saying is that, in my opinion, Ethan is in a similar place to Jake back then. He's been hurt and he can't deal with it, so he's lashing out. He doesn't really hate you, Rae."

"I'm not really sure about—" My argument is cut off before it really gets started.

"Something's happened between the two of you, right?" My cheeks heat, and it must be enough to confirm her suspicions. "Thought so. I'm not telling you to give him a break, to go easy on him. I'm actually telling you the opposite. Fight back, push him. Show him what you're really made of and maybe this thing between you will turn around."

"I don't want him."

"Never said you did. This might not turn out the same as things with Jake and me. But something's got to give at some point, and he needs someone, Rae. He's barely letting the guys in. The other night he turned up at Jake's place in the middle of the night. He was a mess. I probably shouldn't have been eavesdropping but..." She trails off with a shrug. "I should probably get back, Jake will be wondering where I am. I just wanted to reach out. He needs as many people in his corner as possible right now. I know it's not going to be easy, but one day, you'll get to see the real Ethan, and I promise you, it'll be worth it. Beneath that hard exterior is a soft and cuddly teddy bear." I snort a laugh as the image of the tattoo on his ass pops into my mind. "What?" she asks, a genuine smile forming on her lips.

"It's nothing. You'd better go before he sends out a search party."

"I wouldn't put it past him. Just think about what I said." She climbs from the booth and turns to leave but stops herself at the last minute. "You're coming to the party tonight, right?"

I shrug. "I'll probably just hide in my room."

"No way. Don't give him that power. Put on your sexiest... err..." She looks me up and down quickly, probably realizing that I'm not a dress kind of girl. "Fishnets," she finishes with a wink. "And show him what you've got. Drink, dance, make some friends. This is your home now, Rae. And believe it or not, some of us want to make you feel welcome."

Something burns at the back of my throat at her words, but I refuse to acknowledge what it is. "Thank you," I mouth.

She stops at the door, glances at me before watching Cody as he makes his way over. "Thanks for the milkshake. You're coming tonight as well, right?"

"What's tonight?" he asks, like he doesn't already know what's going on.

"Party at Rae's. If you're free, you're more than welcome. Any friend of Rae's is a friend of ours." With one more killer smile, she's out the door and gone as if she never appeared.

"What was all that about?"

"Ugh... high school bullshit. Whatever," I mutter, but I can't deny that her words haven't struck a chord with me. Especially her admitting that Ethan went to Jake's the other night and that he was a mess after we were together. What the hell is that supposed to mean? I tell myself he was just pissed off that he didn't stick around to get any and bury the little voice inside me that tells me it's more than that.

"So party at yours?" Cody digs.

"Yeah, football party. They won, apparently. You up for it?"

"I've not got any other plans. Plus, if it means it'll stop you from hiding in your bedroom then I'm all in."

"You were listening?"

The fucker doesn't even have the audacity to look guilty. "You need to have some fun, Rae. Like *Barbie* said, put on your best fishnets and let's party."

And so that is exactly what I do.

The party is in full swing by the time we finish up for the night and make our way to the Savage mansion. There are cars everywhere, meaning that Cody has to practically park at the end of the street, and there are bodies everywhere celebrating tonight's win. The atmosphere is electric, and it almost makes me glad I'm going to get to experience it. Almost.

"You came," a soft voice sings the second we step foot into the house as Barbie comes around the corner with Camila not far behind. I'm surprised she didn't bring her to Aces, they seem to be joined at the hip.

"This one deserves a night off."

"A-fucking-men," Barbie calls, lifting her drink in the air. "Now, you need help choosing an outfit?" she asks, eyeing my current attire.

"I've been dressing myself for more than a decade, I'm pretty sure I'm capable."

"Nope, no way. Here, it's a fresh one," she says, handing her Solo cup to Cody. "Mason?" she calls behind her, and seconds later the blonde guy appears.

"You rang?"

"Yeah. This is Cody, guy from Aces, Rae's friend. Keep him company while we go and get Rae party ready."

"You really don't need to do anything," I mumble, but it falls on deaf ears because after passing her cup over, Barbie takes me by the shoulders and pushes me toward the stairs. When I look back, I find Sindy right behind her.

Fuck my life. This is why I don't have girlfriends.

The sight of my bedroom door hanging where it should is a welcome one. I wasn't expecting to come home last night to find it back, but I was seriously fucking relieved. Especially now, seeing how crazy this party is.

I'm pushed through it, neither of the girls behind me appreciating its significance. I wonder how I would have explained that to them if it was still missing.

"Sit," Barbie demands, going straight for my closet and pulling the doors open. "Okay, what have we got here?"

Sindy does something similar when she sits down at my dressing table. "You own any makeup that isn't black?" she asks.

"Yeah. There's purple lipstick there somewhere," I quip. It earns me an eye roll, but she doesn't say anything more.

Knowing I'm not getting out of this, I let the girls go to town, with one exception. My hair stays up.

24

ETHAN

I am fucking buzzing as I walk into my house with Jake beside me and the rest of the team hot on our heels. It was a fucking unbelievable game. We smashed the other team and proved that we deserve our place in the state playoffs. Rosewood fucking High is not a team to be messed with.

The crowd erupts when they realize we've arrived. The volume almost takes the fucking roof off the place, and my chest swells with pride. I love this. I love being someone to the rest of the school. I love belonging to something. I fucking love the guys who are standing around me. They are my family, and fuck if they've not proved they've got my back more than my actual family these days.

Drinks are handed to us and the cheer squad descends, mostly still in their uniforms.

"You were on fire tonight," Shelly breathes in my ear, pressing her body temptingly up against mine. I drop my arm around her waist and pull her tighter.

"Fucking right. And it was only the beginning. I've got plenty more fire for the rest of the night."

She smiles at me, a twinkle in her eye that holds promises for what's to come.

I slam my lips down on hers. It's what she—hell, it's what everyone—expects, so I may as well play my part. Only, everything about the kiss is wrong. It's nice, sure. But it doesn't have desire stirring in any part of my body.

"At least get through the door before you get her naked, Savage," someone shouts from behind as they push past us to get into the house.

"Let's go and get more drinks." Shelly slips her hand into mine and I walk us through to the kitchen.

The music pounds and there are people covering every inch of the house. I couldn't think of a better way to drown everything out. It's almost like old times as I knock back shots with the team in the kitchen.

"Sooo," Zayn drawls. "Who's it going to be tonight?" He looks out over the crowd. "You tagging 'em?"

Jesus, we've not done this since the night at dash.

"Shelly," I announce, earning me a few groans.

"That's not even a challenge. One look from you and her legs are open, Savage."

I shrug, lifting my shot to my lips.

"No one said it had to be a challenge. Just that you had to name them."

"Dash night upped the ante, my friend. I'm calling your girl, and you've got until dawn."

Rolling my eyes, I pour myself another shot and knock it back. We just fucking won. No girl at this party is going to be a challenge for any of us tonight.

"I'm out," Shane pipes up from the other side of the group.

"Oh no, Dunn. You wanna hang with the big boys all of a sudden, then you've got to walk the walk. So… who shall we give Dunn?" Zayn looks over the crowd, assessing the girls in his eyeline.

Rich stands beside him, rubbing his palms together. "Victoria?" he asks.

"Nah, a cheerleader is too easy. Even for Dunn." Shane bristles, his lips pressing into a thin line. "That there, who's she?"

"No fucking way. Alyssa's my friend," Shane barks.

"That should be easy for you then, you already know her."

"Yeah, and I also know that she's after the basketball team. There's no fucking way any of you have got a chance with her."

"Zayn will give it a pop," I announce, pissed off that he started this game once again and wanting to give him a challenge.

"Fuck off, not if she's a hoop hooker."

"You called the game, but you don't get to call the shots. Shane can have Victoria, she'll have her sights set higher anyway, and you can have Alyssa."

"Fine. Whatever. I'll break her."

"But…" Shane argues, looking at the three of us.

"Sorry, but Zayn's right. You want to be one of us then you've got to act like it. Now, we've made it easy. So even a virgin like you should get the girl tonight." He pales, making me wonder how true that virgin title is, but I don't dwell on it. If he is, then it's high time he lost it.

"So if Savage is taking control, it's only fair he gets a challenge too."

Silence falls over our group as people start thinking about my target for the night. No single woman in this house is a threat right now. I so much as mention getting on their knees and they'll be down before they've even heard the words.

"Her," Zayn says, lifting his arm to point someone out.

As I look up, the world around me, along with the guys' excitement, fades into nothing because descending the stairs and following Amalie and Camila is Rae. She's wearing the shortest fucking skirt I've ever seen with a simple black tank, but fuck if it doesn't make my cock swell on sight. Her tits are pushed up and are perfectly framed by the low cut of her top. Her hair, like usual, is piled on top of her head, but it's way more intricate than I've ever seen and her makeup, although still heavy and dark, is flawless.

As if she can feel my stare, she turns toward me. Our eyes connect and something crackles between us. The slightest of smiles curls at her lip before her normal scowl falls into place as she continues to descend and gets swallowed by the crowd.

I swallow harshly, knowing that after the shit I gave Shane and Zayn, I can hardly turn her down. Plus, like fuck am I allowing them to tag her for someone else. No other motherfucker touches what's mine.

Thankfully, I've had enough shots now that the fact I just claimed her doesn't really register in my head.

I turn to the excited stares of my teammates and take another shot when it's handed to me. "Fine. I'll have her on her knees in minutes."

"By that, I'm assuming you mean with a knife in her hand so she can cut it off," Rich adds, much to the others' delight.

"Ha ha. She's a pussycat, really. Stroke her right and she'll be putty in my hands." Zayn laughs before he turns his attention to the other guys, giving me the opportunity to slip away.

It takes me forever to get through the house. The place is packed, and with every turn I make someone wants to talk about some part of tonight's game. It's not that I don't want to relive our epic win, but I need her gone. Amalie and Camila might think that she's welcome, but she's really fucking not. I want to celebrate with my friends like old times, not have my reality rubbed in my face.

When I come to a stop in the doorway to the living room, I scan the dancing crowd in front of me.

I find Mason first, his blond hair standing out over the rest, and head over.

"Where is she?" I bark at Camila, interrupting their moment as they move together.

"Don't know what you're talking about."

"Right, like fuck you don't. Where is she?"

"Chill the fuck out, man." I glance at Mason and narrow my eyes. "If your girl tells me where she is, then I'll gladly fuck off."

I'm just looking back to Camila when I spot someone who really doesn't fucking belong here. Her little friend from Aces. He's a college kid. Why the fuck does he want to be at a high school party? Movement to the side of him catches my eye before I get my answer.

He reaches out and pulls *her* into his body. Their hips grind with the music, and he leans down to whisper something in her ear, or worse, to ki—no. Not fucking happening.

Anger swells in my belly and mixes with the one too many shots I've already had tonight. I push my way between Mason and Camila to get to them.

Mason's hand lands on my shoulder. "Think about this, man," he shouts over the music, but I barely register the words. I need to get his fucking hands off her hips. I need to get his eyes off her fucking body.

I barge through the people between us before lifting my hands and forcefully removing the motherfucker from what belongs to me. He stumbles back, the people surrounding us backing up a little to give us some space.

"Get your motherfucking hands off her."

"Or what?" the douchebag says, taking a huge step until he's standing before me.

"Or I'll fucking make you," I spit. I'm not aware that the music in the room has been turned down to almost non-existent or that every single set of eyes has turned on me. All I can focus on is him. Him and the images in my head of his hands on her. His fingers running over her curves, dipping into places only I should be allowed to experience.

"Looks like you're going to have to, because as far as I see it, I'm doing nothing wrong." He holds out his hand, and I follow its movements to find Rae slip hers into it.

I see fucking red.

My arm rears back, my fist clenched, but just as I'm about to throw the punch, hands wrap around my upper arm.

"Don't even fucking think about it, Savage," Jake seethes in my ear, his voice low and menacing.

My chest heaves as he continues to hold me back. If I wanted to, I could break free, and he knows it. But I don't, I just stand there staring at him, warning him that he needs to back the fuck off and get out of my fucking house.

"What the fuck is your problem?" Rae stands between the two of us, her head tipped back so she can look me in the eye from her low position.

"You. You're my fucking problem, haven't you figured that out already?" Her teeth grind and her jaw pops in frustration. "Didn't you get the message last weekend? You're. Not. Invited. Now take this fucking pussy, and get out of my fucking house."

There's a collective gasp from the people behind me, but I don't pay it any attention, my eyes still drilling into hers.

"That's the thing though, Savage. This isn't your house. It's your dad's, and because of his wandering penis, you get the delight of having to live with me. So suck it up, asshole. This is my house too. You think you're king? Well, meet your motherfucking queen." She steps forward, closing the space between us. Her breasts brush my chest, and I don't miss the lowering of her eyelids at the connection. "So what are you going to do about it?" she taunts, her hand on her hips like the defiant trash she is.

Tension crackles between us as silence falls around the room. "Stay out of my fucking way."

I shake off Jake and storm from the room, needing some fucking fresh air.

This time, when I make my way through the house, everyone moves out of my way. Even those not in the room sense that now wouldn't be the time to step up to me. I'm unsure if that's because gossip really does spread that fast around here, or it's just the vibe I'm giving off as I make my way out to the pool area.

Even out here is packed, but as I make my way over to the loungers on the far corner of the pool, the kids who were sitting there scamper.

I fall down, rest my head back, and squeeze my eyes shut, but the only thing I see is them. I see them dancing, their bodies moving together, his lips pressing—

"Argh," I shout into the night.

I don't bother to look up to see if I'm center of attention right now. I don't give a fuck. All I need is her out of my fucking head.

"Here," a familiar voice says. I crack an eye open to find Jake and Mason looming over me, holding beer and shots.

Sitting, I take a shot and a beer and down them in quick succession.

"You've got it bad, huh?" Jake asks, amusement filling his voice.

"Don't fucking start. I didn't get in the middle of shit with you and Amalie, so keep your nose out of mine."

He puts his hands up in surrender. "Maybe not. But he did" —he nods toward Mason— "and I'm fucking glad he did. I may not have wanted to hear a fucking word of it at the time, but fuck, if I didn't need it. So, get comfortable, we're going to have a little chat."

"Sorry, but my dick is still firmly between my legs. You want to have a little girly chat, then I suggest you go and find some girls."

"Suck it up, Savage. You're going fucking nowhere until I've said what I've come to say."

I cast my eyes away from him, not interested in a single word of it.

"You hate her. Fine. You think she's ruined your life. Fine, you think that. But know that the only one fucking up your life right now is you. So get your head out of your fucking ass and act like a normal human being. We're only seeing bits of how you're behaving when it comes to her, and I dread to fucking think how you're treating her behind closed doors. She didn't choose to be here, Ethan. She was dragged, probably kicking and screaming if she had any idea of who she was going to live with. Now for the love of God, will you either go and apologize and make peace, ignore her, or fuck her." I blanch at his final option. "Oh, don't look so shocked. We all know you're hard for her. You've not touched anyone else since she arrived."

"I kissed Shelly earlier," I argue, weakly.

"Oh yeah, because one kiss in a few weeks is totally normal for Ethan Savage when his house is full of pussy." Jake waves his hand around my back yard. There are bikini-clad girls around the pool and others wearing not much more everywhere else. "The Ethan we know wouldn't be sitting here sulking, he'd be in that pool with his hand in some girl's panties and his tongue down her throat."

He's got a fucking point. It only makes all of this worse. The picture he's just painted is exactly what should be happening right now, but as I look at the girls before me, none of them spark even an ounce of interest. I glance up at the house just as a light comes on in her bedroom. Now that, that one small sign of life from her, and I'm drowning in fucking desire.

I bite down on my cheeks as I wait to see if she's going to appear. Unfortunately, the only girls who show their faces are Amalie and Camila as they join the boys. "Oh goodie, two more to join in the lecture."

"Nope, this is your funeral, Ethan. We're not getting involved," Camila says, cuddling into Mason's side and pressing her lips to his neck.

"Although you should probably know," Amalie adds. "She's just gone upstairs with him."

Something unpleasant stirs in my belly before it tracks its way through my veins. My temperature soars and my fists clench.

"So..." Jake taunts. "What are you going to do about it?"

"Fuck you," I bark, pushing from the lounger and storming inside to the sound of his laughter.

Once again, the crowds part as I make my way to the stairs. Taking two at a time, I run up until I'm standing on the other side of her door, praying for his fucking benefit that I'm not about to find him with his hands on her in any way, let alone anything worse.

I grasp the handle and push the door with such force it crashes back against the wall with a loud bang. A startled cry sounds out, but I'm so amped up that it takes me a few seconds to register that she's sitting on her bed. Alone.

Thank fuck for that. I really didn't want tonight to be the night I kill someone.

"Where is he?"

"W hy do you care? You didn't seem to like him all that much."
His chest swells at my response before he reaches out and slams the door so hard my bed actually rattles.

"I don't like him."

"Why? Because he's actually nice to me and that can't possibly be allowed?" I sass, scooting over until my legs are hanging off the bed.

"No. Because he wants you."

I laugh at the serious expression on his face. "Cody? Jesus, Ethan. You really are delusional. Fucking hell," I mutter, pushing to my feet and walking to the other side of the room, needing to put as much space between us as possible. He doesn't move, but I feel his eyes follow every one of my footsteps.

"From the way he was touching you, I'd say he was very much interested."

"We were dancing. Just like everyone else in the room. What's the big fucking deal? You hate me. Why do you care who I dance with? I thought you'd just be glad it wasn't a member of your team who took my interest."

"So you do like him?"

"What? No. Stop twisting my words."

He takes a step toward me, and I immediately take one back. It's clear in his eyes that he's been drinking, and so have I. That combined with the electricity that's crackling between us can't be a good thing.

"Y-you need to leave."

He takes another step, and another, but unless I want to have this exchange on the balcony for everyone to see, then I have nowhere else to escape to.

"Why? So when your little boyfriend comes back from wherever he's gone you can let him fuck you?"

My hand reaches out, and by some miracle, he doesn't see it coming. My palm connects with his cheek with a loud slap. His eyes widen in shock and he bares his teeth at me.

"You're going to fucking regret that, trash." His teeth grind, the muscle in his neck pulses, and he takes a final step toward me. I've no choice but to step back if I don't want to collide with him.

"What are you going to do?" I ask, holding my arms out from my sides. "You going to demand I strip naked again? Humiliate me in front of the kids I sit in class with? Maybe put on another little show out here? Only this time you really will have an audience." I glance over my shoulder at the students below all having a good time, totally oblivious to what's going on up here.

I lift my hands to the hem of my hoodie. "Shall I start with my top? Give them all a good eyeful of my tits. Would you like that? Them all knowing you have this kind of power over me?" I lift the fabric and pull it from my body.

"Sweet cheeks." I barely hear it, his voice is so low.

I hang my arm over the balcony and let it drop, knowing that it'll catch the attention of the people below.

"You think they're looking now?"

"Don't," he warns as I lift my arms to undo my bra.

"But this is what you want, isn't it? You want to show me up. Make me feel small. Worthless." I pop the clasp, feeling weirdly empowered in this moment as he's watching me like he's about to lose control at any moment.

The music is so loud from below that I've no idea if anyone is actually looking, and to be honest, I'd rather not know. I need to prove to Ethan for good that I'm not afraid of him or his little games. If he wants me stripped bare, then that's what he's going to get.

I allow the straps to fall down my arms and take the weight of my breast in my palms. "What is it you want tonight? Are you going to eat me out again with them watching? Or maybe you want to just fuck me while they all appreciate what a fucking king you are for breaking me down."

"No," he shouts at exactly the same time I let go of my bra and allow it to drop to the tiles at my feet. He darts forward, his hand wrapping tightly around my wrist, and I'm pulled into my bedroom before he turns back around and shuts the door behind us, cutting off the outside world from whatever is going to happen next.

His chest heaves as his eyes bounce between my eyes and my exposed chest.

"You're fucking right. I want you to strip, but I'll be fucked if anyone else gets to look at you."

My breath catches at his honesty. Something flashes in his eyes, something I've seen before but not been able to latch onto.

"Now. What the fuck are you waiting for?"

"I don't follow your orders, asshole."

He's on me in seconds. His fingers find their way into my hair and he pulls so I have no choice but to look up at him moments before his lips crash to mine. I stumble back with the force and hit the wall. His large body engulfs mine but not in an intimidating way like I might imagine. His hard planes press against my soft curves, and I can't help the moan that rumbles up my throat when the length of his cock presses into my stomach.

"Jesus. Fuck," he mutters against the sensitive skin of my neck when he eventually releases my lips, allowing me to drag some air into my lungs.

My nipples tighten as his Bears jersey brushes against them, and a bolt of lust heads straight for my clit.

"You going to make me beg again?" I moan, breathlessly.

"No. This is happening with or without you begging. My restraint has its limits, sweet cheeks."

My breath catches at what he's implying. I should stop this now. This shouldn't be how it goes. But then he lifts his hand, cups my breast and pinches my nipple and all my rational thoughts vanish as I turn into a ball of need.

"Ethan, fuck."

He lowers down, pulling one and then the other nipple into his mouth. My fingers thread into his hair in an attempt to hold him there, but I'm no match for his strength, and when he decides to move and continue his trail down my body, I have no choice but to let him.

He pulls the zipper of my skirt down, allowing it to drop to the floor before dragging my fishnets and panties down my legs.

"No one else ever gets to look at this," he says, staring right at my core. "You got that?" He glances up from under his lashes. His blue eyes are dark, darker than I've ever seen. I nod in agreement because there's not much else I can do in that moment other than follow orders. I'm so lost to him it's embarrassing after the way he's treated me, but what he has to offer is too tempting. The escape from reality he can give me is too much to deny.

He reaches around me and lifts as he stands, as if I'm as light as a feather.

"Where shall I fuck you, sweet cheeks? Against the wall? Bed? Over the balcony?" We both know that final one isn't an option, seeing as he's already dragged me inside, but fuck if the idea doesn't turn me on a little.

"Bed," I breathe in his ear.

He does as I suggest and stops when his knees hit the mattress and lowers me down his body. The second his hands leave me, he pulls his jersey over his head, quickly followed by removing his pants and boxers until he's standing before me bare.

He takes his hard length in his hand and strokes slowly as he stares down at me.

Worrying that he's about to insist I come good on our bet, I scoot back on the bed. I'm not against doing it, but not in the mood he's in right now. He wants to punish me, that much is clear in his eyes, let alone his words, and I don't need him taking it out on my throat.

He doesn't seem to care that I back away, because he quickly lies on his front between my legs. He hooks his hands around my thighs and tugs until my center is right in front of his face. He blows a stream of air across my swollen skin, and I buck in his hold.

"I knew you were fucking desperate for me again."

Before I can even consider coming up with a response, his tongue is on me and I lose all ability to function. All I can do is feel.

His tongue teases as his fingers find my entrance. His movements are fast but measured, as if he's done this to me a million times and knows exactly what I like.

"Oh fuck. Ethan. Ethan," I chant.

"That's it. Let everyone know who's doing this to you, baby."

He ups the ante, licking, sucking, and biting until I scream out, my body thrashing about on the bed as I ride out my release.

My chest is still heaving, my breathing erratic, and I'm coming down from my high when the mattress compresses as he crawls over me much like a lion would its prey. If I haven't just been eaten by the king then I'd certainly think he was about to consume me.

His hand slips around the back of my neck and tilts my head so he can crash his lips to mine. The second his tongue parts my lips, my own taste immediately explodes on my in my mouth and my core clenches for more.

His tongue sweeps in, teasing and dancing with mine. Our teeth clash as it gets more and more frantic with our need. My nails scratch down his back, eliciting a growl of approval from him and making me want to do it more, anything to make this man come undone and hand himself over when he craves being in control at all times.

I reach down between our bodies and wrap my fingers around his length, getting my first feel of him. He's hard as a rock but soft and velvety to touch. I run my fingertips over his head and he barks a curse as his arms threaten to give out.

Ripping his lips from mine, he sits up and pushes my knees toward my chest. He stares down at my heated skin as he runs the head of his cock over me.

I fight the fear that wants to take over, that makes my body want to tremble and scamper, but the second I look to where we're about to be connected, I forget all about that. All about the past, all about the nightmares that keep me awake at night.

He builds me high again just with the teasing of his cock. After a few minutes, he dips the tip inside me, and I will myself not to tense at his intrusion. The last thing I need right now is him knowing the truth. I'm sure that'll only feed his need to punish me, to claim something that's not his to have.

He looks up at me and licks his lips. His eyes take in every inch of my face before dropping down my body once again. What I wouldn't give to know what he's thinking right now.

"Birth control?" he asks after a long silence between us.

I shake my head.

He looks down at my pussy again for a few seconds, making me wonder if he's going to do it anyway, but eventually, he leans over the side of the bed and grabs a condom from his pocket.

I watch intently as he rolls it down his shaft and lines himself up again.

His eyes flick up again at the last minute, something dark playing in them, and I swallow down the lump that crawls up my throat.

Just let it happen, Raelynn. It's not a big fucking deal.

"Don't come. This is for me after all the fucking teasing you've been doing, for all the times you've defied me. You got that?" His eyes widen as he says it, making me wonder if he's already regretting it, but I'm not sure if this asshole ever regrets any of the shit that falls from his mouth.

He sucks in two breaths before his grip on my hips tightens and he pushes inside me. In one quick move, I'm so full of him that I can hardly breathe. It stings, burns, exactly like I was expecting, and I slam my eyes shut to hide the tears that are welling within them.

"Fuuuuuuck," he grates out. I expect him to move, to pull out and slam back in, but it's almost like it takes him a few seconds to remember what he's supposed to be doing.

"Ethan." My voice is no more than a whimper, but it's enough to bring him back from whatever daze he'd lost himself in.

"Christ, you're tight." His voice is so deep, so rough that it has desire pulling at my insides, making me desperate for him to move and show me what he's really got. He seems to think he's something special in the bedroom—well, now is the perfect time to prove his skills. To drag me out of my own head, away from my fears and to show me heaven. I could really use a fucking slice of that right now.

He pulls out slowly before pushing back inside. He groans as if it's physically painful, and my need to see the effect this is having on him is too much to bear. I open my eyes. They're still brimming with tears, but I can't not look.

My breath catches when I find him staring down at me. His eyes are dark, but gone is the anger. It's pure desire that's staring back at me.

His full lips are parted to allow his fast breaths to pass. The muscles of his neck are pulled tight, as are his abs. A fine sheen of sweat covers his body. I find where his fingers are digging into the skin of my hips and the sight of him holding onto me so tightly unnerves me. No one's ever held on tight.

A ball of emotion crawls up my throat as his movements continue. His length strokes at places inside me that I didn't know existed, and in only the way that Ethan can, he starts to push away the pain and discomfort that I remember all too well and replace it with something else entirely. Pleasure.

I focus on that, needing it to be the thing I remember about this fucked-up situation. I might forever regret this, but at least I'll always have the lesson it taught me.

"Fuck, baby," he grunts, dragging my eyes back up to his. "So fucking good. You shouldn't feel this good."

He drops down over me, his lips finding mine in a wet and dirty kiss as his hips continue to piston in and out of me.

When both of us are desperate for air, he pulls away, drops his face into the crook of my neck and skirts his hand down my body. He squeezes my breast, pinches my nipple before making his way descending to my core. His fingertips find my clit and he presses down. That, along with the things he's doing inside my body, has me racing toward an orgasm I was already told I wasn't allowed to have.

"Jesus, fuck," he moans as my muscles start to clamp down around him.

"Ethan." His name, a plea for more, falls from my lips without any instruction from my brain. My nails dig into his back with my need for more of him. I need everything he can give me to push the last remaining nightmare from my mind.

Twisting my head so my lips brush his ear, I whisper, "Fuck me, Ethan. Give me everything you have."

He roars into my neck, his body tensing at my demand before he sits, slides his hands under my ass and lifts me to just the right angle before slamming into me. I fly up the bed, my head hitting the wood, but his grip tightens even more, keeping me in place so he can keep up his punishing rhythm.

He pounds into me time and time again as I watch, enthralled, as he comes apart before me.

"Fuck, fuck," he chants, his cock swelling even more inside me, telling me that the end is in sight.

The second he reaches the point of no return, every single muscle in his body tenses before he lets out the most incredible groan and his cock pulsates, buried deep inside me.

I can't drag my eyes away despite the fact that my tears are about to drop at any moment. I refuse to allow this motherfucker to see me cry, but I'm not sure I have a choice right now.

The wave of emotions that engulf my body in that moment are too strong to contend with. The hate I feel for him, and the relief I have that he's just given me that, even though I'm equally ashamed I allowed it to happen. Fuck, my head's a fucking mess.

When he's finished, he releases his hold on me, pulls out, and climbs off the bed. He doesn't look at me, not once. I keep my eyes on him as he turns away from me, drops the condom into the trash and bends to pull on his pants. His teddy bear tattoo catches my eye, but even the sight of such a ridiculous bit of ink on his body doesn't stir anything inside. Now he's released me, I feel numb.

I panic when he reaches for the door. "Ethan?" I hate how pathetic and weak my voice sounds, but I can't help it. I wasn't under the illusion that he'd lie down beside me and pull me into his arms. I didn't expect for this to heal everything that's so broken between us, but watching him just walk out without even acknowledging me? Well, it fucking hurts.

He halts, hearing his name, but he doesn't turn back.

A little strength bubbles up from somewhere, my need to have the last say getting the better of me. "We're done now, Ethan. You got what you wanted. You stripped me bare. Now leave me the fuck alone." My voice cracks on the final sentence, and I know he doesn't miss it. His shoulders tense as the words hit him, but still, they're not enough to pull on the decent part of him that I know is inside somewhere.

He doesn't say anything. He just walks out through my bedroom door with his head slightly hanging in defeat. My first sob erupts long before he's closed the door behind him, and once they start, they don't stop.

26

ETHAN

Forgetting the fact I've got half the school in my house, I run down the stairs in my need for a drink. I need to drown out what I just did.

I fly around the bottom of the stairs and collide with a body, sending her scattering back on the wooden floor.

"Fucking hell," I moan. Am I going to fuck everything up tonight?

I step up to the barely-dressed girl and hold my hand out to help her up. It's not until she's standing before me that I register who it is.

"Does your cousin know you're here?"

Poppy's lips press into a thin line. "I don't know. But this is a school party, and in case you hadn't noticed, I go to Rosewood." She places her hand on her hip, waiting for my response, but I don't really care.

"Don't say I didn't warn you."

Jake might have a fucked-up family but he's protective as hell over Poppy. He'll flip his lid when he spots her dressed like a fucking whore.

I push past her and head for the kitchen. The bottles of whiskey that I know are there are too much to ignore.

I can see my prize, but fucking Zayn gets in my fucking way.

"How's it going with your dark horse?" he slurs, getting in my face.

"Back the fuck off," I bark, my palms connecting with his chest to push him away. I don't want to think about her right now, let alone talk about her.

"Or what, asshole?" Zayn's eyes are wild with the amount of alcohol he's consumed, and it seems to make him think he can take me. Fucking idiot.

Pulling my arm back, landing the punch I was desperate to plow into the dickhead's face earlier. I hit him square on the jaw, but it's not enough. It's nowhere near e-fucking-nough. Grabbing onto his shirt when he starts to stumble away in shock, I throw another and another. His nose explodes, blood pouring down onto his top, but even the sight of that isn't enough to stop me. Pain sears up my arm, but I welcome it. I need it. I deserve it.

"Ethan, what the fuck are you doing?" Jake hollers when the screams and cries for help around us alert him to the ongoings in the kitchen. "Fucking hell."

His arms wrap around my upper body, pinning mine to my sides to stop me from throwing any more punches. The rest of the team descends. Some help Jake move me to the other side of the room while others tend to Zayn, who's now rolling around on the floor in pain.

Everything around me blurs. All I can focus on is the anger that's consuming me. I thought taking it out on her was going to get rid of it, but I realize it's not her I'm angry with. It's me. Everything I've done. All the shit I've pulled.

"What the fuck, Savage?"

"He was in my way."

"Then ask him to fucking move."

"What the hell?" Mason asks, coming to a stop in front of me.

"Whiskey," I groan, holding my arm up, hoping someone will place a bottle in my hand.

"Fine," Jake says seconds before the cold glass hits my fingers. Fucking heaven.

I twist the cap and down as much as my throat can handle.

"Can you and Camila get him the fuck out of here?" Jake asks, but I ignore him, happy to drown myself in whiskey. "Take him to mine. I'll finish things here. We'll meet you there after. This needs to end."

I've no idea if he directs that final statement at me or not, but I ignore him anyway.

I'm none too gently pushed to my feet, and Camila and Mason drag me from the house. It's not all that much of a feat for them because being here, under the same roof as her, is the last place I want to be.

"Get the fuck in," Mason barks, pointing to Camila's Mini, and I do as I'm told.

He hops in the passenger seat while she drops into the driver's seat, and we almost immediately start moving.

I don't look out the window, my only focus the bottle in my hands and the relief it can give me from the memories that are rolling around in my head.

My legs barely work when we pull up outside Jake's aunt and uncle's house. Seeing as he's still suffering with his ribs, Camila ends up being the one trying to support me as I make our way to Jake's trailer.

"Fucking help, will you?" she fumes. "I'll happily just dump you here if that's what you want."

"Oh, Mase. Is she this feisty in the sack?"

"Shut the fuck up, asshole, or I'll let her dump you and not look back."

He doesn't mean that. Does he?

We eventually make it down to the trailer, and before I know it, I'm on Jake's couch finishing off the bottle in my hands.

"Did you think to grab me another?" I ask the couple who are staring at me like I'm a green alien who's sprouted two extra heads.

"No, asshole, we didn't."

"Fucking bullshit. Jake must have—" I try to stand but Mason, being sober, beats me to it and is in my face in seconds.

"Move," I demand, keeping my fists out of it this time.

"No fucking chance."

A growl sounds out around the trailer, but it doesn't register that it comes from my throat.

"I need—"

"No. You don't need whiskey. Or beer. Or fucking weed. What you need is to start talking. We can't fucking help if we don't know, motherfucker."

My fists curl, not knowing another way to deal with his demands. Like fuck am I talking.

"Go on then. Hit me, if it'll make you feel better."

"Mason, no," Camila says in a rush, coming to stand at his side protectively.

"It's fine, Cami. Sit down." She looks between the two of us locked in our stare off but eventually does as she's told.

"Sit," Mason demands, his hands hitting my shoulders just enough to have me falling to the couch.

I watch as he walks into Jake's little kitchenette and grabs three bottles of water from the fridge.

"Drink." He shoves it under my nose and leaves it there until I have to take it if I want him to go the fuck away. "Great, now talk," he says, falling down beside Camila and pulling her into his side. The sight of them has my stomach turning over. So fucking happy and content with each other. It's sickening.

"Fuck you."

"Nah. You fucked her though, didn't you?"

Our eyes lock, a million words passing between us. We've been friends for too long for me to hide shit from either Mason or Jake.

"None of your business."

"It is when you're trying to drown yourself in a bottle of whiskey. You can do this now, or you can do it when Jake and Amalie get here, makes no difference to us. But get one thing straight. You are damn well fucking talking."

My teeth grind as I try to figure out a way to explain what I've done. How I've treated her.

"Fine. I fucked her. Happy?"

"I'm assuming I can safely say that she's now not out of your system." The fact he's almost amused by this situation pisses me off even more.

"No... I... Fuck." I sit forward and hang my head, running the events of the night through my mind.

I have no idea how long the three of us sit there in silence, but, eventually, there are footsteps outside and then the door's opening.

"Sorry. Took fucking ages to clear out," Jake says, walking straight up to me and slapping me around the head. "You sorted this waste of fucking space out yet?"

No one says anything, but I can imagine the looks that are passing between them.

"Amalie tried to see Rae, but she refused to speak, let alone answer the door. What the fuck did you do, Ethan?"

Things that I've said to her over her short time here run through my head. The things I've made her do, tonight included. My need to hurt her, to escape the constant anger that's always threatening to boil over was too much, and I took. I took what I wanted without any thought for her. That's not how I do things. That's not fucking cool.

"I fucked her," I repeat quietly.

"Right. And it was so bad she sent you running to a bottle?" Jake laughs.

"I..." Fuck. "I'm not sure she was totally up for it." I fall back and tip my face to the ceiling, squeezing my eyes shut so I don't have to look at their disapproving faces. The girls gasp but otherwise no one says anything as the reality of the situation presses down so heavily on my chest that I struggle to suck in a fucking breath.

"I've been a fucking asshole since she arrived. Demanding she do shit. I just... I was so... fuck. I don't even know who I am right now. I fucking hate myself. But she... then her... FUCK," I shout, unable to even vocalize what it is I'm feeling, how fucking hurt and angry and fucked-up I am.

"You need to sober the fuck up and talk to her," Amalie suggests after the longest fucking silence of my life. "You were drunk before you even went up there, you might not be seeing things clearly."

"Even if I'm not. All the other stuff. Fuck." I think about the day I made her strip. I watched her body tremble in fucking fear, yet I kept pushing. I remember the other night with her up on the fucking balcony. One wrong move and she'd have gone down. So what she was wet as fuck and begging for me? I made that happen. She didn't. All she did was turn up. She doesn't deserve any of what I threw at her.

"She's stronger than you're giving her credit for, Ethan. If she didn't want something, I'm pretty sure she'd have just told you."

I think back to her biting my fingers in Aces' bathroom. Amalie is right, but she doesn't see what it's like when it's just the two of us together. It's like she hands me the control she always keeps a tight grip onto everywhere else. Why? What stops her kicking back more?

"Get some fucking sleep. Sober up. Then tomorrow, talk to her with a rational head. Maybe apologize for being an epic douchebag since the moment she arrived. The four of us sitting here are proof that asshole actions can be forgiven and things can turn around."

I lie back on the sofa. If the four of them say any more, then I don't hear it because the numbness from the alcohol drags me under.

———

The trailer's still in silence when I wake with a raging hard-on from the dream I was having about being inside Rae yesterday. The tingling of desire lasts all of three seconds after I come to before reality slams into me right before the headache that's pounding at my temples hits as well.

Fuck. I'm a mess.

Regret. Shame. They both threaten to swallow me whole, and I can say with absolute certainty that the bright light of day has not brought me any clarity on the situation. If anything, without the whiskey fueling my thoughts, it's fucking worse.

The guys' advice from last night hits me.

Talk to her.

I drag my cell from my pocket, and my stomach drops when I see I've got a message. Only it's not from her.

Needing a distraction, I swipe it and see what she's sent.

Chelsea: Thank you for thinking of me. That means a lot. Hopefully I'll get to see you soon x

I sigh. If Chelsea of all people is attempting to get her shit together then I guess I'd better make the effort too.

I almost change my mind and curl back up on the couch when I push the door open and am blinded by the almost midday autumn sun. My head swims, and last night's whiskey threatens to make a reappearance. I've no idea what time the guys left me last night, but seeing as it's almost lunchtime and Jake and Amalie are still in bed, they couldn't have called it a night too early.

I pull up my Uber app ready to order a car to get me home, but at the last minute, I cancel the order in favor of walking. The headspace and fresh air might do me a bit of good. Give me some fucking clarity with regards to Rae and everything's that happened. And everything that might happen next.

I scrub my hand down my face as I allow the realization that I don't want what happened with Rae last night to be a one-off to settle. The bullshit that got us there aside, it was fucking mind-blowing and I'm now craving to be inside her again, to feel her body against mine like I never have anyone else. Not that I deserve to feel any of that again after how I've treated her.

I grab some breakfast on the way when I'm confident my stomach can take it, and it's almost two hours later when I walk up the driveway toward the house. It looks exactly like it did before the party, almost as if last night never happened. There's just one difference. Dad's car is here.

Motherfucker. So not only do I have the grovel of my life ahead of me with Rae, but I've got to deal with him.

I don't see any sign of life as I walk into the house. I stop by the kitchen for a bottle of water before making my way toward the stairs. I figure that I'd rather deal with Rae than I would my father, which is really saying something. However, I don't make it to the stairs, because as I approach the family room, their voices ring out and I'm powerless but to stop when I hear Rae's name mentioned.

"I can't believe she just blanked you like that after not seeing you for over a week," Dad says softly to Ash.

"It's fine. I'm used to Rae's temper. She was always such a placid child. If I wasn't so stupid then maybe..." Ash's voice breaks, and I see through the crack in the door as Dad leans toward her.

"Maybe what?"

She blows out a breath. I know I shouldn't be listening in on their private conversation, but it's clear that Ash knows more about Rae than any of us, and hell knows I could use a little light shedding on her before we talk.

Her shoulders shake, the tension surrounding her obvious even from out in the hall. "It was all my fault. I thought he was God's gift. He was so sweet. The perfect boyfriend. Little did I know he—" She sniffles, and it cuts off her words.

Every muscle in my body is locked tight as I wait for what's to come.

"He what, Ash?" Dad asks, his own voice rough and full of emotion. He's clearly having the same thoughts—fears—as me right now.

She sobs, and I damn near march inside the room to demand she finishes that fucking sentence. But when she does say the words, all the fight leaves me.

"Only wanted her. She was only thirteen when he—"

I stumble back, unable to comprehend what she's saying. Refusing to accept it. Everything I've done to her. The way I've treated her. And she's been... no, no.

On shaky legs, I drag myself up the stairs. I need the truth. I need to know if I'm just one in a line of men who haven't treated her as she deserves.

I throw her bedroom door open the second I'm in front of it, the weight of the regret I feel pressing down on me to the point I can't drag in the air I need.

I don't know what I was expecting, but the second I look up and find only an empty room, disappointment floods me. I need to talk to her. I need her to tell me what I just overheard isn't true, even though every fiber of my being knows that it is.

My eyes settle on her bed. It's covered in her diaries, the ones she'd hidden from me. No wonder she looked so terrified when she discovered me reading them.

Fuck. It was him. The asshole I was reading about. The one who was treating her to everything she wanted.

Racing over, I rummage through them until I find the one I was reading. I flick through for any sign for where I should look. All of a sudden the pretty pink writing stops and a more rushed, scratchy handwriting starts. I stare down at the pages, flipping through and picking out important words. In places, the ink has run where she's spilled water on it, but it's not long before I realize that they were probably her tears.

27

RAELYNN

I didn't get a wink of sleep last night despite the party finishing not long after Ethan ran from my room. I can only assume he pulled the whole thing to an abrupt end after what happened between us. He wasn't in a good place when he first appeared in my room; I can't imagine he left any better.

Every time I drifted off, *he* appeared. I'd spent months thinking that he was the best thing that ever happened in my life. That for once, Mom had got it right. Oh how wrong I was. He wasn't treating me like the daughter he never had. It took months for me to accept after the event, but all he was doing was grooming me. Putting in the legwork to ensure I'd trust him when he thought the time was right.

And fuck did I trust him.

I didn't bat an eyelid when he told me he'd run me a bath one night when Mom was working late. Yes, I thought it was odd when he suggested he join me, but he soon soothed my concerns when he reminded me how Mom couldn't afford for us to waste water.

A shudder runs down my spine as I revisit that night. I was so young. So naïve. If I had any idea what he was capable of, I'd have run as fast as I could in the opposite direction that night, but I truly believed that he'd never hurt a fly.

I blow out a shaky, emotional breath as I stare ahead at the waves crashing up onto the beach.

I wanted to get out of the house before Ethan or our parents arrived home this morning. I needed time. Time to get my head together. Time to hopefully push *him* from my thoughts. I wasn't expecting Mom and Eric to be back already. They'd told me they'd be home tomorrow, but I guess things change. I couldn't cope with them, listening to all the wonderful things they'd done while they were away, so I ran. Ran right past Mom as she asked how I was. I felt awful as I did it, and I still feel terrible now.

Obviously, we moved after that horrific event—Mom's coping mechanism for life: running away— and she ensured I had counseling at my next couple of schools to help me with my insomnia and the nightmares that plagued me, but although I told her it helped, I'm not sure it ever really did. It helped me to accept what happened, but I don't ever think I'll understand it or be convinced that it wasn't my fault. He was the master manipulator, and I fell for it like the good little girl I was.

I both lost and found something that night. I lost my childhood, my innocence, but I gained an understanding of how strong I am, what I'm capable of. It was a hard way of learning that I need to be more aware of who I spend time with and look out for the signs I should have seen back then.

I learned that I have a choice, that I can stand up for myself. It taught me that just because it happened once, I don't have to be the victim again. Thankfully, I never came anywhere close to it happening again. Until I moved here and met the asshole across the hall.

But things with him were different. I had a choice. I could see exactly what game he was playing and I either chose to play along or I didn't. I had power. The kind of power I never had back then.

If I truly didn't want him to lay a finger on me, then he wouldn't have.

From the very beginning, I knew that for the first time in my life, I was going to allow him to take what he wanted, what I craved from him. And last night was no exception.

I needed it to be him to show me what sex is, how it should be. I've never cared about anyone enough to hate them, to argue with them like I have Ethan. And, although scary as hell to admit, it's the truth.

It's the reason I cried most of the night. Not because I gave him something that he didn't deserve. But because after the event, he just walked out. He had no idea what a big moment of my life that was, how much I was trusting him with my body in those few moments. He had no reason to. But he walked away.

So either I was totally wrong about him and there being a redeemable human being hiding under all the hate and anger, or what I felt when we connected was totally one-sided. Maybe it was just sex for him. Maybe I was just another girl. Another notch in his bedpost. Rumor around school sure leads me to believe he's got a few.

I sit in that exact spot on the beach until the sun starts to set. My stomach grumbles, having not eaten anything all day, and eventually forces me to stand and move.

I grab a takeout burger from Aces and plaster a fake smile on my face as Bill chats away to me about last night's game, even though he knows I really don't care. If I were in a less somber mood, his excitement might be infectious. But as things stand, it's not.

I walk up toward the house with a ball of dread sitting in my stomach. Eric's car is still here, but Ethan's isn't. Even with it missing, my hands tremble slightly that he'll be home and want a repeat of last night... or worse, to talk about it.

I find Mom and Eric sitting at the table in the kitchen with dinner in front of them.

"Hey, honey. Would you like some dinner?" Mom asks hesitantly when I stop in the doorway.

"No, I've eaten, but thank you. Listen, I'm—"

"It's okay, Rae."

"No, it's not. I'm sorry for this morning. Things have just been... hard starting over here. I'm sorry."

"Oh honey, you should have called if you were having a hard time. You know I've always got time for you."

Have you? The question is on the tip of my tongue, but I don't allow it to slip out. What's the point? If it were true, she wouldn't have run the second we got here and forced me to find my own way.

"Has Ethan helped get you settled at school?" Eric asks, a hopeful look in his eye.

"Oh yeah. He's been great," I lie. More like a baptism of fire than a warm welcoming but whatever. What's done is done. "Where is he?"

"I'm not sure. I hear last night's game was incredible," Eric says, like he's expecting me to have been there.

"So I hear."

"You didn't go?" I have no idea why Mom looks so shocked. I've never been one to go to school events.

"No, I got a job and worked." Unfortunately, admitting that means inviting a load of questions before I'm able to escape to the safety of my bedroom.

My bedroom door is closed—like I left it—when I get upstairs. I push it open, and the memories I tried to outrun when I left for the beach hit me full force. Why I didn't tidy up my diaries before I left, fuck only knows. I rush over and start sorting them out so I can hide them back in the ottoman where they belong when one catches my eye. It's the one I wanted. The one I wrote in after the events of that night. I don't remember how I left it exactly, but something tells me it wasn't open on this page or at this angle. I look at the page, but I refuse to read the words and look around my room.

Was he here?

That thought is only confirmed when I lift my most recent diary where I put my thoughts about last night. I'd left it on some possible song lyrics that seemed to sum up the situation nicely.

You seem to want me gone.

But I've done nothing wrong.

I hate this stupid game.

But I love it all the same.

Underneath those words is his handwriting, and my breath catches when I read the few words he's written.

You should have told me.

I'm sorry.

My heart pounds at having confirmation that he was actually here and that he read this. He knows.

"Fuck." My hands lift to my hair, and I spin on the spot, not knowing what to do. Depending on how he takes this, it could change everything, and as fucked-up as stuff has been, it was becoming normal. I'm not sure I want another change in my life.

Deciding I need to pull up my big girl panties and be the bigger person about this, I drag my bedroom door open once more and march across the hall. I don't bother knocking, not wanting to know if he'd let me in or not if I gave him a warning, and like he's done to me so many times, I throw his door wide open.

Empty.

A huge rush of air passes my lips as I release the breath I didn't know I was holding. I feel totally deflated as I walk back to my room. What am I supposed to do now? Wait until he reappears and discover what he now thinks about this whole situation?

The rest of Saturday passes with radio silence from Ethan. I spend another fitful night's sleep between looking at the ceiling and waking up covered in a cold sweat with *his* eyes staring down on me.

I'm in a foul mood when I wake Sunday morning, but it doesn't stop Mom interrupting my silence and all but forcing me to have breakfast with her and Eric.

Neither of them have a clue where Ethan is, but Eric doesn't seem too bothered, assuming he'll have been at some party last night and still sleeping off the effects of the night before.

I try to be as nonchalant about it as he is, but I can't help something twisting inside me. Everything isn't okay. After Friday night and then him reading my diary, everything is far from being okay.

Digging in my purse for my cell the second I'm able to escape back to my room, I hope to see something from him. But as usual, no one wants me. I don't really know why I bother carrying the thing around with me, it's not like I have friends who want to chat.

I type a message out and delete it a million times. I don't want to look like I care, especially if Eric is right. Me appearing concerned will only be ammunition for him to hit me with later. I can already hear his words. *"Aw, it's so cute you care about me, sweet cheeks. Now how about you do something that really shows me you care."* The image of his naked body and hard cock fill my mind and every muscle south of my waist clenches in memory.

Damn him. Why do I want to do it all over again? I should be the one now wanting to push him over the fucking balcony, not craving that he fucks me over it instead.

I glance out of the doors to the small space and bite down on my bottom lip. I imagine looking out over the beach in the distance as Ethan fills me from behind.

Fuck. Get your head out of the gutter, Raelynn. The guy fucking hates you.

Without putting too much more thought into it, I hit send on the most recent message I typed out.

Where are you? Your dad's home.

I sit and stare at the words, regretting them more and more as they taunt me from the screen. I thought by making it about his dad then it would look less like I'm worried, but I realize the fact I've sent it in the first place shows how I'm feeling. Eric's probably already been in contact to let him know they're home. He doesn't need to hear it from me.

Dropping my cell to the bed, I throw myself back onto the pillows with a groan of frustration. Even not here, he's fucking with my head... *and your body.* My thighs clench at that thought, my temperature increasing as I remember our time together. The look in his eyes. The way his muscles tensed as he was about to come. The fullness of his parted lips as he groaned in pleasure.

Fuck. Fuck. Fuck.

28

RAELYNN

"We need to talk." I look to my left and right where my arms have just been captured and find Barbie and Sindy attached to each one, looking like they're on a mission.

The three of us walk along as if we're best friends. I had a feeling something like this would happen seeing as Ethan never reappeared yesterday or this morning. And if what the rumor mill is saying is correct, then he didn't turn up for morning practice earlier either.

Neither of them stops until the three of us are standing in the girls' locker room. Granted, it's a welcome relief from being dragged into the guys', but it's still not really a place I want to be. At least it smells better.

They both guide me over to the benches in the center of the lockers and the three of us sit, me one side, them opposite.

"I'm pretty sure this could be classed as abduction," I mutter.

Barbie cracks a smile, but Sindy keeps the hard expression on her face. "Cut the shit, Rae. We need to know what's going on with Ethan."

"Then you should probably go and find someone who cares."

"We have," Barbie states, her eyes drilling into mine as if she can read my mind.

I blow out and accept that I can either openly talk or be coerced into it, and I don't have the time or the energy for the latter.

"We know you slept with him."

"Right. And what's the issue? He worried I wasn't all that impressed and that I'll ruin his reputation?"

Both of them stare at me with blank expressions.

"No, he's worried you didn't want it. That he forced you."

My chin drops. "W-what? That's why he's vanished? Because he thinks he..."

"Yeah. We found him laying into Zayn, drunk off his face after the event, and we dragged him back to Jake's. He was a fucking mess."

"So did he..." Sindy adds.

When I don't respond, Barbie tries. "Did he force himself on you, Rae?"

"Do I look like the kind of girl who does things she doesn't want to?"

"No, but with things like this... that often doesn't matter." Barbie's voice gets quieter as she finishes her sentence.

"Ethan might be an asshole, but he's not a fucking rapist." The word is bitter on my tongue, but I refuse to beat around the bush about this, no matter what horrors lie in my past.

They both sag in relief, showing just how worried they both are for their friend.

Deciding I'm in this deep and that I may as well give them a little more, I open my mouth again. "I won't lie, things between the two of us haven't exactly been sunshine and roses since I turned up. He's not exactly been... *welcoming*, shall we say."

They fall silent, obviously sensing that I have more I want to get out. I don't want to tell these two anything, I don't want them thinking I want to be friends or any crazy shit like that, but having the opportunity to get all this off my chest after bottling it up for what feels like forever becomes too much. "I've pushed back against him just as much. I wouldn't say I'm innocent in all this. I also wouldn't say that I've not enjoyed some of it. I've never really had anyone..." I trail off, suddenly realizing I'm giving them too much. They don't need to know that I've been lonely since the one person I trusted ruined everything for me. I've refused to become attached to anyone else since for fear of the past repeating itself.

"Do you... do you know where he is?" Sindy asks, shocking the hell out of me, seeing as I thought he was with them.

"N-no. He's with the guys, isn't he?"

Barbie shakes her head. "None of us have seen him since going to bed Friday night. He was gone when we all got up the next morning. Not seen or heard from him since."

"Fuck," I mutter, the image of his writing in my diary filling my head. "He came back to the house. Our parents are back. He went into my room." I suck in a shaky breath as the feelings from finding out he'd read everything hit me once again. "I'd left something on the bed. It probably freaked him out more than he already was if what you're saying is true."

"What?"

I shake my head, not willing to give these almost strangers any more information on my fucked-up life. "It doesn't matter. Just know that it wouldn't have helped."

"Okay, so..." Sindy starts before trailing off, hoping someone might have an idea.

"Have the guys spoken to the rest of the team? He's probably just crashed on one of their couches or something."

"Nope, no one's seen him. They need him, Rae. The next playoff game is next Friday. He needs to be at training. Needs his head in the right place. Can you reach out to him?"

"I messaged him already. No response."

"Fuck. We need to find him."

"And in the meantime?" Sindy asks.

"We keep Rae here company."

"Oh, um... that's really not necessary."

"I think it is. We still hardly know you, yet you're already important to—"

"Don't say it," I groan, cutting Barbie off.

"You like him, don't you?" Both of their eyes bore into me as I try to come up with an answer.

"N-no, he's an asshole."

"Oh, hun. We know all about assholes and how they have this weird ability to steal your heart when you least expect it."

"No, he's not... I haven't..."

"We need to get to class, but we're hanging out after school."

"Can't. I have work." I'm sure I've never been more relieved that I have to work for my own money.

"Okay, well, how about we come over after? Hang out, do homework?"

"I don't have a choice, do I? If I say no, you're going to show up anyway, aren't you?"

"We sure are."

"Let's go, or Mr. Richards will have us all in detention for skipping," Sindy says, linking her arm through mine.

"Rae, please try reaching out again. We all need him."

I nod to Barbie, who takes off in the opposite direction to her own class.

We walk in silence for a few seconds before Sindy speaks. "You're allowed to have friends here, you know. Ethan might think he wants you to leave, but I have a feeling he'd miss you if he ran you out of town now."

"I'm not sure about that," I mutter as the door we're aiming for appears in front of us, and I sigh in relief.

"This is your home now, Rae. It's time you accepted it and realize that it comes with a side dish of friends, whether you like it or not."

Sindy lets me go as we enter the classroom only a few seconds behind everyone else. The chair at the back of the room beside Jake taunts me, but I keep my eyes down and focus on where I need to go as I walk through the room.

As the day progresses, the rumors get more and more unbelievable as to where he's gone but equally the tension rises, because everyone in this school is relying on the Bears giving them a victory this year. More and more of the students' attention turns on me. Last week I was mostly invisible. But this week, word is starting to spread about who I am, or more so where I live.

By the time the final bell rings, I'm beyond ready to get the hell out of the place and the curious looks of everyone around me.

I walk straight out of school, foregoing a stop at my locker, and head straight for the bus stop that will take me to Aces.

If I thought it was going to give me a reprieve from the questions and stares then I was very wrong, because by the time the bus has stopped a million times on its route, other members of my class have already driven here and got themselves comfortable at their designated tables.

At least the football slash cheer table is empty... for now. I've no doubt they'll all come tumbling through the door soon, looking for answers, just like everyone else.

"So..." Cody says, dragging me from my thoughts. "Friday night was... interesting. What's the deal with you and Savage then?"

"No deal. He hates me."

The fucker has the audacity to laugh at my comment.

"Rae, come on. I had you pegged as one of the smart ones. That boy doesn't hate you."

"Really? Are you sure we're talking about the same guy?"

"Yeah, the one who was about ready to take my head off just because I had my hands on your hips. He was so fucking jealous."

"No, he just wanted us gone. He doesn't think we belong in his world, and I've got to be honest, I can't really argue with that."

"Speak for yourself, sweetheart."

"You want to go back? Be my guest. He's fucked off, it seems, so the coast is clear."

"Where's he gone?"

"No idea. Not that anyone seems to believe me. It's like they all think I've locked him in a dungeon somewhere or something."

"You can be a little scary. I can see where they might get that idea from."

I swat him with my notepad before heading back over to check on my customers.

Bang on the time I'm expecting them, the Rosewood Bears come waltzing into the diner with the cheer team hot on their heels. Jake and Mason are noticeably missing, probably out on an Ethan search party with their girls.

Groaning, I busy myself getting a couple of drink refills before reluctantly heading over.

"What can I get for you all?" I ask, forcing out a polite voice.

A couple of the guys give me their orders before a female interrupts them. "You know you were a bet, right?"

"I'm sorry, what?" I ask, getting a little whiplash from the random subject change.

"You. The guys dared Ethan to sleep with you Friday night."

I tell myself not to react. Not to show that her words have any effect on me. But from her reaction, I don't think I'm successful.

"Oh my god. You did sleep with him. What did he do, shove a bag over your head so he didn't have to look at you?"

My breath catches in my throat, a ball so fucking huge clogging it, stopping any smart-ass response I'd usually hit her back with.

"Enough, Shelly," one of the guys says. His deep voice is enough to bring me back to myself slightly.

"I don't know what you're talking about. The only girls stupid enough to open their legs for the likes of these douchebags are sluts like you."

She gasps, her hand coming up to cover her heart as if I've actually wounded her with my words.

"Oh come off it, love. You know as well as the rest of us that you've got no morals, just a desperate need to have your existence validated by having one of Rosewood's elite on your arm. It's pathetic."

Silence falls over the table as Shelly decides against going up against me and shrinks down in her seat.

"So, humble pie for Shelly," I quip. "What about the rest of you?"

I do the best I can writing down their orders with a trembling hand and run away the second I'm able to.

My head's fucking spinning as I put their orders through to the kitchen. The second I'm done, I turn on my heels, intending on slipping out the back for a little fresh air. I fucking need it after what I had to endure over the past five minutes.

I push through the fire exit and take what feels like my first breath since they all walked in. I'm just about to push a rock into the doorjamb to stop it locking me out when a figure appears. A figure in a Bears jersey. Fucking great.

"Fuck off," I say, not bothering to look up at his face. "I'm not interested in anything you have to say."

"I was just coming to make sure you were okay. Shelly was just being a bitch, trying to push your buttons." It's the genuine concern in his voice that has me looking up.

Kind green eyes stare down at me. His long, messy blonde hair is pulled back from his face in an annoying little top knot that has my fingers twitching to cut off. I recognize him as Sindy's friend. The one who is apparently part of the team even though he looks too... nice.

"I couldn't give a shit what she says."

"Okay, if you say so." It's clear he doesn't believe me, and I can't say I blame him.

Her words are on repeat in my head and only help to confuse me more when it comes to Ethan. *What, this whole thing just a bet?* No, it can't be. *Can it?* "Fuck."

I spin away from his probing eyes, worried that he can see too much. He seems much more perceptive than the others.

"Listen, I'm not here to pry or to tell you what to do. I just wanted to make sure you were okay."

"Was it a bet?" The words are out of my mouth before I have a chance to stop them.

"Err..." He looks away from me briefly, and it's all the answer I need.

"You're all a fucking joke, you know that?" I snap. "Do you have any idea how many girls' lives you ruin with your stupid, fucked-up games?"

"I couldn't agree more," he says, shocking the hell out of me.

"What?"

"I agree. Most of those guys are assholes."

"And you're hanging around with them why?"

"I have my reasons. But don't think they're my friends. They're not."

"But—"

"It doesn't matter. This isn't about me." *No, sadly it's about me and my fucked-up life.* "I just... it wasn't really a bet. There was no prize to win. Just a game the guys play where they pick each other a target for the night, giving them until dawn to... well, you know. I don't think Shelly or any of the girls really know about it. I think she was just trying to push your buttons."

"And I was Ethan's. Nice," I say, ignoring the bit about Shelly, because whether she knew or not, she's a fucking bitch.

"I'm sorry, Rae."

"It's fine. It's not like I'm stupid enough to fall for his charms."

He eyes me curiously, probably seeing right through my lie. "Well, that's... uh... good. I'm Shane, by the way. In case you'd forgotten."

"I'd like to say it was nice to see you again, but—"

"I know. I'd better get back."

I nod and watch him turn back toward the door. "Shane?" I ask before he disappears inside.

"Yeah."

"Maybe stop hanging around with them, eh?"

"I will, when I get what I want." My brows crease, wondering what on earth he could possibly need from assholes like them, but I allow him to go. I've got enough on my plate without worrying about his games.

Leaning back against the wall, I look out over the small courtyard space that mostly consists of old crap that Bill needs to get rid of and take in a deep breath.

He doesn't hold the power for me to care about this, I tell myself over and over before walking back inside with my head held high and ready to deliver food to my favorite table.

Cody eyes me suspiciously as I grab the plates, but thankfully, he doesn't say anything. I'm not sure what my answer would be if he did, because I'm sure as fuck not telling him the truth.

Their attention doesn't leave me until they finally pay their check and leave, and it's only then that I manage to breathe in a real breath.

Shane nods at me before he follows the others out like a sheep, and I wonder once again what he's playing at. He's either playing me by making out that he's a good guy, or something much more interesting is going on. I tell myself that I don't care before getting back to work.

———

When Cody drops me off at the house after our shift, Ethan's car is still missing and his bedroom is in darkness. I guess he hasn't appeared at some point then.

My eyes lock on the Mini sitting in the driveway beside it, and I groan. I guess they didn't get a better offer.

"Friends of yours?" Cody guesses when he looks over to find me staring at the car like I want to set it on fire.

"I don't have friends," I snap and immediately feel awful, because from the second he was thrust into my life by Bill, he's been nothing but a friend to me.

"Ah, yes. I forgot."

"I'm sorry. I didn't mean to snap. It's just been a long day."

"It's fine, I get it. Have a good night."

"You too, see you tomorrow." With that, I climb from his car, dreading what I'm going to have to endure once I get inside.

"Hey, honey. Did you have a good day?" Mom asks the second I step into the kitchen to grab a drink.

"Great," I lie, plastering on a smile as I pull the fridge open for a bottle of water.

"You've got two friends up in your bedroom waiting for you." When I look over, she's got the biggest grin on her face. She's been desperate for me to connect with someone in all the different places we've been, never really understanding why I've not made any friends. What's the point when tomorrow, next week, next month I'm going to be calling a new place home and surrounded by a whole new load of students? "I've already sent up refreshments. They said you've all got a lot of work to do. They seem really wonderful."

She pulls me into her arms, her excitement at me being 'normal' causing a lump to form in my throat. I hate to disappoint her, but she must be aware that she's the reason I'm far from normal.

"I'd better get up there then."

"Rae," she calls when I'm at the door. "They're always welcome. If you want sleepovers or anything." Her eyes shine with emotion, and I can't help returning it as I nod, despite the fact I find her permission hilarious. Does she have any idea what goes on under this roof while Eric is away?

"Thanks, Mom."

There's music playing as I make my way to my room, grateful that I shoved all my diaries back in the ottoman where they belong and not left them out for more prying eyes.

I push the door open and they both look up from their books. I wasn't really expecting them to actually be working, but it seems they really did just want to come here to do homework.

"Hey, we were starting to wonder if you stood us up."

"You're in my bedroom."

"Wouldn't put it past you," Barbie says with a laugh.

Dropping my bag on the end of the bed, I snatch up one of the cookies Mom must have sent up for them.

"Your mom's nice," Sindy says. "She looked kinda shocked when we told her we were meeting you."

"I'm not surprised. Never had friends turn up at my front door before."

Both of their faces turn sad. I hate the pity in their eyes.

"Enough of that. What are we doing?" After kicking my boots off, I grab my books and find myself a spot on the bed for our late homework session.

29

ETHAN

"It's not that I don't like having you here, baby. But don't you think you should head back. You need to be in class. Coach needs you. Jake and Mason need you, not to mention the rest of the guys."

"I know, Mom." I twist the mug in my hands back and forth to give me something to focus on.

"It might help if you talk about it," she encourages for the millionth time since I arrived unexpectedly on my grandparents' porch at the beginning of the week.

The second I read those words in her diary, I knew there was no way I could hang around and look her in the eye. The way I'd treated her, it was inexcusable. Unforgivable. And that was before I knew the horrors of her past.

Slumping back in the chair, I rub my hand over my face and across my rough jaw. I look a mess, I don't need to look up into my mom's caring eyes to know that. I just don't know how to pull myself out of the pit I've fallen into.

Regret consumes me. Memories haunt me. And that's only the daytime. At night it gets so, so much worse because my dreams are full of her. Of the way she smells, the way she sounds as my name falls from her lips, how soft her skin is, how hot and tight her pussy is.

Fuck.

Every morning I wake up, my cock's rock hard and begging for me to go back and beg for another chance. But then my brain kicks in and I know I can't. I can't look into those dark, haunted eyes that I now know are shadowed by what she was forced to endure, and I just can't do it. Every time she looks at me, she's going to remember. If I'm lucky, it'll just be the shit I pulled, or it could be worse.

I could remind her of him. That monster. The cunt who took her childhood away from her. Who made her the closed-off person she is today. I've no doubt that she is the way she is because of him. Her inability to trust, her lack of friends.

"It's a girl." The words fall out of my mouth without instruction from my brain. My need to talk, to tell someone who won't—hopefully—judge me.

"I guessed that much, E."

I blow out a breath. Of course she fucking knows. She always knows. It's one of the reasons why she's left such a big hole in my life with her being gone. One look at me and she always knew what I wanted—what I needed. "And I miss you." I hate the guilt that fills her features.

"I'm so sorry, baby. I want to be there for you, but the thought of seeing them, seeing her..." She visibly shivers at the thought alone. "I still love him. I think I always will, and I'm not sure I'll ever forgive him for this."

"I understand, Mom, I really do. It just fucking sucks." She lifts a brow at my language but doesn't chastise me like she usually would.

"So this girl..."

Placing my elbows on the table, I drop my head into my hands and suck in a breath. "I don't even know where to start."

"Try the beginning."

The truth about who she is is on the tip of my tongue, but I swallow it down, not ready to divulge that information yet. "I don't even like her."

"Yet she's got you so tied up that she's managed to get you to run here. There's a very fine line between love and hate, Ethan."

"It's hate. Definitely hate."

Her eyes drill into me until I'm unable to look into them anymore. "So what did you do?"

"Me? Why do you assume that I did something?"

"I'm sorry, baby. But you're the guy, you're genetically programmed to screw up more than the woman." My chin drops and she laughs. "I'm kidding, I'm kidding." I'm not sure I believe her.

"I've been a right ass to her."

"Because you hate her."

I nod. "Yep. Hate."

"And how does she feel about you?"

I shrug, although not because I don't know, more because there's no way she could feel anything but pure hatred for me. It's what I deserve. "Pretty sure she can't stand the sight of me."

"You kissed her?" Mom asks, leaning in like she's a little too invested in this conversation already.

"Mom," I snap, not wanting to go down this road with her.

"What? Would you prefer I ask if you've slept with her yet? Don't forget who you're talking to. I'm the one who bought you that first pack of condoms and a few more since. And I know for a fact that you're not collecting the things."

I blush, actually fucking blush, and she finds it hilarious.

"Okay fine. Yes to all the things, and you're not getting any more detail than that."

She sits back and thinks for a few seconds, and my stomach twists with what bit of advice could come from her next.

"Okay, I know many women claim to be able to sleep around like men and not allow feelings to get involved. And I'm sure there are women out there who can, but I've yet to meet one. In my experience, if she's let you kiss her, let alone anything else that we won't go into," she winks and I want the ground to swallow me up. When I'm sitting in front of my mom, I'll always be a little boy, no matter how old I actually am, "then I can almost assure you that she doesn't actually hate you."

"No, I'm pretty sure she's one of those who can detach her emotions. I actually think she's a master at it."

"Huh. Well, I guess I'll have to pass judgment on that until I meet her."

I choke on my coffee. Yeah, that's not going to be happening anytime soon.

"No matter what I tell you, my original point still stands. You need to go home. For school, for the team, and to sort things out with your girl."

My girl. That should sound all kinds of wrong, but hearing the words fall from Mom's lips is anything but.

My mind takes me back to Friday night once again as I stared down at her on her bed. My cock swells, thankfully beneath the table, as I remember exactly how it felt as I sank inside her.

"Fucking hell."

"If you learn anything from this disaster with your father and me, let it be that matters of the heart are complicated things. You can be thinking that you're in the middle of one play while the other person is on a total different pitch."

I smile at her. I love it when she tries to bring football analogies into day-to-day life thinking it'll help me understand, despite the fact that she almost always screws it up.

"Thanks, Mom." I refrain from telling her that I was fully aware of how complicated love was before this mess. It's one of the reasons I've never had a girlfriend. I don't have time for that kind of drama in my life.

"Anytime." She falls silent again, and I risk a glance up. It's clear she's deep in thought, so I leave her to it. I'm just about to push from the chair when she speaks. "What's her name?"

"Nice try."

"Fine," she concedes. "I know you'll tell me when you're ready. Have you heard anything from Chelsea? Ohhh, it's not her, is it?"

"No, Mom. It's not Chelsea." I roll my eyes at her. Chelsea's mom and mine have been friends for years. Anything happening with her would be like getting with my sister. A shudder runs down my spine. Rae could be that one day. *Fuck.* I push the thought from my mind. I don't need that shit in my head. "I've messaged her a few times but only had one reply. I just hope she gets what she needs."

"I'm sure she will. Honey said that she's hopeful the time away was exactly what she needed."

I nod, hoping that she's right. Chelsea has always been a little wild, but recently it's like she's lost her grip on reality. "I'm going to have a shower."

"And then you're heading home?"

"Jeez, are you sure you're not trying to get rid of me?"

"Never, you're welcome here as long as you like. I just don't want you falling behind because of it."

"I know. I'll go back... soon." *Maybe.*

30

RAELYNN

When I walked into the kitchen on Tuesday morning, I soon learned of Ethan's whereabouts because Eric announced that he was with his mother. Eric was pissed—rightly so. He was missing classes that he needed and practice that he should be making the most of, but according to him, Ethan was refusing to come home for some unknown reason.

I kept my mouth shut, not wanting to get involved in what was obviously a tense relationship between father and son. Mom kept watching me, making me wonder if she suspected that I knew more than I was letting on, but she never said anything.

I thought my time was up this morning when she knocked on my bedroom door and slipped inside before I left for school.

"Are you glad it's nearly the weekend?"

"I guess," I mutter, dropping some books into my bag. It's been a long-ass week, what with the continuous questions about Ethan and the entire school's building tension over whether he's going to reappear for the all-important game next weekend.

Amalie and Camila have kept up their promise to me and followed me around while trying to strengthen our friendship. I won't be admitting it aloud any time soon, but, not only am I starting to get used to their presence in my life, I'm also actually looking forward to it. When they weren't here after I came home from Aces last night, I actually missed their company. It was a fucking weird feeling after being alone for so long, that's for fucking sure.

"Eric and I are heading out of town this afternoon," she drops this in as if it's our normal.

"Again? I feel like you only just got back."

"I know. There's been some emergency. I don't know. We'll be gone by the time you get home, but I've organized a surprise for you for tomorrow."

"Oh?"

"I can't tell you now, but I think you're going to really enjoy it."

"Okaaaay," I say curiously as she pulls me in for a quick hug.

"Rachel's been shopping. Everything you could want to eat and drink is in the kitchen but if you need anything else then you've got your credit card."

I nod, already knowing that I won't be using it. I've got a little of my own money left before my first payday from Aces at the end of the month. Hopefully it'll see me through. "Any news on Ethan?" I ask, wondering if I should expect him to reappear the second his dad disappears.

"No idea. Eric hasn't spoken to him and only had a few messages from Kelly."

"Okay, well... I'd better head out if I don't want to miss the bus."

"I could take you, if you like." Guilt twists her features. Whatever Eric's emergency is, I'm one hundred percent sure that she doesn't need to follow to help out, but it seems she's doing just that anyway.

"It's fine. I'm sure you need to pack or something. Have a good trip."

"Okay, I'll see you in a few days then. Be good."

"When aren't I?" I ask as I pull my door open and leave her standing in the middle of my room, looking lost.

My heart drops the second I step out of the front door. The last thing I want is to spend the weekend alone in the huge house. I might like my own company, but it's a little different being alone in the tiny apartments Mom and I shared compared to this mansion.

Shaking my head, I make my way down the long driveway on my way to the bus stop.

School is just deja vu of the rest of the week with everyone asking me if there's any news. So much for starting here and blending in; everyone now seems to know my name and my connection to the Savages.

———

By the time I climb out of Cody's car, I'm exhausted and the sight of both Amalie and Camila's cars sitting in the driveway doesn't fill me with any kind of excitement. All I want to do is crawl into bed in the hope that sleep claims me, unlike the rest of the week. My eyes sting and my muscles burn as I walk to the front door, reminding me of the few hours I've managed each night since this time last week.

It's all Ethan's fault. My lips purse as I think of him. If he didn't storm into my room last Friday night then none of this would have happened. He'd still be here, and I might still have some control over my insomnia and the nightmares that are continuing to come thick and fast.

"What the hell is this?" I ask, walking into my bedroom and finding not only my bed like I was expecting but two temporary ones on the floor.

"Your mom invited us to keep you company while she was gone." My chin drops as the cogs in my brain start working. I think back to her words Monday night after she discovered my 'friends.' Something about sleepovers and being normal.

"If you tell me we're having a pillow fight and playing truth or dare then I'm walking straight back out that door."

"No, you're safe," Amalie says.

"Although, we do still need gossip about you and Ethan."

"I told you we fucked."

"Yes, but there are a million and one ways that could have gone down—"

"Oh, he went down," I mutter much to their amusement—and excitement, if the seal clapping is anything to go by.

"Rumor has it he's got mad skills."

"Says who, the entire cheer squad?"

Amalie snorts a laugh, although her face looks anything but amused. "Sadly, those sluts have intimate knowledge of all our guys. Here's hoping they've sucked so many they don't remember which belongs to whom."

"Jesus, they've got some issues." I kick my shoes off and rummage in my drawer for something more comfortable to change into.

"You're telling us. And believe it or not, you haven't met the worst one."

"No?"

"No. Chelsea is the captain and she's—"

"A raging fucking bitch?" Amalie interrupts.

"That works," Camila agrees with a laugh.

"Where's she then?"

"Fuck knows. With Ethan, for all we know. She vanished almost as quickly as he did."

Something stirs in my stomach, and when I turn to look at them both it's clearly written all over my face.

"She didn't actually mean that they're together," Amalie says softly, making Camila wince.

"I don't care if they are."

"Really? So you can honestly say, hand on heart, that you're not missing the asshole from across the hall?"

"No, it's such a relief not to be constantly looking over my shoulder." *Liar.*

"Has anyone ever told you that you're a terrible liar, Rae?"

"No one's ever looked closely enough to notice." Fuck, why do I keep saying shit like this to these two and making myself look like a pathetic loser?

"Well lucky for you, you've got us now to point out all the things you don't want to know."

"Like just how badly you want Ethan back."

"I don't. I—"

"It's probably easier just to concede," Amalie says, elbowing Camila in the ribs. "This one is nothing if not persistent."

"Good to know. I'm just going to..." I hold up the clothes in my hand and move toward the en suite.

"Take your time."

"I hope you're hungry," Camila shouts just as I close the door behind me. "We've ordered enough Chinese to feed the entire football team."

Not needing another reminder of the one person I'm trying not to think about, I lean back against the door and press the heels of my hands into my eyes in an attempt to force him out.

My stomach's still twisting unpleasantly at Camila's suggestion that he might be with the bitchiest of the cheer bitches. I never thought of myself as a jealous person, but I hate to admit that I fear that's what I'm feeling right now. I don't want him, yet why can't I even consider the idea of anyone else having him?

Needing some time to get my head together before I go out and field more questions from my new besties, I turn the shower on and strip down. The water from the power shower above my head soothes my tense muscles, but it's not enough to keep it away because the second I step from the water I'm as uptight as I was before.

"Whoa, your hair is so long," Amalie says when I finally rejoin them and find them both surrounded by a million takeout containers. They weren't joking when they said they'd ordered enough to feed the five thousand.

I shrug before swiping a band from my sideboard and going to pull it back.

"No, don't do that. It's so beautiful."

"It gets in the way," I say. It's my go-to excuse. Has been ever since... no, not going there tonight.

"Trust me, I know." She whips her long blonde mane over her shoulder as evidence. "It just really softens your face. It suits you."

Telling myself it's just me and the girls—something I never thought I'd hear myself say—I put the band back down and continue toward the food.

Although totally out of my comfort zone, we have a good night. And I'm not sure if it's because of their company or not, but when we eventually turn the lights out long after midnight, I fall asleep a hell of a lot quicker than I have the rest of the week, and when I wake, I immediately realize I had a peaceful night and actually feel refreshed for the first time in days.

It's still early when I swing my legs from the bed and quietly make my way to the en suite. Both Amalie and Camila are passed out, so after grabbing a hoodie, I slip from my bedroom.

I make myself a coffee and head out into the morning sun. It's colder than I was expecting as I settle myself on one of the loungers looking out over the infinity pool and beach beyond. I tuck my knees up into my giant hoodie and wrap my palms around the steaming mug, allowing its warmth to seep into me.

I think back over last night and the girl chat. I've never had anyone to discuss things like that with before, and the first time they started talking sex, I'll be honest, I wasn't really sure I should stay in the room. I know their boyfriends; it was a little odd. But it soon became obvious that their conversation was a normal one for them, so I endured listening. It was a whole other ball game when they turned the questions on me and my time with Ethan. They wanted the ins and outs—quite literally—and my cheeks flamed red hot the second they turned their eyes on me.

I gave them the basics, enough that might get them off my back, but even just skimming the surface of what's gone down between us, I could see them both getting ideas in their heads that there might be more to us than I'm letting on. Plans for triple dates with their boys were literally playing out in their minds like a little movie.

I've no idea how long I sit out there, but my coffee has been long drunk and the sun's much higher in the sky when I hear the doorbell ring.

Regretfully untangling myself from my little cocoon, I walk through the house to the front door. I have no idea who it could be, but I can honestly say that I never would have guessed in a million years when I pull the front door open.

"Hi, are you Rae?" asks one of the ladies before me. They're all dressed in black tunics with flawless hair and makeup, and sitting beside them are silver pull-along trollies.

"Um..."

"We've been booked for the day."

Footsteps sound out behind me before they come to a stop on each side of me.

"Come in," Amalie says politely before wrapping her fingers around my upper arm and gently pulling me out of the way.

"Uh... what the hell is going on?"

"Think of it as a welcome to town present."

"This really isn't necessary," I whisper, watching as the three women grab the handles of their trollies and march in.

"Where would you like us to set up?"

"I'll show you," Camila says, pointing down the hallway.

"Would any of you like a drink before we start?" Amalie asks. I watch it all play out like I'm not really here.

"Coffees would be great. Thank you so much."

I watch the four of them disappear around the corner, my stomach in knots.

"What... um... is this really necessary?"

"Looking at how tense you are, yes. It's totally necessary."

"I've... um... never..." I trail off. I've never really thought about what was lacking in my life. I had Mom, I've always been healthy, things and money have never really bothered me, but suddenly I can't help thinking about how much I've missed out on. Something as simple as a girly sleepover like last night is one thing, but a full-on spa day with friends is well out of the norm for me. The closest I've come is a discount face mask I've picked up from the store on occasion.

"Lucky for you, I'm a pro. Come on. It's time to put your feet up, forget all about the world, and relax for a few hours." She links her arm through mine, and together we head for the kitchen for coffee before joining Camila in the family room while the therapists set up in the sun room.

"I'm assuming my mom had something to do with his," I whisper to Amalie and Camila when the three of us are laid out with gunk on our faces and cucumbers over our eyes.

"She might have mentioned a few things that sparked off the idea."

"T-thank you," I whisper, not really wanting to acknowledge that I'm enjoying this but needing to let them know how much I appreciate it.

"Trust us, it's our pleasure. And bonus, you'll be looking extra hot for when Ethan reappears."

I immediately sit up. "Do you know something? Is he coming back?" The rush in which the questions fall from my mouth make it clear to everyone in the room just how desperate I am for him to be here.

"Whoa, calm down. No, still no news. But he's got to be back sooner rather than later. He can't miss too much more school or practice."

I lie back down, a knot tightening my stomach as I think about what our first meeting is going to be like.

I never thought I'd say it, but I actually really enjoy my day of pampering, not that I'm going to tell anyone that.

"So what now?" I ask when the therapists have left and the three of us are lounging around on the couches, thoroughly relaxed.

"Now? Now, we order food, find some drinks, and watch some shit on TV."

"You're both staying again? Don't you have anything better to be doing than babysitting me?"

"One, we're not babysitting you. We're getting to know you. And second, not really. The boys are spending the whole weekend working on plays and shit for Friday, and as hot as it is to watch them, a whole weekend of it is a bit much."

"Okay but—"

"No buts. All you need to worry about is what food you want delivered."

And that's how the rest of our day goes. We order a mountain of food and drink way too much vodka before once again crashing out in my room.

31

ETHAN

I know the guys are spending the weekend putting in extra practice sessions ready for Friday. I see all the messages come through to the group chat that Jake set up, and I feel guilty as I think about all the work they're doing while I'm here wallowing in self-pity after my deplorable actions.

I know Mom's right. I need to go back and face the music, but more than that, I really need to get back for school and the team. They'll never forgive me if I miss any more practices before Friday night's game, and I'll never forgive myself if I get myself benched and miss the final games of my high school football career.

Blowing out a long breath, I push myself from the bed, knowing that if I'm not with them then I should still make some kind of effort to keep myself in shape for Friday. I drag on a pair of sweats, a hoodie, and my sneakers. I swipe my cell from the nightstand and push my earbuds into place.

Mom is in the kitchen with Gran when I pass. They both look up and smile as I head for the front door.

I take off without a destination in mind, just knowing that I need to run until my lungs hurt and my muscles burn. Running away feels too damn good, but I know what I'm doing right now is taking the pussy's way out. I need to get a grip and head back. A feisty, short ass brunette should not hold the power to make me second guess going home, but somewhere along the line, it seems I either handed her my balls or I grew my very own vagina, because just the thought of seeing her again has my heart rate increasing.

By the time I turn back down my grandparents' street, my hoodie is soaked with sweat and I can barely catch my breath. It's exactly what I need.

Mom and Gran are exactly where I left them, both hugging their mugs and shooting the shit.

"Would you like some breakfast?" Mom calls as I come to a stop in the doorway.

"Yeah. Let me shower first."

"Damn right," Gran says, fighting her smile. "I'm not having you dripping sweat in my kitchen. Scram."

I salute her and disappear to my room.

I just shut the door behind me when my cell starts ringing. Assuming it's going to be Mason again trying to find out when I'm coming back—the fucker's been relentless all week—I pull it out and almost answer without looking, but at the last minute my eyes land on the screen.

Shane?

What the fuck is he calling me for?

I almost ignore it and throw it onto my bed, but my need to know why he's reaching out gets the better of me.

"Yeah?" I ask, putting my phone to my ear.

"Uh... hey." Silence surrounds me, and just as I'm about to ask what the fuck he wants, he starts talking. "So... I was just wondering when you were planning on coming back."

"Why the fuck do you care?"

"I don't, but... fuck, she's going to fucking kill me for this," he says quietly, sounding like a crazy man.

"Spit it out or get off my cell," I bark. I'm hot, sweaty, exhausted, and hungry. I don't have the energy for this bullshit.

"Rae. You need to come back for Rae." His words make my breath catch.

"Why? What's wrong with her?" My question comes out in a rush, and any hope I had of sounding unaffected by her goes straight out the window.

"Nothing's wrong but..." He trails off, but it's obvious he has so much more to say.

"But?"

"Shelly's been giving her grief—"

"You've met Rae, right? I'm pretty sure she can handle herself around the likes of Shelly."

"Yeah, yeah of course she can. But... I think she's missing you."

"I highly fucking doubt that, man. She fucking hates me."

"Maybe so, but your parents are gone again and—"

She's alone. I have no idea if those are the words that fall from his lips, because his voice fades away as I picture her in the house with no one.

"And anyway," Shane says, my senses coming back to me once again, "we fucking need you on the field Friday night."

"I'll see what I can do," I mutter, thoughts of her alone still at the forefront of my mind.

"I gotta go, Jake's busting our fucking balls."

"Sure, yeah." I pull my cell from my ear before thinking better of it. "Shane?"

"Yeah?"

"Um... thanks for looking out for her, man."

"No worries. Just do the right thing, yeah?"

I hang up before my mouth runs away with me. I've not exactly been focusing on doing the right thing when it comes to Rae since she arrived. I've just got to home and find out if it's not too little too late.

I shower, pull on some fresh clothes, and pack the little I brought with me. It's time to face the music.

———

It's late Monday evening when I eventually drive through Rosewood. I'm fucking exhausted and wished I'd flown the long ass journey to Connecticut when I first fled town. I'd put my seat back and crashed on the side of the road last night, not wanting to waste time getting a motel, but I'm fucking paying the price for it now.

It's dark when I pull up out front of Jake's aunt and uncle's house. I debated where to go. Home would have been the most sensible place, but call me a pussy, I'm still not ready to look her in the eyes.

Jake's trailer lights are on, and I breathe a sigh of relief even though I know I'm about to get ripped a new one for skipping out on the team.

I knock but don't bother waiting for a response, seeing as it's pouring down with rain. I pull the door open and step up inside.

"Well, he is alive," Jake says after doing a double take. Amalie lifts her head from his shoulder and also looks my way, but unlike Jake's angry eyes, hers are full of sympathy and concern.

"Yeah, look, I'm—"

My apology is cut off when he pushes from the couch and steps toward me. I wince when he lifts his arm, because from the anger rolling off him, I expect him to plant his fist in my face. It's the least of what I deserve for everything, but the pain never comes. Instead, he pulls me in for a quick man-hug and pounds me on the back a few times.

When he pulls back, he barks out a laugh when he looks at my face. "No need to look so freaked out, bro."

"I... uh... thought you were going to rip me a new one."

"Oh don't worry. It's coming. Beer?"

"Yes." One thing about spending time at my grandparents' is that it's an alcohol-free house. Not exactly what I needed after these few weeks, but in hindsight, it was probably for the best.

He walks over to the fridge and pulls two bottles out. I leave him to it and walk over to where Amalie's still sitting on the couch, looking at me.

"Good to have you back," she says softly.

Every inch of my body fills with guilt for leaving, but I couldn't see any other way after what I discovered.

"I'm not sure everyone will think that," I mutter. I know she's been spending time with Rae. Mason let it slip in one of his messages that the girls had been over at my house doing homework with her.

"You need to talk to her, Ethan." Her slim hand lands on my knee and squeezes encouragingly. "I'm not getting in the middle, but I think you might be blowing things a little out of proportion."

"Am I?" I snap. "I doubt she's told you the whole story."

"You're probably right, but she's told me enough that I know that you need to pull your head out of your ass and talk to her."

"And here I was thinking that it would be Jake giving me a tongue lashing."

She quirks a brow at me, but she doesn't say anything else.

32
_____

RAELYNN

T he second I step into school on Tuesday morning, it's obvious
something has happened. The buzz around the students is electric, but
as I make my way to my locker and then to my first class of the day, I
can't get a handle on what it is from the tiny snippets of conversation I hear.

All that changes once the students around me start filling the room.

"Apparently he just turned back up to practice this morning like everything
was normal."

"I heard Coach really laid into him."

"Yeah. He threatened to bench him for Friday night's game."

"Lisa said that Jake had him pinned against the wall."

The gossip goes on and on, but after the first few I'm unable to listen as my
pulse starts to race and nothing but white noise fills my ears.

He's back.

I glance around, noting that none of the team have yet arrived in class but
knowing it doesn't really matter. He's not in any of my classes today.

Blowing out a slow breath and hoping my sudden bout of anxiety over seeing
him again disappears with it, I sink back in my chair and try to ignore the gossip
surrounding me. I have no doubt most of it is bullshit.

I look for him all day, but the closest I get is spotting Jake at the end of the
hallway, presumably heading for the locker room for afternoon practice.

"Have you seen him?" Amalie asks, coming to stand next to where I'm gazing
down the hallway.

"Um... no. You?"

"Yeah."

"And? How is he?"

"Honestly, I've no idea. But it's not really for me to discover. You need to talk to him."

"I know. But I have a suspicion that he's doing everything possible to avoid me."

"He's got a lot going on for the game." It's clear the second the words leave her lips that she believes them as much as I do.

"Whatever. I'm going to be late for work."

"You want me to drop you off?"

"No, it's okay. I'm sure it's well out of your way."

"Shut up. Come on. You can buy me a milkshake to say thank you."

I grab the books I need before following Amalie out toward the parking lot. I don't really have much of an argument as I'd much prefer a lift from her than getting on the bus. It's well worth the milkshake she's after.

I spend all night watching the door and waiting for the team to arrive, but they never do. I tell myself over and over that it's just because they're focused on the Friday night and not because Ethan's demanded they boycott the place.

I expect his car to be sitting outside the house when Cody pulls up to drop me off, but his space is still vacant, like it has been for the for days.

"This is fucking bullshit," I mutter as I storm to my bedroom and dump my bag. If I thought he was driving me crazy by running off after discovering my secrets, it's nothing compared to knowing he's close yet avoiding me. He really must hate me after discovering the truth.

Pulling my clothes angrily from my body, I storm through to my en suite and stand under the shower before turning it on. When I flick the switch, I'm blasted with ice cold water. It's a welcome relief from thinking about that motherfucker all day.

I toss and turn all night as I wonder what the next day is going to hold. Is he going to turn up to the classes I know we have together, or is he more serious about not seeing me than even I think he is?

———

I'm a nervous fucking wreck as I walk into class the next day, knowing that he should also be in it.

I'm the first in the room, so I find my seat and pull my books out, ready to get started.

Students soon begin to fill the room around me. The teacher arrives, and I just start to think that he's not going to show when the door pushes open. Every set of eyes in the room turns to see who it is seeing as we're all silent, ready for class to start. My breath catches as I get my first look at him in almost two weeks. He's just as annoyingly handsome as the first time I laid eyes on him. He's wearing a pair of dark jeans that are teasingly tight across his thighs—and, I'm sure, his ass, should I get a look at his back—and a skin-tight white V-neck t-shirt that shows every ripple of muscle beneath as he closes the door behind him and nods in apology to the teacher.

As he takes a step to the back of the room, I swear to god that I stop breathing. I stare at him, willing him to look at me so I can get a read on him. Is he ashamed of what happened between us, what he thinks he did? Is he just repulsed by me now he knows my past? Does he care more than he's ever let on? That last one is a long shot, but in the long hours I've had awake at night trying to figure this shit out, I've thought of every angle possible.

He steps up to my desk, his scent filling my nose and my mouth watering, but still, he refuses to look at me and instead keeps his eyes on the floor.

Fucking pussy.

I realize there and then that if I want to have this out with him, I'm going to have to be the one to confront him.

I don't get a chance for the rest of the day. He's out of class before I even pick up my book to leave, and he remains irritatingly invisible. Knowing it's too late to do anything seeing as I should be heading for work, I vow to find a way to intercept him tomorrow and head off to find the bus.

"Is there any chance I could get tomorrow night off?" I ask Bill, poking my head into his office.

"Is everything okay?" he asks, concern filling his eyes.

"Y-yes, of course. I'm just falling a little behind this week and—" Thankfully, my rambling is cut off when he agrees, although I can see in his eyes that he doesn't totally believe me. I get out of there before he feels the need to play the part of my dad and sit me down for a talk.

There's still no appearance from the team or the bitch squad. It's a relief as much as it is frustrating that Ethan has so much control over his idiot friends that he can stop them coming here.

"You fallen out with your friends or something?" Cody asks when we pull up to the Savage house later that evening.

Both Amalie and Camila have been busy this week so haven't been here. Amalie's buying a house for her and Jake. I think she's utterly insane, but I guess when you have that kind of money, what else is there to do? And Mason's had doctor appointments. I can't really complain at either of them, and I hate to admit it, but after their almost constant company last week, I miss them.

"They're busy."

"So... I'll see you Friday then?"

"Yeah. Thanks for the lift."

"Always." He turns and gives me a sad smile before I climb from the car. I've been trying to put a brave face on, but I fear that Cody can see right through it. I'm grateful however that he doesn't seem to want to dig into what's put it there.

The rest of the evening drags. I end up getting talked into a late night dinner with Mom and Eric and am forced to listen to their plans for leaving again tomorrow. They've only been back a matter of hours and they're already talking about leaving again. I bite my tongue to stop myself asking if he's ever been here to support Ethan, but it's not my place to get involved.

"Have you seen him?" Eric's voice drags me from my thoughts, making me wonder if I said Ethan's name aloud.

"I've seen him at school," I mutter.

"I keep calling, but it just goes to voicemail. I swear he's not been here yet this week."

I shrug, not wanting to confirm his suspicions.

"Just keep trying. I'm sure he's just busy," Mom adds, like this kind of behavior is normal. Although we've only been here a few weeks, so maybe it is. Maybe Ethan often just fucks off without a word to his parents.

Pushing my dinner around my plate, I try not to focus on the look on his face in class earlier. He was hurting, that much was clear, but why? And why did he even refuse to look at me? Is he that ashamed to even glance my way after learning the truth? That thought causes my heart to constrict. He might be an asshole, but I always thought there was someone redeemable beneath the hardened exterior.

"Can I be excused?" I ask once my dinner is cold and the two of them are reliving a memory from their last trip.

"Of course." I get to the door with my plate when Mom's voice calls me back. "Rae, it's Thanksgiving next week. We'll be back so we can all celebrate as a family." A lump forms in my throat. Are we a family? I almost laugh at the hopeful look on her face.

"Sure thing, Mom. Looking forward to it." They must be the least sincere words I've ever said, but she accepts them and thankfully allows me the escape I'm desperate for.

33

ETHAN

I thought avoiding her would be easy. She's just one person in a huge school full of students, but I swear to fucking god that every time I look up, there she is. Without her even realizing it, she's driving me fucking crazy. Those fucking short shirts she wears that show off the smooth lines of her stomach. Her ridiculous excuse for skirts that make my mouth water to rediscover what's hiding beneath. She's all I can fucking think about, and it's the reason I continue to stay away. I don't need her distracting me more than she already is. Coach, Jake, and the rest of the team deserve my undivided attention for tomorrow night. I can't allow her to take up any more of my headspace, and I know talking to her will do just that. There's so much that's been left unsaid between us, and after everything, she deserves my time to hear her out properly, and I know I can't give her that right now.

Thursday afternoon's practice session is grueling beyond belief. We thought Coach was upping the ante earlier in the week, but nothing could have prepared us for this afternoon. My legs feel like jelly as I pull my bag up onto my shoulder and head for the locker room door.

What I really want to do is go home, relax in the jacuzzi and sleep in my own bed, but I fear that if I do that, sleep won't come for one reason or another. I want to say it'll be because I'll be inside her all night like I keep dreaming of, but realistically, it'll be because I'm in bed on the other side of the hallway, tossing and turning for being a pussy and hiding from her once again.

I need to man the fuck up and get it over with, I know this. But still, I keep telling myself to get the game out of the way and then I can do what needs to be done.

Sadly, those intentions come crashing down around my feet when I pull the locker room door open and find her leaning back against the opposite wall with one foot propped up and a can of soda halfway to her lips.

Our eyes lock. My heart damn near falls out of my chest as something crackles between us.

Someone crashes into my back where I've stopped so suddenly. "Savage, what the fuck, man?" But still, I stand there staring at her.

I'm jostled to the side as a few of the guys leave and head toward the exit.

"What do you want?" I grunt, dragging my eyes from her dark ones in favor of the floor.

"I think it's time we talked, don't you?"

Voices get louder behind me as she pushes from the wall and closes the space between us. As usual, her hair is pulled back from her face, her makeup is heavy, her eyes and lips dark in a stark contrast to her pale skin. She's anything but my type, but as she stands there demanding more from me than I'm willing to give right now, I'm hard-pressed to say I've ever wanted anyone more. Her ripped black shirt has *whatever* scrawled across the front of it in white and her black skirt is almost pointless. When I make it down her pantyhose covered legs and to her biker books, I take my time in heading back up once again. Only now, she's got her hand on her jutted-out hip and one brow raised in question.

"No."

"N-no?" she questions, her head pulling back in surprise.

"No. We're not doing this here."

"Why?" she asks, her chin lifting in defiance in a way I love. I'm not used to girls standing up to me—they're usually heading down to their knees instead. It's a refreshing change to the norm. As she opens her mouth, the voices behind me get louder still. "You ashamed of me now? Now you know the truth?"

The guys come barreling through the doorway and hesitate when they see us together in the empty hallway.

"Fucking hell, Savage. You slumming it tonight?"

The words and their assumptions about Rae piss me off—only, not enough to show her that. They give me the perfect distraction and moment to think to get me out of this situation.

Ignoring them, I turn my stare back on her. "Yeah, actually. I am." I put as much hatred into my voice as I can. "We're done here, *trash*." I narrow my eyes at her as she gasps in shock, a couple of the guys slapping my shoulder as I get to them. Thank fuck it's not Jake or Mason, because they'd call me out on this bullshit in a second.

With her standing there looking like I've just told her I've killed her puppy, I make my retreat. We find the rest of the guys still in the parking lot, and when Zayn suggests heading to his place to watch some old games, I eagerly agree. Anything to attempt to forget the look I just put on her face.

I end up sleeping on Zayn's couch. Thankfully, the girls didn't turn up. Fighting them off was the last thing I needed, especially seeing as there was no alcohol. I offered to get some in, but all I got in return was some seriously pissed-off faces. Their only concern is the game. It should be mine too, but the second I left Rae standing there, I knew I'd made a mistake. I was avoiding talking about it, hoping that it would help clear my head, but in doing so, it's only made it worse. If I'd just taken her up on her offer, or even gone home last night, then all this could be sorted.

I don't spot her until she's carrying a tray toward a table in the cafeteria at lunch. Ignoring the guys around me, I push from my seat and head over.

"Rae." She stills at the sound of my voice but refuses to turn. Instead, she lowers her tray to the empty table in front of her and sits, never once even glancing over her shoulder at me.

Dropping down beside her, I wait to see if she'll even acknowledge she has company. "Rae, I'm sorry. I—"

"Not fucking interested," she barks, staring down at her plate and poking at a fry. "What the fuck are you even doing here? I'd thought you'd be too ashamed to be seen with me."

"I didn't mean it. I'm not—"

"Well, maybe you shouldn't have fucking said it, eh?" She finally turns her dark stare on me and my breath catches when I find tears pooling in her eyes.

Fuck. My chest aches and my hand twitches to reach out to touch her, to do anything to show her that I didn't mean what I said yesterday, that I didn't really mean any of the fucked-up things I've said and done to her since she arrived here. With that, she stands, snatches her uneaten food up and dumps it in the trash on the way out. She passes Camila and Amalie, who don't have a choice but to stand aside. They look to her before their eyes find me. Both sets narrow slightly before they turn on their heels and follow her.

"Fucking hell," I shout, causing a few others to look my way. "What?" I bark, getting up and storming from the cafeteria.

I head straight for the gym, ignoring anyone who calls out to me as I pass. The only person's voice I want to hear just ran away from me as fast as she could. Rightly so. I'm just surprised that her lunch made it to the trash and didn't end up on my head. It's what I deserve. I know that.

I go straight for the weight bench and lie down, ready to distract myself with the burning of my muscles. I wrap my fingers around the cool metal bar, but at the last second, I release it knowing that I'll never forgive myself if I push too hard and fuck up tonight. There's too much riding on it.

"Fuck," I shout, my voice echoing around the empty room.

I pull my cell from my pocket and find her name. I want to call her, demand she tells me where she is so I can find her and ensure she listens to me, but I know it's pointless. Even if she agreed, I have a feeling that Amalie and Camila wouldn't let me within a mile of her right now. They want me to talk to her, sure. But not when we're both this angry.

Instead, I find someone else's number and hit call.

"Ethan?"

"Mom." My voice breaks, and her gasp of shock sounds out loud and clear. "I've fucked up." It's painful to admit, but I need to get it out.

"Go on, I'm listening."

"The girl I mentioned. She's *her* daughter." Mom's breath catches once again, telling me she knows who I mean. "I've... I've done some stuff that I'm really ashamed of. But I was so fucking mad. So fucking angry for how he treated you, then he had the gall to move them in and I made her the target of all my hate. It was wrong, and fucked-up, and... and... fuck." I drop my head into my hands as memories of all the despicable things I've done and said to her play out in my mind.

"Ethan," she says softly, dragging me from my turmoil. "It's going to be okay. The most important thing is that you know you were wrong. You can only right something if you truly accept you made a mistake in the first place."

"She's never going to forgive me... and..." I trail off, not knowing if I should, or even can, voice the next bit.

"And what, sweetheart?"

"I... I need her." My voice is barely a whisper, the honesty behind my words slamming me in the chest and making it hard to breathe.

"You've really fallen for her, huh?"

"I know it's wrong, but... fuck." The image of her laid out naked on her bed before me fills my mind. "She's never going to forgive me. And she shouldn't. I... I..." I can't even bring myself to say the words out loud for what I fear I did that night. "She's got a rough past, and the way I've acted toward her. How I've treated her. I... I think I've..." My chest heaves as I fight to drag in the air I need.

"Ethan. Ethan. Just breathe," Mom says softly. "Calm down. Take a moment and tell me as much as you like. I'm your mom. Judgment free zone here, remember?" It's the same thing she's said to me time and time again over the years when I fuck up. And I know it's true. She's never judged me when I've made a mistake. She's only ever listened and supported me. And fuck if that's not exactly what I need right now.

I squeeze my eyes shut, blocking out everything around me and force the words out. "I think I might have forced myself on her."

The halt in Mom's breathing shatters me. I hate that I've shocked her, that she's now going to think differently of me. That I could be *that* kind of man.

"Okay, start from the beginning. Tell me everything."

And so I do. Much to her horror, I'm sure. I explain about how I've treated her, what I've made her do. I hold nothing back, including what I know about her past.

"I wish you'd have told me this when you were here," Mom says when I've eventually finished.

"I-I just couldn't," I admit. The only reason I can now is because I'm on the phone. It makes it just that little bit easier to handle.

"I understand. You need to talk to her. Not in the middle of school, or before tonight's game. You need her to be somewhere she feels comfortable, safe, and you need to listen to her. I mean really listen to her. There's a very good chance that a lot of this isn't as bad as you're making it out to be."

"And what if it is?" I ask, terrified of what the reality could be.

"We'll deal with that when we get to it. But the facts remain that she's done nothing to show that she thinks you did anything wrong. She could have reported you. This could be a bigger issue than what it appears to be right now."

I blow out a long breath I didn't know I was holding, because she's right. If I really did force her that night, she would've have told someone. Reported it. I'd have been hauled off in the back of a cop car by now and questioned.

"I know it's hard, but focus on the game. It's only hours away. Do what you need to do. Take the win. Then go and find your girl and get everything out on the table."

"Okay." I nod, her words settling into me. I can do that.

"And Ethan?" she quickly adds. "Don't pussyfoot around how you feel. If you're falling for her, then damn well tell her."

"Okay. Okay." My heart pounds at the thought, but I know she's right. "Thanks, Mom."

"Always, sweetheart. I'm always here, no matter how many miles are between us right now."

"I miss you," I admit. I've already laid my heart and fears on the line, I may as well be totally honest.

"I know. I miss you too."

We say an emotional goodbye before I fall back onto the bench once again and allow my eyes to close as I think about everything she just said to me.

34

RAELYNN

"Jesus, it's even quieter than two weeks ago," I complain as we look around at the empty diner. "Guess I'll make the most of the time." I pull a couple of books from my bag and hop up onto one of the stools at the counter to get some work done. "Chocolate milkshake would be a real treat right now," I say, glancing at Cody.

"Guess I've got nothing else to do," he mutters before disappearing back to the kitchen.

I sigh and flip my book open. Half of the town has headed to Thunder Valley to watch the Bears thrash the Bobcats, and those who've not gone apparently don't care for a night out.

Five minutes later, Cody places my drink in front of me. "Thank you," I mumble. Lifting my eyes from my chemistry book, I find a somber look on his face.

"What's wrong?" I ask, feeling guilty that I didn't notice his mood before.

"Nothing." He grabs a cloth and starts cleaning down the already spotless counters.

"Cody?"

He blows out a breath. "I've just got a date after work. I'm... uh..."

"Wait. Are you nervous?"

He stills and looks up at me. "I've been chasing her for a while. I didn't think she'd ever say yes."

My heart swells for the sweet guy before me.

"Why don't you get out of here and head home to get ready?"

"No, no. I can't leave—"

"Of course you can. We haven't had a customer for thirty minutes. We're hardly going to get a mad rush this time of night. Harry is in the kitchen. I'll be fine."

His eyes flick to the door and then back to me. He really wants to do as I suggest, but being the good guy he is, he doesn't want to leave me alone.

"I'll be fine. Go and make yourself sexy."

His chin drops. "You mean I'm not always sexy?"

Laughing at him, I shoo him toward where his stuff is and watch when he returns with it a few moments later.

"Call me if you have any issues," he says, stopping by where I'm still sitting.

"I will," I promise, but like fuck do I mean it. I'm more than capable of closing this empty diner up for the night.

"Thank you."

"Have a good night. Don't do anything I wouldn't do." He looks back over his shoulder and laughs before pushing through the door. I hope the woman he's meeting knows how lucky she is.

As expected, the rest of my shift is dead. Even Harry comes out from the kitchen to sit with me when he gets bored of sorting shit out back.

"This is bullshit," he complains.

"I think we call it a night. No one's going to turn up now, seems like a waste of both of our lives being here."

"I couldn't agree with you more. If we close now, I might get home in time to put my kids to bed."

Smiling at him, I jump up. "Let's do this then. You get your stuff and go. I'll cash out and then head home."

"I can stay."

"No, no. I insist. Your kids will love it." His wide smile as he thinks about them only goes to prove that I'm right.

He helps me sort some closing duties out before I walk with him to the main door with the intention of locking up behind him, putting tonight's measly takings in the safe and heading home myself.

As I stand in the doorway, the moon sits high in the sky and the light reflects in the inky black ocean below. I blow out a breath as I stand there for a few moments, allowing the serenity to seep into me. It was raining earlier in the day, and the scent from that downpour mixes with the fresh sea air. There might be so many things about this place that haven't been all that welcoming since I stepped foot in town, but being down here by the sea, I feel more at home than I can remember feeling in any of our previous places.

I take a step back inside, reaching out to pull the door closed behind me when it happens. A body, dressed head to toe in black, slams into me, sending me careening back into the diner. I slide across the tiles before crashing into one of the booths. My head hits the corner of the wooden benching and my vision blurs from the impact.

Squeezing my eyes shut, I will myself to focus, to try to figure out what the hell to do. Loud footsteps get closer, and I fight to keep my breathing steady. I don't want to show whoever this motherfucker is that I'm scared. I can only assume that he's been watching and now knows I'm alone. Fucking pussy.

Dragging my eyelids open, the bright lights above burn, making the place of impact on the back of my head pound.

He's right in front of me, crouched down by my side, but all I can see is his eyes. The rest of him is covered in black fabric, hiding his identity.

"Give me whatever cash is in this place and I'll have no reason to hurt you, princess." His voice is low and calculating.

I scramble to sit so I'm not in such a vulnerable position.

"Fuck you," I spit.

His eyes crinkle at the sides, making me assume that a smile is currently playing on his lips.

"Oh you're going to regret that."

He reaches behind him and my heart jumps in my chest before he reveals what I was dreading. The spotlights above reflect off the glistening metal of the gun as he moves it toward my head.

My mouth goes dry as he presses it to my temple. Leaning in, his eyes run over every inch of my face. He's looking for my fear, but like fuck am I going to give it to him. I jut my chin out.

"Now... where were we?" The cold metal presses harder into my skin, and I fight not to react. "Oh yes, you were going to direct me to the safe and open the motherfucker for me."

I allow him to lift me when he fists my shirt and drags me from the floor. Although he doesn't lift me enough to be able to find my footing. He pulls to the back as I kick and fight behind him.

When we get to Bill's office, he throws me down on the floor, my shoulder smarting when it hits the tiles.

"Open it." The gun in his hand is still trained on my head, but his eyes flick to where the safe is.

"I can't."

"Don't fucking lie to me."

"I-I'm not." I hate that my voice wavers. It only serves to tell him one of two things. One, I'm scared. And two, I'm lying. Neither of which I want him to know.

"Liar," he bellows.

I don't get to argue my case any more. He steps up to me, his arm lifting before the gun connects with the side of my face. My head snaps to the side with the force, the entire right side instantly burning up. Something cool trickles down and drips from my chin, but I refuse to look to see the blood soaking into my white shirt.

"Now. Open it."

"No."

"You're a real fucking stupid bitch, you know that?"

His gun lifts once more, and, only two seconds later, pain like I've never known explodes in my skull and blackness claims me.

I tell myself to fight. I keep my eyes open, but I have no chance.

35

ETHAN

"Holy fucking shit, that was something fucking else," Jake practically squeals as we bound into the Bobcats visitors' locker room that we'd overtaken for the evening. I can only imagine that the atmosphere in their own is very different, seeing as we just carved them up and served them to their own home supporters.

"Fucking finals, baby," someone calls before Jake is pounced on by almost all of the team as chants and cheers echo in the room around us.

"Cheer the fuck up, dickhead. We've made it." Mason's arm wraps around my shoulder as we watch the scene playing out in front of us. It's basically just a pile of Bears rolling around on the floor.

"You're gonna be with us, aren't you?" I ask, turning to look at him.

Hope shines in his eyes. "I really fucking hope so, bro. The doctors aren't all that happy, but I'll do anything to be on that fucking field with you guys as we win this thing."

"Too fucking right," I shout, and his eyes light up that I'm getting in the spirit of things. "Right, you winning motherfuckers, get your asses up. We've got a party waiting for us," I holler and watch as players begin climbing off of Jake, who's trapped at the bottom of the pile.

"Cheers," he mutters when I reach a hand out to pull him up. The wide smile on his face is contagious, and I pull him straight into me and slam my fist down on his back.

"We're so fucking close, man. How're you feeling?"

"I can't even..." He shakes his head, a delighted laugh falling from his lips. "Fuck, I really fucking need Brit. Right the fuck now."

"Get your horny ass in the shower and you'll be inside her in no time." I push him in the direction of the showers and Mason trails behind us, not wanting to miss any of this.

I was half expecting Amalie and Camila to be waiting for us and to have to come up with some bullshit excuse as to why the five of us weren't getting the team bus back, but when we eventually emerge from the locker room neither of them are in sight.

"Where are your girls?" I ask as we find seats on the bus, ready for the journey back.

"They're meeting us at your place. Insisted we celebrate as a team."

"Fair enough. Hey," I shout to the rest of the guys once they're on board. "Anyone manage to smuggle any beer on this piece of shit?"

A few call back that it was my job before Coach stands from his seat. "Savage, get control of yourself. You've all got one more game. One more game to focus on, and that's what I need. Keep your eyes on that motherfucking trophy and not a can of beer or some skirt. Can you lot do that for me for two fucking weeks?" A series of 'yes, Coach' sounds out despite the fact that the entire team is about to descend on my house for the party of all parties.

A pang hits me in the chest that this is going to be the last post-game party I'm going to hold. Shane's dad announced at the beginning of the season that, should we make it to the state finals, he was holding that party. And with his experience in the NFL and his reputation, no one could really argue with him.

Leaning forward, I hit Shane upside the head. "I hope you're ready for what's going to descend on your house in two weeks."

He turns to look at me, something haunting in his eyes. "It ain't my fucking house. These guys can do whatever, it was Dad's dumb shit idea."

"Okaaay," I mutter. Shane and I still haven't discussed *that* phone call. I was expecting him to accost me when I got home, but he just nodded, gave me the smallest hint of a smile and carried on with his life. It was fucking weird, but then that's Shane in a nutshell. I've never been able to figure that motherfucker out.

The drive back is long as fuck as all of us crave alcohol and girls. Jake is antsy as fuck to get his hands on Amalie, and I can't say I blame him. If I had someone as hot as her waiting to celebrate with me then I'd be impatient as fuck too.

Thoughts of Rae have never been far from my mind. The idea that she could be with Amalie and Camila waiting for me hits me like a fucking truck. I know that Hell is more likely to freeze over than that actually happening, especially after she so easily dismissed me earlier, but a guy can dream, can't he?

Now this game is over, we need to talk. And I don't give a fuck if it's in the middle of tonight's party. I'll cancel the fucking thing if it means I get the chance to attempt to put things right. To tell her how I really feel.

"Thank fuck for that," Jake mutters the second the bus pulls into the school parking lot. The cheer squad's bus was in front of us, and they're all waiting impatiently for us to join them, just as ready to party as we are.

I glance out the window and find Shelly staring right back at me. She winks and bites down on her index finger. I assume she's going for sexy, but after what Shane told me she said to Rae, she can fuck right off. I've fucked up enough when it comes to Rae, I don't need her fucking assistance as well.

The guys at the front start moving before the bus has even stopped, and in only a few minutes the three of us are following Shane down the stairs.

"Ethan." Shelly's high-pitched voice goes straight through me. She comes over, her hand wrapping around my bicep as she presses her tits into me.

"Shelly, I'm not—fuck," I bark when my cell starts ringing in my pocket. I'd finally conceded and spoken to my dad, so I already know he's out of town for this party—not that I'd have cared if he were here. He doesn't seem to give me a second thought when he fucks off, allowing me to use his house however I see fit, so why should I care? Pulling it out, thinking there's an issue, I freeze when I see a name I never expected.

Rae.

Shrugging off Shelly's unwanted attention, I swipe the screen and turn away from the excitement so I can hear her.

"Rae?"

Her sobs fill the line, and my heart drops into my fucking shoes. "Rae, what's wrong? Where are you? Fuck," I ask in a panic. She doesn't cry. Something has to be wrong.

I don't look back. Instead, I pull my keys from my pocket and run toward my car.

"A-Aces Ethan, please—"

"I'm coming, baby. I'm coming. Sit tight." Yanking my car door open, I start the engine and fly from the lot.

"D-don't h-hang up," she whispers through my car speakers once they connect.

"Fuck, no. I'm right here. I'm on my way right now." My heart races as I try to come up with the reason she's calling me in the state she's clearly in. "Are you okay? Are you hurt?"

"Yeah, he—I'm sorry, Miss. We need to assess you," a deep voice says.

"Wait, just wait. I'm coming," I shout into the phone as I pull into the parking lot.

I just about forget to turn the engine off before I jump out and run toward where she is.

There are police cars, an ambulance, flashing lights and officers everywhere. A crowd is starting to form, nosey fuckers.

"Get out of my fucking way," I bark as I shoulder through the bystanders until I come to a line of cops in front of the diner.

The place looks like it always does, police aside, and I relax ever so slightly. At least the place isn't up in flames with her inside.

I rush through them, my desperation to see her getting the better of me.

"Son, you can't go in there," one of the officers says, his hand wrapping around my forearm.

"Like fuck I can't. My girl's in there. She just called me. I need to get to her." Ripping my arm from him, I run before he can reach for me again.

The restaurant is empty aside from a couple of officers at the cash register, so I run toward the kitchen and Bill's office.

There's another small huddle of officers in the office doorway, telling me everything I need to know.

"Excuse me." I storm through them. None of them stop me, I think they're too shocked to react.

"Fucking hell." I come to a grinding halt at the scene before me.

Rae is sitting with her back resting on the back wall of the office, but that's not what stops me. It's the blood that's covering her face and shirt that has me on the verge of a fucking heart attack.

"Fuck, Rae." I drop to my knees beside her, forcing the paramedic to stop whatever it was she was doing as I pull her into my arms.

She trembles against my body, and for the first time since I met her, vulnerability oozes from her. She rests the non-bloody side of her face against my chest and cries. Each gut-wrenching sob is like a fucking spear to my heart.

I hold her tighter, hoping like fuck that I'm helping, that it's what she needs right now. "It's okay. I'm here. You're safe." It feels so fucking weird to comfort her yet at the same time, so natural.

"I'm really sorry, but I need to assess this head wound."

My eyes meet those of the kind-looking paramedic also sitting on the floor.

"You okay?" I whisper to Rae, and she nods slightly.

Reluctantly, I release her and rest her back against the wall. I move back slightly to give the paramedic some space, but a startled cry from Rae stops me. "No." When I look up, her eyes are wide and full of panic as she reaches her hand for me.

Slipping my own into her blood-covered one, I keep our connection while she's patched up. My eyes hold hers and I swear to God that as I look into those brown depths I'm seeing her for the very first fucking time. Gone is the hard-ass bitch part that she plays so well, and staring back at me is just a girl who's as broken and fucked-up as I am.

"I'm so fucking sorry," I whisper, guilt over everything that has gone before hitting me like a fucking sledgehammer. Emotion clogs my throat as even more tears mix with the blood on her face and drop down onto her shirt.

She nods, accepting my apology, but like fuck is that the only one she's going to get from me. I owe her a fucking lifetime's worth before she even considers accepting them.

I sit with her hand in mine, feeling like my heart's going to pound out of my chest as I wait to get her back in my arms. The paramedics finish what they need to do before telling her that she needs to go with them to the hospital for stitches once the police have finished with her. I have to bite my tongue to stop me from refusing and demanding that I just take her home to look after her. She's fucking terrified and exhausted; the last thing she needs is to deal with all these people.

It can't be more than thirty minutes later when Rae's given her statement to the officers and they allow the paramedics to take her.

"Can you walk, sweetheart?" the paramedic asks as they tidy up to leave.

"Fuck that." Standing, I scoop Rae's tiny body up into my arms. "Okay?" I ask once she's wrapped her arms around my neck and lightly pressed her head to my shoulder.

"I will be."

"You're fucking killing me here, you know that, right?"

"I'm sure I can walk."

"I'm not talking about your weight, baby. I could bench press you all fucking day." I drop my nose to her hair as I wait for the ambulance doors to open and breathe her in. "If something fucking happened to you, I never would have—"

"Stop. It wasn't you who robbed the place. You were... fuck." She blows out a breath. "The game. Fuck. Did you win?"

A smile curls at my lips. With the stress of the last hour, it feels like the first one I've pulled in about a year.

"Of course we fucking won. Was there any doubt?"

"With the size of your ego, probably not."

I laugh as I stare down at her. "Good to know he didn't knock the quick wit out of you."

"Never."

I place her down on the gurney in the back, but she still refuses to release my hand.

Sitting in the chair beside her while the paramedic deals with some paperwork at the other end of her bed, I close my eyes and rest my head back for a second.

"Are you okay?" Her soft, concerned voice fills my ears, and I turn to look at her.

"I don't even know where to start to attempt to explain everything that I am."

Her eyes hold mine, and she swallows as she thinks. The smooth skin of her neck ripples, catching my eye, and my need to have my lips on her gets the better of me.

Leaning forward, she gasps as she must realize my intention, but she doesn't move to pull back.

"I'm so fucking sorry," I whisper so quietly that I doubt she even hears it as my lips gently brush hers.

"Enough of that, you two." The paramedic laughs.

I lift my lips from hers but rest my forehead against hers instead. Our eyes hold, her dark to my light as a million things pass between us.

"I could never be ashamed of you, Rae. None of this has been about you. It's all been about me and my fucked-up head."

Her warm palm rests on my cheek, and it makes me wonder how we went from me comforting her to her comforting me in a split second. "Let me get my head sewn back together and we'll talk, yeah?"

I nod, unable to speak around the lump that's formed in my throat. If she's willing to talk then maybe she will forgive me, or at least put up with me so I can continue to apologize.

———

Watching her be tended to and knowing that there's fuck all I can do to help is frustrating as fuck. But I do what is expected of me and sit in the chair beside her bed as everyone but me it seems gets to touch her.

A nurse stitches her up and gives her some pain relief, and a doctor checks her over before writing her a prescription for a load more painkillers. They want to keep her in but Rae refuses point blank, insisting that she's leaving.

"I'm not happy about this," the doctor says, signing off her paperwork. "If anything changes, any extra pain, dizziness, blacking out, anything. You get her back here immediately, you hear me?"

"I will. I've had a concussion a time or two, I know the drill."

"You better, because she's about to be in your care."

"I've got her. I promise."

With a hard stare, he leaves us to it.

"Are you sure about this?"

"Ethan," she sighs, sounding exasperated. "I'm fine. It looks worse than it is with all the blood."

"You'd better be fucking right. Come on."

With my arm around her waist and her clinging on to her bag of pills, we make our way to the exit.

Our Uber is idling in the taxi bay, and after making sure she's settled and comfortable, I run around to the other side and join her.

"What are you doing?" Rae asks when I pull my cell from my pocket.

"There's a raging party going on at home. I'm calling it off."

"No," she snaps, shocking the hell out of me. "You guys won, don't ruin the night for them as well."

"I'm not taking you back there. The music will be loud and—"

"So take me somewhere else."

"Whe—okay." Leaning forward, I give the driver our new destination before sliding into the middle seat and pulling Rae into me. She almost immediately rests her head on my shoulder and sighs in contentment when I wrap my arm around her waist.

"Thank you," she whispers. The sincerity in her voice makes my breath catch.

"Baby, you have nothing to thank me for."

"There wasn't anyone else I wanted to call," she admits, her body noticeably tensing beside me.

"I'm glad it was me."

"Really?"

"Yeah, really." I press my lips into the top of her head and hold them there until the car pulls up in front of a hotel. I've never stayed before, but it's got the best reputation in town, along with being the most exclusive and expensive.

"We're staying here?"

"As long as they've got a room."

I help her from the car before booking us a room for the night. Although I ensure it's not just any room.

"Holy shit, Ethan. This is insane," Rae gasps as I hold the door open for our suite. The far wall is floor to ceiling windows that showcase not only the huge balcony but the beach beyond.

"W-we can't stay here," she says, turning her concerned gaze back to me.

"Why not?"

"Because this place is for..."

"For?" I ask when she trails off.

"Adults." Her brow furrows, and I bark out a laugh.

"I'm not sure there's an age restriction as long as you can afford it."

"Yeah, that's the other issue. You shouldn't be spending this kind of money on me."

Stepping up to her, I press two fingers against her lips to keep her from saying any more.

"I thought you'd learned by now that I do what I like when I like." I wink, and her cheeks heat a little. "And what you've just said is utter bullshit. You deserve this and more. I know I've fucked up, but let me show you how it should be. How you deserve to be treated."

She swallows and bites down on the inside of her lips as she continues to stare at me.

"Tell me what you need, and it's yours."

"I don't—"

"If you say you don't need anything, then I'll just order everything I can think of to make you happy. So unless you want his place filled with everything then I suggest you just be honest. Are you hungry? Thirsty?"

"I need…" I raise a brow as I wait for her to finish her sentence. "A wee."

Barking out a laugh, I drop my hand down to hers and squeeze her fingers. "I think that's the door." I lift my chin over her shoulder and she turns to look.

"I'll just be a few minutes." She takes a step back but doesn't get very far. "You're going to need to let go."

"Are you going to be okay?"

"Ethan, he only hit me on the head. It's nothing."

My eyes flick down to her shirt that's still covered in her blood, and I remember the panic that filled me the second I stepped into that room and saw her.

"It's not nothing. You should be in the hospital right now, not here with me."

"I'm fine. I promise." When I still don't release her, she sighs. "You wanna come?"

"Thought you'd never ask." Rolling her eyes, she walks toward the bathroom with me trailing behind.

"Whoa, it's huge."

"So I hear," I mutter, unable to stop myself.

Ignoring me, she continues. "Most of our apartments have been smaller than this."

I look around the bathroom and realize that it is a bit over the top. A huge walk-in shower with more jets than I've ever seen. A huge roll top bath in the center of the room and a his and hers basin with more worktop space than I'm sure any woman could fill.

"Look at that bath. I bet that's incredible."

"You want to try it out?"

"Um… yes."

"Your wish is my command."

"Aww, you my fairy godmother now?"

"I'll be whatever you want me to be, baby." She stills and stares at me. "What?"

"It's just weird, is all."

"What is?"

"You being nice. It's unnerving."

"Rae," I say on a sigh, stepping up to her and taking her face gently in my hands. "I was a fucking asshole. The things I said to you, the things I did." I cringe. "They're unforgivable. I don't even know how to start apologizing. Then that night, when we… when I… and then I found your diaries. Fuck," I bark, turning away from her. Placing my palms on the marble counter, I hang my head in shame.

"Ethan," she whispers, coming to stand behind me. I flinch when her hands land on my side and slip around to rest on my abs. "I never wanted you to find out like that. What happened in the past, that's... in the past. What happened between the two of us has nothing to do with that."

Her body heat burns as she holds onto me.

"But—"

She spins me until I'm facing her, my butt resting on the counter, but still, I refuse to look at her instead keeping my eyes on the shiny tiles on the floor.

"No buts," she says softly. Her palm cupping my rough cheek. "Look at me," she demands, and I have no choice but to follow orders. My eyes meet hers, and, the same as earlier, everything she's feeling is right there. For some reason, she's dropped her walls and she's willing to let me see her, the real her. "You didn't do anything that I wasn't fully on board with. If I didn't want to, I can assure you that you'd still be trying to retract your balls from your chest now."

The corners of my lips twitch up in a smile. "I love your fucking mouth." My eyes widen as I realize the words that just fell from my lips. "I... uh... never know what's going to come out n—"

Copying my move from earlier, she places her fingers against my lips to stop my rambling. "Every time you touched me, I wanted it. Craved it. That night, I needed you inside me just as much as you wanted to be there. I promise. And if you'd just stuck around or answered your damn phone then I'd have told you that."

"I'm so fucking so—"

Her lips press to mine and my words die as her heat seeps into me. My hands find her hips as her tongue teases my bottom lip. Knowing that she's stretching up, I lift her and spin so she can sit on the counter. Pushing her legs apart, I step between them, our lips still connected.

With one hand on her waist, I wrap the other around the back of her neck to cradle her head and slide my tongue between her lips. The kiss is like none we've shared in the past. It's not full of hate, anger, and a need to hurt. Instead, it's slow, passionate, and full of all the words we're holding back from saying to each other.

Her tongue slides against mine as her taste explodes in my mouth. My fingers tighten against her in my desperation for more, but I can't forget everything she's been through tonight. I need to hold back where I would usually go all in.

Her fingers find the bottom of my jersey and slip inside. My muscles twitch as she lightly scratches over my abs.

"Off," she mutters against my lips as she pushes the fabric up. I'm powerless to do anything but follow her demand, and I reluctantly reach behind my head and pull my jersey up and off. Our lips only part for the few seconds it takes for the fabric to pass.

I step back up to her and pull her to the edge of the counter so she has no choice but to feel just how turned on I am by her. She gasps as I press against her sensitive center, her legs wrapping around my hips and pulling me closer still.

36

RAELYNN

I run my hands over the expanse of his muscular back and lose myself in his touch and kiss. It's the exact distraction I need right now. I hand myself over to him willingly.

When I came to earlier, I found myself curled in the ball in Bill's office, lying in a puddle of my own blood. I thought I was going to pass straight back out as my heart began to race and I fought to drag in the air I needed. But thankfully, after a few minutes, my panic diminished as my fear took over that he was still there somewhere. I strained to hear any movement outside of the office but everything was in silence.

Breathing a sigh of relief, I pulled my phone from my pocket and called 911. I have no idea what came over me, but the second I hung up the phone I felt so alone and only one person's face popped into my head. He was the only one I wanted in that moment to support me.

Before I had a chance to put any more thought into it, I found his number and dialed. I was so disorientated that I had no idea what the time was or where he might be, all I knew was that I needed him. Just like I do right now.

A low moan rumbles up from the back of his throat and my core clenches.

"Jesus, Rae." He moves his lips from mine and kisses across my jaw and down my neck. "Do you have any idea how fucking scary that was? Seeing you covered in blood?" He moves back from my skin slightly, looking at the red-stained shirt.

"Take it off me."

My words seem to bring him back to himself and he puts a little space between us. His eyes widen in panic as his chest continues to heave.

"Ethan?" I ask, wondering what the hell I just said wrong.

"I'm sorry. I'm supposed to be looking after you."

"And you call that *not* looking after me?"

"Oh continuing that could certainly be classified as looking after you, but it's not what you need right now."

"I beg to di—"

"Don't," he says, stepping away even more. "I need to do the right thing, and taking you like an animal on the counter like I want isn't doing that."

"I'm not compl—"

"Rae," he moans, almost as if he's in pain. "Just... just let me look after you."

"Okay," I whisper, my need to experience this softer side of Ethan that I knew was always there almost bigger than my need for him.

Glancing around the room, his gaze locks on the bathtub. He stalks toward it, leans over, and runs the water before grabbing the little bottle that's sitting on the side and pouring it in. Bubbles appear almost instantly, but I pay more attention to his muscular, tattooed back as he moves.

Feeling my stare, he looks over his shoulder. A wicked smirk appears on his lips, but unlike all the times I've seen it before, I'm confident that nothing vicious is going to come out of his mouth. He turns and walks back over, his eyes trained on mine, but instead of dropping his lips back to mine like I want, he just slips his hands around my waist and lifts me from the counter.

"You do your thing while I go order us food for after. Anything you want?" I bite down on my bottom lip as my eyes drop to his torso and then the deep V lines that drop into his pants. *Fuck yeah, there's something I want.* "To eat, Rae. Is there anything you want to eat?"

"N-nothing too heavy," I say, not even bothering to lift my eyes from his body.

"I'll just be a few minutes. Call if you need me."

"I'll be fine."

Reluctantly he leaves me standing in the middle of the ginormous room, feeling a little lost. After a second or two, I remember what I'm supposed to be doing and make use of the toilet before risking a look at myself in the mirror.

I gasp when I first see my reflection. Why the hell he felt the need to kiss me, fuck only knows. I look like a mess. The right side of my face is tinged pink with my blood, my hair is a mess, and I don't even need to mention the patch they had to shave to stitch me back together. I guess it could be seen as intentional, although it's certainly not a look I'd go for. I might hate my hair, but I've still refrained from cutting it all off after all these years, so clearly I'm more attached than I want to admit. My shirt is no longer white, although my skin is paler than I think I've ever seen it in comparison.

Lifting my fingers, I gently touch my new wound. I suck in a sharp breath when it hurts like a bitch.

"Don't," Ethan says, stepping inside the room. "Just leave it alone to heal."

"It's fucking ugly."

"Scars are cool, baby. I thought of anyone you would understand that."

I shrug, allowing what he's really saying seep into me. "All of mine are on the inside. I'm not sure about this one."

"Your hair will cover it," he says, stepping up to me. His arms wrap around my waist and his chin rests on my left shoulder as he stares at me in the mirror. "You're still beautiful. It just makes you even edgier, some might say scary."

I laugh, grateful he steered away from the awkward beautiful comment so quickly. "You think I'm scary?"

"Fucking terrifying, baby. You have no idea."

My chin drops as a million questions run around my head, but I don't get the chance to ask any of them.

"Your bath is ready." He releases my waist, and we both watch his hands as his fingers wrap around the bottom of my shirt and lift. He's very careful when it gets to my head and ensures he removes it without causing me any more pain.

His eyes hold mine for a beat before dropping to my bra covered breasts.

"I never told you before." He drops his lips to the curve of my shoulder. "I was too busy being a dick, but you're so fucking sexy. Your curves. Fuck, Rae."

I gasp at the honesty in his words. I have to avert my eyes. I can't look into his intense stare as he says these things. They make me want to believe him, and that's dangerous.

"Look at me." Without instruction from my brain, my eyes fly back to meet his darkening blue ones. "I wanted you from the moment you arrived. I wanted my hands on you. To know just how soft your skin would be. How you'd taste." He licks up the column of my neck, and I shudder.

I bite down on my bottom lip to stop myself saying anything, and a moan rumbles up instead.

"Then I dared you to get naked. Fuck, baby. You brought me to my fucking knees with your confidence and your defiance. Like fucking kryptonite."

His hands tickle around my back before he releases my bra and lets the straps fall from my shoulders. But his eyes don't drop. They stay firmly on mine.

"Then I tasted you. And fuck if I didn't become addicted."

"But—"

"No buts. Not right now." His hands skim down my stomach and come to a stop on the button of my skirt. He pops it open and pushes the fabric from my hips. His lips tickle against the shell of my ear and goosebumps cover my entire body. "And then... then I slid inside you and that was it. You ruined me, Rae. Fucking ruined me."

His words have my heart thundering against my ribs. I'm waiting for the other shoe to drop. For him to tell me he's currently streaming this to the entire school or some other douchebag move that I'm sure he's capable of, but he never does. Instead, he rips his eyes from mine and kisses a line down my spine as he peels my pantyhose and panties from my body.

I'm left staring at my naked, broken body in the mirror as every touch of his lips sends a bolt of lust straight through my body until my core is aching. It should be the last thing I want after what I've been through tonight, but fuck, Ethan is a law unto himself, and right now I want him. I want him more than my next breath.

I lift each foot when I'm instructed to do so before a squeal leaves my lips when a pain radiates from my ass cheek. "You did not just bite me?" I ask in shock.

Turning, I find him sitting on his haunches, looking at me. His lips are parted and his chest heaves with his increased breathing, and when I drop lower, I find the unmistakable bulge of his erection beneath his jeans.

He swallows, making his neck ripple and his Adam's apple bob. "Th—" He clears his throat before continuing. "The food will be here in an hour. Let's get you cleaned up."

Standing, he holds out his hand for mine. I slip it in, loving the way he squeezes it tight. He continues holding while I climb into the bathtub and sink down into the bubbles.

He loiters awkwardly beside me, deep in thought.

"What are you doing?"

He takes a few seconds to answer. Trepidation fills me, because I can't get a read on him.

"I'm just... I'm just wondering why me? Why did you call me tonight when you could have called others?"

"I didn't want anyone else," I admit. If we're being honest, then I'm going all in.

"But why? I've been nothing but an asshole to you. Why?"

I shrug, because really, I don't have the answer he's after. "I don't know. All I do know is that I came to, terrified that he was going to come back, and the only person I wanted was you. It's fucked-up, I know. But..." I blow out a breath. "Something told me that you'd protect me. That although you've hurt me, that actually, you wouldn't accept anyone else doing it."

He hangs his head in shame. "No one will hurt you again. Me included." His voice is so broken it has a lump forming in my throat. "I know I don't deserve your forgiveness, but I swear to fucking god, I'll do anything to prove to you that I'm not that person. I was angry. I was hurt. I was lashing out because of things I had no control over, and then you appeared: the perfect target. I didn't expect you to fight back. I didn't expect you to push me, to dare me. To make me want you. But fuck, Rae. I want you so fucking bad. And I don't mean to prove a point or to take my hate out on you. I mean, I want to protect you. I want to make you smile, because when you do, it's fucking breathtaking. I want to be the kind of guy you deserve. I want to show you how you should be treated. I want you to be my motherfucking queen."

"Ethan," I whisper, tears streaming down my cheeks at his raw honesty.

When he eventually looks up, his own eyes are full of water threatening to tip over the edge. His breath catches at the look on my face, but I don't miss a little hope seeping into his eyes.

"What the fuck are you waiting for?" His brow quirks in confusion. "Get the fuck in."

Faster than I thought possible, Ethan has his jeans and boxers on the floor and is stepping into the soothing water with me. The bubbles swallow up most of his body, which is a damn fucking shame, but I soon find myself turned so that I can lean back into him and it totally makes up for it.

His legs cage me in while his hands rest teasingly on my stomach. I gently settle my head on his shoulder and tip my chin so I can look up at him. His eyes are closed, his lips pressed into a thin line. He looks like he's in pain.

"Are you okay?"

"Couldn't be better." He opens his eyes, and his dark blue irises find mine. They're so full of need and hunger it makes my stomach clench.

He presses a sweet kiss to my forehead and rests his lips there. I relax, allowing his warmth to soothe me, and I close my eyes.

I've no idea how long I stay there, but sooner than I'd like Ethan speaks behind me. "Baby, you can't fall asleep."

"I'm not," I whisper back.

He laughs. "I'm pretty sure you were just snoring."

"I really doubt that."

"Really?"

Leaning forward, he grabs a washcloth and a bar of soap. "Tell me if it hurts, okay?"

I nod, too busy watching his hands lather up the cloth to pay much attention to what he's saying. He starts on my face before dropping down to my neck and to my shoulder, washing away the evidence tonight has left on my skin. He's so gentle and I feel myself starting to drift off once again as he rubs the cloth over me. That is, until it brushes one of my nipples. My breath catches, and I tense.

"Fuck," he mutters behind me.

"Sorry."

"Never. Never be sorry for that."

"O-okay."

He does it again to the other side, but I'm pretty sure it's not by accident this time.

"Ethan," I moan, wiggling against him as need flows through me. With him wrapped around me like this, his hands on my body, his length quite obviously pressing into my back, all I can think about is him and the way he's able to play my body.

"What do you need?" he whispers in my ear, the deep rasp of his voice not making the situation any better.

"You."

He stills for a second. "Are you sure? Your head..."

"Is perfectly okay, like I keep saying. Please, Ethan. Make me forget."

"Fuck. I don't stand a fucking chance with you, do I?"

I smile but don't reply. I can't, because he abandons the cloth in favor of running his fingers down my stomach. I open my legs when he gets to the apex of my thighs and lean back into him a little more.

His fingers tease over my lips before zeroing in on my clit.

"Jesus, Rae."

"I told you," I moan as he starts pressing harder exactly where I need. "I need you."

"Christ. I don't deserve this."

"Stop thinking. Right here, right now. That's all that exists."

He nods against me before reaching lower to find my entrance.

"Fuck, you're so ready for me."

"Mmm..." I moan, pressing my lips to the thundering pulse in his neck as he works me to a frenzy.

His other hand cups one of my breasts, and he pinches my nipple hard at the same time he thrusts up into me and bends his fingers just so.

"Ethan, fuck, shit," I chant as he pushes me higher.

"I fucking love it when you moan my name," he groans, his entire body locked up tight behind me. "You're so close, I can feel it."

"Oh god," I whimper before crying out his name as I fall over the edge into mind-numbing pleasure. In those few seconds, nothing else exists. There're no gun-wielding robbers, no stitches, no dickhead I'm forced to live with, just the two of us. Me taking what I need and him willingly giving it.

"Fucking hell, Rae." He continues stroking me as I come down from my high.

I lie a limp, exhausted mess on top of him as I try to regain control of both my breathing and my limbs.

"We should probably get out. The water's getting cold and our food will be here soon." The thought of eating makes my stomach growl loudly. "Yeah, see. Your stomach agrees."

I've no idea how long ago it was since I last ate. I've no idea what the time is now, but he's right. Suddenly I'm starving.

After gently pouring some water over my hair in an attempt to get some of the blood out, he releases the drain.

"Sit forward."

I do as I'm told, and in seconds I'm alone in the huge tub as Ethan climbs out. With his back to me, I get a great shot at his ass and that damn teddy bear tattoo that I'm so intrigued about. He reaches for a towel and sadly wraps it around his waist before turning around, although when he does, I smirk, noticing that the fabric does nothing to hide what's happening below his waist.

"What?" he asks innocently when he spots where my eyes are focused. "I just had this hot as shit girl wet and laid out on top of me as she rode my fingers. What else do you expect?"

I hate that his words have color tinting my cheeks, but I can't help it. There's something about him and his dirty words that bring out the innocent little girl within me.

"Check you out, getting all shy. I've already seen it all, baby. It's a little late for that, don't you think?"

"It's different," I admit and then slam my lips shut.

"Oh, how's that?"

You're looking at me different. It's like you see me now, not just your anger. "I don't know. It just is." I lift my hand to his outstretched one so he can pull me from the bath.

"You're lying, but you're also buck naked so at this very second so I'm going to let you get away with it." He watches as some bubbles slide down my body before he reaches out to grab me a towel. He wraps it around my body and tucks it into place before passing me a second for my hair.

A knock sounding out from the main part of our suite stops him asking me the questions that are right on the tip of his tongue. He looks at me for a second longer before turning and leaving me alone.

I gently wring my hair out before drying my body off. Spotting his jersey on the floor where it fell earlier, I carefully pull it over my head and hang the towels back up.

I know we're alone once more because the door to the suite closed a few seconds ago, but Ethan must appreciate that I need a little space because he has not come back yet.

I stare at myself in the mirror, thankfully looking a little more normal now the blood's been washed away, but still nowhere near what I'm used to. But I think that's got more to do with Ethan than it does what happened tonight. My eyes are lighter, my walls are down. It's a weird feeling after being so closed off for so long. I've yet to figure out if it's a good or bad thing, mind you.

Deciding I need go out before he comes back to find me, I pull the door open. I immediately find him sitting on the edge of the couch with the biggest display of fruit sitting on the coffee table behind him.

"Whoa, that's a little much, don't you think?"

He startles at my voice, obviously lost to his own thoughts. "Oh... um... yeah. I just asked for a selection of fruit. There's even chocolate dipping sauce." His eyebrows wiggle suggestively, and I can't help but laugh.

"Give me one orgasm and you think I'm a sure thing, eh?"

I lower myself down on the opposite couch to him. "No, that's no—"

"It was a joke, Ethan. Don't look so worried. I meant what I said in there." I nod to the bathroom. "I was fully on board, every single time. Amalie and Camila said that you—"

"Motherfuckers," he mutters, rubbing his hand over his face.

"They said you thought you forced yourself on me, that it was the reason you left."

"That was part of it..." He blows out a long breath, his eyes focused on the huge windows that look out at the beach beyond.

"And the rest of it was my diaries," I add, filling in the gaps that he seems to be skirting around.

Silence descends around us. The only thing I can hear is his heavy breathing as he tries to form the words he needs.

Sitting forward, he rests his elbows on his knees and drops his head into his hands. "I just... I read some of what you'd been through, and all I could see was me doing the exact same thing. I pushed you until you didn't have a choice but to give me what I wanted."

"Ethan, no—"

"I freaked out," he continues, cutting me off. "I was already ashamed of everything I'd done and knew that no matter what I told myself, I didn't hate you or blame you for how my life had turned upside down. I panicked because I realized that what I felt for you was something very different. That night when I..."

"When we had sex?"

"Yeah. It was different from any other time I have. It was... incredible, mind-blowing, and I knew it was never going to be enough for me. I knew I wanted more. That I wanted you. But I also knew that I didn't deserve you. And then I read all that and... fuck. I don't know, Rae. It was just so much all at once. I freaked."

"I understand. It's a lot to take on board."

"I don't mean what happened to you. I couldn't give a shit about that..." I gasp, and he must realize how what he just said sounded. "Wait... no. That came out wrong."

"Look at me," I demand, needing to see his eyes.

He looks up at me, although he doesn't move his head. His eyes are dark and haunted as he remembers. "Of course I care. I fucking hate that you went through that, and I hope that one day you might be willing to tell me all of it in detail so I can totally understand. But knowing about it... it doesn't change how I feel about you. I'm not ashamed like I made out the other day, that was bullshit to keep you at arm's length. All of it has just been fucking bullshit." He lifts from the couch before dropping down on his haunches before me. He takes my hands in his, his eyes laser-focused on mine. "Can we start again? From tonight. From right now?"

Memories of everything he's said and done to me since I arrived flash through my mind like a movie. "I... I don't know." A huge part of me wants to say yes and jump into his arms, because this side of Ethan Savage is one I can get on board with. But there's that other part, one that I remember all too well still. The wounds are still too raw.

He nods, his eyes full of emotion as he stands and backs away from me. Every muscle in my body aches for me to reach out for him, to pull him into my arms and to tell him that I'd love to start over as of right now, but I know I'm not in the right place after the events of tonight to make that kind of decision. I need food, I need sleep, and I need a hell of a lot more painkillers.

"Okay, okay. I understand." He walks back into the bathroom, his shoulders sagged in defeat, and I hate myself for hurting him but knowing it's the right thing to do and nowhere near what he deserves for how he's treated me.

When he returns only a few moments later, he's picked himself back up and replaced the towel that was still around his waist with his boxer briefs.

My eyes feast on his toned and tanned skin as he makes his way back over to me. But unlike I'm expecting, he doesn't stop at the closest couch to him. Instead, he falls down beside me. "Not hungry?" he asks as if our previous conversation never happened.

"Uh... yeah."

I sit back as he grabs a selection of fruit from the vast arrangement, some of which I've no clue what they are, but I'm not going to point that out. The vast differences between us are already stark; I don't need to remind him of why he spent our first few weeks calling me trailer trash.

"Thank you," I whisper when he hands me a plate.

"Are you feeling okay?"

"Yeah, my head's getting worse though. I think it's time for more pills."

Ethan grabs his cell from the coffee table. "Fuck," he barks, rushing to get up. When he returns, it's with the bag full of pills the doctor insisted I left the hospital with. "I'm already doing a shit job of looking after you," he mutters, pulling the boxes out and reading the instructions to find out which ones I should be taking.

He stills when I rest my hand on his forearm, stopping his movements. "You're doing a great job. Stop worrying."

He sighs and relaxes back. "Why were you even there alone tonight?" He already knows the answer to this—he was there when I answered the officer's questions.

"Because it was quiet and it seemed like a waste of time for us all being there," I repeat.

"I know, but it was fucking stupid."

"Hindsight and all that," I mutter, feeling pretty fucking stupid for allowing it to happen in the first place.

"He could have fucking killed you, Rae."

"I know. But he didn't. I'm here, and aside from an unexpected haircut and a headache, I'm fine."

He glances over at me. His question's written all over his face.

"Really. I'm fine. Stop worrying."

"Not possible."

I smile at him before holding my hands out for the tablets he's holding and accepting a bottle of water when he hands it over for me to take them with.

I awake with a start. My heart pounds as I turn to look at Rae beside me.

"It's okay, I'm still alive."

"Fuck," I bark, first because I was supposed to stay awake to wake her every so often because of the concussion, but also because the last thing I was expecting was to find her wide awake. "You scared the shit out of me."

"Well if you hadn't have fallen asleep on me then you'd have known every so often that I was awake."

"Smart ass."

She shrugs and goes back to staring at the ceiling like she was when I first looked over.

"How are you feeling?"

Dread sits heavy in my stomach, because from just looking at her tense body, I know she's shut back down. I guess I should have expected it. Last night she'd had the shock of her life. I wasn't her biggest concern. She's probably kicking herself for letting me in like she did last night. But it's too late now, because I remember all of it. Every word she said to me and the exact look in her eyes as she did.

She can tell me as much as she likes this morning that she hates me, but I know it's not true. Not really.

"Like shit," she mutters. "We should probably go home and see if the house is still standing."

I know she's right, but that doesn't mean I'm ready to walk out of this suite. I need to know where we stand.

"Rae," I say, turning onto my side so I can look at her.

From here, she looks totally normal, and as if last night never happened. Sadly, I know that's not the case. She's in pain, and that's only confirmed when she briefly glances at me. Her eyes are dark, proving that she didn't get much sleep last night, and the bruising is really starting to appear on the side of her face.

"Fuck." I reach for her, but the second she stills, I pull my hand back, not wanting to push her too much.

Sitting on the edge of her bed, she keeps her back to me. "I shouldn't have called you last night. It was a mistake. Clearly I wasn't thinking straight."

"What? No, baby. No. I'm so glad you did."

She pushes to her feet and walks to the end of the bed. "Why? So you could see me suffering? See me in pain? I bet you fucking loved that after everything, didn't you?"

"What? No. I fucking hated it. What the hell are you talking about?"

"You think I believed a word of what you said last night? The bullshit you spewed about how you *really* feel about me? Like fuck did I. We both know that you were just taking advantage of me when I was at my lowest. Well, congratulations. Last night was probably the second worst in my life. But I doubt even you could beat my worst."

"Rae, stop. Just stop talking." I'm in front of her in seconds, my fingertips running down her arm to find her hand, but she pulls it away as if I've just burned her.

"I'm done with this bullshit. Where's my purse?" My mouth opens to respond, but no words form. "Fuck it. I don't need your help."

She spins on her heels and races around the room until she finds her purse on the dresser. She pulls her cell out and taps on the screen for a few seconds before rushing into the bathroom and slamming the door behind her.

The loud bang is what I need to drag me from my daze. "Rae. You need to hear me out."

I stand on the other side of the door, knowing that she can't hide in there forever and wait.

The toilet flushes, water runs and there's some rustling, but she's silent no matter how many times I knock on the door and beg for her to come out and listen to me.

I pace back and forth, knowing she's going to have to emerge soon. The second the lock clicks open, my heart jumps into my throat. I crowd her in the doorway, my eyes burning into hers, begging her to listen, to believe what I've been saying to her.

"Rae, please. I swear on my life I meant every word I said to you last night. This thing between us, the chemistry, the need, that pull you feel. It's real. Please."

"I'm done, Ethan. There's a car waiting for me outside. Don't follow me." It's only now I notice that she's no longer just wearing my jersey but also her skirt and boots.

She pushes past me. I'm so lost that I allow her to do so, I even stumble a little with the force she uses that's not necessary.

"Rae, please. I'm begging you. Come back and we'll talk. Just give me a chance."

"You had a chance when I first arrived and you were a cunt. You made your bed, Ethan. Now you need to lie in it. Alone." And with those parting words ringing in my ears, the suite door slams behind me and I drop to my knees.

"Rae."

I hang my head, trying to work out what the hell went wrong, allowing myself to wallow in self-pity for two seconds before I make my way back to my feet and rush toward where my pile of clothes still sits on the bathroom floor.

I tug on my jeans, pull my hoodie on, sans jersey seeing as Rae's still wearing it, and shoved my feet into my shoes, foregoing socks because they'll take too long. Emerging from the bathroom, I spot the white bag full of painkillers that Rae will need. I swipe them from the side table and run from the room.

I request an Uber as I race down the stairs, not bothering to wait for the elevator, but I regret it when I see I've got a ten-minute wait for the car to arrive.

Hoping I might find her outside the hotel also waiting, I run out, but she's not there.

"Fuck," I pant, my hands landing on my knees as I stare out over the hotel grounds.

The ten-minute wait for the car is the longest of my life. I've fucked up royally when it comes to Rae, time and time again, but as far as I'm aware, I did nothing but look after her last night. She told me everything was fine and I believed her. I thought I could read her. I thought the way her body responded to me last night was all the evidence I needed. Well, this morning just proves that I could be very, very wrong.

She was just freaked out over what happened to her. She was craving the feeling of safety. She wasn't of sound mind. You took advantage... again.

"Yes," I hiss when what I hope is my car pulls up to the entrance. I jump in the back and bark my address at him. I don't need her going back to the mess my house could be in.

The roads are deserted but still, the journey still takes forever. My knees bounce and I fidget my hands in my lap as nervous energy races through me.

"Thanks," I call to the driver, but I'm already flying up the driveway toward the front door so I have no idea if he hears or not.

The front door is unlocked, and I basically fall through it in my need to find her. There are bodies littered everywhere as expected, but what I'm not prepared for is five people to emerge from the kitchen, each one looking stressed and harassed.

"Ethan, what the fucking hell?" Jake barks, his voice full of anger. "Where the fuck have you been?" He steps up to me, and his palms slam down on my chest, forcing me to take a step back.

Fuck. It's the first time I register that I just took off last night, no explanation, no reason, no destination. I just left them.

"Where's Rae?" Shane asks, standing shoulder to shoulder with Jake, a darkness to his eyes I've never seen before.

"She's... She's..." I stutter, but I don't get a chance to finish it before the front door opens.

"She's here."

"What the fuck?" The question is asked by all of them simultaneously as they turn toward her. The bruise on her face is unmistakable, but when she steps toward us and they get a look at her head, they all gasp in horror.

Everything after that is a blur as Jake's fist connects with my jaw, and I fall back into the wall. I don't make it to the floor before he grasps the front of my shirt and pulls me up to face him.

He cocks his arm back once more before it lands on my cheek and another to my mouth that successfully splits my lip before Amalie manages to pull him away. At no point do I fight back, because I might not have anything to do with Rae's current state, but I deserve a few good hits for what I have done.

The hate in his eyes rivals my own that I've felt over the past few weeks.

"What the fuck?" I ask, lifting my hand to wipe the blood. "That wasn't me. Fucking hell." I shake my head before locking my eyes on Rae, waiting for her to explain. Both Amalie and Camila are now at her sides, checking her over, but the concern's not left her face.

It takes too fucking long for her to say something, but eventually she breaks the silence. "Aces was broken into. The guy had a gun. Thankfully he only hit me with it."

"Jesus. Fuck, Rae. Are you okay?"

"I'll be fine."

"Where have you been?"

"Ethan took us to..." She hesitates, not wanting to admit that we've spent the night together, despite the fact nothing really happened.

"I took her to a hotel so she didn't have to deal with this lot." I gesture to the still passed out bodies surrounding us.

"You better have fucking looked after her," Jake seethes.

"Fucking hell, I know I've been an asshole, but shit, Thorn."

"He did," she whispers. "If you don't mind. I'm going upstairs."

Everyone takes a step back to allow her the space she needs, and we all watch as she climbs the stairs and turns the corner.

Every inch of me aches to follow her, to make sure she's okay, but she's made it more than clear this morning that she doesn't need or want me. The thought is like a baseball bat to the fucking chest.

"Get these motherfuckers out of here."

I push through my little crowd in favor of the kitchen. I might need to follow Rae to make sure she's okay, but I'm not a fucking idiot. She doesn't want me right now, and as hard as the rejection is to take, having it witnessed by half our fucking class is not necessary.

I power up the coffee machine before falling down in one of the chairs to the sound of the five of them waking bodies and pointing them toward the exits.

Dropping my arms to the table, I rest my head on them and try to block everything out. I need sleep.

"Everyone's gone," a voice says, dragging me from my uncomfortable slumber. My back aches and my neck pulls as I try to sit up.

"Yet you're all still here," I snap, looking at them all.

"You can be an asshole to everyone else, Savage. You can push them away until they never return, but you can't fucking get rid of us. We're in this for the long haul, so I suggest you pull up your motherfucking panties and get a grip."

"Fuck you," I spit at Mason as all sets of eyes bore into me. "I've done fuck all wrong. She called me. I went to her. I looked after her. I was fucking nice, did everything for her I can think of, and the second I woke this morning she ran as fast as she fucking could."

"And you blame her?" he bellows. "You've been a fucking cunt to her since the moment she arrived."

"She seemed pretty happy with me being there last night. After all, she called me and not any of you."

"You're a fucking idiot, Ethan."

"Why? What the fuck am I missing?"

Mason shakes his head. "I can't, I just fucking can't."

He spins away from me and shakes his arms out.

"You guys go and... hit the gym or something. We've got this," Camila says, taking a step toward me.

"No, I don't need a fucking girly intervention." I stand and both Camila and Amalie have the balls to stand toe to toe with me.

"Yes. Yes, you fucking do," Camila states.

Our stare holds, my lips pursing in frustration but knowing I can't move them like I would if it were Jake and Mason staring at me like them.

"Fuck, that's hot," Mason mutters, looking his girl up and down, desire filling his eyes.

"Fuck off, you three," Amalie says, waving them off.

After a little hesitation, they leave.

"What the fuck is Shane even doing here?"

"He was helping us look for the two of you last night. He's not the dick you guys think he is, you know. I'd kinda hoped that now it's been proved he had nothing to do with all that shit before that you'd all give him the benefit of the doubt." The reference to Chelsea has me wondering once again how she is and when she's going to reappear.

Not being able to argue with them after he did call me with her concerns about Rae, I shut up, sit down, and take a sip of my cold coffee. "Ugh, that's shit."

The girls make me a fresh one before sitting down opposite me.

"So..." Amalie starts.

"So?" I snark back.

"You're an even bigger fucking idiot than I thought you were." I open my mouth to respond, but Amalie continues. "She likes you, Ethan. Fuck knows why, but she does."

"Oh yeah, that's why she freaked out this morning." I roll my eyes at both of them.

"It was probably exactly that. You're... you're a lot to take at the best of times. After what she'd just been through, I'm sure her head was all fucked-up. Just give her some time. Be there for her like you were last night. Show her the real you, yeah?"

"We know you like her too, and we also know you're scared," Camila adds.

"Who are you, fucking Oprah or some shit?"

"No, I'm just someone who's been watching this all play out. Give. Her. Time."

"What if I don't want to?"

"Tough. If you think she's worth it, then you're going to have to wait. And no, contrary to your beliefs, I'm sure it won't fall off through lack of use." Camila flicks her eyes down to my crotch and lifts a brow. "So how about you try to act like the kind of guy she deserves while you wait, eh?"

"You two are a pain in the fucking ass, you know that, right?"

They both smile innocently. "Now, we're going to make her a coffee and go and make sure she's okay. You go hang with the guys. Soak up their advice, although, you might want to ignore most of it. And like we said, give her time. If it's meant to be, it'll be."

I watch as they make Rae and themselves a coffee and leave me with their words spinning around in my head.

After a few minutes, I wander through the house to find the guys. I hear them before I see them in my home gym.

"The girls chewed you up and spat you out, huh?"

"Something like that," I mutter, sitting on the weight bench.

Jake brings the treadmill to a stop, Mason leans back against the bike while Shane looks totally out of place in the corner.

"You want her?"

I nod at the three of them, no point denying it now. They all know the truth anyway.

"Then you need to fucking show her, bro. Stake your claim."

"But the girls said—"

"Fuck the girls. We got them, didn't we? You want her to believe how you feel, fucking show her."

"How?"

"Fuck knows. You're Ethan Savage. I'm sure you'll figure it out."

38

RAELYNN

I'd been expecting the knock at my door since the moment I shut it. The only thing I wasn't sure of was who'd be on the other side. I'd hoped that Ethan got the message this morning that I needed some space, but he's never exactly been one to figure shit out that easily.

Last night was a mistake. I never should have allowed him to take me to that hotel. I never should have been alone with him. Because now? Now all I want is him. More of his touch, more of his kisses. Just more of him, full stop. I feel like a fucking junkie craving my next hit, and just as much as that shit is bad for you, I know sure as hell that Ethan fucking Savage is bad for me too. He sees me as a plaything. He's made that more than obvious in the past, and just because he whispered some sweet words to me last night and looked after me, it doesn't mean that it wasn't all one big fat lie just to make me trust him. If I trust him, if I let him in even more than he already is, then he will have the power to truly shatter me. And I already know I won't survive it. One man has already tried his best to ruin my life. I will never give another that kind of power, no matter how fucking good he looks with bubbles running down his naked skin or how skilled he is with his fingers. My thighs clench as I remember what he did to me in the bathtub last night. But I soon chastise myself for putting myself in the position in the first place. It's what he wants. He wants to play me.

The knock comes again, only this time it's followed up with a soft female voice and words I can't ignore.

"We've got coffee."

"Fuck's sake."

I pull the door open to find two smiling faces looking back at me, although I don't miss the concern in their eyes. I fucking hate it. It reminds me of the looks I got from the officers and the social workers after Mom came home early that night and discovered what was really going on under her roof.

I shudder at the thought and accept the steaming mug when they pass it over to me.

I stand back and they walk inside. "You don't have to talk if you don't want to. We just wanted to see if you wanted or needed anything and then we'll get out of your hair."

"I really appreciate that," I say, taking a cautious sip of my coffee.

I turn my back on them and walk out to the balcony assuming they'll follow. And they do.

We make ourselves comfortable before the low rumble of male voices sounds out below us as the guys make themselves at home on the loungers around the pool.

"I don't know what you did to him, girl. But he's a fucking mess right now."

"I didn't do anything."

"Yeah, you did. You showed him that for the first time in his life he can't have exactly what he wants. And it's exactly what he needs."

"He doesn't want me. He just wants to hurt me. Prove that he's better, stronger, more powerful."

"You really believe that?"

I shrug, his sweet words from last night coming back to me. "I have no idea what I believe right now," I admit. "Last night was... fuck. It was fucking scary. But I shouldn't have called him to come and help. I don't know what I was thinking."

"You were thinking that he'd look after you in the way only he can. You knew he'd be there in a heartbeat, because beneath all his hard, outer shell is a huge teddy bear who just wants to care for someone and be cared about in return. You knew he'd be mortified if you turned to someone other than him. You knew—"

"I get it," I say, cutting her off, unable to hear any more. Her words are cutting too close to the truth, and it's freaking me out.

"He's been a wanker. We all know this," Amalie says. "But he really likes you, Rae. Now, all you've got to do is decide if you're willing to give him the benefit of the doubt and see if he's worth it."

"I think he is," I whisper so quietly I don't think they hear.

"I fucking knew it," Camila squeals, a huge smile curling at her lips. Amalie shakes her head and laughs at her friend.

"We've told him to back off, but—"

"Ethan doesn't do what he's told," I interrupt.

They both laugh. "Exactly. None of those three do things how they're meant to be done." They both look over the railing at their guys, soft, happy smiles appearing on their faces.

"Ugh, you guys are sickening."

"You can join us. It's not such a bad place to be."

"What's the story with Shane?" I ask after a few moments of silence.

"Honestly, he's a good guy. But as for what he's up to, suddenly hanging with the team and wanting to get involved in stuff he's always run a mile from... we've no idea."

"Probably a girl."

"Ha," Camila barks. "Maybe he's hoping to steal you from under Jake's feet."

"I think he's well aware that won't be happening."

"Yeah, could be fun to watch though."

"Nah, it's something else."

They chat away for a while longer before I start yawning. "We should leave you to rest. Call us if you need anything, even if it's just to put Ethan on a leash."

"I can handle Ethan."

"Oh we know, girl. We know." Camila winks. "Just... make him work for it before you decide to give him a chance."

"Do you not know me at all?"

They both laugh before saying their goodbyes.

I stay where I am for a while and watch as they approach their guys, who both make space for them on their loungers and immediately wrap their arms around them.

Ethan's face, however, drops before he looks up toward my room. His body stills when he finds me staring back at him and his chin drops, his eyes lightening a little with hope.

I stand with his eyes burning into me and shake my head slowly. His shoulders drop once more before I turn my back on him and walk into my room, shutting the door behind me so I don't risk overhearing them talking because I would put money on my name being featured more than once.

Leaving my now empty mug on the side, I walk through to my bathroom with the intention of having a shower before attempting to get some sleep. I know I was supposed to stay awake last night just in case, but it didn't matter what I'd been through and how exhausted I was, at no point did I switch off. With him beside me, I just couldn't relax. It wasn't because I was afraid of him or what he might do, more that I was scared of myself and what I might do. He laid there quite happily in just a pair of boxers, his torso exposed from the waist, his muscles and tanned skin ready for the taking, and fuck if the only thing I could think about was climbing over his body. Those kinds of thoughts should have been the last thing on my mind after the night I'd had, but I couldn't help it. As my frustration grew, so did my doubt about everything he'd told me. My exhausted brain told me that I was imagining things and that he wasn't really that gentle with me, that he didn't whisper the things he did in my ear, that he didn't touch me so delicately and lovingly.

He'd told me that he wasn't going to fall asleep so that he could check on me, but that didn't last very long. It couldn't have been an hour after I pretended to fall asleep that he started snoring lightly. I was tempted to get up and leave then, but I knew he'd freak out in the morning and that kind of drama wasn't worth it. It wasn't until he turned his panicked eyes on me when the sun had risen that I realized I should have done exactly that. The look on his face, the openness, the honesty, the hope, it ripped me wide open and terrified me more than I think I ever have been in my life.

My heart races once again as I think back. I think it was the hope that really did me in. It told me how serious he was about the things he'd said to me about how he really felt, and I panicked.

I have a quick shower. I can't remember if I'm allowed to with my stitches, but there's no way I'm not washing my hair. Ethan attempted it last night, but warm water wasn't much of a match for the dried blood clinging to my hair. I carefully shampoo, making sure I avoid the wound. I immediately feel better knowing that my hair is clean. I have no idea what I'm going to do about my patch that's missing, because I'm certainly not wearing it down to hide it.

Your hair is so beautiful, princess.

His words hit me all of a sudden, and my knees buckle. Thankfully, I manage to catch myself before I end up in a pile on the floor. I tell myself it's a sign that I need some sleep and turn the shower off.

I dry off quickly, my headache that's been throbbing away nicely all morning starting to get the better of me, and I pull on a pair of panties and a tank ready to dive under the covers and hope sleep will claim me now I'm back in my own bed alone.

I just pull the covers back to get in when a knock sounds out. I know who it is, and it's not just because the girls said they'd leave me to rest. I feel it. The chemistry, the connection, even with the door between us.

Knowing that he's not going to leave until I answer, I walk over to the door and pull it open. His eyes find mine for a few seconds and my breath catches at the emotion swimming in them before they drop and take in my body.

A shudder runs down my spine and my nipples instantly pebble under his scrutiny. He growls, clearly not missing my response to him just standing there.

"D-did you want something?" I hate that my voice wavers, but I can't help the effect he has on me.

"Y-you... uh... left these in the hotel. I thought you might need them." He lifts up the white bag containing my painkillers, and the increasing throb in my head suddenly makes so much sense. It was hours ago I last took some.

"Oh, yeah. Thank you." I take them from him, my fingers brushing lightly against his, causing sparks to shoot up my arm. He must feel it too, because his eyes widen and he takes the smallest step toward me.

He hesitates, unsure what my reaction will be. His hand lifts, but he never closes the space between us, and whatever it is he sees in my eyes must tell him to back off because his hand never touches me.

"Rae," he breathes. I hate that my eyes fill with moisture at the broken tone to his voice. "W-what happened this morning?"

"I came to my senses."

He blows out a breath. "Baby, everything I said to you yesterday was true. You're fucking killing me right now."

I still at his admission, and he uses the opportunity to wrap his hand around the back of my neck and drop his forehead to mine. His eyes stay on mine and I fight to hold his stare. I'm so desperate to close mine so he can't read the truth in them about how I really feel.

"Just give me a chance. Let me show you how it can be."

"I-I can't. You don't want me. You just don't want anyone else to have me."

"Fuck, Rae. I want you so fucking bad. Any way I can have you."

I shake my head against his. "No. No, you don't. I'm sorry." I stand back and briefly look at his defeated stance before I close the door. He has to take a step back for me to fully close it, and he refuses.

"P-please. Leave it open. I need to know you're okay."

I don't have the energy to argue, so I do as he says and silently walk over to my bed and climb in. I know he's still watching me, but I refuse to look his way. If I do, it would mean he's seeing the fact that I'm on the verge of breaking down. He saw me broken last night. That was enough.

I keep my back to him and focus on my breathing, hoping it'll relax me enough to send me to sleep. By some miracle, it works, because everything fades away.

———

When I wake, I'm totally disorientated. Sitting up, my head spins before the incessant banging makes itself known. Everything hits me all at once as I squeeze my eyes shut in the hope of blocking it all out. Sadly it doesn't work. Looking to my nightstand, I find my tablets where I left them, but beside them is a new glass of water. I try to convince myself that it was Rachel, but I know it's pointless because it was obviously him making sure I'm okay.

I make use of it to swallow down two tablets before making my way to the bathroom on unsteady legs.

I've no idea what time it is or how long I've been asleep, but it doesn't feel like it's been anywhere near long enough. My stomach grumbles as I sit on the toilet, staring at the wall in a total daze. I haven't eaten anything aside from a bit of fruit in the hotel room yesterday... shit, was that yesterday?

I find my cell the second I get out of the bathroom and discover it's early evening. I slept for longer than I thought.

I put it back in my purse and go to grab something to cover up with when some red fabric folded at the bottom of my bed catches my eye. It's Ethan's Bears jersey, but a different one than the one I stole yesterday seeing as that's in the laundry.

Reaching out, I lift it and bring it to my nose. Breathing in, I allow my eyes to flicker closed as his scent surrounds me. Something within me settles, and I don't even bother to push it down like I usually would.

Slipping the fabric over my head, I very gently run my fingers through my now dry hair and head for the door.

The house is in silence apart from someone rustling around in the kitchen when I get there.

"Rae, there you are," Rachel's soft voice says when I join her. "How are you feeling?"

"I've been better," I admit honestly for the first time since the incident.

"Have a seat." She pulls a chair out for me and I immediately fall into it. "Would you like a drink, food..."

"Yes and yes. As long as you don't mind. I'm more than cap—"

"I'd love to." She squeezes my shoulder gently and walks to the coffee machine. "Ethan told me what happened. That must have been terrifying."

"Yeah, it was." *Although not as terrifying as what happened after in that hotel room.* Just at the mention of his name, my heart begins to race. I know I was the one to send him away, but fuck if I couldn't do with being in his arms again like last night. Tears burn my eyes as I think back before I shake my head, feeling like an emotional rollercoaster. *It must be the head trauma that's causing it,* I tell myself, *nothing to do with the man himself.* "Uh... where is he? Um... Ethan?"

"Said he was going for a swim, so probably in the pool. What would you like to eat?"

My stomach rumbles right on cue. "I know it's evening, but any chance of breakfast?" I ask, suddenly wanting her incredible pancakes.

"Sure thing. Pancakes?"

"Please."

I watch her putter around as she effortlessly makes me some food while trying to keep thoughts of Ethan in the pool from my mind.

"Here you go, sweetie."

"Thank you. Do you mind if I take them up to my room?"

"Of course not. Just shout if you need anything, I won't be far away."

"Thank you." My voice cracks as tears well in my eyes once more. What the hell is wrong with me?

Grabbing the comforter from the bed and dragging it out to the balcony with me, I wrap myself up to keep warm and sit in the seat closest to the edge. I know I shouldn't, but I'm a glutton for punishment. Before looking over the edge, I start work on my plate that's overloaded with pancakes, bacon, and syrup. Exactly what I need.

The water splashes below, and eventually get too much and shift in my seat so I can watch his body cut through the water. He moves so flawlessly as he swims back and forth. I have no idea how he continues for so long, but I'm not complaining. Watching him is almost therapeutic.

I lose count of how many lengths he does, but eventually he comes to a stop and hops over the little underwater wall that separates the main pool from the jacuzzi, and he rests his head back against the tiles behind him.

He shuts his eyes, but he doesn't look relaxed at all. It's clear to see from here that the muscles in his neck and shoulders are pulled tight and he seems to have a permanent frown on his face.

I continue watching him as the sun descends in the sky as the day I've totally missed comes to an end.

I have no idea if he can sense I'm watching him, but when he eventually drags his eyes open, they lock straight onto mine. I still think that he knew I was here all along. It makes me wonder if he feels the same tingles of awareness that I do when he's watching me.

Lifting his arms to rest them on the edge, I can't help but think he's inviting me to join him. But as much as I'd love to, I sit exactly where I am. Our silent exchange continues for some time as we stay locked in our stare. He's begging me to believe him, and I'm trying to keep my walls up in an attempt to stop him from hurting me, although I know it's pointless. I'm pretty sure he's going to smash them down and force his way in eventually.

When my eyes start to get heavy once again. I give him a weak smile before standing with my comforter around me and head back inside, but it's not before I hear a loud splash behind me.

39

ETHAN

My hand slaps the water in frustration. I'm desperate to go up there and pull her into my arms like I did last night to ensure she's safe, but I know she won't allow it. I understand her wanting to keep me at arm's length. Hell, if she were anyone else, I'd be warning her away from me as well. But she's not anyone else. She's mine.

My heart thuds at that thought. Is she, though? Because she seems to be doing everything in her power to stop that from happening.

Frustrated with myself, I push from the water and head inside.

"Would you like some dinner? I just made Rae pancakes and there's some batter left."

"No, I'm good. Thank you, though," I say to Rachel as I pass the kitchen. Could I eat? Yeah, I can always eat, but there's something I want more, and I need to see what she's doing.

I've no idea if she's sleeping, but I make sure I'm quiet as I make my way to her bedroom just in case. I can't help smiling when I find her door open, just like I left it earlier so I could check on her. Maybe she is softening to me after all, because not so long ago, if I asked her to do this, she'd have thrown it back in my face.

I push the door wider and poke my head inside. She's facing away as I walk into the room, but I make quick work of rounding her bed so I can see her. I half expect her to look at me and rip me a new one, much like I did every time I came in here to check on her earlier, but to my surprise, she's asleep once again.

It's dark out now, but I close the curtains she left open and flick off the sidelight so it doesn't disturb her. I desperately want to pull the covers back and slide in, but the scent of chlorine on my body stops me. Not for long though.

After having the quickest shower of my life, I walk straight back into her room and lie down with her. My need to be close and to make sure she's okay is too much to deny. There's a very good chance she'll wake up and freak out, but as I lie there listening to her shallow breathing and being surrounded by her sweet scent, I couldn't care less.

———

She's still out when I stir awake the next morning to head for practice with the guys. I'm not sure what Jake is trying to achieve, but with both him and Coach riding our asses, half the team is going to be dead by Friday. I quickly shut off my cell alarm when it starts blaring, not wanting it to wake her. After everything she's been through, she deserves this time to recharge.

With a gentle kiss to her head, I slip out of her room unnoticed and get ready.

I'm the last one out on to the field, and I get a dirty look from Jake for being late. He soon puts it to one side when Mason asks how Rae is.

"I left her sleeping."

Mason's brow rises. "And you know that how?"

"That's enough, girls. There's plenty of time for gossip later. We've got shit to do," Jake barks, totally focused on the job at hand. He shouts orders for everyone to start warming up, and, like a good little team, everyone hops to it, despite it being the ass crack of Sunday morning and really, we should all still be in bed.

Mason strips his hoodie off and joins me as we start sprints. It's the first time I've seen him join in since his accident.

"Bro, tell me you've been given the all clear to play?"

"Not officially, but I'm not missing it for the fucking world, so I need to get back into shape."

We set off again, and although he covers it well. I still see the pain etched onto his features. I want to tell him that he's pushing too hard and he should still be healing, but I know it's pointless, and I also know that if it were me in his position I'd be doing the same right now, so I can hardly criticize.

We continue until we've got sweat pouring from us and the sun has long risen above the horizon. My muscles ache, not helped by my lack of sleep the last few nights, and my lungs burn as I drag in the air I need.

"All right, ladies. Let's call it a day."

"Thank fuck for that," Mason moans beside me with his hands on his knees. "Are you trying to fucking kill me, Thorn?"

"No, but I want you on that fucking field next Friday. And I know all your asses are going to eat your own fucking body weight in turkey on Thursday so I'm planning ahead."

A series of groans sound out behind me before Jake suggests we all head for breakfast.

"Aces?" Mason asks with trepidation. "Are they open?"

"As far as I know. Let's go check."

We all head off in various cars before descending on Bill. It is open, but it's quiet, and Bill looks a hell of a lot more stressed than usual.

"Savage?" he calls the second I step into the diner. I nod my chin in greeting and walk over while the guys make themselves at home in our booth.

"How is she? I tried calling, but she's not answering her phone."

"She's okay."

He blows out a shaky breath. "She shouldn't have been alone. I should have been here. I should have—"

"It wasn't your fault. The others should have still been here, but I understand more than most just how stubborn she is, so I get why they left. Stop beating yourself up about it, there's nothing you could have done."

"But she's really okay?"

"Yeah, it'll take more than a knock to the head to take her out."

He chuckles, but he's far from amused. "I bought her a bunch of flowers and some chocolates on the way in this morning. You think you could take them home for her?"

"You should do it. I'm sure she'd love to see you."

"Um..." he says awkwardly.

"I can do it. I'll come and grab them before we leave."

"Thank you. I trust you're looking after your girl."

"I'm trying, Bill. I'm fucking trying." He laughs again, but I can't find it in me to do so. How does everyone already know that she belongs to me? It's about time she got the fucking memo.

40

RAELYNN

Stretching out my legs, I roll over and pull my eyes open. I'm shocked to see a huge bunch of flowers on my dresser. It's not the sort of thing I'm used to, and all they do is remind me of what happened. I yawn and stretch out my sore body, I'm not sure I've ever slept quite so hard in my life. My head still hurts, but it's nothing compared to the last time I woke.

I lie there, memories of my dreams fading, feeling embarrassed that I dreamt of him. That he was here. That he crawled into bed with me and pulled my body to his and whispered sweet things in my ear.

Sitting up, I look to the other side of the bed and my body stills. There's an obvious head dent in the pillow, and the covers are a mess.

Holy shit. Was it a dream?

My heart starts to race as I try to distinguish what was dream and what was real, but I've got no clue.

There's once again a fresh glass of water on my nightstand beside my painkillers. Reaching for it all, I swallow two before my being awake makes the pain worse and I curl back into the warmth of my bed, not ready to emerge into the real world yet.

I think back over yesterday and the way Jake laid into Ethan, thinking that he did this to me. I've never had anyone stand up for me like that before, and to his best friend as well. The feelings it drags up unnerve me, but it also makes me wonder if Ethan's friends really have accepted me here. If Amalie and Camila don't just spend time with me because they feel they have to but because they actually want to. Do I actually have friends?

Before I lose my confidence, I climb out of bed and find my purse. My cell is right at the bottom, the battery about to die. Plugging it into the charger beside my bed, I unlock it and find voicemails, missed calls, and messages from Mom, dozens of missed calls from Bill, and a long stream of messages from Cody trying to find out if I'm okay. I feel bad that I've not responded, but I wasn't really in the mood for talking to anyone.

Ignoring them for now, I open up the group chat the girls started that I thought I was just included in to make me feel wanted, and, for the first time, I start a conversation.

Rae: Are you free? Could do with some company.

My heart thunders in my chest as I wait for a sign that either of them are replying. It only takes a few seconds before a message pops up.

Amalie: Free as a bird. Jake's out putting the guys through their paces.

Camila: Yes! What do you want to do?

Seeing as I'm breaking down all kinds of barriers, I reply with the one thing I never ever thought I would suggest, but with a slight tremble to my hands, I go for it.

Rae: I need to chill out. Forget all the bullshit. You guys know of a spa that will have us last minute?

Little dots bounce for longer than last time, and the longer the responses take the more I regret the suggestion.

Amalie: Hell yes! I've just booked us in. I'll leave the house to pick you both up in 30.

Camila: Yesssssss!

The smile that breaks across my face is so wide and genuine that it actually makes my cheeks hurt. Could this place that I hated so much when I first arrived actually be my first real home?

I think about Amalie and Camila, and then I force myself to consider the possibility of Ethan and the things he's said to me recently being true. Could this place really be it for me? Could I have a life and a future here?

With an extra spring in my step, I find some clothes and have a very quick shower to fully wake me up before packing a bag and heading downstairs.

The house is in silence, and I love it. Pulling the front door open, I breathe in the scent of the fresh sea morning air, and I sit in the swing seat and wait.

Grabbing my cell, I hit call on Mom's number. Rachel and Ethan have dealt with her so far, so she's probably going out of her mind not speaking to me in person.

"Raelynn, thank goodness," she breathes the second the call connects. "How are you? We've tried to get back, but we haven't been able to get on an earlier flight."

"I'm fine, Mom. It's nothing."

"It is not nothing, honey. Ethan told me everything, he sounded so concerned."

"Well, he doesn't need to be. I'm fine."

Silence fills the line and I begin to dread what she's going to say next. "Um… Eric said…" She trails off, and my frustration gets the better of me.

"What, Mom?"

"Eric said that Ethan mentioned…"

My eyes roll so hard at her avoidance of whatever she has to say that it makes my head hurt.

"What?" I snap.

"Is something going on with the two of you?" My breathing catches and my cheeks heat, knowing that there's no way she'll have missed it. "It's totally fine if it is. You're both adults now and…"

"Mom, stop rambling."

"I'm sorry, I just hate being so far away when something so awful has happened."

"I'm fine," I repeat for what feels like the millionth time. "Ethan's looked after me. I couldn't—"

"Aw," she says. "And to think I thought you hated each other."

"Oh, I do. He's a total asshole."

She laughs. "Honey, if I've learned anything from all my disastrous relationships, it's that if you feel that strongly for someone then they're most probably worth it."

I mull her words over in my mind for a few seconds before a question falls from my lips that I wasn't intending to ask. "So if something were to happen, that would be okay?"

"Oh, honey. You don't need my permission, you know that. If you've found someone who's managed to weasel his way into your heart, then I already know he's worth it." I nod as her words settle. "I know I've not really been around since we moved, but even from a distance, I can tell the change in you. And the fact that you're letting people in after all this time… well." Her voice cracks. "It makes me hope I haven't totally screwed you up with everything I've put you through."

I laugh at her. "We can only hope, eh?" As I say that, Amalie's car pulls into the driveway. "Mom, I've got to go. I'm going to a spa with the girls." The words feel foreign as they leave my mouth, but they also feel right.

Mom squeals on the other end, delighted that I'm doing something so normal. "Have a great time. I want to hear all about it when I get back."

"Will do, Mom."

I hang up and make my way over toward Amalie's car, sliding into the passenger seat when Camila climbs in the back to save me doing so.

"So not that I'm complaining one bit, but what's this all about?"

"Just really needed to get out and chill out."

"Ethan that annoying?" Camila asks with a laugh.

I'm silent for a few seconds, and it's just enough time for them to jump to conclusions. "Oh my god, something's happened, hasn't it?" Amalie asks excitedly.

"No, no. I mean, yeah, I'm pretty sure he slept in my bed last night to make sure I was okay, but he'd left before I woke."

"And if he hadn't?"

"I don't know," I answer honestly.

I can tell myself all I like that he's playing me and that I need to stay as far away as possible, but having his hot body for the taking beside me, could I have walked away? I really have no idea.

"You so need to go for it with him," Camila encourages.

"Give her a break, Cami. You'll do things at your pace, right Rae?" Amalie asks softly.

"Do you think he really does like me?" I immediately feel stupid and vulnerable for asking the question, but it's too late now. It's out.

"Yes, Rae. Yes, he really does."

Silence hangs heavy in the car around us as I try to figure out what I'm supposed to do with that piece of information.

Thankfully, Amalie pulls up to a fancy hotel and spa, and I'm able to forget about her words in favor of appreciating the lavish building in front of me.

"Should I have given a budget for this?"

"Don't even think about it. The only thing you need to worry about is what color polish you want on your nails. Leave the rest to us."

I open my mouth to argue, but one look from Amalie stops me. "Okay, okay," I concede.

We're directed straight through to a restaurant where we have brunch, followed by every spa treatment imaginable, most of which I never knew even existed. We spend time sitting around the pool and generally chat about random shit. Thankfully, they steer clear of too much Ethan talk and just allow me to think about that in private, and no one even mentions Friday night, which I'm grateful for. I mean, it's not like I'm going to forget any time soon with the steady throb of my head or my bald patch.

By the time Amalie drops me off later that night, I'm once again exhausted, but in such a good way. I've been waxed, scrubbed, plucked, and painted within an inch of my life and I feel like I'm floating on a cloud after all the soft music and essential oils.

Ethan's car is here, but as I make my way to my room, I don't find any evidence of him. After a quick change of clothes, I get myself under the covers and turn the TV on.

I find some chat show to watch, and no sooner has the sun set outside am I asleep once again.

I have no idea what time it is when the mattress compresses beside me, signaling that my nighttime minder has arrived. I keep my body still and my breathing slow as he gets himself comfortable. I'm grateful that my back's to him or he'd be able to tell I was awake, I'm sure.

He lies still for a few seconds before blowing out a long breath and turning toward me. His arm comes around my waist, and he slides his front to my back.

The heat of his bare skin against my barely dressed body burns, and everything in me aches to turn over and see what he'd do. But this isn't the time. What Amalie and Camila said might be true. All the words he's said to me in the last few days might be true, but the middle of the night when I'm still in pain isn't the time to figure our shit out.

"Are you awake?" he whispers.

Fuck. I will my breathing not to falter and for my body not to tense. I've no idea if I pull it off or not, but after a few seconds he speaks again and I relax.

"Goodnight, baby. I'm here if you need me."

A lump forms in my throat and tears burn my eyes as he drops a kiss to my bare shoulder and gets comfortable behind me.

What is wrong with you, Rae? Turn around. Turn the fuck around.

But I never do. Instead, I lie there until my exhaustion claims me once again. Make him work for it, they said. Make him prove it. Don't give in just because he's here protecting you like no one else ever has.

———

He's gone again when I wake the next morning. I'd turned my alarm off, knowing that I wasn't going to school this morning. I've got a follow up with a doctor to check my stitches.

I glance at the clock, and realizing I've still got ages, I intend on rolling over once again but a piece of paper on my nightstand catches my eye.

I'll pick you up at eleven for your appointment x

My hand trembles as I hold the slip of paper. *He's going to skip school for me?* I don't know why I'm shocked, it's not the first time. He's not exactly a model student. But he needs to be there, not escorting me to a bullshit appointment.

Grabbing my cell, I shoot him a message.

It's fine. I'll grab an Uber. My thumb hovers over the send button before I add some more at the last minute. **Thank you, though.**

His reply comes almost immediately, and I'm unsure if I'm more shocked by the speed when he should be in class or his words.

For once, do as you're told. I'll pick you up at eleven. Be ready.

Well... fuck.

I fall back on the bed with a groan. I could reply and tell him to go to hell, but I have a suspicion that he'll just turn up here at eleven anyway. If I've already left then he'll turn up at the appointment. I'd put money on it, so I decide to just take the easy route for once and climb out of bed to shower and dress.

I apply my makeup with extra precision than usual and I very, very carefully blow dry my hair and pull it back in a loose bun. I tell myself that it's just because I've got the time, but deep down, I know that's not the reason. *He is.*

I allow Rachel to make me breakfast, although the thought of spending time with Ethan awake after everything that's passed between us has my stomach in knots, and the last thing I really want to do is eat.

Ten minutes before eleven, the sound of an engine rumbles through me before his giant truck appears at the end of the driveway.

I stand from the swing and take a step toward him. My temperature soars and goosebumps cover my skin the second his eyes lock on me. Something flutters in my stomach, and I try to convince myself it's not nerves. I don't get nervous.

I walk, on wobbly legs, down to his truck, but before I reach him, he's out and running around to the passenger door to open it for me.

"Whoa, who are you, and what have you done with Ethan Savage?"

He chuckles, but it doesn't meet his eyes. They're deadly serious as he stares down at me.

"I told you. I'm a good guy really."

"So you keep saying. But don't you know that most girls like their boys a little bit bad?"

His eyes drop from mine and run down the length of me. That one look has my heart rate picking up and desire knotting in my lower stomach.

"Is that right?"

I swallow loudly as he closes the space between us. The air is thick with tension as I try to drag some in, but under his intense stare, I'm unable to do anything but feel the crackle of chemistry between us.

Reaching out, he tucks a stray lock of hair that's escaped behind my ear. The second we connect, my entire body flinches with the shock. He continues moving his head toward me. I start to wonder if he's going to throw caution to the wind and be the bad boy I just alluded to and kiss me, but at the last minute, he leans to the side so his lips brush the shell of my ear. A shudder runs up my spine as his breath tickles.

"Lucky for you, I can be bad. *Very* bad. Some might even say I've got a bit of a rep."

My mouth goes dry, stopping any words from coming out.

When he pulls back, a smug smirk pulls at his lips.

"I've had better." It's a total barefaced lie, and I'm pretty sure he knows it. He laughs, and this time it lightens his eyes.

"Then I guess I've something to prove. Your chariot awaits."

He waits while I climb in, not an easy feat when I'm basically three foot two. I expect him to help me, any excuse to get his hands on me, but to my surprise, he holds back. Maybe he can be a good boy. I refuse to admit it, but I'm kind of disappointed.

Once he's happy I'm settled, he closes the door on me and jogs around to the driver's side.

"I've got to be honest," he says as he turns the car and heads off the property, "I didn't think you'd be here waiting for me."

"I thought I'd keep you on your toes."

"You certainly do that, baby."

His use of my new nickname does things to my insides that I don't need to be thinking about right now.

"How are you feeling?"

"Fine."

"Are you ever anything other than fine?"

"Yeah. Often I'm angry. Mostly at you."

"Fair enough. Are you angry now?"

"No. Just fine."

I stare out the window in an attempt to seem unaffected by him.

"It's not working, you know."

"What's not working?" I turn to him to see him drag his eyes from me and back to the road.

"Looking out the window and attempting to ignore me. I know you can't ignore me. Ignore this."

He gestures between us.

"Oh? And what is *this* exactly?" I copy his previous arm gesture and raise a brow.

"Us. You can fight it all you want, baby. But we both know it's only going to end one way."

He pulls into the hospital parking lot and straight into a vacant space.

"Oh yeah, and how's that exactly?"

He leans over, the scent of him filling my nose, and I damn near moan in delight. "With you admitting how you really feel and with me so deep inside you that you'll never be able to forget me."

My breath catches at his words. It's something the old Ethan would say, but it's laced with something other than hate now, and I'm not really sure how to deal with it.

"You'd be so lucky," I sass, reaching for the handle, but he catches my wrist.

"I really fucking hope I will be." He tugs my arm, and my body moves forward just enough for him to capture my lips. My brain screams fight, but my entire body sags in relief. It's a teasing kiss, just a simple brush of his lips against mine, and when I think he's going to deepen it and give me what I need but won't admit, he's gone and jumping from the car.

"Motherfucker," I mutter to myself, but when he pulls my door open, the smirk on his face tells me that he knows exactly what he just did.

I take two steps toward the entrance when his fingers tickle against my wrist. My immediate reaction is to pull away, but my curiosity gets the better of me and I leave it to see what he does next.

Not a second later, his fingers tangle with mine and he squeezes. My chin drops. He's holding my fucking hand. My heart begins to race as I fight with myself as to what to do.

He pulls me to a stop, and before I know what's happening, he backs me up against the wall of the reception. He stands staring down at me, amusement shining in his blue eyes.

"Stop over-thinking," he warns. "Just trust me."

A laugh rumbles up. Trust him?

"I told you that I'd prove that all those words I said to you in that hotel room were the truth, and I can't do that if you won't let me." He lifts the hand that's not still gripped onto mine tightly and cups my cheek. "Let me show you how I really feel. What I really want." He presses his body against mine, and I gasp as the unmistakable shape of his hard cock presses into my stomach. He leans down so only I can hear his next words. "Only you do that. No one else in the world could have me hard as we walk into a fucking hospital."

I laugh, because if I don't then I'm afraid I might give the people around us waiting a show.

"W-we're going to be late," I whisper, trying to keep my wits about me.

"We are. Let's go and get your head checked."

Thankfully, the wait to see the doctor isn't all that long. I'm not sure I could have coped with the tension crackling between the two of us if it had been much longer.

He was happy that my wound was healing okay and that there didn't seem to be any other issues. He cleared me to go back to school—not that his word would stop me from showing up in the morning, but it's nice to know it's actually safe.

"I need to be back at school for practice, but do you want to go for lunch first?" Ethan asks once we're back in his car.

"We need to go to school."

"I didn't have you down as a goodie two shoes."

"I'm not, but I intend on graduating and getting into college so it kinda needs to be done."

"Oh yeah. What do you want to do?"

"Honestly, anything. All I've wanted for years was just to be in control of my own life. I don't even know where, all I know is that it's going to be my choice and mine alone."

"I understand that."

"I've been dragged to every corner of the country, or so it feels, in Mom's quest to give me the perfect life, or what she deems as perfect, and I've fucking hated it. This is the only place that's ever felt—" I slam my lips shut, knowing that I've just said too much.

"Ever felt like what?"

"Fuck," I mutter, resting my head back and closing my eyes for a beat. "Home, okay? It's the first place that I could actually see myself making a life. It's fucked-up, but for some reason, I feel like I might just belong here."

"Why's that fucked-up?" he asks, turning to stare at me, but I refuse to look back, knowing that he'll be able to read too much in my eyes.

"Because Mom's barely been here since we moved. It's my gazillionth school in the last decade, and I've had to deal with you."

"Oh come on, I'm not that bad."

"Really?" I ask, now leaning forward to look into his eyes. "You want me to list all the fucked-up things?"

Guilt immediately fills his eyes as he takes a trip down memory lane.

Before I notice his hand move, he takes mine in his and lifts my knuckles to his lips. He places a kiss there but doesn't pull away.

He looks at me through his lashes, and my heart jumps into my chest. "I'm so fucking sorry, Rae. I'll do anything to prove to you that that person back then wasn't me. Name it and I'll do it, just to show you."

"Shut up, Ethan. I don't need you to do something crazy like run through school naked to prove anything."

"Really?" His eyes light up like the idea actually excites him.

"No, don't do that."

"Oh yeah. Why not?" My cheeks heat. "Fuck, I love it when you blush. So come on, tell me why I shouldn't do that. Be brave, Rae. I dare you."

"Y-you s-shouldn't because..." I suck in a breath as I try to come up with a lie that won't expose me too much, but with his eyes boring into mine, begging me to tell the truth, it's exactly what falls from my lips. "I don't want anyone else seeing you naked."

"See, admitting what you really want wasn't that hard, was it?"

"Worse than this gash on my head, I can tell you that for nothing."

He barks out a laugh, and I know there and then that it was worth admitting for that noise alone. I smile and laugh with him.

"So you want to go back to school then?"

"I think we should. We've already missed enough."

"Okay. We'll stop for takeout and head back."

I buckle up while he starts the engine. He drives to a burger place and orders for us before taking the next turn toward Rosewood High.

"Don't," he warns when I start to open the bag of food that's sitting on my lap.

"Why? Did you buy it for us to look at?"

"No, just... do as you're told."

"Not my specialty."

"Don't I fucking know it," he mutters, pulling into a space and hopping out.

He comes around to my side once again and takes the bag from my lap before taking my hand and helping me jump out.

"Where are we going?" I ask when he refuses to release my hand and walks us around the back of the building.

"Trust me."

"You say that a lot."

"Because you need to."

He walks us toward the football stadium and pushes through one of the side doors. We walk through until we begin climbing the stairs. The place is deserted apart from the two of us. I guess that's what he was going for.

It's not until we're right at the top that he turns, pulls a seat down for me and nods for me to sit. He undoes the bag and hands me my half of the food. We begin eating in silence, but it's not uncomfortable.

"I love it here when it's empty. Things are so crazy on game night that it's nice to come up here and reflect on everything during the day."

"The perfect Ethan Savage with the perfect life has things he needs to reflect on," I quip.

"I'm far from perfect, Rae. Just look how I've treated you. My life was falling apart long before I even realized. If I was paying more attention, or just home more, I might have noticed that things hadn't been right between my parents. I should have seen it coming, and I sure as hell shouldn't have taken it out on you."

"Hindsight is a great thing. Sadly, there's not much we can do about the past."

He tenses beside me. "I'm sorry you had to go through what you did, and I'm sorry I invaded your privacy and found out the way I did."

"It's okay. Well... it's not, but it is what it is. And in a weird way, I'm glad you know."

"Me too."

"No one else knows about it. I've never told anyone."

"No one?" he asks, turning to look at me, but I continue to stare ahead at the empty stands.

"Well, obviously the police officers and social workers, but I've never told anyone in day-to-day life."

"Why?"

"Never had anyone to tell."

"Fucking hell, Rae," he says sadly, shaking his head.

"Don't pity me."

"I'm not. I'm not. I'm just so glad you've got people who care now."

"Have I?" I know I'm pushing my luck by asking, but I need to hear it.

"Yeah. Amalie and Camila love you. Jake cares enough to plow his fist into my face," he says lightheartedly, pointing to his split lip. "And I..." He trails off.

"And you?" It's my turn to turn to him, but he avoids my stare as he considers his words.

"I... I think you're kind of incredible."

"Is that right?"

"You're the strongest person I've ever met, Rae. By a fucking mile. After everything you've been through, you're a fucking warrior."

"It was nothing. People deal with worse."

"Yeah, they do, but you're amazing. That kind of shit would break most people but you're... you're..."

"Amazing?" I add, using the last word he said to describe me.

"Yeah. That and some." He turns to me, his eyes soft, his barriers down. His eyes study mine for a few seconds, his lips parting like he has something to say but is unsure if he should let it out or not. I want to push him, but I find I can't, wanting him to offer whatever it is himself. "And... and I'm falling for you harder than I know what to do with."

My breath catches at the honesty in his tone.

"Ethan, I—"

"No. We're done talking."

"Oh."

His hand slips around the side of my neck, his thumb brushing my cheek gently as he leans in. My brain screams to back away, to protect myself, but my body is all in and I find myself closing the space between us.

41

ETHAN

I brush my lips over hers gently, waiting to see how she responds to me. She was more than up for it when I kissed her in the car earlier, but if I've learned anything about Rae, it's that she's unpredictable at the best of times. My fingers twitch against her neck as I wait to see what she's going to do.

It feels like it takes an eternity, but eventually, her soft lips move against mine and my restraint snaps. Her lips part the second my tongue touches them and hers almost instantly meets mine. I explore her mouth like it's the first time, savoring her taste, allowing it to feed my addiction for this woman beside me.

I shift over in my seat to close the space between us, but already knowing that I'm never going to be able to get close enough with an armrest in the middle.

Dropping my hands to her waist, I lift her from her seat. The remaining food and wrappers that were on her lap fall to the ground as I settle her where she belongs: on my lap.

Her legs just fit on either side of mine, and I groan in relief as her weight presses down on me.

Finding the smooth exposed skin of her back, I slide my hands up, delighting in the fact that she shudders as I do so. My lips curl into a smile as she eagerly continues our kiss.

Her hands thread into my hair and pull, the bite of pain only adding fuel to my already out of control fire.

"Rae," I moan into her mouth as they drop to my shoulders and then skim over my pecs and abs. My muscles pull and dance as she runs her light touch over them. "Fuck." Finding the bottom of my shirt, she slips her hands inside. Our skin connects with an explosion of electricity that has my cock threatening to burst through my jeans. Her pussy is right above, and it would be so easy to take her like this for the entire school to see if they were to descend on this place.

That thought is the bucket of cold water I need. This girl is mine, no one else gets to have their eyes on her.

Ripping my lips from hers, I kiss down her neck. "Baby, we need to stop." I hate that the words pass my lips, but this isn't how this is going to go between us. Not now, anyway.

"We really don't," she whispers, throwing her head back to give me better access. My hands slip around to her stomach, and the temptation to push them up to her tits is so fucking strong, but she deserves more than this. She deserves everything and more. Fuck knows if I'm able to deliver it, but I'm gonna give it a fucking good go.

"We do. I want to do this properly. Treat you properly, the way you deserve."

"Didn't stop you before." Her chest is heaving before me, her lips parted to drag in the air she needs. When she looks down, her usually dark eyes are almost black with desire.

"I know," I say, regret filling my tone.

"So make it up to me. I thought you wanted to prove yourself." She tilts her head to the side and her eyebrow quirks in challenge.

"But—"

"Are you man enough, Ethan?" She wiggles in my lap, ensuring I feel every tiny movement. My hands land on her hips, holding her in place, desperate for more of her.

"You fucking know I am."

"So... Prove. It."

The fabric of her fishnets disintegrates beneath my fingers, and in seconds I'm moving her soaked panties aside.

"Fucking hell," I moan as her juices coat my fingers.

"Ethan," she moans in return, throwing her head back once more and thrusting her tits in my face.

Forgetting everything, I push the fabric of her top up and pull the cups of her bra down to give me the access I need.

Pushing my fingers inside her, I lean forward and suck one of her nipples into my mouth.

"Fuck. Fuck."

I suck hard before biting down enough to have her crying out. I pump my fingers inside her, bending them to hit the place she needs before kissing my way toward her other nipple to give it the same treatment.

"Ethan. Shit. Fuck," she moans above me, and my chest swells with everything I feel for the woman. She's so fucking strong. So fucking brave. And needs to be so fucking mine.

I sit back when I sense she's about to fall, because as much as I want her in my mouth, I want to watch her come apart in my hands more.

"Come on, baby. Come for me. Let me see how fucking beautiful you are."

"Oh god."

"Nah, just Ethan Savage, baby."

Her lips curl up as if she's about to laugh, but I graze her G-spot once more and she falls headfirst into her release instead. And it's fucking magical. Her chin drops, her eyes close, and she clenches around me so fucking hard it makes my cock weep to be inside her, to experience just what it'll be like with us connected exactly as we should be.

She falls forward against me as she fights to catch her breath.

"I'm pretty sure that was the hottest thing I've ever seen."

She laughs against me but doesn't say anything for the longest time. When she does speak, I can't help but laugh too.

"I really needed that."

"Glad I could help, baby."

Regretfully, I help her off me and she rights her clothing before falling back down into her own seat. She's too far away, but there's not much I can do about it other than drag her home to bed, but even I know I need to be here for practice. Mason is joining us for the first time to see if he's going to be able to be a part of next week's final.

"So..." Rae starts hesitantly.

"So what?"

"So now what?"

"Well, I think it's safe to say you finished your lunch." I look to where what she had left is now scattered on the ground.

"I meant with us, you idiot."

My heart slams against my chest at her use of the word us. Is there an us? Is she going to allow there to be an us? "I told you. I fully intend to do things right this time. If you'll allow me, that is."

"Hmmm..."

"What's that supposed to mean?"

"It means that I'll consider it." Her lips twitch as she fights her smile.

"You'll consider it?" I ask, arching my brow.

"Yeah. I mean, I have just had quite a significant bump to the head, so there's a very good chance I'm not thinking straight right now."

"I should hope not, after that orgasm."

"Ethan, I'm being serious," she says, swatting my shoulder, but the wide smile on her face tells me otherwise.

"Right. Of course you are."

The school bell rings in the distance, efficiently putting our time to an end.

Jake will castrate me if I miss practice, and I'm in too much of a good mood right now to put up with his angry ass.

Reaching over, I wrap my hand around the back of her neck and gently pull her over to me. "This is what happens next. I'll get Amalie or Camila to take you home. Then you can wait for me there. Clothes optional. I fully intend to spend the entire night proving myself to you."

"Oh yeah?" Her cheeks heat at my words, and it's almost enough to blow off practice in favor of her body.

I shake my head, trying to get the dirty thoughts out of my mind before I go and get sweaty with the guys.

"Yeah. By the end of tonight, there's going to be no doubt who you belong to. I guarantee that by morning there will only be one person's name you remember, and I promise you, it won't be yours." Her cheeks only get redder as her tongue sneaks out to lick her bottom lip. "Sound like a plan?"

"Um... I'll consid—"

I slam my lips down on hers before she gets a chance to finish the word.

Pulling back abruptly before I'm in so deep I'm not going to be able to walk away without being inside her, I stand and pull my cell from my pocket.

"Can you take Rae home?" I bark the second Camila picks up. My voice is rough even to my own ears, and she doesn't miss it.

"Of course. Is everything okay?"

Rearranging myself so that Rae has no choice but to know the state she's left me in, I smile down at her. "Yeah, everything's great. We just came back to school after her appointment."

"Oh, she wasn't in my last class."

"No, she was getting a very different kind of lesson."

"Ethan, what are—"

"She'll meet you by your car," I interrupt when Rae looks like she's about to kick me in the balls and steal my cell. I hang up and give her my most innocent face.

"You're a fucking nightmare."

"I'm your fucking nightmare though, baby."

"I haven't decided if I want you yet."

"Oh, ouch."

"Come on, Savage. You've got practice to get to."

"It's just a warm-up really, for what comes later."

I leave her in the parking lot with a sweet kiss that's sure to tide her over until I get home. Camila walks up to us with Amalie hot on her heels, and both of them witness it. As I walk past them back toward the building, I can tell they want to smile, but instead, they both keep their hard eyes on me in warning.

They don't need to say it. If I hurt her, I'll cause myself some physical pain; they don't need to threaten it.

I walk toward the locker rooms with the widest smile on my face. Jake and Mason take one look at me when I join them and slap me on the shoulder.

"We're happy for you, bro. Now, you ready to smash this shit before you can get back to your girl?"

"Fucking right. Let's do this."

42

RAELYNN

"**B**loody knew you wouldn't be able to fight him," Amalie says as the three of us climb into Camila's Mini.

I sigh. "I tried. I really did. But man, he knows exactly what to say to make me melt."

"Huh, I never had Ethan down as the romantic type, so I'm assuming you're talking about his filthy mouth."

I bark out a laugh. "Yeah, something like that."

"You want a milkshake?" Camila asks the two of us.

"Yeah. I need to see Bill and Cody, show them I'm still alive."

"Awesome. That'll waste some time until the guys finish and Ethan can eat you for dinner."

My entire body heats with the suggestion. "Jeez, he really has worked his charm on you, eh?" Camila asks, glancing at me squirming in her backseat.

"Do you guys think I'm an idiot for even considering this thing with Ethan?" I hate sounding unsure, but I need to know what they think.

"No, not at all. If you feel that connection, then I say go for it."

I nod, a small smile playing on my lips as I think back over the afternoon with him.

Both Bill and Cody race toward me when the three of us enter the diner. Bill's given me two weeks off fully paid after what I went through. It's not necessary, but I appreciate it and will gladly accept. They throw question after question at me but mostly just repeatedly ask me if I'm okay.

Eventually, they leave the three of us in peace to enjoy our milkshakes, but I don't miss their concerned glances my way. It's not helped by the missing hair exposing my wound. It makes me want to take it down to hide it, but I'm not sure I'm ready to fully embrace it yet, or ever.

"What's going on?" I ask Amalie as she furiously taps at her cell with a wide smile on her face.

"Oh, um..."

"What?" Both Camila and I ask simultaneously.

"We just need to wait an hour before delivering Rae back home."

"Why? Has something happened at practice?" Images fill my head of Ethan getting hurt so close to the final game, and I panic.

"No, no everything's fine. Just trust us, yeah?" Amalie winks at Camila as they share a silent best friend conversation over the table and I sigh in frustration.

"Fine, whatever. I want another one of these for it, though."

They both laugh but agree and call Cody back over.

———

It's almost an hour and a half later when we eventually pull up in front of the Savage house. The sun is beginning to set, casting the house in a gorgeous orange hue. Both Jake and Mason are waiting out front, and, after nodding a greeting at me, they climb into the car with their girls.

"Have a great night," Amalie calls out. I look back over my shoulder to find all four of them grinning at me like idiots.

"He's waiting for you," Mason says before Camila revs the engine and they disappear out of the driveway. It's not until I'm alone that my nerves hit.

What the hell am I going to find inside this house?

With a trembling hand, I push the front door open and step inside. There are cases in the hallway, pointing to the fact that Mom and Eric are home. I'm surprised she doesn't come running at me the second I'm in the house, but everything is eerily quiet.

"Hello?" I call out, but really it's not loud enough for anyone to hear me. I find the kitchen and the family room empty when I poke my head inside. Assuming they've gone straight out, I head for the stairs, thinking that it's probably where Ethan is waiting for me. Naked, hopefully. Butterflies take up flight in my stomach at the thought.

My steps quicken as I climb up and race toward my bedroom. My door is ajar when I get there and I push it open eagerly, convinced that he'll be there. Disappointment floods me when I look around and find the room empty, aside from the flowers that I now know came from Bill.

"Where are you?" I mutter, walking farther into the room and dropping my purse to the bed. It's then that a crash comes from outside, followed by a curse in a very familiar voice.

Smiling that I've found him, I walk toward the balcony. The closer I get to the edge, the more my jaw drops as I take in the pool area beneath me.

Twinkling fairy lights are strung up everywhere. There's a little bistro set with candles flickering in the center, and the outside sofa that sits at the edge of the patio overlooking the beach is covered in blankets and pillows. Soft music plays as the scent of the grill floats up to me. Then finally, Ethan appears. He's dressed in a pair of sweats and his usual Bears jersey. I watch him walk to the grill and open the top before he starts poking at the contents. The butterflies that were already fluttering erupt in my belly, and everything below my stomach clenches in anticipation. The memory of his fingers playing me earlier slams into me and spikes my temperature. I can't deny that I need more of that side of Ethan.

I stand and watch him for a few minutes, wanting to take him in while he's not aware he's got company. He looks so relaxed and totally at home. There's nothing pulling the muscles in his shoulders tight, and I'm sure when he finally looks up at me, I won't find any of the shadows haunting his eyes like when we first met. He's like an entirely different person, he's just still wrapped in the same unbelievably hot package.

I don't think I make a noise, so I can only assume that he senses my stare because after another two seconds of my quiet perusal of his body, his head turns and his eyes find mine. I discover that I was right, because even from this distance all I can see is desire and... love? No, that's crazy. Isn't it?

"There you are," he says softly, staring up at me. "I feel like I should be quoting some sappy line from Shakespeare right now."

"It's okay. I think you may have already maxed out on your romance quota tonight." I glance around at what he's done once more in total awe.

"You like it?" The shyness in his tone has my eyes immediately flying back to his. Surely Ethan Savage isn't unsure of himself right now?

"It's incredible. You did it for me?" I ask, just to be sure this isn't his usual way to welcome home his dad.

"All for you, baby. I told you, I'm going to do it right this time. Give you everything you deserve and more."

I shake my head, tears burning my eyes as I take in the sweet guy before me, the one who's a million miles from the one I first met. Some might think I'm crazy for allowing myself to be swept up by him after what he did to me, how he treated me but I can't help myself. Our connection was there from the very beginning. I see that now. We both just dealt with it in the wrong way. I understand that he was hurt and lashing out. Did he push boundaries he shouldn't have? Sure. But I get it. And now, I see the genuine regret and need to make things right every time I look at him. And I might have caved earlier than I was expecting, but I still fully intend on making him work for it. I'm not one to make anyone's life easy, and Ethan's going to have to learn that I also like to play dirty from time to time.

"It's amazing. You're amazing."

"Well if that's the case, why the fuck are you still up there while I'm down here?" He holds his arms out as if to say, *come and get me*, and I spin on my heels and run toward him.

"There she is," he says when I emerge into the garden.

I stop in the doorway and just look at him. Really look at him, as if it's our first time. He really is beautiful. His thick hair flops down into his face, his blue eyes stare into mine, and the square cut of his jaw gives him the edgy look that I know he loves to play up. But it's his smile that that gets me moving. Gone is the cocky, arrogant, full of himself asshole he shows the rest of the world, and in its place is a small, nervous smile as he waits to see what I'm going to do. That one smile tells me so much. He's nervous that after all this I'm going to turn my back on him, and it's the first time I've ever really appreciated that he needs me just as much as I've realized I need him. It sounds corny as fuck, but as I stand here with him waiting for me, I can't help but feel he's the piece that's been missing from my life. It's not been a place that I needed, or the friends that have eluded me all these years. It's just been him. His sexy smirk, the way he refuses to take my shit or believe me when I'm trying to push him away. The way he smashes through my barriers and climbs over my giant wall. The way he forces me to admit to myself how I really feel. Just the way he is: flaws, broken parts, hurt and all. Just him.

His brows furrow in concern, and it's that move, that final show of weakness for me that has me moving. My legs carry me faster than my brain realizes, and in seconds I'm in his arms with his lips pressing down on mine.

One of his hands slides into my hair while the other comes to rest on my hip and ensures there's no space between us whatsoever.

He kisses me for the longest time. We're both breathless when he finally releases me.

"Whoa, that was some welcome."

"Only the best. Are you hungry?"

"Starved, seeing as someone deposited most of my burger on the ground earlier."

"Let me make up for it."

He walks over to the bistro set and pulls one of the chairs out for me. "Thank you," I mouth, totally blown away by all of this. The self-confessed fuck 'em and chuck 'em seems to be hopping aboard the romance train along with his two best friends.

"I've got meat in every variety you could desire." When he turns to me, I make a show of running my eyes down his body.

"Stop it. Stop it right now," he warns. "I promised you I'd do this properly, but when you look at me like that it…"

"It what, Ethan?" I cross one leg across the other, knowing it'll make my skirt rise up.

"It'll… um…"

"What's wrong? Cat got your tongue?" I stand and close the distance between us once again. "Where are our parents?" I breathe into his ear.

"G-Gone out."

"So there's no one here to watch what happens next?"

He shakes his head, eyes locked on mine.

"Good." I press a kiss to his chest before dropping to my knees.

"Rae, what are you…" His words trail off as I pull the tie of his sweats.

"What?" I ask innocently, tilting my head to the side and looking up at him. "I thought you only wanted me on my knees."

He tips his head back and barks out a laugh. To anyone else, this wouldn't be funny, but I can't help but join him as we both take a trip down memory lane. Thinking about how he treated me should hurt, but I can accept that it's just a part of our past and what helped us get to this moment.

"So, Ethan. You got me down here at last. What should I do?" I trail my fingertip over the bulge of his growing erection beneath the fabric and delight when a low growl rumbles up his throat at my touch.

"Rae, you don't have—"

"Shhh…" I interrupt, pushing the fabric of his shirt up and pressing kisses along the waistband of his boxers. His muscles bunch with each connection before I run my tongue up the definition of his V.

"Fuck, Rae." His fingers gently hold on to my head, ever cautious of my healing wound. They flex and I smile, knowing just how desperate for more he is right now. I could feel the length of him when I was on top of him earlier; I can only imagine how painful it was for him to walk away and go to practice with balls that blue.

I pull back, wrap my fingers around the fabric of both his sweats and boxers, and pull. His cock springs free, now totally hard and begging for my touch.

I glance up at him through my lashes. His eyes are locked on me, but they're darker than I've ever seen them, and the muscles in his neck are pulled tight with restraint. It's one seriously impressive sight, and the fact that I hold all the power right now is a serious turn-on. I've never had a man totally at my mercy like this before, and fuck if I don't love it.

His fingers flex again, and I give in. Reaching out, I wrap my hand around his wide length. His entire body shudders at my contact, and the groan that leaves him practically has my panties melting off me.

Leaning forward, I lick the tip of him. His body flinches, and, encouraged by his hand that's still holding my head, I part my lips and take him inside my mouth.

I have no idea what I was expecting, but he's hot, sweet, and silky smooth.

"Fucking hell, baby," he moans, and hearing his enjoyment gives me the confidence I need to continue.

I suck him as far back as I dare before pulling off and starting all over again. His breathing gets erratic above me, and it's not long before his cock gets even harder.

"Rae, I'm gonna come, baby," he warns, giving me time to make a decision, but really, there's not one to make. I'm fully on board with the idea of us now, and I fully intend on giving him everything.

I suck him again, taking him deeper than before, and the second he hits the back of my throat he lets out the most feral moan before his cock twitches violently between my lips and he comes in my mouth.

Sitting back, I wipe my mouth with the back of my hand before risking a look up at him. But the second our eyes connect, I feel stupid for allowing a few nerves to hit me. His eyes are still full of desire, and he's got the laziest smile on his face.

I'm up on my feet in seconds and lifted until I have no choice but to wrap my legs around his still naked waist.

His lips crash down on mine and our tongues duel as our teeth clash.

"So, it was okay?" I ask with a cheeky smile when he releases me.

"Fucking right."

He drops my feet to the ground so he can cover himself up, but his arms soon wrap around my waist once again.

"Good to know. It was my first."

His chin drops. "It was... fuck," he barks. "Could you be any more perfect?"

I laugh. "I'm far from that."

"I don't know. I think you're pretty perfect for me."

I melt at his words, but I don't get the chance to return the sentiment.

"Now, as long as it's not burnt to a crisp, it's time for dinner."

"Sorry," I say with a wince, thinking I've ruined what he's been so lovingly cooking.

I take a step away, but he soon catches my hand and pulls me back into his chest. "Never apologize for that." He kisses my forehead and allows me to take a seat while he plates up.

The food is great and only slightly singed from its few extra minutes in the grill.

"I can't believe you did all this," I say as he pours me a new drink.

"I had some help."

"You're telling me that you didn't make this yourself?" I ask, holding up my glass, gesturing to everything as we make our way over to the sofa.

"No, Rachel helped with the food. The guys helped with the lights and shit."

"Aw, lights and shit, so romantic."

"What you see is what you get, baby."

He takes my drink and places it on the table with his before lying down beside me.

"I'm not sure that's entirely true."

"No?"

"Nope. I'm pretty sure I'm looking at a different Ethan than the one everyone at school sees."

"You might actually be right there."

"Yeah, it seems you do have a heart buried in there somewhere." I place my hand on his chest and he covers it with his own.

"Yeah, and it seems it only beats for you."

I gasp, the honesty in his words taking any I might have to reply with. But instead of waiting for me to say something, he leans over and takes my lips in a sweet kiss. He pulls a blanket over both of us and his hand leisurely trails around my body beneath, slowly driving me crazy with my need for him.

We make out on that sofa for the longest time with our tongues, lips, and hands exploring every inch of each other's bodies, but at no point do either of us take it further. That is, until Ethan's lips brush the shell of my ear.

"Want to continue this upstairs?"

"Like you wouldn't believe."

He chuckles before untangling us from the blanket and standing with his hand out for me to take. His cock tents his sweats, and my core clenches at knowing what's to come. He's right about one thing: we're going to do this properly this time, and there's going to be no doubt in his mind that I'm fully on board with what's about to happen.

He leads me up to my room before shutting the door behind us. Then he turns to me, his eyes dark and hungry, and a wave of nerves sweeps through me. It's crazy, this isn't our first time, but it's so different. Last time it was just sex, with a truckload of anger and desire. This time it's so much more. It's the beginning of something. Something that could be epic if neither of us fuck it up somewhere along the way.

Taking a step toward me, he reaches out and grasps the bottom of my shirt. In the blink of an eye he has it off and on the floor. Reaching behind his head, he pulls his jersey from his body and closes the space between us. His arm wraps around my back, and his fingers unhook my bra before pushing the straps from my arms, allowing it to fall to the floor. His bare chest presses against mine, and I can't help the sigh that falls from my lips. Even when we hated each other, there's no denying that together we were electric.

His fingers grip my chin, and he stares down at me, his eyes searching mine for something, although I have no idea what.

"Eth—" I don't get a chance to finish, because his lips find mine and cut off my question.

He walks us back to the bed, only stopping when my legs hit the mattress and prevent us from going any farther.

"You sure about this?" he asks, his lips brushing against mine.

"Yes. Ethan. A hundred times, yes."

He nods, that lazy smirk that I love spreading across his lips once more before he claims mine again. His fingers brush my stomach as they drop to the waistband of my skirt before he pushes it down. He lowers, kissing every bit of skin he can find as he goes, and pulling my nipples into his mouth one after the other until he's kissing down my stomach and pulling my remaining clothing down my legs and off, quickly followed by his.

Once I'm bare, he stands to full height once again before lowering me to the bed. He's so gentle despite the inferno of need I can see in his eyes. He kisses me once again before repeating his previous journey down my body, only this time, when he gets to my center, he parts my legs and drops to his knees. Wrapping his hands around my thighs, he pulls me right to the edge of the bed before lowering his head and licking up the length of my pussy and making me cry out, the sensation overtaking my body. My hips lift from the bed before his large hands wrap around my hips to keep me in place.

"Now it's my turn to have some fun." He flashes me a wicked smile that's full of dirty promises before dropping back down and doing some seriously crazy shit with his tongue that has me begging for more.

His name is a garbled cry on my lips when he eventually tucks two fingers inside me and allows me to fall over the edge. My heart is racing, my skin flushed, and every muscle in my body pulsates as he crawls over and lifts my weightless body up higher on the bed so he can sit between my thighs.

"Good?" he asks, a cocky grin on his face.

"Your ego doesn't need inflating any more than it already is," I mutter.

"Too late for that. Everyone in the area probably knows just how good I am after that." My cheeks heat even more. It even burns down onto my chest. "Fucking love it when you blush."

He settles himself and wraps his hand around his solid length. I take a moment to appreciate the sight of him sitting there, waiting for what's to come, and although he's only just rocked my world, I can already feel the tingles of another from the sight of him alone.

"Shit," he mutters as he teases my clit with the head of his cock before leaning over the bed and pulling a condom from his pocket.

"Sure thing, was I?"

"A guy can only hope."

I'm enthralled as he rips the packet open and quickly rolls it down his shaft. I gasp when he goes back to teasing my sensitive clit that's still swollen from everything his mouth just did to me.

"You need to get on birth control, baby. I refuse to put up with having a barrier between us for too long." My chin drops. I want to chastise him for his alpha caveman act, but I find it hard to when I totally agree. I don't want anything between us either.

"Okay," I whisper before he lowers his cock and pushes inside me just slightly. My muscles tense at the unusual invasion, despite the fact that I'm more than ready after his talented tongue made me all kinds of relaxed.

"Rae?" he asks, all his movements grinding to a halt.

"Yeah?"

Something crackles between us as our eyes hold, our ultimate connection seemingly on hold for a moment.

"Are you sure you want to do—"

"Yes, I said—" I wrap my legs around his waist in the hope of getting him moving. He laughs lightly before placing two fingers over my lips to stop me saying any more.

"Let me finish. Are you sure you want to do this, because once I'm inside you, that's it. You're it for me. End of. Is that what you want?"

I tilt my head to the side and look at him, really look at him. He chews on his bottom lip as he waits for my response, the softer side of him that I love on full display as he openly tells me what he wants. Me.

"Yes. Yes, that's what I want." I barely get the last word out before he surges forward, filling me to the hilt and forcing me to move up the bed.

"Fuck, yes," he groans, dropping forward so he can claim my mouth as well as my body.

My hands run down his back as he starts to move. And as he does so, he kisses me so sweetly, mutters promises that I never thought I'd hear from him, and loves my body in the way he told me he would.

His slow thrusts build me higher and higher until my nails are raking down his back in my desperate need for release. He knows exactly what I need, but he doesn't up the tempo until we're both right on the edge. Then and only then does he pick up the pace until we're both crying out in pleasure as he brings us both to the edge so we can crash over together.

"Fucking hell," he pants, falling down on top of me, his weight pushing me into the mattress in the most delicious way. "I really needed that," he says, mimicking me from earlier in the day and making me laugh.

Rolling over onto his side, he removes the condom then pulls me into his body. "Are you okay? Is your head okay?"

"I'm fine," I say, brushing my fingertips over his rough jaw.

"It's my job to look after you now, so I need to know the truth." He stares at me like he doesn't believe a word of it.

"Okay, so I'm due some more painkillers. But really, I'm okay."

"Okay enough for another round?" he asks, thrusting his once again hard cock against my stomach.

"I'll consider it."

He laughs before a thought seems to hit him out of nowhere. "What now?"

"What do you mean?"

"Do we just walk into school hand in hand tomorrow and announce it to the world?" The thought has my heart rate increasing. I can already picture the horror on all the cheer sluts' faces.

"Um... maybe we should tell our parents first. Give us a little time to get used to it before everyone else has to."

"I couldn't really give a fuck about anyone else's feelings about it. I'm kinda surprised you do."

"Oh, I don't. I'm just not sure I'm ready for the scrutiny I'll get. I'm not exactly who anyone expected you to end up with."

"True," he says with a wince, knowing exactly what I'm talking about. "But if anyone gives you grief, they'll have me to answer to."

"Is that right?" I laugh.

"Yeah, although I'm pretty sure the cheer sluts are more scared of you than they are me."

I can't help but smile. "I should hope so. I'm scary as fuck."

Ethan barks out a laugh as I sit myself up. "Where do you think you're going?"

"I need painkillers."

"I can get them," he offers, moving to get up.

"It's okay. I... uh... need the bathroom too."

I can see he's torn about letting me go, but really, what's he going to do? Pee for me? I drop a quick kiss to his lips before getting out and walking to the bathroom.

"A man could get used to this," he says as he watches me walk naked across the room. "You're so sexy, baby."

I shake my booty a little as I move, lapping up his praise and unable to keep the smile from my lips at how things have turned out.

I do my thing and take my pills before rejoining him. When I step from the bathroom, I find him lying on his front waiting for me. I run my eyes up the length of his body, taking in his toned muscles and bronzed skin.

"Seems I'm not the only one who appreciates the view around here."

"Damn straight. But what I'm more interested in is..." I walk over and drag my fingertip up his leg before I get to his ass, " how you ended up with this on your ass cheek, teddy."

He laughs, the sound making me smile once again.

"Ugh, that. I lost a bet and for it, I had to have whatever Jake and Mason decided permanently stamped on my ass."

"And they chose a teddy bear, why?"

"We're the Bears." He shrugs. "Although I like to think we're a tad more fearsome than that pansy-ass thing I'm now stuck with."

"It's cute."

"Is it though?"

Shaking my head at the look on his face, I climb back onto the bed with him. "So, lose a lot of bets, do you?" I ask, thinking back to Shelly's bitchy comment about the reason Ethan went after me the night of the party.

"No, I don't make a habit out of it. I don't want any more stupid shit on me."

"So that night we first slept together, was—"

"Stop. Stop right there," he says, moving over me so I have no choice but to roll onto my back and look up at him. "We have a stupid game we play where we name girls for the night. But it's not a bet. There are no prizes to be won. Just a bit of fun. Yes, I was given your name that night." I open my mouth to say something, but he just continues anyway. "But, that bullshit had nothing to do with us or anything that happened. That only happened because I couldn't stay away from you and you were driving me crazy."

"Crazy, huh? Exactly how crazy."

"Fucking insane. Allow me to show you." His lips find mine once again and his fingers plunge inside my more than willing entrance.

And that's how we spend the remainder of the night. I've no idea what time we eventually fall asleep, and I've no idea what happened to our parents, but quite frankly, I really don't give a shit. All I know is that I fall asleep with a wide smile on my lips and have the most peaceful night's sleep ever with him by my side.

43

ETHAN

When I wake up, I think I'm the happiest I've ever been in my life. I've got my girl tucked into my side sleeping soundly, and we're on the cusp of winning the title we've coveted for as long as we've known how to throw a fucking ball. Despite everything with my parents and all the bullshit that came with that shock announcement, things are good. No, things are fucking incredible.

"Morning."

Her quiet, sleepy voice makes my heart tumble in my chest, but it's nothing compared to when I look down into her wide, dark eyes. They've always amazed me. From the very first moment she appeared in my life, she's totally taken over my world. And right now, it's in a way I never could have imagined. This woman fucking owns me, but I don't think she has any idea. My balls are in her hands. Suddenly everything I've witnessed with Amalie and Jake and Camila and Mason makes total sense. The lengths they went to, the bullshit they endured. All of it. One hundred percent fucking worth it. Just like everything the two of us have experienced in our short time together. They say everything happens for a reason—well, I guess I should be thanking my parents for their failed marriage because fuck, if it weren't for them then she wouldn't be in my arms right now and I already know for a fact that she's the best thing about my life.

"Morning, baby. Are you feeling okay?"

"You know, at some point, you're going to have to stop asking me that."

"Maybe. I'll never stop wanting to know though."

"I'm fine. I promise."

"No headache?"

"A little, but it's better with every day."

I smile, knowing that she's probably covering up the truth, but I let her believe she's being brave and pretending like what she went through was nothing. I guess, to her, after what she went through at the hands of that monster years ago, it *was* nothing.

"Are you okay? Your entire body just locked up."

"Yeah, just thinking."

"About?"

"How best to start our day."

She squeals as I flip us over and settle between her legs.

"This is a definite benefit to living in the same house," she says as I drop down to kiss her. "Ew, morning breath."

"Don't give a fuck, give me your lips."

———

By the time we get to school we're both fully sated and had a very brief conversation with our parents which mostly consisted of Ash making sure that Rae was okay. It seems a little late if you ask me, seeing as it happened Friday night and it's now Tuesday, but hey, what do I know about parenting? They keep saying they couldn't get a flight, but they weren't all that far away. Seems like a great excuse just not to come back. Although it meant I got Rae all to myself, so I can't really complain.

As Rae requested, once we step foot from my car we act like nothing's changed. I fucking hate it from the second I close the car door and am unable to reach for her. I hate it even more when I glance at her and find her walls built up so high I worry that she might not drop them again. I understand her reasons for wanting to keep this between us for a while, but that doesn't mean I agree. I want to be able to touch her and kiss her whenever the fuck I like, not having to sneak it like I'm her dirty little secret that she's ashamed for others to know. It's a sobering thought, but one I hope is far from the truth. I have to trust her just like I've asked her to do me. She thinks she's doing what's best for us, so I just need to give her the time she needs to get her head around everything and then I can prove just how serious I am about this.

She walks off ahead of me toward her locker to get her books for her first few classes as I head toward the benches where the football team and cheer squad hang out.

Jake and Mason's eyes are flicking from me to where Rae just disappeared with confused expressions on their faces.

"Jesus, Savage. You fucked up already? I thought you were onto a sure thing with all that romantic shit last night," Jake says, thankfully quiet enough so that the rest of the team don't hear.

My lips twitch up into a smile, one that Mason doesn't miss.

"Wait, look at that smug as fuck grin he's trying to fight. He might have fucked it up, but not before he got what he wanted last night. Was stringing up all those motherfucking lights worth it?"

"Fuck you," I say, but I lose the fight with my grin.

"You fucking get your girl, bro?" Jake asks quietly.

"Yeah, I might just have got myself the girl."

"All fucking right. Good one, bro."

"Keep it on the down-low though, yeah?"

"Sure. But why?"

"Rae," I say with a sigh. "She thinks it's for the best if we keep it between us for a while."

"Why?"

I flick my eyes over to the cheer squad.

"Ah, the pack of hyenas that will no doubt be after her blood for taking the legend that is Ethan Savage off the market."

"Something like that," I mutter.

"What? What aren't you telling us?"

"Nothing," I lie.

"Out with it before we beat it out of you."

"Do you..." I hesitate, not wanting to sound like a pussy. "Do you think it's because she's ashamed?"

Both of their jaws drop in shock at my words. I instantly regret letting my fears pass my lips, but once they recover, Mason slaps my shoulder and smiles.

"What are you talking about, bro? Never. She just doesn't want them on her case. I get it, they're like piranhas."

"Just give her some time. She'll come around."

I nod at their enthusiasm and hope that they're right.

Jake starts talking about training this afternoon before we head off for our first classes.

I don't see Rae again all morning, seeing as we're in different classes, so by the time lunch rolls around I'm damn near desperate. Jake and Mason can sense my separation anxiety and lap it up. After all the shit I've given them about their girls, I know I deserve it, but it doesn't make it any less annoying.

The cheer squad are already at our usual tables, and the second Shelly spots me heading her way, she's up on her feet waiting for me. The noise in the cafeteria is enough to cover my groan.

"Shelly, what do you want?" I snap once I'm close enough she can hear me clearly.

Apparently she misses the warning in my tone because she steps toward me, and the next thing I know she's running her hand over my chest. My body locks up at her unwanted touch.

"Ethan?" she questions when she notices that I don't react to her like I normally would. It's not like she's expecting me to lean down to kiss her or anything, but I'm not usually so averse to her touch.

"Shelly, I'm not—" Something tells me to look up, and when I do, I immediately lock eyes with a pair of very familiar, very angry dark ones.

She flicks her death glare between the two of us. I'm unsure who she wants to hurt more, me for allowing Shelly to touch me, or for Shelly for even attempting to in the first place.

Giving up on trying to explain to Shelly, I push her hand away and step back.

"What the hell, Ethan?"

Ignoring her, I keep my eyes on Rae. She's bristling with anger, but what does she expect when no one knows I'm off the market?

An idea hits me, and before I can talk myself out of it, I'm pushing Zayn out of the way and climbing up on top of our table, kicking a tray of food aside as I garner the attention of more and more students sitting around, eating their lunch.

When I find Rae again, she's taken a couple of steps forward, but her shoulders are still tense and anger and confusion practically vibrate from her.

Her brows draw together as she watches me, but it's not enough to stop me. I've made a decision and I'm throwing caution to the wind and going balls to the wall. True Ethan Savage style. I don't do hiding in the shadows; I live my life in the light and don't give two fucks as to what people think. And right now, I need them all knowing exactly who I belong to.

"I've got an announcement to make," I call out over the cafeteria. The volume in the huge room soon begins to reduce as more and more students turn to see what the hell I'm up to. All the while Rae's eyes get wider and her head starts shaking from side to side. "This is probably going to come as a shock to many of you, but I need everyone to know that that girl over there. Yeah, the cute little feisty one." A few laughs sound out, along with complaints and sniggers from the cheer squad. I just about manage not to kick the tray from the table around me onto their laps. "She's taken me off the market. Ethan Savage is off the fucking market and has officially handed his balls over in the hope that she looks after them."

Rae laughs, but she's still mortified at what I'm doing. She continues shaking her head as I jump down from the table and head her way. Ignoring everyone around me and the catcalls, I walk straight up to her, thread one hand into the non-shaved side of her hair, and pull her lips to mine to seal the deal on the announcement I've just made.

Everything around us fades as she parts her lips and accepts my kiss without second thought. Her tongue strokes mine and I lose myself in her taste, her scent, and her touch as she finds the bottom of my shirt and pushes her hands under until she finds the skin on my back.

A groan rumbles up my throat, and I really fucking wish we weren't currently in the middle of a room surrounded by hundreds of students.

I have no idea how much time passes, but eventually someone slaps me on the back and the world starts to make itself known once again.

"I hate to break up this little love fest, but Coach is expecting us for our afternoon session."

I rip my lips from Rae's and pull back a little. Her eyes are dark and full of the same need that I feel.

"I'm sorry," I whisper, knowing that she's going to rip me a new one later for that little stunt I just pulled.

"You're a fucking nightmare."

"Your nightmare, baby."

"Let's go, lover boy." Jake and Mason flank my sides and all but drag me from the cafeteria. I might have been delighted this morning when I woke with Rae in my arms knowing that we didn't have morning practice, but fuck if I want to get changed and embark on an afternoon-long session with Coach instead.

I never thought I'd put anything above football—okay, well maybe partying—but fuck if that little brunette hasn't flipped my priorities on their head.

"So much for keeping it quiet, eh?"

"What? I gave her three hours. How much more time did she need?"

"Rae needs a fucking medal for agreeing to put up with you," Jake mutters as we make our way toward the lockers.

Practice is endless, or so it seems. It's not so bad while I know that Rae is stuck in class, but once school is out and I know she's home alone, hopefully waiting for me, it's fucking torture.

"A little impatient, are we?" Mason laughs when we make our way toward the showers once Coach lets us go.

"Like you're not desperate to get out of here," I mutter in the hope it covers just how impatient I am. "How are the ribs holding up?" I ask when he looks like he's in agony just pulling his shirt over his head.

"I'm not going to lie, they've been better."

"You going to be okay for next week?"

Coach has been taking it easy on him, but I can still see how much of a toll it's taking on him. He's desperate to be part of the final, but the last thing any of us want is him causing himself more damage by pushing too hard.

"Only time will tell."

We make quick work of washing off an afternoon's worth of mud and sweat before heading out for the parking lot. A few of the guys agree to head to Aces, but the three of us have more important things, or girls, to see. I laugh at myself as I take a step toward my car. I've become one of them, one of the guys I've always laughed at when he'd choose spending time with a girl rather than hanging with the guys.

The drive home is fast even with my growing anticipation for what I'm going to find when I get there. I'm pretty sure she'll still be pissed about what I did earlier, but I couldn't help it. The look on her face when she saw Shelly acting like she had a chance with me, like she owned me. I never want to see it again. Everyone at Rosewood now knows I'm taken and hopefully it'll keep the vultures away.

Jumping from my car, my muscles scream after the hours of practice Coach put us through, but my need for her is bigger than my need to rest. I grab a bottle of water from the kitchen as I pass before heading up the stairs and hoping she's waiting for me.

Her room is empty, but when I step out onto her balcony, I spot her mom sitting outside around the pool.

"Hey, is Rae home?" I ask, stepping up beside her.

Ash pushes her sunglasses to the top of her head and looks up at me from her magazine.

"No, she's not back yet. Your dad's at the office too."

I blow out a sigh and take a step to leave.

"Come and sit down. I think it's probably time we got to know each other a little better."

Guilt hits me as her words flow through my ears. I've not exactly been nice to her since I discovered she existed. I guess I owe her this, especially as I'm now dating her daughter. My stomach twists. What the hell are our parents going to think about this?

After a beat, I sit down on the lounger beside her and rest back, staring out over the pool.

"So you and Rae then?"

"Uh... yeah." I lift my hand to scratch at the back of my neck, already feeling totally out of my depth. It's one thing to meet your girlfriend's mother, but when she already lives in your house, it's only weirder.

"I've got to say, I didn't see that coming. Eric's told me so many wonderful things about you, but I didn't in a million years expect for you to break down Rae's walls. I'm not sure I ever expected anyone to, to be honest."

"Yeah, she's a little... guarded," I say with a wince.

"She's not had it easy. I'm not sure how much you know but—"

"I know everything," I interrupt. I turn toward Ash when I sense her stare burning into me.

"She's... she's told you?"

"Yeah, well. Kind of," I admit, thinking of the morning I found her diaries. "What's important is that I know."

Ash nods. "My daughter's complicated and beautiful. She doesn't let anyone get close, so the fact that she's allowed you in tells me all I need to know. I would tell you to look after her, but I know I don't need to. Rae is more than capable of looking after herself, she doesn't need me warning you. She's been stubbornly independent from the day she was born. It's frustrating as hell, but I can't imagine her any other way."

I laugh, thinking just how true that is from just the short time I've known her.

"I should head inside. Your dad's due back any moment. Would you like another?" Ash asks, nodding to my now empty bottle of water.

"I'm fine, thank you."

She nods and pushes from the lounger before collecting up her things and walking into the house.

Resting back, I run our short conversation through my mind, assuming that was her way of telling me she was fine with us being a couple. I drop my head back and close my eyes, enjoying the peace and the sound of trickling water from the pool.

I must drift off, because the next thing I know, there's a shadow looming over me.

"Well, that was fucking embarrassing." Rae falls down on the lounger her mother vacated however long ago and turns to me.

"Sorry," I say, but it's anything but sincere.

"Really?" She laughs. "You didn't seem all that sorry when you molested me in front of the entire school."

"You didn't seem all that bothered either."

"I was just glad to see that hussy's hands off of what's mine."

"What's yours, eh?" Getting up from my lounger, I lift her and settle us so she's lying on top of me, stomach to stomach.

"Yep. I don't take too kindly to cheer sluts touching my property."

"I'm not an object for you to own."

"No? So I can't do whatever I want to you?" She trails her fingertip around the neck of my shirt and my skin prickles.

"Oh, you can most definitely do that." She leans forward and presses her lips to the underside of my jaw. "I should probably warn you though that your mom's inside and possibly watching us."

"I know. I spoke to her. She'll be busy making herself look pretty for your dad. They're going out for a meal, which means." Another kiss. "We've got." Kiss. "The house." Kiss. "To." Kiss. "Ourselves." Kiss. "Whatever shall we do?"

I run my hands down her back until I can squeeze her ass, pressing her hard into me so she has no choice but to feel exactly what she does to me. "Hmmm... I've got a few ideas. What time are they going out?"

"In about an hour."

"Perfect. How do you fancy a dip in the pool? I've wanted to fuck you in there since I first saw you emerge in your wet, see-through clothes."

"Now that sounds like a perfect way to spend the evening."

44

RAELYNN

nock, knock, knock. "Rae, Ethan, you guys awake yet?" Mom calls hesitantly through my bedroom door. I have no idea if she knows for sure that Ethan's in here with me or if it's her way of finding out. I don't really care either way, mind you. Ethan seems to have moved himself in and I'm not arguing about being able to fall asleep in his arms each night and wake each morning the same way.

"No, we're really not," I call back groggily, wishing she'd leave and allow us a few more hours of peace but I already know it's not going to happen. She laid out all her Thanksgiving plans when I got back from hanging out with Amalie and Camila Tuesday night. That may have been over twenty-four hours ago but I'm still unsure I'm at all prepared for it.

"Well, get your asses out of bed. We've got plans, kiddos."

"Please tell me she's fucking joking," Ethan says, pulling me tighter into my body. "There are things I need way more right now than to spend some one-on-one time with my dad." His erection presses against me and heat floods my core.

"You've got ten minutes to be dressed and downstairs. No excuses."

Ethan groans again and I can't help but laugh. "It's only a few hours, and then we can spend the evening together."

"But I want to be together now," he sulks.

Flipping over in his arms, we lie with our noses touching, our eyes locked on each other's. "Just a couple of hours, then we can have our first Thanksgiving together."

"First of many?" he asks optimistically.

"I hope so." A little zing of excitement races through me at what the future could hold for us. "But right now, we need to go and be good kids for our parents so they don't suddenly start complaining about what we're up to under your dad's roof."

"He's not really in any position to complain, seeing as we know exactly what he's been up to."

"Maybe not, but this is still his house."

He groans. "You know, I prefer it when you're a rule breaker."

"Even bad girls need to toe the line every now and then. Now," I say with a kiss to his nose, "we need to get moving."

"But—"

"No buts, Savage."

I jump from the bed and pull the sheets with me, leaving him totally bare behind me. Glancing over my shoulder, I run my eyes over every solid inch of him. My muscles clench to jump on top of him but I know I can't, so instead, I continue walking toward the bathroom.

He's still in exactly the same place when I emerge and does everything he can to tempt me back into bed.

"You know delayed gratification is a thing, right?"

"I'm too impatient for that. Especially when it comes to you."

"It'll be so worth it later. Now get dressed before your dad drags you out of the house buck naked." I throw his clothes at him in the hope it gets him moving.

Thankfully he does, but when we get downstairs both our parents are waiting not so patiently for us.

"Finally," Eric mutters. "We don't want to know what took you both so long."

"Don't look at me. I've been ready for ages. It was your son who refused to get out of bed."

The four of us head for Eric's car so he can take us out for breakfast before we separate. Mom and I go home to help Rachel with the Thanksgiving preparations. Mom tried to tell her that we didn't need her, but she insisted. I have no idea what her story is, but I can't help but think that the Savages are her family of sorts.

Once everything's sorted and in the oven, we make ourselves a pitcher of margaritas, which is something of a tradition for our Thanksgiving celebrations, and Mom drags me up to her and Eric's bedroom.

"This really isn't necessary."

"Oh, come on. Don't you want to look the part for Ethan?"

"Ethan's more than happy with how I look now. Bald patch and all," I say, pointing to the side of my head.

"I'm sure he is, honey. But how about we surprise him? Show him what you've really got."

"He's aware," I say and then instantly regret it. Heat hits my cheeks as what I've just admitted to her hits me full force.

"Rae, you're an adult, so I'm not going to give you *that* speech, but I will say this…" I groan, wondering what the hell is going to follow. "I am way too young to be a grandmother, so please, I beg you, be safe."

"I'm not intending on being a parent anytime soon, don't worry." I don't tell her that I've already made an appointment to get myself on birth control as Ethan suggested. A girl's got to have some secrets. It's bad enough that Mom and Eric are going to be a front row seat to our relationship. Well, when they're here that is. What happens after high school is still up for discussion. I might be crazy even considering a future together. College is still a long way off, but we need to at least get our ducks in a row, and I need to take a serious look at where I want to go and what I want to study.

By the time Mom has finished with me, my makeup is light and perfect, my hair is hanging around my shoulders, the ends styled in loose curls. I stare at myself in the mirror, wondering who the hell the girl is looking back. I'm not sure I've ever seen myself looking like this. At least I've got my usual clothes on to remind me of who I really am.

"I've got a present for you." The second the words pass her lips my stomach drops. It only gets worse when she pulls out a Macy's bag from her closet.

"Mom, you really didn't need—"

"Oh shush. I wanted to treat you. I hope you like it."

Knowing that Mom has spent most of my teenage years trying to make me a girly girl, hence the Thanksgiving makeover, I dread to think what I'm about to pull out. Probably some frilly, flowery cocktail dress. Something I wouldn't be seen in in a million years, yet something I already know I'm going to wear just to make her happy. There's only ever been one person I'd put my own feelings aside for, and that's her. She might have made my life harder than it's needed to be over the years, but I know deep down she's only ever done it in an attempt to better our lives. She's not always gone the right way about it, but she's tried, I'll give her that.

Sucking in a large breath, I open the bag and pull out the fabric, praying I'm not going to hate it.

Much to my surprise, the material that emerges is a deep purple, exactly the color I'd choose for myself, and as of yet, no frills.

When I finally hold the dress up, I can't believe my eyes. It's a tight-fitting, body con style with a huge feature zipper running down the length of the back. It's got thin spaghetti straps and a really quite low V at the front which I'm sure Ethan is going to love.

"It's stunning. I love it," I say, honestly, totally relieved that she's not about to dress me up like a doll.

"I knew you would the moment I saw it."

"Thank you so much."

"You're welcome, honey. Now go and slip it on. The boys will be back soon."

With a kiss to her cheek, I leave her to get dressed and head to my room with my new dress in hand.

Already knowing there's no chance of wearing a bra under it, I ignore that drawer and instead open the one full of the fancy Victoria's Secret panties I bought with Ethan's credit card. I search through until I find the tiniest pair I bought and then make quick work of changing.

I stand in front of my full-length mirror, wondering who's staring back at me. The shadows I'm so used to seeing in my eyes are gone, my glossy dark hair shines around my shoulders, and my skin looks fresh, not only with Mom's makeover but with the hint of a tan I've managed in my time here, despite it practically being winter. I've never spent so much time outside and it shows.

The new dress shows off my curves to perfection until I get down to my boots. I laugh at myself. They're probably not what Mom had in mind to complete this look, but I still need to have a bit of myself in this outfit.

With a nod of my head, I turn and walk out of my room, butterflies beginning to dance in my stomach as I think about Ethan's reaction to this new and, dare I say it, improved version of myself.

"Honey, that looks incredible." Her nose wrinkles when she sees my feet. "Really?" she asks with a laugh but thankfully doesn't bother arguing.

I shrug, walking over to help her finish setting up the table with Rachel.

"You're staying to eat with us, right?" Mom asks her.

"Oh no, I couldn't."

"Do you have anywhere else to eat?" Mom persists.

"Well, no. But—"

"No buts. You're as much a part of his family, if not more so, than we are. Set yourself a seat."

Rachel nods, her cheeks a little rosy and her eyes glassy.

The front door slams, and my heart jumps into my throat.

Clenching my fists at my side, I listen as their footsteps get louder before they both appear in the doorway. Eric immediately walks over to Mom, but whatever happens past that, I've no idea, because all my attention is solely on Ethan.

With his eyes wide, he slowly runs them over every inch of me. I squirm under his attention. Not knowing what he's thinking unnerves me, but it only lasts so long because his eyes find mine once again and I can read every single thought in his head, and every single one is filthy and should not be thought about with our parents only feet away.

I swallow nervously when he takes a step forward. Time stands still as I watch him, but then he's right there in front of me, my face framed by his hands. I have no choice but to step back until I gently hit the wall behind me.

"Rae," he breathes, his eyes dancing all over my face, down my hair and to my chest for a beat. "Fuck." His eyes find mine once again, and they bounce between them as he fights with the words he wants to say. "Fuck it. Rae... I think I'm falling in love with you." I gasp at the raw honesty in his words. "You turned my world upside down, but it turns out it was in the best way fucking possible. I was nothing before you, and I already know that I never want to go back to being him. You've made me, Rae. You've made me the man I am, and I'll forever be grateful you saw through all the bullshit and gave me a chance." He doesn't give me the opportunity to respond, because his lips find mine and he kisses me much too deeply and passionately for our parents to witness.

"All right, son, put her down. You're even embarrassing the turkey," Eric says lightly.

Both of us pull back with wide smiles on our faces, hunger shining in our eyes.

"I mean it," he whispers.

"I know. I feel the same." The wide smile that stretches across his face is everything. It's so beautiful and honest that it totally makes all of the bullshit we've both endured worth it. "Now, let's go and celebrate our first of many Thanksgivings."

EPILOGUE

Ethan

The rest of Thanksgiving was beyond perfect. We enjoyed our dinner together like the dysfunctional family that we were. We watched the game, Rae and Ash pretending to understand what Dad and I were shouting about as things got tense toward the end, before Dad and Ash disappeared from the family room to enjoy the rest of their evening together and leaving Rae and me alone at last.

I wasn't really up for spending the morning with Dad. We'd only seen each other in passing since the day he dropped the bombshell that was Ash and Rae on me. It's safe to say that life had changed a bit since then, and I had a bit of a different view on life and relationships.

Dad was hesitant to say anything about our current living situation, but he soon realized that things between Rae and I were serious and he relaxed. After breakfast at a diner, we walked down the beach to get a few things off our chests.

It was exactly what we needed. We cleared the air. Dad told me, much like Mom did, that things weren't as black and white as I first thought when it came to the end of their relationship and the beginning of his with Ash. He was more than relieved that I'd let go of my anger and he was very intrigued to discover how much Rae had to do with that. He gave us his blessing, and although I didn't really feel like I needed it, I did feel better about everything for having heard it from his lips.

"This is the start of a new chapter for both of us, son," he said. "The end of your football season. The beginning of a new relationship. The future is yours for the taking."

Those are the words that run around my head as I sit in the locker room of the stadium that's hosting tonight's playoff final while Jake paces back and forth in front of me, a ball of nerves, fire and anticipation.

"Pack it in," I bark at him. The atmosphere in the room is heavy as we all try to get our heads in the game before we walk out onto that field together for the final time.

My fists clench in my lap as I try to get myself together. I don't get nervous. I blow out a breath, willing my stomach to settle and for my hands to stop trembling. This is the biggest night of all our lives. Some of our futures depend on this—college scouts are going to be watching this game. The entire fucking town is watching this game. The. Pressure. Is. On.

Fuck. I need Rae.

Her method of distraction earlier worked at the time, but right now the feeling of her lips sliding down my cock is long forgotten as I watch Jake continue to pace.

"Seriously, bro. You're not helping."

"I don't give a fuck if I'm helping you. It's helping me. Fuck." He shakes his arms out at his sides and jumps up and down a few times as Coach walks over.

"All right, ladies. Get in here," he calls and everyone comes running. Every single face shows the enormity of tonight. Most look nervous, some look downright terrified. "This is it, boys. This is what you've worked all your life for. You will forever remember this night. Now, let's make sure it's for the right fucking reasons, shall we?"

There are a few mutters of agreement, everyone too lost in their own heads, going through plays and focusing.

"I didn't fucking hear you, ladies. Are we going to fucking do this?"

"Yes, Coach."

"Come on, we can do better than that. We're the fucking Rosewood Bears," Jake bellows, coming to a stop beside Coach. "Now, are we going to do this?"

The eruption of noise from the team makes me wince as our nerves begin to give way to our excitement. This win is so close. Jake's dream. The only thing he wanted for so many years is almost in touching distance.

"Let's fucking do this." The floor vibrates beneath us as the team falls into line behind Jake, Mason, and me. I look to my left and find a wide smile splitting Mason's face. I couldn't be happier that he's experiencing this with us.

Jake, who's just in front of us, is totally focused. I doubt he even hears the Billie Eilish song that's booming through the sound system of the stadium or the roar of the crowd that only gets louder as we emerge onto the field.

I look to the stands where I know my girl is. I find her almost immediately, and everything inside me that was unsettled inside that locker room immediately relaxes. Her hair is much like it was the night of Thanksgiving. It's been that way since I expressed how much I liked it. I didn't tell her that to make her change—she could shave it all and I wouldn't give a fuck because it's her I want, the incredible person who's on the inside. The outside is just an added bonus. Her makeup is back to her usual style, dark and edgy. She looks hot as fuck up there, standing like a human barrier between both my mom and dad. I wasn't expecting Mom to turn up to this, despite how much I wanted her here, but she surprised me last night by calling and telling me she was in a car outside the house. I'm pretty sure she was more excited to meet Rae at last than she was to attend this game, not that she'd ever admit that. It means the world to me that she was able to put aside her issues with Dad and be here for this.

Rae's eyes find mine and an encouraging smile spreads across her face before she blows me a kiss that I catch in my hand like the whipped motherfucker that I am. I would be worried that the guys witness it, but when I look their way, I find them locked in their girls' stares as well as they soak up every bit of their optimism that we're going to smash the Rebels and claim our rightful place as state champions.

The cheerleaders do their thing ahead of us, dragging up as much excitement as possible from our Rosewood crowd. We've had a big game or two in the past, but we've never had this many people travel to watch us play. It's a sobering feeling, knowing that they all came here for us.

The roars of excitement continue to ring out around us when Jake suddenly stops his progress out to the middle of the field.

"Motherfucker." I barely hear his voice over the crowd, but when I follow his gaze, I soon find what he's talking about, or I should say who.

A smile twitches at my lips. It's such a great sight to see her back where she belongs.

As if she can feel our attention, she turns. Her light blue eyes find Jake's before she drags them away toward Mason. She smiles weakly, an apology of sorts before she finds me. A more genuine smile pulls at her lips, a thank you for my support before she looks over my shoulder. Someone holds her attention, and I can't help but turn to see who it is, but almost all the guys are staring in her direction, looking shocked to see her leading her squad once more.

"What the fuck is she doing back? Tonight is not the night for her bullshit," Jake snaps when he turns to us.

"Just ignore her, bro. Tonight isn't about her, don't give her the satisfaction. She's clearly making a statement by showing her face," Mason says, anger filling his eyes as he glances back at her.

"That's enough. Let's just focus on this win, yeah?"

"Everyone in," Jake barks, making the guys huddle around. All hands reach into the center of our circle. The stadium might be a hive of activity around us, but in this huddle, only we exist. "Champions on three. One. Two. Three."

"CHAMPIONS."

Rae

I watch as the guys huddle on our side of the field. Excitement knots my stomach. I still know fuck all about football, and I'm not sure I'll leave this place with any more knowledge other than if our Bears have managed to pull it off or not.

I tell myself to keep my eyes on them, but I can't help them from wandering back over to the cheer squad and the girl I've never seen before. There's no doubt she belongs, but I can't miss the angry looks that are constantly being flicked her way.

Leaning forward, I tap Amalie on the shoulder. It takes a few seconds, but she eventually pulls her eyes from Jake to look back at me.

"Who's that?" I nod toward the girl, but Amalie doesn't need to look.

"That? That's Chelsea. Bitch extraordinaire."

My lips form an O, but I don't say any more and Amalie turns back as the guys get ready to start the game.

"Oh my god, I'm so nervous," Ethan's mom, Kelly, whispers in my ear. "I love watching him play almost as much as I hate it."

"This is my first game," I admit.

"Watching them do what they love, watching them win, it's the best feeling in the world, but when one of them goes down, it's like time stops. It doesn't matter if it's Ethan or one of the others, my heart stops every damn time."

I look back to the field as her world settles in my mind. I hadn't even thought about the possibility of him being hurt. That certainly doesn't help settle my nerves any.

The whistle blows, and everyone jumps into action. Kelly reaches out and grabs my hand, hers trembling violently, making me resist from pulling away like I'm desperate to. The crowd around us starts shouting and screaming even louder, and I can't help but wince as I try to figure out when I should be cheering and when I should be worried.

I keep my eyes on number eighty-nine the entire game. They manage to take the lead early on and maintain it for almost the whole game, but fifteen minutes before we're all celebrating, the Rebels manage to score.

The tension around us becomes so thick you could cut it with a knife as the

Rebel crowd at the other side of the stadium start cheering and shouting. They're reigning champions, I know that much, and they're expecting to leave here with their reputation intact.

The shouts get louder, the chants get more aggressive, and Kelly's grip only gets tighter. In front of us, Amalie and Camila shout and scream, their own hands locked together as they pray for a chance to take back the win.

I'm not sure I've ever felt so sick as the clock starts to count down toward the final whistle calling time on the Bears' chances, but then all of a sudden, we take possession of the ball. One of our guys runs at full speed down the field, making everyone who wasn't already on their feet rise from their seats.

Come on. Come on, I chant silently in my head as I struggle to keep my eye on the ball. I glance up at the clock. One minute. One fucking minute. *Come on.* I want to scream, shout, do anything, but as the tension reaches breaking point all I can do is stand and watch, and pray.

Then the almightiest roar, the volume of which I don't think I've ever experienced before, erupts around me. I lift my eyes from where they were locked on Ethan to see the rest of the team running at Jake before he disappears under the pile of red. The final whistle blows and the stadium vibrates with excitement and energy. A delighted cry rumbles up my throat, my cheeks aching with the size of my smile. I have no choice but to turn to Kelly when she pulls me to her. She has tears rolling down her cheeks, her smile almost as wide as mine.

"They did it," she murmurs, wrapping her arms around my shoulders. No sooner has she released me does my own mom pull me into her while Eric hollers next to her.

The excitement is palpable and still vibrating around us once we're able to start making our way out of the stadium. Tonight's party is at Shane's, but before we go there, we're all out for a celebratory family meal, awkwardly with both my mom and Kelly. I'm just hoping that the joy from tonight will be enough for there not to be any tension between them all. They're all there for Ethan, so hopefully they'll remember that.

There's already a massive crowd surrounding the door the guys are going to come out of. Front and center unsurprisingly are Amalie and Camila, along with the entire cheer squad ready to congratulate their team, probably on their knees at the first chance they get.

I run my eyes over them as they bounce in excitement for the guys to appear and notice that Chelsea is standing off to the side, the rest of the squad with their back to her. I've been told some of the history there, but it seems she has bigger issues than she was possibly expecting by turning up tonight of all nights. I guess she wanted to be a part of the fame alongside everyone else.

The door cracks open, and a new round of screams sound out before almost all the team emerges with the biggest smiles on their faces. They eagerly get pulled this way and that as everyone congratulates them. I look to Amalie and Camila when none of our guys appear, and I see a flash of concern pass between them, but it doesn't last long because not even a second later, Jake appears with his two main men on either side of him. Amalie and Camila take off running and immediately jump into their boys' arms while Ethan scans the crowd, a frown forming. I step forward, the connection that's always pulling me to him stronger than ever after the night he's just had. It's that moment that he finds me in the crowd just a little behind the cheerleaders. He pushes them aside when they try to get a piece of him. He's not interested. He's got one destination in mind, and none of them feature.

"Hey, champ," I say, a wide smile spreading across my face.

"Fuck yeah," he barks, his elation oozing from him.

He lunges for me and I squeal as he picks me up and spins me around while laughing in delight.

Everyone around us vanishes. It's just me and him celebrating the epic performance he pulled off tonight. He brings us to a stop, but he doesn't let me down. Instead, he pulls me tighter to him.

"That win was good, but winning you was better." His lips crash down on mine, and I put everything I have into my kiss in an attempt to show him just how I feel, although I fear I'll never be able to communicate the intensity properly.

He pulls back, both of us fighting to catch our breath and stares into my eyes.

"Rae, I—"

I shake my head, stopping him from saying any more. "I love you, Ethan."

"I fucking love you too."

We're dragged from our intimate moment when Jake, Mason, Amalie, and Camila surround us.

"We fucking did it," Jake screams, and the three of them embrace while we stand there and watch, each of us with tears filling our eyes at watching our guys celebrate the win they've been working toward for years.

A flash of red catches my eye, and when I look up, one of the team is pulling Chelsea away from the crowd and into the shadows. I elbow Amalie, who glances at me before following my stare. She just rolls her eyes and turns back to our group.

"You better get your asses to Shane's the second you're done with your family shit," Jake says to Ethan.

"Too fucking right." Ethan says his brief goodbyes before pulling me into his arms. "You ready for this, baby?"

"A meal with our parents? No, probably not."

"No. That'll be a piece of piss. I meant this. Us, our future. You ready for that?"

"Too fucking right. Bring it on, baby. Bring. It. On." With his arm wrapped around my waist, we make our way out to the parking lot to embark on our new lives together with wide smiles on our faces.

Are you ready to properly meet the Queen Bitch?
Fierce is next... keep reading!

FIERCE

1

CHELSEA

I stare out the window at the building I've spent the past eight weeks of my life inside and as much as I hate the place, I can't help but crave being back inside. It's safe in there. People understand me. They don't look at me like I don't belong, like I'm a piece of shit on their shoe after all the mistakes I've made.

My hands tremble in my lap as the gray brick walls disappear in the distance as my driver heads toward my home.

Home. It's a funny word. It's meant to be a place where you feel safe, loved, protected. You're meant to feel like you belong.

I've never felt any of those things. Even before I was old enough to know things around me weren't right, I knew. Even now being somewhere where those feelings should come easily, they don't. My past is too ingrained. The fear too real after all these years.

I blow out a breath as anticipation races through me for what I'll find waiting for me. My parents have visited me weekly after they shipped me off to "have a breather" as they put it. They made it sound like they were doing me a favor, but after the drama I've brought down on them, I'm pretty sure the breather was more for them than me.

Derek and Honey are the perfect parents on paper. I guess that's why they signed up to foster broken kids all those years ago. Shame this broken teenager doesn't fit into their perfect life.

I've done everything I can to become a person people would want to spend time with, to want to be friends with. But I still end up as the outcast. Okay granted, most of that is my fault. I've spent the past eight weeks reflecting on all my mistakes, on my weaknesses. The counselors seem to think I've turned a corner and am strong enough to show my face in a place where everyone hates me. I, on the other hand, am not so sure.

I think back over what my senior year at Rosewood High has been like so far. I've lost the guy I've wanted for as long as I can remember to a freaking supermodel. I drugged said supermodel in my attempt at him noticing me once again like he did that one night in the summer. When that didn't work, I moved on to his best friend in the hope it would make him jealous. Wrong. All that resulted in was my parents sending me away for my breather.

Everyone hates me and I'm about to go walking back into that school like nothing happened. It has disaster written all over it. But what else am I supposed to do?

I refuse to cower down. I'm stronger than that.

I'm Chelsea fucking Fierce.

My parents must have been at the window waiting for my arrival. They wanted to come and get me themselves, but I refused, knowing that I'd need this time to try to adjust.

The smiles on their faces are wide, but I'm not stupid, they're just as worried about this as I am, if not more so.

They've done everything for me. I couldn't ask for better parents really, but their traditional views on things make my rule-breaking all the worse in their eyes. Just coming home drunk is a major sin, let alone some of the other things I've forced them to deal with.

Sucking in a huge lungful of air, I push the door open and step out.

"Chelsea, it's so good to have you home," Mom sings, rushing toward me with her arms out wide.

She engulfs me in her hug and for the first time since I watched that building disappear, a lump crawls up my throat and tears burn my eyes.

I was safe there. No one wanted to hurt me. No one wanted to make me an outcast for my mistakes like I'm sure this entire town does.

I'm not naïve enough to think what happened that final night stayed inside the walls of the Savage's house. I'm sure everyone knows what a disappointment I am, just how screwed up I am.

"Everything's going to be okay," she whispers in my ear, sounding a little emotional herself. She hands me off to my dad who gives me a much briefer one-armed hug. He's not really the touchy-feely type like Mom, so even this gesture is a lot for him.

"We've got a surprise for you inside."

I have a fleeting thought that they might have got some friends to come and meet me, but I push it away instantly. I lost my squad the moment I dropped that pill into Amalie's drink, let alone Mason's. It was stupid. I was desperate. I just wanted someone to want me.

I shake my head. My excuses mean shit. My behavior was inexcusable, which is why none of my squad will be here. They'll have turned their backs on me as fast as I ran from Ethan's house that night.

I might have spent my entire Rosewood High career trying to be the cheer squad captain, needing the title, the accolade to make me feel like I belong, but I'm not stupid enough to think that the rest of the girls weren't doing something similar.

Yes, we had each other's backs. We played the part of being best friends. But the reality was that we were all as fake as each other. None of them will have missed me. I don't need to look any farther than my cell phone to know that's the case. The only person who's bothered to reach out is Ethan. Guilt fills me that I mostly ignored his attempts to check that I was okay, but I wasn't in the right frame of mind to talk to anyone from Rosewood. I'm still not, but I seem to have little choice about it now.

I follow my parents up the steps onto the porch and into the house. They both look excited about whatever is inside for me. I, however, don't feel any of it. Dread is what fills my belly.

The downstairs appears empty—I was right about the squad then—so I expect them to turn toward the stairs. But when we don't do that, I'm thoroughly confused.

Dad steps out of the open back door, and Mom and I follow. I glance around, but everything is as I remember. That is until Dad opens the door to the pool house, it's then I see that things have changed.

So they've decorated the pool house. Am I really supposed to get excited about this?

"Um... I don't understand." My irritation levels are beginning to rise. All I want to do is fall onto my bed and forget that I'm back here. I really don't need to give my opinion on the shade of cream Mom chose for the walls.

"It's for you," Dad says, gesturing to the space beyond.

"You decorated it for me. Why?"

Mom takes my hand and leads me to the new couch in the center of the living area. With both my hands in hers, she blows out a breath.

"This is a fresh start, Chelsea. For all of us. We know we've been hard on you, had unrealistic expectations. We love you, but we also know that we've been a little overbearing in our need to protect you. We neglected to notice that you're a young woman now who's going to be embarking on her life without parents very soon. And as much as we hate that our time together is coming to an end, we know that we need to accept it. You're no longer our little bug, but a beautiful young woman who has the world at her feet.

"So this is for you. We've moved all of your stuff from your room. You've got your own front door key." Dad pulls it from his pocket and hands it over. "There's food and drinks in the fridge along with everything else you might need."

"I... um... I don't understand." I can't deny that this sounds freaking incredible, but I was expecting to come home and find myself locked in my bedroom and only allowed to attend school for classes for the foreseeable future.

"This is for you. We want you to be able to have your space to do as you wish. You're eighteen now, Chelsea," he says, reminding me that I was forced to celebrate my biggest birthday in that place. "We think taking control of your life will help you. We—"

"We'll only be in the house, and it's still your home, we're not kicking you out or anything," Mom adds, clearly not as on board with this plan as Dad.

"Of course. You're our daughter. We love you, but we came to the conclusion while you were away that we're smothering you. So we did this."

I look around, now seeing a few of my ornaments and picture frames that I didn't notice when I first entered.

A genuine smile creeps onto my face. It's an alien feeling as every one I've given for almost as long as I can remember has been fake.

All but that one night, a little voice chirps, but I shoot it down. I don't think about that night. Nothing good can come of what happened that night.

"Are you serious?"

"We are. We know things have been strained, but we hope that by giving you space you'll be able to continue with everything you've been working on without us breathing down your neck."

For the second time in less than fifteen minutes, tears burn my eyes. I'm not used to these overpowering emotions. I much prefer being the hard as nails girl everyone is scared of, not the weak emotional one I've turned into.

"T-thank you," I choke out.

"We'll leave you to get settled. We're both home all day if you need anything. I'll give you a shout when lunch is ready."

They both get up to leave, but Mom turns back before she gets to the door and pulls me into another hug.

"We're so proud of you, sweetie."

"Thanks, Mom."

"Are you going to the game tonight?"

I blow out a breath. Tonight is the final state championship game. Other than the cheer finals, it's the one day I've been looking forward to more than any other. I knew our boys could do it—or more so that Jake could do it—there was never any doubt in my mind, and I'd love nothing more than to watch them lift that trophy.

"I'm not sure."

"Your uniform is washed and pressed in your closet. It's time to restart your life again."

I nod against her, and she releases me to explore my new home.

I spin on the spot, a smile creeping onto my face, and excitement bubbling in my belly. I've basically got my own apartment; this couldn't be any more perfect. Well, actually that's not true, a lot of things could be a lot fucking better right now, but at least I've got some privacy while I try to figure my shit out.

I look around before walking toward the bedroom. They've painted it a deep purple, my favorite color. I run my hand over the comforter and push down on the luxury memory foam mattress. I think I'm going to like that.

Poking my head into the bathroom, I find the purple theme continues and that I've got a brand-new suite and what looks like a waterfall shower.

Maybe this homecoming isn't going to be so bad.

2

SHANE

I sit on the bench in the locker room before our final game. The other guys are pacing, looking nervous, but all I hear is my dad's words from earlier.

"This is the moment we've dreamed of, son. This is our night. Go out there and make me proud. Show those scouts what for."

Everything is about him. About his success and how he can look good. It's fucking exhausting.

I glance at all the others.

I want this as much as they do, of course I do. But the pressure to be the best, to continue the Dunn name, to go to an Ivy League college and then take the NFL by storm is too fucking much. Even if that was what I wanted it would be too much.

I want to go to college, sure. I wouldn't even mind playing college football, but it's not my future. No matter how Dad tries to ignore it, I'm not as much of a natural like him and my brothers.

"All right, ladies. Get in here," Coach calls, and everyone comes running. Some stare at the floor as the pressure of the night gets too much for them, others look pumped and ready for a fight. "This is it, boys. This is what you've worked all your life for. You will forever remember this night. Now, let's make sure it's for the right fucking reasons, shall we?"

The ones who aren't lost in their own heads reply, but that's not enough for Coach.

"I didn't fucking hear you, ladies. Are we going to fucking do this?"

"Yes, Coach."

"Come on, we can do better than that. We're the fucking Rosewood Bears,"

Jake shouts, coming back to life and spurring on his team the way he knows best. I stare at my captain, the one who's led us to this point, and like always my opinions of him duel. He's an asshole, no one would deny that, and other than always taking what I fucking want, I'm pretty sure there's a decent guy in there somewhere. Amalie seems to think so, and she's pretty awesome, so… "Now, are we going to do this?"

The noise from everyone around me is mind-blowing. The excitement is palpable, nerves are running rampant but over all of that is the belief that we can do this.

I can do this.

I can do this for me.

Not for my dad.

Not for the Dunn name or to prove I'm as good as them.

I can do this for me. After all, something's got to go my fucking way for once.

"Let's fucking do this," someone shouts as we move toward the doors that lead us out to the field for our final game together.

Some of us have played together since little league, it's been a long fucking time and we deserve this success.

The pounding of feet reverberates through me before the cheering of the crowd takes over. The guys continue forward, but I can't help slowing down to take in the moment. The stadium is full to the brim, most wearing Bears red but there is a significant mass of blue to the side of me.

Everyone is on their feet shouting and screaming for their team.

It's really quite sobering to be part of something this big.

"Dunn, what the fuck, man?" Zayn bumps into my shoulder as he passes me, forcing me to continue toward the huddle that's forming on our half of the field.

I'm almost there when our cheerleaders catch my eye. My stomach knots like it does every time I see them. But unlike before, now it's for a different reason. The person I look for is no longer there. Her squad has left her behind, most days it's like she never even existed.

Something uncomfortable tugs at my gut, but anger begins to burn through me. I have no idea if it's for the way they've allowed her to vanish like she was nothing, or for how she hurt those I care about, but it's there, nonetheless.

I'm just about to move to where the guys are waiting for me when the cheerleaders part and a familiar flash of dark hair catches my eye.

My breathing falters, and I stop dead in my tracks as I wait for her to turn to see me. But she never does.

"Everyone in," Jake shouts, dragging me from my daze.

I run over to join my team and huddle with them. Normally when we're like this before a game, we're the only people who exist, the outside world stops, the crowd disappears and we focus on the game, on our teammates, on our win. But that's far from how I'm feeling right now. My head's spinning with questions and my blood is boiling with anger. Everyone thinks I'm the quiet one, the calm one, and mostly that's true. But there's something about her that makes me forget all that and lose my goddamn mind.

"Champions on three. One. Two. Three."

I fight to pull my head out of my ass and focus on what I should be doing.

"CHAMPIONS."

We part, take our positions, listen to the sound of the whistle starting the game, but it's all a blur.

Every chance I get, I'm looking toward the squad, desperate to know if she's looking at me, although, I know she's not. I'd feel it if she were. What is obvious every time I glance over is the fact she's no longer front and center of her own squad, but more pushed to the sidelines. I see the way the other girls look at her. It seems they are less than impressed with their captain's reappearance, much like the rest of the school will be when they discover she's back, I would imagine.

A few weeks might have passed, but it hasn't been long enough for anyone to forget what she did. I'm not sure any amount of time will be enough for some.

I struggle to get into the game for the entire sixty minutes, thankfully my body does what it's supposed to be doing while my mind is back in my bedroom all those weeks ago. I told myself that I needed to forget it. That it was a moment of madness that we'd both regret, but I can't. No matter what I do, I can't fucking forget it.

The win is euphoric, especially after it looked like we were going to come away second at one point. The guilt was already beginning to build that it would have been my fault for not being fully focused, but how can I be with her right there?

Winning a game always feels incredible. But nothing can prepare me for the moment that final whistle blows announcing us the state champion winners. It's fucking mind-blowing.

Every single one of us turns and runs for Jake, needing to celebrate as one, as a team. I might have spent a lot of my time trying to separate myself from some of these guys, but right now. We are one. And we just fucking smashed it.

We're all grinning and laughing like idiots as we eventually stumble back into the locker room. We're sweaty, covered in mud, but no one gives a shit. All everyone wants to do is party. I don't blame them, if things were different, I'd want to celebrate in style too. But the euphoria of the win aside, the last thing I want to do is go home to watch my dad soak up the glory as if he just won our final game single-handedly.

So what, he's ex-NFL and might have been the one to first teach me to catch and throw a ball. He wasn't on the field tonight. I was. He shouldn't be soaking up the glory, lapping up the attention. I should. I mean, mostly it's the last thing I want, all attention on me, but still. If I wanted it, it should be mine.

We hit the showers, the excitement for what the rest of the night might hold vibrates around us, how the girls are going to hero-worship us the second we leave this room is all the guys can talk about. And while it might be an exciting prospect. I know that I'm going to have to deal with her. Or worse, she's going to ignore me like I don't exist. Don't get me wrong, it's fairly standard to be invisible. Most days I've thrived on it. But she's ignored me one too many times and made one too many mistakes.

Everyone else might be angry, but it's the quiet one she needs to be worried about.

The crowd erupts once again when the guys push open the double doors that take us out of the stadium. They immediately get swallowed up into the crowd, which unsurprisingly the cheer squad are front and center of.

Jake and Mason are immediately pounced on by their girls before Ethan parts the crowd and makes a beeline for his. Jealousy stirs in my belly. It's not just because I went after Amalie first, despite his asshole ways, even I can see that they're right together. I was just trying to convince myself that I could want someone else. Something more... normal. But I guess that wasn't meant to be.

I'm just about to push my way through to find my parents who no doubt will be somewhere close, my dad most probably signing autographs like he just made the final play to win the game. I roll my eyes and grit my teeth. Nothing ever changes. I'd like to think that when I get out of here in a few months that I'll be able to live my own life, but that's not likely to happen with my dad already having colleges lined up for me. Him and football seem to control every part of my life. Just because my brothers have it flowing through their veins like he does and happily followed his advice to start at Maddison last year, it doesn't mean I want the same.

I step forward, ready to push away the roaming hands of any cheerleader who thinks they've got a chance with me tonight, but before I reach the crowd, warm fingers wrap around my wrist.

I know who it is immediately. I don't need to turn, the tingles that run up my arm are evidence enough.

She tugs and I stupidly follow. I should ignore her and walk on by like she's nothing to me. Only she's not. No matter how much she might deserve it. She's something. Always has been.

She pulls me into the shadows, away from prying eyes of the gathered crowd waiting for their heroes.

"Congrats, champ." Her voice flows over me like fucking silk and it makes my teeth clench. She should not have this effect on me.

I keep my eyes on the ground, afraid of what'll happen when I look into her large, chocolate ones.

"Shane?"

I take a step closer. If she thinks it's because I've missed her and want to be close, then she's wrong. This is nothing but a warning. She's messed with my head long enough. It's time for this bullshit between us to end.

I suck in a breath and prepare to look at her.

Lifting my head, my throat closes slightly when I take in her expression. Gone is the confident girl who thought she ran the school, and in her place is the girl I always knew was hiding beneath.

Where did she go and what exactly has happened to her in the past few weeks?

I push my concern aside. She doesn't deserve it.

"What the fuck are you doing here, Chelsea?"

3

CHELSEA

I knew returning without warning wasn't going to be easy, but I never could have imagined the looks on my squad's faces when I arrived to warm up before the game.

Shelly stood front and center leading the troops. I knew she'd step up, as my assistant captain she was always hungry for power. She was probably barking orders before I was even out of town.

Every single set of eyes stared me up and down, their lips curling in disgust that I dare turn up dressed in my uniform and expecting to join them.

This was my squad. So what I left? I never quit, I never officially handed things over to Shelly, I just had a... break.

They allowed me to cheer for the game, although none of them wanted me there. That was clear enough from the looks alone, but they had clearly put a lot of work into re-choreographing my routines so that I didn't exist. It was embarrassing, I could only hope that people were too excited about the game to notice me looking like a lost puppy while the entire squad appeared to be experts.

I was out of practice, I knew that, but it was even more horrific than I was expecting.

The eyes of the team drilled into me as each one noticed my sudden appearance. A few ran their eyes down my body in the way they do that makes my skin crawl with disgust. I know why they do it. It's my own fault. I know how I acted. What I made them all think of me.

It was stupid. *I'm* stupid.

Once the crowd started dispersing and the squad brings their routine to a close. Shelly turns to me, what was my loyal group of girls standing behind her like an army.

"You can go now. No one wants you here." She looks me up and down as she would one of the nerds we used to mock together and a lump the size of the ball the guys were just throwing around climbs up my throat.

"But—"

"No. You lost any right to this squad when you started drugging our players," Shelly spits, her hands on her hips. "You're nothing here. You. Are. Not. Welcome."

She nods her head to the squad and they immediately follow her lead. They all walk past me. Not one giving me a second glance as they make their way toward where the team will emerge from. A couple even go as far as slamming their shoulders into mine just to really nail the point home.

"Fuck," I bark once they're out of earshot. Tears burn the back of my eyes, but I refuse to cry. I am stronger than this.

They won't break me.

They might think they've dethroned me, but they need to realize that my crown is going nowhere, it's currently just a little crooked.

Sucking in a large breath, I straighten my uniform. It used to fit me like a second skin, but now... I just can't wait to get out of it and into something more comfortable. That's something I never thought I'd say.

I follow the way the squad left a few minutes ago. I might have been dreading seeing them, but their reaction was predictable. There's someone else whose opinion about me being back is a little more up in the air.

I know he's seen me. I felt his eyes drilling into me when he should have been focusing on the game. It was one of the reasons I nearly didn't come. I didn't want to take anyone's focus away from winning this for us, but equally, I wanted to be a part of it. I've worked tirelessly for years for this squad and supporting our team, I wanted to experience it too. Selfish? Yeah, probably after everything I've done, but I'm still a senior at this school. I want these memories too.

The crowd is already huge by the doors where the team will emerge from, so it takes me quite a while to fight my way through. I also successfully drag a few more students' attention my way that clearly weren't watching the squad through the game. Eyes widen and chins drop at my appearance, but I ignore them. Everyone knows me as a stone-faced whore, so that's the mask I'll slip on and give them what they expect.

I stand on the edge of the crowd where I can see the guys emerge and hopefully catch the attention of the one I want. My stomach flutters with nerves as I wait. The excitement around me only increases as the minutes tick by. But nothing could have prepared me for the eruption of noise when the door opens for the first time.

A few of the guys emerge and the crowd goes crazy, engulfing them into the mass of bodies. The noise level only increases when the captain appears with his boys at his sides. The wide smile on Jake's face makes something twist in my stomach. But it's no longer jealousy as he searches for Amalie in the crowd. For many, many years, I thought Jake was it for me. I mean, the captain of the football team and the captain of the cheer squad are meant to be, right? No, apparently not. It didn't stop me from spending the best part of the last few years following him around like a lost puppy while trying to do anything to get his attention. It worked... once. I gave him my V-card one night when he'd had way too much to drink. I don't think he even realized he was my first... or it was even me he was fucking, to be honest.

A sigh passes my lips as I think about that night. It was only a few weeks before Amalie arrived and she swept him straight out from under my feet. Not that he ever showed me there was anything between us, other than that night.

I was gutted. There had only been two guys up until that point that I'd really wanted and although the first one thinks of me as a little sister, the second had used my body and still didn't want me.

Am I really that unlovable?

Zayn appears, quickly followed by the one I want.

My stomach somersaults as I take in his shaggy blond hair that's still wet from his shower and his clean Bear's jersey that clings to his sculpted chest.

My mind takes me back to the one time I got up close and personal to that chest. I vividly remember what my hands looked like as I pressed them against his pecs to get some leverage.

Heat fills my veins as I relive that fateful night.

He takes two steps from the building and my stomach drops thinking that he's going to walk straight out and not see me. Taking matters into my own hands, I reach out and grasp his wrist. He stills for a beat and I panic that he's about to rip himself away before even acknowledging me.

He keeps his eyes on the ground for the longest time. I just start to think that he's going to refuse to look at me when his head lifts.

I gasp when his green eyes connect with mine. But they're not like I remember. They're not soft and kind. They're hard and angry, rightly so. My heart aches as I look into them. Has the boy I've been craving gone?

My skin prickles with awareness as our eyes hold. But the longer it lasts the darker his get and the tingles of excitement I first felt give way to a different kind. Fear. Fear that he's going to break our connection and walk away from me, much like I did that night. I guess it's what I deserve. No. It is what I deserve.

He steps toward me, and my hope rises. He might be angry, but at least he's going to acknowledge me. When he looked away the first time our eyes connected when he was playing, it hurt. Really fucking bad. He's the one person I need on my side right now. I just need to figure out how I'm going to make that happen because right now, he looks like he's barely restraining himself from sending me back to where I just came from.

The second he's before me, he wraps his hand around my wrist and pulls me back into the shadows, away from prying eyes. Oh great, he's ashamed of talking to me. Good start.

I roll my eyes at myself and allow him to drag me to where he wants me.

"What the fuck are you doing here, Chelsea?"

"Waiting for you." My voice is so sickly sweet it hurts my own ears and makes me wince.

"Did you really think that was the best idea? No one wants you here."

My heart drops at the truth in his words. "Even you?"

He stares at me, his jaw popping as his teeth grind before he lets out a sigh. "Chels."

"No," I snap. "Don't *Chels* me. Tell me how it is. Tell me how you really feel."

"You shouldn't have turned up tonight. If we lost, it would have been your fault."

"But you didn't, did you, champ?" I step forward and run my hands up his chest, desperate to know if that connection is still there between us.

Before I get a chance to feel it, my hands are ripped away.

"Not here. Not tonight."

His eyes hold mine, his warning loud and clear.

I open my mouth to say more, but he steps away before any words pass my lips.

His eyes drop down the length of my body, a little heat creeps into them and pushes the anger away.

He remembers as well as I do.

"Go and find a more willing member of the team. They all want to celebrate tonight, and I'm sure they'd be more than happy to get you on your knees."

My chin drops. I'm not shocked by the suggestion, it's the fact the words are coming from his mouth that surprises me.

He's always been the kind one, I always thought the pushover. Maybe I don't know all there is to know about the quietest member of the team.

I don't get to say anymore because when I come back to myself, he's gone. Swallowed by the crowd who are overjoyed to celebrate with their champions.

I stay where I am, watching the excitement that I should be in the center of with a heavy heart.

Before long, everyone starts to disperse. Tonight's celebrations are happening in the Dunn household. We haven't had a proper party there—that I know of—since Shane's eighteenth, but knowing his dad, I'm not surprised he wants to take charge of tonight.

Mom's been friends with Maddie, Shane's mom, since before I arrived in town. Everything that goes on under that roof is football related or somehow a reminder of Brett's success and the future he wants for all his boys. Mom always jokes about what it would have been like if they'd had three girls who weren't at all interested in the game. It doesn't really bear thinking about.

I wait until the area is clear before stepping out of the shadows. After how Shane just was with me, I don't really want the wrath of anyone else.

I had hoped that he would be nice, maybe have some weird understanding that I needed to do this, that I needed time away and that I had to be here for this.

I know it's crazy to ask that of him. He has no idea about anything, well other than the basics.

Mom's friendship with both Maddie and Kelly, Ethan's mom, means they know some things about my life, some of the darkness that my parents rescued me from.

Just because I felt like we had some kind of connection that night, that when he looks at me, he can see deeper than the others, it doesn't mean he knows any of the shit that follows me around and why I do the stuff I do.

He sees me the same as the others do. I'm disposable to him. Just a cheer slut to use and abuse when the time is right.

I thought he was different.

With a sigh, I emerge to find a few students and their families loitering by their cars, but no one gives me a second glance.

I look down at myself. I've never felt more out of place or uncomfortable, but equally, I've never been one to do things to give me an easy life.

I jump in my car and start the engine. The rumble races through me and I can't help feeling a little better. I haven't driven since I left this place, and suddenly having this freedom once again fills me with excitement.

I could drive and just keep going. I could leave Rosewood behind for good. Would anyone besides my parents actually miss me? I very much doubt it.

I could set up my own life and embark on a new future.

I rest my head back and blow out a long breath.

It doesn't really matter if I stay here or if I skip town. Life is going to be unrecognizable for me, it seems, and I can't see it getting any easier any time soon.

I should drive home, make myself a hot chocolate and dive into my bed in the hope that I never have to emerge ever again. But when I pull out of the stadium parking lot, I don't head for home. I turn the same way almost all the others have and in the direction of the Dunn household.

What's the point in hiding, I may as well rip the Band-Aid off in one night, right?

Seeing as I'm probably one of the last to arrive, I can't park anywhere near his house. The Dunn residence isn't a stranger to a party. Hell, it's where I learned that I could drink most guys under the table and that if I touch them the right way, then they'll be like putty in my hands.

Jesus, I sound just like the woman who gave birth to me.

A sobering chill runs down my spine at the thought. I guess it's true what they say, the apple never falls far from the tree.

I told myself I'd never be like her. Never reduce myself to the things she did. I was too young to know what it was she was really doing at the time, but I sensed it. And as I've gotten older, it's become clearer and clearer the reason why she used to take all the random guys back to her bedroom and be high as a fucking kite when they eventually left.

My stomach turns over as I think back to that trailer. I can still remember the smell as if it were yesterday.

I heave as my memories get too much. I've been with my parents for over ten years, yet that life is still as vivid as the day I moved here.

Bringing my car to a stop about a million miles from the Dunn house, I throw my door open and climb out. I tug at my uniform in an attempt to feel like I used to in it, but it's pointless. I fear that I no longer belong in it, and I have no idea what that means for me. Being the captain was who I was. Without it, I'm just some lost girl who seems to have no control over her life despite the fact she's the one who did all the things to make it explode in the first place.

Luca and Leon, Shane's brothers, have thrown some massive parties over the years. But then I guess they never won the state championship when they both played for the Bears because I've never seen anything of this scale before.

I wonder how much Mr. Dunn paid the neighbors to ignore this tonight?

Cars litter their usually quiet street, there are people everywhere, some moving to attend the party, others just watching the commotion and probably wondering what the hell is going on.

As I round the final corner, I have to weave in and out of the cars to even get close to the house.

"Jesus," I mutter when I find a press van and a load of reporters huddled in the front yard. But I'm not surprised to find Brett at the front and center of the attention. He lives for the fame.

As I get closer, I find the twins with wide proud smiles on their faces and their arms thrown around a very reluctant looking Shane.

This is his idea of hell, I don't need to see the pained expression on his face to know that. He's done everything he can to stay out of the spotlight over the years. This is his dad and brothers' thing, it's not his.

Brett chats away despite the fact the questions are most probably about tonight's game.

I stand to the side, hidden in the bushes as Brett continues to take the limelight until four other people join them. The press immediately turns away from Shane's fame-hungry father and to Jake and Mason, who both have their girls pinned tightly to their side.

That pang of jealousy I felt earlier hits me. I want someone to hold me that tightly. Just once. Is that too much to ask?

Jake and Mason answer questions, but they don't look entirely comfortable about it. They need Ethan. He'd lap up this kind of media attention.

It's weird not to see the three of them together.

Regret fills me for not responding to the messages he's sent me over the past few weeks. I know Kelly has left and it was selfish of me not to at least ask how he was handling everything. I need to remember that while my life is falling apart, others' are too.

At some point, Shane manages to slip away because when I drag myself from my thoughts, he's nowhere to be seen.

Taking that as my cue to also head inside, I step around the tree and walk around the back of the house.

There are people everywhere. Most of which I don't recognize as Rosewood students.

As I make my way to the kitchen, I get more than a few dirty looks. I keep my head high and smile in return.

Yes, I've made mistakes. A lot of them. But I refuse to cower down to these people who suddenly seem to think they're better than me.

I find myself a soda in the kitchen and sip it as I look around the room.

Everyone chats and laughs as if they don't have a care in the world.

"I hope you dropped a few of your own pills into that," Shelly barks, coming to stand in front of me.

She has Victoria and Krissy standing right behind her. All three have their hands on their hips and fierce looks on their faces.

"It's funny," Krissy pipes up, breaking the crackling tension between us all. "I thought we'd made it clear that you weren't welcome here."

I push from the counter and get in Shelly's space.

"Oh yeah. And you should probably remember who got you your place on the squad," I spit at Krissy. She was nothing before she tried out. I made her what she is today. I was the one who allowed her to attend these kinds of parties and hang out with the football team.

"Krissy deserves her spot on the squad. Much more than you do right now," Shelly barks, speaking for Krissy, who fumes behind her.

"Ladies, ladies, ladies. Put the claws away, eh?" Zayn says, sliding up beside me and wrapping his arm around my shoulder and making me cringe. I know it's my fault that the guys think they own my body, that they have the right to touch, but they really fucking don't. Not anymore. "I'm sure Chelsea has a reason to be here that doesn't involve drugging us all."

"Fuck you," I spit, pushing his arm from me and stepping away from them.

"Here you go, Chelsea. I made you a drink. It's a special cocktail, especially for you." A wicked smile pulls at Zayn's lips as he holds out a cup for me. "Go on, drink it. See how you like it."

We stand, locked in our stare. Him daring me to take it and me begging him not to make me.

"No," I bark, not taking my eyes from his.

"What's wrong, Chelsea? You too good to drink your own poison?" He lifts a brow.

"I'm not drinking that." My stomach turns over at the thought alone.

"Prove to us that you're sorry, that you belong here. Come on, the Chelsea I used to know never turned down a drink. We'll start to think they're something wrong with you."

My heart pounds, and my hands shake. I can't let these assholes see beneath my mask. I hate to do it, but I know there's no other way out of this.

I stare at Zayn a little longer, really study him. He's not a bad guy. He doesn't go out of his way to hurt people, girls especially. I really doubt he spiked that drink.

I guess I'm about to find out.

"Fine," I spit, taking the drink and downing it in one.

The girls' eyes go wide as Zayn continues staring at me.

Sweetness explodes on my tongue the second the liquid hits and I instantly know it's just fruit juice. It's still yet to be seen if there're any drugs in it though.

I feel weak for doing it. I shouldn't bend to them. I need to stay strong. Focus on what I want and why I'm here.

I look back up to Zayn and hold his dark stare. He's usually the joker, but right now his eyes hold a viciousness that I'm not sure I've ever seen. Would he take things this far? Have I just played right into his hands?

My stomach turns over and I worry I'm about to puke on my own feet.

Not wanting to show any kind of weakness. I take a step forward.

"What are you trying to prove, Hunter?" I sass, popping my hip out.

His top lips curls in a way I'm not used to when I'm this close to him before he dismisses me with a tilt of his chin.

Glancing to the side, I find Shelly and Krissy staring daggers at me.

Needing to get away from their burning, hate-filled stares, I turn on my heels and run.

I push people aside as their too-loud whispers, all directed at me, fill my ears.

"Why the hell is she here?"

"Doesn't she know we don't want her anymore?"

"Karma will kick her ass into next year."

"She looks like a whore."

"She's put on weight."

"Why did we ever think she was that pretty?"

All of them swirl around my head as I fight to find an escape.

I shouldn't have come here.

I should have driven home, or better, just kept going.

Finally, I make it out of the packed room and out into the hallway, reaching for the handle of the first door, I slip inside and breathe a sigh of relief.

4

SHANE

Everything about this party is exactly as I feared. It's meant to be about us celebrating a successful season and taking the championship, but predictably, Dad is making it about him.

"Shane's skills and success are down to me. I made sure he had a ball in his hands from the day he was born. I made him practice. I encouraged him to join the team. I, I, I, me, me, me."

I'm fucking sick of it.

Everything is about him. About his NFL career, about his success as a father, about his wealth.

Fury bubbles in my veins as I push through all the people, most of which I've never seen before in my life to find some space, some peace.

If I knew he was going to have the fucking press here waiting for us, then I never would have come back. But I needed to get away from her. From those large dark eyes that do things to my insides. The way they practically begged for me to give her a chance, to listen to her.

I might be the only one who will do that. She might have never wanted to admit it, but she's been in my life longer than anyone realizes thanks to our mothers. But she needs to realize that I'm not the pushover she thinks I am.

While Chelsea might have spent our entire school careers avoiding me, pretending I'm nothing to her, she's spent hours under this exact roof, mostly hanging out with my brothers, but also me too on occasion. I know the things she keeps hidden from the outside world. I've even had a glimpse of the real girl hiding beneath the hard outer shell on occasion. And it's those little glimpses that keep me going back for more because she calls to me in a way I can't ignore.

I fall down onto the chair behind my dad's desk and stare around the room.

His career is proudly displayed on every single wall as well as lining each shelf. There are jerseys, posters, trophies, everything to remind him of what a success he is every time he looks up. But that's not all. His golden boys' journey to the top is also proudly displayed. Photographs of Luca and Leon in their first jerseys, a ball between them which is bigger than the almost newborn babies. Images of them playing at little league, proudly holding their first trophies, and an array of other similar photos right through to them now playing for the Maddison Panthers.

What's glaringly obvious as I sit here, ignoring the party that's booming on the other side of the door, is any evidence that I even exist.

I let out a long sigh, rest my head back and close my eyes in an attempt to block it all out. It does fuck all though. My reality is still pounding around me. I should be enjoying myself, reveling in our team's success. But no, I'm hiding like a fucking pussy.

The sound of the door opening drags my head down from staring at the ceiling and when I look over, the person who's leaning back against it is the last I expected to see.

The anger that was already beginning to get the better of me reaches all new heights at the sight of her.

"What the fuck are you doing?" I bark, pushing the chair out with so much force that it clatters against the wall behind me.

Her wide, startled eyes find mine. If I weren't so lost in my frustration over tonight, then I might see her shock, but I don't, all I see is red.

Stalking toward her, my fists curl at my sides.

"I asked you a question."

She swallows, the skin of her long slender neck rippling.

"I needed a breather."

I don't stop until I'm right in front of her.

"You weren't welcome in the first place."

Her already dark chocolate eyes darken further with my words.

"I'm pretty sure this is an open house tonight."

"Yeah, to anyone but you," I snap.

"But—"

"There are no buts here, Chelsea. You fucked up. Big fucking time."

"Yeah, and I'm sorry, all right?"

A bitter laugh falls from my lips. "No. It's not fucking all right. First you drugged Amalie, and then not happy with causing all that drama, you had to go for Mason. What the fuck were you even thinking?"

Her eyes narrow. I know I'm getting to her and that the best thing for both of us would be for me to send her away, but now we've started, I can't stop, and it seems she's in the same mood too.

"Ah, I forgot about your obsession with the supermodel."

"I'm not obsessed with her. She's just a decent person, unlike someone else I know."

"Pfft." She rolls her eyes at me and I lose my shit.

Reaching out, I take her chin between my fingers and squeeze.

"You don't get to walk back in here after disappearing out of the blue and expect to fit back in," I seethe.

"No one cares I left." She tries to avert her gaze, but I hold her in place and meet her eyes once more.

"Is that what you really think?" I ask, my eyes drilling into hers.

"Well no one wanted me to come back so clearly no one missed me."

Something twists in my chest, but I refuse to tell her that I spent the past few weeks trying to find out where the hell she was. I was aware that Ethan knew, but he wasn't giving that information up for shit. Nor was my mother.

"Oh, I don't know. I'm sure a few of the guys missed you. There was one less slut to suck their cocks with you gone."

"Fuck you, Shane. You're just jealous."

"Really?" I laugh. "You think I'm jealous of those assholes?"

Tears begin to pool in her eyes, and it feeds something inside me. Something dark that I don't really want to acknowledge, but I'm powerless to keep going.

"That night only happened because I wanted to see what the big deal was about."

She gasps.

I lean in so my lips brush the shell of her ear. She shudders, but she's about to learn there's going to be nothing pleasurable about this. "All I hear is how good you suck, how tight your pussy is. Thought it would be a damn shame to be the only one on the team not to experience it."

"No," she cries.

"What? You think I actually wanted you that night?" A bitter laugh rumbles up my throat. "You offered it to me on a plate. Did you really think I'd refuse?"

"Shane," she warns. "Don't do this."

"Don't do what? Treat you like the cheap slut that you are? You're nothing, Chelsea. No one wants you here. Now fuck off."

A sob rumbles up her throat, but she somehow manages to keep the tears that fill her eyes from dropping.

She stares at me for a beat before pulling her face from my grip and wrenching the door open.

At the last minute, she turns back.

"You're lying, Shane. I know you're fucking lying." It's then her tears fall, but she runs before I get a chance to do anything.

"Fuck," I bellow into the room, but the sound gets swallowed by the loud music coming from the wide-open door.

A huge part of me screams to chase her. To pull her into my arms and tell her that she's right. That I was lying. But I can't. Not tonight. Maybe not ever.

Chelsea doesn't want me. She's made that abundantly clear on many occasions. Hell, most of the time she doesn't even want to be associated with me.

I know as well as she does that that night between us meant nothing. We'd both been drinking. Noah and Tasha had disappeared upstairs, and I was fucking livid that he was screwing around on Camila. Chelsea was just there. A distraction from going and rearranging one of my best friend's face for disrespecting one of my closest friends and the girl I thought he was in love with.

Needing to do something other than just hide in my dad's office. I storm through the open door and go in search of some alcohol. Anything to stop me from chasing after Chelsea and doing what I really want to do.

5

CHELSEA

I manage to keep it together until I'm safely inside my car. Everyone inside that house might not want me there, but I'll be fucked if I'm going to show any of them that they're getting to me.

I blow out a shaky breath and stare ahead through blurry eyes.

I didn't really know what to expect from Shane. He's always been the quiet one, the one who sits back and watches all the drama unfold around him. I thought he'd probably be angry, after all, he was the one who got the blame for drugging Amalie seeing as Jake found them together that night. It had worked out kinda perfect for me because everyone believed Jake and no one even bothered to look for another suspect.

I shouldn't have done it. I knew it at the time and I really know it now. But I was desperate. It's not an excuse, I'm aware of that. I spent a lot of time with counselors while I was away dealing with the guilt and I fully accept that I was wrong and that I have no excuses for my appalling behavior. I just have to apologize and hope that at least someone will forgive me, or I don't know what my future looks like here in Rosewood.

I've applied for colleges out of state. I never intended to hang around once I graduated. But everything's changed now.

My priorities have changed. The easiest thing would be to stay. I've got my new pool house and the support of my parents here. But if I bump into someone who hates me every time I turn a corner, then I'm not sure they're enough to really keep me here.

Once my tears clear enough for me to drive home safely, I make my way back.

It's not all that late, but still the house is in darkness when I pull up into the driveway. I make my way around the back and let myself into my new little home.

I breathe a sigh of relief the second I shut myself inside.

No one can hurt me here.

No one can look at me like they hate me.

And most importantly, while I'm alone, no one can learn my secret.

I don't get much sleep. I spend most of the night tossing and turning, trying to get used to my new bed. It's too soft, too comfortable, and nothing like what I've spent the last eight weeks sleeping on. That was like lying on a fucking rock compared to this.

The sun's only just risen when I give up and go in search of something to drink.

I make myself a cup of coffee and put a Pop-Tart into the toaster that my parents left for me. I do it all with a smile on my face because despite everything that's going on outside my little sanctuary, I'm overjoyed with this little bit of independence my parents have granted me.

I need this breathing space to come to terms with everything.

My life has been turned upside down, by my own doing of course. But that's only the beginning of the changes that are on the horizon.

Dragging on a pair of yoga pants and an oversized hoodie, I pull my curtains open and head out for a morning walk along the beach. I've missed the sea while I've been away. I'd usually run, but I'm not sure I've got it in me this morning.

Finding my favorite playlist, I drop my cell into my pocket and pop my earbuds in to block out the world around me and I take off.

Being so early on a Saturday morning, I have little concern about running into anyone from school who might be tempted to drown me in the ocean.

I feel like I breathe for the first time in weeks when I step down onto the sand. I tug my sneakers off and pull my yoga pants up a little so they don't get wet, and then I walk down to where the waves are crashing onto the beach.

The warm water surrounds my feet and I sigh in relief.

I feel at home here and I can forget all the bullshit and just be me. I can pretend for just a little while that everything is okay. That I still have friends and a life here and that I'm not the biggest fuckup that Rosewood High has ever seen.

I don't keep track of the time or how far I've walked, I just keep going as the sun begins to rise higher and higher. It's late in the year but with the sun beating down, I soon end up shedding my hoodie and tying it around my waist as I continue walking.

I'm lost in my own head, staring at my feet as they splash through the shallow water so I don't see anyone approaching until it's too late.

"I'm going to start assuming that you're stalking me." His familiar voice sends a shudder down my already heated body, but that's nothing compared to when I look up and find him shirtless and in only a pair of low-slung shorts. His golden skin glistens in the sun and his hair is dripping with sweat. I'm fairly sure I've never seen him looking better.

"Oh yeah, I slept outside your house last night and followed you here. Guilty," I say sarcastically, holding my hands up in defeat.

He silently stares at me and I hate that I can't get a read on him.

He shocked me last night with those vicious words he whispered in my ear. It was so unlike him. But then again, I've never really made the effort to get to know him better.

He has every right to hate me. To say the things he did. They were true. I didn't start things with him that night because I wanted him. I was lonely. Bored. Jealous of Tasha finding that connection with someone that I was so desperate for. Even if it was with a nerd like Noah.

Their relationship just showed that we don't have to fall for a football player to find love. Maybe I'd had it wrong all this time.

I remember looking at him on the other end of the sofa after Tasha and Noah stumbled out of the room to find a little privacy, and I wondered if maybe I should try something a little different.

One thing's for sure, he blew me away that night.

It was nothing like the night I lost my V-card with Jake. We'd been drinking but we weren't wasted, and it didn't feel like the only thing he wanted was the release. There was more to his touch, more to the words he whispered to me. He made me think I'd been focusing all my efforts on the wrong guys this whole time.

But there's a good chance that just like everything else in my life, I'm wrong about that too.

"Are—" He stops himself and looks out to the water. His hand comes up and he wraps his fingers around the back of his neck and tugs.

"Are..." I encourage, not wanting this weird exchange to be over quite yet.

"Fucking hell," he mutters to himself. "Are you okay? You know, after yesterday." And there he is, the sweet guy I remember from that night.

"I'll survive. You know me, stone face, hardened heart." I roll my eyes. I'm not naïve to what the rest of the school thinks of me. They think I'm some heartless bitch who only cares about herself. The reality is far from that.

"Chels, you don't need to do that."

"Do what?" I shrug, looking down at my feet.

"Pretend that everything's fine when it's very much not."

"Yeah well. What's the alternative? Everyone hates me. No one wants me here. And I can't see it changing anytime soon."

"Can you blame anyone?"

"I never said they were wrong."

"Me either."

"Ouch."

"What do you want me to say, Chelsea? Everything about what you did was wrong."

"I know."

"And you let me take the fall for it. Because I wasn't already enough of an outcast with the team, you allowed them to think I was capable of that."

"I'm sorry," I whisper, but it's too quiet for him to hear it.

"What was that?" he asks, reaching out so I have no choice but to look at him. The second his fingers connect with my chin, tingles erupt.

I have no idea if he feels it too. I can only hope this isn't a one-sided thing. Even if he never forgives me, I'd like to think that maybe that kind of connection does really exist.

"I'm sorry, okay? I'm sorry I did it. I was in a bad place. I shouldn't have let you take the fall, that wasn't fair."

He steps closer and my heart rate picks up.

His eyes leave mine for the briefest second and when they come back, they're colder, angrier.

"Prove it."

"W-what?"

"Prove. It."

"How?"

"I don't know. Use your imagination. But I know for a fact you have some skills that can make guys do whatever it is you want. Maybe try that." There's no emotion in his voice. The change in him confuses the hell out of me.

"Y-you want me to get on my knees?" I stutter, not quite believing what he's suggesting. I'd expect it from some of the other members of the team, but not Shane.

He quirks an eyebrow impatiently.

"Here? Now?"

"Why not? It's what you deserve."

My chin drops as we engage in a silent battle of wills. Where's the sweet guy from a few moments ago?

It's another second when I hear it. The booming voice that can only be from another member of the team.

"Chelsea, what a fucking surprise to see you here." Zayn's arm wraps around my shoulder and he pulls me into his body.

Shane's eyes narrow at him, but he doesn't say anything.

"I'm surprised you wanted to show your face this morning after the way you left the party last night. Everyone really fucking hates you, girl."

It's only when I turn to look into his eyes that I remember the drink he forced me to have last night. I guess it's safe to assume that there was nothing in it.

"I know," I mutter. "Shane was just suggesting a way I could make it up to the team."

"Oh yeah, what's that then?"

Ripping my eyes from Shane's, I turn to Zayn. He's clearly out on his morning run too, but he's still wearing a shirt.

My eyes hold his for a second before I make a show of running them down his body.

"You know me, Zayn. I've got certain skills that can make up for things." I use similar words to what Shane just said to me to prove a point before licking my lips enticingly.

I take a step toward him and run my fingertips down his chest before slipping them under his shirt to find his abs. They tense as I flatten my palm against them ready to slide it under the waistband of his shorts.

His eyes widen, but I don't miss the heat that fills them. Zayn's never been one to say no to a good offer.

Just as I'm about to push my hand lower and into his boxers, a low growl comes from beside me. Fingers dig into my upper arm and I'm pulled away from Zayn and into a hard, heaving chest.

"I'll catch up with you," he says over my shoulder.

Zayn immediately nods and jogs off down the beach.

"Don't fucking touch him." His large hand lands on my stomach and my breath catches in my throat.

"You jealous, Shane?"

He growls again as something tickles around the shell of my ear. His nose? Lips? I'm not sure, but fuck if my knees don't want to buckle.

"Nah. I just don't want anyone else to get you on your knees before I'm finished with you."

He might be threatening me, but his words send a wave of heat between my legs.

"Is that right? If the first time was so good that you need a repeat, all you need to do is say the words."

"Nah. It's not that easy, Chelsea. This isn't about pleasure. It's about revenge."

"R-revenge?" I stutter, totally thrown for a loop.

"I'm glad you're confused because so am I. My head's a fucking mess and it's all because of you."

Something crackles between us as his hand snakes up my body. My nipples pebble as it brushes over my left breast, but he doesn't stop like I need him to, instead his hand wraps around my neck.

"Oh god," I moan. I don't mean for it to come out loud, but fuck, he's turning me on right now with his dominance. I had no idea that he had it in him, but I am all in with this side of Shane Dunn.

"You might want to lock your door because I'll strike when you least expect it. Things are on my terms now. Not yours."

I shudder in his hold, but instead of giving me more, he releases me with a shove. If I had my wits about me, then I'd be able to catch myself, but he's just rendered me useless and I tumble to the soft sand at his feet.

"You look right at home on your knees."

6

SHANE

I turn away from Chelsea before I do something else I'll regret. I'm not sure what it is about her, but she brings out a different side of me. One that I'm not sure I like. Although if the way her body shuddered against my hold told me anything, I'm pretty sure she liked it.

My lungs burn by the time I catch up with Zayn.

"Hey, man," I pant as he comes to a stop beside me.

"What the fuck was that about?"

"What, Chelsea? Fuck knows. Trying to apologize or some shit," I lie.

His brows draw together. "And what exactly did you have against her grabbing a handful of the goods?" He thrusts his hips forward in a way I never need to see any other guy do.

"We're on the beach. There are kids around."

"Riiight. Is there something you need to tell me?"

"Uh... nope, don't think so."

Since I started hanging out with the team more in my pathetic attempt to find out where she'd gone, Zayn and I struck up an unlikely friendship. We're polar opposites in every way, other than our love of the game, but we just kinda clicked in a way I never have with any of my teammates. I'm not complaining because it's not like I ever got Noah or Wyatt out to train with me. It's kinda nice having some company.

"Okay. Just watch your back, if you're playing games with Chelsea, you're more than likely going to lose."

"I can handle Chelsea."

"Bro, I'm pretty sure there's not a man on this earth who can handle Chelsea Fierce."

I laugh at his comment in a lame-ass attempt to cover up how it really makes me feel.

We workout together on the beach for a little over an hour before I head home to shower.

The house was a disaster when I left first thing this morning, but as I walked down the street, the cleaning company my dad hires were all arriving, so I have no doubt that it will be like a show home again once I get there.

"It was a great night last night, eh son?" Dad says when he strolls into the kitchen as I'm grabbing a bottle of water from the refrigerator.

"Yeah. Great."

Clearly it passed him by that after I disappeared from the press, I only emerged from hiding when I needed more alcohol, something that I seriously regretted when I first woke up this morning knowing that I was meeting Zayn.

He'd wanted to cancel seeing as it was the morning after our big night, but I refused to hear it. Just because the season is over, it doesn't mean I'm letting up. I might not want the football career my father has planned for me, but I still want to play. Plus, it's not like Coach is going to let up on us just because we're state champions. He'll want to send us all off to college in prime condition. My muscles ache just thinking about it.

Leaving him behind, I take my bottle up to my bedroom. I don't have the patience for his self-centered bullshit this morning.

Closing the door behind me, I pull my discarded shirt from the waistband of my shorts and throw it toward the laundry basket. I take a step forward, my eyes land on the bed in the center of the room.

Suddenly it's that night again...

I was so fucking angry having just watched my best friend disappear off upstairs with a girl who wasn't his girlfriend. I'd been suspicious for a while as he just wasn't himself, but until that point, I'd had no evidence to accuse him of anything.

The second she turned up at my house with Chelsea in tow while Noah and I were shooting the shit over an old NFL game, I knew exactly what was going on.

I let them in because, well, I'm not a douchebag, and the second Tasha was in the room she climbed on Noah's lap and started kissing him. There was so much familiarity between the two of them that this wasn't some one-off, random hook-up. They'd been bumping uglies for a while.

My fists curled as he pulled her out of the room, telling me that they were going to make use of one of our many guestrooms. In one respect, I was grateful. It meant I no longer had to watch them, but on the other, I was devastated for Camila.

It wasn't the first time he'd been accused. Mason took him to the ground at

Noah's own birthday party, but Camila waved it off as her ex-childhood best friend throwing his weight around. Turned out, Mason was right.

I had no idea that while I was still sitting there with my head spinning that Chelsea was anonymously messaging Camila to make sure she walked in on them.

Had I known that was the reason Camila randomly turned up not long later, the evening might have gone very differently.

Images of our time together play out in my mind like it only happened days ago, not weeks. I rub at my stubbled jaw, it's not even weeks, it's months since that night. I've watched Camila and Mason reunite, Ethan find Rae, and I'm still here harboring some weird feelings for a girl I should hate for all the shit she's caused. Yet I can't get her out of my fucking head.

I tell myself that it's just because I'm angry with her. She framed me as the one who drugged Amalie, she viciously went after Camila, one of my oldest friends. Yet all I can think about is that night.

Maybe it was just because it was a long time coming. Maybe I've just latched on to her even more than usual because she was my first, not that I have any intention of telling her that.

Chelsea's been in my life for years, she's followed Luca around like a lost puppy for most of that time waiting for him to throw her a bone, but while she was clearly after him, I was in the background wishing she'd give me a chance. I'd have given anything back then for her to look at me like she did him.

That night she did just that and I was powerless but to fall for her charms.

I shouldn't have done it, I knew that. Allowing myself to go there made me no better than the guys on the team that I spend my days moaning about and trying not to be like. It made me like my father. I shudder at the thought.

But the way she touched me, the way she kissed me. It meant something. It wasn't just a meaningless night, a way to pass the time. Of that I was sure, until she was gone anyway.

"Fucking hell." I slam my head back against the solid door, wishing that I could forget all about her and that night. She doesn't deserve my time or my attention. But she calls to me like no one else ever has. She always fucking has.

She's like a fucking drug that I know I shouldn't want, yet I'm powerless to resist even knowing that it'll make me more desperate after another taste.

I push from the door and drop my shorts and boxers as I make my way to my bathroom to wash this morning's sweat and sand from my body.

My semi-hard cock taunts me. The memories of that night threatening to make it go full mast in its need for another round. My cock doesn't care that we should hate her. That she doesn't deserve another chance. It just wants her. The same as the organ beating in my chest, but I manage to ignore that a little easier.

I stand under the hot spray and allow it to soothe my tense muscles, but it does little to help. My head and heart seem to be in a constant battle for how I should handle Chelsea. I spent weeks trying to find where she was, wanting to know she was okay after everything that happened. But one look at her and the anger I should have felt when she disappeared hit me like a truck.

Attempting to push her out of my head, I get dressed and make my way back to the kitchen for some food.

Mom sits at the counter in her yoga outfit and sips on a cup of coffee.

"Morning."

"Morning, baby. How are you feeling this morning?"

"Great, why?"

"Last night was... intense," she says with a wince.

"You can say that again. Did you know he had the press coming?"

"You know your dad. He's in a lane of his own. He gets an idea in his head and he makes it happen." Mom sounds as exhausted as I feel with Dad's antics.

I grunt some unintelligible noise.

"He just wants the best for you."

"And what about what I want?"

Sadness washes over her. She's well aware that I don't want to be forced into the NFL, but she's about as successful at talking Dad out of it as I am.

"He thinks you've got what it takes."

"Maybe I have. That doesn't mean I need to want it though."

"I know. Would you like some breakfast?"

"Yes, please."

I sit as she gets up and pulls the refrigerator open. "Grilled cheese?"

"Sounds good."

"So I was at yoga with Honey this morning," she says, mentioning Chelsea's mom.

"Oh yeah," I mutter.

"Did you know that Chelsea is back? Honey said they've moved her into the pool house to give her some breathing space."

"Yeah, she was here last night," I say, ignoring her comment about her new living arrangements but tucking the information away for later.

"Was she? I didn't see her."

"She didn't stay long. She's not exactly everyone's favorite person right now."

"Understandable. Honey said she's in a better place and ready to get back to reality."

"I don't think it's going to be that easy."

Mom sighs. "I told her that I'd ask you to keep an eye out for her at school next week."

"Mom," I complain. "Chelsea won't want me being her bodyguard."

"I'm not asking you to attach yourself to her hip. Just keep an eye out."

"And what if I don't want to? What if I think she deserves all that's coming to her?"

"Shane, don't be like that."

"She drugged Amalie and Mason, Mom. She hurt Camila." I don't go in to any more about what happened with Camila, she really doesn't need to know the details of what Noah's been up to.

"She made a mistake or two. No one's perfect, son. Sometimes people just need a little forgiveness to be able to turn a corner and make a fresh start."

"And what if I can't forgive her?"

"Then I guess that's up to you. I just hoped you might be a little more mature about it."

"Not forgiving her after she hurt people I care about doesn't make me immature."

"Okay, maybe that was the wrong word. Just... just give her a break. She hasn't always had it easy, and I think she deserves a second chance."

Mom places my breakfast down in front of me before she turns and leaves the room.

"She's had about a million after all the drama she's caused over the years," I mutter to myself.

I drop my plate into the dishwasher before leaving the house in favor of spending the day at Wyatt's on his Xbox. It sounds much more appealing than spending the day at home with either Dad going on about what college team will give me the best shot at the NFL or Mom trying to convince me to give Chelsea the benefit of the doubt.

Thankfully, as usual, Wyatt keeps the conversation away from anything to do with football or last night. As much as I might want to continue celebrating our epic win, I'm also relieved to have a break from it all.

At some point in the early evening, Noah turns up to join us. Sadly, he has other opinions on dissecting last night.

"I can't believe Chelsea dared to show her face. Tash said the squad was less than pleased to see her. She said Shelly was vicious."

I recall the tears that filled her eyes as I gave her a few of my own truths last night and guilt hits me. I knew she hadn't had the best return. The girls' frustration at her sudden reappearance was palpable, but I didn't really put much thought into how they might have spoken to her.

"What did she expect?" Wyatt asks, shocking the hell out of me. He usually steers clear of having any opinions where the cheer squad or the football team are concerned.

"To be welcomed back into their loving arms and be reinstated as captain, I think."

We hang out for a while longer, but now they've mentioned her name, I can't get her shocked face from this morning when I accidentally pushed her to the sand out of my head.

She looked like a scared little mouse that I was about to crush with my foot.

"I need to head out. Thanks for the pizza," I say to Wyatt, nodding at the boxes littering the coffee table of his den that we ordered earlier.

"No worries. See you tomorrow."

I grab my hoodie from the back of Wyatt's couch and make my way out of his house.

If I were to cut through the alley behind Wyatt's house, it only takes me ten minutes to walk home. But instead of turning right, I turn left up the street. I know why, even if I don't want to accept it. This way leads me right to the house I shouldn't be going anywhere near. Only, it's not the house that interests me. It's the pool house.

7

CHELSEA

I spend the afternoon and evening with my parents. My intention was to lock myself away and pretend anything that happened yesterday was just a dream... fucking nightmare more like.

They both try to dig into my time away, but other than the generic 'it was good and exactly what I needed' that they want to hear, I don't go into any more detail.

That place is depressing enough, the last thing I want to do is talk about it.

I'd like to think it's the closest I'm ever going to get to jail, but seeing as I've already done some seriously questionable things in the past few months, I'm not all that confident.

It's regimented with its routines. I understand why, the teenagers inside are fucking up at every possible turn and need some serious boundaries put in place, but fuck, it's hard work.

Wake up at seven-thirty, chores, school, therapy sessions, more chores, bed. Every fucking day.

The girl I was roomed with was the best part about that place. The stories she told me about her past made mine look like child's play, but she got me like no one I've ever met before. I'm not sure how I was lucky enough to be roomed with her, but I'm so fucking grateful. She made my few weeks bearable.

Those routines soon became second nature and unbelievably I miss them even after being home for barely twenty-four hours. Suddenly being free to fuck up my life all over again is a pressure I really don't need.

I have no idea how I'm supposed to go from that kind of life and back to school in only a few hours.

My head spins at the possibility of trying to reenter my life once again. If last night was anything to go by, then it's not going to be smooth sailing.

With my belly full of Mom's cooking, I lay out on my couch watching old episodes of the Kardashians, they make me feel a little better about my life as I take in all their drama.

At some point, I find my eyes shutting and despite the fact my bed is only feet away, I cave to my exhaustion and allow myself the sleep I need.

I have no idea how long I'm out for but when I wake, I can't shake the feeling that I'm being watched.

It's crazy. The only people who know that I'm in here are Mom and Dad and I'd like to think they're not here watching me sleep. I know they're protective, but shit, that would be just creepy.

Cracking my eye open, I expect to find the place empty and prepare for feeling ridiculous, but that's not what happens.

A scream falls from my lips when I find a figure sitting on my coffee table in the dark.

Sitting up so fast my head spins, my eyes focus and I'm able to make out my nocturnal visitor's features despite the dark hoodie he's hiding behind.

"What the hell are you doing? Trying to scare me to death?"

He shrugs. "We've got unfinished business."

Resting his elbows on his knees, he leans forward slightly. His emerald eyes catch the small amount of light that's streaming in from the moon outside and I gasp at the darkness within them.

I have no idea if he's angry or turned on right now. And it's just another of those times where I wish I'd paid more attention to him in the past. I should be able to read him better than this by now.

"H-have we?" I stutter, pushing the blanket from my legs and sitting forward.

If he thinks I'm going to back down, then he's got another thing coming. I'm not some weak girl that he can put in her place. I thought he'd know better than that.

Maybe he does.

Pushing from the couch, I turn my back on him and walk to my kitchen for a drink.

A low growl rumbles from behind me. It confuses me for a second, that is until the short hemline of my Bear's jersey catches my eye.

"You like my shirt, Shane?" I ask, knowing exactly what he's looking at right now. A smile twitches my lips that he cares enough that he's unable to keep his feelings about it locked down.

"Take it off," he demands.

Bending over slightly, I pull a bottle from the refrigerator and twist the top, making a show of drinking some down.

"Why? You want your number on my back?" I ask innocently as I place the bottle on the counter.

When I spin around, I find him standing halfway between where I am and the coffee table where I left him.

"You don't deserve my number. You don't even deserve to be wearing that shirt after the shit you pulled."

I shrug once again. I can't argue with his words. I know what I did and I won't hide from the mistakes I made.

"So because of my questionable judgment, you think I should forget the team I've supported for years like I don't care?"

His eyes burn down my body, but linger for a little longer than necessary on my bare legs. The hem of the jersey kisses the top of my thighs so there's not much of my skin that's not on show below my waist right now. I may have chosen a different shirt had I known I was going to have company.

Although, when his dark, hungry eyes come back to mine, I wonder if it's actually had a pretty desirable effect.

"What are you going to do, Shane? Rip it from my body?"

One side of his lip curls up in a sinister smirk as he takes a step toward me.

"I'm not going to make you do anything, Chelsea. We both know you get yourself in enough trouble without any encouragement."

"Things are different now," I argue, thinking of the hours of counseling sessions I've had over the past few weeks.

"Is that right? So you're not willing to do anything to reclaim your place at school?"

He tilts his head to the side, usually I'd describe it as cute but with the intense look on his face that I'm not sure I've ever seen before, it's far from cute. If anything, it's... hot.

Fuck.

Heat races through my body as memories of how his hands felt on my body slam into me.

"N-no," I stutter, trying to remember what it was he just said to me as he takes another step forward. His scent fills my nose and does nothing to tamp down my desire.

I've always wanted the bad boys, the assholes. It's a weakness I've never been able to rid myself of. I always dismissed Shane because he was a good guy. But this Shane standing before me right now is anything but a good guy. He warned me on the beach earlier that he was after revenge. Have I stirred something inside him that I never should have been close enough to in the first place?

I should regret that night.

I was desperate. Lonely. Lost. But he gave me something that I'd never experienced before and fuck if I don't want to find out if it was a one-off thing or if it really exists.

"No?" he asks.

"No. If I get my place back, my squad back, it's because I deserve it, because I've earned it."

"Pfft. Little chance of that happening."

"So be it."

"You're lucky, you know."

"How's that?"

"Because you could be dealing with a lot worse than me right now."

A shudder runs down my spine as images from my past flash through my eyes. I've dealt with worse.

"You don't scare me, Shane."

"I wasn't expecting to. Now," he says, closing the final bit of space between us.

My breathing increases with his proximity and when his eyes drop to my heaving chest, I know he doesn't miss it.

"Take. It. Off."

"Fuck you." I laugh, although the serious look in his eyes makes me think this is anything but a joke.

"Been there, done that, Chelsea. Or did your time with me just blur into all the time you've spent with the rest of the team with your legs open?"

"No," I argue, my fingers gripping the hem of my jersey tightly.

His eyebrow quirks. "Tell me, what number was I? How many team members came before me?"

I shake my head, refusing to answer that question.

"Or was that night just about you getting a full house? Was I the last one? One more ride so you could score a home run."

"No," I cry. He's so far from the truth, but I don't want to confess all my secrets.

Turning away from his angry stare, I look toward the house, but all I see is our reflection in the glass doors.

"I'm waiting, Chelsea. I've been waiting a long time."

"You wanted a repeat, you should have just said."

"No, that's not what I was waiting for." Something flashes in his eyes and I wonder how true that statement really is. "I've been waiting to hear what you've got to say for yourself. To hear your excuses. To understand why you happily walked around while allowing people to think that I was capable of the things you did."

"I've said I'm so—"

"I don't want your fucking apologies. Your words mean nothing. As you're aware, actions speak much, much louder."

I swallow nervously, but still heat fills my veins.

His eyes roam my body once more. "Come on, Chels. It's not like I haven't seen it before. Hell, our entire class has seen your naked body more times than we can count. You never used to be shy about showing anyone who'd look what you're rocking."

Fed up with his taunting, and knowing that he's right, I pull my jersey over my head and throw it at him.

"Better? You got what you wanted now? Remove my armor and hope that it makes me weak? Well, let me tell you something, Shane." I push from the wall with my head held high. He's right after all, I've spent way too much time at parties naked and trying to tempt guys to like me. I shouldn't care that I'm standing here in just a small pair of panties. But unlike when I've had half the class looking at me, standing here before Shane right now, I feel bare and it's not just because of my lack of clothes.

My breasts press against his chest and he gasps. "You might think you're in charge here. You can spit your vile words, tell me what a whore I am, make assumptions about the things I've done, but we both know that right now, I'm the one who holds all the power."

I drop my hand to his crotch and just like I suspected, he's hard as fuck.

8

SHANE

"**F**uck," I groan as she wraps her fingers around my length.

It was probably no secret what her naked body was doing to me, I'm wearing sweats for fuck's sake. All she had to do was glance down to see the imprint of my cock against the fabric.

"Tables have turned now, huh, Shane?"

My brain misfires as she presses the length of her body against me, her hand trapped between us as she continues to hold me.

Suddenly my revenge mission seems so far from my mind with the scent of her floral perfume filling my nose and the heat of her skin against my body.

"I warned you, I'm not the kind of girl who's going to play your games, Dunn. I set the rules around here."

She strokes me over the fabric and my head spins.

"That night, you didn't stand a chance. I got exactly what I needed. You were like putty in my hands, very much like right now."

Finding some strength from somewhere, I lift my hand and manage to wrap my fingers around her wrist, stopping her movement before I come in my pants like a fucking kid.

I tell myself it's not her, that it's just the touch I haven't had since she was in my room that night. The second she left me with nothing but memories, I craved more, but I knew I wasn't going to get it. She played me, I knew that. Just like she's trying to now. She didn't want me. She just wanted someone, a distraction while her friend was busy elsewhere.

"What are you doing, Chelsea?" My voice is rough and deep, and it gives away what I really want.

Fuck.

I shouldn't even be here right now, let alone even considering allowing her to do this.

I probably well deserve all she can give me after what she did. I told her I was coming after revenge, but I wasn't really expecting this. I didn't think she'd turn the tables like this.

How naïve I was.

I wanted to tell her how it felt being on the other end of her betrayal. To have the entire school look at me like I was the fucking Devil while she swanned around ruling the school like she always has.

"Trying to make you feel good. Isn't it obvious? I'm trying to make up for everything, just like you suggested on the beach this morning."

I squeeze my eyes shut in an attempt to keep my focus, but it's really fucking hard with her fingers gripping me so tightly.

"I wouldn't have—" My words are cut off by her bitter laugh.

"Oh really? So you would have said no if I had pushed my hand inside your shorts like I did Zayn's?"

The thought of her touching him has jealousy eating at me. It's ridiculous, she was only doing it to make a point but still, I hated the idea that he might have actually gone through with it.

"No."

"Why not? I deserve it. I deserve to be the whore on her knees in front of everyone who was on that beach."

My teeth grind as I try to keep the truth hidden. "Chelsea," I warn.

"Come on, Shane. You had so much to say earlier. Cat got your tongue all of a sudden?"

She releases me and I breathe a sigh of relief, but it only lasts the briefest of seconds because before I have a chance to get my head straight, she wrapped her fingers around the sides of my sweats and pulled harshly.

My length is in her hand in a second and she strokes slowly, her huge chocolate eyes staring up at me.

"Is this what you wanted when you came here tonight, Shane? Did you want a quick thrill so you could say you'd fucked me when I was down?"

I open my mouth to answer, but no intelligible words come out. My head screams at me to move, but I'm trapped between the counter and Chelsea's parted lips. My muscles are fucking frozen to the spot.

"How badly do you want my mouth, Shane? How desperate are you to feel my lips wrap around your cock? To have me suck you until you're dry?"

"Fuuuck."

"Well, it seems tonight really isn't your lucky night."

"Huh? What? Chels—"

She pushes away from me and stands, a triumphant smile on her face.

"Shane, put your fucking cock away and get out of my pool house. You're not welcome here."

My jaw drops.

"What?" She chuckles. "You thought you could walk in here, threaten me and that I'd drop to my knees and make up for my mistakes? Fuck off, Shane. I might have regrets, but they don't make me weak. Especially where you are concerned."

I swallow harshly as I pull my sweats back up. With her arms crossed over her breasts in a way that only makes them look more appealing, she takes a step toward me.

"If you want to play, Shane." Her eyes drop down the length of my body, tingles erupt in their wake. "Then let's play. But I can assure you that you'll lose."

Why do I get the idea that she's right? I came here tonight to have it out with her, yet I'm the one leaving after being chewed a new one.

"I'm not playing your games. I wanted you to understand what your mistakes did to me." My eyes trail down her body much like she just did to me. "But I see it was pointless. You don't care about anyone but yourself. Goodbye, Chelsea." I push from the counter and march through her pool house toward the door I entered through not so long ago.

"Hey, Shane?" her soft voice calls out to me. I shouldn't turn back. I should keep walking with my head held high and not give her the satisfaction. Of course, that's what I should do. Just like the night I became Chelsea's newest victim; I do the opposite of what would be sensible.

I look back over my shoulder to find her holding her arms out at her sides. Except for her tiny pair of panties, her body is bare for me.

"Get a good look. It's the last time you're going to see it."

I keep my eyes on hers. I've already fallen for too many of her games tonight.

"Get rid of Jake Thorn's jersey, Chelsea. His number doesn't belong to you," I demand before ripping the door open and stepping out into the night beyond.

"Fuck you, Shane," she shouts at me, and despite the fact I'm still hard as fuck from her touch and the sight of her body, a triumphant smile tugs at one side of my lips.

I might have played right into her hands back there, but there's one thing I'm certain of. If I made the right move tonight, I could have taken back power.

She wanted me as much as I wanted her. And it's only a matter of time until it's going to happen again.

My cock throbs and my mouth waters.

She might think she's fierce, but I'm going to prove that she has more weaknesses than just her need for power.

9

CHELSEA

A sob erupts the second he closes the door behind him. Tears burn my eyes and I'm unable to stop them from falling as I wrap my arms around my middle in an attempt to hold myself together.

This isn't what I wanted for us when I came back. I know it's what I deserve. Probably less than what I deserve. But the fact he's talking to me, turning up here even, shows me that there's a chance I can rediscover the sweet guy that I know is hiding inside from that night.

Thoughts of how he touched me, the things he whispered in my ear cause another sob to rumble up.

I need that Shane. I need the boy who's going to pull me into his arms and make me feel safe. Not the cruel replacement that turned up here tonight looking for revenge.

With my head spinning, I take a step toward my bedroom, bending down to pick up my discarded jersey as I go. It's the one I've always worn with Jake's number on the back. Why would I wear any other when he was the one I wanted? But Shane is right. It's wrong of me to wear it now. Even in private. Jake's not mine, he never was, and he never will be.

He rejected me, just like so many others in my life before him. I guess it's something I should be used to by now.

I drop it in the laundry basket as I pass with a sigh. It's time I moved on with my life and start focusing on the future instead of everything I've fucked up in my past.

Pulling open a drawer, I find a tank and pair of sleep shorts and curl up in the center of my bed in a ball as my tears soak my pillow.

I shouldn't have come back here. It's been barely twenty-four hours of my fresh start and I'm already fucking everything up.

The guy I want more than anything to pull me into his arms and tell me that everything is going to be okay has just slammed the door in my face and walked away without looking back. None of my squad wants me, and the rest of the school looked at me as if I was a piece of trash.

I deserve it, I know that, I do. But I couldn't help hoping it wouldn't be quite this bad.

It was delusional.

I'm delusional.

I blow out a shaky breath as I come up with a plan. Just finish school and then start over somewhere else, anywhere else. The thought of leaving my parents at a time when I'm going to need them the most terrifies me, but I know they'll be better off without me. It might have been their choice to allow me into their home all those years ago, and then to keep me when they thought they saw something redeemable inside me or some bullshit, but they don't need the drama I bring to their lives. I bet they had a great time the past few weeks without me being here. They could go to bed at night not wondering if they were going to get a drunken wake up call, or worse, blue and white flashing lights on the doorstep again as Dad's cop friend dragged my ass home.

Jesus. I was a mess.

When I wake the next morning, my eyes are sore from crying and my chest still aches as I remember watching Shane walk away. But knowing I need to do something, anything to try to feel normal once again, I find my cell and risk a message to someone who's always picked me up in the past.

Chelsea: Hey! Are you still in town?

Luca: Yeah, heading back to MKU later. Breakfast?

A smile twitches at my lips that he knows exactly what I need.

Chelsea: Would love to. Pick me up in an hour?

Luca: I'll be there x

I bite down on my lip as a little bit of the old me creeps in. Luca has always been my go-to Dunn brother. I can't lie, I gravitated to him at the beginning because he was so hot. He was the older brother that all the girls fancied but would never have a chance with. As much as I didn't want to accept it, I didn't have a chance either, but unlike my friends, I got to spend time with him and in my naïve little head, attempt to convince him I was the one for him. Reality was that I was a prepubescent girl who he saw as a sister of some sort.

He's always been so sweet and always ignored my advances despite my best attempts over the years. I never really gave up, but as my boobs grew and I found my place as a varsity cheerleader, I discovered I could get the attention of almost every other boy in our class, so I shifted my attention.

Luca's always been there though, acting like the brother I never had and helping to steer me in the right direction more often than not.

I have a quick shower, blow dry my hair, and apply my makeup just like I always do. I do it without thinking about my reality as I focus on such mundane tasks.

It's not until I pull my closet open and stare at all my clothes that I allow reality to seep in.

My cheer uniforms hang proudly at one end beside shelves of sports bras and yoga pants. It's only been a few weeks really, but even still, I feel different. I still want the same things, I want my squad, my future, I want to find love, but all of that suddenly seems a little less important these days.

Reaching in, I pull out my favorite pair of pants and pull the hot pink fabric up my legs before grabbing the matching sports bra and dragging an oversized tank over the top. I'll go for pancakes with Luca then head to the beach for a run after, burn off the excess sugar.

There was a gym at the center, but it was nowhere near as kitted out as I needed it to be in order to attempt to stay in shape. I might not be rejoining my squad anytime soon, but I'm not losing the years of hard work I've put in.

I give myself one final glance in the mirror before I head for the door. I look the same on the outside. My large eyes still hold the dark memories from my past that I'll forever hold inside, only now, there's an extra secret to keep to myself, for now at least.

I'm just closing the pool house door when the beep of his horn sounds out. Mom and Dad are sitting at the dining table when I pass through the kitchen.

"Morning, Chelsea. Did you sleep well?"

I think about my late-night visitor but quickly push him aside. "It was great," I lie easily.

"Have you got plans for today? I was thinking we could head to the mall and start our Christmas shopping." The hopeful look in her eyes damn near kills me. She's so desperate for us to be a normal family.

"Sure," I concede, unable to disappoint her once again. "I'm going for breakfast with Luca, then I'll come straight back."

"Okay. Have fun, sweetie."

After swiping a strawberry from her plate, I make my way to the front of the house when Luca beeps again.

Jogging down the steps from the house, I almost feel like my old self when I find him smiling at me through the driver's window of his truck.

"Looking good, beautiful." He makes a show of checking me out as I jog around the front and pull the door open. I'm sure a few years ago I'd have died a million deaths if he ever looked at me like that, but that's not how things are between us now. He's off killing it at MKU and I'm here pulling the pin out of the grenade on my life.

"Hey. Is that a bit of girl on your face?" I joke, reaching over to wipe an invisible mark off his cheek.

"Glad to see they didn't take away your smart ass."

"There's nothing to worry about where my ass is concerned, Dunn."

He chuckles at me before putting the car in reverse and backing out of my parents' driveway.

"And if you must know, there was no girl last night. I just hung out with Leon, Shane, and Dad watching old NFL games."

The mention of Shane is like a baseball bat to the gut.

"You okay?" he asks, glancing over when he pulls up at an intersection. "All the color's just drained from your face."

"Yeah, yeah. I'm good."

"You hanging, Chels? That why you needed this breakfast?"

"Something like that," I mutter.

"So what? You head to the beach with your squad and celebrate returning to your tribe?"

I look over expecting to find that he's joking, but I do a double take when I find him looking deadly serious.

"What?" he asks when the silence between us gets a little too much.

"I don't have a squad, Luc. The only celebrating my *tribe* will be doing is that they've gotten rid of me."

"What the fuck?" he barks.

"Oh come on, you've heard the rumors. You know why I left. Don't tell me you really expected me to be able to turn back up and reenter my old life like nothing happened." I take from the opening and closing of his mouth that he did. "We're not like guys, we don't have a fight and get over it. I'm done as far as the squad, hell the school, are concerned."

"You made a mistake, Chels. It'll blow over."

"I drugged the new girl, let your brother take the fall, and then went after one of our players. There's no coming back from that, Luc. I should just be glad I don't have a criminal record to go along with it."

He blows out a long breath as we make our way to the other side of town and our usual diner for the best pancakes in Rosewood.

"You fucked up. We all do it. They'll forgive you. They have to, that squad is nothing without you."

"They seem to be coping fine." I think of my butchered routines on Friday night. I mean, it wasn't the kind of performance that'll get them anywhere at regionals, but equally, it wasn't terrible.

"You've got this, Chels. I have faith in you."

"I'm glad someone does. Fancy coming to school with me tomorrow to hold my hand?" I ask with a laugh.

Luca pulls the car to a stop in the parking lot behind the diner and turns to me. His eyes are full of sympathy that I really don't want to see. Sitting back, I stare at the brick wall ahead instead of his familiar green eyes.

"Chelsea, you don't need anyone to hold your hand. You never have. Fierce isn't just your last name, girl. It runs through your fucking veins. You need to pick yourself up and walk back into that school like you fucking own it. But you really don't need me to tell you this, do you?"

For the first time since I can really remember, I think I do need to hear it.

Since I turned up in Rosewood after being dragged from my old life, I've made a point of showing everyone a certain side of me. And right now, I need to find that girl that Luca is talking about once again. It's no good being this broken girl who's been beaten down by her past and her mistakes. That won't get me anywhere.

I've got to hold my head high. Even if it is easier said than done.

"Come on, let's go eat our weight in pancakes."

I follow into the diner and we take a seat in our usual booth. The waitress comes over immediately, but she doesn't need to ask for our orders we're here so much.

I thought that when Luca left for college that it would be the end of our mornings, but apparently, he enjoyed them as much as me because at least once a month I'll wake on a weekend to find a message from him.

"The usual for both of you?"

"Please," Luca answers for us.

"A-actually, could I get an orange juice instead?"

"Of course, sweetie."

"Thank you."

"What, no black coffee this morning to go with your black heart?" he asks lightly, repeating the joke I've made on many occasions.

"Nah. So how's things been? I missed this."

Luca smiles before recollecting his tales from college while I've been away and successfully distracting me from my own life. It's the exact escape I need.

With stomachs full of pancakes and syrup, we make our way back toward our side of Rosewood and back to real life.

"You heading back to MKU this afternoon?"

"Yeah. Only a couple of weeks and I'll be back for the holidays," he says, clearly sensing where my thoughts are at. I need an ally in Rosewood right now, not all the way over in Maddison.

The thought of the holiday joy I'm going to have to spend the rest of the day faking with my mom doesn't fill me with happiness, but I guess it's better than the alternative being alone and miserable. I may as well have some company.

"Thank you for this morning. I really needed it," I say, leaning in to give him a hug.

"You've got this, Chels. You know where I am if you need me."

"I really appreciate that, Luc. But you've got a life to live, you don't need me cock blocking you."

He looks me up and down, his eyebrow quirking. "You think you could stop me getting some. Now that I'd like to see."

"On that note." I jump down from his truck and wave him off when he disappears from my view.

With a sigh, I make my way inside to find Mom and discover what plans she has for us for the rest of the day.

10

SHANE

The last thing I want to do when I get back from my excruciating time with Chelsea is to be forced to sit dissecting old NFL games like it would actually help me with my future progression. Luca and Leon don't give a shit, they'll happily watch games for hours with Dad and point out everyone's mistakes.

Thankfully, the obvious effect Chelsea had on my body has long vanished by the time I fall down on the couch, but that doesn't mean my muscles still aren't pulled tight or that my balls aren't blue as fuck.

That one night with Chelsea might be the only real experience I have, but fuck, I know enough to know exactly what I need right now.

I shift in my seat as images of that night threaten to reignite my earlier desire.

"You all good over there?" Leon asks, amusement curling at his lips. "You enjoying this a little too much, bro?" He nods to my crotch and to the TV.

My lack of female action is something that both my brothers like to rip me for. Just because I'm not like them with a different girl bouncing on my cock every night, it doesn't mean I'm not interested. Both of them have sat me down before now to tell me it's okay if I'm gay and that it shouldn't stop my football career, like it should even need fucking saying. It's twenty fucking twenty, it shouldn't matter who I chose to love. They just don't understand that I don't get all that excited about testing out every available pussy while I have the chance.

"Fuck you. I'm going to bed."

"Oooh someone's touchy."

I flip Leon off over my shoulder as I walk out. Luca looks over but he just rolls his eyes at the two of us.

I lie in bed staring at the ceiling running the events since she showed her face last night through my mind. Did I play it all wrong?

I think about her dark eyes begging for me to listen to her in the shadows after the game, I think about the tears that filled them while we were in Dad's office. Was I too harsh? Or, not enough?

I remember what she did, how she could so easily hurt people I—she—cares about.

One thing is for sure. I shouldn't have gone there tonight. I shouldn't have gone anywhere near their house. I shouldn't have stepped foot inside her pool house, and I certainly shouldn't have gotten her to take that fucking jersey off.

The sight of her standing before me, confident as anything is burned into my eyelids. She's so fucking perfect and I remember all too well how that body lined up with mine, how we moved together, how soft her skin was.

Groaning to myself, I shove my hand under the sheets and wrap my fingers around my length. It's got nothing on Chelsea's gentle touch but it's all I've got.

Resting back, I close my eyes and put myself back in that pool house. I forget everything, the vile words we hurled at each other, her reputation, the fact I should hate her, and I just focus on how good I know she can make me feel.

All too soon, my cock jerks in my hand and I stifle the groan that wants to erupt. Knowing my luck, Leon will walk past the door at the exact same time and think I'm jacking off to a football poster on my wall or some shit.

Unable to sleep and not wanting to lie in the dark with thoughts of a girl who shouldn't take up my headspace, I turn my Xbox on and spend almost all night playing online with Wyatt who is more than happy to give up a night's sleep to gaming.

I have no idea what time I eventually crash. All I do know is that when I wake the sun is high and my dad and brothers' voices boom from downstairs.

Groaning, I turn over and grab my cell from the nightstand.

Finding no messages, I open up Instagram and start scrolling, anything so that I don't have to crawl out of bed yet. I soon regret it though when I find a photo of none other than Chelsea with my fucking brother out to breakfast this morning.

Anger stirs in my belly as I grip my phone tighter. How dare he take her out like everything is normal.

Hearing footsteps pounding up the stairs, I throw the covers off and march for the door.

Ripping it open, I wait to see which one of them is about to appear around the corner.

Something explodes within me when it's the one I want.

"What the fuck do you think you're playing at?" I bark at Luca as he gets closer.

"What the fuck?" he asks in shock as I stand in the middle of the hallway, effectively stopping him from getting to his room. "Get the fuck out of the way, Shane."

"No. What the fuck were you doing with her this morning?"

"Oooh," he sings as realization dawns. "We went for breakfast. So what?"

"So what? Don't you know what she did?" I balk.

"Yeah. She fucked up. She's been gone weeks. She's paid for it. She doesn't need shit from me too."

I stare at him, my mouth hanging open. "You're fucking serious?"

"Yeah. She fucked up, Shane. We all do. Give her a fucking break."

I look him up and down, my lip curling in disgust. "You've fucked her, haven't you?"

"What? No. of course I haven't fucked her. She's like my little fucking sister. What the hell is wron—oh."

"What?" I spit.

"Jealousy doesn't look good on you, little brother."

My teeth grind. "I'm not jealous."

"No. That why you're stalking her Instagram? Finding out where she's been? That's why you kept ringing me while she was gone, wasn't it? I thought you were concerned about her, but no, you just wanted to fuck her."

"No. No. She's been around half the team, I'm not going there too." He lifts his brow and all it does is piss me off further.

"Get the fuck out of my way. I need to go back to college. And you, you need to sort your shit out."

"I don't fucking want her," I argue after he pushes me aside and storms past.

"I didn't say anything about wanting her. I said sort your shit out, but I'm glad you just admitted that she's the issue. She's lonely, Shane. Go see her. Be nice to her. You might even get what you want." I watch him stop when he gets to his door and turn back. "But don't fucking hurt her. She's been through enough."

"Don't hurt... fucking hell. What line has she spun you this morning?"

"The truth, Shane. She needs some friends right now, how about you try to be one."

"What the fuck ever." Marching into my room, I slam the door behind me, hoping that I can leave his words out in the hallway.

How can he say that? Be her fucking friend. I've never been her friend. She's followed Luca around for years like a fucking puppy, she never had any intention of ever being my friend.

I was just a means to an end. A toy for her to enjoy when she was bored. She said it herself last night.

I am nothing to her.

I shouldn't even fucking care.

I open up my cell again, ready to unfollow her. My finger hovers over the button as her large chocolate eyes stare up at me.

"Motherfucker," I bark, throwing my cell onto the bed and storming toward the shower.

I don't fucking need this bullshit.

After showering off the lingering scent of her perfume from last night that continued to taunt me even while I was sleeping, I head to the gym to work out some of my frustrations.

I could stay at home and use Dad's state of the art home gym but the second he discovers me in there he usually insists on 'helping' and his brand of helping usually means pushing me until I can no longer feel my legs. I might need the burn right now, but I also need to be able to walk into school tomorrow.

I shoot Zayn a message as I jump in the car, and he agrees to meet me there.

We hit the gym for a little over an hour before finding ourselves in the sauna.

"You coming to mine tonight? Mom's away?"

"Uh… I guess."

"The rest of the guys are coming, the girls too."

The fact that he means the squad, minus Chelsea, makes my chest clench in a way it shouldn't. I shouldn't feel bad for her missing out on this stuff after she was the one who fucked it all up, but I can't help it. It's her squad, her senior year. Shelly can make out that she's taken over all she likes, but we all know Chelsea made them what they are. Their coach sure didn't do it.

"Sure thing, man," I say, pushing thoughts of Chelsea to the back of my head. If she can go out for breakfast with my brother like everything is normal, then I can have a night with the team and her squad of bitches.

"Yo, catch," Rich shouts the second I walk into Zayn's den later that night as a bottle of beer comes flying for my head.

"Fucking hell. A little warning would have been nice."

"You don't get no warning in the NFL, my friend," Rich says, making me want to turn around and walk straight back out again. I've already had to endure one of Dad's pep talks before I managed to leave the house this evening, I really don't need it from them too.

Twisting the cap, I throw it at him and it bounces off his temple.

"Someone needs to get laid," he mutters. My entire body freezes and suddenly my head is back in Chelsea's pool house last night.

Shaking her from my head, I fall down onto one of Zayn's beanbags and tip the bottle to my lips.

"It's all right, bro. The girls will be here soon and they all wanna fuck a champ."

"Shut the fuck up, man," Zayn says, attempting to come to my rescue.

As far as they are concerned, I haven't gone past second base with any of the cheer bitches that throw themselves at us at every available opportunity.

I used to be happy to watch it all from the sidelines while hanging out with my other friends, but then she happened, and I found myself in the middle of this world.

I just wanted to find out where she was, I needed to know that she was okay, all the while wishing that I didn't care that much.

That's the thing with Chelsea Fierce, she fucks with my head until I don't know which way is up.

A ruckus is raised at the door behind me, and when I glance over, I find the rest of the team and the cheer squad piling into the room.

"To the state fucking champions," someone shouts before a round of hollers and cheers sound out.

Fucking hell, was that only Friday night? It already feels like a lifetime ago.

Everyone grabs a drink, someone turns the music up and the party really gets started.

I'm more than happy watching everyone enjoy themselves from my seat, but Victoria gets other ideas and pulls me up to join everyone else.

"There's nothing wrong with enjoying yourself, Dunn."

"I am," I argue, although I'm not sure my face matches my words.

"Dance with me," she demands, pressing her body up against mine. She moves in time with the music and I forget everything and move with her.

The next thing I know, I'm rolling over on Zayn's sofa and falling flat on my face on his wooden floor. I have no idea how much I had to drink last night, but everything is pretty hazy.

Ow my fucking head.

I rest it on my forearm and I'm pretty sure I fall back to sleep.

"Rise and shine, ladies," someone announces way too loudly before the blinds are opened and the sun comes streaming in. "The bitches are waiting."

Glancing at the owner of the noise, I find Zayn standing with a shit-eating grin on his face as he looks between Rich and I who are both groaning in frustration. Why the fuck does he look so good this morning?

"Fuck. Off," Rich grunts, clearly sharing my thoughts.

"No can do, girls. School is calling."

Fucking hell, it's Monday.

"And you know that Rosewood High needs its champion Bears to show their faces this morning."

"This is all your fucking fault, Hunter," I mumble, pushing myself so I'm sitting against the edge of the couch.

"Me? I didn't pin you down and poor that vodka down your throat, Dunn."

"No, I'm pretty sure that was Victoria right before you did a body shot off her—"

"Enough," I bark. The events of last night are fuzzy at best, I really don't need a first thing refresher of the bad decisions I made.

11

CHELSEA

I'd hardly looked at my cell while I was away, and I certainly didn't open any social media apps. I could only imagine the exaggeration and lies that were flying around on there about what happened and where I'd gone to. The only messages I opened were from Ethan, but even then, I mostly didn't respond. It was nice to know that someone other than my parents did actually miss me.

After a fitful night's sleep full of nightmares about what the next day might hold, I sit up in bed and lift my cell from the nightstand.

Six a.m. The mornings I'm usually up this early, it's because I requested the squad start the day with a morning workout session. That's far from my reality today though. I'd love to don my sports bra and yoga pants and burn off some of my excess fat until my legs feel like jelly and all of us help each other limp back to the locker rooms to put ourselves back together.

I blow out a long sigh, wondering if I'll ever get a chance to return to that life. Cheerleading is everything to me. It was always my plan to secure a scholarship so my parents didn't need to bankroll my future, hell knows they've already done more for me than I deserve. But now, with no squad and my future up in the air, I have no idea what my plan is.

Unlocking my cell, I hesitantly open Instagram. I'm hit with more notifications than I can deal with, and not wanting to see what people are saying about me, I focus my attention on my feed. It's fine, just the usual high school images until one makes me stop. My stomach turns over at the sight of Victoria with her hands all over Shane.

My lips purse as I scroll through the many variations of the same photography. My hands shake. I want to scream at her to get her hands off him, he's mine. But I know he's not. All we had was one intense night. I can't stake any claim.

Unable to continue looking at the familiarity of their touch, I slam my cell facedown on the bed.

I've been gone weeks. I'd be stupid to assume that he's not moved on. That another member of the squad hasn't got her claws into him. He's always acted like he wasn't interested in what we had to offer, but then he wasn't exactly turning me away that night. Maybe I was just the one to give him the push and the confidence he needed to turn into one of them.

Tears burn my eyes, but I refused to cry over whatever this weird infatuation is I have with Shane Dunn. We had one night, one that I'm sure he probably regrets after everything that happened after it.

I need to forget about all of that. Forget about the past. I need to focus on the future and trying to find myself some kind of a life as I figure out what comes next. I once thought it was easy. Go to school, cheer, win regionals, get a scholarship and get the hell out of Rosewood. I still want to leave, to get away from those who'll continue to whisper things about me, but suddenly disappearing off on my own somewhere across the country is less appealing.

With a sigh, I climb out of bed and set about getting ready for my big return to Rosewood High.

Dread rolls around in my stomach as I think about what the day might hold. I guess, I've already had it out with the squad, they're going to be expecting me. Fuck, that could be worse.

I try to focus on other things but it's impossible. By the time I walk through the kitchen of the main house where Mom is having her morning coffee, I'm worried I might puke at any moment. The second I pull the door open, her beloved festive music sounds out and I stifle a groan.

"Aw, it's so good to have you back again. This place just isn't the same without you," she says, smiling softly at me.

"It must be like I'm not here being out in the pool house," I mutter, raiding their refrigerator instead of mine.

"Not at all. I feel your presence even if you are out there." A silence falls between us as I swipe an apple from the bowl in the center of the island. "Thank you for yesterday. I know it wasn't exactly your idea of fun, but..." She trails off, leaving me to think about our afternoon at the mall. Mom loves the holidays, almost to an obsessive level. Every room of the house gets decorated within an inch of its life, and Dad and I are forced to endure hours of Christmas music throughout the entire house. Usually she'd have done it all this weekend, and I can't help but feel relieved that I didn't come home to the chaos of Mom bossing Dad around in her quest to make everything perfect.

"It was great, Mom." It's a lie, and she knows it. She had this huge list of gifts to buy and I had no one. Well, that's not true, I had the two of them but I couldn't exactly buy them with Mom there.

The look of sympathy on her face when I told her I had no one to buy for was one I remember all too well from my former years when people discovered just what a disaster my life was. It's a look that had mostly vanished from my life once I was adopted.

The squad and I had always done secret Santa. I have no idea whether they're doing it again this year or not, but I do know that I'm not going to be invited to take part.

With a sigh, I say goodbye to Mom and regretfully leave the house.

My stomach is in knots. I should eat the apple that I picked up, I know that, but I feel like all I'll do is puke it back up if I even attempt to eat it.

As I sit in the parking lot behind the wheel of my car with my classmates loitering around and heading for the buildings to start their days, I can't force my muscles to move.

This place has been my playground for years. I ruled this school along with my squad and the team. I shouldn't now be afraid to step foot inside.

It's all my own fault. I know that. If I hadn't made such stupid, fucked-up decisions then none of this would have happened. I'd still have my position, my future, my friends.

A few students eventually notice me sitting here, and I'm forced to move before I change my mind and drive back home again to hide in my pool house. That's not the girl I am. I don't hide. I stand proud with my head held high and my shoulders back. It's time to rediscover the old Chelsea, the one I pushed aside in my time away. It's time to take back control of my life.

Throwing the door open, I climb out and pull my purse over my shoulder. I focus on the building ahead and ignore the burning stares of everyone around me.

The voices start out as whispers but as I get closer to the main building to find my locker the gossip surrounding me becomes loud enough that I've got no choice but to hear it.

"Did you hear the cheer squad refused to take her back?"

"Can you believe she had the audacity to turn up to the game on Friday night. Like she supports them, pfft. She probably just wanted to drug them again."

"Does she really think she's welcome back here?"

"She needs to watch her back. I've heard the squad are gunning for her."

A shiver runs down my spine. No one in Rosewood, other than my parents, know the real me. So the threat of the squad coming after me doesn't really scare me, but out of everyone, they know me the best. They would know how to hurt me. Hell, they already have. They know the only thing I want is to cheer, and they've already taken that away from me. So what's left?

This should have been my year, but from the get-go it's been anything but.

First Amalie stole Jake, not that he was ever really mine, then my ankle stopped me from cheering and now this.

Most will probably tell me it's karma and that I deserve it, they'd probably be right, but it doesn't stop it hurting like a bitch. I've spent all my life working toward this point, toward regionals and my future and to watch it just fall away hurts like hell.

The whispers and gossip only get worse and I make my way inside the building. My only saving grace is that I haven't seen any members of the squad. They'll be outside in our usual spot trying to bag a player. I roll my eyes at the kind of behavior I was front and center of not so long ago. It's amazing how quickly things can change.

Students' stares burn into my back as I make my way toward my locker. In the past I've always loved that it's close to the girls' locker rooms, it made my life easier but as I get closer to possibly bumping into the squad, I start to wish it was situated at the other side of the school.

I'm just sorting my books out when a shadow falls over me. Swallowing down my nerves, I risk a look over my shoulder.

"Chelsea," Miss Kelly, our cheer coach, says on a sigh. "I think we need to go and have a chat, don't you?"

Dread churns in my stomach that she's going to attempt a therapy session with me. If she thinks that she's going to unearth any more than the counselors did at the center then she needs to think again. I'm not sure there's a counselor on earth who could sort out the mess that my head and life is right now.

Grabbing the couple of books I need, I slam my locker closed and follow Kelly toward her office within the girls' locker room.

I have serious mixed feelings where our cheer coach is concerned. She's got a great reputation from her own cheer career and the teams she's coached in the past. But I can't help feeling like she's lost her enthusiasm. That or it's been misplaced onto Mr. Knight, one of the other gym staff. He's married with a couple of kids but we're all convinced they're having an affair. She spends more of our training sessions either in the office with him or just markedly absent. It's how I've ended up being more than just the squad captain, a role that I'm more than happy to take on board. I've been choreographing routines for as long as I can remember. Even before I lived here, dancing was my escape. I'd take my radio out to the fields behind where we lived and lose hours making up routines, teaching myself moves. I used to watch the cheer team at my school, when I was there, in awe. I wanted to be them so badly, but most days it was all I could do to get to class let alone anything else that would take up my time. But I wanted it, so fucking badly.

When I moved here, the cheer squad was the first thing I looked into. I was desperate to at least make something of my new life, hell knows I needed something to keep me from drowning as my world once again was flipped upside down. I might have found myself with incredible new parents who had enough money to give me everything I could need, but that was far from going to fix my issues. I had more of those fuckers on the day I was born than Derek and Honey had probably had all their lives.

Pushing away thoughts of my past from my mind, I drop down on the chair in front of Kelly's desk.

"It's so nice to have you back, Chelsea. It hasn't been the same without you."

"Really? It seemed to me on Friday night that no one had noticed I wasn't there."

"You've always been my best flyer, Chels. Of course we missed you."

I quirk a brow at her. I don't even remember seeing her on Friday night. She clearly has no idea what when down.

"Whatever. I want my squad back."

"Um... I understand that, Chelsea. I know how much this squad means to you."

"Do you? How? You're never here. There wouldn't even be a squad if it weren't for me, let alone one that's going to regionals in a few months," I seethe.

"I'm sure you of all people can understand that life can be... complicated."

"Yeah, I sure as fuck know that. Look," I say, standing from the chair and pacing back and forth in front of her desk. "I know I fucked up. I'm willing to take responsibility for my actions and I'll apologize to anyone, however you'd like me to. But I need my squad."

Kelly stares at me, her eyes narrowing.

She can't possibly know that I'm hiding things, can she? She probably knows me as well as my parents after all these years working side by side, but she can't know.

"I know you do, Chelsea. But I don't think it's going to be that easy. You've been gone weeks and the girls have—"

"I don't give a fuck. They were a mess on Friday night. They've trashed my routines, they were out of time, uncoordinated."

"They've worked hard to compensate for you not being there."

"Well, I'm here now."

"Look, Chelsea—"

"No," I interrupt. "Don't *Look, Chelsea,* me. This is my squad, Kelly. My fucking squad." I hate that my voice cracks and my bottom lip starts to tremble.

"I'm sorry, Chelsea. I need to focus on you, and right now, you need to get back into class and make sure you're going to graduate."

"Jesus, I didn't go on an extended holiday. I went to school every day. I haven't fallen behind. I will graduate."

"Prove it. Meanwhile, I'll speak to the squad, to Shelly, and see how they feel."

"This is bullshit," I spit, knowing full well that Shelly won't take me back. She wants the fame and attention of being captain and to be able to control my life. *Just like you used to,* a little voice in my head says, but I push her down. There's no point in focusing on the past. I need to fight for my future.

"Go to class, get those grades up. We've still got a few months before regionals. We'll be ready no matter what."

"You can't go to regionals without me. I am this squad. They never would have had a shot without me."

"Chelsea, I hate to say it, but maybe you should have been focused on that during the past few months instead of..." She waves her hand around not wanting to finish the sentence.

"Yeah well, shit happens, Kelly. I thought you of all people would understand that. How is Mr. Knight's wife, by the way?"

Kelly turns beet red with anger. "Get to class, Chelsea, before you cause even more damage to your cheer career."

"Whatever." I pull the door open so hard it slams back against the wall.

Every set of eyes now filling the locker room now turn to me and who should be front and center but Shelly.

"Aw, you having a little tantrum because you didn't get your way. Such a shame, right, girls? The all-powerful Chelsea Fierce has fallen from her throne, losing her crown on the way down. Mind you don't hurt your ass when you hit the floor."

"Fuck you, Shelly. This is my squad and you know it. You don't have what it takes to make it anywhere near regionals. You're unorganized, lacking dedication, you spend more time on your back with your legs open than you do training." By the time I've finished, we're practically nose to nose.

"Pfft, that's rich. You're the one who's been with almost the entire football team."

"Is that right?" I seethe. I know how I've made it look over the years, but everyone's opinion of me is far from the truth.

"Who's left? Just Shane probably, and I know for a fact that he wouldn't touch you with a barge pole."

"Is that right? I'd put money on having a better chance than you."

An evil smile curls at her lips. "Of course, you just drug the ones who aren't willing."

My arm has moved before I even register, and my palm stings against her cheek.

"You bitch," she squeals as the squad surrounds her. "You're finished here, Chelsea. Get. Out."

"I'm fucking leaving. But I'll be waiting."

"Waiting for what?" Victoria asks.

"For you to all be begging me to come back. I know you all want to win, and you know as well as I do that you need me."

"No one needs you, Chelsea. You're nothing but a raging bitch."

"Just wait," I repeat as I back out of the locker room.

I keep my head high and my eyes locked on Shelly's but inside I'm crumbling faster than I can control.

The hallway is empty when I stumble out, thank fuck because I'm on the verge of breaking.

No one needs you, Chelsea.

Shelly's words run on repeat in my head and mix with those of my past that I've locked down in a little box.

My chest heaves as I fight not to lose control. I make it to the bathroom without anyone seeing me. I'm just about to push inside when a figure at the other end of the hallway catches my eye, but whoever it is disappears around the corner before I get a chance to see who it is.

Standing in front of the mirrors, I fight my need to cry. I refuse to allow them to break me, especially only minutes into my first day back.

I'm better than this. I'm stronger than this.

I refuse to be beaten down by Shelly and her band of bitches who should have my back, not hers.

After fixing my makeup, I walk out to the deserted hallway and make my way to the first class of the day.

It seems that if I had any ideas of slipping in unnoticed today then it's all been shot to shit when I knock on my physics class door and walk inside.

Every single set of eyes drill into me, including that of the teacher.

"Oh... um... welcome back," he stutters. "Please take your seat. We've only just got started."

I nod, trying to appear totally unfazed by everyone's attention. After all, attention is what I've craved all these years, it should come naturally. But as I make my way across the room toward an empty desk, all I want is for the ground to swallow me up.

I keep my eyes on the one person I know I'm safe beside. Ethan.

Our teacher continues with whatever he's talking about as I fall into my chair and blow out a breath.

I've lost the attention of some, I can feel it, but the majority are still staring at me like I'm some alien creature they've never seen before.

"It'll get better," Ethan says, turning his back on most of the class. "It's good to see you back, Chels."

"I wish I could say it was good to be back." I blow out a breath as I pull my book from my purse. "Thank you, Ethan. For the messages. For thinking of me."

A sad smile pulls at my lips as he reaches over and squeezes my hand.

"Life can be tough. Sometimes we all need a friend." A lump forms in my throat at his kindness. He could quite easily be the leader of the Chelsea hate campaign seeing as it was one of his best friends I stupidly went after, but thankfully, Ethan sees a little deeper than my bullshit decisions.

"I think you might be the only one I have left," I mutter, more to myself than him, but he still hears.

"Just give everyone time. They're pissed, rightly so. But this is your home, Chels. You'll find your footing again."

"But what if I don't?"

"Then you'll find new footing. Be a new you. Everything will be okay."

I nod, wishing that I could feel just an ounce of his positivity.

I look at him, his kind eyes sparkle in a way I've never seen before and he looks happier than I think I've ever experienced.

"We looked for you at the party on Friday night."

"I didn't stay long, it was... intense."

"One day at a time. Things will be fine, you'll see."

"Mr. Savage, Miss Fierce, I'm sure you've got loads to catch up on, but if you could please save it for lunch."

"Sorry," we both mutter, turning to focus on whatever it is we should be doing.

I sit back in my chair, aware that I've still got one too many sets of eyes on me and trying to block them out to focus. Kelly might have been right about one thing this morning. I really fucking need to graduate. And as the next few months go on, it's only going to get harder, that I'm sure of.

12

SHANE

A s I watched her all but run toward the girls' bathroom, every muscle in my body ached for me to follow her. She was upset, that much was obvious. I'd watched the squad run back into the locker rooms not long after she was dragged in there by Miss Kelly. There was never going to be a good outcome for her.

I'm just about to take a step toward where she disappeared when Zayn appears around the corner.

Taking a step back, I walk his way.

"Hey, man. How's the hangover?"

"Fucking great," I complain. "No better way to start a Monday at school."

"So I hear that Chelsea has shown her face."

I focus on the hallway ahead, but he keeps his eyes firmly on the side of my face. I know he's suspicious from Saturday morning. He might not have said anything last night, but I saw the look on his face when I was dancing with Victoria.

"Well, I guess she couldn't hide forever."

"So you haven't seen her?"

"Uh no. I went home for a shower and now here I am."

"Right."

"Right what?" I bark, already fed up with this conversation and his suspicion. I don't need anyone digging into my history with Chelsea. The fewer people who know about that night and my fucked-up head, the better.

"Oh nothing. I'm just watching you, that's all." He gestures between his eyes and mine.

I raise a brow at him.

"Don't act all innocent. I saw that thing between the two of you on the beach. You're hiding shit."

"Whatever. We're late." I turn away from him and toward my first class of the day, the sound of his laughter filters down to me. I don't need him looking too closely, I really fucking don't.

Grateful that she's not in my class, I find my seat and slump down in the hope I can be ignored while I drown in my hangover and the memories of my bad decisions. Sadly, those bad decisions all include one person who stirs something inside me she shouldn't.

Whispers and gossip ripple around the room and I hear her name mentioned more than once proving that no matter how hard I try, I can't escape her. Maybe I should have followed her earlier and just got it over with.

She thinks she's won sending me away like that on Saturday night. I should leave it there, but there's this nagging voice within me that demands I don't let her have the last word.

By some miracle, I get through the entire morning without seeing her. I was expecting her in math, but rumor had it that she was with the guidance counselor. Fine by me seeing as Zayn was sitting beside me just waiting to discover something. He's like a fucking dog with a bone, and I fear he's not going to stop until I give him something.

"Can you believe she just walked in like nothing ever happened?" Camila asks Amalie when I drop down beside them with my lunch.

"Jesus, not you too," I complain. "She's all anyone's talked about all morning."

"Well, it's quite big news. What's got your panties in a twist?" Camila asks, studying me.

"Nothing. I'm just sick of hearing it all. Of course she turned up, this is her school."

"We know that. She's just not said anything about anything. You'd think she could at least apologize."

"I'm sure she will. I can't imagine walking back in after everything was easy. Give her a break."

"Whoa," Camila says, holding her hands up in shock. "Are you actually defending her after what she did to you?"

"No, I'm just saying that it must be hard. I'm bored with hearing it, imagine how she feels."

"I don't really give a shit how she feels, Shane. She hurt three of the most important people in my life not so long ago. I couldn't have cared less if she never returned."

"Bit harsh?" Amalie asks, making Camila shrug.

"Don't say you agree with him."

"I've been the school outcast. It's not something I'd wish on anyone."

"Even your worst enemy?"

"She's not exactly my worst enemy. She's just... lost, I guess."

I nod because I have a feeling that Amalie has just hit the nail on the head perfectly.

"Well, I think you're both fucking crazy and should be heading up the *we hate Chelsea* movement that's sweeping through the school." Camila is soon distracted when Mason steps up behind her and drops a kiss to her temple. "Hey, baby. You'll back me up here..." she goes on to explain her point of view and when Mason sides with Amalie and I, Camila's face starts to turn pink with frustration.

"Just give her a break. She fucked up."

"Fucked up. She fucking drugged you."

"Yeah, I know. But no one died, we're all good. Stop getting involved and maybe just focus on your own life."

"Ugh, please. We don't need to see that much tongue," Amalie complains when Mason pulls Camila onto his lap and drops his lips to hers. Camila flips her off over Mason's shoulder.

"Because you're so much better with Jake?"

"Meh. Anyway, it doesn't look like you're one to talk. Care to explain this?" Amalie asks, pulling her cell out and opening Instagram on an image of Victoria climbing me like a tree.

"If I knew there was going to be photographic evidence, then I might have put up a bit more of a fight."

Amalie looks from her cell to me and back again, her face full of amusement. "You put up any kind of fight?"

I think back to my fuzzy memories of the night before. "I have no idea. There was too much vodka."

"Shane, Shane, Shane. I thought you were better than them."

I shrug. "Boys will be boys."

"Ain't that the truth. I just thought you had better taste than a cheer slut."

"Me too," I admit. "Sadly, there wasn't much choice."

An eruption of noise at the cafeteria entrance cuts off our conversation and when we look over we find none other than Amalie's boyfriend lapping up the congratulations from our win on Friday night. Ethan is beside him with the entire cheer squad behind them.

"Oh look, the entertainment has arrived," Amalie mutters.

I watch as Jake looks around, the second he finds her, his eyes light up and he marches over. The moment he's in touching distance, he pulls her from the bench and straight into his arms.

A smile forms on my lips as I watch them. I always thought Jake was an asshole, I mean, he is an asshole, but when he's with Amalie, he's a totally different guy. A guy that I'm starting to discover that I actually like. Although I'm never going to tell him that.

Excitement vibrates through the students as they recall Friday night. The noise level becomes deafening as we celebrate the win we've waited all our lives for.

Everyone is laughing and enjoying themselves when suddenly the room quietens down. People turn toward the entrance and when I follow, I find the reason for the break in excitement.

Chelsea is standing in the wide doorway. She looks beautiful, like she always does. Her long dark hair is pulled over one shoulder, her dark eyes are wide as she takes in the view before her and her full red lips are parted. But the confidence she usually wears is disappearing faster than I can compute as the cheer squad turns on her.

A few people call out that she's not welcome, that she should go back into hiding.

"Jesus, people are cruel," Mason mutters as he stands from the bench.

I do the same, my need to protect one of our own overriding my need to see her get some justice.

A second before she's surrounded by the cheer squad, our eyes lock. Fear fills hers and it hits me right in the chest.

I don't think I breathe as she's swallowed up by the girls who used to support her every move.

"Fucking hell," Mason barks before both him and Jake take off for the crowd.

They quickly force their way into the huddle, but my legs refuse to move.

That is until a scream sounds out, one I recognize all too well. Then my body moves without any instruction from my brain. My need to go to her, to help her, is too much to ignore.

By the time I break through the now much larger crowd, it seems the show is over because Shelly is standing front and center with a shit-eating grin on her face. Her loyal followers standing behind her and backing her all the way.

Glancing up to the hallway beyond, I find the girl they've just sent away running as fast as her legs will carry her.

I'm pushing through the rest of the crowd before I even know what I'm doing, and I run after her.

"Chelsea?" She doesn't stop, her movements don't falter as she flees from whatever just happened with Shelly. "Chelsea stop, please."

She flies into the girls' bathroom and slams the door behind her.

"Chelsea?" I ask, poking my head inside.

"Go away." Her voice is broken and rough and it pulls at me.

Ignoring her warning, I step farther into the room.

"Chels?"

"I said go away, Shane. I can't do this. I can't—"

Placing my hand on her shoulder, I spin her around and gasp.

There are bright red scratch marks across her cheeks, but surprisingly that's not the most shocking thing because what has my eyes widening is her tears.

"Fuck, Chels." Before I know what I'm doing, I have her in my arms.

Her small frame trembles as I hold her tight.

"No, no," she fights, trying to push me away from her. "Shane, no."

I hold tight, knowing that she needs this right now, but when she reaches up and twists my nipple, I have no choice but to release her.

"Ow," I complain, rubbing at the sting.

"You should have let go," she snaps.

"You should have let me hold you."

"Why?" she asks, wiping at her wet cheeks. "So you could say that you helped me when I broke. So that you could go back to your little friends and tell them how weak I am? So you can tell them that they're winning, that they're ruining my life?" The fire that I'm so used to starts to burn in her eyes.

"No, I was coming to make sure you were okay."

"Jesus, you really are pathetic. You that desperate for another round?"

I close the space between us so she has no choice but to back up until she hits the wall.

Our bodies are only an inch apart and her heat burns into me.

"You may have left me on the edge the other night, but no, that wasn't my intention."

I stare down into her tear-filled chocolate eyes.

She swallows nervously before biting down on her bottom lip. My eyes flit between them and her quickly darkening eyes.

"Go on then. Take whatever you want. You might as well kick me when I'm down."

As much as I might want to take her in my arms and look after her, I won't. Not like this.

Lifting my hand, I gently touch my fingertip to the scratches down her cheek. She startles and gasps at my contact.

"They have no right laying a hand on you," I whisper, ignoring her previous comment.

She shrugs one shoulder. "I deserve it for all the people I've hurt."

"Many would probably agree."

"You don't?"

"I don't know what I think when it comes to you."

Her breathing catches at my honesty.

"One thing I do know though, I don't just take. I don't take things that aren't offered to me, and I certainly don't take from others when they're down."

I take a step back and suck in a lungful of air now that I'm not surrounded by her scent.

"You want something from me, this isn't how you get it."

She opens her mouth to respond, but I'm done. I came in here with good intentions and I'm not going to stand here while she unleashes more hate and frustration my way.

Turning my back on her, I'm almost out the door when her voice stops me.

"Shane?" Resting my hand on the doorframe, I stop and hang my head, waiting for whatever she has to say. "I'm... I'm sorry." If the room weren't so silent, I would think I misheard.

"I know," I say before disappearing from her sight and allowing the door to close behind me.

13

CHELSEA

A sob rumbles up the second the door slams behind him.

I shouldn't have said those things. I knew the moment I looked into his eyes that he didn't follow me for a fight, but I freaked out.

I didn't want him to see me broken, to see me cry, but he was standing before me while I crumbled.

Shelly shouldn't have this power over me, but she ambushed me, spurred on by the girls who used to stand behind my every move.

As she raised her hand to get her revenge for the slap I gave her earlier, all I could do was stand there and take it.

I expected the slap, I didn't anticipate her nails as they clawed at my cheek.

"Fuck," I bark, turning to look in the mirror to inspect the damage.

I run my finger over the deepest gouge and hiss when it stings.

Movement over my shoulder has my heart jumping into my throat. My first thought is that he came back without me hearing but I soon realize it's not him.

"What?" I bark at the short, dark-haired girl who clearly was hiding in one of the cubicles this whole time.

"Nothing," she says, walking toward the sinks to wash her hands. "You're welcome, by the way."

I give her a double-take. "Um... for what, exactly?"

"For giving you some kind of privacy. I must say though, I was disappointed that he didn't kiss you. That would have been hot."

"Fucking hell, creepy much. You were watching?"

"No, just listening."

We stare at each other, other than our dark hair we're opposites in every way. I might not be currently wearing my preppy cheer uniform but that's the persona I try to give off whereas everything about this girl is dark. The exact kind I'd usually steer clear of. So why I feel drawn to her, I have no fucking clue.

"They've all got you very wrong, don't they?"

"They? Who? What?"

She finishes washing her hands before coming to stand in front of me.

"I've heard so much about you, it's good to finally meet the woman behind all the stories." I narrow my eyes at her. Who the fuck is this girl? "Rae," she says as if she can read my mind. "Ethan's girlfriend. He's told me all about you."

A laugh rumbles up my throat. "You're Ethan's girl? For real?"

She smiles, gesturing at herself. "I know. Shocking right? I don't even own a cheer uniform."

"Maybe not," I muse. "But I think I'm already understanding why he didn't stand a chance."

"Oh yeah?"

"Ethan always loved a challenge, and why do I think you're the ultimate one?"

She pops her hip and rests her hand on it. "Because I am."

"I think I like you already."

"That's good because most people are just scared, or jealous."

"You bagged Ethan Savage. Girl, that group out there will be about as jealous as it comes."

"I fucking love it. Seeing the frustration in their eyes on a daily basis is what gets me up in the morning. Well, that and Ethan's co—"

"Okay," I say with a laugh, halting any more words. "Ethan and I might be close, but there's always been a line between us."

"More than you have with the rest of the team, I hear."

"Fucking hell. You don't hold back, do you?"

"What's the point? What you see is what you get. Like it or fucking lump it."

I shake my head at her in total amazement.

"You fancy getting out of here. I'm not really feeling it, plus I've got gym later and I really don't have the patience for that."

"You want to skip?"

"Yeah. You don't actually want to be here after that, do you?" she asks, nodding at my cheek.

"No, I really fucking don't."

"Perfect, come on then. Let's head to the beach, I'm sure your tan could use some work after weeks of being locked up."

I follow her out of the bathroom and for the first time today, I'm able to ignore the stares and harsh words that are muttered as we pass.

"You know, I wasn't in prison, right?"

"Some center full of fucked-up teenagers and counselors who want to know your deepest thoughts and feelings? Sounds like prison to me."

I can't really argue because she does kinda have a point.

"You've got a car, right? I rode with Ethan?"

"Um... yeah. Over there." I point to my white convertible BMW.

"Wow, of course."

"What?" I ask.

"Just wondering if you could be any more stereotypical. You must have looked like something out of the movies getting out of this in your cheer uniform."

"I guess you won't find out seeing as they've kicked me out."

"I'm sure you'll get over it."

We climb in and in seconds we're heading out of the parking lot and away from Rosewood High.

"So how much has Ethan told you exactly?"

"Adopted, cheer bitch... sorry, head cheer bitch, team bike, life of the party, drink spiker, did I mention bitch?" She ticks each item off on her fingers.

"Oh my god," I mutter.

"What? Did I miss something?"

"No, no, I think you nailed it."

"If it makes you feel any better, I'm about as screwed up. You're in good company."

I've never really had what I would class as a close girlfriend. I spent all my time with the squad, but I never really connected with any of them, not in a way I would hope. I guess I wasn't the only one who felt that way, seeing as they all turned their backs on me at the first possible opportunity.

I glance over at Rae, someone who I never would have considered spending time with and much like with Shane, I start to wonder if I had everything wrong.

I clung to the squad, thinking they were what would make me happy. I attached myself to the football team thinking that I was destined to be with the best of the bunch, but was I just trying too hard?

Cheer is always going to be my life. But maybe I can have that and not the toxic relationships that come with it.

It's a sobering thought.

"Everything okay?" she asks after a few seconds.

"Yeah. You're... I'm not even sure what you are. But I needed this, so... thank you, I guess."

"You're welcome. Shall we?" she asks, gesturing to the beach outside.

"Yes." I grab a hoodie from the back of my car before following her down toward the shore.

We walk along in silence until we find a spot between the dunes where we're hidden from the world and we sit our asses down.

I wrap my hoodie around my body while Rae happily stretches her fishnet-clad legs out in the sun.

"How aren't you cold?"

"How are you? This is like summer in some of the places I've lived."

"Where have you lived?"

"Most recently, Washington. Before that, everywhere."

"So what's your story then. And don't even try to tell me you don't have one."

"Oh, I have one. Much like I believe you do. I'll just skim the basics. Desperate mother, too many almost stepdads to count, some of which were more questionable than others. We moved. A lot. She ended up fucking Ethan's dad and here we are."

"Wow, okay then." She raises her brows at me, waiting for me to return the favor. "So... crack whore mother, some very dodgy men, in the system by seven, moved here by eight and been with my new parents ever since."

"Well, aren't we a pair." She laughs.

"It must be boring having the perfect life. Imagine not dealing with all that baggage on a daily basis."

"I literally have no idea what that must be like."

We lose the afternoon chatting about bullshit and steering away from our pasts. I know that I shared more than I have with almost anyone in Rosewood since the day I arrived, and I have a feeling that Rae might have done the same.

Hearing her talk about her past, albeit briefly, made me wonder if that was the connection between us, why I felt instantly at ease with her unlike most others. I think... I think she might get me in a way that no one else does. She's been through hell, she knows what it's like to try to rebuild a life after that kind of nightmare.

"We should probably get back. Ethan will wonder where I am if I'm not waiting for him after practice."

We stand and brush the sand from our bodies before heading back toward my car.

"I never thought I'd see the day that Ethan Savage settled for one woman, you know."

"From what I've heard, you're not the only one to think that."

"He was a whore. Sorry." I wince.

"No need. I'm fully aware of that side of Ethan. We all have pasts, Chelsea. We know that more than most. I refuse to judge someone based on what's happened before."

"And that is why we're going to get along. Everyone else can't see past my mistakes."

"I understand why, you hurt people they care about. But one day they'll fuck up and they'll need a friend. You just need to hope karma works her magic and they get back what they gave to you."

Her words are on repeat in my head as we climb back into the car, ready to return to school.

"So, tell me about Shane," Rae asks, sitting back and waiting for me to reverse the car out of the space. "Chelsea?" she prompts when I don't do anything.

"Shit, sorry." I don't say anything else until we're on the road. "Shane is... Shane," I say on a sigh.

"There's history there, though, right? The tension in that bathroom, shit you could have cut it with a knife."

"Yes, no. I don't know. There was something. I don't know," I repeat. "My head was so fucked up back then. Hell, it still is now, possibly worse actually. I've got no idea what's going on."

"It sounded to me like he cared."

"We're toxic. We'll never work."

I shrug it off and thankfully she leaves it there.

We're just about to get out once we're back in the school parking lot when I find my voice again.

"Rae, please don't... please don't say anything about Shane and me. I think it's for the best if it all just stays in the past."

"Whatever you want. I won't tell a soul, not that you really told me anything."

"Nothing to tell."

"Fair enough. I'll see you tomorrow then, yeah?"

"Sure. Thank you for today. I really needed it."

"Anytime. Us fucked-up folk need to be normal sometimes too."

I laugh as she climbs from the car.

She turns back when she's halfway across the parking lot.

"Chelsea?"

"Yeah."

"Don't let the past define you. Only you have the power to change your future."

I nod and watch as she disappears toward the boys' locker room to meet Ethan.

I should just drive home and spend the night hiding in my pool house, but some part of me that's a glutton for punishment has me pushing the car door open and walking toward the gym where the squad will be practicing.

I pull the door open and silently make my way down.

The sound of them counting as they work through the routine is painful to hear. I should be doing that. I should be leading them.

I stand slightly back of the open doors and keep hidden in the shadows as I watch them. Kelly is nowhere to be seen, as usual, and Shelly is at the front barking her orders. Although she misses all the important things that need to be picked up like Victoria not locking her knees out on the lift she's working on.

"All in. We're going to hit it from the top. Harley," she barks, referring to one of our JV cheerleaders. "You're going to be our flyer."

Fucking bitch. You can't replace me with a JV.

Harley swallows nervously and looks around at the girls. "B-but I thought Tasha was doing it."

"Yeah well, Tasha keeps fucking it up." Tasha huffs out her frustration, but this is one decision I can't help but agree with Shelly on. Tasha is no flyer.

"Just get in position. You're the best we've got and you know it."

A few of the varsity girls turn their noses up at the decision, but I get where Shelly is coming from.

I stand watching them with a lump in my throat and my fists clenched so tightly that my nails dig into my palms.

My need to go marching in there and set them straight is all-consuming, but nothing good will come of it.

Watching Harley do what I should be doing, and doing it well, is the final straw. With tears once again filling my eyes, I turn and run.

Unfortunately, I barely get around the corner before I collide with a very hard and warm wall.

"Fuck. I'm sorry."

"Chels?" Large hands wrap around my upper arms, but I have no intention of breaking down in front of anyone else today.

"No. Just no." I spin out of Ethan's grip and run for my car so I can fall apart in private.

I run past a few other members of the team, some of whom offer to cheer me up. My stomach turns over at the thought. The second I'm in my car, I put it in drive and speed home to the safety of my pool house.

The second I'm inside, I strip out of my shirt and skinny jeans and pull on some yoga pants and a sports bra. I shove my earbuds in and hit play on my usual workout playlist and I take off.

I don't allow thoughts to enter my head about what today has been like. I just run. I focus on the pulling of my muscles, on the movement of my limbs, of the music in my ears. I keep it all bottled up until I hit the park that I usually run around before heading back.

Seeing as schools out, it's full of happy, laughing kids and it's the last thing I need to see after my short conversation about my past with Rae earlier.

I fall down onto a bench and watch as a couple of small children chase each other around as their mother watches with a smile on her face.

I never had this growing up. I never had this kind of freedom to just be a kid. To forget about the stresses of young life and to play like my life depended on it. Survival was my only focus as a young kid.

I wrap my arms around myself and fight to keep the tears that are threatening in my eyes.

Was I always destined to be a fuck-up? Is it laced through my genes from my birth mother, just like the poison of her drugs?

Not wanting to draw attention to myself, I drag my already sore body from the bench and force myself to run back home. I've had nowhere near the exercise I need, and I'm already suffering the consequences.

I have a shower the second I get back and intend on heading up to the house to find out what Mom's cooked for dinner, only when I emerge from the shower voices filter down from the living area.

Dread fills my veins.

Who the hell would willingly turn up and wait for me?

I quickly pull on some clothes and reluctantly poke my head out of the bedroom.

"Here she is," Ethan announces, making Rae look in my direction.

"Hey," she says as if she belongs in my pool house.

"Hey... um... what are you...?"

"We figured that you'd kinda had a rough day, so we ordered pizza. Thought we'd come and entertain you."

"Aren't you lucky?" Rae adds with a wink.

"You're just here to hang out?"

Ethan's brows draw together in confusion. "Uh... yeah. Is that okay?"

A smile curls at my lips and just for a moment, all of the weight I've been carrying around lifts from my shoulders.

"Yeah, it's really great. Thank you."

"We brought beer too."

I stare at it before shaking my head. "Nah, not on a school night."

"What the hell did they do to you in that place?" Ethan jokes. I laugh along with him because I understand how different this is for me. But everything is different now. I'm different now.

After grabbing myself a soda, I fall onto the other couch just as the food arrives, and for the first time in what feels like forever, I have somewhat of a normal night hanging out with friends.

14

SHANE

"You not going to go chasing after her this time?" Zayn asks, his arms resting on my shoulder as Chelsea flies past us and out of the building.

I tense at the question, and I have no doubt that he feels it.

"Shelly dragged her nails across her face, someone needed to make sure she was okay?"

"Did they though? Chelsea is more than capable of looking after herself."

I agree, but that's not the point, she shouldn't have to.

"You coming to Aces?" Rich calls from in front of us.

"Sure thing," Zayn shouts. "You're coming, right?"

"Yep. Wouldn't want to be anywhere else." As I say it, the image of Chelsea's pool house pops into my head.

I know she skipped this afternoon. She was meant to be in both my classes. I'd be lying if I said I wasn't nervous as I waited for her to walk through the door, only she never did.

I was disappointed, I wanted to see if she was okay after what happened in the bathroom and her fight with Shelly, but mostly I was worried.

She must have been dreading coming back here. No amount of time away was going to erase what happened before she left. No one has forgotten, even if some like Amalie and Mason are happy to let things lie and move on with their lives, the likes of Shelly certainly are not.

Cheer to Chelsea is like football to Jake and the other guys. It's their life. It's their purpose. It's why they get out of bed every morning. But have that taken away and what's left, other than the broken shell of a person who's full of regrets.

"Fucking hell," I mutter, scrubbing my hand over my rough jaw. I need to get her out of my fucking head.

"What's wrong?" Zayn asks, dropping down into my passenger seat.

"Nothing," I grunt.

After waiting a few seconds to see if any others are going to join us, I start to back out of the space.

"Nothing, yeah sure. That's why you're acting like a moody motherfucker. This morning I assumed it was the hangover, or the fact you allowed yourself to get up close and personal to a cheer slut, but it's only gotten worse. So what gives, Shane?"

"I don't wanna talk about it," I mutter under my breath.

"Well that really fucking sucks for you because I think you're gonna have to."

I blow out a breath. Even if I did want to talk about it, I have no idea where I'd start. Luckily—or unluckily, I'm not so sure—Zayn seems to know exactly where to kick off his questioning.

"Something happened with Chelsea, didn't it?"

My grip on the steering wheel tightens, turning my knuckles white. I haven't told anyone about that night. As far as I'm aware, only the two of us know about it.

"Yeah," I admit.

"So what's the big fucking deal? You're just another notch on her... wait..." He holds his hand up in the space between us. Thankfully, I need to focus on the road, so I don't have to see him connecting the dots. "You... you like her, don't you?"

"No. No. No, I fucking hate her for what she did," I argue, but even to my ears, it's weak at best.

"So what are we talking here. She just suck you off, or did you get further?"

"Does it matter?" I ask, not really wanting to get into the details. Mostly because I have no idea if he's already been there and has first-hand experience himself. The thought has heat racing through my veins that all the guys I spend time with have seen her like I have.

"Of course it matters. When and how many times?" I glance over to find a shit-eating grin on Zayn's face. "What?" he asks.

"You're acting like you didn't get laid last night."

"Who said I did?"

"Uh... the girl crying out your name in the next room most of the night."

"The girl?" he asks, amusement filling his voice. "That wasn't one, Dunn."

"Fucking hell," I mutter.

"Why have one when you can have two? Laurie and Ruby together. Whoa, man. I'm telling you that you haven't lived until you've had one suc—"

"Okay," I say, cutting off whatever he was about to describe. "Ruby is a junior, man. Not to mention your sister's friend. Don't you think you should lay off the young ones a little?"

"What? I didn't stand a chance."

"Whatever. You're a dog."

"At least I'm not hung up on one pussy."

"I'm not... fuck."

"Bro, the fact you're even trying to deny it is highly amusing. So what's the real issue here? You hate her, yet you want to fuck her again? I don't see the issue, there's nothing wrong with a good old hate fuck. They're the hottest kind if you ask me."

"Says the expert," I mutter, rolling my eyes.

"Two in one night, bro. Two in one night," he repeats as we climb from the car.

"Zayn," I say, my voice suddenly taking on a serious tone. "Please don't—"

"Your secret's safe, man. You don't even need to ask. But do us both a favor, yeah?"

"What?"

"Go and fucking bang her. Fuck this asshole mood out of your system."

I can't help but laugh as we make our way toward Aces. It's either that or I spin on my heel and go and find exactly what he just suggested. The temptation to do just that is almost too high to ignore.

The squad turned up not long after us and filled the final spaces in the team's usual booths. Just like since she disappeared, her absence is ever noticeable when we all hang out, and similarly, no one Except for me seems to care or even notice.

Although it shouldn't, my heart aches for her that she's been so easily forgotten by the people who were meant to be her friends.

Would Noah, Wyatt, Camila and now Zayn miss me as little if I were to suddenly up and leave? I'd like to think I'd had a little more impact on their lives and that they would notice my sudden disappearance. It makes me wonder what Chelsea's life is really like if those who are meant to be her friends just don't care.

Burgers and shakes are delivered to our table via Rae's friend Cody. I eat and try to join in with the others, but my head's not in it. I'm too busy wondering what she's doing and if she's sitting at home alone while all her so-called friends are out enjoying themselves as if she doesn't even exist.

When my cell rings, it's the perfect excuse to make my excuses and head home, although the second I pull it out and find my dad's name staring back at me, I start to wonder if I should be so relieved or not.

"I need to go," I say, turning to Zayn. "You okay getting back or do you want a ride?"

"I'm good. You go and get what you need." He winks at me.

"What? No. My dad," I say, waving my still ringing cell at him.

"Sure. Sure. I'm good. See you tomorrow."

I nod at him and the rest of the team who are huddled around our table before heading out.

Deciding against calling him back, I put my car in drive and set off on the short distance home.

I don't bother calling out for him, or even looking for him. I know exactly where he'll be. He only ever calls me for one thing and that means he'll be in his office talking 'business', aka my dreaded future.

"Ah there you are. I was calling you."

"I know and here I am," I mutter, falling down onto one of the giant leather couches in the center of the room.

"Right, well... I spent the afternoon on a call with the Steelers' coach. He is very interested. I've sent him some extra footage of you in action. He's going to look it over, but he thinks you might be a great fit for their team. Do you know how many players left his team last year and walked straight into the NFL?" Dad asks, his brows raised in excitement.

"I have no idea, but I'm sure you're about to tell me."

"What's wrong? This team is one of my top picks for you. It could take you all the way."

"All the way where? To your dream. I'm not interested, Dad." Standing, I walk toward the door, already over his conversation.

"Shane, get back here."

"No, we're done."

With my teeth grinding in frustration, I fly through the door, slamming it behind me and marching straight for the front door.

Anger swirls in my belly as I storm for my car. I'm so fucking fed up with having this same conversation. Why can't he just hear me?

I don't want the fucking NFL. I'm not good enough and I don't have the desire. I love football, I do. But it's not my future. Although I've got no idea what is.

I am not my dad. I am not my brothers. The NFL is their dreams and I'll support them all the way, but it is not mine and I just wish he would listen to me.

I drive around town as the sun sets with nowhere to go. I could go to Wyatt's and lose myself in a game, or I'm sure Zayn would welcome me in, his mom is never there to care what he does. But neither of those places hold any kind of appeal right now. I don't want to hang out with friends. I just want to... forget. I want a few moments of quiet where everything in my head just stops.

I find myself pulling into Chelsea's driveway.

I shouldn't be here. I should just go home and lock myself in my room away from Dad and his unrealistic ideas, but I can't get her out of my fucking head.

She's the one who makes everything go away. And I need that. I need that more than anything right now.

The sun has almost totally set by the time I slip around the side of her house, her parents are in their living room watching the TV but thankfully don't notice me.

As I approach the pool house, movement inside has me jumping into the bushes slightly.

I stand in the shadows, watching as both Ethan and Rae emerge. Chelsea smiles at them. It's a real genuine smile that she doesn't give out very often, and my own lips twitch slightly at the sight. That is until they disappear off around the edge of the pool and toward the driveway, thankfully the opposite way that I came. The second they're out of sight, her face drops. Sadness washes through her as she closes the door behind them and walks back into her pool house. Her shoulders are down and her head lowered as she falls onto the couch.

Stepping from the shadows, I make my way over, keeping my eyes on her defeated form.

I come to a stop at the door and just watch her as she lifts her fingers to her cheek to wipe away a tear.

My fists clench with my need to storm inside and pull her to me. I might have wanted to see her suffer after what she did, but watching her fall apart is ripping me open.

As if she knows I'm here, her eyes lift.

Her lips part in shock and I can only imagine a squeal of shock leaves them as our eyes hold.

She stands, she makes no move to invite me in, but she doesn't send me away either.

When another tear drops, she doesn't wipe it away this time, and it's my undoing.

Pulling the door open, I march inside and take her in my arms.

"Shane, what the hell are you doing?" she asks, her eyes wide as I wrap one arm around her waist and pull her into my body. Lifting my other hand, I wipe away the wet trail her tear left behind with my thumb.

"What I should have done earlier."

Leaning forward, I press my lips to hers. I want to give her a chance to pull away, to tell me where to go, but the second we connect I lose all restraint.

Walking her backward, she bumps up against the counter. Her hands slide down my back before slipping inside my jersey.

Dropping my hands to her thighs, I make quick work of lifting her onto the counter, her legs instantly part allowing me to stand between them.

"Shane," she moans when I begin kissing across her jaw and down her neck. "Off," she demands, pulling at the fabric around my body.

Releasing her for a beat, I drag it over my head and drop it to the floor beside us.

Her eyes land on my chest before she lifts them to meet mine. They're dark, hungry, and it only spurs me on. My need to lose myself in her is too much to deny her. Being here right now with her hands on me and her legs locked around my waist, nothing else exists. There's no bullshit outside of these four walls. We're just two people who need to escape everything that's going on in their lives that's totally out of their control.

"I shouldn't be doing this," I whisper, taking her cheeks in my hands. I don't know why I say it, some fucked-up need to make sure she knows there's nothing more here than what I'm about to give her.

"So are you planning on stopping?" She tilts her head to the side and bites down on her bottom lip.

"Fuck no."

I've got her in my arms in a heartbeat and carrying her toward the back of the pool house where I'm hoping her bedroom is.

As I walk, her lips trail across my neck, only increasing my need for her.

The second I find her bed, I lower her down onto it and crawl over her body.

"Shane, what are—"

"No," I say, placing my finger against her lips, cutting off any more words she might want to say to me. "No talking or I'll leave. No bullshit, I just... I just need..." She raises her brows, waiting for me to finish. I swallow down my pride because I need this too much right now to do anything but tell the truth. "You, okay? I just need you."

Her heels dig into my lower back and I fall on top of her, pressing her tiny frame into the mattress.

"Give me everything," she moans when I release her lips once again.

Gathering up the fabric of her tank, I push it up her stomach, my lips kissing across the smooth skin as I do.

Once I've got it over her breasts, she takes over and rips it from her body.

Her chest heaves as her breaths race past her parted lips.

She needs this as much as I do. I have no idea what I'd have done if she'd have turned me away like she did the other night. Hell, she might still do so.

That thought spurs me on.

The second she arches her back for me, I slip my hand behind her to unhook her bra.

She moans loudly as I pull the fabric from her body.

Her nipples are pert and ready for me.

Fuck, this girl has my head all kinds of fucked-up.

I hate her.

I want her.

I shouldn't have her.

I can't help myself.

"Shane," she moans. "Please."

I stare up at her as she looks down at me.

I should walk away and not look back. There's no way that this is anything short of a disaster waiting to happen. But I fear after just one taste all those weeks ago that I'm already in too deep.

Tension crackles between us as neither of us moves and only the sound of our heavy, labored breathing can be heard.

"Shane? I thought you came here with a plan in mind," she taunts. "Or aren't you man enou—fuck," she cries when I dive forward and suck one of her rosy nipples into my mouth.

Her fingers dive into my hair to hold me in place and she groans in pleasure under me. I switch to the other side as my fingers trail down her sides to pull at her pants.

My lips leave her as she lifts her hips, allowing me to drag the fabric down her legs. She kicks her pants from her feet so I don't have to pull away to rid her of the clothing.

Sitting up, I stare down at her laid bare before me.

She's so fucking beautiful. Her slim body is flawless perfection and clearly shows all the hours she puts into her sport.

I can't get e-fucking-nough.

Skimming my hands down her thighs, her hips writhe with her need for more.

"What do you need?"

"You," she moans. "Y-your mouth."

I swallow nervously. She has no idea—I don't think—that our time together before was a first for me. Unlike most of the rest of the team, I don't spend every night of the week with a different girl. I wasn't waiting for anyone in particular. I just knew that I didn't want it to be just anyone. I never in a million years would have thought Chelsea would have been the one to take my V-card, but now it's happened, I can't imagine it any other way.

"What's wrong? You going to leave me high and dry?"

I stare at her, my head spinning with my need.

"I deserve it. You should get up and walk out now and not look back. Everyone else would."

"Enough," I bark, ensuring her lips slam shut immediately. "I said no talking."

Lowering to my stomach, I wrap my hands around her thighs and focus on her core.

She's so ready for this, and the sight has desire racing through me. My cock is impossibly hard and desperate for her touch, but for some fucked-up reason, I want to give this to her first. I want to help her leave everything behind just like I'm craving for myself.

Closing the space between us, I flatten my tongue and press it against her. I'll be the first to admit that I don't really know what I'm doing, but as she moans, her fingers once again find their way into my hair and pull painfully hard. Not that I'm about to complain. With her taste on my tongue and her sweet scent surrounding me, I'm so fucking lost I barely know my own name. It's exactly what I needed. What I knew she could give me.

"Shane, fuck," she moans, her back arching in her need for more.

Releasing one of her hips, I find her entrance and slide one finger inside her.

"Yes, yes. Fuck yes," she chants, spurring me on. I lick faster before grazing her with my teeth and add another finger stretching her open. "Oh god. Oh god."

Her muscles clamp down on me and I keep my rhythm, desperate to feel her fall apart against me.

I remember all too well how tight she was when she came around me last time, the little noises she made as she came down from her high. It was fucking mind-blowing and I need to experience it again more than I need my next breath.

"Shane. Shane. Shannnnnne," she screams as her body quakes beneath me. Her thighs clamp around my ears as she falls.

Standing from the bed, I drop my hands to the waistband of my pants and pop the button. My eyes stay on Chelsea as she lies lax on the bed, trying to catch her breath.

"Shane, I—" Propping herself up on her elbows, her words are cut off as she watches me push both my pants and boxers down my thighs and take myself in hand. "Fuck."

"What?" I ask, kicking the fabric from my ankles and taking a step toward her. "You thought that was all I came for?"

She shakes her head, her eyes still locked on me. "N-no. I just thought..." She trails off as I place one knee on the edge of her bed and then the other.

"You just thought..." I prompt, reminding her that she was in the middle of saying something.

"I thought you were about to leave."

"Not yet. I need to take what I came for first."

Something flashes in her eyes, the fire I'm so used to as she rips me a new one, but the words don't follow. She knows full well that she'll only be denying herself if she turns on me right now.

However fucked-up this might be. However much we might hate each other. This right now is happening because we both need it too much. We need each other too much.

That thought is fucking terrifying.

I shouldn't need anyone, let alone Chelsea.

Forcing the thought from my head, I crawl between her legs and find her entrance.

"Condom?" I ask, realizing that I don't have one. *Fuck.*

"It's okay, it's safe."

"But…"

"I haven't been with anyone, Shane. Not since…"

My eyes fly up to meet hers. All I see is honesty staring back at me.

"Contrary to popular belief, I'm not actually a whore."

"No, that wasn't…" She quirks a brow. "I was just surprised."

"No talking, remember?" she sasses, wrapping her legs around my hips and dragging me closer.

"I didn't forget."

She squeals as I thrust my hips forward, filling her in one swift move.

Fuck. My eyes squeeze tight as I give myself a second. She's so hot, so tight, so fucking incredible.

Leaning over her, I wrap my hand around the back of her neck and tilt her up so I can capture her lips. I thrust again as my tongue delves into her mouth and my hand comes up to cup her breast, my fingers pinching her nipple.

"Oh god, Shane," she mumbles against my lips as I play her body.

I was nervous as fuck that first time. I had no idea what I was doing and she was, well… Chelsea, expert at all the things. But the second I got my hands on her, everything just fell into place. It was like my body just knew what to do and the nerves fell away as she moaned and writhed against my touch.

Our tongues duel as our bodies find a rhythm that has me racing toward my release long before I'm ready for this to be over.

Chelsea's nails scratch down my back as her slick walls ripple around me, telling me that she's about to fall over the edge with me.

"Chelsea," I groan. It's half in awe and half just to remind myself that it's her, that this is happening again.

Dropping my hand down her body, I find her clit and circle it.

She cries out, her nails digging into my skin, but the bite of pain only adds to the pleasure that's coursing through my veins.

"Fuck. Fuck," I groan against her lips, desperate for air but refusing to pull away from her.

"Shane," she cries. "Oh god, Shane."

Her entire body locks up as her pleasure slams into her. Her back arches and she throws her head back. I miss her lips immediately, but the second I open my eyes and get a look at her, it's soon forgotten.

With her eyes squeezed shut, her swollen lips are parted in pleasure as she rides out her climax. Her pussy clamps down on me impossibly tight and I can't help but fall over the edge with her.

Falling to the side of her, we both lie lax and trying to catch our breath.

The silence surrounding us becomes heavy, but it's not with the tension that was filling the room not so long ago, it's quickly becoming more and more awkward as neither of us says anything.

Chelsea is the first to break it, but I never could have guessed the words that fall from her lips.

"Well, that was unexpected but enjoyable." A laugh bubbles up my throat. "But you can leave now."

Sitting up, I stare down at her. Her hair is all over the place, her cheeks pink with exertion and her lips red from my kisses. She doesn't make any attempt to hide the fact she's naked and if her words weren't so final, I'd probably have a job keeping my eyes on her face, but as it is, I'm too shocked to really notice.

"I can leave now. Wow."

"What? Did you expect to spend the night cuddling? You got what you came for. You can go now."

She rolls on her side, turning her back toward me.

"What? I didn't... Chels?"

"Just go, Shane. We both know you don't want to actually spend time with me. You just wanted that revenge fuck you talked about Saturday night. Well, you got it so off you fuck."

"You don't actually believe that, do you?" I place my hand on her waist and her body locks up at my touch.

"Leave."

Knowing that I've got no chance of getting through to her. I reluctantly push from her bed and drag my clothes on.

She doesn't move an inch as I prepare to leave.

With a sigh, I walk to the door, bending down to pick up my jersey as I do. Unable to stop myself, I look over my shoulder. She's staring at the wall, but I know she's aware of my attention because her body tenses as my eyes run up the length of her.

"Here," I say, throwing my jersey at her. "This isn't over."

She opens her mouth to respond but doesn't say anything. Assuming she's done, I turn to leave. I'm halfway across her living area when her sob sounds out.

My fists clench, my nails digging into my palms, but I don't turn back. I might not know her all that well, but I do know that I wasn't meant to hear that.

The second I get in my car, I regret it.

15

CHELSEA

I shouldn't have let him go. I knew that the moment he stepped out of the room. I should have called him back, allowed him to spend some more time distracting me.

While he was here, I forgot about everything that happened today. For those few moments, I felt like me once again. Like I belonged somewhere, like someone wanted me.

I'm not stupid enough to believe it's the truth. He might have said it wasn't about revenge, but I'm sure he would have said anything in those few seconds before getting what he came for to make sure I agreed.

When I wake, my eyes are sore from crying once again and my muscles ache from our short time together, but that's not the most noticeable thing.

That's his scent.

It's everywhere and for the briefest of moments, I believe I dreamed that he left, I allow myself to believe he's still here with me.

But the second I open my eyes, it all comes crashing down. The bed beside me is empty, just like the rest of my pool house.

He left. He left after getting what he wanted. He's just like the rest of the guys on the team, only he's left more of a mark. He's the only one—other than Jake—that I've ever wanted more from, needed more from. Only he has no idea. Because just like the rest of the team, he just sees me as an easy piece of ass. I allowed him to have me and now he thinks it's his God-given right. He's probably enjoying that everyone else hates me. It means he's got no competition. I now really am a sure thing.

My chest aches as those short few moments from last night run through my mind. I don't want to think about it, but I can't stop. It's like my brain just wants to torture me.

I think about the gentleness of his touch, the way he played my body like he had a fucking map. The way he moved, the softness of his lips. None of those actions screamed revenge and hate fuck, but it couldn't have been anything else or he would still damn well be here.

Wouldn't he?

If he cared, he wouldn't just walk away. If it were anything more than a quick release, a way to prove to me that he has the power then he wouldn't have left.

You told him to, a little voice says, and I remember the exact words that fell from my lips as I dismissed him like he was nothing.

I cover my mouth with my hand, wanting to stop the sob from erupting.

What the hell was I thinking?

Sitting up, I discover the reason for his slightly overpowering and mind-spinning scent. I'm wearing his jersey.

I should have showered after he left, but I didn't have it in me. Instead, I pulled his shirt over my head and curled up in bed, willing my body to sleep to take me away from the memory of his touch. Only when it did claim me it was filled with vivid memories of him.

This is such a fucking mess.

Pushing from the bed, I set about getting myself ready for another shit show of a day at Rosewood High where I'm sure I'll be chewed out by Shelly and the squad and ignored by Shane like I'm nothing more than a piece of trash he threw away.

With a sigh, I pull his jersey over my head, but before dropping it to the laundry, I can't help but gather the fabric up to my nose and breathe him in.

I want to cling to the feelings that race around my body while I'm surrounded by him. The safety, the contentment, the belonging. But what's the point? They're all lies.

I'm sitting in English later that morning, my many regrets spinning around my head. I seem to be adding more to my already endless collection.

Will I ever make the right decision?

I was first in, much to our teacher's surprise. I'm not sure I've ever been early to class in my life, but right now it sure beats risking running into Shelly or anyone else in the school who wants me gone, which sadly is almost all of them.

She starts talking to me about what I've missed while I was gone after expressing her half-hearted delight at having me back. I half listen. I know I should be more interested in what she's telling me, but right now, as I wait for the rest of the class to appear and turn their hate stares on me, I really can't find it in me.

A few students start to file in, most of which I don't really know, although each and every one looks my way, even if for a very brief second.

I keep my head down, but it doesn't mean that I don't feel their stares or hear their constant whispers.

The class must be about half full when the atmosphere changes. I don't want to look, I already know the cause but I'm powerless but to lift my head.

The second I do, my eyes lock with his green ones. His face is blank and I have no idea what he's thinking or feeling. I hate it.

Does he regret last night? The lack of expression or care seems to hint at that.

My stomach knots. No matter how naïve, I was still hopeful things might be different this morning.

Dragging my eyes from Shane's, I focus on the guys standing behind him. Zayn's standing with his usual smirk playing on his lips as he looks between the two of us. Great, seems another person knows our secret. How long until the rest of the school finds out? Shane will be lynched for even talking to me, let alone touching me.

But it's not Zayn's amusement that really catches my attention because that's the furious eyes of their captain who's standing just behind Shane's shoulder.

I gasp at the darkness of the blue eyes I used to think I knew better than my own. His stare pins me to my chair and a shudder of fear runs down my spine.

Jake Thorn might be an asshole, but he'd never hurt me on purpose, of that I'm sure. But I hurt the one person who means more to him than anything else, and I know that I'm going to have to accept whatever consequences he has for me.

I know it won't make much difference, but my lips part anyway.

"I'm sorry," I mouth to him.

His lips purse in anger as his stare holds but it's only a few second later when our teacher barks at them for blocking the entrance and the three of them are forced to move.

He holds my stare until he's got no choice but to look toward his desk.

My stomach rolls and I worry that I'm going to end up running to the bathroom any minute. Thankfully, the rest of the class arrives, the teacher starts and I'm able to breathe through the nausea.

Regrets are horrible things. I hate that I hurt people that were my friends. I hate the way they look at me now with disappointment and anger laced through their features. But other than apologize, I have no idea how to fix everything I did. I know it was wrong. I know it was a massive mistake. I was just... I am... lost. I'm so desperate for those connections that I see everyone has around me. The friendships, the relationships. I've never had them. Never.

It should have been a natural thing with my mother, but she was too concerned about getting her next hit than she ever was about me. Honey and Derek are great, I love them in my own way, but they're not my real parents. I don't feel that natural bond with them. Our relationship has taken years to evolve to what it is now, and at times it wasn't easy, but together we found our way through. They have proved to me that people don't always let you down. They could have so easily given up on me over the years. Hell, I've given them enough reason to, but they've stood by me through every one of my mistakes and bad decisions.

I let out a sigh, wishing I had all the answers and that one day I won't feel like such an outcast. Everyone walks around the hallways here like they belong, like they've found their place, but even before all of this, I never felt at home. It's why I forced the relationships I did form. The girls in the squad needed to be friends with me if they wanted to keep their place, the football team accepted me because I had something to offer. Not one of them wanted me for me. I'm pretty sure no one has ever wanted me for me.

A smile curls at my lips as I think about the time I spent with Rae yesterday. Despite everything she'd heard about me in my absence, she genuinely seemed to want to spend time with me yesterday, genuinely seemed like she wanted to know the real me, not the bullshit Barbie doll persona I give everyone else. She saw the cracks, the dents and the broken parts of me that I keep locked inside, just like I did in her.

We'd be the most unlikely of friends, her with her goth look and me pining after my cheer uniform, but then I guess the connection that I've always craved runs deeper than our preferences and our style. Its strength comes from our fears, our nightmares, the things we keep hidden from the outside world.

As our teacher continues, I start to wonder how trustworthy she is. Could she be the one I confide in? Fuck knows I need to tell someone my secret.

The last thing I expected last night was Ethan and Rae to turn up to keep me company because they were concerned about me. Okay that's a lie, the last thing I expected was what happened after that, but I need to not think about him right now. It's bad enough that his stare is burning into the back of my head.

Ethan's words resonated with me. He's not usually one to be so wise, but I guess Rae must be having a good influence on him.

"You're Chelsea fucking Fierce. When have you ever sat back and allowed shit to happen around you? You want your old life back? Get out there and fucking take it."

He had a point. The only issue is that I'm not sure I'm that same person anymore.

My time away certainly gave me the opportunity to reflect. It gave me much more than that, and it changed my life in ways I'm not sure the counselors could even imagine.

I want my old life back. Well... I want my squad back. Everything else. The fake friendships, the bending over backward to keep my position at the top of the school and the bullshit that came with that, not so much.

I just want my team. My future. The rest is so up in the air right now.

I'm still lost in my thoughts when the bell rings. I make quick work of packing everything up and trying to get out of the room as soon as possible. I might be keen to make amends for all my wrongdoings, but I don't want to have it out with Jake in the middle of a classroom with an audience.

"Get out of my way," a familiar voice barks from behind me as I take a step from behind my desk. My shoulder gets banged and when I look up, I find one of my previously loyal cheerleaders pushing me out of the way so she can get past.

I want to say something, but I bite my tongue. Making a scene isn't going to help anyone right now.

I eventually manage to make it out of the room before Shane and Jake even get up from their desks, clearly neither of them have any desire to talk to me. Right now, that is fine by me. I just want to get through the day without any more scratches or bruises.

My next class is just a repeat of the previous one. Constant stares and gossip. I'm actually starting to get used to it in a weird way. The old me would have loved all the attention, it's a shame that the new me mostly just wants to hide in the closet until they're all bored with me.

I'm surrounded by students and heading toward the cafeteria for lunch when the chatter around me suddenly drops out. The second I look up, I know why. Shelly and her bitches are walking this way, and every set of eyes is drilling into me.

Blowing out a frustrated breath, I take a step to go down the stairs to escape them. I'm hungry and I really don't have the patience for their bullshit right now.

"You're supposed to be staying out of my way," Shelly spits, coming to a stop in front of me and placing her hands on her hips.

The hallway around us falls almost deadly silent as they wait for a repeat of yesterday's fight. I had no intention of partaking in that one, I really don't want to be standing here now.

"I'm not in your way. I'm just going for lunch."

"You're not welcome."

"I'm not welcome in the cafeteria? Fuck off, Shelly, no one made you God."

She takes a step forward, a scowl on her face.

"Careful, those lines will set and you'll need to beg daddy for some more Botox." She gasps, as do the rest of the squad, although I have no idea why, it's no secret that Shelly's looks aren't all natural.

"You bitch," she squeals, raising her hand, much like she did yesterday, and I move to avoid her. I forget that I'm standing at the top of the stairwell. That is until I place my foot down and there is no floor for it to land on.

"Fuck," I squeal a beat before I begin to fall.

My arm releases the books I was holding to my chest like a shield from Shelly, but I don't manage to find anything to stop myself.

The last thing I hear is a collective gasp as my back hit the wall before I was tumbling down the stairs.

I vaguely remember hitting people's legs, but I'd pick up so much speed that none of the hands that reach for me successfully stop me.

16

CHELSEA

The pounding of my head is the first thing I feel when I come back to myself. I wiggle my toes and then my fingers and breathe a sigh of relief. At least they still work.

"Chelsea?" a soft female voice says from beside me but I can't register who it belongs too.

A warm hand slips into mine and squeezes.

"Everything's okay. You're in the hospital."

"Should we get a doctor?"

I know that voice. The English accent is a dead giveaway.

"Amalie?" My voice is a rough whisper, but the shock is clear.

Dragging my eyes open, I have to blink a few times to make my vision clear, but when they do, there she is sitting at my bedside.

"What are you..."

"Doing here? I've been asking myself the same question to be honest."

"I'm..." I swallow and lick my lips. "I'm sorry."

She nods but I'm positive it's not to accept my apology more so just to prove she heard it.

"Here, have a drink." I turn to the sound of the other voice and find Rae.

A smile pulls at my lips despite the blinding pain in my head.

"T-thank you," I say once I've had a sip of the water. "W-what happened?"

"Shelly pushed you down the stairs."

I allow her words to run around my head for a second or two as I try to drag up my hazy memory of what happened today.

"N-no she did—fuck," I shout.

"What? What's wrong?" Rae is up off her chair, her eyes wide as she looks me over.

"Fuck, fuck, fuck," I chant, trying to push myself up to a sitting position. "What's wrong with me? What have the doctors said?" I ask in a rush.

"Nothing much, just that you had quite the hit to the head. Why, does something hurt?"

"No... um... I'm... fuck." I drop my head into my hands as both of them come in closer, intrigued by my freak out I'd imagine. "I'm pregnant," I mumble into my hands.

"What?" Amalie screeches in total disbelief.

"I need the doctor. I need to know. Fuck." I press my hand to my stomach, praying that Shelly hasn't just ruined the one good thing in my life. The one good thing to come out of all of this.

"Okay, yes. I'll go find her." Rae pulls the curtain back and runs from the room.

Amalie's attention stays on me. "You're not joking... are you?"

I shake my head. "No, I'm not. If I've lo—fuck. I can't. Fuck." My voice cracks and my chin trembles at the thought of losing this as well as everything else in my life.

To my utter disbelief, Amalie wraps her arm around my shoulder and holds me to her.

"I'm sure it'll be fine."

I want to agree, but all I feel right now is dread. I haven't even had the chance to fully accept my reality and it might already be over. No. No, it can't be. I need this. I need everything to be okay.

By the time Rae reappears with a kind looking doctor trailing behind her, I've got tears running down my cheeks faster than I can control.

"Good afternoon, Chelsea. I'm Dr. Francis. Your friend here tells me that you think you might be pregnant."

"There's no might. I am."

"Okay, we've done blood work but it hasn't come back from the lab yet. How far along do you think you are?"

"About eleven weeks."

I might not be looking at either Rae or Amalie, but I don't miss their chins dropping in shock.

"Okay. Have you had an ultrasound?"

I shake my head. I visited a doctor at the center who had set the ball rolling but I don't have a date or anything although I know it must be soon.

"Okay." She reaches for my hand and squeezes in support. "Do you have any abdominal pain, any reason to believe something may not be right?"

I focus on my body for a moment, but other than my head and a few aches and pains, nothing seems wrong.

"N-no, I don't think so."

"Right, let me go and make a call or two and I'll see what I can do to get an ultrasound machine brought in."

With a soft smile and a glance at my shocked audience, she disappears back through the curtain.

"You're pregnant?"

Rae asks as if she needs to hear me say it again just to believe it.

"Yeah, but no one knows. I haven't even told my parents. You're the only ones."

"Jesus, Chelsea. You really know how to bring the drama don't you?"

"It wasn't meant to happen."

"For the love of God, please tell me that it's not Jake's." I'm not sure if she's asking that as a joke or not, but as I look at Amalie, I see a flicker of fear in her eyes.

"Of course it's not. That boy hasn't looked at me twice since you turned up."

"G-good. That's good." She lowers herself back to the chair, deep in thought.

"So whose is it?" Rae asks.

I shake my head. "Now's really not the time. Plus, I have a feeling he's not going to want anything to do with it."

"You haven't told him?"

"Not yet."

I was intending on telling my parents when I first got back from the center. But they were so happy to have me home and hopefully in a more positive place that I didn't have it in me to confess.

I know they're going to be disappointed in me. I see the way they look at me when I've been out partying. They're not stupid, they know the things we all get up to, and I've always promised Mom that I'd be sensible. I had a future, a cheer career to think of. Having this kind of accident certainly wasn't part of my plan.

"I-I know that I have no right to ask anything of you," I say directly to Amalie. "But I'd really appreciate it if you kept this to yourself."

She blows out a breath. Her eyes leaving mine for a beat. "You're right. I don't owe you anything. I should go straight back to Rosewood and shout through the PA system." Every muscle in my body locks up at the thought. "But I won't. That's not the kind of person I am."

"Okay," the doctor sings, reappearing with a machine and another woman who I unfortunately recognize behind her. "Let's see what's going on then, shall we? This is—"

"We already know each other," the other lady says, and I just about manage to stifle a groan. "Nice to see you, Chelsea."

"You too," I say tightly, staring at the older version of the person who put me in this place. Shelly might not have actually pushed me, but she was the catalyst for this whole disaster.

Of all the people, the woman who turns up to do my first ultrasound has to be Shelly's mom. I have no fucking chance of keeping this secret now.

The doctor pulls the sheet from me and I discover that I'm still in my skirt and top that I put on this morning.

"If you could lift your top and lower your waistband a little. I'll get this all set up."

"Would you like some privacy?" Dr. Francis asks, nodding to Rae and Amalie.

"N-no. They can stay if they like."

Smiling, Rae moves closer to my side and takes my hand in hers. Amalie remains standing somewhat awkwardly at the end of the bed.

"I'm going to squeeze some gel on your tummy and we'll have a little look."

The gel is warmer than I'm expecting, and in only seconds a plastic wand thing is being pressed against my skin.

Shelly's mom tilts her head this way and that as she stares at the screen I can't see while tapping away at a few buttons.

My heart pounds in my chest and my hands begin to sweat, not knowing which way this is going to go.

"Right, Chelsea." She turns the screen to me and a fuzzy black and white image flickers on the screen. "Everything looks good. Can you see that there?" She points at a little blob in the middle of the screen. "That's your baby."

A sob erupts from my throat. "It's okay?"

"Yes, everything looks good. All the measurements line up with your eleven-week prediction. Congratulations, I guess."

"Oh my god." Tears pool in my eyes as I stare at my baby. My baby.

It's surreal.

I knew this day was coming. I knew I'd get to see it, but it's utterly mind-blowing.

"I can't believe you're growing a person," Rae mutters, equally as mesmerized by the screen.

"Trust me. I know."

"Would you like a printout?"

"Yes, please."

Sadly, Shelly's mom removes the wand from my stomach and the image of my baby disappears from the screen. I miss it almost immediately. It's the weirdest feeling that has me on the verge of a breakdown.

The doctor hands me some tissue to wipe my belly and before long I'm being handed a strip of paper with a range of images of my baby on it.

"Are we all okay here?" Shelly's mom asks before wheeling the machine out and leaving us to it. I don't see her go, I'm too fascinated by the images before me to even consider warning her about not saying anything.

"Your parents are in the waiting room. They're getting a little frantic," Dr. Francis says with a wince.

"We'll go and leave you to talk to your parents," Rae says.

"Uh... okay."

Fear fills my veins at the thought of admitting all of this to them. They're going to be so disappointed in me.

Just before Amalie and Rae pull the curtain back to leave, I call out.

"Amalie?"

She looks back over her shoulder at me, but she doesn't say anything.

"I really am sorry."

She nods, her eyes softening as she accepts it before they both continue through the curtain.

I'm alone, left alone with my own thoughts for all of three minutes. The entire time I have the ultrasound images grasped tightly in my hand.

Everything is okay. She didn't ruin the only bit of positive in my life.

"Chelsea, thank god you are okay. Principal Hartmann said you'd been pushed down the stairs, what on earth..." Mom comes rushing over and carefully pulls me in for a hug.

"I'm okay. And she didn't actually push me. I thought she was going to." I gesture to my face that she has yet to notice, seeing as I hid in the pool house from the second I got in from school last night.

"Jesus, Chelsea. Shelly did that?"

"I had it coming. I thought she was going to do it again, I stepped back and, well... here I am." I shrug, playing it down. Yes, my head throbs, but I'm okay. We're okay.

"You might want to sit down though. I've got something I need to tell you both."

Mom pulls back and looks at me suspiciously.

"I'm okay, I promise. It's just that..." I trail off until they're both in the chairs beside my bed. "I'm pregnant."

If I weren't so terrified by their reaction then the cartoon wide eyes and dropped chins might be amusing but as it is the sight only tightens the knot of dread sitting heavy in my stomach.

"Y-you're pregnant. Like... having a baby pregnant?" Mom asks in total disbelief.

"Yes. I'm so sorry. I should have told you sooner, but I was scared."

"You're having a baby now?"

"What? No, no. Not yet. Here." I reluctantly release my ultrasound pictures and allow her to look at them.

"Oh my god," she gasps, her own eyes getting a little wet.

"How far along?"

"Eleven weeks."

They're both silent as they stare at the images, and I sit nervously for the anger to come once the shock has worn off.

"How long have you known?"

"Quite a while."

"And you've kept it secret all this time? Even in the center?"

"Well, I saw a doctor, but yeah."

"Oh, Chelsea," Mom says, standing back up and pulling me into a hug. She sobs on my shoulder and although I hate that I've made her cry, I'm just glad neither of them are shouting at me. "You should have told us."

I look between the two of them, not missing that Dad is yet to say anything about this. "I was—I am—terrified."

"Oh, sweetie. You don't need to be scared of us. You know we'll support you no matter what." Mom runs her hand gently over my hair and a lump forms in my throat.

"I-I really want this baby, Mom. I want..." I blow out a breath, trying not to break down. "I want something of my own, you know. I didn't plan it. I was too focused on my future to even consider it. But now it's happened... I wouldn't have it any other way."

"I know, baby. I know." Mom holds me tighter as she cries.

She had a baby when she was not that much older than I am now. I remember the day she told me about it, the joy as she talked about discovering that she was pregnant was clear in her eyes all these years later. Despite her parents' opinion about things, she was excited about what her future held but sadly, it wasn't meant to be and the baby was born with a genetic disorder and died before he was six months old. She's never been able to conceive again.

I know that it's something that rips her apart to this day. She and Dad have always been desperate to have their own kids. But thankfully they decided to give back and started fostering kids about ten years before they were lucky enough to find me standing at their front door.

To this day, I've got no idea what it was about me that made them decide to go through all the legal stuff and adopt me unlike all the others they'd cared for, but I can't really argue because they've given me everything I was missing in my former years.

When Dad does speak his voice is so loud compared to the soft sound of Mom's sobs that it startles me.

"Who... um... who's the father."

"Derek," Mom chastises. "That's not the most important thing right now. When she's ready, I'm sure she'll tell us," Mom says, squeezing my hand and thankfully giving me a way out of this conversation. "Everything is okay with the baby though, yeah?"

"It seems that way."

She takes my hand and sits on the bed beside me.

"I know I probably should be mad, you are still in high school after all, but I think this could well be the best thing that's ever happened to you."

Dad looks at her like she's just grown an extra head, whereas all I do is smile because I can't help but agree.

"I know things are scary and unknown right now. But I do know that you are going to be a fantastic mother. I do wish you'd told us sooner, just so we could have supported you. But I need you to know how proud I am of you."

She smiles at me and I look from her kind eyes to my dad's. He doesn't seem quite so thrilled by this turn of events, but they both know me well enough to know that when I set my mind to something that nothing is going to stop me.

"What about college? Cheer? The scholarship you were so desperate for?" he asks, always the voice of reason.

"Oh Derek, give her a break."

"I'm just curious."

"I'll figure it all out. Everything happens for a reason, right, Dad?" I lift a brow and wait for him to agree.

"I guess," he mutters, but we all know he believes the words. He's said them himself enough times over the years.

17

SHANE

"What the fuck is going on?" I ask Zayn as we make our way toward the cafeteria for lunch. The kids around us are buzzing with something. Excited chatter and gossip get louder and louder.

"She pushed her right down. It was brutal."

"She fell top to bottom like a rag doll."

"No one knows if she's alive."

What the actual fuck?

I may be clueless, but it doesn't stop a trickle of dread from running down my spine. After yesterday's public fight, my imagination is running on overdrive right now.

"I have no clue but it sounds dramatic whatever it is," Zayn mutters.

We're almost at the cafeteria when the crowd in front of us parts and Principal Hartmann appears along with three other teachers all frog-marching Shelly, Krissy, and Aria, down the hallway.

Something uncomfortable sits heavy in my stomach as realization starts to hit. There really is only one person those students could have been talking about.

"Chelsea," I mutter to myself before running for the cafeteria to find some answers.

I have to fight my way through the crowds that seem to have appeared out of nowhere to watch Shelly, but in seconds I'm through and running toward someone who'll know.

"Cami, what's happened?"

"That," she says, glancing over her shoulder. "Fuck knows. Some cheer slut drama probably. I don't have time for that bullshit."

I purse my lips. I want to shout at her that that bullshit she's talking about could very well mean something to me, but I can't.

Instead I force out, "Yeah you're probably right."

"Shane." Spinning on my heel, I find Zayn talking to Ruby and Harley. Ruby blushes bright red just looking at him, whereas Harley looks bored by having to stand in her brother's vicinity. "Go on," Zayn encourages once I join them.

Harley rolls her eyes in frustration before turning to me. "Shelly pushed Chelsea down the stairs."

"What? Is she okay?" I ask in a rush, probably looking like I care too much, but I really don't give a shit right now.

"I have no idea. She's been taken to the hospital."

I'm out of the school building before I've even realized I've moved. My need to get to her is all-consuming, but the second I turn the engine on, I freeze.

There's a very good chance she won't want me there. She's shown me time and time again that she doesn't care, that she doesn't want me, and I keep running back like a sad little puppy.

My grip on the wheel tightens until my knuckles turn white. I need to go there. I need to know she's okay.

"Motherfucker," I bark, slamming my palm down on the wheel and resting my head back.

My head spins as it screams at me to get out of the car and continue with my day as if nothing's happened.

It's what she would want.

But what about what I want? What I need?

"Fuck it."

I put the car in drive and speed out of the school parking lot. Only, when I get to the turn for the hospital, I don't take it.

My head's too fucked-up after last night and everything else that's happened in the past few weeks.

I just need it all to stop.

I breathe a sigh of relief when I find our driveway empty. The last thing I need right now is another lecture from my dad.

Thankfully, I managed to sneak back into the house last night without him spotting me. I didn't need a rehash of our previous conversation. Nothing he can say to me can change my mind. I don't care about the fame, the success, the money. Professional football and the NFL will not make me happy. The pressure he puts on me for high school football is bad enough. I watch what he's like with my brothers. He's relentless in his need for them to be the best. It's exhausting.

I blow through the house, not stopping as I descend the stairs to the basement and Dad's home gym. I hate being in it but needs must and all that.

Pulling my hoodie and shirt off, I drop them to the bench before coming to a stop in front of what I really need.

The punching bag.

I run my fingers over the smooth black leather before pulling my other arm back and plowing my fists into it over and over.

I didn't bother wrapping them, so after only a couple of hits, they split open.

I punch over and over, taking everything out on the bag. I picture my dad and all his bullshit demands, Chelsea and the way she repeatedly keeps turning me away. I'd never hit a woman, but Shelly's face pops into my head as I throw another. How fucking dare she lay her hands on Chelsea. Who the fuck does she think she is? She's already taken away her captaincy and enjoys rubbing it in her face. Isn't that enough?

My hair sticks to my forehead, my chest heaves with exertion as I fight through the pain of my exhausted muscles to continue. But no matter how many times my fists connect with the leather, it's not enough.

The door opens behind me and breaks through my angry haze. I throw one more punch at the bag before turning to find the inevitable. My furious father because I'm not at school where I should be. But to my surprise, when I turn around, I find Luca staring back at me.

"What are you doing here?"

"I left a textbook in my room. More importantly, why are you here? Shouldn't you be in class?"

"Fuck off," I grunt, turning my back on him and giving the punching bag my attention once again.

"You need a partner to take that out on?"

By the time I look over my shoulder, he's dropped his bags and pulled his shirt over his head.

He stands a few feet in front of me and puts his fists up, ready to fight.

"I'm not fighting you," I mutter, taking a step back. We might have fought many times over the years but I'm not taking this out on him.

"Yeah you are," he taunts, coming closer and jabbing me in the shoulder. "So what's wrong? Dad riding your ass about the NFL again?"

"When isn't he?"

I move around him to get some space, but he's not having it and follows, continuing to taunt me.

"So if it's not Dad then it can only be one other thing."

"Oh yeah, what's the...?" I ask, better his arm away when he starts to hit me harder.

"A girl."

"Luca, will you just leave me the fuck alone?"

"No can do, brother. You need to get this out and I'm offering it to you. Plus, I could use a good workout and seeing as your fists are already busted up, I stand a pretty good chance of winning."

I don't point out that he always wins. He's bigger and stronger than me. Both of them are which is why they're better at the game.

Wiping my face with my discarded shirt, I turn back to him.

"It's her, isn't it?"

"Who?" I bark.

"Chelsea," he practically sings her name in delight and it reawakens my anger once again. "Don't think I don't see it, little brother. You've pined after her for years."

"What does it matter? She's only ever had eyes for greater things. You..." I roll my eyes. "Jake fucking Thorn." I regret my admission the second his lips twitch in achievement. "Oh, just fuck off back to college."

"So what? You think you're not good enough for her, is that it?" Luca's fist connects with my cheek but it's not a punch, more a tap to get me worked up and make me fight back. "It's what Dad says, right? You need to push hard, play harder, work harder if you're going to make it. He wants it for you, but he doesn't really think you can do it."

Fury races through my veins. I know he's just saying it to rile me up, but fuck if it's not working.

"And as for Chelsea, she wants a winner, Shane. Someone she can be proud of. Someone she can show off to make her feel better about herself. That's not you, is it?"

"Motherfucker." I fly at him, but not before I see the smirk on his face.

My fist connects with his jaw and his head snaps to the side before he comes back at me.

"That's better, little brother. Let it out. Show me how you really feel."

He pushes me back, but I don't let it put me off.

Fists fly, bodies connect and unlike when I hit the bag, I actually get some relief from the stress that's been pulling at my muscles.

"Fuck, fuck," I say, stumbling back from him after a few minutes. I'm dripping in sweat and my body is aching.

I'm fairly sure he didn't hit me with everything he's capable of, but still, it hurts.

I fall down onto the bench a second before a bottle of water is thrust in my face.

"Drink."

"Who are you, my fucking father?"

"No, thank fuck."

He drops down beside me, equally out of breath as he rests his elbows on his knees and sucks in a few deep breaths.

"You've got better, faster. I'll give you that."

"Fuck you."

He chuckles. "Nah, save it for Chels."

"That's not–"

"Cut the bullshit, Shane. You're fucking good enough for her and you know it. You want her? Take her. You want the NFL? Have at it, you're good enough. You want to be a fucking ballet dancer? Go for it. What I said earlier was bullshit and you know it. Don't listen to that asshole, nothing you ever do will be good enough for him, it's just something that you need to accept. But you don't need to be good enough for him. You just need to be good enough for you."

I sit back and let his words sink in.

"Chelsea's a good girl, Shane. But it's no secret that she's been screwed up by her past. She's... complex. And just like you, she doesn't feel like she's good enough. You manage to see beneath the mask she wears, you know the vulnerable girl that's beneath. The one that hardly anyone else sees. She's not as strong as she makes out but she won't accept it. She'll fight until the bitter end, until she gets what she wants. Rightly or wrongly.

"You want her. You're gonna have to fucking fight too, bro. Because she won't drop those walls easily."

"Fucking hell, Luc. How did Mr. Fuck 'em and Chuck 'em get so wise when it comes to women?"

"I'm not fucking wise. I just know her. And you're wrong. She never wanted me. She just wanted me to want her. She's lost, Shane. The question is, are you strong enough to help find her?"

I blow out a breath, not even knowing where to start with all of that information he's just unloaded on me.

"I need to get out of here. Dad'll bust my ass if he finds me here. You too. I suggest you get washed up and disappear. Maybe go and visit that girl that's got you all tied up in knots."

"The new cheer captain pushed her down the stairs today."

"She fucking what?" he booms, anger rolling through him in an instant. "Is she okay?"

I shrug. "I have no idea. She was taken to the hospital."

"And you're here fighting with me because..."

"Because I have no idea what to do. She keeps sending me away. She doesn't want me."

"And you're going to allow that? She needs you. Be there." He collects his stuff and looks over his shoulder at me before he disappears. "Call me if you need anything, yeah?"

"Thanks, man. Sorry about your eye," I say, nodding to where it's starting to swell.

"Nah, the girls will love it. They get all kinds of wet for a bad boy."

"Fucking hell. Go. Please, just go."

I'm still shaking my head when the door slams behind him. He might be a fucking idiot, but he's kinda got a point.

Collecting any of the evidence I was here, I take myself up to my room for a shower. I can hardly walk into the hospital with my knuckles in the state they're in now.

Turning the shower on, I avoid looking at myself in the mirror. Luca might not have gone full force on me, but that doesn't mean I can't feel myself bruising from his hits.

My hands sting like a bitch when the hot water hits them. Gritting my teeth, I stare down as the water washes the blood away.

Scrubbing them down my face, I make quick work of washing myself before getting ready to go and find out what happened to Chelsea.

The drive to the hospital is quick and as I park, I can't help regretting not just coming here first. Although I think I needed that time with Luca more than I'm willing to admit.

With a sigh, I push open the door and head toward the ER. I have no idea if that's where she'll be or if she's even still here, but it seems like the best place to start.

I've barely walked through the doors when I see two people I wasn't expecting heading my way.

"Hey, what are you doing here?" I ask Amalie and Rae when they come to a stop in front of me.

"We came with Chelsea. Did you hear what happened?"

"Yeah, Shelly pushed her down the stairs or something."

"She said that Shelly didn't actually push her, but whatever happened, Chelsea ended up at the bottom unconscious."

"I-is she okay?"

The two of them share a look and dread twists in my stomach.

"Yeah, just a bang to the head. She'll be back to her usual delightful self in a few days, I'm sure," Amalie says with a roll of her eyes.

"I'm surprised you helped," I say.

"What was I supposed to do? Feed her to the wolves so they could have another go? Shelly is taking it a bit far now, even if she didn't push her."

"We should go. Ethan and Jake are going to be waiting." Thoughts of school and missing practice with the guys should concern me, but now I know she's here, my need to see her has only increased. "Why are you here anyway? Shouldn't you be with the team?"

"Oh yeah, I... uh... I've got an appointment," I lie, badly.

"In the ER?"

"No, I'm cutting through."

They both eye me curiously, but when I take a step forward, they both stand aside and let me pass.

"I'll see you tomorrow," I say, waving them off and disappearing into the building, grateful that they can't see me walk straight up to the reception desk.

"Um... hi," I say when the woman eventually looks up from her computer. "I'm looking for Chelsea Fierce."

"And you are?"

"I'm... um... her boyfriend?" I cringe as I say the word, and I can't help that it comes out like a question.

"Her parents are with her. You're more than welcome to go through as long as it's only you. Or you can wait." She points with her pen to the chairs behind me and I look over my shoulder.

"I'll wait, thank you. Wouldn't want to overwhelm her if she's not feeling great." Plus, the last thing I need is a grilling from Honey and Derek.

I find a seat in the corner but where I can keep an eye on the exit.

Pulling my cell from my pocket I open my Snapchat notifications. My eyes almost pop out when I find images and videos of Chelsea as she tumbled down the stairs and was left helpless at the bottom.

What the fuck is wrong with people?

I end up waiting so long that I begin to wonder if I missed her parents leaving, but only a few minutes later I spot them emerging from the ER doors. Derek pulls his crying wife into his side as they move toward the entrance.

My heart is heavy as I stand and make my way through the doors.

I have no idea what I'm going to find on the other side, and my pulse begins to race as I get closer to where I know she is.

18

CHELSEA

W hen the painkillers I've been given start to kick in, my parents say their goodbyes so that I can rest. The doctor reappeared while Mom sat holding my hand and explained that although everything looked perfectly fine that they wanted to keep me overnight just to keep an eye on me.

I hated the idea of a night in the hospital, but I could hardly argue. I had just had a flight down a set of stairs.

My arms ache where I must have hit them, my hip smarts when I shift in the bed but it's my head that is still throbbing and if I look around the room too fast, it starts to spin. Maybe a night here where I know I'll be looked after should anything go wrong won't be so bad.

I place my hand to my belly, feeling like a huge weight has been lifted now that people know about my little secret.

I hadn't even registered that my period was late while I was in the center. It wasn't until I'd been there three weeks and realized that I hadn't had one for ages that I started to panic. Turns out I was right to because when I did the test, it almost immediately turned positive.

I panicked for about two minutes as I sat there on the closed toilet seat, but as I thought about it, I soon realized that it might not be such a bad thing. Yeah, I was young, I'd only celebrated my eighteenth birthday the week before, but I knew I could do it. I could be a mom. I might not be able to look after myself at the best of times but even in those few moments, I knew that I loved the small person growing inside me more than anything.

I'd lived through hell as a child. I could be a better mother than the one I was forced upon. I could give a child a better start in life than that bitch gave me.

Hell, I've already done a better job seeing as no drugs or alcohol have passed my lips since I found out. I'm sure that's more than she could have said during any of her pregnancy with me.

I have no idea how much time has passed before I come back to again. The sound of people milling around outside the curtain fills my ears. It's so loud at times I wonder how I slept through it, or the pain that's still pounding away in my head.

Knowing that it was the pain that woke me, I reach out to find the buzzer for the doctor to see if I can get some more Tylenol. When I don't immediately find it resting on my pillow where I left it, I drag my eyes open to look for it.

"Fucking hell," I gasp, not expecting to find someone staring at me. "You're turning into a stalker," I snap, my heart racing in fright.

His eyes burn into mine. There's an intensity within them that makes me panic.

Fuck. Does he know?

My heart races so fast that my head begins to spin.

I quickly locate the call button and press my finger on it.

My stomach turns like I might be about to puke and my mouth waters.

"Are you okay? Can I get you anything?" He sits forward in the chair and reaches for my hand.

My entire body locks up. I can't do this. Not now and certainly not here.

"No, and you shouldn't be here."

"W-what?" he asks, his eyes widening in shock.

"Shane." I suck in a breath and focus on the curtain in front of me. If I so much as look at him, I'll break and I can't afford for that to happen. "What I need is for you to leave."

"That's bullshit and you know it," he says, getting closer but I hold my nerve despite the scent of him filling my nose and begging me to turn to his green eyes that I know are going to be dark like when he's hungry or well... hungry.

I blow out a shaky breath and pray that he doesn't notice.

"Thank you for coming to check on me. As you can see, I'm fine, but I need you to leave."

His entire body tenses before he moves even closer. The heat of his breath hits my cheek and my traitorous body shudders with his proximity.

"This is the last time you're going to get to send me away, Chelsea." His voice is low and angry, and it has a ball of emotion crawling up my throat. "You make me walk out now and I'm not coming back. Ever. I've tried to be nice, to reach out to you when others dismissed you, but you've turned me away every time. Well, this is it." He holds his arms out. "You tell me to go now and we're done."

Every single part of me wants to break down and tell him to stay, to be honest about everything and be brave. But I can't. I'm terrified that he won't want me. Won't want us. And I can't allow that to happen. I've been rejected over and over my whole life. That needs to stop now, so I'll send him away before he gets the chance.

I might have wanted to see him when I first came back but he's proved to me that anything between us wouldn't be a good idea. I've got to focus on me right now, not everyone else. I've got something more precious to look after.

My fists clench, my nails digging into my palms as I try to muster up the strength to say the word I need to.

"G-go."

An unamused laugh falls from him as he takes a huge step back from the bed.

"You know, I thought you were different from what they all said. I thought it was all an act. I thought that beneath it all you were different. That you didn't mean to hurt people, that all that shit was just you being hugely misguided, but it seems that I'm the idiot because they're all right, aren't they? You really are just a bitch who doesn't care about anyone but herself." At those words, my eyes search his out. I regret it instantly because the green is darker than I've ever seen and they're full of unshed tears.

Fuck.

"Whatever this was. It's done. Goodbye, Chelsea."

Without a second glance in my direction, he disappears through the curtain. I swallow the sob that erupts from my throat because I need to know he's gone before I fall apart.

Curling in on myself. I wrap my arms around my belly and cry. "I'm sorry, I'm so sorry," I whisper to my baby. "It's for the best, I promise."

It's not until the next afternoon that I'm finally discharged and able to leave the hospital. Everything is still fine and finally they've got the pain in my head to subside a little.

Mom insists on holding on to me all the way out to the car as if I'm going to drop to the floor any moment. She tried to get me to sit in a wheelchair. I wasn't having any of that. Everything is fine, I'm just a little sore with a bump to the head, there's no need for the mollycoddling.

"We've got your room all ready for you," she says once I'm settled in the back of the car and she's in the front beside Dad.

"I'm fine to go back to the pool house."

"Nonsense. We need to keep an eye on you for a few days at least."

I catch Dad's eyes in the mirror and they crinkle at the edges. I know it's his way of begging me just to comply to make both our lives easier.

I do, but mostly because I'm too exhausted to do anything but.

I spent what felt like all of last night crying after sending Shane away and with the constant noise of the ER outside the curtain, I got hardly any sleep. I would prefer to hide in my pool house, but to be honest, any comfortable bed in a quiet room would be hard to refuse right now.

The ride home is tense. I know it's because they're both worried about me and what my plans are now that college is clearly out of the question but they seem to both be avoiding bringing it up, which really is fine by me because I don't have any answers.

The second we get home, I'm escorted up to my old bedroom and told to get in bed. I do because I'm exhausted, but I really don't need Mom fussing around me like I'm about to break any moment.

"Mom, I'm really okay. You don't need to do any of this."

"I know. I just want to make sure you're comfortable."

"I just hit my head."

"Chelsea," she sighs. "Someone pushed you down the stairs."

"She didn't push me and the second I'm back at school I'll tell Hartmann that. I'm not exactly innocent here. I brought all this crap on myself. I've just got to see it through. Everyone will get bored with me eventually and move on to someone else."

"Do you really believe that?"

I shrug. If I don't believe it then what hope do I have?

"You're not stupid, Chelsea. All of this might blow over, but then what? You'll turn up at school one day no longer able to hide your secret and you'll be hot gossip again."

"What are you suggesting here, Mom?"

"I... I don't know. I just hate that you're going through all this."

"It's fine. It's karma."

She opens her mouth to argue once again. She might be fully aware of my misdemeanors, but that doesn't stop her from trying to defend me. It's admirable, but I'd rather she just call a spade a spade. I was wrong. I hurt people that I should have cared about, and I'm just learning my lesson. They're fighting back, and rightly so. It might be misplaced because the people who should hate me, Amalie, Mason, S-Shane—I can't even think his name without getting emotional—seem to be fine. It's those who are fighting for their honor, like Shelly, who seem to have the biggest issue.

"Any chance we could get takeout pizza for dinner?" I ask, attempting to change the subject.

"Of course. Anything you want." She sits on the edge of my bed. "How have you been, you know, with the pregnancy? Any morning sickness or cravings or anything? Is there anything you need? Prenatal vitamins?"

I smile at her enthusiasm. Why I was ever scared to tell her I don't know. I should have known she'd be nothing but supportive.

"I've felt a little nauseous but nothing much. I've been a bit off food to be honest, although I wake up in the night starving some days. I've got all the vitamins I need. Thank you." I take her hand and squeeze it in both of mine. "Thank you for being okay with this."

"Oh, Chelsea. Sometimes things in life are out of our control. We just have to trust that someone up there has our best interest at heart." She glances out the window. Over the years, Mom's battled with her faith. She really wants to believe there's something out there, but then she'll remember all the hard times and it'll make her question everything. She was brought up in a religious household and I know she feels guilty for questioning her parents' beliefs and the way she was brought up. I just hope she finds the answers she craves one day.

"It's crazy," I say, dropping my hand to my belly. "But it feels right. I know everything about it is far from perfect, but it just feels... right," I repeat, unable to explain it any better. Once the shock wore off, something within me settled. I've got something that's mine. Something that's going to rely on me and look at me like I'm the most important person in the world. Something to give me purpose, a reason for being. It already fills me with more joy than anything in my previous eighteen years.

"I understand. Being pregnant is a wonderful gift and a beautiful thing. I'm so glad you've shared it with me. Anything you need, all you need to do is ask. I'll leave you to get some sleep." She drops a kiss to my cheek and leaves the room, closing the door behind her.

Climbing out of bed, I find my purse that Dad dropped to the chair when we first got in here and I dig out my ultrasound pictures. I lay in bed just staring at them for the longest time before sleep eventually claims me.

Everything in my life might be all kinds of fucked-up right now but I've got my little one. Everything will be okay.

When I wake again, it's to a gentle knock on the door.

"Sweetie, are you awake? You've got a visitor." Mom pokes her head around the door as I pull myself up to sit against the headboard.

My first thought is that it's Shane and hope swells in my chest that he's ignored my words once again and is going to fight for me. But the second she stands aside and I spot a pair of fishnet-clad legs behind her, I know it was wishful thinking. After what I said, I have no reason to think he'll ever speak to me again. Although, I guess he's going to have to because at some point we're going to have to have a serious conversation.

"Hey, how are you feeling?" Rae asks, walking into the room with a box of donuts in hand.

"All the better for seeing those."

"I'm glad I could be of assistance."

"We were going to order pizza for dinner. Would you like to stay, Rae?" Mom asks.

Rae looks to me and I nod at both of them.

"That would be great, thank you, Mrs. Fi—"

"It's Honey," Mom says with a smile.

Rae walks into the room but waits until Mom has shut the door behind her before she drops down onto the end of my bed and places the box between us.

"So..." she starts. "You're pregnant."

"Can I at least get some sugar in me before you start on the hard stuff?"

She laughs, pulling the lid off and giving me first choice.

I fight a moan of delight when the sweetness explodes on my tongue. It's a million times better than the crap they gave me in the hospital.

"You can come again," I mumble around a mouthful.

"You might change your mind in a minute, I want all the details. Tell me everything. How did it happen?"

It doesn't escape me that we only met on Monday and yet this feels like the most natural conversation I've ever had with another girl despite the fact I really don't want to talk about this.

"Well, I spent the night with this guy. Now, I don't know what you do with Ethan but he stuck his pen—" One of the cushions that was on the bed gently hits me in the shoulder.

"That wasn't what I meant. I don't need all the ins and outs." We're both silent for a beat before we simultaneously bursts out laughing.

Tears fill my eyes and joy fills my heart. I can't remember the last time I laughed like this, and it feels so incredibly good.

Once the giggles subside, a silence falls around us and Rae blows out a breath. "I might be way off the mark here but..." I look up at her, my breath catching as I wait for whatever it is that she thinks she's figured out. "It's Shane's, isn't it?"

I gasp in shock. I barely know this girl, we've spent no more than a few hours together, how has she figured this out?

"Um... how... um... what makes you say that?" I ask, trying and failing to sound like she hasn't just knocked my world off-balance.

"There was just something he said while you were away that stuck with me. Then I saw his reaction to you on Friday night. He was meant to be focused on the game, but at every opportunity, his eyes searched you out." My heart starts to race. Surely, she must have been imagining things. "Then we saw him at the hospital. He made up some bullshit excuse about having an appointment. I think Amalie might have fallen for it, but I saw right through his lie. He came to see you, didn't he?"

I swallow nervously as I try to come up with any words to answer her.

"Y-yes." I hold her eyes as she absorbs that one simple word. Mine fill with tears whereas hers brighten with accomplishment. "You don't need to look so pleased with yourself."

"When I was a kid, I used to imagine what it might be like to be a detective."

"Well, congrats, Sherlock. You seem to have this case all figured out," I mutter, reaching out for another donut just to give me something to do instead of stew on the admission I just made.

"Fucking hell, it's really Shane? I thought the idea was a little left field, but... fuck."

I shrug, what is there to say.

"He's..." She trails off, trying to find the right words. "He's different from the rest of the guys. He seems more... sensible, thoughtful, kind."

A lump forms in my throat and tears sting the back of my eyes, desperate to be released.

"H-he is. He's a really great guy, actually. Just... don't tell anyone I told you that." I laugh, but it's far from the joyous one that fell from my lips not so long ago.

"But you've still not told him?"

I shake my head. "I can't. What if he doesn't want us?"

19

SHANE

"Here, drink this," Zayn says, shoving a bottle into my hand.

"Doesn't Ethan have anything stronger?"

I'm in a bitch of a mood. Have been since she sent me away from the hospital like a fucking spare part on Tuesday evening.

By the time I go home, Dad had somehow discovered that I'd skipped school and ripped me a new one, claiming that I had no idea how good I had it and that I should appreciate everything he's given to me. As per usual, there was no mention of anyone other than him. I have no idea how Mom puts up with his bullshit. Anyone overhearing would think he was a fucking single dad who had to do everything alone. Truth of it is that he was absent for most of my childhood while he swanned around the country chasing fame and fortune. Mom was the one to bring me up, he just supplied the money in an attempt to make up for his absence.

Asshole.

"Vodka?" Zayn asks.

"Yes." Reaching out, I take it from his hand instead of the beer.

I'm not in the mood for a party but Zayn insisted that I show my face and at least attempt to enjoy myself while drowning my sorrows with the copious amounts of alcohol Mr. Savage always supplies for Ethan's parties.

"Cheer up," he says, falling down beside me. "So she blew you off? There's plenty of other pussy here tonight to distract you."

"Who said she blew me off?"

"Uh... have you seen your face?" I'm assuming he doesn't mean the bruises that Luca left behind.

"Fuck off," I grunt, twisting the lid of the bottle and lifting it to my lips.

The vodka burns as I swallow a shot, but I welcome it. It's better than the ache in my chest that's been consuming all my thoughts since I walked away from her.

Part of me thinks I should have fought, should have stood my ground and made her hear me out for once, but then another part of me thinks it's probably for the best. If she's not interested now, then why should I bother?

Zayn falls into conversation with Justin who's sitting beside him and they both ignore me as Ethan's house fills with more and more kids ready to see in the weekend in style.

The music is turned up in the other room and the rest of the team descends on the couches. As is usual these days, Jake, Mason, and Ethan are absent, probably too busy with their girls to bother with us. I get it. I'd rather hang with my girl—if I had one—than these assholes given the chance.

All of a sudden Zayn stops talking mid-sentence and stands, totally ignoring whatever he and Justin were discussing.

"Ruby, baby. You are looking fine tonight." His eyes drop down her body and I roll mine at him before glancing over my shoulder.

She's wearing the smallest red dress that I think I've ever seen. No wonder Zayn's eyes look like they might pop out.

He stalks toward her but stops abruptly when two others walk into the room.

"Harley, what the fuck are you wearing?" he asks, turning to his sister who's dressed similarly to Ruby.

"So it's okay for you to eye fuck my friend but I can't possibly show any skin?"

"It's not the same, Ruby is..."

Ruby, Harley, and Poppy's eyes rise as they wait to find out how Zayn's going to dig himself out of this hole. He looks between the three of them.

"She's not my sister."

"Nor is Poppy, but I doubt you'd look at her like you just did Ruby."

"Ew no, why would I look at her like that?" He curls his lip up in disgust as he turns to Jake's cousin.

"You're a pig. Come on, let's go and get a drink."

"But—" Ruby complains as Harley slips her arm through hers and drags her away from her brother.

"No buts. You don't want to touch him with a barge pole. He's probably diseased by the number of skanks he's touched." Ruby blushes red. It seems she hasn't confessed about her time with Zayn last weekend.

The three of them disappear, but Ruby doesn't lose Zayn's attention until she's slipped around the corner.

"Fucking Harley," he mutters, dropping down onto the couch. "Things were easier when Mom refused to let her attend."

"She just needs someone to distract her," Justin suggests. "I can offer my services." He wiggles his eyebrows and Zayn's shoulders visibly tense.

"Don't even think about touching her, asshole. Anyone goes near my sister and I cut your balls off and feed them to you, got it?" he barks.

A couple of the team nod in agreement, but most just roll their eyes at him. I'm not sure why he's bothering, he knows full well that most of these assholes don't do as they're told. Ever. If one of them sets their sights on Harley, then they'll fucking have her, I've no doubt.

Conversation turns to college applications and I almost walk off when someone asks me if I've made a decision about which team I want to play for when our missing captain and team members join us with their girls.

"Ah, about time the captain showed his face," Zayn shouts, earning him the finger from Jake.

"What the fuck is she doing here?" Justin barks and when I look to the doorway, I find Chelsea standing with Rae.

Good question. What the fuck is she doing here?

She's not dressed like I'm used to. Instead of the barely-there outfits she used to select for this kind of party, she's wearing a decent length skirt and a shirt that covers almost everything she used to show off to get attention.

She looks good. Too fucking good and it has desire that I shouldn't feel filling my veins.

She hovers by the door as Rae tries to talk her into joining us.

"Come on, Chels. What's wrong? Forgotten how to make us compliant?" someone calls. My teeth grind as I think about them all having detailed knowledge of her body.

Her eyes lock with whoever said it for a beat. Before she rolls them and looks around the room. She visibly flinches the second she finds me. Her lips part and she takes a step back. Rae reaches for her but the second she looks at me, she seems to understand.

Great. If someone knows then no doubt everyone will before long. I'll just be another idiot who's fallen for Chelsea's charm and beauty.

She whispers something to Rae before backing out of the room.

I swear I don't breathe until she's gone from my sight.

"Okay, you two need to sort whatever that was out," Zayn whispers to me once everyone is distracted.

"Nah. We're done."

"Really?" he asks, quirking an eyebrow.

"Yeah. She's expressed her true feelings. Time to move on." I sit forward, resting my elbows on my knees and glance around at the girls littering the room, most of whom are on the cheer squad and totally out of the question. I've been burned once by one of them, I'm going nowhere near another.

There is one who's noticeably absent though. Shelly hasn't been seen since being marched to the Principal's office on Tuesday. It turns out that she was already on Hartmann's shit list and he suspended her. With her gone and Chelsea at home recovering, it's been a quiet few days for Rosewood High which is unusual to say the least.

"Right, we need to set tonight's challenge," Zayn announces. Jake, Mason and Ethan all excuse themselves, not needing any kind of challenge to make sure they get laid tonight, leaving the rest of us waiting to hear what he's got to say. "Our little tagging game is fun and all, but how about we up the ante?"

"Go on," Justin says, leaning forward, intrigue filling his eyes. A few of the other guys follow the move. I, however, stay exactly where I am knowing that I won't be getting involved, just like every other time they've done this shit.

I have no intention of hooking up with a girl just for bragging rights. It's not really my style.

"Fuck the tags, let's make this a dare."

"Ohhhhh," someone says as more and more of the guys listen in to Zayn's plan.

"We name the girls, you must get some kind of evidence that you succeed or…"

"Or?" Rich asks.

"Or… winter formal is just around the corner." Zayn rubs at his chin in thought. "I'm sure none of you want the public humiliation that could come with failing."

Shaking my head, I entertain myself with my bottle of vodka while Zayn starts dishing out names.

"Shane," he barks, turning to me. His eyes twinkling with delight.

"Oh no, not a fucking chance, man."

"Oh, I don't know. I think you might like this particular challenge," he whispers so only I can hear. I quirk a brow at him, wondering if he's going where I think he is with this.

I take another shot of vodka. The strength of the alcohol no longer burning my throat, but it's having the exact effect I needed it to on the rest of my body.

"Go on then," I taunt, leaning forward much like the others did. I don't look to the guys, but I feel their eyes on me. They're used to me running away from these challenges, so I understand why they'd be surprised.

Zayn smiles, and excitement explodes in my belly. "Chelsea."

A couple of the guys gasp and a few laugh. "Oh fuck off, Shane isn't going to go for that," Rich barks.

"Well, there's no point in him being the only member of the team she's not been with." My lips purse in anger and I fight to stop my reaction from showing on my face.

"Fine," I say, much to their surprise. "What?" I ask when a few of them question me. "A dare is a dare, right?"

I take another shot and sit back, ideas forming in my head faster than they should as Zayn rattles off a few more names.

"Happy?" he says, turning to me once everyone has their target for the night.

"Yet to be determined," I say, pushing from the couch and walking away.

"Don't forget the evidence." I flip him off over my shoulder and head for the kitchen in search of Chelsea.

It takes me longer than I'd like to find her, but the second I step foot into Ethan's den, I know she's there. I feel her.

Looking to my right, I find her curled up into the opposite corner of the couch to where Rae and Ethan are. Jake and Amalie are on another, along with Mason and Camila, who are making out on a beanbag.

"Everyone out," I bark, successfully earning everyone's attention.

I lift the bottle again as all eyes turn on me.

Ethan barks out a laugh like it's the most ludicrous thing he's ever heard.

"What was that, Dunn?"

"I said," I repeat with a roll of my eyes. "Everyone. Out." Taking a step forward, I lock my eyes on Chelsea's. She swallows nervously as she sits motionless on the couch. "Except you. Chelsea and I need to have a little chat. Don't we, Chels."

"Oh my god," Amalie gasps from behind me. I know this is a little out of character for me. But the girl brings out the crazy in me, that plus the alcohol that's currently racing through my veins.

"I don't think so," Ethan says, standing in front of me and blocking my view of her.

We stand chest to chest, nose to nose. Ethan's not the kind of guy I'd go up against willingly. My brothers might have taught me to fight fairly well, but I have no reason to believe that he wouldn't squash me like a fly should he wish.

"I-it's okay, Ethan." Her soft voice fills the room before her slender hand wraps around his upper arm.

I want to rip it away. She shouldn't get to touch him with such familiarity. Red hot jealousy burns through me that every guy I know has had a taste of what I want.

Glancing to my left, I find Jake staring between the two of us. There's no love lost between him and Chelsea these days, but he was the one she pined after for all that time and he was the one who got her first. He always gets what he wants.

After a beat, Ethan stands down and allows Rae to pull him from the room, although it's not before she whispers a warning in my ear.

"Hurt her and I'll hurt you."

If it had come from any other five-foot nothing girl, I might not bat an eyelid, but Rae is kinda scary. I nod at her, although I don't take my eyes from Chelsea's.

They all leave the room, and soon the door is closed behind them, leaving the two of us alone with the tension crackling between us.

The silence is heavy as our connection holds. My heart races as I try to come up with the words I need to say to her, but being this close, and this drunk, all I can think about is kissing her.

"What?" she barks after a few long, quiet seconds. "What do you want?"

I take a step closer, running my eyes down her body. "I think you know what I want."

"And I think you know my opinion on that."

I lift the bottle to my lips before offering it to her. She pushes it away, refusing my gesture.

"How much have you had?"

"Enough," I say, placing in on the coffee table and taking another step toward her.

"So I see. I'm almost impressed that you had the balls to kick Ethan out of his own den."

"Almost impressed. Wow. I wonder what I'd have to do to really impress you," I tease, stalking toward her until she has to start backing up.

"To leave. I don't know how many times I need to—" Her words are cut off with a gasp as her back connects with the wall. "Shane?" Her voice is barely a whimper, I might be concerned if it weren't for the fact her eyes drop to my lips.

"Careful, Chelsea, that almost sounded needy," I warn.

The heat of her body burns against my skin, but I don't touch her. Not yet.

"No, I-I don't want you. You need to—"

"Is that right? So your heart isn't racing right now?" I ask, knowing full well that it's pounding just like my own. I can tell by the fast movement of her chest. Her breath catches at my words as I look down at her breasts. "And your nipples..." I reach out a finger and very gently tease around one. "They're not hard and desperate for my touch?"

"Fuck you, Shane," she spits, but she's only angry because she knows I'm right.

My eyes find hers once again. Excitement fills me at the fire I see shining in hers. It's been diminished more than not recently, and I hate it. There might be things that Chelsea has done that are less than desirable, but her passion, her desire. Fuck, it brings me to my fucking knees.

"That was kind of the idea, baby," I say, my cheek brushing against her so I can whisper it in her ear. She shudders and I can't help but smile.

She turns to me, and I pull back to meet her eyes, too intrigued to find out what she's about to say no to.

"Why me, Shane?"

A laugh falls from my lips. I wish I had the answer to that question. I could be going after any girl right now, but she's the only one I want, the only one I can think about even when I beg for my mind to stop.

"I have no idea."

"You've got a thing about being second best, don't you?"

"W-what?" I stutter.

"You're always the little brother, the one who's never quite good enough, always watching your big brother's get what they want while standing on the sidelines."

Anger swirls in my belly, filling my veins with red hot fury. This is the thing about Chelsea. She knows me better than anyone because she's been in my life just that long, not that she'd ever admit it. We're closer than anyone imagines. "That's not true," I argue, and she quirks a brow at me.

"No? And with me? You're once again picking up sloppy seconds, and Jake's no less. The guy you've had to follow for as long as you can remember."

"Enough," I bark, my fingers gripping her jaw, my eyes staring down into hers.

"Why? Can't handle the truth?" Our stare holds, anger, desire, passion crackling between us. "Cat got your tongue, Shane? I thought you were here to rip me a new one."

"No. You're wrong."

"Oh?"

"I came here to prove you wrong."

"About what?"

"About what you want."

"Wha—" I assume she's going to ask what I'm talking about, but she doesn't get the chance because I make the most of her parted lips and press mine to them.

She stills to start with and we stand with just our lips connected but then it's like someone flips her switch and her hands come up to tangle in my hair and I lean forward, pressing her body into the wall.

My tongue sweeps into her mouth and hers eagerly joins in. My hands run up her sides and slip into the fabric of her t-shirt. I skim up her soft skin until I find the swell of her breasts. Her head falls back, banging against the wall as I squeeze, and I panic. A moment of reality through my drunken, angry haze.

"Y-your head. Are you okay?" The healing scratch marks the only visible reminder of what she's been through this week.

Her fingers tighten in my hair and she moves my head so I have no choice but to look at her.

"Don't do that."

"Don't do what?"

"Pretend that you care. That this is anything more than what it is."

I want to argue, to tell her that this is way more than she's willing to accept, but the words die on my tongue as I remember exactly why I searched her out in the first place.

The challenge. The dare.

Hurt her like she repeatedly does you and prove that she wants more than she'll admit.

With a nod to myself, I pull my cell from my pocket. She huffs in impatience, but I don't stop. I won't film it, I wouldn't do that to her. But there were no rules. Pulling up the microphone, I press play and place it on the dresser beside us.

"Okay, fine," I say, turning my attention back on her. Her eyes are dark with desire, her lips already swollen from my kiss. My cock strains against the fabric of my pants, desperate to be inside her once more. My hands drop to her thighs and after pushing her skirt up around her waist, I lift her.

"Oh god," she squeals as my fingers dig into the skin of her thighs.

"You don't want me to care? You want rough. I'll give you whatever you need, baby."

"Oh fuck, Shane," she squeals, as I lift her higher and press my lips to her neck.

Her thighs clamp around me as I run my tongue up her sweet skin. She shudders, her fingers once again diving for my hair.

I bite, suck and kiss hard enough that there's going to be no forgetting I was here the second it's over.

She might like to keep pretending that there's nothing here, that she doesn't want me, but we both know it's a lie.

When we're together like this. It's like nothing else exists. It's just us and it's fucking explosive.

Lifting the fabric of her shirt up her belly, she helps me out by pulling it off and dropping it to the floor as I drop my lips to the swell of her breast.

I smile in delight when I find the front fastener and make quick work of undoing it so her tits spill out.

"Shane, Shane, please," she chants above me as I kiss and lick everywhere but where she needs me.

"You don't want this remember?" I remind her.

"Fuck you, Shane," she groans, trying to direct me with my hair.

"All in good time. I want to hear you admit it first."

"Admit what?"

"That you want me. This. That you made a mistake every time you sent me away."

I lick up the underside of her breast and allow my nose to brush over her peak. She gasps as the sensation races through her. But the stubborn bitch still resists.

"No. I just want this."

"You just want me for sex?"

"Yes. Now please. Give me what I need."

"Why not one of the others? I'm sure they'd be up for it."

"No," she cries as my teeth sink into the softness of her breast.

I look up at her as I suck and lick at the bite. Her eyes are black, her cheeks red with desire.

"No, I don't want..."

"Go on. You don't want...?"

"I don't want any of them, okay?"

"So, say it. Say those three little words and I'll give you what you need."

My tongue brushes the very tip of her nipple and her eyes shutter with pleasure.

"Fuck," she barks. "I want you, okay. I fucking want you. Argh," she screams when my lips wrap around her tip and I suck her deep into my mouth.

Her heels dig into my ass, her nails scratch at my scalp as her back arches against the wall, giving all of herself to me.

Her chests heaves and my name leaves her lips with her cries of pleasure as I switch to the other side.

Just when I think it might be taking her too close to the edge, I drop her back to the ground.

"What the fuck are you doing?" she asks when I take a step back.

Rubbing at my jaw, I run my eyes down the length of her. Her neck, chest, and breasts are covered in my bite and suck marks, my cock weeps as I take in the sight. Her skirt is bunched around her waist, exposing her tiny black panties.

Shaking my head, I push my hair away from my face, pulling my shirt over my head and drop to my knees before her.

Sucking her bottom lip into her mouth, she watches me with heat filling her eyes.

Reaching forward, I wrap my fingers around the sides of her panties and pull until they come away from her body.

"Shane, fuck." Her eyes widen in shock as I ball up the lace and shove it deep in my pocket.

"For later, then you inevitably send me away." I'm only half-joking. I have no intention of sleeping with them under my pillow or anything fucking crazy but I'm not against a little memento of tonight, alongside the recording of course.

Tapping against the inside of her thigh, she widens her stance for me, giving me just enough space to lean forward and find her clit with my tongue.

Her taste explodes in my mouth, making my head spin with my need to sink inside her. I could do that right now, hell knows she's ready, but I'm not okay with this being over too quickly. I already know that it'll never be long enough.

Her fingers return to my hair as I lift her leg over my shoulder to give me more access.

I'm a little more confident this time, helped by my recent experience but more so the vodka. Just like that first night, my inhibitions are a hell of a lot lower than usual.

Parting her lips, I suck on her clit as she chants above me. My fingers find her soaked entrance and I groan in delight as I slide them into her slick channel.

"Oh god," she moans as the vibrations of my low groan rumbles through her and she only gets wetter.

I lap at her and my fingers increase speed inside her. The one leg she's standing on begins to tremble as her pussy begins to clamp down on my digits.

As much as I want her to come like this, I won't allow it. There's no way I'm risking giving her what she needs only for her to walk out without looking back once again.

Just as I sense she's on the brink of falling over the edge, I pull back and wipe my mouth with the back of my hand.

"What the fuck are you doing?" she barks as she realizes that I've stopped and drags her head from where it was resting back against the wall.

"Changed my mind," I say with a shrug.

"You fucking what?"

Falling down onto the couch, I stretch my legs out in front of me. The bulge of my hard cock obvious beneath the fabric of my pants.

"If it's good enough for you, then it's good enough for me, baby."

"I've never left you like that."

"As good as every time you send me away."

"No. No, that's nothing like—"

"Say it again," I demand.

"Say wha—oh." She places her hands on her hips. She's still totally on display for me to enjoy despite the patch of skin around her waist that's covered by her skirt.

"Say. It. Tell me you want me."

Her lips purse and her teeth grind.

"Tell me that you feel this. This thing between us when we're together."

"It's just sex, Shane."

"Is it? So it was like this with all of them, was it?"

Something passes across her face but she covers it before I get a chance to attempt to make it out.

She opens her mouth to respond but no words come out. I already knew I was right, but that's all the confirmation I need to know that this thing isn't one-sided. She feels it too.

"Strip."

20

CHELSEA

"Strip."

It's hardly the demand of the century, seeing as I'm basically standing here naked anyway.

I make quick work of undoing the button around my waist and shimmying the fabric down my legs.

Shane watches my every move, his eyes almost black with desire.

I stare at him resting back on the couch like he doesn't have a care in the world, but I know that's far from the truth. The darkening bruises around his eye and jaw, and his cut lip are just the beginning.

I really thought after I sent him away from the hospital that it would be the end of us. I know that Shane is nicer than most guys, that he's already given me one too many chances to admit that I want him but I really didn't think he'd come back for more once again.

He's drunk, a little voice in my head says, and as if he can read my mind, he leans forward for the bottle he abandoned not so long ago.

He swallows down a couple of mouthfuls like it's water, only I know from the slight slur of his voice and the confidence in his touch that it's not.

I really fucking want some. But I can't. Not that he offers me any.

"So now what? I told you what you wanted to hear." Although, we both know I didn't. I might have said I wanted him in that moment but there is so much left unsaid between us. I should have told him the truth a few moments ago when he asked about this being like me with the others.

He has no idea that really, there aren't any others. Just like everyone else at

Rosewood High, he has me marked as some kind of whore who puts out to everyone who shows any kind of interest, only it's not quite the truth.

"Show me. Show me what all the others rave about. I think I've forgotten the last time, maybe you're not that good after all."

He places the bottle on the floor after opening his fly temptingly.

I should walk away from what he's insinuating, but I know I've only got myself to blame. It may not be as bad as he thinks, but I can't lie, I've touched one too many of his teammates in the past. Those I haven't are happy enough to brag along with the others making out like they know. I should have set them straight the first time someone claimed to have had me on my knees, but I couldn't. Fucked-up, I know, but they were talking about me like I was something, like they cared and had a reason to keep me around. Like I said, fucked-up. But it is what it is.

I expect him to push his pants down, but he never does. He just keeps his eyes on me, daring me to give him what he needs.

"I should walk out right now," I say, although my body betrays me and takes me a step closer to him.

"Go on then. I'm getting used to seeing your back."

I hate this side of him. The angry at the world persona he's playing to try to hurt me like I have him. But as much as I might hate it and crave the sweet guy that I know he really is, I can't help but be turned on. Something inside me just can't resist that hint of a bad boy that I suspect only I've had the pleasure of witnessing.

I think back to him ripping my panties from my body not so long ago and a wave of desire washes through me. Who knew he had it in him?

"I never back away from a challenge, Shane. You want to play games, then you've chosen the wrong opponent if you want to win."

He swallows as he takes in my body as I close the space between us.

Once I'm right in front of him, I place my hands on the back of the couch on either side of his head.

He stares up at me, his eyes dark and his chest heaving.

"What are you waiting for? You owe me."

I can't really argue with that. I owe him a hell of a lot more than a blowjob though after all the bullshit I caused him.

"Oh yeah. What exactly do I owe you?"

"Everything. Now..." He shoves his thumbs into the waistband of his boxers and pushes.

"Stop," I demand, making his eyes widen in shock.

Backing away from him, I drop to my knees.

The sight of me before him has the vein in his neck pulsating.

"Allow me, I *owe you* after all."

His lips part to respond, but no words come out as I wrap my own fingers around the fabric and tug.

He lifts his hips to help and I pull his pants and boxers over his ass and down his thighs. His already hard cock rests against his stomach and I can't help but bite down on my bottom lip at the thought of taking him in my mouth again. He wasn't wrong with what he said earlier, it's been so long I have almost forgotten.

Once he's free of his pants, I discard the fabric on the floor and push his legs wider so I can settle between them.

I drop my lips to the side of his knee and slowly kiss up his thigh. His fingers slide into my hair as his impatience starts to get the better of him, but I refuse to be rushed.

Leaning forward, he reaches for the bottle of vodka he left on the floor and lifts it to his lips.

"Want some?" he offers this time.

I shake my head.

"Your loss." He drains the bottle before throwing it to the other side of the couch and resting back.

He stares down at me, his impatience obvious in his eyes as I continue teasing him.

"Chels," he moans as I scratch my nails down his abs. "I need—"

"I know what you need, Shane."

His hands tighten in my hair, leaving me little choice but to look up at him. His eyes are still dark with desire but there's more there now. His usual softness has returned.

"No, I really don't think you do."

A lump forms in my throat and tears burn the backs of my eyes as our connection holds. Damn pregnancy hormones. I desperately want to believe that there could be something between us, but it would be dangerous to even allow a little bit of hope in. He doesn't want me. He can't, not after everything. There's a reason why no one knows about this situation we keep finding ourselves in. I'm his dirty little secret. One that he's happy to enjoy behind closed doors, but is probably ashamed to admit to the outside world. I'm not the kind of girl guys like Shane deserve. He should have a nice girl on his arm. Not one with a tarnished reputation who everyone hates.

Needing to break whatever weird connection has developed, I do the only thing I know that will distract him. I lean forward and lick up the length of him. His cock pulsates beneath my gentle touch, his hips lift as he seeks more and his fingers tighten until his grip is almost too painful to bear.

"Fuck, Chelsea."

Spurred on by his words and reaction to my simple touch, I wrap my fingers around him and lick around the head of his cock.

He groans, the noise at the back of his throat reawakening my own lost pleasure from earlier.

Parting my lips, I suck him as deep as he'll go, loving the growl that rumbles up his throat.

Glancing up at him, I find his head resting back on the couch, his blond hair is a mess after having my hands in it not so long ago, his eyes are shut, his cheeks flushed and his lips parted.

I run my eyes down his body, taking in his chest and cut abs. Fuck, I want to run my tongue over every indentation. I want to be able to take my time, to enjoy this thing between us not just have stolen moments full of anger and hate as we battle against each other and what we really feel.

"Fuck, fuck," he chants when I lift my hand and cup his balls.

His length swells between my lips and I know he's almost at the end.

I suck him once more before releasing him with a pop and standing.

"What the fuck?" His head lifts, his eyes wide in shock.

He must realize my intention the second he sees the smirk on my lips.

Tit for tat, baby. You leave me hanging, then you can expect the exact same treatment in return.

"You set the rules, baby," I say in a sickly-sweet voice that I usually reserve for hooking up with the assholes he plays with. "Not my fault if you can't handle the consequences."

I step back, but he's quicker than I give him credit for. His fingers find mine and I'm pulled toward him with such force that I have no choice but to fall into his lap.

"Going somewhere?" he asks, his eyes glittering with amusement.

"Yeah, leaving."

"Not this time. I'm not finished with you. And for once... I'm calling the shots."

I stare at him, enjoying his more dominant side.

In seconds he's moved me so that I'm sitting astride his lap and his large hands wrap around my waist, holding me in place.

"Go on then, I think we've both waited long enough."

Reaching down, I grasp him. His eyelids lower at the sensation and I delight in the fact that even now, I hold all the power. It's how I need it to be. I need to be the one who can call the shots in an attempt to protect myself.

The moment I have us lined up, I sink down and watch as the muscles in Shane's neck strain with pleasure. His jaw pops as I drop lower and his fingertips dig into my skin.

"Fuck," he barks once I'm fully seated.

His eyes hold mine and I lift slowly and drop back down.

"Fucking hell, Chelsea," he groans, suddenly sounding much more sober.

"What?" I ask, confused by the change in him.

"It's not supposed to be like this." His voice is low and almost a whisper, and I lift once again.

"Like what?"

"This fucking good. This fucking addictive."

I fall silent, but I fear my feelings about what he just said are written all over my face. He's right. It shouldn't be like this.

It was supposed to be one night of distraction. It wasn't supposed to turn into needing each other quite like this. It wasn't supposed to turn into this toxic thing that I can't help craving as much as I hate it.

Unable to look at the honesty in his eyes, I drop my head to the crook of his neck and push all thoughts aside as I ride him.

His hands help me move, but it's not long until his need for release has his hips pistoning up into me.

My fingers curl around the back of the couch and my nails dig in as I race toward my own orgasm.

"Fuck, Chelsea, fuck."

Sitting up straight, I throw my head back and cry his name as my body crashes over the edge.

Only seconds later, he pulls me down against his body, and with his face tucked in my neck, he stills as he growls out his release, his cock twitching deep inside me and igniting some of my own aftershocks.

His increased breaths tickle across my heated skin as he comes down from his high.

Knowing that I need to move, that our time together is over, I push away from him but his arms lock around me, holding me in place.

"Shane?" I question, needing him to release me before I start allowing myself to believe there could be more here.

"Just need a minute. That was…" He trails off.

"Yeah," I agree. What else is there to say? It was pretty incredible. Almost enough to make me believe that there could be something between us.

"Chelsea?" he asks, a weird emotion filling his voice that I can't place.

"Yeah?" I whisper, enjoying being in his arms a little too much.

His fingers thread into my hair and hold me in place as he moves his lips to my ear.

"That was a dare," he whispers.

For a second, the words don't register. But the moment they do, my entire body tenses in his hold.

Allowing me to move, his arms drop from around me and I sit up.

He's got a smug as fuck grin on his face as his eyes bounce between mine.

Something hot explodes inside me as I stare back. "You're a fucking asshole. You're no better than any of them, you know that?"

"Can't beat them, join them," he says with a shrug.

"Fucking prick." I climb off him, hating that him slipping from inside me feels so good it's almost a distraction from reality.

"You feel better now that you got one over on me? You win, Shane. You fucking win."

I tug my clothes on while he remains motionless on the couch. I don't look at him, I don't dare look to see that smirk again because I know how much it's going to piss me off.

I don't even have the energy to say anything as I blow through the door. I slam it as hard as I can behind me as I run from the house.

I didn't want to fucking be here in the first place, but knowing I was almost as good as new, Rae insisted I attempt to rejoin the world and Mom couldn't do much but agree. She couldn't keep me locked up in that bedroom forever.

I keep my head down as I push through the students all enjoying their Friday night. Seeing as I'm now the social pariah, hardly anyone even glances my way as I make my way to the front door.

Thankfully, Rae is nowhere to be seen or I know I'd never make it out. Thankfully, I do because by the time I dig inside my purse for my car keys, tears are streaming down my cheeks.

"You motherfucker," I scream, slamming my hands down on the steering wheel in an attempt to get some of my anger out.

I was the one warning him not to play games, that he'd be the one to lose. How fucking wrong was I?

He's supposed to be the nice one. The sweet one. Yet he just played me at my own game. Although I'm not sure it was ever my game to begin with.

It's not until I'm halfway home that I realize the car behind me has been trailing me since leaving Ethan's house.

My heart races knowing that he's followed me and is driving drunk. I have no idea if I'm angrier at the thought of having to see him once again or that he's put himself in danger. I'm tempted to say it's the latter, but I push it aside, not wanting to deal with how I really feel about him.

It's dark so I can't really make out the car other than its bright as fuck headlights, but it makes every single turn I do, even to the point of signaling a turn on the street I live on.

My fingers tighten on the wheel and my heart pounds in my chest. I'm tempted to lock myself in the car for fear of getting out and having to deal with him again. But after blowing out a breath, I find some balls, turn off the ignition and push the door open.

The car is still there, idling by the sidewalk, but now I'm able to see it, I realize it's a truck and not one I recognize.

I take a step toward it to see who the driver is, but before I get a chance to see inside, it speeds off.

Weird.

Telling myself it's just someone from school trying to freak me out, most likely Shelly. I shake my head and walk to the house. I'm desperate to go to my pool house but all my stuff is in my old bedroom. That's all going to be changing tomorrow. No matter what my parents think, I'm perfectly fine and I'm going back to my little haven to get away from the world.

Thankfully, the house is in silence, so after grabbing myself a bottle of water, I head up to my room.

I walk over to the window to close the curtains but a set of lights outside once again catches my eye. Fear trickles through me, but I push it aside. Plenty of people hate me now, it could easily be any number of them as they watched me flee from Ethan's.

21

SHANE

The second the words are out of my mouth, I regret them.

It's the reason I sit there and watch her dress without saying a word. She should walk out after learning what I'd done.

I'm no better than her. Playing games to win points.

I wanted to prove that she wanted me. I guess I achieved that. She told me as much. So why doesn't it give me any sense of achievement? *Because you hurt her, asshole,* a little voice says in my head.

"Fuck," I bark into the quiet room. The bass of the music pounding through the walls tells me that the party is still going strong outside. Thankfully, everyone knows the rule that if Ethan's den door is shut then no one enters.

Pushing myself from the couch, I sway a little as I get to my feet, proving just how much I've had to drink already. Sadly, it's not enough to help me forget that look in her eyes as realization hit her.

I'm such a fucking asshole. Yeah, she's pulled some dickhead moves in the past, but she didn't deserve that.

She's wrong. I'm not one of *them.* They walk around taking whatever they think they deserve, much like my dad. I am not like them.

I pull my clothes on with the intention of getting out of here. A huge part of me wants to find her and tell her that it was a mistake, tell her how I really feel but I know she wouldn't accept it, it would be pointless and probably lead to us doing something else we'll regret.

"Shane, my man. Where've you been, bro?"

"Busy," I grunt at Zayn as both him and Justin wrap their arms around my shoulders.

"Oh, getting busy with Chelsea?" His eyes light up as my entire body tenses. "You know we need evidence, right? Your word alone won't stand tonight."

"Not that it ever would. There's no way you'd get a shot with Chelsea," Justin slurs.

They navigate me toward the kitchen where some of the team are still loitering with drinks in their hand.

I grab a beer from the counter as we pass before falling down onto the same couch I was on before all this shit kicked off.

"So..." Justin prompts, causing everyone to turn to look at me. "Shane thinks he's completed his challenge."

"I didn't say that," I argue.

"You didn't need to, man. So come on, let's see the evidence. Give these assholes something to aim for."

Her panties burn in my pocket and the recording on my cell taunts me. But I don't move to grab either.

"I don't have any."

"No proof means it didn't happen, and if it didn't happen, then you lose."

Getting more and more frustrated with these douchebags, I push from the couch.

"I don't give a fuck. Do your worst," I say, lifting my hands from my sides. "Some things are more important than your fucking bullshit games. How about you stop playing for just a moment and find something more meaningful in your fucking lives."

I don't hang around to hear their response, I storm from the room and toward the front door.

Sadly, I don't make it that far before I'm collared.

"Shane, what happened to Chelsea? I can't find her."

Rae's concerned eyes stare up into mine. "I have no idea."

Her eyes narrow in frustration. "What did you do?"

I want to fire back at her that Chelsea deserves whatever comes her way, but I think we'd both know it would be a lie.

"Something I regret," I admit quietly.

"Jesus. You two are a fucking nightmare."

"And you need to keep your nose out. You have no idea what's happened between us, you've only heard her side of the story, I assume."

"I'm pretty sure I understand fairly well. I know she fucked up, but people make mistakes, Shane. Much like tonight." She lifts a knowing brow. "So how about you put all of that aside and do the right thing."

"I have no idea what that is," I admit.

"Well you'd better fucking figure it out before it's too late."

She spins on her heels and marches away from me, her cell in her hand, I assume calling Chelsea.

I double back on myself, grab a bottle of whatever I can find on the kitchen counter before finally leaving the house.

Ethan's place is almost on the beach so in only minutes, me and my new friend Jack find ourselves on the sand and watching the waves crash onto the beach.

The stars twinkle above in the inky black sky and I wonder what it would be like to lay here with Chelsea beside me. All the bullshit banished and to just be us.

Could there be an us, or are we toxic to even consider?

I don't drag my ass from the beach until the sun is beginning to rise. I don't want to go home, I know it'll only end up in an inevitable argument with my dad.

With a sigh, I walk that way. What I really want to do is go to Chelsea. But even in my drunken state, I know that's a really fucking bad idea.

The house is in darkness, and I breathe a sigh of relief. It wouldn't be unusual for Dad to be up working through the night. Hell knows he's caught the three of us sneaking in before now.

I make it to the stairs before I realize someone else is awake. Light comes from the basement and footsteps head my way.

"What fucking time do you call this?" Dad barks. He's wearing only a pair of shorts with a towel hanging around his neck.

"Too fucking early for you to be working out. Be fucking normal for once in your life and sleep."

His eyes widen in shock. "You've been drinking." It's a statement, not a question, so I don't bother answering it. "What the fuck is wrong with you? Skipping school, getting drunk, staying out all night. This isn't you, Shane, and this kind of behavior isn't going to help get you into—"

"Don't fucking say it," I bark, knowing exactly what's about to fall from his lips.

"No coach is going to want a fuckup, Shane."

"So, what about Luca and Leon? Did you give them this kind of shit every time they threw a party and got so drunk everyone trashed the house?" I already know the answer, he had the place cleaned up and ignored it ever happened. "What about when they used to sneak in late every weekend? Did you accuse them of fucking everything up? No, of course you fucking didn't because they can do no fucking wrong. Your fucking golden boys who hang on your every word. It's fucking pathetic."

"That's enough," he barks. "I will not accept this kind of behavior from you."

"What, suddenly acting like this is unacceptable? Unbelievable. You're a fucking joke, you know that?"

"Shane, that's enough," Mom's soft voice calls from down the stairs.

Dad and I stand in our silent stare off for a few more seconds before I dismiss him with a lift of my chin and head up the stairs.

"What's happened?" Mom asks as I pass her at the top of the stairs. It's obvious that we've woken her.

"Nothing. Go back to bed."

"Shane, what—"

"I said it's nothing."

This time she lets me go and the second I'm in my room I fall face-first on the bed and pass out.

By the time I wake the next morning, the sun has long risen and it's so late that I've got a ton of missed calls from Zayn telling me that I missed our morning workout. It's probably for the best, he would have spent the entire time grilling me over what happened last night. He's the only one out of the guys who'll believe me without the evidence they apparently require.

I might have set up that recording last night, but I don't know why I bothered, I was never going to allow anyone to hear it. This thing between me and Chelsea is just that, between us. It's our fucked-up, messy, toxic little secret.

My head throbs as I drag my body to the bathroom to freshen up in the hope I'll feel a little more human once again.

I'm more than happy to spend the day hidden in my room, stepping out means I'll probably have to see someone and deal with the regrets and memories from the night before.

I think about the argument with Dad, that's one thing I don't regret. It's about time someone stood up to him, I just never really thought it would be me. I recall my time with Chelsea and the ache that's been in my chest since she walked out only gets more persistent.

I shake my head. After our first time together, I told myself that I'd be able to just forget her, and I did to a point. I sat back and watched her be her usual self at school afterward when all I wanted was for her to look my way and give me even a hint that she remembered our time together, that it meant anything to her like it did me.

Then the truth came out, and I wanted to look at her once again for a very different reason. I wanted to tell her what I really thought of her. I wanted to accuse her of setting me up, of using me as a scapegoat and not giving two fucks.

But she disappeared, and everything changed once again. Yes, I still wanted to rip her a new one, but concern soon overtook. It was stupid, I knew that. I shouldn't have been concerned after everything but somehow she'd wiggled her way under my skin and no matter how hard I tried, I couldn't get her out.

My need for coffee and food eventually cause me to leave the safety of my bedroom. Thankfully, when I get down to the kitchen, it's only Mom who's sitting with a cup of coffee and her tablet.

"Afternoon," she says with a smile. "How are you feeling?"

"Better than I should," I mutter, thinking of the vodka and whiskey mix from last night.

"Your dad's out of town for a few days."

"Great," I grunt, pulling a bag of chips from the cupboard and throwing a couple into my mouth.

"I know he gives you a hard time, but it's only because he cares."

"Oh yeah, that's why." I roll my eyes at her.

"Baby," she starts with a sigh, but I hold my hand up to stop her.

"Can we not? I'm too hungover to talk about him."

"Sure." She falls silent as she watches me crash around in the kitchen, making a sandwich and my much-needed coffee.

After a few minutes, I fall down beside her.

"What's wrong?" she asks.

"Other than what we're not talking about, I assume?"

"Yeah. What's eating you? I have no problem with you going out and partying with your friends but over the past few weeks, you haven't been yourself. I know he's giving you a hard time, but it's more than that, isn't it?"

I stare down at my sandwich as I consider how to answer her question. I'm suddenly feeling much less hungry.

"It's a girl," I mutter quietly. I don't really want to have this conversation with her but I know it's better to just come out with it or she'll be like a dog with a bone until I confess.

"Thought as much. Anyone I know."

"Yeah, but I'm not telling you who so don't bother asking."

She chuckles. "Okay then. So what's the issue?"

"It's just... it's fucked-up. I shouldn't like her. We shouldn't work. It's a disaster waiting to happen..."

"But you can't walk away," Mom finishes for me.

I can't help but laugh. "Oh, I've walked away plenty. Doesn't stop me going straight back though." I think of all the times she's sent me away, and I told myself that that was it. No more. But every time, I've gone right back for more. I'm like a fucking addict needing my next hit.

"Love's a funny thing."

"Calm down there, no one mentioned the L-word," I joke.

"No, but the heart wants what it wants regardless of what our heads think."

"Helpful, thanks."

"Is she worth it?"

I open my mouth to respond, but I soon realize that I have no answer. Most people would say absolutely not. Chelsea Fierce is a force to be reckoned with and whoever she touches ends up burned. I know, I've experienced it. But that doesn't stop me from wanting to jump back into the fire.

I think of the soft broken side of her that I've had glimpses of over the years. *That* Chelsea is worth it. The one who allows her walls to drop and shows who she really is beneath the mask and armor she wears on a daily basis.

"Yeah, I think she is," I answer.

"Then you've got to fight for what you want."

"What if it'll only end in disaster?"

"Sometimes it's a risk we've got to take. You want her, then there's always a chance it won't work and you'll end up getting hurt. It's part of the territory, unfortunately. You've just got to trust yourself, and if you think she's worth it then you owe it to yourself to try."

"Thanks, Mom."

"No problem," she says, getting up and rinsing her mug out. "Just promise me one thing."

"Sure."

"Be safe."

I nod, really not wanting to get into that kind of conversation with her. Plus, I can hardly tell her I have been. The last two times I've been with Chelsea, we haven't used protection. I trusted her when she said she was covered. I shake my head at myself.

I might still be none the wiser about what to do with her, but I do know one thing. We need to draw a line under whatever this thing is. Whether that's to put a stop to it or just to quit the bullshit games we're playing, I'm not sure. But I need to be the bigger man here. I need to go and apologize for last night and we need to sit down and talk, something that we haven't done... ever.

Butterflies flutter in my belly as I head out the front door. I'm more nervous walking over there to have a conversation than I have been for anything else we've done. It's fucking crazy.

I park beside her and her mom's car and kill the engine. My hand trembles as I reach out for the button, and I chastise myself for being such a pussy.

It's just Chelsea. A girl I've spent countless hours with over the years. Okay, so she spent most of them avoiding me until recently when all we've tried to do is hurt each other, but she's still the same girl.

She's not though. She's different and you know it.

Fuck. I scrub my hand down my face and climb from the car. There's no backing out now. There's a chance she's already seen that I'm here, so I need to man the fuck up and do what I came to do.

Walking around the house, the sound of soft relaxing music filters through the air, and when I get around to the back, I find both Chelsea and Honey bent in half on yoga mats beside the pool.

Chelsea's wearing a pink pair of pants and a small matching top, but I hardly notice with the way her ass is stuck up in the air as it is.

Now this wasn't what I was expecting.

Her mom softly says something and both of them move simultaneously into their next position.

I have no idea how long I stand there watching her, it's kind of hypnotic, but all too soon, a dark pair of eyes lock on mine. There's no shock on her face, making me wonder if she knew I was here all along.

Honey notices that Chelsea is distracted and follows her gaze.

"Oh, Shane. What a nice surprise. Fancy joining us?" she asks with a hopeful look on her face.

"Um..."

"I think we're done here anyway, right, Mom?" Chelsea says, helping me out.

Honey checks her watch. "Yes, you're right. I need to get moving. I've got a meeting in an hour. I probably won't be back until late and your dad is away on business overnight. Help yourself to whatever, order yourselves food if you want some," she offers, looking between the two of us like she's trying to figure this out. The two of us may have spent plenty of time together in the past but I'm not sure this has ever happened before.

"Thanks, Mom," Chelsea says. "Have a great day."

After looking between us for another second, Honey smiles and heads for the house.

"What are you doing here?" Chelsea barks, her demeanor changing the second her mom is out of earshot.

"We need to talk."

"Talk?" she asks, her eyes widening. "We don't talk, Shane. Plus, I've got nothing to say to you."

"That's a shame, because I've got plenty to say to you."

Her lips purse and she grinds her teeth in frustration as she stares at me.

"And it seems like you've got nothing better planned since you're about to be home alone, so shall we?" I gesture toward the sun loungers that sit around the pool.

She huffs when I walk over and drop down into one. I stretch my legs out and place my hands behind my head, making a show out of getting comfortable.

It might be late in the year but the sun warms my skin as I sit here.

"Jesus fucking Christ," she mutters, spinning on her heels and walking away from me.

I sit forward, ready to chase her but decide against it. She marches through the door to her pool house but in seconds she returns with a zip-up hoodie over her shoulders. Apparently, I'm the only one who thinks it feels like summer.

I run my eyes down her body as she makes her way back over to me.

"What?" she barks.

"N-nothing." I swallow how disappointed I am that she's covered herself up, I don't think she'd want to hear it right now anyway.

"I hope you've got the hangover from hell," she mutters, sitting beside me and folding her arms over her chest.

"Not as bad as I deserve."

She looks over at me but quickly averts her gaze when she finds me staring back at her.

"That's a shame."

"I'm sorry, Chels."

"Really? That's all you got?"

"Uh... yeah. I was pissed at you for continually sending me away. I wanted to hurt you back. It was stupid. But when Zayn dared me, I couldn't think of anything else but making you admit that this is... something."

"Fucking Zayn," Chelsea mutters to herself.

"He knows about... us—"

"There is no us, Shane."

"Yeah, no, yeah... I know. I meant, he knows we slept together, and he knew I was pissed. He thought he was doing us a favor."

"Great. So the whole team knows by now then," she huffs.

"He hasn't told anyone."

"Pfft. It doesn't matter. Everyone already thinks we probably have anyway."

"What's that supposed to mean?" I ask.

"Nothing." She sits back and stares ahead. "Anything else?"

I'm silent for a moment as I consider what I want to say to her. When I don't respond she turns her eyes back on me. My mouth waters as I take in her flawless beauty. "I... uh... I like you." Unable to hold her eyes, I glance down at my feet.

She gasps as she moves to sit on the edge of the lounger like me, our knees are only a breath apart.

Reaching out, she gently touches her fingers to my chin and I have no choice but to look up at her. I didn't intend to say those words, the admission just kind of fell out, and now I'm feeling like an idiot.

Our eyes connect, her chocolate to my green, and something crackles between us.

She shakes her head, a small smile playing on her lips.

"What you did last night. I deserved it. I deserved it and so much more for everything I've done to you and the others."

"Maybe so, but I shouldn't have done it. I hate myself for setting out to hurt you. It's not who I am, Chels."

"I know, you're the sweet one." One side of her lip twitches.

"Oh yeah, real nice."

"If you weren't, you wouldn't be here right now."

Pushing to stand, I have no choice but to look up at her once she's at full height.

"Mom made smoothies. You want one?"

"Um... sure."

Before I have time to blink, she's making her way to the kitchen. I blow out a long breath, chastising myself for being such an idiot. I know I said I wanted to talk, but I didn't want to come across like a total pussy.

"Fuck," I bark into the quiet of the back yard, dropping my head into my hands.

"Everything okay?" Her soft voice flows through me and my spine stiffens. Fucking hell, there's no way I'm leaving here today without convincing her that I'm a total fucking idiot.

"Yeah, everything is fine." I turn to look at her, she's holding two fancy glasses with straws sticking out the top with the front of her hoodie wide open. Just that bit of skin makes my mouth water. I already know that she'll be sweeter than whatever is in those glasses.

"Uh... here." Heat hits her cheeks, and I relax for a moment. Is she as unsure about this as I am?

I watch her as she moves to her seat and lowers down. I have no idea if she's aware of my attention or not but at no point does she look my way. Instead she takes the straw between her lips and sucks.

My cock swells as I remember just how hot and smooth those lips feel wrapped around my cock. Fuck. I came here to apologize not to sit here with a raging hard-on.

"You weren't that drunk then?" Chelsea asks suddenly, startling me from my little trip down memory lane.

"Uh... w-what?"

"I can read you, Shane. I know exactly where your thoughts are at."

"Can you blame me, you give good—"

"I'm off now," Honey's voice cuts through what I was about to say and my face flushes with color while Chelsea barks out a laugh.

Honey appears in the kitchen doorway and looks between the two of us.

"Have a good day, you two." She smiles at Chelsea and then me before turning and disappearing.

Silence stretches out between the two of us until the sound of an engine revving hits our ears and a car backs out of the driveway.

"So... we've got the whole house to ourselves," Chelsea says, putting her now empty glass down on the side table and looking to me. "What shall we do?"

22

CHELSEA

My heart thunders in my chest as Shane's honest eyes stare back at me. I was not expecting him to apologize, let alone admit that he does feel something for me.

I should fall back to my usual protective measure and send him away for fear of him getting too close and finding out the truth but the thought of spending time with him like two normal people who aren't constantly fighting is too tempting.

I don't deserve his apology, especially when I'm the one lying to him right now. I should confess, tell him everything that I'm hiding. But the words get stuck on my tongue.

If I drop that bomb then everything is going to change again, and this right now, it feels... right. And I crave a normal day more than anything.

Should I forgive him so easily for that stunt he pulled yesterday? Maybe not. But after all the times I hurt him, I can't really say that he was wrong for doing it. I deserved it.

Pushing from my lounger, I stand beside Shane's. He's still holding his full smoothie in his hands and staring up at me with desire in his eyes.

I know he was watching as I drank my own drink and I know exactly what he was thinking. I don't need to see the shape of his cock beneath his pants to confirm it. And I also can't deny that it turned me on too.

I have no idea what it is about Shane. I've had guys in this position time and time again, but I've never wanted to climb them like I do him right now. Every single part of my body craves him, craves his touch, his kiss, his caress.

Fuck.

"I-I just came here to talk, Chels." He swallows, the tendons in his neck strain and his Adam's apple bobs.

"And we have. You told me you're sorry, I told you I deserved it and you admitted you like me. What else is there to discuss?" The question tastes bitter on my tongue. There is so much more we need to discuss but I can't do it right now. I need this. I need him.

"Um... e-everything. We've barely scratched the surface. Chels?" he asks as I straddle his lounger and lower myself to his lap.

His eyes darken as I settle myself and place my hands on his shoulders.

"We've got plenty of time. You heard Mom, she'll..." I place a kiss to his jaw. "Be." Kiss. "Gone." Kiss. "All." Kiss. "Day." My final kiss is to the corner of his mouth and seems to be the end of his restraint because his hand slides up my back and his fingers thread into my hair as his tongue sweeps into my mouth.

I whimper above him because being close, having his hands on me is just that good.

His kiss is addictive, all-consuming, and as I hand myself over to him completely, I don't ever want to stop.

My hands roam around his chest, desperate to find his bare skin. After a few seconds, I slip my hands under the hem of his shirt and brush my fingertips up his abs. His entire body flinches at my contact.

"Fuck, Chelsea. What are you doing to me?" he groans against my lips, sending red hot lust straight through my veins.

His hands grip on to my ass, pulling me down harder onto him. His length presses against me and the temptation to take what we both clearly need is almost unbearable.

Torturing both of us, I reluctantly stand and back away from him.

As my heart races, I run my eyes down the length of him. His hair is a disheveled mess, his eyes are unbelievably dark, his lips swollen and his chest heaves as he tries to catch his breath. He looks incredible and makes me wonder how I've managed to turn him away so many times.

"Ches?" he asks, panic starting to set in that I'm about to end this once again. Fortunately for him, he couldn't be more wrong. I couldn't send him away now even if I wanted to.

"I was wondering," I say, slipping the hoodie down my arms so it falls to the floor at my feet. He sits forward, eager to hear what I've got to say next.

I lift my hands to my bra and as smoothly as possible pull it over my head.

Shane's eyes drop and he swallows as he stares at my swollen breasts.

"If you wanted..." I shove my thumbs into the waistband of my yoga pants and panties and push them down my thighs. "A swim."

Before he has a chance to respond, I turn and dive into the warm water behind me.

I have no idea how he sheds his clothes so quickly but I'm still under the water when I sense him join me.

Just as I break the surface, his arms slip around my waist and he pulls me up against his hard, naked body.

Opening my eyes, I find his green ones staring back at me.

"Hey," I say, nerves assaulting me from somewhere.

A wide smile spreads across his face. "Hey."

I wrap my arms around his shoulders and my legs around his waist. His already hard cock teasing my entrance and reawakening the desire that was coursing through me not so long ago.

He walks me backward until my back hits the pool wall.

When he drops his head, I lower my eyelids, preparing to resume our earlier kiss but his lips don't find mine, instead they brush my ear.

"I thought we were done with the games." A shudder runs through me as his breath tickles my sensitive skin.

"Mind games, yeah," I breathe. "Sex games, I'm all in."

He growls in response and his mouth latches on to my neck. My head falls back, giving him all the access he needs. But he doesn't continue long enough before he speaks again.

"If we're doing this..." Just the thought of this being a thing has my stomach somersaulting. "I need you to promise me something."

"And what's that?" I ask, playing with the hair at the nape of his neck.

"I'm the only member of the team that gets to touch you, look at you, have you. You want me. You give them all up." It's hardly the demand of the century. I've used them over the years, just like they have me. Jake was the only one I ever thought I wanted more with. Not playing games with them isn't exactly a hardship, especially if I can have Shane.

Gripping on to his hair, I pull his head from the crook of my neck so I can look into his eyes. So he can see the honesty in my words.

"I don't want them. I've never wanted them."

His eyes bounce between mine as he thinks about my words. "So, what do you want?" His voice cracks slightly as his nerves creep in.

"You."

"Fuck."

His lips find mine once again as he pins me back harder against the wall. His kiss is bruising, but I can't get enough. Our teeth clash as our tongues duel, desperately trying to get enough of each other but both knowing that we'll never achieve it.

He lifts me higher before lining his cock up with my entrance.

"Okay?" he mumbles against my lips before pushing inside.

"Yes, Shane. Always."

I love that he's sweet enough to ask. That he doesn't just take like so many of the others. But he needs to know that he already owns me. He can take exactly what he likes and I'll meet him move for move.

"Fuuuuck," he grates out as he stretches me open.

"Oh god."

The water laps around us as we move together. His hands grip on to my ass almost painfully as he thrusts up into me, taking what he needs and giving me exactly what I'm craving.

Seeking out my lips, his tongue plunges into my mouth, mimicking what's happening below the water as my body starts to race toward the end. I don't want this to be over. This connection, I want to feel it forever.

"You feel so good, baby."

"Yeah," I moan as he brushes his lips across my neck.

"So tight, so hot, so perfect."

One of his hands leaves my ass in favor of roaming over my body. He squeezes each breast, pinching each nipple and sending shockwaves of pleasure racing through me. Then he brushes his fingertips down my stomach to find my clit.

"Oh shit," I moan, my eyes closing as pleasure explodes within me.

"Look at me, Chelsea. Don't hide. Don't run."

I do as I'm told, and my eyes fly open. It's the first time I accept that he's as vulnerable as me right now. He's laid on the line how he feels, what he wants, and just like me, he's terrified that I'll reject him. Fuck, what I've been doing since I came back. Continually walking away, or sending him away like I don't care.

Admitting that I want him, that what we have here means something to me terrifies the shit out of me. What if I tell him the truth and he walks away from me? From us? The thought alone has a lump forming in my throat.

People always abandon me. Leave me. Why should I believe that he'd be any different? The only people who've stuck around are Honey and Derek and even all these years later, I have no idea why they chose me.

"Jesus, fuck, Chelsea." Shane's low, husky voice drags me from my inner turmoil and brings me back to the here and now. He stares at me, his eyes telling me more than his lips do and I can only hope that mine are doing the same. That he can read everything I'm too scared to put into words.

"Come, Chelsea." As he says it, he pinches my clit and thrusts up higher.

"Oh fuck," I cry not two seconds later, following his order.

I just register his smirk of achievement before I have no choice but to slam my eyes closed and ride out the waves of pleasure.

Shane thrusts three more times before his grip on my hips becomes almost painful as his entire body stills. A groan of pleasure rumbles up his throat as his cock twitches violently inside me.

His arms wrap around me and he holds me tight, our chests crushed together as we fight to gain control of our racing hearts.

After long silent minutes with my ear pressed against his chest listening to his heart thunder, he releases me slightly.

Reluctantly, I pull my face away and glance up at him.

Reality comes crashing down that this is over now. Every other time we've been together, things have gone very wrong from this moment on.

Biting down on the inside of my cheek, I risk a glance up at him. His eyes are soft, full of something I'm not used to seeing on the guys I've spent time with in the past.

Reaching out, he brushes a wet lock of hair from my cheek and tucks it behind my ear.

"Stop waiting for something to go wrong," he murmurs.

"But... it always does."

"Not today. Today, we just enjoy." He leans forward and brushes his lips against mine. "No games, no bullshit. Just... us."

A smile curls at my lips. "Yeah?" I ask, hopeful that we could at least attempt to do this.

"Yeah. If you want me." That little bit of vulnerability I saw earlier creeps back into his eyes.

Cupping his cheek in my hand, I sigh when he leans into my touch.

"I do."

"Perfect," he says before dropping his hands to my waist and scaring the shit out of me when he lifts and launches me into the pool. I squeal before I go under but can't help laughing once I come back up.

It's been too long since I let go of everything and just had some fun.

With my past and bad decisions weighing me down, it's easy to forget that I am only eighteen and that I can have this.

We play around in the pool for the longest time. Our hands barely leave each other's bodies as we enjoy ourselves and laugh like we've got no worries in the world. It's incredible and although we don't go any farther than a few naughty gropes and the odd kiss or two, I'm desperate for him to pull me to him once again so he can consume me. But he never does. I know it's not because he doesn't want to. He's been hard almost since he pulled out of me earlier, but he's made no move to take me again.

"We should probably get out," I say when our splashing comes to a stop. I hold my hands up above the water and inspect my wrinkled fingertips.

"Yeah, you're probably right. I'm hungry," he says, crowding me into the corner.

"O-okay, we can shower and order food."

"Food? Hmmm..." he mumbles into the crook of my neck. "I wasn't talking about food."

Heat floods my body as his front presses against me, his cock prodding me in the stomach.

"Then we definitely need to get out so you can get what you need."

His hands slide up the sides of my body before tucking under my arms and lifting me from the water as if I weigh no more than a feather.

Water runs down my bare body as his eyes follow its movement.

The cool air and his stare have my nipples pebbling.

"Oh yeah, I'm definitely starving."

Feeling brazen under his attention, I part my knees. His eyes immediately drop to my core and he licks his bottom lip. My muscles clench as I remember exactly how it feels with his tongue against me.

He leans forward. My fingers dive into his hair, halting his movement.

"Shane?"

"Lie back," he demands, pulling at my legs so my ass slides toward the edge of the pool.

I glance around at the houses surrounding us. None of them directly overlooks our back yard, but that doesn't mean they can't see what's going on right now.

"Chels?" He follows my line of sight. "You think they'll get off watching the show?"

My eyes widen at his words. I thought I knew the kind of guy that Shane was. It seems I was very wrong. He might not be a dog like the majority of his teammates, but fuck. His confidence is hot.

"Shane?" I repeat, my head spinning with lust, unable to think straight.

Do I want him to eat me right here for everyone to see how he owns me? Fuck yes.

Doing as I'm told, I rest back on my elbows. Placing my heels on the edge of the pool, I watch as his pupils dilate as he stares at me.

"I thought you said no games," I quip. "This definitely feels like you're playing me right now."

My words eventually cut through his daze and his eyes come back to mine.

"I don't mind these games so much."

Without wasting another second, he dives for me.

I fall back down, my back arching against the hard tiles beneath me, my shoulder blades smarting with pain as I writhe, but I couldn't give a fuck. Shane licks, sucks, and drives me fucking crazy with his fingers teasing my entrance.

Any thoughts of nosy neighbors evaporate from my mind as I focus on what he's doing to my body.

"Shane, Shane, Shane," I cry in pleasure as he pushes me over the edge. My fingers find his hair and I hold him in place until I've ridden out the final seconds of my orgasm. "Fucking hell," I pant when I eventually let up my hold and he moves away from me.

I'm still laying out on the tiles a sated mess when he jumps from the pool and stands over me. Water drips from his body, splashing over my now mostly dry one.

"Come on," he says, holding his hand out for me. "I think we've given your neighbors enough of a treat for the day. I'll save fucking you over the table for another time."

Despite the fact he's only just made me come, my thighs clench as the image of him thrusting into me from behind fills my mind.

Shaking the thoughts away before I tell him that it's exactly what happens next, I lift my hand up and allow him to pull me to my feet.

"Shower?" I ask, standing so close that my breasts brush against his chest.

"Sounds perfect. You do look really dirty."

I tilt my head to the side and look up at him through my lashes.

"What?" he asks.

"Where did the sweet, shy guy go?"

He chuckles. "You just weren't looking in the right places, baby."

"So it seems," I mutter as he pulls me along behind him toward my pool house.

"Just because I don't always act like them," he says, and I assume he means his teammates. "It doesn't mean that I don't want the same things."

"Me on my knees?"

The muscles in his shoulders tense as he continues dragging me through the living room and then the bedroom. He doesn't stop until we're in the walk-in shower, and then he spins me and backs me up against the wall. He takes my chin in his fingers and lowers his face so his nose is almost brushing mine. His eyes are hard, much like they were last night and nothing like the easy-going, fun-loving guy I've spent the last few hours with.

"Don't. Don't ever compare me to them like that. I don't want you for a cheap ride. And I'd really prefer not having the constant reminder that they did."

"Shane, that's not—"

"You're mine, but they all had you first. It makes me want to kill every last one of them."

I take his clenched fists in my hands and lift them to my lips.

I hold his eyes, hoping that he can read the truth in them. "Most of them are lying, Shane," I whisper.

His jaw pops and his eyes remain angry and hard.

"Shane," I repeat, knowing that he didn't hear a word I just said. I wrap my hand around his neck and brush my thumb along the line of his jaw. "I haven't touched most of them. They're bragging to make themselves look like a big man. I promise you, it's nowhere near as bad as it seems."

He blinks a few times, but he doesn't relax, and I worry for a second that my stupid comment has ruined this and that he's about to realize his mistake and walk away.

I might have forced him to do so in the past, but now I've somewhat allowed myself to believe that there could be something between us, it would kill me to watch him turn his back on me, on this.

"I hope to fuck that you are right." I don't get a chance to respond because as he says it, he reaches out and turns the shower on. We're both blasted with ice cold water for a few seconds before it begins to warm up.

I open my mouth to say more, although I'm not sure what exactly, but I don't get the chance because the second my lips part, his tongue sweeps inside.

23

SHANE

Just the thought of what she might have done with the guys I'm forced to spend time with has anger racing through my veins.

She can tell me that it's bullshit on their part all she likes. Hell, I believe her. I know what braggers and bullshitters they are, I experience it daily. But still, it doesn't do much to get the images I don't need out of my head.

I want her to be mine and mine alone. I hate that others have experienced this. Her.

"Stop overthinking," she warns, her soap covered hands rubbing across my abs and getting dangerously close to where I really need them. "Stop worrying about what's already been done. We can't change the past, Shane. I know that better than anyone."

She looks up at me, her dark eyes open and honest in a way I'm not sure I've seen before.

"Why did you do it, Chels? Why hurt everyone?"

"It was stupid," she says, bowing her head, too ashamed of her actions to hold my eyes.

"Explain it to me. Please. Help me understand."

She blows out a breath as she considers her words.

"You know my past, Shane. It was... bad. I was a nuisance, this unwanted, unloved small person who only got in the way. I had no use, well not until I grew up a little, not that that stopped some of the guys leering..." A shudder runs down her spine as she remembers.

Wrapping my arms around her, I gather her close in the hope it helps her to feel the opposite of those things she just described.

"I've just always wanted to be wanted," she says so quietly that I almost think I imagined it. "I know I had Honey and Derek, but they didn't choose me, not really. They had no choice but to take me in when I first turned up on their doorstep.

"I've watched everyone for years, finding their best friend. That person they can have a conversation with without even saying words. I've watched those around me fall in love. And I've always just felt alone.

"I was jealous. I won't lie, I thought Jake was it for me. Two broken souls who could fix each other or some bullshit. Then Amalie turned up and shattered anything I believed. He wanted her, *you* wanted her.

"Then Mason and Camila sorted their shit out, and one by one I was watching everyone find what I wanted so fucking badly.

"I lashed out. I was jealous and drowning in other's happiness. I've got no real excuse because it was a fucking stupid thing to do. It was misguided, immature, unnecessary, selfish, the list goes on.

"I'll never forgive myself for it. To this day I'm not sure what I was trying to achieve other than to stop everyone being so happy and moving on with their lives while I seemed to be forever stuck in misery. I was so fucking lonely, Shane. So fed up with everything. Of pretending, of trying to be the person everyone had to like. All of it was fucking bullshit."

We're both silent for a beat before she speaks again.

"I never set out to hurt you or to make it look like it was you. But once everyone assumed, I couldn't exactly scream it from the rooftops that it was me. Well, I guess I could have but..." she sighs. "I'm so sorry. So fucking sorry. Somehow, I intend on making it up to the others too. I don't know how; I just hope I'll figure something out."

"I'm pretty sure you just need to say the words, Chels."

Taking her cheek in my hand, I move her head so she has no choice but to look at me. Her eyes are full of tears, but I have no idea if any have fallen with the water pouring down over both of us.

"I'm sorry," she whispers, her voice cracking. "There are so many things I'd do differently if I could go back."

"You can't. You've got to accept it for what it was and move on. We all have."

She nods sadly.

Silence falls between us once again as her words from moments ago run around in my head.

"What about the squad?" I ask.

"What about them?" Her brow creases in confusion.

"I thought they were your friends."

"Like the team are your friends?"

"But—"

"My squad are my squad," she says, cutting me off. "I decided a long time ago that cheer was going to be my life. I love it. I live it. Becoming captain was never a question for me. It's in my blood.

"Those girls, they don't hang around with me because they like me, because we're friends, they do it because they have to. I'm their leader, the reason they're on that squad, the reason they have the position in the school they do.

"They're not my friends," she repeats. "Just look how quickly they turned their backs on me when I fucked up. Real friends don't do that. They should be there no matter how bad you screw everything up, even if they're angry. L-like you," she whispers.

"The only people I've ever had any kind of real friendship with is Luca and Ethan. They both see beneath the act, they see me, not just the cheer bitch everyone else gets."

"So you and Ethan, you've never..."

Her lips curl in disgust before she chuckles. "Never. He's kinda like my brother. Luca too."

"And me?" I ask, running my thumb along her bottom lip and stepping closer.

"Are not like my brother," she says with a smirk.

"Thank fuck for that," I mutter with a laugh.

Tension crackles between us but no words are said as we continue to stare at each other.

Chelsea's lips part, but she doesn't say anything for the longest time.

"I-I think you might have been what I was searching for all along." Her eyes widen the second she realizes she said it aloud.

"Is that right?" I close in on her, pushing her up against the cold tiled wall.

"I'm not sure, you might need to show me again."

I have no idea what time it is when we emerge from her bathroom, but I do know that I'm hungry, and for actual food this time.

"Where are you going?" Chelsea asks in shock when I walk toward the door to her pool house naked.

"Well, I wasn't going to walk home like this if that's what you're worried about."

"Good. You're not the only one who gets to claim ownership, you know." Her eyes run down my body, staking her claim.

"All yours, baby."

I'm only gone seconds as I grab my abandoned clothes but when I get back, what I find is almost as good as her still being naked.

She's standing at her refrigerator wearing the jersey I left behind the night she sent me away.

"I sure hope there's nothing underneath that."

"You'll have to find out for yourself," she says, turning to me with two sodas in hand. "What do you want to eat?"

"Whatever. I'm easy."

"You sure are." She winks.

"Being corrupted by the chief cheer slut. I must say, it has its benefits." A brief flash of hurt flickers in her eyes and I feel awful for joking about it. I step up to her and take her hand in mine. "Hey, I didn't mean…"

"It's okay. Chinese?" she asks, grabbing her cell and opening it up to change the subject.

"Sure. Sounds perfect."

We spend a few minutes debating dishes before she places the order and we fall down onto her couch.

She turns the TV on and opens Netflix.

"Any preference?"

"Nope, whatever you want."

Her recommended programs open up and I can't help but laugh.

"What?"

"You're such a girl." I take in the cheer series that she's halfway through and all the chick flicks and romance that fills the screen.

"Yeah, and?"

"I was kinda expecting it to be full of phycological thrillers and murder documentaries."

"Fucking hell, Shane. I'm not a total psychopath. I do have a… softer side."

"I know, I know. I'm only joking. And I happen to like getting beneath your hard outer shell."

"Oh yeah?"

I wrap my arm around her shoulder once she's chosen some series to watch that I've never even heard of and tucks herself into my side.

It's really fucking comfortable.

"I believe you, you know," I say after a few quiet moments as the theme tune to the program plays out. "If you say it's not as it seems then, I believe you. Those guys can be real assholes."

"They can. Which leads me to my burning question," she says, looking up at me. "Why are you suddenly hanging out with them? You used to stay as far away from the team as possible but since I've come back, you seem to always be with them."

"Hmm… it wasn't by choice, I figured that I might be able to find the information I needed from one of them."

"Information? What could you possibly need from them?"

"I thought they might have known where you went."

Her chin drops. "Y-you were looking for me?"

"You just disappeared. I was still desperate for a repeat of that night and then everything blew up and you were gone. I didn't know what to think. I wanted to shout at you for what you did, I wanted to hurt you for allowing me to take the fall, but mostly, I just wanted you. I wanted to know you were okay, that you were safe.

"Mom refused to tell me where you'd gone despite the fact I knew she knew. I had no idea if you'd run or what."

"I was sent," she admits. "I'd already fucked up one too many times and when I got home that night and confessed to my parents they got straight on the phone and booked me a place at the center. They'd threatened time and time again but I didn't think they'd do it. It had been years since I'd been there, I was more than happy to never return. But looking back now, I think it was the best thing they could have done. I needed that time. I needed the space to figure out who I was and what I really wanted."

"What did you do there? What's it like?"

"It's basically a group home but they have teachers and counselors on site to work with all the kids. It's one of the better places to end up when you've got no home, that's for sure.

"I did schoolwork every morning, therapy sessions and exercise in the afternoons. It was regimented and structured, everything I needed to sort my head out."

"Did you speak to anyone from home?" I ask, thinking about how lonely that sounds.

"My parents called regularly, and Ethan messaged a couple of times. I needed the space."

I pull her tighter into my body. "I'm glad it helped. But I'm even more glad you're back."

"It gave me perspective. Helped me figure out what I want."

"And what do you want?"

She lets out a sigh and is silent for so long that I'm not sure if she's going to answer me. "I want to focus on my future. I want to forge meaningful relationships and if that means I distance myself from the squad and the team, then so be it. I'm done making myself miserable trying to be what others expect of me."

"But what about college? If you give up on the squad then..." I trail off, she doesn't need me to spell it out for her.

"What will be will be."

Her cell buzzes on the coffee table, telling us that dinner has arrived.

She jumps up and heads for the door.

"You can't go like that," I say, hopping up behind her.

"Then you can answer the door. Come on."

We make our way through her house. She stands to the side a little as I pull the door open to take our food.

I'm just about to close it behind the guy when her fingers wrap around the wood and she peers outside.

"What's wrong?" I ask, looking out in the same direction as her.

"Do you recognize that truck?" she asks, pointing to a black truck idling at the end of her driveway.

"No, why?"

She waves me off and closes the door when I try to see who's in the driver's seat.

"I'm sure it's nothing. I've just seen it a few times. Probably waiting for a neighbor or something."

Taking the food back out to her pool house, we put all the containers out on the coffee table and sit on the floor to eat.

We have the most incredibly relaxed night, eating, chatting and watching her girly TV. We both steer away from the hard conversations that we'd brushed on previously. Chelsea had a point when she talked about leaving the past where it was. It was time for fresh starts for both of us.

The sun has barely set when I look down to find Chelsea asleep. As smoothly as I can, I slip out from under her and sweep her into my arms. I carry her through to the bedroom and peel back the sheet before dropping her down and crawling in behind her.

She sighs and snuggles her ass back into my crotch as she gets settled.

I lay there for the longest time with her in my arms, thinking about all the things she told me today and trying to imagine what her previous life was really like. Eventually, I find myself drifting off with her and I swear to God, I have the best night's sleep of my life.

24

CHELSEA

The second I wake, a smile breaks across my lips.

Sighing in contentment, I tighten my hold around Shane's waist and snuggle closer.

"Morning," he whispers before pressing his lips against the top of my head.

Unable to resist looking at him, I tilt my head up. His hair is all over the place and he has a pillow crease in his cheek. I'm pretty sure he's never looked better.

"Hey."

"Why do you look so surprised to see me?" he asks, his eyes bouncing between mine.

"Thought you might have changed your mind and snuck out in the middle of the night," I admit.

"You're kidding, right? Why would I leave when I could be curled around you?"

"Many reasons," I say, looking away from his soft eyes.

"Chels," he warns.

"I'm sorry, this... this is just going to take a bit of getting used to. No one usually wants to hang around this long."

"That's because you haven't allowed them to get to know you."

I think about his words. They're true. For the last... well, forever, I've put on this act. Pretended to be exactly what I thought everyone wanted from me, and I've kept everyone at arm's length.

"What do you want to do today?" I ask, wanting to turn the conversation away from me.

"I could do with working out this morning."

"Why? Didn't you get enough exercise yesterday?" I ask with a wink.

His eyes darken before me and my core clenches with need.

Reaching forward, he tucks a lock of hair behind my ear.

"I could go for another day of that kind of exercise." A smirk curls at his lips. "After a real workout. Just because the season is over, it doesn't mean I can get out of shape."

Pushing the covers down to expose his abs, I trail my finger over them and smile when his body flinches beneath my touch.

"Looks pretty impressive to me."

"Oh yeah? I'm not sure how they look will help me with college football somehow."

"If the coach was a woman, it might."

"And you'd be okay with that, would you? Me showing off the goods to get my place."

"Hmm... on second thought."

"Exactly."

"Can I come work out with you?"

"You think you can keep up?" he asks, teasingly.

"Cheer is a sport, you know. I put a lot of hours in to stay in peak condition."

"As many hours as we do?"

Propping myself up on my elbow, I stare down at him.

"I guess we're about to find out."

I don't know why I'm baiting him. I'm sure he could outrun me any day of the week, but I'm not one to back down from a challenge.

"Seems like we are."

He slips from beneath me and sits on the edge of the bed.

"Hey," I complain, rolling over onto my stomach.

Standing, he turns and rips the covers away from me.

"You won't win by laz– fuck, I think I changed my mind."

I glance down at myself. His jersey is hitched up around my waist, exposing my bare ass.

"Oh yeah? Why's that?" I ask innocently, rolling over to my back and parting my knees just slightly.

Shane clears his throat as he stares down at me, his cock trying to break free from his boxer briefs.

"You wearing only my number. Fuck. Do you know how many times I've fantasized about this?"

"Nope. But I think you should tell me all about it." Lifting my hand, I trail my fingertip down my thigh. "Was I just like this?" He watches my movement, his lips parted and his chest already heaving.

"Fuck, Chels."

"Was I totally bare beneath?" I part my legs wider and hook my finger under the hem of the jersey so he can see beneath. My nipples pebble and heat floods my core, my own words and his stare enough to turn me on.

Slipping one hand up my stomach, I make a show of pinching my own nipples and moaning in pleasure. It's over the top but I can't deny that they're not a lot more sensitive since... no. I lock that down. Guilt hits me full force that I'm keeping this little–or huge–secret from him. He deserves to know, but spending this time together, getting to know each other, I don't want it to end and I know that's what'll happen when I admit the truth.

I just need this right now. I need him and I'm too selfish right now to give him up.

"Yeah." His voice is low and husky, it's exactly what I need to help push those thoughts away and focus on right now.

"And did I touch myself like this?" Running my hand back down my stomach, I shamelessly part myself and run my fingers over my clit.

I arch my back and moan, keeping my eyes on him, fascinated by the way the muscle in his neck pulsates.

"Mmm..."

"Did you get yourself off while thinking about this?"

"What the fuck do you think?" he barks before diving forward and ripping my hand away from myself and replacing it with this tongue.

"Oh fuck, Shane," I cry, my back arching for real this time as pleasure races through me.

Before we even leave the pool house to embark on our morning workout session, I already feel like I've run a few miles. My knees feel a little weak and my muscles pull from our earlier activity.

"We'll leave my car at home and run down the beach?" Shane asks as he backs out of my driveway. Mom's car is already gone but that's not a surprise. She and Maddie have probably met for a morning yoga session. I'm sure they're busy gossiping about the fact Shane turned up to see me yesterday afternoon by surprise.

"Yeah, sounds perfect," I say, looking around for that truck but thankfully it's nowhere to be seen.

"You okay?" he asks, obviously noticing that I'm not really with him.

"Yeah, yeah, I'm good."

"If you're worried that you're not going to be able to keep up then all you've got to do is say so, I can go easy on you."

"Shut up. I'll run circles around you, Dunn."

"That right?"

"Just wait and see."

His driveway is equally as empty as mine, confirming my suspicion that our moms are together.

"I'll get changed and then we can head out the back."

"Sure."

I follow him through his house but only once before have I followed him toward his bedroom. That night. The night when all this started and sealed our fate. My hand comes up to rest on my belly.

It was just meant to be a bit of fun. I was bored, lonely and pissed off that Tasha had left me alone to hook up. Tormenting Camila had been the wrong thing to do, so was sleeping with Shane some might say. But I can hardly regret it now. I'm pretty sure that decision might be the best of my life. No matter what happens when I tell him about what we created that night. I can't regret it. Excitement and anticipation swirl in my stomach as I think about what the coming months will hold.

"Didn't think I'd get invited back in here," I say as I take a seat on the end of his bed.

"I didn't think you'd ever be in here in the first place."

"I can understand that."

"You rocked my fucking world that night, you know that?" he asks as he pulls some clothes from a drawer and goes about changing.

"Oh yeah? You weren't too bad either."

"Whoa, thanks for the glowing report."

"I'm joking. You were amazing. I was shocked. I'd have put money on you being a virgin," I say with a laugh, but I soon stop when he stills and looks over his shoulder at me.

"I was," he admits, making my chin drop.

"Fuck off you were. You knew exactly what you were doing," I say like I was an expert that night. I'd only been with Jake before him, and that was forgettable at best. I had such high hopes for my first time and when I got the chance for it to be with Jake, I thought all my dreams were coming true. Well, a drunken, painful fumble wasn't exactly what my fantasies were made of.

I watch as he pulls a clean shirt over his head. "I'm not lying, Chels. You were my first."

"Well, shit." *And what a first that was.*

"Well, your male ego will be pleased to know that I had no idea."

"It wasn't exactly hard."

"I think you'll find it was," I say with a wink.

He chuckles. "What the fuck am I going to do with you?" He walks over to the bed and reaches for my hand.

I stand the second he tugs and our chests brush.

"So I stood up to the guys from your past then?" he whispers in my ear.

"Shane," I say on a sigh. "I told you, it wasn't like that. I'm not like that."

"You're not going to try to tell me that you were a virgin too, are you?"

"Um... no. But I have less experience than you think."

He pulls back and looks into my eyes. He studies me for a moment and I expect him to ask me to explain, but he doesn't. Instead he drops his lips to mine for a brief kiss before he pulls me from the room.

We make our way to the end of his yard and out to an alleyway that eventually leads us to the beach.

We warm up on the dry sand before taking off.

The sun beams down on us and sparkles on the calm sea to our side. The beach is almost empty with it still being a little chilly despite the bright morning sun.

I breathe in lungfuls of fresh sea air and smile. I really fucking needed this.

When I first discovered I was pregnant, I did a lot of research on what I was and wasn't allowed to do. I was terrified that I'd lose the escape I got when I was working out and that I'd have to give up all my favorite foods. I had no real clue what growing a person entailed, but I was relieved to read that I could mostly continue as normal, for now at least.

My heart pounds as my muscles burn.

Shane runs right beside me, every few seconds he glances over to make sure I'm still keeping up.

He really does underestimate me. What does he think I did when I wasn't barking orders at the squad or partying?

I have no idea how long we run, but eventually Shane slows to a stop.

"That all you got, Dunn?" I ask as he bends at the waist and places his hands on his knees.

He looks up at me, a smile breaks across his face as he shakes his head.

"What?"

"You really are full of surprises, aren't you?"

"I told you. Cheer is hardcore, and I work out... hard."

"So I see."

Standing up straight, he steps toward me. His fingers wrap around my ponytail and tugs so I've got no choice but to look up at him.

He stares down at me, his green eyes sparkling with something I can't quite read.

"I really fucking like you," he admits.

He looks nervous when I don't immediately respond.

"That's good." He lifts an eyebrow. "Because I really fucking like you too."

He seals his lips over mine and kisses the life out of me in the middle of the beach.

"Get a fucking room," a familiar voice calls.

"Fucking hell," Shane mutters against my lips before pressing his forehead against mine. "Sorry."

"I can handle these guys," I say, turning to see who our visitors are. "Morning, Zayn, Ethan." I can't help but laugh at the shocked look on Ethan's face. Fair play to Rae because she clearly didn't share my secret with her boy like I expected her to.

"Should have fucking known you were otherwise engaged when you bailed yesterday morning," Zayn says with a laugh. "Thought you'd fucked it up on Friday night, man."

"It's going to take more than a stupid fucking dare to get to me, Zayn. You should know that by now."

Ethan remains mute as he looks between the two of us like he can't believe what he's seeing.

"I'm sorry but have I walked into the fucking twilight zone or something. You two?" he asks, pointing between us. "You and you?"

Shane laughs as he pulls me into his side and possessively wraps an arm around my waist. I fucking love it.

"Yeh," Shane agrees. "Us two."

"Fucking hell. I thought the most shocking thing to happen this year was me handing Rae my balls. Clearly, I was wrong. Shane Dunn and Chelsea Fierce. Fuck me," he mutters to himself, making us all laugh.

"I'm glad you weren't too hard on him. He was a miserable fuck without you," Zayn says, making me very happy.

"Oh, is that right?" I ask, looking up at Shane.

"And you need to shut the fuck up," he barks back, but the smile on his face counteracts his harsh words. He really couldn't give a fuck about Zayn's teasing.

"So when exactly did this happen?"

"Uh..." I start, not really sure how to answer that.

"She dug her claws in before she went away and left me wanting more."

"And here we all were thinking you hated her."

"Yeah, I kinda did, she can be pretty convincing though."

Reaching up, I twist his nipple, laughing when he squeals like a little bitch.

When I look back to the guys, Ethan is nodding like he's figuring something out. "I guess that makes sense."

"What does?"

"That motherfucker started being our friend after you left. Digging to get information on you. Guess I should have seen straight through it."

"You were otherwise distracted if I remember rightly," Shane points out.

"True that. You do know that the rest of the school is going to have a field day with this, right?"

A ball of dread forms in my stomach at just the thought. But it's not for me, it's for Shane. He's the one who's going to be on the end of the bullshit. Everyone hates me. They're not going to understand why he doesn't.

"It'll be fine," he says with a confidence that I really don't feel.

"Well, we've got your back."

"Thank you, Ethan. I really appreciate it."

"Tell me, did Rae know about this?"

"Um..."

"She's in so much trouble." A wicked smile curls at his lips as ideas form in his head.

"Well, this has been fun and all, but we need to get going," Shane says, releasing me and taking a step forward.

"Do we?" I ask. He looks back over his shoulder at me and winks. "Oh yeah, we do. See you both tomorrow?"

"Already looking forward to it," Zayn says with a smile.

"Zayn, we'd appreciate it if—"

"He won't say anything until you're ready, will you, Hunter?" Shane finishes for me.

"My lips are sealed."

We say our goodbyes before taking off down the beach back toward Shane's house.

We're both silent as we run, but I can't help but wonder if Shane's head is full of thoughts about how we'll handle this once tomorrow and school comes around.

There's no way we're going to keep it secret, we've already been discovered once, it's only a matter of time before it happens again. But I hate to think what kind of backlash he's going to get from this.

I must admit that by the time his house is visible in the distance that I'm more than ready to stop. My legs burn and my muscles ache, but I refuse to let him know that I'm starting to struggle.

"You ready to admit defeat yet?" he asks, getting ahead of me and turning to face me just to show off.

"Never."

He must be able to see that I'm lying but he doesn't say anything, instead he slows to a walk and comes back beside me. He reaches for my hand and tangles our fingers together as we make our way from the beach.

"I think I might have found my new favorite workout partner."

"Oh yeah?"

"You're much better to look at than Zayn."

"I'm glad you think so," I say with a laugh.

His house is still in silence as we make our way back up to his room.

"I need to shower then get food."

"How about you pack some stuff, we get food then shower at mine."

"You mean together?"

"I'm sure that can be arranged."

"Can we get burgers?"

"If you want," I say with a laugh.

"Okay, deal."

I fall back on his bed while he pulls out a bag and starts shoving stuff inside.

"Fancy packing enough stuff for the night?"

He stops and looks my way.

"I like you on my bed," he says, running his eyes down the length of me.

"I prefer you in mine. There's no one who can overhear while I corrupt you."

"I shouldn't have admitted that earlier, should I?"

I'm silent for a moment while I think. "Did I give you all your firsts?"

His cheeks heat, it's utterly adorable, although I don't tell him that.

"Yeah," he admits, not that he needed to, it was written all over his face.

"Mmm... I like that only I've touched you."

"I hate that others have touched you." He looks away and back to what he was packing.

"Hardly," I admit.

He stops immediately and finds my eyes. He wants to ask, he wants to know the truth, but he's scared of my answer.

"There was only Jake, and then you."

His mouth opens and then closes as he takes on board what I've just said.

"But..."

"It's all bullshit. Yeah, I've done more with them than I should," I say with a wince. "But they've not touched me."

"None of them?" he asks, his brows drawing together.

"Just one."

"Jake." He rolls his eyes.

Scrambling from the bed, I come to a stop in front of him and take both his hands in mine.

"Yeah, but let me tell you something." I reach up on my tiptoes and kiss his lips. "You're much better."

He can't fight the smile that pulls at the corners of his lips, and I'm so glad because it knocks me for a loop.

"Oh yeah?"

"Yeah. You might not want to tell him that though."

He barks a laugh and pulls me into his arms. "I know, that's all that matters."

"He was really drunk. It probably wasn't his finest performance."

Lifting his fingers, he presses two against my lips. "I'm glad to know I'm better, but I don't need the details."

"Okay," I say with a laugh, dropping his other hand so he can finish packing.

25

SHANE

I can't lie, knowing that Jake Thorn didn't rock her world makes me feel better about life than I have in a long time. It also helps that half, or more, of the guys I spend time with haven't had a taste of what's mine, like I once thought.

"Why are you smiling at me?" Chelsea asks from the other side of her coffee table.

We stopped off to get burgers after leaving my house and ate them in the front of my car. It's not exactly the kind of first date she deserves, but it was pretty perfect for us. One day soon I'll take her out and treat her right, but not when we're both covered in sweat and sand from our run.

"Just thinking about what you said earlier," I admit with a smirk.

"Wha– oh, I didn't tell you to stroke your ego," she mutters, rolling her eyes.

"Maybe not, but I like it."

"Fucking hell, I've created a monster." She throws her pen at me, but I easily catch it before it connects with my face.

We both continue with our homework, but I can't wipe the smile off my face, or refrain from glancing up at her where she types away on her laptop every few seconds.

"You're never going to get that finished," she says, without looking up from the screen. "I can feel you watching me."

"Can't help it."

With a sigh, she closes the lid and looks at me. I swear just the sight of her takes my fucking breath away. She's so beautiful.

Color hits her cheeks and she smiles in a way that only a few see. It's unsure and shy and I freaking love it. I love that I can see under the mask, the act, the bullshit. Yeah, she's fucked up, but she knows that. She's opened up and I'm so fucking grateful she has because what I've found inside is exactly what I always hoped was in there. A really sweet, funny and warm-hearted girl.

"So what did you win the other night then?"

Her question confuses me. "Huh?"

"The dare you won when you fucked me, what did you win or get out of it?"

"Uh um... nothing."

"What kind of shit dare was it if there weren't any benefits or consequences?"

"There were consequences, something about the winter formal but I didn't get anything out of it."

"How come? You got me." Her brows draw together in confusion.

"There had to be evidence, or it didn't happen," I say with a wince. She's aware of how the guys act, I'm sure she's been in the middle of their games and tags before now but admitting that she was used in this doesn't make me very comfortable and only points out how wrong their stupid game is and why I've never gotten involved before.

"You didn't get any?"

I swallow nervously. I hate that I caved to their fucking demands that night. I blame the alcohol. "Yeah, I recorded it."

"So show them and get out of whatever bullshit they want you to do." She doesn't even look shocked, which amazes me.

"It wasn't a video, just a sound recording." She nods. "And no fucker is listening to that."

"But—" She starts to argue.

"You're mine, Chelsea. No one gets to hear you like that. I'll take whatever they throw at me, I don't care."

Pushing to her feet, she walks over to me and drops into my lap. She's once again wearing my jersey but thankfully she's wearing a pair of shorts underneath, making it almost possible to look at her without losing my goddamn mind.

She takes my cheeks in her hands and stares into my eyes.

"I don't deserve you."

She drops her lips to mine and I'm powerless but to kiss her back.

All too soon she's standing once again and walking to her kitchen.

"Drink?"

"Soda would be great," I mutter, rearranging myself in my pants.

Sadly, after handing me a can, she retakes her seat at her computer and opens it back up.

"Are you behind after being away?" I ask as she starts clicking around.

"Not really. All my teachers sent work, I spent most evenings doing it.

Contrary to popular belief, I'm not actually an idiot," she says it lightheartedly, but I hear the underlying anger in that statement.

"Did I ever say I thought you were?"

"No, but I know what people think of me."

"Good thing I'm not *people* then, isn't it?"

"It really is."

We both get back to what we were doing, well, she does. I mostly stare down at the paper in front of me while my thoughts run at a million miles a minute.

"What changed?" I ask, my thoughts spilling from my lips without permission.

She finishes what she's doing before looking up at me.

"What changed with what?"

"After that first night, you left like I'd set your ass on fire and you ignored me from then on. I just assumed I was shit and that you were disappointed."

"I'm fairly sure I remember you making me cry out your name that night."

"Chelsea," I sigh. "You're the queen of playing the game. I had no idea back then if it was one or not. Seeing as you'd never looked twice at me before, I could only assume it was."

"Honestly," she whispers. "A lot changed." She looks down at her hands that are twisting in her lap. "I made some stupid decisions, and one of them was leaving that night. Going away made me realize a lot of things, and one of the biggest was that I wanted you. It's why I came to you first. Why I sought you out after the game. I needed to apologize. I... I needed you."

She looks up at me, her dark eyes full of honesty and regrets.

"Shane, I—"

Whatever she's about to say is cut off when the door behind me opens.

"Hey, I was just wondering... oh, hello, Shane. I wasn't expecting to see you again."

"We're just doing homework," Chelsea says in a rush.

When I glance over my shoulder to say hello, Honey is looking between us with a weird expression on her face.

"Mom, can we talk... outside."

"Sure, sweetie." Chelsea gets up and ushers her mom outside.

I watch the two of them interact but I'm unable to lip read any of what they're saying to each other, although when Honey points at me it makes it clear who they're talking about.

The conversation gets a little heated before Honey walks back to the house. Chelsea looks to the sky, sucking in a deep breath before reaching out for the handle and pulling it open.

"Everything okay?" I ask the second she's inside.

"Yeah, it's..." She takes one look at me and bursts into tears.

"Shit."

I'm up off the floor and have her in my arms in seconds.

"Shhh, it's okay," I whisper into her hair.

"I'm sorry, I'm just being stupid. She offered to make us dinner. I hope you're hungry."

We spend the rest of the afternoon working before heading into the main house to have dinner with Honey.

It's all very normal. Despite the look I keep getting from Chelsea's mom. I almost expect her to launch into the 'what are your intentions with my daughter' speech but it never comes.

Her eyes are soft as she looks between the two of us, but I can see questions swimming in them. Just like I'm sure everyone will tomorrow when we walk into school together.

The thought alone has my stomach in knots.

I've never exactly been in the spotlight like Chelsea. I might be on the team, but I've spent as much time hidden in the shadows as possible, much to my dad's annoyance. He wanted me to be just like him and my brothers and go after the top spot. Shame he couldn't see that his youngest son was too shy and happy being hidden.

But thanks to the girl beside me, I've spent a few weeks as the topic of everyone's gossip as they blamed me for drugging Amalie all those weeks ago.

Walking into that place with the real culprit on my arm is going to cause a stir, that's for sure.

Ideas for the things people might say, accuse me of, fill my mind but one glance at the girl beside me and I know it's worth it.

Our relationship might not be what anyone expected, it might have come from nothing but games and lies, but there's something so right about it. I don't expect anyone else to understand. They don't need to. All that matters is that we're on the same page, and as she meets my eyes, hers twinkle with delight and I know that we are.

We're us going forward and things can only get better... right?

26

CHELSEA

"Are you sure about this?" I ask Shane who's sitting in the driver's seat of his car beside me.

My stomach turns and I worry I might vomit in the footwell.

I blow out what I hope is a calming breath, but it does little to settle the nerves racing around me.

I'm not worried about me. They can throw whatever they like at me and I'll let it wash over me as if it doesn't sting. I'm worried about Shane. He doesn't deserve what they're inevitably going to say about him because of me.

"Yes, Chels. I'm sure. I refuse to hide this because of those assholes." Reaching over, he laces our fingers together and tugs me over to him.

His lips brush against mine, and I immediately relax.

"How about we just go back to the pool house for the day?" I ask against him.

Hanging out in there together yesterday was so incredible. I'm not sure I've ever felt so relaxed in my own home. Him being there with me was just so natural.

Everything was great until Mom turned up and jumped to conclusions about Shane's sudden appearance. Okay so they're correct conclusions and she was not impressed when I admitted that I haven't told him the truth yet.

To be fair, I was trying to work up the courage when she interrupted us. I tell myself that if she didn't choose that exact moment to storm in then I would have confessed all. Although, a huge part of me knows that I'm only lying to myself.

I'm living in denial right now because I know once the truth is out that everything is going to change all over again.

This normal we've found is going to be shattered, and I'm terrified of losing him now that I've found him.

Someone knocking on the window scares the shit out of me and causes us to jump apart in fright.

When I turn to the window, I find a smiling Rae looking back at me with an amused looking Ethan behind her.

"Fucking hell, was that necessary?" I ask, pushing the door open.

"Good morning to you too."

I grunt at her as I climb from the car and grab my purse.

"Are you ready for this?" she asks as Shane walks around and takes my hand.

"No," I state.

"It'll be fine. I'm sure you've dealt with worse in the past," Rae says knowingly.

"Me? Yes, it's him I'm worried about."

"He's a big boy and can make his own decisions," Shane mutters.

"Is that right?" Rae looks up at him, wiggling her eyebrows in delight.

"Really?" Ethan barks. "Don't you think it's bad enough that you withheld information about those two from me, now you're checking him out?"

Rae winces. "I'm in trouble." She winks before Ethan lifts her over his shoulder and marches away from us.

"She's really good for him," I say to Shane as we watch her struggle and squeal against his hold.

"It's amazing what the right woman can do, don't you think?"

"You think I'm the right one?"

Tingles erupt within me as he drops his lips to whisper in my ear. "Yep, in all the wrong ways."

As we get closer to the school building, my skin starts to prickle. I don't need to look up to know that we're gathering attention.

"Huh, looks like the newest gossip just arrived," Shane mutters, clearly braver than me and looking around at our growing audience.

Sucking in some confidence, I lift my head.

Every set of eyes in the vicinity is trained on us.

"Fucking hell. This is going to be hell."

"Only if we let it. Come on."

Much to my horror, Shane guides me to where the team and the squad hang out. They're all too busy in their own conversations to notice us at first. But the second Rich looks up, he elbows Justin and in seconds all of them are glancing our way.

"Well, this isn't what I was expecting to see on a Monday morning," Rich announces, ensuring anyone who hadn't noticed turns our way.

Whispered comments filter around us. My heart hammers in my chest as I wait for the first attack to come.

Shane must get bored waiting for any kind of reaction, either that or he just really wants to nail the point home because he pulls on my arm until I have no choice but to step into his body. He threads his fingers into my hair and lowers his mouth.

Just before they brush against mine, he says, "Might as well give them something to stare at."

His lips press against mine and I forget that we're standing here in the middle of the school with almost everyone watching us. His tongue slips into my mouth and tangles with mine as he pulls me tighter against him.

"Well, fuck me. I didn't think Shane had that in him," Justin hollers when he eventually releases me.

Shane chuckles but doesn't look their way.

"Can I walk you to class?"

"I'd love you to."

Leaving our spectators and the comments they make loud enough for us to hear, we turn our backs and walk away.

While I'm with him, they can't hurt me.

"I wish I was in your classes this morning," Shane says, coming to a stop outside my first class of the day.

"I'll be fine." Reaching out, I cup his cheek in my palm, loving that he's worried about me.

"I'll see you at lunch though, yeah?"

"You can count on it."

I nod as he captures my lips in a sweet kiss before turning away and marching down the hallway.

My heart melts as I watch him move. I had no idea I could feel quite this strongly about another person, other than the one I'm currently growing. That thought has my guilt hitting me full force again.

I'll tell him soon, I say to myself as I make my way into the empty classroom with a goofy smile on my face.

As each class passes, I ignore the comments that I was expecting, the gossip that I hear happening around me. It means little to me, my reputation in Rosewood High was ruined all those weeks ago, I just don't want to bring Shane down with me.

For the first time since I came back, I find myself actually eating lunch in the cafeteria. But I'm not at the table I'm used to with the team and the squad, I'm at one I never thought I would be. I look up at Shane and then to his friends who surround us. Camila and Mason are opposite with Amalie beside her and Ethan and Rae next to me.

Camila doesn't hide the fact that's she's not happy about this, and I can't blame her. Knowing she's only looking out for Shane makes me like her that much more. Amalie, however, hasn't really batted an eyelid about my appearance.

She should be the one who's angry at me, much like Mason but it seems they've accepted it for what it was, a mistake, and moved on. I couldn't be more grateful, but that doesn't mean I won't speak to both of them when I get a chance to apologize.

They all chat around me as if my presence by Shane's side is normal. While the rest of the school looked shocked, if not slightly horrified by this turn of events, these guys just seem to roll with it. It makes me wonder if Rae had given them the heads up.

She told me that she and Amalie had seen Shane at the hospital last week and it was how she figured it out, maybe Amalie had similar thoughts.

While the football team mostly ignores us, I feel the cheer squad's attention throughout lunch.

I haven't spoken to any of them since my final run-in with Shelly and quite frankly, I don't have any intention of changing that.

I might not be happy about leaving my squad behind but if that's how it's going to be then so be it. I've got more important things to worry about right now.

I slip my hand into Shane's and squeeze.

Dropping his lips to my ear, his breath makes me shudder. "Are you okay? You wanna get out of here?"

"No, I'm fine. Your friends are nice."

"You've just got to give people a chance, Chels."

I want the ground to swallow me up as how I've acted in the past flashes through my mind. I've been such a bitch.

"I'm just going to the bathroom," I say as I stand, needing to get away and have a moment.

I head for the bathrooms that he chased me to last week, but when I glance back over my shoulder, I find he's not doing the same today, his eyes are firmly fixed on me though, concern laced through them.

I push inside and suck in a deep, calming breath, willing the tears filling my eyes to subside. I really don't need to break down and give anyone any more reason to gossip about me.

I get a few dirty looks from the girls inside, but thanks to my previous reputation, none of them actually say anything to my face. I guess it's one benefit of being known as the queen bitch.

"Hey, are you okay?" a familiar voice asks as I waste time washing my hands.

"Yeah, I just needed a breather."

"You haven't told him, have you?"

Turning, I find Rae's dark eyes and immediately look away.

"Not yet. I'm scared."

She walks over to the mirror and wipes at the dark makeup under her eyes.

"I understand that. But don't you think it's going to get worse the longer you keep it inside. Today must have been huge for him. What he's done for you takes some serious balls. You owe him the truth."

My stomach twists and I lift my hand to it in the hope it stops it. "I know. But what if he hates me?"

"He'll hate you more for lying to him."

"Touché."

"I can't imagine how scary it must be. But you need him. Both of you," she says, glancing down to my stomach.

I blow out a breath.

"I know. I know. Things have just been so... incredible. I don't want to ruin it."

"Who says it will ruin it? Yeah, it's gonna be a shock, but things might be okay."

I like her positive thinking, but I'm a little more realistic about the whole thing.

By the time it gets to the end of the day, I'm just about ready to go home and have a nap while Shane is at practice.

I'm standing at my locker, grabbing the books I need for tonight when a shadow falls over me.

A shiver runs down my spine as I slam my locker and turn on whoever it is that's brave enough to approach me. I might have been the hot topic around school today but at least everyone has kept their distance.

My eyes widen when I find Victoria, Tasha, and Aria standing before me.

"Shouldn't you be at practice?" I ask, pushing away from the lockers and moving for the exit.

"That's what we need to talk to you about."

I pause with my back to them. "Why?" I ask over my shoulder.

"Um... things aren't going so well."

I turn around and look at the three of them. They look nervous and it piques my interest.

"And that's my issue because...? I've been kicked out, remember?"

"Yeah but... we need you."

Something that I can only describe as hope blooms within me.

"You... need me? For what exactly."

"Ugh, cut the bullshit," Aria says, stepping forward. "Shelly was a shit captain. She can't organize shit. Kelly, well fuck knows where Kelly is, she's not turned up to practice since Wednesday and everything's falling apart."

I open my mouth to respond but no words come out.

"Please," Victoria adds. "Come back. We know things are... awkward, but Shelly was the one who didn't want you. We all know that we need you if we're going to stand a chance at regionals. Please, Chels."

"Wow, okay," I mutter in surprise.

"So what do you say?"

The thought of following them and doing what I love most fills me with joy, but then my reality slams into me. I can hardly climb onto a pyramid and be thrown around like I used to.

"I can't cheer," I admit. "After the accident last week, it's not a good idea for me to..." I trail off before I say too much and can be caught lying.

"But you can captain, you can lead us, right? One of the JV girls can take your place. Harley is really good."

"Um..." A smile twitches at my lips. "I'd love to." I try to contain my excitement, but it breaks across my face as they squeal in delight and run at me.

"Shelly is going to be really pissed when she gets back to school," I say as I walk in the opposite direction from where I expected to be going.

"Shelly can fuck off," Victoria mutters. "She doesn't have what it takes to be captain. Her head's gotten so big I'm surprised she can fit in the fucking gym."

I allow the three of them to go ahead of me as I pull my cell out to shoot Shane a message to tell him that I'm not heading straight home. He'd given me his keys so I could drive his car, telling me that he'd get a lift from one of the guys but it seems we're going to get to travel together after all.

The girls are all gathered in the center of the mats when I walk in.

"She said yes," Victoria squeals as they all turn my way.

Delight lights up their faces as I walk toward them and the final piece of my puzzle slots into place. This gym is my home. I belong here, and it's not until right now that I really accept just how much I'd missed it. I might not be able to cheer like before, but that's not an issue. I'm with my squad.

Dropping my purse and books to the side of the gym, I take my place at the front of the girls.

"You guys ready to fucking kill regionals?" I shout, a wide smile on my face as they all start jumping up and down and cheering.

27

SHANE

Chelsea: I'm in the gym with the squad. Meet me when you're done xx
I stare at my message with wide eyes and fear filling my veins. I know that Shelly is still suspended, but nothing good can come of her being with those girls. They pushed her down the fucking stairs for Christ's sake. She can tell me all she likes that Shelly didn't touch her but if it weren't for her, then Chelsea never would have ended up in the hospital like she did.

I dress as quickly as I can after showering off the session's mud and sweat. Our usual practice might be over along with the season but Coach isn't letting up with our conditioning. I'm glad, I need it. Although less so now I've got Chelsea to keep me active.

"You on a fucking promise or something?" Zayn asks as he watches me hop around trying to dress at the speed of light.

"Something like that."

"I hate to say this, but you two are seriously fucking cute together."

"Aw, Zayn. You jealous?"

"Of regular pussy? Hell yeah," he states as I roll my eyes.

"You might meet someone who'll put up with your brand of asshole one day."

"Someone? Nah, I want at least two regulars. One could never keep up with me."

"You're a fucking dog. This is why you have zero regular girls. They're worried they'll catch something."

"You're moody when you need to get laid."

"I don't need..." I trail off, and he laughs. "Whatever. I'm outta here. Not coming to Aces?"

"I'll see if Chelsea wants to."

As I leave, he makes whipping noises behind me. All I do is smile. I fucking love it.

Jogging toward the gym, I pray that I'm not about to walk into some kind of cheer torture scene. But to my surprise, what I find is very much the opposite. Thank fuck.

Music booms around the gym and Chelsea is front and center counting and barking orders at the girls who are somersaulting, cartwheeling, and flying through the air.

She's got the biggest smile on her face and I can't help but share her joy. I have no idea what's happened to get her here again, the one place she wanted to be more than anything but she looks right at home.

"Lock your arms, Aria. If Ruby drops, it's your fault," she barks as the JV wobbles on top of the pyramid looking terrified. "That's it. Better."

I stand and watch them all for long minutes before one of the girls spots me and causes Chelsea to also look my way.

"Hey," she says, bounding over to me and throwing her arms around my shoulders. Her eyes sparkle in delight.

"I wasn't expecting to find this," I say into the top of her hair.

"I know. Isn't it incredible? Let me just finish up with these guys and we can get out of here."

I release her from my hold and watch her lead her squad in a cool down before dismissing them to the locker rooms.

Pride oozes from my chest as I watch her taking back the role that was always meant to be hers.

"Okay, let's get the fuck out of here," she says, walking to me and swiping her purse from the floor.

"Don't you wanna..." I gesture to the locker rooms where the others disappeared.

"I'm sure they can shower without me." She laughs, reaching up and brushing a wet lock of my hair from my face. That's not exactly what I meant, but I'm not going to complain that she's not about to leave me waiting for her.

"The guys wanted to know if you wanted to go to Aces."

"They want me there?" she asks, and I hate that she even has to question it.

"Well, they invited me, I told them that we come as a package."

She smiles up at me. "You don't have to do that, you know. You shouldn't be punished for my mistakes."

"I'm not. I just don't want to go without you. You belong there more than I do."

She looks back to the now empty and quiet gym and lets out a sigh.

"What happened here exactly?"

"I'll tell you on the way. I could really use a burger and milkshake."

The team looks a little hesitant as we walk toward our usual table, that is everyone apart from Ethan who immediately makes sure there's enough space for us to join.

Chelsea gets a few looks that I'm not all that impressed by, but on the whole, the team are on their best behavior, which is unusual. They're too busy planning for winter formal and the party that follows.

It's not until we're joined by the squad and they engage with Chelsea like everything is normal that I start to relax.

Pulling her tighter into my side, I kiss the top of her head and she looks up at me and smiles. My chest aches and three little words that I know she's nowhere ready to hear almost fall from my lips.

My cell vibrating in my pocket thankfully stops any more crazy thoughts.

Mom: Dad's back and wants you here for dinner.

I groan and Chelsea doesn't miss it.

"Everything okay?" she asks, looking up at me with those huge eyes of hers.

I show her my cell.

"Want me to come too?"

My lips curl at her offer but the thought of having her there to hear Dad and I argue about my future isn't exactly my idea of fun.

"I really appreciate that, but I think it's probably best if I do it alone."

"Okay," she says snuggling into my side.

"Do you want a lift home or are you going to hang out with the squad?"

She looks up at them. "I think I'll stay for a bit. Call me later though, yeah?"

"Try and stop me."

Tilting her head back, I sweep my tongue into her mouth, not giving two fucks about our audience.

Hoots and hollers sound out around us but I barely hear any of them. As always, I'm too lost in her.

The last thing I want to do is leave her here, especially to go and spend time with my dad, but I don't really have much of a choice. If I don't go now, then it'll only make it worse.

With one final kiss, I leave her behind. She has a huge smile on her face, so I don't doubt that she's exactly where she wants to be. Ethan winks at me as I look back over my shoulder telling me that he'll keep an eye on her. I never thought I'd happily rely on him for anything, but it's weird how things change.

Dread fills me as I make the short drive home. The closer I get, the more I wish I took Chelsea up on her offer to come with me. She would have made this a little more bearable.

Both Mom and Dad are already in the dining room when I get there, waiting for me.

"What time do you call this?" Dad barks the second I step into the room.

"I got Mom's message twenty minutes ago. I came as fast as I could."

Dad tuts while Mom mutters that it's okay as she rushes from the room, I guess to get the dinner.

"You look like shit."

"Wow, thanks, Dad. It's nice to see you too."

"You need to take better care of yourself if you're—"

"Don't," I warn.

"Oh, you wouldn't believe who I ran into yesterday."

I roll my eyes but keep my attention on my empty plate.

"I did a speech at Penn. Do you know who their new coach is going to be next season?"

"I've got no idea, but I'm assuming you're about to tell me," I mutter.

Thankfully before he can launch into his story, Mom reappears with armfuls of food. Jumping up from the table, I help her lay it all out in the center.

"Kit Anderson," Dad continues as if Mom isn't currently acting like a servant and loading his plate with food. "Can you believe that?"

I shrug, helping myself to some chicken. I'm not hungry after the burger I had at Aces but I know better than to sit here and refuse food.

"He gave me some great insight into who's tipped for the top next year. I've reevaluated our options and I think..." He pauses as he reaches into his pocket and pulls out a list.

"Do we need to do this now?" Mom asks softly.

"It's important, Maddie. Shane's choice now will determine his future career. I have to make the right decision."

And that statement right there just about says it all.

"I know you just want the best for him, but don't you think it should be Shane's decision to make, not yours?"

Dad cuts her a seething look and she pales slightly. Dad's a force to be reckoned with, I think she learned years ago that trying to persuade him in a different direction is pointless.

"He doesn't have all the information. I do."

"He is also sitting right here," I mutter. "You can give me all the information you like, but I'm the one filling out the applications, and I'll apply wherever I see fit." Pushing my chair out behind me, I stand. "I'm sorry, Mom. I'm sure this is delicious, but I'm not sitting here and putting up with his bullshit."

"Shane, get back in here right this second," he barks from behind me as I race from the room and up the stairs.

I pace back and forth in my bedroom as the sound of my parents arguing downstairs filters up to me.

I can't fucking wait to get out of here and start my own life.

Sitting down at my desk, I pull open my bottom drawer and wrap my fingers around the college applications I've been working on. A couple are the same as the ones Dad wants me to apply to, but he's not the reason.

I flick through the brochures for the millionth time, hoping that something will jump out at me and tell me that it's the one. Nothing does.

Part of me wants to get as far away from here as possible, as far away from him as possible. But the other part wants to stay. I could apply to Maddison or Florida U and be close for Mom.

With a sigh, I rest back in my chair. I wonder where Chelsea is planning to go. We might have spent quite a bit of time together over the past few days, but talk about our futures hasn't really come up.

Even thinking about this is crazy. It's only been a few days and here I am allowing thoughts of her future to influence mine.

Unable to resist, I grab my cell from the side and shoot her a message.

It's fucking crazy, but I miss her.

If I thought I had some weird obsession before when she barely spoke to me or looked my way, then I know I do now. She's given me a taste, shown me what she hides beneath the mask she wears, and fuck, I never want to let her go.

28

CHELSEA

I hated seeing the dejected look on his face as he walked out of Aces, but I knew he was right. He needed to deal with his family alone. It's not my place to turn up and play peacekeeper between him and his dad.

My lips curl in disgust as I think about how his dad treats him and what he expects from him. Shane doesn't talk about it much, he doesn't need to. I've seen it with my own eyes over the years, heard his crazy unrealistic expectations. Shane's avoidance when it comes to talking about the future and what college he wants to go to is understandable.

His dad wants him to be the NFL's next big star, but anyone who knows Shane even a little bit can tell that's not who he is. Hell, I knew that even before anything happened between us.

Pushing thoughts of Shane from my mind for now, I focus on my squad as they sit and gossip around me.

The last thing I was expecting was to end the day back in my beloved role as captain, I thought that ship had long sailed but it turned out that I just had to be patient.

"Shelly is back tomorrow," Aria says. "She's not going to be happy about this."

A shiver of dread runs down my spine at the thought. I can't imagine she was too thrilled to be suspended when she didn't so much as touch me last week but it seemed that she was already on Hartmann's shit list and that it was the exact excuse he needed to give her some time out.

I can't really complain. It's been nice without her. I can't help but wonder though if my easy return to the squad is going to be very short-lived. She's going to come back gunning for me, that's for sure.

Our afternoon in Aces is just like old times, only now, I feel like I might actually belong. The squad wants me, whereas before I was sure they just put up with me because they had to, and I now know that I've got someone who's going to stand beside me no matter what tomorrow and Shelly bring.

Nerves flutter in my belly and remind me that those aren't the only differences. In a few weeks, I know I'm not going to be able to hide this secret anymore. I've been lucky this far with keeping it to myself but I know I'm on borrowed time, especially with Shane.

I need to tell him before someone else beats me to it.

"Hey, Chels. You want a lift home?" Ethan asks, dragging me from my thoughts.

Looking up, I find him standing with his arm around Rae. He's not looking at her yet he's got this smile playing on his lips that I don't think existed until she turned up in his life.

"Yeah, that would be great," I say.

After saying goodbye to the squad, I follow Ethan and Rae from the diner.

I'm too busy chatting to them to pay much attention to the parking lot and I jump into the back of Ethan's truck without much thought.

That is until we pull out and I spot that truck again, idling by the exit.

"Hey," I say, poking my head between the two front seats. "You have any idea who drives that truck?"

I know it's a long shot, but I figure it's worth asking because I don't have a fucking clue. I've racked my brain to come up with the answer but other than one possibility that I don't even want to consider, I've got no idea who it could be. They seem pretty interested in me, mind you.

Ethan looks in his mirror as we pull out in front of them and shakes his head.

"I have no idea. Why?"

"No reason," I lie, looking back over my shoulder to see if I can get a look at the driver. Sadly, the reflection of the windshield means I can't see shit other than the sun lowering in the sky.

Sitting back, I cross my arms and blow out a breath.

It's just a coincidence that I keep seeing it, I tell myself. But it doesn't settle the unease that's churning in my stomach.

I try not to look back, knowing that I'll drive myself crazy, but I do. The truck follows us all the way to the end of my street before it continues forward when Ethan signals to turn. He doesn't seem bothered after I pointed it out earlier. But why should he? He's not aware that it's been following me around like a fucking psycho stalker for the past few days.

I breathe a little easier knowing that he's gone as I wave goodbye to Ethan and Rae and slip into the house.

The sound of Christmas music fills my ears and unlike the past few years, instead of groaning, I actually smile.

"Hey, sweetie," Mom says when I poke my head into the living room. "I was hoping you'd be back soon. Want to help me?" she asks, gesturing to the bare tree.

She's been slowly decorating the house since I got back from the center, but I'm surprised it's taken her this long to tackle the tree.

I was intending on having a shower and starting on my homework, but for once, hanging out with Mom and getting in the festive spirit seems more appealing.

"Sure," I say, dropping my purse to the couch and going to join her.

"Did you have a good day?" she asks as we wrap the fairy lights around the branches.

"Yes, actually." I go on to tell her about the squad.

"You know you probably shouldn't be cheering now, don't you?"

I stare at her for a beat, clearly my expression saying exactly what my words aren't.

"I'm sorry, I'm sorry. I can't help worrying."

"I know what I'm doing, Mom," I say, reaching into the box of decorations and pulling an ornament out.

"Is that why you haven't told Shane yet, because you know what you're doing?" She stops what she's doing and stares at me.

There was no hiding Shane's involvement in this whole thing when he turned up over the weekend and then never left.

"Things are complicated."

"You're telling me."

I let out a sigh and sit on the edge of the couch. "The time we spent together before I went away... it was... I thought it was a mistake. I was lonely, he was there. I don't need to spell that out for you," I say with a roll of my eyes.

"But then I found myself in that place again, and I started allowing myself to reflect and consider what I really wanted, and things started to change for me. The time I'd spent with him, albeit short, it was different. He was different.

"Then I found out about..." I gesture to myself. "And I knew I needed to do something about it. I didn't for a second think he'd give me the time of day when I got back. I'd dragged him down along with the others I'd hurt. He had every right to throw my attempts at making up for it back in my face. Well, actually he did to start with but..." I trail off, not really needing to go into all of that.

"By some miracle, he forgave me and he showed me the real him and what life could be like if I just let someone in.

"He's..." I pause, thinking of our time together and trying to come up with a word to describe it. "He's been incredible. Everything I never knew I needed but always wanted. I don't know," I say with a shake of my head. "Everything just feels right."

Mom looks at me with soft, tear-filled eyes. "Chelsea," she says, dropping down beside me and taking my hands in hers. "Don't get me wrong, I'm thrilled you've found that in him. He's a really good kid and I don't think I could have chosen someone better for you if I tried. But," she says, and I groan. "You need to tell him. The longer this goes on and he doesn't know the truth, the more it's going to hurt him. If he's the kind of guy you think he is, then he's going to want to know."

"What if he's not that guy?" I ask, terrified of even saying the words aloud.

"If he's not, then you don't need him in your life. You are a strong, *fierce*, young woman, Chelsea. You don't need a man. You are more than capable of doing things yourself."

"I... I know that. Believe it or not, I'm not actually scared of doing this alone if I have to. I just... I don't want to. I know what it's like to come from a broken home, I don't want that." I pull my hand from hers and drop it to my belly.

"You need to trust that he'll do the right thing. And if that's not what you want, then you need to make the best of it. You're going to be an incredible mother, Chelsea. Just don't waste time and risk Shane not being the kind of dad he could be because he's too angry to see what's important."

"You're right." I nod. "I just don't know how I'm supposed to tell him."

"You'll figure it out. I have faith in you."

We spend the next hour finishing up the tree before Mom offers to make us both hot chocolates. I leave her to it so I can go shower and change.

The second I walk into the pool house, I can smell him. Disappointment floods me that he's not here and I pull my cell from my purse. I find a message from him from ten minutes ago.

Shane: I miss you. What are you doing?

Chelsea: Putting up decs with Mom. Did everything go okay?

It shows that he's read the message, but he doesn't respond. Dread sits heavy in my stomach that he's still in the middle of dealing with whatever his dad's got to be throwing at him.

With a sigh, I drop down on the edge of my bed and place my cell on my nightstand, hoping that I'll hear from him again soon.

Pulling the top drawer open, I lift up the notebooks and scraps of paper to find what I'd hidden beneath.

I pull my ultrasound pictures out and stare at my little person. Excitement races through me and I press my palm to my stomach, hoping that they know how much I love it already.

I run my finger over the tiny black and white image, wondering what the baby might look like. If it is going to have dark hair and eyes like me, or light like Shane. If it is going to be a little cheerleader or a football player.

I know I've got so many things to be worried or apprehensive about but excitement is my overriding emotion whenever I think about what the future holds for me.

Placing my pictures on the nightstand, I push from the bed in favor of stripping off and getting in the shower.

I intend to pull on a pair of sweats and a hoodie and spend the evening chilling out with Mom and some Christmas movie she's sure to find on the TV.

I'm just rinsing the conditioner from my hair when I hear a crash.

My heart jumps into my throat as I think about the truck with the dark windows and beaming headlights.

"Fuck," I mutter, making quick work of finishing up and wrapping a towel around my body, feeling grateful that no one's walked in here with a knife or anything crazy.

With my heart almost pounding out of my chest, I poke my head from the bathroom. But there's no one there.

"Hello," I shout out as I tiptoe to the living area. But when I get there, I find it as empty as the bedroom.

I glance around, looking for something out of place that could have caused the crash, but I find nothing.

Assuming it was just Mom coming to get something, I walk back to the bedroom. Something on the floor by my bed catches my eye. The second I take a step toward it, I know exactly what it is. My ultrasound pictures.

I look around again, although I already know there's no one here but fear skates through me, nonetheless.

Who just walked in here and saw this?

Picking up my cell, I pray that there will be a reply from Shane letting me know that he's still at home.

Please, please, please, I beg silently as I tap the screen.

Nothing.

"Fuck."

Dropping the towel to the floor, I make quick work of pulling on some clothes, although with how violently my hands are trembling, I'm not very successful.

The second I'm dressed, I grab my cell and car keys and run from the pool house.

"I'm sorry, Mom. I need to be somewhere," I call as I run through the main house.

"Is everything okay?" she calls back from her position in the kitchen.

"I hope so."

She shouts something back, but I'm already out the door, too far away to make out the words.

I don't bother looking around for my stalker, instead I wrench the door open and drop down into the driver's seat.

I fly out of the driveway and in seconds, I'm heading for the Dunn house.

If it was him, there's a very good chance that he didn't go straight home.

Fuck.

My hands tremble against the wheel and my stomach turns over as I think about him finding out like that.

He's going to fucking hate me.

My mouth waters like I'm about to throw up and for a moment I think I'm going to have to pull over so I can do just that. But after sucking in some deep breaths, it passes and I'm able to continue.

The second I turn on his street, I'm craning my neck to see if his car is parked in the driveway.

Please be here. Please be here.

"Oh my god," I cry when I get closer and see the back end of his car parked in the driveway.

Pulling my car to a stop on the street, I rest my head back and close my eyes for a second.

Maybe there was no one there. Maybe it was just my imagination and I didn't put the pictures on the nightstand like I thought.

I almost turn around and head home, feeling stupid for overreacting. But what if I'm wrong? What if my first instinct was right and he's in there now hating me because he knows my—our—secret.

"Shit, shit, shit."

Letting out my breath in a long exhale, I push the door open and step out.

Walking up to the front door, I knock and wait. But nothing happens despite the fact I can hear voices—raised voices—inside. Hearing an argument in full force doesn't help settle my nerves at all.

Gripping the door handle, I push down to see if it'll allow me inside. Surprisingly, it does.

I silently slip into the house and peer around the kitchen door where the shouting is coming from.

Inside, I find Maddie and Brett barking at each other, arms flailing around in frustration. Moving before I'm caught, I turn for the stairs and quietly run up.

I pass the closed bedroom doors until I get to the one I want.

Okay, here goes nothing.

I push it open and step inside, but the room is empty.

My heart rate increases once more as I hesitantly take a step inside and look around.

I relax the second the sound of running water hits my ears and I turn toward Shane's bathroom.

Steam billows out from the adjoining room and a smile pulls at my lips, knowing that I'm going to find him naked behind that door. Things are definitely turning out better than I was expecting.

Placing my cell and keys on the dresser, I make my way over.

The heat hits me the second I step into the room. It's clear he's been in here for some time. Everything is steamed up and I can barely see him behind the glass door.

He's standing with his face tipped up to the water, totally still.

I make the most of my few minutes to rake my eyes down his sculpted body. He's not as bulky as some of the other guys on the team, but he's no less cut.

My mouth waters as I think about stripping naked and joining him. About running my hands over his smooth, taut skin.

I trail my eyes back up, enjoying my view. As if he knows I'm here, when I get to his chin, his head drops and our eyes connect.

As his eyes widen in shock, something crackles between us.

His lips part in surprise before a smile tugs at one corner.

Reaching out, he cuts off the water and steps out from behind the screen.

His eyes drop from mine to take in my body and my temperature soars.

"Fuck," is all he says before he closes the space between us and finds my lips.

His hands grip my ass as he lifts me and places me on the counter. My knees part and he steps between them, soaking me with his wet body.

His kiss is bruising as he slides his fingers into my still wet hair so he can tilt my face to just the right angle. His tongue sweeps into my mouth, tangling with my own as he claims me.

My hands run down his back, my nails scratching lightly until I find his ass and squeeze. It presses us closer together, his hard cock teasing at my core.

Heat floods me at the thought of him taking me here like this.

"Shane," I moan when he rips his lips from mine in favor of kissing down my neck.

His teeth graze as he kisses and sucks the sensitive skin into his mouth.

His hand finds its way under my shirt and he groans when he finds me bare beneath. His hot touch is a hint of a reminder of the panic I felt as I dressed and left the pool house.

But all that floats away when he pinches my nipple so hard I swear it has me on the edge of release.

"Shane, I need you."

"Fuck, Chels."

Gripping the hem of my shirt, he rips it over my head, throwing it haphazardly behind him somewhere. He continues kissing down to the swell of my breasts as he pushes my already high skirt up my thighs so it's around my waist.

He makes quick work of ripping the sides of my panties so they fall from my body before pulling me to the edge of the counter.

He's in a frenzy of need, but right before he pushes inside me, he rests his forehead against mine and looks into my eyes.

My breath catches at the emotions staring back at me. I can't decipher most of them, but one thing I do know. He needs this right now.

"Fuck me," I demand and he surges forward.

A garbled cry falls from my lips as he fills me in one swift move.

Thankfully, he stills for a beat to allow me to adjust before he pulls out, shifts me forward a little more and thrusts back in.

"Oh god."

I lean back on my palms and watch where we connect.

So. Fucking. Hot.

"Chelsea," he groans, forcing me to look up at him.

His lids are heavy, he's desperate to close them, to allow the pleasure to take him away from whatever it is that's causing the frown lines to crease his forehead.

"I'm here. Take what you need."

His fingers dig into my hips with a painful grip as he pulls out.

"How did you know?" His voice is so low that I almost don't make out the words.

"Know what?"

"That I needed you. Fuuuuck."

He hits me so deep that I lose all train of thought as he slams into me over and over, building me up for one incredible fall.

"Shane. Fuck. Fuck." My head falls back as he keeps going.

The only thing that can be heard is that of our heavy breathing and our skin connecting. The scent of his shower gel gives way to the smell of sex as the heat of the room has our skin slick with sweat.

"Lips. Chelsea. Need your lips."

Dragging my head up, I find him staring at me. His eyes almost black with his need. Sitting up, I wrap my hand around the back of his neck and crash my lips to his.

The new angle is mind-blowing and in only seconds I am racing toward my release.

Our kiss is messy as we try to get as much of each other as we can but soon our need for air as we both fall over the edge halts our movements.

"Oh fuuuuuck," he grates out as his cock twitches violently inside me.

Dropping my head to his shoulder, I fight to catch my breath, but he doesn't let up.

With his fingers once again in my hair, he pulls my head back and finds my lips.

He kisses me like it might be the last chance he gets. It's wet, dirty, and full of emotion. It's like he's trying to tell me just how he feels, how desperate he is without saying the actual words. I accept all of it because the feeling is most definitely mutual. I may have told Mom earlier that I know what I'm doing. But the truth of it is that I have no fucking idea. I'm on the cusp of something so life-changing that I can't really even begin to comprehend what my future looks like. But being with Shane like this. All of it floats away and I know he needs this just as much as I do right now.

Lifting me into his arms, I wrap my legs around his waist, and he carries me into his bedroom before lowering me to the bed.

He stands back up and stares down at me. His chest heaves as droplets continue to fall from his hair and run down his defined muscles. His cock is hard once again and twitches under my stare.

"How'd you know?" he asks, repeating his question from earlier. "How'd you know I needed you?"

I bite down on my bottom lip, unsure of how to answer that question.

"D-did you come to the pool house tonight?" His brows pull together at my sudden change of topic.

"What? No, I was here. Wishing I was with you."

I can't fight the smile that spreads across my lips.

"Is everything okay?" he asks, clearly sensing that something is off with me.

"Y-yeah." I should come clean. I should tell him everything now.

I open my mouth to say something, anything, but at the same time, he falls on top of me and takes advantage of my parted lips.

"I wanted to come to you. But you were hanging with your mom. Fuck, Chels."

"What happened with your dad?"

"Normal bullshit. I'm not good enough. Will never make it. Need to decide which team I want to play for. He just won't fucking listen."

"Shane," I say, placing my palm on his rough cheek.

"You are good enough. You are more than good enough. You're incredible."

A smile twitches at his lips.

He shakes his head like he can't believe what I'm saying.

"Fucking hell, I can't get enough of you."

He quickly tugs my skirt down my legs and drops it to the floor so we're both bare before he rolls me on top of him.

"Your turn," he says with a wink, taking his length in hand and holding it so all I have to do is sink down.

"Jeez, I'm not your sex slave."

"The position is available should you want y..." His words trail off as I lower down onto him. "Fuck. Will I ever get used to this feeling?"

"I hope not."

I drop down until I've taken every inch of him.

He stares up at me with such adoration, such, dare I say it... love, that it brings tears to my eyes.

"Chels," he says, reaching for my hands and pulling me forward.

His eyes search mine. I have no doubt he can see my threatening tears but like always when I'm around him, I don't want to hide how I feel. My mask is well and truly shed when it's just the two of us. He sees me. The real me. And yet he's still here.

"I know," I whisper. "I know."

"You fucking slay me, you know that."

"The feeling is mutual."

Dropping my lips to his, I cut off whatever his response was going to be. I fear he's on the edge of admitting something he's going to regret when I'm finally brave enough to tell him the truth.

I'll do it after this, I tell myself, once again putting it off.

I move against him, keeping the pace slow this time. Trying to show him exactly how I feel about him with my body instead of my words. I need him to know how real this is, how much it means to me. Words are nothing. They get thrown around all the time. Lies are too easy. But this. This feeling of us together. There is no lie there. It's impossible.

Our tongues slide against one another's as I continue to grind against him. His hands find my hips, attempting to get me to go faster but I resist. I'm in charge this time and I set the pace.

Dragging my lips from his, I kiss across his jaw, sucking his earlobe into my mouth before dropping down his neck.

"So good," I groan in his ear. "Your cock feels so good inside me."

A low growl comes from the back of his throat.

"Do you feel it?" His fingers grip the nape of my neck.

"Every fucking time I look at you. Touch you. Think of you."

"Fuck, Shane," I pant, his words pushing me closer to release.

"You're it for me, Chels. This is it for me. Whatever happens from here on out, college, our futures. It's us, baby. Promise me."

His words make my heart swell to the point I worry it might burst. "It's us. Always."

The first clench of my release hits me and I just start to fall when there's a commotion at the door.

"Shane, I need—fuck." Brett's eyes go impossibly wide as they land on us before he lifts his hands to his hair and spins around. "What the fuck, boy? This is our house. Our fucking house. Get her fucking out of here," he bellows so loud I can't help but wince as I jump from Shane.

"Get the fuck out, Dad."

"What the hell—oh," Maddie says, racing in to see what's going on.

Her eyes land on me and although I register the shock that was in Brett's she looks nowhere near as murderous at finding me here.

"Get the fuck out," Brett barks at me, risking turning around. Thankfully, I'm now wrapped in one of Shane's sheets. He however is still standing naked with just a pillow covering his junk.

"Dad, stop. Don't fucking talk to her like that."

"You are a fucking joke. A fucking joke." He marches toward Shane with his finger pointing at him.

Shame races through Shane's features.

"No," I cry, attempting to run over, but Maddie catches my arm and stops me from getting between the two of them.

"Just go, Chels." Shane's voice is empty, cold, and it makes a sob erupt from my throat.

"No, I'm not leaving you with him like this."

"It's fine. I'll see you tomorrow."

"No. Shane."

It takes a few seconds, but eventually he rips his eyes from his father's and turns them on me.

"Please," he whispers, his eyes pleading with me not to make this harder than it already is.

The tears that were filling my eyes spill over.

"O-okay."

"Here." He throws a shirt at me that's on the chair beside him and after a second, I follow Maddie out of the room.

She shuts the door behind us.

"What are you doing? You need to stop them, stop him," I plead.

"I will. Don't worry about him. I'll tell him to call you."

Not worrying that she's standing before me, I drop the sheet and pull Shane's shirt over my head. His scent relaxes me instantly, well that is until there's a loud crash from his bedroom.

"Go," she says. "Everything will be okay."

I want to scream at her. How is it going to be okay? She saw the look in Brett's eyes just like I did. I want to run in there and drag Shane out with me. But I can't. I'm powerless to do anything but what I'm told.

With a nod, I turn and head for the stairs.

"Chelsea." My name is no more than a whisper.

Turning, I look over my shoulder at her sad expression.

"I'm glad it's you," is all she says before slipping back into the room seconds before shouts erupt and something else smashes.

I race down the stairs, tears streaming down my face as I flee their house. I don't want to leave without him, I want to stand beside him and fight his battles with him, but I know I can't. This is a family thing and I need to back away and let him deal with it in his own way.

I don't realize that I left my shoes on his bathroom floor until I step foot on his driveway and the stones dig into my skin.

"Motherfucker," I spit as I run toward my car.

I fire up the engine and speed away from his house. If I sit out here, I know the temptation to go back inside will be too strong to ignore.

I'm almost back at my house before I notice the lights behind me.

Fire burns in my belly as my grip tightens on the wheel. Now really isn't the time for this asshole.

Unlike earlier, when I turn onto my street, he follows.

Slamming my foot on the break, I bring my car to an abrupt stop before jumping out and running toward the truck following me.

To my surprise, it slows to a stop in front of my house despite the fact I'm getting closer.

The passenger window lowers as I approach.

"What the fuck is your problem? Why the fuck do you keep following me, asshole?" I scream. I lost control of my emotions about the time I was sent away from Shane's room.

The car is in darkness as I approach but my eyes soon adjust.

"What is it you want from m..." My final word trails off as I look into a familiar set of eyes. "No," I cry, fear like I haven't felt for years filling my veins. "No. No." I stumble back, tripping over my own feet as I run for the house.

This time I don't feel the stones cutting through my skin as I fly around the back of the house and race toward the safety of my pool house.

I fumble with the lock and after what feels like the longest time, I fall through the door. My breaths come in harsh pants as I try to drag in the air I need.

Slamming the door behind me, I run for the bedroom and then through to the bathroom, the door closing behind me with a loud crash.

Those blue eyes are a permanent image in my head.

"No. No. No," I chant as I turn the shower on and drop to the floor beneath the spray.

The water soaks Shane's shirt but I barely notice. I just need the quiet that comes with the water.

It's the only place I used to feel safe. Safe from them.

A shudder runs down my spine.

I thought I'd left them all behind. I thought the men of my past were only in my occasional nightmare now. I had no idea one would be stalking me.

I have no idea who those eyes belong to. I never took the time to learn any of their names. They were just one scumbag after the other who turned up for my whore of a mother. Some barely looked my way, some looked too hard. Some... my blood runs cold and I fight to keep the memories down.

Nothing good can come from recalling that time of my life. A time when no one cared what happened to me. When they forced themselves on me, thinking they could take things that weren't theirs to take.

Fuck. I want Shane.

Pulling my knees up to my chest, I wrap my arms around them and drop my head to my arms as I try to push away the images that have haunted me for years. It's only been in the past few months that I've mostly rid them from my life.

29

SHANE

"Are you trying to intentionally fuck everything up?" Dad barks, but I'm already tired of his bullshit.

As Mom slips back into the room, hopefully to help calm him the fuck down, I find a pair of boxers and pull them up my legs.

My muscles are pulled tight with anger, and unmoving when all I want to be doing is punching him, is physically painful.

The look on Chelsea's face as I sent her away haunts me. I didn't want to hurt her. I just needed her away from this, from him.

Dragging on a pair of sweats, I pull a clean shirt from my drawer and grab a bag.

"Are you even listening to me?"

I don't give him so much as an acknowledgment, and it only adds fuel to his already raging fire.

"Brett, that's enough," Mom tries soothing as I begin shoving clothes into the bag, preparing to leave.

Sadly, her words have little effect on him.

"So is that it then? You're going to throw away a chance at everything for a pair of tits and a nice ass?"

I turn on him, fire burning through my body to retaliate. It would be so easy to lash out. But that would make me as bad as him. And I'm nothing like him.

"That would involve me having something to throw away. I don't want it. Any of it. How many times do I need to say it before it registers in your dense head? I'm not throwing away anything for her. She *is* my future."

His chin drops. "That's bullshit. You're eighteen, you don't know what you want."

"And you do? How could you possibly know what I want?"

"Because I know best," he roars.

I don't think he expects me to laugh, but that's exactly what I do. His fists curl at his sides as his frustration gets too much to take.

"Go on, old man, hit me. See if it helps knock some sense into me," I taunt, taking a step toward him so I'm right in his face.

"Shane, stop," Mom begs. She knows as well as I do that Dad has a temper that can snap at any moment.

"Why? I think it's time we saw him for who he really is. Come on, show me how much of a disappointment I am."

His teeth grind as I prepare for the pain I know is coming.

Only it never does.

After long seconds, he takes a step back.

"Fucking pussy," I mutter, turning around and swiping the bag I'd haphazardly packed.

"Where the fuck are you going?" he barks at me.

"Someplace where someone wants me. The real me. Not the one they're forcing me to be."

With that, I storm past Mom, who sobs as I leave and race through the house.

The moment I'm in my car, I allow myself to breathe and take a moment to think about what just happened.

"Motherfucker," I scream, slamming my hands down on the steering wheel.

A huge part of me wishes he would have hit me, just so I could retaliate. Hell knows I've wanted to a million times over the years.

Once my hands have stopped trembling enough to start the car, I back out of the drive with my chest heaving and one thought in my mind.

I need her. I need Chelsea.

I tell myself it's to make sure she's okay. But I know that selfishly, it's more for me than her.

She gives me a calm that I don't feel all that often, especially not at home. I need it. I need some kind of sign that this bullshit is going to come to an end. I need to have some hope that I'm going to be able to make my own choice and not be my dad's puppet to do with as he wishes for the rest of my life.

The journey to her house only takes minutes and before I know it, I am pushing my car door open and jogging around the side of the house with my bag in hand.

I have no idea if she wants me here, but there's no fucking way I'm staying in that house and allowing him to rip me in two. I've put up with it for long enough.

I'm eighteen. I can do what I fucking want.

The pool house is in darkness and I worry that maybe she's not here. But where would she have gone? She left wearing nothing but my shirt.

When I get to the door, I find it ajar and it has my already racing heart picking up speed once again.

"Chelsea?" I call, pushing it open and stepping inside.

I make my way to the bedroom, dropping my bag to the bed as I pass.

A sliver of light from the bathroom and the sound of water running indicates where she is and a little excitement starts to push away the anger that's still running rampant.

Wrapping my fingers around the door handle, I push, expecting it to open and be met by hopefully a naked and wet Chelsea. Only, when I push, the door doesn't move.

I try again, thinking it's stuck and a swear to God a scream of fear comes from the bathroom.

"Chelsea?" I ask, concern snaking through my veins. "It's just me. Are you okay?"

Movement sounds come from inside before the lock clicks and she cracks the door open.

She's soaking wet, her hair stuck to her face, her makeup running down her cheeks but I can see from the redness of her eyes that it's not from the shower.

I drop lower and see that she's still in my shirt and that it's soaked through.

Pushing through the door, I take her in my arms.

She's ice cold and shivers against my hold.

"What the hell, Chels?"

Holding her tight, I walk us to the shower. As expected, when I put my hand under the water it's freezing cold. What the hell happened? This can't be because of my dad, surely.

Turning the shower off, I lead her from the room, grabbing a towel on my way out.

She clings to me as if I might disappear any moment. Her slim body trembling against mine, her wet through shirt, soaking my own.

"I'm just going to set you on the bed."

Thankfully, she releases me and drops down when I encourage her to do so.

I make quick work of peeling the wet fabric from her body and dropping it to the floor. I dry her off, squeezing the water from her hair before finding my discarded jersey tangled in the sheets and pulling it over her head.

"Get in," I say, nodding to the bed and she scrambles to do so, quickly covering herself.

I shed my clothes and climb in with her, pulling her cold body to mine and wrapping myself around her like a blanket.

She trembles in my hold, as she fights the tears I know are threatening.

"It's okay," I say, holding her to me as tight as I can.

She shakes her head, her breathing ragged as she tries to get control of herself.

She's silent for the longest time and although it kills me not to ask, not to know what's wrong with her, I know she needs this.

Hell, I need this.

Dropping my nose to her hair, I breathe her in. Reminding myself of why I came here. Why being here with her means so much to me.

I think back to the connection between us before we were interrupted and tonight went to hell. My heart swells as I remember the look in her eyes as she stared down at me. I remember the heat that raced through my veins as she told me she felt it too. I mean, I knew, I feel it in her touch, see it in her eyes but to hear her admit that I'm not the only crazy one here felt fucking amazing.

I'm so lost in my thoughts that when she finally breaks her silence, it takes me a second to register her words.

"That truck... the one that's been following me..."

Every muscle in my body tenses as I wait to hear what's coming next. Did he stop her? Has he hurt her?

"He's a man from my past." Her words are so quiet, muffled against my chest, that I hardly hear her. "One of my birth mother's... v-visitors."

My body jolts at her words. I remember all too well the things she told me about her past. She didn't go into detail, understandably, and I was happy to allow her the time she needed to tell me, if she even wanted to.

"I-I..." She blows out a breath. "I don't remember which one he is exactly. They all kind of blurred into one. But I remember his eyes. They're so bright, I always used to think they were fake." She pulls back from me a little and looks up to me.

Her large, dark eyes are red-rimmed from crying and the sight is like a baseball bat to my chest.

"Did he..." I trail off, not able to say the words to form the question I need to ask.

"I-I don't know. Like I said, they all blur into one. Some of them were more interested than others. Some of them were even nice to me, but I was so young and stupid. I can't distinguish which was which from my memories. The good fades away and only the darkness stays with me."

"Fucking hell, Chels." I pull her back into my arms and hold her tight.

"How did he find me?" she whispers.

"I don't know, baby. But nothing's going to happen to you. I promise you."

She blows out a shaky breath before looking up at me again.

"How'd it go with your dad?"

"That doesn't matter right now."

"It does. This isn't just about me and my past, Shane. I want to be here for you too."

"I know and you are. This," I say, squeezing her tight. "Is all I need right now."

"All you need?" She raises a brow and her usual sparkle begins to come back.

"You're in my arms. What more could I need?"

She smiles, but it doesn't meet her eyes like it usually would. I hate that something from so long ago, a lifetime ago, can cause her this much pain. I'd do anything to take it away but as I lie here holding her to me as tight as I can, I know there's nothing more that I can do.

Silence falls around us and eventually, her breathing evens out and I know she's fallen asleep.

I smile to myself, knowing that she feels safe enough to do so, and I know in that moment that I made the right decision tonight. Coming here and leaving that cunt behind was the right thing to do. I'm not sure I've ever said truer words in my life than when I told him that Chelsea was my future, and tomorrow I intend to tell her.

It's time we stopped thinking about the past, about the nightmares and the mistakes and start looking forward to our future together because that's exactly how it should be.

"No. Don't touch me. No."

Chelsea's fear-filled cries startle me awake seconds before her elbow connects with my eye socket.

Ignoring the pain, I push myself up on my elbow and stare down at her. There's a deep crease between her brows as she thrashes about, fighting her nighttime demons.

"Chelsea, it's okay," I say, taking her face in my hands. "It's just me. You're safe."

Her eyes fly open, finding mine immediately. It takes a second, but the fear filling them starts to subside.

"Shane," she says on a sigh before her eyes close once again and she falls back to sleep.

This is repeated over and over as the minutes tick by.

It feels like every time I begin to drift off to sleep, she's crying out in terror.

By the fourth or fifth time, I decide it's time to wake her to drag her from her nightmares.

"Chelsea, Chelsea," I repeat until her eyes flicker open once more. "Hey," I say softly, leaning down to brush my lips against hers.

"Shane?" she asks, sounding confused.

"Shhh... it was a nightmare. Everything is okay. I'm right here," I soothe, my lips brushing against hers.

Slipping my hand under the hem of my jersey that she's still wearing, she noticeably relaxes against me.

"Make it go away, Shane. Please." Her plea guts me, fucking slays me.

"Anything." Sweeping my tongue into her mouth, I move my hand up her ribs until I find her breast. Her nipple is already pebbled for me and I pinch it, making her gasp into our kiss.

I tease her with my hands and lips until she's moaning, writhing and begging for more.

When I can restrain myself no longer, I settle myself between her thighs and slide myself into her.

We both moan as I move so slowly and gently inside her.

"Better?" I groan against the soft skin of her neck.

"Yes. More, Shane, give me more."

Lifting her hands, I take both her wrists in one of mine and stare down at her.

A tear trickles from one of her eyes and it wrecks me. Reaching out, I wipe it with my thumb.

"Shane, I..." She hesitates and I shake my head slightly. She doesn't need to talk right now. "I think I've fallen in love with you."

My breathing catches and I swear that my heart stops in my chest. The world around us ceases to exist as I stare down into her dark, haunted eyes.

"Chelsea, I—"

"No," she says after slipping one hand from my grasp and placing her fingers against my lips. "Don't. Not just because I did."

My eyes plead with her, but I know she's right. She's not ready to hear the words, especially straight off the back of her admitting it.

"Fucking hell, Chelsea."

Dropping my lips to hers I kiss her as deep as I can, trying to put everything I feel into my actions.

No sooner have we found our releases than we fall back asleep in each other's arms. Thankfully, the next time I wake, the sun is shining through from the living room and Chelsea's stare is burning into me.

Cracking an eye open, I look to the other side of the bed.

"Morning," I croak when I find her staring back at me like I was expecting.

"I thought it was all a dream," she says softly.

I shake my head. "Sadly not."

She blows out a long breath. "What are you going to do about your dad?"

"No idea. Quite honestly, I don't care."

"But college."

I shrug. "I'd rather not go than have my life dictated by him."

"What about you?" I ask, thinking about my crazy thoughts for the future yesterday.

"I don't know. I've applied a ton of places, have a shot at a scholarship at a couple. But..." she sighs, looking nervous all of a sudden. "After school, can we... talk?"

My eyes bounce between hers, trying to read what she's not telling me.

"Chels?" I pull her toward me, hoping that she'll say something to squash the lump of dread that's just formed in my belly.

"It's okay, I'm not ending this or anything. I just think we need to talk about the future."

"You mean where we go to college."

"Yeah," she says, looking away from my eyes. "Stuff like that."

Her words don't make me feel better and I almost suggest that we blow off school and just do the talking now. But knowing that's not going to help at all with my dad, I drag my exhausted body up until I'm sitting back against her headboard and pull her onto my lap.

"Whatever you need, baby."

30

CHELSEA

The lingering fear from my recurring nightmare clings to me as Shane and I get ready for school. The nerves fluttering in my belly about the conversation we need to have later help to distract me but the revulsion I remember all too well from their touch refuses to leave me.

"Everything's going to be okay," Shane says as we walk hand in and around my house to find his car.

Every muscle in my body is pulled tight as I wait to see if *his* truck is going to be there.

Some movement at the window in the living room tells me that Mom is aware that Shane's here once again and he's the reason I ran like I did last night.

Thankfully, when we get to the front of the house, there's no sign of him.

I breathe a sigh of relief and drop down into Shane's passenger seat.

He's right. Everything is going to be okay.

By the time we're pulling into the school parking lot, I almost believe myself. Shane will accept what I have to tell him and we can continue on as we have been with our shared little secret for now and the guy will just disappear as fast as he appeared now that he's seen me.

It's wishful thinking, I know, but it's all I've got right now.

"Looks like we're still hot gossip, baby," Shane mutters as we walk toward the main building to go to our lockers.

My skin prickles as all eyes burn into us. It's much the same as yesterday morning but if anything, everyone is even more intrigued.

I really thought something else would have happened by now to take the heat off us. Someone does something stupid every hour here at Rosewood High. None of are hot gossip for all that long.

Students whisper things to each other as we pass but I don't make out what they're saying.

"What the hell is going on?" I mutter. Sensing that I don't need an answer, Shane continues walking silently beside me.

We step in through the open doors and I get my first look at what has everyone talking and my world falls out from beneath me.

Pinned to every locker and every available surface are posters with an image I'd recognize from a mile away.

The words start to blur before me as reality hits.

Who's baby Fierce's daddy?

The world spins around me and as Shane drops my hand, I feel like I'm going to be swallowed whole.

No. No. No. This is not happening.

It's like I'm in a dream and watching this whole thing play out as all eyes burn into me and kids laugh and gossip.

"Tell me this is a joke." Shane's voice breaks through the haze, it's rough and deep and I know that if I were to turn around and look at him the expression on his face would devastate me.

This wasn't how it was meant to happen.

"Um..." I stare at the image of our baby that surrounds me.

My little secret out in the world for everyone else to look at.

That should be mine—ours—not all of theirs.

My breaths start to increase as I try to make sense of all of this and what I'm meant to say to him with everyone watching us.

"Chelsea," he warns, his voice telling me that he's on the verge of losing his shit, but as I open my mouth to respond nothing comes out, instead my knees buckle and I begin to drop.

"I've got you," a familiar friendly voice says in my ear as large hands grasp my upper arms. "Let's go. Dunn, you too." I'm pushed forward before we halt for a second. "Get fucking rid of all this." People start moving behind me as paper starts ripping and getting wadded up.

"Wait," I cry, stepping forward to pull one of the posters from the wall. I stare down at my baby.

I'm so sorry, I screwed this up.

I squeeze my eyes shut, praying that I can keep the tears at bay, for now at least.

Ethan directs me toward and empty classroom but just before we walk through the door, someone steps from the crowd with a triumphant smile on her fake face.

"You," I bark, staring into the evil eyes of a girl I once trusted.

Shelly smiles back at me sweetly as if she has no idea what I could be accusing her of.

"You need to watch your fucking back."

Her smile doesn't falter, and it only serves to irritate me further.

All she does is laugh before she slips back into the crowd and disappears.

Anger races through me and I fight to pull away from Ethan's grip to run after her, but he refuses to release me and instead directs me to the classroom.

I have no idea if it's just the two of us or if Shane followed orders, but as I stand there staring at the ultrasound picture, I'm too scared to turn around and find out.

The door opens and then closes behind me and the tension grows.

Losing the fight with my tears, they spill over as I continue staring at the ultrasound. I've done all kinds of unmentionable things over the years, but this makes me feel totally violated. This is my baby. Mine. No one should have the power to spread him or her all over the school. This image is mine to look at, mine to choose who I show.

A sob erupts and I lift my hand to cover my mouth in the hope it keeps more down.

This is what she wanted. Me broken. I refuse to allow her to see it happen.

"Chelsea?" His voice is weak, rough, and full of emotion.

"Oh god," I whisper, looking up at the ceiling in the hope of finding the right words.

"Is it true? Are you... is that... fuck."

Turning to look at him, I gasp at the tortured look on his face. His eyes are wide, staring right at me as he tugs at his hair.

Our eyes lock and his shoulders tense even more. He doesn't need my words. He knows me enough by now to read it in my eyes.

"I'm so sorry."

His hands drop as his body turns rigid. His lips press into a thin line and his eyes harden. If the situation wasn't what it was, I'd say it was hot, but that's the last thing on my mind right now.

He takes a step forward and I have to fight not to retreat. I know he won't hurt me but my need to escape just in case almost gets the better of me.

"Whose is it?"

My chin drops. Of all the things I was expecting him to say, that wasn't it.

"W-what?"

"I said... Whose. Is. It?" His eyes drop from mine, pure disgust dripping from them as he stares down at my stomach.

"It's yours, Shane."

A bitter laugh falls from his lips. "You really expect me to believe that?"

"Uh... ye—"

"You're nothing but a fucking whore, Chelsea. That could be any one of the teams', and you know it. Hell, you've probably been through the fucking chess club and the band for all I know."

"What? No," I cry. "It's yours. It can only be yours."

"Bullshit. Everyone knows what you get up to. All the guys on the team brag about what you let them do. You're a fucking liar."

His cold words rip me in two. He has every right to be angry, I know that. But the person standing before me isn't my Shane. He's cold, cruel, evil.

I did this. I turned my soft, sweet guy into this monster. All because I was too weak, too afraid to tell him the truth.

"W-what I said was true. There's only been you and Jake."

"So it's his then."

"No, that was too long ago. It was that night, Shane. That first night."

"We used protection," he spits, as if that makes it a sure thing. I'm growing the evidence right now to prove otherwise.

"It happens," I say with a shrug.

"You're fucking unbelievable, you know that? I can't believe I've fallen for your lies and bullshit. I can't believe..." He trails off, his hands returning to his hair as he spins away from me.

When his eyes come back to mine, the sparkling green I'm used to is gone, they're dark and empty.

"You promised me the games were over. But you've been playing me this whole time."

He reaches out and swipes the contents of the teacher's desk to the floor before storming toward the door.

"Shane," I cry. "Please. I need you."

He looks over his shoulder and for the briefest second, I think I've got him. Then his eyes drop from mine once more before he says. "You should have thought about that before lying to me all this time." And then he's gone.

I stumble back, lose my footing and crash to the ground in a heap.

When I open my eyes, I find two concerned sets staring back at me.

"I'm so sorry," I whimper.

"Let's get you out of here."

Ethan and Rae each take one of my arms and together they lift me from the floor.

There are still hordes of students filling the hallway, all waiting to witness the fallout from this no doubt.

"All right douchebags, the show is over," Ethan bellows the second he emerges and the majority of the students scatter.

Looking around, I notice that almost all the posters have disappeared and the second we step outside of the building, I discover why. Jake, Amalie, Mason and Camila stand at the benches with their hands full of them.

The four of them rush over when they spot us.

I wince, waiting for the backlash from them but all they do is give me small sympathetic smiles.

To be fair, nothing they could say right now could make me hate myself more than I already do.

"We thought that maybe you'd want to dispose of these," Amalie says softly, handing over her stack of posters.

"T-thank you." I look from her to Camila. "Will you find him, please. Make sure he's okay. It wasn't meant to happen like this."

They both nod.

"Come on, we're taking you home."

Ethan and Rae gently push me in the direction of the parking lot but before we're out of earshot of the others, I stop and turn around.

As expected, I find their eyes on me.

"I..." I hesitate, not really wanting this to be the way I say the words but feeling compelled to express just how much he means to me. "I really love him. Please, please tell him that."

I sob as I turn around and accept the embrace that Ethan gives me as we walk. Rae slips her hand into mine.

Their support right now means everything to me. But they're not who I want.

A parking space two spots down from Ethan's taunts me.

He's already left.

The emptiness that I was already feeling as he blew through that door threatens to engulf me.

I press my hand to my chest as the ache radiates from it.

"I... I need to find him. I need to explain."

Ethan and Rae exchange a look.

"We're taking you home, Chels. I think you need to give him some space."

"But I need to explain."

"We know you do, but right now, you need to let him cool down and you need to take a breath."

I nod, knowing they're right but hating it at the same time.

The drive back home passes me by in a blur.

All I can see is Shane's devastated, furious face.

I need to fix this. Only, I have no idea how.

31

SHANE

I don't see the students who are eagerly waiting for something to happen as I storm from that classroom.

Things are shouted. Accusations are made but I don't hear a single one. Blood rushes past my ears so fast that just a buzzing fills them.

Out of the corner of my eye, I spot Jake, Amalie, Mason, and Cami furiously ripping the posters from the lockers and walls.

Amalie spots me over her shoulder and runs to me.

"Shane, are you okay?" Looking from her concerned eyes to the posters in her hand, I reach out and snatch one. The rest flutter to the ground but I don't stop to help her pick them up. All I can think about is getting out of here. Getting away from the gossip, the prying eyes, the knowing looks.

I didn't give a fuck when I walked in with her on my arm yesterday. It was what I wanted. They could tell me whatever they wanted, give me all their bullshit opinions. As far as I was concerned, she was everything I wanted.

But now... I've just had exactly what they all expected rubbed in my face.

How can this even be true? How could she have kept something so huge from me?

Pulling my keys from my pocket, I jump in my car and start the engine the second I'm inside. I need to get away from here right now.

I can't deal with all of them, and I certainly can't deal with her right now.

My head spins as I drive and I have no clue if I run any lights or almost kill anyone at the intersections I pass through. I have no fucking idea how but somehow I manage to get myself to the beachside parking lot by Aces in one piece.

The piece of paper on my lap flutters and catches my eye. Any chance I had of this being a really bad joke stares back at me.

Grabbing it once again, I shoulder the door and climb out.

I'm on the sand in seconds and I take off running until I find a secluded dune in the distance.

It's only then that I stop, fall to the sand and hold the poster up in front of me.

The wording at the top taunts me and I make quick work of ripping it off and stuffing it into the soft sand beside me.

I don't need a reminder of the doubt over this. I don't need a reminder of the person almost everyone else thinks Chelsea is.

Or is she?

"Fuuuuuck," I scream into the surrounding silence.

I'm so fucking confused.

Is this a game? Has she been playing me this entire time? My heart constricts as I even think about that possibility. Everything felt so real, so raw. When she told me last night that she loved me... fuck.

My fingers tighten on the paper and it crinkles in my hold.

With my heart pounding and my head warring, I look down at the image on the paper.

My breath catches as I focus on the small black and white person in the middle.

"Fucking hell."

A ball so fucking huge clogs my throat and my eyes burn.

Is this mine? Did we fucking do this?

My hands tremble as my eyes remain locked on the small person before me.

Everything is so clear, I can make out all the important parts.

Then I spot the date printed in the corner.

Last Tuesday.

I think back to my visit to the hospital to make sure she was okay.

Did she know then?

Has she known all along?

Is that why she sent me away?

My teeth grind as all these questions fill my head.

Only one person can answer all of them. But right now, the last thing I want to do is look at her.

I'm fucking terrified. Although I'm not sure of what.

Her telling me that this is real. That it's mine and that our lives are about to change forever. Or that it's not, and it's someone else's.

That thought is like a knife straight through my heart.

I want to believe her. That she's only been with me, that it can only be mine.

But for years the evidence has pointed toward her being much less innocent. Should I believe her, or the gossip from the locker room?

Falling back on the sand, I use the paper to block the sun as I continue to stare at it.

If this is mine, if this is really happening, what does that mean for my future? A future that was already up in the air and surrounded by arguments and disagreements. What's going to happen now?

I lie there for hours running everything over in my head again and again desperately trying to come up with answers that continue to elude me. Only one person holds the answers, and I have yet to decide if I can trust anything that comes out of her mouth.

Eventually, clouds gather overhead and everything darkens, much like my mood.

Knowing I need to move before I get soaked, I carefully fold the paper and slide it into my pocket before climbing to my feet.

Every step is hard work as I make my way back down the beach.

My stomach grumbles as the smell from Aces hits it telling me that it's now long past lunch.

What happened to Chelsea? Is she still at school lapping up the attention from all of this? Something tells me that she's not.

A huge part of me wants to go and find her, to see if she's okay, to hear her out. But then I remember everything, and I change my mind. She might just fill me with more lies. How am I supposed to know?

"Shouldn't you be at school?" Bill chastises when I walk inside the diner and take a seat at one of the stools at the bar.

"Yep." I don't even bother trying to hide the truth.

"Everything okay?"

"Oh yeah. Perfect. That's why I'm here in the middle of the day," I mutter.

His eyes widen at my attitude. He's used to getting shit off the rest of the guys, but not from me.

"You want to talk about it?"

"Not really. Just a girl."

"Isn't it always?" He chuckles. "What did you do?" I look up at him and he must read the truth in my eyes. "Oh, what did she do?"

"Made me trust her."

"Ouch." He must know who we're talking about. He was here last night while she sat beside me with my arm wrapped around her. "Maybe things aren't as they seem."

"Yeah, maybe. Any chance of takeout?" I ask, already fed up with talking about this.

"Sure thing, you want your usual?"

"Please."

Thankfully, Bill takes off to place my order before a group of what looks like college kids pour through the doors and take him away from me.

The second my food is ready, I'm out of there.

I eat it in the car while the rain pours down around me.

I watch as the small rivers of water pour down the windshield and I can't help but compare their descent into nothingness to my life.

I'm drowning right now. It was bad enough with just the bullshit with my dad, but now this.

Fuck. I don't know which way is up.

I should probably drive home but the thought of bumping into that asshole puts me off immediately. I told him that I was done last night, that I chose Chelsea. Now look at me.

Starting the car, I head for a house that I hope I'll be welcome in and will give me the escape that I need.

The driveway is empty but I abandon my car nonetheless and walk around the back.

As always, I find a key hidden under a plant pot in the back yard and I use it to let myself in.

Knowing where the alcohol is stashed in this place, I swipe a bottle of Jack and make my way toward the den.

The guys are at practice, so I've probably got a little while longer with my own fucked-up thoughts before I get hit with a barrage of questions. I can only hope that when he gets home that he's alone. I can't be dealing with a team gathering this afternoon, that's for sure.

By the time I have company, half the bottle is gone and I'm half passed out on the couch with music pounding around me.

"Jesus fucking Christ, Shane," Zayn says, walking in, turning the music down and ripping the bottle from my hands.

"What?" I slur. "I couldn't stay there."

"I wasn't suggesting you could. I was also wasn't thinking that breaking into my house was the best idea either. If Mom came home first—"

"Did she?"

"Well, no, but—"

"But nothing. Give me that back."

"What the fuck are you doing?"

"Getting wasted and forgetting my problems. What does it look like I'm fucking doing, asshole?"

Zayn drops down on the coffee table in front of me, the bottle hanging temptingly from his hands.

"And what good is it going to do?"

I blow out a breath. "It's making me feel better."

"Do you think you should be sorting this shit out?"

"Talk to her? No thanks." An unamused laugh falls from my lips. "She's a lying fucking cunt."

Zayn's brow rises. "You really believe that?"

"I don't fucking know what to believe." Pushing from his couch, I stumble over to the floor to ceiling windows that showcase his back yard. "I've spent years listening to you guys talk about being with her. Then she tells me that she's not really been with any of you and that it's all lies and bullshit." I fall silent for a moment. "Have you fucked her?"

"No," he states, although I can make out a little guilt in his eyes.

"She's sucked you off though I'm assuming."

He hesitates for a second, and that slight pause is all the answer I need. "Motherfucker," I shout, slamming my palms down on the glass before me.

"It was ages ago, Shane. And it meant nothing. We were both drunk, one thing led to another."

"Did you touch her?"

"W-what?"

"Did. You. Touch. Her?"

"Uh... no. I k-kissed her," he admits with a wince. "But that was it. I fucking swear to you."

Although I'm fucking mortified, he's just admitted to having his cock and tongue in her mouth, I must say I'm relieved it didn't go any farther.

"Shane," he sighs. "As far as I know, none of the guys have actually slept with her."

"Bullshit, it's all they brag about."

"Yeah, exactly. Brag about. Justin's the fucking loudest but I know for a fact that's bullshit."

I spin to look at him so fast that the room moves around me. "Fuck," I bark, grabbing my head in the hope it stops the spinning.

"Why does it even matter? Even if she has slept with the entire team, which she hasn't," he quickly adds. "All that's in the past. I've seen the way she looks at you, man. She's never looked at any other fucker like that. Well... other than Jake, but that's old news. He's so fucking smitten with Amalie that he's never going to see his balls again."

Falling back down on the couch, I rest my elbows on my knees and hang my head.

"She's fucking pregnant, Zayn," I admit out loud for the first time. "She's growing a baby. A fucking baby."

"So I heard."

"This is so fucked up."

I look up at him. His usual easy-going smirk is long gone as he stares back at me looking deadly serious. It's an unnerving look on him.

"So what are you going to do about it?"

Reaching for the remote, I turn the volume back up and reach for the bottle he's placed beside him. He doesn't even try to stop me this time.

I lift the bottle to my lips and fall back on the couch.

"I'm going to get fucked up."

"Fair enough. I just so happen to have the exact thing you need."

Standing, Zayn reaches into his pocket and pulls out a blunt quickly followed by a lighter.

Lifting it to his lips, he lights up and takes a pull.

I know the rules of this house, and I know he's breaking the biggest one by doing this but I'm so relieved to have his support right now and so desperate for the escape that I don't say a word.

He passes it over and I waste no time in taking a hit.

I've only done it a few times. It's not something I want to make a habit of, but desperate times call for desperate measures.

"All right, calm down. You're meant to be sharing," he says, snatching it back before falling down beside me.

I pass him the bottle and he takes a shot after having another pull on the blunt.

"To worrying about our issues tomorrow."

"What the fuck are you worrying about?"

"Whose pussy I'm claiming Friday night."

"Oh to be you," I mutter, trying to push images of Friday night's winter formal out of my head.

School dances are not my thing, but I was intending to ask Chelsea. I guess that's off now.

One song rolls into the next as we sit here passing the alcohol and weed back and forth. That is until a shrill voice cuts through the bass.

"Mom is going to fucking kill you, asshole."

Looking to the door I find Harley, Zayn's little sister standing with her hand on her hips and drilling Zayn with a death glare.

"Oh look, the goody-two-shoes and her friends have arrived."

Looking behind Harley, I find Ruby and Poppy, Jake's cousin, loitering behind her.

"No weed in the house, how many times?" She marches in and makes a show of attempting to take it from him but he's not interested, he's got his sights on someone else.

He dodges Harley and she crashes to the couch beside me, growling in frustration as he stalks toward the door.

"Hey, baby," he coos at Ruby who shamelessly arches her back to push her tits in his direction. He wraps his hand around her bare waist and pins her to the wall, lowering his head but not enough to kiss her. She stares up at him as if he just hung the moon. It's sickening.

Poppy watches with her top lip curled in disgust.

"Careful, Ruby. That mongrel has probably got fleas, or worse."

Zayn glances up at her and blows a kiss in her direction. She shudders before turning her back on the two of them.

"Get your fucking hands off her," Harley snaps, physically pulling her friend from Zayn's clutches. "Cut that shit out or I'll tell Mom."

"Ohhh I'm so scared," Zayn taunts.

Harley rolls her eyes. "We're going to do homework in the back yard."

Harley and Poppy march off but Ruby hangs back for a few minutes.

"You're more than welcome to join our party, baby."

"Ruby," Harley calls.

She bites down on her bottom lip and lets her eyes roam down Zayn's body. "Maybe next time, big boy."

Zayn groans as if in physical pain as she disappears from view.

"Damn, that girl is a motherfucking tease," he complains as he falls back to the couch and reaches for the bottle.

"I thought you..." I trail off, vague recollections of that night last weekend filling my mind.

"A guy never kisses and tells, bro. But Ruby and I, we've got unfinished business."

The three of them walk in front of the glass wall, Ruby's hips swinging seductively purely for Zayn's benefit. When she looks over her shoulder, she smiles and winks, but when I look back to Zayn, I swear his eyes are elsewhere for a second.

"Poppy was right, you're a fucking dog," I mutter, reclaiming the bottle and draining what's left.

32

CHELSEA

"Thank you," I whisper as Ethan pulls up in my driveway beside Mom's car.

I barely looked up the entire journey here, not even the fear of being followed by my past was strong enough to drag my eyes up.

"Do you want us to come in or..." Rae asks.

"No, it's okay. You head back to school. I don't need to drag anyone else into this disaster."

"If you need us," she says, turning to look at me. "We're only a phone call away."

"Thank you. I really appreciate it."

Part of me wants to walk around the side of the house and go and hide in my little sanctuary, but it's the other part of me that wins out, the part that desperately needs a hug from Mom.

Slamming the front door behind me, I race toward where I expect her to be.

I'm right, because as I turn the corner into the kitchen, she stands from her stool.

"Chelsea?"

A sob rips from my throat as I run to her.

She gathers me up in her arms exactly as I need and she holds me so tight. Almost as tightly as Shane did last night when he found me mid-freak-out over the ghost from my past. That thought has my cries getting louder and my tears flowing faster.

"What on Earth has happened?" she asks once I've calmed down a little. "Is everything okay with the—"

"H-he found out, Mom. Shelly told the entire school and totally ambushed him. God, it's such a mess. You should have seen his fa–fuck," I say when I pull back and find Maddie sitting on the stool opposite where Mom was when I rushed in.

"Um..." Mom says, looking between the two of us.

My heart swells with the knowledge that she's kept my secret from her best friend, her friend who just so happens to be this baby's other grandmother.

"What's happened with Shane?" Maddie asks in a rush, standing with us and correctly guessing who we're talking about.

"You might want to sit down," Mom suggests, reaching out and taking my hand for support.

I really want her to say the words, but I know that this needs to come from me. Someone needs to hear it the way it should be said.

"I'm..." My voice trembles, giving away my fragile state. Maddie's eyes bore into mine, fear and apprehension lacing through. "I'm p-pregnant."

"What?" she asks on a gasp.

"I'm sorry, I'm so sorry." My tears reappear and I furiously wipe at my cheeks getting fed up with my overflowing emotions.

"I'm assuming you're telling me this because it's Shane's."

"Oh my god, this is such a mess."

"Sit down, I'll get you a drink," Mom says, pushing me toward an empty stool.

Maddie's eyes don't leave me as I move and after sucking a deep breath, I turn to her.

"Yes, it's Shane's. He didn't know. It happened before I went away, I found out while I was there. Then I came back and we reconnected in a way I never could have imagined. I should have told him right away, but I was so scared I'd lose him. I've wanted to tell him so many times but things between us have been so incredible that I just couldn't ruin that."

"What did Shelly do?" she asks hesitantly.

"I-I think she snuck into the pool house last night and took a photograph of my ultrasound picture. She stuck these all around the school."

Not wanting to hold anything back, I pull the poster from my purse and slide it over so they can both look at it.

"What a bitch," Maddie mutters.

"It can only be Shane's; I swear to you. What she's implying. It's not true."

They both nod at me.

"Where is he?"

I blow out a breath, pulling the poster back and staring at my baby once again.

"I don't know. He ran. His car was gone from the lot by the time I got there."

Maddie hops down from the stool to collect her purse and pulls her cell out.

"I'm just going to..." She trails off. We don't need an explanation as she taps the screen and then puts it to her ear.

"I'm so sorry, sweetie. I know this isn't how you wanted it to go." She holds me to her again and thankfully refrains from saying any kind of I told you so.

I should have told him that first night when I found him in Brett's office at the after-party. I should have been brave and just laid out all my truths right there. But instead I got swept away by him and actually started to believe that we could have something.

"Nothing," Maddie says, dropping her cell and shaking her head sadly. "I should probably go in case he goes home. Things are already tense enough with him and Brett, this is the last thing either of them need."

"I think that's probably for the best," Mom agrees.

They both share a look, having a silent conversation that only lifelong friends can before Maddie turns to leave.

"Maddie," I call before she disappears. "I'm sorry. This really was an accident."

"Chelsea," she sighs. "Some things in life are never planned, but that doesn't always mean they're going to be a disaster. You'll get through this, we all will. Just have faith." With one final smile, she walks away.

Faith.

I wonder if that's what has kept her with Brett all this time.

"Do you mind if I just go to the pool house so I can be alone for a bit?"

"Of course, sweetie. You do whatever you need. I'll be here if you need me."

"Thank you, Mom. Thank you for everything."

"You're welcome."

Her eyes don't leave me until I slip inside the pool house and turn to the bedroom.

I don't even bother kicking my shoes off, I just curl up in the center of my bed and allow more tears to come.

The next thing I know, Mom is gently shaking my shoulder to wake me.

When I drag my sore eyes open, I find she's brought a tray of dinner out for me.

"You need to eat, sweetie." And just to prove that she's right, my stomach rumbles right on cue.

"Thank you." I pull myself so I'm sitting against the headboard and she places the tray on my lap.

I stare down at my favorite, Mom's homemade mac and cheese, and my stomach growls once again.

"Do you mind?" she asks, pointing to the other side of the bed.

"Of course not." As she gets settled, I reach for the fork. "Did Maddie find him?"

"She messaged about an hour ago and still hadn't then."

"Jesus. This is all my fault."

Mom doesn't say anything. She doesn't need to. We both know my statement is true.

All of it is my fault.

If I were on birth control, this would never have happened. If I were brave enough to confess all then this wouldn't have happened.

I'm a fucking mess, and all I've done is prove to him once again how untrustworthy I am.

He'd be stupid to ever look twice at me, at either of us again after this.

I blow out a frustrated breath.

"He'll be fine. Shane's got a sensible head on his shoulders. He's probably just taking a bit of time to get his head around everything. Don't forget, you've had weeks to get used to this huge change in your life, he's just had it dropped on him. That must be some kind of shock."

I nod because there's not really anything else to do.

What I really want to do is get out and start searching for him. But what good would that do? He clearly doesn't want to see me or talk about it because he would be here if he did.

"Are you going to school tomorrow?" Mom asks, dragging me from my plans of driving to the houses of everyone I know in the hope of finding him.

"I have no idea right now."

"I trust you to do the right thing for you. If you need a few days, then take them. Just please try not to fall behind. I know things are up in the air right now, but not graduating won't help."

"Don't worry, I have every intention of graduating and still going to college, even if it's a couple of years late."

"One step at a time."

Once I've finished eating, Mom kisses my cheek and takes the tray, leaving me to my own misery. After using the bathroom, I shed my clothes and pull Shane's jersey over my head before climbing back into bed and almost immediately falling back to sleep again.

I'm awake before my alarm the next morning but as it starts blaring, I make no move to get out of bed. The thought of walking into school where everyone knows my secret fills me with dread.

I probably should go just in case Shane does, but something tells me that he's going to avoid that place just like I am.

Rubbing at my sore eyes, I smooth my bed hair down with my fingers.

I need to see someone, I need to talk to someone. Someone who understands me.

When I woke in the middle of the night to pee, I found the strength to pull my cell from my purse.

I had so many messages, none of which I opened other than the couple from Rae checking in on me. No one else cared when I wasn't in the middle of the next big drama to hit Rosewood High so they can fuck off.

As expected, I had nothing from Shane. I almost shut it down without reaching out but in the end, I decided that I at least needed to try.

I found his name and typed out a million different messages to send him but, in the end, I deleted them all and went with something simple.

Chelsea: I'm sorry. Please let me explain x

I wanted to tell him again that I loved him, try to explain how much both he and this baby mean to me, but there's no way I could express it in a message, so I'll have to wait until I see him again.

When I light it up, I find a lot more messages but the only one I care about sits unread just like it did after I sent it last night.

With a sigh, I find the next best person.

Chelsea: Do you have classes all day? I need you.

The little blue ticks appear almost immediately, and the typing bubble pops up.

Luca: Breakfast? I'll be there in a couple of hours.

Chelsea: Thank you x

He sends me back a hugging gif. I have no idea if he knows, if he's spoken to either Shane or his mom, but whether it's my simple message or the big news, he knows I need him and he's dropping everything for me.

I want to feel guilty. It's the last week of the semester. He really should be in class but instead he's coming to rescue me from myself. I guess he's used to it at this point.

With two hours to waste, I have a shower and do my hair and makeup. On the outside, it makes me look almost normal but inside I'm still a broken mess and I fear I will be until I get the chance to be in his arms again.

Standing in front of the mirror in just my underwear, I stare down at my belly. I swear it's bigger today.

I run my hands over the smooth skin and try to imagine what it might look like in a few months' time when there is no more hiding it.

I turn to the side and I can't help but smile at the slight bulge that never used to be there.

When I first found out, I thought I'd hate my body changing. I've spent years working on it, to be strong enough to do everything cheer required of me, but standing here right now, I don't care all that much. All I want is for the little person I'm growing to be happy and healthy. There are plenty of women out there who have a baby and get back to their sport, that's my aim. My cheer dream is far from dead, just postponed a little while I do something more important.

Glancing at the time, I jump into action knowing that he's going to be here soon. I pull on a pair of yoga pants and an oversized hoodie before slipping my feet into my sneakers.

A knock on my pool house door has my heart jumping into my throat. I assumed he'd wait in the driveway. Thoughts of it being Shane standing there has my pulse racing as I practically run for the door.

My face drops the second I find Luca.

"Hey," I say, my usual cheer long gone.

"Seeing as you were expecting me, you don't look all that pleased about me being here."

"I-it's not that. I'm really glad to see you, I just thought..."

"It might have been Shane," he finishes for me.

"You know?"

He shakes his head. "I know something is going on. Mom rang to see if I'd seen or heard from him, but I have no idea what's actually going on. I'm hoping you're going to tell me though."

Grabbing my purse, I look up at his kind face and into those eyes that are so like the ones I so desperately need.

"Shall we? I'll explain on the way."

I wave at Mom who's watching us from the kitchen door. Luca nods at her so I can only assume they've already spoken.

"Your carriage awaits," he says, opening the passenger door for me.

"Thank you."

After jogging around to the driver's side, he makes quick work of turning the engine over and backing out.

"Go on then. Hit me with the drama."

"I'm pregnant."

"Fuuuuck, girl."

"It's Shane's."

"Jesus, no wonder he's gone MIA. I think I'd leave the country if the girl I was banging came out with that."

"Nice, Luc. Real nice." Crossing my arms over my chest, I stare out the window. I was kinda hoping he'd be a little more supportive.

"Shit, I'm sorry. I didn't mean... I mean, it's just my worst nightmare. But... fuck. I'm sorry. Ignore me. So, how'd it happen?" I turn to look at him. "No, shit. I didn't mean how, I meant... how far along are you?"

I laugh at him and it feels so good after the hours of stress I've had.

"Twelve weeks."

"Whoa, so really pregnant."

"I'm not sure anyone at nine months would agree with that, but yeah, it's not new."

"So you've known a while."

"Yeah. I should have told him by now but... it was just so huge, I didn't even know where to start."

"I get that, but yeah, you should have told him. So I'm assuming from his disappearing act that he's found out."

"One of the squad pinned my ultrasound picture all over school."

"What?" he spits. "Why would she do that?"

"She hates me," I mutter, rolling my eyes. "He freaked out, rightly so, and left school."

"Shit. No wonder Mom's losing her mind."

"Uh huh."

"Jesus, Dad's going to have a field day with this."

I tell Luca about their dad finding us together the other night and losing the plot, the grimace on his face as I explain has dread sitting heavy in my stomach for what's going to happen when he discovers this.

Luca takes us to our usual diner and we slide into our booth before we order the same food, the only difference is my hot chocolate.

"That's why you didn't have coffee last time," Luca says, figuring me out.

"Guilty," I say with a laugh.

"Don't take this the wrong way, I'm just asking because I care but..." I hold my breath as I wait for what's to come. "Are you keeping it?"

"Yes," I say without any hesitation. "I knew the second I found out that there wasn't any other option."

"Okay." He smiles softly at me. "I think you're going to be a great mom."

"I sure hope so."

Silence settles between us but it's not uncomfortable.

"Do you think he'll come around? Do you think he'll want this with me?" I ask, hoping like hell I get the answer I want.

"Honestly, I have no idea what he's going to do or want with this."

My heart sinks, it was the response I was expecting but equally the one I didn't want.

The bell above the door to the diner chimes making Luca look up but I don't bother, the chances of it being the guy I want is slim to none and I guarantee that if it were Shane, Luca would have said something instantly.

"Can you message him, see if he's okay?"

"I'll try but I sent one last night after Mom phoned and it's gone unread."

Our breakfast is brought over and I mostly poke it around my plate.

"You really should be eating that, you know."

"I know. I'm just worried."

"It will be okay. Just give him some time. He'll be back."

I sigh, hoping that he's right. But while his cell sits on the table, silent, I can't help thinking the worst. That things are done between us.

33

SHANE

Zayn's attempts to get me to school this morning we're pointless, there was no way I was showing my face. Not until I knew the truth, and that meant talking to Chelsea, and I can't see that happening anytime soon.

The alcohol did its job last night and by the time we'd drained that first bottle everything started to get a little hazy. It was exactly what I needed.

That being said though, when I woke this morning it was with a raging hangover and a massive reality check.

Other than a trip to the bathroom, I remain on Zayn's den couch. He and Harley disappeared to school over an hour ago and his mom's away on business, so I've got the peaceful house to myself to wallow in my misery.

Well, that is until the doorbell starts ringing.

"Ugh, go away," I call out, not that they'd be able to hear me from the back of the house.

It rings a few times before stopping and I breathe a sigh of relief that whoever it is has left. That's soon ruined though when it starts up again.

"For fuck's sake."

Assuming it's a delivery or something important, I pull on my pants and head for the front of the house.

I don't bother looking out, I just grasp the handle and twist.

"What?" I bark much to the surprise of the visitor. "Mom?"

"Hey," she says, almost shyly, rocking back on her heels holding a tray of takeout coffee.

"How'd you find—" It's a stupid question, everyone in this town talks, especially the moms, and I overheard Zayn telling his last night that I was here so I should have expected this really. I feel like an idiot for not even considering it would be her.

"Can I..." She gestures into the house. It feels weird inviting her into someone else's house but I stand aside regardless and allow her in.

She follows me through to the kitchen where I take a seat at the island, I can't take her back to the den, it probably still smells vaguely of last night's weed. I'm surprised she can't smell it on me to be honest since I haven't bothered showering or anything yet.

She sits opposite me, her eyes never leaving my face. Concern is written all over hers. I don't need to hear a word to know that she knows.

"How are you doing?" she asks softly.

"I have no idea," I reply honestly, dropping my attention to the counter in front of me.

"Here, I brought your favorite."

I take the cup when she hands it over but don't say anything. I have no idea where to even start.

"I saw her yesterday." That gets my attention. My heart slams against my ribcage as I wait for her to say more.

I might have lost myself in my own despair yesterday but at no point did I forget her and how she might be dealing with all this. It pissed me off that after everything, all the games and lies that I could still be concerned about her but I think it's time I accepted that it's just how this thing between us works. She's worked her way so deep inside me that I fear I'm never going to be rid of her.

"How is she?" I hate myself for asking but I know that if I don't, it'll only eat at me.

"Mortified. Embarrassed. Angry. Hating herself."

"Good."

"Shane," Mom warns.

"What? Do you have any idea what that was like yesterday? I thought we were..." I blow out a breath. "I thought it was serious. That she felt like I did." I feel like a pussy admitting this but I need to tell someone.

"Things aren't always quite so black and white, baby."

"You're defending her?"

"No. I'm just saying that she probably had her reasons. People make mistakes all the time, Shane. You just have to—"

"Like Dad?" I ask, spinning this back on her.

"Um... yeah, him especially. All I'm saying is that hiding in here isn't going to help with anything. You're both hurting and the only way to get all the facts is to talk." I run my hand down my face and rub at my jaw. I really don't need this little pep talk on top of the hangover pounding at my temples.

"How are you feeling, about... about the baby?"

My chest compresses as she says that one word.

Baby.

It's the realization I don't need that this is all very real and not the nightmare I hope I'd conjured up in my sleep when I first woke.

I shake my head, struggling to comprehend what all this really means for me. For us.

"She's really pregnant?" I ask, ever hopeful that yesterday was a really bad joke.

Mom reaches into her purse and pulls out the poster that started this whole thing. I stare down at the image which is almost as familiar as the back of my hand after all the time I spent staring at it yesterday.

My breath catches as I stare down at it once again. My copy is folded in my pocket for when I feel the need to remind myself that this is all real.

"She is. Twelve weeks."

"Fucking hell."

"And it's... m-mine?"

"She assured me that there was no other option."

I blow out a shaky breath.

Flying off the handle and accusing her of lying was so easy. But even as I shouted those things at her, I remembered how sincere she was when she told me the truth about the other guys, about how she'd only been with Jake.

My hands tremble as I finally allow the truth to settle within me. I'm going to be a fucking dad. A fucking eighteen-year-old dad.

This was certainly not part of the plan.

Dad is going to lose his shit.

"Does he know?"

Mom shakes her head. "I haven't told anyone. But this is going to be hot gossip, it'll get back to him sooner than you think."

I see the same fear and trepidation flicker through her eyes as I feel.

"Shane, no matter what..." She reaches over, takes my hand and squeezes. "I'm here to support you. I'll do as much or as little as you need."

Tears burn my eyes as I stare at her.

"I'm not sure I'm ready for this," I admit, emotion clogging my throat.

"Oh baby." She gets up from her stool and comes to stand in front of me, wrapping her arms around me. "I'll let you in on a secret. No one is ever ready for a baby. Even those couples who appear to have it all together. They're just as scared. It's a huge unknown and even after having one, or two, the next is always different. It's the most challenging, but equally the most incredible, most rewarding thing you'll do in your life."

"But school, college..."

"We'll figure it out," she says, pulling back and cupping my cheek in her palm.

"I can't believe you're not angry," I mutter, pulling my cup closer before lifting it to my lips.

"What's the point? The deed has been done, quite literally." I groan as my face heats. I really don't need Mom thinking about what I've been up to with Chelsea, although she is sporting the evidence of our interactions, or will be very soon. "Plus, I think your dad might handle that all by himself."

Dread sits heavy in my stomach.

"I'll talk to him, okay. Soften the blow, if I can. But he's not going to be happy."

"Mom," I sigh. "I really hate him. I don't want anything he wants for me and I'm exhausted listening to it all."

"I know, baby."

"How do you put up with it?"

She shrugs, a sad look passing over her face.

"Are you happy?"

"This isn't meant to be about me."

"If you're not happy, you need to do something about it." She swallows nervously and I wonder just how close to home I've just hit. "Don't worry about us, we're all old enough to deal with whatever you need to do."

She looks up at me, tears filling her eyes. "When did you get so wise?"

"About the time I learned I was going to be a father maybe. Fuck," I bark. "How is this happening?"

She squeezes my hand again. "Come home, please. Your dad's out of town until Saturday, maybe even Sunday. It'll be safe. You can at least be in our own space while you try to get your head around all of this."

The thought of spending another night of Zayn's couch doesn't fill me with joy.

"Okay. But if he goes off the second he's back. I'm gone again. I don't need his bullshit right now." Or ever, but I don't add that bit.

"That's fair. Go and get your stuff."

I don't have any stuff but I go back to the den just to make sure I haven't left anything before following her out of the house and driving back home.

"Are you hungry?" she asks when we step through the front door.

"Yeah."

"Pancakes?"

"That would be awesome. I need to take a shower really quick though."

"Please do, you smell like stale whiskey."

"Thanks," I say with a laugh.

I have a quick shower before heading back down to the kitchen, the smell of the sweet pancakes and salty bacon assaults my nose and makes my stomach growl. When did I last eat?

"So what are you going to do now? You can't hide forever."

I shrug.

"Shane, it's only Wednesday. You really—"

I fix her with a look that has her words faltering. If I ever deserved a few days off, then now is the time.

"Okay, fine. But can you do something for me?"

"What is it?"

"Can you talk to her?"

"I'll consider it, if you promise to do something for me."

"Go on."

"Think about your future too."

She sighs. "Deal. I guess it's time for both of us to grow up a little."

"Everything will work out," I say, my voice full of confidence that I don't really feel.

She smiles weakly at me before plating up our breakfast and we fall into a comfortable silence, both too lost in thoughts about our futures and what they might hold.

Eventually, I leave her and escape to the peace of my room. I know she's right. I need to see Chelsea. We certainly can't leave things like we did in that classroom. We're connected now whether we like it or not.

Mom gives me the space I need for a few hours before she pokes her head around the door, asking if it's okay for her to enter. I nod at her and when she pushes the door open, I find she's carrying a fresh mug of coffee and has a bag of chips in her hand.

"Thought you might need something."

"Thank you," I say, sitting myself up from where I was lying on my bed staring up at the ceiling.

"I was just thinking, isn't it winter formal on Friday?"

"Yeah and..."

"No reason," she says with an innocent shrug before backing out of the room.

34

CHELSEA

I don't pay any attention to the other diners around us until I stand and turn to leave. It's then that I lock eyes with a very familiar pair that I never want to see again.

My blood runs cold, just like it did when I looked into his car and found those icy blues staring back at me.

He pushes to stand as I start to run.

"Wait, please," he calls, but there's no way I'm sticking around to hear anything that asshole has to say, no matter how politely he asks me.

I don't realize that Luca isn't behind me until I'm outside of the diner and I risk a look back.

The only person who's there is him. He's standing in the doorway with his brows pulled together.

"W-what do you want from me?" I stutter, trying like hell not to show him that I'm scared and failing miserably.

"Please, Rose. I just want to talk to you."

"I'm not Rose. You've got the wrong person," I say, turning my back on him, hoping that Luca will appear at any moment and take me away before this gets out of hand.

"It's you, I know it is."

"Is everything okay?" Luca asks, finally emerging from behind the man. "Is this asshole giving you grief?"

"N-no, it's fine. Can we just go, please?"

"Of course." Luca looks between me and the guy, confusion written all over his face.

FIERCE 947

The second his car beeps to signal that it's unlocked, I jump in and lock it once again behind me.

My chest heaves as my breaths rush past my lips in my panic.

"What the fuck was that? Who was he? Fuck, are you okay?" he asks when he notices that I'm on the verge of a panic attack.

I nod, focusing on my breathing until things start to return to normal. His concerned eyes never leave me though.

"Do I need to go and beat the shit out of him for something?"

I can't help the laugh that falls from my lips. It's probably the least of what that guy deserves.

He's still looking at us from his place in the doorway of the diner, I don't need to look up to know he's there. I can feel his stare prickling my skin.

"It's fine. It's nothing."

"I beg to fucking differ. You're anything but fine."

"It's just a ghost from my past. One I hope to never see again."

"Your past? You mean before Rosewood?"

"Yeah. Can you just take me home, please?"

"Of course."

He starts the engine, and with the guy's eyes watching our every move, he pulls out of his space and onto the road.

I hold his eyes, I don't want to, but I'd be lying if I said his insistence to see me, to talk to me, didn't intrigue me.

Now my fear has subsided knowing that I'm safe in the car beside Luca, I see something else in his eyes. But before I get a chance to figure out what it is, we've turned the corner and he's no longer in sight.

"Are you sure you're okay?"

"Yeah." My hands tremble in my lap and my heart is still galloping in my chest but I'm fine.

What I need is to be in the pool house with the outside world safely locked on the other side of the door.

We drive back to my house in silence. I can sense the million and one questions Luca has for me, but thankfully, he manages to keep them inside.

"What are you doing for the rest of the day?" he asks me when he's brought the car to a stop on the driveway.

"Homework. What about you?"

"I should probably attempt to attend at least one of my classes today."

"Luca," I say on a sigh. "I said to come if you didn't have class."

Reaching over, he takes my hand in his. "You needed me, Chels. Shane needs me. There's nowhere else I'd rather be."

Emotion burns at the back of my eyes and I fight to blink the tears away.

"Oh no no. No crying, you know I can't deal with that."

I laugh at him as I tug his arm so I can give him an awkward car hug.

"I'll see you soon, yeah?" I nod as I push the door open. "And if you need me, just call me. Any time."

"Thank you, Luc. I really appreciate it."

"You take good care of my niece or nephew." He nods to my belly and butterflies take flight.

"I will. Thank you." He salutes me before backing out of the driveway.

Panic hits me as he drives off and I realize I should have told him not to tell Shane that he's seen me. I don't want him going to find him and attempt to fight my battles for me. Not that I think for a second that he would listen to me. With a smile, I hurry to the front door and let myself in.

I end up spending the afternoon with Mom wrapping presents. It's not exactly what I would have chosen to spend the rest of my day doing but I can't deny that the mundane task does relax me somewhat.

"Are you planning on going back to school this week?" she asks as she adds another present to the perfectly wrapped pile beside her.

"I have no idea what I'm doing. I used to thrive on the attention but now, I just want to hide."

"Understandable. I was just thinking that if you're off tomorrow, we could go to the mall. You're going to need new clothes soon and it might be nice to get you out of the house."

I sit and think about her offer for a few seconds. "That sounds really good, I'd like that."

"It's a date then. Just make sure you touch base with your teachers and get the work you're missing, young lady."

"I will, I promise."

It's late by the time I get to do what I craved so badly earlier and lock myself in my pool house. Mom and I made homemade pizzas for when Dad got home from work and we sat and ate like a real family. It was nice. Exactly what I needed.

After promising to meet Mom in the morning for our day out, I head to my sanctuary and let out a sigh.

The stress from the last two days pulls my muscles tight, all I want to do is curl up in a ball once more and fall asleep.

I'd left my cell in my purse on silent and told myself time and time again throughout the day not to check it but once I'm alone, my restraint snaps and I pull it out and wake it up.

I keep my eyes shut for a beat, praying that he'll have reached out, but there's nothing. Well, not from him. There's plenty from others.

I reply to Luca to thank him again for dropping everything for me this morning, and I also send an apology back to Rae for ignoring her all day when she's just worried about me. She replies immediately saying that she understands and that she's sorry for not coming to see me today, but they had forced family stuff after school. I get it, it's fine. I don't expect everyone to stop their lives because mine is falling apart.

I ignore everyone else, they're just gossip hunting.

After pulling on Shane's jersey once more, I climb into bed wishing that he'd turn up and pull me into his arms.

It never happens, and when I wake the next morning, I'm still alone.

Shopping with Mom is better than I expected it to be. I pick up some maternity clothes that I'm going to need before she drags me into a baby shop to start looking at things.

I'll admit that I don't know the first thing about looking after a baby, but I figure I've still got a bit of time to work it out and I hear people say all the time that it's something that usually comes fairly naturally once the time comes, so I'm hoping that is the case.

She's not happy about it, but I stop her from buying anything. Other than maternity clothes, I refuse to buy anything until after my next ultrasound. I think I'd like to find out the gender, and I really have no idea what Shane thinks about it, so until we've made that decision, hopefully together, I'll refrain from any of the cute stuff that Mom waved under my nose in her attempt to sway me.

I need to think of him. I've already been through so much of this pregnancy without him being a part of it. I want to at least give him the chance to be there for everything that's still to come, should he want to of course.

I'm still putting everything into my closet when there's a knock at my pool house door later that afternoon.

With my heart in my throat, I once again run through to the living area in the hope it's him, but just like yesterday morning, my hopes are dashed when I find Rae staring back at me.

"Hey," I say, opening the door for her.

I never used to lock it, but since seeing *him* I've started being a little more cautious. He clearly wants something from me and a late-night visit like he used to give my birth mother is certainly not on the cards.

I shudder at the thought.

"Are you okay? All the color just drained from your face."

"Yeah, yeah, I'm good. Especially now that I've seen this," I say, my eyes widening at the sight of the box of donuts she has in her hand.

"You seemed to like them last time."

"They're donuts, who doesn't like them?" I take the box, place them on the coffee table and immediately pull the lid off to make my selection.

"Was he in school today?" I mumble around a mouthful of sugary goodness in the hope she can't make out the words. But when her lips curl up into a smile, I know she didn't miss it.

"Nope."

"And was everyone still talking about what a whore I am."

"Pretty much."

"Wow, don't sugarcoat it, will you?"

"I can if you want, I just thought you'd prefer to hear the truth."

I groan. "I would, I just equally don't want to deal with it all."

"There's nothing to deal with where they're concerned. They're a bunch of gossips. Who cares what they think?"

"I know. I do know that. It's just hard sometimes."

"I heard someone taking bets on if it was Shane's or not," she admits quietly.

"They fucking what?"

"Kids are assholes. Just let them get on with it. So I'm assuming you haven't heard from him then?"

I shake my head. "I've sent messages, but they've not even been read. I've seen his mom and brother though."

"What did they have to say?"

"To be patient."

"Helpful."

"Patience isn't really my specialty."

"They're right though. That must have been one hell of a shock to find out like that." Guilt twists my stomach that I allowed it to happen. "He'll come around. He's a good guy and he'll want to do right by you."

"He has every reason not to."

"Chels, that boy loves you. He'll be back."

"You think?"

"I know."

I narrow my eyes at her. "What aren't you telling me?"

"Nothing," she says, raising her hands in surrender. "I know nothing."

She leaves me after getting a message from Ethan to say he's finished with the team.

I flick through the TV channels but not finding anything that captures my attention, I pull out a book I picked up this afternoon with Mom about what to expect from childbirth and having a newborn and take it to bed with me along with a hot chocolate. It's not the kind of book I thought I'd be reading for a few years yet, but here we go.

When I wake the next morning, it's with the book poking me in the arm and still open on a page I vaguely remember reading.

I'd turned my alarm off last night knowing that there was no way I was going to school again today, so when I look to my cell, I'm surprised to see how late it is.

I'll go back next semester. It'll have given them plenty of time to get over the drama, and hopefully someone else will have done something that takes the heat off me.

I still haven't received a reply from Shane, but I send him another one anyway. I need him to know how much I miss him.

I get up, shower, do my hair, generally waste time because it's not like I've got a lot to do today. I should get out and go for a run but the thought of seeing someone when I'm alone doesn't sit right with me.

Eventually, I grab my laptop and get immersed in some work.

Mom pops in and out with food and drinks throughout the day to check on me, but other than that, I stay locked in my own little world, keeping everything and everyone else at bay.

That is until sometime after six o'clock.

Mom told me that dinner would be at seven so once I finished the assignment I'd been working on, I head to the bathroom to freshen up and get ready to meet them.

I'm just about to slip my shoes on when there's a knock at the door.

Knowing that I've only been disappointed when my imagination has run away with me over the past couple of days, I don't even bother hoping that it's him because I know it's not.

I'm staring down at my cell, praying for a response as I walk into the living area so I don't look up to the door until I'm right in front of it.

And when I do, I can't help but gasp in shock.

35

CHELSEA

S tanding on the other side of the glass door is Shane.

He looks exactly as I remember, his shaggy blond hair styled in its usual messy style, his emerald eyes staring at me as if he sees all the way into my soul and his full lips that make my stomach clench with desire. But that's where the similarities end because he's wearing a crisp white shirt and a pair of slim black dress pants, and in his hands is a giant box.

My hand trembles as I fumble with the lock to allow him inside.

"Hey," I say in a rush the second there's a gap in the door. "You look... amazing."

"Thanks. Can I come in?"

"Oh shit, yeah," I say jumping out of the way and holding the door open for him.

I stand, awkwardly rocking on the spot as I fiddle with my fingers, not knowing what to do.

Fuck, I've missed him.

I watch silently as he places the box on the coffee table and turns to me.

His eyes run down the length of my body, I have no idea why, I'm just wearing a massive hoodie and a pair of yoga pants, it's not sexy in the slightest.

"Shane." Just being able to say his name gives me tingles. "Fuck. I'm so fucking sorry. I had no idea... I should have told you... shit... I don't even..."

"Stop," he demands, reaching forward and taking my hand in his, tugging me into his body.

His heat burns, but in such a good way. My knees threaten to give way as his scent fills my nose.

"Oh god," I whimper as he stares down at me. "I've missed you so much."

"Chels, will you go to winter formal with me?"

My chin drops as his words register. "Y-you want to go to the dance?" One side of my lip twitches with the beginning of a smile.

"If you still want me."

A laugh bubbles up my throat, but not because there's anything funny about this situation but because it's so unbelievable.

"You're serious?"

"Deadly."

"Um…" I look around, my head spinning with this unexpected little visit. "I don't have anything to wear." I think about the dresses I've worn to previous dances and even though I'm not showing, I know they're not suitable.

"I've got you covered." He stands aside and allows me to see the box that I'd forgotten he carried in.

"What have you done?"

Without saying a word, he walks over to the box and pulls the top off. Inside is an abundance of tissue paper.

"Go on then. Let's see how well I know you."

I step up to the box and peer inside, but the contents are totally hidden.

"You chose it all by yourself?"

"Sure did. Go on the suspense is killing me."

Pulling back the tissue, I find fire engine red fabric staring back at me.

Tingles erupt in my stomach as I reach in and pull the dress free.

"Oh my god, Shane. It's stunning."

It's full-length with a deep V and a high split up one leg. It has a lot more fabric than the dresses I'm used to wearing, but it's so freaking sexy.

"Yeah?" I look to his hesitant eyes.

I relax for the first time in days, and a sob erupts from my throat out of nowhere. The relief of seeing him after not knowing what he was thinking, what he was doing, or even where he was the last few days is suddenly just too much to take.

"Shit," he mutters, gathering me up in his arms and pulling me tightly into his chest.

I breathe him in and it only makes me cry harder. Having him here, being able to wrap my arms around him. It's everything.

"Shush, it's okay."

"I'm so sorry. I'm so so sorry."

"Hey," he says, tucking his thumb under my chin and lifting my face up so I can look at him. "We'll do that later. Right now, I want to take my girl to formal. So dry those eyes, put on that sexy dress and let's enjoy our night together."

I swallow down my emotions and nod at him, a wide smile on my face.

"Sounds incredible."

He releases me, picks up the dress I'd dropped back into the box and with his hand in mine, pulls me toward my bedroom.

He settles himself in the middle of my bed. He looks fucking breathtaking and all I want to do is crawl into it with him.

"You've got thirty minutes. You also need to pack an overnight bag."

"Shane Dunn, have you been holding out on me?"

"What?" he asks innocently. "You think you're the only one who can have secrets?"

"I guess not," I say lightly, ignoring the ball of dread that threatens to fill my stomach at the mention of my secret.

He said he wants to talk later. We can do that.

"Come on, time's ticking."

"Okay, okay."

With his eyes burning into me, I pull the zipper down on the hoodie I'm wearing, revealing the bra I've got on underneath. After peeling my pants down my legs, I turn to him and he groans.

"I should probably go and wait out there, shouldn't I?"

With his gaze locked on my covered breasts, I reach behind me and drop the fabric.

"This was a really bad idea."

"Too late now. If only you came sooner and gave me more than thirty minutes to get ready. Just imagine how we could have used the time."

I push my panties from my hips and smile when his teeth sink into his bottom lip.

"Now I know, I can see it."

My brows furrow for a moment before I realize that he's looking at my belly.

I turn to the side, looking at myself in the mirror, and run my hand over my stomach.

"You think?"

"Yeah."

Anticipation crackles between us. The possessive look in his eyes has heat flooding my core.

Pulling my eyes away from his in the mirror, I force myself to focus on what I should be doing.

Pulling a drawer open, I find a suitable pair of panties for that dress and pull them on before sitting at my dressing table and making quick work of my hair and makeup.

"You could do that with more clothes on you know," Shane grumbles behind me.

"And what would be the fun in that?"

"If you're trying to make a point by showing me what I've been missing, trust me when I say it's really not necessary."

"Been a *hard* few days, has it?"

"Like you wouldn't believe."

I know I shouldn't be winding him up right now but I can't help it. I'm so happy that he's here and happy to joke with me once again that it's too much to ignore.

I know we've got a lot of heavy stuff to talk about but he's come offering a little fun first and I'll grab on to that with two hands.

The fact he's here at all means everything to me, let alone the rest of it.

"How about you help me cover it up?"

I step up to the bed and hold my dress out for him.

He makes quick work of sliding to the edge of the mattress and holding it out so I can step into it.

I turn so my breasts aren't right in his face, feeling like that might be a tease too much.

He pulls the fabric up my legs before I feel the soft brush of his lips on the small of my back.

"Shane?" I moan as they begin trailing up my spine as the fabric encases my body.

Slipping my arms into the holes, he pulls them up until the straps are resting over my shoulders.

I shudder as the tip of his nose runs along the line of my shoulder until his lips brush against the column of my neck.

"Oh god." My nipples pebble against the fabric they're now hidden behind, and all I can think about is taking it back off again.

Pressing the length of his body against my back, the obvious bulge of his cock presses against my ass and his hand slides around to my stomach, resting gently on the very slight bump he pointed out earlier.

"You're mine, Chelsea. Are you ready to go and show the world?"

"Yes," I whimper, too overcome with happiness at having his hand possessively on my stomach.

Lacing his fingers with mine, he spins me away from him so I can face him.

"Whoa." His eyes rush around my body, not knowing where to look first. "I knew it would be perfect but... fuck."

As I find some suitable shoes in my closet, he takes hold of the small bag I'd packed as I was getting ready and we leave the pool house.

Clearly, he wasn't the only one in on this little surprise because I find Mom, Dad, and Maddie standing in our backyard ready to take pictures.

"Jeez, it's not prom night or anything," I say with a laugh when both Mom and Maddie get a little choked up at the sight of us.

The thought of prom suddenly terrifies me. How big will I be by then? Will I still even be pregnant, or will I have had the baby?

A shudder of fear races down my spine. Shane squeezes my hand and I wonder if he's having similar thoughts.

Our lives are about to change so rapidly, and although I'm excited and sure that it's what I want, it's still scary. Everything we'd planned for the rest of our lives has potentially been turned upside down.

We smile for a couple of photographs before our teary-eyed moms wave us off, wishing us a fun night. I'm assuming they're aware that Shane's just told me to pack a bag and that we're spending the night together. Although, I guess they've not got much to worry about now, the worst has already happened.

The second we're settled in his car, Shane reaches over and takes my hand.

"Are you ready for this?"

I think of almost our entire class in the gym enjoying themselves. The last thing they are probably expecting is for the two of us to turn up hand in hand.

I think back to when we walked into school together on Monday and he openly kissed me in front of everyone. Hell, how was that only four days ago? It feels like a lifetime.

Might as well give them something to stare at. His words hit me and I can't help but smile.

"Yes. I think I am."

He glances over at me with a smile playing on his lips.

"You always wanted the attention, looks like you're doing a good job of getting it, hey?"

"Yeah, once I decided that I no longer wanted it. Go figure."

"They'll soon get over it."

"What? When I've got a belly the size of a basketball? Yeah, that should really take the heat off me."

"A basketball, bit small don't you think. More like one of those exercise ball things."

I gasp in mock horror and swat his shoulder.

"Carry on and you won't be capable of making any more."

"You want more?"

"Who knows. It's not like I planned this one."

"Good to know," he mutters.

"Shane," I say, reaching over to rest my hand on his thigh. "I didn't... I wouldn't..."

"I know, Chels. That wasn't why I said it."

"I fucked this all up so bad."

"Not now. Let's just enjoy the evening."

I love his idea. It's so sweet and thoughtful after the way we left things the other day. Although I can't help but feel the huge elephant in the corner of the room—or car.

As much as I want to lose myself in him, in the connection between us and how electric it is when we touch, I know we're only masking our issues. Just like I've done since I came back.

It's time I ripped that Band-Aid off and expressed all my truths, my fears, and what I want for the future.

36

SHANE

I thought I was crazy doing this. I didn't think anyone would understand but the second I told Mom my plans, she was fully on board. Her eyes went all soft and I thought she was going to burst into tears on me.

She immediately sent me back up to my room to get dressed so we could go out shopping. She didn't take me to the Rosewood Mall but her favorite one a few towns over. She might have been there to help me, but I knew the dress the second I saw it. I didn't bother looking at any others. After taking a chance on the size, I walked out of that store with the first genuine smile playing on my face that I'd had in days. Something just isn't right without her. I'm not right without her.

That being said, walking up to her pool house with the hope she'd agree to this plan was one of the most nerve-wracking things I've ever done in my life.

She could easily have said no. I told myself time and time again that she probably would just so I could be prepared. But I knew the moment I looked in her eyes that she needed me there just as much as I needed to be.

The relief that flooded me was all-consuming. I desperately wanted to pull her to me and make her mine once again, but I knew I had to wait.

There're a lot of things that need to be said between us. And yeah, maybe we should have the conversations before spending the evening together at the formal, but fuck it. I just want a normal night with my girl. Is that too much to ask? I want to push everything aside, just for a few hours so we can enjoy each other's company before we allow reality back in again and accept that everything is about to change for us.

The parking lot at school is mostly full when we turn up. I know we're late, it's how I planned it.

I've always been the one to hide in the shadows, to shrug off the attention being part of the team brought me, but not tonight. Tonight I was going to hold my head high and show the world what I wanted.

After telling her to stay put, I jog around the front of the car and open her door for her.

Reaching in, I tighten my fingers around hers and pull her from the car. I don't step back so when she stands to full height her breasts brush against my chest and with her heels on her lips are in the perfect position.

It would be so easy. Every muscle in my body screams for me to close that little bit of space.

Her dark eyes stare up into mine, begging me to make the move because she knows she can't.

I've got to be the one to make the move tonight. I'm calling the shots.

"Ready to show that dress off?"

I feel the shudder that runs through her body at my question.

"You're not scared, are you?"

"I..." She hesitates, and I hate the apprehensive look in her eyes.

Leaning in, my lips brush against her ear, this time her shudder is for a whole nother reason as my breath races past her skin. "You're Chelsea fucking Fierce, baby. Walk in there with your shoulders back and show them that you will never hide from them."

She gasps at my words but after a beat, she nods.

"Only if you're by my side."

"I wouldn't want to be anywhere else."

"Okay. Come on then, let's do this."

She slips her hand into mine and after slamming the door behind her, we set off toward the gym where Rosewood High hosts all their events.

The music booms out long before we get there. A few students loiter around outside, probably trying to locate the alcohol that stashed throughout the week in the hope of sneaking some in.

A few of them look our way, but no one says anything.

As we approach the door, Chelsea's hand begins to squeeze mine harder.

I can't help but smile to myself. Only a few months ago, I wondered if she really was an ice queen. Nothing ever affected her. Everything anyone said or did just washed over her like water off a duck's back. But I see it now. I see her vulnerable side, her fears, her nerves, and I fucking love it because I know full well that I am the only one who can.

She sucks in a deep breath before we both push the double doors open and walk inside.

We go straight through to where all the action is. As if they're expecting us, the music bottoms out for a beat as we step inside and almost everyone in the room turns our way.

"Fuck," she squeaks beside me. But only a second later, she sets her shoulders and follows my lead toward the center of the room.

All eyes follow us as I pull Chelsea in front of me. As if on cue, the song changes and I pull her into my body.

"Might as well give them something to stare at," I say as she stares at me in total awe.

A shy smile appears on her lips as she shakes her head.

"You're amazing. You know that?"

I shrug. "You bring it out in me."

Unable to resist her any longer, I lower my head. It starts as a soft brush of lips knowing that our entire class, hell, the entire school, is watching. But I'm unable to leave it at that when she presses the length of her body tighter against mine.

With my hands on the bare skin of her back, I part my lips and lick into her mouth. She eagerly accepts my kiss as if it's just the two of us inside her pool house.

I can only assume that everyone gets bored with us because when we eventually part, a little breathless and dizzy a few songs later, most kids have gone back to their own conversations and dancing.

Chelsea laughs, and it makes my heart clench. "I can't believe you just did that."

"It was time for some new gossip around this place, don't you think?"

"It still focuses on us, though."

"Maybe, but at least it's different."

"Well, well, well," a familiar deep voice says making its way over. "Didn't think you had that in you, Dunn."

Looking up, I find Ethan's amused face with Rae tucked into his side.

"You don't need to worry about Shane. He's got plenty in him."

"Huh, I thought that was you," Ethan deadpans, looking at Chelsea and making Rae snort with laughter.

"I wasn't expecting to see you here tonight. I didn't really have you down as a school dance kinda girl," Chelsea says to Rae.

"Now whatever gave you that impression?"

I take in her dark makeup, black skater dress, fishnets, and combat boots.

"I have no idea," she says, having similar thoughts.

"It was Sindy and Barbie," she says with a roll of her eyes.

"Who?" My brows pinch at not having a clue who she's talking about.

"Them." She nods her chin over my shoulder and when I glance over, I find Amalie and Camila walking our way with my reluctant looking teammates trailing behind.

"So this is a torture-your-boyfriend kinda night, is it?"

"You'd think so looking at their faces, right?"

"Dunn, Chelsea," Jake says when he gets to us.

"Hey. Um…" Chelsea says, tensing beside me. "Can we talk for a minute?"

Jake looks between the two of us. It's as if he's asking my permission, a part of me wants to laugh. How the hell did we get to this?

"I've just got a few things I need to say to him," Chelsea whispers in my ear.

"I trust you," I whisper back. "But please, make sure you tell him that I'm the best you've ever had."

"Shane," she squeals, slapping my chest playfully.

She drops a quick kiss to my cheek before leading Jake over to a quieter corner.

"What's that all about?" Amalie asks me, watching my girl lead her guy away.

"I have no idea, but I doubt she's about to jump him."

We both watch as Chelsea says whatever it is she needs to say to him. Jake shakes his head, a soft smile playing on his lips.

She's apologizing, that much is obvious, and I couldn't be more fucking proud of her right now.

"So you two—or three—really going for it then?" Amalie asks, turning away to give him some privacy.

"Yeah, I think we are."

"I would say that I think you need your head checked, but I'm not blind. You two are pretty perfect for each other. Even if I never in a million years would have put you together when I first arrived."

"Can't help who you fall for."

"You don't need to tell me that. I could have gone for the nice guy, but instead I ended up with—" She squeals as Jake wraps his hands around her waist and pulls her back into him. "That," she says with a laugh.

"Why do I get the feeling you're talking about me?"

"Because we are," Amalie says. "I was just saying what an asshole you are."

"Yeah, well, it's a good thing you fucking love it."

Averting my gaze as he pushes his tongue into her mouth, I look to Chelsea when she slips her arm around my waist and tucks herself into my side.

"Everything okay?"

"Yeah. I just needed to say my piece after…"

"I get it," I say, dropping my lips to her temple.

"I need to talk to Mase too, but he's otherwise occupied right now."

I look over to find him grinding away with Camila to the beat of the music.

"Shall we join them?"

"I'd prefer to do it in private with less clothes on," Chelsea murmurs, making my cock twitch with excitement.

"We've got plenty of time for that."

Despite everything and the unknowns hanging between us, we have the most incredible, normal, night.

We dance, drink, chat, and laugh with friends. At some point, Zayn and a few others from the team joined us but after Zayn's tagging announcement for the night, they mostly spent their time trying to win their chosen girls while the eight of us watched with delight as most of them got turned down time and time again.

Zayn eventually got bored trying to capture the nerd he'd been challenged to and ended up dancing with a thrilled looking Ruby while his sister and Poppy glanced at their antics with disgust on their faces.

"Shall we get out of here," Chelsea eventually whispers in my ear when everyone around us is lost in their own conversations.

"Hmmm... that sounds like a perfect idea. Ready to see what else I've got planned?"

"So ready."

We say our goodbyes to those around us before leaving the dance behind.

It's not until we're both back in my car that I think I take a breath.

"That was kinda crazy," Chelsea says, her thoughts mirroring my own.

"Yeah, it was. It needed to happen though."

"Why do you say that?"

"Everyone knows now."

"Knows what?" she asks, nerves laced through her voice.

"That you're it for me." Reaching over, I take her hand and lift her knuckles to my lips. "Right, let's go."

With her hand resting on my thigh, I back out of the space and toward our weekend destination. I was going to book us a hotel, but Mom called in a few favors and she managed to find the perfect place for us to have the privacy we need to sort everything out once and for all.

"I'm hungry," Chelsea complains when I've been driving for about an hour.

"What do you want?"

"Er... burger and milkshake."

I chuckle at her. "Next diner we pass, we'll stop."

"Aren't we nearly there? We've been driving for ages."

"Hardly."

"Maybe I'm just impatient."

I glance over at her; her usually dark eyes are almost black. She sucks her bottom lip into her mouth, knowing that I'm watching, and it makes my cock swell. Dropping my eyes to her chest, I find her swollen breasts that are temptingly exposed by the dress.

"Eyes on the road, Shane," she says with a laugh, pointing forward.

I do as I'm told, but only because I don't want to kill us all before I tell her what I've been planning for days.

"There," Chelsea shouts, pointing to an illuminated building up ahead, proving just how hungry she really is.

I signal to pull off the road and slow to a stop in the diner parking lot.

Chelsea is pushing the door open and climbing out before I've even had a chance to turn the engine off.

"I think we're a little overdressed," she murmurs to me as we walk inside the tired diner. I glance around at the two other customers in old ripped jeans and oil-stained shirts and I can't help but agree.

Their eyes, along with the sole waitress' follow us over to a booth in the window. I expect Chelsea to reach for the menu the second we're seated, but she doesn't. Instead, she just waits until the waitress comes over.

"Hey there, what can I get you both?"

"A cheeseburger, please. The biggest you've got. And a strawberry milkshake," Chelsea says without taking a breath.

"Okay, and you, dear?"

"I'll take the same. Thank you."

She scurries off as I silently laugh at Chelsea.

"What?"

"It's a good thing she didn't hang around, you might have eaten her."

"It's not funny. Every now and then I just get so ravenous, it's like I haven't eaten anything ever and I suddenly need to consume everything in sight."

"Tell me about it. Tell me everything," I demand.

She opens her mouth and then closes it again. "I don't know where to start," she admits.

"When did you find out?"

Picking up one of the salt packets from the holder, she fiddles with it as she thinks back. "About three weeks after I left.

"I didn't want to be there to start with and my entire focus was getting back. But after a while, I settled in and realized that actually, my parents were right to send me.

"I woke up one morning and the realization that I'd not had my period in a really long time just slammed into me out of nowhere.

"I'm not the kind of girl who tracked that sort of thing, but I didn't need to try to work it out. I knew. I can't explain how I felt different, I just did. It was weird.

"I got myself a test, and there it was. That positive result stared back at me."

"Did you tell anyone?"

"Other than the doctor." She shakes her head. "Nope."

"Jesus, Chels."

She shrugs like it's not a big deal. "I knew in that moment that I'd keep it. I don't even really remember panicking that much. It just felt right. It still does. Yeah, I was nervous as hell about having to tell people, you. But I knew I wanted it." Her hand drops beneath the table, her palm pressing against her belly.

It's a sight I didn't expect to see, not for many years yet anyway but excitement begins to bubble up within me.

We might be young. People might think we're crazy, but I already know that I want this with her.

Is it going to be easy? No. I'm not under any illusion that it's going to be easy in any sense of the word, but that's not enough to scare me off. Nothing worthwhile is easy. And if I had to embark on this challenge with anyone, then I can't imagine it being with anyone but Chelsea.

"I should have told you. I wanted to tell you, but then that first night you were so..."

"Horrible?"

"Yeah, something like that. I deserved it though. What I did, it was... unforgivable. You had every right to treat me like that, worse if I'm honest.

"But then as things changed between us, it got harder. You were quickly becoming everything I'd ever wanted, and I knew that admitting the truth would potentially ruin everything we were building.

"I was scared. No, terrified, that you would hate me, that you would leave me, and then I'd be back to square one once again with no one."

Reaching across the table, I take her hand in mine. "You should have told me. Hearing it from you would have been a hell of a lot better than what happened."

She swallows nervously. "I know. I was going to tell you that night, remember I said we needed to talk? I knew I had to do it. I just never got the chance."

"Who was it?"

"Shelly."

"What? Why would she do that? Wasn't kicking you out of the squad and pushing you down the stairs enough?"

She shrugs. "They let me back in without her permission. We all knew she'd be pissed."

"How'd she find out?"

"The woman who did my ultrasound in the hospital was her mom. I can only assume it came from her."

"Fucking hell." I think back to her being in the hospital and a thought hits me. "That's why you kicked me out of the hospital. You thought I was going to find out."

Guilt washes over her features. "Things were... complicated between us back then."

"Only because you made them that way. If you didn't keep sending me—"

"I was scared, Shane," she interrupts. "I was confused. I spent the whole time I was away thinking about you, about that night, about all the reasons you had to hate me but praying that by some miracle that you didn't. Then I came back, and it seemed you did hate me. But then there were these little moments when you didn't and..." she sighs. "I didn't know which way was up. Everything was different. My life had totally changed in ways that no one knew about and although I had much more clarity about what I wanted since going away, I was drowning."

"I never hated you, Chels. I tried to, trust me, I did. I was so angry that you let me take the fall for all of that. That you allowed what happened between us, instigated it even, when you knew the truth. But still, I couldn't hate you."

I look down at the table for a beat.

"I've wanted you for too long." She gasps and I look up at her from under my lashes. "I watched you for years look at anyone but me. But suddenly you saw me, wanted me. I don't even..." I shake my head unsure of how to vocalize what I'm trying to say to her but the waitress chooses that exact moment to bring our plates over.

"Thank you," we both say as she hovers around asking if we need anything else.

Once she's gone, I look at Chelsea, who has already started on her fries, and I smile.

"What?" she asks, shyly.

"You're so much more than I ever imagined."

"I will be after I've eaten all this. It's the size of my head," she says, nodding to the burger.

"That's not what I meant and you know it. For someone who always wanted to be front and center, you're not very good with compliments."

"I didn't get them very often," she admits.

"Well, you'd better get used to it."

Chelsea demolishes her dinner, I have no idea where she puts it, especially as I struggle to clear my own plate, but she claims to feel better for it as she sits back and places her hand on her belly.

"Should we go? We don't have far to go."

We both slide out from the booth and I'm almost at the door when I realize she's not behind me.

"Chel—" My word is cut off when I find her staring at the desserts on show.

"Want a donut?" she asks like we haven't just eaten our body weight in food.

"No, I really don't," I say with a laugh.

"I'll get you one just in case you change your mind."

I'm still chuckling at her as she takes the box the waitress passes over and we make our way back to the car.

Only twenty minutes later, we're pulling up into a parking lot for an apartment building that overlooks the bay. The moon glitters in the dark sea. I can only imagine how stunning it might be in daylight.

"We're staying here?"

"We are. Come on." I jump out excitedly and grab both our bags from the trunk before joining her at her side of the car as she stares out at the sea beyond.

Silently we make our way inside the building.

"Wow, this is fancy," she says, taking in the lavish surroundings.

The entrance is impressive with its huge artwork and solid oak desk for security to sit behind.

After giving the guy my name like Mom instructed. He gives me a card before gesturing toward the elevators and we make our way over.

I tap the card to the panel and the second the doors close behind us we begin to move.

Chelsea is silent but her excitement is palpable as the elevator keeps rising.

When we step out, our feet sink into the plushest carpet that I've ever stood on.

There is only one set of doors in this huge entrance hall.

"I guess this is us then."

Tapping the card to the box beside the wall, the doors click and I push them open.

"Oh wow," Chelsea gasps, coming to stand beside me as we take in the view of the entire bay through the wall of floor to ceiling windows. "That's incredible."

Dropping our bags, I pull her forward toward the doors.

The moon shines bright and the stars twinkle in the black sky above.

Pulling her in front of me, I wrap my arms around her middle and rest my chin on her shoulder.

Everything might be up in the air right now, but with her in my arms, everything also feels right.

37

CHELSEA

My heart races as I stand in Shane's arms, looking out over the tranquil night view before us.

I thought I'd be in my pool house alone tonight while everyone enjoyed winter formal. I never could have imagined any of this.

Him, the dress, this incredible penthouse apartment. All of it has been way beyond anything I could have ever wished for.

Spinning in his arms, I look up at him.

He stares back at me, his green eyes dark and full of emotion.

"Chelsea, I—"

Cupping his cheek in my hand, I shake my head. "I'm really sorry, Shane. But what I said the other night is true. I love you, and I want this with you, if you'll have me... have us."

Dropping his forehead to mine, he continues to stare into my eyes.

"I wouldn't have it any other way."

One minute I'm on my feet staring at him and the next my legs are around his waist and my back is pressed against the window behind me.

"Shit, that's cold," I gasp as the cold glass bites into my exposed skin.

He takes advantage of my parted lips and plunges his tongue past them and deep into my mouth.

I sag in his hold as I give myself over to him but his hold on me doesn't falter.

He kisses me as if he's making up for the past few days. As his tongue caresses mine, tears burn my eyes. I can feel everything he's trying to tell me, and it's totally overwhelming.

I don't deserve this guy. I'm fully aware of that, and I intend on trying to prove to him every day that I'm worthy of him.

The fire that's been burning in my belly all night begins to roar to the point that just being pinned here kissing him isn't enough.

"Shane," I mumble against his lips.

"I know, baby."

He pulls his lips from mine but only gets as far as my jaw as he lowers my feet to the floor once more.

The length of his body presses me against the glass, and I feel every inch of him. He needs this just as badly as I do.

"Bedroom, now," I moan as his hand comes up to squeeze my breast.

Without missing a beat, he takes my hand and tugs me from the glass.

I'm assuming that he's not been here before, but that doesn't stop him navigating us straight to the ginormous master bedroom, again with a view out over the bay.

"This is beautiful," I say, taking in all the cream and gold hues around the room.

"You're beautiful."

When I turn, I find Shane's eyes on me. Something tells me he's barely even noticed the room.

A smile tugs at my lips as heat hits my cheeks.

"This dress is hot as fuck," he says, taking a step toward me. He lifts his finger and runs it along the deep V, teasing me as it tickles over the swollen swell of my breasts. "But I think it might look even better on the floor."

"I guess you'd better find out."

Tucking his fingers under the shoulder straps, he pushes them until the entire top of the dress falls from my body.

He bites down on his bottom lip as he stares down at my breasts, my nipples hard and begging for attention.

Reaching forward, I take the top button on his shirt between my fingers and make quick work of popping them all open until I'm able to push the fabric from his shoulders.

It falls to the floor before he steps up to me once again. The hot skin of his chest almost burning against my sensitive breasts. His fingers thread into my hair as he crashes our lips together once again.

My nails scratch down his back before finding their way to his abs and dropping lower.

He's rock hard beneath his pants. I rub him and he groans into my mouth.

"Fuck, Chels." His lips trail down my neck as I open his fly and push my hand inside both his pants and boxers.

He growls, sinking his teeth into my soft skin as I wrap my fingers around his length.

Kissing down his chest, I run my tongue along the indentations of his abs, before pushing both his pants and boxers down his thighs. His cock springs free, teasingly close as I sit on the edge of the bed.

Reaching out, I wrap my fingers around him once more and look up at him through my lashes.

His lids are heavy, half covering his dark emerald eyes, his lips parted as his increased breaths race past.

I stroke him slowly and his jaw tics as his teeth grind.

"Good?" I ask. I don't need to, his body is giving me all the answers, but I need to hear his voice.

"So good." It's rough, sexy, needy. I fucking love it.

Leaning forward, I lick the precum that had leaked from the tip. His entire body flinches at my soft contact, his fingers lacing through my hair as if he's going to take control, but he never does.

Parting my lips once again, I take him in my mouth.

"Jesus, fuck."

I watch as his head falls back, sucking him deeper until he hits the back of my throat.

I know he hates that I've got a bit of a reputation for this, but I'm hoping that I can make him forget all about it now he's the only one reaping the rewards.

Pulling back, I lick around the head before sucking him back down again.

His head drops and our eyes connect as I continue working him.

Before long, he gets even harder in my mouth and I work him faster knowing that he's getting closer to his release.

"Chels," he warns, his fingers tightening in my hair as if he's about to pull me back. But I have other ideas because I don't let up for a second.

Lifting my hand, I cup his balls and squeeze gently.

He groans a beat before he twitches in my mouth and his salty cum hit's my tongue.

I suck him until he's finished, then sit back and wipe my mouth with the back of my hand, a smug smile on my face.

Resting back on my elbows, I watch him. His chest heaves with his exertion, his hair falls over his face and a sated smile plays on his lips.

After a second, he kicks his shoes off before allowing the fabric around his hips to drop to the floor.

Scooting back on the bed when he steps toward me, he climbs onto the bed, straddling my legs.

His hands land on my waist and slide up until he's palming both of my breasts. My back arches, offering him up more of me. He pinches my nipples before dropping to find my lips.

The second we connect once again, I lose myself to him. I forget everything that got us to this point in our lives, and I just take everything he's offering.

His lips trail down my neck, leaving goose bumps in their wake before he licks along the line of my collarbone and descends to my nipples.

"Shane," I moan, both of my hands diving into his hair to hold him in place.

He sucks and licks, sending fire straight down between my thighs.

"Oh god, Shane, please."

His fingers wrap around the waist of my dress that's still in place before he begins to pull. I lift my hips to help him out and in no time at all, it drops to the floor, leaving me in only my red lace panties.

He stares at them for a beat, before his dark eyes flick up to mine, a smirk playing on his lips before he reaches out and rips them from my body.

I gasp, desire for him pulling all my muscles tight.

Pushing my knees apart, he settles himself between them and rubs his cock through my wetness.

"I can't wait any longer to be inside of you," he admits.

"So don't." And he doesn't. Before I've even finished talking, he surges forward, filling me to the hilt in one smooth move.

"Fuck. I'm fucking addicted to this feeling."

"That good, huh?" I ask with a smirk.

"Yeah, but I don't just mean your body. I mean this," he says, gesturing between the two of us. "It's not just sex, is it? This... this is bigger than that."

A lump forms in my throat, because I know exactly what he means. Neither of us has much experience with this, but even with my lack thereof, I know that this is bigger than anything in my past.

I nod. "I know. I feel it."

"Fuck, Chelsea." He stops moving and just stares at me, his hand sliding up my body until he grips on to the back of my neck. "I love you so much."

I gasp at hearing the words and tears fill my eyes. My chest swells to the point I swear that my heart's going to stop right there.

"Shit, I didn't mean to make you cry," he says, reaching up to wipe my tears as they slip from my eyes.

"It- it's okay. They're happy tears. I love you too."

"Jesus. I don't think I'll ever get used to hearing you say that."

"I hope you never do."

Unable to stay still any longer, he slowly pulls out of me before sliding back in.

"Shane," I moan, my back arching as he hits every single nerve inside me, pushing me toward another high that I know I'll never get used to.

Sitting back, he wraps my legs around his hips and picks up speed. In only a
seconds sweat is glistening on my skin as he thrusts into me hard, building
higher and higher.

"Come, Chels. I need to feel you."

He drops his thumb to my clit, and I detonate around him. My eyes slam closed as my back arches and I cry out his name.

Seconds later, his own growl fills the room before he jerks inside me and gives me everything he has.

We both still, the only sounds that can be heard is that of our heavy breathing.

Still inside me, he stares down at me. Something crackles between us despite what only just happened. Aftershocks from my recent orgasm fire off, revving me up for another.

Hesitantly, he moves his hand forward from where they were resting on my knees. I'm confused by the move for a moment, he's just had his hands everywhere, why is he suddenly unsure. But then his large palm lands on my belly.

I probably look more pregnant than I did before, thanks to the giant burger from not so long ago.

He continues to stare, his thumb rubbing back and forth over the taut skin.

"Our baby is growing in there." The awe in his voice has emotions hitting me full force once again.

"I know," I whisper. It blows my mind every time I think about it too.

"When's your due date?"

"July seventh."

He shakes his head as he tries to process it all.

Placing my hand on his distracts him a little and his eyes find mine.

"Lie with me?"

I move my leg to the side, and he pulls out of me and falls down on the bed, facing me.

His eyes search my face as if he can't believe I'm really here.

"Are you sure you want this?"

His brows draw together.

"It's going to change everything. Your entire life. I would understand if you didn't—"

"Stop. Stop talking right now," he says, placing two fingers against my lips. "We did this together. So we will continue to do this together."

"But your future, college, your career."

"And yours too. This isn't just about me having to make changes."

"I know but I chose this. I didn't have to..." I trail off, not able to even say the words. "You didn't choose this, you were ambushed with it."

"It doesn't matter. No matter how I found out, my feelings about it would have been the same."

A smile tugs at my lips.

"Clearly someone up there thinks this is meant to be so I think it's only fair we give it a good shot."

"I figure that I can screw it up as much as I am so..." I trail off, it's meant to be a joke but I can tell by the look of Shane's face that he's not amused one bit by it.

"You're not screwed up, Chels. You're just dealing with the fallout from all of that."

His words remind me of yesterday morning.

"What? What is it?"

"I went to breakfast with Luca yesterday morning."

He tenses at my word. "I know, he called me. Ripped me a new one for not being there for you."

"He didn't." *Of course he did.* "I told him not to. I needed someone to talk to, not someone to get to you from the inside."

"He cares about you, baby. He was only trying to help."

"I know. Anyway, we get to the same diner we always do and *he* was there."

"He? Who's... oh. Shit. What happened?"

"He told me that he just wanted to talk but I ran. But I saw something different in him, I can't figure it out but something is telling me that he might not be the man I remember him as. My memories from that time are so fucked up. I don't know what's nightmares and what's real anymore."

"Maybe you should talk to him," he says with a wince, making my heart rate pick up.

I know he's right. It's the only way to find out the truth, to discover why he's sought me out all of a sudden.

"Is there anything else you need to tell me? Any other secrets you been too scared to admit?"

I think for a minute, sucking my bottom lip into my mouth.

"I hate peanut butter," I say seriously.

"I already know that."

"Really? I try not to tell people because they think there must be something wrong with me."

"Chels, you've spent countless hours in my house. I've spent longer than I want to admit watching you. I know these stupid little things, I've seen them."

I open my mouth to respond, but I find I have no words.

"Um... how about... I want you to fuck me again."

He chuckles. "I don't think that's a secret, baby."

Rolling onto his back, he pulls me with him so I have no choice but to straddle his waist. His hands once again come to my belly before sliding down to my hips, ready to help me move.

"Go on then, rock my world."

"I'm pretty sure I've already done that." I smirk.

"I can fucking guarantee it, baby. But it's time to do it again."

38

SHANE

When I wake, the other side of the bed is empty and cold. I sit up in a panic that she might have left in the middle of the night. I feel stupid for it the second I see her curled up in the love seat in front of the windows staring out at the sea crashing onto the beach wearing my shirt from last night.

She looks so peaceful with her head tilted to the side, lost in thought and her hand resting on her belly. I bet she doesn't even realize she's doing it, but it fills me with joy. It's clear how fiercely she loves that baby already and I can't wait to see her with him or her in her arms.

Something possessive washes through me and my teeth grind. Thoughts of the man who's been trailing her have my fists curling in the sheets. Now more than ever I need to make sure she's safe, and I don't know how to do that with some random guy clearly stalking her.

Blowing out a calming breath, I climb from the bed and make my way over to her.

"Hey, baby," I say, dropping a kiss to the top of her head.

She startles as I touch her, showing just how lost in her own head she really was.

"Morning. Sorry, did I wake you?"

"Sitting here silently?" I ask with a laugh. "No, I just missed you."

She turns to look at me, running her eyes down my naked body.

"Hmm... I missed you too, but I was hungry."

I glance at the coffee table and gasp. "You ate my donut?"

"Well, you didn't really want it in the first place, so..." She shrugs.

"You know the kitchen is full of food for us, right?"

"Yeah, but I wasn't sure if I was allowed to eat it or not. I just took a bottle of water."

"It's all ours. Would you like a real breakfast?"

Her eyes drop to my semi. "That all depends on what you're offering."

"I was going to offer to make you pancakes, but now that you put it like that."

It must be over an hour later when we eventually make it to the kitchen. Both freshly showered, Chelsea still wears my shirt, her long bare legs sticking temptingly out the bottom and one too few buttons done up, giving me the perfect tease as to what's underneath.

She perches herself on a kitchen stool while I get everything out to make our breakfast.

"I didn't have you down as a chef."

"I'm not sure I'd describe myself quite like that, but I can knock out a few things. Pancakes being one."

"I guess it's a good thing that one of us can cook seeing as we're starting a family and will need to fend for ourselves."

My stomach twists, but I'm not sure if it's with fear for what's to come or excitement.

"You want us to live together and do this right?" I ask.

"Why do you look so surprised? I don't want you at your parents while I'm at mine. I don't want you to be a part-time dad like we're not a couple just because we're young."

"Okay, but how the hell are we going to afford all this. We're still in school. I know my dad's loaded, but I highly doubt he's going to put up any cash when he finds out about this."

"Good, your dad's a cunt." I spin to Chelsea just in time to see her lips slam shut and her eyes widen in horror. "Fuck, that wasn't meant to be out loud. I'm sorry."

"Don't be. He is a cunt. I fucking hate him."

"He's gonna lose it when he hears about this, isn't he?"

"I can't imagine him doing anything else. I only have to breathe the wrong way and he goes off. I don't know what I did to make him hate me so much."

I turn back to the pan I'd put on the stove so she doesn't have a front-row seat to the emotion that I'm sure if filling my face as I think of my dysfunctional family. Mom and my brothers are incredible, I couldn't ask for better, but he just poisons everything.

"Hey," she says, slipping her delicate hands around my waist, her breasts pressing against my back. Her touch makes me shudder and I relax into her.

"You haven't done anything wrong." Her lips brush against my shoulder blade as she says the words and my skin erupts in goose bumps. "He's the one with the issue. And if he doesn't support us, then he'll be the one missing out. He won't get to see his grandbaby grow up. That will be on him, not you."

"I think my mom wants to leave him."

"And you're surprised?"

"No, not at all. I don't know how she's put up with him for so long. I just worry about what she'll do."

"She'll be fine."

I turn in her arms and take her face in my hands. "I know she will. Thankfully, they're not my biggest concern right now."

"Oh?" she asks as I brush the tip of my nose against her.

"Nope, that would be you two. My parents are capable of sorting their own lives out. We need to figure out how to start ours."

"We'll figure it out."

"I'm going to get a job," I announce. It's been something I've been thinking about since finding out about the baby, and I know that I need to step up to the plate. We can't expect handouts from our parents to help fund this. We're old enough for this to happen, so we need to be grown up enough to accept responsibility.

"Me too," Chelsea agrees.

"You don't need to. You just need to focus on this little one," I say, dropping my hand to her belly.

"We're a team now. I want to do my part too. Plus, there will be times once the baby is here that I won't be able to do much, and I want us to be prepared."

After dropping a chaste kiss to her lips, I push her back in the direction of the stool she was previously on so I can continue with breakfast.

"What are you going to do about college?" I ask as I pour some batter in to the now scorching hot pan.

"I'm thinking I might take a year off. Get used to being a mom and then see if I could maybe start part-time after that. What about you?"

"I don't know. We might need for me to just get a job."

"No, Shane. I refused to allow you to do that."

"I'll do whatever I need to to make sure you and our baby are looked after."

"You have no idea how much that means to me, but still, I refuse to let you sacrifice your future."

"I don't even know what I want from my future, besides you."

"Forget about your dad and everything he wants for you, what can you see yourself doing?"

"I want to be involved with football, but I don't want to play professional. I want to be in the background. Trainer maybe, something like that."

"You've got a little time, applications aren't due for a few weeks yet. Think about what *you* want, and I'll support you all the way."

I look over my shoulder at her and smile. "I love you."

"I love you too, but please, don't burn my pancakes."

By the time Sunday morning rolls around, I'm nowhere near ready to leave our little penthouse of heaven but I know that real life is waiting. Christmas might only be a few days away but with the number of things we need to deal with, my father being the most pressing, it feels like a million years away.

"I don't want to go," Chelsea whines as I hold both our bags in one hand and hold my other out to pull her from the love seat where she's enjoying the last few seconds of the view.

"I know, but it's the holidays."

A smile twitches at her lips. "We're spending it together, right?"

"Too fucking right. I can't imagine I'll be welcome at the Dunn family Christmas dinner. You think your parents will be okay with me gate-crashing?"

"He might surprise you, Shane."

"Yeah, and he might not," I say sadly.

I know he's home, I've had messages from Mom. What I don't know yet is if he knows, although unless he's come home and locked himself in the house, I can't imagine he doesn't. This gossip isn't contained to Rosewood High, it's all over the town now that the kids have had plenty of time to go home and tell their parents.

The infamous Brett Dunn's son has got his teenage girlfriend pregnant, I bet they're all fucking loving it.

With a sad sigh and one last look at our weekend escape, Chelsea and I make our way down to my car.

The drive home is much more somber than the one here, the tension in the car is palpable and I hate that we have no idea what we're about to arrive back to.

My intention is to take Chelsea home, make sure she's happy before going and facing the music. I know she's going to want to come with me, but much like the last time, I need to do this alone. She's got enough to worry about right now, she doesn't need my broken relationship with my dad weighing down on her more than it probably already is.

All those plans are shattered though when I pull into Chelsea's driveway to find a truck parked in it that has her tensing in fear.

"W-why is that h-here?" she asks, her wide eyes locked on the black truck that I recognize immediately.

"Should I drive away?" I offer, not being able to get a read on what she wants me to do.

"N-no. I think it's time to get to the bottom of this. Find out what the asshole wants. If he's brazen enough to turn up at my house like this, then I need to find out what his issue is."

"Okay, let's go."

I'm at her door before she's even got one foot out.

"I'll be right beside you, baby."

She nods but no words pass her lips as hand in hand we make our way to the front door.

"Chelsea, is that you?" her mom calls from the living room and Chelsea's grip becomes almost painful.

"It'll be okay. I'm here, your parents are here. They're not stupid enough to put you at risk."

"I know, I know," she says, blowing out a slow breath.

The second we turn the corner, my eyes lock on the man that I haven't seen before, I've only ever seen his shadow behind the windshield of his truck.

He stands the second he sees Chelsea and I get a second to study him. I've never seen him before, of that I'm positive, but I can't help thinking there's something familiar about him.

Chelsea gasps despite knowing that he was here, and stumbles back a little.

Reaching out, I wrap my arm around her waist and pull her into my side.

"It's okay. I've got you," I whisper down to her as her eyes remain locked on the man.

"Chelsea, this is Greg—"

She tenses in my arms before cutting her mom off.

"What the hell are you doing in my house? Isn't it enough that you've been stalking me everywhere I've been for the past week, now you've got to force your way into my home, my family?"

He swallows nervously, his lips parting to say something but no words come out. I have no idea who he is or what he wants but it's blatantly obvious that he's out of his depth right now.

"I'm sorry. I didn't mean to scare you. I just... I didn't know how to go about it."

"Go about what?" Chelsea spits. "Thought I was grown up now so it would be okay to take whatever you wanted?" She stands forward, finding her courage from somewhere, and holds her arms out at her side. "You're sick. All of you. The best thing that ever could have happened to me was being taken away from that place. From scumbags like you."

"What? No, no... I wasn't... I didn't..."

He looks to Honey and Derek for support.

"Chelsea, sweetie. Greg isn't one of them. He's your father."

"What?" Chelsea barks, her body rigid as she stares at the three of them, disbelief written all over her face.

I stare at the man she's been so scared of the past few days and it suddenly dawns on me why he looked familiar, although his eyes are blue and Chelsea's dark, they're almost identical.

Holy shit.

Chelsea shakes her head.

"No. I remember you. You used to take her to her bedroom like all the others. You're just one of them who used to fund her drug habit."

"No, I was trying to help."

"Help? If what you're saying is true. You left me there. You left me with all those disgusting men who used to..." She trails off as the blood drains from Greg's face. "Helping me would have been taking me away, feeding me, clothing me, caring for me. But you did none of that."

"I did what I could at the time."

"Well clearly it wasn't good enough. Do you have any idea what it was like for me? That place was hell on earth. And you left me there."

Guilt covers his face. He reaches up and rubs at his jaw as he tries to find the words to reply.

"I brought you food, clothes every time I came. I gave her money but no doubt she blew it all on drugs. I did what I could."

"Bullshit," Chelsea spits.

"If I could have taken you away, given you a better life, I would have. But I couldn't."

"Why? What so important you couldn't help a vulnerable child?"

"If I could go back, I would have done things so differently," he admits.

"But you can't, so tell me, why? Why couldn't you be the man that I needed?"

"Your mother was my student. Admitting you were mine, it would have exposed our affair and I couldn't risk my career. It was the only thing I had."

Shaking her head, Chelsea rubs her hands over her face.

"Your job? Your fucking job. You left me there, knowing exactly what she was doing, what the men were capable of because of your fucking job," she screams, her body visibly trembling with her anger. "Those men they..." She shudders as the memories hit her. "You need to leave. You need to leave and never come back. I'm not interested in anyone who could do that to me or any other child. Not doing anything makes you as bad as them. No, do you know what, it makes you worse. You actively left me there. Left me there to be neglected and abused. You're a fucking monster, just like them."

"No, Rose, please."

Rose?

"That's not who I am. That girl, that one you abandoned, is long gone. I'm no longer that weak and vulnerable child that you forgot about. My name is Chelsea, Chelsea Fierce and I will not forget about all of that, everything you have done or failed to do, just because you've now decided to try to make amends for all your wrongdoings.

"I don't need a father. I've got the most incredible parents now who have given me everything you failed to. You're too late. I don't need you."

The tension in the room is heavy as they continue to stare at each other. The weight of Chelsea's words pressing down on all of us.

"You're right. About all of that, you're right. I just needed to..." he sighs. "I needed to see you. To know that despite all my mistakes that you survived."

"Yeah, I survived. I'm fucked-up beyond belief, but I survived."

Both her mom and dad gasp at her words, both of them obviously wanting to argue but wisely they keep their mouths shut.

"Please, R—Chelsea. I need—" She cuts him a scathing look and he backs down. "Okay, I'm going to go. I'm going to leave this here, just in case you ever want to reach out, even if it's to yell at me. I'd really like to get to know you, if you'd ever consider giving me the time of day." He drops a business card on the table. The room is so silent the sound of it hitting the glass is like a gunshot through the house.

He turns to Honey and Derek. "Thank you for allowing me to do this, welcoming me into your home. I know it's more than I deserve."

With one last look at his daughter, he walks from the room and soon after the house.

The second the front door slams. Chelsea breaks.

The three of us rush to her, thankfully I get to her before her parents and gather her up in my arms as she cries.

I move us to the couch and sit down with her on my lap.

Glancing at her parents, I find a similar look of guilt on their faces that was on Greg's not so long ago.

They think they did the wrong thing. And although I understand, I can't help but think that it needed to happen.

He's been weighing on Chelsea's mind since she first saw his truck, she needed to know the truth, no matter how painful it might be.

Long agonizing minutes pass as we all wait for Chelsea to calm herself down.

As I rub my hand up and down her back, her mom goes to make us all some coffee.

Eventually, she pulls her head from the crook of my neck and wipes the tears from her cheeks.

"I'm sorry," she says weakly.

"Oh, sweetie. You've got nothing to be sorry about," Honey soothes.

"I should have told you about him following me."

"He told us before you came back."

"Is he really my father?"

They both nod. "Yeah. It seems that he's been looking for you for a while. I know it's easy to say, but I really do think he wants to try to make amends."

Chelsea blows out a shaky breath.

"You have no idea what it was like," she says quietly. "The things I've told you all, they're just the tip of the iceberg."

"We know, sweetie. And we won't tell you what to do here. If you decide to never see him again, then we'll respect your decision, he will too. He just had to try."

She nods, holding me a little tighter as she falls silent once again.

"I hate that he can take me right back there as if it was yesterday."

No one speaks. Not a single one of us can take any of that away, make it any better. Although I really fucking wish I could.

After long excruciating minutes, Honey attempts to lighten the mood with a subject change.

"Did you two have a nice weekend?"

"Yeah, it was amazing," Chelsea says.

"I'm glad you've sorted things out."

"We have. This is it now, right?" she asks, her big eyes looking up at me.

"It is."

"Well, welcome to the family then, I guess," Derek says, lifting his mug in our direction.

"We'll leave you to it."

Derek and Honey take their coffee and close the door behind them.

Chelsea snuggles back into me and breathes me in. The move, the knowledge that she feels safe in my arms like this makes my chest ache.

"I love you, Chelsea," I whisper into the top of her head.

"I love you too."

39

CHELSEA

I can only assume that somehow Shane managed to carry me out to the pool house because when I wake a while later, that's exactly where I am.

Thankfully, the second I crack my eyes open, I find him sitting beside me playing on his phone.

Reaching out, I place my hand on his thigh and squeeze.

"Hey, how are you feeling?"

"I'm fine," I say, although the memories of what happened when we got back here aren't far away, nor are the images of my past that I try to keep locked in a little box in my head.

"You don't need to put on a brave face for me, baby."

"I know. I just... I don't know what else to do right now. Talking about all that, it just makes it all come back... even after all this time, it's so raw."

He slides down until he's lying on his side facing me.

"You know you can tell me anything and I won't think any different of you, right?"

I nod, the size of the lump in my throat making it impossible to say any words.

He reaches out, wrapping his hand around the back of my neck and squeezing possessively. I love it so much, a smile starts to twitch at my lips.

"So, you were called Rose?" Hearing the name makes my spine stiffen. I always hated it. I don't think I've ever been as happy as the day my parents told me that I could change it.

To me, Rose signaled someone who was weak, defenseless, and that wasn't who I was by the time Honey and Derek took me in. I was stronger, braver, I could look after myself to some extent. I was fierce. Or at least I wanted to be. Finding out that was their last name was the first time I realized that I was where I belonged.

It didn't take me all that long to settle on a new name. The second Chelsea hit me, I knew it was right. Chelsea Fierce was the perfect name for the new me. The girl who took no shit, gave zero fucks and got everything she wanted.

It was great until I realized those things didn't really make me happy. I isolated myself from everyone, put walls up even with those who were meant to be my friends. I see that now, and I vow to never allow myself to fall back into that old life. I've got Shane now, and hopefully a real friend in Rae. Things are definitely looking up.

"Yep. That's what the woman who pushed me out decided I should be called. She probably couldn't spell anything longer." It's meant to be a joke, but the expression on Shane's face tells me he finds the whole thing anything but funny.

"It's pretty, but I can't imagine calling that. You're definitely a Chelsea."

"I agree. Although I didn't lose it completely. I'm now Chelsea Rose. I figured that my past was always going to be a part of me, so I may as well embrace it to some extent."

"Although it's horrible, hearing just some of the things you experienced makes me feel murderous, it did make you who you are. And I, for one, think you're pretty incredible."

"Yeah?"

"Yeah."

We stare at each other for the longest time. No words are said, they're not needed. That connection I craved is right there, and it's everything I need.

"Are you hungry?"

"Is that a serious question?" I ask with a laugh.

"Your mom came down to ask if we wanted to join them for dinner. You were asleep, so I declined. Thought we could order pizza or something. What?" he asks when I fall silent.

"I kind of fancy going out. We've been inside the whole weekend."

"Okay. What do you want to do?"

Thirty minutes later, we're both changed and heading out of the pool house.

We embark on the long walk from my parents' house to the seafront. The sun is setting, casting a stunning orange hue all over the bay as the moon makes an appearance for the night.

We stop at a diner and order takeout slices of pizza. We steered clear of Aces end of the beach, knowing the chances of bumping into someone from school would be high. I don't want to avoid them really, but equally, I want to keep Shane to myself while I can. I'm not ready for our weekend to be over.

"How are you feeling?" Shane asks once we've both finished eating.

We're sitting on the sea wall, our legs dangling over with the sand below, watching the waves crash in.

"Honestly, I have no idea. I always assumed that my dad was just some random guy who donated his sperm. I didn't think I had a father, as such, let alone one who was present in my early years."

"Did you mean what you said about not wanting anything to do with him?"

Did I? I think back to what I said to him and I wince. My words might have been true, he shouldn't have left me there, but now some time has passed, and I feel less ambushed by the whole thing, I know that the situation probably wasn't that simple. Things rarely are.

My biological father taking me in his arms and carrying me away from hell was a fantasy I had many times as a child. I imagined him being some wealthy businessman who desperately wanted me but for some reason couldn't get to me. It was one of the stories I formulated in my head to escape my reality. Sadly, that one, nor any of the others ever materialized and when I was taken away, it was by the state and I was dumped in some kids home, not a wealthy man's penthouse.

I sigh. "I don't know."

Reaching over, he takes my hand and lifts my knuckles to his lips.

"Well, whatever you decide. I'm here for you."

A sob erupts from my throat without warning.

"Chels?"

"I'm okay. You just really don't know how much that means to me."

I wipe away the tear that drops before he notices and breathe in a deep breath.

I don't deserve this. I don't deserve him. But fuck, I'm going to do everything I can from now on to keep him.

"I can come with you, it might soften the blow," I offer as Shane puts his sneakers on the next morning, ready to go home and face the music with his father.

"No, it's okay. Just be here waiting for when I get back. There's a good chance I'll need you." His eyes darken as he says the words and my insides clench with desire.

As much as I hate it when he argues with his dad, I can't deny that it fires him up in the perfect way and I do love helping to take his mind off it after.

"How do you want me?" I say in what I hope is a seductive voice.

"Hmm... in my jersey with nothing beneath."

"Done. Message me when you're leaving."

Standing, he stalks toward me. "I've changed my mind. I think I'll stay and take that right now."

"As much as I want to agree. You need to do this. The last thing you want is it hanging over your head during the holidays."

"I know," he mutters, brushing his lips against mine.

As much as I hate to do it, I push my palms against his chest to put a stop to his attempt to put it off.

"Go, Shane. I'll be here when you get back."

"Ugh, fine."

Falling down onto the couch, I watch as he pushes the door open but instead of walking straight through it and disappearing around the house, he still for a beat.

"What?" I ask when the color drains from his face.

"Can you hear shouting?"

Sitting up, I listen.

"Fuck," Shane barks before running to the house. I jump from the couch, hot on his heels as he runs through the open kitchen doors and into the hallway.

The shouting ceases as he comes to an abrupt halt when his eyes land on the people before us.

"Brett, no," Maddie cries, pulling at his arm as he storms toward Shane.

"I told you that you were going to fuck everything up," he bellows at Shane.

I want to do something, say something, but I'm frozen on the spot as I stare at the fury rolling off him in waves.

"How do you expect to be successful now? No one will want you with a kid attached to you. You're a fucking disgrace, boy. Fucking disgrace."

"I don't give a fuck, Dad. I don't want the NFL. I don't want your dream."

"No? Am I not good enough for you? Is all the legwork I've done to get you a chance at the best college teams in the country not up to your standard?"

"I don't want it. I never have, but you refuse to listen to me."

"No? So tell me now, what do you want?"

There's a beat of utter silence, the calm before the storm because all of us know that this is going to get worse before it gets better.

"I want Chelsea. I want Chelsea and our baby."

Brett lets out a laugh, but it's nowhere near amused. It's menacing, and it makes a shiver run down my spine.

"You're fucking delusional. You think you're able to look after a baby? And with her?" Disapproval drips from his features as he turns to look at me. "She's nothing but a cheap slut."

"Brett," Dad barks, his fists curled in anger. He steps forward, but Mom places her hand on his arm and stops him.

Shane's chest swells with anger as he steps up to his dad, his fists clenched, ready to fight.

"Leave it, please," I beg, reaching out to touch his arm but he doesn't acknowledge my touch, he's too lost to his anger.

"Take that back."

His dad laughs again. "You're a fucking idiot, boy. You're throwing everything away. You choose her and you're giving up everything I can offer you. Everything."

"How many times? I don't fucking want it."

Brett's eyes turn black, cold, as his lips press into a thin line and the vein in his neck pulsates menacingly.

"You ungrateful little..."

"Nooo," I cry as Brett's arm suddenly flies toward Shane.

"Brett, no," Maddie screams racing forward.

Dad jumps into action, but we're all too late.

Brett's fist connects with Shane's cheek. The crack is so loud it makes my stomach turn over.

Shane stumbles back, his shoulder connecting with the wall before he falls back.

"Shane," I shout. There's a commotion behind me as I drop to my knees beside him. "Shane? Shane?"

"Fucking animal," Maddie spits before joining me at his other side.

"Baby, wake up. Shane. Fuck." Her eyes are wide and full of fear as she stares at him.

Jumping to her feet, she marches over to Brett who's now being restrained by my dad as he attempts to push him to the front door. His lip split open and blood trickling down his chin from where my dad must have retaliated on Shane's behalf.

"If you've fucking hurt him, I'll kill you." She pokes him in the chest as spittle flies from her mouth. "I'll fucking kill you."

"I'd like to see you try."

"Who are you? What happened to the man I married, huh? When did he turn into such a vile asshole?"

Brett doesn't say anything, he just stares at his wife as if she's lost her goddamn mind. Anger and frustration burn in my stomach for her.

"We're done. Expect to hear from my lawyer. I can't spend another day pretending I love you." She turns away, her back to him, unable to even look at his face. "Get him the hell out of here before I call the police."

After putting up a bit of a fight, Dad eventually gets Brett out of the front door and slams it behind him.

Fucking hell.

Remembering that Shane's laid out next to me, I rip my eyes from Maddie and down to him. The most incredible sight greets me. His beautiful green eyes.

"Shane, oh my god," I wail, dropping down to him and wrapping my arms around his shoulders.

"I'm fine. I'm okay," he says into my hair as his arms come around me as if I'm the one who needs it right now.

Who am I kidding? I fucking do. That was terrifying.

After a few seconds, I release him, and he pushes himself so he's sitting against the wall.

"Well, that went well," he jokes, looking up at the concerned, traumatized faces staring down at him.

Maddie bursts into tears before Mom ushers her toward the kitchen. Dad walks toward us and holds his hand out to Shane to pull him up, who in turn does the same to me seeing as I'm still on the floor.

"I'll go get you some ice," I say, looking at Shane's swelling face.

"I need a drink," Dad announces, shaking his hand out and marching in the same direction Mom and Maddie just left.

We follow to find Mom pouring Maddie a glass of whiskey before Dad takes it from her and tips the bottle to his lips.

"Can I?" Shane asks once Dad's lowered the bottle, and he reluctantly passes it over, clearly deciding that it's okay to break his no alcohol for minors rule after what just went down.

Shane swallows a shot before passing the bottle back.

Ten minutes later, we all find ourselves sitting around the dining table. Shane with an ice pack pressed to his face and the adults all nursing their drinks. No one seems to have noticed that it's only just past midday. Although, to be fair, if I weren't pregnant, I think I'd want a drink right now.

"I'll make up the guest room for you tonight," Mom offers to Maddie. You're more than welcome to stay as long as you like.

"T-thank you. I should go to the house to get some stuff before he burns it all."

"I don't think he'd—" Maddie's look cuts Mom's words off.

"What about..." Maddie flicks a look to Shane and me and I swallow nervously.

Mom chuckles, the sound of it feels so good after the stress and tension of the past hour. "I think he's already moved in, don't you?"

They all turn to us.

"You've both proved to us that you're adults now who can make your own decisions. So what do you two want to do?"

"Honey was right," Shane says before I get a chance. "I'm pretty sure I've already moved in." A wide smile spreads across my face. "Of course, that's if it's okay with you both." He looks to Mom and Dad, who both smile at him.

"You're going to be parents in a few months. I'm not sure we're in any position to stop you."

"I'm going to get a job, part-time obviously, so we've got our own money. I'm not sure what I'm going to do about college yet, but I will be going—"

"We both will. We're going to make this work. All we ask is for your support. If we can stay in the pool house for now, that would be great, but we'll get our own place as soon as we can. We want to do this the right way, for us, and for this little one."

Both Mom and Maddie's eyes fill with tears once again.

"We'll be here for all of you, no matter what," Mom says.

"You're both going to be incredible parents," Maddie adds.

"Only time will tell," I say with a laugh.

40

CHELSEA

"We're going to be late," Shane says, dropping down on the edge of the bed, looking hot in his button-down and dress pants. His hair is styled and just waiting for his hands to run through it to mess it up, or I might in a minute because I've got a thing about his messy, just-fucked hair. That just shows the one-eighty my life has taken because his long shaggy locks used to be one of the things I used to mock him for. It might be shorter now than it used to be, but it's no less of a mess. Now I just spend my time running my fingers through it and using it to hold him against me instead of telling him to cut it off.

"I'm nearly ready," I say, but I'm too focused on his reflection in my mirror to finish off my makeup. "Are you sure they want me to go?"

"Of course. Amalie and Jake invited both of us. They know we come as a package deal now."

"Oh god, we're one of them now, aren't we?"

"What do you mean?"

"You know how annoyingly sweet Amalie, Jake, Camila, and Mason are? That's us now too."

"I should hope so," he says with a shit-eating grin on his face. "I was always jealous of them."

"Ah, I forgot that you wanted Amalie first."

"I thought I did, I was just trying to distract myself from wanting what I couldn't have."

"Who was that?" I ask innocently, batting my eyelashes at him.

"Oh, just this insanely hot cheerleader. She wasn't interested though."

I make quick work of applying my lipstick, the kind that doesn't immediately rub off at the first touch of a kiss, good thing really seeing as I intend on doing just that the second I get to him.

Pushing from the stool, I stalk over to him. He watches me, fire burning in his eyes as I get closer.

"That dress," he says, biting down on his bottom lip. I'm wearing a skintight, burgundy body con dress that shows off every one of my curves, including my very small baby bump. Anyone who didn't know I was pregnant wouldn't see it, but I can and I'm so ready to embrace it.

I stop in front of him and reach for his shirt. I wrap my fingers in the soft cotton and pull him from the bed until he's standing before me.

"I'm glad you like it, one of your gifts is hiding beneath it. If you're lucky, you can unwrap it later."

He groans as if he's in physical pain.

"Maybe we should cancel on the party."

"Nope, you said we were invited." Reaching up on my tiptoes, I brush my lips against his as I slide my hand down my body to find his already hard cock. "Down boy, you've got a few hours yet."

"You're killing me. Get your shoes on and let's go before I really do change my mind."

Regretfully, I take a step back from him and turn to get my shoes.

"Come on then, let's go," I announce once I'm ready.

I glance around the room, which is now filled with his possessions as well as my own. I loved this place before, but since he officially moved in and made the space ours, I love it that much more.

The day after the showdown with Brett, my dad escorted both Shane and Maddie to their house. It turned out not to be necessary as he wasn't there, we've since discovered that he's in New York, but there was plenty of evidence that he had been there because the place was smashed to pieces. They didn't stay long enough to do anything about it though. They just grabbed what they wanted and left without looking back.

Maddie hasn't decided what she's going to do next, whether she'll eventually move back in, or not. She's said that she'll get through the holidays and then try to make some decisions for her future.

Thankfully, our house is big enough so now not only is Shane in here with me, his mom is in a guest room and we've got Luca and Leon too so that we can all celebrate the holidays as one big family. It might not be perfect for some of them, but to me, it's everything and for the first time in possibly forever, I'm actually excited.

I've got Shane's gifts all wrapped and ready for tomorrow, and I can't wait to see if he likes them. Plus, there's the little sexy set I've got on under this dress as an extra treat of course.

The drive to Amalie and Jake's new house takes a little over thirty minutes. Seeing as they're both planning on going to Maddison once Amalie graduates next year, they wanted to be on the right side of town.

I shake my head at how crazy this all is. They've bought a house, we're having a baby. Shit, someone will get engaged next. It's insane seeing as we're all eighteen or thereabout, but like I've said many times before, it just feels right. I guess what they say is true, when you know, you know.

"This place is cute, although not your average house for two eighteen-year-olds to own," I say as we pull up on the street the GPS brought us to.

It's a stylish gray and white modern duplex with huge windows and a cute front yard.

My mind runs away with me as I picture Shane and me in a place like this with a toddler running around. Butterflies erupt at the thought.

"It's impressive, that's for sure."

"I bet Jake doesn't know what to do with himself after that shitty trailer."

Shane turns to me, his brows drawn together. "Jake lived in a trailer? I thought he lived with his aunt and uncle."

"Yeah until they banished him to the back of their property in a damn old trailer that you wouldn't wish on your worst enemy."

"How didn't I know this?"

"It's a closely guarded secret. He used to want you all to think he had it all, but the reality was that being captain was about all he had. Until Amalie, of course."

"Wow, I never would have guessed."

"Exactly as he intended."

Movement inside catches my eye and I watch for a second as Mason and Jake talk and laugh with each other.

Happiness tugs at my stomach that they've found their forever with their girls.

"Are you planning on getting out?" Shane asks, opening my door for me. I hadn't even realized he'd left the car.

"Yeah, sorry."

I can't help the nerves that assault me as we stand at their front door. The majority of the people inside have every right to hate me, yet here I am invited to their housewarming cum Christmas Eve party like I'm one of them.

"Alright," Jake says eloquently when he pulls the door open. He looks as gorgeous as ever, but unlike all the years in the past, it does nothing for me.

"Nice place," I say, stepping inside when he moves aside and Shane gestures for me to do so.

"It's going to take some getting used to, that's for sure."

"Hey," Amalie says, rushing down the hall to greet us, looking totally harassed.

"Hi. Is everything okay?"

"Yeah, just trying to get the food ready. Excuse me." She races back off in the same direction she came.

"Ignore her, she just wanted everything to be perfect. I keep telling her to chill out but she won't have it."

I stifle a laugh. I bet him telling her that is really not helping.

"I'll go and see if she wants some help."

"Rather you than me."

Leaving Shane with Jake, I go in the direction Amalie disappeared, assuming it's to the kitchen.

When I get there, I find her flitting around counters full of food and drink.

"Can I help with anything?" She startles and turns to me with wide eyes. "Sorry, I didn't mean to scare you."

"Sorry, it's me. I'm just... gah. I know I'm putting too much pressure on myself. It's just..." She looks away from me. "I'm sorry, you don't care about all this."

"Of course I do. What's wrong?"

"It's just my first Christmas without them," she says, tears filling her eyes before she averts them.

Of course, I should have thought of that before now. The first Christmas without your parents must be so tough.

Reaching out, I take her hand in mine. "It's okay to be sad. No one expects you to be okay during this time."

"I know, I just need to keep busy so I don't spend the entire time thinking about what I would be doing with them if they were still h-here." Her chin trembles, her voice cracking at the end of her words.

I have no idea if she wants one from me, but without putting much thought into it, I pull her into my arms for a hug.

It's only brief, but when she pulls back, she's got a small smile on her lips.

"Thank you. I needed that."

"Put me to work, what can I do to help?"

"Can you make me a drink, a strong one?"

"Sure. Any preference?"

"Surprise me."

Walking over to the counter with the bottles, I find everything from beers to spirits and mixers. Pulling my phone from my purse, I look up cocktail recipes and mix one up for her.

"What is it?" she asks when I pass it over.

"A Screaming Orgasm. I thought it might help right now."

She stares at me for a beat before she burst out laughing.

"Shit, I needed that," she says, taking a sip as we're joined by two others.

"We've been sent for more beer," Mason says, pulling the refrigerator open like it's his house.

"Ugh, why couldn't he do it himself?" Amalie grumbles before putting her glass down and stalking from the room. I wince, feeling a little sorry for Jake. Amalie's in a bad place right now, and he's about to be the one to feel the force of it. I'm sure he's more than capable though.

"Oh, looks like he's in the doghouse."

"Leave her alone," Camila says, stepping up to Mason.

"What? I'm just saying."

"Could I have a word with you two?" I ask, stepping forward.

Both of their heads spin my way and they stare at me as if they didn't know I was in the room.

"Of course," Mason says softly while his girl places her hands on her hips and raises her brows.

I'm not surprised, I knew which of the two of them was likely to make me work for it. Rightly so I guess after I sent her after her cheating boyfriend. Although it might have been a bitch move, at least she found of the truth before it went on any longer.

"I just wanted to say that I'm sorry, I really am. How I behaved before was unforgivable—"

"Yet here you are asking for it," Camila snaps.

"No, no, I'm not. I'd understand if you never did. I just want you to know how much I regret all of it. My head was a mess, and I was making stupid decisions."

"Like sleeping with Shane?"

I can't help but laugh. "No, that was probably the only sensible thing I did back then."

Camila opens her mouth to say more, but she must change her mind because she soon closes it again.

Mason, however, just gives me a soft smile. "You're all good, girl." Stepping up to me, he gives me a brief hug. Camila gives him death stares the entire time, making me wonder why he thought it was a good idea.

"Stand down, Cami bear. It's over." He chuckles.

Camila steps forward, but it's nothing like the friendly way her boyfriend did. She frowns and points at me. "If you hurt him. If a few weeks down the line this all turns out to be one of your sick games, I swear I'll... I'll fucking kill you."

"Okay, baby. That's enough." Mason wraps his hand around Camila's upper arms and pulls her back into his chest and wraps his arms around her.

"What Camila is trying to say is that we're glad you're back and we hope things work out for you from here on out."

"No, I wasn't—" Camila protests until Mason spins her and cuts off her words with his lips.

While they're distracted, I take a handful of the beers they came in for and go to join the others.

Amalie is still busying herself arranging the food she's prepared on the dining table while Jake looks at her with concern in his eyes.

"Here she is," Ethan announces, distracting me from the obvious tension in the room as I place the bottles down. "How's Rosewood's next star doing," he drawls, clearly already one too many beers down as he places his hand on my belly.

I notice Shane tense as he watches Ethan touch me, but a quick shake of my head and he soon relaxes. Ethan is anything but a threat.

"Keep your hands to yourself, Savage," Rae barks, swatting his forearm to make him release me. "I'm sorry, please ignore him."

"It's okay, I'm used to him by now."

"Yeah, Chelsea has been my wing-woman for years, she knows the drill."

"Oh yeah?" Rae stands to her full height, all of about five foot two, and stares at him. "On the prowl tonight, are you?"

"Uh huh, got my sights on this feisty little thing."

"Jesus," I mutter, slipping around them and joining Shane on the couch.

"Everything okay?" he asks as I pass him one of the beers I kept hold of.

"Yeah, just a normal day in Rosewood," I say with a chuckle.

"What's up with Amalie?"

"It's her first Christmas since her parents died. She's struggling."

"Ah of course."

"Brit, come and sit down. None of these fuckers care how you've arranged the sausage rolls, baby."

Amalie shoots Jake a scathing look from where she's still moving things around, but she must see something in him because after a second she backs away and out of the room.

Jake sits forward as if he's about to follow her, but it's not necessary because in only seconds she returns with the drink I made her.

"What have you got there?" Jake asks, making Amalie smirk as she sits beside him.

"It's a Screaming Orgasm. Chelsea made it for me." She grins.

"Careful if she made it," Camila pipes up, earning herself the attention of the entire room. Alcohol sure does give her a loose tongue.

"That's enough," Mason says as the awkward tension begins to lift.

"No, it's okay. I deserve it," I admit as Shane's grip on me tightens.

Amalie shrugs. "I trust her," she says, lifting the glass to her lips and taking a huge mouthful.

Something inside me swells. The regret for what I did is still there, I think it always will be, but the happiness I now feel starts to push it down somewhat.

The drinks flow, well for everyone bar me, and thankfully everyone begins to relax into the evening. Everyone gets drunker and drunker and for once, I get to watch as they begin stumbling their way to the toilet and clumsily missing their mouths as they try to have another drink. I never realized quite how stupid we all look as the alcohol takes over.

I enjoy myself more than I should just watching them all, and unlike I was expecting, I don't really miss not being a part of it. There's something very sobering about being the sensible one.

"I really fucking love you," Shane slurs as he pulls me onto his lap and pushes my skirt up my thighs so I can straddle him.

"What are you doing?" My argument is weak at best, I might not be under the influence right now, but any touch from him has a similar effect. He makes me lose my mind with need.

"Kiss me," he demands.

I stare into his desire filled eyes and I'm powerless, unable to deny him anything he asks. Leaning forward, I press my lips to his. His tongue immediately darts out and pushes past my lips.

I have no idea what the others are doing around us, not that I care. My entire focus is on Shane as I shamelessly grind my hips down on his growing cock.

"Get a room." Ethan's booming voice eventually cuts through my lust and I pull back, my chest heaving and my body strung tight to continue.

"Don't even think about taking his advice and having sex in our new house," Jake barks, earning himself a look from Amalie. I'm not sure if she's just annoyed in general with everything to do with this time of year because of the memories it's bringing up for her or if she's just pissed off at him, but there's a definite tension between the two of them. And the words that fall from Shane's drunken lips next sure don't help.

"Oh yeah, you worried someone will do a better job of it? You do know I'm the best she's ever had, right?" His final words are muffled as I place my palm over his mouth.

"Shane!" I whisper-squeal, mortified that he's just said that out loud for everyone to hear.

Ethan, Mason, and Rae burst out laughing, but Amalie and Jake are much less amused.

I turn to look at the couple as Amalie's face turns beet red before she pushes from the couch and storms from the room.

"Bro, I think you'd better go and prove your worth. Give her a real one of those screaming orgasms," Ethan says, a smirk firmly in place as he talks.

"I'm so sorry," I say to Jake as he looks at the door, torn over what to do.

With a sigh, he stands from the couch and follows, but he stops at the door and looks back at me.

"I was really, really drunk. I'm surprised I stayed awake long enough to finish that night."

Shame burns at my insides and colors my cheeks. Great, the night I'd dreamed of for years really was one big drunken mistake to him.

"Well, I know for a fact that one of us didn't finish," I mutter, my need to have the last word getting the better of me.

"Oh burn, bro. Burn," Ethan barks while the others snigger around us.

"Fucking hell," Jake mutters before ducking out of the room to go and find his girl.

"We should probably leave now."

"Why? Things just got interesting," Ethan says, his voice still full of amusement. "I want to hear more about sex god Jake Thorn not completing his duties."

Shane's hands grip my ass reminding me that I'm still straddling him like a hussy.

"Yeah, it's definitely time for us to go."

Climbing from his lap, I make quick work of pulling my dress down. It's not like they haven't seen my ass before, but I'm a different person now and the only one I want looking at me is currently half asleep on the couch.

"Shane," I shout, startling him awake. "Let's go."

He mumbles something incoherent as he rearranges himself in his pants. As glad as I am that he can keep it up while plastered, now really isn't the time to show it off.

Reaching for his hand, I pull him from the couch.

He stumbles a little before steadying himself and wrapping his arm around my shoulder.

"I love you Chelsea Fierce," he slurs.

"I love you too. Now let's go before I can't move you."

"Do you want help?" Both Ethan and Mason stand, but I shake my head.

"I've got him. You carry on enjoying yourselves."

"Because listening to those two make up will be so much fun," Rae complains with a roll of her eyes.

"Have a great Christmas," I say, ignoring her comment. "We'll see you New Year's Eve at Zayn's?"

"Sure thing. Have a good one."

With a few more goodbyes, I eventually manage to get Shane out of the house and into the car.

"If you pass out before we get home, you're going to have to sleep in the car," I warn him. I'm lying, of course. I wouldn't be able to sleep knowing he was out there alone, but I hope my words are enough to keep him with me.

Shane keeps me amused all the way home, muttering mostly incoherent things but every now and then he'll drop in how much he loves me, or how badly he wants to fuck me and explain in vivid detail the things he wants to do to me. I can't deny that by the time I pull up on my parents' driveway that I'm a ball of need.

Sadly, by that time, he's also fallen asleep and is snoring lightly beside me.

"Shane. Shane," I say, shaking his shoulder to wake him. "Come on, or I'll have to go and get your brothers to get you out."

Still he snores.

"For fuck's sake, Shane."

Trying a different tact to get him alert, I pop his seatbelt and skim my hand up his thigh, rubbing his cock through his pants. In only seconds, it starts to harden under my touch.

"Wake up, baby. You've got promises to fulfill," I purr in his ear.

He groans, thrusting his hips up to get more.

"Chelsea." His voice is slurred, rough and deep.

"Wake up and get to the pool house and you can have whatever you want."

Suddenly, his eyes fly open.

"Fuck," he barks, his chest heaving and his eyes almost black with desire.

"Hey."

"Hey." A smile curls at his lips as he stares at me and lust curls at my insides.

"Shall we go inside?"

"Yes."

He somewhat clumsily manages to get himself out of the car before I wrap my arm around his waist in an attempt to steady him.

We sway our way around the back of the house. He trips and stumbles but thankfully stays on his feet. It makes me think of all the times my parents have collected me in a similar state and had to deal with getting me to bed. This is making me realize that I should probably get them a better Christmas present.

Finally, we get to the pool house. Shane leans against the wall, his eyelids getting heavy once again.

The second we're inside, he heads for the bedroom before falling face-first onto the bed and almost immediately starts snoring.

I can't help but laugh at him, and I drop to my knees and slip his shoes off. Not exactly what I thought I'd be doing on my knees tonight, but hey. He deserves this. After everything both his father and I have put him through the past few weeks, he needed to lose himself for a night.

I manage to roll him over and get his pants off, but after undoing the buttons on his shirt, I give up trying to get it off him. He's totally out of it and no help at all.

Kicking my shoes off, I peel my dress from my body and look at the black lace underwear I'd bought especially for tonight. Not wanting to waste it, I find my cell in my purse and open the camera. I snap a couple of pictures before sending them to Shane with a sarcastic comment about what he's missed out on. I'm sure he'll enjoy those when he looks at his cell tomorrow.

After finding his jersey, I pull it over my head and make use of the bathroom before crawling into bed beside him.

He might be out of it, but the second I press my back against him, his arm wraps around my waist and I'm pulled back so that were connected in every way possible.

"I love you, Chels."

"I love you too, Shane. Merry Christmas."

41

SHANE

I have no idea what time it is when I wake, but the sun is streaming through from the living area and my head pounds.

It takes me a second to remember the night before.

Fucking Ethan insisting we all do shots.

I want to curl back into Chelsea and sleep away the rest of the day, but my need for the bathroom and painkillers are too pressing.

Sitting from the bed, I find I'm just wearing my boxers and open shirt from the night before. I glance over at Chelsea and smile. She tried to look after me last night.

My pressing need for the bathroom keeps me from watching her peacefully sleeping any longer and I stand from the bed, shedding my shirt as I go.

I do my thing before brushing my teeth in the hope it'll make me feel a little more human before going in search of some Advil.

I down a bottle of water with the tablets before heading back to sleep, but when I walk into the bedroom, a very different idea pops into my head.

Chelsea's shifted since I left and she's now lying on her stomach, the sheets pushed aside with my jersey up around her waist. Her round ass is on full display with the scrap of lace she's wearing.

My cock swells as my mouth waters.

Time for her first present of the day, I think,

Starting at her ankle, I kiss up her leg until I get to the swell of her ass. Palming one side, I bite down on the other.

"What the—oh," she cries, quickly relaxing beneath me. "As you were."

She rests her head on her arm and looks down at me as I continue.

Slipping my finger beneath the lace, she parts her legs a little to give me better access and I slide it through her wetness.

"Hmm... were you dreaming about this?"

"Always," she says on a gasp as I slide one finger inside her. Her muscles clamp down, hungrily trying to suck me deeper. "You promised me all these dirty things last night and then you went and passed out."

"I'd better make it up to you then."

She moans when I pull my finger from her and instead wrap my hands around her hips. I lift her until she's on all fours and wrap my fingers around the sides of her panties.

I pull them down until they fall to her knees but I make no move to remove them further, I'm too desperate for her.

Leaning forward, I lick up her seam.

She cries out and I spear my tongue inside her.

"Oh god," she whimpers as I focus my attention on her clit. She pushes back into me, needing more. Sliding two fingers deep inside her, I suck, lick and bite until she's crying out my name, her legs trembling as she reaches her climax.

"Fuck, Shane." Her arms give out and she falls down onto the pillow, her ass still temptingly up in the air.

Crawling forward, I push the waist of my boxer briefs down just enough to release my cock. I run the head through her wetness before slowly pushing inside her.

She groans as I stretch her open until she's full of me.

Gliding my hand down her spine, I slide my fingers into her hair and tug gently. Her back arches, allowing me to slide a little deeper.

"So good," I groan, slowly pulling out before sliding straight back in.

"More, Shane. More."

Picking up the tempo, I give her exactly what she craves until the only sounds that fill the pool house are those of our heavy breathing and our skin connecting as we both chase our orgasms.

The second her pussy clenches with the beginnings of her release, I fall headfirst into my own.

"Fucking hell, that was some wake up," Chelsea says between heaving breaths as I fall down beside her, trying to catch my own breath.

"Merry Christmas, baby."

A wide smile spreads across her face as it occurs to her what day it is.

"Merry Christmas."

Turning over, she pulls open the drawer of her nightstand before placing two beautifully wrapped presents in front of me.

"I was wearing your first present, but you seem to have removed the bottom half."

She lifts my jersey up to show me the matching bra to the set she was wearing.

"You'll just have to wear it for me another time."

"I'm sure that can be arranged. Go on," she prompts, nudging the gifts closer.

Taking hold of the biggest one first, I make quick work of ripping the paper away to find a nondescript black box. Narrowing my eyes at her, I lift the top off to find a stunning silver watch staring back at me.

"Chels," I say, knowing that it's more than she can probably afford right now.

"Look at the back."

Pulling the timepiece from its cushion, I flip it over.

Shane. My one and only x

Emotion clogs my throat as I stare down at her words.

"Thank you so much," I manage to say around the lump after a few seconds.

"You're welcome."

Removing my old one, I drop it on the nightstand and place the new one on my wrist.

"It's perfect."

"And this one."

Wondering what else she's done for me, I rip it open but soon realize that this one is even more sentimental because it's a photo frame with 'I love my daddy' engraved in the dark wood, and in the center, our ultrasound picture.

Reaching out, I run my fingertip over our baby.

"It still blows my mind," I whisper.

"Me too. I'm not sure I'll believe it until he or she is in my arms."

I nod, totally understanding where she's coming from.

Resting it on my pillow, I climb from the bed so I can get her gift.

"This is for you," I say, crawling back on the bed to sit beside her.

She smiles at me before taking the small gift. My stomach is in knots, it's nothing huge, but I really want her to like it. It took me long enough to find it.

I bite down on the inside of my cheek as she rips into the paper and flips open the lid of the jewelry box.

"Oh, it's beautiful," she gushes as she stares down at the necklace and I breathe out a huge sigh of relief.

"Yeah?"

"Yeah."

"Can I?" I hold my hand out and she places the box in it.

I have the necklace out in seconds and I hold up the three interlocked bands and turn them over.

"Look closer." I hold it out for her and she gasps the moment she sees our names engraved in it. "And we can add the third once we decide on a name."

"Oh my god," she sobs, her hand comes up to cover her mouth as tears fill her eyes.

She quickly pushes from the headboard and holds her hair out of the way so that I can place it around her neck. Turning back around to me, she holds the pendant between her fingers.

"Thank you so much. I love it."

"I love you," I say, leaning forward and capturing her lips.

"I'm not sure you've ever gotten ready so fast," I say when Chelsea stands from her dressing table in record time.

"I'm excited," she says with a beaming smile. "I think this is the first Christmas in, well ever, that I've looked forward to."

Like me, she's wearing a novelty Christmas sweater that our mothers insisted on, hers has "baking my little pudding" stitched across the front whereas mine is a standard Santa design.

"You look cute."

"I feel like I should shove a pillow up my sweater so it makes sense. My minute bump doesn't really do it any justice."

"You'll regret even saying that in a few months." I laugh, pulling her into my arms and tucking a lock of her hair behind her ear. "Are you ready for the craziness?"

"More than ready. This is the first of loads of amazing Christmases. Just think, this time next year, we'll be surrounded by toys and hopefully an excited baby."

"I'm not sure he or she will be all that excited at six months old."

"Well, we can be excited enough for the baby too."

"That sounds like a plan, baby. Shall we?"

"Yes," she squeals with delight before we grab the couple of bags of presents we have for our families and make our way to the main house.

Honey and Mom are busy in the kitchen making waffles, there's already a stack high enough to feed the five thousand.

Derek, Luca, and Leon sit at the table eagerly waiting for their food delivery.

"At fucking last," Luca barks when he spots us. "We're not allowed to eat until you two show your faces. Mom wanted to come and get you, we thought it probably wasn't a good idea."

Chelsea's hand squeezes mine and when I glance over her cheeks are a little red.

"We were exchanging gifts before heading up."

"Sure you were," Luca says with a wink. "Gifts. Seems to be that you gave her your gift a few months ago."

"That's enough you two. I want to have some appetite left for the waffles," Derek complains.

We take our seats and not two seconds later, Honey and Mom bring over breakfast.

Luca and Leon dive in as if they've not eaten in a month while the rest of us watch them in fascination.

"What?" Leon mumbles around a mouthful. "I'm hungry."

Laughing at them, I grab a waffle for Chelsea before placing another on my plate.

"How was the party last night?" Mom asks, reminding me about the hangover that's still thudding away nicely at my temples.

"I'm not sure Shane remembers much of it." Chelsea chuckles.

"Overdo it all, did you, son?" Derek asks.

"Something like that."

Thankfully the conversation takes a different turn and I'm able to put aside the fact I don't remember how I got back into the pool house last night, let alone how the evening at Amalie and Jake's might have ended.

I shrug to myself as I look around the table at those I love. Things might be crazy right now. Chelsea and I might not have a clue what the next few months and years might hold for us, but at this moment surrounded by all these incredible people that I know will support us no matter what, I couldn't be happier.

We have the best Christmas I think I've ever had. We laugh, joke, eat incredible food, thanks to our mothers, and we enjoy each other's company. It's the exact kind of Christmas I've already dreamed of and I can only hope that those in our future are as heartwarming.

The sun's long set when I find myself alone with Chelsea in her parents' kitchen as she gets herself a snack. How she's still hungry after everything we've consumed today, I have no idea.

"Hey," I say, wrapping my arms around her middle and holding her tight.

"Hey."

"Have you had a good day?" I ask.

"Yeah. The best. Thank you."

"What are you thanking me for?"

She spins in my arms and stares up into my eyes.

"For everything. For just being you and making all my dreams come true."

I open my mouth to respond, but I have no words. Instead, I put everything I feel for her into my kiss.

"I love you, Chelsea Fierce," I whisper against her lips, my palm pressing tenderly against her swollen stomach.

"I love you too."

42

CHELSEA

"I'm not sure how I feel about saying goodbye to this year," I admit as we walk through Zayn's front door.

All our parents—minus Brett, who's still in New York—are at Rosewood's annual New Year's Eve celebration that Camila's mom organizes every year and tonight is Zayn's turn to host our party.

A huge part of me is ready to see the back of a lot of things that have happened this year, but another part of me wants to cherish them. Yeah, I fucked up. Yeah, I did things I'll regret for the rest of my life, but equally, I got the two best things in my life.

I glance at Shane as he leads us toward the back of the house and Zayn's den. I can't help but smile as I think of all the things he's taught me. How he's shown me that it is possible to have exactly what I always wanted. Someone in my corner. Someone who would fight for me no matter what and love me so hard that it's almost unfathomable.

"I know you're staring."

"As you should. You look hot tonight."

"I'm nothing compared to you. At least every guy at Rosewood and beyond knows you're taken now," he says, and when I follow his gaze, I find almost everyone looking our way.

It seems that despite everyone being at home for the holidays, they've not forgotten the hottest gossip to hit Rosewood High in a while.

"Ignore them. They're just jealous that I got you and they didn't."

"I'm not sure anyone had any interest in me before you, baby."

I shrug, none of it matters. That's all in the past. We've got so much to focus on for our future, and that's where I intend on putting all my energy.

A cheer erupts as we enter Zayn's den, and when I look up, I find almost all of the team and the majority of the squad.

I haven't seen any of them since running from school the day Shelly exposed my secret.

Victoria, Tash, Aria, and a couple of the JV girls immediately see us and come over to congratulate me before taking great pleasure in explaining that Shelly is off the squad for good after that last stunt. Hartmann is on her case big time, one more wrong move and she's out of Rosewood for good.

Part of me is glad, she's clearly a conniving bitch with a seriously dodgy moral compass, but another part of me knows that it could so easily have been me. If my parents hadn't intervened when they did and force a reality check on me, who knows how far things might have gone.

I'd like to think that after finding out about being pregnant that it would have reined me in, but honestly, I have no idea what might have happened if I didn't spend those weeks at the center.

When I glance over to find Shane, he's been swallowed up by the team in a series of guy hugs and slaps on the back.

My heart swells that we're now able to celebrate our news with our teams.

"You're still going to lead us next year, right?" Aria asks once the excitement has died down.

"If you'll still have me."

"Hell yes. You're our way to regional success, girl."

A wide smile spreads across my face that my squad have that kind of faith in me.

After a few minutes, Shane finds me once again and hands me a drink while he takes a pull from his bottle of beer.

He's sworn to take it easier tonight after his Christmas Eve excess. He was mortified when I told him what happened that evening, although secretly I think he loves that he's not only got one up on Jake but that Jake knows about it as well.

Looking around the room, I find the six of them sitting on one of Zayn's couches. I breathe a sigh of relief when I see a genuine smile light up Amalie's face once again. Hopefully, now Christmas is done, she's been able to turn a corner and look forward to the year ahead.

We've all got so much to look forward to. Graduation, college, moving out, babies—well, that's just Shane and me as far as we know.

"Right, boys! Gather around," Zayn bellows around the room, totally unaware of what shenanigans are going on elsewhere in his house. It seems he thinks the only party is in this room while the rest of our class party outside the door. "It's time to set out the last challenge of the year."

Shane groans beside me as the excitement level skyrockets around the team. He leads me over to the couches to join the others who are no longer interested in the Bears games.

"You guys are all pigs, you know that, right?" Amalie asks, watching the action along with the rest of us as Zayn starts dishing out names.

"What?" Mason says as if he's going to argue. "If you're going to accuse anyone, it should be the guy whose lap you're currently sitting on. He started this whole thing."

"Why am I not surprised?" she says with a roll of her eyes.

"You set me up with some stinkers one too many times, I know that for a fact," I say with a laugh. Shane doesn't react to my comment like he once used to. It seems that he's come to terms with my past and believes me when I say that it's really not as shady as everyone makes out. "Some of the pickup lines those guys use are appalling. It's no wonder they're over there still single."

"Look at the expression on Justin's face," Ethan says, pointing. "I wonder who he's just been given." He laughs.

We watch their delight and horror as all the names continue to be dished out until all eyes turn on the ringleader. At the same time, the door opens and Harley, Ruby, and Poppy walk through the door. Since Harley and Ruby became JV members of the squad, they've been spending more and more time with the team and it seems tonight that Poppy is being dragged along, despite the fact she clearly looks like she wants to be anywhere else on earth right now.

Rich and Justin watch the three of them enter before they share a look.

"Oh fuck," Shane says, clearly thinking the same as me. "This is not going to go well."

Looking to Amalie and Jake, I find that they got bored with the action and are busy entertaining themselves. That can only be a good thing because I don't think he's going to like what's about to happen.

Wide smiles spread across Justin and Rich's faces before they both point at Poppy.

Zayn follows their fingers before all the color drains from his face. He shakes his head, but I know as well as he does that his refusal is futile. The rules of the game state that you don't get a second pick.

Zayn barks something at the two of them, the only words I make out are a series of swears before he storms from the room, much to the amusement of everyone who was watching the exchange.

"Well, tonight might have just gotten more interesting," Ethan states, having just watched the same thing we did. He glances to Jake, who's still oblivious to what's just happened. He's going to lose his shit when he discovers his team is using the only family member he actually likes as a pawn in their games.

All the guys disperse, probably heading off to find their conquests for the night. We might not have been involved in all that, but we all know that they have until the sun comes up to score their girl.

Jake eventually allows Amalie up for air, but no one fills him in on what he missed. Instead, we break off into a series of different conversations about the upcoming year as they all drink and I sip on my fruit juice.

Before I know it, the final countdown is on and we're speeding toward putting this dramatic year behind us.

"Come on, let's get out of here," Shane whispers in my ear before pushing from the couch and pulling me with him.

I follow him, my hand firmly grasped in his, as he makes his way outside to Zayn's back yard.

There's a big crowd out here knowing that we'll soon be able to enjoy the fireworks that are going to light up the sky.

Ignoring everyone around us, Shane pulls me into his body, his hands resting on my hips as he stares down into my eyes.

"I can't wait to find out what the future holds for us," he whispers, his voice rough with emotion. I know he's worried about his Mom, she's adamant that the moment the holidays are over that she's filing for divorce from Brett and moving on with her life. Without his dad breathing down his neck, he's had the space to be able to really think about what he wants. He's got applications written up in the pool house ready to send off to start college in September. He's still insistent that he's going to study part-time so that he can work to support us. As much as I hate that he's having to put his future on hold for us, I've learned that nothing I say is going to change his mind. He wants to do right by us, and I really can't argue with that.

"I know, me too. We're soon going to be able to say that we'll meet our baby this year."

His lips brush mine as people around us start counting down to midnight.

Our kiss deepens right as the cheer goes up around us. I forget where I am, that we're surrounded by our entire class and just hand myself over to him, showing him that I am his and that I want this for many, many years to come.

Shane rips his lips from mine right as the first of the fireworks display cracks above us. He turns me in his arms, rests his hands on my belly as his chin lands on my shoulder. We look up as color explodes in the inky night sky, signaling the start of a fresh new year.

It's time to start anew, to put our past and our mistakes behind us and look forward to our future together and our new family.

Before the fireworks end, I lower my eyes and look around at all my classmates around us. I see them all differently now. I no longer need to be the center of their attention, I no longer need to be Chelsea Fierce, queen bitch, head cheerleader, and the girl no one liked. I'm now Chelsea Fierce, girlfriend,

friend, and soon-to-be mother. I smile to myself, happiness washing over me once again.

My eyes land on two people in the crowd and I gasp.

"What is it?" Shane asks, noticing my reaction.

"There in the doorway."

I keep my eyes on the unlikely couple to see if Zayn's going to win his challenge tonight. He's got Poppy pinned up against the wall with his forearms caging her in.

He lowers his head, but before we get to see if his lips meet hers, the crowd moves, and our view is blocked.

"Looks like this year is going to be just as dramatic as the last one."

"That's fine as long as it doesn't involve us."

Shane turns me back around. "How about we keep our drama inside the pool house?"

"Sounds perfect. Fancy going there right now?"

"Have you all to myself to celebrate the new year? Hell yes, let's go."

He takes my hand and leads me from Zayn's house so that we can bring in the new year as we intend on spending the rest of our lives, together.

EPILOGUE

Shane
Six months later...

"Chelsea, are you okay?" I call through to the bedroom after the sound of something heavy hitting the floor rings out through the pool house. "Chelsea?" I shout again, panic starting to filter through me.

Her due date was four days ago and every weird noise she makes has me on edge.

I'm so fucking excited to finally meet our little person, but equally, I'm more terrified than I have been in my entire life.

I glance around at all the baby stuff that covers every available surface of our small home as I push from the couch to make sure she's okay.

"Chels—" My words are cut off the second I push the bedroom door open. "What the hell are you doing?" I ask, although I can't deny that the sight before me is fucking incredible.

"Please, Shane. I'm fucking dying here. I need this baby out of me," she says, looking over her shoulder, her tired eyes begging for me to do the thing she's been asking of me for the past week.

I know I should just do it. But our baby is so low now, ready to come out, it freaks me out a little just thinking about pushing myself inside her.

However, the sight of her on all fours totally bare for the taking does have my cock swelling with my need for her.

I think she thinks I've refused because I don't find her attractive like she is right now. She couldn't be farther from the truth. She's even more beautiful and sexy to me now carrying our baby. There's no doubt that I want her, it's just my fucked-up head that keeps stopping me.

"Come on. All the articles say that sex is the best way to bring on labor. Something about a chemical in sperm or something, I don't know. I just know it can help. Please. The raspberry tea, the pineapple, none of them have worked. Let's try it, please."

Unable to take her begging any longer, I drop my hand to my waistband and pop open my fly.

"Yesss," she hisses as she watches me push both my pants and boxer briefs down my legs and kick them off.

My hard cock bobs in front of me and I take it in hand as I step up to her.

Teasing her pussy with my fingers, I find her wet and ready for me.

"Oh god," she moans, spurring me on even more than I already was. Now I've decided to do this, I'm damn near desperate to slide into her.

I work her for a few more seconds, but as she starts pushing her ass higher in the air, I know she needs more.

Sweeping the head of my cock through her juices, I slowly push inside her.

My teeth clench as the familiar, yet always mind-blowing sensation consumes me until she's as full of me as she can get.

"Fucking hell, Chelsea. So good, so fucking good."

"Yes, yes," she cries as I pull slowly before thrusting back in.

My intention is to take it slow, to be gentle. But the second her heat engulfs me, I lose all control.

All too soon, her pussy is squeezing me tight, her entire body trembling as she starts to fall over the edge.

"Oh god, oh god," she chants, her fingers twisting in the sheets as pleasure washes over her.

"Fuuuuck," I groan as the tightening of her walls pushes me over the edge. I stay deep inside her long after I've come, just trying to catch my breath and give her what she wanted, something to get things moving.

Eventually, she awkwardly drops to her side, her round belly making movements hard for her.

"Fuck. I needed that," she says with a grin. "If it doesn't do the job, we're doing it again after I've had a nap."

Flipping the fabric of her skirt over her ass, she rests her hand on her bulging belly and rubs lovingly.

"You've woken him up," she says with a laugh.

I'm hardly surprised. He's probably got a headache.

We say he, but really, we have no idea what the sex is. She wanted to find out, but I liked the idea of it being a surprise. I was happy to give her what she wanted and told the sonographer—not Shelly's mom—that we wanted to know. But our baby is clearly Chelsea's child because the stubborn little thing kept its legs closed and was at such an awkward angle that the sonographer wasn't confident enough to say either way.

I thought Chelsea would be pissed, she was adamant that she wanted to know, but we found out what was really important, that everything was progressing well and that there were no concerns, so she was happy. She's since told me she's glad we didn't find out because it makes what's about to come that much more exciting.

After pulling my boxers back on, I crawl onto the bed behind her. I press my front to her back and rest my hand over hers on her belly.

"He's kicking like crazy."

She slips her hand away and allows me to feel the foot, or knee, pushing against her skin. It's the weirdest fucking feeling ever, but as much as it freaks me out to know that it's an actual person in there, it makes my heart ache. I had no idea it was possible to love someone you'd never met, but apparently it is because I love our little person something fierce.

After long silent minutes, Chelsea's breathing evens out and she relaxes into sleep.

It's still early evening and after lying in this morning, I'm nowhere near ready to go to sleep but I don't move, I'm too content with her and our baby in my arms.

Despite not thinking I'd doze off, the next thing I know I'm jostled awake as Chelsea pushes herself up on the bad.

"Ow fuck," she moans. Assuming she's got a back or hip ache once again, I don't think much of it as I open my eyes and reach to do whatever I can to help her but then she says my name and her voice is like I've never heard it before.

It has me sitting up faster than I knew possible before I look up to her wide, terrified eyes.

"Chels?"

"I... uh... I think it's time."

"Oh fuck. Fuck. Fuck," I chant, trying like hell to remember what we're supposed to do right now.

I scramble so I'm sitting between her legs and place my hands beside hers on her belly.

"Did you have a contraction?"

"I think so. I mean, I have no idea what they're meant to feel like but it was like a period pain on steroids."

"Okay. So we need to wait for the next one and see how much time is between them."

"Yeah, okay. We can do that."

She rests her head back against the wall as she keeps her breathing slow.

"Shane?" she asks.

"Yeah, baby?"

"I'm really fucking scared."

"It's okay. I'm right here. I'm not leaving your side." She nods, but I have no idea how much comfort my words give her.

The silence stretches out between us for long, excruciating minutes. I'm just starting to think that maybe it was a false alarm when Chelsea's entire body tenses. She lifts her head from the wall, the fear in her eyes stronger than ever.

"Another one?"

It takes her a few seconds to respond, but eventually, she nods her head.

"Can you call up to the house, let them know this is happening."

"Yes, I'm on it."

"Get the bags out of the closet, I double checked everything yesterday so everything should be ready." There's a quiver in her voice that I don't like, but I know that other than being beside her and holding her hand right now, there's nothing I can do.

The next four hours of my life are like a whirlwind. Despite being told that a first labor can take a very long time, Chelsea's contractions come closer and closer faster than we're expecting.

In only two hours they were down to four minutes apart and with the help of Honey at the other side of her, we make our way to the hospital.

Chelsea had already expressed her wish to have a water birth and thankfully, when we arrive at the maternity ward, there's a room and a pool free for us.

Once the midwife has done all her initial checks, I hold Chelsea's hand as she climbs into the pool.

She sighs in relief the second the warm water surrounds her and I sit there beside her, with her hand in mine throughout the rest of her labor.

Watching her in agonizing pain is possibly the worst experience of my life. In those couple of hours, I'd give anything to take her pain away, to experience it for her.

But then, a little over two hours after we first arrive, the most incredible thing happens.

Chelsea gives birth to our utterly perfect daughter.

I watch every moment of it and I'm crying long before the midwife lifts her tiny body from the water and places her on Chelsea's chest for her first cuddle with her little girl.

"Oh my god," she sobs as she stares down at a full head of dark hair. "Oh my god, I did it."

"You did, baby, and she's perfect."

"She's a she?" Chelsea asks, sounding shocked, as if she missed the midwife's announcement only a few moments ago.

"Yeah. We have a little girl. You've got yourself a little cheerleader."

"Oh my god," she repeats, breaking down as she holds our baby to her chest.

After a few minutes, the midwife gently lifts our little person from Chelsea and places her in a crib to the side of us so they can check her over.

"Dad, would you like to come and stand with her while we sort Mom out?"

I look between the two of them, totally torn for which one needs me the most right now.

"I'm fine. Go and be with her, she might be scared." That's the only encouragement I need. After dropping a kiss to Chelsea's lips and telling her how fucking incredible she is, I walk over to our baby.

I run my eyes over every inch of her. From her dark hair and equally dark eyes, just like her mommy's, all the way down her little body.

The midwife weighs her, measures her, before putting a tiny diaper on her and taking the outfit we'd chosen as the first she'd wear from the side.

She makes quick work of putting her in it and slipping a hat on her head, she does a much better job than I'm sure I'll do when they allow me to do it.

"Are you ready for your first cuddle, Daddy?"

My heart constricts as she calls me that.

I'm a fucking dad.

I knew it was coming. I've had six months to get used to the idea, but fuck, I feel totally unprepared in those moments as the midwife passes my daughter to me.

Walking back slowly, I lower us both down onto the small couch behind me.

"Hey, baby girl. How are you doing?"

Her wide eyes stare up at me. So innocent, so vulnerable. Tears form in my eyes as I stare at her.

"I'm your daddy," I mouth silently, unsure if I'm reminding myself that she's mine or making sure she knows who I am.

A sob has me dragging my eyes from my little girl and when I look up, I find Chelsea watching us with tears streaming down her cheeks and a wide smile on her face.

"I can't believe how perfect she is."

"I can, she's half you," Chelsea whispers.

The midwife breaks our moment, instructing Chelsea to lie down so she can check her over. "We won't be long, sweetie, and then that gorgeous baby is all yours."

With everything as it should be with both Chelsea and our little girl, they're discharged six hours later.

I'd texted everyone to let them know that she was here and that both mother and baby were doing great, but as we requested, everyone stayed away. We wanted this moment to be just about us. We might be young, but we're doing this together, as a family. This moment is about us and is one we'll never be able to repeat.

My car is outside exactly where Honey parked it when we arrived. I click the car seat into the base and triple-check that it's secure before turning to help Chelsea into the car.

"I can't," she says, pausing before dropping down into the passenger seat.

"Why? What's wrong?" I ask in a panic.

"N-nothing. I just can't be that far away from her."

With a smile, I watch as she makes her way around the back of the car and pulls the door open. She climbs inside and immediately slides over to be right beside our daughter.

Closing the door behind her, I climb in and look at Chelsea in the rearview mirror.

"Ready to go home, Mommy?"

"I am if you are, Daddy."

"Christ, this is weird."

"I'm sure we'll get used to it."

"I'm not sure we've got a choice."

I'm not sure I've ever driven more like my granddad in my life, and I make my way across town toward our home.

After the holidays, Luca and Leon went back to college and after another couple of weeks, Mom moved back in our house.

As she said she would, she got in touch with a lawyer the second they reopened and filed for divorce from my father. Much to all our shock, he signed the second he was served with the papers and he agreed to let her have the house. She's undecided as to whether she wants to stay there or not, but right now, she's turned it into her home.

She invited Chelsea and me to join her, but we're both more than happy in our pool house until we can afford to get a place of our own. That might not be for a few years as we find our feet as parents, college students, and part-time employees as we try to build a life for ourselves, but I have every confidence that it'll all work out in the end.

The house remains silent as we make our way around the back with our new arrival. It might barely be dawn, but I know for a fact that Honey is at a window somewhere watching us. She must be so desperate to come down and meet her grandchild, but much to her annoyance, I'm sure, she's holding back.

Chelsea walks ahead to open the door while I carry the bags and the car seat with our precious cargo.

Placing her down on the coffee table, we both take a seat on the edge of the couch, just staring at her.

"I can't believe we made her."

"She's beautiful."

The time stretches out as we both stare at our peacefully sleeping baby.

"Are you still happy with the name we picked?" I ask.

"Are you?"

"Yeah, it feels right."

"I agree."

I wrap my arm around Chelsea's shoulders and pull her to me, pressing my lips against her hair.

"You were incredible, Chels."

"I'm glad you think so. I knew it was going to hurt. But fuck, no one can prepare you for that."

I hold her tighter.

"She was worth it though. And I'd totally do it again."

I turn to stare at her. "One thing at a time, yeah?"

"Oh, I didn't mean anytime soon, I was just saying. Even only hours after, it's not put me off."

"You're something else, you know that?"

She shrugs, suddenly sitting forward when a dark pair of eyes flutter open.

"Hey, Nadine," Chelsea coos, reaching forward and hesitantly unstrapping her. In a matter of seconds, she has her in her arms and is cradling her like a pro.

Standing with her, I brush my finger over Nadine's cheek. "It really suits her."

"Welcome to the world, Nadine Dunn," Chelsea says, her voice cracking with emotion.

We haven't talked about marriage, our focus has been our baby, but Chelsea was adamant that she was going to have my last name so that one day we'd all have the same one.

We might have a million and one things going on in our lives right now, and I know the right thing to do is wait, but fuck if I don't want to get on one knee and demand that she become mine right now.

"You think she's hungry?" Chelsea asks, dragging me from my crazy thoughts.

"Only one way to find out."

Chelsea had some lessons in feeding in the hospital and she's quick to do exactly as she was told.

"I'm just going to put all this away while you do that."

I put everything in its new home while Chelsea nurses. When I come back out, Nadine is already asleep again in Chelsea's arms and Chelsea doesn't look too far behind.

"We should get some sleep while she is."

Chelsea nods, seemingly too exhausted to even speak. "Can you message everyone? Tell them we're home and let them know that we'll message again once we've had some rest so they can come and meet her. Message Greg too, he'll want to know."

Chelsea didn't mention her paternal dad again until almost the end of January when she decided that she was curious enough to reach out to him via text. Since then, they've only met twice. They're taking things slow, but she's decided that she'd like to get to know him, the him now, not the one from her childhood. I couldn't be prouder of her, fighting her demons and embracing a new family member.

"Of course."

I take Nadine from Chelsea's arms so she can get up easier. Even a few hours in, it feels natural to hold her in my arms.

I follow Chelsea through to our bedroom and lower Nadine to her bassinet next to Chelsea's side of the bed as Chelsea drops down onto it.

"I don't think I've ever been this exhausted."

"Get some sleep. I'll join you in a few minutes."

I send out a few messages as Chelsea lies watching Nadine sleep beside her, but when I come back, she's fast asleep.

I'm tired, although nowhere near as tired as Chelsea must be after going through all that, but I can't help but pull a chair over and sit and watch both of them sleep.

One reckless night that I never in a million years thought would happen changed my life forever.

It brought me the most important person in my life, and in turn, she just gave me another.

I shake my head as I try to process everything I'm feeling watching my entire world before me.

Eventually, my eyes get too heavy to sit any longer. Standing, I lean over the bassinet and drop a gentle kiss to Nadine's forehead before walking around the bed and crawling in behind Chelsea once again.

I wrap my arm around her waist like I did all those hours ago, but this time there is no kicking baby in her belly because our little bundle is sleeping soundly beside us.

"I love you so much. You fucking blew me away today."

"Thank you," she mumbles in her sleep. "You saved me. You both did."

With emotion clogging my throat, I hold her tighter to me and close my eyes, ready to start our lives as parents when we next wake up.

Are you ready for Poppy and Zayn?
HUNTER is now live.

ABOUT THE AUTHOR

Tracy Lorraine is a *USA Today* and *Wall Street Journal* bestselling new adult and contemporary romance author. Tracy has recently turned thirty and lives in a cute Cotswold village in England with her husband, baby girl and lovable but slightly crazy dog. Having always been a bookaholic with her head stuck in her Kindle, Tracy decided to try her hand at a story idea she dreamt up and hasn't looked back since.

Be the first to find out about new releases and offers. Sign up to my newsletter here.

If you want to know what I'm up to and see teasers and snippets of what I'm working on, then you need to be in my Facebook group. Join Tracy's Angels here.

Keep up to date with Tracy's books at
www.tracylorraine.com

ALSO BY TRACY LORRAINE

Fierce #4

Hunter #5

Faze (#6 Prequel)

Fury #6

Legend #7

Maddison Kings University Series

TMYM: Prequel

TRYS #1

TDYW #2

TBYS #3

TVYC #4

TDYD #5

Ruined Series

Ruined Plans #1

Ruined by Lies #2

Ruined Promises #3

Never Forget Series

Never Forget Him #1

Never Forget Us #2

Everywhere & Nowhere #3

Chasing Series

Chasing Logan

The Cocktail Girls

His Manhattan

Her Kensington

HUNTER SNEAK PEEK
PROLOGUE

Poppy
Three years ago...

"Zayn, your turn," Ethan says, his eyes moving around the circle until he finds Zayn's excited dark eyes.

It's his birthday, he should be excited. Unlike me, who's been forced to attend a fifteen-year-old boy's party while ignoring the fact he doesn't want me, Ruby, or his sister here.

We stand out like a sore thumb among his football friends, but for some crazy reason Jada, Zayn and Harley's mom, seemed to think it was a good idea.

I roll my eyes at her naïve plans. At least Scarlett, their older sister, had the sense to argue and has hidden herself in her room.

The tension in the room ticks up a notch as everyone stares at the empty bottle that Zayn spins in the middle of the circle we're all sitting in.

All the girls around me, bar Harley, seem to hold their breath in the hope of getting a chance at seven seconds in heaven with Zayn.

I try to keep my breathing steady in the hope of covering up that I'd also be more than willing to lock myself in the closet with Zayn.

He's hot, and I can't deny that I haven't had a crush on him since they first arrived in Rosewood last year.

It's just a shame he's one of Jake's football buddies. They might all only be sophomores, but I only have to take one look at the varsity team to see what they're going to be like in two years. Their egos and wannabe god-like personas are already growing larger than life.

I have no interest in getting tangled up with that. I'm not a popular girl, I'm not destined for the cheer squad or one of the sport teams. I'll just hide in the shadows while doing my thing and counting down the days until I can leave for college and finally take charge of my own life.

I let out a sigh, lost in thoughts of a future without the weight of my family weighing down on me. Being fourteen shouldn't be like this. I shouldn't be worrying about everyone else more than myself, but sadly it's my reality.

The bottle slows to a stop and my heart jumps into my throat as realization dawns that it could be about to land on me. I glance to Harley at my side and smile, imagining everyone's irritation—mostly Zayn's—should it land on his sister.

It misses her though, and when the bottle comes to a stop, it's pointed directly at me.

My eyes fly up in shock as I look up at Zayn.

"No. No fucking way," Jake, my cousin barks, his eyes narrowing on Zayn.

"Calm down, man. It's just some fun. Poppy, you're up for it, right?" Ethan looks at me expectantly.

"I... um..." I hesitate as all the sophomore girls' eyes drill into me.

"Just let him spin it again," Shelly pipes up, one of the cheer wannabes. "Zayn doesn't want to kiss a freshman anyway. She probably doesn't have the first clue about what she's doing."

I part my lips to argue, but really, she has a point. My experience with kissing is limited to an awkward lip press with Christopher back in junior high during a game of kiss chase.

"No second spins," Ethan spits, reiterating the rules that he laid out at the beginning of this stupid game. "You get in the closet or you forfeit, and I'm pretty sure none of you want to do the dares that I've got running around in my head." He smiles wickedly and Shelly pales slightly. I've heard all about Ethan Savage's dares, and so has everyone else in the room looking at their faces. "So..." He waves his hand between the two of us and the closet being used for this game.

My nerves quadruple to the point I worry if I'm going to be able to actually walk over there.

I push to stand, feeling the stares of everyone around me but no more so than Harley's shock and my cousin's death stare.

I manage to take two steps to where Ethan is now holding the door open before a hand wraps around my wrist.

"If he tries anything with you, tell me and I'll lay him out."

"It's fine, Jake. It's just for fun," I tell him, but I don't meet his eyes. The last thing I need him to see are my nerves and, dare I say it, excitement about this.

"It better be. You're worth more than any of this group has to offer." I don't miss the sounds of the rest of the team ribbing Zayn for having to kiss his little sister's friend, but I zone them out and focus on Jake.

"They're your friends, Jake."

"Yeah, and you're my family. The only decent one I got. I want the best for you, Popsicle."

I roll my eyes at his overprotectiveness, although I can't help but feel loved. It's something I don't feel all that often where my family is concerned. I think Jake is the only person who actually understands, who gets me. And for that, I'll forever be grateful.

"It's all good. You've got nothing to worry about."

He releases me, allowing me to slip into the closet.

I wait in the shadows for Zayn to join me while the hoots and hollers from his friends continue.

"Make sure she gives you one hell of a present, Hunter," someone calls, making me swallow down the lump of anxiety that's climbed up my throat.

It's only a kiss. I can do that. It's no biggie.

Right?

There's no doubt in my mind that he's only doing this because it's a game. There's no way in hell he'd ever willingly kiss me. I might have imagined what it would be like a time or two, but I suspect it never so much as crossed his mind, let alone in this capacity.

The door widens, allowing a sliver of light to illuminate me before it clicks shut, bathing us both in darkness.

My heart beats so wildly I swear he must be able to hear it. My hands tremble and my temperature spikes.

Every noise he makes sounds incredibly loud despite the fact I have blood rushing in my ears faster than I'm sure is natural as he closes the space between us.

"Poppy?" he asks, his voice sounding calm, like this is just an everyday occurrence for him.

I remind myself that it probably is. Jake, Zayn, and the others have girls hanging off them wherever they go. He's probably well-practiced in this sort of thing.

"Y-yeah," I whisper, hating that my voice cracks, showing my nerves.

The heat of his body hits mine. "Do you have any idea how long I've wanted to do this?"

His words throw me off for a second and it takes me longer than it should to register them.

"Y-you want to k-kiss me?" I sound pathetic and I kick myself for not sounding more confident.

"Yeah. There was no one else I wanted that bottle to land on. This is the only birthday present I wanted."

"Oh God," I practically whimper when his fingers find mine.

He steps into my body, pressing me back into the wall. I gasp at the feeling of his hard body against mine as his fingers tickle up my bare arm before he grasps the back of my neck.

"Ready?" he asks, his voice deeper than it was only moments ago.

My head spins as I fight to remember to breathe.

"Y-yeah, I—" I don't get to finish my thought because his soft, full lips brush mine.

At just that small contact, my knees go weak. He must sense it because his other hand lands on my waist. It feels huge as his touch burns my skin, causing sensations to swell within me that I've never felt before.

His lips stay on mine, unmoving for what feels like forever but in reality, it's probably not more than a second before his tongue teases at the seam of my lips.

I have no idea what I'm doing, but it doesn't seem to matter because my body seems to know what's expected of me and my lips part, allowing him entry.

If I didn't already know he'd had experience, then I did in that moment as he took control of the kiss. His tongue sweeping against mine.

My arms stay rigid at my sides as his fingers twitch at my waist, obviously wanting to move, but he never moves.

He kisses me like I've seen on TV, but it feels nothing like I imagined. I'm not nervous. Not self-conscious. I just let myself go and allow him to sweep me away.

All too soon, he places a chaste kiss on my lips and backs away from me. I miss him almost instantly, to the point I actually reach out for him, but despite my eyes having adjusted to the darkness, I don't manage to make contact with him.

"Poppy?" he asks again, his voice husky and rough, it does things to my insides I can't explain.

"Yeah?" I ask eagerly, desperate to hear it again.

"Don't repeat a word I said to you."

Lead fills my veins at his warning. I should have known he was lying.

I'm too devastated to respond, desperately trying to fight the tears that are already burning the backs of my eyes.

I thought he really meant it. That he's been thinking about kissing me like I have him.

Stupid, stupid girl.

He pushes the door open, the sudden light makes me close my eyes as a chorus of cheers erupts from the other side.

My heart sinks into my feet as I wonder how the hell I'm supposed to walk out of here with my head held high.

You're not, a little voice in my head says. *You just totally screwed up.*

The ruckus only gets louder as a victorious Zayn steps from the closet after his few seconds in heaven.

"So..." someone prompts. "Did she give you the gift you've been dreaming of?"

Before he answers, he looks back at me. I might be back in the shadows but he sees me and our eyes connect for the briefest moment.

"Nah, she's a frigid bitch." He walks away as his friends erupt in laughter and a couple of the girls descend on him, probably offering to do everything I apparently couldn't. All the while, I pray for the ground to swallow me up while continuing to hide in the shadows.

How long can I stay in here? Will anyone even notice?

HUNTER SNEAK PEEK
CHAPTER ONE

Poppy

I rush out of the Hunter's kitchen with a drink in hand, ready to find Harley and Ruby to celebrate the New Year together.

Butterflies erupt in my stomach, despite all the crap in my life, this is an exciting moment. One year closer to finishing school. One year closer to taking control of my life. One year closer to leaving this place and everything I despise about it behind. This year we're going to become seniors, we get to start seriously thinking about our futures and what we want from life. I might not have it all figured out yet, but I know one thing. My future isn't here. There are too many memories and demons lurking in the shadows for me to ever want to stay.

But while I'm stuck here, I figure I'd better make the most of it.

I see a flash of Harley's bright red hair and I can't help but smile. At least I have a couple of good things in my life, my two best friends are definitely that. I have no idea how I'd survive this place without them.

The sound of the party around me begins to lessen as kids head outside, ready to watch the fireworks that are about to illuminate the sky.

I shouldn't have come tonight but despite my parents' obvious irritation that I was going to spend the night enjoying myself and they weren't, I packed a bag and walked straight out the front door. Most days I allow them to blackmail me into doing as they wish, tonight wasn't one of those nights.

I knew it was safe being here. It's mostly the seniors who are partying at the

Hunter's, the majority of our junior class are elsewhere, thank God. It means that for once, I'm able to let my hair down and attempt to enjoy being a seventeen-year-old girl if just for a couple of hours, forget about the weight that presses down on my shoulders every other day of the year.

I'm almost at the door when a warm hand wraps around my wrist. The grip is hard, meaningful, and my heart jumps into my throat. A shiver of fear runs down my spine.

He's not here, I remind myself. *You're safe right now. He is not here.* It doesn't matter how many times I repeat those words in the millisecond I have before whoever has touched me makes themselves known, the fear threatens to swallow me whole regardless.

I kick myself for letting my guard down tonight, for allowing myself to think that I could have just one normal night. For once, just enjoy a party like everyone around me does without constantly looking over my shoulder, waiting for the devil to strike.

"You're looking hot tonight, Pops."

His deep, rough voice flows over me, and instantly my shiver returns, only this time it's not with fear.

Steeling myself, I lift my chin, ready to fight.

"Get your hands off me, Zayn."

I try to pull myself from his grip but he's holding too tightly. Before I've even had a chance to plan my next move, he's taken control and pulled me back until the cool of the wall bites into my skin.

He stares into my eyes and as always, I hate that he can see so deep.

"Why aren't you enjoying yourself like everyone else?"

"I... um... I am. See?" I lift my drink and tip it toward my mouth, only it doesn't meet my lips. Instead, it's taken from my fingers and pressed against his full lips in a heartbeat.

"That's soda," he states, his brows drawn.

"So?"

"Don't you want to let go, have a little fun? You're always so uptight."

I flinch at his words. I spend most of my life trying to cover up how I really feel, what's really going on with me. I really don't need him digging and finding the ugly things that I try to keep away from everyone else.

"Don't you want to have fun?"

"Who says I'm not?"

"Aside from the soda, your face."

My lips part to respond but I fear I have no argument.

"The others don't see it, do they?" His fingers lift and he tucks a lock of hair behind my ear, his touch burning all the way down to my toes.

"Don't see what, Zayn?" I snap. I shouldn't ask. I'm terrified to hear the answer, to know what he really thinks of me but that's the thing about my best friend's older brother. He affects me in a way that no one else ever has. It annoys the crap out of me.

"I don't know," he muses, staring deep into my eyes. "But I want to find out."

"Fuck you, Zayn," I spit.

"Now there's an idea. You think that'll help loosen you up a little?" His eyebrows wiggle in excitement as I will all of my muscles below my waist not to clench at the thought.

I told myself years ago that I wasn't ever allowed to lose myself in Zayn's smooth lines. He shattered my young heart all those years ago in that closet. I may never have forgiven him for that, but hell if I don't still dream about it. I tell myself that should the situation arise ever again that I'd tell him to go to hell, but I'm pretty sure I'm only lying to myself because even now, I can feel that kiss.

"Let me go," I damn near beg.

"Why, so you can go and pretend to be happy? Tell me how to make it better, Poppy. Tell me how to put a genuine smile on your face."

"Why do you care?" I ask, my eyes narrowing on his sparkling ones.

"I've always cared. I watch you, you know, when you're not looking."

"No," I argue, knowing that it can't be true. The thought of it being true and him discovering what I keep hidden is scarier than him admitting that he might actually care.

"These frown lines," he says, his finger gently running between my brows, smoothing them out. "I want to know what puts them there." His finger continues down over my nose until it connects with my lips.

I suck in a ragged breath as I watch his eyes follow its journey. It lingers on my bottom lip for a beat before pulling it out. His eyes darken as he sucks on his own bottom lip like he's imagining all kinds of dirty things.

I've seen the look on him before. Usually right before he makes a play for a cheer slut. But despite the fact I know that, it doesn't make me move. In fact, right now, with his scent filling my nose and the heat of his body seeping into mine, all it does is make me want to find out where he's going with this.

I don't need to look up to know we're alone right now, someone has turned the music down and all the voices that can be heard are coming from the garden.

I should push him away. Harley, or worse, Jake could see us and jump to conclusions. What I really don't need in my life right now is more drama. But as I remain locked in his stare, I'm powerless to move.

His hand wraps around the back of my neck, his fingers squeezing in the most incredible way.

"What keeps these muscles so tense, Pops? What are you hiding?"

My lips part to respond as he rests his forearm against the wall beside my head. He steps closer, completely surrounds me with his size and I feel like a little girl once again. I feel like I'm fourteen once more and about to experience everything I'd been dreaming about.

"Zayn," I warn as he slowly closes the space between us, the crowd from outside beginning their countdown to the New Year.

"Celebrate the New Year with me, Pops. Let's bring it in style."

He steps closer still. His hard, powerful body pressing mine back into the wall. His muscles meld with my softness and my knees threaten to give out.

Right as the first firework explodes, his lips connect with mine. His grip on my neck gets tighter and my lips part without any instruction from my brain.

You shouldn't be doing this, the little voice in my head screams. But I already know I don't have the strength in me to stop it. Not now that I can taste him, feel his tongue dancing with mine, feel his hardness pressing against my stomach.

Fuck, he actually wants me.

His tongue delves past my lips once more, searching mine out. This kiss is different to the previous one we shared. There's no hesitation whatsoever. He knows what he's doing this time.

As he should, he's been with half of the senior girls according to the gossip.

"Oh God," I mumble against his lips, the realization of what I'm doing slamming into me full force.

Pressing my palms against his solid chest, I push in the hope of making him back up.

"Zayn, stop," I beg the second his lips part from mine.

Keeping my eyes on the fabric of my shirt, I fight down my need to pull him straight back to me.

I miss him already. It's crazy.

"You shouldn't have done that," I whisper, needing to at least attempt to tell him how wrong it was.

"Why?" His voice hits me exactly where I don't need it to. That combined with how ferociously his chest is heaving doesn't help my resolve at all.

"Because nothing good happens when we..."

"When we?"

I roll my eyes at myself, at the fact he needs me to say the words out loud. "When we kiss." I lift my eyes to him, needing him to know how serious I am.

"I don't have a black eye yet, do I?" he says, referring to what happened after that horrendous experience of our last kiss.

I might have wanted to hide in that closet for the rest of eternity but the second I heard Jake's angry growl and the girls start screaming, I didn't have a choice but to step into the light and watch as Jake rained hell down on Zayn's face for what he said about me.

"Give it time."

Our eyes hold, mine hold a warning whereas I swear his hold a promise, although I'm not entirely sure what he's trying to promise me. All I do know is that the tingles continue to race through me and my temperature doesn't decrease at all with his stare burning into me.

When the fireworks are over, the crowd starts to disperse and their chatter and laughter filter down to me. I know I need to move. I can't be standing here in this stare-off with Zayn when Jake or Harley emerges.

Thankfully, loud footsteps approaching us sound as I drag my eyes away from his dark and hungry stare.

I look up in time to see Justin clap his hand down on Zayn's shoulder. His eyes are wild and he sways a little on his feet. The guy's wasted.

I'm about to roll my eyes at the state of him when he says the words that rips the rug from beneath me once again.

"Sweet, man. I didn't think you were going to pull off your tag tonight. Right at the stroke of midnight, too."

My eyes widen as understanding washes through me. The team's little games aren't a secret around the girls of Rosewood High.

"What?" I ask, forcing the word out through the lump in my throat.

"Pop, it's not—"

"Don't lie to me, Zayn," I hiss back. "Tell me I wasn't a dare," I demand.

He swallows nervously but his lips remain sealed.

"Tell me," I damn near plead, not knowing how I'm going to deal with this again. The first rejection hurt like hell. But this time, it's so different.

That kiss, those few seconds of escape from reality, there's no way he can have any idea how much it meant to me, how much I needed it.

He gave me something that took me away, even if for a few seconds and now it's all crumbling around my feet once again.

"Pops, I—"

"No," I bark, shoving at his chest. "Don't *Pops* me. You're a fucking joke. You know that, right? The group of you are a fucking joke," I scream, briefly meeting Justin's eyes who doesn't so much as flinch at my volume.

Assholes.

Zayn takes a step back, his eyes still trained on me. Something akin to regret filling them but I refuse to acknowledge it.

Stepping past him, my arm collides with his, sending a pain right down to my fingers but despite my gasp, he doesn't react.

"I told you, nothing good comes from us kissing. It's time you realized that," I hiss at him before I storm past.

"And what if I don't?"

Shaking my head, I march from the kitchen and head toward the stairs.

What I really want to do is walk straight out of the Hunter's front door and leave this party and his games behind me. But where would I go?

Home?

I almost laugh to myself at the thought. I think I'd rather be Zayn's plaything, the pawn in his games, than being at home tonight.

I fly up the stairs, my legs burning as I take two at a time in my need to get away. I ignore all the doors until I get to the penultimate one and I swing it open.

The safety of Harley's room makes me sigh with relief. I slam it behind me, feeling the vibrations of the force I used before I throw myself at the bed.

I tell myself not to cry. Not to waste any more tears on that asshole, but it's not a fight I can win because the harder I try to keep them in, the more they insist on being released until I'm sobbing into Harley's pillow.

Need more?
HUNTER is now live.

Printed in the USA
CPSIA information can be obtained
at www.ICGtesting.com
LVHW061412180823
755499LV00015B/278/J